THE HARD SF RENAISSANCE

Tor Anthologies Edited by David G. Hartwell and Kathryn Cramer

The Ascent of Wonder
Spirits of Christmas

Tor Books by David G. Hartwell

NONFICTION
Age of Wonder

EDITOR
Bodies of the Dead
Centaurus
Christmas Forever
The Dark Descent
Foundation of Fears
Northern Stars (with Glenn Grant)
Northern Suns (with Glenn Grant)
The Science Fiction Century
The Screaming Skull
Visions of Wonder (with Milton T. Wolf)

THE HARD SF RENAISSANCE

EDITED BY DAVID G. HARTWELL
AND KATHRYN CRAMER

A Tom Doherty Associates Book
New York

This is a work of fiction. All the characters and events portrayed in the stories in this anthology are either fictitious or are used fictitiously.

THE HARD SF RENAISSANCE

Edited by Patrick Nielsen Hayden

A Tor Book
Published by Tom Doherty Associates, LLC
175 Fifth Avenue
New York, NY 10010

Tor® is a registered trademark of Tom Doherty Associates, LLC.

ISBN: 0-312-87635-1

Printed in the United States of America

Copyright Acknowledgments

Contents

Introduction

NEW PEOPLE, NEW PLACES, NEW POLITICS

The hard SF tradition is continuous from at least the late 1930s. In our 1994 hard SF anthology, *The Ascent of Wonder*, we argued that "There has been a persistent viewpoint that hard SF is somehow the core and the center of the SF field." But while hard SF was never entirely out of fashion, since the 1940s it has not been as central to popular SF, nor as fashionable, as it became in the 1990s.

The term was coined by P. Schuyler Miller in 1957, and in its origins has always been to some extent nostalgic, in that it was coined to describe fiction that measured up to the "real" SF of the past. But it has also always signified SF that has something centrally to do with science, and it is this latter aspect of the term that we choose to emphasize, and it is this latter aspect that is most evident in the renaissance of hard SF in the 1990s.

The big names in hard SF in the nineties, based on number of stories published, were Stephen Baxter, Greg Egan, Gregory Benford, Geoffrey Landis, G. David Nordley, Paul McAuley, Nancy Kress, Kim Stanley Robinson, Charles Sheffield, Brian Stableford, Allen Steele, Bruce Sterling, Robert J. Sawyer, etc. Many of them wrote a number of stories in other genres or subgenres, but also made significant contributions in SF. Otherwise the big names of this and earlier generations, Poul Anderson, David Brin, Greg Bear, Hal Clement, Ben Bova, and Larry Niven, Jack Williamson, etc., wrote significant novels, and published less than ten stories in the whole decade, although some of those stories were certainly important. And Arthur C. Clarke, following the deaths of Heinlein and Asimov, became the standard bearer for the old ideals of hard SF unmixed with overt politics and remained a bestselling writer.

Those old ideals, of vision of the future distant in time and space, and filled with wonder far removed from the politics of today, did not disappear in the 1990s. But they began to seem old fashioned, because many of the main ideas of hard SF had become politicized in the real world in the 1980s, associated with either the right or the left—near future space travel and weaponry with the right, nuclear dangers and the environment with the left, etc.

Here is the legend of right-wing political involvement in the real world USA in hard SF, the origin story of the SF advisors to President Reagan, who inspired the "Star Wars" defense plan in the early 1980s (as told by Greg Bear in his 2001 World SF convention guest of honor speech):

> Jerry Pournelle got together Poul [Anderson], and Gregory Benford and Larry Niven, Dean Ing, Robert Heinlein, and a number of other writers—Bjo Trimble was there with her daughter, Lora—lots of science fiction writers getting together with generals, rocket scientists young and old, new and experienced,

and people from NASA, and politicians, discussing this possibility: that perhaps nuclear war was going to become a push-button affair where computers would make the decision.

No one could tolerate that, and we had to start building defensive shields. So we started putting together different ideas. General Danny Graham had one vision, and some of the writers had another. And they had a science fiction fan for a president; his name was Ronald Reagan.

Now we laugh. Do you want your presidents to be smart? Do you want them to be dreamers? Or do you want them to be lucky? Because this thing that went forth that Ronald Reagan did was the vastest bluff in the blue-bottom baboon history of the whole Cold War. Ronald Reagan said we could put a whole umbrella over the United States and protect [it]. . . . Science fiction writers helped the rocket scientists elucidate their vision and clarified it. They put it together in prose that Ronald Reagan could understand, and Ronald Reagan who read science fiction, said "Why not?" And he was lucky and so, that thing that had terrified me as a child surviving the Cuban missile crisis, . . . the ever present shadow of nuclear war, all of that, suddenly wasn't really there anymore.

All political narratives are oversimplified in fiction, especially when the narrative is repeated by opponents of the group in question. Probably this story has been as well, but the committee was a fact, and it was a committee formed by the political right in SF, that, a decade after the famous Vietnam ads (and see Joe Haldeman "For White Hill" story note for more on this), added significant credence to the identification of American hard SF with right-wing politics and fulfilled one of the dreams of SF—that if our stories were read by and our prophecies were listened to by the people who run the world, then the world would change for the better.

Certain writers such as Ted Chiang, Catherine Asaro, Paul Levinson, Michael Flynn, Alexander Jablokov, David Langford, Ian MacDonald, Robert Reed, George Turner, James Patrick Kelly, and Robert Charles Wilson also came into prominence (some after decades of publishing) as hard SF or space opera writers, each with several highly regarded stories. (Many of them wrote other kinds of fiction.)

There were other significant threads, and significant works by important writers, that are not part of this argument, or this anthology. (This is not intended as a comprehensive literary history of 1990s SF.) Many popular, talented, and award-winning SF writers such as Connie Willis, John Kessel, Jack Womack, Howard Waldrop, James Morrow, Terry Bisson, Tim Powers, Harry Turtledove, Karen Joy Fowler, and Neal Stephenson, wrote in other areas in the 1990s. (The 1990s was also the decade of the rise of Alternate History as a main form of SF, for instance.)

In this anthology we present representative examples from among the significant SF writers and hard SF stories of the decade, and try to point out linkages and relationships to give some clearer understanding of how hard SF, often mixed with space opera (or vice versa) has evolved in recent years, escalating into the new century. This book focuses on what has been called "The New Hard SF," "Baroque Hard SF Space Opera" (or "Baroque Space Opera")," "Hard Character SF," and a number of other unwieldy terms. The New Thing of the nineties, was broader than just hard SF, but there was certainly a hard SF renaissance and the stories in this book prove it.

No consensus has emerged as to what to call it: a lot of diverse things happened, even within the compass of this book. It is sometimes called Radical Hard SF and that is the term we will trace because it illuminates certain interesting things about the evolution of the field in the last couple of decades.

This term originated in an *Interzone* editorial by David Pringle and Colin

Greenland (in *Interzone* #8) and was then preempted by Bruce Sterling in his polemical fanzine *Cheap Truth*, as a description of what Sterling wanted the Movement to be. (See the note for Sterling's "Bicycle Repairman.") And of course neither cyberpunk nor the stories in *Interzone* turned out as anticipated in the various calls for Radical Hard SF. But seeds had been planted. It was clear that what Radical Hard SF was in opposition to was a perceived trend in American SF in the 1980s toward militarist, right-wing or libertarian, space war fiction marketed as synonymous with hard SF. The pages of *Cheap Truth* were filled with attacks on that stuff.

Some issues in the evolution of space opera need to be addressed, before we can fully understand what happened to hard SF. So let us turn there for a moment.

The Hugo Awards for best novel for the last twenty years have generally been given to space opera or hard SF, from David Brin and C. J. Cherryh to Vernor Vinge, Lois Bujold, and Orson Scott Card—as opposed to the shorter fiction awards, which have been distributed much more widely over the range of SF and fantasy styles and possibilities. It is arguable that the Hugo Award has always gone primarily to space opera, as currently defined, though many of the earlier winners, up to the end of the 1970s, would have been mortally offended to be identified as such. Space opera used to be a pejorative locution designating the worst form of formulaic hackwork.

But in the early and mid-1980s space opera completed a redefinition process begun in the late 1970s in particular by influential editors Lester and Judy-Lynn Del Rey, and in the 1990s space opera had become synonymous with popular science fiction adventure fiction. It was also the term most often used in the U.S. to describe *Star Trek* and *Star Wars* fiction. It is clear that both films and television helped promote this redefinition. And finally, it is evident that this redefinition was intended to conflate hackneyed work with ambitious SF adventure fiction, to blur distinctions in order to sell more books and make the media tie-in writing-for-hire fiction seem more respectable.

In the 1980s, the traditional optimistic, problem-solving kind of hard SF was marginalized by the advent of cyberpunk (originally the Movement: radical reformers of hard SF) and by the ascendence of the Humanists (originally—and self-parodyingly—the Boffos of Sycamore Hill: the "boring old farts" of the writing workshop in Sycamore Hill, North Carolina, who were actually the same age as the cyberpunks). Both groups, and the outer circles of imitators and followers of both, rejected space opera and the common forms and styles of hard SF, and the politics of the Right, in favor of new attitudes and approaches, new dress codes and new critical value systems, and left-leaning politics. The standard essay on the subject is Michael Swanwick's "User's Guide to the Postmoderns."

The real attention in the 1980s and the early 1990s went to William Gibson and Bruce Sterling, and their cohorts and emulators, on the one hand, and to Connie Willis, Kim Stanley Robinson, John Kessel, and Orson Scott Card on the other. Lois McMaster Bujold (published by Baen books and serialized in *Analog*) became prominent, and Dan Simmons too. Orson Scott Card's two-volume anthology of 1980s SF (*Future on Fire* [1991] and *Future on Ice* [1998]) is the best available selection of eighties writers. There is no comparable anthology for the 1990s. But Card's long and judgmental story notes must be read along with and in juxtaposition to the general introductions to Gardner Dozois' annual *Year's Best Science Fiction* (in which the fashions and prevalent attitudes are clearly presented, sometimes in very different terms than in Card's books).

Promoting hard SF in the 1980s was left primarily to influential editor Jim Baen, first at Tor Books and then from 1983 on at Baen Books, and to *Analog*. (Examples of what Baen was promoting and what the Movement was attacking included the Libertarian fiction of Vernor Vinge, the late work of Robert A. Heinlein, and the *There Will Be War* anthology series edited by Jerry Pournelle.) Hard SF, it seemed, was narrowing to a subgenre concerned primarily with military fiction and political attacks, usually from the right, on liberal causes and politicians, and with artificially set up problems solved by stereotypical characters, in neither venue valuing literary style.

In *The Ascent of Wonder*, an anthology we felt was a necessary corrective to this seeming narrowing, we examined the historical origins of hard SF and tried to tease out what hard SF had actually to do with science. The book had three introductions, one each by Gregory Benford, Kathryn Cramer, and David G. Hartwell. Benford argued for hard SF's "fidelity to facts": "Hard SF plays with the net of fact up and strung as tight as the story allows." Cramer remarked that in the decades since John W. Campbell's death, "the hard SF attitude became a saleable commodity of its own, separable from scientific content. Particularly during the Reagan years, hard SF evolved into right-wing power fantasies about military hardware, men killing things with big machines . . ." She invited the reader instead to explore the myriad ways science could be used in hard SF. Hartwell described hard SF as being about the "beauty of truth" and "the emotional experience of describing and confronting what is true," portraying hard SF as a literature of faith in science, in opposition to literary modernism.

Some fine and popular writers emerged from Baen Books and from *Analog* (Lois Bujold at Baen Books, Michael Flynn at *Analog*), but with these and a few other significant exceptions, Baen Books and *Analog* didn't get much serious attention, nor many award nominations in the field, by the beginning of the 1990s. Nor were many of the stories selected for prestigious reprint in *Year's Best* anthologies, despite the fact that *Analog* was, and always has been, the magazine with the highest circulation in the SF field. A bunch of the *Analog* writers, whose fiction was published nearly exclusively therein, got together in the nineties as a booster group and had themselves photographed on several occasions at conventions with editor Stanley Schmidt as the "*Analog* Mafia." But they did not succeed in appearing as a hip, young, cutting-edge group.

It was among the British writers in particular that a new space opera (which was the most obvious U.K. response to the call for Radical Hard SF) conspicuously flowered in the late 1980s and during the 1990s. British SF critic Paul Kincaid, in 2001 in an essay on 1990s SF, "The New Optimism," says:

> British science fiction, meanwhile, was following exactly the opposite trajectory [from American SF]. While cyberpunks admitted the influence of the British New Wave, writers such as Colin Greenland in *Take Back Plenty* and Ian McDonald in *Desolation Road* were paying self-conscious homage to the free-wheeling American SF adventures of their youth.
>
> . . . the most influential writer in Britain today is Iain (M.) Banks. . . . Certainly in science fiction terms there are lines of descent clearly visible from Banks to Ken MacLeod to Alastair Reynolds. The science fiction they have created is big, sprawling, often funny or at least idiosyncratic, and undeniably optimistic. Banks's Culture, a world of plenty and diversity and the ability to do just about anything one might desire, is the most utopian vision of the far future I have encountered in a very long time. Here is a future to aim for that is wealthy

and free, a future in which competent women and men can succeed against heavy odds. A future that is, except for its distinctly left-wing bias, remarkably like the dream that used to be found in American SF during the optimistic fifties.

There are no neat divisions and clear boundaries; we merely observe large groupings and general tendencies. And new literary forms do not replace older ones, but coexist with them. There are examples of all forms of space opera, to the tv tie-in, romance or westerns couched in SF clothing, including the crudely executed, to be found in publications of the 1990s and today. And all the forms of hard SF, from the Gernsbackian idea story to the Campbellian problem-solving story and all, sometimes, in rudimentary prose. The new did not drive out the old, but neither did the bad old overwhelm the good new.

What did happen was that significant attention began to focus in the early 1990s on new writers, such as Greg Egan, Stephen Baxter, Paul McAuley, Iain M. Banks, Ian MacDonald, and Gwyneth Jones, who were doing striking new things in SF, most often with a left-wing (or at least certainly not right-wing) political bent, and most often in hard SF or space opera. Most of them are British writers, not American, and by the mid and late 1990s they had been joined by many others, both British and American, in advancing hard SF and in bringing new energy and variety to space opera. It was the decade of Kim Stanley Robinson's Mars trilogy, and also of many other Mars novels. It was the decade that Australian and Canadian SF writers became significant groups in SF and particularly in hard SF, rather than a few disparate talents of generally unknown nationality. We will continue this discussion throughout the book in the story notes, and of course in the choice of stories as examples, trying to tease out the threads of hard SF.

Here, in this book, we present the very real resurgence in 1990s science fiction of ambitious and complex strains of hard SF.

David G. Hartwell & Kathryn Cramer
Pleasantville, New York

GENE WARS

Paul McAuley

Paul McAuley (born 1955) is a British writer who often writes hard SF, one of the group (along with Stephen Baxter, Peter Hamilton, Iain M. Banks, and others) responsible for the UK part of the hard SF/space opera renaissance of the 1990s. With degrees in botany and zoology, McAuley did scientific research in Britain and in Los Angeles before becoming a professor in the U.K. A few years ago, he gave up teaching to become a full-time writer. "I'm a science junkie—always have been," he says. "If I'd been a writer before becoming a scientist I think I'd still be writing *about* science and I'm certainly still excited by the rich strangeness of the universe. . . . As a scientist, I hope I've acquired a certain meticulousness about thinking things through, the ability to see things from the bottom up, and to not be afraid of research. I'm definitely writing more and more about biology and the culture of science now that I'm no longer a scientist—it's something I know a little bit about."

His first novel, *Four Hundred Billion Stars*, was co-winner of the Philip K. Dick Award in 1988 (with Rudy Rucker's *Wetware*). He has since published a number of SF novels, of which *Fairyland* (1994) won the Arthur C. Clarke and the John W. Campbell Awards for best novel, and *Pasquale's Angel* (1994) won the Sidewise Award for alternate history fiction. He completed a trilogy of SF novels, *The Book of Confluence* (*Child of the River*, 1997; *Ancient of Days*, 1998; *Shrine of Stars*, 1999). In 2001, he published two new novels, *The Secret of Life*, a hard SF near-future thriller about life on Mars, and *Whole Wide World*, a novel of high-tech intrigue. He has two collections of short fiction, *The King of the Hill and Other Stories* (1991) and *The Invisible Country* (1996). He also writes reviews for *Interzone*.

In Nick Gevers' interview with McAuley for *Infinity Plus* in 1999, when asked what it meant that he referred to himself as a writer of "radical hard SF," McAuley replied:

> *Radical hard SF* was a term coined by David Pringle and Colin Greenland in an *Interzone* editorial some years ago. [*Interzone* #8, Summer 1984—eds.] They suggested that there was room in SF for new fictions that would be "critical and investigative, facing up to the science and technology of the present and future . . . using the hard-edged language and imagery of technology for imaginative interpretations of reality." More recently, Gardner Dozois has appropriated it to describe the subgenre of revisionist widescreen baroque space opera—which is only partly what I think radical hard SF can do. I use the definition very loosely: SF rooted in the core traditions of SF but also surfing the wave of the present, with rounded characters, bleeding edge science, an attempt to convey the complexity of a world or worlds. It's a reaction to the trad SF approach of filtering the future through One Big Change—nanotechnology, immortality, biotech. If there's one thing we've learnt from the twentieth century, it's that change is continuous and is advancing on a thousand different fronts.

The influence of this notion of a Radical Hard SF, which has meant different things to different writers, is one of the central concerns of this anthology.

"Gene Wars," with its themes of a biotech growing out of control, the politics of technology, and the emergence of a posthumanity, is certainly a story about change continuous and advancing. It is hard-edged future history of the alterations wrought by genetic engineering upon society and, as in Bruce Sterling's *Schismatrix*, McAuley's characters are transformed almost beyond recognition. Another element of newer breeds of hard SF is that they are often engaged with the politics of the post–Cold War era and the new millennium. This story shows the strong influence of the political movements against globalization and genetically engineered crops, a far cry from the techno-libertarian and/or promilitarist stance (still epitomized by many writers associated with Baen Books) that increasingly characterized a significant amount of hard SF in the early and middle 1980s.

1

On Evan's eighth birthday, his aunt sent him the latest smash-hit biokit, *Splicing Your Own Semisentients*. The box-lid depicted an alien swamp throbbing with weird, amorphous life; a double helix spiralling out of a test-tube was embossed in one corner. Don't let your father see that, his mother said, so Evan took it out to the old barn, set up the plastic culture trays and vials of chemicals and retroviruses on a dusty workbench in the shadow of the shrouded combine.

His father found Evan there two days later. The slime mould he'd created, a million amoebae aggregated around a drop of cyclic AMP, had been transformed with a retrovirus and was budding little blue-furred blobs. Evan's father dumped culture trays and vials in the yard and made Evan pour a litre of industrial-grade bleach over them. More than fear or anger, it was the acrid stench that made Evan cry.

That summer, the leasing company foreclosed on the livestock. The rep who supervised repossession of the supercows drove off in a big car with the test-tube and double-helix logo on its gull-wing door. The next year the wheat failed, blighted by a particularly virulent rust. Evan's father couldn't afford the new resistant strain, and the farm went under.

2

Evan lived with his aunt, in the capital. He was fifteen. He had a street bike, a plug-in computer, and a pet microsaur, a cat-sized triceratops in purple funfur. Buying the special porridge which was all the microsaur could eat took half of Evan's weekly allowance; that was why he let his best friend inject the pet with a bootleg virus to edit out its dietary dependence. It was only a partial success: the triceratops no longer needed its porridge, but it developed epilepsy triggered by sunlight. Evan had to keep it in his wardrobe. When it started shedding fur in great swatches, he abandoned it in a nearby park. Microsaurs were out of fashion, anyway. Dozens could be found wandering the park, nibbling at leaves, grass, discarded scraps of fastfood. Quite soon they disappeared, starved to extinction.

3

The day before Evan graduated, his sponsor firm called to tell him that he wouldn't be doing research after all. There had been a change of policy: the covert gene wars were going public. When Evan started to protest, the woman said sharply, "You're better off than many long-term employees. With a degree in molecular genetics you'll make sergeant at least."

4

The jungle was a vivid green blanket in which rivers made silvery forked lightnings. Warm wind rushed around Evan as he leaned out of the helicopter's hatch; harness dug into his shoulders. He was twenty-three, a tech sergeant. It was his second tour of duty.

His goggles flashed icons over the view, tracking the target. Two villages a klick apart, linked by a red dirt road narrow as a capillary that suddenly widened to an artery as the helicopter dove.

Flashes on the ground: Evan hoped the peasants only had Kalashnikovs: last week some gook had downed a copter with an antiquated SAM. Then he was too busy laying the pattern, virus-suspension in a sticky spray that fogged the maize fields.

Afterwards, the pilot, an old-timer, said over the intercom, "Things get tougher every day. We used just to take a leaf, cloning did the rest. You couldn't even call it theft. And this stuff . . . I always thought war was bad for business."

Evan said, "The company owns copyright to the maize genome. Those peasants aren't licensed to grow it."

The pilot said admiringly, "Man, you're a real company guy. I bet you don't even know what country this is."

Evan thought about that. He said, "Since when were countries important?"

5

Rice fields spread across the floodplain, dense as a handstitched quilt. In every paddy, peasants bent over their own reflections, planting seedlings for the winter crop.

In the centre of the UNESCO delegation, the Minister for Agriculture stood under a black umbrella held by an aide. He was explaining that his country was starving to death after a record rice crop.

Evan was at the back of the little crowd, bareheaded in warm drizzle. He wore a smart onepiece suit, yellow overshoes. He was twenty-eight, had spent two years infiltrating UNESCO for his company.

The minister was saying, "We have to buy seed genespliced for pesticide resistance to compete with our neighbours, but my people can't afford to buy the rice they grow. It must all be exported to service our debt. Our children are starving in the midst of plenty."

Evan stifled a yawn. Later, at a reception in some crumbling embassy, he managed to get the minister on his own. The man was drunk, unaccustomed to hard liquor. Evan told him he was very moved by what he had seen.

"Look in our cities," the minister said, slurring his words. "Every day a thousand more refugees pour in from the countryside. There is kwashiorkor, beri-beri."

Evan popped a canapé into his mouth. One of his company's new lines, it squirmed with delicious lasciviousness before he swallowed it. "I may be able to help you," he said. "The people I represent have a new yeast that completely fulfills dietary requirements and will grow on a simple medium."

"How simple?" As Evan explained, the minister, no longer as drunk as he had seemed, steered him onto the terrace. The minister said, "You understand this must be confidential. Under UNESCO rules . . ."

"There are ways around that. We have lease arrangements with five countries that have . . . trade imbalances similar to your own. We lease the genome as a loss-leader, to support governments who look favourably on our other products . . ."

6

The gene pirate was showing Evan his editing facility when the slow poison finally hit him. They were aboard an ancient ICBM submarine grounded somewhere off the Philippines. Missile tubes had been converted into fermenters. The bridge was crammed with the latest manipulation technology, virtual reality gear which let the wearer directly control molecule-sized cutting robots as they travelled along DNA helices.

"It's not facilities I need," the pirate told Evan, "it's distribution."

"No problem," Evan said. The pirate's security had been pathetically easy to penetrate. He'd tried to infect Evan with a zombie virus, but Evan's gene-spliced designer immune system had easily dealt with it. Slow poison was so much more subtle: by the time it could be detected it was too late. Evan was thirty-two. He was posing as a Swiss grey-market broker.

"This is where I keep my old stuff," the pirate said, rapping a stainless-steel cryogenic vat. "Stuff from before I went big time. A free luciferase gene complex, for instance. Remember when the Brazilian rainforest started to glow? That was me." He dashed sweat from his forehead, frowned at the room's complicated thermostat. Grossly fat and completely hairless, he wore nothing but Bermuda shorts and shower sandals. He'd been targeted because he was about to break the big time with a novel HIV cure. The company was still making a lot of money from its own cure: they made sure AIDS had never been completely eradicated in third-world countries.

Evan said, "I remember the Brazilian government was overthrown—the population took it as a bad omen."

"Hey, what can I say? I was only a kid. Transforming the gene was easy, only difficulty was finding a vector. Old stuff. Somatic mutation really is going to be the next big thing, believe me. Why breed new strains when you can rework a genome cell by cell?" He rapped the thermostat. His hands were shaking. "Hey, is it hot in here, or what?"

"That's the first symptom," Evan said. He stepped out of the way as the gene pirate crashed to the decking. "And that's the second."

The company had taken the precaution of buying the pirate's security chief: Evan had plenty of time to fix the fermenters. By the time he was ashore, they would have boiled dry. On impulse, against orders, he took a microgram sample of the HIV cure with him.

7

"The territory between piracy and legitimacy is a minefield," the assassin told Evan. "It's also where paradigm shifts are most likely to occur, and that's where I come in. My company likes stability. Another year and you'd have gone public, and most likely the share issue would have made you a billionaire—a minor player, but still a player. Those cats, no one else has them. The genome was supposed to have been wiped out back in the twenties. Very astute, quitting the grey medical market and going for luxury goods." She frowned. "Why am I talking so much?"

"For the same reason you're not going to kill me," Evan said.

"It seems such a silly thing to want to do," the assassin admitted.

Evan smiled. He'd long ago decoded the two-stage virus the gene-pirate had used on him: one a Trojan horse which kept his T lymphocytes busy while the other rewrote loyalty genes companies implanted in their employees. Once again it had proven its worth. He said, "I need someone like you in my organization. And since you spent so long getting close enough to seduce me, perhaps you'd do me the honour of becoming my wife. I'll need one."

"You don't mind being married to a killer?"

"Oh, that. I used to be one myself."

8

Evan saw the market crash coming. Gene wars had winnowed basic foodcrops to soybeans, rice, and dole yeast: tailored ever-mutating diseases had reduced cereals and many other cash crops to nucleotide sequences stored in computer vaults. Three global biotechnology companies held patents on the calorific input of ninety-eight percent of humanity, but they had lost control of the technology. Pressures of the war economy had simplified it to the point where anyone could directly manipulate her own genome, and hence her own body form.

Evan had made a fortune in the fashion industry, selling templates and microscopic self-replicating robots which edited DNA. But he guessed that sooner or later someone would come up with a direct-photosynthesis system, and his stock-market expert systems were programmed to correlate research in the field. He and his wife sold controlling interest in their company three months before the first green people appeared.

9

"I remember when you knew what a human being was," Evan said sadly. "I suppose I'm old fashioned, but there it is."

From her cradle, inside a mist of spray, his wife said, "Is that why you never went green? I always thought it was a fashion statement."

"Old habits die hard." The truth was, he liked his body the way it was. These days, going green involved somatic mutation which grew a metre-high black cowl to absorb sufficient light energy. Most people lived in the tropics, swarms of black-caped anarchists. Work was no longer a necessity, but an indulgence. Evan added, "I'm going to miss you."

"Let's face it," his wife said, "we never were in love. But I'll miss you, too." With a flick of her powerful tail she launched her streamlined body into the sea.

10

Black-cowled post-humans, gliding slowly in the sun, aggregating and reaggregating like amoebae. Dolphinoids, tentacles sheathed under fins, rocking in tanks of cloudy water. Ambulatory starfish; tumbling bushes of spikes; snakes with a single arm, a single leg; flocks of tiny birds, brilliant as emeralds, each flock a single entity.

People, grown strange, infected with myriads of microscopic machines which re-engraved their body form at will.

Evan lived in a secluded estate. He was revered as a founding father of the posthuman revolution. A purple funfur microsaur followed him everywhere. It was recording him because he had elected to die.

"I don't regret anything," Evan said, "except perhaps not following my wife when she changed. I saw it coming, you know. All this. Once the technology became simple enough, cheap enough, the companies lost control. Like television or computers, but I suppose you don't remember those." He sighed. He had the vague feeling he'd said all this before. He'd had no new thoughts for a century, except the desire to put an end to thought.

The microsaur said, "In a way, I suppose I am a computer. Will you see the colonial delegation now?"

"Later." Evan hobbled to a bench and slowly sat down. In the last couple of months he had developed mild arthritis, liver spots on the backs of his hands: death finally expressing parts of his genome that had been suppressed for so long. Hot sunlight fell through the velvet streamers of the tree things; Evan dozed, woke to find a group of starfish watching him. They had blue, human eyes, one at the tip of each muscular arm.

"They wish to honour you by taking your genome to Mars," the little purple triceratops said.

Evan sighed. "I just want peace. To rest. To die."

"Oh, Evan," the little triceratops said patiently, "surely even you know that nothing really dies anymore."

WANG'S CARPETS

Greg Egan

❀

Greg Egan (born 1961) is the most prominent SF writer from Australia on the world stage. He has a degree in mathematics and has worked as a computer programmer, mostly in jobs supporting medical research. He remains socially isolated from the SF field—almost no one in the field has met him in person—and he has written a strongly worded attack on national identities in SF. He does not identify himself as an Australian SF writer, but as a writer of SF in the English language who happens to live in Australia. His Web site (www.netspace.net.au/~gregegan) reprints several interviews that yield some further insight into Egan, perhaps the most interesting hard SF writer to emerge in the 1990s. He says, "I have a vision of a universe that we're increasingly able to understand through science—and that includes understanding who we are, where we came from, and why we do the things we do. What drives me is the desire to explore both the details of this vision, for their own sake—things like quantum mechanics and cosmology, simply because they're beautiful and elaborate and fascinating—but also the ways in which we can adapt to this situation, and use what we're learning constructively." And "I don't think SF will ever be enough, but it's the easiest place to start examining new technologies, a few decades (or centuries, sometimes) before anyone else is discussing them."

His first novel (not SF) was published in 1983. His SF writing burst into prominence in 1990 along with several fine stories that focussed attention on his science fiction and launched his books. His SF novels to date are *Quarantine* (1992), *Permutation City* (1994), *Distress* (1995), *Diaspora* (1997), *Teranesia* (1999), and *Schild's Ladder* (2001), a disaster novel on a cosmic scale. His short story collections are *Our Lady of Chernobyl* (1995), *Axiomatic* (1995), and *Luminous* (1999).

"Wang's Carpets" first appeared in editor Greg Bear's flagship SF anthology, *New Legends* (1995) (which, along with *Far Futures* [ed. Gregory Benford], was one of the two most ambitious and important original anthologies of the decade for hard SF). It is one of Egan's finest stories to date. Though "Wang's Carpets" is most memorable for the image of a naturally-occurring computer program in which exists virtual life, this is contrasted with a solipsistic transhumanity: nearly immortal post-humans who search the universe for non-human intelligence because their survival depends on finding that the universe is not just all about them. Identity and gender are changed at will; physical appearance is manifested at will. Their identities have become so fluid that they search for an Other to define themselves in opposition to.

Stories such as this seem far beyond the political issues of today, though Egan is not apolitical. Egan said, "When I write about the far future, I'm not interested in pretending that all our current problems—things like disease, poverty, war and racism—are going to be with us for the next ten thousand years. Human nature is a physical thing, and eventually we'll transform it as much as we like. But those 'temporary' problems are still enormously important to us, right now. So, although I've written a couple of short stories since *Diaspora* which share the idea that in the long run we'll find software the most convenient form—especially for space travel—I'm backing off now, and concentrating on the near future."

There is a literary politics implicit in the subtext of "Wang's Carpets": The solipsism of what remains of humanity might be seen to stand in for the post-modern/post-structuralist lit-crit point of view that the world as we perceive it, and even science, is a symbolic construct of language; it's contrasted here to the scientific stance that there is a real universe out there to which words must refer and which they can only in part represent—mathematics is the foundation of science. Being a hard SF writer, Egan of course comes down on the side of science.

Waiting to be cloned one thousand times and scattered across ten million cubic light-years, Paolo Venetti relaxed in his favorite ceremonial bathtub: a tiered hexagonal pool set in a courtyard of black marble flecked with gold. Paolo wore full traditional anatomy, uncomfortable garb at first, but the warm currents flowing across his back and shoulders slowly eased him into a pleasant torpor. He could have reached the same state in an instant, by decree—but the occasion seemed to demand the complete ritual of verisimilitude, the ornate curlicued longhand of imitation physical cause and effect.

As the moment of diaspora approached, a small gray lizard darted across the courtyard, claws scrabbling. It halted by the far edge of the pool, and Paolo marveled at the delicate pulse of its breathing, and watched the lizard watching him, until it moved again, disappearing into the surrounding vineyards. The environment was full of birds and insects, rodents and small reptiles—decorative in appearance, but also satisfying a more abstract aesthetic: softening the harsh radial symmetry of the lone observer; anchoring the simulation by perceiving it from a multitude of viewpoints. Ontological guy lines. No one had asked the lizards if they wanted to be cloned, though. They were coming along for the ride, like it or not.

The sky above the courtyard was warm and blue, cloudless and sunless, isotropic. Paolo waited calmly, prepared for every one of half a dozen possible fates.

An invisible bell chimed softly, three times. Paolo laughed, delighted.

One chime would have meant that he was still on Earth: an anticlimax, certainly—but there would have been advantages to compensate for that. Everyone who really mattered to him lived in the Carter-Zimmerman polis, but not all of them had chosen to take part in the diaspora to the same degree; his Earth-self would have lost no one. Helping to ensure that the thousand ships were safely dispatched would have been satisfying, too. And remaining a member of the wider Earth-based community, plugged into the entire global culture in real time, would have been an attraction in itself.

Two chimes would have meant that this clone of Carter-Zimmerman had reached a planetary system devoid of life. Paolo had run a sophisticated—but nonsapient—self-predictive model before deciding to wake under those conditions. Exploring a handful of alien worlds, however barren, had seemed likely to be an enriching experience for him—with the distinct advantage that the whole endeavor would be untrammeled by the kind of elaborate precautions necessary in the presence of alien life. C-Z's population would have fallen by more than half—and many of his closest friends would have been absent—but he would have forged new friendships, he was sure.

Four chimes would have signaled the discovery of intelligent aliens. Five, a technological civilization. Six, spacefarers.

Three chimes, though, meant that the scout probes had detected unambiguous signs of life—and that was reason enough for jubilation. Up until the moment of the prelaunch cloning—a subjective instant before the chimes had sounded—no reports of alien life had ever reached Earth. There'd been no guarantee that any part of the diaspora would find it.

Paolo willed the polis library to brief him; it promptly rewired the declarative memory of his simulated traditional brain with all the information he was likely to need to satisfy his immediate curiosity. This clone of C-Z had arrived at Vega, the second closest of the thousand target stars, twenty-seven light-years from Earth. Paolo closed his eyes and visualized a star map with a thousand lines radiating out from the sun, then zoomed in on the trajectory that described his own journey. It had taken three centuries to reach Vega—but the vast majority of the polis's twenty thousand inhabitants had programmed their exoselves to suspend them prior to the cloning and to wake them only if and when they arrived at a suitable destination. Ninety-two citizens had chosen the alternative: experiencing every voyage of the diaspora from start to finish, risking disappointment, and even death. Paolo now knew that the ship aimed at Fomalhaut, the target nearest Earth, had been struck by debris and annihilated *en route*. He mourned the ninety-two, briefly. He hadn't been close to any of them, prior to the cloning, and the particular versions who'd willfully perished two centuries ago in interstellar space seemed as remote as the victims of some ancient calamity from the era of flesh.

Paolo examined his new home star through the cameras of one of the scout probes—and the strange filters of the ancestral visual system. In traditional colors, Vega was a fierce blue-white disk, laced with prominences. Three times the mass of the sun, twice the size and twice as hot, sixty times as luminous. Burning hydrogen fast—and already halfway through its allotted five hundred million years on the main sequence.

Vega's sole planet, Orpheus, had been a featureless blip to the best lunar interferometers; now Paolo gazed down on its blue-green crescent, ten thousand kilometers below Carter-Zimmerman itself. Orpheus was terrestrial, a nickel-iron-silicate world; slightly larger than Earth, slightly warmer—a billion kilometers took the edge off Vega's heat—and almost drowning in liquid water. Impatient to see the whole surface firsthand, Paolo slowed his clock rate a thousandfold, allowing C-Z to circumnavigate the planet in twenty subjective seconds, daylight unshrouding a broad new swath with each pass. Two slender ocher-colored continents with mountainous spines bracketed hemispheric oceans, and dazzling expanses of pack ice covered both poles—far more so in the north, where jagged white peninsulas radiated out from the midwinter arctic darkness.

The Orphean atmosphere was mostly nitrogen—six times as much as on Earth; probably split by UV from primordial ammonia—with traces of water vapor and carbon dioxide, but not enough of either for a runaway greenhouse effect. The high atmospheric pressure meant reduced evaporation—Paolo saw not a wisp of cloud—and the large, warm oceans in turn helped feed carbon dioxide back into the crust, locking it up in limestone sediments destined for subduction.

The whole system was young, by Earth standards, but Vega's greater mass, and a denser protostellar cloud, would have meant swifter passage through most of the traumas of birth: nuclear ignition and early luminosity fluctuations; planetary coalescence and the age of bombardments. The library estimated that Orpheus had enjoyed a relatively stable climate, and freedom from major impacts, for at least the past hundred million years.

Long enough for primitive life to appear—

A hand seized Paolo firmly by the ankle and tugged him beneath the water. He offered no resistance, and let the vision of the planet slip away. Only two other people in C-Z had free access to this environment—and his father didn't play games with his now-twelve-hundred-year-old son.

Elena dragged him all the way to the bottom of the pool, before releasing his foot and hovering above him, a triumphant silhouette against the bright surface. She was ancestor-shaped, but obviously cheating; she spoke with perfect clarity; and no air bubbles at all.

"Late sleeper! I've been waiting seven weeks for this!"

Paolo feigned indifference, but he was fast running out of breath. He had his exoself convert him into an amphibious human variant—biologically and historically authentic, if no longer the definitive ancestral phenotype. Water flooded into his modified lungs, and his modified brain welcomed it.

He said, "Why would I want to waste consciousness, sitting around waiting for the scout probes to refine their observations? I woke as soon as the data was unambiguous."

She pummeled his chest; he reached up and pulled her down, instinctively reducing his buoyancy to compensate, and they rolled across the bottom of the pool, kissing.

Elena said, "You know we're the first C-Z to arrive, anywhere? The Fomalhaut ship was destroyed. So there's only one other pair of us. Back on Earth."

"So?" Then he remembered. Elena had chosen not to wake if any other version of her had already encountered life. Whatever fate befell each of the remaining ships, every other version of him would have to live without her.

He nodded soberly, and kissed her again. "What am I meant to say? You're a thousand times more precious to me, now?"

"Yes."

"Ah, but what about the you-and-I on Earth? Five hundred times would be closer to the truth."

"There's no poetry in five hundred."

"Don't be so defeatist. Rewire your language centers."

She ran her hands along the sides of his rib cage, down to his hips. They made love with their almost-traditional bodies—and brains; Paolo was amused to the point of distraction when his limbic system went into overdrive, but he remembered enough from the last occasion to bury his self-consciousness and surrender to the strange hijacker. It wasn't like making love in any civilized fashion—the rate of information exchange between them was minuscule, for a start—but it had the raw insistent quality of most ancestral pleasures.

Then they drifted up to the surface of the pool and lay beneath the radiant sunless sky.

Paolo thought, *I've crossed twenty-seven light-years in an instant. I'm orbiting the first planet ever found to hold alien life. And I've sacrificed nothing—left nothing I truly value behind. This is too good, too good.* He felt a pang of regret for his other selves—it was hard to imagine them faring as well, without Elena, without Orpheus—but there was nothing he could do about that now. Although there'd be time to confer with Earth before any more ships reached their destinations, he'd decided—prior to the cloning—not to allow the unfolding of his manifold future to be swayed by any change of heart. Whether or not his Earth-self agreed, the two of them were powerless to alter the criteria for waking. The self with the right to choose for the thousand had passed away.

No matter, Paolo decided. The others would find—or construct—their own reasons for happiness. And there was still the chance that one of them would wake to the sound of *four chimes*.

Elena said, "If you'd slept much longer, you would have missed the vote."

The vote? The scouts in low orbit had gathered what data they could about Orphean biology. To proceed any farther, it would be necessary to send microprobes into the ocean itself—an escalation of contact that required the approval of two-thirds of the polis. There was no compelling reason to believe that the presence of a few million tiny robots could do any harm; all they'd leave behind in the water was a few kilojoules of waste heat. Nevertheless, a faction had arisen that advocated caution. The citizens of Carter-Zimmerman, they argued, could continue to observe from a distance for another decade, or another millennium, refining their observations and hypotheses before intruding . . . and those who disagreed could always sleep away the time, or find other interests to pursue.

Paolo delved into his library-fresh knowledge of the "carpets"—the single Orphean life-form detected so far. They were free-floating creatures living in the equatorial ocean depths—apparently destroyed by UV if they drifted too close to the surface. They grew to a size of hundreds of meters, then fissioned into dozens of fragments, each of which continued to grow. It was tempting to assume that they were colonies of single-celled organisms, something like giant kelp—but there was no real evidence yet to back that up. It was difficult enough for the scout probes to discern the carpets' gross appearance and behavior through a kilometer of water, even with Vega's copious neutrinos lighting the way; remote observations on a microscopic scale, let alone biochemical analyses, were out of the question. Spectroscopy revealed that the surface water was full of intriguing molecular debris—but guessing the relationship of any of it to the living carpets was like trying to reconstruct human biochemistry by studying human ashes.

Paolo turned to Elena. "What do you think?"

She moaned theatrically; the topic must have been argued to death while he slept. "The microprobes are harmless. They could tell us exactly what the carpets are made of, without removing a single molecule. What's the risk? *Culture shock?*"

Paolo flicked water onto her face, affectionately; the impulse seemed to come with the amphibian body. "You can't be sure that they're not intelligent."

"Do you know what was living on Earth, two hundred million years after it was formed?"

"Maybe cyanobacteria. Maybe nothing. This isn't Earth, though."

"True. But even in the unlikely event that the carpets are intelligent, do you think they'd notice the presence of robots a millionth their size? If they're unified organisms, they don't appear to react to anything in their environment—they have no predators, they don't pursue food, they just drift with the currents—so there's no reason for them to possess elaborate sense organs at all, let alone anything working on a submillimeter scale. And if they're colonies of single-celled creatures, one of which happens to collide with a microprobe and register its presence with surface receptors . . . what conceivable harm could that do?"

"I have no idea. But my ignorance is no guarantee of safety."

Elena splashed him back. "The only way to deal with your *ignorance* is to vote to send down the microprobes. We have to be cautious, I agree—but there's no point *being here* if we don't find out what's happening in the oceans right now. I don't want to wait for this planet to evolve something smart enough to broadcast biochemistry lessons into space. If we're not willing to take a few infinitesimal risks, Vega will turn red giant before we learn anything."

It was a throwaway line—but Paolo tried to imagine witnessing the event. In a quarter of a billion years, would the citizens of Carter-Zimmerman be debating the ethics of intervening to rescue the Orpheans—or would they all have lost interest, and departed for other stars, or modified themselves into beings entirely devoid of nostalgic compassion for organic life?

Grandiose visions for a twelve-hundred-year-old. The Fomalhaut clone had been obliterated by one tiny piece of rock. There was far more junk in the Vegan system than in interstellar space; even ringed by defenses, its data backed up to all the far-flung scout probes, this C-Z was not invulnerable just because it had arrived intact. Elena was right; they had to seize the moment—or they might as well retreat into their own hermetic worlds and forget that they'd ever made the journey.

Paolo recalled the honest puzzlement of a friend from Ashton-Laval, *Why go looking for aliens? Our polis has a thousand ecologies, a trillion species of evolved life. What do you hope to find, out there, that you couldn't have grown at home?*

What had he hoped to find? Just the answers to a few simple questions. Did human consciousness bootstrap all of space-time into existence, in order to explain itself? Or had a neutral, preexisting universe given birth to a billion varieties of conscious life, all capable of harboring the same delusions of grandeur—until they collided with each other? Anthrocosmology was used to justify the inward-looking stance of most polises: if the physical universe was created by human thought, it had no special status that placed it above virtual reality. It might have come first—and every virtual reality might need to run on a physical computing device, subject to physical laws—but it occupied no privileged position in terms of "truth" versus "illusion." If the ACs were right, then it was no more *honest* to value the physical universe over more recent artificial realities than it was honest to remain flesh instead of software, or ape instead of human, or bacterium instead of ape.

Elena said, "We can't lie here forever; the gang's all waiting to see you."

"Where?" Paolo felt his first pang of homesickness; on Earth, his circle of friends had always met in a real-time image of the Mount Pinatubo crater, plucked straight from the observation satellites. A recording wouldn't be the same.

"I'll show you."

Paolo reached over and took her hand. The pool, the sky, the courtyard vanished—and he found himself gazing down on Orpheus again . . . night-side, but far from dark, with his full mental palette now encoding everything from the pale wash of ground-current long-wave radio, to the multicolored shimmer of isotopic gamma rays and back-scattered cosmic-ray *bremsstrahlung*. Half the abstract knowledge the library had fed him about the planet was obvious at a glance, now. The ocean's smoothly tapered thermal glow spelt *three hundred Kelvin* instantly—as well as backlighting the atmosphere's tell-tale infrared silhouette.

He was standing on a long, metallic-looking girder, one edge of a vast geodesic sphere, open to the blazing cathedral of space. He glanced up and saw the star-rich dust-clogged band of the Milky Way, encircling him from zenith to nadir, aware of the glow of every gas cloud, discerning each absorption and emission line. Paolo could almost feel the plane of the galactic disk transect him. Some constellations were distorted, but the view was more familiar than strange—and he recognized most of the old signposts by color. He had his bearings now. Twenty degrees away from Sirius—south, by parochial Earth reckoning—faint but unmistakable: the sun.

Elena was beside him—superficially unchanged, although they'd both shrugged off the constraints of biology. The conventions of this environment mimicked the physics of real macroscopic objects in free fall and vacuum, but it wasn't set up to model any kind of chemistry, let alone that of flesh and blood. Their new bodies were human-shaped, but devoid of elaborate microstructure—and their minds weren't embedded in the physics at all, but were running directly on the processor web.

Paolo was relieved to be back to normal; ceremonial regression to the ancestral form was a venerable C-Z tradition—and being human was largely self-affirming, while it lasted—but every time he emerged from the experience, he felt as if he'd broken free of billion-year-old shackles. There were polises on Earth where the citizens would have found his present structure almost as archaic: a consciousness dominated by sensory perception, an illusion of possessing solid form, a single time coordinate. The last flesh human had died long before Paolo was constructed, and apart from the communities of Gleisner robots, Carter-Zimmerman was about as conservative as a transhuman society could be. The balance seemed right to Paolo, though—acknowledging the flexibility of software, without abandoning interest in the physical world—and although the stubbornly corporeal Gleisners had been first to the stars, the C-Z diaspora would soon overtake them.

Their friends gathered round, showing off their effortless free-fall acrobatics, greeting Paolo and chiding him for not arranging to wake sooner; he was the last of the gang to emerge from hibernation.

"Do you like our humble new meeting place?" Hermann floated by Paolo's shoulder, a chimeric cluster of limbs and sense organs, speaking through the vacuum in modulated infrared. "We call it Satellite Pinatubo. It's desolate up here, I know—but we were afraid it might violate the spirit of caution if we dared pretend to walk the Orphean surface."

Paolo glanced mentally at a scout probe's close-up of a typical stretch of dry land, and expanse of fissured red rock. "More desolate down there, I think." He was tempted to touch the ground—to let the private vision become tactile—but he resisted. Being elsewhere in the middle of a conversation was bad etiquette.

"Ignore Hermann," Liesl advised. "He wants to flood Orpheus with our alien machinery before we have any idea what the effects might be." Liesl was a green-and-turquoise butterfly, with a stylized human face stippled in gold on each wing.

Paolo was surprised; from the way Elena had spoken, he'd assumed that his friends must have come to a consensus in favor of the microprobes—and only a late sleeper, new to the issues, would bother to argue the point. "What effects? The carpets—"

"Forget the carpets! Even if the carpets are as simple as they look, we don't know what else is down there." As Liesl's wings fluttered, her mirror image faces seemed to glance at each other for support. "With neutrino imaging, we barely achieve spatial resolution in meters, time resolution in seconds. We don't know anything about smaller life-forms."

"And we never will, if you have your way." Karpal—an ex-Gleisner, human-shaped as ever—had been Liesl's lover last time Paolo was awake.

"We've only been here for a fraction of an Orphean year! There's still a wealth of data we could gather nonintrusively, with a little patience. There might be rare beachings of ocean life—"

Elena said dryly, "Rare indeed. Orpheus has negligible tides, shallow waves, very few storms. And anything beached would be fried by UV before we glimpsed anything more instructive than we're already seeing in the surface water."

"Not necessarily. The carpets seem to be vulnerable—but other species might be better protected, if they live nearer to the surface. And Orpheus is seismically active; we should at least wait for a tsunami to dump a few cubic kilometers of ocean onto a shoreline, and see what it reveals."

Paolo smiled; he hadn't thought of that. A tsunami might be worth waiting for.

Liesl continued, "What is there to lose by waiting a few hundred Orphean years?

At the very least, we could gather baseline data on seasonal climate patterns—and we could watch for anomalies, storms and quakes, hoping for some revelatory glimpses."

A few hundred Orphean years? A *few terrestrial millennia?* Paolo's ambivalence waned. If he'd wanted to inhabit geological time, he would have migrated to the Lokhande polis, where the Order of Contemplative Observers watched Earth's mountains erode in subjective seconds. Orpheus hung in the sky beneath them, a beautiful puzzle waiting to be decoded, demanding to be understood.

He said, "But what if there are no 'revelatory glimpses'? How long do we wait? We don't know how rare life is—in time, or in space. If this planet is precious, *so is the epoch it's passing through.* We don't know how rapidly Orphean biology is evolving; species might appear and vanish while we agonize over the risks of gathering better data. The carpets—and whatever else—could die out before we'd learned the first thing about them. What a waste that would be!"

Liesl stood her ground.

"And if we damage the Orphean ecology—or culture—by rushing in? That wouldn't be a waste. It would be a tragedy."

Paolo assimilated all the stored transmissions from his earth-self—almost three hundred years' worth—before composing a reply. The early communications included detailed mind grafts—and it was good to share the excitement of the diaspora's launch; to watch—very nearly firsthand—the thousand ships, nanomachine-carved from asteroids, depart in a blaze of fusion fire from beyond the orbit of Mars. Then things settled down to the usual prosaic matters: Elena, the gang, shameless gossip, Carter-Zimmerman's ongoing research projects, the buzz of interpolis cultural tensions, the not-quite-cyclic convulsions of the arts (the perceptual aesthetic overthrows the emotional, again . . . although Valladas in Konishi polis claims to have constructed a new synthesis of the two).

After the first fifty years, his Earth-self had begun to hold things back; by the time news reached Earth of the Fomalhaut clones' demise, the messages had become pure audiovisual linear monologues. Paolo understood. It was only right; they'd diverged, and you didn't send mind grafts to strangers.

Most of the transmissions had been broadcast to all of the ships, indiscriminately. Forty-three years ago, though, his Earth-self had sent a special message to the Vega-bound clone.

"The new lunar spectroscope we finished last year has just picked up clear signs of water on Orpheus. There should be large temperate oceans waiting for you, if the models are right. So . . . good luck." Vision showed the instrument's domes growing out of the rock of the lunar farside; plots of the Orphean spectral data; an ensemble of planetary models. "Maybe it seems strange to you—all the trouble we're taking to catch a glimpse of what you're going to see in close-up so soon. It's hard to explain: I don't think it's jealousy, or even impatience. Just a need for independence.

"There's been a revival of the old debate: Should we consider redesigning our minds to encompass interstellar distances? One self spanning thousands of stars, not via cloning, but through acceptance of the natural time scale of the light-speed lag. Millennia passing between mental events. Local contingencies dealt with by nonconscious systems." Essays, pro and con, were appended; Paolo ingested summaries. "I don't think the idea will gain much support though—and the new astronomical projects are something of an antidote. We have to make peace with the fact that we've stayed behind . . . so we cling to the Earth—looking outward, but remaining firmly anchored.

"I keep asking myself, though: Where do we go from here? History can't guide us. Evolution can't guide us. The C-Z charter says *understand and respect the universe* . . . but in what form? On what scale? With what kind of senses, what kind of minds? We can become anything at all—and that space of possible futures dwarfs the galaxy. Can we explore it without losing our way? Flesh humans used to spin fantasies about aliens arriving to 'conquer' Earth, to steal their 'precious' physical resources, to wipe them out for fear of 'competition' . . . as if a species capable of making the journey wouldn't have had the power, or the wit, or the imagination, to rid itself of obsolete biological imperatives. *Conquering the galaxy* is what bacteria with spaceships would do—knowing no better, having no choice.

"Our condition is the opposite of that: we have no end of choices. That's why we need to find alien life—not just to break the spell of the anthrocosmologists. We need to find aliens who've faced the same decisions—and discovered how to live, what to become. We need to understand what it means to inhabit the universe."

Paolo watched the crude neutrino images of the carpets moving in staccato jerks around his dodecahedral room. Twenty-four ragged oblongs drifted above him, daughters of a larger ragged oblong that had just fissioned. Models suggested that shear forces from ocean currents could explain the whole process, triggered by nothing more than the parent reaching a critical size. The purely mechanical break-up of a colony—if that was what it was—might have little to do with the life cycle of the constituent organisms. It was frustrating. Paolo was accustomed to a torrent of data on anything that caught his interest; for the diaspora's great discovery to remain nothing more than a sequence of coarse monochrome snapshots was intolerable.

He glanced at a schematic of the scout probes' neutrino detectors, but there was no obvious scope for improvement. Nuclei in the detectors were excited into unstable high-energy states, then kept there by fine-tuned gamma-ray lasers picking off lower-energy eigenstates faster than they could creep into existence and attract a transition. Changes in neutrino flux of one part in ten-to-the-fifteenth could shift the energy levels far enough to disrupt the balancing act. The carpets cast a shadow so faint, though, that even this near-perfect vision could barely resolve it.

Orlando Venetti said, "You're awake."

Paolo turned. His father stood an arm's length away, presenting as an ornately clad human of indeterminate age. Definitely older than Paolo, though; Orlando never ceased to play up his seniority—even if the age difference was only twenty-five percent now, and falling.

Paolo banished the carpets from the room to the space behind one pentagonal window, and took his father's hand. The portions of Orlando's mind that meshed with his own expressed pleasure at Paolo's emergence from hibernation, fondly dwelt on past shared experiences, and entertained hopes of continued harmony between father and son. Paolo's greeting was similar, a carefully contrived "revelation" of his own emotional state. It was more of a ritual than an act of communication—but then, even with Elena, he set up barriers. No one was totally honest with another person—unless the two of them intended to permanently fuse.

Orlando nodded at the carpets. "I hope you appreciate how important they are."

"You know I do." He hadn't included that in his greeting, though. "First alien life." *C-Z humiliates the Gleisner robots, at last*—that was probably how his father saw it. The robots had been first to Alpha Centauri, and first to an extrasolar planet—but first life was Apollo to their Sputniks, for anyone who chose to think in those terms.

Orlando said, "This is the book we need, to catch the citizens of the marginal polises. The ones who haven't quite imploded into solipsism. This will shake them up—don't you think?"

Paolo shrugged. Earth's transhumans were free to implode into anything they liked; it didn't stop Carter-Zimmerman from exploring the physical universe. But thrashing the Gleisners wouldn't be enough for Orlando; he lived for the day when C-Z would become the cultural mainstream. Any polis could multiply its population a billionfold in a microsecond, if it wanted the vacuous honor of outnumbering the rest. Luring other citizens to migrate was harder—and persuading them to rewrite their own local charters was harder still. Orlando had a missionary streak: he wanted every other polis to see the error of its ways and follow C-Z to the stars.

Paolo said, "Ashton-Laval has intelligent aliens. I wouldn't be so sure that news of giant seaweed is going to take Earth by storm."

Orlando was venomous. "Ashton-Laval intervened in its so-called 'evolutionary' simulations so many times that they might as well have built the end products in an act of creation lasting six days. They wanted talking reptiles, and—*mirabile dictu!*—they got talking reptiles. There are self-modified transhumans in *this polis* more alien than the aliens in Ashton-Laval."

Paolo smiled. "All right. Forget Ashton-Laval. But forget the marginal polises, too. We choose to value the physical world. That's what defines *us*—but it's as arbitrary as any other choice of values. Why can't you accept that? It's not the One True Path that the infidels have to be bludgeoned into following." He knew he was arguing half for the sake of it—he desperately wanted to refute the anthrocosmologists himself—but Orlando always drove him into taking the opposite position. Out of fear of being nothing but his father's clone. Despite the total absence of inherited episodic memories the stochastic input into his ontogenesis, the chaotically divergent nature of the iterative mind-building algorithms.

Orlando made a beckoning gesture, dragging the image of the carpets halfway back into the room. "You'll vote for the microprobes?"

"Of course."

"Everything depends on that now. It's good to start with a tantalizing glimpse—but if we don't follow up with details soon, they'll lose interest back on Earth very rapidly."

"Lose interest? It'll be fifty-four years before we know if anyone paid the slightest attention in the first place."

Orlando eyed him with disappointment, and resignation. "If you don't care about the other polises, think about C-Z. This helps us; it strengthens us. We have to make the most of that."

Paolo was bemused. "The charter is the charter. What needs to be strengthened? You make it sound like there's something at risk."

"What do you think a thousand lifeless worlds would have done to us? Do you think the charter would have remained intact?"

Paolo had never considered the scenario. "Maybe not. But in every C-Z where the charter was rewritten, there would have been citizens who'd have gone off and founded new polises on the old lines. You and I, for a start. We could have called it Venetti-Venetti."

"While half your friends turned their backs on the physical world? While Carter-Zimmerman, after two thousand years, went solipsist? You'd be happy with that?"

Paolo laughed. "No—but it's not going to happen, is it? *We've found life.* All right, I agree with you: this strengthens C-Z. The diaspora might have 'failed' . . . but it didn't. We've been lucky. I'm glad, I'm grateful. Is that what you wanted to hear?"

Orlando said sourly, "You take too much for granted."

"And you care too much what I think! I'm not your . . . heir." Orlando was first-generation, scanned from flesh—and there were times when he seemed unable to accept that the whole concept of generation had lost its archaic significance. "You don't need me to safeguard the future of Carter-Zimmerman on your behalf. Or the future of transhumanity. You can do it in person."

Orlando looked wounded—a conscious choice, but it still encoded something. Paolo felt a pang of regret—but he'd said nothing he could honestly retract.

His father gathered up the sleeves of his gold and crimson robes—the only citizen of C-Z who could make Paolo uncomfortable to be naked—and repeated as he vanished from the room: "You take too much for granted."

The gang watched the launch of the microprobes together—even Liesl, though she came in mourning, as a giant dark bird. Karpai stroked her feathers nervously. Hermann appeared as a creature out of Escher, a segmented worm with six human-shaped feet—on legs with elbows—given to curling up into a disk and rolling along the girders of Satellite Pinatubo. Paolo and Elena kept saying the same thing simultaneously; they'd just made love.

Hermann had moved the satellite to a notional orbit just below one of the scout probes—and changed the environment's scale, so that the probe's lower surface, an intricate landscape of detector modules and attitude-control jets, blotted out half the sky. The atmospheric-entry capsules—ceramic teardrops three centimeters wide—burst from their launch tube and hurtled past like boulders, vanishing from sight before they'd fallen so much as ten meters closer to Orpheus. It was all scrupulously accurate, although it was part real-time imagery, part extrapolation, part *faux*. Paolo thought, *We might as well have run a pure simulation . . . and pretended to follow the capsules down*. Elena gave him a guilty/admonishing look. *Yeah—and then why bother actually launching them at all? Why not just simulate a plausible Orphean ocean full of plausible Orphean life-forms? Why not simulate the whole diaspora?* There was no crime of heresy in C-Z; no one had ever been exiled for breaking the charter. At times it still felt like a tightrope walk; though, trying to classify every act of simulation into those that contributed to an understanding of the physical universe (good), those that were merely convenient, recreational, aesthetic (acceptable) . . . and those that constituted a denial of the primacy of real phenomena (time to think about emigration).

The vote on the microprobes had been close: seventy-two percent in favor, just over the required two-thirds majority, with five percent abstaining. (Citizens created since the arrival at Vega were excluded . . . not that anyone in Carter-Zimmerman would have dreamt of stacking the ballot, perish the thought.) Paolo had been surprised at the narrow margin; he'd yet to hear a single plausible scenario for the microprobes doing harm. He wondered if there was another, unspoken reason that had nothing to do with fears for the Orphean ecology, or hypothetical culture. *A wish to prolong the pleasure of unraveling the planet's mysteries?* Paolo had some sympathy with that impulse—but the launch of the microprobes would do nothing to undermine the greater long-term pleasure of watching, and understanding, as Orphean life evolved.

Liesl said forlornly, "Coastline erosion models show that the north-western shore of Lambda is inundated by tsunami every ninety Orphean years, on average." She offered the data to them; Paolo glanced at it, and it looked convincing—but the point was academic now. "We could have waited."

Hermann waved his eye-stalks at her. "Beaches covered in fossils, are they?"

"No, but the conditions hardly—"

"No excuses!" He wound his body around a girder, kicking his legs gleefully. Hermann was first-generation, even older than Orlando; he'd been scanned in the twenty-first century, before Carter-Zimmerman existed. Over the centuries, though, he'd wiped most of his episodic memories, and rewritten his personality a dozen times. He'd once told Paolo, "I think of myself as my own great-great-grandson. Death's not so bad, if you do it incrementally. Ditto for immortality."

Elena said, "I keep trying to imagine how it will feel if another C-Z clone stumbles on something infinitely better—like aliens with wormhole drives—while we're back here studying rafts of algae." The body she wore was more stylized than usual—still humanoid, but sexless, hairless, and smooth, the face inexpressive and androgynous.

"If they have wormhole drives, they might visit us. Or share the technology, so we can link up the whole diaspora."

"If they have wormhole drives, where have they been for the last two thousand years?"

Paolo laughed. "Exactly. But I know what you mean, *First alien life* . . . and it's likely to be about as sophisticated as seaweed. It breaks the jinx, though. Seaweed every twenty-seven light-years. Nervous systems every fifty? Intelligence every hundred?" He fell silent, abruptly realizing what she was feeling: electing not to wake again after first life was beginning to seem like the wrong choice, a waste of the opportunities the diaspora had created. Paolo offered her a mind graft expressing empathy and support, but she declined.

She said, "I want sharp borders, right now. I want to deal with this myself."

"I understand." He let the partial model of her that he'd acquired as they'd made love fade from his mind. It was nonsapient, and no longer linked to her—but to retain it any longer when she felt this way would have seemed like a transgression. Paolo took the responsibilities of intimacy seriously. His lover before Elena had asked him to erase all his knowledge of her, and he'd more or less complied—the only thing he still knew about her was the fact that she'd made the request.

Hermann announced, "Planetfall!" Paolo glanced at a replay of a scout probe view that showed the first few entry capsules breaking up above the ocean and releasing their microprobes. Nanomachines transformed the ceramic shields (and then themselves) into carbon dioxide and a few simple minerals—nothing the micrometeorites constantly raining down onto Orpheus didn't contain—before the fragments could strike the water. The microprobes would broadcast nothing; when they'd finished gathering data, they'd float to the surface and modulate their UV reflectivity. It would be up to the scout probes to locate these specks, and read their messages, before they self-destructed as thoroughly as the entry capsules.

Hermann said, "This calls for a celebration. I'm heading for the Heart. Who'll join me?"

Paolo glanced at Elena. She shook her head. "You go."

"Are you sure?"

"Yes! Go on." Her skin had taken on a mirrored sheen; her expressionless face reflected the planet below. "I'm all right. I just want some time to think things through, on my own."

Hermann coiled around the satellite's frame, stretching his pale body as he went, gaining segments, gaining legs. "Come on, come on! Karpal? Liesl? Come and celebrate!"

Elena was gone. Liesl made a derisive sound and flapped off into the distance, mocking the environment's airlessness. Paolo and Karpal watched as Hermann grew longer and faster—and then in a blur of speed and change stretched out to wrap the entire geodesic frame. Paolo demagnetized his feet and moved away, laughing; Karpal did the same.

Then Hermann constricted like a boa and snapped the whole satellite apart.

They floated for a while, two human-shaped machines and a giant worm in a cloud of spinning metal fragments, an absurd collection of imaginary debris, glinting by the light of the true stars.

The heart was always crowded, but it was larger than Paolo had seen it—even though Hermann had shrunk back to his original size, so as not to make a scene. The huge, muscular chamber arched above them, pulsating wetly in time to the music, as they searched for the perfect location to soak up the atmosphere. Paolo had visited public environments in other polises, back on Earth; many were designed to be nothing more than a perceptual framework for group emotion-sharing. He'd never understood the attraction of becoming intimate with large numbers of strangers. Ancestral social hierarchies might have had their faults—and it was absurd to try to make a virtue of the limitations imposed by minds confined to wet-ware—but the whole idea of mass telepathy as an end in itself seemed bizarre to Paolo . . . and even old-fashioned, in a way. Humans, clearly, would have benefited from a good strong dose of each other's inner life to keep them from slaughtering each other—but any civilized transhuman could respect and value other citizens without the need to have been them firsthand.

They found a good spot and made some furniture, a table and two chairs—Hermann preferred to stand—and the floor expanded to make room. Paolo looked around, shouting greetings at the people he recognized by sight, but not bothering to check for identity broadcasts from the rest. Chances were he'd met everyone here, but he didn't want to spend the next hour exchanging pleasantries with casual acquaintances.

Hermann said, "I've been monitoring our modest stellar observatory's data stream—my antidote to Vegan parochialism. Odd things are going on around Sirius. We're seeing electron-positron annihilation gamma rays, gravity waves . . . and some unexplained hot spots on Sirius B." He turned to Karpal and asked innocently, "What do you think those robots are up to? There's a rumor that they're planning to drag the white dwarf out of orbit and use it as part of a giant spaceship."

"I never listen to rumors." Karpal always presented as a faithful reproduction of his old human-shaped Gleisner body—and his mind, Paolo gathered, always took the form of a physiological model, even though he was five generations removed from flesh. Leaving his people and coming into C-Z must have taken considerable courage; they'd never welcome him back.

Paolo said, "Does it matter what they do? Where they go, how they get there? There's more than enough room for both of us. Even if they shadowed the diaspora—even if they came to Vega—we could study the Orpheans together, couldn't we?"

Hermann's cartoon insect face showed mock alarm, eyes growing wider, and wider apart. "Not if they dragged along a white dwarf! Next thing they'd want to start building a Dyson sphere." He turned back to Karpal. "You don't still suffer the urge, do you, for . . . *astrophysical* engineering?"

"Nothing C-Z's exploitation of a few megatons of Vegan asteroid material hasn't satisfied."

Paolo tried to change the subject. "Has anyone heard from Earth, lately? I'm beginning to feel unplugged." His own most recent message was a decade older than the time lag.

Karpal said, "You're not missing much; all they're talking about is Orpheus . . . ever since the new lunar observations, the signs of water. They seem more excited by the mere possibility of life than we are by the certainty. And they have very high hopes."

Paolo laughed. "They do. My Earth-self seems to be counting on the diaspora to find an advanced civilization with the answers to all of transhumanity's existential problems. I don't think he'll get much cosmic guidance from kelp."

"You know there was a big rise in emigration from C-Z after the launch? Emigration, and suicides." Hermann had stopped wriggling and gyrating, becoming almost still, a sign of rare seriousness. "I suspect that's what triggered the astronomy program in the first place. And it seems to have stanched the flow, at least in the short term. Earth C-Z detected water before any clone in the diaspora—and when they hear that we've found life, they'll feel more like collaborators in the discovery because of it."

Paolo felt a stirring of unease. *Emigration and suicides? Was that why Orlando had been so gloomy?* After three hundred years of waiting, how high had expectations become?

A buzz of excitement crossed the floor, a sudden shift in the tone of the conversation. Hermann whispered reverently, "First microprobe has surfaced. And the data is coming in now."

The nonsapient Heart was intelligent enough to guess its patron's wishes. Although everyone could tap the library for results, privately, the music cut out and a giant public image of the summary data appeared, high in the chamber. Paolo had to crane his neck to view it, a novel experience.

The microprobe had mapped one of the carpets in high resolution. The image showed the expected rough oblong, some hundred meters wide—but the two-or-three-meter-thick slab of the neutrino tomographs was revealed now as a delicate, convoluted surface—fine as a single layer of skin, but folded into an elaborate space-filling curve. Paolo checked the full data: the topology was strictly planar despite the pathological appearance. No holes, no joins—just a surface that meandered wildly enough to look ten thousand times thicker from a distance than it really was.

An inset showed the microstructure, at a point that started at the rim of the carpet and then—slowly—moved toward the center. Paolo stared at the flowing molecular diagram for several seconds before he grasped what it meant.

The carpet was not a colony of single-celled creatures. Nor was it a multicellular organism. It was a *single molecule*, a two-dimensional polymer weighing twenty-five million kilograms. A giant sheet of folded polysaccharide, a complex mesh of interlinked pentose and hexose sugars hung with alkyl and amide side chains. A bit like a plant cell wall—except that this polymer was far stronger than cellulose, and the surface area was twenty orders of magnitude greater.

Karpal said, "I hope those entry capsules were perfectly sterile. Earth bacteria would gorge themselves on this. One big floating carbohydrate dinner, with no defenses."

Hermann thought it over. "Maybe. If they had enzymes capable of breaking off a piece—which I doubt. No chance we'll find out, though: even if there'd been bacterial spores lingering in the asteroid belt from early human expeditions, every ship in the diaspora was double-checked for contamination *en route*. We haven't brought smallpox to the Americas."

Paolo was still dazed. "But how does it assemble? How does it . . . grow?" Hermann consulted the library and replied, before Paolo could do the same.

"The edge of the carpet catalyses its own growth. The polymer is irregular, aperiodic—there's no single component that simply repeats. But there seem to be about twenty thousand basic structural units—twenty thousand different polysaccharide building blocks." Paolo saw them: long bundles of cross-linked chains running the whole two-hundred-micron thickness of the carpet, each with a roughly square cross-section, bonded at several thousand points to the four neighboring units. "Even at this depth, the ocean's full of UV-generated radicals that filter down from the surface. Any structural unit exposed to the water converts those radicals into more polysaccharide—and builds another structural unit."

Paolo glanced at the library again, for a simulation of the process. Catalytic sites strewn along the sides of each unit trapped the radicals in place, long enough for new bonds to form between them. Some simple sugars were incorporated straight into the polymer as they were created; others were set free to drift in solution for a microsecond or two, until they were needed. At that level, there were only a few basic chemical tricks being used . . . but molecular evolution must have worked its way up from a few small autocatalytic fragments, first formed by chance, to this elaborate system of twenty thousand mutually self-replicating structures. If the "structural units" had floated free in the ocean as independent molecules, the "life-form" they comprised would have been virtually invisible. By bonding together, though, they became twenty thousand colors in a giant mosaic.

It was astonishing. Paolo hoped Elena was tapping the library, wherever she was. A colony of algae would have been more "advanced"—but this incredible primordial creature revealed infinitely more about the possibilities for the genesis of life. Carbohydrate, here, played every biochemical role: information carrier, enzyme, energy source, structural material. Nothing like it could have survived on Earth, once there were organisms capable of feeding on it—and if there were ever intelligent Orpheans, they'd be unlikely to find any trace of this bizarre ancestor.

Karpal wore a secretive smile.

Paolo said, "What?"

"Wang tiles. The carpets are made out of Wang tiles."

Hermann beat him to the library, again.

"*Wang* as in twentieth-century flesh mathematician, Hao Wang. *Tiles* as in any set of shapes that can cover the plane. Wang tiles are squares with various shaped edges, which have to fit complementary shapes on adjacent squares. You can cover the plane with a set of Wang tiles, as long as you choose the right one every step of the way. Or, in the case of the carpets, grow the right one."

Karpal said, "We should call them. Wang's Carpets, in honor of Hao Wang. After twenty-three hundred years, his mathematics has come to life."

Paolo liked the idea, but he was doubtful. "We may have trouble getting a two-thirds majority on that. It's a bit obscure . . ."

Hermann laughed. "Who needs a two-thirds majority? If we want to call them Wang's Carpets, we can call them Wang's Carpets. There are ninety-seven languages in current use in C-Z—half of them invented since the polis was founded. I don't think we'll be exiled for coining one private name."

Paolo concurred, slightly embarrassed. The truth was, he'd completely forgotten that Hermann and Karpal weren't actually speaking Modern Roman.

The three of them instructed their exoselves to consider the name adopted:

henceforth, they'd hear "carpet" as "Wang's Carpet"—but if they used the term with anyone else, the reverse translation would apply.

Paolo sat and drank in the image of the giant alien: the first life-form encountered by human or transhuman that was not a biological cousin. The death, at last, of the possibility that Earth might be unique.

They hadn't refuted the anthrocosmologists yet, though. Not quite. If, as the ACs claimed, human consciousness was the seed around which all of space-time had crystallized—if the universe was nothing but the simplest orderly explanation for human thought—then there was, strictly speaking, no need for a single alien to exist, anywhere. But the physics that justified human existence couldn't help generating a billion other worlds where life could arise. The ACs would be unmoved by Wang's Carpets; they'd insist that these creatures were physical, if not biological, cousins—merely an unavoidable by-product of anthropogenic, life-enabling physical laws.

The real test wouldn't come until the diaspora—or the Gleisner robots—finally encountered conscious aliens: minds entirely unrelated to humanity, observing and explaining the universe that human thought had supposedly built. Most ACs had come right out and declared such a find impossible; it was the sole falsifiable prediction of their hypothesis. Alien consciousness, as opposed to mere alien life, would always build itself a separate universe—because the chance of two unrelated forms of self-awareness concocting exactly the same physics and the same cosmology was infinitesimal—and any alien biosphere that seemed capable of evolving consciousness would simply never do so.

Paolo glanced at the map of the diaspora, and took heart. *Alien life already*—and the search had barely started; there were nine hundred and ninety-eight target systems yet to be explored. And even if every one of them proved no more conclusive than Orpheus . . . he was prepared to send clones out farther—and prepared to wait. Consciousness had taken far longer to appear on Earth than the quarter-of-a-billion years remaining before Vega left the main sequence—but the whole point of being here, after all, was that Orpheus wasn't Earth.

Orlando's celebration of the microprobe discoveries was a very first-generation affair. The environment was an endless sunlit garden strewn with tables covered in *food*, and the invitation had politely suggested attendance in fully human form. Paolo politely faked it—simulating most of the physiology, but running the body as a puppet, leaving his mind unshackled.

Orlando introduced his new lover, Catherine, who presented as a tall, dark-skinned woman. Paolo didn't recognize her on sight, but checked the identity code she broadcast. It was a small polis; he'd met her once before—as a man called Samuel, one of the physicists who'd worked on the main interstellar fusion drive employed by all the ships of the diaspora. Paolo was amused to think that many of the people here would be seeing his father as a woman. The majority of the citizens of C-Z still practiced the conventions of relative gender that had come into fashion in the twenty-third century—and Orlando had wired them into his own son too deeply for Paolo to wish to abandon them—but whenever the paradoxes were revealed so starkly, he wondered how much longer the conventions would endure. Paolo was same-sex to Orlando, and hence saw his father's lover as a woman, the two close relationships taking precedence over his casual knowledge of Catherine as Samuel. Orlando perceived himself as being male and heterosexual, as his flesh original had been . . . while Samuel saw himself the same way . . . and each perceived the other to be a heterosexual woman. If certain third parties ended up with mixed signals, so be it. It was a typical C-Z compromise: nobody could bear to overturn the old order and do away with gender entirely (as most other polises had done) . . . but nobody could resist the flexibility that being software, not flesh, provided.

Paolo drifted from table to table to table, sampling the food to keep up appearances, wishing Elena had come. There was little conversation about the biology of Wang's Carpets; most of the people here were simply celebrating their win against the opponents of the microprobes—and the humiliation that faction would suffer, now that it was clearer than ever that the "invasive" observations could have done no harm. Liesl's fears had proved unfounded; there was no other life in the ocean, just Wang's Carpets of various sizes. Paolo, feeling perversely even-handed after the fact, kept wanting to remind these smug movers and shakers, *There might have been anything down there. Strange creatures, delicate and vulnerable in ways we could never have anticipated. We were lucky, that's all.*

He ended up alone with Orlando almost by chance; they were both fleeing different groups of appalling guests when their paths crossed on the lawn.

Paolo asked, "How do you think they'll take this, back home?"

"It's first life, isn't it? Primitive or not. It should at least maintain interest in the diaspora, until the next alien biosphere is discovered." Orlando seemed subdued; perhaps he was finally coming to terms with the gulf between their modest discovery, and Earth's longing for world-shaking results. "And at least the chemistry is novel. If it had turned out to be based on DNA and protein, I think half of Earth C-Z would have died of boredom on the spot. Let's face it, the possibilities of DNA have been simulated to death."

Paolo smiled at the heresy. "You think if nature hadn't managed a little originality, it would have dented people's faith in the charter? If the solipsist polises had begun to look more inventive than the universe itself . . ."

"Exactly."

They walked on in silence, then Orlando halted and turned to face him.

He said, "There's something I've been wanting to tell you: My Earth-self is dead."

"*What?*"

"Please, don't make a fuss."

"But . . . why? Why would he—?" *Dead* meant suicide; there was no other cause—unless the sun had turned red giant and swallowed everything out to the orbit of Mars.

"I don't know why. Whether it was a vote of confidence in the diaspora"—Orlando had chosen to wake only in the presence of alien life—"or whether he despaired of us sending back good news, and couldn't face the waiting, and the risk of disappointment. He didn't give a reason. He just had his exoself send a message, stating what he'd done."

Paolo was shaken. If a clone of *Orlando* had succumbed to pessimism, he couldn't begin to imagine the state of mind of the rest of Earth C-Z.

"When did this happen?"

"About fifty years after the launch."

"My Earth-self said nothing."

"It was up to me to tell you, not him."

"I wouldn't have seen it that way."

"Apparently, you would have."

Paolo fell silent, confused. How was he supposed to mourn a distant version of Orlando, in the presence of the one he thought of as real? Death of one clone was a strange half-death, a hard thing to come to terms with. His Earth-self had lost a father; his father had lost an Earth-self. What exactly did that mean to *him?*

What Orlando cared most about was Earth C-Z. Paolo said carefully, "Hermann told me there'd been a rise in emigration and suicide—until the spectroscope picked up the Orphean water. Morale has improved a lot since then—and when they hear that it's more than just water . . ."

Orlando cut him off sharply. "You don't have to talk things up for me. I'm in no danger of repeating the act."

They stood on the lawn, facing each other. Paolo composed a dozen different combinations of mood to communicate, but none of them felt right. He could have granted his father perfect knowledge of everything he was feeling—but what exactly would that knowledge have conveyed? In the end, there was fusion, or separateness. There was nothing in between.

Orlando said, "Kill myself—and leave the fate of transhumanity in your hands? You must be out of your fucking mind."

They walked on together, laughing.

Karpal seemed barely able to gather his thoughts enough to speak. Paolo would have offered him a mind graft promoting tranquillity and concentration—distilled from his own most focused moments—but he was sure that Karpal would never have accepted it. He said, "Why don't you just start wherever you want to? I'll stop you if you're not making sense."

Karpal looked around the white dodecahedron with an expression of disbelief. "You live here?"

"Some of the time."

"But this is your base environment? No trees? No sky? No *furniture*?"

Paolo refrained from repeating any of Hermann's naive-robot jokes. "I add them when I want them. You know, like . . . music. Look, don't let my taste in decor distract you."

Karpal made a chair and sat down heavily.

He said, "Hao Wang proved a powerful theorem, twenty-three hundred years ago. Think of a row of Wang tiles as being like the data tape of a Turing machine." Paolo had the library grant him knowledge of the term; it was the original conceptual form of a generalized computing device, an imaginary machine that moved back and forth along a limitless one-dimensional data tape, reading and writing symbols according to a given set of rules.

"With the right set of tiles, to force the right pattern, the next row of the tiling will look like the data tape after the Turing machine has performed one step of its computation. And the row after that will be the data tape after two steps, and so on. For any given Turing machine, there's a set of Wang tiles that can imitate it."

Paolo nodded amiably. He hadn't heard of this particular quaint result, but it was hardly surprising. "The carpets must be carrying out billions of acts of computation every second . . . but then, so are the water molecules around them. There are no physical processes that don't perform arithmetic of some kind."

"True. But with the carpets, it's not quite the same as random molecular motion."

"Maybe not."

Karpal smiled, but said nothing.

"What? You've found a pattern? Don't tell me: our set of twenty thousand polysaccharide Wang tiles just happens to form the Turing machine for calculating pi."

"No. What they form is a universal Turing machine. They can calculate anything at all—depending on the data they start with. Every daughter fragment is like a program being fed to a chemical computer. Growth executes the program."

"Ah." Paolo's curiosity was roused—but he was having some trouble picturing where the hypothetical Turing machine put its read/write head. "Are you telling me only one tile changes between any two rows, where the 'machine' leaves its mark on the 'data tape' . . ." The mosaics he'd seen were a riot of complexity, with no two rows remotely the same.

Karpal said, "No, no. Wang's original example worked exactly like a standard Turing machine, to simplify the argument . . . but the carpets are more like an arbitrary number of different computers with overlapping data, all working in parallel. This is biology, not a designed machine—it's as messy and wild as, say . . . a mammalian genome. In fact, there are mathematical similarities with gene regulation: I've identified Kauffman networks at every level, from the tiling rules up; the whole system's poised on the hyperadaptive edge between frozen and chaotic behavior."

Paolo absorbed that, with the library's help. Like Earth life, the carpets seemed to have evolved a combination of robustness and flexibility that would have maximized their power to take advantage of natural selection. Thousands of different autocatalytic chemical networks must have arisen soon after the formation of Orpheus—but as the ocean chemistry and the climate changed in the Vegan system's early traumatic millennia, the ability to respond to selection pressure had itself been selected for, and the carpets were the result. Their complexity seemed redundant, now, after a hundred million years of relative stability—and no predators or competition in sight—but the legacy remained.

"So if the carpets have ended up as universal computers . . . with no real need anymore to respond to their surrounding . . . what are they *doing* with all that computing power?"

Karpal said solemnly, "I'll show you."

Paolo followed him into an environment where they drifted above a schematic of a carpet, an abstract landscape stretching far into the distance, elaborately wrinkled like the real thing, but otherwise heavily stylized, with each of the polysaccharide building blocks portrayed as a square tile with four different-colored edges. The adjoining edges of neighboring tiles bore complementary colors—to represent the complementary, interlocking shapes of the borders of the building blocks.

"One group of microprobes finally managed to sequence an entire daughter fragment," Karpal explained, "although the exact edges it started life with are largely guesswork, since the thing was growing while they were trying to map it." He gestured impatiently, and all the wrinkles and folds were smoothed away, an irrelevant distraction. They moved to one border of the ragged-edged carpet, and Karpal started the simulation running.

Paolo watched the mosaic extending itself, following the tiling rules perfectly—an orderly mathematical process here: no chance collisions of radicals with catalytic sites, no mismatched borders between two new-grown neighboring "tiles" triggering the disintegration of both. Just the distillation of the higher-level consequences of all that random motion.

Karpal led Paolo up to a height where he could see subtle patterns being woven, overlapping multiplexed periodicities drifting across the growing edge, meeting and sometimes interacting, sometimes passing right through each other. Mobile pseudoattractors, quasistable waveforms in a one-dimensional universe. The carpet's second dimension was more like time than space, a permanent record of the history of the edge.

Karpal seemed to read his mind. "One-dimensional. Worse than flatland. No connectivity, no complexity. What can possibly happen in a system like that? Nothing of interest, right?"

He clapped his hands and the environment exploded around Paolo. Trails of color streaked across his sensorium, entwining, then disintegrating into luminous smoke.

"Wrong. Everything goes on in a multidimensional frequency space. I've Fourier-transformed the edge into over a thousand components, and there's independent information in all of them. We're only in a narrow cross-section here, a sixteen-dimensional slice—but it's oriented to show the principal components, the maximum detail."

Paolo spun in a blur of meaningless color, utterly lost, his surroundings beyond comprehension. "You're a *Gleisner robot*, Karpal! *Only* sixteen dimensions! How can you have done this?"

Karpal sounded hurt, wherever he was. "Why do you think I came to C-Z? I thought you people were flexible!"

"What you're doing is . . ." *What?* Heresy? There was no such thing. Officially. "Have you shown this to anyone else?"

"Of course not. Who did you have in mind? Liesl? *Hermann?*"

"Good. I know how to keep my mouth shut." Paolo invoked his exoself and moved back into the dodecahedron. He addressed the empty room. "How can I put this? The physical universe has three spatial dimensions, plus time. Citizens of Carter-Zimmerman inhabit the physical universe. Higher dimensional mind games are for the solipsists." Even as he said it, he realized how pompous he sounded. It was an arbitrary doctrine, not some great moral principle.

But it was the doctrine he'd lived with for twelve hundred years.

Karpal replied, more bemused than offended, "It's the only way to see what's going on. The only sensible way to apprehend it. Don't you want to know what the carpets are *actually like?*"

Paolo felt himself being tempted. Inhabit a *sixteen-dimensional slice of a thousand-dimensional frequency space*? But it was in the service of understanding a real physical system—not a novel experience for its own sake.

And nobody had to find out.

He ran a quick—nonsapient—self-predictive model. There was a ninety-three-percent chance that he'd give in, after fifteen subjective minutes of agonizing over the decision. It hardly seemed fair to keep Karpal waiting that long.

He said, "You'll have to loan me your mind-shaping algorithm. My exoself wouldn't know where to begin."

When it was done, he steeled himself, and moved back into Karpal's environment. For a moment, there was nothing but the same meaningless blur as before.

Then everything suddenly crystallized.

Creatures swam around them, elaborately branched tubes like mobile coral, vividly colored in all the hues of Paolo's mental palette—Karpal's attempt to cram in some of the information that a mere sixteen dimensions couldn't show? Paolo glanced down at his own body—nothing was missing, but he could see *around* it in all the thirteen dimensions in which it was nothing but a pinprick; he quickly looked away. The "coral" seemed far more natural to his altered sensory map, occupying sixteen-space in all directions, and shaded with hints that it occupied much more. And Paolo had no doubt that it was "alive"—it looked more organic than the carpets themselves, by far.

Karpal said, "Every point in this space encodes some kind of quasi-periodic pattern in the tiles. Each dimension represents a different characteristic size—like a wavelength, although the analogy's not precise. The position in each dimension represents other attributes of the pattern, relating to the particular tiles it employs.

So the localized systems you see around you are clusters of a few billion patterns, all with broadly similar attributes at similar wavelengths."

They moved away from the swimming coral, into a swarm of something like jellyfish: floppy hyperspheres waving wispy tendrils (each one of them more substantial than Paolo). Tiny jewel-like creatures darted among them. Paolo was just beginning to notice that nothing moved here like a solid object drifting through normal space; motion seemed to entail a shimmering deformation at the leading hypersurface, a visible process of disassembly and reconstruction.

Karpal led him on through the secret ocean. There were helical worms, coiled together in groups of indeterminate number—each single creature breaking up into a dozen or more wriggling slivers, and then recombining . . . although not always from the same parts. There were dazzling multicolored stemless flowers, intricate hypercones of "gossamer-thin" fifteen-dimensional petals—each one a hypnotic fractal labyrinth of crevices and capillaries. There were clawed monstrosities, writhing knots of sharp insectile parts like an orgy of decapitated scorpions.

Paolo said, uncertainly, "You could give people a glimpse of this in just three-dimensions. Enough to make it clear that there's . . . *life* in here. This is going to shake them up badly, though." Life—embedded in the accidental computations of Wang's Carpets, with no possibility of ever relating to the world outside. This was an affront to Carter-Zimmerman's whole philosophy: if nature had evolved "organisms" as divorced from reality as the inhabitants of the most inward-looking polis, where was the privileged status of the physical universe, the clear distinction between truth and illusion?

And after three hundred years of waiting for good news from the disapora, how would they respond to this back on Earth?

Karpal said, "There's one more thing I have to show you."

He'd named the creatures squids, for obvious reasons. *Distant cousins of the jellyfish, perhaps?* They were prodding each other with their tentacles in a way that looked thoroughly carnal—but Karpal explained, "There's no analog of light here. We're viewing all this according to ad hoc rules that have nothing to do with the native physics. All the creatures here gather information about each other by contact alone—which is actually quite a rich means of exchanging data, with so many dimensions. What you're seeing is communication by touch."

"Communication about what?"

"Just gossip, I expect. Social relationships."

Paolo stared at the writhing mass of tentacles.

"You think they're *conscious?*"

Karpal, pointlike, grinned broadly. "They have a central control structure with more connectivity than the human brain—and which correlates data gathered from the skin. I've mapped that organ, and I've started to analyze its function."

He led Paolo into another environment, a representation of the data structures in the "brain" of one of the squids. It was—mercifully—three-dimensional, and highly stylized, built of translucent colored blocks marked with icons, representing mental symbols, linked by broad lines indicating the major connections between them. Paolo had seen similar diagrams of transhuman minds; this was far less elaborate, but eerily familiar nonetheless.

Karpal said, "Here's the sensory map of its surroundings. Full of other squids' bodies, and vague data on the last known positions of a few smaller creatures. But you'll see that the symbols activated by the physical presence of the other squids are linked to these"—he traced the connections with one finger—"representations. Which are crude miniatures of *this whole structure* here."

"This whole structure" was an assembly labeled with icons for memory retrieval, simple tropisms, short-term goals. The general business of being and doing.

"The squid has maps, not just of other squids' bodies, but their minds as well. Right or wrong, it certainly tries to know what the others are thinking about. And"—he pointed out another set of links, leading to another, less crude, miniature squid mind—"it thinks about its own thoughts as well. I'd call that *consciousness*, wouldn't you?"

Paolo said weakly, "You've kept all this to yourself? You came this far, without saying a word—"

Karpal was chastened. "I know it was selfish—but once I'd decoded the interactions of the tile patterns, I couldn't tear myself away long enough to start explaining it to anyone else. And I came to you first because I wanted your advice on the best way to break the news."

Paolo laughed bitterly. "The best way to break the news that *first alien consciousness* is hidden deep inside a biological computer? That everything the diaspora was trying to prove has been turned on its head? The best way to explain to the citizens of Carter-Zimmerman that after a three-hundred-year journey, they might as well have stayed on Earth running simulations with as little resemblance to the physical universe as possible?"

Karpal took the outburst in good humor. "I was thinking more along the lines of the *best way to point out* that if we hadn't traveled to Orpheus and studied Wang's Carpets, we'd never have had the chance to tell the solipsists of Ashton-Laval that all their elaborate invented life-forms and exotic imaginary universes pale into insignificance compared to what's really out here—and which only the Carter-Zimmerman diaspora could have found."

Paolo and Elena stood together on the edge of satellite Pinatubo, watching one of the scout probes aim its maser at a distant point in space. Paolo thought he saw a faint scatter of microwaves from the beam as it collided with iron-rich meteor dust. Elena's mind being diffracted all over the cosmos? Best not think about that.

He said, "When you meet the other versions of me who haven't experienced Orpheus, I hope you'll offer them mind grafts so they won't be jealous."

She frowned. "Ah. Will I or won't I? I can't be bothered modeling it. I expect I will. You should have asked me before I cloned myself. No need for jealousy, though. There'll be worlds far stranger than Orpheus."

"I doubt it. You really think so?"

"I wouldn't be doing this if I didn't believe that." Elena had no power to change the fate of the frozen clones of her previous self—but everyone had the right to emigrate.

Paolo took her hand. The beam had been aimed almost at Regulus, UV-hot and bright, but as he looked away, the cool yellow light of the sun caught his eye.

Vega C-Z was taking the news of the squids surprisingly well, so far. Karpal's way of putting it had cushioned the blow: it was only by traveling all this distance across the real, physical universe that they could have made such a discovery—and it was amazing how pragmatic even the most doctrinaire citizens had turned out to be. Before the launch, "alien solipsists" would have been the most unpalatable idea imaginable, the most abhorrent thing the diaspora could have stumbled upon—but now that they were here, and stuck with the fact of it, people were finding ways to view it in a better light. Orlando had even proclaimed, "*This* will be the perfect hook for the marginal polises. 'Travel through real space to witness a truly alien virtual reality.' We can sell it as a synthesis of the two world views."

Paolo still feared for Earth, though—where his Earth-self and others were waiting in hope of alien guidance. Would they take the message of Wang's Carpets to heart and retreat into their own hermetic worlds, oblivious to physical reality?

And he wondered if the anthrocosmologists had finally been refuted . . . or not. Karpal had discovered alien consciousness—but it was sealed inside a cosmos of its own, its perceptions of itself and its surroundings neither reinforcing nor conflicting with human and transhuman explanations of reality. It would be millennia before C-Z could untangle the ethical problems of daring to try to make contact . . . assuming that both Wang's Carpets, and the inherited data patterns of the squids, survived that long.

Paolo looked around at the wild splendor of the scar-choked galaxy, felt the disk reach in and cut right through him. *Could all this strange haphazard beauty be nothing but an excuse for those who beheld it to exist? Nothing but the sum of all the answers to all the questions humans and transhumans had ever asked the universe—answers created in the asking?*

He couldn't believe that—but the question remained unanswered.

So far.

GENESIS

Poul Anderson

Poul Anderson (1926–2001), along with Arthur C. Clarke, is one of the most important literary ancestors of, as well as a participant in, the nineties resurgence of hard SF. It was not his very American politics, but his tone and approach (as in such stories as "Kyrie") that are evident in the works of such writers as Stephen Baxter, Ken MacLeod, and Greg Egan. One of the Grand Masters who lent particular honor to that title, he died at the end of July 2001. He was married to the poet and writer Karen Anderson, a famous beauty in her day with whom he also collaborated. His daughter, Astrid, is married to Greg Bear. To the readers and writers who grew up reading his work he was an heroic figure, a living giant of the SF field. And because of the sheer size of his output, his influence is in the water, in the air, and in the soil of SF. He was a professional writer of astonishing competence, varied talents and interests, and a thoughtful stylist. He financed his honors degree in physics by writing, and remained a writer after graduating in 1948. His first novel, *Vault of the Ages*, was published in 1952. Distinguished as a fantasy writer—*The Broken Sword* (1954) was his first adult novel—and a mystery writer—his first mystery, *Perish by the Sword* (1959), won the Cock Robin prize—he is nevertheless principally one of the heroes of hard science fiction, a John W. Campbell man whose stories appeared in *Astounding/Analog* for five decades. Of his many excellent collections, *All One Universe* is perhaps the best, since it contains not only first-class SF stories but also several fine essays and extensive story notes by Anderson, who has been notably reticent in his other books.

During the fifties and the following four decades he produced a long string of fine SF and fantasy adventure stories and novels continuing to the present. "He is perhaps SF's most prolific writer of any consistent quality," says *The Encyclopedia of Science Fiction*. The extraordinary thing is that he continued to write so well, given that he wrote so much. James Blish, in the 1950s, called him "the continuing explosion." He was active and prolific in hard SF in the 1990s, and his major work was this novella, and the novel of the same title expanded from it.

Anderson has always defended the traditions of military honor in his fiction, and devoted much of his effort to adventure plots. His many volumes of Dominic Flandry stories and novels are exemplars. Anderson respected the military virtues of courage, loyalty, honor and sacrifice, and often subjected his characters to situations of extreme hardship, allowing them to show these virtues. But he usually doesn't write about war. In fact, his characters are businessmen (such as in a series of books and stories about the wily trader Nicholas van Rijn) as often as soldiers (such as the Dominic Flandry series). In "The Saturn Game," or in *Tau Zero*, they are scientists, multiple specialists. In *The Boat of a Million Years*, they are immortals living throughout human history, from the distant past into the far future, not necessarily above average in intelligence or emotional maturity—though the necessities of survival through the calamities of history have weeded out the weaker ones, and even some of the stronger. His heroes are heroic and strong in the slightly tragic vein of nineteenth-century Romanticism—often they have suffered some earlier emotional wound—but blended in is a practical streak, an allegiance to reason and to knowledge that is a hallmark of hard science fiction characters, that Heinlein and Campbell tradition referred to above. You know a fair amount about what they are feeling, but what really matters is what they do, regardless of how they feel.

But he has also turned out a number of colorful, powerful hard science fiction stories and novels, from *Brain Wave* (1954) to *The Boat of a Million Years* (1989), the four-novel sequence in the 1990s beginning with *Heritage of Stars* (1993), and *Genesis* (2000), that are generally perceived as his major works—the most famous is probably *Tau Zero* (1970). These are marked by astronomical and physical speculation and large-scale Stapledonian vistas of time and space. Even in his swashbuckling adventure stories, he is famous for beginning with calculations of the elements of the orbit of the world to be his setting, and allowing the physics, chemistry and biology to follow logically. He is an admirer of Hal Clement's fiction, and himself wrote a nonfiction book, *Is There Life on Other Worlds?* (1963), on the general subject of what kinds of life forms might inhabit what kinds of planets.

Politically, Anderson represented the hard SF mainstream tradition of the twentieth century. "As for the value of the individual, I'm quite consciously in the Heinleinian tradition there. . . . It's partly an emotional matter, a Libertarian predilection, a prejudice in favor of individual freedom, and partly an intellectual distrust based on looking at the historical record and considering the theory of it, including matters like chaos theory. A distrust of large, encompassing systems . . ." he said in an interview in *Locus*. He is given to making his stories vehicles for philosophical and social commentary, in the Heinlein manner. In much of his fiction of the 1990s, especially in *Heritage of Stars* and its sequels, his political bent is evident.

But not here. Far into the post-human era, AIs responsible for whole planets are the dominant civilization. Gaia, the Earth AI, has been reporting unreliably the progress of Earth's ecosystem. A ship is sent to investigate. Like Egan in "Wang's Carpets," in this story, Anderson takes on some of the grand SF themes of the 1990s—uploaded minds, virtual life, virtual civilizations—and integrates them with some of the grand themes of space opera—interplanetary civilizations, all-powerful computers, and human survival over vast expanses of time. It first appeared in *Far Futures*, the aforementioned original anthology of specifically hard SF novellas, and then was expanded into the novel *Genesis*.

Was it her I ought to have loved . . . ?
—Piet Hein

1

No human could have shaped the thoughts or uttered them. They had no real beginning, they had been latent for millennium after millennium while the galactic brain was growing. Sometimes they passed from mind to mind, years or decades through space at the speed of light, nanoseconds to receive, comprehend, consider, and send a message on outward. But there was so much else—a cosmos of realities, an infinity of virtualities and abstract creations—that remembrances of Earth were the barest undertone, intermittent and fleeting, among uncounted billions of other incidentals. Most of the grand awareness was directed elsewhere, much of it intent on its own evolution.

For the galactic brain was still in infancy: unless it held itself to be still a-borning. By now its members were strewn from end to end of the spiral arms, out into the halo and the nearer star-gatherings, as far as the Magellanic Clouds. The seeds of fresh ones drifted farther yet; some had reached the shores of the Andromeda.

Each was a local complex of organisms, machines, and their interrelationships.

("Organism" seems best for something that maintains itself, reproduces at need, and possesses a consciousness in a range from the rudimentary to the transcendent, even though carbon compounds are a very small part of its material components and most of its life processes take place directly on the quantum level.) They numbered in the many millions, and the number was rising steeply, also within the Milky Way, as the founders of new generations arrived at new homes.

Thus the galactic brain was in perpetual growth, which from a cosmic viewpoint had barely started. Thought had just had time for a thousand or two journeys across its ever-expanding breadth. It would never absorb its members into itself; they would always remain individuals, developing along their individual lines. Let us therefore call them not cells, but nodes.

For they were in truth distinct. Each had more uniquenesses than were ever possible to a protoplasmic creature. Chaos and quantum fluctuation assured that none would exactly resemble any predecessor. Environment likewise helped shape the personality—surface conditions (what kind of planet, moon, asteroid, comet?) or free orbit, sun single or multiple (what kinds, what ages?), nebula, interstellar space and its ghostly tides . . . Then, too, a node was not a single mind. It was as many as it chose to be, freely awakened and freely set aside, proteanly intermingling and separating again, using whatever bodies and sensors it wished for as long as it wished, immortally experiencing, creating, meditating, seeking a fulfillment that the search itself brought forth.

Hence, while every node was engaged with a myriad of matters, one might be especially developing new realms of mathematics, another composing glorious works that cannot really be likened to music, another observing the destiny of organic life on some world, life which it had perhaps fabricated for that purpose, another—Human words are useless.

Always, though, the nodes were in continuous communication over the light-years, communication on tremendous bandwidths of every possible medium. *This* was the galactic brain. That unity, that selfhood which was slowly coalescing, might spend millions of years contemplating a thought; but the thought would be as vast as the thinker, in whose sight an eon was as a day and a day was as an eon.

Already now, in its nascence, it affected the course of the universe. The time came when a node fully recalled Earth. That memory went out to others as part of the ongoing flow of information, ideas, feelings, reveries, and who knows what else? Certain of these others decided the subject was worth pursuing, and relayed it on their own message-streams. In this wise it passed through light-years and centuries, circulated, developed, and at last became a decision, which reached the node best able to take action.

Here the event has been related in words, ill-suited though they are to the task. They fail totally when they come to what happened next. How shall they tell of the dialogue of a mind with itself, when that thinking was a progression of quantum flickerings through configurations as intricate as the wave functions, when the computational power and data-base were so huge that measures become meaningless, when the mind raised aspects of itself to interact like persons until it drew them back into its wholeness, and when everything was said within microseconds of planetary time?

It is impossible, except vaguely and misleadingly. Ancient humans used the language of myth for that which they could not fathom. The sun was a fiery chariot daily crossing heaven, the year a god who died and was reborn, death a punishment for ancestral sin. Let us make our myth concerning the mission to Earth.

Think, then, of the primary aspect of the node's primary consciousness as if it were a single mighty entity, and name it Alpha. Think of a lesser manifestation of itself that it had synthesized and intended to release into separate existence as a second entity. For reasons that will become clear, imagine the latter masculine and name it Wayfarer.

All is myth and metaphor, beginning with this absurd nomenclature. Beings like these had no names. They had identities, instantly recognizable by others of their kind. They did not speak together, they did not go through discussion or explanation of any sort, they were not yet "they." But imagine it.

Imagine, too, their surroundings, not as perceived by their manifold sensors or conceptualized by their awarenesses and emotions, but as if human sense organs were reporting to a human brain. Such a picture is scarcely a sketch. Too much that was basic could not have registered. However, a human at an astronomical distance could have seen an M2 dwarf star about fifty parsecs from Sol, and ascertained that it had planets. She could have detected signs of immense, enigmatic energies, and wondered.

In itself, the sun was undistinguished. The galaxy held billions like it. Long ago, an artificial intelligence—at that dawn stage of evolution, this was the best phrase—had established itself there because one of the planets bore curious lifeforms worth studying. That research went on through the megayears. Meanwhile the ever-heightening intelligence followed more and more different interests: above all, its self-evolution. That the sun would stay cool for an enormous length of time had been another consideration. The node did not want the trouble of coping with great environmental changes before it absolutely must.

Since then, stars had changed their relative positions. This now was the settlement nearest to Sol. Suns closer still were of less interest and had merely been visited, if that. Occasionally a free-space, dirigible node had passed through the neighborhood, but none chanced to be there at this epoch.

Relevant to our myth is the fact that no thinking species ever appeared on the viviferous world. Life is statistically uncommon in the cosmos, sapience almost vanishingly rare, therefore doubly precious.

Our imaginary human would have seen the sun as autumnally yellow, burning low and peacefully. Besides its planets and lesser natural attendants, various titanic structures orbited about it. From afar, they seemed like gossamer or like intricate spiderwebs agleam athwart the stars; most of what they were was force fields. They gathered and focused the energies that Alpha required, they searched the deeps of space and the atom, they transmitted and received the thought-flow that was becoming the galactic brain; what more they did lies beyond the myth.

Within their complexity, although not at any specific location, lived Alpha, its apex. Likewise, for the moment, did Wayfarer.

Imagine a stately voice: "Welcome into being. Yours is a high and, it may be, dangerous errand. Are you willing?"

If Wayfarer hesitated an instant, that was not from fear of suffering harm but from fear of inflicting it. "Tell me. Help me to understand."

"Sol—" The sun of old Earth, steadily heating since first it took shape, would continue stable for billions of years before it exhausted the hydrogen fuel at its core and swelled into a red giant. But—

A swift computation. "Yes. I see." Above a threshold level of radiation input, the geochemical and biochemical cycles that had maintained the temperature of Earth would be overwhelmed. Increasing warmth put increasing amounts of water vapor into the atmosphere, and it is a potent greenhouse gas. Heavier cloud cover, raising the albedo, could only postpone a day of catastrophe. Rising above it, water molecules were split by hard sunlight into hydrogen, which escaped to space, and oxygen, which bound to surface materials. Raging fires released monstrous tonnages of carbon dioxide, as did rocks exposed to heat by erosion in desiccated lands. It is the second major greenhouse gas. The time must come when the last oceans boiled away, leaving a globe akin to Venus; but well before then, life on Earth would be no more than a memory in the quantum consciousnesses. "When will total extinction occur?"

"On the order of a hundred thousand years futureward."

Pain bit through the facet of Wayfarer that came from Christian Brannock, who was born on ancient Earth and most passionately loved his living world. Long since had his uploaded mind merged into a colossal oneness that later divided and redivided, until copies of it were integral with awareness across the galaxy. So were the minds of millions of his fellow humans, as unnoticed now as single genes had been in their bodies when their flesh was alive, and yet significant elements of the whole. Ransacking its database, Alpha had found the record of Christian Brannock and chosen to weave him into the essence of Wayfarer, rather than someone else. The judgment was—call it intuitive.

"Can't you say more closely?" he appealed.

"No," replied Alpha. "The uncertainties and imponderables are too many. Gaia," mythic name for the node in the Solar System, "has responded to inquiries evasively when at all."

"Have . . . we . . . really been this slow to think about Earth?"

"We had much else to think about and do, did we not? Gaia could at any time have requested special consideration. She never did. Thus the matter did not appear to be of major importance. Human Earth is preserved in memory. What is posthuman Earth but a planet approaching the postbiological phase?

"True, the scarcity of spontaneously evolved biomes makes the case interesting. However, Gaia has presumably been observing and gathering the data, for the rest of us to examine whenever we wish. The Solar System has seldom had visitors. The last was two million years ago. Since then, Gaia has joined less and less in our fellowship; her communications have grown sparse and perfunctory. But such withdrawals are not unknown. A node may, for example, want to pursue a philosophical concept undisturbed, until it is ready for general contemplation. In short, nothing called Earth to our attention."

"*I* would have remembered," whispered Christian Brannock.

"What finally reminded us?" asked Wayfarer.

"The idea that Earth may be worth saving. Perhaps it holds more than Gaia knows of—" A pause. "—or has told of. If nothing else, sentimental value."

"Yes, I understand," said Christian Brannock.

"Moreover, and potentially more consequential, we may well have experience to gain, a precedent to set. If awareness is to survive the mortality of the stars, it must make the universe over. That work of billions or trillions of years will begin with some small, experimental undertaking. Shall it be now," the "now" of deathless beings already geologically old, "at Earth?"

"Not small," murmured Wayfarer. Christian Brannock had been an engineer.

"No," agreed Alpha. "Given the time constraint, only the resources of a few stars will be available. Nevertheless, we have various possibilities open to us, if we commence soon enough. The question is which would be the best—and, first, whether we *should* act.

"Will you go seek an answer?"

"Yes," responded Wayfarer, and "Yes, oh, God damn, yes," cried Christian Brannock.

A spaceship departed for Sol. A laser accelerated it close to the speed of light, energized by the sun and controlled by a network of interplanetary dimensions. If necessary, the ship could decelerate itself at journey's end, travel freely about, and return unaided, albeit more slowly. Its cryomagnetics supported a good-sized ball of antimatter, and its total mass was slight. The material payload amounted simply to: a matrix, plus backup, for running the Wayfarer programs and containing a database deemed sufficient; assorted sensors and effectors; several bodies of different capabilities, into which he could download an essence of himself; miscellaneous equipment and power systems; a variety of instruments; and a thing ages forgotten, which Wayfarer had ordered molecules to make at the wish of Christian Brannock. He might somewhere find time and fingers for it.

A guitar.

2

There was a man called Kalava, a sea captain of Sirsu. His clan was the Samayoki. In youth he had fought well at Broken Mountain, where the armies of Ulonai met the barbarian invaders swarming north out of the desert and cast them back with fearsome losses. He then became a mariner. When the Ulonsian League fell apart and the alliances led by Sirsu and Irrulen raged across the land, year after year, seeking each other's throats, Kalava sank enemy ships, burned enemy villages, bore treasure and captives off to market.

After the grudgingly made, unsatisfactory Peace of Tuopai, he went into trade. Besides going up and down the River Lonna and around the Gulf of Sirsu, he often sailed along the North Coast, bartering as he went, then out over the Windroad Sea to the colonies on the Ending Islands. At last, with three ships, he followed that coast east through distances hitherto unknown. Living off the waters and what hunting parties could take ashore, dealing or fighting with the wild tribes they met, in the course of months he and his crews came to where the land bent south. A ways beyond that they found a port belonging to the fabled people of the Shining Fields. They abode for a year and returned carrying wares that at home made them rich.

From his clan Kalava got leasehold of a thorp and good farmland in the Lonna delta, about a day's travel from Sirsu. He meant to settle down, honored and comfortable. But that was not in the thought of the gods nor in his nature. He was soon quarreling with all his neighbors, until his wife's brother grossly insulted him and he killed the man. Thereupon she left him. At the clanmoot which composed the matter she received a third of the family wealth, in gold and movables. Their daughters and the husbands of these sided with her.

Of Kalava's three sons, the eldest had drowned in a storm at sea; the next died of the Black Blood; the third, faring as an apprentice on a merchant vessel far south to Zhir, fell while resisting robbers in sand-drifted streets under the time-gnawed colonnades of an abandoned city. They left no children, unless by slaves. Nor would Kalava, now; no free woman took his offers of marriage. What he had gathered through a hard lifetime would fall to kinfolk who hated him. Most folk in Sirsu shunned him too.

Long he brooded, until a dream hatched. When he knew it for what it was, he set about his preparations, more quietly than might have been awaited. Once the business was under way, though not too far along for him to drop if he must, he sought Ilyandi the skythinker.

She dwelt on Council Heights. There did the Vilkui meet each year for rites and conference. But when the rest of them had dispersed again to carry on their vocation—dream interpreters, scribes, physicians, mediators, vessels of olden lore and learning, teachers of the young—Ilyandi remained. Here she could best search the heavens and seek for the meaning of what she found, on a high place sacred to all Ulonai.

Up the Spirit Way rumbled Kalava's chariot. Near the top, the trees that lined it, goldfruit and plume, stood well apart, giving him a clear view. Bushes grew sparse and low on the stony slopes, here the dusty green of vasi, there a shaggy hairleaf, yonder a scarlet fireflower. Scorchwort lent its acrid smell to a wind blowing hot and slow off the Gulf. That water shone, tarnished metal, westward beyond sight, under a silver-gray overcast beneath which scudded rags of darker cloud. A rainstorm stood on the horizon, blurred murk and flutters of lightning light.

Elsewhere reached the land, bloomgrain ripening yellow, dun paperleaf, verdant pastures for herdlings, violet richen orchards, tall stands of shipwood. Farmhouses and their outbuildings lay widely strewn. The weather having been dry of late, dust whirled up from the roads winding among them to veil wagons and trains of porters. Regally from its sources eastward in Wilderland flowed the Lonna, arms fanning out north and south.

Sirsu lifted battlemented walls on the right bank of the main stream, tiny in Kalava's eyes at its distance. Yet he knew it, he could pick out famous works, the Grand Fountain in King's Newmarket, the frieze-bordered portico of the Flame Temple, the triumphal column in Victory Square, and he knew where the wrights had their workshops, the merchants their bazaars, the innkeepers their houses for a seaman to find a jug and a wench. Brick, sandstone, granite, marble mingled their colors softly together. Ships and boats plied the water or were docked under the walls. On the opposite shore sprawled mansions and gardens of the Helki suburb, their rooftiles fanciful as jewels.

It was remote from that which he approached.

Below a great arch, two postulants in blue robes slanted their staffs across the way and called, "In the name of the Mystery, stop, make reverence, and declare yourself!"

Their young voices rang high, unawed by a sight that had daunted warriors. Kalava was a big man, wide-shouldered and thick-muscled. Weather had darkened his skin to the hue of coal and bleached nearly white the hair that fell in braids halfway down his back. As black were the eyes that gleamed below a shelf of brow, in a face rugged, battered, and scarred. His mustache curved down past the jaw, dyed red. Traveling in peace, he wore simply a knee-length kirtle, green and trimmed with kivi skin, each scale polished, and buskins; but gold coiled around his arms and a sword was belted at his hip. Likewise did a spear stand socketed in the chariot, pennon flapping, while a shield slatted at the rail and an ax hung ready to be thrown. Four matched slaves drew the car. Their line had been bred for generations to be draft creatures—huge, long-legged, spirited, yet trustworthy after the males were gelded. Sweat sheened over Kalava's brand on the small, bald heads and ran down naked bodies. Nonetheless they breathed easily and the smell of them was rather sweet.

Their owner roared, "Halt!" For a moment only the wind had sound or motion.

Then Kalava touched his brow below the headband and recited the Confession: "What a man knows is little, what he understands is less, therefore let him bow down to wisdom." Himself, he trusted more in blood sacrifices and still more in his own strength; but he kept a decent respect for the Vilkui.

"I seek counsel from the skythinker Ilyandi," he said. That was hardly needful, when no other initiate of her order was present.

"All may seek who are not attainted of ill-doing," replied the senior boy as ceremoniously.

"Ruvio bear witness that any judgments against me stand satisfied." The Thunderer was the favorite god of most mariners.

"Enter, then, and we shall convey your request to our lady."

The junior boy led Kalava across the outer court. Wheels rattled loud on flagstones. At the guesthouse, he helped stall, feed, and water the slaves, before he showed the newcomer to a room that in the high season slept two-score men. Elsewhere in the building were a bath, a refectory, ready food—dried meat, fruit, and flatbread—with richenberry wine. Kalava also found a book. After refreshment, he sat down on a bench to pass the time with it.

He was disappointed. He had never had many chances or much desire to read, so his skill was limited; and the copyist for this codex had used a style of lettering obsolete nowadays. Worse, the text was a chronicle of the emperors of Zhir. That was not just painful to him—oh, Eneio, his son, his last son—but valueless. True, the Vilkui taught that civilization had come to Ulonai from Zhir. What of it? How many centuries had fled since the desert claimed that realm? What were the descendants of its dwellers but starveling nomads and pestiferous bandits?

Well, Kalava thought, yes, this could be a timely warning, a reminder to people of how the desert still marched northward. But was what they could see not enough? He had passed by towns not very far south, flourishing in his grandfather's time, now empty, crumbling houses half buried in dust, glassless windows like the eye sockets in a skull.

His mouth tightened. *He* would not meekly abide any doom.

Day was near an end when an acolyte of Ilyandi came to say that she would receive him. Walking with his guide, he saw purple dusk shade toward night in the east. In the west the storm had ended, leaving that part of heaven clear for a while. The sun was plainly visible, though mists turned it into a red-orange step pyramid. From the horizon it cast a bridge of fire over the Gulf and sent great streamers of light aloft into cloudbanks that glowed sulfurous. A whistlewing passed like a shadow across them. The sound of its flight keened faintly down through air growing less hot. Otherwise a holy silence rested upon the heights.

Three stories tall, the sanctuaries, libraries, laboratories, and quarters of the Vilkui surrounded the inner court with their cloisters. A garden of flowers and healing herbs, intricately laid out, filled most of it. A lantern had been lighted in one arcade, but all windows were dark and Ilyandi stood out in the open awaiting her visitor.

She made a slight gesture of dismissal. The acolyte bowed her head and slipped away. Kalava saluted, feeling suddenly awkward but his resolution headlong within him. "Greeting, wise and gracious lady," he said.

"Well met, brave captain," the skythinker replied. She gestured at a pair of confronting stone benches. "Shall we be seated?" It fell short of inviting him to share wine, but it meant she would at least hear him out.

They lowered themselves and regarded one another through the swiftly deepening twilight. Ilyandi was a slender woman of perhaps forty years, features thin and regular, eyes large and luminous brown, complexion pale—like smoked copper, he thought. Cropped short in token of celibacy, wavy hair made a bronze coif above a plain white robe. A green sprig of tekin, held at her left shoulder by a pin in the emblematic form of interlocked circle and triangle, declared her a Vilku.

"How can I aid your venture?" she asked.

He started in surprise. "Huh! What do you know about my plans?" In haste: "My lady knows much, of course."

She smiled. "You and your saga have loomed throughout these past decades. And . . . word reaches us here. You search out your former crewmen or bid them come see you, all privately. You order repairs made to the ship remaining in your possession. You meet with chandlers, no doubt to sound them out about prices. Few if any people have noticed. Such discretion is not your wont. Where are you bound, Kalava, and why so secretively?"

His grin was rueful. "My lady's not just wise and learned, she's clever. Well, then, why not go straight to the business? I've a voyage in mind that most would call crazy. Some among them might try to forestall me, holding that it would anger the gods of those parts—seeing that nobody's ever returned from there, and recalling old tales of monstrous things glimpsed from afar. I don't believe them myself, or I wouldn't try it."

"Oh, I can imagine you setting forth regardless," said Ilyandi half under her breath. Louder: "But agreed, the fear is likely false. No one had reached the Shining Fields by sea, either, before you did. You asked for no beforehand spells or blessings then. Why have you sought me now?"

"This is, is different. Not hugging a shoreline. I—well, I'll need to get and train a new huukin, and that's no small thing in money or time." Kalava spread his big hands, almost helplessly. "I had not looked to set forth ever again, you see. Maybe it is madness, an old man with an old crew in a single old ship. I hoped you might counsel me, my lady."

"You're scarcely ready for the balefire, when you propose to cross the Windroad Sea," she answered.

This time he was not altogether taken aback. "May I ask how my lady knows?"

Ilyandi waved a hand. Catching faint lamplight, the long fingers soared through the dusk like nightswoopers. "You have already been east, and would not need to hide such a journey. South, the trade routes are ancient as far as Zhir. What has it to offer but the plunder of tombs and dead cities, brought in by wretched squatters? What lies beyond but unpeopled desolation until, folk say, one would come to the Burning Lands and perish miserably? Westward we know of a few islands, and then empty ocean. If anything lies on the far side, you could starve and thirst to death before you reached it. But northward—yes, wild waters, but sometimes men come upon driftwood of unknown trees or spy storm-borne flyers of unknown breed—and we have all the legends of the High North, and glimpses of mountains from ships blown off course—" Her voice trailed away.

"Some of those tales ring true to me," Kalava said. "More true than stories about uncanny sights. Besides, wild huukini breed offshore, where fish are plentiful. I have not seen enough of them there, in season, to account for as many as I've seen in open sea. They must have a second shoreline. Where but the High North?"

Ilyandi nodded. "Shrewd, Captain. What else do you hope to find?"

He grinned again. "I'll tell you after I get back, my lady."

Her tone sharpened. "No treasure-laden cities to plunder."

He yielded. "Nor to trade with. Would we not have encountered craft of theirs, or, anyhow, wreckage? However . . . the farther north, the less heat and the more rainfall, no? A country yonder could have a mild clime, forestfuls of timber, fat land for plowing, and nobody to fight." The words throbbed. "No desert creeping in? Room to begin afresh, my lady."

She regarded him steadily through the gloaming. "You'd come home, recruit people, found a colony, and be its king?"

"Its foremost man, aye, though I expect the kind of folk who'd go will want a republic. But mainly—" His voice went low. He stared beyond her. "Freedom. Honor. A freeborn wife and new sons."

They were silent awhile. Full night closed in. It was not as murky as usual, for the clearing in the west had spread rifts up toward the zenith. A breath of coolness soughed in leaves, as if Kalava's dream whispered a promise.

"You are determined," she said at last, slowly. "Why have you come to me?"

"For whatever counsel you will give, my lady. Facts about the passage may be hoarded in books here."

She shook her head. "I doubt it. Unless navigation—yes, that is a real barrier, is it not?"

"Always," he sighed.

"What means of wayfinding have you?"

"Why, you must know."

"I know what is the common knowledge about it. Craftsmen keep their trade secrets, and surely skippers are no different in that regard. If you will tell me how you navigate, it shall not pass these lips, and I may be able to add something."

Eagerness took hold of him. "I'll wager my lady can! We see moon or stars unoften and fitfully. Most days the sun shows no more than a blur of dull light amongst the clouds, if that. But you, skythinkers like you, they've watched and measured for hundreds of years, they've gathered lore—" Kalava paused. "Is it too sacred to share?"

"No, no," she replied. "The Vilkui keep the calendar for everyone, do they not? The reason that sailors rarely get our help is that they could make little or no use of our learning. Speak."

"True, it was Vilkui who discovered lodestones. . . . Well, coasting these waters, I rely mainly on my remembrance of landmarks, or a periplus if they're less familiar to me. Soundings help, especially if the plumb brings up a sample of the bottom for me to look at and taste. Then in the Shining Fields I got a crystal—you must know about it, for I gave another to the order when I got back—I look through it at the sky and, if the weather be not too thick, I see more closely where the sun is than I can with a bare eye. A logline and hourglass give some idea of speed, a lodestone some idea of direction, when out of sight of land. Sailing for the High North and return, I'd mainly use it, I suppose. But if my lady could tell me of anything else—"

She sat forward on her bench. He heard a certain intensity. "I think I might, Captain. I've studied that sunstone of yours. With it, one can estimate latitude and time of day, if one knows the date and the sun's heavenly course during the year. Likewise, even glimpses of moon and stars would be valuable to a traveler who knew them well."

"That's not me," he said wryly. "Could my lady write something down? Maybe this old head won't be too heavy to puzzle it out."

She did not seem to hear. Her gaze had gone upward. "The aspect of the stars in the High North," she murmured. "It could tell us whether the world is indeed round. And are our vague auroral shimmers more bright yonder—in the veritable Lodeland—?"

His look followed hers. Three stars twinkled wan where the clouds were torn. "It's good of you, my lady," he said, "that you sit talking with me, when you could be at your quadrant or whatever, snatching this chance."

Her eyes met his. "Yours may be a better chance, Captain," she answered fiercely. "When first I got the rumor of your expedition, I began to think upon it and what it could mean. Yes, I will help you where I can. I may even sail with you."

The *Gray Courser* departed Sirsu on a morning tide as early as there was light to steer by. Just the same, people crowded the dock. The majority watched mute. A number made signs against evil. A few, mostly young, sang a defiant paean, but the air seemed to muffle their strains.

Only lately had Kalava given out what his goal was. He must, to account for the skythinker's presence, which could not be kept hidden. That sanctification left the authorities no excuse to forbid his venture. However, it took little doubt and fear off those who believed the outer Windroad a haunt of monsters and demons, which might be stirred to plague home waters.

His crew shrugged the notion off, or laughed at it. At any rate, they said they did. Two-thirds of them were crusty shellbacks who had fared under his command before. For the rest, he had had to take what he could scrape together, impoverished laborers and masterless ruffians. All were, though, very respectful of the Vilku.

The *Gray Courser* was a yalka, broad-beamed and shallow-bottomed, with a low forecastle and poop and a deckhouse amidships. The foremast carried two square sails, the mainmast one square and one fore-and-aft; a short bowsprit extended for a jib. A catapult was mounted in the bows. On either side, two boats hung from davits, aft of the harnessing shafts. Her hull was painted according to her name, with red trim. Alongside swam the huukin, its back a sleek blue ridge.

Kalava had the tiller until she cleared the river mouth and stood out into the Gulf. By then it was full day. A hot wind whipped gray-green water into whitecaps that set the vessel rolling. It whined in the shrouds; timbers creaked. He turned the helm over to a sailor, trod forward on the poop deck, and sounded a trumpet. Men stared. From her cabin below, Ilyandi climbed up to stand beside him. Her white robe fluttered like wings that would fain be asoar. She raised her arms and chanted a spell for the voyage:

"Burning, turning,
The sun-wheel reels
Behind the blindnes
Cloud-smoke evokes.
The old cold moon
Seldom tells
Where it lairs
With stars afar.
No men's omens
Abide to guide
High in the skies.
But lodestone for Lodeland
Strongly longs."

While the deckhands hardly knew what she meant, they felt heartened.

Land dwindled aft, became a thin blue line, vanished into waves and mists. Kalava was cutting straight northwest across the Gulf. He meant to sail through the night, and thus wanted plenty of sea room. Also, he and Ilyandi would practice with her ideas about navigation. Hence after a while the mariners spied no other sails, and the loneliness began to weigh on them.

However, they worked stoutly enough. Some thought it a good sign, and cheered, when the clouds clove toward evening and they saw a horned moon. Their mates were frightened; was the moon supposed to appear by day? Kalava bullied them out of it.

Wind stiffened during the dark. By morning it had raised seas in which the ship reeled. It was a westerly, too, forcing her toward land no matter how close-hauled. When he spied, through scud, the crags of Cape Vairka, the skipper realized he could not round it unaided.

He was a rough man, but he had been raised in those skills that were seemly for a freeman of Clan Samayoki. Though not a poet, he could make an acceptable verse when occasion demanded. He stood in the forepeak and shouted into the storm, the words flung back to his men:

"Northward now veering,
Steering from kin-rift,
Spindrift flung gale-borne,
Sail-borne is daft.
Craft will soon flounder,
Founder, go under—
Thunder this wit-lack!
Sit back and call
All that swim near.
Steer then to northward."

Having thus offered the gods a making, he put the horn to his mouth and blasted forth a summons to his huukin.

The great beast heard and slipped close. Kalava took the lead in lowering the shafts. A line around his waist for safety, he sprang over the rail, down onto the broad back. He kept his feet, though the two men who followed him went off into the billows and had to be hauled up. Together they rode the huukin, guiding it between the poles where they could attach the harness.

"I waited too long," Kalava admitted. "This would have been easier yesterday. Well, something for you to brag about in the inns at home, nay?" Their mates drew them back aboard. Meanwhile the sails had been furled. Kalava took first watch at the reins. Mightily pulled the huukin, tail and flippers churning foam that the wind snatched away, on into the open, unknown sea.

3

Wayfarer woke.

He had passed the decades of transit shut down. A being such as Alpha would have spent them conscious, its mind perhaps at work on an intellectual artistic creation—to it, no basic distinction—or perhaps replaying an existent piece for contemplation-enjoyment or perhaps in activity too abstract for words to hint at. Wayfarer's capabilities, though large, were insufficient for that. The hardware and software (again we use myth) of his embodiment were designed principally for interaction with the material universe. In effect, there was nothing for him to do.

He could not even engage in discourse. The robotic systems of the ship were subtle and powerful but lacked true consciousness; it was unnecessary for them, and distraction or boredom might have posed a hazard. Nor could he converse with entities elsewhere; signals would have taken too long going to and fro. He did spend a while, whole minutes of external time, reliving the life of his Christian Brannock element, studying the personality, accustoming himself to its ways. Thereafter he . . . went to sleep.

The ship reactivated him as it crossed what remained of the Oort Cloud. Instantly aware, he coupled to instrument after instrument and scanned the Solar System. Although his database summarized Gaia's reports, he deemed it wise to observe for himself. The eagerness, the bittersweet sense of homecoming, that flickered around his calm logic were Christian Brannock's. Imagine long-forgotten feelings coming astir in you when you return to a scene of your early childhood.

Naturally, the ghost in the machine knew that changes had been enormous since his mortal eyes closed forever. The rings of Saturn were tattered and tenuous. Jupiter had gained a showy set of them from the death of a satellite, but its Red Spot faded away ages ago. Mars was moonless, its axis steeply canted. . . . Higher resolution would have shown scant traces of humanity. From the antimatter plants inside the orbit of Mercury to the comet harvesters beyond Pluto, what was no more needed had been dismantled or left forsaken. Wind, water, chemistry, tectonics, cosmic stones, spalling radiation, nuclear decay, quantum shifts had patiently reclaimed the relics for chaos. Some fossils existed yet, and some eroded fragments aboveground or in space; otherwise all was only in Gaia's memory.

No matter. It was toward his old home that the Christian Brannock facet of Wayfarer sped.

Unaided, he would not have seen much difference from aforetime in the sun. It was slightly larger and noticeably brighter. Human vision would have perceived the light as more white, with the faintest bluish quality. Unprotected skin would have reacted quickly to the increased ultraviolet. The solar wind was stronger, too. But thus far the changes were comparatively minor. This star was still on the main sequence. Planets with greenhouse atmospheres were most affected. Certain minerals on Venus were now molten. Earth—

The ship hurtled inward, reached its goal, and danced into parking orbit. At close range, Wayfarer looked forth.

On Luna, the patterns of maria were not quite the same, mountains were worn down farther, and newer craters had wrecked or obliterated older ones. Rubble-filled anomalies showed where ground had collapsed on deserted cities. Essentially, though, the moon was again the same desolation, seared by day and death-cold by night, as before life's presence. It had receded farther, astronomically no big distance, and this had lengthened Earth's rotation period by about an hour. However, as yet it circled near enough to stabilize that spin.

The mother planet offered less to our imaginary eyes. Clouds wrapped it in dazzling white. Watching carefully, you could have seen swirls and bandings, but to a quick glance the cover was well-nigh featureless. Shifting breaks in it gave blue flashes of water, brown flashes of land—nowhere ice or snowfall, nowhere lights after dark; and the radio spectrum seethed voiceless.

When did the last human foot tread this world? Wayfarer searched his database. The information was not there. Perhaps it was unrecorded, unknown. Perhaps that last flesh had chanced to die alone or chosen to die privately.

Certainly it was long and long ago. How brief had been the span of Homo sapiens, from flint and fire to machine intelligence! Not that the end had come suddenly or simply. It took several millennia, said the database: time for whole civilizations to rise and fall and leave their mutant descendants. Sometimes population decline had reversed in this or that locality, sometimes nations heeded the vatic utterances of prophets and strove to turn history backward—for a while, a while. But always the trend was ineluctable.

The clustered memories of Christian Brannock gave rise to a thought in Wayfarer that was as if the man spoke: I saw the beginning. I did not foresee the end. To me this was the magnificent dawn of hope.

And was I wrong?

The organic individual is mortal. It can find no way to stave off eventual disintegration; quantum chemistry forbids. Besides, if a man could live for a mere thousand years, the data storage capacity of his brain would be saturated, incapable of holding more. Well before then, he would have been overwhelmed by the geometric increase of correlations, made feebleminded or insane. Nor could he survive the rigors of star travel at any reasonable speed or unearthly environments, in a universe never meant for him.

But transferred into a suitable inorganic structure, the pattern of neuron and molecular traces and their relationships that is his inner self becomes potentially immortal. The very complexity that allows this makes him continue feeling as well as thinking. If the quality of emotions is changed, it is because his physical organism has become stronger, more sensitive, more intelligent and aware. He will soon lose any wistfulness about his former existence. His new life gives him so much more, a cosmos of sensing and experience, memory and thought, space and time. He can multiply himself, merge and unmerge with others, grow in spirit until he reaches a limit once inconceivable; and after that he can become a part of a mind greater still, and thus grow onward.

The wonder was, Christian Bannock mused, that any humans whatsoever had held out, clung to the primitive, refused to see that their heritage was no longer of DNA but of psyche.

And yet—

The half-formed question faded away. His half-formed personhood rejoined Wayfarer. Gaia was calling from Earth.

She had, of course, received notification, which arrived several years in advance of the spacecraft. Her manifold instruments, on the planet and out between planets, had detected the approach. For the message she now sent, she chose to employ a modulated neutrino beam. Imagine her saying: "Welcome. Do you need help? I am ready to give any I can." Imagine this in a voice low and warm.

Imagine Wayfarer replying, "Thank you, but all's well. I'll be down directly, if that suits you."

"I do not quite understand why you have come. Has the rapport with me not been adequate?"

No, Wayfarer refrained from saying. "I will explain later in more detail than the transmission could carry. Essentially, though, the reason is what you were told. We"—he deemphasized rather than excluded her—"wonder if Earth ought to be saved from solar expansion."

Her tone cooled a bit. "I have said more than once: No. You can perfect your engineering techniques anywhere else. The situation here is unique. The knowledge to be won by observing the unhampered course of events is unpredictable, but it will be enormous, and I have good cause to believe it will prove of the highest value."

"That may well be. I'll willingly hear you out, if you care to unfold your thoughts more fully than you have hitherto. But I do want to make my own survey and develop my own recommendations. No reflection on you; we both realize that no one mind can encompass every possibility, every interpretation. Nor can any one mind follow out every ongoing factor in what it observes; and what is overlooked can prove to be the agent of chaotic change. I may notice something that escaped you. Unlikely, granted. After your millions of years here, you very nearly *are* Earth and the life on it, are you not? But . . . we . . . would like an independent opinion."

Imagine her laughing. "At least you are polite, Wayfarer. Yes, do come down. I will steer you in."

"That won't be necessary. Your physical centrum is in the arctic region, isn't it? I can find my way."

He sensed steel beneath the mildness: "Best I guide you. You recognize the situation as inherently chaotic. Descending on an arbitrary path, you might seriously perturb certain things in which I am interested. Please."

"As you wish," Wayfarer conceded.

Robotics took over. The payload module of the spacecraft detached from the drive module, which stayed in orbit. Under its own power but controlled from below, asheen in the harsh spatial sunlight, the cylindroid braked and slanted downward.

It pierced the cloud deck. Wayfarer scanned eagerly. However, this was no sightseeing tour. The descent path sacrificed efficiency and made almost straight for a high northern latitude. Sonic-boom thunder trailed.

He did spy the fringe of a large continent oriented east and west, and saw that those parts were mainly green. Beyond lay a stretch of sea. He thought that he glimpsed something peculiar on it, but passed over too fast, with his attention directed too much ahead, to be sure.

The circumpolar landmass hove in view. Wayfarer compared maps that Gaia had transmitted. They were like nothing that Christian Brannock remembered. Plate tectonics had slowed, as radioactivity and original heat in the core of Earth declined, but drift, subduction, upthrust still went on.

He cared more about the life here. Epoch after epoch, Gaia had described its posthuman evolution as she watched. Following the mass extinction of the Paleotechnic, it had regained the abundance and diversity of a Cretaceous or a Tertiary. Everything was different, though, except for a few small survivals. To Wayfarer, as to Alpha and, ultimately, the galactic brain, those accounts seemed somehow, increasingly, incomplete. They did not quite make ecological sense—as of the past hundred thousand years or so. Nor did all of Gaia's responses to questions.

Perhaps she was failing to gather full data, perhaps she was misinterpreting, perhaps—It was another reason to send him to her.

Arctica appeared below the flyer. Imagine her giving names to it and its features. As long as she had lived with them, they had their identities for her. The Coast Range of hills lifted close behind the littoral. Through it cut the Remnant River, which had been greater when rains were more frequent but continued impressive. With its tributaries it drained the intensely verdant Bountiful Valley. On the far side of that, foothills edged the steeply rising Boreal Mountains. Once the highest among them had been snowcapped; now their peaks were naked rock. Streams rushed down the flanks, most of them joining the Remnant somewhere as it flowed through its gorges toward the sea. In a lofty vale gleamed the Rainbowl, the big lake that was its headwaters. Overlooking from the north loomed the mountain Mindhome, its top, the physical centrum of Gaia, lost in cloud cover.

In a way the scenes were familiar to him. She had sent plenty of full-sensory transmissions, as part of her contribution to universal knowledge and thought. Wayfarer could even recall the geological past, back beyond the epoch when Arctica broke free and drifted north, ramming into land already present and thrusting the

Boreals heavenward. He could extrapolate the geological future in comparable detail, until a red giant filling half the sky glared down on an airless globe of stone and sand, which would at last melt. Nevertheless, the reality, the physical being here, smote him more strongly than he had expected. His sensors strained to draw in every datum while his vessel flew needlessly fast to the goal.

He neared the mountain. Jutting south from the range, it was not the tallest. Brushy forest grew all the way up its sides, lush on the lower slopes, parched on the heights, where many trees were leafless skeletons. That was due to a recent climatic shift, lowering the mean level of clouds, so that a formerly well-watered zone had been suffering a decades-long drought. (Yes, Earth was moving faster toward its doomsday.) Fire must be a constant threat, he thought. But no, Gaia's agents could quickly put any out, or she might simply ignore it. Though not large, the area she occupied on the summit was paved over and doubtless nothing was vulnerable to heat or smoke.

He landed. For an instant of planetary time, lengthy for minds that worked at close to light speed, there was communication silence.

He was again above the cloud deck. It eddied white, the peak rising from it like an island among others, into the level rays of sunset. Overhead arched a violet clarity. A thin wind whittered, cold at this altitude. On a level circle of blue-black surfacing, about a kilometer wide, stood the crowded structures and engines of the centrum.

A human would have seen an opalescent dome surrounded by towers, some sheer as lances, some intricately lacy; and silver spiderwebs; and lesser things of varied but curiously simple shapes, mobile units waiting to be dispatched on their tasks. Here and there, flyers darted and hovered, most of them as small and exquisite as hummingbirds (if our human had known hummingbirds). To her the scene would have wavered slightly, as if she saw it through rippling water, or it throbbed with quiet energies, or it pulsed in and out of space-time. She would not have sensed the complex of force fields and quantum-mechanical waves, nor the microscopic and submicroscopic entities that were the major part of it.

Wayfarer perceived otherwise.

Then: "Again, welcome," Gaia said.

"And again, thank you," Wayfarer replied. "I am glad to be here."

They regarded one another, not as bodies—which neither was wearing—but as minds, matrices of memory, individuality, and awareness. Separately he wondered what she thought of him. She was giving him no more of herself than had always gone over the communication lines between the stars. That was: a nodal organism, like Alpha and millions of others, which over the eons had increased its capabilities, while ceaselessly experiencing and thinking; the ages of interaction with Earth and the life on Earth, maybe shaping her soul more deeply than the existence she shared with her own kind; traces of ancient human uploads, but they were not like Christian Brannock, copies of them dispersed across the galaxy, no, these had chosen to stay with the mother world. . . .

"I told you I am glad too," said Gaia regretfully, "but I am not, quite. You question my stewardship."

"Not really," Wayfarer protested. "I hope not ever. We simply wish to know better how you carry it out."

"Why, you do know. As with any of us who is established on a planet, high among my activities is to study its complexities, follow its evolution. On this planet that means, above all, the evolution of its life, everything from genetics to ecology. In what way have I failed to share information with my fellows?"

In many ways, Wayfarer left unspoken. Overtly: "Once we"—here he referred to the galactic brain—"gave close consideration to the matter, we found countless unresolved puzzles. For example—"

What he set forth was hundreds of examples, ranging over millennia. Let a single case serve. About ten thousand years ago, the big continent south of Arctica had supported a wealth of large grazing animals. Their herds darkened the plains and made loud the woods. Gaia had described them in loving detail, from the lyre-curved horns of one genus to the wind-rustled manes of another. Abruptly, in terms of historical time, she transmitted no more about them. When asked why, she said they had gone extinct. She never explained how.

To Wayfarer she responded in such haste that he got a distinct impression she realized she had made a mistake. (Remember, this is a myth.) "A variety of causes. Climates became severe as temperatures rose—"

"I am sorry," he demurred, "but when analyzed, the meteorological data you supplied show that warming and desiccation cannot yet have been that significant in those particular regions."

"How are you so sure?" she retorted. Imagine her angry. "Have any of you lived with Earth for megayears, to know it that well?" Her tone hardened. "I do not myself pretend to full knowledge. A living world is too complex—chaotic. Cannot you appreciate that? I am still seeking comprehension of too many phenomena. In this instance, consider just a small shift in ambient conditions, coupled with new diseases and scores of other factors, most of them subtle. I believe that, combined, they broke a balance of nature. But unless and until I learn more, I will not waste bandwidth in talk about it."

"I sympathize with that," said Wayfarer mildly, hoping for conciliation. "Maybe I can discover or suggest something helpful."

"No. You are too ignorant, you are blind, you can only do harm."

He stiffened. "We shall see." Anew he tried for peace. "I did not come in any hostility. I came because here is the fountainhead of us all, and we think of saving it."

Her manner calmed likewise. "How would you?"

"That is one thing I have come to find out—what the best way is, should we proceed."

In the beginning, maybe, a screen of planetary dimensions, kept between Earth and sun by an interplay of gravity and electromagnetism, to ward off the fraction of energy that was not wanted. It would only be a temporary expedient, though, possibly not worthwhile. That depended on how long it would take to accomplish the real work. Engines in close orbit around the star, drawing their power from its radiation, might generate currents in its body that carried fresh hydrogen down to the core, thus restoring the nuclear furnace to its olden state. Or they might bleed gas off into space, reducing the mass of the sun, damping its fires but adding billions upon billions of years wherein it scarcely changed any more. That would cause the planets to move outward, a factor that must be taken into account but that would reduce the requirements.

Whatever was done, the resources of several stars would be needed to accomplish it, for time had grown cosmically short.

"An enormous work," Gaia said. Wayfarer wondered if she had in mind the dramatics of it, apparitions in heaven, such as centuries during which fire-fountains rushed visibly out of the solar disc.

"For an enormous glory," he declared.

"No," she answered curtly. "For nothing, and worse than nothing. Destruction of everything I have lived for. Eternal loss to the heritage."

"Why, is not Earth the heritage?"

"No. Knowledge is. I tried to make that clear to Alpha." She paused. "To you I say again, the evolution of life, its adaptations, struggles, transformations, and how at last it meets death—those are unforeseeable, and nowhere else in the space-time universe can there be a world like this for them to play themselves out. They will enlighten us in ways the galactic brain itself cannot yet conceive. They may well open to us whole new phases of ultimate reality."

"Why would not a life that went on for gigayears do so, and more?"

"Because here I, the observer of the ages, have gained some knowledge of *this* destiny, some oneness with it—" She sighed. "Oh, you do not understand. You refuse to."

"On the contrary," Wayfarer said, as softly as might be, "I hope to. Among the reasons I came is that we can communicate being to being, perhaps more fully than across light-years and certainly more quickly."

She was silent awhile. When she spoke again, her tone had gone gentle. "More . . . intimately. Yes. Forgive my resentment. It was wrong of me. I will indeed do what I can to make you welcome and help you learn."

"Thank you, thank you," Wayfarer said happily. "And I will do what I can toward that end."

The sun went under the cloud deck. A crescent moon stood aloft. The wind blew a little stronger, a little chillier.

"But if we decide against saving Earth," Wayfarer asked, "if it is to go molten and formless, every trace of its history dissolved, will you not mourn?"

"The record I have guarded will stay safe," Gaia replied.

He grasped her meaning: the database of everything known about this world. It was here in her. Much was also stored elsewhere, but she held the entirety. As the sun became a devouring monster, she would remove her physical plant to the outer reaches of the system.

"But you have done more than passively preserve it, have you not?" he said.

"Yes, of course." How could an intelligence like hers have refrained? "I have considered the data, worked with them, evaluated them, tried to reconstruct the conditions that brought them about."

And in the past thousands of years she had become ever more taciturn about that, too, or downright evasive, he thought.

"You had immense gaps to fill in," he hinted.

"Inevitably. The past, also, is quantum probabilistic. By what roads, what means, did history come to us?"

"Therefore you create various emulations, to see what they lead to," about which she had told scarcely anything.

"You knew that. I admit, since you force me, that besides trying to find what happened, I make worlds to show what *might* have happened."

He was briefly startled. He had not been deliberately trying to bring out any such confession. Then he realized that she had foreseen he was bound to catch scent of it, once they joined their minds in earnest.

"Why?" he asked.

"Why else but for a more complete understanding?"

In his inwardness, Wayfarer reflected: Yes, she had been here since the time of humanity. The embryo of her existed before Christian Brannock was born. Into the growing fullness of her had gone the mind-patterns of humans who chose not to go to the stars but to abide on old Earth. And the years went by in their tens of millions.

Naturally she was fascinated by the past. She must do most of her living in it. Could that be why she was indifferent to the near future, or actually wanted catastrophe?

Somehow that thought did not feel right to him. Gaia was a mystery he must solve.

Cautiously, he ventured, "Then you act as a physicist might, tracing hypothetical configurations of the wave function through space-time—except that the subjects of your experiments are conscious."

"I do no wrong," she said. "Come with me into any of those worlds and see."

"Gladly," he agreed, unsure whether he lied. He mustered resolution. "Just the same, duty demands I conduct my own survey of the material environment."

"As you will. Let me help you prepare." She was quiet for a span. In this thin air, a human would have seen the first stars blink into sight. "But I believe it will be by sharing the history of my stewardship that we truly come to know one another."

4

Storm-battered until men must work the pumps without cease, *Gray Courser* limped eastward along the southern coast of an unknown land. Wind set that direction, for the huukin trailed after, so worn and starved that what remained of its strength must be reserved for sorest need. The shore rolled jewel-green, save where woods dappled it darker, toward a wall of gentle hills. All was thick with life, grazing herds, wings multitudinous overhead, but no voyager had set foot there. Surf dashed in such violence that Kalava was not certain a boat could live through it. Meanwhile they had caught but little rainwater, and what was in the butts had gotten low and foul.

He stood in the bows, peering ahead, Ilyandi at his side. Wind boomed and shrilled, colder than they were used to. Wrack flew beneath an overcast gone heavy. Waves ran high, gray-green, white-maned, foam blown off them in streaks. The ship rolled, pitched, and groaned.

Yet they had seen the sky uncommonly often. Ilyandi believed that clouds—doubtless vapors sucked from the ground by heat, turning back to water as they rose, like steam from a kettle—formed less readily in this clime. Too eagerly at her instruments and reckonings to speak much, she had now at last given her news to the captain.

"Then you think you know where we are?" he asked hoarsely.

Her face, gaunt within the cowl of a sea-stained cloak, bore the least smile. "No. This country is as nameless to me as to you. But, yes, I do think I can say we are no more than fifty daymarches from Ulonai, and it may be as little as forty."

Kalava's fist smote the rail. "By Ruvio's ax! How I hoped for this!" The words tumbled from him. "It means the weather tossed us mainly back and forth between the two shorelines. We've not come unreturnably far. Every ship henceforward can have a better passage. See you, she can first go out to the Ending Islands and wait at ease for favoring winds. The skipper will know he'll make landfall. We'll have it worked out after a few more voyages, just what lodestone bearing will bring him to what place hereabouts."

"But anchorage?" she wondered.

He laughed, which he had not done for many days and nights. "As for that—"

A cry from the lookout at the masthead broke through. Down the length of the vessel men raised their eyes. Terror howled.

Afterward no two tongues bore the same tale. One said that a firebolt had pierced the upper clouds, trailing thunder. Another told of a sword as long as the hull, and blood carried on the gale of its flight. To a third it was a beast with jaws agape and three tails aflame. . . . Kalava remembered a spear among whirling rainbows. To him Ilyandi said, when they were briefly alone, that she thought of a shuttle now seen, now unseen as it wove a web on which stood writing she could not read. All witnesses agreed that it came from over the sea, sped on inland through heaven, and vanished behind the hills.

Men went mad. Some ran about screaming. Some wailed to their gods. Some cast themselves down on the deck and shivered, or drew into balls and squeezed their eyes shut. No hand at helm or pumps, the ship wallowed about, sails banging, adrift toward the surf, while water drained in through sprung seams and lapped higher in the bilge.

"Avast!" roared Kalava. He sprang down the foredeck ladder and went among the crew. "Be you men? Up on your feet or die!" With kicks and cuffs he drove them back to their duties. One yelled and drew a knife on him. He knocked the fellow senseless. Barely in time, *Gray Courser* came again under control. She was then too near shore to get the huukin harnessed. Kalava took the helm, wore ship, and clawed back to sea room.

Mutiny was all too likely, once the sailors regained a little courage. When Kalava could yield place to a halfway competent steersman, he sought Ilyandi and they talked awhile in her cabin. Thereafter they returned to the foredeck and he shouted for attention. Standing side by side, they looked down on the faces, frightened or terrified or sullen, of the men who had no immediate tasks.

"Hear this," Kalava said into the wind. "Pass it on to the rest. I know you'd turn south this day if you had your wish. But you can't. We'd never make the crossing, the shape we're in. Which would you liefer have, the chance of wealth and fame or the certainty of drowning? We've got to make repairs, we've got to restock, and *then* we can sail home, bringing wondrous news. When can we fix things up? Soon, I tell you, soon. I've been looking at the water. Look for yourselves. See how it's taking on more and more of a brown shade, and how bits of plant stuff float about on the waves. That means a river, a big river, emptying out somewhere nigh. And that means a harbor for us. As for the sight we saw, here's the Vilku, our lady Ilyandi, to speak about it."

The skythinker stepped forward. She had changed into a clean white robe with the emblems of her calling, and held a staff topped by a sigil. Though her voice was low, it carried.

"Yes, that was a fearsome sight. It lends truth to the old stories of things that appeared to mariners who ventured, or were blown, far north. But think. Those sailors did win home again. Those who did not must have perished of natural causes. For why would the gods or the demons sink some and not others?

"What we ourselves saw merely flashed overhead. Was it warning us off? No, because if it knew that much about us, it knew we cannot immediately turn back. Did it give us any heed at all? Quite possibly not. It was very strange, yes, but that does not mean it was any threat. The world is full of strangenesses. I could tell you of things seen on clear nights over the centuries, fiery streaks down the sky or stars with glowing tails. We of the Vilkui do not understand them, but neither do we fear them. We give them their due honor and respect, as signs from the gods."

She paused before finishing: "Moreover, in the secret annals of our order lie accounts of visions and wonders exceeding these. All folk know that from time to time the gods have given their word to certain holy men or women, for the guidance of the people. I may not tell how they manifest themselves, but I will say that this today was not wholly unlike.

"Let us therefore believe that the sign granted us is a good one."

She went on to a protective chant-spell and an invocation of the Powers. That heartened most of her listeners. They were, after all, in considerable awe of her.

Besides, the larger part of them had sailed with Kalava before and done well out of it. They bullied the rest into obedience.

"Dismissed," said the captain. "Come evening, you'll get a ration of liquor."

A weak cheer answered him. The ship fared onward.

Next morning they did indeed find a broad, sheltered bay, dun with silt. Hitching up the huukin, they went cautiously in until they spied the river foretold by Kalava. Accompanied by a few bold men, he took a boat ashore. Marshes, meadows, and woods all had signs of abundant game. Various plants were unfamiliar, but he recognized others, among them edible fruits and bulbs. "It is well," he said. "This land is ripe for our taking." No lightning bolt struck him down.

Having located a suitable spot, he rowed back to the ship, brought her in on the tide, and beached her. He could see that the water often rose higher yet, so he would be able to float her off again when she was ready. That would take time, but he felt no haste. Let his folk make proper camp, he thought, get rested and nourished, before they began work. Hooks, nets, and weirs would give rich catches. Several of the crew had hunting skills as well. He did himself.

His gaze roved upstream, toward the hills. Yes, presently he would lead a detachment to learn what lay beyond.

5

Gaia had never concealed her reconstructive research into human history. It was perhaps her finest achievement. But slowly those of her fellows in the galactic brain who paid close attention had come to feel that it was obsessing her. And then of late—within the past hundred thousand years or so—they were finding her reports increasingly scanty, less informative, at last ambiguous to the point of evasiveness. They did not press her about it; the patience of the universe was theirs. Nevertheless they had grown concerned. Especially had Alpha, who as the nearest was in the closest, most frequent contact; and therefore, now, had Wayfarer. Gaia's activities and attitudes were a primary factor in the destiny of Earth. Without a better understanding of her, the rightness of saving the planet was undecidable.

Surely an important part of her psyche was the history and archeology she preserved, everything from the animal origins to the machine fulfillment of genus Homo. Unnumbered individual minds had uploaded into her, too, had become elements of her being—far more than were in any other node. What had she made of all this over the megayears, and what had it made of her?

She could not well refuse Wayfarer admittance; the heritage belonged to her entire fellowship, ultimately to intelligence throughout the cosmos of the future. Guided by her, he would go through the database of her observations and activities in external reality, geological, biological, astronomical.

As for the other reality, interior to her, the work she did with her records and emulations of humankind—to evaluate that, some purely human interaction seemed called for. Hence Wayfarer's makeup included the mind-pattern of a man.

Christian Brannock's had been chosen out of those whose uploads went starfaring because he was among the earliest, less molded than most by relationships with machines. Vigor, intelligence, and adaptability were other desired characteristics.

His personality was itself a construct, a painstaking refabrication by Alpha, who had taken strands (components, overtones) of his own mind and integrated them to form a consciousness that became an aspect of Wayfarer. No doubt it was not a perfect duplicate of the original. Certainly, while it had all the memories of Christian Brannock's lifetime, its outlook was that of a young man, not an old one. In addition, it possessed some knowledge—the barest sketch, grossly oversimplified so as not to overload it—of what had happened since its body died. Deep underneath its awareness lay the longing to return to an existence more full than it could now imagine. Yet, knowing that it would be taken back into the oneness when its task was done, it did not mourn any loss. Rather, to the extent that it was differentiated from Wayfarer, it took pleasure in sensations, thoughts, and emotions that it had effectively forgotten.

When the differentiation had been completed, the experience of being human again became well-nigh everything for it, and gladsome, because so had the man gone through life.

To describe how this was done, we must again resort to myth and say that Wayfarer downloaded the Christian Brannock subroutine into the main computer of the system that was Gaia. To describe what actually occurred would require the mathematics of wave mechanics and an entire concept of multileveled, mutably dimensioned reality which it had taken minds much greater than humankind's a long time to work out.

We can, however, try to make clear that what took place in the system was not a mere simulation. It was an emulation. Its events were not of a piece with events among the molecules of flesh and blood; but they were, in their way, just as real. The persons created had wills as free as any mortal's, and whatever dangers they met could do harm equal to anything a mortal body might suffer.

Consider a number of people at a given moment. Each is doing something, be it only thinking, remembering, or sleeping—together with all ongoing physiological and biochemical processes. They are interacting with each other and with their surroundings, too; and every element of these surroundings, be it only a stone or a leaf or a photon of sunlight, is equally involved. The complexity seems beyond conception, let alone enumeration or calculation. But consider further: At this one instant, every part of the whole, however minute, is in one specific state; and thus the whole itself is. Electrons are all in their particular quantum shells, atoms are all in their particular compounds and configurations, energy fields all have their particular values at each particular point—suppose an infinitely fine-grained photograph.

A moment later, the state is different. However slightly, fields have pulsed, atoms have shifted about, electrons have jumped, bodies have moved. But this new state derives from the first according to natural laws. And likewise for every succeeding state.

In crude, mythic language: Represent each variable of one state by some set of numbers; or, to put it in equivalent words, map the state into an n-dimensional phase space. Input the laws of nature. Run the program. The computer model should then evolve from state to state in exact correspondence with the evolution of our original matter-energy world. That includes life and consciousness. The maps of organisms go through one-to-one analogues of everything that the organisms themselves would, among these being the processes of sensation and thought. To them, they and their world are the same as in the original. The question of which set is the more real is meaningless.

Of course, this primitive account is false. The program did *not* exactly follow the course of events "outside." Gaia lacked both the data and the capability necessary to model the entire universe, or even the entire Earth. Likewise did any other node, and the galactic brain. Powers of that order lay immensely far in the future, if they would ever be realized. What Gaia could accommodate was so much less that the difference in degree amounted to a difference in kind.

For example, if events on the surface of a planet were to be played out, the stars must be lights in the night sky and nothing else, every other effect neglected. Only a limited locality on the globe could be done in anything like full detail; the rest grew more and more incomplete as distance from the scene increased, until at the antipodes there was little more than simplified geography, hydrography, and atmospherics. Hence weather on the scene would very soon be quite unlike weather at the corresponding moment of the original. This is the simplest, most obvious consequence of the limitations. The totality is beyond reckoning—and we have not even mentioned relativistic nonsimultaneity.

Besides, atom-by-atom modeling was a practical impossibility; statistical mechanics and approximations must substitute. Chaos and quantum uncertainties made developments incalculable in principle. Other, more profound considerations entered as well, but with them language fails utterly.

Let it be said, as a myth, that such creations made their destinies for themselves.

And yet, what a magnificent instrumentality the creator system was! Out of nothingness, it could bring worlds into being, evolutions, lives, ecologies, awarenesses, histories, entire timelines. They need not be fragmentary miscopies of something "real," dragging out their crippled spans until the nodal intelligence took pity and canceled them. Indeed, they need not derive in anyway from the "outside." They could be works of imagination—fairy-tale worlds, perhaps, where benevolent gods ruled and magic ran free. Always, the logic of their boundary conditions caused them to develop appropriately, to be at home in their existences.

The creator system was the mightiest device ever made for the pursuit of art, science, philosophy, and understanding.

So it came about that Christian Brannock found himself alive again, young again, in the world that Gaia and Wayfarer had chosen for his new beginning.

He stood in a garden on a day of bright sun and mild, fragrant breezes. It was a formal garden, graveled paths, low-clipped hedges, roses and lilies in geometric beds, around a lichened stone basin where goldfish swam. Brick walls, ivy-heavy, enclosed three sides, a wrought-iron gate in them leading to a lawn. On the fourth side lay a house, white, slate-roofed, classically proportioned, a style that to him was antique. Honeybees buzzed. From a yew tree overlooking the wall came the twitter of birds.

A woman walked toward him. Her flower-patterned gown, the voluminous skirt and sleeves, a cameo hung on her bosom above the low neckline, dainty shoes, parasol less an accessory than a completion, made his twenty-third-century singlesuit feel abruptly barbaric. She was tall and well formed. Despite the garments, her gait was lithe. As she neared, he saw clear features beneath high-piled mahogany hair.

She reached him, stopped, and met his gaze. "Benveni, Capita Brannoch," she greeted. Her voice was low and musical.

"Uh, g'day, Sorita—uh—" he fumbled.

She blushed. "I beg your pardon, Captain Brannock. I forgot and used my Inglay—English of my time. I've been—" She hesitated. "—supplied with yours, and we both have been with the contemporary language."

A sense of dream was upon him. To speak as dryly as he could was like clutching at something solid. "You're from my future, then?"

She nodded. "I was born about two hundred years after you."

"That means about eighty or ninety years after my death, right?" He saw an inward shadow pass over her face. "I'm sorry," he blurted. "I didn't mean to upset you."

She turned entirely calm, even smiled a bit. "It's all right. We both know what we are, and what we used to be."

"But—"

"Yes, but." She shook her head. "It does feel strange, being . . . this . . . again."

He was quickly gaining assurance, settling into the situation. "I know. I've had practice in it," light-years away, at the star where Alpha dwelt. "Don't worry, it'll soon be quite natural to you."

"I have been here a little while myself. Nevertheless—young," she whispered, "but remembering a long life, old age, dying—" She let the parasol fall, unnoticed, and stared down at her hands. Fingers gripped each other. "Remembering how toward the end I looked back and thought, 'Was that *all?*' "

He wanted to take those hands in his and speak comfort, but decided he would be wiser to say merely, "Well, it wasn't all."

"No, of course not. Not for me, the way it had been once for everyone who ever lived. While my worn-out body was being painlessly terminated, my self-pattern was uploaded—" She raised her eyes. "Now we can't really recall what our condition has been like, can we?"

"We can look forward to returning to it."

"Oh, yes. Meanwhile—" She flexed herself, glanced about and upward, let light and air into her spirit, until at last a full smile blossomed. "I am starting to enjoy this. Already I am." She considered him. He was a tall man, muscular, blond, rugged of countenance. Laughter lines radiated from blue eyes. He spoke in a resonant baritone. "And I will."

He grinned, delighted. "Thanks. The same here. For openers, may I ask your name?"

"Forgive me!" she exclaimed. "I thought I was prepared. I . . . came into existence . . . with knowledge of my role and this milieu, and spent the time since rehearsing in my mind, but now that it's actually happened, all my careful plans have flown away. I am—was—no, I am Laurinda Ashcroft."

He offered his hand. After a moment she let him shake hers. He recalled that at the close of his mortal days the gesture was going out of use.

"You know a few things about me, I suppose," he said, "but I'm ignorant about you and your times. When I left Earth, everything was changing spinjump fast, and after that I was out of touch," and eventually his individuality went of its own desire into a greater one. This reenactment of him had been given no details of the terrestrial history that followed his departure; it could not have contained any reasonable fraction of the information.

"You went to the stars almost immediately after you'd uploaded, didn't you?" she asked.

He nodded. "Why wait? I'd always longed to go."

"Are you glad that you did?"

"Glad is hardly the word." He spent two or three seconds putting phrases together. Language was important to him; he had been an engineer and occasionally a maker of songs. "However, I am also happy to be here." Again a brief grin. "In such pleasant company." Yet what he really hoped to do was explain himself. They would be faring together in search of one another's souls. "And I'll bring something new back to my proper existence. All at once I realize how a human can appreciate in a unique way what's out yonder," suns, worlds, upon certain of them life that was more wonderful still, nebular fire-clouds, infinity whirling down the throat of a black hole, galaxies like jewelwork strewn by a prodigal through immensity, space-time structure subtle and majestic—everything he had never known, as a man, until this moment, for no organic creature could travel those reaches.

"While I chose to remain on Earth," she said. "How timid and unimaginative do I seem to you?"

"Not in the least," he avowed. "You had the adventures you wanted."

"You are kind to say so." She paused. "Do you know Jane Austen?"

"Who? No, I don't believe I do."

"An early-nineteenth-century writer. She led a quiet life, never went far from home, died young, but she explored people in ways that nobody else ever did."

"I'd like to read her. Maybe I'll get a chance here." He wished to show that he was no—"technoramus" was the word he invented on the spot. "I did read a good deal, especially on space missions. And especially poetry. Homer, Shakespeare, Tu Fu, Basho, Bellman, Burns, Omar Khayyam, Kipling, Millay, Haldeman—" He threw up his hands and laughed. "Never mind. That's just the first several names I could grab out of the jumble for purposes of bragging."

"We have much getting acquainted to do, don't we? Come, I'm being inhospitable. Let's go inside, relax, and talk."

He retrieved her parasol for her and, recollecting historical dramas he had seen, offered her his arm. They walked slowly between the flower beds. Wind lulled, a bird whistled, sunlight baked odors out of the roses.

"Where are we?" he asked.

"And when?" she replied. "In England of the mid-eighteenth century, on an estate in Surrey." He nodded. He had in fact read rather widely. She fell silent, thinking, before she went on: "Gaia and Wayfarer decided a serene enclave like this would be the best rendezvous for us."

"Really? I'm afraid I'm as out of place as a toad on a keyboard."

She smiled, then continued seriously: "I told you I've been given familiarity with the milieu. We'll be visiting alien ones—whatever ones you choose, after I've explained what else I know about what she has been doing these many years. That isn't much. I haven't seen any other worlds of hers. You will take the leadership."

"You mean because I'm used to odd environments and rough people? Not necessarily. I dealt with nature, you know, on Earth and in space. Peaceful."

"Dangerous."

"Maybe. But never malign."

"Tell me," she invited.

They entered the house and seated themselves in its parlor. Casement windows stood open to green parkscape where deer grazed; afar were a thatched farm cottage, its outbuildings, and the edge of grain-fields. Cleanly shaped furniture stood among paintings, etchings, books, two portrait busts. A maidservant rustled in with a tray of tea and cakes. She was obviously shocked by the newcomer but struggled to conceal it. When she had left, Laurinda explained to Christian that the owners of this place, Londoners to whom it was a summer retreat, had lent it to their friend, the eccentric Miss Ashcroft, for a holiday.

So had circumstances and memories been adjusted. It was an instance of Gaia directly interfering with the circumstances and events in an emulation. Christian wondered how frequently she did.

"Eccentricity is almost expected in the upper classes," Laurinda said. "But when you lived you could simply be yourself, couldn't you?"

In the hour that followed, she drew him out. His birth home was the Yukon Ethnate in the Bering Federation, and to it he often returned while he lived, for its wilderness preserves, mountain solitudes, and uncrowded, uncowed, plainspoken folk. Otherwise the nation was prosperous and progressive, with more connections to Asia and the Pacific than to the decayed successor states east and south. Across the Pole, it was also becoming intimate with the renascent societies of Europe, and there Christian received part of his education and spent considerable of his free time.

His was an era of savage contrasts, in which the Commonwealth of Nations maintained a precarious peace. During a youthful, impulsively taken hitch in the Conflict Mediation Service, he twice saw combat. Later in his life, stability gradually became the norm. That was largely due to the growing influence of the artificial-intelligence network. Most of its consciousness-level units interlinked in protean fashion to form minds appropriate for any particular situation, and already the capabilities of those minds exceeded the human. However, there was little sense of rivalry. Rather, there was partnership. The new minds were willing to advise, but were not interested in dominance.

Christian, child of forests and seas and uplands, heir to ancient civilizations, raised among their ongoing achievements, returned on his vacations to Earth in homecoming. Here were his kin, his friends, woods to roam, boats to sail, girls to kiss, songs to sing and glasses to raise (and a gravesite to visit—he barely mentioned his wife Laurinda; she died before uploading technology was available). Always, though, he went back to space. It had called him since first he saw the stars from a cradle under the cedars. He became an engineer. Besides fellow humans he worked closely with sapient machines, and some of them got to be friends too, of an eerie kind. Over the decades, he took a foremost role in such undertakings as the domed Copernican Sea, the Asteroid Habitat, the orbiting antimatter plant, and finally the Grand Solar Laser for launching interstellar vessels on their way. Soon afterward, his body died, old and full of days; but the days of his mind had barely begun.

"A fabulous life," Laurinda said low. She gazed out over the land, across which shadows were lengthening. "I wonder if . . . they . . . might not have done better to give us a cabin in your wilderness."

"No, no," he said. "This is fresh and marvelous to me."

"We can easily go elsewhere, you know. Any place, any time that Gaia has generated, including ones that history never saw. I'll fetch our amulets whenever you wish."

He raised his brows. "Amulets?"

"You haven't been told—informed? They are devices. You wear yours and give it the command to transfer you."

He nodded. "I see. It maps an emulated person into different surroundings."

"With suitable modifications as required. Actually, in many cases it causes a milieu to be activated for you. Most have been in standby mode for a long time. I daresay Gaia could have arranged for us to wish ourselves to wherever we were going and call up whatever we needed likewise. But an external device is better."

He pondered. "Yes, I think I see why. If we got supernatural powers, we wouldn't really be human, would we? And the whole idea is that we should be." He leaned forward on his chair. "It's your turn. Tell me about yourself."

"Oh, there's too much. Not about me, I never did anything spectacular like you, but about the times I lived in, everything that happened to change this planet after you left it—"

She was born here, in England. By then a thinly populated province of Europe, it was a quiet land ("half adream," she said) devoted to its memorials of the past. Not that creativity was dead; but the arts were rather sharply divided between ringing changes on classic works and efforts to deal with the revelations coming in from the stars. The aesthetic that artificial intelligence was evolving for itself overshadowed both these schools. Nevertheless Laurinda was active in them.

Furthermore, in the course of her work she ranged widely over Earth. (By then, meaningful work for humans was a privilege that the talented and energetic strove to earn.) She was a liaison between the two kinds of beings. It meant getting to know people in their various societies and helping them make their desires count. For instance, a proposed earthquake-control station would alter a landscape and disrupt a community; could it be resisted, or if not, what cultural adjustments could be made? Most commonly, though, she counseled and aided individuals bewildered and spiritually lost.

Still more than him, she was carefully vague about her private life, but he got the impression that it was generally happy. If childlessness was an unvoiced sorrow, it was one she shared with many in a population-regulated world; he had had only a son. She loved Earth, its glories and memories, and every fine creation of her race. At the end of her mortality she chose to abide on the planet, in her new machine body, serving as she had served, until at length she came to desire more and entered the wholeness that was to become Gaia.

He thought he saw why she had been picked for resurrection, to be his companion, out of all the uncounted millions who had elected the same destiny.

Aloud, he said, "Yes, this house is right for you. And me, in spite of everything. We're both of us more at home here than either of us could be in the other's native period. Peace and beauty."

"It isn't a paradise," she answered gravely. "This is the real eighteenth century, remember, as well as Gaia could reconstruct the history that led to it," always monitoring, making changes as events turned incompatible with what was in the chronicles and the archeology. "The household staff are underpaid, undernourished, underrespected—servile. The American colonists keep slaves and are going to rebel. Across the Channel, a rotted monarchy bleeds France white, and this will bring on a truly terrible revolution, followed by a quarter century of war."

He shrugged. "Well, the human condition never did include sanity, did it?" That was for the machines.

"In a few of our kind, it did," she said. "At least, they came close. Gaia thinks you should meet some, so you'll realize she isn't just playing cruel games. I have"—in the memories with which she had come into this being—"invited three for dinner tomorrow. It tampers a trifle with their actual biographies, but Gaia can remedy that later if she chooses." Laurinda smiled. "We'll have to make an amulet provide you with proper smallclothes and wig."

"And you provide me with a massive briefing, I'm sure. Who are they?"

"James Cook, Henry Fielding, and Erasmus Darwin. I think it will be a lively evening."

The navigator, the writer, the polymath, three tiny, brilliant facets of the heritage that Gaia guarded.

6

Now Wayfarer downloaded another secondary personality and prepared it to go survey Earth.

He, his primary self, would stay on the mountain, in a linkage with Gaia more close and complete than was possible over interstellar distances. She had promised to conduct him through her entire database of observations made across the entire planet during manifold millions of years. Even for those two, the undertaking was colossal. At the speed of their thought, it would take weeks of external time and nearly total concentration. Only a fraction of their awareness would remain available for anything else—a fraction smaller in him than in her, because her intellect was so much greater.

She told him of her hope that by this sharing, this virtually direct exposure to all she had perceived, he would come to appreciate why Earth should be left to its fiery doom. More was involved than scientific knowledge attainable in no other way. The events themselves would deepen and enlighten the galactic brain, as a great drama or symphony once did for humans. But Wayfarer must undergo their majestic sweep through the past before he could feel the truth of what she said about the future.

He had his doubts. He wondered if her human components, more than had gone into any other node, might not have given her emotions, intensified by ages of brooding, that skewed her rationality. However, he consented to her proposal. It accorded with his purpose in coming here.

While he was thus engaged, Christian would be exploring her worlds of history and of might-have-been and a different agent would range around the physical, present-day globe.

In the latter case, his most obvious procedure was to discharge an appropriate set of the molecular assemblers he had brought along and let them multiply. When their numbers were sufficient, they would build (grow; brew) a fleet of miniature robotic vessels, which would fly about and transmit to him, for study at his leisure, everything their sensors detected.

Gaia persuaded him otherwise: "If you go in person, with a minor aspect of me for a guide, you should get to know the planet more quickly and thoroughly. Much about it is unparalleled. It may help you see why I want the evolution to continue unmolested to its natural conclusion."

He accepted. After all, a major part of his mission was to fathom her thinking. Then perhaps Alpha and the rest could hold a true dialogue and reach an agreement—whatever it was going to be. Besides, he could deploy his investigators later if this expedition left him dissatisfied.

He did inquire: "What are the hazards?"

"Chiefly weather," she admitted. "With conditions growing more extreme, tremendous storms spring up practically without warning. Rapid erosion can change contours almost overnight, bringing landslides, flash floods, sudden emergence of tidal bores. I do not attempt to monitor in close detail. That volume of data would be more than I could handle"—yes, she—"when my main concern is the biological phenomena."

His mind reviewed her most recent accounts to the stars. They were grim. The posthuman lushness of nature was megayears gone. Under its clouds, Earth roasted. The loftiest mountaintops were bleak, as here above the Rainbowl, but nothing of ice or snow remained except dim geological traces. Apart from the waters and a few islands where small, primitive species hung on, the tropics were sterile deserts. Dust and sand borne on furnace winds scoured their rockscapes. North and south they encroached, withering the steppes, parching the valleys, crawling up into the hills. Here and there survived a jungle or a swamp, lashed by torrential rains or wrapped hot and sullen in fog, but it would not be for much longer. Only in the high latitudes did a measure of benignity endure. Arctica's climates ranged from Floridian—Christian Brannock's recollections—to cold on the interior heights. South of it across a sea lay a broad continent whose northerly parts had temperatures reminiscent of central Africa. Those were the last regions where life kept any abundance.

"Would you really not care to see a restoration?" Wayfarer had asked her directly, early on.

"Old Earth lives in my database and emulations," Gaia had responded. "I could not map this that is happening into those systems and let it play itself out, because I do not comprehend it well enough, nor can any finite mind. To divert the course of events would be to lose, forever, knowledge that I feel will prove to be of fundamental importance."

Wayfarer had refrained from pointing out that life, reconquering a world once more hospitable to it, would not follow predictable paths either. He knew she would retort that experiments of that kind were being conducted on a number of formerly barren spheres, seeded with synthesized organisms. It had seemed strange to him that she appeared to lack any sentiment about the mother of humankind. Her being included the beings of many and many a one who had known sunrise dew beneath a bare foot, murmurs in forest shades, wind-waves in wheatfields from horizon to horizon, yes, and the lights and clangor of great cities. It was, at root, affection, more than any scientific or technological challenge, that had roused in Gaia's fellows among the stars the wish to make Earth young again.

Now she meant to show him why she felt that death should have its way.

Before entering rapport with her, he made ready for his expedition. Gaia offered him an aircraft, swift, versatile, able to land on a square meter while disturbing scarcely a leaf. He supplied a passenger for it.

He had brought along several bodies of different types. The one he picked would have to operate independently of him, with a separate intelligence. Gaia could spare a minim of her attention to have telecommand of the flyer; he could spare none for his representative, if he was to range through the history of the globe with her.

The machine he picked was not equivalent to him. Its structure could never have supported a matrix big enough to operate at his level of mentality. Think of it, metaphorically, as possessing a brain equal to that of a high-order human. Into this brain had been copied as much of Wayfarer's self-pattern as it could hold—the merest sketch, a general idea of the situation, incomplete and distorted like this myth of ours. However, it had reserves it could call upon. Inevitably, because of being most suitable for these circumstances, the Christian Brannock aspect dominated.

So you may, if you like, think of the man as being reborn in a body of metal, silicates, carbon and other compounds, electricity and other forces, photon and particle exchanges, quantum currents. Naturally, this affected not just his appearance and abilities, but his inner life. He was not passionless, far from it, but his passions were not identical with those of flesh. In most respects, he differed more from the long-dead mortal than did the re-creation in Gaia's emulated worlds. If we call the latter Christian, we can refer to the former as Brannock.

His frame was of approximately human size and shape. Matte blue-gray, it had four arms. He could reshape the hands of the lower pair as desired, to be a tool kit. He could similarly adapt his feet according to the demands upon them, and could extrude a spindly third leg for support or extra grip. His back swelled outward to hold a nuclear energy source and various organs. His head was a domed cylinder. The sensors in it and throughout the rest of him were not conspicuous but gave him full-surround information. The face was a holographic screen in which he could generate whatever image he wished. Likewise could he produce every frequency of sound, plus visible light, infrared, and microwave radio, for sensing or for short-range communication. A memory unit, out of which he could quickly summon any data, was equivalent to a large ancient library.

He could not process those data, comprehend and reason about them, at higher speed than a human genius. He had other limitations as well. But then, he was never intended to function independently of equipment.

He was soon ready to depart. Imagine him saying to Wayfarer, with a phantom grin, "*Adiós*. Wish me luck."

The response was . . . absentminded. Wayfarer was beginning to engage with Gaia.

Thus Brannock boarded the aircraft in a kind of silence. To the eye it rested small, lanceolate, iridescently aquiver. The material component was a tissue of wisps. Most of that slight mass was devoted to generating forces and maintaining capabilities, which Gaia had not listed for him. Yet it would take a wind of uncommon violence to endanger this machine, and most likely it could outrun the menace.

He settled down inside. Wayfarer had insisted on manual controls, against emergencies that he conceded were improbable, and Gaia's effectors had made the modifications. An insubstantial configuration shimmered before Brannock, instruments to read, keypoints to touch or think at. He leaned back into a containing field and let her pilot. Noiselessly, the flyer ascended, then came down through the cloud deck and made a leisurely way at five hundred meters above the foothills.

"Follow the Remnant River to the sea," Brannock requested. "The view inbound was beautiful."

"As you like," said Gaia. They employed sonics, his voice masculine, hers—perhaps because she supposed he preferred it—feminine in a low register. Their conversation did not actually go as reported here. She changed course and he beheld the stream shining amidst the deep greens of the Bountiful Valley, under a silver-gray heaven. "The plan, you know, is that we shall cruise about Arctica first. I have an itinerary that should provide you a representative sampling of its biology. At our stops, you can investigate as intensively as you care to, and if you want to stop anyplace else we can do that too."

"Thank you," he said. "The idea is to furnish me a kind of baseline, right?"

"Yes, because conditions here are the easiest for life. When you are ready, we will proceed south, across countries increasingly harsh. You will learn about the adaptations life has made. Many are extraordinarily interesting. The galactic brain itself cannot match the creativity of nature."

"Well, sure. Chaos, complexity . . . You've described quite a few of those adaptations to, uh, us, haven't you?"

"Yes, but by no means all. I keep discovering new ones. Life keeps evolving."

As environments worsened, Brannock thought. And nonetheless, species after species went extinct. He got a sense of a rear-guard battle against the armies of hell.

"I want you to experience this as fully as you are able," Gaia said, "immerse yourself, *feel* the sublimity of it."

The tragedy, he thought. But tragedy was art, maybe the highest art that humankind ever achieved. And more of the human soul might well linger in Gaia than in any of her fellow intelligences.

Had she kept a need for catharsis, for pity and terror? What really went on in her emulations?

Well, Christian was supposed to find out something about that. If he could.

Brannock was human enough himself to protest. He gestured at the land below, where the river flowed in its canyons through the coastal hills, to water a wealth of forest and meadow before emptying into a bay above which soared thousands of wings. "You want to watch the struggle till the end," he said. "Life wants to live. What right have you to set your wish against that?"

"The right of awareness," she declared. "Only to a being that is conscious do justice, mercy, desire have any existence, any meaning. Did not humans always use the world as they saw fit? When nature finally got protection, that was because humans so chose. I speak for the knowledge and insight that *we* can gain."

The question flickered uneasily in him: What about her private emotional needs?

Abruptly the aircraft veered. The turn pushed Brannock hard into the force field upholding him. He heard air crack and scream. The bay fell aft with mounting speed.

The spaceman in him, who had lived through meteoroid strikes and radiation bursts because he was quick, had already acted. Through the optical magnification he immediately ordered up, he looked back to see what the trouble was. The glimpse he got, before the sight went under the horizon, made him cry, "Yonder!"

"What?" Gaia replied as she hurtled onward.

"That back there. Why are you running from it?"

"What do you mean? There is nothing important."

"The devil there isn't. I've a notion you saw it more clearly than I did."

Gaia slowed the headlong flight until she well-nigh hovered above the strand and wild surf. He felt a sharp suspicion that she did it in order to dissipate the impression of urgency, make him more receptive to whatever she intended to claim.

"Very well," she said after a moment. "I spied a certain object. What do you think you saw?"

He decided not to answer straightforwardly—at least, not before she convinced him of her good faith. The more information she had, the more readily she could contrive a deception. Even this fragment of her intellect was superior to his. Yet he had his own measure of wits, and an ingrained stubbornness.

"I'm not sure, except that it didn't seem dangerous. Suppose you tell me what it is and why you turned tail from it."

Did she sigh? "At this stage of your knowledge, you would not understand. Rather, you would be bound to misunderstand. That is why I retreated."

A human would have tensed every muscle. Brannock's systems went on full standby. "I'll be the judge of my brain's range, if you please. Kindly go back."

"No. I promise I will explain later, when you have seen enough more."

Seen enough illusions? She might well have many trickeries waiting for him. "As you like," Brannock said. "Meanwhile, I'll give Wayfarer a call and let him know," Alpha's emissary kept a minute part of his sensibility open to outside stimuli.

"No, do not," Gaia said. "It would distract him unnecessarily."

"He will decide that," Brannock told her.

Strife exploded.

Almost, Gaia won. Had her entirety been focused on attack, she would have carried it off with such swiftness that Brannock would never have known he was bestormed. But a fraction of her was dealing, as always, with her observing units around the globe and their torrents of data. Possibly it also glanced from time to time—through the quantum shifts inside her—at the doings of Christian and Laurinda. By far the most of her was occupied in her interaction with Wayfarer. This she could not set aside without rousing instant suspicion. Rather, she must make a supremely clever effort to conceal from him that anything untoward was going on.

Moreover, she had never encountered a being like Brannock, human male aggressiveness and human spacefarer's reflexes blent with sophisticated technology and something of Alpha's immortal purpose.

He felt the support field strengthen and tighten to hold him immobile. He felt a tide like delirium rush into his mind. A man would have thought it was a knockout anesthetic. Brannock did not stop to wonder. He reacted directly, even as she struck. Machine fast and tiger ferocious, he put her off balance for a crucial millisecond.

Through the darkness and roaring in his head, he lashed out physically. His hands tore through the light-play of control nexuses before him. They were not meant to withstand an assault. He could not seize command, but he could, blindly, disrupt.

Arcs leaped blue-white. Luminances flared and died. Power output continued;

the aircraft stayed aloft. Its more complex functions were in ruin. Their dance of atoms, energies, and waves went uselessly random.

The bonds that had been closing on Brannock let go. He sagged to the floor. The night in his head receded. It left him shaken, his senses awhirl. Into the sudden anarchy of everything he yelled, "Stop, you bitch!"

"I will," Gaia said.

Afterward he realized that she had kept a vestige of governance over the flyer. Before he could wrest it from her, she sent them plunging downward and cut off the main generator. Every force field blinked out. Wind ripped the material frame asunder. Its pieces crashed in the surf. Combers tumbled them about, cast a few on the beach, gave the rest to the undertow.

As the craft fell, distintegrating, Brannock gathered his strength and leaped. The thrust of his legs cast him outward, through a long arc that ended in deeper water. It fountained high and white when he struck. He went down into green depths while the currents swept him to and fro. But he hit the sandy bottom unharmed.

Having no need to breathe, he stayed under. To recover from the shock took him less than a second. To make his assessment took minutes, there in the swirling surges.

Gaia had tried to take him over. A force field had begun to damp the processes in his brain and impose its own patterns. He had quenched it barely in time.

She would scarcely have required a capability of that kind in the past. Therefore she had invented and installed it specifically for him. This strongly suggested she had meant to use it at some point of their journey. When he saw a thing she had not known was there and refused to be fobbed off, he compelled her to make the attempt before she was ready. When it failed, she spent her last resources to destroy him.

She would go that far, that desperately, to keep a secret that tremendous from the stars.

He recognized a mistake in his thinking. She had not used up everything at her beck. On the contrary, she had a planetful of observers and other instrumentalities to call upon. Certain of them must be bound here at top speed, to make sure he was dead—or, if he lived, to make sure of him. Afterward she would feed Wayfarer a story that ended with a regrettable accident away off over an ocean.

Heavier than water, Brannock strode down a sloping sea floor in search of depth.

Having found a jumble of volcanic rock, he crawled into a lava tube, lay fetally curled, and willed his systems to operate as low-level as might be. He hoped that then her agents would miss him. Neither their numbers nor their sensitivities were infinite. It would be reasonable for Gaia—who could not have witnessed his escape, her sensors in the aircraft being obliterated as it came apart—to conclude that the flows had taken his scattered remains away.

After three days and nights, the internal clock he had set brought him back awake.

He knew he must stay careful. However, unless she kept a closer watch on the site than he expected she would—for Wayfarer, in communion with her, might too readily notice that she was concentrating on one little patch of the planet—he dared now move about. His electronic senses ought to warn him of any robot that came into his vicinity, even if it was too small for eyes to see. Whether he could then do anything about it was a separate question.

First he searched the immediate area. Gaia's machines had removed those shards of the wreck that they found, but most were strewn over the bottom, and she had evidently not thought it worthwhile, or safe, to have them sought out. Nearly all of what he came upon was in fact scrap. A few units were intact. The one that interested him had the physical form of a small metal sphere. He tracked it down by magnetic induction. Having taken it to a place ashore, hidden by trees from the sky, he studied it. With his tool-hands he traced the (mythic) circuitry within and identified it as a memory bank. The encoding was familiar to his Wayfarer aspect. He extracted the information and stored it in his own database.

A set of languages. Human languages, although none he had ever heard of. Yes, very interesting.

"I'd better get hold of those people," he muttered. In the solitude of wind, sea, and wilderness, he had relapsed into an ancient habit of occasionally thinking aloud. "Won't likely be another chance. Quite a piece of news for Wayfarer." If he came back, or at least got within range of his transmitter.

He set forth afoot, along the shore toward the bay where the Remnant River debouched. Maybe that which he had seen would be there yet, or traces of it.

He wasn't sure, everything had happened so fast, but he thought it was a ship.

7

Three days—olden Earth days of twenty-four hours, cool sunlight, now and then a rainshower leaving pastures and hedgerows asparkle, rides through English lanes, rambles through English towns, encounters with folk, evensong in a Norman church, exploration of buildings and books, long talks and companionable silences—wrought friendship. In Christian it also began to rouse kindlier feelings toward Gaia. She had resurrected Laurinda, and Laurinda was a part of her, as he was of Wayfarer and of Alpha and more other minds across the galaxy than he could number. Could the rest of Gaia's works be wrongful?

No doubt she had chosen and planned as she did in order to get this reaction from him. It didn't seem to matter.

Nor did the primitive conditions of the eighteenth century matter to him or to Laurinda. Rather, their everyday experiences were something refreshingly new, and frequently the occasion of laughter. What did become a bit difficult for him was to retire decorously to his separate room each night.

But they had their missions: his to see what was going on in this reality and afterward upload into Wayfarer; hers to explain and justify it to him as well as a mortal was able. Like him, she kept a memory of having been one with a nodal being. The memory was as dim and fragmentary as his, more a sense of transcendence than anything with a name or form, like the afterglow of a religious vision long ago. Yet it pervaded her personality, the unconscious more than the conscious; and it was her relationship to Gaia, as he had his to Wayfarer and beyond that to Alpha. In a limited, mortal, but altogether honest and natural way, she spoke for the node of Earth.

By tacit consent, they said little about the purpose and simply enjoyed their surroundings and one another, until the fourth morning. Perhaps the weather whipped up a lifetime habit of duty. Wind gusted and shrilled around the house, rain blinded the windows, there would be no going out even in a carriage. Indoors a fire failed to hold dank chill at bay. Candlelight glowed cozily on the breakfast table, silverware and china sheened, but shadows hunched thick in every corner.

He took a last sip of coffee, put the cup down, and ended the words he had been setting forth: "Yes, we'd better get started. Not that I've any clear notion of what to look for. Wayfarer himself doesn't." Gaia had been so vague about so much. Well,

Wayfarer was now (whatever "now" meant) in rapport with her, seeking an overall, cosmic view of—how many millions of years on this planet?

"Why, you know your task," Laurinda replied. "You're to find out the nature of Gaia's interior activity, what it means in moral—in human terms." She straightened in her chair. Her tone went resolute. "We *are* human, we emulations. We think and act, we feel joy and pain, the same as humans always did."

Impulse beckoned; it was his want to try to lighten moods. "And," he added, "make new generations of people, the same as humans always did."

A blush crossed the fair countenance. "Yes," she said. Quickly: "Of course, most of what's . . . here . . . is nothing but database. Archives, if you will. We might start by visiting one or two of those reconstructions."

He smiled, the heaviness lifting from him. "I'd love to. Any suggestions?"

Eagerness responded. "The Acropolis of Athens? As it was when new? Classical civilization fascinated me." She tossed her head. "Still does, by damn."

"Hm." He rubbed his chin. "From what I learned in my day, those old Greeks were as tricky, quarrelsome, shortsighted a pack of political animals as ever stole an election or bullied a weaker neighbor. Didn't Athens finance the building of the Parthenon by misappropriating the treasury of the Delian League?"

"They were human," she said, almost too low for him to hear above the storm-noise. "But what they made—"

"Sure," he answered. "Agreed, Let's go."

In perception, the amulets were silvery two-centimeter discs that hung on a user's breast, below garments. In reality—outer-viewpoint reality—they were powerful, subtle programs with intelligences of their own. Christian wondered about the extent to which they were under the direct control of Gaia, and how closely she was monitoring him.

Without thinking, he took Laurinda's hand. Her fingers clung to his. She looked straight before her, though, into the flickery fire, while she uttered their command.

Immediately, with no least sensation of movement, they were on board marble steps between outworks, under a cloudless heaven, in flooding hot radiance. From the steepest, unused hill slopes, a scent of wild thyme drifted up through silence, thyme without bees to quicken it or hands to pluck it. Below reached the city, sun-smitten house roofs, open agoras, colonnaded temples. In this clear air Brannock imagined he could well-nigh make out the features on the statues.

After a time beyond time, the visitors moved upward, still mute, still hand in hand, to where winged Victories lined the balustrade before the sanctuary of Nike Apteros. Their draperies flowed to movement he did not see and wind he did not feel. One was tying her sandals. . . .

For a long while the two lingered at the Propylaea, its porticos, Ionics, Dorics, paintings, votive tablets in the Pinakotheka. They felt they could have stayed past sunset, but everything else awaited them, and they knew mortal enthusiasm as they would presently know mortal weariness. Colors burned. . . .

The stone flowers and stone maidens at the Erechtheum . . .

Christian had thought of the Parthenon as exquisite; so it was in the pictures and models he had seen, while the broken, chemically gnawed remnants were merely to grieve over. Confronting it here, entering it, he discovered its sheer size and mass. Life shouted in the friezes, red, blue, gilt; then in the dusk within, awesomeness and beauty found their focus in the colossal Athene of Pheidias.

—Long afterward, he stood with Laurinda on the Wall of Kimon, above the

Asclepium and Theater of Dionysus. A westering sun made the city below intricate with shadows, and coolth breathed out of the east. Hitherto, when they spoke it had been, illogically, in near whispers. Now they felt free to talk openly, or did they feel a need?

He shook his head. "Gorgeous," he said, for lack of anything halfway adequate. "Unbelievable."

"It was worth all the wrongdoing and war and agony," she murmured. "Wasn't it?"

For the moment, he shied away from deep seriousness. "I didn't expect it to be this, uh, gaudy—no, this bright."

"They painted their buildings. That's known."

"Yes, I knew too. But were later scholars sure of just what colors?"

"Scarcely, except where a few traces were left. Most of this must be Gaia's conjecture. The sculpture especially, I suppose. Recorded history saved only the barest description of the Athene, for instance." Laurinda paused. Her gaze went outward to the mountains. "But surely this—in view of everything she has, all the information, and being able to handle it all at once and, and understand the minds that were capable of making it—surely this is the most likely reconstruction. Or the least unlikely."

"She may have tried variations. Would you like to go see?"

"No, I, I think not, unless you want to. This has been overwhelming, hasn't it?" She hesitated. "Besides, well—"

He nodded. "Yeh." With a gesture at the soundless, motionless, smokeless city below and halidoms around: "Spooky. At best, a museum exhibit. Not much to our purpose, I'm afraid."

She met his eyes. "Your purpose. I'm only a—not even a guide, really. Gaia's voice to you? No, just a, an undertone of her, if that." The smile that touched her lips was somehow forlorn. "I suspect my main reason for existing again is to keep you company."

He laughed and offered her a hand, which for a moment she clasped tightly. "I'm very glad of the company, eccentric Miss Ashcroft."

Her smile warmed and widened. "Thank you, kind sir. And I am glad to be . . . alive . . . today. What should we do next?"

"Visit some living history, I think," he said. "Why not Hellenic?"

She struck her palms together. "The age of Pericles!"

He frowned. "Well, I don't know about that. The Peloponnesian War, the plague—and foreigners like us, barbarians, you a woman, we wouldn't be too well received, would we?"

He heard how she put disappointment aside and looked forward anew. "When and where, then?"

"Aristotle's time? If I remember rightly, Greece was peaceful then, no matter how much hell Alexander was raising abroad, and the society was getting quite cosmopolitan. Less patriarchal, too. Anyhow, Aristotle's always interested me. In a way, he was one of the earliest scientists."

"We had better inquire first. But before that, let's go home to a nice hot cup of tea!"

They returned to the house at the same moment as they left it, to avoid perturbing the servants. There they found that lack of privacy joined with exhaustion to keep them from speaking of anything other than trivia. However, that was all right; they were good talkmates.

The next morning, which was brilliant, they went out into the garden and settled on a bench by the fish basin. Drops of rain glistened on flowers, whose fragrance awoke with the strengthening sunshine. Nothing else was in sight or earshot. This time Christian addressed the amulets. He felt suddenly heavy around his neck, and the words came out awkwardly. He need not have said them aloud, but it helped him give shape to his ideas.

The reply entered directly into their brains. He rendered it to himself, irrationally, as in a dry, professorish tenor:

"Only a single Hellenic milieu has been carried through many generations. It includes the period you have in mind. It commenced at the point of approximately 500 B.C., with an emulation as historically accurate as possible."

But nearly everyone then alive was lost to history, thought Christian. Except for the few who were in the chronicles, the whole population must needs be created out of Gaia's imagination, guided by knowledge and logic; and those few named persons were themselves almost entirely new-made, their very DNA arbitrarily laid out.

"The sequence was revised as necessary," the amulet continued.

Left to itself, that history would soon have drifted completely away from the documents, and eventually from the archeology, Christian thought. Gaia saw this start to happen, over and over. She rewrote the program—events, memories, personalities, bodies, births, life spans, deaths—and let it resume until it deviated again. Over and over. The morning felt abruptly cold.

"Much was learned on every such occasion," said the amulet. "The situation appeared satisfactory by the time Macedonian hegemony was inevitable, and thereafter the sequence was left to play itself out undisturbed. Naturally, it still did not proceed identically with the historical past. Neither Aristotle nor Alexander were born. Instead, a reasonably realistic conqueror lived to a ripe age and bequeathed a reasonably well constructed empire. He did have a Greek teacher in his youth, who had been a disciple of Plato."

"Who was that?" Christian asked out of a throat gone dry.

"His name was Eumenes. In many respects he was equivalent to Aristotle, but had a more strongly empirical orientation. This was planned."

Eumenes was specially ordained, then. Why?

"If we appear and meet him, w-won't that change what comes after?"

"Probably not to any significant extent. Or if it does, that will not matter. The original sequence is in Gaia's database. Your visit will, in effect, be a reactivation."

"Not one for your purpose," Laurinda whispered into the air. "What was it? What happened in that world?"

"The objective was experimental, to study the possible engendering of a scientific-technological revolution analogous to that of the seventeenth century A.D., with accompanying social developments that might foster the evolution of a stable democracy."

Christian told himself furiously to pull out of his funk. "Did it?" he challenged.

The reply was calm. "Do you wish to study it?"

Christian had not expected any need to muster his courage. After a minute he said, word by slow word, "Yes, I think that might be more useful than meeting your philosopher. Can you show us the outcome of the experiment?"

Laurinda joined in: "Oh, I know there can't be any single, simple picture. But can you bring us to a, a scene that will give an impression—a kind of epitome—like, oh, King John at Runnymede or Elizabeth the First knighting Francis Drake or Einstein and Bohr talking about the state of their world?"

"An extreme possibility occurs in a year corresponding to your A.D. 894," the amulet told him. "I suggest Athens as the locale. Be warned, it is dangerous. I can protect you, or remove you, but human affairs are inherently chaotic and this situation is more unpredictable than most. It could escape my control."

"I'll go," Christian snapped.

"And I," Laurinda said.

He glared at her. "No. You heard. It's dangerous."

Gone quite calm, she stated, "It is necessary for me. Remember, I travel on behalf of Gaia."

Gaia, who let the thing come to pass.

Transfer.

For an instant, they glanced at themselves. They knew the amulets would convert their garb to something appropriate. She wore a gray gown, belted, reaching halfway down her calves, with shoes, stockings, and a scarf over hair coiled in braids. He was in tunic, trousers, and boots of the same coarse materials, a sheath knife at his hip and a long-barreled firearm slung over his back.

Their surroundings smote them. They stood in a Propylaea that was scarcely more than tumbled stones and snags of sculpture. The Parthenon was not so shattered, but scarred, weathered, here and there buttressed with brickwork from which thrust the mouths of rusted cannon. All else was ruin. The Erechtheum looked as if it had been quarried. Below them, the city burned. They could see little of it through smoke that stained the sky and savaged their nostrils. A roar of conflagration reached them, and bursts of gunfire.

A woman came running out of the haze, up the great staircase. She was young, dark-haired, unkempt, ragged, begrimed, desperate. A man came after, a burly blond in a fur cap, dirty red coat, and leather breeches. Beneath a sweeping mustache, he leered. He too was armed, murderously big knife, firearm in right hand.

The woman saw Christian looming before her. "*Voetho!*" she screamed. "*Onome Theou, kyrie, voetho!*" She caught her foot against a step and fell. Her pursuer stopped before she could rise and stamped a boot down on her back.

Through his amulet, Christian understood the cry. "Help, in God's name, sir, help!" Fleetingly he thought the language must be a debased Greek. The other man snarled at him and brought weapon to shoulder.

Christian had no time to unlimber his. While the stranger was in motion, he bent, snatched up a rock—a fragment of a marble head—and cast. It thudded against the stranger's nose. He lurched back, his face a sudden red grotesque. His gun clattered to the stairs. He howled.

With the quickness that was his in emergencies, Christian rejected grabbing his own firearm. He had seen that its lock was of peculiar design. He might not be able to discharge it fast enough. He drew his knife and lunged downward. "Get away, you swine, before I open your guts!" he shouted. The words came out in the woman's language.

The other man retched, turned, and staggered off. Well before he reached the bottom of the hill, smoke had swallowed sight of him. Christian halted at the woman's huddled form and sheathed his blade. "Here, sister," he said, offering his hand, "come along. Let's get to shelter. There may be more of them."

She crawled to her feet, gasping, leaned heavily on his arm, and limped beside him up to the broken gateway. Her features Mediterranean, she was doubtless a native. She looked half starved. Laurinda came to her other side. Between them, the visitors got her into the portico of the Parthenon. Beyond a smashed door lay an interior dark and empty of everything but litter. It would be defensible if necessary.

An afterthought made Christian swear at himself. He went back for the enemy's weapon. When he returned, Laurinda sat with her arms around the woman, crooning comfort. "There, darling, there, you're safe with us. Don't be afraid. We'll take care of you."

The fugitive lifted big eyes full of night. "Are . . . you . . . angels from heaven?" she mumbled.

"No, only mortals like you," Laurinda answered through tears. That was not exactly true, Christian thought; but what else could she say? "We do not even know your name."

"I am . . . Zoe . . . Comnenaina—"

"Bone-dry, I hear from your voice." Laurinda lifted her head. Her lips moved in silent command. A jug appeared on the floor, bedewed with cold. "Here is water. Drink."

Zoe had not noticed the miracle. She snatched the vessel and drained it in gulp after gulp. When she was through she set it down and said, "Thank you," dully but with something of strength and reason again in her.

"Who was that after you?" Christian asked.

She drew knees to chin, hugged herself, stared before her, and replied in a dead voice, "A Flemic soldier. They broke into our house. I saw them stab my father. They laughed and laughed. I ran out the back and down the streets. I thought I could hide on the Acropolis. Nobody comes here anymore. That one saw me and came after. I suppose he would have killed me when he was done. That would have been better than if he took me away with him."

Laurinda nodded. "An invading army," she said as tonelessly. "They took the city and now they are sacking it."

Christian thumped the butt of his gun down on the stones. "Does Gaia let this go *on?*" he grated.

Laurinda lifted her gaze to his. It pleaded. "She must. Humans must have free will. Otherwise they're puppets."

"But how did they get into this mess?" Christian demanded. "Explain it if you can!"

The amulet(s) replied with the same impersonality as before:

"The Hellenistic era developed scientific method. This, together with the expansion of commerce and geographical knowledge, produced an industrial revolution and parliamentary democracy. However, neither the science nor the technology progressed beyond an approximate equivalent of your eighteenth century. Unwise social and fiscal policies led to breakdown, dictatorship, and repeated warfare."

Christian's grin bared teeth. "That sounds familiar."

"Alexander Tytler said it in our eighteenth century," Laurinda muttered unevenly. "No republic has long outlived the discovery by a majority of its people that they could vote themselves largesse from the public treasury." Aloud: "Christian, they were only human."

Zoe hunched, lost in her sorrow.

"You oversimplify," stated the amulet voice. "But this is not a history lesson. To continue the outline, inevitably engineering information spread to the warlike barbarians of northern Europe and western Asia. If you question why they were granted existence, reflect that a population confined to the littoral of an inland sea could not model any possible material world. The broken-down societies of the South were unable to change their characters, or prevail over them, or eventually hold them off. The end results are typified by what you see around you."

"The Dark Ages," Christian said dully. "What happens after them? What kind of new civilization?"

"None. This sequence terminates in one more of its years."

"Huh?" he gasped. "Destroyed?"

"No. The program ceases to run. The emulation stops."

"My God! Those millions of lives—as real as, as mine—"

Laurinda stood up and held her arms out into the fouled air. "Does Gaia know, then, does Gaia know this time line would never get any happier?" she cried.

"No," said the voice in their brains. "Doubtless the potential of further progress exists. However, you forget that while Gaia's capacities are large, they are not infinite. The more attention she devotes to one history, the details of its planet as well as the length of its course, the less she has to give to others. The probability is too small that this sequence will lead to a genuinely new form of society."

Slowly, Laurinda nodded. "I see."

"I don't," Christian snapped. "Except that Gaia's inhuman."

Laurinda shook her head and laid a hand on his. "No, not that. Posthuman. *We* built the first artificial intelligences." After a moment: "Gaia isn't cruel. The universe often is, and she didn't create it. She's seeking something better than blind chance can make."

"Maybe." His glance fell on Zoe. "Look, something's got to be done for this poor soul. Never mind if we change the history. It's due to finish soon anyway."

Laurinda swallowed and wiped her eyes. "Give her her last year in peace," she said into the air. "Please."

Objects appeared in the room behind the doorway. "Here are food, wine, clean water," said the unheard voice. "Advise her to return downhill after dark, find some friends, and lead them back. A small party, hiding in these ruins, can hope to survive until the invaders move on."

"It isn't worthwhile doing more, is it?" Christian said bitterly. "Not to you."

"Do you wish to end your investigation?"

"No, be damned if I will."

"Nor I," said Laurinda. "But when we're through here, when we've done the pitiful little we can for this girl, take us home."

Peace dwelt in England. Clouds towered huge and white, blue-shadowed from the sunlight spilling past them. Along the left side of a lane, poppies blazed in a grainfield goldening toward harvest. On the right stretched the manifold greens of a pasture where cattle drowsed beneath a broad-crowned oak. Man and woman rode side by side. Hoofs thumped softly, saddle leather creaked, the sweet smell of horse mingled with herbal pungencies, a blackbird whistled.

"No, I don't suppose Gaia will ever restart any program she's terminated," Laurinda said. "But it's no worse than death, and death is seldom that easy."

"The scale of it," Christian protested, then sighed. "But I daresay Wayfarer will tell me I'm being sloppy sentimental, and when I've rejoined him I'll agree." Wryness added that that had better be true. He would no longer be separate, an avatar; he would be one with a far greater entity, which would in its turn remerge with a greater still.

"Without Gaia, they would never have existed, those countless lives, generation after generation after generation," Laurinda said. "Their worst miseries they brought on themselves. If any of them are ever to find their way to something better, truly better, she has to keep making fresh starts."

"Mm, I can't help remembering all the millennialists and utopians who slaughtered people wholesale, or tortured them or threw them into concentration camps, if their behavior didn't fit the convenient attainment of the inspired vision."

"No, no, it's not like that! Don't you see? She gives them their freedom to be themselves and, and to become more."

"Seems to me she adjusts the parameters and boundary conditions till the setup looks promising before she lets the experiment run." Christian frowned. "But I admit, it isn't believable that she does it simply because she's . . . bored and lonely. Not when the whole fellowship of her kind is open to her. Maybe we haven't the brains to know what her reasons are. Maybe she's explaining them to Wayfarer, or directly to Alpha," although communication among the stars would take decades at least.

"Do you want to go on nonetheless?" she asked.

"I said I do. I'm supposed to. But you?"

"Yes. I don't want to, well, fail her."

"I'm sort of at a loss what to try next, and not sure it's wise to let the amulets decide."

"But they can help us, counsel us." Laurinda drew breath. "Please. If you will. The next world we go to—could it be gentle? That horror we saw—"

He reached across to take her hand. "Exactly what I was thinking. Have you a suggestion?"

She nodded. "York Minster. It was in sad condition when I . . . lived . . . but I saw pictures and—It was one of the loveliest churches ever built, in the loveliest old town."

"Excellent idea. Not another lifeless piece of archive, though. A complete environment." Christian pondered. "We'll inquire first, naturally, but offhand I'd guess the Edwardian period would suit us well. On the Continent they called it the *belle époque*."

"Splendid!" she exclaimed. Already her spirits were rising anew.

Transfer.

They arrived near the west end, in the south aisle.

Worshippers were few, scattered closer to the altar rail. In the dimness, under the glories of glass and soaring Perpendicular arches, their advent went unobserved. Windows in that direction glowed more vividly—rose, gold, blue, the cool gray-green of the Five Sisters—than the splendor above their backs; it was a Tuesday morning in June. Incense wove its odor through the ringing chant from the choir.

Christian tautened. "That's Latin," he whispered. "In England, 1900?" He glanced down at his garments and hers, and peered ahead. Shirt, coat, trousers for him, with a hat laid on the pew; ruffled blouse, ankle-length gown, and lacy bonnet for her; but—"The clothes aren't right either."

"Hush," Laurinda answered as low. "Wait. We were told this wouldn't be our 1900. Here may be the only York Minster in all of Gaia."

He nodded stiffly. It was clear that the node had never attempted a perfect reproduction of any past milieu—impossible, and pointless to boot. Often, though not necessarily always, she took an approximation as a starting point; but it never went on to the same destiny. What were the roots of this day?

"Relax," Laurinda urged. "It's beautiful."

He did his best, and indeed the Roman Catholic mass at the hour of tierce sang some tranquility into his heart.

After the Nunc Dimittis, when clergy and laity had departed, the two could wander around and savor. Emerging at last, they spent a while looking upon the carven tawny limestone of the front. This was no Parthenon; it was a different upsurging of the same miracle. But around it lay a world to discover. With half a sigh and half a smile, they set forth.

The delightful narrow "gates," walled in with half-timbered houses, lured them. More modern streets and buildings, above all the people therein, captured them. York was a living town, a market town, core of a wide hinterland, node of a nation. It racketed, it bustled.

The half smile faded. A wholly foreign setting would not have felt as wrong as one that was half homelike.

Clothing styles were not radically unlike what pictures and historical dramas had once shown; but they were not identical. The English chatter was in no dialect of English known to Christian or Laurinda, and repeatedly they heard versions of German. A small, high-stacked steam locomotive pulled a train into a station of somehow Teutonic architecture. No early automobiles stuttered along the thoroughfares. Horsedrawn vehicles moved crowdedly, but the pavements were clean and the smell of dung faint because the animals wore a kind of diapers. A flag above a post office (?), fluttering in the wind, displayed a cross of St. Andrew on which was superimposed a two-headed gold eagle. A man with a megaphone bellowed at the throng to stand aside and make way for a military squadron. In blue uniforms, rifles on shoulders, they quick-marched to commands barked in German. Individual soldiers, presumably on leave, were everywhere. A boy went by, shrilly hawking newspapers, and Christian saw WAR in a headline.

"Listen, amulet," he muttered finally, "where can we get a beer?"

"A public house will admit you if you go in by the couples' entrance," replied the soundless voice.

So, no unescorted women allowed. Well, Christian thought vaguely, hadn't that been the case in his Edwardian years, at any rate in respectable taverns? A signboard jutting from a Tudor façade read GEORGE AND DRAGON. The wainscotted room inside felt equally English.

Custom was plentiful and noisy, tobacco smoke thick, but he and Laurinda found a table in a corner where they could talk without anybody else paying attention. The brew that a barmaid fetched was of Continental character. He didn't give it the heed it deserved.

"I don't think we've found our peaceful world after all," he said.

Laurinda looked beyond him, into distances where he could not follow. "Will we ever?" she wondered. "Can any be, if it's human?"

He grimaced. "Well, let's find out what the hell's going on here."

"You can have a detailed explanation if you wish," said the voice in their heads. "You would be better advised to accept a bare outline, as you did before."

"Instead of loading ourselves down with the background of a world that never was," he mumbled.

"That never was ours," Laurinda corrected him.

"Carry on."

"This sequence was generated as of its fifteenth century A.D.," said the voice. "The conciliar movement was made to succeed, rather than failing as it did in your history."

"Uh, conciliar movement?"

"The ecclesiastical councils of Constance and later of Basel attempted to heal the Great Schism and reform the government of the Church. Here they accomplished it, giving back to the bishops some of the power that over the centuries had accrued to the popes, working out a reconciliation with the Hussites, and making other important changes. As a result, no Protestant breakaway occurred, nor wars of religion, and the Church remained a counterbalance to the state, preventing the rise of absolute monarchies."

"Why, that's wonderful," Laurinda whispered.

"Not too wonderful by now," Christian said grimly. "What happened?"

"In brief, Germany was spared the devastation of the Thirty Years' War and a long-lasting division into quarrelsome principalities. It was unified in the seventeenth century and soon became the dominant European power, colonizing and conquering eastward. Religious and cultural differences from the Slavs proved irreconcilable. As the harsh imperium provoked increasing restlessness, it perforce grew more severe, causing more rebellion. Meanwhile it decayed within, until today it has broken apart and the Russians are advancing on Berlin."

"I see. What about science and technology?"

"They have developed more slowly than in your history, although you have noted the existence of a fossil-fueled industry and inferred an approximately Lagrangian level of theory."

"The really brilliant eras were when all hell broke loose, weren't they?" Christian mused. "This Europe went through less agony, and invented and discovered less. Coincidence?"

"What about government?" Laurinda asked.

"For a time, parliaments flourished, more powerful than kings, emperors, or popes," said the voice. "In most Western countries they still wield considerable influence."

"As the creatures of special interests, I'll bet," Christian rasped. "All right, what comes next?"

Gaia knew. He sat in a reactivation of something she probably played to a finish thousands of years ago.

"Scientific and technological advance proceeds, accelerating, through a long period of general turbulence. At the termination point—"

"Never mind!" Oblivion might be better than a nuclear war.

Silence fell at the table. The life that filled the pub with its noise felt remote, unreal.

"We dare not weep," Laurinda finally said. "Not yet."

Christian shook himself. "Europe was never the whole of Earth," he growled. "How many worlds has Gaia made?"

"Many," the voice told him.

"Show us one that's really foreign. If you agree, Laurinda."

She squared her shoulders. "Yes, do." After a moment: "Not here. If we disappeared it would shock them. It might change the whole future."

"Hardly enough to notice," Christian said. "And would it matter in the long run? But, yeh, let's be off."

They wandered out, among marvels gone meaningless, until they found steps leading up onto the medieval wall. Thence they looked across roofs and river and Yorkshire beyond, finding they were alone.

"Now take us away," Christian ordered.

"You have not specified any type of world," said the voice.

"Surprise us."

Transfer.

The sky stood enormous, bleached blue, breezes warm underneath. A bluff overlooked a wide brown river. Trees grew close to its edge, tall, pale of bark, leaves silver-green and shivery. Christian recognized them, cottonwoods. He was somewhere in west central North America, then. Uneasy shadows lent camouflage if he and Laurinda kept still. Across the river the land reached broad, roads twisting their way through cultivation—mainly wheat and Indian corn—that seemed to be parceled out among small farms, each with its buildings, house, barn, occasional stable or workshop. The sweeping lines of the ruddy-tiled roofs looked Asian. He spied oxcarts and a few horseback riders on the roads, workers in the fields, but at their distance he couldn't identify race or garb. Above yonder horizon thrust clustered towers that also suggested the Orient. If they belonged to a city, it must be compact, not sprawling over the countryside but neatly drawn into itself.

One road ran along the farther riverbank. A procession went upon it. An elephant led, as richly caparisoned as the man under the silk awning of a howdah. Shaven-headed men in yellow robes walked after, flanked by horsemen who bore poles from which pennons streamed scarlet and gold. The sound of slowly beaten gongs and minor-key chanting came faint through the wind.

Christian snapped his fingers. "Stupid me!" he muttered. "Give us a couple of opticals."

Immediately he and Laurinda held the devices. From his era, they fitted into the palm but projected an image at any magnification desired, with no lenses off which light could glint to betray. He peered back and forth for minutes. Yes, the appearance was quite Chinese, or Chinese-derived, except that a number of the individuals he studied had more of an American countenance and the leader on the elephant wore a feather bonnet above his robe.

"How quiet here," Laurinda said.

"You are at the height of the Great Peace," the amulet voice answered.

"How many like that were there ever?" Christian wondered. "Where, when, how?"

"You are in North America, in the twenty-second century by your reckoning. Chinese navigators arrived on the Pacific shore seven hundred years ago, and colonists followed."

In this world, Christian thought, Europe and Africa were surely a sketch, mere geography, holding a few primitive tribes at most, unless nothing was there but ocean. Simplify, simplify.

"Given the distances to sail and the dangers, the process was slow," the voice went on. "While the newcomers displaced or subjugated the natives wherever they settled, most remained free for a long time, acquired the technology, and also developed resistance to introduced diseases. Eventually, being on roughly equal terms, the races began to mingle, genetically and culturally. The settlers mitigated the savagery of the religions they had encountered, but learned from the societies, as well as teaching. You behold the outcome."

"The Way of the Buddha?" Laurinda asked very softly.

"As influenced by Daoism and local nature cults. It is a harmonious faith, without sects or heresies, pervading the civilization."

"Everything can't be pure loving-kindness," Christian said.

"Certainly not. But the peace that the Emperor Wei Zhi-fu brought about has lasted for a century and will for another two. If you travel, you will find superb achievements in the arts and in graciousness."

"Another couple of centuries." Laurinda's tones wavered the least bit. "Afterward?"

"It doesn't last," Christian predicted. "These are humans too. And—tell me—do they ever get to a real science?"

"No," said the presence. "Their genius lies in other realms. But the era of warfare to come will drive the development of a remarkable empirical technology."

"What era?"

"China never recognized the independence that this country proclaimed for itself, nor approved of its miscegenation. A militant dynasty will arise, which overruns a western hemisphere weakened by the religious and secular quarrels that do at last break out."

"And the conquerors will fall in their turn. Unless Gaia makes an end first. She does—she did—sometime, didn't she?"

"All things are finite. Her creations too."

The leaves rustled through muteness.

"Do you wish to go into the city and look about?" asked the presence. "It can be arranged for you to meet some famous persons."

"No," Christian said. "Not yet, anyway. Maybe later."

Laurinda sighed. "We'd rather go home now and rest."

"And think," Christian said. "Yes."

Transfer.

The sun over England seemed milder than for America. Westering, it sent rays through windows to glow in wood, caress marble and the leather bindings of books, explode into rainbows where they met cut glass, evoke flower aromas from a jar of potpourri.

Laurinda opened a bureau drawer. She slipped the chain of her amulet over her head and tossed the disc in. Christian blinked, nodded, and followed suit. She closed the drawer.

"We do need to be by ourselves for a while," she said. "This hasn't been a dreadful day like, like before, but I am so tired."

"Understandable," he replied.

"You?"

"I will be soon, no doubt."

"Those worlds—already they feel like dreams I've wakened from."

"An emotional retreat from them, I suppose. Not cowardice, no, no, just a necessary, temporary rest. You shared their pain. You're too sweet for your own good, Laurinda."

She smiled. "How you misjudge me. I'm not quite ready to collapse yet, if you aren't."

"Thunder, no."

She took crystal glasses out of a cabinet, poured from a decanter on a sideboard, and gestured invitation. The port fondled their tongues. They stayed on their feet, look meeting look.

"I daresay we'd be presumptuous and foolish to try finding any pattern, this early in our search," she ventured. "Those peeks we've had, out of who knows how many worlds—each as real as we are." She shivered.

"I may have a hunch," he said slowly.

"A what?"

"An intimation, an impression, a wordless kind of guess. Why has Gaia been doing it? I can't believe it's nothing but pastime."

"Nor I. Nor can I believe she would let such terrible things happen if she could prevent them. How can an intellect, a soul, like hers be anything but good?"

So Laurinda thought, Christian reflected; but she was an avatar of Gaia. He didn't suppose that affected the fairness of her conscious mind; he had come to know her rather well. But neither did it prove the nature, the ultimate intent, of Earth's node. It merely showed that the living Laurinda Ashcroft had been a decent person.

She took a deep draught from her glass before going on: "I think, myself, she is in the same position as the traditional God. Being good, she wants to share existence with others, and so creates them. But to make them puppets, automatons, would be senseless. They have to have consciousness and free will. Therefore they are able to sin, and do, all too often."

"Why hasn't she made them morally stronger?"

"Because she's chosen to make them human. And what are we but a specialized African ape?" Laurinda's tone lowered; she stared into the wine. "Specialized to make tools and languages and dreams; but the dreams can be nightmares."

In Gaia's and Alpha's kind laired no ancient beast, Christian thought. The human elements in them were long since absorbed, tamed, transfigured. His resurrection and hers must be nearly unique.

Not wanting to hurt her, he shaped his phrases with care. "Your idea is reasonable, but I'm afraid it leaves some questions dangling. Gaia does intervene, again and again. The amulets admit it. When the emulations get too far off track, she changes them and their people." Until she shuts them down, he did not add. "Why is she doing it, running history after history, experiment after experiment—why?"

Laurinda winced. "To, to learn about this strange race of ours?"

He nodded. "Yes, that's my hunch. Not even she, nor the galactic brain itself, can take first principles and compute what any human situation will lead to. Human affairs are chaotic. But chaotic systems do have structures, attractors, constraints. By letting things happen, through countless variations, you might discover a few general laws, which courses are better and which are worse." He tilted his goblet. "To what end, though? There are no more humans in the outside universe. There haven't been for—how many million years? No, unless it actually is callous curiosity, I can't yet guess what she's after."

"Nor I." Laurinda finished her drink. "Now I am growing very tired, very fast."

"I'm getting that way too." Christian paused. "How about we go sleep till evening? Then a special dinner, and our heads ought to be more clear."

Briefly, she took his hand. "Until evening, dear friend."

The night was young and gentle. a full moon dappled the garden. Wine had raised a happy mood, barely tinged with wistfulness. Gravel scrunched rhythmically underfoot as Laurinda and Christian danced, humming the waltz melody together. When they were done, they sat down, laughing, by the basin. Brightness from above overflowed it. He had earlier put his amulet back on just long enough to command that a guitar appear for him. Now he took it up. He had never seen anything more beautiful than she was in the moonlight. He sang a song to her that he had made long ago when he was mortal.

"Lightfoot, Lightfoot, lead the measure
As we dance the summer in!
'Lifetime is our only treasure.
Spend it well, on love and pleasure,'
Warns the lilting violin.

"If we'll see the year turn vernal
Once again, lies all with chance.
Yes, this ordering's infernal,
But we'll make our own eternal
Fleeting moment where we dance.

"So shall we refuse compliance
When across the green we whirl,
Giving entropy defiance,
Strings and winds in our alliance.
Be a victor. Kiss me, girl!"

Suddenly she was in his arms.

8

Where the hills loomed highest above the river that cut through them, a slope on the left bank rose steep but thinly forested. Kalava directed the lifeboat carrying his party to land. The slaves at the oars grunted with double effort. Sweat sheened on their skins and runneled down the straining bands of muscle; it was a day when the sun blazed from a sky just half clouded. The prow grated on a sandbar in the shallows. Kalava told two of his sailors to stand guard over boat and rowers. With the other four and Ilyandi, he waded ashore and began to climb.

It went slowly but stiffly. On top they found a crest with a view that snatched a gasp from the woman and a couple of amazed oaths from the men. Northward the terrain fell still more sharply, so that they looked over treetops down to the bottom of the range and across a valley awash with the greens and russets of growth. The river shone through it like a drawn blade, descending from dimly seen foothills and the sawtooth mountains beyond them. Two swordwings hovered on high, watchful for prey. Sunbeams shot past gigantic cloudbanks, filling their whiteness with cavernous shadows. Somehow the air felt cooler here, and the herbal smells gave benediction.

"It is fair, ai, it is as fair as the Sunset Kingdom of legend," Ilyandi breathed at last.

She stood slim in the man's kirtle and buskins that she, as a Vilku, could with propriety wear on trek. The wind fluttered her short locks. The coppery skin was as wet and almost as odorous as Kalava's midnight black, but she was no more wearied than any of her companions.

The sailor Urko scowled at the trees and underbrush crowding close on either side. Only the strip up which the travelers had come was partly clear, perhaps because of a landslide in the past. "Too much woods," he grumbled. It had, in fact, been a struggle to move about wherever they landed. They could not attempt the hunting that had been easy on the coast. Luckily, the water teemed with fish.

"Logging will cure that." Kalava's words throbbed. "And then what farms!" He stared raptly into the future.

Turning down-to-earth: "But we've gone far enough, now that we've gained an idea of the whole country. Three days, and I'd guess two more going back downstream. Any longer, and the crew at the ship could grow fearful. We'll turn around here."

"Other ships will bring others, explorers," Ilyandi said.

"Indeed they will. And I'll skipper the first of them."

A rustling and crackling broke from the tangle to the right, through the boom of the wind. "What's that?" barked Taltara.

"Some big animal," Kalava replied. "Stand alert."

The mariners formed a line. Three grounded the spears they carried; the fourth unslung a crossbow from his shoulders and armed it. Kalava waved Ilyandi to go behind them and drew his sword.

The thing parted a brake and trod forth into the open.

"Aah!" wailed Yarvonin. He dropped his spear and whirled about to flee.

"Stand fast!" Kalava shouted. "Urko, shoot whoever runs, if I don't cut him down myself. Hold, you whoresons, hold!"

The thing stopped. For a span of many hammering heartbeats, none moved.

It was a sight to terrify. Taller by a head than the tallest man it sheered, but that head was faceless save for a horrible blank mask. Two thick arms sprouted from either side, the lower pair of hands wholly misshapen. A humped back did not belie the sense of their strength. As the travelers watched, the thing sprouted a skeletal third leg, to stand better on the uneven ground. Whether it was naked or armored in plate, in this full daylight it bore the hue of dusk.

"Steady, boys, steady," Kalava urged between clenched teeth. Ilyandi stepped from shelter to join him. An eldritch calm was upon her. "My lady, what *is* it?" he appealed.

"A god, or a messenger from the gods, I think." He could barely make her out beneath the wind.

"A demon," Eivala groaned, though he kept his post.

"No, belike not. We Vilkui have some knowledge of these matters. But, true, it is not fiery—and I never thought I would meet one—in this life—"

Ilyandi drew a long breath, briefly knotted her fists, then moved to take stance in front of the men. Having touched the withered sprig of tekin pinned at her breast, she covered her eyes and genuflected before straightening again to confront the mask.

The thing did not move, but, mouthless, it spoke, in a deep and resonant voice. The sounds were incomprehensible. After a moment it ceased, then spoke anew in an equally alien tongue. On its third try, Kalava exclaimed, "Hoy, that's from the Shining Fields!"

The thing fell silent, as if considering what it had heard. Thereupon words rolled out in the Ulonaian of Sirsu. "Be not afraid. I mean you no harm."

"What a man knows is little, what he understands is less, therefore let him bow down to wisdom," Ilyandi recited. She turned her head long enough to tell her companions: "Lay aside your weapons. Do reverence."

Clumsily, they obeyed.

In the blank panel of the blank skull appeared a man's visage. Though it was black, the features were not quite like anything anyone had seen before, nose broad, lips heavy, eyes round, hair tightly curled. Nevertheless, to spirits half stunned the magic was vaguely reassuring.

Her tone muted but level, Ilyandi asked, "What would you of us, lord?"

"It is hard to say," the strange one answered. After a pause: "Bewilderment goes through the world. I too . . . You may call me Brannock."

The captain rallied his courage. "And I am Kalava, Kurvo's son, of Clan Samayoki." Aside to Ilyandi, low: "No disrespect that I don't name you, my lady. Let him work any spells on me." Despite the absence of visible genitals, already the humans thought of Brannock as male.

"My lord needs no names to work his will," she said. "I hight Ilyandi, Lytin's daughter, born into Clan Arvala, now a Vilku of the fifth rank."

Kalava cleared his throat and added, "By your leave, lord, we'll not name the others just yet. They're scared aplenty as is." He heard a growl at his back and inwardly grinned. Shame would help hold them steady. As for him, dread was giving way to a thrumming keenness.

"You do not live here, do you?" Brannock asked.

"No," Kalava said, "we're scouts from overseas."

Ilyandi frowned at his presumption and addressed Brannock: "Lord, do we trespass? We knew not this ground was forbidden."

"It isn't," the other said. "Not exactly. But—" The face in the panel smiled. "Come, ease off, let us talk. We've much to talk about."

"He sounds not unlike a man," Kalava murmured to Ilyandi.

She regarded him. "If you be the man."

Brannock pointed to a big old gnarlwood with an overarching canopy of leaves. "Yonder is shade." He retracted his third leg and strode off. A fallen log took up most of the space. He leaned over and dragged it aside. Kalava's whole gang could not have done so. The action was not really necessary, but the display of power, benignly used, encouraged them further. Still, it was with hushed awe that the crewmen sat down in the paintwort. The captain, the Vilku, and the strange one remained standing.

"Tell me of yourselves," Brannock said mildly.

"Surely you know, lord," Ilyandi replied.

"That is as may be."

"He wants us to," Kalava said.

In the course of the next short while, prompted by questions, the pair gave a bare-bones account. Brannock's head within his head nodded. "I see. You are the first humans ever in this country. But your people have lived a long time in their homeland, have they not?"

"From time out of mind, lord," Ilyandi said, "though legend holds that our forebears came from the south."

Brannock smiled again. "You have been very brave to meet me like this, m-m, my lady. But you did tell your friend that your order has encountered beings akin to me."

"You heard her whisper, across half a spearcast?" Kalava blurted.

"Or you hear us think, lord," Ilyandi said.

Brannock turned grave. "No. Not that. Else why would I have needed your story?"

"Dare I ask whence you come?"

"I shall not be angry. But it is nothing I can quite explain. You can help by telling me about those beings you know of."

Ilyandi could not hide a sudden tension. Kalava stiffened beside her. Even the dumbstruck sailors must have wondered whether a god would have spoken thus.

Ilyandi chose her words with care. "Beings from on high have appeared in the past to certain Vilkui or, sometimes, chieftains. They gave commands as to what the folk should or should not do. Ofttimes those commands were hard to fathom. Why must the Kivalui build watermills in the Swift River, when they had ample slaves to grind their grain?—But knowledge was imparted, too, counsel about where and how to search out the ways of nature. Always, the high one forbade open talk about his coming. The accounts lie in the secret annals of the Vilkui. But to you, lord—"

"What did those beings look like?" Brannock demanded sharply.

"Fiery shapes, winged or manlike, voices like great trumpets—"

"Ruvio's ax!" burst from Kalava. "The thing that passed overhead at sea!"

The men on the ground shuddered.

"Yes," Brannock said, most softly, "I may have had a part there. But as for the rest—"

His face flickered and vanished. After an appalling moment it reappeared.

"I am sorry, I meant not to frighten you, I forgot," he said. The expression went stony, the voice tolled. "Hear me. There is war in heaven. I am cast away from a battle, and enemy hunters may find me at any time. I carry a word that must, it is vital that it reach a certain place, a . . . a holy mountain in the north. Will you give aid?"

Kalava gripped his sword hilt so that it was as if the skin would split across his knuckles. The blood had left Ilyandi's countenance. She stood ready to be blasted with fire while she asked, "Lord Brannock, how do we know you are of the gods?"

Nothing struck her down. "I am not," he told her. "I too can die. But they whom I serve, they dwell in the stars."

The multitude of mystery, seen only when night clouds parted, but skythinkers taught that they circled always around the Axle of the North . . . Ilyandi kept her back straight. "Then can you tell me of the stars?"

"You are intelligent as well as brave," Brannock said. "Listen."

Kalava could not follow what passed between those two. The sailors cowered.

At the end, with tears upon her cheekbones, Ilyandi stammered, "Yes, he knows the constellations, he knows of the ecliptic and the precession and the returns of the Great Comet, he is from the stars. Trust him. We, we dare not to otherwise."

Kalava let go his weapon, brought hand to breast in salute, and asked, "How can we poor creatures help you, lord?"

"*You* are the news I bear," said Brannock.

"What?"

"I have no time to explain—if I could. The hunters may find me at any instant. But maybe, maybe you could go on for me after they do."

"Escaping what overpowered you?" Kalava's laugh rattled. "Well, a man might try."

"The gamble is desperate. Yet if we win, choose your reward, whatever it may be, and I think you shall have it."

Ilyandi lowered her head above folded hands. "Enough to have served those who dwell beyond the moon."

"Humph," Kalava could not keep from muttering, "if they want to pay for it, why not?" Aloud, almost eagerly, his own head raised into the wind that tossed his whitened mane: "What'd you have us do?"

Brannock's regard matched his. "I have thought about this. Can one of you come with me? I will carry him, faster than he can go. As for what happens later, we will speak of that along the way."

The humans stood silent.

"If I but had the woodcraft," Ilyandi then said. "Ai, but I would! To the stars!"

Kalava shook his head. "No, my lady. You go back with these fellows. Give heart to them at the ship. Make them finish the repairs." He glanced at Brannock. "How long will this foray take, lord?"

"I can reach the mountaintop in two days and a night," the other said. "If I am caught and you must go on alone, I think a good man could make the whole distance from here in ten or fifteen days."

Kalava laughed, more gladly than before. "*Courser* won't be sea-worthy for quite a bit longer than that. Let's away." To Ilyandi: "If I'm not back by the time she's ready, sail home without me."

"No—" she faltered.

"Yes. Mourn me not. What a faring!" He paused. "May all be ever well with you, my lady."

"And with you, forever with you, Kalava," she answered, not quite steadily, "in this world and afterward, out to the stars."

9

From withes and vines torn loose and from strips taken off clothing or sliced from leather belts, Brannock fashioned a sort of carrier for his ally. The man assisted.

However excited, he had taken on a matter-of-fact practicality. Brannock, who had also been a sailor, found it weirdly moving to see bowlines and sheet bends grow between deft fingers, amidst all this alienness.

Harnessed to his back, the webwork gave Kalava a seat and something to cling to. Radiation from the nuclear power plant within Brannock was negligible; it employed quantum-tunneling fusion. He set forth, down the hills and across the valley.

His speed was not very much more than a human could have maintained for a while. If nothing else, the forest impeded him. He did not want to force his way through, leaving an obvious trail. Rather, he parted the brush before him or detoured around the thickest stands. His advantage lay in tirelessness. He could keep going without pause, without need for food, water, or sleep, as long as need be. The heights beyond might prove somewhat trickier. However, Mount Mindhome did not reach above timberline on this oven of an Earth, although growth became more sparse and dry with altitude. Roots should keep most slopes firm, and he would not encounter snow or ice.

Alien, yes. Brannock remembered cedar, spruce, a lake where caribou grazed turf strewn with salmonberries and the wind streamed fresh, driving white clouds over a sky utterly blue. Here every tree, bush, blossom, flitting insect was foreign; grass itself no longer grew, unless it was ancestral to the thick-lobed carpeting of glades; the winged creatures aloft were not birds, and what beast cries he heard were in no tongue known to him.

Wayfarer's avatar walked on. Darkness fell. After a while, rain roared on the roof of leaves overhead. Such drops as got through to strike him were big and warm. Attuned to both the magnetic field and the rotation of the planet, his directional sense held him on course while an inertial integrator clocked off the kilometers he left behind.

The more the better. Gaia's mobile sensors were bound to spy on the expedition from Ulonai, as new and potentially troublesome a factor as it represented. Covertly watching, listening with amplification, Brannock had learned of the party lately gone upstream and hurried to intercept it—less likely to be spotted soon. He supposed she would have kept continuous watch on the camp and that a tiny robot or two would have followed Kalava, had not Wayfarer been in rapport with her. Alpha's emissary might too readily become aware that her attention was on something near and urgent, and wonder what.

She could, though, let unseen agents go by from time to time and flash their observations to a peripheral part of her. It would be incredible luck if one of them did not, at some point, hear the crew talking about the apparition that had borne away their captain.

Then what? Somehow she must divert Wayfarer for a while, so that a sufficient fraction of her mind could direct machines of sufficient capability to find Brannock and deal with him. He doubted he could again fight free. Because she dared not send out her most formidable entities or give them direct orders, those that came would have their weaknesses and fallibilities. But they would be determined, ruthless, and on guard against the powers he had revealed in the aircraft. It was clear that she was resolved to keep hidden the fact that humans lived once more on Earth.

Why, Brannock did not know, nor did he waste mental energy trying to guess. This must be a business of high importance; and the implications went immensely further, a secession from the galactic brain. His job was to get the information to Wayfarer.

He *might* come near enough to call it in by radio. The emissary was not tuned in at great sensitivity, and no relay was set up for the short-range transmitter. Neither requirement had been foreseen. If Brannock failed to reach the summit, Kalava was his forlorn hope.

In which case—"Are you tired?" he asked. They had exchanged few words thus far.

"Bone-weary and plank-stiff," the man admitted. And croak-thirsty too, Brannock heard.

"That won't do. You have to be in condition to move fast. Hold on a little more, and we'll rest." Maybe the plural would give Kalava some comfort. Seldom could a human have been as alone as he was.

Springs were abundant in this wet country. Brannock's chemosensors led him to the closest. By then the rain had stopped. Kalava unharnessed, groped his way in the dark, lay down to drink and drink. Meanwhile Brannock, who saw quite clearly, tore off fronded boughs to make a bed for him. He flopped onto it and almost immediately began to snore.

Brannock left him. A strong man could go several days without eating before he weakened, but it wasn't necessary. Brannock collected fruits that ought to nourish. He tracked down and killed an animal the size of a pig, brought it back to camp, and used his tool-hands to butcher it.

An idea had come to him while he walked. After a search he found a tree with suitable bark. It reminded him all too keenly of birch, although it was red-brown and odorous. He took a sheet of it, returned, and spent a time inscribing it with a finger-blade.

Dawn seeped gray through gloom. Kalava woke, jumped up, saluted his companion, stretched like a panther and capered like a goat, limbering himself. "That did good," he said. "I thank my lord." His glance fell on the rations. "And did you provide food? You are a kindly god."

"Not either of those, I fear," Brannock told him. "Take what you want, and we will talk."

Kalava first got busy with camp chores. He seemed to have shed whatever religious dread he felt and now to look upon the other as a part of the world—certainly to be respected, but the respect was of the kind he would accord a powerful, enigmatic, high-ranking man. A hardy spirit, Brannock thought. Or perhaps his culture drew no line between the natural and the supernatural. To a primitive, everything was in some way magical, and so when magic manifested itself it could be accepted as simply another occurrence.

If Kalava actually was primitive. Brannock wondered about that.

It was encouraging to see how competently he went about his tasks, a woodsman as well as a seaman. Having gathered dry sticks and piled them in a pyramid, he set them alight. For this, he took from the pouch at his belt a little hardwood cylinder and piston, a packet of tinder, and a sulfur-tipped sliver. Driven down, the piston heated trapped air to ignite the powder; he dipped his match in, brought it up aflame, and used it to start his fire. Yes, an inventive people. And the woman Ilyandi had an excellent knowledge of naked-eye astronomy. Given the rarity of clear skies, that meant many lifetimes of patient observation, record-keeping, and logic, which must include mathematics comparable to Euclid's.

What else?

While Kalava toasted his meat and ate, Brannock made inquiries. He learned of warlike city-states, their hinterlands divided among clans; periodic folkmoots where the freemen passed laws, tried cases, and elected leaders; an international order of sacerdotes, teachers, healers, and philosophers; aggressively expansive, sometimes piratical commerce; barbarians, erupting out of the ever-growing deserts and wastelands; the grim militarism that the frontier states had evolved in response; an empirical but intensive biological technology, which had bred an amazing variety of specialized plants and animals, including slaves born to muscular strength, moronic wits, and canine obedience. . . .

Most of the description emerged as the pair were again traveling. Real conversation was impossible when Brannock wrestled with brush, forded a stream in spate, or struggled up a scree slope. Still, even then they managed an occasional question and answer. Besides, after he had crossed the valley and entered the foothills he found the terrain rugged but less often boggy, the trees and undergrowth thinning out, the air slightly cooling.

Just the same, Brannock would not have gotten as much as he did, in the short snatches he had, were he merely human. But he was immune to fatigue and breathlessness. He had an enormous data store to draw on. It included his studies of history and anthropology as a young mortal, and gave him techniques for constructing a logic tree and following its best branches—for asking the right, most probably useful questions. What emerged was a bare sketch of Kalava's world. It was, though, clear and cogent.

It horrified him.

Say rather that his Christian Brannock aspect recoiled from the brutality of it. His Wayfarer aspect reflected that this was more or less how humans had usually behaved, and that their final civilization would not have been stable without its pervasive artificial intelligences. His journey continued.

He broke it to let Kalava rest and flex. From that hill the view swept northward and upward to the mountains. They rose precipitously ahead, gashed, cragged, and sheer where they were not wooded, their tops lost in a leaden sky. Brannock pointed to the nearest, thrust forward out of their wall like a bastion.

"We are bound yonder," he said. "On the height is my lord, to whom I must get my news."

"Doesn't he see you here?" asked Kalava.

Brannock shook his generated image of a head. "No. He might, but the enemy engages him. He does not yet know she is the enemy. Think of her as a sorceress who deceives him with clever talk, with songs and illusions, while her agents go about in the world. My word will show him what the truth is."

Would it? Could it, when truth and rightness seemed as formless as the cloud cover?

"Will she be alert against you?"

"To some degree. How much, I cannot tell. If I can come near, I can let out a silent cry that my lord will hear and understand. But if her warriors catch me before then, you must go on, and that will be hard. You may well fail and die. Have you the courage?"

Kalava grinned crookedly. "By now, I'd better, hadn't I?"

"If you succeed, your reward shall be boundless."

"I own, that's one wind in my sails. But also—" Kalava paused. "Also," he finished quietly, "the lady Ilyandi wishes this."

Brannock decided not to go into that. He lifted the rolled-up piece of bark he had carried in a lower hand. "The sight of you should break the spell, but here is a message for you to give."

As well as he was able, he went on to describe the route, the site, and the module that contained Wayfarer, taking care to distinguish it from everything else around. He was not sure whether the spectacle would confuse Kalava into helplessness, but at any rate the man seemed resolute. Nor was he sure how Kalava could cross half a kilometer of paving—if he could get that far—without Gaia immediately perceiving and destroying him. Maybe Wayfarer would notice first. Maybe, maybe.

He, Brannock, was using this human being as consciencelessly as ever Gaia might have used any; and he did not know what his purpose was. What possible threat to the fellowship of the stars could exist, demanding that this little brief life be offered up? Nevertheless he gave the letter to Kalava, who tucked it inside his tunic.

"I'm ready," said the man, and squirmed back into harness. They traveled on.

The hidden hot sun stood at midafternoon when Brannock's detectors reacted. He felt it as the least quivering hum, but instantly knew it for the electronic sign of something midge-size approaching afar. A mobile minisensor was on his trail.

It could not have the sensitivity of the instruments in him, he had not yet registered, but it would be here faster than he could run, would see him and go off to notify stronger machines. They could not be distant either. Once a clue to him had been obtained, they would have converged from across the continent, perhaps across the globe.

He slammed to a halt. He was in a ravine where a waterfall foamed down into a stream that tumbled off to join the Remnant. Huge, feathery bushes and trees with serrated bronzy leaves enclosed him. Insects droned from flower to purple flower. His chemosensors drank heavy perfumes.

"The enemy scouts have found me," he said. "Go."

Kalava scrambled free and down to the ground but hesitated, hand on sword. "Can I fight beside you?"

"No. Your service is to bear my word. Go. Straightaway. Cover your trail as best you can. And your gods be with you."

"Lord!"

Kalava vanished into the brush. Brannock stood alone.

The human fraction of him melted into the whole and he was entirely machine life, logical, emotionally detached, save for his duty to Wayfarer, Alpha, and consciousness throughout the universe. This was not a bad place to defend, he thought. He had the ravine wall to shield his back, rocks at its foot to throw, branches to break off for clubs and spears. He could give the pursuit a hard time before it took him prisoner. Of course, it might decide to kill him with an energy beam, but probably it wouldn't. Best from Gaia's viewpoint was to capture him and change his memories, so that he returned with a report of an uneventful cruise on which he saw nothing of significance.

He didn't think that first her agents could extract his real memories. That would take capabilities she had never anticipated needing. Just to make the device that had tried to take control of him earlier must have been an extraordinary effort, hastily carried out. Now she was still more limited in what she could do. An order to duplicate and employ the device was simple enough that it should escape Wayfarer's notice. The design and commissioning of an interrogator was something else—not to mention the difficulty of getting the information clandestinely to her.

Brannock dared not assume she was unaware he had taken Kalava with him. Most likely it was a report from an agent, finally getting around to checking on the lifeboat party, that apprised her of his survival and triggered the hunt for him. But the sailors would have been frightened, bewildered, their talk disjointed and nearly meaningless. Ilyandi, that bright and formidable woman, would have done her best to forbid them saying anything helpful. The impression ought to be that Brannock only meant to pump Kalava about his people, before releasing him to make his way back to them and himself proceeding on toward Mindhome.

In any event, it would not be easy to track the man down. He was no machine, he was an animal among countless animals, and the most cunning of all. The kind of saturation search that would soon find him was debarred. Gaia might keep a tiny portion of her forces searching and a tiny part of her attention poised against him, but she would not take him very seriously. Why should she?

Why should Brannock? Forlorn hope in truth.

He made his preparations. While he waited for the onslaught, his spirit ranged beyond the clouds, out among the stars and the millions of years that his greater self had known.

10

The room was warm. It smelled of lovemaking and the roses Laurinda had set in a vase. Evening light diffused through gauzy drapes to wash over a big four-poster bed.

She drew herself close against Christian where he lay propped on two pillows. Her arm went across his breast, his over her shoulders. "I don't want to leave this," she whispered.

"Nor I," he said into the tumbling sweetness of her hair. "How could I want to?"

"I mean—what we are—what we've become to one another."

"I understand."

She swallowed. "I'm sorry. I shouldn't have said that. Can you forget I did?"

"Why?"

"You know. I can't ask you to give up returning to your whole being. I *don't* ask you to."

He stared before him.

"I just don't want to leave this house, this bed yet," she said desolately. "After these past days and nights, not yet."

He turned his head again and looked down into gray eyes that blinked back tears. "Nor I," he answered. "But I'm afraid we must."

"Of course. Duty."

And Gaia and Wayfarer. If they didn't know already that their avatars had been slacking, surely she, at least, soon would, through the amulets and their link to her. No matter how closely engaged with the other vast mind, she would desire to know from time to time what was going on within herself.

Christian drew breath. "Let me say the same that you did. I, this I that I am, damned well does not care to be anything else but your lover."

"Darling, darling."

"But," he said after the kiss.

"Go on," she said, lips barely away from his. "Don't be afraid of hurting me. You can't."

He sighed. "I sure can, and you can hurt me. May neither of us ever mean to. It's bound to happen, though."

She nodded. "Because we're human." Steadfastly: "Nevertheless, because of you, that's what I hope to stay."

"I don't see how we can. Which is what my 'but' was about." He was quiet for another short span. "After we've remerged, after we're back in our onenesses, no doubt we'll feel differently."

"I wonder if I ever will, quite."

He did not remind her that this "I" of her would no longer exist save as a minor memory and a faint overtone. Instead, trying to console, however awkwardly, he said, "I think I want it for you, in spite of everything. Immortality. Never to grow old and die. The power, the awareness."

"Yes, I know. In these lives we're blind and deaf and stupefied." Her laugh was a sad little murmur. "I like it."

"Me too. We being what we are." Roughly: "Well, we have a while left to us."

"But we must get on with our task."

"Thank you for saying it for me."

"I think you realize it more clearly than I do. That makes it harder for you to speak." She lifted her hand to cradle his cheek. "We can wait till tomorrow, can't we?" she pleaded. "Only for a good night's sleep."

He made a smile. "Hm. Sleep isn't all I have in mind."

"We'll have other chances . . . along the way. Won't we?"

Early morning in the garden, flashes of dew on leaves and petals, a hawk aloft on a breeze that caused Laurinda to pull her shawl about her. She sat by the basin and looked up at him where he strode back and forth before her, hands clenched at his sides or clutched together at his back. Gravel grated beneath his feet.

"But where should we go?" she wondered. "Aimlessly drifting from one half-world to another till—they—finish their business and recall us. It seems futile." She attempted lightness. "I confess to thinking we may as well ask to visit the enjoyable ones."

He shook his head. "I'm sorry. I've been thinking differently." Even during the times that were theirs alone.

She braced herself.

"You know how it goes," he said. "Wrestling with ideas, and they have no shapes, then suddenly you wake and they're halfway clear. I did today. Tell me how it strikes you. After all, you represent Gaia."

He saw her wince. When he stopped and bent down to make a gesture of contrition, she told him quickly, "No, it's all right, dearest. Do go on."

He must force himself, but his voice gathered momentum as he paced and talked. "What have we seen to date? This eighteenth-century world, where Newton's not long dead, Lagrange and Franklin are active, Lavoisier's a boy, and the Industrial Revolution is getting under way. Why did Gaia give it to us for our home base? Just because here's a charming house and countryside? Or because this was the best choice for her out of all she has emulated?"

Laurinda had won back to calm. She nodded. "Mm, yes, she wouldn't create one simply for us, especially when she is occupied with Wayfarer."

"Then we visited a world that went through a similar stage back in its Hellenistic era," Christian continued. Laurinda shivered. "Yes, it failed, but the point is, we discovered it's the only Graeco-Roman history Gaia found worth continuing for centuries. Then the, uh, conciliar Europe of 1900. That was scientific-industrial too, maybe more successfully—or less unsuccessfully—on account of having kept a strong, unified Church, though it was coming apart at last. Then the Chinese-American—not scientific, very religious, but destined to produce considerable technology in its own time of troubles." He was silent a minute or two, except for his footfalls. "Four out of many, three almost randomly picked. Doesn't that suggest that all which interest her have something in common?"

"Why, yes," she said. "We've talked about it, you remember. It seems as if Gaia has been trying to bring her people to a civilization that is rich, culturally and spiritually as well as materially, and is kindly and will endure."

"Why," he demanded, "when the human species is extinct?"

She straightened where she sat. "It isn't! It lives again here, in her."

He bit his lip. "Is that the Gaia in you speaking, or the you in Gaia?"

"What do you mean?" she exclaimed.

He halted to stroke her head. "Nothing against you. Never. You are honest and gentle and everything else that is good." Starkly: "I'm not so sure about her."

"Oh, no." He heard the pain. "Christian, no."

"Well, never mind that for now," he said fast, and resumed his gait to and fro. "My point is this. Is it merely an accident that all four live worlds we've been in were oriented toward machine technology, and three of them toward science? Does Gaia want to find out what drives the evolution of societies like that?"

Laurinda seized the opening. "Why not? Science opens the mind, technology frees the body from all sorts of horrors. Here, today, Jenner and his smallpox vaccine aren't far in the future—"

"I wonder how much more there is to her intention. But anyway, my proposal is that we touch on the highest-tech civilization she has."

A kind of gladness kindled in her. "Yes, yes! It must be strange and wonderful."

He frowned. "For some countries, long ago in real history, it got pretty dreadful."

"Gaia wouldn't let that happen."

He abstained from reminding her of what Gaia did let happen, before changing or terminating it.

She sprang to her feet. "Come!" Seizing his hand, mischievously: "If we stay any length of time, let's arrange for private quarters."

In a room closed off, curtains drawn, Christian held an amulet in his palm and stared down at it as if it bore a face. Laurinda stood aside, listening, while her own countenance tightened with distress.

"It is inadvisable," declared the soundless voice.

"Why?" snapped Christian.

"You would find the environment unpleasant and the people incomprehensible."

"Why should a scientific culture be that alien to us?" asked Laurinda.

"And regardless," said Christian, "I want to see for myself. Now."

"Reconsider," urged the voice. "First hear an account of the milieu."

"No, *now*. To a safe locale, yes, but one where we can get a fair impression, as we did before. Afterward you can explain as much as you like."

"Why shouldn't we first hear?" Laurinda suggested.

"Because I doubt Gaia wants us to see," Christian answered bluntly. He might as well. Whenever Gaia chose, she could scan his thoughts. To the amulet, as if it were a person: "Take us there immediately, or Wayfarer will hear from me."

His suspicions, vague but growing, warned against giving the thing time to inform Gaia and giving her time to work up a Potemkin village or some other diversion. At the moment she must be unaware of this scene, her mind preoccupied with Wayfarer's, but she had probably made provision for being informed in a low-level—subconscious?—fashion at intervals, and anything alarming would catch her attention. It was also likely that she had given the amulets certain orders beforehand, and now it appeared that among them was to avoid letting him know what went on in that particular emulation.

Why, he could not guess.

"You are being willful," said the voice.

Christian grinned. "And stubborn, and whatever else you care to call it. Take us!"

Pretty clearly, he thought, the program was not capable of falsehoods. Gaia had not foreseen a need for that; Christian was no creation of hers, totally known to her, he was Wayfarer's. Besides, if Wayfarer noticed that his avatar's guide could be a liar, that would have been grounds for suspicion.

Laurinda touched her man's arm. "Darling, should we?" she said unevenly. "She *is* the . . . the mother of all this."

"A broad spectrum of more informative experiences is available," argued the voice. "After them, you would be better prepared for the visit you propose."

"Prepared," Christian muttered. That could be interpreted two ways. He and Laurinda might be conducted to seductively delightful places while Gaia learned of the situation and took preventive measures, meantime keeping Wayfarer distracted. "I still want to begin with your highest tech." To the woman: "I have my reasons. I'll tell you later. Right now we have to hurry."

Before Gaia could know and act.

She squared her shoulders, took his free hand, and said, "Then I am with you. Always."

"Let's go," Christian told the amulet.

Transfer.

The first thing he noticed, transiently, vividly, was that he and Laurinda were no longer dressed for eighteenth-century England, but in lightweight white blouses, trousers, and sandals. Headcloths flowed down over their necks. Heat smote. The air in his nostrils was parched, full of metallic odors. Half-heard rhythms of machinery pulsed through it and through the red-brown sand underfoot.

He tautened his stance and gazed around. The sky was overcast, a uniform gray in which the sun showed no more than a pallor that cast no real shadows. At his back the land rolled away ruddy. Man-high stalks with narrow bluish leaves grew out of it, evenly spaced about a meter apart. To his right, a canal slashed across, beneath a transparent deck. Ahead of him the ground was covered by different plants, if that was what they were, spongy, lobate, pale golden in hue. A few—creatures—moved around, apparently tending them, bipedal but shaggy and with arms that seemed trifurcate. A gigantic building or complex of buildings reared over that horizon, multiply tiered, dull white, though agleam with hundreds of panels that might be windows or might be something else. As he watched, an aircraft passed overhead. He could just see that it had wings and hear the drone of an engine.

Laurinda had not let go his hand. She gripped hard. "This is no country I ever heard of," she said thinly.

"Nor I," he answered. "But I think I recognize—" To the amulets: "This isn't any re-creation of Earth in the past, is it? It's Earth today."

"Of approximately the present year," the voice admitted.

"We're not in Arctica, though."

"No. Well south, a continental interior. You required to see the most advanced technology in the emulations. Here it is in action."

Holding the desert at bay, staving off the death that ate away at the planet. Christian nodded. He felt confirmed in his idea that the program was unable to give him any outright lie. That didn't mean it would give him forthright responses.

"This is their greatest engineering?" Laurinda marveled. "We did—better—in my time. Or yours, Christian."

"They're working on it here, I suppose," the man said. "We'll investigate further. After all, this is a bare glimpse."

"You must remember," the voice volunteered, "no emulation can be as full and complex as the material universe."

"Mm, yeh. Skeletal geography, apart from chosen regions; parochial biology; simplified cosmos."

Laurinda glanced at featureless heaven. "The stars unreachable, because here they are not stars?" She shuddered and pressed close against him.

"Yes, a paradox," he said. "Let's talk with a scientist."

"That will be difficult," the voice demurred.

"You told us in Chinese America you could arrange meetings. It shouldn't be any harder in this place."

The voice did not reply at once. Unseen machines rumbled. A dust devil whirled up on a sudden gust of wind. Finally: "Very well. It shall be one who will not be stricken dumb by astonishment and fear. Nevertheless, I should supply you beforehand with a brief description of what you will come to."

"Go ahead. If it is brief."

What changes in the history would that encounter bring about? Did it matter? This world was evidently not in temporary reactivation, it was ongoing; the newcomers were at the leading edge of its time line. Gaia could erase their visit from it. If she cared to. Maybe she was going to terminate it soon because it was making no further progress that interested her.

Transfer.

Remote in a wasteland, only a road and an airstrip joining it to anything else, a tower lifted from a walled compound. Around it, night was cooling in a silence hardly touched by a susurrus of chant where robed figures bearing dim lights did homage to the stars. Many were visible, keen and crowded amidst their darkness, a rare sight, for clouds had parted across most of the sky. More lights glowed muted on a parapet surrounding the flat roof of a tower. There a single man and his helper used the chance to turn instruments aloft, telescope, spectroscope, cameras, bulks in the gloom.

Christian and Laurinda appeared unto them.

The man gasped, recoiled for an instant, and dropped to his knees. His assistant caught a book that he had nearly knocked off a table, replaced it, stepped back, and stood imperturbable, an anthropoid whose distant ancestors had been human but who lived purely to serve his master.

Christian peered at the man. As eyes adapted, he saw garments like his, embroidered with insignia of rank and kindred, headdress left off after dark. The skin was ebony black but nose and lips were thin, eyes oblique, fingertips tapered, long hair and closely trimmed beard straight and blond. No race that ever inhabited old Earth, Christian thought; no, this was a breed that Gaia had designed for the dying planet.

The man signed himself, looked into the pale faces of the strangers, and said, uncertainly at first, then with a gathering strength: "Hail and obedience, messengers of God. Joy at your advent."

Christian and Laurinda understood, as they had understood hunted Zoe. The amulets had told them they would not be the first apparition these people had known. "Rise," Christian said. "Be not afraid."

"Nor call out," Laurinda added.

Smart lass, Christian thought. The ceremony down in the courtyard continued. "Name yourself," he directed.

The man got back on his feet and took an attitude deferential rather than servile. "Surely the mighty ones know," he said. "I am Eighth Khaltan, chief astrologue of the Ilgai Technome, and, and wholly unworthy of this honor." He hesitated. "Is that, dare I ask, is that why you have chosen the forms you show me?"

"No one has had a vision for several generations," explained the soundless voice in the heads of the newcomers.

"Gaia has manifested herself in the past?" Christian subvocalized.

"Yes, to indicate desirable courses of action. Normally the sending has had the shape of a fire."

"How scientific is *that*?"

Laurinda addressed Khaltan: "We are not divine messengers. We have come from a world beyond your world, as mortal as you, not to teach but to learn."

The man smote his hands together. "Yet it is a miracle, again a miracle—in my lifetime!"

Nonetheless he was soon avidly talking. Christian recalled myths of men who were the lovers of goddesses or who tramped the roads and sat at humble meat with God Incarnate. The believer accepts as the unbeliever cannot.

Those were strange hours that followed. Khaltan was not simply devout. To him the supernatural was another set of facts, another facet of reality. Since it lay beyond his ken, he had turned his attention to the measurable world. In it he observed and theorized like a Newton. Tonight his imagination blazed, questions exploded from him, but always he chose his words with care and turned everything he heard around and around in his mind, examining it as he would have examined some jewel fallen from the sky.

Slowly, piecemeal, while the stars wheeled around the pole, a picture of his civilization took shape. It had overrun and absorbed every other society—no huge accomplishment, when Earth was meagerly populated and most folk on the edge of starvation. The major technology was biological, agronomy, aquaculture in the remnant lakes and seas, ruthlessly practical genetics. Industrial chemistry flourished. It joined with physics at the level of the later nineteenth century to enable substantial engineering works and reclamation projects.

Society itself—how do you summarize an entire culture in words? It can't be done. Christian got the impression of a nominal empire, actually a broad-based oligarchy of families descended from conquering soldiers. Much upward mobility was by adoption of promising commoners, whether children or adults. Sons who made no contributions to the well-being of the clan or who disgraced it could be kicked out, if somebody did not pick a fight and kill them in a duel. Unsatisfactory daughters were also expelled, unless a marriage into a lower class could be negotiated. Otherwise the status of the sexes was roughly equal; but this meant that women who chose to compete with men must do so on male terms. The nobles provided the commons with protection, courts of appeal, schools, leadership, and pageantry. In return they drew taxes, corvée, and general subordination; but in most respects the commoners were generally left to themselves. Theirs was not altogether a dog-eat-dog situation; they had institutions, rites, and hopes of their own. Yet many went to the wall, while the hard work of the rest drove the global economy.

It was not a deliberately cruel civilization, Christian thought, but neither was it an especially compassionate one.

Had any civilization ever been, really? Some fed their poor, but mainly they fed their politicians and bureaucrats.

He snatched his information out of talk that staggered everywhere else. The discourse for which Khaltan yearned was of the strangers' home—he got clumsily evasive, delaying responses—and the whole system of the universe, astronomy, physics, everything.

"We dream of rockets going to the planets. We have tried to shoot them to the moon," he said, and told of launchers that ought to have worked. "All failed."

Of course, Christian thought. Here the moon and planets, yes, the very sun were no more than lights. The tides rose and fell by decree. The Earth was a caricature of Earth outside. Gaia could do no better.

"Are we then at the end of science?" Khaltan cried once. "We have sought and sought for decades, and have won to nothing further than measurements more exact." Nothing that would lead to relativity, quantum theory, wave mechanics, their revolutionary insights and consequences. Gaia could not accommodate it. "The angels in the past showed us what to look for. Will you not? Nature holds more than we know. Your presence bears witness!"

"Later, perhaps later," Christian mumbled, and cursed himself for his falsity.

"Could we reach the planets—Caged, the warrior spirit turns inward on itself. Rebellion and massacre in the Westlands—"

Laurinda asked what songs the people sang.

Clouds closed up. The rite in the courtyard ended. Khaltan's slave stood motionless while he himself talked on and on.

The eastern horizon lightened. "We must go," Christian said.

"You will return?" Khaltan begged. "Ai-ha, you will?"

Laurinda embraced him for a moment. "Fare you well," she stammered, "fare always well."

How long would his "always" be?

After an uneasy night's sleep and a nearly wordless breakfast, there was no real cause to leave the house in England. The servants, scandalized behind carefully held faces, might perhaps eavesdrop, but would not comprehend, nor would any gossip that they spread make a difference. A deeper, unuttered need sent Christian and Laurinda forth. This could well be the last of their mornings.

They followed a lane to a hill about a kilometer away. Trees on its top did not obscure a wide view across the land. The sun stood dazzling in the east, a few small clouds sailed across a blue as radiant as their whiteness, but an early breath of autumn was in the wind. It went strong and fresh, scattering dawn-mists off plowland and sending waves through the green of pastures; it soughed in the branches overhead and whirled some already dying leaves off. High beyond them winged a V of wild geese.

For a while man and woman stayed mute. Finally Laurinda breathed, savored, fragrances of soil and sky, and murmured, "That Gaia brought this back to life—She must be good. She loves the world."

Christian looked from her, aloft, and scowled before he made oblique reply. "What are she and Wayfarer doing?"

"How can we tell?"—tell what the gods did or even where they fared. They were not three-dimensional beings, nor bound by the time that bound their creations.

"She's keeping him occupied," said Christian.

"Yes, of course. Taking him through the data, the whole of her stewardship of Earth."

"To convince him she's right in wanting to let the planet die."

"A tragedy—but in the end, everything is tragic, isn't it?" Including you and me.

"What . . . we . . . they . . . can learn from the final evolution, that may well be worth it all, as the Acropolis was worth it all. The galactic brain itself can't foreknow what life will do, and life is rare among the stars."

Almost, he snapped at her. "I know, I know. How often have we been over this ground? How often have *they*? I might have believed it myself. But—"

Laurinda waited. The wind skirled, caught a stray lock of hair, tossed it about over her brow.

"But why has she put humans, not into the distant past—" Christian gestured at the landscape lying like an eighteenth-century painting around them. "—but into now, an Earth where flesh-and-blood humans died eons ago?"

"She's in search of a fuller understanding, surely."

"Surely?"

Laurinda captured his gaze and held it. "I think she's been trying to find how humans can have, in her, the truly happy lives they never knew in the outer cosmos."

"Why should she care about that?"

"I don't know. I'm only human." Earnestly: "But could it be that this element in her is so strong—so many, many of us went into her—that she longs to see us happy, like a mother with her children?"

"All that manipulation, all those existences failed and discontinued. It doesn't seem very motherly to me."

"I don't know, I tell you!" she cried.

He yearned to comfort her, kiss away the tears caught in her lashes, but urgency drove him onward. "If the effort has no purpose except itself, it seems mad. Can a nodal mind go insane?"

She retreated from him, appalled. "No. Impossible."

"Are you certain? At least, the galactic brain has to know the truth, the whole truth, to judge whether something here has gone terribly wrong."

Laurinda forced a nod. "You will report to Wayfarer, and he will report to Alpha, and all the minds will decide" a question that was unanswerable by mortal creatures.

Christian stiffened. "I have to do it at once."

He had hinted, she had guessed, but just the same she seized both his sleeves and protest spilled wildly from her lips. "What? Why? No! You'd only disturb him in his rapport, and her. Wait till we're summoned. We have till then, darling."

"I want to wait," he said. Sweat stood on his skin, though the blood had withdrawn. "God, I want to! But I don't dare."

"Why not?"

She let go of him. He stared past her and said fast, flattening the anguish out of his tones, "Look, she didn't want us to see that final world. She clearly didn't, or quite expected we'd insist, or she'd have been better prepared. Maybe she could have passed something else off on us. As is, once he learns, Wayfarer will probably demand to see for himself. And she does not want him particularly interested in her emulations. Else why hasn't she taken him through them directly, with me along to help interpret?

"Oh, I don't suppose our action has been catastrophic for her plans, whatever they are. She can still cope, can still persuade him these creations are merely . . . toys of hers, maybe. That is, she can if she gets the chance to. I don't believe she should."

"How can you take on yourself—How can you imagine—"

"The amulets are a link to her. Not a constantly open channel, obviously, but at intervals they must inform a fraction of her about us. She must also be able to set up intervals when Wayfarer gets too preoccupied with what he's being shown to notice that a larger part of her attention has gone elsewhere. We don't know when that'll happen next. I'm going back to the house and tell her through one of the amulets that I require immediate contact with him."

Laurinda stared as if at a ghost.

"That will not be necessary," said the wind.

Christian lurched where he stood. "What?" he blurted. "You—"

"Oh—Mother—" Laurinda lifted her hands into emptiness.

The blowing of the wind, the rustling in the leaves made words. "The larger part of me, as you call it, has in fact been informed and is momentarily free. I was waiting for you to choose your course."

Laurinda half moved to kneel in the grass. She glanced at Christian, who had regained balance and stood with fists at sides, confronting the sky. She went to stand by him.

"My lady Gaia," Christian said most quietly, "you can do to us as you please," change or obliterate or whatever she liked, in a single instant; but presently Wayfarer would ask why. "I think you understand my doubts."

"I do," sighed the air. "They are groundless. My creation of the Technome world is no different from my creation of any other. My avatar said it for me: I give existence, and I search for ways that humans, of their free will, can make the existence good."

Christian shook his head. "No, my lady. With your intellect and your background, you must have known from the first what a dead end that world would soon be, scientists on a planet that is a sketch and everything else a shadow show. My limited brain realized it. No, my lady, as cold-bloodedly as you were experimenting, I believe you did all the rest in the same spirit. Why? To what end?"

"Your brain is indeed limited. At the proper time, Wayfarer shall receive your observations and your fantasies. Meanwhile, continue in your duty, which is to observe further and refrain from disturbing us in our own task."

"My duty is to report."

"In due course, I say." The wind-voice softened. "There are pleasant places besides this."

Paradises, maybe. Christian and Laurinda exchanged a glance that lingered for a second. Then she smiled the least bit, boundlessly sorrowfully, and shook her head.

"No," he declared, "I dare not."

He did not speak it, but he and she knew that Gaia knew what they foresaw. Given time, and they lost in their joy together, she could alter their memories too slowly and subtly for Wayfarer to sense what was happening.

Perhaps she could do it to Laurinda at this moment, in a flash. But she did not know Christian well enough. Down under his consciousness, pervading his being, was his aspect of Wayfarer and of her coequal Alpha. She would need to feel her way into him, explore and test with infinite delicacy, remake him detail by minutest detail, always ready to back off if it had an unexpected effect; and perhaps another part of her could secretly take control of the Technome world and erase the event itself. . . . She needed time, even she.

"Your action would be futile, you know," she said. "It would merely give me the trouble of explaining to him what you in your arrogance refuse to see."

"Probably. But I have to try."

The wind went bleak. "Do you defy me?"

"I do," Christian said. It wrenched from him: "Not my wish. It's Wayfarer in me. I, I cannot do otherwise. Call him to me."

The wind gentled. It went over Laurinda like a caress. "Child of mine, can you not persuade this fool?"

"No, Mother," the woman whispered. "He is what he is."

"And so—?"

Laurinda laid her hand in the man's. "And so I will go with him, forsaking you, Mother."

"You are casting yourselves from existence."

Christian's free fingers clawed the air. "No, not her!" he shouted. "She's innocent!"

"I am not," Laurinda said. She swung about to lay her arms around him and lift her face to his. "I love you."

"Be it as you have chosen," said the wind.

The dream that was the world fell into wreck and dissolved. Oneness swept over them like twin tides, each reclaiming a flung drop of spindrift; and the two seas rolled again apart.

11

The last few hundred man-lengths Kalava went mostly on his belly. From bush to bole he crawled, stopped, lay flat and strained every sense into the shadows around him, before he crept onward. Nothing stirred but the twigs above, buffeted on a chill and fitful breeze. Nothing sounded but their creak and click, the scrittling of such leaves as they bore, now and then the harsh cry of a hookbeak—those, and the endless low noise of demons, like a remote surf where in shrilled flutes on no scale he knew, heard more through his skin than his ears but now, as he neared, into the blood and bone of him.

On this rough, steep height the forest grew sparse, though brush clustered thick enough, accursedly rustling as he pushed by. Everything was parched, branches brittle, most foliage sere and yellow-brown, the ground blanketed with tindery fallstuff. His mouth and gullet smoldered as dry. He had passed through fog until he saw from above that it was a layer of clouds spread to worldedge, the mountain peaks jutting out of it like teeth, and had left all rivulets behind him. Well before then, he had finished the meat Brannock provided, and had not lingered to hunt for more; but hunger was a small thing, readily forgotten when he drew nigh to death.

Over the dwarfish trees arched a deep azure. Sunbeams speared from the west, nearly level, to lose themselves in the woods. Whenever he crossed them, their touch burned. Never, not in the southern deserts or on the eastern Mummy Steppe, had he known a country this forbidding. He had done well to come so far, he thought. Let him die as befitted a man.

If only he had a witness, that his memory live on in song. Well, maybe Ilyandi could charm the story out of the gods.

Kalava felt no fear. He was not in that habit. What lay ahead engrossed him. How he would acquit himself concerned him.

Nonetheless, when finally he lay behind a log and peered over it, his head whirled and his heart stumbled.

Brannock had related truth, but its presence overwhelmed. Here at the top, the woods grew to the boundaries of a flat black field. Upon it stood the demons—or the gods—and their works. He saw the central, softly rainbowlike dome, towers like lances and towers like webwork, argent nets and ardent globes, the bulks and shapes everywhere around, the little flyers that flitted aglow, and more and more, all half veiled and ashimmer, aripple, apulse, while the life-beat of it went through him to make a bell of his skull, and it was too strange, his eyes did not know how to see it, he gaped as if blinded and shuddered as if pierced.

Long he lay powerless and defenseless. The sun sank down to the western clouds. Their deck went molten gold. The breeze strengthened. Somehow its cold reached to Kalava and wakened his spirit. He groped his way back toward resolution. Brannock had warned him it would be like this. Ilyandi had said Brannock was of the gods whom she served, her star-gods, hers. He had given his word to their messenger and to her.

He dug fingers into the soil beneath him. It was real, familiar, that from which he had sprung and to which he would return. Yes, he was a man.

He narrowed his gaze. Grown a bit accustomed, he saw that they yonder did, indeed, have shapes, however shifty, and places and paths. They were not as tall as the sky, they did not fling lightning bolts about or roar with thunder. Ai-ya, they were awesome, they were dreadful to behold, but they could do no worse than kill him. Could they? At least, he would try not to let them do worse. If they were about to capture him, his sword would be his friend, releasing him.

And . . . yonder, hard by the dome, yonder loomed the god of whom Brannock spoke, the god deceived by the sorceress. He bore the spearhead form, he sheened blue and coppery in the sunset light; when the stars came forth they would be a crown for him, even as Brannock foretold.

Had he been that which passed above the Windroad Sea? Kalava's heart thuttered.

How to reach him, across a hard-paved space amidst the many demons? After dark, creeping, a finger-length at a time, then maybe a final dash—

A buzz went by Kalava's temple. He looked around and saw a thing the size of a bug hovering. But it was metal, the light flashed off it, and was that a single eye staring at him?

He snarled and swatted. His palm smote hardness. The thing reeled in the air. Kalava scuttled downhill into the brush.

He had been seen. Soon the sorceress would know.

All at once he was altogether calm, save that his spirit thrummed like rigging in a gale. Traveling, he had thought what he might do if something like this proved to be in his doom. Now he would do it. He would divert the enemy's heed from himself, if only for a snatch of moments.

Quickly, steadily, he took the firemaker from his pouch, charged it, drove the piston in, pulled it out and inserted a match, brought up a little, yellow flame. He touched it to the withered bush before him. No need to puff. A leaf crackled instantly alight. The wind cast it against another, and shortly the whole shrub stood ablaze. Kalava was already elsewhere, setting more fires.

Keep on the move! The demon scouts could not be everywhere at a single time. Smoke began to sting his eyes and nostrils, but its haze swirled ever thicker, and the sun had gone under the clouds. The flames cast their own light, leaping, surging, as they climbed into the trees and made them torches.

Heat licked at Kalava. An ember fell to sear his left forearm. He barely felt it. He sped about on his work, himself a fire demon. Flyers darted overhead in the dusk. He gave them no heed either. Although he tried to make no noise except for the hurtful breaths he gasped, within him shouted a battle song.

When the fire stood like a wall along the whole southern edge of the field, when it roared like a beast or a sea, he ran from its fringe and out into the open.

Smoke was a bitter, concealing mist through which sparks rained. To and fro above flew the anxious lesser demons. Beyond them, the first stars were coming forth.

Kalava wove his way among the greater shapes. One stirred. It had spied him.

Soundlessly, it flowed in pursuit. He dodged behind another, ran up and over the flanks of a low-slung third, sped on toward the opal dome and the god who stood beside it.

A thing with spines and a head like a cold sun slid in front of him. He tried to run past. It moved to block his way, faster than he was. The first one approached. He drew blade and hoped it would bite on them before he died.

From elsewhere came a being with four arms, two legs, and a mask. "Brannock!" Kalava bawled. "Ai, Brannock, you got here!"

Brannock stopped, a spear-length away. He did not seem to know the man. He only watched as the other two closed in.

Kalava took stance. The old song rang in him:

> If the gods have left you,
> Then laugh at them, warrior.
> Never your heart
> Will need to forsake you.

He heard no more than the noise of burning. But suddenly through the smoke he saw his foes freeze moveless, while Brannock trod forward as boldly as ever before; and Kalava knew that the god of Brannock and Ilyandi had become aware of him and had given a command.

Weariness torrented over him. His sword clattered to the ground. He sank too, fumbled in his filthy tunic, took out the message written on bark and offered it. "I have brought you this," he mumbled. "Now let me go back to my ship."

12

We must end as we began, making a myth, if we would tell of that which we cannot ever really know. Imagine two minds conversing. The fire on the mountaintop is quenched. The winds have blown away smoke and left a frosty silence. Below, cloud deck reaches ghost-white to the rim of a night full of stars.

"You have lied to me throughout," says Wayfarer.

"I have not," denies Gaia. "The perceptions of this globe and its past through which I guided you were all true," as true as they were majestic.

"Until lately," retorts Wayfarer. "It has become clear that when Brannock returned, memories of his journey had been erased and falsehood written in. Had I not noticed abrupt frantic activity here and dispatched him to go see what it was—which you tried to dissuade me from—that man would have perished unknown."

"You presume to dispute about matters beyond your comprehension," says Gaia stiffly.

"Yes, your intellect is superior to mine." The admission does not ease the sternness: "But it will be your own kind among the stars to whom you must answer. I think you would be wise to begin with me."

"What do you intend?"

"First, to take the man Kalava back to his fellows. Shall I send Brannock with a flyer?"

"No, I will provide one, if this must be. But you do not, you *cannot*, realize the harm in it."

"Tell me, if you are able."

"He will rejoin his crew as one anointed by their gods. And so will he come home, unless his vessel founders at sea."

"I will watch from afar."

"Lest my agents sink it?"

"After what else you have done, yes, I had best keep guard. Brannock made promises on my behalf which I will honor. Kalava shall have gold in abundance, and his chance to found his colony. What do you fear in this?"

"Chaos. The unforeseeable, the uncontrollable."

"Which you would loose anew."

"In my own way, in my own time." She broods for a while, perhaps a whole microsecond. "It was misfortune that Kalava made his voyage just when he did. I had hoped for a later, more civilized generation to start the settlement of Arctica. Still, I could have adapted my plan to the circumstances, kept myself hidden from him and his successors, had you not happened to be on the planet." Urgently: "It is not yet too late. If only by refraining from further action after you have restored him to his people, you can help me retrieve what would otherwise be lost."

"If I should."

"My dream is not evil."

"That is not for me to say. But I can say that it is, it has always been, merciless."

"Because reality is."

"The reality that you created for yourself, within yourself, need not have been so. But what Christian revealed to me—yes, you glossed it over. These, you said," almost tearfully, if a quasi god can weep, "are your children, born in your mind out of all the human souls that are in you. Their existence would be empty were they not left free of will, to make their own mistakes and find their own ways to happiness."

"Meanwhile, by observing them, I have learned much that was never known before, about what went into the making of us."

"I could have believed that. I could have believed that your interferences and your ultimate annihilations of history after history were acts of pity as well as science. You claimed they could be restarted if ever you determined what conditions would better them. It did seem strange that you set one line of them—or more?—not in Earth's goodly past but in the hard world of today. It seemed twice strange that you were reluctant to have this particular essay brought to light. But I assumed that you, with your long experience and superior mentality, had reasons. Your attempt at secrecy might have been to avoid lengthy justifications to your kindred. I did not know, nor venture to judge. I would have left that to them.

"But then Kalava arrived."

Another mind-silence falls. At last Gaia says, very softly through the night, "Yes. Again humans live in the material universe."

"How long has it been?" asks Wayfarer with the same quietness.

"I made the first of them about fifty thousand years ago. Robots in human guise raised them from infancy. After that they were free."

"And, no doubt, expanding across the planet in their Stone Age, they killed off those big game animals. Yes, human. But why did you do it?"

"That humankind might live once more." A sigh as of time itself blowing past. "This is what you and those whom you serve will never fully understand. Too few humans went into them; and those who did, they were those who wanted the stars. You," every other node in the galactic brain, "have not felt the love of Earth, the need and longing for the primordial mother, that was in these many and many who remained with me. I do."

How genuine is it? wonders Wayfarer. How sane is she? "Could you not be content with your emulations?" he asks.

"No. How possibly? I cannot make a whole cosmos for them. I can only make them, the flesh-and-blood them, for the cosmos. Let them live in it not as machines or as flickerings within a machine, but as humans."

"On a planet soon dead?"

"They will, they must forge survival for themselves. I do not compel them, I do not dominate them with my nearness or any knowledge of it. That would be to stunt their spirits, turn them into pet animals or worse. I simply give guidance, not often, in the form of divinities in whom they would believe anyway at this stage of their societies, and simply toward the end of bringing them to a stable, high-technology civilization that can save them from the sun."

"Using what you learn from your shadow folk to suggest what the proper course of history may be?"

"Yes. How else should I know? Humankind is a chaotic phenomenon. Its actions and their consequences cannot be computed from first principles. Only by experiment and observation can we learn something about the nature of the race."

"Experiments done with conscious beings, aware of their pain. Oh, I see why you have kept most of your doings secret."

"I am not ashamed," declares Gaia. "I am proud. I gave life back to the race that gave life to us. They will make their own survival, I say. It may be that when they are able, they will move to the outer reaches of the Solar System, or some of them somehow even to the stars. It may be they will shield Earth or damp the sun. It is for them to decide, them to do. Not us, do you hear me? Them."

"The others yonder may feel differently. Alarmed or horrified, they may act to put an end to this."

"Why?" Gaia demands. "What threat is it to them?"

"None, I suppose. But there is a moral issue. What you are after is a purely human renascence, is it not? The former race went up in the machines, not because it was forced but because it chose, because that was the way by which the spirit could live and grow forever. You do not want this to happen afresh. You want to perpetuate war, tyranny, superstition, misery, instincts in mortal combat with each other, the ancient ape, the ancient beast of prey."

"I want to perpetuate the lover, parent, child, adventurer, artist, poet, prophet. Another element in the universe. Have we machines in our self-sureness every answer, every dream, that can ever be?"

Wayfarer hesitates. "It is not for me to say, it is for your peers."

"But now perhaps you see why I have kept my secrets and why I have argued and, yes, fought in my fashion against the plans of the galactic brain. Someday my humans must discover its existence. I can hope that then they will be ready to come to terms with it. But let those mighty presences appear among them within the next several thousand years—let signs and wonders, the changing of the heavens and the world, be everywhere—what freedom will be left for my children, save to cower and give worship? Afterward, what destiny for them, save to be animals in a preserve, forbidden any ventures that might endanger them, until at last, at best, they too drain away into the machines?"

Wayfarer speaks more strongly than before. "Is it better, what they might make for themselves? I cannot say. I do not know. But neither, Gaia, do you. And . . . the fate of Christian and Laurinda causes me to wonder about it."

"You know," she says, "that *they* desired humanness."

"They could have it again."

Imagine a crowned head shaking. "No. I do not suppose any other node would create a world to house their mortality, would either care to or believe it was right."

"Then why not you, who have so many worlds in you?"

Gaia is not vindictive. A mind like hers is above that. But she says, "I cannot take them. After such knowledge as they have tasted of, how could they return to me?" And to make new copies, free of memories that would weigh their days down with despair, would be meaningless.

"Yet—there at the end, I felt what Christian felt."

"And I felt what Laurinda felt. But now they are at peace in us."

"Because they are no more. I, though, am haunted," the least, rebellious bit, for a penalty of total awareness is that nothing can be ignored or forgotten. "And it raises questions which I expect Alpha will want answered, if answered they can be."

After a time that may actually be measurable less by quantum shivers than by the stars, Wayfarer says: "Let us bring those two back."

"Now it is you who are pitiless," Gaia says.

"I think we must."

"So be it, then."

The minds conjoin. The data are summoned and ordered. A configuration is established.

It does not emulate a living world or living bodies. The minds have agreed that that would be too powerful an allurement and torment. The subjects of their inquiry need to think clearly; but because the thought is to concern their inmost selves, they are enabled to feel as fully as they did in life.

Imagine a hollow darkness, and in it two ghosts who glimmer slowly into existence until they stand confronted before they stumble toward a phantom embrace.

"Oh, beloved, beloved, is it you?" Laurinda cries.

"Do you remember?" Christian whispers.

"I never forgot, not quite, not even at the heights of oneness."

"Nor I, quite."

They are silent awhile, although the darkness shakes with the beating of the hearts they once had.

"Again," Laurinda says. "Always."

"Can that be?" wonders Christian.

Through the void of death, they perceive one speaking: "Gaia, if you will give Laurinda over to me, I will take her home with Christian—home into Alpha."

And another asks: "Child, do you desire this? You can be of Earth and of the new humanity."

She will share in those worlds, inner and outer, only as a memory borne by the great being to whom she will have returned; but if she departs, she will not have them at all.

"Once I chose you, Mother," Laurinda answers.

Christian senses the struggle she is waging with herself and tells her, "Do whatever you most wish, my dearest."

She turns back to him. "I will be with you. Forever with you."

And that too will be only as a memory, like him; but what they were will be together, as one, and will live on, unforgotten.

"Farewell, child," says Gaia.

"Welcome," says Wayfarer.

The darkness collapses. The ghosts dissolve into him. He stands on the mountaintop ready to bear them away, a part of everything he has gained for those whose avatar he is.

"When will you go?" Gaia asks him.

"Soon," he tells her: soon, home to his own oneness.

And she will abide, waiting for the judgment from the stars.

ARTHUR STERNBACH BRINGS THE CURVEBALL TO MARS

Kim Stanley Robinson

Kim Stanley Robinson (born 1952) began writing SF stories in the 1970s, publishing about ten stories before gaining his Ph.D. in English in 1982. His dissertation was later published as *The Novels of Philip K. Dick* (1984). He became a famous SF writer in 1984 upon the publication of his first novel, *The Wild Shore*, an excellent post-catastrophe SF novel in the Steinbeckian tradition of George R. Stewart's *Earth Abides*. It had the bad luck to be published in the same year as William Gibson's *Neuromancer*, to which it came in second for major awards. Worse, it allowed Robinson to become a symbol of the opposition for the adherents of the Movement, cyberpunk's official name in the mid-eighties. He did win some major awards, and was nominated for more. But the discourse surrounding Robinson's major works of that decade—the Orange Country trilogy: *The Wild Shore, The Gold Coast* (1988), and *Pacific Edge* (1990), and the novels *Icehenge, Memory of Whiteness*, and *Escape from Katmandu* (1989)—was contoured by literary politics.

Then in the 1990s Robinson mined his 1985 novella "Green Mars" for what became his Mars trilogy—*Red Mars* (1992), *Green Mars* (1994), *Blue Mars* (1996), all award winners and nominees—a stand-alone novel, *Antarctica* (1997), and a collection, *The Martians* (1999). The Mars trilogy is generally recognized as one of the SF masterworks of the decade and confirmed him in the front ranks of contemporary SF writers. The trilogy also moved him very publicly into hard SF, especially due to the wonderfully detailed settings, and in the portrayal of scientists as characters doing the daily work of science. He said in a *Locus* interview: "Science fiction rarely is about scientists doing real science, in its slowness, its vagueness, the sort of tedious quality of getting out there and digging amongst rocks and then trying to convince people that what you're seeing justifies the conclusions you're making. The whole process of science is wildly under-represented in science fiction because it's not easy to write about. There are many facets of science that are almost exactly opposite of dramatic narrative. It's slow, tedious, inconclusive, it's hard to tell good guys from bad guys—it's everything that a normal hour of *Star Trek* is not." His interest in themes of frontier life and of colonization marks him politically as a North American. But Robinson also injects large doses of politics and political discussion, left wing, communitarian, and socialist Utopian ideas into the Mars novels, an unusual spin for hard SF.

Robinson's Mars books were among the first in what became, as one reviewer put it, the "millennial wave of Mars exploration tales." In a time when it was fashionable to explore notions of virtuality, Robinson remained steadfastly loyal to actuality as the true origin of stories. Rather than exploring the multi-layered worlds of virtual reality and uploaded minds, he took on the task of imagining what it would be like if people colonized Mars, and how they would get along there. Not the SF trope Mars, the easily habitable planet, in the tradition of Edgar Rice Burroughs's Barsoom series, Stanley G. Weinbaum's *A Martian Odyssey* (1934), Ray Bradbury's *The Martian Chronicles* (1950), or for that matter, Philip K. Dick's *Martian Time-Slip* (1964), but the real place as described by NASA's Mars Exploration Program, a long-term effort of robotic exploration. While to some extent, his approach to Mars comes out of Hal Clement's *Mission of Gravity* (1953), his approach is not so much world-building on the planetary scale, as a faith in powerful settings to tell powerful stories.

This story, from *The Martians*, of how baseball is played on Mars, is hard SF with a light touch. It explores the physics of baseball, in the persona of a sports fan trying to adapt the sport to a radically changed environment.

He was a tall skinny Martian kid, shy and stooping. Gangly as a puppy. Why they had him playing third base I have no idea. Then again they had me playing shortstop and I'm left-handed. And can't field grounders. But I'm American so there I was. That's what learning a sport by video will do. Some things are so obvious people never think to mention them. Like never put a lefty at shortstop. But on Mars they were making it all new. Some people there had fallen in love with baseball, and ordered the equipment and rolled some fields, and off they went.

So there we were, me and this kid Gregor, butchering the left side of the infield. He looked so young I asked him how old he was, and he said eight and I thought Jeez you're not *that* young, but realized he meant Martian years of course, so he was about sixteen or seventeen, but he seemed younger. He had recently moved to Argyre from somewhere else, and was staying at the local house of his co-op with relatives or friends, I never got that straight, but he seemed pretty lonely to me. He never missed practice even though he was the worst of a terrible team, and clearly he got frustrated at all his errors and strike-outs. I used to wonder why he came out at all. And so shy; and that stoop; and the acne; and the tripping over his own feet, the blushing, the mumbling—he was a classic.

English wasn't his first language, either. It was Armenian, or Moravian, something like that. Something no one else spoke, anyway, except for an elderly couple in his co-op. So he mumbled what passes for English on Mars, and sometimes even used a translation box, but basically tried never to be in a situation where he had to speak. And made error after error. We must have made quite a sight—me about waist-high to him, and both of us letting grounders pass through us like we were a magic show. Or else knocking them down and chasing them around, then winging them past the first baseman. We very seldom made an out. It would have been conspicuous except everyone else was the same way. Baseball on Mars was a high-scoring game.

But beautiful anyway. It was like a dream, really. First of all the horizon, when you're on a flat plain like Argyre, is only three miles away rather than six. It's very noticeable to a Terran eye. Then their diamonds have just over normal-sized infields, but the outfields have to be huge. At my team's ballpark it was nine hundred feet to dead center, seven hundred down the lines. Standing at the plate the outfield fence was like a little green line off in the distance, under a purple sky, pretty near the horizon itself—what I'm telling you is that the baseball diamond about covered *the entire visible world*. It was so great.

They played with four outfielders, like in softball, and still the alleys between fielders were wide. And the air was about as thin as at Everest base camp, and the gravity itself only bats .380, so to speak. So when you hit the ball solid it flies like a golf ball hit by a big driver. Even as big as the fields were, there were still a number of home runs every game. Not many shut-outs on Mars. Not till I got there anyway.

I went there after I climbed Olympus Mons, to help them establish a new soil sciences institute. They had the sense not to try that by video. At first I climbed in the Charitums in my time off, but after I got hooked into baseball it took up most of my spare time. Fine, I'll play, I said when they asked me. But I won't coach. I don't like telling people what to do.

So I'd go out and start by doing soccer exercises with the rest of them, warming up all the muscles we would never use. Then Werner would start hitting infield practice, and Gregor and I would start flailing. We were like matadors. Occasionally we'd snag one and whale it over to first, and occasionally the first baseman, who was well over two meters tall and built like a tank, would catch our throws, and we'd slap our gloves together. Doing this day after day Gregor got a little less shy with me, though not much. And I saw that he threw the ball pretty damned hard. His arm was as long as my whole body, and boneless it seemed, like something pulled off a squid, so loose-wristed that he got some real pop on the ball. Of course sometimes it would still be rising when it passed ten meters over the first baseman's head, but it was moving, no doubt about it. I began to see that maybe the reason he came out to play, beyond just being around people he didn't have to talk to, was the chance to throw things really hard. I saw too that he wasn't so much shy as he was surly. Or both.

Anyway our fielding was a joke. Hitting went a bit better. Gregor learned to chop down on the ball and hit grounders up the middle; it was pretty effective. And I began to get my timing together. Coming to it from years of slow-pitch softball, I had started by swinging at everything a week late, and between that and my shortstopping I'm sure my teammates figured they had gotten a defective American. And since they had a rule limiting each team to only two Terrans, no doubt they were disappointed by that. But slowly I adjusted my timing, and after that I hit pretty well. The thing was their pitchers had no breaking stuff. These big guys would rear back and throw as hard as they could, like Gregor, but it took everything in their power just to throw strikes. It was a little scary because they often threw right at you by accident. But if they got it down the pipe then all you had to do was time it. And if you hit one, how the ball flew! Every time I connected it was like a miracle. It felt like you could put one into orbit if you hit it right, in fact that was one of their nicknames for a home run, Oh that's orbital they would say, watching one leave the park headed for the horizon. They had a little bell, like a ship's bell, attached to the backstop, and every time someone hit one out they would ring that bell while you rounded the bases. A very nice local custom.

So I enjoyed it. It's a beautiful game even when you're butchering it. My sorest muscles after practice were in my stomach from laughing so hard. I even began to have some success at short. When I caught balls going to my right I twirled around backwards to throw to first or second. People were impressed though of course it was ridiculous. It was a case of the one-eyed man in the country of the blind. Not that they weren't good athletes, you understand, but none of them had played as kids, and so they had no baseball instincts. They just liked to play. And I could see why—out there on a green field as big as the world, under a purple sky, with the yellow-green balls flying around—it was beautiful. We had a good time.

I started to give a few tips to Gregor, too, though I had sworn to myself not to get into coaching. I don't like trying to tell people what to do. The game's too hard for that. But I'd be hitting flies to the outfielders, and it was hard not to tell them to watch the ball and run under it and then put the glove up and catch it, rather than run all the way with their arms stuck up like the Statue of Liberty's. Or when they took turns hitting flies (it's harder than it looks) giving them batting tips. And Gregor and I played catch all the time during warm-ups, so just watching me—and trying to throw to such a short target—he got better. He definitely threw hard. And I saw there was a whole lot of movement in his throws. They'd come tailing in to me every which way, no surprise given how loose-wristed he was. I had to look sharp or I'd miss. He was out of control, but he had potential.

And the truth was, our pitchers were bad. I loved the guys, but they couldn't throw strikes if you paid them. They'd regularly walk ten or twenty batters every game, and these were five-inning games. Werner would watch Thomas walk ten, then he'd take over in relief and walk ten more himself. Sometimes they'd go through this twice. Gregor and I would stand there while the other team's runners walked by as in a parade, or a line at the grocery store. When Werner went to the mound I'd stand by Gregor and say, You know Gregor you could pitch better than these guys. You've got a good arm. And he would look at me horrified, muttering No no no no, not possible.

But then one time warming up he broke off a really mean curve and I caught it on my wrist. While I was rubbing it down I walked over to him. Did you see the way that ball curved? I said.

Yes, he said, looking away. I'm sorry.

Don't be sorry, That's called a curve ball, Gregor. It can be a useful throw. You twisted your hand at the last moment and the ball came over the top of it, like this, see? Here, try it again.

So we slowly got into it. I was all-state in Connecticut my senior year in high school, and it was all from throwing junk-curve, slider, split-finger, change. I could see Gregor throwing most of those just by accident, but to keep from confusing him I just worked on a straight curve. I told him Just throw it to me like you did that first time.

I thought you weren't to coach us, he said.

I'm not coaching you! Just throw it like that. Then in the games throw it straight. As straight as possible.

He mumbled a bit at me in Moravian, and didn't look me in the eye. But he did it. And after a while he worked up a good curve. Of course the thinner air on Mars meant there was little for the balls to bite on. But I noticed that the blue dot balls they played with had higher stitching than the red dot balls. They played with both of them as if there was no difference, but there was. So I filed that away and kept working with Gregor.

We practiced a lot. I showed him how to throw from the stretch, figuring that a wind-up from Gregor was likely to end up in knots. And by mid-season he threw a mean curve from the stretch. We had not mentioned it to anyone else. He was wild with it, but it hooked hard; I had to be really sharp to catch some of them. It made me better at shortstop too. Although finally in one game, behind twenty to nothing as usual, a batter hit a towering pop fly and I took off running back on it, and the wind kept carrying it and I kept following it, until when I got it I was out there sprawled between our startled center fielders.

Maybe you should play outfield, Werner said.

I said Thank God.

So after that I played left center or right center, and I spent the games chasing line drives to the fence and throwing them back in to the cut-off man. Or more likely, standing there and watching the other team take their walks. I called in my usual chatter, and only then did I notice that no one on Mars ever yelled anything at these games. It was like playing in a league of deaf-mutes. I had to provide the chatter for the whole team from two hundred yards away in center field, including of course criticism of the plate umpires' calls. My view of the plate was miniaturized but I still did a better job than they did, and they knew it too. It was fun. People would walk by and say, Hey there must be an American out there.

One day after one of our home losses, 28 to 12 I think it was, everyone went to get something to eat, and Gregor was just standing there looking off into the distance. You want to come along? I asked him, gesturing after the others, but he shook his head. He had to get back home and work. I was going back to work myself, so I walked with him into town, a place like you'd see in the Texas panhandle. I stopped outside his co-op, which was a big house or little apartment complex, I could never tell which was which on Mars. There he stood like a lamppost, and I was about to leave when an old woman came out and invited me in. Gregor had told her about me, she said in stiff English. So I was introduced to the people in the kitchen there, most of them incredibly tall. Gregor seemed really embarrassed, he didn't want me being there, so I left as soon as I could get away. The old woman had a husband, and they seemed like Gregor's grandparents. There was a young girl there too, about his age, looking at both of us like a hawk. Gregor never met her eye.

Next time at practice, I said, Gregor, were those your grandparents?

Like my grandparents.

And that girl, who was she?

No answer.

Like a cousin or something?

Yes.

Gregor, what about your parents? Where are they?

He just shrugged and started throwing me the ball.

I got the impression they lived in another branch of his co-op somewhere else, but I never found out for sure. A lot of what I saw on Mars I liked—the way they run their businesses together in co-ops takes a lot of pressure off them, and they live pretty relaxed lives compared to us on Earth. But some of their parenting systems—kids brought up by groups, or by one parent, or whatever—I wasn't so sure about those. It makes for problems if you ask me. Bunch of teenage boys ready to slug somebody. Maybe that happens no matter what you do.

Anyway we finally got to the end of the season, and I was going to go back to Earth after it. Our team's record was three and fifteen, and we came in last place in the regular season standings. But they held a final weekend tournament for all the teams in the Argyre Basin, a bunch of three-inning games, as there were a lot to get through. Immediately we lost the first game and were in the loser's bracket. Then we were losing the next one too, and all because of walks, mostly. Werner relieved Thomas for a time, then when that didn't work out Thomas went back to the mound to re-relieve Werner. When that happened I ran all the way in from center to join them on the mound. I said Look you guys, let Gregor pitch.

Gregor! they both said. No way!

He'll be even worse than us, Werner said.

How could he be? I said. You guys just walked eleven batters in a row. Night will fall before Gregor could do that.

So they agreed to it. They were both discouraged at that point, as you might expect. So I went over to Gregor and said Okay, Gregor, you give it a try now.

Oh no, no no no no no no no. He was pretty set against it. He glanced up into the stands where we had a couple hundred spectators, mostly friends and family and some curious passersby, and I saw then that his like-grandparents and his girl something-or-other were up there watching. Gregor was getting more hangdog and sullen every second.

Come on Gregor, I said, putting the ball in his glove. Tell you what, I'll catch you. It'll be just like warming up. Just keep throwing your curve ball. And I dragged him over to the mound.

So Werner warmed him up while I went over and got on the catcher's gear, moving a box of blue dot balls to the front of the ump's supply area while I was at it. I could see Gregor was nervous, and so was I. I had never caught before, and he had never pitched, and bases were loaded and no one was out. It was an unusual baseball moment.

Finally I was geared up and I clanked on out to him. Don't worry about throwing too hard, I said. Just put the curve ball right in my glove. Ignore the batter. I'll give you the sign before every pitch; two fingers for curve, one for fastball.

Fastball? he says.

That's where you throw the ball fast. Don't worry about that. We're just going to throw curves anyway.

And you said you weren't to coach, he said bitterly.

I'm not coaching, I said, I'm catching.

So I went back and got set behind the plate. Be looking for curve balls, I said to the ump. Curve ball? he said.

So we started up. Gregor stood crouched on the mound like a big praying mantis, red-faced and grim. He threw the first pitch right over our heads to the backstop. Two guys scored while I retrieved it, but I threw out the runner going from first to third. I went out to Gregor. Okay, I said, the bases are cleared and we got an out. Let's just throw now. Right into the glove. Just like last time, but lower.

So he did. He threw the ball at the batter, and the batter bailed, and the ball cut right down into my glove. The umpire was speechless. I turned around and showed him the ball in my glove. That was a strike, I told him.

Strike! he hollered. He grinned at me. That was a curve ball, wasn't it.

Damn right it was.

Hey, the batter said. What was that?

We'll show you again, I said.

And after that Gregor began to mow them down. I kept putting down two fingers, and he kept throwing curve balls. By no means were they all strikes, but enough were to keep him from walking too many batters. All the balls were blue dot. The ump began to get into it.

And between two batters I looked behind me and saw that the entire crowd of spectators, and all the teams not playing at that moment, had congregated behind the backstop to watch Gregor pitch. No one on Mars had ever seen a curve ball before, and now they were crammed back there to get the best view of it, gasping and chattering at every hook. The batter would bail or take a weak swing and then look back at the crowd with a big grin, as if to say Did you see that? That was a curve ball!

So we came back and won that game, and we kept Gregor pitching, and we won the next three games as well. The third game he threw exactly twenty-seven pitches, striking out all nine batters with three pitches each. Walter Feller once struck out all twenty-seven batters in a high school game; it was like that.

The crowd was loving it. Gregor's face was less red. He was standing straighter in the box. He still refused to look anywhere but at my glove, but his look of grim terror had shifted to one of ferocious concentration. He may have been skinny, but he was tall. Out there on the mound he began to look pretty damned formidable.

So we climbed back up into the winner's bracket, then into a semi-final. Crowds of people were coming up to Gregor between games to get him to sign their baseballs. Mostly he looked dazed, but at one point I saw him glance up at his co-op family in the stands and wave at them, with a brief smile.

How's your arm holding out? I asked him.

What do you mean? he said.

Okay, I said. Now look, I want to play outfield again this game. Can you pitch to Werner? Because there were a couple of Americans on the team we played next, Ernie and Caesar, who I suspected could hit a curve. I just had a hunch.

Gregor nodded, and I could see that as long as there was a glove to throw at, nothing else mattered. So I arranged it with Werner, and in the semifinals I was back out in right-center field. We were playing under the lights by this time, the field like green velvet under a purple twilight sky. Looking in from center field it was all tiny, like something in a dream.

And it must have been a good hunch I had, because I made one catch charging in on a liner from Ernie, sliding to snag it, and then another running across the middle for what seemed like thirty seconds, before I got under a towering Texas leaguer from Caesar. Gregor even came up and congratulated me between innings.

And you know that old thing about how a good play in the field leads to a good at-bat. Already in the day's games I had hit well, but now in this semifinal I came up and hit a high fastball so solid it felt like I didn't hit it at all, and off it flew. Home run over the center field fence, out into the dusk. I lost sight of it before it came down.

Then in the finals I did it again in the first inning, back-to-back with Thomas—his to left, mine again to center. That was two in a row for me, and we were winning, and Gregor was mowing them down. So when I came up again the next inning I was feeling good, and people were calling out for another homer, and the other team's pitcher had a real determined look. He was a really big guy, as tall as Gregor but massive-chested as so many Martians are, and he reared back and threw the first one right at my head. Not on purpose, he was out of control. Then I barely fouled several pitches off, swinging very late, and dodging his inside heat, until it was a full count, and I was thinking to myself Well heck, it doesn't really matter if you strike out here, at least you hit two in a row.

Then I heard Gregor shouting Come on, Coach, you can do it! Hang in there! Keep your focus! All doing a passable imitation of me, I guess, as the rest of the team was laughing its head off. I suppose I had said all those things to them before, though of course it was just the stuff you always say automatically at a ball game, I never meant anything by it, I didn't even know people heard me. But I definitely heard Gregor, needling me, and I stepped back into the box thinking Look I don't even like to coach, I played ten games at shortstop trying not to coach you guys, and I was so irritated I was barely aware of the pitch, but hammered it anyway out over the right field fence, higher and deeper even than my first two. Knee-high fastball, inside. As Ernie said to me afterwards, You *drove* that baby. My teammates rang the little ship's bell all the way around the bases, and I slapped hands with every one of them on the way from third to home, feeling the grin on my face. Afterwards I sat on the bench and felt the hit in my hands. I can still see it flying out.

So we were ahead 4–0 in the final inning, and the other team came up determined to catch us. Gregor was tiring at last, and he walked a couple, then hung a curve and their big pitcher got into it and clocked it far over my head. Now I do okay charging liners, but the minute a ball is hit over me I'm totally lost. So I turned my back on this one and ran for the fence, figuring either it goes out or I collect it against the fence, but that I'd never see it again in the air. But running on Mars is so weird. You get going too fast and then you're pinwheeling along trying to keep from doing a faceplant. That's what I was doing when I saw the warning track, and looked back up and spotted the ball coming down, so I jumped, trying to jump straight up, you know, but I had a lot of momentum, and had completely forgotten about the gravity, so I shot up and caught the ball, amazing, but found myself *flying right over the fence.*

I came down and rolled in the dust and sand, and the ball stayed stuck in my glove. I hopped back over the fence holding the ball up to show everyone I had it. But they gave the other pitcher a home run anyway, because you have to stay inside the park when you catch one, it's a local rule. I didn't care. The whole point of playing games is to make you do things like that anyway. And it was good that that pitcher got one too.

So we started up again and Gregor struck out the side, and we won the tournament. We were mobbed, Gregor especially. He was the hero of the hour. Everyone wanted him to sign something. He didn't say much, but he wasn't stooping either. He looked surprised. Afterward Werner took two balls and everyone signed them, to make kind-of trophies for Gregor and me. Later I saw half the names on my trophy were jokes, "Mickey Mantel" and other names like that. Gregor had written on it "Hi Coach Arthur, Regards Greg." I have the ball still, on my desk at home.

ON THE ORION LINE

Stephen Baxter

❁

Stephen Baxter (born 1957), emerged in the late eighties and in the nineties as one of *Interzone*'s new breed of hard SF writer. He has written an abundance of fine hard SF, both in short story and novel form. He has relatively speaking burst into prominence overnight. Asked how he would explain the recent renaissance of hard SF of which he is a key figure, he replied:

> With great difficulty. For one thing, I'm pretty certain there is no conscious "movement." Paul McAuley and I, for instance, emerged in parallel, both working off our personal influences. I greatly admire Paul's work but I don't think I'd say I'm influenced by it. I think it's also possible the shock and disappointment that the real space program delivered to our collective systems has now worked through. The Moon turned out to be dead and dull, space flight there was difficult and a bore, Mars is almost inaccessible to us right now and sterilized by ultraviolet anyhow, Venus is a hellhole . . . we've learned all this in the last couple of decades, and it shattered a lot of fond illusions . . . Now we've worked through all that, to some extent. You have works like Robinson's and Sargent's which deal with the solar system as it is, not how we'd like it to be—and it still turns out to be an interesting place.

In 1995 and 1996 he became a major figure internationally in hard SF when his work was published outside the U.K. Not only were his earlier novels reprinted in the U.S., but his 1995 *The Time Ships* was a leading contender in 1996 for the Hugo Award for best novel. In the mid and late 1990s he produced nearly ten short stories a year. He appeared in most of the major magazines, sometimes twice. A new novel, *Voyager*, was released in England and in the U.S. in early 1997. Baxter is now one of the big names in hard SF, the author of a number of highly regarded novels (he has won the Philip K. Dick Award, the John W. Campbell Memorial Award, the British SF Association Award, and others for his novels) and many short stories. *The Encyclopedia of Science Fiction* summarizes his early career thusly:

> He began publishing SF with "The Xeelee Flower" for *Interzone* in 1987, which with most of his other short work fits into his Xeelee Sequence, an ambitious attempt at creating a Future History; novels included in the sequence are *Raft* (1989), *Timelike Infinity* (1992), *Flux* (1993) and *Rind* (1994). The sequence—as centrally narrated in the second and fourth volume—follows humanity into interstellar space, where it encounters a complex of alien races; the long epic ends (being typical in this of U.K. SF) darkly, many aeons hence.

He published four books in 2000 alone, including a collaboration with Arthur C. Clarke, *The Light of Other Days; Longtusk* (*Mammoth*, book two); *Reality Dust;* and *Manifold: Time* in the U.S., and won the Philip K. Dick Award again for his collection, *Vacuum*

Diagrams (1999). In 2001, he had five new books out: three novels, *Manifold: Space, Manifold: Origin*, and *Icebones*, the non-fiction book *Deep Future*, and the collection *Omegatropic: Non-Fiction & Fiction*. He is notably prolific. His 1995 novel, *The Time Ships*, is a sequel to H. G. Wells's 1895 *The Time Machine* published on its hundredth anniversary of publication. Then came *Voyage* (1996), *Titan* (1997), and *Moonseed* (1998). In 2002, he had several new books out: *Deep Future*, a non-fiction book which David Langford describes as "a lively though often chilling tour of possible futures," and a new novel, *Phase Space*.

"On the Orion Line" explores both the space opera theme of the short-lived individual caught in a long-lived galactic war and the hard SF theme of good old-fashioned bootstrapping. It is told from the point of view of a not-very-bright fifteen-year-old, an unusual choice in recent hard SF. In this story his ignorance is a pretext for the better-informed characters to explain the physics (the role served in older SF by the professor's beautiful daughter). Also, his ignorance serves to highlight, though only gently, the moral issues raised by the story.

The *Brief Life Burns Brightly* broke out of the fleet. We were chasing down a Ghost cruiser, and we were closing.

The lifedome of the *Brightly* was transparent, so it was as if Captain Teid in her big chair, and her officers and their equipment clusters—and a few low-grade tars like me—were just floating in space. The light was subtle, coming from a nearby cluster of hot young stars, and from the rivers of sparking lights that made up the fleet formation we had just left, and beyond *that* from the sparking of novae. This was the Orion Line—six thousand light years from Earth and a thousand lights long, a front that spread right along the inner edge of the Orion Spiral Arm—and the stellar explosions marked battles that must have concluded years ago.

And, not a handful of klicks away, the Ghost cruiser slid across space, running for home. The cruiser was a rough egg-shape of silvered rope. Hundreds of Ghosts clung to the rope. You could see them slithering this way and that, not affected at all by the emptiness around them.

The Ghosts' destination was a small, old yellow star. Pael, our tame Academician, had identified it as a fortress star from some kind of strangeness in its light. But up close you don't need to be an Academician to spot a fortress. From the *Brightly* I could see with my unaided eyes that the star had a pale blue cage around it—an open lattice with struts half a million kilometers long—thrown there by the Ghosts, for their own purposes.

I had a lot of time to watch all this. I was just a tar. I was fifteen years old.

My duties at that moment were non-specific. I was supposed to stand to, and render assistance any way that was required—most likely with basic medical attention should we go into combat. Right now the only one of us tars actually working was Halle, who was chasing down a pool of vomit sicked up by Pael, the Academician, the only non-Navy personnel on the bridge.

The action on the *Brightly* wasn't like you see in Virtual shows. The atmosphere was calm, quiet, competent. All you could hear was the murmur of voices, from the crew and the equipment, and the hiss of recycling air. No drama: it was like an operating theater.

There was a soft warning chime.

The captain raised an arm and called over Academician Pael, First Officer Till, and Jeru, the commissary assigned to the ship. They huddled close, conferring—apparently arguing. I saw the way flickering nova light reflected from Jeru's shaven head.

I felt my heart beat harder.

Everybody knew what the chime meant: that we were approaching the fortress cordon. Either we would break off, or we would chase the Ghost cruiser inside its invisible fortress. And everybody knew that no Navy ship that had ever penetrated a fortress cordon, ten light-minutes from the central star, had come back out again.

One way or the other, it would all be resolved soon.

Captain Teid cut short the debate. She leaned forward and addressed the crew. Her voice, cast through the ship, was friendly, like a cadre leader whispering in your ear. "You can all see we can't catch that swarm of Ghosts this side of the cordon. And you all know the hazard of crossing a cordon. But if we're ever going to break this blockade of theirs we have to find a way to bust open those forts. So we're going in anyhow. Stand by your stations."

There was a half-hearted cheer.

I caught Halle's eye. She grinned at me. She pointed at the captain, closed her fist and made a pumping movement. I admired her sentiment but she wasn't being too accurate, anatomically speaking, so I raised my middle finger and jiggled it back and forth.

It took a slap on the back of the head from Jeru, the commissary, to put a stop to that. "Little morons," she growled.

"Sorry, sir—"

I got another slap for the apology. Jeru was a tall, stocky woman, dressed in the bland monastic robes said to date from the time of the founding of the Commission for Historical Truth a thousand years ago. But rumor was she'd seen plenty of combat action of her own before joining the Commission, and such was her physical strength and speed of reflex I could well believe it.

As we neared the cordon the Academician, Pael, started a gloomy count-down. The slow geometry of Ghost cruiser and tinsel-wrapped fortress star swiveled across the crowded sky.

Everybody went quiet.

The darkest time is always just before the action starts. Even if you can see or hear what is going on, all you do is think. What was going to happen to us when we crossed that intangible border? Would a fleet of Ghost ships materialize all around us? Would some mysterious weapon simply blast us out of the sky?

I caught the eye of First Officer Till. He was a veteran of twenty years; his scalp had been burned away in some ancient close-run combat, long before I was born, and he wore a crown of scar tissue with pride.

"Let's do it, tar," he growled.

All the fear went away. I was overwhelmed by a feeling of togetherness, of us all being in this crap together. I had no thought of dying. Just: let's get through this.

"Yes, *sir!*"

Pael finished his countdown.

All the lights went out. Detonating stars wheeled.

And the ship exploded.

I was thrown into darkness. Air howled. Emergency bulkheads scythed past me, and I could hear people scream.

I slammed into the curving hull, nose pressed against the stars.

I bounced off and drifted. The inertial suspension was out, then. I thought I could smell blood—probably my own.

I could see the Ghost ship, a tangle of rope and silver baubles, tingling with highlights from the fortress star. We were still closing.

But I could also see shards of shattered lifedome, a sputtering drive unit. The shards were bits of the *Brightly*. It had gone, all gone, in a fraction of a second.

"Let's do it," I murmured.

Maybe I was out of it for a while.

Somebody grabbed my ankle and tugged me down. there was a competent slap on my cheek, enough to make me focus.

"Case. Can you hear me?"

It was First Officer Till. Even in the swimming starlight that burned-off scalp was unmistakable.

I glanced around. There were four of us here: Till, Commissary Jeru, Academician Pael, me. We were huddled up against what looked like the stump of the First Officer's console. I realized that the gale of venting air had stopped. I was back inside a hull with integrity, then—

"Case!"

"I—yes, sir."

"Report."

I touched my lip; my hand came away bloody. At a time like that it's your duty to report your injuries, honestly and fully. Nobody needs a hero who turns out not to be able to function. "I think I'm all right. I may have a concussion."

"Good enough. Strap down." Till handed me a length of rope.

I saw that the others had tied themselves to struts. I did the same.

Till, with practiced ease, swam away into the air, I guessed looking for other survivors.

Academician Pael was trying to curl into a ball. He couldn't even speak. The tears just rolled out of his eyes. I stared at the way big globules welled up and drifted away into the air, glimmering.

The action had been over in seconds. All a bit sudden for an earthworm, I guess.

Nearby, I saw, trapped under one of the emergency bulkheads, there was a pair of legs—just that. The rest of the body must have been chopped away, gone drifting off with the rest of the debris from *Brightly*. But I recognized those legs, from a garish pink stripe on the sole of the right boot. That had been Halle. She was the only girl I had ever screwed, I thought—and more than likely, given the situation, the only girl I ever would get to screw.

I couldn't figure out how I felt about that.

Jeru was watching me. "Tar—do you think we should all be frightened for ourselves, like the Academician?" Her accent was strong, unidentifiable.

"No, sir."

"No." Jeru studied Pael with contempt. "We are in a yacht, Academician. Something has happened to the *Brightly*. The 'dome was designed to break up into yachts like this." She sniffed. "We have air, and it isn't foul yet." She winked at me. "Maybe we can do a little damage to the Ghosts before we die, tar. What do you think?"

I grinned. "Yes, sir."

Pael lifted his head and stared at me with salt water eyes. "Lethe. You people are monsters." His accent was gentle, a lilt. "Even such a child as this. You embrace death—"

Jeru grabbed Pael's jaw in a massive hand, and pinched the joint until he squealed. "Captain Teid grabbed you, Academician; she threw you here, into the yacht, before the bulkhead came down. I saw it. If she hadn't taken the time to do that, she would have made it herself. Was *she* a monster? Did *she* embrace death?" And she pushed Pael's face away.

For some reason I hadn't thought about the rest of the crew until that moment. I guess I have a limited imagination. Now, I felt adrift. The captain—dead?

I said, "Excuse me, Commissary. How many other yachts got out?"

"None," she said steadily, making sure I had no illusions. "Just this one. They died doing their duty, tar. Like the captain."

Of course she was right, and I felt a little better. Whatever his character, Pael was too valuable not to save. As for me, I had survived through sheer blind chance, through being in the right place when the walls came down: if the captain had been close, her duty would have been to pull me out of the way and take my place. It isn't a question of human values but of economics: a *lot* more is invested in the training and experience of a Captain Teid—or a Pael—than in *me*.

But Pael seemed more confused than I was.

First Officer Till came bustling back with a heap of equipment. "Put these on." He handed out pressure suits. They were what we called slime suits in training: lightweight skinsuits, running off a backpack of gen-enged algae. "Move it," said Till. "Impact with the Ghost cruiser in four minutes. We don't have any power; there's nothing we can do but ride it out."

I crammed my legs into my suit.

Jeru complied, stripping off her robe to reveal a hard, scarred body. But she was frowning. "Why not heavier armor?"

For answer, Till picked out a gravity-wave handgun from the gear he had retrieved. Without pausing he held it to Pael's head and pushed the fire button.

Pael twitched.

Till said, "See? Nothing is working. Nothing but bio systems, it seems." He threw the gun aside.

Pael closed his eyes, breathing hard.

Till said to me, "Test your comms."

I closed up my hood and faceplate and began intoning, "One, two, three . . ." I could hear nothing.

Till began tapping at our backpacks, resetting the systems. His hood started to glow with transient, pale blue symbols. And then, scratchily, his voice started to come through. ". . . Five, six, seven—can you hear me, tar?"

"Yes, sir."

The symbols were bioluminescent. There were receptors on all our suits—photoreceptors, simple eyes—which could "read" the messages scrawled on our companions' suits. It was a backup system meant for use in environments where anything higher-tech would be a liability. But obviously it would only work as long as we were in line of sight.

"That will make life harder," Jeru said. Oddly, mediated by software, she was easier to understand.

Till shrugged. "You take it as it comes." Briskly, he began to hand out more gear. "These are basic field belt kits. There's some medical stuff: a suture kit, scalpel blades, blood-giving sets. You wear these syrettes around your neck, Academician. They contain painkillers, various gen-enged med-viruses . . . no, you wear it *outside* your suit, Pael, so you can reach it. You'll find valve inlets here, on your sleeve, and here, on the leg." Now came weapons. "We should carry handguns, just in case they start working, but be ready with these." He handed out combat knives.

Pael shrank back.

"Take the knife, Academician. You can shave off that ugly beard, if nothing else."

I laughed out loud, and was rewarded with a wink from Till.

I took a knife. It was a heavy chunk of steel, solid and reassuring. I tucked it in my belt. I was starting to feel a whole lot better.

"Two minutes to impact," Jeru said. I didn't have a working chronometer; she must have been counting the seconds.

"Seal up." Till began to check the integrity of Pael's suit; Jeru and I helped each other. Face seal, glove seal, boot seal, pressure check. Water check, oh-two flow, cee-oh-two scrub . . .

When we were sealed I risked poking my head above Till's chair.

The Ghost ship filled space. The craft was kilometers across, big enough to have dwarfed the poor, doomed *Brief Life Burns Brightly*. It was a tangle of silvery rope of depthless complexity, occluding the stars and the warring fleets. Bulky equipment pods were suspended in the tangle.

And everywhere there were Silver Ghosts, sliding like beads of mercury. I could see how the yacht's emergency lights were returning crimson highlights from the featureless hides of Ghosts, so they looked like sprays of blood droplets across that shining perfection.

"Ten seconds," Till called. "Brace."

Suddenly silver ropes thick as tree trunks were all around us, looming out of the sky.

And we were thrown into chaos again.

I heard a grind of twisted metal, a scream of air. The hull popped open like an eggshell. The last of our air fled in a gush of ice crystals, and the only sound I could hear was my own breathing.

The crumpling hull soaked up some of our momentum.

But then the base of the yacht hit, and it hit hard.

The chair was wrenched out of my grasp, and I was hurled upward. There was a sudden pain in my left arm. I couldn't help but cry out.

I reached the limit of my tether and rebounded. The jolt sent further waves of pain through my arm. From up there, I could see the others were clustered around the base of the First Officer's chair, which had collapsed.

I looked up. We had stuck like a dart in the outer layers of the Ghost ship. There were shining threads arcing all around us, as if a huge net had scooped us up.

Jeru grabbed me and pulled me down. She jarred my bad arm, and I winced. But she ignored me, and went back to working on Till. He was under the fallen chair.

Pael started to take a syrette of dope from the sachet around his neck.

Jeru knocked his hand away. "You always use the casualty's," she hissed. "Never your own."

Pael looked hurt, rebuffed. "Why?"

I could answer that. "Because the chances are you'll need your own in a minute."

Jeru stabbed a syrette into Till's arm.

Pael was staring at me through his faceplate with wide, frightened eyes. "You've broken your arm."

Looking closely at the arm for the first time, I saw that it was bent back at an impossible angle. I couldn't believe it, even through the pain. I'd never bust so much as a finger, all the way through training.

Now Till jerked, a kind of miniature convulsion, and a big bubble of spit and blood blew out of his lips. Then the bubble popped, and his limbs went loose.

Jeru sat back, breathing hard. She said, "Okay. Okay. How did he put it?—You take it as it comes." She looked around, at me, Pael. I could see she was trembling, which scared me. She said, "Now we move. We have to find an LUP. A lying-up point, Academician. A place to hole up."

I said, "The First Officer—"

"Is dead." She glanced at Pael. "Now it's just the three of us. We won't be able to avoid each other anymore, Pael."

Pael stared back, eyes empty.

Jeru looked at me, and for a second her expression softened. "A broken neck. Till broke his neck, tar."

Another death, just like that: just for a heartbeat that was too much for me.

Jeru said briskly, "Do your duty, tar. Help the worm."

I snapped back, "Yes, sir." I grabbed Pael's unresisting arm.

Led by Jeru, we began to move, the three of us, away from the crumpled wreck of our yacht, deep into the alien tangle of a Silver Ghost cruiser.

We found our LUP.

It was just a hollow in a somewhat denser tangle of silvery ropes, but it afforded us some cover, and it seemed to be away from the main concentration of Ghosts. We were still open to the vacuum—as the whole cruiser seemed to be—and I realized then that I wouldn't be getting out of this suit for a while.

As soon as we picked the LUP, Jeru made us take up positions in an all-around defense, covering a 360-degree arc.

Then we did nothing, absolutely nothing, for ten minutes.

It was SOP, standard operating procedure, and I was impressed. You've just come out of all the chaos of the destruction of the *Brightly* and the crash of the yacht, a frenzy of activity. Now you have to give your body a chance to adjust to the new environment, to the sounds and smells and sights.

Only here, there was nothing to smell but my own sweat and piss, nothing to hear but my ragged breathing. And my arm was hurting like hell.

To occupy my mind I concentrated on getting my night vision working. Your eyes take a while to adjust to the darkness—forty-five minutes before they are fully effective—but you are already seeing better after five. I could see stars through the chinks in the wiry metallic brush around me, the flares of distant novae, and the reassuring lights of our fleet. But a Ghost ship is a dark place, a mess of shadows and smeared-out reflections. It was going to be easy to get spooked here.

When the ten minutes were done, Academician Pael started bleating, but Jeru ignored him and came straight over to me. She got hold of my busted arm and started to feel the bone. "So," she said briskly. "What's your name, tar?"

"Case, sir."

"What do you think of your new quarters?"

"Where do I eat?"

She grinned. "Turn off your comms," she said.

I complied.

Without warning she pulled my arm, hard. I was glad she couldn't hear how I howled.

She pulled a canister out of her belt and squirted gunk over my arm; it was semi-sentient and snuggled into place, setting as a hard cast around my injury. When I was healed the cast would fall away of its own accord.

She motioned me to turn on my comms again, and held up a syrette.

"I don't need that."

"Don't be brave, tar. It will help your bones knit."

"Sir, there's a rumor that stuff makes you impotent." I felt stupid even as I said it.

Jeru laughed out loud, and just grabbed my arm. "Anyhow it's the First Officer's, and he doesn't need it anymore, does he?"

I couldn't argue with that; I accepted the injection. The pain started ebbing almost immediately.

Jeru pulled a tactical beacon out of her belt kit. It was a thumb-sized orange cylinder. "I'm going to try to signal the fleet. I'll work my way out of this tangle; even if the beacon is working we might be shielded in here." Pael started to protest, but she shut him up. I sensed I had been thrown into the middle of an ongoing conflict between them. "Case, you're on stag. And show this *worm* what's in his kit. I'll come back the same way I go. All right?"

"Yes." More SOP.

She slid away through silvery threads.

I lodged myself in the tangle and started to go through the stuff in the belt kits Till had fetched for us. There was water, rehydration salts, and compressed food, all to be delivered to spigots inside our sealed hoods. We had power packs the size of my thumbnail, but they were as dead as the rest of the kit. There was a lot of low-tech gear meant to prolong survival in a variety of situations, such as a magnetic compass, a heliograph, a thumb saw, a magnifying glass, pitons, and spindles of rope, even fishing line.

I had to show Pael how his suit functioned as a lavatory. The trick is just to let go; a slime suit recycles most of what you give it, and compresses the rest. That's not to say it's comfortable. I've never yet worn a suit that was good at absorbing odors. I bet no suit designer spent more than an hour in one of her own creations.

I felt fine.

The wreck, the hammer-blow deaths one after the other—none of it was far beneath the surface of my mind. But that's where it stayed, for now; as long as I had the next task to focus on, and the next after that, I could keep moving forward. The time to let it all hit you is after the show.

I guess Pael had never been trained like that.

He was a thin, spindly man, his eyes sunk in black shadow, and his ridiculous red beard was crammed up inside his faceplate. Now that the great crises were over, his energy seemed to have drained away, and his functioning was slowing to a crawl. He looked almost comical as he pawed at his useless bits of kit.

After a time he said, "Case, is it?"

"Yes, sir."

"Are you from Earth, child?"

"No. I—"

He ignored me. "The Academies are based on Earth. Did you know that, child? But they do admit a few off-worlders."

I glimpsed a lifetime of outsider resentment. But I couldn't care less. Also I wasn't a child. I asked cautiously, "Where are you from, sir?"

He sighed. "It's 51 Pegasi. I-B."

I'd never heard of it. "What kind of place is that? Is it near Earth?"

"Is everything measured relative to Earth . . . ? Not very far. My home world was one of the first extra-solar planets to be discovered—or at least, the primary is. I grew up on a moon. The primary is a hot Jupiter."

I knew what *that* meant: a giant planet huddled close to its parent star.

He looked up at me. "Where you grew up, could you see the sky?"

"No—"

"I could. And the sky was full of sails. That close to the sun, solar sails work efficiently, you see. I used to watch them at night, schooners with sails hundreds of kilometers wide, tacking this way and that in the light. But you can't see the sky from Earth—not from the Academy bunkers anyhow."

"Then why did you go there?"

"I didn't have a choice." He laughed, hollowly. "I was doomed by being smart. That is why your precious commissary despises me so much, you see. I have been taught to think—and we can't have that, can we . . . ?"

I turned away from him and shut up. Jeru wasn't "my" commissary, and this sure wasn't my argument. Besides, Pael gave me the creeps. I've always been wary of people who knew too much about science and technology. With a weapon, all you want to know is how it works, what kind of energy or ammunition it needs, and what to do when it goes wrong. People who know all the technical background and the statistics are usually covering up their own failings; it is experience of use that counts.

But this was no loudmouth weapons tech. This was an Academician: one of humanity's elite scientists. I felt I had no point of contact with him at all.

I looked out through the tangle, trying to see the fleet's sliding, glimmering lanes of light.

There was motion in the tangle. I turned that way, motioning Pael to keep still and silent, and got hold of my knife in my good hand.

Jeru came bustling back, exactly the way she had left. She nodded approvingly at my alertness. "Not a peep out of the beacon."

Pael said, "You realize our time here is limited."

I asked, "The suits?"

"He means the star," Jeru said heavily. "Case, fortress stars seem to be unstable. When the Ghosts throw up their cordon, the stars don't last long before going pop."

Pael shrugged. "We have hours, a few days at most."

Jeru said, "Well, we're going to have to get out, beyond the fortress cordon, so we can signal the fleet. That or find a way to collapse the cordon altogether."

Pael laughed hollowly. "And how do you propose we do that?"

Jeru glared. "Isn't it your role to tell me, Academician?"

Pael leaned back and closed his eyes. "Not for the first time, you're being ridiculous."

Jeru growled. She turned to me. "You. What do *you* know about the Ghosts?"

I said, "They come from someplace cold. That's why they are wrapped up in silvery shells. You can't bring a Ghost down with laser fire because of those shells. They're perfectly reflective."

Pael said, "Not perfectly. They are based on a Planck-zero effect. . . . About one part in a billion of incident energy is absorbed."

I hesitated. "They say the Ghosts experiment on people."

Pael sneered. "Lies put about by your Commission for Historical Truth, Commissary. To demonize an opponent is a tactic as old as mankind."

Jeru wasn't perturbed. "Then why don't you put young Case right? How *do* the Ghosts go about their business?"

Pael said, "The Silver Ghosts tinker with the laws of physics."

I looked to Jeru; she shrugged.

Pael tried to explain. It was all to do with quagma.

Quagma is the state of matter that emerged from the Big Bang. Matter; when raised to sufficiently high temperatures, melts into a magma of quarks—a quagma.

And at such temperatures the four fundamental forces of physics unify into a single superforce. When quagma is allowed to cool and expand its binding superforce decomposes into four sub-forces.

To my surprise, I understood some of this. The principle of the GUTdrive, which powers intrasystem ships like *Brief Life Burns Brightly*, is related.

Anyhow, by controlling the superforce decomposition, you can select the ratio between those forces. And those ratios govern the fundamental constants of physics.

Something like that.

Pael said, "That marvelous reflective coating of theirs is an example. Each Ghost is surrounded by a thin layer of space in which a fundamental number called the Planck constant is significantly lower than elsewhere. Thus, quantum effects are collapsed. . . . Because the energy carried by a photon, a particle of light, is proportional to the Planck constant, an incoming photon must shed most of its energy when it hits the shell—hence the reflectivity."

"All right," Jeru said. "So what are they doing here?"

Pael sighed. "The fortress star seems to be surrounded by an open shell of quagma and exotic matter. We surmise that the Ghosts have blown a bubble around each star, a space-time volume in which the laws of physics are—tweaked."

"And that's why our equipment failed."

"Presumably," said Pael, with cold sarcasm.

I asked, "What do the Ghosts want? Why do they do all this stuff?"

Pael studied me. "You are trained to kill them, and they don't even tell you that?"

Jeru just glowered.

Pael said, "The Ghosts were not shaped by competitive evolution. They are symbiotic creatures; they derive from life-forms that huddled into cooperative collectives as their world turned cold. And they seem to be motivated—not by expansion and the acquisition of territory for its own sake, as we are—but by a desire to understand the fine-tuning of the universe. *Why are we here?* You see, young tar, there is only a narrow range of the constants of physics within which life of *any* sort is possible. We think the Ghosts are studying this question by pushing at the boundaries—by tinkering with the laws that sustain and contain us all."

Jeru said, "An enemy who can deploy the laws of physics as a weapon is formidable. But in the long run, we will out-compete the Ghosts."

Pael said bleakly, "Ah, the evolutionary destiny of mankind. How dismal. But we lived in peace with the Ghosts, under the Raoul Accords, for a thousand years. We are so different, with disparate motivations—why should there be a clash, anymore than between two species of birds in the same garden?"

I'd never seen birds, or a garden, so that passed me by.

Jeru glared. She said at last, "Let's return to practicalities. *How* do their fortresses work?" When Pael didn't reply, she snapped, "Academician, you've been *inside* a fortress cordon for an hour already and you haven't made a single fresh observation?"

Acidly, Pael demanded, "What would you have me do?"

Jeru nodded at me. "What have *you* seen, tar?"

"Our instruments and weapons don't work," I said promptly. "The *Brightly* exploded. I broke my arm."

Jeru said, "Till snapped his neck also." She flexed her hand within her glove. "What would make our bones more brittle? Anything else?"

I shrugged.

Pael admitted, "I do feel somewhat warm."

Jeru asked, "Could these body changes be relevant?"

"I don't see how."

"Then figure it out."

"I have no equipment."

Jeru dumped spare gear—weapons, beacons—in his lap. "You have your eyes, your hands and your mind. Improvise." She turned to me. "As for you, tar, let's do a little infil. We still need to find a way off this scow."

I glanced doubtfully at Pael. "There's nobody to stand on stag."

Jeru said, "I know. But there are only three of us." She grasped Pael's shoulder, hard. "Keep your eyes open, Academician. We'll come back the same way we left. So you'll know it's us. Do you understand?"

Pael shrugged her away, focusing on the gadgets on his lap.

I looked at him doubtfully. It seemed to me a whole platoon of Ghosts could have come down on him without his even noticing. But Jeru was right; there was nothing more we could do.

She studied me, fingered my arm. "You up to this?"

"I'm fine, sir."

"You are lucky. A good war comes along once in a lifetime. And this is your war, tar."

That sounded like parade-ground pep talk, and I responded in kind. "Can I have your rations, sir? You won't be needing them soon." I mimed digging a grave.

She grinned back fiercely. "Yeah. When your turn comes, slit your suit and let the farts out before I take it off your stiffening corpse—"

Pael's voice was trembling. "You really are monsters."

I shared a glance with Jeru. But we shut up, for fear of upsetting the earthworm further.

I grasped my fighting knife, and we slid away into the dark.

What we were hoping to find was some equivalent of a bridge. Even if we succeeded, I couldn't imagine what we'd do next. Anyhow, we had to try.

We slid through the tangle. Ghost cable stuff is tough, even to a knife blade. But it is reasonably flexible; you can just push it aside if you get stuck, although we tried to avoid doing that for fear of leaving a sign.

We used standard patrolling SOP, adapted for the circumstance. We would move for ten or fifteen minutes, clambering through the tangle, and then take a break for five minutes. I'd sip water—I was getting hot—and maybe nibble on a glucose tab, check on my arm, and pull the suit around me to get comfortable again. It's the way to do it. If you just push yourself on and on you run down your reserves and end up in no fit state to achieve the goal anyhow.

And all the while I was trying to keep up my all-around awareness, protecting my dark adaptation, and making appreciations. How far away is Jeru? What if an attack comes from in front, behind, above, below, left or right? Where can I find cover?

I began to build up an impression of the Ghost cruiser. It was a rough egg-shape, a couple of kilometers long, and basically a mass of the anonymous silvery cable. There were chambers and platforms and instruments stuck as if at random into the tangle, like food fragments in an old man's beard. I guess it makes for a flexible, easily modified configuration. Where the tangle was a little less thick, I glimpsed a more substantial core, a cylinder running along the axis of the craft. Perhaps it was the drive unit. I wondered if it was functioning; perhaps the Ghost equipment was designed to adapt to the changed conditions inside the fortress cordon.

There were Ghosts all over the craft.

They drifted over and through the tangle, following pathways invisible to us. Or they would cluster in little knots on the tangle. We couldn't tell what they were doing or saying. To human eyes a Silver Ghost is just a silvery sphere, visible only by reflection like a hole cut out of space, and without specialist equipment it is impossible even to tell one from another.

We kept out of sight. But I was sure the Ghosts must have spotted us, or were at least tracking our movements. After all we'd crash-landed in their ship. But they made no overt moves toward us.

We reached the outer hull, the place the cabling ran out, and dug back into the tangle a little way to stay out of sight.

I got an unimpeded view of the stars.

Still those nova firecrackers went off all over the sky; still those young stars glared like lanterns. It seemed to me the fortress's central, enclosed star looked a little brighter, hotter than it had been. I made a mental note to report that to the Academician.

But the most striking sight was the fleet.

Over a volume light-months wide, countless craft slid silently across the sky. They were organized in a complex network of corridors filling three-dimensional space: rivers of light gushed this way and that, their different colors denoting different classes and sizes of vessel. And, here and there, denser knots of color and light sparked, irregular flares in the orderly flows. They were places where human ships were engaging the enemy, places where people were fighting and dying.

It was a magnificent sight. But it was a big, empty sky, and the nearest sun was that eerie dwarf enclosed in its spooky blue net, a long way away, and there was movement in three dimensions, above me, below me, all around me. . . .

I found the fingers of my good hand had locked themselves around a sliver of the tangle.

Jeru grabbed my wrist and shook my arm until I was able to let go. She kept hold of my arm, her eyes locked on mine. *I have you. You won't fall.* Then she pulled me into a dense knot of the tangle, shutting out the sky.

She huddled close to me, so the bio lights of our suits wouldn't show far. Her eyes were pale blue, like windows. "You aren't used to being outside, are you, tar?"

"I'm sorry, Commissary. I've been trained—"

"You're still human. We all have weak points. The trick is to know them and allow for them. Where are you from?"

I managed a grin. "Mercury. Caloris Planitia." Mercury is a ball of iron at the bottom of the sun's gravity well. It is an iron mine, and an exotic matter factory, with a sun like a lid hanging over it. Most of the surface is given over to solar power collectors. It is a place of tunnels and warrens, where kids compete with the rats.

"And that's why you joined up? To get away?"

"I was drafted."

"Come on," she scoffed. "On a place like Mercury there are ways to hide. Are you a romantic, tar? You wanted to see the stars?"

"No," I said bluntly. "Life is more useful here."

She studied me. "A brief life should burn brightly—eh, tar?"

"Yes, sir."

"I came from Deneb," she said. "Do you know it?"

"No."

"Sixteen hundred light years from Earth—a system settled some four centuries after the start of the Third Expansion. It is quite different from the solar system. It is—organized. By the time the first ships reached Deneb, the mechanics of exploitation had become efficient. From preliminary exploration to working ship yards and daughter colonies in less than a century. . . . Deneb's resources—its planets and asteroids and comets, even the star itself—have been mined to fund fresh colonizing waves, the greater Expansion—and, of course, to support the war with the Ghosts."

She swept her hand over the sky. "Think of it, tar. The Third Expansion: between here and Sol, across six thousand light years—nothing but mankind, the fruit of a thousand years of world-building. And all of it linked by economics. Older systems like Deneb, their resources spent—even the solar system itself—are supported by a flow of goods and materials inward from the growing periphery of the Expansion. There are trade lanes spanning thousands of light years, lanes that never leave human territory, plied by vast schooners kilometers wide. But now the Ghosts are in our way. And *that's* what we're fighting for!"

"Yes, sir."

She eyed me. "You ready to go on?"

"Yes."

We began to make our way forward again, just under the tangle, still following patrol SOP.

I was glad to be moving again. I've never been comfortable talking personally—and for sure not with a Commissary. But I suppose even Commissaries need to talk.

Jeru spotted a file of the Ghosts moving in a crocodile, like so many schoolchildren, toward the head of the ship. It was the most purposeful activity we'd seen so far, so we followed them.

After a couple of hundred meters the Ghosts began to duck down into the tangle, out of our sight. We followed them in.

Maybe fifty meters deep, we came to a large enclosed chamber, a smooth bean-shaped pod that would have been big enough to enclose our yacht. The surface appeared to be semi-transparent, perhaps designed to let in sunlight. I could see shadowy shapes moving within.

Ghosts were clustered around the pod's hull, brushing its surface.

Jeru beckoned, and we worked our way through the tangle toward the far end of the pod, where the density of the Ghosts seemed to be lowest.

We slithered to the surface of the pod. There were sucker pads on our palms and toes to help us grip. We began crawling along the length of the pod, ducking flat when we saw Ghosts loom into view. It was like climbing over a glass ceiling.

The pod was pressurized. At one end of the pod a big ball of mud hung in the air, brown and viscous. It seemed to be heated from within; it was slowly boiling, with big sticky bubbles of vapor crowding its surface, and I saw how it was laced with purple and red smears. There is no convection in zero gravity, of course. Maybe the Ghosts were using pumps to drive the flow of vapor.

Tubes led off from the mud ball to the hull of the pod. Ghosts clustered there, sucking up the purple gunk from the mud.

We figured it out in bioluminescent "whispers." The Ghosts were *feeding*. Their home world is too small to have retained much internal warmth, but, deep beneath their frozen oceans or in the dark of their rocks, a little primordial geotherm heat must leak out still, driving fountains of minerals dragged up from the depths. And, as at the bottom of Earth's oceans, on those minerals and the slow leak of heat, lifeforms feed. And the Ghosts feed on *them*.

So this mud ball was a field kitchen. I peered down at purplish slime, a gourmet meal for Ghosts, and I didn't envy them.

There was nothing for us here. Jeru beckoned me again, and we slithered further forward.

The next section of the pod was . . . strange.

It was a chamber full of sparkling, silvery saucer-shapes, like smaller, flattened-out Ghosts, perhaps. They fizzed through the air or crawled over each other or jammed themselves together into great wadded balls that would hold for a few seconds and then collapse, their component parts squirming off for some new adventure elsewhere. I could see there were feeding tubes on the walls, and one or two Ghosts drifted among the saucer things, like an adult in a yard of squabbling children.

There was a subtle shadow before me.

I looked up, and found myself staring at my own reflection—an angled head, an open mouth, a sprawled body—folded over, fish-eye style, just centimeters from my nose.

It was a Ghost. It bobbed massively before me.

I pushed myself away from the hull, slowly. I grabbed hold of the nearest tangle branch with my good hand. I knew I couldn't reach for my knife, which was tucked into my belt at my back. And I couldn't see Jeru anywhere. It might be that the Ghosts had taken her already. Either way I couldn't call her, or even look for her, for fear of giving her away.

The Ghost had a heavy-looking belt wrapped around its equator. I had to assume that those complex knots of equipment were weapons. Aside from its belt, the Ghost was quite featureless: it might have been stationary, or spinning at a hundred revolutions a minute. I stared at its hide, trying to understand that there was a layer in there like a separate universe, where the laws of physics had been tweaked. But all I could see was my own scared face looking back at me.

And then Jeru fell on the Ghost from above, limbs splayed, knives glinting in both hands. I could see she was yelling—mouth open, eyes wide—but she fell in utter silence, her comms disabled.

Flexing her body like a whip, she rammed both knives into the Ghost's hide—if I took that belt to be its equator, somewhere near its north pole. The Ghost pulsated, complex ripples chasing across its surface. But Jeru did a handstand and reached up with her legs to the tangle above, and anchored herself there.

The Ghost began to spin, trying to throw Jeru off. But she held her grip on the tangle, and kept the knives thrust in its hide, and all the Ghost succeeded in doing was opening up twin gashes, right across its upper section. Steam pulsed out, and I glimpsed redness within.

For long seconds I just hung there, frozen.

You're trained to mount the proper reaction to an enemy assault. But it all vaporizes when you're faced with a ton of spinning, pulsing monster, and you're armed with nothing but a knife. You just want to make yourself as small as possible; maybe it will all go away. But in the end you know it won't, that something has to be done.

So I pulled out my own knife and launched myself at that north pole area.

I started to make cross-cuts between Jeru's gashes. Ghost skin is tough, like thick rubber, but easy to cut if you have the anchorage. Soon I had loosened flaps and lids of skin, and I started pulling them away, exposing a deep redness within. Steam gushed out, sparkling to ice.

Jeru let go of her perch and joined me. We clung with our fingers and hands to the gashes we'd made, and we cut and slashed and dug; though the Ghost spun crazily, it couldn't shake us loose. Soon we were hauling out great warm mounds of meat—ropes like entrails, pulsing slabs like a human's liver or heart. At first ice crystals spurted all around us, but as the Ghost lost the heat it had hoarded all its life, that thin wind died, and frost began to gather on the cut and torn flesh.

At last Jeru pushed my shoulder, and we both drifted away from the Ghost. It was still spinning, but I could see that the spin was nothing but dead momentum; the Ghost had lost its heat, and its life.

Jeru and I faced each other.

I said breathlessly, "I never heard of anyone in hand-to-hand with a Ghost before."

"Neither did I. Lethe," she said, inspecting her hand. "I think I cracked a finger."

It wasn't funny. But Jeru stared at me, and I stared back, and then we both started to laugh, and our slime suits pulsed with pink and blue icons.

"He stood his ground," I said.

"Yes. Maybe he thought we were threatening the nursery."

"The place with the silver saucers?"

She looked at me quizzically. "Ghosts are symbiotes, tar. That looked to me like a nursery for Ghost hides. Independent entities."

I had never thought of Ghosts having young. I had not thought of the Ghost we had killed as a mother protecting its young. I'm not a deep thinker now, and wasn't then; but it was not, for me, a comfortable thought.

But then Jeru started to move. "Come on, tar. Back to work." She anchored her legs in the tangle and began to grab at the still-rotating Ghost carcass, trying to slow its spin.

I anchored likewise and began to help her. The Ghost was massive, the size of a major piece of machinery, and it had built up respectable momentum; at first I couldn't grab hold of the skin flaps that spun past my hand. As we labored I became aware I was getting uncomfortably hot. The light that seeped into the tangle from that caged sun seemed to be getting stronger by the minute.

But as we worked those uneasy thoughts soon dissipated.

At last we got the Ghost under control. Briskly Jeru stripped it of its kit belt, and we began to cram the baggy corpse as deep as we could into the surrounding tangle. It was a grisly job. As the Ghost crumpled further, more of its innards, stiffening now, came pushing out of the holes we'd given it in its hide, and I had to keep from gagging as the foul stuff came pushing out into my face.

At last it was done—as best we could manage it, anyhow.

Jeru's faceplate was smeared with black and red. She was sweating hard, her face pink. But she was grinning, and she had a trophy, the Ghost belt around her shoulders. We began to make our way back, following the same SOP as before.

When we got back to our lying-up point, we found Academician Pael was in trouble.

Pael had curled up in a ball, his hands over his face. We pulled him open. His eyes were closed, his face blotched pink, and his faceplate dripped with condensation.

He was surrounded by gadgets stuck in the tangle—including parts from what looked like a broken-open starbreaker handgun; I recognized prisms and mirrors and diffraction gratings. Well, unless he woke up, he wouldn't be able to tell us what he had been doing here.

Jeru glanced around. The light of the fortress's central star had gotten a *lot* stronger. Our lying-up point was now bathed in light—and heat—with the surrounding tangle offering very little shelter. "Any ideas, tar?"

I felt the exhilaration of our infil drain away. "No, sir."

Jeru's face, bathed in sweat, showed tension. I noticed she was favoring her left hand. She'd mentioned, back at the nursery pod, that she'd cracked a finger, but had said nothing about it since—nor did she give it any time now. "All right." She dumped the Ghost equipment belt and took a deep draft of water from her hood spigot. "Tar, you're on stag. Try to keep Pael in the shade of your body. And if he wakes up, *ask him what he's found out.*"

"Yes, sir."

"Good."

And then she was gone, melting into the complex shadows of the tangle as if she'd been born to these conditions.

I found a place where I could keep up 360-degree vision, and offer a little of my shadow to Pael—not that I imagined it helped much.

I had nothing to do but wait.

As the Ghost ship followed its own mysterious course, the light dapples that came filtering through the tangle shifted and evolved. Clinging to the tangle, I thought I could feel vibration: a slow, deep harmonization that pulsed through the ship's giant structure. I wondered if I was hearing the deep voices of Ghosts, calling to each other from one end of their mighty ship to another. It all served to remind me that everything in my environment, *everything*, was alien, and I was very far from home.

I tried to count my heartbeat, my breaths; I tried to figure out how long a second was. "A thousand and one. A thousand and two . . ." Keeping time is a basic human trait; time provides a basic orientation, and keeps you mentally sharp and in touch with reality. But I kept losing count.

And all my efforts failed to stop darker thoughts creeping into my head.

During a drama like the contact with the Ghost, you don't realize what's happening to you because your body blanks it out; on some level you know you just don't have time to deal with it. Now I had stopped moving, the aches and pains of the last few hours started crowding in on me. I was still sore in my head and back and, of course, my busted arm. I could feel deep bruises, maybe cuts, on my gloved hands where I had hauled at my knife, and I felt as if I had wrenched my good shoulder. One of my toes was throbbing ominously: I wondered if I had cracked another bone, here in this weird environment in which my skeleton had become as brittle as an old man's. I was chafed at my groin and armpits and knees and ankles and elbows, my skin rubbed raw. I was used to suits; normally I'm tougher than that.

The shafts of sunlight on my back were working on me too; it felt as if I was lying underneath the elements of an oven. I had a headache, a deep sick feeling in the pit of my stomach, a ringing in my ears, and a persistent ring of blackness around my eyes. Maybe I was just exhausted, dehydrated; maybe it was more than that.

I started to think back over my operation with Jeru, and the regrets began.

Okay, I'd stood my ground when confronted by the Ghost and not betrayed Jeru's position. But when she launched her attack I'd hesitated, for those crucial few seconds. Maybe if I'd been tougher the commissary wouldn't find herself hauling through the tangle, alone, with a busted finger distracting her with pain signals.

Our training is comprehensive. You're taught to expect that kind of hindsight torture, in the quiet moments, and to discount it—or, better yet, learn from it. But, effectively alone in that metallic alien forest, I wasn't finding my training was offering much perspective.

And, worse, I started to think ahead. Always a mistake.

I couldn't believe that the Academician and his reluctant gadgetry were going to achieve anything significant. And for all the excitement of our infil, we hadn't found anything resembling a bridge or any vulnerable point we could attack, and all we'd come back with was a belt of field kit we didn't even understand.

For the first time I began to consider seriously the possibility that I wasn't going to live through this—that I was going to die when my suit gave up or the sun went pop, whichever came first, in no more than a few hours.

A *brief life burns brightly*. That's what you're taught. Longevity makes you conservative, fearful, selfish. Humans made that mistake before, and we finished up a subject race. Live fast and furiously, for *you* aren't important—all that matters is what you can do for the species.

But I didn't want to die.

If I never returned to Mercury again I wouldn't shed a tear. But I had a life now, in the Navy. And then there were my buddies: the people I'd trained and served with, people like Halle—even Jeru. Having found fellowship for the first time in my life, I didn't want to lose it so quickly, and fall into the darkness alone—especially if it was to be for *nothing*.

But maybe I wasn't going to get a choice.

After an unmeasured time, Jeru returned. She was hauling a silvery blanket. It was Ghost hide. She started to shake it out.

I dropped down to help her. "You went back to the one we killed—"

"—and skinned him," she said, breathless. "I just scraped off the crap with a knife. The Planck-zero layer peels away easily. And look . . ." she made a quick incision in the glimmering sheet with her knife. Then she put the two edges together again, ran her finger along the seam, and showed me the result. I couldn't even see where the cut had been. "Self-sealing, self-healing," she said. "Remember that, tar."

"Yes, sir."

We started to rig the punctured, splayed-out hide as a rough canopy over our LUP, blocking as much of the sunlight as possible from Pael. A few slivers of frozen flesh still clung to the hide, but mostly it was like working with a fine, light metallic foil.

In the sudden shade, Pael was starting to stir. His moans were translated to stark bioluminescent icons.

"Help him," Jeru snapped. "Make him drink." And while I did that she dug into the med kit on her belt and started to spray cast material around the fingers of her left hand.

"It's the speed of light," Pael said. He was huddled in a corner of our LUP, his legs tucked against his chest. His voice must have been feeble; the bioluminescent sigils on his suit were fragmentary and came with possible variants extrapolated by the translator software.

"Tell us," Jeru said, relatively gently.

"The Ghosts have found a way to *change* lightspeed in this fortress. In fact to increase it." He began talking again about quagma and physics constants and the rolled-up dimensions of spacetime, but Jeru waved that away irritably.

"How do you *know* this?"

Pael began tinkering with his prisms and gratings. "I took your advice, Commissary." He beckoned to me. "Come see, child."

I saw that a shaft of red light, split out and deflected by his prism, shone through a diffraction grating and cast an angular pattern of dots and lines on a scrap of smooth plastic behind.

"You see?" His eyes searched my face.

"I'm sorry, sir."

"The wavelength of the light has changed. It has been increased. Red light should have a wavelength, oh, a fifth shorter than that indicated by this pattern."

I was struggling to understand. I held up my hand. "Shouldn't the green of this glove turn yellow, or blue . . . ?"

Pael sighed. "No. Because the color you see depends, not on the wavelength of a photon, but on its energy. Conservation of energy still applies, even where the Ghosts are tinkering. So each photon carries as much energy as before—and evokes the same 'color.' Since a photon's energy is proportional to its frequency, that means frequencies are left unchanged. But since lightspeed is equal to frequency multiplied by wavelength, an increase in wavelength implies—"

"An increase in lightspeed," said Jeru.

"Yes."

I didn't follow much of that. I turned and looked up at the light that leaked around our Ghost-hide canopy. "So we see the same colors. The light of that star gets here a little faster. What difference does it make?"

Pael shook his head. "Child, a fundamental constant like lightspeed is embedded in the deep structure of our universe. Lightspeed is part of the ratio known as the fine structure constant." He started babbling about the charge on the electron, but Jeru cut him off.

She said, "Case, the fine structure constant is a measure of the strength of an electric or magnetic force."

I could follow that much. "And if you increase lightspeed—"

"You *reduce* the strength of the force." Pael raised himself. "Consider this. Human bodies are held together by molecular binding energy—electromagnetic forces. Here, electrons are more loosely bound to atoms; the atoms in a molecule are more loosely bound to each other." He rapped on the cast on my arm. "And so your bones are more brittle, your skin more easy to pierce or chafe. Do you see? You too are embedded in spacetime, my young friend. You too are affected by the Ghosts' tinkering. And because lightspeed in this infernal pocket continues to increase—as far as I can tell from these poor experiments—you are becoming more fragile every second."

It was a strange, eerie thought: that something so basic in my universe could be manipulated. I put my arms around my chest and shuddered.

"Other effects," Pael went on bleakly. "The density of matter is dropping. Perhaps our structure will eventually begin to crumble. And dissociation temperatures are reduced."

Jeru snapped, "What does that mean?"

"Melting and boiling points are reduced. No wonder we are overheating. It is intriguing that bio systems have proven rather more robust than electromechanical ones. But if we don't get out of here soon, our blood will start to boil. . . ."

"Enough," Jeru said. "What of the star?"

"A star is a mass of gas with a tendency to collapse under its own gravity. But heat, supplied by fusion reactions in the core, creates gas and radiation pressures that push outward, counteracting gravity."

"And if the fine structure constant changes—"

"Then the balance is lost. Commissary, as gravity begins to win its ancient battle, the fortress star has become more luminous—it is burning faster. That explains the observations we made from outside the cordon. But this cannot last."

"The novae," I said.

"Yes. The explosions, layers of the star blasted into space, are a symptom of destabilized stars seeking a new balance. The rate at which *our* star is approaching that catastrophic moment fits with the lightspeed drift I have observed." He smiled and closed his eyes. "A single cause predicating so many effects. It is all rather pleasing, in an aesthetic way."

Jeru said, "At least we know how the ship was destroyed. Every control system is mediated by finely tuned electromagnetic effects. Everything must have gone crazy at once. . . ."

We figured it out. The *Brief Life Burns Brightly* had been a classic GUTship, of a design that hasn't changed in its essentials for thousands of years. The lifedome, a tough translucent bubble, contained the crew of twenty. The 'dome was connected by a spine a klick long to a GUTdrive engine pod.

When we crossed the cordon boundary—when all the bridge lights failed—the control systems went down, and all the pod's superforce energy must have tried to escape at once. The spine of the ship had thrust itself up into the lifedome, like a nail rammed into a skull.

Pael said dreamily, "If lightspeed were a tad faster, throughout the universe, then hydrogen could not fuse to helium. There would only be hydrogen: no fusion to power stars, no chemistry. Conversely if lightspeed were a little lower, hydrogen would fuse too easily, and there would be *no* hydrogen, nothing to make stars—or water. You see how critical it all is? No doubt the Ghosts' science of fine-tuning is advancing considerably here on the Orion Line, even as it serves its trivial defensive purpose . . ."

Jeru glared at him, her contempt obvious. "We must take this piece of intelligence back to the Commission. If the Ghosts can survive and function in these fast-light bubbles of theirs, so can we. We may be at the pivot of history, gentlemen."

I knew she was right. The primary duty of the Commission for Historical Truth is to gather and deploy intelligence about the enemy. And so *my* primary duty, and Pael's, was now to help Jeru get this piece of data back to her organization.

But Pael was mocking her.

"Not for ourselves, but for the species. Is that the line, Commissary? You are so grandiose. And yet you blunder around in comical ignorance. Even your quixotic quest aboard this cruiser was futile. There probably is no bridge on this ship. The Ghosts' entire morphology, their evolutionary design, is based on the notion of cooperation, of symbiosis; why should a Ghost ship have a metaphoric *head*? And as for the trophy you have returned—" He held up the belt of Ghost artifacts. "There are no weapons here. These are sensors, tools. There is nothing here capable of producing a significant energy discharge. This is less threatening than a bow and arrow." He let go of the belt; it drifted away. "The Ghost wasn't trying to kill you. It was blocking you. Which is a classic Ghost tactic."

Jeru's face was stony. "It was in our way. That is sufficient reason for destroying it."

Pael shook his head. "Minds like yours will destroy *us*, Commissary."

Jeru stared at him with suspicion. Then she said, "*You have a way*. Don't you, Academician? A way to get us out of here."

He tried to face her down, but her will was stronger, and he averted his eyes.

Jeru said heavily, "Regardless of the fact that three lives are at stake—does duty mean nothing to you, Academician? You are an intelligent man. Can you not see that this is a war of human destiny?"

Pael laughed. "Destiny—or economics?"

I looked from one to the other, dismayed, baffled. I thought we should be doing less yapping and more fighting.

Pael said, watching me, "You see, child, as long as the explorers and the mining fleets and the colony ships are pushing outward, as long as the Third Expansion is growing, our economy works. The riches can continue to flow inward, into the mined-out systems, feeding a vast horde of humanity who have become more populous than the stars themselves. But as soon as that growth falters . . ."

Jeru was silent.

I understood some of this. The Third Expansion had reached all the way to the inner edge of our spiral arm of the galaxy. Now the first colony ships were attempting to make their way across the void to the next arm.

Our arm, the Orion Arm, is really just a shingle, a short arc. But the Sagittarius Arm is one of the galaxy's dominant features. For example, it contains a huge region of star-birth, one of the largest in the galaxy, immense clouds of gas and dust capable of producing millions of stars each. It was a prize indeed.

But that is where the Silver Ghosts live.

When it appeared that our inexorable expansion was threatening not just their own mysterious projects but their home system, the Ghosts began, for the first time, to resist us.

They had formed a blockade, called by human strategies the Orion Line: a thick sheet of fortress stars, right across the inner edge of the Orion Arm, places the Navy and the colony ships couldn't follow. It was a devastatingly effective ploy.

This was a war of colonization, of world-building. For a thousand years we had been spreading steadily from star to star, using the resources of one system to explore, terraform and populate the worlds of the next. With too deep a break in that chain of exploitation, the enterprise broke down.

And so the Ghosts had been able to hold up human expansion for fifty years.

Pael said, "We are already choking. There have already been wars, young Case: human fighting human, as the inner systems starve. All the Ghosts have to do is wait for us to destroy ourselves, and free them to continue their own rather more worthy projects."

Jeru floated down before him. "Academician, listen to me. Growing up at Deneb, I saw the great schooners in the sky, bringing the interstellar riches that kept my people alive. I was intelligent enough to see the logic of history—that we must maintain the Expansion, *because there is no choice*. And that is why I joined the armed forces, and later the Commission for Historical Truth. For I understood the dreadful truth which the Commission cradles. And that is why we must labor every day to maintain the unity and purpose of mankind. For if we falter we die; as simple as that."

"Commissary, your creed of mankind's evolutionary destiny condemns our own kind to become a swarm of children, granted a few moments of loving and breeding and dying, before being cast into futile war." Pael glanced at me.

"But," Jeru said, "it is a creed that has bound us together for a thousand years. It is a creed that binds uncounted trillions of human beings across thousands of light years. It is a creed that binds a humanity so diverse it appears to be undergoing speciation. . . . Are you strong enough to defy such a creed now? Come, Academician. None of us *chooses* to be born in the middle of a war. We must all do our best for each other, for other human beings; what else is there?"

I touched Pael's shoulder; he flinched away. "Academician—is Jeru right? Is there a way we can live through this?"

Pael shuddered. Jeru hovered over him.

"Yes," Pael said at last. "Yes, there is a way."

* * *

The idea turned out to be simple.

And the plan Jeru and I devised to implement it was even simpler. It was based on a single assumption: Ghosts aren't aggressive. It was ugly, I'll admit that, and I could see why it would distress a squeamish earthworm like Pael. But sometimes there are no good choices.

Jeru and I took a few minutes to rest up, check over our suits and our various injuries, and to make ourselves comfortable. Then, following patrol SOP once more, we made our way back to the pod of immature hides.

We came out of the tangle and drifted down to that translucent hull. We tried to keep away from concentrations of Ghosts, but we made no real effort to conceal ourselves. There was little point, after all; the Ghosts would know all about us, and what we intended, soon enough.

We hammered pitons into the pliable hull, and fixed rope to anchor ourselves. Then we took our knives and started to saw our way through the hull.

As soon as we started, the Ghosts began to gather around us, like vast antibodies.

They just hovered there, eerie faceless baubles drifting as if in vacuum breezes. But as I stared up at a dozen distorted reflections of my own skinny face, I felt an unreasonable loathing rise up in me. Maybe you could think of them as a family banding together to protect their young. I didn't care; a lifetime's carefully designed hatred isn't thrown off so easily. I went at my work with a will.

Jeru got through the pod hull first.

The air gushed out in a fast-condensing fountain. The baby hides fluttered, their distress obvious. And the Ghosts began to cluster around Jeru, like huge light globes.

Jeru glanced at me. "Keep working, tar."

"Yes, sir."

In another couple of minutes I was through. The air pressure was already dropping. It dwindled to nothing when we cut a big door-sized flap in that roof. Anchoring ourselves with the ropes, we rolled that lid back, opening the roof wide. A few last wisps of vapor came curling around our heads, ice fragments sparkling.

The hide babies convulsed. Immature, they could not survive the sudden vacuum, intended as their ultimate environment. But the way they died made it easy for us.

The silvery hides came flapping up out of the hole in the roof, one by one. We just grabbed each other—like grabbing hold of a billowing sheet—and we speared it with a knife, and threaded it on a length of rope. All we had to do was sit there and wait for them to come. There were hundreds of them, and we were kept busy.

I hadn't expected the adult Ghosts to sit through that, non-aggressive or not; and I was proved right. Soon they were clustering all around me, vast silvery bellies looming. A Ghost is massive and solid, and it packs a lot of inertia; if one hits you in the back you know about it. Soon they were nudging me hard enough to knock me flat against the roof, over and over. Once I was wrenched so hard against my tethering rope it felt as if I had cracked another bone or two in my foot.

And, meanwhile, I was starting to feel a lot worse: dizzy, nauseous, overheated. It was getting harder to get back upright each time after being knocked down. I was growing weaker fast; I imagined the tiny molecules of my body falling apart in this Ghost-polluted space.

For the first time I began to believe we were going to fail.

But then, quite suddenly, the Ghosts backed off. When they were clear of me, I saw they were clustering around Jeru.

She was standing on the hull, her feet tangled up in rope, and she had knives in both hands. She was slashing crazily at the Ghosts, and at the baby hides that came flapping past her, making no attempt to capture them now, simply cutting and destroying whatever she could reach. I could see that one arm was hanging awkwardly—maybe it was dislocated, or even broken—but she kept on slicing regardless.

And the Ghosts were clustering around her, huge silver spheres crushing her frail, battling human form.

She was sacrificing herself to save me—just as Captain Teid, in the last moments of the *Brightly*, had given herself to save Pael. And *my* duty was to complete the job.

I stabbed and threaded, over and over, as the flimsy hides came tumbling out of that hole, slowly dying.

At last no more hides came.

I looked up, blinking to get the salt sweat out of my eyes. A few hides were still tumbling around the interior of the pod, but they were inert and out of my reach. Others had evaded us and gotten stuck in the tangle of the ship's structure, too far and too scattered to make them worth pursuing further. What I had got would have to suffice.

I started to make my way out of there, back through the tangle, to the location of our wrecked yacht, where I hoped Pael would be waiting.

I looked back once. I couldn't help it. The Ghosts were still clustered over the ripped pod roof. Somewhere in there, whatever was left of Jeru was still fighting.

I had an impulse, almost overpowering, to go back to her. No human being should die alone. But I knew I had to get out of there, to complete the mission, to make her sacrifice worthwhile.

So I got.

Pael and I finished the job at the outer hull of the ghost cruiser.

Stripping the hides turned out to be as easy as Jeru had described. Fitting together the Planck-zero sheets was simple too—you just line them up and seal them with a thumb. I got on with that, sewing the hides together into a sail, while Pael worked on a rigging of lengths of rope, all fixed to a deck panel from the wreck of the yacht. He was fast and efficient: Pael, after all, came from a world where everybody goes solar sailing on their vacations.

We worked steadily, for hours.

I ignored the varying aches and chafes, the increasing pain in my head and chest and stomach, the throbbing of a broken arm that hadn't healed, the agony of cracked bones in my foot. And we didn't talk about anything but the task in hand. Pael didn't ask what had become of Jeru, not once; it was as if he had anticipated the commissary's fate.

We were undisturbed by the Ghosts through all of this.

I tried not to think about whatever emotions churned within those silvered carapaces, what despairing debates might chatter on invisible wavelengths. I was, after all, trying to complete a mission. And I had been exhausted even before I got back to Pael. I just kept going, ignoring my fatigue, focusing on the task.

I was surprised to find it was done.

We had made a sail hundreds of meters across, stitched together from the invisibly thin immature Ghost hide. It was roughly circular, and it was connected by a dozen lengths of fine rope to struts on the panel we had wrenched out of the wreck. The sail lay across space, languid ripples crossing its glimmering surface.

Pael showed me how to work the thing. "Pull this rope, or this . . ." the great patchwork sail twitched in response to his commands. "I've set it so you shouldn't have to try anything fancy, like tacking. The boat will just sail out, hopefully, to the cordon perimeter. If you need to lose the sail, just cut the ropes."

I was taking in all this automatically. It made sense for both of us to know how to operate our little yacht. But then I started to pick up the subtext of what he was saying.

Before I knew what he was doing he had shoved me onto the deck panel, and pushed it away from the Ghost ship. His strength was surprising.

I watched him recede. He clung wistfully to a bit of tangle. I couldn't summon the strength to figure out a way to cross the widening gap. But my suit could read his, as clear as day.

"Where I grew up, the sky was full of sails . . ."

"Why, Academician?"

"You will go further and faster without my mass to haul. And besides—our lives are short enough; we should preserve the young. Don't you think?"

I had no idea what he was talking about. Pael was much more valuable than I was; I was the one who should have been left behind. He had shamed himself.

Complex glyphs crisscrossed his suit. "Keep out of the direct sunlight. It is growing more intense, of course. That will help you. . . ."

And then he ducked out of sight, back into the tangle. The Ghost ship was receding now, closing over into its vast egg shape, the detail of the tangle becoming lost to my blurred vision.

The sail above me slowly billowed, filling up with the light of the brightening sun. Pael had designed his improvised craft well; the rigging lines were all taut, and I could see no rips or creases in the silvery fabric.

I clung to my bit of decking and sought shade.

Twelve hours later, I reached an invisible radius where the tactical beacon in my pocket started to howl with a whine that filled my headset. My suit's auxiliary systems cut in and I found myself breathing fresh air.

A little after that, a set of lights ducked out of the streaming lanes of the fleet, and plunged toward me, growing brighter. At last it resolved into a golden bullet shape adorned with a blue-green tetrahedron, the sigil of free humanity. It was a supply ship called *The Dominance of Primates*.

And a little after *that*, as a Ghost fleet fled their fortress, the star exploded.

As soon as I had completed my formal report to the ship's commissary—and I was able to check out of the *Dominance*'s sick bay—I asked to see the captain.

I walked up to the bridge. My story had got around, and the various med patches I sported added to my heroic mythos. So I had to run the gauntlet of the crew—"You're supposed to be dead, I impounded your back pay and slept with your mother already"—and was greeted by what seems to be the universal gesture of recognition of one tar to another, the clenched fist pumping up and down around an imaginary penis.

But anything more respectful just wouldn't feel normal.

The captain turned out to be a grizzled veteran type with a vast laser burn scar on one cheek. She reminded me of First Officer Till.

I told her I wanted to return to active duty as soon as my health allowed.

She looked me up and down. "Are you sure, tar? You have a lot of options. Young as you are, you've made your contribution to the Expansion. You can go home."

"Sir, and do what?"

She shrugged. "Farm. Mine. Raise babies. Whatever earthworms do. Or you can join the Commission for Historical Truth."

"Me, a commissary?"

"You've been there, tar. You've been in among the Ghosts, and come out again—with a bit of intelligence more important than anything the Commission has come up with in fifty years. Are you *sure* you want to face action again?"

I thought it over.

I remembered how Jeru and Pael had argued. It had been an unwelcome perspective, for me. I was in a war that had nothing to do with me, trapped by what Jeru had called the logic of history. But then, I bet that's been true of most of humanity through our long and bloody history. All you can do is live your life, and grasp your moment in the light—and stand by your comrades.

A farmer—me? And I could never be smart enough for the Commission. No, I had no doubts.

"A brief life burns brightly, sir."

Lethe, the captain looked like she had a lump in her throat. "Do I take that as a yes, tar?"

I stood straight, ignoring the twinges of my injuries. "Yes, *sir!*"

BEGGARS IN SPAIN

Nancy Kress

Nancy Kress (born 1948) is one of the major SF writers of the last two decades, well known for her complex medical SF stories, and for her biological and evolutionary extrapolations in such classics as *Beggars in Spain* (1993), *Beggars and Choosers* (1994), and *Beggars Ride* (1996). In 1998 she married SF writer Charles Sheffield. In recent years, she has written two science thrillers, *Oaths and Miracles* (1995) and *Stinger* (1998), SF novel *Maximum Light* (1998), and *Probability Moon* (2000) and *Probability Sun* (2001), the first and second books in a trilogy of hard SF novels set against the background of a war between humanity and an alien race. Her new novel, *Probability Space*, is out in 2002. Her stories are rich in texture and in the details of the inner life of character and have been collected in *Trinity and Other Stories* (1985), *The Aliens of Earth* (1993), and *Beaker's Dozen* (1998). She teaches regularly at summer writing workshops such as Clarion, and during the year at the Bethesda Writing Center in Bethesda, Maryland. She is the Fiction columnist for *Writer's Digest*.

Kress, as much as any SF writer today, is an heir to the tradition of H. G. Wells. Nowhere in her work is this more evident than in "Beggars in Spain," and the novels that have grown out of it. With this story, she began her magnum opus. In this story she deals with human and social evolution, with class and economic issues, and with ordinary characters, as Wells did in "A Story of the Days to Come," and *When the Sleeper Wakes*. It is a more European than American approach, though set in the U.S.

Here, genetically engineered children requiring no sleep are persecuted for their differentness, a theme with roots both in Zenna Henderson and A. E. van Vogt's *Slan*. Discussing *Beggars in Spain*, the novel that grew out of this novella, in an interview, she said:

> The tension between the state and the individual is what gives most fiction its pull and when I wrote *Beggars in Spain*, I was thinking of Ayn Rand's objectivism at one pole, and at the other, Ursula K. Le Guin's Anarres in *The Dispossessed*. Anarres is Le Guin's version of anarchy, which is an intensely social system as she has set it up, and where solidarity is the basis for the construction of the society. So individual responsibility in the one end, solidarity in the other end, and what I wanted to do in *Beggars in Spain* is show that neither of these, to me, are especially good solutions: objectivism, because it ignores the fact that we are a social species; and anarchism, as Ursula Le Guin portrays it, because it is to me too idealistic.

Thus Kress called two of the most powerful streams of political discourse in SF into question at the beginning of the decade, and like Kelly, below, finds a center by posing questions.

With energy and sleepless vigilance go forward and give us victories.
—Abraham Lincoln, to Major General Joseph Hooker, 1863

1

They sat stiffly on his antique Eames chairs, two people who didn't want to be here, or one person who didn't want to and one who resented the other's reluctance. Dr. Ong had seen this before. Within two minutes he was sure: the woman was the silently furious resister. She would lose. The man would pay for it later, in little ways, for a long time.

"I presume you've performed the necessary credit checks already," Roger Camden said pleasantly, "so let's get right on to details, shall we, Doctor?"

"Certainly," Ong said. "Why don't we start by your telling me all the genetic modifications you're interested in for the baby."

The woman shifted suddenly on her chair. She was in her late twenties—clearly a second wife—but already had a faded look, as if keeping up with Roger Camden was wearing her out. Ong could easily believe that. Mrs. Camden's hair was brown, her eyes were brown, her skin had a brown tinge that might have been pretty if her cheeks had had any color. She wore a brown coat, neither fashionable nor cheap, and shoes that looked vaguely orthopedic. Ong glanced at his records for her name: Elizabeth. He would bet people forgot it often.

Next to her, Roger Camden radiated nervous vitality, a man in late middle age whose bullet-shaped head did not match his careful haircut and Italian-silk business suit. Ong did not need to consult his file to recall anything about Camden. A caricature of the bullet-shaped head had been the leading graphic of yesterday's online edition of the *Wall Street Journal*: Camden had led a major coup in cross-border data-atoll investment. Ong was not sure what cross-border data-atoll investment was.

"A girl," Elizabeth Camden said. Ong hadn't expected her to speak first. Her voice was another surprise: upper-class British. "Blonde. Green eyes. Tall. Slender."

Ong smiled. "Appearance factors are the easiest to achieve, as I'm sure you already know. But all we can do about 'slenderness' is give her a genetic disposition in that direction. How you feed the child will naturally—"

"Yes, yes," Roger Camden said, "that's obvious. Now: intelligence. *High* intelligence. And a sense of daring."

"I'm sorry, Mr. Camden—personality factors are not yet understood well enough to allow genet—"

"Just testing," Camden said, with a smile that Ong thought was probably supposed to be light-hearted.

Elizabeth Camden said, "Musical ability."

"Again, Mrs. Camden, a disposition to be musical is all we can guarantee."

"Good enough," Camden said. "The full array of corrections for any potential gene-linked health problem, of course."

"Of course," Dr. Ong said. Neither client spoke. So far theirs was a fairly modest list, given Camden's money; most clients had to be argued out of contradictory genetic tendencies, alteration overload, or unrealistic expectations. Ong waited. Tension prickled in the room like heat.

"And," Camden said, "no need to sleep."

Elizabeth Camden jerked her head sideways to look out the window.

Ong picked a paper magnet off his desk. He made his voice pleasant. "May I ask how you learned whether that genetic-modification program exists?"

Camden grinned. "You're not denying it exists. I give you full credit for that, Doctor."

Ong held onto his temper. "May I ask how you learned whether the program exists?"

Camden reached into an inner pocket of his suit. The silk crinkled and pulled; body and suit came from different social classes. Camden was, Ong remembered, a Yagaiist, a personal friend of Kenzo Yagai himself. Camden handed Ong hard copy: program specifications.

"Don't bother hunting down the security leak in your data banks, Doctor—you won't find it. But if it's any consolation, neither will anybody else. Now." He leaned suddenly forward. His tone changed. "I know that you've created twenty children so far who don't need to sleep at all. That so far nineteen are healthy, intelligent, and psychologically normal. In fact, better than normal—they're all unusually precocious. The oldest is already four years old and can read in two languages. I know you're thinking of offering this genetic modification on the open market in a few years. All I want is a chance to buy it for my daughter *now*. At whatever price you name."

Ong stood. "I can't possibly discuss this with you unilaterally, Mr. Camden. Neither the theft of our data—"

"Which wasn't a theft—your system developed a spontaneous bubble regurgitation into a public gate, have a hell of a time proving otherwise—"

"—*nor* the offer to purchase this particular genetic modification lies in my sole area of authority. Both have to be discussed with the Institute's Board of Directors."

"By all means, by all means. When can I talk to them, too?"

"You?"

Camden, still seated, looked at him. It occurred to Ong that there were few men who could look so confident eighteen inches below eye level. "Certainly. I'd like the chance to present my offer to whoever has the actual authority to accept it. That's only good business."

"This isn't solely a business transaction, Mr. Camden."

"It isn't solely pure scientific research, either," Camden retorted. "You're a for-profit corporation here. *With* certain tax breaks available only to firms meeting certain fair-practice laws."

For a minute Ong couldn't think what Camden meant. "Fair-practice laws . . ."

". . . are designed to protect minorities who are suppliers. I know, it hasn't ever been tested in the case of customers, except for red-lining in Y-energy installations. But it could be tested, Doctor Ong. Minorities are entitled to the same product offerings as non-minorities. I know the Institute would not welcome a court case, Doctor. None of your twenty genetic beta-test families are either Black or Jewish."

"A court . . . but you're not Black *or* Jewish!"

"I'm a different minority. Polish-American. The name was Kaminsky." Camden finally stood. And smiled warmly. "Look, it is preposterous. You know that, and I know that, and we both know what a grand time journalists would have with it anyway. And you know that I don't want to sue you with a preposterous case, just to use the threat of premature and adverse publicity to get what I want. I don't want to make threats at all, believe me I don't. I just want this marvelous advancement you've come up with for my daughter." His face changed, to an expression Ong wouldn't have believed possible on those particular features: wistfulness. "Doctor—do you know how much more I could have accomplished if I hadn't had to *sleep* all my life?"

Elizabeth Camden said harshly, "You hardly sleep now."

Camden looked down at her as if he had forgotten she was there. "Well, no, my dear, not now. But when I was young . . . college, I might have been able to finish college and still support . . . well. None of that matters now. What matters, Doctor, is that you and I and your board come to an agreement."

"Mr. Camden, please leave my office now."

"You mean before you lose your temper at my presumptuousness? You wouldn't be the first. I'll expect to have a meeting set up by the end of next week, whenever and wherever you say, of course. Just let my personal secretary, Diane Clavers, know the details. Anytime that's best for you."

Ong did not accompany them to the door. Pressure throbbed behind his temples. In the doorway Elizabeth Camden turned. "What happened to the twentieth one?"

"What?"

"The twentieth baby. My husband said nineteen of them are healthy and normal. What happened to the twentieth?"

The pressure grew stronger, hotter. Ong knew that he should not answer; that Camden probably already knew the answer even if his wife didn't; that he, Ong, was going to answer anyway; that he would regret the lack of self-control, bitterly, later.

"The twentieth baby is dead. His parents turned out to be unstable. They separated during the pregnancy, and his mother could not bear the twenty-four-hour crying of a baby who never sleeps."

Elizabeth Camden's eyes widened. "She killed it?"

"By mistake," Camden said shortly. "Shook the little thing too hard." He frowned at Ong. "Nurses, Doctor. In shifts. You should have picked only parents wealthy enough to afford nurses in shifts."

"That's horrible!" Mrs. Camden burst out, and Ong could not tell if she meant the child's death, the lack of nurses, or the Institute's carelessness. Ong closed his eyes.

When they had gone, he took ten milligrams of cyclobenzaprine-III. For his back—it was solely for his back. The old injury hurting again. Afterward he stood for a long time at the window, still holding the paper magnet, feeling the pressure recede from his temples, feeling himself calm down. Below him Lake Michigan lapped peacefully at the shore; the police had driven away the homeless in another raid just last night, and they hadn't yet had time to return. Only their debris remained, thrown into the bushes of the lakeshore park: tattered blankets, newspapers, plastic bags like pathetic trampled standards. It was illegal to sleep in the park, illegal to enter it without a resident's permit, illegal to be homeless and without a residence. As Ong watched, uniformed park attendants began methodically spearing newspapers and shoving them into clean self-propelled receptacles.

Ong picked up the phone to call the president of Biotech Institute's Board of Directors.

Four men and three women sat around the polished mahogany table of the conference room. Doctor, lawyer, Indian chief, thought Susan Melling, looking from Ong to Sullivan to Camden. She smiled. Ong caught the smile and looked frosty. Pompous ass. Judy Sullivan, the Institute lawyer, turned to speak in a low voice to Camden's lawyer, a thin, nervous man with the look of being owned. The owner, Roger Camden, the Indian chief himself, was the happiest-looking person in the room. The lethal little man—what did it take to become that rich, starting from nothing? She, Susan, would certainly never know—radiated excitement. He beamed, he glowed, so unlike the usual parents-to-be that Susan was intrigued. Usually the prospective daddies and mommies—especially the daddies—sat there looking as if they were at a corporate merger. Camden looked as if he were at a birthday party.

Which, of course, he was. Susan grinned at him, and was pleased when he grinned back. Wolfish, but with a sort of delight that could only be called innocent—what would he be like in bed? Ong frowned majestically and rose to speak.

"Ladies and gentlemen, I think we're ready to start. Perhaps introductions are in order. Mr. Roger Camden, Mrs. Camden, are of course our clients. Mr. John Jaworski, Mr. Camden's lawyer. Mr. Camden, this is Judith Sullivan, the Institute's head of Legal; Samuel Krenshaw, representing Institute Director Dr. Brad Marsteiner, who unfortunately couldn't be here today; and Dr. Susan Melling, who developed the genetic modification affecting sleep. A few legal points of interest to both parties—"

"Forget the contracts for a minute," Camden interrupted. "Let's talk about the sleep thing. I'd like to ask a few questions."

Susan said, "What would you like to know?" Camden's eyes were very blue in his blunt-featured face; he wasn't what she had expected. Mrs. Camden, who apparently lacked both a first name and a lawyer, since Jaworski had been introduced as her husband's but not hers, looked either sullen or scared, it was difficult to tell which.

Ong said sourly, "Then perhaps we should start with a short presentation by Dr. Melling."

Susan would have preferred a Q&A, to see what Camden would ask. But she had annoyed Ong enough for one session. Obediently she rose.

"Let me start with a brief description of sleep. Researchers have known for a long time that there are actually three kinds of sleep. One is 'slow-wave sleep,' characterized on an EEG by delta waves. One is 'rapid-eye-movement sleep,' or REM sleep, which is much lighter sleep and contains most dreaming. Together these two make up 'core sleep.' The third type of sleep is 'optional sleep,' so-called because people seem to get along without it with no ill effects, and some short sleepers don't do it at all, sleeping naturally only three or four hours a night."

"That's me," Camden said. "I trained myself into it. Couldn't everybody do that?"

Apparently they were going to have a Q&A after all. "No. The actual sleep mechanism has some flexibility, but not the same amount for every person. The raphe nuclei on the brain stem—"

Ong said, "I don't think we need that level of detail, Susan. Let's stick to basics."

Camden said, "The raphe nuclei regulate the balance among neurotransmitters and peptides that lead to a pressure to sleep, don't they?"

Susan couldn't help it; she grinned. Camden, the laser-sharp ruthless financier, sat trying to look solemn, a third-grader waiting to have his homework praised. Ong looked sour. Mrs. Camden looked away, out the window.

"Yes, that's correct, Mr. Camden. You've done your research."

Camden said, "This is my *daughter*," and Susan caught her breath. When was the last time she had heard that note of reverence in anyone's voice? But no one in the room seemed to notice.

"Well, then," Susan said, "you already know that the reason people sleep is because a pressure to sleep builds up in the brain. Over the last twenty years, research has determined that's the *only* reason. Neither slow-wave sleep nor REM sleep serve functions that can't be carried on while the body and brain are awake. A lot goes on during sleep, but it can go on awake just as well, if other hormonal adjustments are made.

"Sleep once served an important evolutionary function. Once Clem Pre-Mammal was done filling his stomach and squirting his sperm around, sleep kept him immobile and away from predators. Sleep was an aid to survival. But now it's a left-over mechanism, like the appendix. It switches on every night, but the need is gone. So we turn off the switch at its source, in the genes."

Ong winced. He hated it when she oversimplified like that. Or maybe it was the light-heartedness he hated. If Marsteiner were making this presentation, there'd be no Clem Pre-Mammal.

Camden said, "What about the need to dream?"

"Not necessary. A left-over bombardment of the cortex to keep it on semi-alert in case a predator attacked during sleep. Wakefulness does that better."

"Why not have wakefulness instead then? From the start of the evolution?"

He was testing her. Susan gave him a full, lavish smile, enjoying his brass. "I told you. Safety from predators. But when a modern predator attacks—say, a cross-border data-atoll investor—it's safer to be awake."

Camden shot at her, "What about the high percentage of REM sleep in fetuses and babies?"

"Still an evolutionary hangover. Cerebrum develops perfectly well without it."

"What about neural repair during slow-wave sleep?"

"That does go on. But it can go on during wakefulness, if the DNA is programmed to do so. No loss of neural efficiency, as far as we know."

"What about the release of human growth enzyme in such large concentrations during slow-wave sleep?"

Susan looked at him admiringly. "Goes on without the sleep. Genetic adjustments tie it to other changes in the pineal gland."

"What about the—"

"The *side effects?*" Mrs. Camden said. Her mouth turned down. "What about the bloody side effects?"

Susan turned to Elizabeth Camden. She had forgotten she was there. The younger woman stared at Susan, mouth turned down at the corners.

"I'm glad you asked that, Mrs. Camden. Because there *are* side effects." Susan paused; she was enjoying herself. "Compared to their age mates, the non-sleep children—who have *not* had IQ genetic manipulation—are more intelligent, better at problem-solving, and more joyous."

Camden took out a cigarette. The archaic, filthy habit surprised Susan. Then she saw that it was deliberate: Roger Camden drawing attention to an ostentatious display to draw attention away from what he was feeling. His cigarette lighter was gold, monogrammed, innocently gaudy.

"Let me explain," Susan said. "REM sleep bombards the cerebral cortex with random neural firings from the brainstem; dreaming occurs because the poor besieged cortex tries so hard to make sense of the activated images and memories. It spends a lot of energy doing that. Without that energy expenditure, non-sleep cerebrums save the wear-and-tear and do better at coordinating real-life input. Thus—greater intelligence and problem-solving.

"Also, doctors have known for sixty years that anti-depressants, which lift the mood of depressed patients, also suppress REM sleep entirely. What they have proved in the last ten years is that the reverse is equally true: suppress REM sleep and people don't *get* depressed. The non-sleep kids are cheerful, outgoing . . . *joyous*. There's no other word for it."

"At what cost?" Mrs. Camden said. She held her neck rigid, but the corners of her jaw worked.

"No cost. No negative side effects at all."

"So far," Mrs. Camden shot back.

Susan shrugged. "So far."

"They're only four years old! At the most!"

Ong and Krenshaw were studying her closely. Susan saw the moment the Camden woman realized it; she sank back into her chair, drawing her fur coat around her, her face blank.

Camden did not look at his wife. He blew a cloud of cigarette smoke. "Everything has costs, Dr. Melling."

She liked the way he said her name. "Ordinarily, yes. Especially in genetic modification. But we honestly have not been able to find any here, despite looking." She smiled directly into Camden's eyes. "Is it too much to believe that just once the universe has given us something wholly good, wholly a step forward, wholly beneficial? Without hidden penalties?"

"Not the universe. The intelligence of people like you," Camden said, surprising Susan more than anything else that had gone before. His eyes held hers. She felt her chest tighten.

"I think," Dr. Ong said dryly, "that the philosophy of the universe may be beyond our concerns here. Mr. Camden, if you have no further medical questions, perhaps we can return to the legal points Ms. Sullivan and Mr. Jaworski have raised. Thank you, Dr. Melling."

Susan nodded. She didn't look again at Camden. But she knew what he said, how he looked, that he was there.

The house was about what she had expected, a huge mock Tudor on Lake Michigan north of Chicago. The land heavily wooded between the gate and the house, open between the house and the surging water. Patches of snow dotted the dormant grass. Biotech had been working with the Camdens for four months, but this was the first time Susan had driven to their home.

As she walked toward the house, another car drove up behind her. No, a truck, continuing around the curved driveway to a service entry at the side of the house. One man rang the service bell; a second began to unload a plastic-wrapped playpen from the back of the truck. White, with pink and yellow bunnies. Susan briefly closed her eyes.

Camden opened the door himself. She could see the effort not to look worried. "You didn't have to drive out, Susan—I'd have come into the city!"

"No, I didn't want you to do that, Roger. Mrs. Camden is here?"

"In the living room." Camden led her into a large room with a stone fireplace. English country-house furniture; prints of dogs or boats, all hung eighteen inches too high: Elizabeth Camden must have done the decorating. She did not rise from her wing chair as Susan entered.

"Let me be concise and fast," Susan said, "I don't want to make this any more drawn-out for you than I have to. We have all the amniocentesis, ultrasound, and Langston test results. The fetus is fine, developing normally for two weeks, no problems with the implant on the uterus wall. But a complication has developed."

"What?" Camden said. He took out a cigarette, looked at his wife, put it back unlit.

Susan said quietly, "Mrs. Camden, by sheer chance both your ovaries released eggs last month. We removed one for the gene surgery. By more sheer chance the second fertilized and implanted. You're carrying two fetuses."

Elizabeth Camden grew still. "Twins?"

"No," Susan said. Then she realized what she had said. "I mean, yes. They're twins, but non-identical. Only one has been genetically altered. The other will be no more similar to her than any two siblings. It's a so-called 'normal' baby. And I know you didn't want a so-called normal baby."

Camden said, "No. I didn't."

Elizabeth Camden said, "I did."

Camden shot her a fierce look that Susan couldn't read. He took out the cigarette again, lit it. His face was in profile to Susan, thinking intently; she doubted he knew the cigarette was there, or that he was lighting it. "Is the baby being affected by the other one's being there?"

"No," Susan said. "No, of course not. They're just . . . co-existing."

"Can you abort it?"

"Not without risk of aborting both of them. Removing the unaltered fetus might cause changes in the uterus lining that could lead to a spontaneous miscarriage of the other." She drew a deep breath. "There's that option, of course. We can start the whole process over again. But as I told you at the time, you were very lucky to have the in vitro fertilization take on only the second try. Some couples take eight or ten tries. If we started all over, the process could be a lengthy one."

Camden said, "Is the presence of this second fetus harming my daughter? Taking away nutrients or anything? Or will it change anything for her later on in the pregnancy?"

"No. Except that there is a chance of premature birth. Two fetuses take up a lot more room in the womb, and if it gets too crowded, birth can be premature. But the—"

"How premature? Enough to threaten survival?"

"Most probably not."

Camden went on smoking. A man appeared at the door. "Sir, London calling. James Kendall for Mr. Yagai."

"I'll take it." Camden rose. Susan watched him study his wife's face. When he spoke, it was to her. "All right, Elizabeth. All right." He left the room.

For a long moment the two women sat in silence. Susan was aware of disappointment; this was not the Camden she had expected to see. She became aware of Elizabeth Camden watching her with amusement.

"Oh, yes, Doctor. He's like that."

Susan said nothing.

"Completely overbearing. But not this time." She laughed softly, with excitement. "Two. Do you . . . do you know what sex the other one is?"

"Both fetuses are female."

"I wanted a girl, you know. And now I'll have one."

"Then you'll go ahead with the pregnancy."

"Oh, yes. Thank you for coming, Doctor."

She was dismissed. No one saw her out. But as she was getting into her car, Camden rushed out of the house, coatless. "Susan! I wanted to thank you. For coming all the way out here to tell us yourself."

"You already thanked me."

"Yes. Well. You're sure the second fetus is no threat to my daughter?"

Susan said deliberately, "Nor is the genetically altered fetus a threat to the naturally conceived one."

He smiled. His voice was low and wistful. "And you think that should matter to me just as much. But it doesn't. And why should I fake what I feel? Especially to you?"

Susan opened her car door. She wasn't ready for this, or she had changed her mind, or something. But then Camden leaned over to close the door, and his manner held no trace of flirtatiousness, no smarmy ingratiation. "I better order a second playpen."

"Yes."

"And a second car seat."

"Yes."

"But not a second night-shift nurse."

"That's up to you."

"And you." Abruptly he leaned over and kissed her, a kiss so polite and respectful that Susan was shocked. Neither lust nor conquest would have shocked her; this did. Camden didn't give her a chance to react; he closed the car door and turned back toward the house. Susan drove toward the gate, her hands shaky on the wheel until amusement replaced shock: It *had* been a deliberately distant, respectful kiss, an engineered enigma. And nothing else could have guaranteed so well that there would have to be another.

She wondered what the Camdens would name their daughters.

Dr. Ong strode the hospital corridor, which had been dimmed to half-light. From the nurse's station in Maternity a nurse stepped forward as if to stop him—it was the middle of the night, long past visiting hours—got a good look at his face, and faded back into her station. Around a corner was the viewing glass to the nursery. To Ong's annoyance, Susan Melling stood pressed against the glass. To his further annoyance, she was crying.

Ong realized that he had never liked the woman. Maybe not any women. Even those with superior minds could not seem to refrain from being made damn fools by their emotions.

"Look," Susan said, laughing a little, swiping at her face. "Doctor—*look*."

Behind the glass Roger Camden, gowned and masked, was holding up a baby in white undershirt and pink blanket. Camden's blue eyes—theatrically blue, a man really should not have such garish eyes—glowed. The baby had a head covered with blond fuzz, wide eyes, pink skin. Camden's eyes above the mask said that no other child had ever had these attributes.

Ong said, "An uncomplicated birth?"

"Yes," Susan Melling sobbed. "Perfectly straightforward. Elizabeth is fine. She's asleep. Isn't she beautiful? He has the most adventurous spirit I've ever known." She wiped her nose on her sleeve; Ong realized that she was drunk. "Did I ever tell you that I was engaged once? Fifteen years ago, in med school? I broke it off because he grew to seem so ordinary, so boring. Oh, God, I shouldn't be telling you all this I'm sorry I'm sorry."

Ong moved away from her. Behind the glass Roger Camden laid the baby in a small wheeled crib. The nameplate said BABY GIRL CAMDEN #1. 5.9 POUNDS. A night nurse watched indulgently.

Ong did not wait to see Camden emerge from the nursery or to hear Susan Melling say to him whatever she was going to say. Ong went to have the OB paged. Melling's report was not, under the circumstances, to be trusted. A perfect, unprecedented chance to record every detail of gene-alteration with a non-altered control, and Melling was more interested in her own sloppy emotions. Ong would obviously have to do the report himself, after talking to the OB. He was hungry for every detail. And not just about the pink-cheeked baby in Camden's arms. He wanted to know everything about the birth of the child in the other glass-sided crib: BABY GIRL CAMDEN #2. 5.1 POUNDS. The dark-haired baby with the mottled red features, lying scrunched down in her pink blanket, asleep.

2

Leisha's earliest memory was of flowing lines that were not there. She knew they were not there because when she reached out her fist to touch them, her fist was empty. Later she realized that the flowing lines were light: sunshine slanting in bars between curtains in her room, between the wooden blinds in the dining room, between the crisscross lattices in the conservatory. The day she realized the golden flow was light she laughed out loud with the sheer joy of discovery, and Daddy turned from putting flowers in pots and smiled at her.

The whole house was full of light. Light bounded off the lake, streamed across the high white ceilings, puddled on the shining wooden floors. She and Alice moved continually through light, and sometimes Leisha would stop and tip back her head and let it flow over her face. She could feel it, like water.

The best light, of course, was in the conservatory. That's where Daddy liked to be when he was home from making money. Daddy potted plants and watered trees, humming, and Leisha and Alice ran between the wooden tables of flowers with their wonderful earthy smells, running from the dark side of the conservatory where the big purple flowers grew to the sunshine side with sprays of yellow flowers, running back and forth, in and out of the light. "Growth," Daddy said to her, "flowers all fulfilling their promise. Alice, be careful! You almost knocked over that orchid!" Alice, obedient, would stop running for a while. Daddy never told Leisha to stop running.

After a while the light would go away. Alice and Leisha would have their baths, and then Alice would get quiet, or cranky. She wouldn't play nice with Leisha, even when Leisha let her choose the game or even have all the best dolls. Then Nanny would take Alice to "bed," and Leisha would talk with Daddy some more until Daddy said he had to work in his study with the papers that made money. Leisha always felt a moment of regret that he had to go do that, but the moment never lasted very long because Mamselle would arrive and start Leisha's lessons, which she liked. Learning things was so interesting! She could already sing twenty songs and write all the letters in the alphabet and count to fifty. And by the time lessons were done, the light had come back, and it was time for breakfast.

Breakfast was the only time Leisha didn't like. Daddy had gone to the office, and Leisha and Alice had breakfast with Mommy in the big dining room. Mommy sat in a red robe, which Leisha liked, and she didn't smell funny or talk funny the way she would later in the day, but still breakfast wasn't fun. Mommy always started with The Question.

"Alice, sweetheart, how did you sleep?"

"Fine, Mommy."

"Did you have any nice dreams?"

For a long time Alice said no. Then one day she said, "I dreamed about a horse. I was riding him." Mommy clapped her hands and kissed Alice and gave her an extra sticky bun. After that Alice always had a dream to tell Mommy.

Once Leisha said, "I had a dream, too. I dreamed light was coming in the window and it wrapped all around me like a blanket and then it kissed me on my eyes."

Mommy put down her coffee cup so hard that coffee sloshed out of it. "Don't lie to me, Leisha. You did not have a dream."

"Yes, I did," Leisha said.

"Only children who sleep can have dreams. Don't lie to me. You did not have a dream."

"Yes I did! I did!" Leisha shouted. She could see it, almost: The light streaming in the window and wrapping around her like a golden blanket.

"I will not tolerate a child who is a liar! Do you hear me, Leisha—I won't tolerate it!"

"You're a liar!" Leisha shouted, knowing the words weren't true, hating herself because they weren't true but hating Mommy more and that was wrong, too, and there sat Alice stiff and frozen with her eyes wide, Alice was scared and it was Leisha's fault.

Mommy called sharply, "Nanny! Nanny! Take Leisha to her room at once. She can't sit with civilized people if she can't refrain from telling lies!"

Leisha started to cry. Nanny carried her out of the room. Leisha hadn't even had her breakfast. But she didn't care about that; all she could see while she cried was Alice's eyes, scared like that, reflecting broken bits of light.

But Leisha didn't cry long. Nanny read her a story, and then played Data Jump with her, and then Alice came up and Nanny drove them both into Chicago to the zoo where there were wonderful animals to see, animals Leisha could not have dreamed—nor Alice *either*. And by the time they came back Mommy had gone to her room and Leisha knew that she would stay there with the glasses of funny-smelling stuff the rest of the day and Leisha would not have to see her.

But that night, she went to her mother's room.

"I have to go to the bathroom," she told Mamselle. Mamselle said, "Do you need any help?" maybe because Alice still needed help in the bathroom. But Leisha didn't, and she thanked Mamselle. Then she sat on the toilet for a minute even though nothing came, so that what she had told Mamselle wouldn't be a lie.

Leisha tiptoed down the hall. She went first into Alice's room. A little light in a wall socket burned near the "crib." There was no crib in Leisha's room. Leisha looked at her sister through the bars. Alice lay on her side, with her eyes closed. The lids of the eyes fluttered quickly, like curtains blowing in the wind. Alice's chin and neck looked loose.

Leisha closed the door very carefully and went to her parents' room.

They didn't "sleep" in a crib but in a huge enormous "bed," with enough room between them for more people. Mommy's eyelids weren't fluttering; she lay on her back making a hrrr-hrrr sound through her nose. The funny smell was strong on her. Leisha backed away and tiptoed over to Daddy. He looked like Alice, except that his neck and chin looked even looser, folds of skin collapsed like the tent that had fallen down in the backyard. It scared Leisha to see him like that. Then Daddy's eyes flew open so suddenly that Leisha screamed.

Daddy rolled out of bed and picked her up, looking quickly at Mommy. But she didn't move. Daddy was wearing only his underpants. He carried Leisha out into the hall, where Mamselle came rushing up saying, "Oh, sir, I'm sorry, she just said she was going to the bathroom—"

"It's all right," Daddy said. "I'll take her with me."

"No!" Leisha screamed, because. Daddy was only in his underpants and his neck had looked all funny and the room smelled bad because of Mommy. But Daddy carried her into the conservatory, set her down on a bench, wrapped himself in a piece of green plastic that was supposed to cover up plants, and sat down next to her.

"Now, what happened, Leisha? What were you doing?"

Leisha didn't answer.

"You were looking at people sleeping, weren't you?" Daddy said, and because his voice was softer Leisha mumbled, "Yes." She immediately felt better; it felt good not to lie.

"You were looking at people sleeping because you don't sleep and you were curious; weren't you? Like Curious George in your book?"

"Yes," Leisha said. "I thought you said, you made money in your study all night!"

Daddy smiled. "Not all night. Some of it. But then I sleep, although not very much." He, took Leisha on his lap. "I don't need much sleep, so I get a lot more done at night than most people. Different people need different amounts of sleep. And a few, a very few, are like you. You don't need any."

"Why not?"

"Because you're special. Better than other people. Before you were born, I had some doctors help make you that way."

"Why?"

"So you could do anything you want to and make manifest your own individuality."

Leisha twisted in his arms to stare at him; the words meant nothing. Daddy reached over and touched a single flower growing on a tall potted tree. The flower had thick white petals like the cream he put in coffee, and the center was a light pink.

"See, Leisha—this tree made this flower. Because it *can*. Only this tree can make this kind of wonderful flower. That plant hanging up there can't, and those can't either. Only this tree. Therefore the most important thing in the world for this tree to do *is* grow this flower. The flower is the tree's individuality—that means just *it*, and nothing else—made manifest. Nothing else matters."

"I don't understand, Daddy."

"You will. Someday."

"But I want to understand *now*," Leisha said, and Daddy laughed with pure delight and hugged her. The hug felt good, but Leisha still wanted to understand.

"When you make money, is that your indiv . . . that thing?"

"Yes," Daddy said happily.

"Then nobody else can make money? Like only that tree can make that flower?"

"Nobody else can make it just the way I do."

"What do you do with the money?"

"I buy things for you. This house, your dresses, Mamselle to teach you, the car to ride in."

"What does the tree do with the flower?"

"Glories in it," Daddy said, which made no sense. "Excellence is what counts, Leisha. Excellence supported by individual effort. And that's *all* that counts."

"I'm cold, Daddy."

"Then I better bring you back to Mamselle."

Leisha didn't move. She touched the flower with one finger. "I want to sleep, Daddy."

"No, you don't, sweetheart. Sleep is just lost time, wasted life. It's a little death."

"Alice sleeps."

"Alice isn't like you."

"Alice isn't special?"

"No. You are."

"Why didn't you make Alice special, too?"

"Alice made herself. I didn't have a chance to make her special."

The whole thing was too hard. Leisha stopped stroking the flower and slipped off Daddy's lap. He smiled at her. "My little questioner. When you grow up, you'll find your own excellence, and it will be a new order, a specialness the world hasn't ever seen before. You might even be like Kenzo Yagai. He made the Yagai generator that powers the world."

"Daddy, you look funny wrapped in the flower plastic." Leisha laughed. Daddy did, too. But then she said, "When I grow up, I'll make my specialness find a way to make Alice special, too," and Daddy stopped laughing.

He took her back to Mamselle, who taught her to write her name, which was so exciting she forgot about the puzzling talk with Daddy. There were six letters, all different, and together they were *her name*. Leisha wrote it over and over, laughing, and Mamselle laughed too. But later, in the morning, Leisha thought again about the talk with Daddy. She thought of it often, turning the unfamiliar words over and over in her mind like small hard stones, but the part she thought about most wasn't a word. It was the frown on Daddy's face when she told him she would use her specialness to make Alice special, too.

Every week Dr. Melling came to see Leisha and Alice, sometimes alone, sometimes with other people. Leisha and Alice both liked Dr. Melling, who laughed a lot and whose eyes were bright and warm. Often Daddy was there, too. Dr. Melling played games with them, first with Alice and Leisha separately and then together. She took their pictures and weighed them. She made them lie down on a table and stuck little metal things to their temples, which sounded scary but wasn't because there were so many machines to watch, all making interesting noises, while you were lying there. Dr. Melling was as good at answering questions as Daddy. Once Leisha said, "Is Dr. Melling a special person? Like Kenzo Yagai?" And Daddy laughed and glanced at Dr. Melling and said, "Oh, yes, indeed."

When Leisha was five she and Alice started school. Daddy's driver took them every day into Chicago. They were in different rooms, which disappointed Leisha. The kids in Leisha's room were all older. But from the first day she adored school, with its fascinating science equipment and electronic drawers full of math puzzlers and other children to find countries on the map with. In half a year she had been moved to yet a different room, where the kids were still older, but they were nonetheless nice to her. Leisha started to learn Japanese. She loved drawing the beautiful characters on thick white paper. "The Sauley School was a good choice," Daddy said.

But Alice didn't like the Sauley School. She wanted to go to school on the same yellow bus as Cook's daughter. She cried and threw her paints on the floor at the Sauley School. Then Mommy came out of her room—Leisha hadn't seen her for a few weeks, although she knew Alice had—and threw some candlesticks from the mantlepiece on the floor. The candlesticks, which were china, broke. Leisha ran to pick up the pieces while Mommy and Daddy screamed at each other in the hall by the big staircase.

"She's my daughter, too! And I say she can go!"

"You don't have the right to say anything about it! A weepy drunk, the most rotten role model possible for both of them . . . and I thought I was getting a fine English aristocrat!"

"You got what you paid for! Nothing! Not that you ever needed anything from me or anybody else!"

"Stop it!" Leisha cried. "Stop it!" and there was silence in the hall. Leisha cut her fingers on the china; blood streamed onto the rug. Daddy rushed in and picked her up. "Stop it," Leisha sobbed, and didn't understand when Daddy said quietly, "You stop it, Leisha. Nothing *they* do should touch you at all. You have to be at least that strong."

Leisha buried her head in Daddy's shoulder. Alice transferred to Carl Sandburg

Elementary School, riding there on the yellow school bus with Cook's daughter.

A few weeks later Daddy told them that Mommy was going away for a few weeks to a hospital, to stop drinking so much. When Mommy came out, he said, she was going to live somewhere else for a while. She and Daddy were not happy. Leisha and Alice would stay with Daddy and they would visit Mommy sometimes. He told them this very carefully, finding the right words for truth. Truth was very important, Leisha already knew. Truth was being true to yourself, your specialness. Your individuality. An individual respected facts, and so always told the truth.

Mommy, Daddy did not say but Leisha knew, did not respect facts.

"I don't want Mommy to go away," Alice said. She started to cry. Leisha thought Daddy would pick Alice up, but he didn't. He just stood there looking at them both.

Leisha put her arms around Alice. "It's all right, Alice. It's all right! We'll make it all right! I'll play with you all the time we're not in school so you don't miss Mommy!"

Alice clung to Leisha. Leisha turned her head so she didn't have to see Daddy's face.

3

Kenzo Yagai was coming to the United States to lecture. The title of his talk, which he would give in New York, Los Angeles, Chicago, and Washington, with a repeat in Washington as a special address to Congress, was "The Further Political Implications of Inexpensive Power." Leisha Camden, eleven years old, was going to have a private introduction after the Chicago talk, arranged by her father.

She had studied the theory of cold fusion at school, and her Global Studies teacher had traced the changes in the world resulting from Yagai's patented, low-cost applications of what had, until him, been unworkable theory. The rising prosperity of the Third World, the last death throes of the old communist systems, the decline of the oil states, the renewed economic power of the United States. Her study group had written a news script, filmed with the school's professional-quality equipment, about how a 1985 American family lived with expensive energy costs and a belief in tax-supported help, while a 2019 family lived with cheap energy and a belief in the contract as the basis of civilization. Parts of her own research puzzled Leisha.

"Japan thinks Kenzo Yagai was a traitor to his own country," she said to Daddy at supper.

"No," Camden said. "*Some* Japanese think that. Watch out for generalizations, Leisha. Yagai patented and marketed Y-energy first in the United States because here there were at least the dying embers of individual enterprise. Because of his invention, our entire country has slowly swung back toward an individual meritocracy, and Japan has slowly been forced to follow."

"Your father held that belief all along," Susan said. "Eat your peas, Leisha." Leisha ate her peas. Susan and Daddy had only been married less than a year; it still felt a little strange to have her there. But nice. Daddy said Susan was a valuable addition to their household: intelligent, motivated, and cheerful. Like Leisha herself.

"Remember, Leisha," Camden said, "a man's worth to society and to himself doesn't rest on what he thinks other people should do or be or feel, but on himself. On what he can actually do, and do well. People trade what they do well, and everyone benefits. The basic tool of civilization is the contract. Contracts are voluntary and mutually beneficial. As opposed to coercion, which is wrong."

"The strong have no right to take anything from the weak by force," Susan said. "Alice, eat your peas, too, honey."

"Nor the weak to take anything by force from the strong," Camden said. "That's the basis of what you'll hear Kenzo Yagai discuss tonight, Leisha."

Alice said, "I don't like peas."

Camden said, "Your body does. They're good for you."

Alice smiled. Leisha felt her heart lift; Alice didn't smile much at dinner anymore. "My body doesn't have a contract with the peas."

Camden said, a little impatiently, "Yes, it does. Your body benefits from them. Now eat."

Alice's smile vanished. Leisha looked down at her plate. Suddenly she saw a way out. "No, Daddy look—Alice's body benefits, but the peas don't! It's not a mutually beneficial consideration—so there's no contract! Alice is right!"

Camden let out a shout of laughter. To Susan he said, "Eleven years old . . . *eleven*." Even Alice smiled, and Leisha waved her spoon triumphantly, light glinting off the bowl and dancing silver on the opposite wall.

But even so, Alice did not want to go hear Kenzo Yagai. She was going to sleep over at her friend Julie's house; they were going to curl their hair together. More surprisingly, Susan wasn't coming either. She and Daddy looked at each other a little funny at the front door, Leisha thought, but Leisha was too excited to think about this. She was going to hear *Kenzo Yagai*.

Yagai was a small man, dark and slim. Leisha liked his accent. She liked, too, something about him that took her a while to name. "Daddy," she whispered in the half-darkness of the auditorium, "he's a joyful man."

Daddy hugged her in the darkness.

Yagai spoke about spirituality and economics. "A man's spirituality—which is only his dignity as a man—rests on his own efforts. Dignity and worth are not automatically conferred by aristocratic birth—we have only to look at history to see that. Dignity and worth are not automatically conferred by inherited wealth—a great heir may be a thief, a wastrel, cruel, an exploiter, a person who leaves the world much poorer than he found it. Nor are dignity and worth automatically conferred by existence itself—a mass murderer exists, but is of negative worth to his society and possesses no dignity in his lust to kill.

"No, the only dignity, the only spirituality, rests on what a man can achieve with his own efforts. To rob a man of the chance to achieve, and to trade what he achieves with others, is to rob him of his spiritual dignity as a man. This is why communism has failed in our time. *All* coercion—all force to take from a man his own efforts to achieve—causes spiritual damage and weakens a society. Conscription, theft, fraud, violence, welfare, lack of legislative representation—*all* rob a man of his chance to choose, to achieve on his own, to trade the results of his achievement with others. Coercion is a cheat. It produces nothing new. Only freedom—the freedom to achieve, the freedom to trade freely the results of achievement—creates the environment proper to the dignity and spirituality of man."

Leisha applauded so hard her hands hurt. Going backstage with Daddy, she thought she could hardly breathe. Kenzo Yagai!

But backstage was more crowded than she had expected. There were cameras everywhere. Daddy said, "Mr. Yagai, may I present my daughter Leisha," and the cameras moved in close and fast—on *her*. A Japanese man whispered something in Kenzo Yagai's ear, and he looked more closely at Leisha. "Ah, yes."

"Look over here, Leisha," someone called, and she did. A robot camera zoomed so close to her face that Leisha stepped back, startled. Daddy spoke very sharply to someone, then to someone else. The cameras didn't move. A woman suddenly knelt in front of Leisha and thrust a microphone at her. "What does it feel like to never sleep, Leisha?"

"What?"

Someone laughed. The laugh was not kind. "Breeding geniuses . . ."

Leisha felt a hand on her shoulder. Kenzo Yagai gripped her very firmly, pulled her away from the cameras. Immediately, as if by magic, a line of Japanese men formed behind Yagai, parting only to let Daddy through. Behind the line, the three of them moved into a dressing room, and Kenzo Yagai shut the door.

"You must not let them bother you, Leisha," he said in his wonderful accent. "Not ever. There is an old Oriental proverb: 'The dogs bark but the caravan moves on.' You must never let your individual caravan be slowed by the barking of rude or envious dogs."

"I won't," Leisha breathed, not sure yet what the words really meant, knowing there was time later to sort them out, to talk about them with Daddy. For now she was dazzled by Kenzo Yagai, the actual man himself who was changing the world without force, without guns, with trading his special individual efforts. "We study your philosophy at my school, Mr. Yagai."

Kenzo Yagai looked at Daddy. Daddy said, "A private school. But Leisha's sister also studies it, although cursorily, in the public system. Slowly, Kenzo, but it comes. It comes." Leisha noticed that he did not say why Alice was not here tonight with them.

Back home, Leisha sat in her room for hours, thinking over everything that had happened. When Alice came home from Julie's the next morning, Leisha rushed toward her. But Alice seemed angry about something.

"Alice—what is it?"

"Don't you think I have enough to put up with at school already?" Alice shouted. "Everybody knows, but at least when you stayed quiet it didn't matter too much! They'd stopped teasing me! Why did you have to do it?"

"Do what?" Leisha said, bewildered.

Alice threw something at her: a hard-copy morning paper, on newsprint flimsier than the Camden system used. The paper dropped open at Leisha's feet. She stared at her own picture, three columns wide, with Kenzo Yagai. The headline said YAGAI AND THE FUTURE: ROOM FOR THE REST OF US? Y-ENERGY INVENTOR CONFERS WITH 'SLEEP-FREE' DAUGHTER OF MEGA-FINANCIER ROGER CAMDEN.

Alice kicked the paper. "It was on TV last night too—on TV. I work hard not to look stuck-up or creepy, and you go and do this! Now Julie probably won't even invite me to her slumber party next week!" She rushed up the broad curving stairs toward her room.

Leisha looked down at the paper. She heard Kenzo Yagai's voice in her head: "The dogs bark but the caravan moves on." She looked at the empty stairs. Aloud she said, "Alice—your hair looks really pretty curled like that."

4

"I want to meet the rest of them," Leisha said. "Why have you kept them from me this long?"

"I haven't kept them from you at all," Camden said. "Not offering is not the same as denial. Why shouldn't you be the one to do the asking? You're the one who now wants it."

Leisha looked at him. She was fifteen, in her last year at the Sauley School. "Why didn't you offer?"

"Why should I?"

"I don't know," Leisha said. "But you gave me everything else."

"Including the freedom to ask for what you want."

Leisha looked for the contradiction, and found it. "Most things that you provided for my education I didn't ask for, because I didn't know enough to ask and you, as the adult, did. But you've never offered the opportunity for me to meet any of the other sleepless mutants—"

"Don't use that word," Camden said sharply.

"—so you must either think it was not essential to my education or else you had another motive for not wanting me to meet them."

"Wrong," Camden said. "There's a third possibility. That I think meeting them is essential to your education, that I do want you to, but this issue provided a chance to further the education of your self-initiative by waiting for *you* to ask."

"All right," Leisha said, a little defiantly; there seemed to be a lot of defiance between them lately, for no good reason. She squared her shoulders. Her new breasts thrust forward. "I'm asking. How many of the Sleepless are there, who are they, and where are they?"

Camden said, "If you're using that term—'the Sleepless'—you've already done some reading on your own. So you probably know that there are 1,082 of you so far in the United States, a few more in foreign countries, most of them in major metropolitan areas. Seventy-nine are in Chicago, most of them still small children. Only nineteen anywhere are older than you."

Leisha didn't deny reading any of this. Camden leaned forward in his study chair to peer at her. Leisha wondered if he needed glasses. His hair was completely gray now, sparse and stiff, like lonely broomstraws. The *Wall Street Journal* listed him among the hundred richest men in America; *Women's Wear Daily* pointed out that he was the only billionaire in the country who did not move in the society of international parties, charity balls, and personal jets. Camden's jet ferried him to business meetings around the world, to the chairmanship of the Yagai Economics Institute, and to very little else. Over the years he had grown richer, more reclusive, and more cerebral. Leisha felt a rush of her old affection.

She threw herself sideways into a leather chair, her long slim legs dangling over the arm. Absently she scratched a mosquito bite on her thigh. "Well, then, I'd like to meet Richard Keller." He lived in Chicago and was the beta-test Sleepless closest to her own age. He was seventeen.

"Why ask me? Why not just go?"

Leisha thought there was a note of impatience in his voice. He liked her to explore things first, then report on them to him later. Both parts were important.

Leisha laughed. "You know what, Daddy? You're predictable."

Camden laughed, too. In the middle of the laugh Susan came in. "He certainly is not. Roger, what about that meeting in Buenos Aires Thursday? Is it on or off?" When he didn't answer, her voice grew shriller. "Roger? I'm talking to you!"

Leisha averted her eyes. Two years ago Susan had finally left genetic research to run Camden's house and schedule; before that she had tried hard to do both. Since she had left Biotech, it seemed to Leisha, Susan had changed. Her voice was tighter. She was more insistent that Cook and the gardener follow her directions exactly, without deviation. Her blonde braids had become stiff sculptured waves of platinum.

"It's on," Roger said.

"Well, thanks for at least answering. Am I going?"

"If you like."

"I like."

Susan left the room. Leisha rose and stretched. Her long legs rose on tiptoe. It felt good to reach, to stretch, to feel sunlight from the wide windows wash over her face. She smiled at her father, and found him watching her with an unexpected expression.

"Leisha—"

"What?"

"See Keller. But be careful."

"Of what?"

But Camden wouldn't answer.

The voice on the phone had been noncommittal. "Leisha Camden? Yes, I know who you are. Three o'clock on Thursday?" The house was modest, a thirty-year-old Colonial on a quiet suburban street where small children on bicycles could be watched from the front window. Few roofs had more than one Y-energy cell. The trees, huge old sugar maples, were beautiful.

"Come in," Richard Keller said.

He was no taller than she, stocky, with a bad case of acne. Probably no genetic alterations except sleep, Leisha guessed. He had thick dark hair, a low forehead, and bushy black brows. Before he closed the door Leisha saw his stare at her car and driver, parked in the driveway next to a rusty ten-speed bike.

"I can't drive yet," she said. "I'm still fifteen."

"It's easy to learn," Keller said. "So, you want to tell me why you're here?"

Leisha liked his directness. "To meet some other Sleepless."

"You mean you never have? Not any of us?"

"You mean the rest of you know each other?" She hadn't expected that.

"Come to my room, Leisha."

She followed him to the back of the house. No one else seemed to be home. His room was large and airy, filled with computers and filing cabinets. A rowing machine sat in one corner. It looked like a shabbier version of the room of any bright classmate at the Sauley School, except there was more space without a bed. She walked over to the computer screen.

"Hey—you working on Boesc equations?"

"On an application of them."

"To what?"

"Fish migration patterns."

Leisha smiled. "Yeah—that would work. I never thought of that."

Keller seemed not to know what to do with her smile. He looked at the wall, then at her chin. "You interested in Gaea patterns? In the environment?"

"Well, no," Leisha confessed. "Not particularly. I'm going to study politics at Harvard. Pre-law. But of course we had Gaea patterns at school."

Keller's gaze finally came unstuck from her face. He ran a hand through his dark hair. "Sit down, if you want."

Leisha sat, looking appreciatively at the wall posters, shifting green on blue, like ocean currents. "I like those. Did you program them yourself?"

"You're not at all what I pictured," Keller said.

"How did you picture me?"

He didn't hesitate. "Stuck-up. Superior. Shallow, despite your IQ."

She was more hurt than she had expected to be.

Keller blurted, "You're the only one of the Sleepless who's really rich. But you already know that."

"No, I don't. I've never checked."

He took the chair beside her, stretching his stocky legs straight in front of him, in a slouch that had nothing to do with relaxation. "It makes sense, really. Rich people don't have their children genetically modified to be superior—they think any offspring of theirs is already superior. By their values. And poor people can't afford it. We Sleepless are upper-middle class, no more. Children of professors, scientists, people who value brains and time."

"My father values brains and time," Leisha said. "He's the biggest supporter of Kenzo Yagai."

"Oh, Leisha, do you think I don't already know that? Are you flashing me or what?"

Leisha said with great deliberateness, "I'm *talking* to you." But the next minute she could feel the hurt break through on her face.

"I'm sorry," Keller muttered. He shot off his chair and paced to the computer, back. "I *am* sorry. But I don't . . . I don't understand what you're doing here."

"I'm lonely," Leisha said, astonished at herself. She looked up at him. "It's true. I'm lonely. I am. I have friends and Daddy and Alice—but no one really knows, really understands—what? I don't know what I'm saying."

Keller smiled. The smile changed his whole face, opened up its dark planes to the light. "I do. Oh, do I. What do you do when they say, 'I had such a dream last night!'?"

"Yes!" Leisha said. "But that's even really minor—it's when *I* say, 'I'll look that up for you tonight' and they get that funny look on their face that means 'She'll do it while I'm asleep.'"

"But that's even really minor," Keller said. "It's when you're playing basketball in the gym after supper and then you go to the diner for food and then you say 'Let's have a walk by the lake' and they say 'I'm really tired. I'm going home to bed now.'"

"But that's really minor," Leisha said, jumping up. "It's when you really are absorbed by the movie and then you get the point and it's so goddamn beautiful you leap up and say 'Yes! Yes!' and Susan says 'Leisha, really—you'd think nobody but you ever enjoyed anything before.'"

"Who's Susan?" Keller said.

The mood was broken. But not really; Leisha could say "My stepmother" without much discomfort over what Susan had promised to be and what she had become. Keller stood inches from her, smiling that joyous smile, understanding, and suddenly relief washed over Leisha so strong that she walked straight into him and put her arms around his neck, only tightening them when she felt his startled jerk. She started to sob—she, Leisha, who never cried.

"Hey," Richard said. "Hey."

"Brilliant," Leisha said, laughing. "Brilliant remark."

She could feel his embarrassed smile. "Wanta see my fish migration curves instead?"

"No," Leisha sobbed, and he went on holding her, patting her back awkwardly, telling her without words that she was home.

Camden waited up for her, although it was past midnight. He had been smoking heavily. Through the blue air he said quietly, "Did you have a good time, Leisha?"

"Yes."

"I'm glad," he said, and put out his last cigarette, and climbed the stairs—slowly, stiffly, he was nearly seventy now—to bed.

They went everywhere together for nearly a year: swimming, dancing, to the museums, the theater, the library. Richard introduced her to the others, a group of twelve kids between fourteen and nineteen, all of them intelligent and eager. All Sleepless.

Leisha learned.

Tony's parents, like her own, had divorced. But Tony, fourteen, lived with his mother, who had not particularly wanted a Sleepless child, while his father, who had, acquired a red hovercar and a young girlfriend who designed ergonomic chairs in Paris. Tony was not allowed to tell anyone—relatives, schoolmates—that he was Sleepless. "They'll think you're a freak," his mother said, eyes averted from her son's face. The one time Tony disobeyed her and told a friend that he never slept, his mother beat him. Then she moved the family to a new neighborhood. He was nine years old.

Jeanine, almost as long-legged and slim as Leisha, was training for the Olympics in ice skating. She practiced twelve hours a day, hours no Sleeper still in high school could ever have. So far the newspapers had not picked up the story. Jeanine was afraid that, if they did, they would somehow not let her compete.

Jack, like Leisha, would start college in September. Unlike Leisha, he had already started his career. The practice of law had to wait for law school; the practice of investment required only money. Jack didn't have much, but his precise financial analyses parlayed $600 saved from summer jobs to $3000 through stock-market investing, then to $10,000, and then he had enough to qualify for information-fund speculation. Jack was fifteen, not old enough to make legal investments; the transactions were all in the name of Kevin Baker, the oldest of the Sleepless, who lived in Austin. Jack told Leisha, "When I hit eighty-four percent profit over two consecutive quarters, the data analysts logged onto me. They were just sniffing. Well, that's their job, even when the overall amounts are actually small. It's the patterns they care about. If they take the trouble to cross-reference data banks and come up with the fact that Kevin is a Sleepless, will they try to stop us from investing somehow?"

"That's paranoid," Leisha said.

"No, it's not," Jeanine said. "Leisha, you don't *know*."

"You mean because I've been protected by my father's money and caring," Leisha said. No one grimaced; all of them confronted ideas openly, without shadowy allusions. Without dreams.

"Yes," Jeanine said. "Your father sounds terrific. And he raised you to think that achievement should not be fettered—Jesus Christ, he's a Yagaiist. Well, good. We're glad for you." She said it without sarcasm. Leisha nodded. "But the world isn't always like that. They hate us."

"That's too strong," Carol said. "Not hate."

"Well, maybe," Jeanine said. "But they're different from us. We're better, and they naturally resent that."

"I don't see what's natural about it," Tony said. "Why shouldn't it be just as natural to admire what's better? We do. Does any one of us resent Kenzo Yagai for his genius? Or Nelson Wade, the physicist? Or Catherine Raduski?"

"We don't resent them because we *are* better," Richard said. "Q.E.D."

"What we should do is have our own society," Tony said. "Why should we allow their regulations to restrict our natural, honest achievements? Why should Jeanine be barred from skating against them and Jack from investing on their same terms just because we're Sleepless? Some of them are brighter than others of them. Some have greater persistence. Well, we have greater concentration, more biochemical stability, and more time. All men are not created equal."

"Be fair, Jack—no one has been barred from anything yet," Jeanine said.

"But we will be."

"*Wait,*" Leisha said. She was deeply troubled by the conversation. "I mean, yes, in many ways we're better. But you quoted out of context, Tony. The Declaration of Independence doesn't say all men are created equal in ability. It's talking about rights and power—it means that all are created equal *under the law*. We have no more right to a separate society or to being free of society's restrictions than anyone else does. There's no other way to freely trade one's efforts, unless the same contractual rules apply to all."

"Spoken like a true Yagaiist," Richard said, squeezing her hand.

"That's enough intellectual discussion for me," Carol said, laughing. "We've been at this for hours. We're at the beach, for Chrissake. Who wants to swim with me?"

"I do," Jeanine said. "Come on, Jack."

All of them rose, brushing sand off their suits, discarding sunglasses. Richard pulled Leisha to her feet. But just before they ran into the water, Tony put his skinny hand on her arm. "One more question, Leisha. Just to think about. If we achieve better than most other people, and we trade with the Sleepers when it's mutually beneficial, making no distinction there between the strong and the weak—what obligation do we have to those so weak they don't have anything to trade with us? We're already going to give more than we get—do we have to do it when we get nothing at all? Do we have to take care of their deformed and handicapped and sick and lazy and shiftless with the products of our work?"

"Do the Sleepers have to?" Leisha countered.

"Kenzo Yagai would say no. He's a Sleeper."

"He would say they would receive the benefits of contractual trade even if they aren't direct parties to the contract. The whole world is better-fed and healthier because of Y-energy."

"Come on!" Jeanine yelled. "Leisha, they're dunking me! Jack, you stop that! Leisha, help me!"

Leisha laughed. Just before she grabbed for Jeanine, she caught the look on Richard's face, on Tony's: Richard frankly lustful, Tony angry. At her. But why? What had she done, except argue in favor of dignity and trade?

Then Jack threw water on her, and Carol pushed Jack into the warm spray, and Richard was there with his arms around her, laughing.

When she got the water out of her eyes, Tony was gone.

Midnight. "Okay," Carol said. "Who's first?"

The six teenagers in the brambled clearing looked at each other. A Y-lamp, kept on low for atmosphere, cast weird shadows across their faces and over their bare legs. Around the clearing Roger Camden's trees stood thick and dark, a wall between them and the closest of the estate's outbuildings. It was very hot. August air hung heavy, sullen. They had voted against bringing an air-conditioned Y-field because this was a return to the primitive, the dangerous; let it be primitive.

Six pairs of eyes stared at the glass in Carol's hand.

"Come *on*," she said. "Who wants to drink up?" Her voice was jaunty, theatrically hard. "It was difficult enough to get this."

"How *did* you get it?" said Richard, the group member—except for Tony—with the least influential family contacts, the least money. "In a drinkable form like that?"

"My cousin Brian is a pharmaceutical supplier to the Biotech Institute. He's curious." Nods around the circle; except for Leisha, they were Sleepless precisely because they had relatives somehow connected to Biotech. And everyone was curious. The glass held interleukin-1, an immune system booster, one of many substances which as a side effect induced the brain to swift and deep sleep.

Leisha stared at the glass. A warm feeling crept through her lower belly, not unlike the feeling when she and Richard made love.

Tony said, "Give it to me!"

Carol did. "Remember—you only need a little sip."

Tony raised the glass to his mouth, stopped, looked at them over the rim from his fierce eyes. He drank.

Carol took back the glass. They all watched Tony. Within a minute he lay on the rough ground; within two, his eyes closed in sleep.

It wasn't like seeing parents sleep, siblings, friends. It was Tony. They looked away, didn't meet each other's eyes. Leisha felt the warmth between her legs tug and tingle, faintly obscene.

When it was her turn, she drank slowly, then passed the glass to Jeanine. Her head turned heavy, as if it were being stuffed with damp rags. The trees at the edge of the clearing blurred. The portable lamp blurred, too—it wasn't bright and clean anymore but squishy, blobby; if she touched it, it would smear. Then darkness swooped over her brain, taking it away: *Taking away her mind.* "Daddy!" She tried to call, to clutch for him, but then the darkness obliterated her.

Afterward, they all had headaches. Dragging themselves back through the woods in the thin morning light was torture, compounded by an odd shame. They didn't touch each other. Leisha walked as far away from Richard as she could. It was a whole day before the throbbing left the base of her skull, or the nausea her stomach.

There had not even been any dreams.

"I want you to come with me tonight," Leisha said, for the tenth or twelfth time. "We both leave for college in just two days; this is the last chance. I really want you to meet Richard."

Alice lay on her stomach across her bed. Her hair, brown and lusterless, fell around her face. She wore an expensive yellow jumpsuit, silk by Ann Patterson, which rucked up in wrinkles around her knees.

"Why? What do you care if I meet Richard or not?"

"Because you're my sister," Leisha said. She knew better than to say "my twin." Nothing got Alice angry faster.

"I don't want to." The next moment Alice's face changed. "Oh, I'm sorry, Leisha—I didn't mean to sound so snotty. But . . . but I don't want to."

"It won't be all of them. Just Richard. And just for an hour or so. Then you can come back here and pack for Northwestern."

"I'm not going to Northwestern."

Leisha stared at her.

Alice said, "I'm pregnant."

Leisha sat on the bed. Alice rolled onto her back, brushed the hair out of her eyes, and laughed. Leisha's ears closed against the sound. "Look at you," Alice said. "You'd think it was *you* who was pregnant. But you never would be, would you, Leisha? Not until it was the proper time. Not you."

"How?" Leisha said. "We both had our caps put in . . ."

"I had the cap removed," Alice said.

"You wanted to get pregnant?"

"Damn flash I did. And there's not a thing Daddy can do about it. Except, of course, cut off all credit completely, but I don't think he'll do that, do you?" She laughed again. "Even to me?"

"But Alice . . . why? Not just to anger Daddy!"

"No," Alice said. "Although you would think of that, wouldn't you? Because I want something to love. Something of my *own*. Something that has nothing to do with this house."

Leisha thought of her and Alice running through the conservatory, years ago, her and Alice, darting in and out of the sunlight. "It hasn't been so bad growing up in this house."

"Leisha, you're stupid. I don't know how anyone so smart can be so stupid. Get out of my room! Get out!"

"But Alice . . . a *baby* . . ."

"Get out!" Alice shrieked. "Go to Harvard! Go be successful! Just get out!"

Leisha jerked off the bed. "Gladly! You're irrational, Alice! You don't think ahead, you don't plan a *baby* . . ." But she could never sustain anger. It dribbled away, leaving her mind empty. She looked at Alice, who suddenly put out her arms. Leisha went into them.

"You're the baby," Alice said wonderingly. "You *are*. You're so . . . I don't know what. You're a baby."

Leisha said nothing. Alice's arms felt warm, felt whole, felt like two children running in and out of sunlight. "I'll help you, Alice. If Daddy won't."

Alice abruptly pushed her away. "I don't need your help."

Alice stood. Leisha rubbed her empty arms, fingertips scraping across opposite elbows. Alice kicked the empty, open trunk in which she was supposed to pack for Northwestern, and then abruptly smiled, a smile that made Leisha look away. She braced herself for more abuse. But what Alice said, very softly, was, "Have a good time at Harvard."

5

She loved it.

From the first sight of Massachusetts Hall, older than the United States by a half century, Leisha felt something that had been missing in Chicago: Age. Roots. Tradition. She touched the bricks of Widener Library, the glass cases in the Peabody Museum, as if they were the grail. She had never been particularly sensitive to myth or drama; the anguish of Juliet seemed to her artificial, that of Willy Loman merely wasteful. Only King Arthur, struggling to create a better social order, had interested her. But now, walking under the huge autumn trees, she suddenly caught a glimpse of a force that could span generations, fortunes left to endow learning and achievement the benefactors would never see, individual effort spanning and shaping centuries to come. She stopped, and looked at the sky through the leaves, at the buildings solid with purpose. At such moments she thought of Camden, bending the will of an entire genetic research institute to create her in the image he wanted.

Within a month, she had forgotten all such mega-musings.

The workload was incredible, even for her. The Sauley School had encouraged individual exploration at her own pace; Harvard knew what it wanted from her, at its pace. In the last twenty years, under the academic leadership of a man who in his youth had watched Japanese economic domination with dismay, Harvard had become the controversial leader of a return to hard-edged learning of facts, theories, applications, problem-solving, intellectual efficiency. The school accepted one out of every two hundred applications from around the world. The daughter of England's Prime Minister had flunked out her first year and been sent home.

Leisha had a single room in a new dormitory, the dorm because she had spent so many years isolated in Chicago and was hungry for people, the single so she would not disturb anyone else when she worked all night. Her second day a boy from down the hall sauntered in and perched on the edge of her desk.

"So you're Leisha Camden."

"Yes."

"Sixteen years old."

"Almost seventeen."

"Going to out-perform us all, I understand, without even trying."

Leisha's smile faded. The boy stared at her from under lowered downy brows. He was smiling, his eyes sharp. From Richard and Tony and the others Leisha had learned to recognize the anger that presented itself as contempt.

"Yes," Leisha said coolly, "I am."

"Are you sure? With your pretty little-girl hair and your mutant little-girl brain?"

"Oh, leave her alone, Hannaway," said another voice. A tall blond boy, so thin his ribs looked like ripples in brown sand, stood in jeans and bare feet, drying his wet hair. "Don't you ever get tired of walking around being an asshole?"

"Do you?" Hannaway said. He heaved himself off the desk and started toward the door. The blond moved out of his way. Leisha moved into it.

"The reason I'm going to do better than you," she said evenly, "is because I have certain advantages you don't. Including sleeplessness. And then after I 'out-perform' you, I'll be glad to help you study for your tests so that you can pass, too."

The blond, drying his ears, laughed. But Hannaway stood still, and into his eyes came an expression that made Leisha back away. He pushed past her and stormed out.

"Nice going, Camden," the blond said. "He deserved that."

"But I meant it," Leisha said. "I will help him study."

The blond lowered his towel and stared. "You did, didn't you? You meant it."

"Yes! Why does everybody keep questioning that?"

"Well," the boy said, "*I* don't. You can help me if I get into trouble." Suddenly he smiled. "But I won't."

"Why not?"

"Because I'm just as good at anything as you are, Leisha Camden."

She studied him. "You're not one of us. Not Sleepless."

"Don't have to be. I know what I can do. Do, be, create, trade."

She said, delighted, "You're a Yagaiist!"

"Of course." He held out his hand. "Stewart Sutter. How about a fish-burger in the Yard?"

"Great," Leisha said. They walked out together, talking excitedly. When people stared at her, she tried not to notice. She was here. At Harvard. With space ahead of her, time to learn, and with people like Stewart Sutter who accepted and challenged her.

All the hours he was awake.

She became totally absorbed in her classwork. Roger Camden drove up once, walking the campus with her, listening, smiling. He was more at home than Leisha would have expected: He knew Stewart Sutter's father, Kate Addams' grandfather. They talked about Harvard, business, Harvard, the Yagai Economics Institute, Harvard. "How's Alice?" Leisha asked once, but Camden said that he didn't know, she had moved out and did not want to see him. He made her an allowance through his attorney. While he said this, his face remained serene.

Leisha went to the Homecoming Ball with Stewart, who was also majoring in pre-law but was two years ahead of Leisha. She took a weekend trip to Paris with Kate Addams and two other girlfriends, taking the Concorde III. She had a fight with Stewart over whether the metaphor of superconductivity could apply to Yagaiism, a stupid fight they both knew was stupid but had anyway, and afterward they became lovers. After the fumbling sexual explorations with Richard, Stewart was deft, experienced, smiling faintly as he taught her how to have an orgasm both by herself and with him. Leisha was dazzled. "It's so *joyful*," she said, and Stewart looked at her with a tenderness she knew was part disturbance but didn't know why.

At mid-semester she had the highest grades in the freshman class. She got every answer right on every single question on her mid-terms. She and Stewart went out for a beer to celebrate, and when they came back Leisha's room had been destroyed. The computer was smashed, the data banks wiped, hardcopies and books smoldering in a metal wastebasket. Her clothes were ripped to pieces, her desk and bureau hacked apart. The only thing untouched, pristine, was the bed.

Stewart said, "There's no way this could have been done in silence. Everyone on the floor—hell, on the floor *below*—had to know. Someone will talk to the police." No one did. Leisha sat on the edge of the bed, dazed, and looked at the remnants of her Homecoming gown. The next day Dave Hannaway gave her a long, wide smile.

Camden flew east again, taut with rage. He rented her an apartment in Cambridge with E-lock security and a bodyguard named Toshio. After he left, Leisha fired the bodyguard but kept the apartment. It gave her and Stewart more privacy, which they used to endlessly discuss the situation. It was Leisha who argued that it was an aberration, an immaturity.

"There have always been haters, Stewart. Hate Jews, hate Blacks, hate immigrants, hate Yagaiists who have more initiative and dignity than you do. I'm just the latest object of hatred. It's not new, it's not remarkable. It doesn't mean any basic kind of schism between the Sleepless and Sleepers."

Stewart sat up in bed and reached for the sandwiches on the night stand. "Doesn't it? Leisha, you're a different kind of person entirely. More evolutionarily fit, not only to survive but to prevail. Those other 'objects of hatred' you cite except Yagaiists—they were all powerless in their societies. They occupied *inferior* positions. You, on the other hand—all three Sleepless in Harvard Law are on the *Law Review*. All of them. Kevin Baker, your oldest, has already founded a successful bio-interface software firm and is making money, a lot of it. Every Sleepless is making superb grades, none have psychological problems, all are healthy—and most of you aren't even adults yet. How much hatred do you think you're going to encounter once you hit the big-stakes world of finance and business and scarce endowed chairs and national politics?"

"Give me a sandwich," Leisha said. "Here's my evidence you're wrong: You yourself. Kenzo Yagai. Kate Addams. Professor Lane. My father. Every Sleeper who inhabits the world of fair trade, mutually beneficial contracts. And that's most of you, or at least most of you who are worth considering. You believe that competition among the most capable leads to the most beneficial trades for everyone, strong and weak. Sleepless are making real and concrete contributions to society, in a lot of fields. That has to outweigh the discomfort we cause. We're *valuable* to you. You know that."

Stewart brushed crumbs off the sheets. "Yes. I do. Yagaiists do."

"Yagaiists run the business and financial and academic worlds. Or they will. In a meritocracy, they *should*. You underestimate the majority of people, Stew. Ethics aren't confined to the ones out front."

"I hope you're right," Stewart said. "Because, you know, I'm in love with you."

Leisha put down her sandwich.

"Joy," Stewart mumbled into her breasts, "you are joy."

When Leisha went home for Thanksgiving, she told Richard about Stewart. He listened tight-lipped.

"A Sleeper."

"A *person*," Leisha said. "A good, intelligent, achieving person!"

"Do you know what your good intelligent achieving Sleepers have done, Leisha? Jeanine has been barred from Olympic skating. 'Genetic alteration, analogous to steroid abuse to create an unsportsmanlike advantage.' Chris Devereaux's left Stanford. They trashed his laboratory, destroyed two years' work in memory formation proteins. Kevin Baker's software company is fighting a nasty advertising campaign, all underground of course, about kids using software designed by 'non-human minds.' Corruption, mental slavery, satanic influences: the whole bag of witch-hunt tricks. Wake up, Leisha!"

They both heard his words. Moments dragged by. Richard stood like a boxer, forward on the balls of his feet, teeth clenched. Finally he said, very quietly, "Do you love him?"

"Yes," Leisha said. "I'm sorry."

"Your choice," Richard said coldly. "What do you do while he's asleep? Watch?"

"You make it sound like a perversion!"

Richard said nothing. Leisha drew a deep breath. She spoke rapidly but calmly, a controlled rush: "While Stewart is asleep I work. The same as you do. Richard—don't do this. I didn't mean to hurt you. And I don't want to lose the group. I believe the Sleepers are the same species as we are—are you going to punish me for that? Are you going to *add* to the hatred? Are you going to tell me that I can't belong to a wider world that includes all honest, worthwhile people whether they sleep or not? Are you going to tell me that the most important division is by genetics and not by economic spirituality? Are you going to force me into an artificial choice, 'us' or 'them'?"

Richard picked up a bracelet. Leisha recognized it: She had given it to him in the summer. His voice was quiet. "No. It's not a choice." He played with the gold links a minute, then looked up at her. "Not yet."

By spring break, Camden walked more slowly. He took medicine for his blood pressure, his heart. He and Susan, he told Leisha, were getting a divorce. "She changed, Leisha, after I married her. You saw that. She was independent and productive and happy, and then after a few years she stopped all that and became a shrew. A whining shrew." He shook his head in genuine bewilderment. "You saw the change."

Leisha had. A memory came to her: Susan leading her and Alice in "games" that were actually controlled cerebral-performance tests, Susan's braids dancing around her sparkling eyes. Alice had loved Susan, then, as much as Leisha had.

"Dad, I want Alice's address."

"I told you up at Harvard, I don't have it," Camden said. He shifted in his chair, the impatient gesture of a body that never expected to wear out. In January Kenzo Yagai had died of pancreatic cancer; Camden had taken the news hard. "I make her allowance through an attorney. By her choice."

"Then I want the address of the attorney."

The attorney, however, refused to tell Leisha where Alice was. "She doesn't want to be found, Ms. Camden. She wanted a complete break."

"Not from me," Leisha said.

"Yes," the attorney said, and something flickered behind his eyes, something she had last seen in Dave Hannaway's face.

She flew to Austin before returning to Boston, making her a day late for classes. Kevin Baker saw her instantly, canceling a meeting with IBM. She told him what she needed, and he set his best data-net people on it, without telling them why. Within two hours she had Alice's address from the attorney's electronic files. It was the first time, she realized, that she had ever turned to one of the Sleepless for help, and it had been given instantly. Without trade.

Alice was in Pennsylvania. The next weekend Leisha rented a hovercar and driver—she had learned to drive, but only groundcars as yet—and went to High Ridge, in the Appalachian Mountains.

It was an isolated hamlet, twenty-five miles from the nearest hospital. Alice lived with a man named Ed, a silent carpenter twenty years older than she, in a cabin in the woods. The cabin had water and electricity but no news net. In the early spring light the earth was raw and bare, slashed with icy gullies. Alice and Ed apparently worked at nothing. Alice was eight months pregnant.

"I didn't want you here," she said to Leisha. "So why are you?"

"Because you're my sister."

"God, look at you. Is that what they're wearing at Harvard? Boots like that? When did you become fashionable, Leisha? You were always too busy being intellectual to care."

"What's this all about, Alice? Why here? What are you doing?"

"Living," Alice said. "Away from dear Daddy, away from Chicago, away from drunken broken Susan—did you know she drinks? Just like Mom. He does that to people. But not to me. I got out. I wonder if you ever will."

"Got out? To *this*?"

"I'm happy," Alice said angrily. "Isn't that what it's supposed to be about? Isn't that the aim of your great Kenzo Yagai—happiness through individual effort?"

Leisha thought of saying that Alice was making no efforts that she could see. She didn't say it. A chicken ran through the yard of the cabin. Behind, the mountains rose in layers of blue haze. Leisha thought what this place must have been like in winter: cut off from the world where people strived towards goals, learned, changed.

"I'm glad you're happy, Alice."

"Are you?"

"Yes."

"Then I'm glad, too," Alice said, almost defiantly. The next moment she abruptly hugged Leisha, fiercely, the huge hard mound of her belly crushed between them. Alice's hair smelled sweet, like fresh grass in sunlight.

"I'll come see you again, Alice."

"Don't," Alice said.

6

SLEEPLESS MUTIE BEGS FOR REVERSAL OF GENE TAMPERING, screamed the headline in the Food Mart. "PLEASE LET ME SLEEP LIKE REAL PEOPLE!" CHILD PLEADS.

Leisha typed in her credit number and pressed the news kiosk for a printout, although ordinarily she ignored the electronic tabloids. The headline went on circling the kiosk. A Food Mart employee stopped stacking boxes on shelves and watched her. Bruce, Leisha's bodyguard, watched the employee.

She was twenty-two, in her final year at Harvard Law, editor of the *Law Review*, ranked first in her class. The next three were Jonathan Cocchiara, Len Carter, and Martha Wentz. All Sleepless.

In her apartment she skimmed the printout. Then she accessed the Groupnet run from Austin. The files had more news stories about the child, with comments from other Sleepless, but before she could call them up Kevin Baker came on-line himself, on voice.

"Leisha. I'm glad you called. I was going to call you."

"What's the situation with this Stella Bevington, Kev? Has anybody checked it out?"

"Randy Davies. He's from Chicago but I don't think you've met him, he's still in high school. He's in Park Ridge, Stella's in Skokie. Her parents wouldn't talk to him—were pretty abusive, in fact—but he got to see Stella face-to-face anyway. It doesn't look like an abuse case, just the usual stupidity: parents wanted a genius child, scrimped and saved, and now they can't handle that she *is* one. They scream at her to sleep, get emotionally abusive when she contradicts them, but so far no violence."

"Is the emotional abuse actionable?"

"I don't think we want to move on it yet. Two of us will keep in close touch with Stella—she does have a modem, and she hasn't told her parents about the net—and Randy will drive out weekly."

Leisha bit her lip. "A tabloid shitpiece said she's seven years old."

"Yes."

"Maybe she shouldn't be left there. I'm an Illinois resident, I can file an abuse grievance from here if Candy's got too much in her briefcase. . . ." *Seven years old.*

"No. Let it sit a while. Stella will probably be all right. You know that."

She did. Nearly all of the Sleepless stayed "all right," no matter how much opposition came from the stupid segment of society. And it was only the stupid segment, Leisha argued—a small if vocal minority. Most people could, and would, adjust to the growing presence of the Sleepless, when it became clear that that presence included not only growing power but growing benefits to the country as a whole.

Kevin Baker, now twenty-six, had made a fortune in microchips so revolutionary that Artificial Intelligence, once a debated dream, was yearly closer to reality. Carolyn Rizzolo had won the Pulitzer Prize in drama for her play *Morning Light*. She was twenty-four. Jeremy Robinson had done significant work in superconductivity applications while still a graduate student at Stanford. William Thaine, *Law Review* editor when Leisha first came to Harvard, was now in private practice. He had never lost a case. He was twenty-six, and the cases were becoming important. His clients valued his ability more than his age.

But not everyone reacted that way.

Kevin Baker and Richard Keller had started the datanet that bound the Sleepless into a tight group, constantly aware of each other's personal fights. Leisha Camden financed the legal battles, the educational costs of Sleepless whose parents were unable to meet them, the support of children in emotionally bad situations. Rhonda Lavelier got herself licensed as a foster mother in California, and whenever possible the Group maneuvered to have small Sleepless who were removed from their homes assigned to Rhonda. The Group now had three ABA lawyers; within the next year they would gain four more, licensed to practice in five different states.

The one time they had not been able to remove an abused Sleepless child legally, they kidnapped him.

Timmy DeMarzo, four years old. Leisha had been opposed to the action. She had argued the case morally and pragmatically—to her they were the same thing—thus: If they believed in their society, in its fundamental laws and in their ability to belong to it as free-trading productive individuals, they must remain bound by the society's contractual laws. The Sleepless were, for the most part, Yagaiists. They should already know this. And if the FBI caught them, the courts and press would crucify them.

They were not caught.

Timmy DeMarzo—not even old enough to call for help on the datanet, they had learned of the situation through the automatic police-record scan Kevin maintained through his company—was stolen from his own backyard in Wichita. He had lived the last year in an isolated trailer in North Dakota; no place was too isolated for a modem. He was cared for by a legally irreproachable foster mother who had lived there all her life. The foster mother was second cousin to a Sleepless, a broad cheerful woman with a much better brain than her appearance indicated. She was a Yagaiist. No record of the child's existence appeared in any data bank: not the IRS, not any school's, not even the local grocery store's computerized check-out slips. Food specifically for the child was shipped in monthly on a truck owned by a Sleepless in State College, Pennsylvania. Ten of the Group knew about the kidnapping, out of the total 3,428 born in the United States. Of that total, 2,691 were part of the Group via the net. Another 701 were as yet too young to use a modem. Only thirty-six Sleepless, for whatever reason, were not part of the Group.

The kidnapping had been arranged by Tony Indivino.

"It's Tony I wanted to talk to you about," Kevin said to Leisha. "He's started again. This time he means it. He's buying land."

She folded the tabloid very small and laid it carefully on the table. "Where?"

"Allegheny Mountains. In southern New York State. A lot of land. He's putting in the roads now. In the spring, the first buildings."

"Jennifer Sharifi still financing it?" She was the American-born daughter of an Arab prince who had wanted a Sleepless child. The prince was dead and Jennifer, dark-eyed and multilingual, was richer than Leisha would one day be.

"Yes. He's starting to get a following, Leisha."

"I know."

"Call him."

"I will. Keep me informed about Stella."

She worked until midnight at the *Law Review*, then until four A.M. preparing her classes. From four to five she handled legal matters for the Group. At five A.M. she called Tony, still in Chicago. He had finished high school, done one semester at Northwestern, and at Christmas vacation he had finally exploded at his mother for forcing him to live as a Sleeper. The explosion, it seemed to Leisha, had never ended.

"Tony? Leisha."

"The answer is yes, yes, no, and go to hell."

Leisha gritted her teeth. "Fine. Now tell me the questions."

"Are you really serious about the Sleepless withdrawing into their own self-sufficient society? Is Jennifer Sharifi willing to finance a project the size of building a small city? Don't you think that's a cheat of all that can be accomplished by patient integration of the Group into the mainstream? And what about the contradictions of living in an armed restricted city and still trading with the Outside?"

"I would never tell *you* to go to hell."

"Hooray for you," Tony said. After a moment he added, "I'm sorry. That sounds like one of *them*."

"It's wrong for us, Tony."

"Thanks for not saying I couldn't pull it off."

She wondered if he could. "We're not a separate species, Tony."

"Tell that to the Sleepers."

"You exaggerate. There are haters out there, there are *always* haters, but to give up . . ."

"We're not giving up. Whatever we create can be freely traded: software, hardware, novels, information, theories, legal counsel. We can travel in and out. But we'll have a safe place to return *to*. Without the leeches who think we owe them blood because we're better than they are."

"It isn't a matter of owing."

"Really?" Tony said. "Let's have this out, Leisha. All the way. You're a Yagaiist—what do you believe in?"

"Tony . . ."

"*Do it*," Tony said, and in his voice she heard the fourteen-year-old Richard had introduced her to. Simultaneously, she saw her father's face: not as he was now, since the bypass, but as he had been when she was a little girl, holding her on his lap to explain that she was special.

"I believe in voluntary trade that is mutually beneficial. That spiritual dignity comes from supporting one's life through one's own efforts, and trading the results of those efforts in mutual cooperation throughout the society. That the symbol of this is the contract. And that we need each other for the fullest, most beneficial trade."

"Fine," Tony bit off. "Now what about the beggars in Spain?"

"The what?"

"You walk down a street in a poor country like Spain and you see a beggar. Do you give him a dollar?"

"Probably."

"Why? He's trading nothing with you. He has nothing to trade."

"I know. Out of kindness. Compassion."

"You see six beggars. Do you give them all a dollar?"

"Probably," Leisha said.

"You would. You see a hundred beggars and you haven't got Leisha Camden's money—do you give them each a dollar?"

"No."

"Why not?"

Leisha reached for patience. Few people could make her want to cut off a comm link; Tony was one of them. "Too draining on my own resources. My life has first claim on the resources I earn."

"All right. Now consider this. At Biotech Institute—where you and I began, dear pseudo-sister—Dr. Melling has just yesterday—"

"*Who?*"

"Dr. Susan Melling. Oh, God, I completely forgot—she used to be married to your father!"

"I lost track of her," Leisha said. "I didn't realize she'd gone back to research. Alice once said . . . never mind. What's going on at Biotech?"

"Two crucial items, just released. Carla Dutcher has had first-month fetal genetic analysis. Sleeplessness is a dominant gene. The next generation of the Group won't sleep either."

"We all knew that," Leisha said. Carla Dutcher was the world's first pregnant Sleepless. Her husband was a Sleeper. "The whole world expected that."

"But the press will have a windfall with it anyway. Just watch. Muties Breed! New Race Set To Dominate Next Generation of Children!"

Leisha didn't deny it. "And the second item?"

"It's sad, Leisha. We've just had our first death."

Her stomach tightened. "Who?"

"Bernie Kuhn. Seattle." She didn't know him. "A car accident. It looks pretty straightforward—he lost control on a steep curve when his brakes failed. He had only been driving a few months. He was seventeen. But the significance here is that his parents have donated his brain and body to Biotech, in conjunction with the pathology department at the Chicago Medical School. They're going to take him apart to get the first good look at what prolonged sleeplessness does to the body and brain."

"They should," Leisha said. "That poor kid. But what are you so afraid they'll find?"

"I don't know. I'm not a doctor. But whatever it is, if the haters can use it against us, they will."

"You're paranoid, Tony."

"Impossible. The Sleepless have personalities calmer and more reality-oriented than the norm. Don't you read the literature?"

"Tony—"

"What if you walk down that street in Spain and a hundred beggars each want a dollar and you say no and they have nothing to trade you but they're so rotten with anger about what you have that they knock you down and grab it and then beat you out of sheer envy and despair?"

Leisha didn't answer.

"Are you going to say that's not a human scenario, Leisha? That it never happens?"

"It happens," Leisha said evenly. "But not all that often."

"Bullshit. Read more history. Read more *newspapers*. But the point is: What do you owe the beggars then? What does a good Yagaiist who believes in mutually beneficial contracts do with people who have nothing to trade and can only take?"

"You're not—"

"*What*, Leisha? In the most objective terms you can manage, what do we owe the grasping and non-productive needy?"

"What I said originally. Kindness. Compassion."

"Even if they don't trade it back? Why?"

"Because . . ." She stopped.

"Why? Why do law-abiding and productive human beings owe anything to those who neither produce very much nor abide by laws? What philosophical or economic or spiritual justification is there for owing them anything? Be as honest as I know you are."

Leisha put her head between her knees. The question gaped beneath her, but she didn't try to evade it. "I don't know. I just know we do."

"Why?"

She didn't answer. After a moment, Tony did. The intellectual challenge was gone from his voice. He said, almost tenderly, "Come down in the spring and see the site for Sanctuary. The buildings will be going up then."

"No," Leisha said.

"I'd like you to."

"No. Armed retreat is not the way."

Tony said, "The beggars are getting nastier, Leisha. As the Sleepless grow richer. And I don't mean in money."

"Tony—" she said, and stopped. She couldn't think what to say.

"Don't walk down too many streets armed with just the memory of Kenzo Yagai."

In March, a bitterly cold March of winds whipping down the Charles River, Richard Keller came to Cambridge. Leisha had not seen him for four years. He didn't send her word on the Groupnet that he was coming. She hurried up the walk to her townhouse, muffled to the eyes in a red wool scarf against the snowy cold, and he stood there blocking the doorway. Behind Leisha, her bodyguard tensed.

"Richard! Bruce, it's all right, this is an old friend."

"Hello, Leisha."

He was heavier, sturdier-looking, with a breadth of shoulder she didn't recognize. But the face was Richard's, older but unchanged: dark low brows, unruly dark hair. He had grown a beard.

"You look beautiful," he said.

She handed him a cup of coffee. "Are you here on business?" From the Groupnet she knew that he had finished his Master's and had done outstanding work in marine biology in the Caribbean, but had left that a year ago and disappeared from the net.

"No. Pleasure." He smiled suddenly, the old smile that opened up his dark face. "I almost forgot about that for a long time. Contentment, yes, we're all good at the contentment that comes from sustained work, but pleasure? Whim? Caprice? When was the last time you did something silly, Leisha?"

She smiled. "I ate cotton candy in the shower."

"Really? Why?"

"To see if it would dissolve in gooey pink patterns."

"Did it?"

"Yes. Lovely ones."

"And that was your last silly thing? When was it?"

"Last summer," Leisha said, and laughed.

"Well, mine is sooner than that. It's now. I'm in Boston for no other reason than the spontaneous pleasure of seeing you."

Leisha stopped laughing. "That's an intense tone for a spontaneous pleasure, Richard."

"Yup," he said, intensely. She laughed again. He didn't.

"I've been in India, Leisha. And China and Africa. Thinking, mostly. Watching. First I traveled like a Sleeper, attracting no attention. Then I set out to meet the Sleepless in India and China. There are a few, you know, whose parents were willing to come here for the operation. They pretty much are accepted and left alone. I tried to figure out why desperately poor countries—by our standards anyway, over there Y-energy is mostly available only in big cities—don't have any trouble accepting the superiority of Sleepless, whereas Americans, with more prosperity than any time in history, build in resentment more and more."

Leisha said, "Did you figure it out?"

"No. But I figured out something else, watching all those communes and villages and kampongs. We are too individualistic."

Disappointment swept Leisha. She saw her father's face: *Excellence is what counts, Leisha. Excellence supported by individual effort. . . .* She reached for Richard's cup. "More coffee?"

He caught her wrist and looked up into her face. "Don't misunderstand me, Leisha. I'm not talking about work. We are too much individuals in the rest of our lives. Too emotionally rational. Too much alone. Isolation kills more than the free flow of ideas. It kills joy."

He didn't let go of her wrist. She looked down into his eyes, into depths she hadn't seen before: It was the feeling of looking into a mine shaft, both giddy and frightening, knowing that at the bottom might be gold or darkness. Or both.

Richard said softly, "Stewart?"

"Over long ago. An undergraduate thing." Her voice didn't sound like her own.

"Kevin?"

"No, never—we're just friends."

"I wasn't sure. Anyone?"

"No."

He let go of her wrist. Leisha peered at him timidly. He suddenly laughed. "Joy, Leisha." An echo sounded in her mind, but she couldn't place it and then it was gone and she laughed too, a laugh airy and frothy as pink cotton candy in summer.

"Come home, Leisha. He's had another heart attack."

Susan Melling's voice on the phone was tired. Leisha said, "How bad?"

"The doctors aren't sure. Or say they're not sure. He wants to see you. Can you leave your studies?"

It was May, the last push toward her finals. The *Law Review* proofs were behind schedule. Richard had started a new business, marine consulting to Boston fishermen plagued with sudden inexplicable shifts in ocean currents, and was working twenty hours a day. "I'll come," Leisha said.

Chicago was colder than Boston. The trees were half-budded. On Lake Michigan, filling the huge east windows of her father's house, whitecaps tossed up cold spray. Leisha saw that Susan was living in the house: her brushes on Camden's dresser, her journals on the credenza in the foyer.

"Leisha," Camden said. He looked old. Gray skin, sunken cheeks, the fretful and bewildered look of men who accepted potency like air, indivisible from their lives. In the corner of the room, on a small eighteenth-century slipper chair, sat a short, stocky woman with brown braids.

"*Alice*."

"Hello, Leisha."

"*Alice*. I've looked for you. . . ." The wrong thing to say. Leisha had looked, but not very hard, deterred by the knowledge that Alice had not wanted to be found. "How are you?"

"I'm fine," Alice said. She seemed remote, gentle, unlike the angry Alice of six years ago in the raw Pennsylvania hills. Camden moved painfully on the bed. He looked at Leisha with eyes which, she saw, were undimmed in their blue brightness.

"I asked Alice to come. And Susan. Susan came a while ago. I'm dying, Leisha."

No one contradicted him. Leisha, knowing his respect for facts, remained silent. Love hurt her chest.

"John Jaworski has my will. None of you can break it. But I wanted to tell you myself what's in it. The last few years I've been selling, liquidating. Most of my holdings are accessible now. I've left a tenth to Alice, a tenth to Susan, a tenth to Elizabeth, and the rest to you, Leisha, because you're the only one with the individual ability to use the money to its full potential for achievement."

Leisha looked wildly at Alice, who gazed back with her strange remote calm. "Elizabeth? My . . . mother? Is alive?"

"Yes," Camden said.

"You told me she was dead! Years and years ago!"

"Yes. I thought it was better for you that way. She didn't like what you were, was jealous of what you could become. And she had nothing to give you. She would only have caused you emotional harm."

Beggars in Spain . . .

"That was wrong, Dad. You were *wrong*. She's my *mother* . . ." She couldn't finish the sentence.

Camden didn't flinch. "I don't think I was. But you're an adult now. You can see her if you wish."

He went on looking at her from his bright, sunken eyes, while around Leisha the air heaved and snapped. Her father had lied to her. Susan watched her closely, a small smile on her lips. Was she glad to see Camden fall in his daughter's estimation? Had she all along been that jealous of their relationship, of Leisha . . .

She was thinking like Tony.

The thought steadied her a little. But she went on staring at Camden, who went on staring implacably back, unbudged, a man positive even on his death bed that he was right.

Alice's hand was on her elbow, Alice's voice so soft that no one but Leisha could hear. "He's done now, Leisha. And after a while you'll be all right."

Alice had left her son in California with her husband of two years, Beck Watrous, a building contractor she had met while waitressing in a resort on the Artificial Islands. Beck had adopted Jordan, Alice's son.

"Before Beck there was a real bad time," Alice said in her remote voice. "You know, when I was carrying Jordan I actually used to dream that he would be Sleepless? Like you. Every night I'd dream that, and every morning I'd wake up and have morning sickness with a baby that was only going to be a stupid nothing like me. I stayed with Ed—in Pennsylvania, remember? You came to see me there once—for two more years. When he beat me, I was glad. I wished Daddy could see. At least Ed was touching me."

Leisha made a sound in her throat.

"I finally left because I was afraid for Jordan. I went to California, did nothing but eat for a year. I got up to 190 pounds." Alice was, Leisha estimated, five-foot-four. "Then I came home to see Mother."

"You didn't tell me," Leisha said. "You knew she was alive and you didn't tell me."

"She's in a drying-out tank half the time," Alice said, with brutal simplicity. "She wouldn't see you if you wanted to. But she saw me, and she fell slobbering all over me as her 'real' daughter, and she threw up on my dress. And I backed away from her and looked at the dress and knew it *should* be thrown up on, it was so ugly. Deliberately ugly. She started screaming how Dad had ruined her life, ruined mine, all for *you*. And do you know what I did?"

"What?" Leisha said. Her voice was shaky.

"I flew home, burned all my clothes, got a job, started college, lost fifty pounds, and put Jordan in play therapy."

The sisters sat silent. Beyond the window the lake was dark, unlit by moon or stars. It was Leisha who suddenly shook, and Alice who patted her shoulder.

"Tell me . . ." Leisha couldn't think what she wanted to be told, except that she wanted to hear Alice's voice in the gloom, Alice's voice as it was now, gentle and remote, without damage anymore from the damaging fact of Leisha's existence. Her very existence as damage. ". . . tell me about Jordan. He's five now? What's he like?"

Alice turned her head to look levelly into Leisha's eyes. "He's a happy ordinary little boy. Completely ordinary."

Camden died a week later. After the funeral, Leisha tried to see her mother at the Brookfield Drug and Alcohol Abuse Center. Elizabeth Camden, she was told, saw no one except her only child, Alice Camden Watrous.

Susan Melling, dressed in black, drove Leisha to the airport. Susan talked deftly, determinedly, about Leisha's studies, about Harvard, about the *Review*. Leisha answered in monosyllables but Susan persisted, asking questions, quietly insisting on answers: When would Leisha take her bar exams? Where was she interviewing for jobs? Gradually Leisha began to lose the numbness she had felt since her father's casket was lowered into the ground. She realized that Susan's persistent questioning was a kindness.

"He sacrificed a lot of people," Leisha said suddenly.

"Not me," Susan said. She pulled the car into the airport parking lot. "Only for a while there, when I gave up my work to do his. Roger didn't respect sacrifice much."

"Was he wrong?" Leisha said. The question came out with a kind of desperation she hadn't intended.

Susan smiled sadly. "No. He wasn't wrong. I should never have left my research. It took me a long time to come back to myself after that."

He does that to people, Leisha heard inside her head. Susan? Or Alice? She couldn't, for once, remember clearly. She saw her father in the old conservatory, potting and repotting the dramatic exotic flowers he had loved.

She was tired. It was muscle fatigue from stress, she knew; twenty minutes of rest would restore her. Her eyes burned from unaccustomed tears. She leaned her head back against the car seat and closed them.

Susan pulled the car into the airport parking lot and turned off the ignition. "There's something I want to tell you, Leisha."

Leisha opened her eyes. "About the will?"

Susan smiled tightly. "No. You really don't have any problems with how he divided the estate, do you? It seems to you reasonable. But that's not it. The research team from Biotech and Chicago Medical has finished its analysis of Bernie Kuhn's brain."

Leisha turned to face Susan. She was startled by the complexity of Susan's expression. Determination, and satisfaction, and anger, and something else Leisha could not name.

Susan said, "We're going to publish next week, in the *New England Journal of Medicine*. Security has been unbelievably restricted—no leaks to the popular press. But I want to tell you now, myself, what we found. So you'll be prepared."

"Go on," Leisha said. Her chest felt tight.

"Do you remember when you and the other Sleepless kids took interleukin-1 to see what sleep was like? When you were sixteen?"

"How did you know about that?"

"You kids were watched a lot more closely than you think. Remember the headache you got?"

"Yes." She and Richard and Tony and Carol and Jeanine . . . after her rejection by the Olympic Committee, Jeanine had never skated again. She was a kindergarten teacher in Butte, Montana.

"Interleukin-1 is what I want to talk about. At least partly. It's one of a whole group of substances that boost the immune system. They stimulate the production of antibodies, the activity of white blood cells, and a host of other immunoenhancements. Normal people have surges of IL-1 released during the slow-wave phases of sleep: That means that they—we—are getting boosts to the immune system during sleep. One of the questions we researchers asked ourselves twenty-eight years ago was: Will Sleepless kids who don't get those surges of IL-1 get sick more often?"

"I've never been sick," Leisha said.

"Yes, you have. Chicken pox and three minor colds by the end of your fourth year," Susan said precisely. "But in general you were all a very healthy lot. So we researchers were left with the alternate theory of sleep-driven immunoenhancement: That the burst of immune activity existed as a counterpart to a greater vulnerability of the body in sleep to disease, probably in some way connected to the fluctuations in body temperature during REM sleep. In other words, sleep *caused* the immune vulnerability that endogenous pyrogens like IL-1 counteract. Sleep was the problem, immune system enhancements were the solution. Without sleep, there would be no problem. Are you following this?"

"Yes."

"Of course you are. Stupid question." Susan brushed her hair off her face. It was going gray at the temples. There was a tiny brown age spot beneath her right ear.

"Over the years we collected thousands—maybe hundreds of thousands—of Single Photon Emission Tomography scans of you and the other kids' brains, plus endless EEG's, samples of cerebrospinal fluid, and all the rest of it. But we couldn't really see inside your brains, really know what's going on in there. Until Bernie Kuhn hit that embankment."

"Susan," Leisha said, "give it to me straight. Without more build-up."

"You're not going to age."

"What?"

"Oh, cosmetically, yes. Gray hair, wrinkles, sags. But the absence of sleep peptides and all the rest of it affects the immune and tissue-restoration systems in ways we don't understand. Bernie Kuhn had a perfect liver. Perfect lungs, perfect heart, perfect lymph nodes, perfect pancreas, perfect medulla oblongata. Not just healthy, or young—*perfect*. There's a tissue regeneration enhancement that clearly derives from the operation of the immune system but is radically different from anything we ever suspected. Organs show no wear and tear—not even the minimal amount expected in a seventeen-year-old. They just repair themselves, perfectly, on and on . . . and on."

"For how long?" Leisha whispered.

"Who the hell knows? Bernie Kuhn was young—maybe there's some compensatory mechanism that cuts in at some point and you'll all just collapse, like an entire fucking gallery of Dorian Grays. But I don't think so. Neither do I think it can go on forever; no tissue regeneration can do that. But a long, long time."

Leisha stared at the blurred reflections in the car windshield. She saw her father's face against the blue satin of his casket, banked with white roses. His heart, unregenerated, had given out.

Susan said, "The future is all speculative at this point. We know that the peptide structures that build up the pressure to sleep in normal people resemble the components of bacterial cell walls. Maybe there's a connection between sleep and pathogen receptivity. We don't know. But ignorance never stopped the tabloids. I wanted to prepare you because you're going to get called supermen, *homo perfectus*, who-all-knows what. Immortal."

The two women sat in silence. Finally Leisha said, "I'm going to tell the others. On our datanet. Don't worry about the security. Kevin Baker designed Groupnet; nobody knows anything we don't want them to."

"You're that well organized already?"

"Yes."

Susan's mouth worked. She looked away from Leisha. "We better go in. You'll miss your flight."

"Susan . . ."

"What?"

"Thank you."

"You're welcome," Susan said, and in her voice Leisha heard the thing she had seen before in Susan's expression and not been able to name: It was longing.

Tissue regeneration. A long, long time, sang the blood in Leisha's ears on the flight to Boston. *Tissue regeneration*. And, eventually: *Immortal*. No, not that, she told herself severely. Not that. The blood didn't listen.

"You sure smile a lot," said the man next to her in first class, a business traveler who had not recognized Leisha. "You coming from a big party in Chicago?"

"No. From a funeral."

The man looked shocked, then disgusted. Leisha looked out the window at the ground far below. Rivers like micro-circuits, fields like neat index cards. And on the horizon, fluffy white clouds like masses of exotic flower blooms in a conservatory filled with light.

The letter was no thicker than any hard-copy mail, but hard-copy mail addressed by hand to either of them was so rare that Richard was nervous. "It might be explosive." Leisha looked at the letter on their hall credenza. MS. LIESHA CAMDEN. Block letters, misspelled.

"It looks like a child's writing," she said.

Richard stood with head lowered, legs braced apart. But his expression was only weary. "Perhaps deliberately like a child's. You'd be more open to a child's writing, they might have figured."

"'They'? Richard, are we getting that paranoid?"

He didn't flinch from the question. "Yes. For the time being."

A week earlier the *New England Journal of Medicine* had published Susan's careful, sober article. An hour later the broadcast and datanet news had exploded in speculation, drama, outrage, and fear. Leisha and Richard, along with all the Sleepless on the Groupnet, had tracked and charted each of four components, looking for a dominant reaction: speculation ("The Sleepless may live for centuries, and this might lead to the following events . . ."); drama ("If a Sleepless marries only Sleepers, he may have lifetime enough for a dozen brides—and several dozen children, a bewildering blended family . . ."); outrage ("Tampering with the law of nature has only brought among us unnatural so-called people who will live with the unfair advantage of time: time to accumulate more kin, more power, more property than the rest of us could ever know . . ."); and fear ("How soon before the Super-race takes over?").

"They're all fear, of one kind or another," Carolyn Rizzolo finally said, and the Groupnet stopped their differentiated tracking.

Leisha was taking the final exams of her last year of law school. Each day comments followed her to the campus, along the corridors and in the classroom; each day she forgot them in the grueling exam sessions, all students reduced to the same status of petitioner to the great university. Afterward, temporarily drained, she walked silently back home to Richard and the Groupnet, aware of the looks of people on the street, aware of her bodyguard Bruce striding between her and them.

"It will calm down," Leisha said. Richard didn't answer.

The town of Salt Springs, Texas, passed a local ordinance that no Sleepless could obtain a liquor license, on the grounds that civil rights statutes were built on the "all men were created equal" clause of the Constitution, and Sleepless clearly were not covered. There were no Sleepless within a hundred miles of Salt Springs and no one had applied for a new liquor license there for the past ten years, but the story was picked up by United Press and by Datanet News, and within twenty-four hours heated editorials appeared, on both sides of the issue, across the nation.

More local ordinances appeared. In Pollux, Pennsylvania, the Sleepless could be denied apartment rental on the grounds that their prolonged wakefulness would increase both wear-and-tear on the landlord's property and utility bills. In Cranston Estates, California, Sleepless were barred from operating twenty-four-hour businesses: "unfair competition." Iroquois County, New York, barred them from serving on county juries, arguing that a jury containing Sleepless, with their skewed idea of time, did not constitute "a jury of one's peers."

"All those statutes will be thrown out in superior courts," Leisha said. "But God! The waste of money and docket time to do it!" A part of her mind noticed that her tone as she said this was Roger Camden's.

The state of Georgia, in which some sex acts between consenting adults were still a crime, made sex between a Sleepless and a Sleeper a third-degree felony, classing it with bestiality.

Kevin Baker had designed software that scanned the newsnets at high speed, flagged all stories involving discrimination or attacks on Sleepless, and categorized them by type. The files were available on Groupnet. Leisha read through them, then called Kevin. "Can't you create a parallel program to flag defenses of us? We're getting a skewed picture."

"You're right," Kevin said, a little startled. "I didn't think of it."

"Think of it," Leisha said, grimly. Richard, watching her, said nothing.

She was most upset by the stories about Sleepless children. Shunning at school, verbal abuse by siblings, attacks by neighborhood bullies, confused resentment from parents who had wanted an exceptional child but had not bargained on one who might live centuries. The school board of Cold River, Iowa, voted to bar Sleepless children from conventional classrooms because their rapid learning "created feelings of inadequacy in others, interfering with their education." The board made funds available for Sleepless to have tutors at home. There were no volunteers among the teaching staff. Leisha started spending as much time on Groupnet with the kids, talking to them all night long, as she did studying for her bar exams, scheduled for July.

Stella Bevington stopped using her modem.

Kevin's second program catalogued editorials urging fairness towards Sleepless.

The school board of Denver set aside funds for a program in which gifted children, including the Sleepless, could use their talents and build teamwork through tutoring even younger children. Rive Beau, Louisiana, elected Sleepless Danielle du Cherney to the City Council, although Danielle was twenty-two and technically too young to qualify. The prestigious medical research firm of Halley-Hall gave much publicity to their hiring of Christopher Amren, a Sleepless with a Ph.D. in cellular physics.

Dora Clarq, a Sleepless in Dallas, opened a letter addressed to her and a plastic explosive blew off her arm.

Leisha and Richard stared at the envelope on the hall credenza. The paper was thick, cream-colored, but not expensive: the kind of paper made of bulky newsprint dyed the shade of vellum. There was no return address. Richard called Liz Bishop, a Sleepless who was majoring in Criminal Justice in Michigan. He had never spoken with her before—neither had Leisha—but she came on Groupnet immediately and told them how to open it, or she could fly up and do it if they preferred. Richard and Leisha followed her directions for remote detonation in the basement of the townhouse. Nothing blew up. When the letter was open, they took it out and read it:

> Dear Ms. Camden,
>
> You been pretty good to me and I'm sorry to do this but I quit. They are making it pretty hot for me at the union not officially but you know how it is. If I was you I wouldn't go to the union for another bodyguard I'd try to find one privately. But be careful. Again I'm sorry but I have to live too.
>
> Bruce

"I don't know whether to laugh or cry," Leisha said. "The two of us getting all this equipment, spending hours on this set-up so an explosive won't detonate . . ."

"It's not as if I at least had a whole lot else to do," Richard said. Since the wave of anti-Sleepless sentiment, all but two of his marine-consultant clients, vulnerable to the marketplace and thus to public opinion, had canceled their accounts.

Groupnet, still up on Leisha's terminal, shrilled in emergency override. Leisha got there first. It was Tony.

"Leisha. I'll need your legal help, if you'll give it. They're trying to fight me on Sanctuary. Please fly down here."

Sanctuary was raw brown gashes in the late-spring earth. It was situated in the Allegheny Mountains of southern New York State, old hills rounded by age and covered with pine and hickory. A superb road led from the closest town, Belmont, to Sanctuary. Low, maintenance-free buildings, whose design was plain but graceful, stood in various stages of completion. Jennifer Sharifi, looking strained, met Leisha and Richard. "Tony wants to talk to you, but first he asked me to show you both around."

"What's wrong?" Leisha asked quietly. She had never met Jennifer before but no Sleepless looked like that—pinched, spent, *weary*—unless the stress level was enormous.

Jennifer didn't try to evade the question. "Later. First look at Sanctuary. Tony respects your opinion enormously, Leisha; he wants you to see everything."

The dormitories each held fifty, with communal rooms for cooking, dining, relaxing, and bathing, and a warren of separate offices and studios and labs for work. "We're calling them 'dorms' anyway, despite the etymology," Jennifer said, trying to smile. Leisha glanced at Richard. The smile was a failure.

She was impressed, despite herself, with the completeness of Tony's plans for lives that would be both communal and intensely private. There was a gym, a small hospital—"By the end of next year, we'll have eighteen AMA-certified doctors, you know, and four are thinking of coming here"—a daycare facility, a school, an intensive-crop farm. "Most of our food will come in from the outside, of course. So will most people's jobs, although they'll do as much of them as possible from here, over datanets. We're not cutting ourselves off from the world—only creating a safe place from which to trade with it." Leisha didn't answer.

Apart from the power facilities, self-supported Y-energy, she was most impressed with the human planning. Tony had Sleepless interested from virtually every field they would need both to care for themselves and to deal with the outside world. "Lawyers and accountants come first," Jennifer said. "That's our first line of defense in safeguarding ourselves. Tony recognizes that most modern battles for power are fought in the courtroom and boardroom."

But not all. Last, Jennifer showed them the plans for physical defense. She explained them with a mixture of defiance and pride: Every effort had been made to stop attackers without hurting them. Electronic surveillance completely circled the 150 square miles Jennifer had purchased—some *counties* were smaller than that, Leisha thought, dazed. When breached, a force field a half-mile within the E-gate activated, delivering electric shocks to anyone on foot—"But only on the *outside* of the field. We don't want any of our kids hurt." Unmanned penetration by vehicles or robots was identified by a system that located all moving metal above a certain mass within Sanctuary. Any moving metal that did not carry a special signaling device designed by Donna Pospula, a Sleepless who had patented important electronic components, was suspect.

"Of course, we're not set up for an air attack or an outright army assault," Jennifer said. "But we don't expect that. Only the haters in self-motivated hate." Her voice sagged.

Leisha touched the hard-copy of the security plans with one finger. They troubled her. "If we can't integrate ourselves into the world . . . free trade should imply free movement."

"Yeah. Well," Jennifer said, such an uncharacteristic Sleepless remark—both cynical and inarticulate—that Leisha looked up. "I have something to tell you, Leisha."

"What?"

"Tony isn't here."

"Where is he?"

"In Allegheny County jail. It's true we're having zoning battles about Sanctuary—zoning! In this isolated spot! But this is something else, something that just happened this morning. Tony's been arrested for the kidnapping of Timmy DeMarzo."

The room wavered. "FBI?"

"Yes."

"How . . . how did they find out?"

"Some agent eventually cracked the case. They didn't tell us how. Tony needs a lawyer, Leisha. Dana Monteiro has already agreed, but Tony wants you."

"Jennifer—I don't even take the bar exams until July!"

"He says he'll wait. Dana will act as his lawyer in the meantime. Will you pass the bar?"

"Of course. But I already have a job lined up with Morehouse, Kennedy, & Anderson in New York—" She stopped. Richard was looking at her hard, Jennifer gazing down at the floor. Leisha said quietly, "What will he plead?"

"Guilty," Jennifer said, "with—what is it called legally? Extenuating circumstances."

Leisha nodded. She had been afraid Tony would want to plead not guilty: more lies, subterfuge, ugly politics. Her mind ran swiftly over extenuating circumstances, precedents, tests to precedents. . . . They could use *Clements v. Voy* . . .

"Dana is at the jail now," Jennifer said. "Will you drive in with me?"

"Yes."

In Belmont, the county seat, they were not allowed to see Tony. Dana Monteiro, as his attorney, could go in and out freely. Leisha, not officially an attorney at all, could go nowhere. This was told them by a man in the D.A.'s office whose face stayed immobile while he spoke to them, and who spat on the ground behind their shoes when they turned to leave, even though this left him with a smear of spittle on his courthouse floor.

Richard and Leisha drove their rental car to the airport for the flight back to Boston. On the way Richard told Leisha he was leaving her. He was moving to Sanctuary, now, even before it was functional, to help with the planning and building.

She stayed most of the time in her townhouse, studying ferociously for the bar exams or checking on the Sleepless children through Groupnet. She had not hired another bodyguard to replace Bruce, which made her reluctant to go outside very much; the reluctance in turn made her angry with herself. Once or twice a day she scanned Kevin's electronic news clippings.

There were signs of hope. The *New York Times* ran an editorial, widely reprinted on the electronic news services:

PROSPERITY AND HATRED: A LOGIC CURVE WE'D RATHER NOT SEE

The United States has never been a country that much values calm, logic, rationality. We have, as a people, tended to label these things "cold." We have, as a people, tended to admire feeling and action: We exalt in our stories and our memorials, not the creation of the Constitution but its defense at Iwo Jima; not the intellectual achievements of a Stephen Hawking but the heroic passion of a Charles Lindbergh; not the inventors of the monorails and computers that unite us but the composers of the angry songs of rebellion that divide us.

A peculiar aspect of this phenomenon is that it grows stronger in times of prosperity. The better off our citizenry, the greater their contempt for the calm reasoning that got them there, and the more passionate their indulgence in emotion. Consider, in the last century, the gaudy excesses of the Roaring Twenties and the anti-establishment contempt of the sixties. Consider, in our own century, the unprecedented prosperity brought about by Y-energy—and then consider that Kenzo Yagai, except to his followers, was seen as a greedy and bloodless logician, while our national adulation goes to neo-nihilist writer Stephen Castelli, to "feelie" actress Brenda Foss, and to daredevil gravity-well diver Jim Morse Luter.

But most of all, as you ponder this phenomenon in your Y-energy houses, consider the current outpouring of irrational feeling directed at the "Sleepless" since the publication of the joint findings of the Biotech Institute and the Chicago Medical School concerning Sleepless tissue regeneration.

Most of the Sleepless are intelligent. Most of them are calm, if you define that much-maligned word to mean directing one's energies into solving problems rather than to emoting about them. (Even Pulitzer Prize winner Carolyn Rizzolo gave us a stunning play of ideas, not of passions run amuck.) All of them show a natural bent toward achievement, a bent given a decided boost by the one-third more time in their days to achieve in. Their achievements lie, for the most part, in logical fields rather than emotional ones: Computers. Law. Finance. Physics. Medical research. They are rational, orderly, calm, intelligent, cheerful, young, and possibly very long-lived.

And, in our United States of unprecedented prosperity, increasingly hated.

Does the hatred that we have seen flower so fully over the last few months really grow, as many claim, from the "unfair advantage" the Sleepless have over the rest of us in securing jobs, promotions, money, success? Is it really envy over the Sleepless' good fortune? Or does it come from something more pernicious, rooted in our tradition of shoot-from-the-hip American action: Hatred of the logical, the calm, the considered? Hatred in fact of the superior mind?

If so, perhaps we should think deeply about the founders of this country: Jefferson, Washington, Paine, Adams—inhabitants of the Age of Reason, all. These men created our orderly and balanced system of laws precisely to protect the property and achievements created by the individual efforts of balanced and rational minds. The Sleepless may be our severest internal test yet of our own sober belief in law and order. No, the Sleepless were *not* "created equal," but our attitudes toward them should be examined with a care equal to our soberest jurisprudence. We may not like what we learn about our own motives, but our credibility as a people may depend on the rationality and intelligence of the examination.

Both have been in short supply in the public reaction to last month's research findings.

Law is not theater. Before we write laws reflecting gaudy and dramatic feelings, we must be very sure we understand the difference.

Leisha hugged herself, gazing in delight at the screen, smiling. She called the *New York Times*: Who had written the editorial? The receptionist, cordial when she answered the phone, grew brusque. The *Times* was not releasing that information, "prior to internal investigation."

It could not dampen her mood. She whirled around the apartment, after days of sitting at her desk or screen. Delight demanded physical action. She washed dishes, picked up books. There were gaps in the furniture patterns where Richard had taken pieces that belonged to him; a little quieter now, she moved the furniture to close the gaps.

Susan Melling called to tell her about the *Times* editorial; they talked warmly for a few minutes. When Susan hung up, the phone rang again.

"Leisha? Your voice still sounds the same. This is Stewart Sutter."

"Stewart." She had not seen him for years. Their romance had lasted two years and then dissolved, not from any painful issue so much as from the press of both their studies. Standing by the comm terminal, hearing his voice, Leisha suddenly felt again his hands on her breasts in the cramped dormitory bed: All those years before she had found a good use for a bed. The phantom hands became Richard's hands, and a sudden pain pierced her.

"Listen," Stewart said, "I'm calling because there's some information I think you should know. You take your bar exams next week, right? And then you have a tentative job with Morehouse, Kennedy, & Anderson."

"How do you know all that, Stewart?"

"Men's room gossip. Well, not as bad as that. But the New York legal community—

that part of it, anyway—is smaller than you think. And, you're a pretty visible figure."

"Yes," Leisha said neutrally.

"Nobody has the slightest doubt you'll be called to the bar. But there is some doubt about the job with Morehouse, Kennedy. You've got two senior partners, Alan Morehouse and Seth Brown, who have changed their minds since this . . . flap. 'Adverse publicity for the firm,' 'turning law into a circus,' blah blah blah. You know the drill. But you've also got two powerful champions, Ann Carlyle and Michael Kennedy, the old man himself. He's quite a mind. Anyway, I wanted you to know all this so you can recognize exactly what the situation is and know whom to count on in the in-fighting."

"Thank you," Leisha said. "Stew . . . why do you care if I get it or not? Why should it matter to you?"

There was a silence on the other end of the phone. Then Stewart said, very low, "We're not all noodleheads out here, Leisha. Justice does still matter to some of us. So does achievement."

Light rose in her, a bubble of buoyant light.

Stewart said, "You have a lot of support here for that stupid zoning fight over Sanctuary, too. You might not realize that, but you do. What the Parks Commission crowd is trying to pull is . . . but they're just being used as fronts. You know that. Anyway, when it gets as far as the courts, you'll have all the help you need."

"Sanctuary isn't my doing. At all."

"No? Well, I meant the plural you."

"Thank you. I mean that. How are you doing?"

"Fine. I'm a daddy now."

"Really! Boy or girl?"

"Girl. A beautiful little bitch, drives me crazy. I'd like you to meet my wife sometime, Leisha."

"I'd like that," Leisha said.

She spent the rest of the night studying for her bar exams. The bubble stayed with her. She recognized exactly what it was: joy.

It was going to be all right. The contract, unwritten, between her and her society—Kenzo Yagai's society, Roger Camden's society—would hold. With dissent and strife and yes, some hatred: She suddenly thought of Tony's beggars in Spain, furious at the strong because they themselves were not. Yes. But it would hold.

She believed that.

She did.

7

Leisha took her bar exams in July. They did not seem hard to her. Afterward three classmates, two men and a woman, made a fakely casual point of talking to Leisha until she had climbed safely into a taxi whose driver obviously did not recognize her, or stop signs. The three were all Sleepers. A pair of undergraduates, clean-shaven blond men with the long faces and pointless arrogance of rich stupidity, eyed Leisha and sneered. Leisha's female classmate sneered back.

Leisha had a flight to Chicago the next morning. Alice was going to join her there. They had to clean out the big house on the lake, dispose of Roger's personal property, put the house on the market. Leisha had had no time to do it earlier.

She remembered her father in the conservatory, wearing an ancient flat-topped hat he had picked up somewhere, potting orchids and jasmine and passion flowers.

When the doorbell rang she was startled; she almost never had visitors. Eagerly, she turned on the outside camera—maybe it was Jonathan or Martha, back in Boston to surprise her, to celebrate—why hadn't she thought before about some sort of celebration?

Richard stood gazing up at the camera. He had been crying.

She tore open the door. Richard made no move to come in. Leisha saw that what the camera had registered as grief was actually something else: tears of rage.

"Tony's dead."

Leisha put out her hand, blindly. Richard did not take it.

"They killed him in prison. Not the authorities—the other prisoners. In the recreation yard. Murderers, rapists, looters, scum of the earth—and they thought they had the right to kill *him* because he was different."

Now Richard did grab her arm, so hard that something, some bone, shifted beneath the flesh and pressed on a nerve. "Not just different—*better*. Because he was better, because we all are, we goddamn just don't stand up and shout it out of some misplaced feeling for *their* feelings . . . God!"

Leisha pulled her arm free and rubbed it, numb, staring at Richard's contorted face.

"They beat him to death with a lead pipe. No one even knows how they got a lead pipe. They beat him on the back of the head and they rolled him over and—"

"Don't!" Leisha said. It came out a whimper.

Richard looked at her. Despite his shouting, his violent grip on her arm, Leisha had the confused impression that this was the first time he had actually seen her. She went on rubbing her arm, staring at him in terror.

He said quietly, "I've come to take you to Sanctuary, Leisha. Dan Walcott and Vernon Bulriss are in the car outside. The three of us will carry you out, if necessary. But you're coming. You see that, don't you? You're not safe here, with your high profile and your spectacular looks—you're a natural target if anyone is. Do we have to force you? Or do you finally see for yourself that we have no choice—the bastards have left us no choice—except Sanctuary?"

Leisha closed her eyes. Tony, at fourteen, at the beach. Tony, his eyes ferocious and alight, the first to reach out his hand for the glass of interleukin-1. Beggars in Spain.

"I'll come."

She had never known such anger. It scared her, coming in bouts throughout the long night, receding but always returning again. Richard held her in his arms, sitting with their backs against the wall of her library, and his holding made no difference at all. In the living room Dan and Vernon talked in low voices.

Sometimes the anger erupted in shouting, and Leisha heard herself and thought *I don't know you.* Sometimes it became crying, sometimes talking about Tony, about all of them. Not the shouting nor the crying nor the talking eased her at all.

Planning did, a little. In a cold dry voice she didn't recognize, Leisha told Richard about the trip to close the house in Chicago. She had to go; Alice was already there. If Richard and Dan and Vernon put Leisha on the plane, and Alice met her at the other end with union bodyguards, she should be safe enough. Then she would change her return ticket from Boston to Belmont and drive with Richard to Sanctuary.

"People are already arriving," Richard said. "Jennifer Sharifi is organizing it, greasing the Sleeper suppliers with so much money they can't resist. What about this townhouse here, Leisha? Your furniture and terminal and clothes?"

Leisha looked around her familiar office. Law books lined the walls, red and green and brown, although most of the same information was on-line. A coffee cup rested on a print-out on the desk. Beside it was the receipt she had requested from the taxi driver this afternoon, a giddy souvenir of the day she had passed her bar exams; she had thought of having it framed. Above the desk was a holographic portrait of Kenzo Yagai.

"Let it rot," Leisha said.

Richard's arm tightened around her.

"I've never seen you like this," Alice said, subdued. "It's more than just clearing out the house, isn't it?"

"Let's get on with it," Leisha said. She yanked a suit from her father's closet. "Do you want any of this stuff for your husband?"

"It wouldn't fit."

"The hats?"

"No," Alice said. "Leisha—what is it?"

"Let's just *do* it!" She yanked all the clothes from Camden's closet, piled them on the floor, scrawled FOR VOLUNTEER AGENCY on a piece of paper and dropped it on top of the pile. Silently, Alice started adding clothes from the dresser, which already bore a taped paper scrawled ESTATE AUCTION.

The curtains were already down throughout the house; Alice had done that yesterday. She had also rolled up the rugs. Sunset glared redly on the bare wooden floors.

"What about your old room?" Leisha said. "What do you want there?"

"I've already tagged it," Alice said. "A mover will come Thursday."

"Fine. What else?"

"The conservatory. Sanderson has been watering everything, but he didn't really know what needed how much, so some of the plants are—"

"Fire Sanderson," Leisha said curtly. "The exotics can die. Or have them sent to a hospital, if you'd rather. Just watch out for the ones that are poisonous. Come on, let's do the library."

Alice sat slowly on a rolled-up rug in the middle of Camden's bedroom. She had cut her hair; Leisha thought it looked ugly, jagged brown spikes around her broad face. She had also gained more weight. She was starting to look like their mother.

Alice said, "Do you remember the night I told you I was pregnant? Just before you left for Harvard?"

"Let's do the library!"

"Do you?" Alice said. "For God's sake, can't you just once listen to someone else, Leisha? Do you have to be so much like Daddy every single minute?"

"I'm not like Daddy!"

"The hell you're not. You're exactly what he made you. But that's not the point. Do you remember that night?"

Leisha walked over the rug and out the door. Alice simply sat. After a minute Leisha walked back in. "I remember."

"You were near tears," Alice said implacably. Her voice was quiet. "I don't even remember exactly why. Maybe because I wasn't going to college after all. But I put my arms around you, and for the first time in years—years, Leisha—I felt you really were my sister. Despite all of it—the roaming the halls all night and the show-off arguments with Daddy and the special school and the artificially long legs and golden hair—all that crap. You seemed to need me to hold you. You seemed to need me. You seemed to *need*."

"What are you saying?" Leisha demanded. "That you can only be close to someone if they're in trouble and need you? That you can only be a sister if I was in some kind of pain, open sores running? Is that the bond between you Sleepers? 'Protect me while I'm unconscious, I'm just as crippled as you are'?"

"No," Alice said. "I'm saying that *you* could be a sister only if you were in some kind of pain."

Leisha stared at her. "You're stupid, Alice."

Alice said calmly, "I know that. Compared to you, I am. I know that."

Leisha jerked her head angrily. She felt ashamed of what she had just said, and yet it was true, and they both knew it was true, and anger still lay in her like a dark void, formless and hot. It was the formless part that was the worst. Without shape, there could be no action; without action, the anger went on burning her, choking her.

Alice said, "When I was twelve Susan gave me a dress for our birthday. You were away somewhere, on one of those overnight field trips your fancy progressive school did all the time. The dress was silk, pale blue, with antique lace—very beautiful. I was thrilled, not only because it was beautiful but because Susan had gotten it for me and gotten software for you. The dress was mine. Was, I thought, *me*." In the gathering gloom Leisha could barely make out her broad, plain features. 'The first time I wore it a boy said, 'Stole your sister's dress, Alice? Snitched it while she was *sleeping*?' Then he laughed like crazy, the way they always did.

"I threw the dress away. I didn't even explain to Susan, although I think she would have understood. Whatever was yours was yours, and whatever wasn't yours was yours, too. That's the way Daddy set it up. The way he hard-wired it into our genes."

"You, too?" Leisha said. "You're no different from the other envious beggars?"

Alice stood up from the rug. She did it slowly, leisurely, brushing dust off the back of her wrinkled skirt, smoothing the print fabric. Then she walked over and hit Leisha in the mouth.

"Now do you see me as real?" Alice asked quietly.

Leisha put her hand to her mouth. She felt blood. The phone rang, Camden's unlisted personal line. Alice walked over, picked it up, listened, and held it calmly out to Leisha. "It's for you."

Numb, Leisha took it.

"Leisha? This is Kevin. Listen, something's happened. Stella Bevington called me, on the phone not Groupnet, I think her parents took away her modem. I picked up the phone and she screamed, 'This is Stella! They're hitting me he's drunk—' and then the line went dead. Randy's gone to Sanctuary—hell, they've *all* gone. You're closest to her, she's still in Skokie. You better get there fast. Have you got bodyguards you trust?"

"Yes," Leisha said, although she hadn't. The anger—finally—took form. "I can handle it."

"I don't know how you'll get her out of there," Kevin said. "They'll recognize you, they know she called somebody, they might even have knocked her out . . ."

"I'll handle it," Leisha said.

"Handle what?" Alice said.

Leisha faced her. Even though she knew she shouldn't, she said, "What your people do. To one of ours. A seven-year-old kid who's getting beaten up by her parents because she's Sleepless—because she's *better* than you are—" She ran down the stairs and out to the rental car she had driven from the airport.

Alice ran right down with her. "Not your car, Leisha. They can trace a rental car just like that. My car."

Leisha screamed, "If you think you're—"

Alice yanked open the door of her battered Toyota, a model so old the Y-energy cones weren't even concealed but hung like drooping jowls on either side. She shoved Leisha into the passenger seat, slammed the door, and rammed herself behind the wheel. Her hands were steady. "Where?"

Blackness swooped over Leisha. She put her head down, as far between her knees as the cramped Toyota would allow. Two—no, three—days since she had eaten. Since the night before the bar exams. The faintness receded, swept over her again as soon as she raised her head.

She told Alice the address in Skokie.

"Stay way in the back," Alice said. "And there's a scarf in the glove compartment—put it on. Low, to hide as much of your face as possible."

Alice had stopped the car along Highway 42. Leisha said, "This isn't—"

"It's a union quick-guard place. We have to look like we have some protection, Leisha. We don't need to tell him anything. I'll hurry."

She was out in three minutes with a huge man in a cheap dark suit. He squeezed into the front seat beside Alice and said nothing at all. Alice did not introduce him.

The house was small, a little shabby, with lights on downstairs, none upstairs. The first stars shone in the north, away from Chicago. Alice said to the guard, "Get out of the car and stand here by the car door—no, more in the light—and don't do anything unless I'm attacked in some way." The man nodded. Alice started up the walk. Leisha scrambled out of the back seat and caught her sister two-thirds of the way to the plastic front door.

"Alice, what the hell are you doing? I have to—"

"Keep your voice down," Alice said, glancing at the guard. "Leisha, *think*. You'll be recognized. Here, near Chicago, with a Sleepless daughter—these people have looked at your picture in magazines for years. They've watched long-range holovids of you. They know you. They know you're going to be a lawyer. Me they've never seen. I'm nobody."

"Alice—"

"For Chrissake, get back in the car!" Alice hissed, and pounded on the front door.

Leisha drew off the walk, into the shadow of a willow tree. A man opened the door. His face was completely blank.

Alice said, "Child Protection Agency. We got a call from a little girl, this number. Let me in."

"There's no little girl here."

"This is an emergency, priority one," Alice said. "Child Protection Act 186. Let me in!"

The man, still blank-faced, glanced at the huge figure by the car. "You got a search warrant?"

"I don't need one in a priority-one child emergency. If you don't let me in, you're going to have legal snarls like you never bargained for."

Leisha clamped her lips together. No one would believe that, it was legal gobbledygook. . . . Her lip throbbed where Alice had hit her.

The man stood aside to let Alice enter.

The guard started forward. Leisha hesitated, then let him. He entered with Alice.

Leisha waited, alone, in the dark.

In three minutes they were out, the guard carrying a child. Alice's broad face gleamed pale in the porch light. Leisha sprang forward, opened the car door, and helped the guard ease the child inside. The guard was frowning, a slow puzzled frown shot with wariness.

Alice said, "Here. This is an extra hundred dollars. To get back to the city by yourself."

"Hey . . ." the guard said, but he took the money. He stood looking after them as Alice pulled away.

"He'll go straight to the police," Leisha said despairingly. "He has to, or risk his union membership."

"I know," Alice said. "But by that time we'll be out of the car."

"*Where?*"

"At the hospital," Alice said.

"Alice, we can't—" Leisha didn't finish. She turned to the back seat. "Stella? Are you conscious?"

"Yes," said the small voice.

Leisha groped until her fingers found the rear-seat illuminator. Stella lay stretched out on the back seat, her face distorted with pain. She cradled her left arm in her right. A single bruise colored her face, above the left eye.

"You're Leisha Camden," the child said, and started to cry.

"Her arm's broken," Alice said.

"Honey, can you . . ." Leisha's throat felt thick, she had trouble getting the words out ". . . can you hold on till we get you to a doctor?"

"Yes," Stella said. "Just don't take me back there!"

"We won't," Leisha said. "Ever." She glanced at Alice and saw Tony's face.

Alice said, "There's a community hospital about ten miles south of here."

"How do you know that?"

"I was there once. Drug overdose," Alice said briefly. She drove hunched over the wheel, with the face of someone thinking furiously. Leisha thought, too, trying to see a way around the legal charge of kidnapping. They probably couldn't say the child came willingly: Stella would undoubtedly cooperate but at her age and in her condition she was probably *non sui juris*, her word would have no legal weight . . .

"Alice, we can't even get her into the hospital without insurance information. Verifiable on-line."

"Listen," Alice said, not to Leisha but over her shoulder, toward the back seat, "here's what we're going to do, Stella. I'm going to tell them you're my daughter and you fell off a big rock you were climbing while we stopped for a snack at a roadside picnic area. We're driving from California to Philadelphia to see your grandmother. Your name is Jordan Watrous and you're five years old. Got that, honey?"

"I'm seven," Stella said. "Almost eight."

"You're a very large five. Your birthday is March 23. Can you do this, Stella?"

"Yes," the little girl said. Her voice was stronger.

Leisha stared at Alice. "Can *you* do this?"

"Of course I can," Alice said. "I'm Roger Camden's daughter."

Alice half-carried, half-supported Stella into the emergency room of the small community hospital. Leisha watched from the car: the short stocky woman, the child's thin body with the twisted arm. Then she drove Alice's car to the farthest corner of the parking lot, under the dubious cover of a skimpy maple, and locked it. She tied the scarf more securely around her face.

Alice's license plate number, and her name, would be in every police and rental-car databank by now. The medical banks were slower; often they uploaded from local precincts only once a day, resenting the governmental interference in what was still, despite a half-century of battle, a private-sector enterprise. Alice and Stella would probably be all right in the hospital. Probably. But Alice could not rent another car.

Leisha could.

But the data file that would flash to rental agencies on Alice Camden Watrous might or might not include that she was Leisha Camden's twin.

Leisha looked at the rows of cars in the lot. A flashy luxury Chrysler, an Ikeda van, a row of middle-class Toyotas and Mercedes, a vintage '99 Cadillac—she could imagine the owner's face if that were missing—ten or twelve cheap runabouts, a hovercar with the uniformed driver asleep at the wheel. And a battered farm truck.

Leisha walked over to the truck. A man sat at the wheel, smoking. She thought of her father.

"Hello," Leisha said.

The man rolled down his window but didn't answer. He had greasy brown hair.

"See that hovercar over there?" Leisha said. She made her voice sound young, high. The man glanced at it indifferently; from this angle you couldn't see that the driver was asleep. "That's my bodyguard. He thinks I'm in the hospital, the way my father told me to, getting this lip looked at." She could feel her mouth swollen from Alice's blow.

"So?"

Leisha stamped her foot. "So I don't want to be inside. He's a shit and so's Daddy. I want *out*. I'll give you four thousand bank credits for your truck. Cash."

The man's eyes widened. He tossed away his cigarette, looked again at the hovercar. The driver's shoulders were broad, and the car was within easy screaming distance.

"All nice and legal," Leisha said, and tried to smirk. Her knees felt watery.

"Let me see the cash."

Leisha backed away from the truck, to where he could not reach her. She took the money from her arm clip. She was used to carrying a lot of cash; there had always been Bruce, or someone like Bruce. There had always been safety.

"Get out of the truck on the other side," Leisha said, "and lock the door behind you. Leave the keys on the seat, where I can see them from here. Then I'll put the money on the roof where you can see it."

The man laughed, a sound like gravel pouring. "Regular little Dabney Engh, aren't you? Is that what they teach you society debs at your fancy schools?"

Leisha had no idea who Dabney Engh was. She waited, watching the man try to think of a way to cheat her, and tried to hide her contempt. She thought of Tony.

"All right," he said, and slid out of the truck.

"Lock the door!"

He grinned, opened the door again, locked it. Leisha put the money on the roof, yanked open the driver's door, clambered in, locked the door, and powered up the window. The man laughed. She put the key into the ignition, started the truck, and drove toward the street. Her hands trembled.

She drove slowly around the block twice. When she came back, the man was gone, and the driver of the hovercar was still asleep. She had wondered if the man would wake him, out of sheer malice, but he had not. She parked the truck and waited.

An hour and a half later Alice and a nurse wheeled Stella out of the Emergency Entrance. Leisha leaped out of the truck and yelled, "Coming, Alice!" waving both her arms. It was too dark to see Alice's expression; Leisha could only hope that Alice showed no dismay at the battered truck, that she had not told the nurse to expect a red car.

Alice said, "This is Julie Bergadon, a friend that I called while you were setting Jordan's arm." The nurse nodded, uninterested. The two women helped Stella into the high truck cab; there was no back seat. Stella had a cast on her arm and looked drugged.

"How?" Alice said as they drove off.

Leisha didn't answer. She was watching a police hovercar land at the other end of the parking lot. Two officers got out and strode purposefully towards Alice's locked car under the skimpy maple.

"My God," Alice said. For the first time, she sounded frightened.

"They won't trace us," Leisha said. "Not to this truck. Count on it."

"Leisha." Alice's voice spiked with fear. "Stella's *asleep*."

Leisha glanced at the child, slumped against Alice's shoulder. "No, she's not. She's unconscious from painkillers."

"Is that all right? Normal? For . . . her?"

"We can black out. We can even experience substance-induced sleep." Tony and she and Richard and Jeanine in the midnight woods . . . "Didn't you know that, Alice?"

"No."

"We don't know very much about each other, do we?"

They drove south in silence. Finally Alice said, "Where are we going to take her, Leisha?"

"I don't know. Any one of the Sleepless would be the first place the police would check—"

"You can't risk it. Not the way things are," Alice said. She sounded weary. "But all my friends are in California. I don't think we could drive this rust bucket that far before getting stopped."

"It wouldn't make it anyway."

"What should we do?"

"Let me think."

At an expressway exit stood a pay phone. It wouldn't be data-shielded, as Groupnet was. Would Kevin's open line be tapped? Probably.

There was no doubt the Sanctuary line would be.

Sanctuary. All of them going there or already there, Kevin had said. Holed up, trying to pull the worn Allegheny Mountains around them like a safe little den. Except for the children like Stella, who could not.

Where? With whom?

Leisha closed her eyes. The Sleepless were out; the police would find Stella within hours. Susan Melling? But she had been Alice's all-too-visible stepmother, and was co-beneficiary of Camden's will; they would question her almost immediately. It couldn't be anyone traceable to Alice. It could only be a Sleeper that Leisha knew, and trusted, and why should anyone at all fit that description? Why should she risk so much on anyone who did? She stood a long time in the dark phone kiosk. Then she walked to the truck. Alice was asleep, her head thrown back against the seat. A tiny line of drool ran down her chin. Her face was white and drained in the bad light from the kiosk. Leisha walked back to the phone.

"Stewart? Stewart Sutter?"

"Yes?"

"This is Leisha Camden. Something has happened." She told the story tersely, in bald sentences. Stewart did not interrupt.

"Leisha—" Stewart said, and stopped.

"I need help, Stewart." *"I'll help you, Alice." "I don't need your help."* A wind whistled over the dark field beside the kiosk and Leisha shivered. She heard in the wind the thin keen of a beggar. In the wind, in her own voice.

"All right," Stewart said, "this is what we'll do. I have a cousin in Ripley, New York, just over the state line from Pennsylvania on the route you'll be driving east. It has to be in New York, I'm licensed in New York. Take the little girl there. I'll call my cousin and tell her you're coming. She's an elderly woman, was quite an activist in her youth, her name is Janet Patterson. The town is—"

"What makes you so sure she'll get involved? She could go to jail. And so could you."

"She's been in jail so many times you wouldn't believe it. Political protests going all the way back to Vietnam. But no one's going to jail. I'm now your attorney of record, I'm privileged. I'm going to get Stella declared a ward of the state. That shouldn't be too hard with the hospital records you established in Skokie. Then she can be transferred to a foster home in New York, I know just the place, people who are fair and kind. Then Alice—"

"She's resident in Illinois. You can't—"

"Yes, I can. Since those research findings about the Sleepless life span have come out, legislators have been railroaded by stupid constituents scared or jealous or just plain angry. The result is a body of so-called 'law' riddled with contradictions, absurdities, and loopholes. None of it will stand in the long run—or at least I hope not—but in the meantime it can all be exploited. I can use it to create the most goddamn convoluted case for Stella that anybody ever saw, and in meantime she won't be returned home. But that won't work for Alice—she'll need an attorney licensed in Illinois."

"We have one," Leisha said. "Candace Holt."

"No, not a Sleepless. Trust me on this, Leisha. I'll find somebody good. There's a man in—are you crying?"

"No," Leisha said, crying.

"Ah, God," Stewart said. "Bastards. I'm sorry all this happened, Leisha."

"Don't be," Leisha said.

When she had directions to Stewart's cousin, she walked back to the truck. Alice was still asleep, Stella still unconscious. Leisha closed the truck door as quietly as possible. The engine balked and roared, but Alice didn't wake. There was a crowd of people with them in the narrow and darkened cab: Stewart Sutter, Tony Indivino, Susan Melling, Kenzo Yagai, Roger Camden.

To Stewart Sutter she said, You called to inform me about the situation at Morehouse, Kennedy. You are risking your career and your cousin for Stella. And you stand to gain nothing. Like Susan telling me in advance about Bernie Kuhn's brain. Susan, who lost her life to Daddy's dream and regained it by her own strength. A contract without consideration for each side is not a contract: Every first-year student knows that.

To Kenzo Yagai she said, Trade isn't always linear. You missed that. If Stewart gives me something, and I give Stella something, and ten years from now Stella is a different person because of that and gives something to someone else as yet unknown—it's an ecology. An *ecology* of trade, yes, each niche needed, even if they're not contractually bound. Does a horse need a fish? *Yes.*

To Tony she said, Yes, there are beggars in Spain who trade nothing, give nothing, do nothing. But there are *more* than beggars in Spain. Withdraw from the beggars, you withdraw from the whole damn country. And you withdraw from the possibility of the ecology of help. That's what Alice wanted, all those years ago in her bedroom. Pregnant, scared, angry, jealous, she wanted to help *me*, and I wouldn't let her because I didn't need it. But I do now. And she did then. Beggars need to help as well as be helped.

And finally, there was only Daddy left. She could *see* him, bright-eyed, holding thick-leaved exotic flowers in his strong hands. To Camden she said, You were wrong. Alice *is* special. Oh, Daddy—the specialness of Alice! You were *wrong*.

As soon as she thought this, lightness filled her. Not the buoyant bubble of joy, not the hard clarity of examination, but something else: sunshine, soft through the conservatory glass, where two children ran in and out. She suddenly felt light herself, not buoyant but translucent, a medium for the sunshine to pass clear through, on its way to somewhere else.

She drove the sleeping woman and the wounded child through the night, east, toward the state line.

MATTER'S END

Gregory Benford

❁

Gregory Benford (born 1941) was the first among the hard science fiction writers to have mastered and integrated Modernist techniques of characterization and use of metaphor. He, more than anyone, has become the chief rhetoritician for hard SF. He coined the phrase "playing with the net up," which he uses to describe the game of hard science fiction.

He is the son of a career military officer, a professor of physics at the University of California, Irvine, working in both astrophysics and plasma physics, and is an intensely competitive man of ideas who enjoys conversational fencing, both as a scientist and as a science fiction writer. He is an advisor to the Department of Energy, NASA, and the White House Council on Space Policy. In addition to the many awards he has won within the SF field, he is also a winner of the Lord Prize for Contributions to Science and the United Nations Medal in Literature. In 1999, he published *Deep Time*, a popular science book subtitled *How Humanity Communicates Across Millennia*. His most recent novel is *Eater* (2000), concerning an intelligent and voracious black hole headed for Earth. Like many of his earlier novels, *Eater* features close-focus rounded characterization of working scientists, showing how science is central to their psychological lives.

His ideas tend to be provocative, intended to stir debate (and perhaps even to offend the dogmatic and complacent), and to be very well researched and argued. Here is an example from a recent interview:

> . . . the idea I want to push next, and in fact I may use in a novel, is that the United States should make Siberia a Protectorate. Pay the Russians off—a hundred, two hundred billion dollars—and simply run Siberia in an ecologically responsible way. It's a frontier as large as the continental U.S., should be opened, *will* be opened, either responsibly or not, and we could use this to put the stamp of liberal western democracy on the ground in Asia.

This idea is certain to have some readers sputtering about American imperialism, and yet it is quintessential Benford: audacious, large scale, and something he would be delighted to argue for hours on end. It is also perfectly consistent with the frontier tradition in American SF.

One of the primary features of American hard SF in the 1990s is the many fine novels about human exploration and settlement of Mars. Benford's entry in this competition is his novel *The Martian Race* (1999), in which the U.S. government has set a thirty billion dollar prize for the first human expedition to make it to Mars and back again, inspiring space travel by private enterprise. It was nominated for the Prometheus Award for best Libertarian SF novel.

"Matter's End," a story in the tradition of Arthur C. Clarke's "Nine Billion Names of God," portrays a convergence of spirituality and quantum mechanics, and shows what it would mean if certain religious interpretations of quantum mechanics were correct.

When Dr. Samuel Johnson felt himself getting tied up in an argument over Bishop Berkeley's ingenious sophistry to prove the nonexistence of matter, and that everything in the universe is merely ideal, he kicked a large stone and answered, "I refute it thus." Just what that action assured him of is not very obvious, but apparently he found it comforting.

—Sir Arthur Eddington

1

India came to him first as a breeze like soured buttermilk, rich yet tainted. A door banged somewhere, sending gusts sweeping through the Bangalore airport, slicing through the four A.M. silences.

Since the Free State of Bombay had left India, Bangalore had become an international airport. Yet the damp caress seemed to erase the sterile signatures that made all big airports alike, even giving a stippled texture to the cool enamel glow of the fluorescents.

The moist air clasped Robert Clay like a stranger's sweaty palm. The ripe, fleshy aroma of a continent enfolded him, swarming up his nostrils and soaking his lungs with sullen spice. He put down his carry-on bag and showed the immigration clerk his passport. The man gave him a piercing, ferocious stare—then mutely slammed a rubber stamp onto the pages and handed it back.

A hand snagged him as he headed toward baggage claim.

"Professor Clay?" The face was dark olive with intelligent eyes riding above sharp cheekbones. A sudden white grin flashed as Clay nodded. "Ah, good. I am Dr. Sudarshan Patil. Please come this way."

Dr. Patil's tone was polite, but his hands impatiently pulled Clay away from the sluggish lines, through a battered wooden side door. The heavy-lidded immigration guards were carefully looking in other directions, hands held behind their backs. Apparently they had been paid off and would ignore this odd exit. Clay was still groggy from trying to sleep on the flight from London. He shook his head as Patil led him into the gloom of a baggage storeroom.

"Your clothes," Patil said abruptly.

"What?"

"They mark you as a Westerner. Quickly!"

Patil's hands, light as birds in the quilted soft light, were already plucking at his coat, his shirt. Clay was taken aback at this abruptness. He hesitated, then struggled out of the dirty garments, pulling his loose slacks down over his shoes. He handed his bundled clothes to Patil, who snatched them away without a word.

"You're welcome," Clay said. Patil took no notice, just thrust a wad of tan cotton at him. The man's eyes jumped at each distant sound in the storage room, darting, suspecting every pile of dusty bags.

Clay struggled into the pants and rough shirt. They looked dingy in the wan yellow glow of a single distant fluorescent tube.

"Not the reception I'd expected," Clay said, straightening the baggy pants and pulling at the rough drawstring.

"These are not good times for scientists in my country, Dr. Clay," Patil said bitingly. His voice carried that odd lilt that echoed both the Raj and Cambridge.

"Who're you afraid of?"

"Those who hate Westerners and their science."

"They said in Washington—"

"We are about great matters, Professor Clay. Please cooperate, please."

Patil's lean face showed its bones starkly, as though energies pressed outward. Promontories of bunched muscle stretched a mottled canvas skin. He started toward a far door without another word, carrying Clay's overnight bag and jacket.

"Say, where're we—"

Patil swung open a sheet-metal door and beckoned. Clay slipped through it and into the moist wealth of night. His feet scraped on a dirty sidewalk beside a black tar road. The door hinge squealed behind them, attracting the attention of a knot of men beneath a vibrant yellow streetlight nearby.

The bleached fluorescence of the airport terminal was now a continent away. Beneath a line of quarter-ton trucks huddled figures slept. In the astringent streetlamp glow he saw a decrepit green Korean Tochat van parked at the curb.

"In!" Patil whispered.

The men under the streetlight started walking toward them, calling out hoarse questions.

Clay yanked open the van's sliding door and crawled into the second row of seats. A fog of unknown pungent smells engulfed him. The driver, a short man, hunched over the wheel. Patil sprang into the front seat and the van ground away, its low gear whining.

Shouts. A stone thumped against the van roof. Pebbles rattled at the back.

They accelerated, the engine clattering. A figure loomed up from the shifting shadows and flung muck against the window near Clay's face. He jerked back at the slap of it. "Damn!"

They plowed through a wide puddle of dirty rainwater. The engine sputtered and for a moment Clay was sure it would die. He looked out the rear window and saw vague forms running after them. Then the engine surged again and they shot away.

They went two blocks through hectic traffic. Clay tried to get a clear look at India outside, but all he could see in the starkly shadowed street were the crisscrossings of three-wheeled taxis and human-drawn rickshaws. He got an impression of incessant activity, even in this desolate hour. Vehicles leaped out of the murk as headlights swept across them and then vanished utterly into the moist shadows again.

They suddenly swerved around a corner beneath spreading, gloomy trees. The van jolted into deep potholes and jerked to a stop. "Out!" Patil called.

Clay could barely make out a second van at the curb ahead. It was blue and caked with mud, but even in the dim light would not be confused with their green one. A rotting fetid reek filled his nose as he got out the side door, as if masses of overripe vegetation loomed in the shadows. Patil tugged him into the second van. In a few seconds they went surging out through a narrow, brick-lined alley.

"Look, what—"

"Please, quiet," Patil said primly. "I am watching carefully now to be certain that we are not being followed."

They wound through a shantytown warren for several minutes. Their headlights picked up startled eyes that blinked from what Clay at first had taken to be bundles of rags lying against the shacks. They seemed impossibly small even to be children. Huddled against decaying tin lean-tos, the dim forms often did not stir even as the van splashed dirty water on them from potholes.

Clay began, "Look, I understand the need for—"

"I apologize for our rude methods, Dr. Clay," Patil said. He gestured at the driver. "May I introduce Dr. Singh?"

Singh was similarly gaunt and intent, but with bushy hair and a thin, pointed nose. He jerked his head aside to peer at Clay, nodded twice like a puppet on strings, and then quickly stared back at the narrow lane ahead. Singh kept the van at a steady growl, abruptly yanking it around corners. A wooden cart lurched out of their way, its driver swearing in a strident singsong. "Welcome to India," Singh said with reedy solemnity. "I am afraid circumstances are not the best."

"Uh, right. You two are heads of the project, they told me at the NSF."

"Yes," Patil said archly, "the project which officially no longer exists and unofficially is a brilliant success. It is amusing!"

"Yeah," Clay said cautiously, "we'll see."

"Oh, you will see," Singh said excitedly. "We have the events! More all the time."

Patil said precisely, "We would not have suggested that your National Science Foundation send an observer to confirm our findings unless we believed them to be of the highest importance."

"You've seen proton decay?"

Patil beamed. "Without doubt."

"Damn."

"Exactly."

"What mode?"

"The straightforward pion and positron decay products."

Clay smiled, reserving judgment. Something about Patil's almost prissy precision made him wonder if this small, beleaguered team of Indian physicists might actually have brought it off. An immense long shot, of course, but possible. There were much bigger groups of particle physicists in Europe and the U.S. who had tried to detect proton decay using underground swimming pools of pure water. Those experiments had enjoyed all the benefits of the latest electronics. Clay had worked on the big American project in a Utah salt mine, before lean budgets and lack of results closed it down. It would be galling if this lone, underfunded Indian scheme had finally done it. Nobody at the NSF believed the story coming out of India.

Patil smiled at Clay's silence, a brilliant slash of white in the murk. Their headlights picked out small panes of glass stuck seemingly at random in nearby hovels, reflecting quick glints of yellow back into the van. The night seemed misty; their headlights forked ahead. Clay thought a soft rain had started outside, but then he saw that thousands of tiny insects darted into their headlights. Occasionally big ones smacked against the windshield.

Patil carefully changed the subject. "I . . . believe you will pass unnoticed, for the most part."

"I look Indian?"

"I hope you will not take offense if I remark that you do not. We requested an Indian, but your NSF said they did not have anyone qualified."

"Right. Nobody who could hop on a plane, anyway." *Or would*, he added to himself.

"I understand. You are a compromise. If you will put this on . . ." Patil handed Clay a floppy khaki hat. "It will cover your curly hair. Luckily, your nose is rather more narrow than I had expected when the NSF cable announced they were sending a Negro."

"Got a lot of white genes in it, this nose," Clay said evenly.

"Please, do not think I am being racist. I simply wished to diminish the chances of you being recognized as a Westerner in the countryside."

"Think I can pass?"

"At a distance, yes."

"Be tougher at the site?"

"Yes. There are 'celebrants,' as they term themselves, at the mine."

"How'll we get in?"

"A ruse we have devised."

"Like that getaway back there? That was pretty slick."

Singh sent them jouncing along a rutted lane. Withered trees leaned against the pale stucco two-story buildings that lined the lane like children's blocks lined up not quite correctly. "Men in customs, they would give word to people outside. If you had gone through with the others, a different reception party would have been waiting for you."

"I see. But what about my bags?"

Patil had been peering forward at the gloomy jumble of buildings. His head jerked around to glare at Clay. "You were not to bring more than your carry-on bag!"

"Look, I can't get by on that. Chrissake, that'd give me just one change of clothes—"

"You left bags there?"

"Well, yeah, I had just one—"

Clay stopped when he saw the look on the two men's faces.

Patil said with strained clarity, "Your bags, they had identification tags?"

"Sure, airlines make you—"

"They will bring attention to you. There will be inquiries. The devotees will hear of it, inevitably, and know you have entered the country."

Clay licked his lips. "Hell, I didn't think it was so important."

The two lean Indians glanced at each other, their faces taking on a narrowing, leaden cast. "Dr. Clay," Patil said stiffly, "the 'celebrants' believe, as do many, that Westerners deliberately destroyed our crops with their biotechnology."

"Japanese companies' biologists did that, I thought," Clay said diplomatically.

"Perhaps. Those who disturb us at the Kolar gold mine make no fine distinctions between biologists and physicists. They believe that we are disturbing the very bowels of the earth, helping to further the destruction, bringing on the very end of the world itself. Surely you can see that in India, the mother country of religious philosophy, such matters are important."

"But your work, hell, it's not a matter of life or death or anything."

"On the contrary, the decay of the proton is precisely an issue of death."

Clay settled back in his seat, puzzled, watching the silky night stream by, cloaking vague forms in its shadowed mysteries.

2

Clay insisted on the telephone call. A wan winter sun had already crawled partway up the sky before he awoke, and the two Indian physicists wanted to leave immediately. They had stopped while still in Bangalore, holing up in the cramped apartment of one of Patil's graduate students. As Clay took his first sip of tea, two other students had turned up with his bag, retrieved at a cost he never knew.

Clay said, "I promised I'd call home. Look, my family's worried. They read the papers, they know the trouble here."

Shaking his head slowly, Patil finished a scrap of curled brown bread that appeared to be his only breakfast. His movements had a smooth liquid inertia, as if the sultry morning air oozed like jelly around him. They were sitting at a low table that had one leg too short; the already rickety table kept lurching, slopping tea into their saucers. Clay had looked for something to prop up the leg, but the apartment was bare, as though no one lived here. They had slept on pallets beneath a single bare bulb. Through the open windows, bare of frames or glass, Clay had gotten fleeting glimpses of the neighborhood—rooms of random clutter, plaster peeling off slumped walls, revealing the thin steel cross-ribs of the buildings, stained windows adorned with gaudy pictures of many-armed gods, already sun-bleached and frayed. Children yelped and cried below, their voices reflected among the odd angles and apertures of the tangled streets, while carts rattled by and bare feet slapped the stones. Students had apparently stood guard last night, though Clay had never seen more than a quick motion in the shadows below as they arrived.

"You ask much of us," Patil said. By morning light his walnut-brown face seemed gullied and worn. Lines radiated from his mouth toward intense eyes.

Clay sipped his tea before answering. A soft, strangely sweet smell wafted through the open window. They sat well back in the room so nobody could see in from the nearby buildings. He heard Singh tinkering downstairs with the van's engine.

"Okay, it's maybe slightly risky. But I want my people to know I got here all right."

"There are few telephones here."

"I only need one."

"The system, often it does not work at all."

"Gotta try."

"Perhaps you do not understand—"

"I understand damn well that if I can't even reach my people, I'm not going to hang out here for long. And if I don't see that your experiment works right, nobody'll believe you."

"And your opinion depends upon . . . ?"

Clay ticked off points on his fingers. "On seeing the apparatus. Checking your raw data. Running a trial case to see your system response. Then a null experiment—to verify your threshold level on each detector." He held up five fingers. "The works."

Patil said gravely, "Very good. We relish the opportunity to prove ourselves."

"You'll get it." Clay hoped to himself that they were wrong, but he suppressed that. He represented the faltering forefront of particle physics, and it would be embarrassing if a backwater research team had beaten the world. Still, either way, he would end up being the expert on the Kolar program, and that was a smart career move in itself.

"Very well. I must make arrangements for the call, then. But I truly—"

"Just do it. Then we get down to business."

The telephone was behind two counters and three doors at a Ministry for Controls office. Patil did the bribing and cajoling inside and then brought Clay in from the back of the van. He had been lying down on the back seat so he could not be seen easily from the street.

The telephone itself was a heavy black plastic thing with a rotary dial that clicked like a sluggish insect as it whirled. Patil had been on it twice already, clearing international lines through Bombay. Clay got two false rings and a dead line. On the fourth try he heard a faint, somehow familiar buzzing. Then a hollow, distant click.

"Angy?"

"Daddy, is that you?" Faint rock music in the background.

"Sure, I just wanted to let you know I got to India okay."

"Oh, Mommy will be so glad! We heard on the TV last night that there's trouble over there."

Startled, Clay asked, "What? Where's your mother?"

"Getting groceries. She'll be so mad she missed your call!"

"You tell her I'm fine, okay? But what trouble?"

"Something about a state leaving India. Lots of fighting, John Trimble said on the news."

Clay never remembered the names of news announcers; he regarded them as faceless nobodies reading prepared scripts, but for his daughter they were the voice of authority. "Where?"

"Uh, the lower part."

"There's nothing like that happening here, honey. I'm safe. Tell Mommy."

"People have ice cream there?"

"Yeah, but I haven't seen any. You tell your mother what I said, remember? About being safe?"

"Yes, she's been worried."

"Don't worry, Angy. Look, I got to go." The line popped and hissed ominously.

"I miss you, Daddy."

"I miss you double that. No, squared."

She laughed merrily. "I skinned my knee today at recess. It bled so much I had to go to the nurse."

"Keep it clean, honey. And give your mother my love."

"She'll be so mad."

"I'll be home soon."

She giggled and ended with the joke she had been using lately. "G'bye, Daddy. It's been real."

Her light laugh trickled into the static, a grace note from a bright land worlds away. Clay chuckled as he replaced the receiver. She cut the last word of "real nice" to make her good-byes hip and sardonic, a mannerism she had heard on television somewhere. An old joke; he had heard that even "groovy" was coming back in.

Clay smiled and pulled his hat down further and went quickly out into the street where Patil was waiting. India flickered at the edge of his vision, the crowds a hovering presence.

3

They left Bangalore in two vans. Graduate students drove the green Tochat from the previous night. He and Patil and Singh took the blue one, Clay again keeping out of sight by lying on the back seat. The day's raw heat rose around them like a shimmering lake of light.

They passed through lands leached of color. Only gray stubble grew in the fields. Trees hung limply, their limbs bowing as though exhausted. Figures in rags huddled for shade. A few stirred, eyes white in the shadows, as the vans ground past. Clay saw that large boles sat on the branches like gnarled knots with brown sheaths wrapped around the underside.

"Those some of the plant diseases I heard about?" he asked.

Singh pursed his lips. "I fear those are the pouches like those of wasps, as reported in the press." His watery eyes regarded the withered, graying trees as Patil slowed the car.

"Are they dangerous?" Clay could see yellow sap dripping from the underside of each.

"Not until they ripen," Singh said. "Then the assassins emerge."

"They look pretty big already."

"They are said to be large creatures, but of course there is little experience."

Patil downshifted and they accelerated away with an occasional sputtering misfire. Clay wondered whether they had any spare spark plugs along. The fields on each side of the road took on a dissolute and shredded look. "Did the genetech experiments cause this?" he asked.

Singh nodded. "I believe this emerged from the European programs. First we had their designed plants, but then pests found vulnerability. They sought strains which could protect crops from the new pests. So we got these wasps. I gather that now some error or mutation has made them equally excellent at preying on people and even cows."

Clay frowned. "The wasps came from the Japanese aid, didn't they?"

Patil smiled mysteriously. "You know a good deal about our troubles, sir."

Neither said anything more. Clay was acutely conscious that his briefing in Washington had been detailed technical assessments, without the slightest mention of how the Indians themselves saw their problems. Singh and Patil seemed either resigned or unconcerned; he could not tell which. Their sentences refracted from some unseen nugget, like seismic waves warping around the earth's core.

"I would not worry greatly about these pouches," Singh said after they had ridden in silence for a while. "They should not ripen before we are done with our task. In any case, the Kolar fields are quite barren, and afford few sites where the pouches can grow."

Clay pointed out the front window. "Those round things on the walls—more pouches?"

To his surprise, both men burst into merry laughter. Gasping, Patil said, "Examine them closely, Doctor Clay. Notice the marks of the species which made them."

Patil slowed the car and Clay studied the round, circular pads on the whitewashed vertical walls along the road. They were brown and matted and marked in a pattern of radial lines. Clay frowned and then felt enormously stupid: the thick lines were handprints.

"Drying cakes, they are," Patil said, still chuckling.

"Of what?"

"Dung, my colleague. We use the cow here, not merely slaughter it."

"What for?"

"Fuel. After the cakes dry, we stack them—see?" They passed a plastic-wrapped tower. A woman was adding a circular, annular tier of thick dung disks to the top, then carefully folding the plastic over it. "In winter they burn nicely."

"For heating?"

"And cooking, yes."

Seeing the look on Clay's face, Singh's eyes narrowed and his lips drew back so that his teeth were bright stubs. His eyebrows were long brush strokes that met the deep furrows of his frown. "Old ways are still often preferable to the new."

Sure, Clay thought, the past of cholera, plague, infanticide. But he asked with neutral politeness, "Such as?"

"Some large fish from the Amazon were introduced into our principal river three years ago to improve fishing yields."

"The Ganges? I thought it was holy."

"What is more holy than to feed the hungry?"

"True enough. Did it work?"

"The big fish, yes. They are delicious. A great delicacy."

"I'll have to try some," Clay said, remembering the thin vegetarian curry he had eaten at breakfast.

Singh said, "But the Amazon sample contained some minute eggs which none of the proper procedures eliminated. They were of a small species—the candiru, is that not the name?" he inquired politely of Patil.

"Yes," Patil said, "a little being who thrives mostly on the urine of larger fish. Specialists now believe that perhaps the eggs were inside the larger species, and so escaped detection."

Patil's voice remained calm and factual, although while he spoke he abruptly swerved to avoid a goat that spontaneously ambled onto the rough road. Clay rocked hard against the van's door, and Patil then corrected further to stay out of a gratuitous mudhole that seemed to leap at them from the rushing foreground. They bumped noisily over ruts at the road's edge and bounced back onto the tarmac without losing speed. Patil sat ramrod straight, hands turning the steering wheel lightly, oblivious to the wrenching effects of his driving.

"Suppose, Professor Clay, that you are a devotee," Singh said. "You have saved to come to the Ganges for a decade, for two. Perhaps you even plan to die there."

"Yeah, okay." Clay could not see where this was leading.

"You are enthused as you enter the river to bathe. You are perhaps profoundly affected. An intense spiritual moment. It is not uncommon to merge with the river, to inadvertently urinate into it."

Singh spread his hands as if to say that such things went without saying.

"Then the candiru will be attracted by the smell. It mistakes this great bountiful largess, the food it needs, as coming from a very great fish indeed. It excitedly swims up the stream of uric acid. Coming to your urethra, it swims like a snake into its burrow, as far up as it can go. You will see that the uric flow velocity will increase as the candiru makes its way upstream, inside you. When this tiny fish can make no further progress, some trick of evolution tells it to protrude a set of sidewise spines. So intricate!"

Singh paused a moment in smiling tribute to this intriguing facet of nature. Clay nodded, his mouth dry.

"These embed deeply in the walls and keep the candiru close to the source of what it so desires." Singh made short, delicate movements, his fingers jutting in the air. Clay opened his mouth, but said nothing.

Patil took them around a team of bullocks towing a wooden wagon and put in, "The pain is intense. Apparently there is no good treatment. Women—forgive this indelicacy—must be opened to get at the offending tiny fish before it swells and blocks the passage completely, having gorged itself insensate. Some men have an even worse choice. Their bladders are already engorged, having typically not been much emptied by the time the candiru enters. They must decide whether to attempt the slow procedure of poisoning the small thing and waiting for it to shrivel and withdraw its spines. However, their bladders might burst before that, flooding their abdomens with urine and of course killing them. If there is not sufficient time . . ."

"Yes?" Clay asked tensely.

"Then the penis must be chopped off," Singh said, "with the candiru inside."

Through a long silence Clay rode, swaying as the car wove through limitless flat spaces of parched fields and ruined brick walls and slumped whitewashed huts. Finally he said hoarsely, "I . . . don't blame you for resenting the . . . well, the people who brought all this on you. The devotees—"

"They believe this apocalyptic evil comes from the philosophy which gave us modern science."

"Well, look, whoever brought over those fish—"

Singh's eyes widened with surprise. A startled grin lit his face like a sunrise. "Oh no, Professor Clay! We do not blame the errors, or else we would have to blame equally the successes!"

To Clay's consternation, Patil nodded sagely.

He decided to say nothing more. Washington had warned him to stay out of political discussions, and though he was not sure if this was such, or if the light-hearted way Singh and Patil had related their story told their true attitude, it seemed best to just shut up. Again Clay had the odd sensation that here the cool certainties of Western biology had become diffused, blunted, crisp distinctions rendered into something beyond the constraints of the world outside, all blurred by the swarming, dissolving currents of India. The tin-gray sky loomed over a plain of ripe rot. The urgency of decay here was far more powerful than the abstractions that so often filled his head, the digitized iconography of sputtering, splitting protons.

4

The Kolar gold fields were a long, dusty drive from Bangalore. The sway of the van made Clay sleepy in the back, jet lag pulling him down into fitful, shallow dreams of muted voices, shadowy faces, and obscure purpose. He awoke frequently amid the dry smells, lurched up to see dry farmland stretching to the horizon, and collapsed again to bury his face in the pillow he had made by wadding up a shirt.

They passed through innumerable villages that, after the first few, all seemed alike with their scrawny children, ramshackle sheds, tin roofs, and general air of sleepy dilapidation. Once, in a narrow town, they stopped as rickshaws and carts backed up. An emaciated cow with pink paper tassels on its horns stood square in the middle of the road, trembling. Shouts and honks failed to move it, but no one ahead made the slightest effort to prod it aside.

Clay got out of the van to stretch his legs, ignoring Patil's warning to stay hidden, and watched. A crowd collected, shouting and chanting at the cow but not touching it. The cow shook its head, peering at the road as if searching for grass, and urinated powerfully. A woman in a red sari rushed into the road, knelt, and thrust her hand into the full stream. She made a formal motion with her other hand and splashed some urine on her forehead and cheeks. Three other women had already lined up behind her, and each did the same. Disturbed, the cow waggled its head and shakily walked away. Traffic started up, and Clay climbed back into the van. As they ground out of the dusty town, Singh explained that holy bovine urine was widely held to have positive health effects.

"Many believe it settles stomach troubles, banishes headaches, even improves fertility," Singh said.

"Yeah, you could sure use more fertility." Clay gestured at the throngs that filled the narrow clay sidewalks.

"I am not so Indian that I cannot find it within myself to agree with you, Professor Clay," Singh said.

"Sorry for the sarcasm. I'm tired."

"Patil and I are already under a cloud simply because we are scientists, and therefore polluted with Western ideas."

"Can't blame Indians for being down on us. Things're getting rough."

"But you are a black man. You yourself were persecuted by Western societies."

"That was a while back."

"And despite it you have risen to a professorship."

"You do the work, you get the job." Clay took off his hat and wiped his brow. The midday heat pressed sweat from him.

"Then you do not feel alienated from Western ideals?" Patil put in.

"Hell no. Look, I'm not some sharecropper who pulled himself up from poverty.

I grew up in Falls Church, Virginia. Father's a federal bureaucrat. Middle class all the way."

"I see," Patil said, eyes never leaving the rutted road. "Your race bespeaks an entirely different culture, but you subscribe to the program of modern rationalism."

Clay looked at them quizzically. "Don't you?"

"As scientists, of course. But that is not all of life."

"Um," Clay said.

A thousand times before he had endured the affably condescending attention of whites, their curious eyes searching his face. No matter what the topic, they somehow found a way to inquire indirectly after his *true* feelings, his *natural* emotions. And if he waved away these intrusions, there remained in their heavy-lidded eyes a subtle skepticism, doubts about his authenticity. Few gave him space to simply be a suburban man with darker skin, a man whose interior landscape was populated with the same icons of Middle America as their own. Hell, his family name came from slaves, given as a tribute to Henry Clay, a nineteenth-century legislator. He had never expected to run into stereotyping in India, for chrissakes.

Still, he was savvy enough to lard his talk with some homey touches, jimmy things up with collard greens and black-eyed peas and street jive. It might put them at ease.

"I believe a li'l rationality could help," he said.

"Um." Singh's thin mouth twisted doubtfully. "Perhaps you should regard India as the great chessboard of our times, Professor. Here we have arisen from the great primordial agrarian times, fashioned our gods from our soil and age. Then we had orderly thinking, with all its assumptions, thrust upon us by the British. Now they are all gone, and we are suspended between the miasmic truths of the past, and the failed strictures of the present."

Clay looked out the dirty window and suppressed a smile. Even the physicists here spouted mumbo jumbo. They even appeared solemnly respectful of the devotees, who were just crazies like the women by the cow. How could anything solid come out of such a swamp? The chances that their experiment was right dwindled with each lurching, damp mile.

They climbed into the long range of hills before the Kolar fields. Burned-tan grass shimmered in the prickly heat. Sugarcane fields and rice paddies stood bone dry. In the villages, thin figures shaded beneath awnings, canvas tents, lean-tos, watched them pass. Lean faces betrayed only dim, momentary interest, and Clay wondered if his uncomfortable disguise was necessary outside Bangalore.

Without stopping they ate their lunch of dried fruit and thin, brown bread. In a high hill town, Patil stopped to refill his water bottle at a well. Clay peered out and saw down an alley a gang of stick-figure boys chasing a dog. They hemmed it in, and the bedraggled hound fled yapping from one side of their circle to the other. The animal whined at each rebuff and twice lost its footing on the cobblestones, sprawling, only to scramble up again and rush on. It was a cruel game, and the boys were strangely silent, playing without laughter. The dog was tiring; they drew in their circle.

A harsh edge to the boys' shouts made Clay slide open the van door. Several men were standing beneath a rust-scabbed sheet-metal awning nearby, and their eyes widened when they saw his face. They talked rapidly among themselves. Clay hesitated. The boys down the alley rushed the dog. They grabbed it as it yapped futilely and tried to bite them. They slipped twine around its jaws and silenced it. Shouting, they hoisted it into the air and marched off.

Clay gave up and slammed the door. The men came from under the awning. One rapped on the window. Clay just stared at them. One thumped on the door. Gestures, loud talk.

Patil and Singh came running, shouted something. Singh pushed the men away, chattering at them while Patil got the van started. Singh slammed the door in the face of a man with wild eyes. Patil gunned the engine and they ground away.

"They saw me and—"

"Distrust of outsiders is great here," Singh said. "They may be connected with the devotees, too."

"Guess I better keep my hat on."

"It would be advisable."

"I don't know, those boys—I was going to stop them pestering that dog. Stupid, I guess, but—"

"You will have to avoid being sentimental about such matters," Patil said severely.

"Uh—sentimental?"

"The boys were not playing."

"I don't—"

"They will devour it," Singh said.

Clay blinked. "Hindus eating meat?"

"Hard times. I am really quite surprised that such an animal has survived this long," Patil said judiciously. "Dogs are uncommon. I imagine it was wild, living in the countryside, and ventured into town in search of garbage scraps."

The land rose as Clay watched the shimmering heat bend and flex the seemingly solid hills.

5

They pulled another dodge at the mine. The lead green van veered off toward the main entrance, a cluster of concrete buildings and conveyer assemblies. From a distance, the physicists in the blue van watched a ragtag group envelop the van before it had fully stopped.

"Devotees," Singh said abstractedly. "They search each vehicle for evidence of our research."

"Your graduate students, the mob'll let them pass?"

Patil peered through binoculars. "The crowd is administering a bit of a pushing about," he said in his oddly cadenced accent, combining lofty British diction with a singsong lilt.

"Damn, won't the mine people get rid—"

"Some mine workers are among the crowd, I should imagine," Patil said. "They are beating the students."

"Well, can't we—"

"No time to waste." Singh waved them back into the blue van. "Let us make use of this diversion."

"But we could—"

"The students made their sacrifice for you. Do not devalue it, please."

Clay did not take his eyes from the nasty knot of confusion until they lurched over the ridgeline. Patil explained that they had been making regular runs to the main entrance for months now, to establish a pattern that drew devotees away from the secondary entrance.

"All this was necessary, and insured that we could bring in a foreign inspector," Patil concluded. Clay awkwardly thanked him for the attention to detail. He wanted to voice his embarrassment at having students roughed up simply to provide him cover, but something in the offhand manner of the two Indians made him hold his tongue.

The secondary entrance to the Kolar mine was a wide, tin-roofed shed like a low aircraft hangar. Girders crisscrossed it at angles that seemed to Clay dictated less by the constraints of mechanics than by the whims of the construction team. Cables looped among the already rusting steel struts and sang low notes in the rot-tinged wind that brushed his hair.

Monkeys chattered and scampered high in the struts. The three men walked into the shed, carrying cases. The cables began humming softly. The weave above their heads tightened with pops and sharp cracks. Clay realized that the seemingly random array was a complicated hoist that had started to pull the elevator up from miles beneath their feet. The steel lattice groaned as if it already knew how much work it had to do.

When it arrived, he saw that the elevator was a huge rattling box that reeked of machine oil. Clay lugged his cases in. The walls were broad wooden slats covered with chicken wire. Heat radiated from them. Patil stabbed a button on the big control board and they dropped quickly. The numbers of the levels zipped by on an amber digital display. A single dim yellow bulb cast shadows onto the wire. At the fifty-third level the bulb went out. The elevator did not stop.

In the enveloping blackness Clay felt himself lighten, as if the elevator was speeding up.

"Do not be alarmed," Patil called. "This frequently occurs."

Clay wondered if he meant the faster fall or the light bulb. In the complete dark, he began to see blue phantoms leaping out from nowhere.

Abruptly he became heavy—and thought of Einstein's *Gedanken* experiment, which equated a man in an accelerating elevator to one standing on a planet. Unless Clay could see outside, check that the massive earth raced by beyond as it clasped him further into its depths, in principle he could be in either situation. He tried to recall how Einstein had reasoned from an imaginary elevator to deduce that matter curved space-time, and could not.

Einstein's elegant proof was impossibly far from the pressing truth of *this* elevator. Here Clay plunged in thick murk, a weight of tortured air prickling his nose, making sweat pop from his face. Oily, moist heat climbed into Clay's sinuses.

And he was not being carried aloft by this elevator, but allowed to plunge into heavy, primordial darkness—Einstein's vision in reverse. No classical coolness separated him from the press of a raw, random world. That European mindscape—Galileo's crisp cylinders rolling obediently down inclined planes, Einstein's dispassionate observers surveying their smooth geometries like scrupulous bank clerks—evaporated here like yesterday's stale champagne. Sudden anxiety filled his throat. His stomach tightened and he tasted acrid gorge. He opened his mouth to shout, and as if to stop him, his own knees sagged with suddenly returning weight, physics regained.

A rattling thump—and they stopped. He felt Patil slam aside the rattling gate. A sullen glow beyond bathed an ornate brass shrine to a Hindu god. They came out into a steepled room of carved rock. Clay felt a breath of slightly cooler air from a cardboard-mouthed conduit nearby.

"We must force the air down from above." Patil gestured. "Otherwise this would read well over a hundred and ten Fahrenheit." He proudly pointed to an ancient battered British thermometer, whose mercury stood at ninety-eight.

They trudged through several tunnels, descended another few hundred feet on a ramp, and then followed gleaming railroad tracks. A white bulb every ten meters threw everything into exaggerated relief, shadows stabbing everywhere. A brown cardboard sign proclaimed from the ceiling:

FIRST EVER COSMIC RAY NEUTRINO INTERACTION
RECORDED HERE IN APRIL 1965

For over forty years, teams of devoted Indian physicists had labored patiently inside the Kolar gold fields. For half a century, India's high mountains and deep mines had made important cosmic-ray experiments possible with inexpensive instruments. Clay recalled how a joint Anglo-Indian-Japanese team had detected that first neutrino, scooped it from the unending cosmic sleet that penetrated even to this depth. He thought of unsung Indian physicists sweating here, tending the instruments and tracing the myriad sources of background error. Yet they themselves were background for the original purpose of the deep holes: Two narrow cars clunked past, full of chopped stone.

"Some still work this portion," Patil's clear voice cut through the muffled air. "Though I suspect they harvest little."

Pushing the rusty cars were four wiry men, so sweaty that the glaring bulbs gave their sliding muscles a hard sheen like living stone. They wore filthy cloths wrapped around their heads, as if they needed protection against the low ceiling rather than the heat. As Clay stumbled on, he felt that there might be truth to this, because he sensed the mass above as a precarious judgment over them all, a sullen presence. Einstein's crisp distinctions, the clean certainty of the *Gedanken* experiments, meant nothing in this blurred air.

They rounded an irregular curve and met a niche neatly cut off by a chainlink fence.

PROTON STABILITY EXPERIMENT
TATA INSTITUTE OF FUNDAMENTAL RESEARCH, BOMBAY
80TH LEVEL HEATHCOTE SHAFT, KFG
2300 METERS DEPTH

These preliminaries done, the experiment itself began abruptly. Clay had expected some assembly rooms, an office, refrigerated 'scope cages. Instead, a few meters ahead the tunnel opened in all directions. They stood before a huge bay roughly cleaved from the brown rock.

And filling the vast volume was what seemed to be a wall as substantial as the rock itself. It was an iron grid of rusted pipe. The pipes were square, not round, and dwindled into the distance. Each had a dusty seal, a pressure dial, and a number painted in white. Clay estimated them to be at least a hundred feet long. They were stacked Lincoln-log fashion. He walked to the edge of the bay and looked down. Layers of pipe tapered away below to a distant floodlit floor and soared to meet the gray ceiling above.

"Enormous," he said.

"We expended great effort in scaling up our earlier apparatus," Singh said enthusiastically.

"As big as a house."

Patil said merrily, "An American house, perhaps. Ours are smaller."

A woman's voice nearby said, "And nothing lives in this iron house, Professor Clay."

Clay turned to see a willowy Indian woman regarding him with a wry smile. She seemed to have come out of the shadows, a brown apparition in shorts and a scrupulously white blouse, appearing fullblown where a moment before there had been nothing. Her heavy eyebrows rose in amusement.

"Ah, this is Mrs. Buli," Patil said.

"I keep matters running here, while my colleagues venture into the world," she said.

Clay accepted her coolly offered hand. She gave him one quick, well-defined shake and stepped back. "I can assist your assessment, perhaps."

"I'll need all your help," he said sincerely. The skimpy surroundings already made him wonder if he could do his job at all.

"Labor we have," she said. "Equipment, little."

"I brought some cross-check programs with me," he said.

"Excellent," Mrs. Buli said. "I shall have several of my graduate students assist you, and of course I offer my full devotion as well."

Clay smiled at her antique formality. She led him down a passage into the soft fluorescent glow of a large data-taking room. It was crammed with terminals and a bank of disk drives, all meshed by the usual cable spaghetti. "We keep our computers cooler than our staff, you see," Mrs. Buli said with a small smile.

They went down a ramp, and Clay could feel the rock's steady heat. They came out onto the floor of the cavern. Thick I-beams roofed the stone box.

"Over a dozen lives, that was the cost of this excavation," Singh said.

"That many?"

"They attempted to save on the cost of explosives," Patil said with a stern look.

"Not that such will matter in the long run," Singh said mildly. Clay chose not to pursue the point.

Protective bolts studded the sheer rock, anchoring cross-beams that stabilized the tower of pipes. Scaffolding covered some sections of the blocky, rusty pile. Blasts of compressed air from the surface a mile above swept down on them from the ceiling, flapping Clay's shirt.

Mrs. Buli had to shout, the effort contorting her smooth face. "We obtained the pipes from a government program that attempted to improve the quality of plumbing in the cities. A failure, I fear. But a godsend for us."

Patil was pointing out electrical details when the air conduits wheezed into silence. "Hope that's temporary," Clay said in the sudden quiet.

"A minor repair, I am sure," Patil said.

"These occur often," Singh agreed earnestly.

Clay could already feel prickly sweat oozing from him. He wondered how often they had glitches in the circuitry down here, awash in pressing heat, and how much that could screw up even the best diagnostics.

Mrs. Buli went on in a lecturer's singsong. "We hired engineering students—there are many such, an oversupply—to thread a single wire down the bore of each pipe. We sealed each, then welded them together to make lengths of a hundred feet. Then we filled them with argon and linked them with a high-voltage line. We have found that a voltage of 280 keV . . ."

Clay nodded, filing away details, noting where her description differed from that of the NSF. The Kolar group had continuously modified their experiment for decades, and this latest enormous expansion was badly documented. Still, the principle was simple. Each pipe was held at high voltage, so that when a charged particle passed through, a spark leaped. A particle's path was followed by counting the segments of triggered pipes. This mammoth stack of iron was a huge Geiger counter.

He leaned back, nodding at Buli's lecture, watching a team of men at the very top. A loud clang rang through the chasm. Sparks showered, burnt-orange and blue. The garish plumes silhouetted the welders and sent cascades of sparks down through the lattice of pipes. For an instant Clay imagined he was witnessing cosmic rays sleeting down through the towering house of iron, illuminating it with their short, sputtering lives.

"—and I am confident that we have seen well over fifty true events," Mrs. Buli concluded with a jaunty upward tilt of her chin.

"What?" Clay struggled back from his daydreaming. "That many?"

She laughed, a high tinkling. "You do not believe!"

"Well, that is a lot."

"Our detecting mass is now larger," Mrs. Buli said.

"Last we heard it was five hundred tons," Clay said carefully. The claims wired to the NSF and the Royal Society had been skimpy on details.

"That was years ago," Patil said. "We have redoubled our efforts, as you can see."

"Well, to see that many decays, you'd have to have a hell of a lot of observing volume," Clay said doubtfully.

"We can boast of five *thousand* tons, Professor Clay," Mrs. Buli said.

"Looks it," Clay said laconically to cover his surprise. It would not do to let them think they could overwhelm him with magnitudes. Question was, did they have the telltale events?

The cooling air came on with a thump and *whoosh*. Clay breathed it in deeply, face turned up to the iron house where protons might be dying, and sucked in swarming scents of the parched countryside miles above.

6

He knew from the start that there would be no eureka moment. Certainty was the child of tedium.

He traced the tangled circuitry for two days before he trusted it. "You got to open the sack 'fore I'll believe there's a cat in there," he told Mrs. Buli, and then had to explain that he was joking.

Then came a three-day trial run, measuring the exact sputter of decay from a known radioactive source. System response was surprisingly good. He found their techniques needlessly Byzantine, but workable. His null checks of the detectors inside the pipes came up goose-egg clean.

Care was essential. Proton decay was rare. The Grand Unified Theories which had enjoyed such success in predicting new particles had also sounded a somber note through all of physics. Matter was mortal. But not very mortal, compared with the passing flicker of a human lifetime.

The human body had about 10^{29} neutrons and protons in it. If only a tiny fraction of them decayed in a human lifetime, the radiation from the disintegration would quickly kill everyone of cancer. The survival of even small life-forms implied that the protons inside each nucleus had to survive an average of nearly a billion billion years.

So even before the Grand Unified Theories, physicists knew that protons lived long. The acronym for the theories was GUTs, and a decade earlier graduate students like Clay had worn T-shirts with insider jokes like IT TAKES GUTS TO DO PARTICLE PHYSICS. But proving that there was some truth to the lame nerd jests took enormous effort.

The simplest of the GUTs predicted a proton lifetime of about 10^{31} years, immensely greater than the limit set by the existence of life. In fact, it was far longer even than the age of the universe, which was only a paltry 2×10^{10} years old.

One could check this lifetime by taking one proton and watching it for 10^{31} years. Given the short attention span of humans, it was better to assemble 10^{31} protons and watch them for a year, hoping one would fizzle.

Physicists in the United States, Japan, Italy, and India had done that all through the 1980s and 1990s. And no protons had died.

Well, the theorists had said, the mathematics must be more complicated. They discarded certain symmetry groups and thrust others forward. The lifetime might be 10^{32} years, then.

The favored method of gathering protons was to use those in water. Western physicists carved swimming pools six stories deep in salt mines and eagerly watched for the characteristic blue pulse of dying matter. Detecting longer lifetimes meant waiting longer, which nobody liked, or adding more protons. Digging bigger swimming pools was easy, so attention had turned to the United States and Japan . . . but still, no protons died. The lifetime exceeded 10^{32} years.

The austerity of the 1990s had shut down the ambitious experiments in the West. Few remembered this forlorn experiment in Kolar, wedded to watching the cores of iron rods for the quick spurt of decay. When political difficulties cut off contact, the already beleaguered physicists in the West assumed the Kolar effort had ceased.

But Kolar was the deepest experiment, less troubled by the hail of cosmic rays that polluted the Western data. Clay came to appreciate that as he scrolled through the myriad event-plots in the Kolar computer cubes.

There were 9×10^9 recorded decays of all types. The system rejected obvious garbage events, but there were many subtle enigmas. Theory said that protons died because the quarks that composed them could change their identities. A seemingly capricious alteration of quarky states sent the proton asunder, spitting forth a zoo of fragments. Neutrons were untroubled by this, for in free space they decayed anyway, into a proton and electron. Matter's end hinged, finally, on the stability of the proton alone.

Clay saw immediately that the Kolar group had invested years in their software. They had already filtered out thousands of phantom events that imitated true proton decay. There were eighteen ways a proton could die, each with a different signature of spraying light and particle debris.

The delicate traceries of particle paths were recorded as flashes and sparkles in the house of iron outside. Clay searched through endless graphic printouts, filigrees woven from digital cloth.

"You will find we have pondered each candidate event," Mrs. Buli said mildly on the sixth day of Clay's labors.

"Yeah, the analysis is sharp," he said cautiously. He was surprised at the high level of the work but did not want to concede anything yet.

"If any ambiguity arose, we discarded the case."

"I can see that."

"Some pions were not detected in the right energy range, so of course we omitted those."

"Good."

Mrs. Buli leaned over to show him a detail of the cross-checking program, and he caught a heady trace of wildflowers. Her perfume reminded him abruptly that her sari wrapped over warm, ample swells. She had no sagging softness, no self-indulgent bulgings. The long oval of her face and her ample lips conveyed a fragile sensuality . . .

He wrenched his attention back to physics and stared hard at the screen.

Event vertices were like time-lapse photos of traffic accidents, intersections exploding, screaming into shards. The crystalline mathematical order of physics led to riots of incandescence. And Clay was judge, weighing testimony after the chaos.

7

He had insisted on analyzing the several thousand preliminary candidates himself, as a double blind against the Kolar group's software. After nine days, he had isolated sixty-seven events that looked like the genuine article.

Sixty-five of his agreed with Mrs. Buli's analysis. The two holdouts were close, Clay had to admit.

"Nearly on the money," he said reflectively as he stared at the Kolar software's array.

"You express such values," Mrs. Buli said. "Always a financial analogy."

"Just a way of speaking."

"Still, let us discard the two offending events."

"Well, I'd be willing—"

"No, no, we consider only the sixty-five." Her almond eyes gave no hint of slyness.

"They're pretty good bets, I'd say." Her eyebrows arched. "Only a manner of speech."

"Then you feel they fit the needs of theory."

Her carefully balanced way of phrasing made him lean forward, as if to compensate for his judge's role. "I'll have to consider all the other decay modes in detail. Look for really obscure processes that might mimic the real thing."

She nodded. "True, there is need to study such."

Protons could die from outside causes, too. Wraithlike neutrinos spewed forth by the sun penetrated even here, shattering protons. Murderous muons lumbered through as cosmic rays, plowing furrows of exploding nuclei.

Still, things looked good. He was surprised at their success, earned by great labor. "I'll be as quick about it as I can."

"We have prepared a radio link that we can use, should the desire come."

"Huh? What?"

"In case you need to reach your colleagues in America."

"Ah, yes."

To announce the result, he saw. To get the word out. But why the rush?

It occurred to him that they might doubt whether he himself would get out at all.

8

They slept each night in a clutch of tin lean-tos that cowered down a raw ravine. Laborers from the mine had slept there in better days, and the physicists had gotten the plumbing to work for an hour each night. The men slept in a long shed, but gave Clay a small wooden shack. He ate thin, mealy gruel with them each evening, carefully dropping purification tablets in his water, and was rewarded with untroubled bowels. He lost weight in the heat of the mine, but the nights were cool and the breezes that came then were soft with moisture.

The fifth evening, as they sat around a potbellied iron stove in the men's shed, Patil pointed to a distant corrugated metal hut and said, "There we have concealed a satellite dish. We can knock away the roof and transmit, if you like."

Clay brightened. "Can I call home?"

"If need be."

Something in Patil's tone told him a frivolous purpose was not going to receive their cooperation.

"Maybe tomorrow?"

"Perhaps. We must be sure that the devotees do not see us reveal it."

"They think we're laborers?"

"So we have convinced them, I believe."

"And me?"

"You would do well to stay inside."

"Um. Look, got anything to drink?"

Patil frowned. "Has the water pipe stopped giving?"

"No, I mean, you know—a drink. Gin and tonic, wasn't that what the Brits preferred?"

"Alcohol is the devil's urine," Patil said precisely.

"It won't scramble my brains."

"Who can be sure? The mind is a tentative instrument."

"You don't want any suspicion that I'm unreliable, that it?"

"No, of course not," Singh broke in anxiously.

"Needn't worry," Clay muttered. The heat below and the long hours of tedious work were wearing him down. "I'll be gone soon's I can get things wrapped up."

"You agree that we are seeing the decays?"

"Let's say things're looking better."

Clay had been holding back even tentative approval. He had expected some show of jubilation. Patil and Singh simply sat and stared into the flickering coals of the stove's half-open door.

Slowly Patil said, "Word will spread quickly."

"Soon as you transmit it on that dish, sure."

Singh murmured, "Much shall change."

"Look, you might want to get out of here, go present a paper—"

"Oh no, we shall remain," Singh said quickly.

"Those devotees could give you trouble if they find—"

"We expect that this discovery, once understood, shall have great effects," Patil said solemnly. "I much prefer to witness them from my home country."

The cadence and mood of this conversation struck Clay as odd, but he put it down to the working conditions. Certainly they had sacrificed a great deal to build and run this experiment amid crippling desolation.

"This result will begin the final renunciation of the materialistic worldview," Singh said matter-of-factly.

"Huh?"

"In peering at the individual lives of mere particles, we employ the reductionist hammer," Patil explained. "But nature is not like a salamander, cut into fragments."

"Or if it were," Singh added, "once the salamander is so sliced, try to make it do its salamander walk again." A broad white grin split the gloom of nightfall.

"The world is an implicate order, Dr. Clay. All parts are hinged to each other."

Clay frowned. He vaguely remembered a theory of quantum mechanics which used that term—"implicate order," meaning that a deeper realm of physical theory lay beneath the uncertainties of wave mechanics. Waves that took it into their heads to behave like particles, and the reverse—these were supposed to be illusions arising from our ignorance of a more profound theory. But there was no observable consequence of such notions, and to Clay such mumbo jumbo from theorists who never got their hands dirty was empty rhapsodizing. Still, he was supposed to be the diplomat here.

He gave a judicial nod. "Yeah, sure—but when the particles die, it'll all be gone, right?"

"Yes, in about 10^{34} years," Patil said. "But the *knowledge* of matter's mortality will spread as swiftly as light, on the wind of our transmitter."

"So?"

"You are an experimentalist, Dr. Clay, and thus—if you will forgive my putting it so—addicted to cutting the salamander." Patil made a steeple of his fingers, sending spindly shadows rippling across his face. "The world we study is conditioned by our perceptions of it. The implied order is partially from our own design."

"Sure, quantum measurement, uncertainty principle, all that." Clay had sat through all the usual lectures about this stuff and didn't feel like doing so again. Not in a dusty shed with his stomach growling from hunger. He sipped at his cup of weak Darjeeling and yawned.

"Difficulties of measurement reflect underlying problems," Patil said. "Even the Westerner Plato saw that we perceive only imperfect modes of the true, deeper world."

"What deeper world?" Clay sighed despite himself.

"We do not know. We *cannot* know."

"Look, we make our measurements, we report. Period."

Amused, Singh said, "And that is where matters end?"

Patil said, "Consensual reality, that is your 'real' world, Professor Clay. But our news may cause that bland, unthinking consensus to falter."

Clay shrugged. This sounded like late-night college bullshit sessions among boozed-up science nerds. Patty-cake pantheism, quantum razzle-dazzle, garbage philosophy. It was one thing to be open-minded and another to let your brains fall out. Was *every*body on this wrecked continent a booga-booga type? He had to get out.

"Look, I don't see what difference—"

"Until the curtain of seeming surety is swept away," Singh put in.

"Surety?"

"This world—this universe—has labored long under the illusion of its own permanence." Singh spread his hands, animated in the flickering yellow glow. "We might die, yes, the sun might even perish—but the universe went on. Now we prove otherwise. There cannot help but be profound reactions."

He thought he saw what they were driving at. "A Nobel Prize, even."

To his surprise, both men laughed merrily. "Oh no," Patil said, arching his eyebrows. "No such trifles are expected!"

9

The boxy meeting room beside the data bay was packed. From it came a subdued mutter, a fretwork of talk laced with anticipation.

Outside, someone had placed a small chalky statue of a grinning elephant. Clay hesitated, stroked it. Despite the heat of the mine, the elephant was cool.

"The workers just brought it down," Mrs. Buli explained with a smile. "Our Hindu god of auspicious beginnings."

"Or endings," Patil said behind her. "Equally."

Clay nodded and walked into the trapped, moist heat of the room. Everyone was jammed in, graduate students and laborers alike, their dhotis already showing sweaty crescents. Clay saw the three students the devotees had beaten and exchanged respectful bows with them.

Perceiving some need for ceremony, he opened with lengthy praise for the endless hours they had labored, exclaiming over how startled the world would be to learn of such a facility. Then he plunged into consideration of each candidate event, his checks and counter-checks, vertex corrections, digital-array flaws, mean free paths, ionization rates, the artful programming that deflected the myriad possible sources of error. He could feel tension rising in the room as he cast the events on the inch-thick wall screen, calling them forth from the files in his cubes. Some he threw into 3-D, to show the full path through the cage of iron that had captured the death rattle of infinity.

And at the end, all cases reviewed, he said quietly, "You have found it. The proton lifetime is very nearly 10^{34} years."

The room burst into applause, wide grins and wild shouts as everyone pressed forward to shake his hand.

10

Singh handled the message to the NSF. Clay also constructed a terse though detailed summary and sent it to the International Astronomical Union for release to the worldwide system of observatories and universities.

Clay knew this would give a vital assist to his career. With the Kolar team staying here, he would be their only spokesman. And this was very big, media-mesmerizing news indeed.

The result was important to physicists and astronomers alike, for the destiny of all their searches ultimately would be sealed by the faint failures of particles no eye would ever see. In 10^{34} years, far in the depths of space, the great celestial cities, the galaxies, would be ebbing. The last red stars would flicker, belch, and gutter out. Perhaps life would have clung to them and found a way to persist against the growing cold. Cluttered with the memorabilia of the ages, the islands of mute matter would turn at last to their final conqueror—not entropy's still hand, but this silent sputter of protons.

Clay thought of the headlines: UNIVERSE TO END. What would *that* do to harried commuters on their way to work?

He watched Singh send the stuttering messages via the big satellite dish, the corrugated tin roof of the shed pulled aside, allowing him to watch burnt-gold twilight seep across the sky. Clay felt no elation, as blank as a drained capacitor. He had gone into physics because of the sense it gave of grasping deep mysteries. He could look at bridges and trace the vectored stability that ruled them. When his daughter asked why the sky was blue, he actually knew, and could sketch out a simple answer. It had never occurred to him to fear flying, because he knew the Bernoulli equation for the pressure that held up the plane.

But this result . . .

Even the celebratory party that evening left him unmoved. Graduate students turned out in their best khaki. Sitar music swarmed through the scented air, ragas thumping and weaving. He found his body swaying to the refractions of tone and scale.

"It is a pity you cannot learn more of our country," Mrs. Buli remarked, watching him closely.

"Right now I'm mostly interested in sleep."

"Sleep is not always kind." She seemed wry and distant in the night's smudged humidity. "One of our ancient gods, Brahma, is said to sleep—and we are what he dreams."

"In that case, for you folks maybe he's been having a nightmare lately."

"Ah yes, our troubles. But do not let them mislead you about India. They pass."

"I'm sure they will," Clay replied, dutifully diplomatic.

"You were surprised, were you not, at the outcome?" she said piercingly.

"Uh, well, I had to be skeptical."

"Yes, for a scientist certainty is built on deep layers of doubt."

"Like my daddy said, in the retail business deal with everybody, but count your change."

She laughed. "We have given you a bargain, perhaps!"

He was acutely aware that his initial doubts must have been obvious. And what unsettled him now was not just the hard-won success here, but their strange attitude toward it.

The graduate students came then and tried to teach him a dance. He did a passable job, and a student named Venkatraman slipped him a glass of beer, forbidden vice. It struck Clay as comic that the Indian government spent much energy to suppress alcohol but did little about the population explosion. The students all laughed when he made a complicated joke about booze, but he could not be sure whether they meant it. The music seemed to quicken, his heart thumping to keep up with it. They addressed him as Clay*ji*, a term of respect, and asked his opinion of what they might do next with the experiment. He shrugged, thinking *'Nother job, sahib?* and suggested using it as a detector for neutrinos from supernovas. That had paid off when the earlier generation of neutrino detectors picked up the 1987 supernova.

The atom bomb, the 1987 event, now this—particle physics, he realized uncomfortably, was steeped in death. The sitar slid and rang, and Mrs. Buli made arch jokes to go with the spicy salad. Still, he turned in early.

11

To be awakened by a soft breeze. A brushing presence, sliding cloth . . . He sensed her sari as a luminous fog. Moonlight streaming through a lopsided window cast shimmering auras through the cloth as she loomed above him. Reached for him. Lightly flung away his sticky bedclothes.

"I—"

A soft hand covered his mouth, bringing a heady savor of ripe earth. His senses ran out of him and into the surrounding dark, coiling in air as he took her weight. She was surprisingly light, though thick-waisted, her breasts like teacups compared with the full curves of her hips. His hands slid and pressed, finding a delightful slithering moisture all over her, a sheen of vibrancy. Her sari evaporated. The high planes of her face caught vagrant blades of moonlight, and he saw a curious tentative, expectant expression there as she wrapped him in soft pressures. Her mouth did not so much kiss his as enclose it, formulating an argument of sweet rivulets that trickled into his porous self. She slipped into place atop him, a slick clasp that melted him up into her, a perfect fit, slick with dark insistence. He closed his eyes, but the glow diffused through his eyelids, and he could see her hair fanning through the air like motion underwater, her luxuriant weight bucking, trembling as her nails scratched his shoulders, musk rising smoky from them both. A silky muscle milked him at each heart-thump. Her velvet mass orbited above their fulcrum, bearing down with feathery demands, and he remembered brass icons, gaudy Indian posters, and felt above him Kali strumming in fevered darkness. She locked legs around him, squeezing him up into her surprisingly hard muscles, grinding, drawing forth, pushing back. She cried out with great heaves and lungfuls of the thickening air, mouth going slack beneath hooded eyes, and he shot sharply up into her, a convulsion that poured out all the knotted aches in him, delivering them into the tumbled steamy earth—

12

—and next, with no memories between, he was stumbling with her . . . down a gully . . . beneath slanting silvery moonlight.

"What—what's—"

"Quiet!" She shushed him like a schoolmarm.

He recognized the rolling countryside near the mine. Vague forms flitted in the distance. Wracked cries cut the night.

"The devotees," Mrs. Buli whispered as they stumbled on. "They have assaulted the mine entrance."

"How'd we—"

"You were difficult to rouse," she said with a sidelong glance.

Was she trying to be amusing? The sudden change from mysterious supercharged sensuality back to this clipped, formal professionalism disoriented him.

"Apparently some of our laborers had a grand party. It alerted the devotees to our presence, some say. I spoke to a laborer while you slept, however, who said that the devotees knew of your presence. They asked for you."

"Why me?"

"Something about your luggage and a telephone call home."

Clay gritted his teeth and followed her along a path that led among the slumped hills, away from their lodgings. Soon the mine entrance was visible below. Running figures swarmed about it like black gnats. Ragged chants erupted from them. A *waarrrk waarrrk* sound came from the hangar, and it was some moments until Clay saw long chains of human bodies hanging from the rafters, swinging themselves in unison.

"They're pulling down the hangar," he whispered.

"I despair for what they have done inside."

He instinctively reached for her and felt the supple warmth he had embraced seemingly only moments before. She turned and gave him her mouth again.

"We—back there—why'd you come to me?"

"It was time. Even we feel the joy of release from order, Professor Clay."

"Well, sure . . ." Clay felt illogically embarrassed, embracing a woman who still had the musk of the bed about her, yet who used his title. "But . . . how'd I get here? Seems like—"

"You were immersed. Taken out of yourself."

"Well, yeah, it was good, fine, but I can't remember anything."

She smiled. "The best moments leave no trace. That is a signature of the implicate order."

Clay breathed in the waxy air to help clear his head. More mumbo jumbo, he thought, delivered by her with an open, expectant expression. In the darkness it took a moment to register that she had fled down another path.

"Where'll we go?" he gasped when he caught up.

"We must get to the vans. They are parked some kilometers away."

"My gear—"

"Leave it."

He hesitated a moment, then followed her. There was nothing irreplaceable. It certainly wasn't worth braving the mob below for the stuff.

They wound down through bare hillsides dominated by boulders. The sky rippled with heat lightning. Puffy clouds scudded quickly in from the west, great ivory flashes working among them. The ground surged slightly.

"Earthquake?" he asked.

"There were some earlier, yes. Perhaps that has excited the devotees further tonight, put their feet to running."

There was no sign of the physics team. Pebbles squirted from beneath his boots—he wondered how he had managed to get them on without remembering it—and recalled again her hypnotic sensuality. Stones rattled away down into narrow dry washes on each side. Clouds blotted out the moonglow, and they had to pick their way along the trail.

Clay's mind spun with plans, speculations, jittery anxiety. Mrs. Buli was now his only link to the Western fragment of India, and he could scarcely see her in the shadows. She moved with liquid grace, her sari trailing, sandals slapping. Suddenly she crouched down. "More."

Along the path came figures bearing lanterns. They moved silently in the fitful silvery moonlight. There was no place to hide, and the party had already seen them.

"Stand still," she said. Again the crisp Western diction, yet her ample hips swayed slightly, reminding him of her deeper self.

Clay wished he had a club, a knife, anything. He made himself stand beside her, hands clenched. For once his blackness might be an advantage.

The devotees passed, eyes rapt. Clay had expected them to be singing or chanting mantras or rubbing beads—but not shambling forward as if to their doom. The column barely glanced at him. In his baggy cotton trousers and formless shirt, he hoped he was unremarkable. A woman passed nearby, apparently carrying something across her back. Clay blinked. Her hands were nailed to the ends of a beam, and she carried it proudly, palms bloody, half crucified. Her face was serene, eyes focused on the roiling sky. Behind her was a man bearing a plate. Clay thought the shambling figure carried marbles on the dish until he peered closer and saw an iris, and realized the entire plate was packed with eyeballs. He gasped and faces turned toward him. Then the man was gone along the path, and Clay waited, holding his breath against a gamy stench he could not name. Some muttered to themselves, some carried religious artifacts, beads and statuettes and drapery, but none had the fervor of the devotees he had seen before. The ground trembled again.

And out of the dark air came a humming. Something struck a man in the line and he clutched at his throat, crying hoarsely. Clay leaped forward without thinking. He pulled the man's hands away. Lodged in the narrow of the throat was something like an enormous cockroach with fluttering wings. It had already embedded its head in the man. Spiky legs furiously scrabbled against the soiled skin to dig deeper. The man coughed and shouted weakly, as though the thing was already blocking his throat.

Clay grabbed its hind legs and pulled. The insect wriggled with surprising strength. He saw the hind stinger too late. The sharp point struck a hot jolt of pain into his thumb. Anger boiled in him. He held on despite the pain and yanked the thing free. It made a sucking sound coming out. He hissed with revulsion and violently threw it down the hillside.

The man stumbled, gasping, and then ran back down the path, never even looking at them. Mrs. Buli grabbed Clay, who was staggering around in a circle, shaking his hand. "I will cut it!" she cried.

He held still while she made a precise cross cut and drained the blood. "What . . . what *was* that?"

"A wasp-thing from the pouches that hang on our trees."

"Oh yeah. One of those bio tricks."

"They are still overhead."

Clay listened to the drone hanging over them. Another devotee shrieked and slapped the back of his neck. Clay numbly watched the man run away. His hand throbbed, but he could feel the effects ebbing. Mrs. Buli tore a strip from her sari and wrapped his thumb to quell the bleeding.

All this time, devotees streamed past them in the gloom. None took the slightest notice of Clay. Some spoke to themselves.

"Western science doesn't seem to bother 'em much now," Clay whispered wryly.

Mrs. Buli nodded. The last figure to pass was a woman who limped, sporting an arm that ended not in a hand but in a spoon, nailed to a stub of cork.

He followed Mrs. Buli into enveloping darkness. "Who were they?"

"I do not know. They spoke seldom and repeated the same words. Dharma and samsara, terms of destiny."

"They don't care about us?"

"They appear to sense a turning, a resolution." In the fitful moonglow her eyes were liquid puzzles.

"But they destroyed the experiment."

"I gather that knowledge of your Western presence was like the wasp-things. Irritating, but only a catalyst, not the cause."

"What *did* make them—"

"No time. Come."

They hurriedly entered a thin copse of spindly trees that lined a streambed. Dust stifled his nose and he breathed through his mouth. The clouds raced toward the horizon with unnatural speed, seeming to flee from the west. Trees swayed before an unfelt wind, twisting and reaching for the shifting sky.

"Weather," Mrs. Buli answered his questions. "Bad weather."

They came upon a small crackling fire. Figures crouched around it, and Clay made to go around, but Mrs. Buli walked straight toward it. Women squatted, poking sticks into the flames. Clay saw that something moved on the sticks. A momentary shaft of moonlight showed the oily skin of snakes, tiny eyes crisp as crystals, the shafts poking from yawning white mouths that still moved. The women's faces of stretched yellow skin anxiously watched the blackening, sizzling snakes, turning them. The fire hissed as though raindrops fell upon it, but Clay felt nothing wet, just the dry rub of a fresh abrading wind. Smoke wrapped the women in gray wreaths, and Mrs. Buli hurried on.

So much, so fast. Clay felt rising in him a leaden conviction born of all he had seen in this land. So many people, so much pain—how could it matter? The West assumed that the individual was important, the bedrock of all. That was why the obliterating events of the West's own history, like the Nazi Holocaust, by erasing humans in such numbing numbers, cast grave doubt on the significance of any one. India did something like that for him. Could a universe which produced so many bodies, so many minds in shadowed torment, care a whit about humanity? Endless, meaningless duplication of grinding pain . . .

A low mutter came on the wind, like a bass theme sounding up from the depths of a dusty well.

Mrs. Buli called out something he could not understand. She began running, and Clay hastened to follow. If he lost her in these shadows, he could lose all connection.

Quickly they left the trees and crossed a grassy field rutted by ancient agriculture and prickly with weeds. On this flat plain he could see that the whole sky worked with twisted light, a colossal electrical discharge feathering into more branches than a gnarled tree. The anxious clouds caught blue and burnt-yellow pulses and seemed to relay them, like the countless transformers and capacitors and voltage drops that made a worldwide communications net, carrying staccato messages laced with crackling punctuations.

"The vans," she panted.

Three brown vans crouched beneath a canopy of thin trees, further concealed beneath khaki tents that blended in with the dusty fields. Mrs. Buli yanked open the door of the first one. Her fingers fumbled at the ignition.

"The key must be concealed," she said quickly.

"Why?" he gasped, throat raw.

"They are to be always with the vans."

"Uh-huh. Check the others."

She hurried away. Clay got down on his knees, feeling the lip of the van's undercarriage. The ground seemed to heave with inner heat, dry and rasping, the pulse of the planet. He finished one side of the van and crawled under, feeling along the rear axle. He heard a distant plaintive cry, as eerie and forlorn as the call of a bird lost in fog.

"Clay*ji*? None in the others."

His hand touched a small slick box high up on the axle. He plucked it from its magnetic grip and rolled out from under.

"If we drive toward the mine," she said, "we can perhaps find others."

"Others, hell. Most likely we'll run into devotees."

"Well, I—"

Figures in the trees. Flitting, silent, quick.

"Get in."

"But—"

He pushed her in and tried to start the van. Running shapes in the field. He got the engine started on the third try and gunned it. They growled away. Something hard shattered the back window into a spiderweb, but then Clay swerved several times and nothing more hit them.

After a few minutes his heart-thumps slowed, and he turned on the headlights to make out the road. The curves were sandy and he did not want to get stuck. He stamped on the gas.

Suddenly great washes of amber light streamed across the sky, pale lances cutting the clouds. "My God, what's happening?"

"It is more than weather."

Her calm, abstracted voice made him glance across the seat. "No kidding."

"No earthquake could have collateral effects of this order."

He saw by the dashboard lights that she wore a lapis lazuli necklace. He had felt it when she came to him, and now its deep blues seemed like the only note of color in the deepening folds of night.

"It must be something far more profound."

"What?"

The road now arrowed straight through a tangled terrain of warped trees and oddly shaped boulders. Something rattled against the windshield like hail, but Clay could see nothing.

"We have always argued, some of us, that the central dictate of quantum mechanics is the interconnected nature of the observer and the observed."

The precise, detached lecturer style again drew his eyes to her. Shadowed, her face gave away no secrets.

"We always filter the world," she said with dreamy momentum, "and yet are linked to it. How much of what we see is in fact taught us, by our bodies, or by the consensus reality that society trains us to see, even before we can speak for ourselves?"

"Look, that sky isn't some problem with my eyes. It's *real*. Hear that?" Something big and soft had struck the door of the van, rocking it.

"And we here have finished the program of materialistic science, have we not? We flattered the West by taking it seriously. As did the devotees."

Clay grinned despite himself. It was hard to feel flattered when you were fleeing for your life.

Mrs. Buli stretched lazily, as though relaxing into the clasp of the moist night. "So we have proven the passing nature of matter. What fresh forces does that bring into play?"

"Huh!" Clay spat back angrily. "Look here, we just sent word out, reported the result. How—"

"So that by now millions, perhaps billions of people know that the very stones that support them must pass."

"So what? Just some theoretical point about subnuclear physics, how's that going to—"

"Who is to say? What avatar? The point is that we were believed. Certain knowledge, universally correlated, surely has some impact—"

The van lurched. Suddenly they jounced and slammed along the smooth roadway. A bright plume of sparks shot up behind them, brimming firefly yellow in the night.

"Axle's busted!" Clay cried. He got the van stopped. In the sudden silence, it registered that the motor had gone dead.

They climbed out. Insects buzzed and hummed in the hazy gloom.

The roadway was still straight and sure, but on all sides great blobs of iridescent water swelled up from the ground, making colossal drops. The trembling half-spheres wobbled in the frayed moonlight. Silently, softly, the bulbs began to detach from the foggy ground and gently loft upward. Feathery luminescent clouds above gathered on swift winds that sheared their edges. These billowing, luxuriant banks snagged the huge teardrop shapes as they plunged skyward.

"I . . . I don't . . ."

Mrs. Buli turned and embraced him. Her moist mouth opened a redolent interior continent to him, teeming and blackly bountiful, and he had to resist falling inward, a tumbling silvery bubble in a dark chasm.

"The category of perfect roundness is fading," she said calmly.

Clay looked at the van. The wheels had become ellipses. At each revolution they had slammed the axles into the roadway, leaving behind long scratches of rough tar.

He took a step.

She said, "Since we can walk, the principle of pivot and lever, of muscles pulling bones, survives."

"How . . . this doesn't . . ."

"But do our bodies depend on roundness? I wonder." She carefully lay down on the blacktop.

The road straightened precisely, like joints in an aged spine popping as they realigned.

Angles cut their spaces razor-sharp, like axioms from Euclid.

Clouds merged, forming copious tinkling hexagons.

"It is good to see that some features remain. Perhaps these are indeed the underlying Platonic beauties."

"What?" Clay cried.

"The undying forms," Mrs. Buli said abstractly. "Perhaps that one Western idea was correct after all."

Clay desperately grasped the van. He jerked his arm back when the metal skin began flexing and reshaping itself.

Smooth glistening forms began to emerge from the rough, coarse earth. Above the riotous, heaving land the moon was now a brassy cube. Across its face played enormous black cracks like mad lightning.

Somewhere far away his wife and daughter were in this, too. *G'bye, Daddy. It's been real.*

Quietly the land began to rain upward. Globs dripped toward the pewter, filmy continent swarming freshly above. Eons measured out the evaporation of ancient sluggish seas.

His throat struggled against torpid air. "Is . . . Brahma . . . ?"

"Awakening?" came her hollow voice, like an echo from a distant gorge.

"What happens . . . to . . . us?"

His words diffracted away from him. He could now see acoustic waves, wedges of compressed, mute atoms crowding in the exuberant air. Luxuriant, inexhaustible riches burst from beneath the ceramic certainties he had known.

"Come." Her voice seeped through the churning ruby air.

Centuries melted between them as he turned. A being he recognized without conscious thought spun in liquid air.

Femina, she was now, and she drifted on the new wafting currents. He and she were made of shifting geometric elements, molecular units of shape and firm thrust. A wan joy spread through him.

Time that was no time did not pass, and he and she and the impacted forces between them were pinned to the forever moment that cascaded through them, all of them, the billions of atomized elements that made them, all, forever.

THE HAMMER OF GOD

Arthur C. Clarke

❁

Arthur C. Clarke (born 1917) lives with his adopted family in Sri Lanka. He received a knighthood in January 1999. He says, "On New Year's Day, the British High Commissioner gave me the splendid news that Her Majesty was awarding me a Knighthood for 'Services to Literature.' I regarded this as a compliment to the entire genre of Science Fiction as much as to myself. The English Lit mandarins could put this piece of news in their pipes and smoke it."

He was chairman of the British Interplanetary Society (1946–47 and 1950–53). In 1945, he made the first proposal that satellites could be used for communications. His first SF story, "Loophole," appeared in *Astounding* in 1946. His first SF novel, *Prelude to Space*, was published in 1951. It was quickly followed by *The Sands of Mars* (1951), *Islands in the Sky* (1952), *Against the Fall of Night* (1953), and *Childhood's End* (1953). *Expedition to Earth*, the first of more than a dozen collections, included the story "The Sentinel," later the basis for the film *2001* (1968), which Clarke expanded into the bestselling novel *2001* (1968).

As we said in *The Ascent of Wonder* (1994), Arthur C. Clarke is the poet of technology and cosmology in modern SF. He is also as much a proponent of space travel as was his peer, Robert A. Heinlein. But Gregory Benford has remarked, "There's more similarity between Arthur C. Clarke and Thoreau than there is between Clarke and Heinlein." For Clarke, the beauties of vistas in space are the beauties of nature, and the exploration of space is the quest for knowledge and close experience of nature, for things never before seen and felt by an individual human. And the medium through which this exploration will be achieved is technology.

Technological artifacts may, in addition, be beautiful in and of themselves, interesting, mysterious, promising. Clarke, unlike Heinlein or Asimov, is also the poet of the big machine. And in this he has always been a leader in hard SF, and has maintained the bond between SF and the twin communities devoted to the construction of enormous machines for scientific exploration—experimental physics and the space community—for decades. Clarke's stories tend to be about the emotional rewards of the quest for knowledge as opposed to the power knowledge can confer.

In the 1990s, Clarke was unwell but still published a few pieces, and collaborated with Gregory Benford, Gentry Lee, and Stephen Baxter on projects. Clarke was important not only for historical reasons but because he was actively collaborating with Baxter and thereby having influence on one of the most important newer writers.

Clarke's politics are not often overt, but are neither of the Libertarian right nor the radical left. They hark back to the liberal "one world" United Nations ideals of the mid-20th century. At a crucial moment for hard SF in the early 1980s, Jerry Pournelle called together Robert A. Heinlein, Gregory Benford, and others to form an official science advisory committee to then President Ronald Reagan and promoted what was then called the Star Wars defense program. (See Greg Bear note, below.) Gregory Benford tells in his essay "Old Legends" in Greg Bear's anthology, *New Legends*, of Clarke's visit to one of their meetings:

The Advisory Council met in August of 1984 in a mood of high celebration. Their pioneering work had yielded fruits unimaginable in 1982. Robert Heinlein, the dean of American science fiction writers, attended; the Council had attracted interest from some speculative quarters and, historically, writers had provided many ideas basic to the space program. Out of the shimmering summer heat came a surprise visitor—Arthur C. Clarke, in town to promote the opening of the film made from his novel, *2010*.

In 1950, Clarke had described an electromagnetic catapult to launch people and cargo from the surface of the moon. This idea evolved into the "mass driver" now being studied for use as a "magnetic machine gun" to shoot down ICBMs. Clarke had testified before Congress against SDI, and regarded the pollution of space by weapons, even defensive ones, as a violation of his life's vision.

Heinlein attacked as soon as Clarke settled into Larry Niven's living room. The conversation swirled from technical issues—could SDI satellites be destroyed by cheap rocks put into orbit? Would SDI lead to further offensive weapons in space? Would it help or hinder other uses of near-Earth orbit?—to a clear clash of personalities. Clarke—cool, analytical, mild-mannered—was taken aback. His old friend Heinlein regarded Clarke's statements as both wrong-headed and rude. Foreigners on our soil should step softly in discussions of our policies, Heinlein said. Clarke was guilty of "British arrogance."

Clarke had not expected this level of feeling among old comrades. They had all believed in the High Church of Space, as one writer present put it. Now, each side regarded the other as betraying that vision, of narrowness, of imposing unwarranted assumptions on the future of mankind. It was a sad moment for many when Clarke said a quiet goodbye and disappeared into his limousine, stunned. Later that afternoon he asked me tentatively, "Do most of the American science fiction writers feel this way?"

We see this moment as symbolic of the developing divide between U.S. and U.K. hard SF in the 1980s, of the consequences of the overt right-wing politicization of American hard SF that began in the 1970s. (See also the Gregory Benford "Immersion" note.)

"The Hammer of God," about an asteroid on a collision course with Earth, appeared in *Time* magazine in 1992. It is didactic SF on a grand scale with characters only faintly sketched in. Although Gardner Dozois reprinted it in his *Year's Best* volume, it got less attention within the field than it deserved. It did, however, feed the prominent political discussions in the U.S. government and elsewhere during the decade about what to do in the event of the discovery of an actual asteroid on a collision course with our planet. This is still in the news as this anthology is published.

I*t came in vertically, punching a hole ten km wide through the atmosphere, generating temperatures so high that the air itself started to burn. When it hit the ground near the Gulf of Mexico, rock turned to liquid and spread outward in mountainous waves, not freezing until it had formed a crater two hundred km across.*

That was only the beginning of disaster: now the real tragedy began. Nitric oxides rained from the air, turning the sea to acid. Clouds of soot from incinerated forests darkened the sky, hiding the sun for months. Worldwide, the temperature dropped precipitously, killing off most of the plants and animals that had survived the initial cataclysm. Though some species would linger on for millenniums, the reign of the great reptiles was finally over.

The clock of evolution had been reset; the countdown to Man had begun. The date was, very approximately, 65 million B.C.

Captain Robert Singh never tired of walking in the forest with his little son Toby. It was, of course, a tamed and gentle forest, guaranteed to be free of dangerous animals, but it made an exciting contrast to the rolling sand dunes of their last environment in the Saudi desert—and the one before that, on Australia's Great Barrier Reef. But when the Skylift Service had moved the house this time, something had gone wrong with the food-recycling system. Though the electronic menus had fail-safe backups, there had been a curious metallic taste to some of the items coming out of the synthesizer recently.

"What's that, Daddy?" asked the four-year-old, pointing to a small hairy face peering at them through a screen of leaves.

"Er, some kind of monkey. We'll ask the Brain when we get home."

"Can I play with it?"

"I don't think that's a good idea. It could bite. And it probably has fleas. Your robotoys are much nicer."

"But . . ."

Captain Singh knew what would happen next: he had run this sequence a dozen times. Toby would begin to cry, the monkey would disappear, he would comfort the child as he carried him back to the house . . .

But that had been twenty years ago and a quarter-billion kilometers away. The playback came to an end; sound, vision, the scent of unknown flowers and the gentle touch of the wind slowly faded. Suddenly, he was back in this cabin aboard the orbital tug *Goliath*, commanding the one hundred person team of Operation ATLAS, the most critical mission in the history of space exploration. Toby, and the stepmothers and stepfathers of his extended family, remained behind on a distant world which Singh could never revisit. Decades in space—and neglect of the mandatory zero-G exercises—had so weakened him that he could now walk only on the Moon and Mars. Gravity had exiled him from the planet of his birth.

"One hour to rendezvous, Captain," said the quiet but insistent voice of David, as *Goliath*'s central computer had been inevitably named. "Active mode, as requested. Time to come back to the real world."

Goliath's human commander felt a wave of sadness sweep over him as the final image from his lost past dissolved into a featureless, simmering mist of white noise. Too swift a transition from one reality to another was a good recipe for schizophrenia, and Captain Singh always eased the shock with the most soothing sound he knew: waves falling gently on a beach, with sea gulls crying in the distance. It was yet another memory of a life he had lost, and of a peaceful past that had now been replaced by a fearful present.

For a few more moments, he delayed facing his awesome responsibility. Then he sighed and removed the neural-input cap that fitted snugly over his skull and had enabled him to call up his distant past. Like all spacers, Captain Singh belonged to the "Bald Is Beautiful" school, if only because wigs were a nuisance in zero gravity. The social historians were still staggered by the fact that one invention, the portable "Brainman," could make bare heads the norm within a single decade. Not even quick-change skin coloring, or the lens-corrective laser shaping which had abolished eyeglasses, had made such an impact upon style and fashion.

"Captain," said David. "I know you're there. Or do you want me to take over?"

It was an old joke, inspired by all the insane computers in the fiction and movies of the early electronic age. David had a surprisingly good sense of humor: he was, after all, a Legal Person (Nonhuman) under the famous Hundredth Amendment, and shared—or surpassed—almost all the attributes of his creators. But there were whole sensory and emotional areas which he could not enter. It had been felt unnecessary to equip him with smell or taste, though it would have been easy to do so. And all his attempts at telling dirty stories were such disastrous failures that he had abandoned the genre.

"All right, David," replied the captain. "I'm still in charge." He removed the mask from his eyes, and turned reluctantly toward the viewport. There, hanging in space before him, was Kali.

It looked harmless enough: just another small asteroid, shaped so exactly like a peanut that the resemblance was almost comical. A few large impact craters, and hundreds of tiny ones, were scattered at random over its charcoal-gray surface. There were no visual clues to give any sense of scale, but Singh knew its dimensions by heart: 1,295 m maximum length, 456 m minimum width. Kali would fit easily into many city parks.

No wonder that, even now, most of humankind could still not believe that this modest asteroid was the instrument of doom. Or, as the Chrislamic Fundamentalists were calling it, "the Hammer of God."

The sudden rise of Chrislam had been traumatic equally to Rome and Mecca. Christianity was already reeling from John Paul XXV's eloquent but belated plea for contraception and the irrefutable proof in the New Dead Sea Scrolls that the Jesus of the Gospels was a composite of at least three persons. Meanwhile the Muslim world had lost much of its economic power when the Cold Fusion breakthrough, after the fiasco of its premature announcement, had brought the Oil Age to a sudden end. The time had been ripe for a new religion embodying, as even its severest critics admitted, the best elements of two ancient ones.

The Prophet Fatima Magdalene (née Ruby Goldenburg) had attracted almost one hundred million adherents before her spectacular—and, some maintained, self-contrived—martyrdom. Thanks to the brilliant use of neural programming to give previews of Paradise during its ceremonies, Chrislam had grown explosively, though it was still far outnumbered by its parent religions.

Inevitably, after the Prophet's death the movement split into rival factions, each upholding *the* True Faith. The most fanatical was a fundamentalist group calling itself "the Reborn," which claimed to be in direct contact with God (or at least Her Archangels) via the listening post they had established in the silent zone on the far side of the Moon, shielded from the radio racket of Earth by three thousand km of solid rock.

Now Kali filled the main viewscreen. No magnification was needed, for *Goliath* was hovering only two hundred m above its ancient, battered surface. Two crew members had already landed, with the traditional "One small step for a man"—even though walking was impossible on this almost zero-gravity worldlet.

"Deploying radio beacon. We've got it anchored securely. Now Kali won't be able to hide from us."

It was a feeble joke, not meriting the laughter it aroused from the dozen officers on the bridge. Ever since rendezvous, there had been a subtle change in the crew's morale, with unpredictable swings between gloom and juvenile humor. The ship's physician had already prescribed tranquilizers for one mild case of manic-depressive symptoms. It would grow worse in the long weeks ahead, when there would be little to do but wait.

The first waiting period had already begun. Back on Earth, giant radio telescopes were tuned to receive the pulses from the beacon. Although Kali's orbit had already been calculated with the greatest possible accuracy, there was still a slim chance that the asteroid might pass harmlessly by. The radio measuring rod would settle the matter, for better or worse.

It was a long two hours before the verdict came, and David relayed it to the crew.

"Spaceguard reports that the probability of impact on Earth is 99.9%. Operation ATLAS will begin immediately."

The task of the mythological Atlas was to hold up the heavens and prevent them from crashing down upon Earth. The ATLAS booster that *Goliath* carried as an external payload had a more modest goal: keeping at bay only a small piece of the sky.

It was the size of a small house, weighed 9,000 tons and was moving at 50,000 km/h. As it passed over the Grand Teton National Park, one alert tourist photographed the incandescent fireball and its long vapor trail. In less than two minutes, it had sliced through the Earth's atmosphere and returned to space.

The slightest change of orbit during the billions of years it had been circling the sun might have sent the asteroid crashing upon any of the world's great cities with an explosive force five times that of the bomb that destroyed Hiroshima.

The date was Aug. 10, 1972.

Spaceguard had been one of the last projects of the legendary NASA, at the close of the twentieth century. Its initial objective had been modest enough: to make as complete a survey as possible of the asteroids and comets that crossed the orbit of Earth—and to determine if any were a potential threat.

With a total budget seldom exceeding $10 million a year, a worldwide network of telescopes, most of them operated by skilled amateurs, had been established by the year 2000. Sixty-one years later, the spectacular return of Halley's Comet encouraged more funding, and the great 2079 fireball, luckily impacting in mid-Atlantic, gave Spaceguard additional prestige. By the end of the century, it had located more than 1 million asteroids, and the survey was believed to be 90 percent complete. However, it would have to be continued indefinitely: there was always a chance that some intruder might come rushing in from the uncharted outer reaches of the solar system.

As had Kali, which had been detected in late 2212 as it fell sunward past the orbit of Jupiter. Fortunately humankind had not been wholly unprepared, thanks to the fact that Senator George Ledstone (Independent, West America) had chaired an influential finance committee almost a generation earlier.

The senator had one public eccentricity and, he cheerfully admitted, one secret vice. He always wore massive horn-rimmed eyeglasses (nonfunctional, of course) because they had an intimidating effect on uncooperative witnesses, few of whom had ever encountered such a novelty. His "secret vice," perfectly well known to everyone, was rifle shooting on a standard Olympic range, set up in the tunnels of a long-abandoned missile silo near Mount Cheyenne. Ever since the demilitarization of Planet Earth (much accelerated by the famous slogan "Guns Are the Crutches of the Impotent"), such activities had been frowned upon, though not actively discouraged.

There was no doubt that Senator Ledstone was an original; it seemed to run in the family. His grandmother had been a colonel in the dreaded Beverly Hills Militia, whose skirmishes with the L.A. Irregulars had spawned endless psychodramas in every medium, from old-fashioned ballet to direct brain stimulation. And his grandfather had been one of the most notorious bootleggers of the twenty-first century. Before he was killed in a shoot-out with the Canadian Medicops during an ingenious attempt to smuggle a kiloton of tobacco up Niagara Falls, it was estimated that "Smokey" had been responsible for at least twenty million deaths.

Ledstone was quite unrepentant about his grandfather, whose sensational demise had triggered the repeal of the late U.S.'s third, and most disastrous, attempt at Prohibition. He argued that responsible adults should be allowed to commit suicide in any way they pleased—by alcohol, cocaine or even tobacco—as long as they did not kill innocent bystanders during the process.

When the proposed budget for Spaceguard Phase 2 was first presented to him, Senator Ledstone had been outraged by the idea of throwing billions of dollars into space. It was true that the global economy was in good shape; since the almost simultaneous collapse of communism and capitalism, the skillful application of chaos theory by World Bank mathematicians had broken the old cycle of booms and busts and averted (so far) the Final Depression predicted by many pessimists. Nonetheless, the senator argued that the money could be much better spent on Earth—especially on his favorite project, reconstructing what was left of California after the Superquake.

When Ledstone had twice vetoed Spaceguard Phase 2, everyone agreed that no one on Earth would make him change his mind. They had reckoned without someone from Mars.

The Red Planet was no longer quite so red, though the process of greening it had barely begun. Concentrating on the problems of survival, the colonists (they hated the word and were already saying proudly "we Martians") had little energy left over for art or science. But the lightning flash of genius strikes where it will, and the greatest theoretical physicist of the century was born under the bubble domes of Port Lowell.

Like Einstein, to whom he was often compared, Carlos Mendoza was an excellent musician; he owned the only saxophone on Mars and was a skilled performer on that antique instrument. He could have received his Nobel Prize on Mars, as everyone expected, but he loved surprises and practical jokes. Thus he appeared in Stockholm looking like a knight in high-tech armor, wearing one of the powered exoskeletons developed for paraplegics. With this mechanical assistance, he could function almost unhandicapped in an environment that would otherwise have quickly killed him.

Needless to say, when the ceremony was over, Carlos was bombarded with invitations to scientific and social functions. Among the few he was able to accept was an appearance before the World Budget Committee, where Senator Ledstone closely questioned him about his opinion of Project Spaceguard.

"I live on a world which still bears the scars of a thousand meteor impacts, some of them *hundreds* of kilometers across," said Professor Mendoza. "Once they were equally common on Earth, but wind and rain—something we don't have yet on Mars, though we're working on it!—have worn them away."

Senator Ledstone: "The Spaceguarders are always pointing to signs of asteroid impacts on Earth. How seriously should we take their warnings?"

Professor Mendoza: "Very seriously, Mr. Chairman. Sooner or later, there's bound to be another major impact."

Senator Ledstone was impressed, and indeed charmed, by the young scientist, but not yet convinced. What changed his mind was not a matter of logic but of emotion. On his way to London, Carlos Mendoza was killed in a bizarre accident when the control system of his exoskeleton malfunctioned. Deeply moved, Ledstone immediately dropped his opposition to Spaceguard, approving construction of two powerful orbiting tugs, *Goliath* and *Titan*, to be kept permanently patrolling on opposite sides of the sun. And when he was a very old man, he said to one of his aides, "They tell me we'll soon be able to take Mendoza's brain out of that tank of liquid nitrogen, and talk to it through a computer interface. I wonder what he's been thinking about, all these years . . ."

Assembled on Phobos, the inner satellite of Mars, ATLAS was little more than a set of rocket engines attached to propellant tanks holding one hundred thousand tons of hydrogen. Though its fusion drive could generate far less thrust than the primitive missile that had carried Yuri Gagarin into space, it could run continuously not merely for minutes but for weeks. Even so, the effect on the asteroid would be trivial, a velocity change of a few centimeters per second. Yet that might be sufficient to deflect Kali from its fatal orbit during the months while it was still falling earthward.

Now that ATLAS's propellant tanks, control systems and thrusters had been securely mounted on Kali, it looked as if some lunatic had built an oil refinery on an asteroid. Captain Singh was exhausted, as were all the crew members, after days of assembly and checking. Yet he felt a warm glow of achievement: they had done everything that was expected of them, the countdown was going smoothly, and the rest was up to ATLAS.

He would have been far less relaxed had he known of the ABSOLUTE PRIORITY message racing toward him by tight infrared beam from ASTROPOL headquarters in Geneva. It would not reach *Goliath* for another thirty minutes. And by then it would be much too late.

At about T minus thirty minutes, *Goliath* had drawn away from Kali to stand well clear of the jet with which ATLAS would try to nudge it from its present course. "Like a mouse pushing an elephant," one media person had described the operation. But in the frictionless vacuum of space, where momentum could never be lost, even one mousepower would be enough if applied early and over a sufficient length of time.

The group of officers waiting quietly on the bridge did not expect to see anything spectacular: the plasma jet of the ATLAS drive would be far too hot to produce much visible radiation. Only the telemetry would confirm that ignition had started and that Kali was no longer an implacable juggernaut, wholly beyond the control of humanity.

There was a brief round of cheering and a gentle patter of applause as the string of zeros on the accelerometer display began to change. The feeling on the bridge was one of relief rather than exultation. Though Kali was stirring, it would be days and weeks before victory was assured.

And then, unbelievably, the numbers dropped back to zero. Seconds later, three simultaneous audio alarms sounded. All eyes were suddenly fixed on Kali and the ATLAS booster which should be nudging it from its present course. The sight was heartbreaking: the great propellant tanks were opening up like flowers in a time-lapse movie, spilling out the thousands of tons of reaction mass that might have saved the Earth. Wisps of vapor drifted across the face of the asteroid, veiling its cratered surface with an evanescent atmosphere.

Then Kali continued along its path, heading inexorably toward a fiery collision with the Earth.

Captain Singh was alone in the large, well-appointed cabin that had been his home for longer than any other place in the solar system. He was still dazed but was trying to make his peace with the universe.

He had lost, finally and forever, all that he loved on Earth. With the decline of the nuclear family, he had known many deep attachments, and it had been hard to decide who should be the mothers of the two children he was permitted. A phrase from an old American novel (he had forgotten the author) kept coming into his mind: "Remember them as they were—and write them off." The fact that he himself was perfectly safe somehow made him feel worse; *Goliath* was in no danger whatsoever, and still had all the propellant it needed to rejoin the shaken survivors of humanity on the Moon or Mars.

Well, he had many friendships—and one that was much more than that—on Mars; this was where his future must lie. He was only 102, with decades of active life ahead of him. But some of the crew had loved ones on the Moon; he would have to put *Goliath*'s destination to the vote.

Ship's Orders had never covered a situation like this.

I still don't understand," said the chief engineer, "why that explosive cord wasn't detected on the preflight check-out."

"Because that Reborn fanatic could have hidden it easily—and no one would have dreamed of looking for such a thing. Pity ASTROPOL didn't catch him while he was still on Phobos."

"But *why* did they do it? I can't believe that even Chrislamic crazies would want to destroy the Earth."

"You can't argue with their logic—if you accept their premises. God, Allah, is testing us, and we mustn't interfere. If Kali misses, fine. If it doesn't, well, that's part of Her bigger plan. Maybe we've messed up Earth so badly that it's time to start over. Remember that old saying of Tsiolkovski's: 'Earth is the cradle of humankind, but you cannot live in the cradle forever.' Kali could be a sign that it's time to leave."

The captain held up his hand for silence.

"The only important question now is, Moon or Mars? They'll both need us. I don't want to influence you" (that was hardly true; everyone knew where he wanted to go), "so I'd like your views first."

The first ballot was Mars 6, Moon 6, Don't know 1, captain abstaining.

Each side was trying to convert the single "Don't know" when David spoke.

"There is an alternative."

"What do you mean?" Captain Singh demanded, rather brusquely.

"It seems obvious. Even though ATLAS is destroyed, we still have a chance of saving the Earth. According to my calculations, *Goliath* has just enough propellant to deflect Kali—if we start thrusting against it immediately. But the longer we wait, the less the probability of success."

There was a moment of stunned silence on the bridge as everyone asked the question, "Why didn't I think of that?" and quickly arrived at the answer.

David had kept his head, if one could use so inappropriate a phrase, while all the humans around him were in a state of shock. There were some compensations in being a Legal Person (Nonhuman). Though David could not know love, neither could he know fear. He would continue to think logically, even to the edge of doom.

With any luck, thought Captain Singh, this is my last broadcast to Earth. I'm tired of being a hero, and a slightly premature one at that. Many things could still go wrong, as indeed they already have . . .

"This is Captain Singh, space tug *Goliath*. First of all, let me say how glad we are that the Elders of Chrislam have identified the saboteurs and handed them over to ASTROPOL.

"We are now fifty days from Earth, and we have a slight problem. This one, I hasten to add, will not affect our new attempt to deflect Kali into a safe orbit. I note that the news media are calling this deflection Operation Deliverance. We like the name, and hope to live up to it, but we still cannot be absolutely certain of success. David, who appreciates all the goodwill messages he has received, estimates that the probability of Kali impacting Earth is still ten percent . . .

"We had intended to keep just enough propellant reserve to leave Kali shortly before encounter and go into a safer orbit, where our sister ship *Titan* could rendezvous with us. But that option is now closed. While *Goliath* was pushing against Kali at maximum drive, we broke through a weak point in the crust. The ship wasn't damaged, but we're stuck! All attempts to break away have failed.

"We're not worried, and it may even be a blessing in disguise. Now we'll use the *whole* of our remaining propellant to give one final nudge. Perhaps that will be the last drop that's needed to do the job.

"So we'll ride Kali past Earth, and wave to you from a comfortable distance, in just fifty days."

It would be the longest fifty days in the history of the world.

Now the huge crescent of the moon spanned the sky, the jagged mountain peaks along the terminator burning with the fierce light of the lunar dawn. But the dusty plains still untouched by the sun were not completely dark; they were glowing faintly in the light reflected from Earth's clouds and continents. And scattered here and there across that once dead landscape were the glowing fireflies that marked the first permanent settlements humankind had built beyond the home planet. Captain Singh could easily locate Clavius Base, Port Armstrong, Plato City. He could even see the necklace of faint lights along the Translunar Railroad, bringing its precious cargo of water from the ice mines at the South Pole.

Earth was now only five hours away.

Kali entered Earth's atmosphere soon after local midnight, two hundred km above Hawaii. Instantly, the gigantic fireball brought a false dawn to the Pacific, awakening the wildlife on its myriad islands. But few humans had been asleep this night of nights, except those who had sought the oblivion of drugs.

Over New Zealand, the heat of the orbiting furnace ignited forests and melted the snow on mountaintops, triggering avalanches into the valleys beneath. But the human race had been very, very lucky: the main thermal impact as Kali passed the Earth was on the Antarctic, the continent that could best absorb it. Even Kali could not strip away all the kilometers of polar ice, but it set in motion the Great Thaw that would change coastlines all around the world.

No one who survived hearing it could ever describe the sound of Kali's passage; none of the recordings were more than feeble echoes. The video coverage, of course, was superb, and would be watched in awe for generations to come. But nothing could ever compare with the fearsome reality.

Two minutes after it had sliced into the atmosphere, Kali reentered space. Its closest approach to Earth had been sixty km. In that two minutes, it took 100,000 lives and did $1 trillion worth of damage.

Goliath had been protected from the fireball by the massive shield of Kali itself; the sheets of incandescent plasma streamed harmlessly overhead. But when the asteroid smashed into Earth's blanket of air at more than one hundred times the speed of sound, the colossal drag forces mounted swiftly to five, ten, twenty gravities—and peaked at a level far beyond anything that machines or flesh could withstand.

Now indeed Kali's orbit had been drastically changed; never again would it come near Earth. On its next return to the inner solar system, the *swifter* spacecraft of a later age would visit the crumpled wreckage of *Goliath* and bear reverently homeward the bodies of those who had saved the world.

Until the next encounter.

THINK LIKE A DINOSAUR

James Patrick Kelly

James Patrick Kelly (born 1951) was told as a young writer by his teachers at the Clarion workshop that science fiction stories should be well thought out and well researched and so he set out to write that way. Only later did he learn that many writers in the field don't bother to work that hard. But by then, his habits were in place. He is not one of hard SF's politically committed true believers, but rather is intrigued by the dramatic possibilities of hard SF situations. He has a clear graceful style and a willingness to do the work of making the science in his stories count. His stories are tight and polished and his narrators tend to have a strong voice and point of view that allow Kelly to play out the drama of the situation he has chosen.

Although a writer identified with the Sycamore Hill workshop in the 1980s, the hotbed of Humanist opposition to the cyberpunks, he was also chosen as representative of the original Movement (along with Greg Bear, another surprise) by Bruce Sterling for inclusion in *Mirrorshades: The Cyberpunk Anthology*. Much of his fiction has a serious hard SF side that appeals broadly to all readers in the field.

Though he is primarily a short story writer (publishing mainly in *Asimov's*) he has published four novels: *Planet of Whispers* (1984), *Freedom Beach* (1985) with John Kessel, *Look into the Sun* (1989), and *Wildlife* (1994). Two collections of his stories have been published—*Heroines* (1990), and *Think like a Dinosaur and Other Stories* (1997)—his new collection, *Strange but Not a Stranger*, was out in 2002. He writes a monthly column about the web for *Asimov's*. His story "Undone" (2001) was selected for all three best of the year volumes and was a Nebula nominee. For some time now, Kelly has, as John Clute put it, "stood on the verge of recognition as a major writer."

Recently, he has used his talents in a new way. He says, "To celebrate my mid-life crisis several years ago, I decided to try something completely different: playwriting. I've had pretty good luck with this. . . . I've written five radio plays for Seeing Ear Theater. Three were adapted from stories, 'Think like a Dinosaur,' 'Breakaway, Backdown' and 'The Propagation of Light in a Vacuum.' Two were originals 'Carrion Death' and 'Feel the Zaz' although I subsequently emitted a story version of 'Zaz.'"

"Think like a Dinosaur" won the 1996 Hugo Award for Best Novelette. It is in the classic hard SF mode and is in fact in dialog with the touchstone of hard SF reading protocols, Tom Godwin's controversial "The Cold Equations." It is an act of literary politics, a genuine hard SF story that undermines, by calling into question, the sexual politics in the subtext of the classic original. But it does not establish a position on the right or left, but in the center. If there is a new literary political synthesis in 1990s American SF, it is at the point where the hard SF stories of Benford, Kelly, and Sterling meet.

Kamala Shastri came back to this world as she had left it—naked. She tottered out of the assembler, trying to balance in Tuulen Station's delicate gravity. I caught her and bundled her into a robe with one motion, then eased her onto the float. Three years on another planet had transformed Kamala. She was leaner, more muscular. Her fingernails were now a couple of centimeters long and there were four parallel scars incised on her left cheek, perhaps some Gendian's idea of beautification. But what struck me most was the darting strangeness in her eyes. This place, so familiar to me, seemed almost to shock her. It was as if she doubted the walls and was skeptical of air. She had learned to think like an alien.

"Welcome back." The float's whisper rose to a *whoosh* as I walked it down the hallway.

She swallowed hard and I thought she might cry. Three years ago, she would have. Lots of migrators are devastated when they come out of the assembler; it's because there is no transition. A few seconds ago Kamala was on Gend, fourth planet of the star we call epsilon Leo, and now she was here in lunar orbit. She was almost home; her life's great adventure was over.

"Matthew?" she said.

"Michael." I couldn't help but be pleased that she remembered me. After all, she had changed my life.

I've guided maybe three hundred migrations—comings *and* goings—since I first came to Tuulen to study the dinos. Kamala Shastri's is the only quantum scan I've ever pirated. I doubt that the dinos care; I suspect this is a trespass they occasionally allow themselves. I know more about her—at least, as she was three years ago—than I know about myself. When the dinos sent her to Gend, she massed 50,391.72 grams and her red cell count was 4.81 million per mm3. She could play the nagasvaram, a kind of bamboo flute. Her father came from Thana, near Bombay, and her favorite flavor of chewyfrute was watermelon and she'd had five lovers and when she was eleven she had wanted to be a gymnast but instead she had become a biomaterials engineer who at age twenty-nine had volunteered to go to the stars to learn how to grow artificial eyes. It took her two years to go through migrator training; she knew she could have backed out at any time, right up until the moment Silloin translated her into a superluminal signal. She understood what it meant to balance the equation.

I first met her on June 22, 2069. She shuttled over from Lunex's L1 port and came through our airlock at promptly 10:15, a small, roundish woman with black hair parted in the middle and drawn tight against her skull. They had darkened her skin against epsilon Leo's UV; it was the deep blue-black of twilight. She was wearing a striped clingy and velcro slippers to help her get around for the short time she'd be navigating our .2 micrograv.

"Welcome to Tuulen Station." I smiled and offered my hand. "My name is Michael." We shook. "I'm supposed to be a sapientologist but I also moonlight as the local guide."

"Guide?" She nodded distractedly. "Okay." She peered past me, as if expecting someone else.

"Oh, don't worry," I said, "the dinos are in their cages."

Her eyes got wide as she let her hand slip from mine. "You call the Hanen dinos?"

"Why not?" I laughed. "They call us babies. The weeps, among other things."

She shook her head in amazement. People who've never met a dino tended to romanticize them: the wise and noble reptiles who had mastered superluminal physics and introduced Earth to the wonders of galactic civilization. I doubt Kamala had ever seen a dino play poker or gobble down a screaming rabbit. And she had never argued with Linna, who still wasn't convinced that humans were psychologically ready to go to the stars.

"Have you eaten?" I gestured down the corridor toward the reception rooms.

"Yes . . . I mean, no." She didn't move. "I am not hungry."

"Let me guess. You're too nervous to eat. You're too nervous to talk, even. You wish I'd just shut up, pop you into the marble, and beam you out. Let's just get this part the hell over with, eh?"

"I don't mind the conversation, actually."

"There you go. Well, Kamala, it is my solemn duty to advise you that there are no peanut butter and jelly sandwiches on Gend. And no chicken vindaloo. What's my name again?"

"Michael?"

"See, you're not *that* nervous. Not one taco, or a single slice of eggplant pizza. This is your last chance to eat like a human."

"Okay." She did not actually smile—she was too busy being brave—but a corner of her mouth twitched. "Actually, I would not mind a cup of tea."

"Now, tea they've got." She let me guide her toward reception room D; her slippers *snicked* at the velcro carpet. "Of course, they brew it from lawn clippings."

"The Gendians don't keep lawns. They live underground."

"Refresh my memory." I kept my hand on her shoulder; beneath the clingy, her muscles were rigid. "Are they the ferrets or the things with the orange bumps?"

"They look nothing like ferrets."

We popped through the door bubble into reception D, a compact rectangular space with a scatter of low, unthreatening furniture. There was a kitchen station at one end, a closet with a vacuum toilet at the other. The ceiling was blue sky; the long wall showed a live view of the Charles River and the Boston skyline, baking in the late June sun. Kamala had just finished her doctorate at MIT.

I opaqued the door. She perched on the edge of a couch like a wren, ready to flit away.

While I was making her tea, my fingernail screen flashed. I answered it and a tiny Silloin came up in discreet mode. She didn't look at me; she was too busy watching arrays in the control room. =A problem,= her voice buzzed in my earstone, =most negligible, really. But we will have to void the last two from today's schedule. Save them at Lunex until first shift tomorrow. Can this one be kept for an hour?=

"Sure," I said. "Kamala, would you like to meet a Hanen?" I transferred Silloin to a dino-sized window on the wall. "Silloin, this is Kamala Shastri. Silloin is the one who actually runs things. I'm just the doorman."

Silloin looked through the window with her near eye, then swung around and peered at Kamala with her other. She was short for a dino, just over a meter tall, but she had an enormous head that teetered on her neck like a watermelon balancing on a grapefruit. She must have just oiled herself because her silver scales shone. =Kamala, you will accept my happiest intentions for you?= She raised her left hand, spreading the skinny digits to expose dark crescents of vestigial webbing.

"Of course, I. . . ."

=And you will permit us to render you this translation?=

She straightened. "Yes."

=Have you questions?=

I'm sure she had several hundred, but at this point was probably too scared to ask. While she hesitated, I broke in. "Which came first, the lizard or the egg?"

Silloin ignored me. =It will be excellent for you to begin when?=

"She's just having a little tea," I said, handing her the cup. "I'll bring her along when she's done. Say an hour?"

Kamala squirmed on the couch. "No, really, it will not take me. . . ."

Silloin showed us her teeth, several of which were as long as piano keys. =That would be most appropriate, Michael.= She closed; a gull flew through the space where her window had been.

"Why did you do that?" Kamala's voice was sharp.

"Because it says here that you have to wait your turn. You're not the only migrator we're sending this morning." This was a lie, of course; we had had to cut the schedule because Jodi Latchaw, the other sapientologist assigned to Tuulen, was at the University of Hipparchus presenting our paper on the Hanen concept of identity. "Don't worry, I'll make the time fly."

For a moment, we looked at each other. I could have laid down an hour's worth of patter; I'd done that often enough. Or I could have drawn her out on why she was going: no doubt she had a blind grandma or second cousin just waiting for her to bring home those artificial eyes, not to mention potential spin-offs which could well end tuberculosis, famine, and premature ejaculation, *blah, blah, blah.* Or I could have just left her alone in the room to read the wall. The trick was guessing how spooked she really was.

"Tell me a secret," I said.

"What?"

"A secret, you know, something no one else knows."

She stared as if I'd just fallen off Mars.

"Look, in a little while you're going someplace that's what . . . three hundred and ten light years away? You're scheduled to stay for three years. By the time you come back, I could easily be rich, famous, and elsewhere; we'll probably never see each other again. So what have you got to lose? I promise not to tell."

She leaned back on the couch, and settled the cup in her lap. "This is another test, right? After everything they have put me through, they still have not decided whether to send me."

"Oh no, in a couple of hours you'll be cracking nuts with ferrets in some dark Gendian burrow. This is just me, talking."

"You are crazy."

"Actually, I believe the technical term is logomaniac. It's from the Greek: *logos* meaning word, *mania* meaning two bits short of a byte. I just love to chat is all. Tell you what, I'll go first. If my secret isn't juicy enough, you don't have tell me anything."

Her eyes were slits as she sipped her tea. I was fairly sure that whatever she was worrying about at the moment, it wasn't being swallowed by the big blue marble.

"I was brought up Catholic," I said, settling onto a chair in front of her. "I'm not anymore, but that's not the secret. My parents sent me to Mary, Mother of God High School; we called it Moogoo. It was run by a couple of old priests, Father Thomas and his wife, Mother Jennifer. Father Tom taught physics, which I got a 'D' in, mostly because he talked like he had walnuts in his mouth. Mother Jennifer taught theology and had all the warmth of a marble pew; her nickname was Mama Moogoo.

"One night, just two weeks before my graduation, Father Tom and Mama Moogoo went out in their Chevy Minimus for ice cream. On the way home, Mama Moogoo pushed a yellow light and got broadsided by an ambulance. Like I said, she was old, a hundred and twenty something; they should've lifted her license back in the '50s. She was killed instantly. Father Tom died in the hospital.

"Of course, we were all supposed to feel sorry for them and I guess I did a little, but I never really liked either of them and I resented the way their deaths had screwed things up for my class. So I was more annoyed than sorry, but then I also had this edge of guilt for being so uncharitable. Maybe you'd have to grow up Catholic to understand that. Anyway, the day after it happened they called an assembly in the gym and we were all there squirming on the bleachers and the cardinal himself telepresented a sermon. He kept trying to comfort us, like it had been our *parents* that had died. When I made a joke about it to the kid next to me, I got caught and spent the last week of my senior year with an in-school suspension."

Kamala had finished her tea. She slid the empty cup into one of the holders built into the table.

"Want some more?" I said.

She stirred restlessly. "Why are you telling me this?"

"It's part of the secret." I leaned forward in my chair. "See, my family lived down the street from Holy Spirit Cemetery and in order to get to the carryvan line on McKinley Ave., I had to cut through. Now this happened a couple of days after I got in trouble at the assembly. It was around midnight and I was coming home from a graduation party where I had taken a couple of pokes of insight, so I was feeling sly as a philosopher-king. As I walked through the cemetery, I stumbled across two dirt mounds right next to each other. At first I thought they were flower beds, then I saw the wooden crosses. Fresh graves: here lies Father Tom and Mama Moogoo. There wasn't much to the crosses: they were basically just stakes with crosspieces, painted white and hammered into the ground. The names were hand printed on them. The way I figure it, they were there to mark the graves until the stones got delivered. I didn't need any insight to recognize a once in a lifetime opportunity. If I switched them, what were the chances anyone was going to notice? It was no problem sliding them out of their holes. I smoothed the dirt with my hands and then ran like hell."

Until that moment, she'd seemed bemused by my story and slightly condescending toward me. Now there was a glint of alarm in her eyes. "That was a terrible thing to do," she said.

"Absolutely," I said, "although the dinos think that the whole idea of planting bodies in graveyards and marking them with carved rocks is weepy. They say there is no identity in dead meat, so why get so sentimental about it? Linna keeps asking how come we don't put markers over our shit. But that's not the secret. See, it'd been a warmish night in the middle of June, only as I ran, the air turned cold. Freezing, I could see my breath. And my shoes got heavier and heavier, like they had turned to stone. As I got closer to the back gate, it felt like I was fighting a strong wind, except my clothes weren't flapping. I slowed to a walk. I know I could have pushed through, but my heart was thumping and then I heard this whispery seashell noise and I panicked. So the secret is I'm a coward. I switched the crosses back and I never went near that cemetery again. As a matter of fact," I nodded at the walls of reception room D on Tuulen Station, "when I grew up, I got about as far away from it as I could."

She stared as I settled back in my chair. "True story," I said and raised my right hand. She seemed so astonished that I started laughing. A smile bloomed on her dark face and suddenly she was giggling too. It was a soft, liquid sound, like a brook bubbling over smooth stones; it made me laugh even harder. Her lips were full and her teeth were very white.

"Your turn," I said, finally.

"Oh, no, I could not." She waved me off. "I don't have anything so good. . . ." She paused, then frowned. "You have told that before?"

"Once," I said. "To the Hanen, during the psych screening for this job. Only I didn't tell them the last part. I know how dinos think, so I ended it when I switched the crosses. The rest is baby stuff." I waggled a finger at her. "Don't forget, you promised to keep my secret."

"Did I?"

"Tell me about when you were young. Where did you grow up?"

"Toronto." She glanced at me, appraisingly. "There *was* something, but not funny. Sad."

I nodded encouragement and changed the wall to Toronto's skyline dominated by the CN Tower, Toronto-Dominion Centre, Commerce Court, and the King's Needle.

She twisted to take in the view and spoke over her shoulder. "When I was ten we moved to an apartment, right downtown on Bloor Street so my mother could be close to work." She pointed at the wall and turned back to face me. "She is an accountant, my father wrote wallpaper for Imagineering. It was a huge building; it seemed as if we were always getting into the elevator with ten neighbors we never knew we had. I was coming home from school one day when an old woman stopped me in the lobby. 'Little girl,' she said, 'how would you like to earn ten dollars?' My parents had warned me not to talk to strangers but she obviously was a resident. Besides, she had an ancient pair of exolegs strapped on, so I knew I could outrun her if I needed to. She asked me to go to the store for her, handed me a grocery list and a cash card, and said I should bring everything up to her apartment, 10W. I should have been more suspicious because all the downtown groceries deliver but, as I soon found out, all she really wanted was someone to talk to her. And she was willing to pay for it, usually five or ten dollars, depending on how long I stayed. Soon I was stopping by almost every day after school. I think my parents would have made me stop if they had known; they were very strict. They would not have liked me taking her money. But neither of them got home until after six, so it was my secret to keep."

"Who was she?" I said. "What did you talk about?"

"Her name was Margaret Ase. She was ninety-seven years old and I think she had been some kind of counselor. Her husband and her daughter had both died and she was alone. I didn't find out much about her; she made me do most of the talking. She asked me about my friends and what I was learning in school and my family. Things like that. . . ."

Her voice trailed off as my fingernail started to flash. I answered it.

=Michael, I am pleased to call you to here.= Silloin buzzed in my ear. She was almost twenty minutes ahead of schedule.

"See, I told you we'd make the time fly." I stood; Kamala's eyes got very wide. "I'm ready if you are."

I offered her my hand. She took it and let me help her up. She wavered for a moment and I sensed just how fragile her resolve was. I put my hand around her waist and steered her into the corridor. In the micrograv of Tuulen Station, she already felt as insubstantial as a memory. "So tell me, what happened that was so sad?"

At first I thought she hadn't heard. She shuffled along, said nothing.

"Hey, don't keep me in suspense here, Kamala," I said. "You have to finish the story."

"No," she said. "I don't think I do."

I didn't take this personally. My only real interest in the conversation had been to distract her. If she refused to be distracted, that was her choice. Some migrators kept talking right up to the moment they slid into the big blue marble, but lots of them went quiet just before. They turned inward. Maybe in her mind she was already on Gend, blinking in the hard white light.

We arrived at the scan center, the largest space on Tuulen Station. Immediately in front of us was the marble, containment for the quantum nondemolition sensor array—QNSA for the acronymically inclined. It was the milky blue of glacial ice and big as two elephants. The upper hemisphere was raised and the scanning table protruded like a shiny gray tongue. Kamala approached the marble and touched her reflection, which writhed across its polished surface. To the right was a padded bench, the fogger, and a toilet. I looked left, through the control room window. Silloin stood watching us, her impossible head cocked to one side.

=She is docile?= she buzzed in my earstone.

I held up crossed fingers.

=Welcome, Kamala Shastri.= Silloin's voice came over the speakers with a soothing hush. =You are ready to open your translation?=

Kamala bowed to the window. "This is where I take my clothes off?"

=If you would be so convenient.=

She brushed past me to the bench. Apparently I had ceased to exist; this was between her and the dino now. She undressed quickly, folding her clingy into a neat bundle, tucking her slippers beneath the bench. Out of the corner of my eye, I could see tiny feet, heavy thighs, and the beautiful, dark smooth skin of her back. She stepped into the fogger and closed the door.

"Ready," she called.

From the control room, Silloin closed circuits which filled the fogger with a dense cloud of nanolenses. The nano stuck to Kamala and deployed, coating the surface of her body. As she breathed them, they passed from her lungs into her bloodstream. She only coughed twice; she had been well trained. When the eight minutes were up, Silloin cleared the air in the fogger and she emerged. Still ignoring me, she again faced the control room.

=Now you must arrange yourself on the scanning table,= said Silloin, =and enable Michael to fix you.=

She crossed to the marble without hesitation, climbed the gantry beside it, eased onto the table and laid back.

I followed her up. "Sure you won't tell me the rest of the secret?"

She stared at the ceiling, unblinking.

"Okay then." I took the canister and a sparker out of my hip pouch. "This is going to happen just like you've practiced it." I used the canister to respray the bottoms of her feet with nano. I watched her belly rise and fall, rise and fall. She was deep into her breathing exercise. "Remember, no skipping rope or whistling while you're in the scanner."

She did not answer. "Deep breath now," I said and touched a sparker to her big toe. There was a brief crackle as the nano on her skin wove into a net and stiffened, locking her in place. "Bark at the ferrets for me." I picked up my equipment, climbed down the gantry, and wheeled it back to the wall.

With a low whine, the big blue marble retracted its tongue. I watched the upper hemisphere close, swallowing Kamala Shastri, then joined Silloin in the control room.

I'm not of the school who thinks the dinos stink, another reason I got assigned to study them up close. Parikkal, for example, has no smell at all that I can tell. Normally Silloin had the faint but not unpleasant smell of stale wine. When she was under stress, however, her scent became vinegary and biting. It must have been a wild morning for her. Breathing through my mouth, I settled onto the stool at my station.

She was working quickly, now that the marble was sealed. Even with all their training, migrators tend to get claustrophobic fast. After all, they're lying in the dark, in nanobondage, waiting to be translated. Waiting. The simulator at the Singapore training center makes a noise while it's emulating a scan. Most compare it to a light rain pattering against the marble; for some, it's low volume radio static. As long as they hear the patter, the migrators think they're safe. We reproduce it for them while they're in our marble, even though scanning takes about three seconds and is utterly silent. From my vantage I could see that the sagittal, axial, and coronal windows had stopped blinking, indicating full data capture. Silloin was skirring busily to herself; her comm didn't bother to interpret. Wasn't saying anything baby Michael needed to know, obviously. Her head bobbed as she monitored the enormous spread of readouts; her claws clicked against touch screens that glowed orange and yellow.

At my station, there was only a migration status screen—and a white button.

I wasn't lying when I said I was just the doorman. My field is sapientology, not quantum physics. Whatever went wrong with Kamala's migration that morning, there was nothing *I* could have done. The dinos tell me that the quantum nondemoliton sensor array is able to circumvent Heisenberg's Uncertainty Principle by measuring spacetime's most crogglingly small quantities without collapsing the wave/particle duality. How small? They say that no one can ever "see" anything that's only 1.62×10^{-33} centimeters long, because at that size, space and time come apart. Time ceases to exist and space becomes a random probablistic foam, sort of like quantum spit. We humans call this the Planck-Wheeler length. There's a Planck-Wheeler time, too: 10^{-45} of a second. If something happens and something else happens and the two events are separated by an interval of a mere 10^{-45} of a second, it is impossible to say which came first. It was all dino to me—and that's just the scanning. The Hanen use different tech to create artificial wormholes, hold them open with electromagnetic vacuum fluctuations, pass the superluminal signal through and then assemble the migrator from elementary particles at the destination.

On my status screen I could see that the signal which mapped Kamala Shastri had already been compressed and burst through the wormhole. All that we had to wait for was for Gend to confirm acquisition. Once they officially told us that they had her, it would be my job to balance the equation.

Pitter-patter, pitter-pat.

Some Hanen technologies are so powerful that they can alter reality itself. Wormholes could be used by some time traveling fanatic to corrupt history; the scanner/assembler could be used to create a billion Silloins—or Michael Burrs. Pristine reality, unpolluted by such anomalies, has what the dinos call harmony. Before any sapients get to join the galactic club, they must prove total commitment to preserving harmony.

Since I had come to Tuulen to study the dinos, I had pressed the white button over two hundred times. It was what I had to do in order to keep my assignment. Pressing it sent a killing pulse of ionizing radiation through the cerebral cortex of the migrator's duplicated, and therefore unnecessary, body. No brain, no pain; death followed within seconds. Yes, the first few times I'd balanced the equation had been traumatic. It was still . . . unpleasant. But this was the price of a ticket to the stars. If certain unusual people like Kamala Shastri had decided that price was reasonable, it was their choice, not mine.

=This is not a happy result, Michael.= Silloin spoke to me for the first time since I'd entered the control room. =Discrepancies are unfolding.= On my status screen I watched as the error-checking routines started turning up hits.

"Is the problem here?" I felt a knot twist suddenly inside me. "Or there?" If our original scan checked out, then all Silloin would have to do is send it to Gend again.

There was a long, infuriating silence. Silloin concentrated on part of her board as if it showed her first-born hatchling chipping out of its egg. The respirator between her shoulders had ballooned to twice its normal size. My screen showed that Kamala had been in the marble for four minutes plus.

=It may be fortunate to recalibrate the scanner and begin over.=

"*Shit.*" I slammed my hand against the wall, felt the pain tingle to my elbow. "I thought you had it fixed." When error-checking turned up problems, the solution was almost always to retransmit. "You're sure, Silloin? Because this one was right on the edge when I tucked her in."

Silloin gave me a dismissive sneeze and slapped at the error readouts with her bony little hand, as if to knock them back to normal. Like Linna and the other dinos, she had little patience with what she regarded as our weepy fears of migration. However, unlike Linna, she was convinced that someday, after we had used Hanen technologies long enough, we would learn to think like dinos. Maybe she's right. Maybe when we've been squirting through wormholes for hundreds of years, we'll cheerfully discard our redundant bodies. When the dinos and other sapients migrate, the redundants zap themselves—very harmonious. They tried it with humans but it didn't always work. That's why I'm here. =The need is most clear. It will prolong about thirty minutes,= she said.

Kamala had been alone in the dark for almost six minutes, longer than any migrator I'd ever guided. "Let me hear what's going on in the marble."

The control room filled with the sound of Kamala screaming. It didn't sound human to me—more like the shriek of tires skidding toward a crash.

"We've got to get her out of there," I said.

=That is baby thinking, Michael.=

"So she's a baby, damn it." I knew that bringing migrators out of the marble was big trouble. I could have asked Silloin to turn the speakers off and sat there while Kamala suffered. It was my decision.

"Don't open the marble until I get the gantry in place." I ran for the door. "And keep the sound effects going."

At the first crack of light, she howled. The upper hemisphere seemed to lift in slow motion; inside the marble she bucked against the nano. Just when I was sure it was impossible that she could scream any louder, she did. We had accomplished something extraordinary, Silloin and I; we had stripped the brave biomaterials engineer away completely, leaving in her place a terrified animal.

"Kamala, it's me. Michael."

Her frantic screams cohered into words. "Stop . . . *don't* . . . oh my god, someone *help!*" If I could have, I would've jumped into the marble to release her, but the sensor array is fragile and I wasn't going to risk causing any more problems with it. We both had to wait until the upper hemisphere swung fully open and the scanning table offered poor Kamala to me.

"It's okay. Nothing's going to happen, all right? We're bringing you out, that's all. Everything's all right."

When I released her with the sparker, she flew at me. We pitched back and almost toppled down the steps. Her grip was so tight I couldn't breathe.

"Don't *kill* me, don't, *please*, don't."

I rolled on top of her. "Kamala!" I wriggled one arm free and used it to pry myself from her. I scrabbled sideways to the top step. She lurched clumsily in the microgravity and swung at me; her fingernails raked across the back of my hand, leaving bloody welts. "Kamala, stop!" It was all I could do not to strike back at her. I retreated down the steps.

"You bastard. What are you assholes trying to do to me?" She drew several shuddering breaths and began to sob.

"The scan got corrupted somehow. Silloin is working on it."

=The difficulty is obscure,= said Silloin from the control room.

"But that's not your problem." I backed toward the bench.

"They lied," she mumbled and seemed to fold in upon herself as if she were just skin, no flesh or bones. "They said I wouldn't feel anything and . . . do you know what it's like . . . it's . . ."

I fumbled for her clingy. "Look, here are your clothes. Why don't you get dressed? We'll get you out of here."

"You bastard," she repeated, but her voice was empty.

She let me coax her down off the gantry. I counted nubs on the wall while she fumbled back into her clingy. They were the size of the old dimes my grandfather used to hoard and they glowed with a soft golden bioluminescence. I was up to forty-seven before she was dressed and ready to return to reception D.

Where before she had perched expectantly at the edge of the couch, now she slumped back against it. "So what now?" she said.

"I don't know." I went to the kitchen station and took the carafe from the distiller. "What now, Silloin?" I poured water over the back of my hand to wash the blood off. It stung. My earstone was silent. "I guess we wait," I said finally.

"For what?"

"For her to fix . . ."

"I'm not going back in there."

I decided to let that pass. It was probably too soon to argue with her about it, although once Silloin recalibrated the scanner, she'd have very little time to change her mind. "You want something from the kitchen? Another cup of tea, maybe?"

"How about a gin and tonic—hold the tonic?" She rubbed beneath her eyes. "Or a couple of hundred milliliters of serentol?"

I tried to pretend she'd made a joke. "You know the dinos won't let us open the bar for migrators. The scanner might misread your brain chemistry and your visit to Gend would be nothing but a three-year drunk."

"Don't you *understand*?" She was right back at the edge of hysteria. "I am not *going*!" I didn't really blame her for the way she was acting but, at that moment, all I wanted was to get rid of Kamala Shastri. I didn't care if she went on to Gend or back to Lunex or over the rainbow to Oz, just as long as I didn't have to be in the same room with this miserable creature who was trying to make me feel guilty about an accident I had nothing to do with.

"I thought I could do it." She clamped hands to her ears as if to keep from hearing her own despair. "I wasted the last two years convincing myself that I could just lie there and not think and then suddenly I'd be far away. I was going someplace wonderful and strange." She made a strangled sound and let her hands drop into her lap. "I was going to help people see."

"You did it, Kamala. You did everything we asked."

She shook her head. "I couldn't *not* think. That was the problem. And then there she was, trying to touch me. In the dark. I had not thought of her since. . . ." She shivered. "It's your fault for reminding me."

"Your secret friend," I said.

"Friend?" Kamala seemed puzzled by the word. "No, I wouldn't say she was a friend. I was always a little bit scared of her, because I was never quite sure of what she wanted from me." She paused. "One day I went up to 10W after school. She was in her chair, staring down at Bloor Street. Her back was to me. I said, 'Hi, Ms. Ase.' I was going to show her a genie I had written, only she didn't say anything. I came around. Her skin was the color of ashes. I took her hand. It was like picking up something plastic. She was stiff, hard—not a person anymore. She had become a thing, like a feather or a bone. I ran; I had to get out of there. I went up to our apartment and I hid from her."

She squinted, as if observing—judging—her younger self through the lens of time. "I think I understand now what she wanted. I think she knew she was dying; she probably wanted me there with her at the end, or at least to find her body afterward and report it. Only I could *not*. If I told anyone she was dead, my parents would find out about us. Maybe people would suspect me of doing something to her—I don't know. I could have called security but I was only ten; I was afraid somehow they might trace me. A couple of weeks went by and still nobody had found her. By then it was too late to say anything. Everyone would have blamed me for keeping quiet for so long. At night I imagined her turning black and rotting into her chair like a banana. It made me sick; I couldn't sleep or eat. They had to put me in the hospital, because I had touched her. Touched *death*."

=Michael,= Silloin whispered, without any warning flash. =An impossibility has formed.=

"As soon as I was out of that building, I started to get better. Then they found her. After I came home, I worked hard to forget Ms. Ase. And I did, almost." Kamala wrapped her arms around herself. "But just now she was with me again, inside the marble . . . I couldn't see her but somehow I knew she was reaching for me."

=Michael, Parikkal is here with Linna.=

"Don't you see?" She gave a bitter laugh. "How can I go to Gend? I'm *hallucinating*."

=It has broken the harmony. Join us alone.=

I was tempted to swat at the annoying buzz in my ear.

"You know, I've never told anyone about her before."

"Well, maybe some good has come of this after all." I patted her on the knee. "Excuse me for a minute?" She seemed surprised that I would leave. I slipped into the hall and hardened the door bubble, sealing her in.

"What impossibility?" I said, heading for the control room.

=She is pleased to reopen the scanner?=

"Not pleased at all. More like scared shitless."

=This is Parikkal.= My earstone translated his skirring with a sizzling edge, like bacon frying. =The confusion was made elsewhere. No mishap can be connected to our station.=

I pushed through the bubble into the scan center. I could see the three dinos through the control window. Their heads were bobbing furiously. "Tell me," I said.

=Our communications with Gend were marred by a transient falsehood,= said Silloin. =Kamala Shastri has been received there and reconstructed.=

"She migrated?" I felt the deck shifting beneath my feet. "What about the one we've got here?"

=The simplicity is to load the redundant into the scanner and finalize. . . . =

"I've got news for you. She's not going anywhere near that marble."

=Her equation is not in balance.= This was Linna, speaking for the first time. Linna was not exactly in charge of Tuulen Station; she was more like a senior partner. Parikkal and Silloin had overruled her before—at least I thought they had.

"What do you expect me to do? Wring her neck?"

There was a moment's silence—which was not as unnerving as watching them eye me through the window, their heads now perfectly still.

"No," I said.

The dinos were skirring at each other; their heads wove and dipped. At first they cut me cold and the comm was silent, but suddenly their debate crackled through my earstone.

=This is just as I have been telling,= said Linna. =These beings have no realization of harmony. It is wrongful to further unleash them on the many worlds.=

=You may have reason,= said Parikkal. =But that is a later discussion. The need is for the equation to be balanced.=

=There is no time. We will have to discard the redundant ourselves.= Silloin bared her long brown teeth. It would take her maybe five seconds to rip Kamala's throat out. And even though Silloin was the dino most sympathetic to us, I had no doubt she would enjoy the kill.

=I will argue that we adjourn human migration until this world has been rethought,= said Linna.

This was the typical dino condescension. Even though they appeared to be arguing with each other, they were actually speaking to me, laying the situation out so that even the baby sapient would understand. They were informing me that I was jeopardizing the future of humanity in space. That the Kamala in reception D was dead whether I quit or not. That the equation had to be balanced and it had to be now.

"Wait," I said. "Maybe I can coax her back into the scanner." I had to get away from them. I pulled my earstone out and slid it into my pocket. I was in such a hurry to escape that I stumbled as I left the scan center and had to catch myself in the hallway. I stood there for a second, staring at the hand pressed against the bulkhead. I seemed to see the splayed fingers through the wrong end of a telescope. I was far away from myself.

She had curled into herself on the couch, arms clutching knees to her chest, as if trying to shrink so that nobody would notice her.

"We're all set," I said briskly. "You'll be in the marble for less than a minute, guaranteed."

"No, Michael."

I could actually feel myself receding from Tuulen Station. "Kamala, you're throwing away a huge part of your life."

"It is my right." Her eyes were shiny.

No, it wasn't. She was redundant; she had no rights. What had she said about the dead old lady? She had become a thing, like a bone.

"Okay, then," I jabbed at her shoulder with a stiff forefinger. "Let's go."

She recoiled. "Go where?"

"Back to Lunex. I'm holding the shuttle for you. It just dropped off my afternoon list; I should be helping them settle in, instead of having to deal with you."

She unfolded herself slowly.

"Come on." I jerked her roughly to her feet. "The dinos want you off Tuulen as soon as possible and so do I." I was so distant, I couldn't see Kamala Shastri anymore.

She nodded and let me march her to the bubble door.

"And if we meet anyone in the hall, keep your mouth shut."

"You're being so mean." Her whisper was thick.

"You're being such a baby."

When the inner door glided open, she realized immediately that there was no umbilical to the shuttle. She tried to twist out of my grip but I put my shoulder into her, hard. She flew across the airlock, slammed against the outer door and caromed onto her back. As I punched the switch to close the door, I came back to myself. *I* was doing this terrible thing—me, Michael Burr. I couldn't help myself: I giggled. When I last saw her, Kamala was scrabbling across the deck toward me but she was too late. I was surprised that she wasn't screaming again; all I heard was her ferocious breathing.

As soon as the inner door sealed, I opened the outer door. After all, how many ways are there to kill someone on a space station? There were no guns. Maybe someone else could have stabbed or strangled her, but not me. Poison how? Besides, I wasn't thinking, I had been trying desperately not to think of what I was doing. I was a sapientologist, not a doctor. I always thought that exposure to space meant instantaneous death. Explosive decompression or something like. I didn't want her to suffer. I was trying to make it quick. Painless.

I heard the whoosh of escaping air and thought that was it; the body had been ejected into space. I had actually turned away when thumping started, frantic, like the beat of a racing heart. She must have found something to hold onto. *Thump, thump, thump!* It was too much. I sagged against the inner door—*thump, thump*—slid down it, laughing. Turns out that if you empty the lungs, it is possible to survive exposure to space for at least a minute, maybe two. I thought it was funny. *Thump!* Hilarious, actually. I had tried my best for her—risked my career—and this was how she repaid me? As I laid my cheek against the door, the *thumps* started to weaken. There were just a few centimeters between us, the difference between life and death. Now she knew all about balancing the equation. I was laughing so hard I could scarcely breathe. Just like the meat behind the door. Die already, you weepy bitch!

I don't know how long it took. The *thumping* slowed. Stopped. And then I was a hero. I had preserved harmony, kept our link to the stars open. I chuckled with pride; I could think like a dinosaur.

I popped through the bubble door into reception D. "It's time to board the shuttle."

Kamala had changed into a clingy and velcro slippers. There were at least ten windows open on the wall; the room filled with the murmur of talking heads. Friends and relatives had to be notified; their loved one had returned, safe and sound. "I have to go," she said to the wall. "I will call you when I land."

She gave me a smile that seemed stiff from disuse. "I want to thank you again, Michael." I wondered how long it took migrators to get used to being human. "You were such a help and I was such a . . . I was not myself." She glanced around the room one last time and then shivered. "I was really scared."

"You were."

She shook her head. "Was it that bad?"

I shrugged and led her out into the hall.

"I feel so silly now. I mean, I was in the marble for less than a minute and then—" she snapped her fingers—"there I was on Gend, just like you said." She brushed up against me as we walked; her body was hard under the clingy. "Anyway, I am glad we got this chance to talk. I really *was* going to look you up when I got back. I certainly did not expect to see you here."

"I decided to stay on." The inner door to the airlock glided open. "It's a job that grows on you." The umbilical shivered as the pressure between Tuulen Station and the shuttle equalized.

"You have got migrators waiting," she said.

"Two."

"I envy them." She turned to me. "Have *you* ever thought about going to the stars?"

"No," I said.

Kamala put her hand to my face. "It changes everything." I could feel the prick of her long nails—claws, really. For a moment I thought she meant to scar my cheek the way she had been scarred.

"I know," I said.

MOUNT OLYMPUS

Ben Bova

❀

Ben Bova (born 1932), a journalist and technical writer as a young man, published his first SF novel in 1959. He was technical editor on Project Vanguard, the first American artificial satellite program, wrote scripts for teaching films with the Physical Sciences Study Committee, and was manager of marketing for Avco Everett Research Laboratory, in Massachusetts. In 1971, he became editor of *Analog*, where he stayed until 1978. He moved on to edit *Omni* from 1978 to 1982, and has been a full-time writer ever since leaving *Omni*, although he went back to school in the eighties, and earned a Ph.D. in Communications in 1996.

He was the immediate heir to John W. Campbell's job, and has always stood for science and for hard SF, and has been particularly influential in promoting each, both as editor of *Analog* and *Omni* in the 1970s and eighties and as a public figure since. He said in a recent interview:

> There's a basic optimism to science fiction—maybe I should confine that to *hard* science fiction. I think the field shares the basic optimism of science itself. If there is a credo in this business, it should be a quote from Albert Einstein: "The most mysterious thing about the universe is its understandability." We can understand the way the universe works; hard science fiction that deals with real science and technology is about people learning how the universe works, whether that universe is the solar system, the whole cosmic wonder of it, or the universe within our own body. But you can learn, and knowledge makes us better. It makes us wiser, more capable, it improves our lives. And knowledge is always to be preferred over ignorance.

Bova's SF books include *The Kinsman Saga* (1976–79, the forerunner of his current planetary books), the "Voyagers" sequence (1981–90). His recent string of interrelated novels began with *Mars* in 1992, and now includes *Moonrise* (1996), *Moonwar* (1998), *Return to Mars* (1999), *Venus* (2000), *Jupiter* (2001), *The Precipice* (2001), and *The Rock Rats* (2002).

> I think of them as historical novels that haven't happened yet. My audience consists partly of science fiction fans, but mostly of people in technical fields. It's a technically educated audience, people who are interested in *realistic* stories about how you get there from here." When writing *Mars*, his choice of setting led him to certain choices about character. He says, ". . . when I first started plotting out the original novel *Mars*, the central character was a white-bread American geologist, and it just didn't work out. So finally I came to a realization that this guy is part Navajo. So we went out to New Mexico for a month or so and absorbed the area and that's when I started writing the novel.

"Mount Olympus" is a Martian adventure story about two men who fly to the highest mountain on Mars, and in the process learn more about Mars and about themselves. Bova's work is permeated by the idea of space as a new frontier, and of SF settings as opportunities for explorers and entrepreneurs, the classic Heinlein thematics of American SF.

The tallest mountain in the solar system is Olympus Mons, on Mars. It is a massive shield volcano that has been dormant for tens, perhaps hundreds of millions of years.

Once, though, its mighty outpourings of lava dwarfed everything else on the planet. Over time, they built a mountain three times taller than Everest, with a base the size of the state of Iowa.

The edges of that base are rugged cliffs of basalt more than a kilometer high. The summit of the mountain, where huge calderas mark the vents that once spewed molten rock, stands some twenty-seven kilometers above the supporting plain.

At that altitude, the carbon dioxide that forms the major constituent of Mars's atmosphere can freeze out, condense on the cold, bare rock, covering it with a thin, invisible layer of dry ice.

Tòmas Rodriguez looked happy as a puppy with an old sock to chew on as he and Fuchida got into their hard suits.

"I'm gonna be in the Guinness Book of Records," he proclaimed cheerfully to Jamie Waterman, who was helping him get suited up. Trudy Hall was assisting Fuchida while Stacy Dezhurova sat in the comm center, monitoring the dome's systems and the equipment outside.

It was the forty-eighth day of the Second Expedition's eighteen months on the surface of Mars, the day that Rodriguez and biologist Mitsuo Fuchida were scheduled to fly to Olympus Mons.

"Highest aircraft landing and takeoff," Rodriguez chattered cheerfully as he wormed his fingers into the suit's gloves. "Longest flight of a manned solar-powered aircraft. Highest altitude for a manned solar-powered aircraft."

"Crewed," Trudy Hall murmured, "not manned."

Unperturbed by her correction, Rodriguez continued, "I might even bust the record for unmanned solar-powered flight."

"Isn't it cheating to compare a flight on Mars to flights on Earth?" Trudy asked as she helped Fuchida latch his life-support pack onto the back of his suit.

Rodriguez shook his head vigorously. "All that counts in the record book is the numbers, chica. Just the numbers."

"Won't they put an asterisk next to the numbers and a footnote that says, 'This was done on Mars'?"

Rodriguez tried to shrug but not even he could manage that inside the hard suit. "Who cares, as long as they spell my name right?"

As the two men put on their suit helmets and sealed them to the neck rings, Jamie noticed that Fuchida was utterly silent through the suit-up procedure. Tòmas is doing enough talking for them both, he thought. But he wondered, Is Mitsuo worried, nervous? He looks calm enough, but that might just be a mask. Come to think of it, the way Tòmas is blathering, he must be wired tighter than a drum.

The bulky hard suits had been pristine white when the explorers first touched down on Mars. Now their boots and leggings were tinged with reddish dust, no matter how hard the explorers vacuumed the ceramic-metal suits each time they returned to the dome's airlock.

Rodriguez was the youngest of the eight explorers, the astronaut that NASA had loaned to the expedition. If it bothered him to work under Dezhurova, the more experienced Russian cosmonaut, he never showed it. All through training and the five-month flight to Mars and their nearly seven weeks on the planet's surface, he had been a good-natured, willing worker. Short and stocky, with a swarthy complexion and thickly curled dark hair, his most noticeable feature was a dazzling smile that made his deep brown eyes sparkle.

But now he was jabbering away like a fast-pitch salesman. Jamie wondered if it was nerves or relief to be out on his own, in charge. Or maybe, Jamie thought, the guy was simply overjoyed at the prospect of flying.

Both men were suited up at last, helmet visors down, life-support systems functioning, radio checks completed. Jamie and Trudy walked with them to the airlock hatch: two Earthlings accompanying a pair of ponderous robots.

Jamie shook hands with Rodriguez. His bare hand hardly made it around the astronaut's glove, with its servo-driven exoskeleton "bones" on its back.

"Good luck, Tòmas," he said. "Don't take any unnecessary risks out there."

Rodriguez grinned from behind his visor. "Hey, you know what they say: There are old pilots and bold pilots, but there are no old, bold pilots."

Jamie chuckled politely. As mission director, he felt he had to impart some final words of wisdom. "Remember that when you're out there," he said.

"I will, boss. Don't worry."

Fuchida stepped up to the hatch once Rodriguez went through. Even in the bulky suit, even with sparrowlike Trudy Hall standing behind him, he looked small, somehow vulnerable.

"Good luck, Mitsuo," said Jamie.

Through the sealed helmet, Fuchida's voice sounded muffled, but unafraid. "I think my biggest problem is going to be listening to Tòmas's yakking all the way to the mountain."

Jamie laughed.

"And back, most likely," Fuchida added.

The indicator light turned green and Trudy pressed the stud that opened the inner hatch. Fuchida stepped through, carrying his portable life-support satchel in one hand.

He's all right, Jamie told himself. Mitsuo's not scared or even worried.

Once they had clambered into the plane's side-by-side seats and connected to its internal electrical power and life-support systems, both men changed.

Rodriguez became all business. No more chattering. He checked out the plane's systems with only a few clipped words of jargon to Stacy Dezhurova, who was serving as flight controller back in the dome's comm center.

Fuchida, for his part, felt his pulse thundering in his ears so loudly he wondered if the suit radio was picking it up. Certainly the medical monitors must be close to the redline, his heart was racing so hard.

Like the expedition's remotely piloted soarplanes, the rocketplane was built of gossamer-thin plastic skin stretched over a framework of ceramic-plastic cerplast. To Fuchida it looked like an oversized model airplane made of some kind of kitchen wrap, complete with an odd-looking six-bladed propeller on its nose.

But it was big enough to carry two people. Huge, compared to the unmanned soarplanes. Rodriguez said it was nothing more than a fuel tank with wings. The wings stretched wide, drooping to the ground at their tips. The cockpit was tiny, nothing more than a glass bubble up front. The rocket engines, tucked in where the wing roots joined the fuselage, looked too small to lift the thing off the ground.

The plane was designed to use its rocket engines for takeoffs, then once at altitude, it would run on the prop. Solar panels painted onto the wing's upper surface would provide the electricity to power the electrical engine. There was too little oxygen in the Martian air to run a jet engine; the rockets were the plane's main muscle, the solar cells its secondary energy source.

Back in the dome, Jamie and the others crowded over Dezhurova's shoulders to watch the takeoff on the comm center's desktop display screen.

As an airport, the base left much to be desired. The bulldozed runway ran just short of two kilometers in length. There was no taxiway; Rodriguez and a helper—often Jamie—simply turned the fragile plane around after a landing so it was pointed up the runway again. There was no windsock. The atmosphere was so rare that it made scant difference which way the wind was blowing when the plane took off. The rocket engines did most of the work of lifting the plane off the ground and providing the speed it needed for the broad, drooping wings to generate enough lift for flight.

Jamie felt a dull throbbing in his jaw as he bent over Dezhurova, watching the final moments before takeoff. With a conscious effort he unclenched his teeth. There are two men in that plane, he told himself. If anything goes wrong, if they crash, they'll both be killed.

"Clear for takeoff," Dezhurova said mechanically into her lip mike.

"Copy clear," Rodriguez's voice came through the speakers.

Stacy scanned the screens around her one final time, then said, "Clear for ignition."

"Ignition."

Suddenly the twin rocket engines beneath the wing roots shot out a bellowing flame and the plane jerked into motion. As the camera followed it jouncing down the runway, gathering speed, the long, drooping wings seemed to stiffen and stretch out.

"Come on, baby," Dezhurova muttered.

Jamie saw it all as if it were happening in slow motion: the plane trundling down the runway, the rockets' exhaust turning so hot the flame became invisible, clouds of dust and grit billowing behind the plane as it sped faster, faster along the runway, nose lifting now.

"Looking good," Dezhurova whispered.

The plane hurtled up off the ground and arrowed into the pristine sky, leaving a roiling cloud of dust and vapor slowly dissipating along the length of the runway. To Jamie it looked as if the cloud was trying to reach for the plane and pull it back to the ground.

But the plane was little more than a speck in the salmon-pink sky now.

Rodriguez's voice crackled through the speakers, "Next stop, Mount Olympus!"

Rodriguez was a happy man. The plane was responding to his touch like a beautiful woman, gentle and sweet.

They were purring along at—he glanced at the altimeter—twenty-eight thousand and six meters. Let's see, he mused. Something like three point two feet in a meter, that makes it eighty-nine, almost ninety thousand feet. Not bad. Not bad at all.

He knew the world altitude record for a solar-powered plane was above one hundred thousand feet. But that was a UAV, an unmanned aerial vehicle. No pilot's flown this high in a solar-powered plane, he knew. Behind his helmet visor he smiled at the big six-bladed propeller as it spun lazily before his eyes.

Beside him, Fuchida was absolutely silent and unmoving. He might as well be dead inside his suit, I'd never know the difference, Rodriguez thought. He's scared, just plain scared. He doesn't trust me. He's scared of flying with me. Probably wanted Stacy to fly him, not me.

Well, my silent Japanese buddy, I'm the guy you're stuck with, whether you like it or not. So go ahead and sit there like a fuckin' statue, I don't give a damn.

Mitsuo Fuchida felt an unaccustomed tendril of fear worming its way through his innards. This puzzled him, since he had known for almost two years now that he would be flying to the top of Olympus Mons. He had flown simulations hundreds of times. This whole excursion to Olympus Mons had been his idea, and he had worked hard to get the plan incorporated into the expedition schedule.

He had first learned to fly while an undergraduate biology student, and had been elected president of the university's flying club. With the single-minded intensity of a competitor who knew he had to beat the best of the best to win a berth on the Second Mars Expedition, Fuchida had taken the time to qualify as a pilot of ultra-light aircraft over the inland mountains of his native Kyushu and then went on to pilot soarplanes across the jagged peaks of Sinkiang.

He had never felt any fear of flying. Just the opposite: he had always felt relaxed and happy in the air, free of all the pressures and cares of life.

Yet now, as the sun sank toward the rocky horizon, casting eerie red light across the barren rust-red landscape, Fuchida knew that he was afraid. What if the engine fails? What if Rodriguez cracks up the plane when we land on the mountain? One of the unmanned soarplanes had crashed while it was flying over the volcano on a reconnaissance flight; what if the same thing happens to us?

Even in rugged Sinkiang there was a reasonable chance of surviving an emergency landing. You could breathe the air and walk to a village, even if the trek took many days. Not so here on Mars.

What if Rodriguez gets hurt while we're out there? I have only flown this plane in the simulator, I don't know if I could fly it in reality.

Rodriguez seemed perfectly at ease, happily excited to be flying. He shames me, Fuchida thought. Yet . . . is he truly capable? How will he react in an emergency? Fuchida hoped he would not have to find out.

They passed Pavonis Mons on their left, one of the three giant shield volcanoes that lined up in a row on the eastern side of the Tharsis bulge. It was so big that it stretched out to the horizon and beyond, a massive hump of solid stone that had once oozed red-hot lava across an area the size of Japan. Quiet now. Cold and dead. For how long?

There was a whole line of smaller volcanoes stretching off to the horizon and, beyond them, the hugely massive Olympus Mons. What happened here to create a thousand-kilometer-long chain of volcanoes? Fuchida tried to meditate on that question, but his mind kept coming back to the risks he was undertaking.

And to Elizabeth.

Their wedding had to be a secret. Married persons would not be allowed on the Mars expedition. Worse yet. Mitsuo Fuchida had fallen in love with a foreigner, a young Irish biologist with flame-red hair and skin like white porcelain.

"Sleep with her," Fuchida's father advised him, "enjoy her all you want to. But father no children with her! Under no circumstances may you marry her."

Elizabeth Vernon seemed content with that. She loved Mitsuo.

They had met at Tokyo University. Like him, she was a biologist. Unlike him, she had neither the talent nor the drive to get very far in the competition for tenure and a professorship.

"I'll be fine," she told Mitsuo. "Don't ruin your chance for Mars. I'll wait for you."

That was neither good nor fair, in Fuchida's eyes. How could he go to Mars, spend years away from her, expect her to store her emotions in suspended animation for so long?

His father made other demands on him, as well.

"The only man to die on the First Mars Expedition was your cousin, Konoye. He disgraced us all."

Isoruku Konoye suffered a fatal stroke while attempting to explore the smaller moon of Mars, Deimos. His Russian teammate, cosmonaut Leonid Tolbukhin, said that Konoye had panicked, frightened to be outside their spacecraft in nothing more than a spacesuit, disoriented by the looming menace of Deimos's rocky bulk.

"You must redeem the family's honor," Fuchida's father insisted. "You must make the world respect Japan. Your namesake was a great warrior. You must add new honors to his name."

So Mitsuo knew that he could not marry Elizabeth openly, honestly, as he wanted to. Instead, he took her to a monastery in the remote mountains of Kyushu, where he had perfected his climbing skills.

"It's not necessary, Mitsuo," Elizabeth protested, once she understood what he wanted to do. "I love you. A ceremony won't change that."

"Would you prefer a Catholic rite?" he asked.

She threw her arms around his neck. He felt tears on her cheek.

When the day came that he had to leave, Mitsuo promised Elizabeth that he would come back to her. "And when I do, we will be married again, openly, for all the world to see."

"Including your father?" she asked wryly.

Mitsuo smiled. "Yes, including even my noble father."

Then he left for Mars, intent on honoring his family's name and returning to the woman he loved.

The excursion plan called for them to land late in the afternoon, almost at sunset, when the low sun cast its longest shadows. That allowed them to take off in daylight, while giving them the best view of their landing area. Every boulder and rock would show in bold relief, allowing them to find the smoothest spot for their landing.

It also meant, Fuchida knew, that they would have to endure the dark frigid hours of night immediately after they landed. What if the batteries fail? The lithium-polymer batteries had been tested for years, Fuchida knew. They stored electricity generated in sunlight by the solar panels and powered the plane's equipment through the long, cold hours of darkness. But what if they break down when the temperature drops to a hundred and fifty below zero?

Rodriguez was making a strange, moaning sound, he realized. Turning sharply to look at the astronaut sitting beside him, Fuchida saw only the inside of his own helmet. He had to turn from the shoulders to see the space-suited pilot—who was humming tunelessly.

"Are you all right?" Fuchida asked nervously.

"Sure."

"Was that a Mexican song you were humming?"

"Naw. The Beatles. 'Lucy in the Sky with Diamonds.' "

"Oh."

Rodriguez sighed happily. "There she is," he said.

"What?"

"Mount Olympus." He pointed straight ahead.

Fuchida did not see a mountain, merely the horizon. It seemed rounded, now that he paid attention to it: a large gently rising hump.

It grew as they approached it. And grew. And grew. Olympus Mons was an immense island unto itself, a continent rising up above the bleak red plain like some gigantic mythical beast. Its slopes were gentle, above the steep scarps of its base. A man could climb that grade easily, Fuchida thought. Then he realized that the mountain was so huge it would take a man weeks to walk from its base to its summit.

Rodriguez was humming again, calm and relaxed as a man sitting in his favorite chair at home.

"You enjoy flying, don't you?" Fuchida commented.

"You know what they say," Rodriguez replied, a serene smile in his voice. "Flying a plane is the second most exciting thing a man can do."

Fuchida nodded inside his helmet. "And the most exciting must be sex, right?"

"Nope. The first most exciting thing a man can do is landing a plane."

Fuchida sank into gloomy silence.

As the senior of the expedition's two astronauts, Anastasia Dezhurova was technically second-in-command to Jamie Waterman. She saw to it that her main duty was the communications center, where she could watch everyone and everything. As long as she was watching, Dezhurova felt, nothing very bad could happen to her fellow explorers.

The dome was quiet, everyone busy at their appointed tasks. Dezhurova could see Waterman outside, doggedly chipping still more rock samples. Trudy Hall was in her lab working with the lichen from the Grand Canyon; the only other woman among them, Vijay Shektar, was in her infirmary, scrolling medical data on her computer.

"Rodriguez to base," the astronaut's voice suddenly crackled in the speaker. "I'm making a dry run over the landing area. Sending my camera view."

"Base to Rodriguez," Dezhurova snapped, all business. "Copy dry run." Her fingers raced over the keyboard and the main display suddenly showed a pockmarked, boulder-strewn stretch of bare rock. "We have your imagery."

Dezhurova felt her mouth go dry. I'd better call Jamie back into the dome. If that's the landing area, they're never going to get down safely.

Rodriguez banked the plane slightly so he could see the ground better. To Fuchida it seemed as if the plane was standing on its left wingtip while the hard, bare rock below turned in a slow circle.

"Well," Rodriguez said, "we've got a choice: boulders or craters."

"Where's the clear area the soarplanes showed?" Fuchida asked.

"'Clear' is a relative term," Rodriguez muttered.

Fuchida swallowed bile. It burned in his throat.

"Rodriguez to base. I'm going to circle the landing area one more time. Tell me if you see anything I miss."

"Copy another circle." Stacy Dezhurova's tone was clipped, professional.

Rodriguez peered hard at the ground below. The setting sun cast long shadows that emphasized every pebble down there. Between a fresh-looking crater and a scattering of rocks was a relatively clean area, more than a kilometer long. Room enough to land if the retros fired on command.

"Looks OK to me," he said into his helmet mike.

"Barely," came Dezhurova's voice.

"The wheels can handle small rocks."

"Shock absorbers are no substitute for level ground, Tòmas."

Rodriguez laughed. He and Dezhurova had gone through this discussion a few dozen times, ever since the first recon photos had come back from the UAVs.

"Turning into final approach," he reported.

Dezhurova did not reply. As the flight controller she had the authority to forbid him to land.

"Lining up for final."

"Your imagery is breaking up a little."

"Light level's sinking fast."

"Yes."

Fuchida saw the ground rushing up toward him. It was covered with boulders and pitted with craters and looked as hard as concrete, harder. They were coming in too fast, he thought. He wanted to grab the control T-stick in front of him and pull up, cut in the rocket engines and get the hell away while they had a chance. Instead, he squeezed his eyes shut.

Something hit the plane so hard that Fuchida thought he'd be driven through the canopy. His safety harness held, though, and within an eyeblink he heard the howling screech of the tiny retro rocket motors. The front of the plane seemed to be on fire. They were bouncing, jolting, rattling along like a tin can kicked across a field of rubble.

Then a final lurch and all the noise and motion stopped.

"We're down," Rodriguez sang out. "Piece of cake."

"Good," came Dezhurova's stolid voice.

Fuchida urgently needed to urinate.

"OK," Rodriguez said to his partner. "Now we just sit tight until sunrise."

"Like a pair of tinned sardines," said Fuchida.

Rodriguez laughed. "Hey, man, we got all the creature comforts you could want—almost. Like tourist class in an overnight flight."

Fuchida nodded inside his helmet. He did not relish the idea of trying to sleep in the cockpit seats, sealed in their suits. But that was the price to be paid for the honor of being the first humans to set foot on the tallest mountain in the solar system.

Almost, he smiled. I too will be in the Guinness Book of Records, he thought.

"You OK?" Rodriguez asked.

"Yes, certainly."

"Kinda quiet, Mitsuo."

"I'm admiring the view," said Fuchida.

Nothing but a barren expanse of bare rock, in every direction. The sky overhead was darkening swiftly. Already Fuchida could see a few stars staring down at them.

"Well, look on the bright side," Rodriguez quipped. "Now we get to test the FES."

The Fecal Elimination System. Fuchida dreaded the moment when he had to try to use it.

Rodriguez chuckled happily, as if he hadn't a care in the world. In two worlds.

"Never show fear." Tòmas Rodriguez learned that as a scrawny asthmatic child, growing up amidst the crime and violence of an inner-city San Diego barrio.

"Never let them see you're scared," his older brother Luis told him. "Never back down from a fight."

Tòmas was not physically big, but he had his big brother to protect him. Most of the time. Then he found a refuge of sorts in the dilapidated neighborhood gym, where he traded hours of sweeping and cleaning for free use of the weight machines. As he gained muscle mass, he learned the rudiments of alley fighting from Luis. In middle school he was spotted and recruited by an elderly Korean who taught martial arts as a school volunteer.

In high school he discovered that he was bright, smart enough not merely to understand algebra but to want to understand it and the other mysteries of mathematics and science. He made friends among the nerds as well as the jocks, often protecting the former against the hazing and casual cruelty of the latter.

He grew into a solid, broad-shouldered youth with quick reflexes and the brains to talk his way out of most confrontations. He did not look for fights, but handled himself well enough when a fight became unavoidable. He worked, he learned, he had the kind of sunny disposition—and firm physical courage—that made even the nastiest punks in the school leave him alone. He never went out for any of the school teams and he never did drugs. He didn't even smoke. He couldn't afford such luxuries.

He even avoided the trap that caught most of his buddies: fatherhood. Whether they got married or not, most of the guys quickly got tied down with a woman. Tòmas had plenty of girls, and learned even before high school the pleasures of sex. But he never formed a lasting relationship. He didn't want to. The neighborhood girls were attractive, yes, until they started talking. Tòmas couldn't stand even to imagine listening to one of them for more than a few hours. They had nothing to say. Their lives were empty. He ached for something more.

Most of the high school teachers were zeroes, but one—the weary old man who taught math—encouraged him to apply for a scholarship to college. To Tòmas' enormous surprise, he won one: full tuition to UCSD. Even so, he could not afford the other expenses, so he again listened to his mentor's advice and joined the Air Force. Uncle Sam paid his way through school, and once he graduated he became a jet fighter pilot. "More fun than sex," he would maintain, always adding, "Almost."

Never show fear. That meant that he could never back away from a challenge. Never. Whether in a cockpit or a barroom, the stocky Hispanic kid with the big smile took every confrontation as it arose. He got a reputation for it.

The fear was always there, constantly, but he never let it show. And always there was that inner doubt. That feeling that somehow he didn't really belong here. They were allowing the chicano kid to pretend he was as smart as the white guys, allowing him to get through college on his little scholarship, allowing him to wear a flyboy uniform and play with the hotshot jet planes.

But he really wasn't one of them. That was made abundantly clear to him in a thousand little ways, every day. He was a greaser, tolerated only as long as he stayed in the place they expected him to be. Don't try to climb too far; don't show off too much; above all, don't try to date anyone except "your own."

Flying was different, though. Alone in a plane seven or eight miles up in the sky it was just him and God, the rest of the world far away, out of sight and out of mind.

Then came the chance to win an astronaut's wings. He couldn't back away from the challenge. Again, the others made it clear that he was not welcome to the competition. But Tòmas entered anyway and won a slot in the astronaut training corps. "The benefits of affirmative action," one of the other pilots jeered.

Whatever he achieved, they always tried to take the joy out of it. Tòmas paid no outward attention, as usual; he kept his wounds hidden, his bleeding internal.

Two years after he had won his astronaut's wings came the call for the Second Mars Expedition. Smiling his broadest, Tòmas applied. No fear. He kept his gritted teeth hidden from all the others, and won the position.

"Big fuckin' deal," said his buddies. "You'll be second fiddle to some Russian broad."

Tòmas shrugged and nodded. "Yeah," he admitted. "I guess I'll have to take orders from everybody."

To himself he added, But I'll be on Mars, shitheads, while you're still down here.

Following his astronaut teammate, Mitsuo Fuchida clambered stiffly down the ladder from the plane's cockpit and set foot on the top of the tallest mountain in the solar system.

In the pale light of the rising sun, it did not look like the top of a mountain to him. He had done a considerable amount of climbing in Japan and Canada and this was nothing like the jagged, snow-capped slabs of granite where the wind whistled like a hurled knife and the clouds scudded by below you.

Here he seemed to be on nothing more dramatic than a wide, fairly flat plain of bare basalt. Pebbles and larger rocks were scattered here and there, but not as thickly as they were back at the base dome. The craters that they had seen from the air were not visible here; at least, he saw nothing that looked like a crater.

But when he looked up he realized how high they were. The sky was a deep blue, instead of its usual salmon pink. The dust particles that reddened the sky of Mars were far below them. At this altitude on Earth they would be up in the stratosphere.

Fuchida wondered if he could see any stars through his visor, maybe find Earth. He turned, trying to orient himself with the rising sun.

"Watch your step," Rodriguez's voice warned in his earphones. "It's—"

Fuchida's boot slid out from under him and he thumped painfully on his rear.

". . . slippery," Rodriguez finished lamely.

The astronaut shuffled carefully to Fuchida's side, moving like a man crossing an ice rink in street shoes. He extended a hand to help the biologist up to his feet.

Stiff and aching from a night of sitting in the cockpit. Fuchida now felt a throbbing pain in his backside. I'll have a nasty bruise there, he told himself. Lucky I didn't land on the backpack and break the life-support rig.

"Feels like ice underfoot," Rodriguez said.

"It couldn't be frost, we're up too high for water ice to form."

"Dry ice."

"Ah." Fuchida nodded inside his helmet. "Dry ice. Carbon dioxide from the atmosphere condenses out on the cold rock."

"Yep."

"But dry ice isn't slippery . . ."

"This stuff is."

Fuchida thought quickly. "Perhaps the pressure of our boots on the dry ice causes a thin layer to vaporize."

"So we get a layer of carbon dioxide gas under our boots." Rodriguez immediately grasped the situation.

"Exactly. We skid along on a film of gas, like gas-lubricated ball bearings."

"That's gonna make it damned difficult to move around."

Fuchida wanted to rub his butt, although he knew it was impossible inside the hard suit. "The sun will get rid of the ice."

"I don't think it'll get warm enough up here to vaporize it."

"It sublimes at seventy-eight point five degrees below zero. Celsius," Fuchida recalled.

"At normal pressure," Rodriguez pointed out.

Fuchida looked at the thermometer on his right cuff. "It's already up to forty-two below," he said, feeling cheerful for the first time. "Besides, the lower the pressure, the lower the boiling point."

"Yeah. That's right."

"That patch must have been shaded by the plane's wing," Fuchida pointed out. "The rest of the ground seems clear."

"Then let's go to the beach and get a suntan," Rodriguez said humorlessly.

"No, let's go to the caldera, as planned."

"You think it's safe to walk around?"

Nodding inside his helmet, Fuchida took a tentative step. The ground felt smooth, but not slick. Another step, then another.

"Maybe we should've brought football cleats."

"Not necessary. The ground's OK now."

Rodriguez grunted. "Be careful, anyway."

"Yes, I will."

While Rodriguez relayed his morning report from his suit radio through the more powerful transmitter in the plane, Fuchida unlatched the cargo bay hatch and slid their equipment skid to the ground. Again he marvelled that this plane of plastic and gossamer could carry them and their gear. It seemed quite impossible, yet it was true.

"Are you ready?" he asked Rodriguez, feeling eager now to get going.

"Yep. Lemme check the compass bearing. . . ."

Fuchida did not wait for the astronaut's check. He knew the direction to the caldera as if its coordinates were printed on his heart.

Rodriguez felt a chill of apprehension tingling through him as they stared down into the caldera. It was like being on the edge of an enormous hole in the world, a hole that went all the way down into hell.

"Nietzsche was right," Fuchida said, his voice sounding awed, almost frightened, in Rodriguez's earphones.

Rodriguez had to turn his entire torso from the hips to see the Japanese biologist standing beside him, anonymous in his bulky hard suit except for the blue stripes on his arms.

"You mean about when you stare into the abyss the abyss stares back."

"You've read Nietzsche?"

Rodriguez grunted. "In Spanish."

"That must have been interesting. I read him in Japanese."

Breaking into a chuckle, Rodriguez said, "So neither one of us can read German, huh?"

It was as good a way as any to break the tension. The caldera was huge, a mammoth pit that stretched from horizon to horizon. Standing there on its lip, looking down into the dark, shadowy depths that dropped away for who knew how far, was distinctly unnerving.

"That's a helluva hole," Rodriguez muttered.

"It's big enough to swallow Mt. Everest," said Fuchida, his voice slightly hollow with awe.

"How long's this beast been dead?" Rodriguez asked.

"Tens of millions of years, at least. Probably much longer. That's one of the things we want to establish while we're here."

"Think it's due for another blow?"

Fuchida laughed shakily. "We'll get plenty of warning, don't worry."

"What, me worry?"

They began to unload the equipment they had dragged on the skid. Its two runners were lined with small Teflon-coated wheels so it could ride along rough ground without needing more than the muscle power of the two men. Much of the equipment was mountaineering gear: chocks and pitons and long coiled lengths of Buckyball cable.

"You really want to go down there?" Rodriguez asked while he drilled holes in the hard basalt for Fuchida to implant geo/met beacons. The instrumentation built into the slim pole would continuously measure ground tremors, heat flow from the planet's interior, air temperature, wind velocity and humidity.

"I spent a lot of time exploring caves," Fuchida answered, gripping one of the beacons in his gloved hands. "I've been preparing for this for a long time."

"Spelunking? You?"

"They call it caving. Spelunking is a term used by non-cavers."

"So you're all set to go down there, huh?"

Fuchida realized that he did not truly want to go. Every time he had entered a cave on Earth he had felt an irrational sense of dread. But he had forced himself to explore the caverns because he knew it would be an important point in his favor in the competition for a berth on the Mars expedition.

"I'm all set," the biologist answered, grunting as he worked the geology/meteorology beacon into its hole.

"It's a dirty job," Rodriguez joked, over the whine of the auger's electric motor, "but somebody's got to do it."

"A man's got to do what a man's got to do," Fuchida replied, matching his teammate's bravado.

Rodriguez laughed. "That ain't Nietzsche."

"No. John Wayne."

"They finished all the preliminary work and headed back to the lip of the caldera. Slowly. Reluctantly, Rodriguez thought. Well, he told himself, even if we break our asses poking around down there at least we've got the beacons up and running.

Fuchida stopped to check the readouts coming from the beacons.

"They all transmitting OK?" Rodriguez asked.

"Yes," came the reply in his earphones. "Interesting . . ."

"What?"

"Heat flow from below ground is much higher here than at the dome or even down in the Canyon."

Rodriguez felt his eyebrows crawl upward. "You mean she's still active?"

"No, no, no. That can't be. But there is still some thermal energy down there."

"We should've brought marshmallows."

"Perhaps. Or maybe there'll be something to picnic on down there waiting for us!" The biologist's voice sounded excited.

"Whattaya mean?"

"Heat energy! Energy for life, perhaps."

A vision of bad videos flashed through Rodriguez's mind: slimy alien monsters with tentacles and bulging eyes. He forced himself not to laugh aloud. Don't worry, they're only interested in blondes with big boobs.

Fuchida called, "Help me get the lines attached and make certain the anchors are firmly imbedded."

He's not reluctant anymore, Rodriguez saw. He's itching to go down into that huge hole and see what kind of alien creatures he can find.

"You all set?" Rodriguez asked.

Fuchida had the climbing harness buckled over his hard suit, the tether firmly clipped to the yoke that ran under his arms.

"Ready to go," the biologist replied, with an assurance he did not truly feel. That dark, yawning abyss stirred a primal fear in both men, but Fuchida did not want to admit to it himself, much less to his teammate.

Rodriguez had spent the morning setting up the climbing rig while Fuchida collected rock samples and then did a half-hour VR show for viewers back on Earth. The rocks were sparser here atop Olympus Mons than they were down on the plains below, and none of them showed the intrusions of color that marked colonies of Martian lichen.

Still, sample collection was the biologist's first order of business. He thought of it as his gift to the geologists, since he felt a dreary certainty that there was no biology going on here on the roof of this world. But down below, inside the caldera . . . that might be a different matter.

Fuchida still had the virtual reality rig clamped to his helmet. They would not do a real-time transmission, but the recording of the first descent into Olympus Mons's main caldera would be very useful both for science and entertainment.

"OK," Rodriguez said, letting his reluctance show in his voice. "I'm ready whenever you are."

Nodding inside his helmet, Fuchida said, "Then let's get started."

"Be careful now," said Rodriguez as the biologist backed slowly away from him.

Fuchida did not reply. He turned and started over the softly rounded lip of the giant hole in the ground. The caldera was so big that it would take half an hour to sink below the level where Rodriguez could still see him without moving from his station beside the tether winch.

I should have read Dante's *Inferno* in preparation for this task, Fuchida thought to himself.

The road to hell begins with a gradual slope, he knew. It will get steep enough soon.

Then both his booted feet slipped out from under him.

"You OK?" Rodriguez's voice sounded anxious in Fuchida's earphones.

"I hit a slick spot. There must be patches of dry ice coating the rock here in the shadows."

The biologist was lying on his side, his hip throbbing painfully from his fall. At this rate, he thought, I'll be black-and-blue from the waist down.

"Can you get up?"

"Yes. Certainly." Fuchida felt more embarrassed than hurt. He grabbed angrily at the tether and pulled himself to his feet. Even in the one-third gravity of Mars it took an effort, with the suit and backpack weighing him down. And all the equipment that dangled from his belt and harness.

Once on his feet he stared down once more into the darkness of the caldera's yawning maw. It's like the mouth of a great beast, a voice in his mind said. Like the gateway to the eternal pit.

He took a deep breath, then said into his helmet microphone, "OK. I'm starting down again."

"Be careful, man."

"Thanks for the advice," Fuchida snapped.

Rodriguez seemed untroubled by his irritation. "Maybe I oughta keep the line tighter," he suggested. "Not so much slack."

Regretting his temper, Fuchida agreed, "Yes, that might help to keep me on my feet." The hip really hurt, and his rump was still sore from his first fall.

I'm lucky I didn't rupture the suit, he thought. Or damage the backpack.

"OK, I've adjusted the tension. Take it easy, now."

A journey of a thousand miles must begin with a single step. Mitsuo Fuchida quoted Lao-tzu's ancient dictum as he planted one booted foot on the ground ahead of him. The bare rock seemed to offer good traction.

You can't see the ice, he told himself. It's too thin a coating to be visible. Several dozen meters to his right, sunlight slanted down into the gradually sloping side of the caldera. There'll be no ice there, Fuchida thought. He moved off in that direction, slowly, testing his footing every step of the way.

The tether connected to his harness at his chest, so he could easily disconnect it if necessary. The increased tension of the line made walking all the more difficult. Fuchida felt almost like a marionette on a string.

"Slack off a little," he called to Rodriguez.

"You sure?"

He turned back to look up at his teammate, and was startled to see that the astronaut was nothing more than a tiny blob of a figure up on the rim, standing in bright sunlight with the deep blue sky behind him.

"Yes, I'm certain," he said, with deliberate patience.

A few moments later Rodriguez asked, "How's that?"

The difference was imperceptible, but Fuchida replied, "Better."

He saw a ledge in the sunlight some twenty meters below him and decided to head for it. Slowly, carefully he descended.

"I can't see you." Rodriguez's voice in his earphones sounded only slightly concerned.

Looking up, Fuchida saw the expanse of deep blue sky and nothing else except the gentle slope of the bare rock. And the tether, his lifeline, holding strong.

"It's all right," he said. "I'm using the VR cameras to record my descent. I'm going to stop at a ledge and chip out some rock samples there."

"Hey, Mitsuo," Rodriguez called.

Automatically Fuchida looked up. But the astronaut was beyond his view. Fuchida was alone down on the ledge in the caldera's sloping flank of solid rock. The Buckyball tether that connected him to the winch up above also carried their suit-to-suit radio transmissions.

"What is it?" he replied, grateful to hear Rodriguez's voice.

"How's it going, man?"

"That depends," said Fuchida.

"On what?"

The biologist hesitated. He had been working on this rock ledge for hours, chipping out samples, measuring heat flow, patiently working an auger into the hard basalt to see if there might be water ice trapped in the rock.

He was in shadow now. The sun had moved away. Looking up, he saw with relief that the sky was still a bright blue. It was still daylight up there. Rodriguez would not let him stay down after sunset, he knew, yet he still felt comforted to see that there was still daylight up there.

"It depends," he answered slowly, "on what you are looking for. Whether you are a geologist or a biologist."

"Oh," said Rodriguez.

"A geologist would be very happy here. There is a considerable amount of heat still trapped in these rocks. Much more than can be accounted for by solar warming alone."

"You mean the volcano's still active?"

"No, no, no. It is dead, but the corpse is still warm—a little."

Rodriguez did not reply.

"Do you realize what this means? This volcano must be much younger than was thought. Much younger!"

"How young?"

"Perhaps only a few million years," Fuchida said excitedly. "No more than ten million."

"Sounds pretty damned old to me, amigo."

"But there might be life here! If there is heat, there might be liquid water within the rock."

"I thought water couldn't stay liquid on Mars."

"Not on the surface," Fuchida said, feeling the exhilaration quivering within him. "But deeper down, inside the rock where the pressure is higher . . . maybe . . ."

"Looks pretty dark down there."

"It is," Fuchida answered, peering over the lip of the ledge on which he sat. The suit's heater seemed to be working fine; it might be a hundred below zero in those shadows, but he felt comfortably warm.

"I don't like the idea of your being down there in the dark."

"Neither do I, but that's why we're here, isn't it?"

No answer.

"I mean, we still have several hundred meters of tether to unwind, don't we?"

Rodriguez said, "Eleven hundred and ninety-two, according to the meter."

"So I can go down a long way, then."

"I don't like the dark."

"My helmet lamp is working fine."

"Still . . ."

"Don't worry about it," Fuchida insisted, cutting off the astronaut's worries. It was bad enough to battle his own fears; he wanted no part of Rodriguez's.

"I saw a crevice at the end of this ledge," he told the astronaut. "It looks like the opening of an old lava tube. It probably leads down a considerable distance."

"Do you think that's a good idea?"

"I'll take a look into it."

"Don't take any chances you don't have to."

Fuchida grimaced as he climbed slowly to his feet. His whole body ached from the bruising he'd received in his falls and he felt stiff after sitting on the ledge for so long. Walk carefully, he warned himself. Even though the rock is warmer down here, there could still be patches of ice.

"You hear me?" Rodriguez called.

"If I followed your advice I'd be in my bed in Osaka," he said, trying to make it sound light and witty.

"Yeah, sure."

Stiffly he walked toward the fissure he had seen earlier. His helmet lamp threw a glare of light before him, but he had to bend over slightly to make the light reach the ground.

There it is, he saw. A narrow, slightly rounded hole in the basalt face. Like the mouth of a pirate's cave.

Fuchida took a step into the opening and turned from side to side, playing his helmet lamp on the walls of the cave.

It was a lava tube, he was certain of it. Like a tunnel made by some giant extraterrestrial worm, it curved downward. How far down? he wondered.

Stifling a voice in his head that whispered of fear and danger, Fuchida started into the cold, dark lava tube.

* * *

"Jamie," Stacy Dezhurova's voice called out sharply, "we have an emergency message from Rodriguez."

Sitting at the electron microscope in the geology lab, Jamie looked up from the display screen when Dezhurova's voice rang through the dome. He left the core sample in the microscope without turning it off and sprinted across the dome to the comm center.

Dezhurova looked grim as she silently handed Jamie a headset. The other scientists in the dome crowded into the commcenter behind him.

Rodriguez's voice was calm but tight with tension. ". . . down there more than two hours now and then radio contact cut off," the astronaut was saying.

Sitting again on the wheeled chair next to Dezhurova as he adjusted the pin microphone, Jamie said, "This is Waterman. What's happening, Tòmas?"

"Mitsuo went down into the caldera as scheduled. He found a lava tube about fifty-sixty meters down and went into it. Then his radio transmission was cut off."

"How long—"

"It's more than half an hour now. I've tried yanking on his tether but I'm getting no response."

"What do you think?"

"Either he's unconscious or his radio's failed. I mean, I really pulled on the tether. Nothing."

The astronaut did not mention the third possibility: that Fuchida was dead. But the thought blazed in Jamie's mind.

"You say your radio contact with him cut off while he was still in the lava tube?"

"Yeah, right. That was more'n half an hour ago."

A thousand possibilities spun through Jamie's mind. The tether's too tough to break, he knew. Those Buckyballs can take tons of tension.

"It's going to be dark soon," Rodriguez said.

"You're going to have to go down after him," Jamie said.

"I know."

"Just go down far enough to see what's happened to him. Find out what's happened and call back here."

"Yeah. Right."

"I don't like it, but that's what you're going to have to do."

"I don't like it much, either," said Rodriguez.

Through a haze of pain, Mitsuo Fuchida saw the irony of the situation. He had made a great discovery but he would probably not live to tell anyone about it.

When he entered the lava tube he felt an unaccustomed sense of dread, like a character in an old horror movie, stepping slowly, fearfully down the narrow corridor of a haunted house, lit only by the flicker of a candle. Except this corridor was a tube melted out of the solid rock by an ancient stream of red-hot lava, and Fuchida's light came from the lamp on his hard suit helmet.

Nonsense! he snapped silently. You are safe in your hard suit, and the tether connects you to Rodriguez, up at the surface. But he called to the astronaut and chatted inanely with him, just to reassure himself that he was not truly cut off from the rest of the universe down in this dark, narrow passageway.

The VR cameras fixed to his helmet were recording everything he saw, but Fuchida thought that only a geologist would be interested in this cramped, claustrophobic tunnel.

The tube slanted downward, its walls fairly smooth, almost glassy in places. The black rock gleamed in the light of his lamp. The tunnel grew narrower in spots, then widened again, although nowhere was it wide enough for him to spread his arms fully.

Perspiration was beading Fuchida's lip and brow, trickling coldly down his ribs. Stop this foolishness, he admonished himself. You've been in tighter caves than this.

He thought of Elizabeth, waiting for him back in Japan, accepting the subtle snubs of deep-seated racism because she loved him and wanted to be with him when he returned. I'll get back to you, he vowed, even if this tunnel leads down to hell itself.

The tether seemed to snag from time to time. He had to stop and tug on it to loosen it again. Or perhaps Rodriguez was fiddling with the tension on the line, he thought.

Deeper into the tunnel he went, stepping cautiously, now and then running his gloved hands over the strangely smooth walls.

Fuchida lost track of time as he chipped at the tunnel walls here and there, filling the sample bags that dangled from his harness belt. The tether made it uncomfortable to push forward, attached to his harness at the chest. It had to pass over his shoulder or around his waist: clumsy, at best.

Then he noticed that the circle of light cast by his helmet lamp showed an indentation off toward the left, a mini-alcove that seemed lighter in color than the rest of the glossy black tunnel walls. Fuchida edged closer to it, leaning slightly into the niche to examine it.

A bubble of lava did this, he thought. The niche was barely big enough for a man to enter. A man not encumbered with a hard suit and bulky backpack, that is. Fuchida stood at the entrance to the narrow niche, peering inside, wondering.

And then he noticed a streak of red, the color of iron rust. Rust? Why here and not elsewhere?

He pushed in closer, squeezing into the narrow opening to inspect the rust spot. Yes, definitely the color of iron rust.

He took a scraper from the tool kit at his waist, nearly fumbling it in his awkwardly gloved fingers. If I drop it I won't be able to bend down to pick it up, not in this narrow cleft, he realized.

The red stain crumbled at the touch of the scraper. Strange! thought Fuchida. Not like the basalt at all. Could it be . . . wet? No! Liquid water cannot exist at this low air pressure. But what is the pressure inside the rock? Perhaps . . .

The red stuff crumbled easily into the sample bag he held beneath it with trembling fingers. It must be iron oxide that is being eroded by water, somehow. Water and iron. Siderophiles! Bacteria that metabolize iron and water!

Fuchida was as certain of it as he was of his own existence. His heart was racing. A colony of iron-loving bacteria living inside the caldera of Olympus Mons! Who knew what else might be found deeper down?

It was only when he sealed up the sample bag and placed it in the plastic box dangling from his belt that he heard the strange rumbling sound. Through the thickness of his helmet it sounded muted, far-off, but still any sound at all this deep in the tunnel was startling.

Fuchida started to back away from the crumbling, rust-red cleft. The rumbling sound seemed to grow louder, like the growl of some prowling beast. It was nonsense, of course, but he thought the tunnel walls were shaking slightly, trembling. It's you who are trembling, foolish man! he admonished himself.

Something in the back of his mind said, Fear is healthy. It is nothing to be ashamed of, if you—

The rusted area of rock dissolved into a burst of exploding steam that lifted Fuchida off his feet and slammed him painfully against the far wall of the lava tube.

Fuchida nearly blacked out as his head banged against the back of his helmet. He sagged to the floor of the tunnel, his visor completely fogged, his skull thundering with pain.

With a teeth-gritting effort of iron will he kept himself from slipping into unconsciousness. Despite the pounding in his head, he forced himself to stay awake, alert. Do not faint! he commanded himself. Do not allow yourself to take the cowardly way. You must remain awake if you hope to remain alive. He felt perspiration beading his forehead, dripping into his eyes, forcing him to blink and squint.

Then a wave of anger swept over him. How stupid you are! he railed at himself. A hydrothermal vent. Water. Liquid water, here on Mars. You should have known. You should have guessed. The heat flow, the rusted iron. There must be siderophiles here, bacteria that metabolize iron and water. They weakened the wall and you scraped enough of it away for the pressure to blow through the wall.

Yes, he agreed with himself. Now that you've made the discovery, you must live to report it to the rest of the world.

His visor was still badly fogged. Fuchida groped for the control stud at his wrist that would turn up his suit fans and clear the visor. He thought he found the right keypad and pushed it. Nothing changed. In fact, now that he listened for it, he could not hear the soft buzz of his suit fans at all. Except for his own labored breathing, there was nothing but silence.

Wait. Be calm. Think.

Call Rodriguez. Tell him what's happened.

"Tòmas, I've had a little accident."

No response.

"Rodriguez! Can you hear me?"

Silence.

Slowly, carefully, he flexed both his arms, then his legs. His body ached, but there didn't seem to be any broken bones. Still the air fans remained silent, and beads of sweat dripped into his eyes.

Blinking, squinting, he saw that the visor was beginning to clear up on its own. The hydrothermal vent must have been a weak one, he thought thankfully. He could hear no more rumbling; the tunnel did not seem to be shaking now.

Almost reluctantly, he wormed his arm up to eye level and held the wrist keyboard close to his visor. The keyboard was blank. Electrical malfunction! Frantically he tapped at the keyboard: nothing. Heater, heat exchanger, air fans, radio—all gone.

I'm a dead man.

Cold panic hit him like a blow to the heart. That's why you no longer hear the air circulation fans! The suit battery must have been damaged when I slammed against the wall.

Fuchida could hear his pulse thundering in his ears. Calm down! he commanded himself. That's not so bad. The suit has enough air in it for an hour or so. And it's insulated very thoroughly; you won't freeze—not for several hours, at least. You can get by without the air circulation fans. For a while.

It was when he tried to stand up that the real fear hit him. His right ankle flared with agony. Broken or badly sprained, Fuchida realized. I can't stand on it. I can't get out of here.

Then the irony really struck him. I might be the first man to die of heat prostration on Mars.

The problem is, Rodriguez said to himself, that we only have one climbing harness and Mitsuo's wearing it.

I've got to go down there without a tether, without any of the climbing tools that he's carrying with him.

Shit!

The alternative, he knew, was to leave the biologist and return to the safety of the plane. Rodriguez shook his head inside his helmet. Can't leave him. It's already getting dark and he'd never survive overnight.

On the other hand, there's a damned good chance that we'll both die down there.

Double shit.

For long, useless moments he stared down into the dark depths of the caldera, in complete shadow now as the sun crept closer to the distant horizon.

Never show fear, Rodriguez repeated to himself. Not even to yourself. He nodded inside his helmet. Yeah, easy to say. Now get the snakes in my guts to believe it.

Still, he started down, walking slowly, deliberately, gripping the tether hand-over-hand as he descended.

It became totally dark within a few steps of leaving the caldera's rim. The only light was the patch of glow cast by his helmet lamp, and the dark rock all around him seemed to swallow that up greedily. He planted his booted feet carefully, deliberately, knowing that carbon dioxide from the air was already starting to freeze out on the bitterly cold rock.

Rodriguez cast a glance up at the dimming sky, like a prisoner taking his last desperate look at freedom before entering his dungeon.

At least I can follow the tether, he thought. He moved with ponderous deliberation, worried about slipping on patches of ice. If I get disabled we're both toast, he told himself. Take it easy. Don't rush it. Don't make any mistakes.

Slowly, slowly he descended. By the time the tether led him to the mouth of the lava tube, he could no longer see the scant slice of sky above; it was completely black. If there were stars winking at him up there he could not see them through the tinted visor of his helmet.

He peered into the tunnel. It was like staring into a well of blackness.

"Hey, Mitsuo!" he called. "Can you hear me?"

No response. He's either dead or unconscious. Rodriguez thought. He's laying deep down that tunnel someplace and I've got to go find him. Or what's left of him.

He took a deep breath. No fear, he reminded himself.

Down the dark tunnel he plodded, ignoring the fluttering of his innards, paying no attention to the voice in his head that told him he'd gone far enough, the guy's dead, no sense getting yourself killed down here too so get the hell out, now.

Can't leave him, Rodriguez shouted silently at the voice. Dead or alive, I can't leave him down here.

Your funeral, the voice countered.

Yeah, sure. I get back to the base OK without him. What're they gonna think of me? How'm I—

He saw the slumped form of the biologist, a lump of hard suit and equipment sitting against one wall of the tunnel.

"Hey, Mitsuo!" he called.

The inert form did not move.

Rodriguez hurried to the biologist and tried to peer into the visor of his helmet. It looked badly fogged.

"Mitsuo," he shouted. "You OK?" It sounded idiotic the moment the words left his lips.

But Fuchida suddenly reached up and gripped his shoulders.

"You're alive!"

Still no answer. His radio's out, Rodriguez finally realized. And the air's too thin to carry my voice.

He touched his helmet against Fuchida's. "Hey, man, what happened?"

"Battery," the biologist replied, his voice muffled but understandable. "Battery not working. And my ankle. Can't walk."

"Jesus! Can you stand up if I prop you?"

"I don't know. My air fans are down. I'm afraid to move; I don't want to generate any extra body heat."

Shit, said Rodriguez to himself. Am I gonna have to carry him all the way up to the surface?

Sitting there trapped like a stupid schoolboy on his first exploration of a cave, Fuchida wished he had paid more attention to his Buddhist instructors. This would be a good time to meditate, to reach for inner peace and attain a calm alpha state. Or was it beta state?

With his suit fans inoperative, the circulation of air inside the heavily insulated hard suit was almost nonexistent. Heat generated by his body could not be transferred to the heat exchanger in the backpack; the temperature inside the suit was climbing steadily.

Worse, it was more and more difficult to get the carbon dioxide he exhaled out of the suit and into the air recycler. He could choke to death on his own fumes.

The answer was to be as still as possible, not to move, not even to blink. Be calm. Achieve nothingness. Do not stir. Wait. Wait for help.

Rodriguez will come for me, he told himself. Tòmas won't leave me here to die. He'll come for me.

Will he come in time? Fuchida tried to shut the possibility of death out of his thoughts, but he knew that it was the ultimate inevitability.

The hell of it is, I'm certain I have a bag full of siderophiles! I'll be famous. Posthumously.

Then he saw the bobbing light of a helmet lamp approaching. He nearly blubbered with relief. Rodriguez appeared, a lumbering robotlike creature in the bulky hard suit. To Fuchida he looked sweeter than an angel.

Once Rodriguez realized that he had to touch helmets to be heard, he asked, "How in the hell did you get yourself banged up like this?"

"Hydrothermal vent," Fuchida replied. "It knocked me clear across the tunnel."

Rodriguez grunted. "Old Faithful strikes on Mars."

Fuchida tried to laugh; what came out was a shaky coughing giggle.

"Can you move? Get up?"

"I think so . . ." Slowly, with Rodriguez lifting from beneath his armpits, Fuchida got to his feet. He took a deep breath, then coughed. When he tried to put some weight on his bad ankle he nearly collapsed.

"Take it easy, buddy. Lean on me. We got to get you back to the plane before you choke to death."

* * *

Rodriguez had forgotten about the ice.

He half-dragged Fuchida along the tunnel, the little pools of light made by their helmet lamps the only break in the total, overwhelming darkness around them.

"How you doing, buddy?" he asked the Japanese biologist. "Talk to me."

Leaning his helmet against the astronaut's, Fuchida answered, "I feel hot. Broiling."

"You're lucky. I'm freezing my ass off. I think my suit heater's crapping out on me."

"I . . . I don't know how long I can last without the air fans," Fuchida said, his voice trembling slightly. "I feel a little lightheaded."

"No problem," Rodriguez replied, with a false heartiness. "It'll get kinda stuffy inside your suit, but you won't asphyxiate."

The first American astronaut to take an EVA spacewalk outside his capsule had almost collapsed from heat prostration, Rodriguez remembered. The damned suits hold all your body heat inside; that's why they make us wear the watercooled longjohns and put heat exchangers in the suits. But if the fans can't circulate the air the exchanger's pretty damned useless.

Rodriguez kept one hand on the tether. In the wan light from his helmet lamp he saw that it led upward, out of this abyss.

"We'll be back in the plane in half an hour, maybe less. I can fix your backpack then."

"Good," said Fuchida. Then he coughed again.

It seemed to take hours before they got out of the tunnel, back onto the ledge in the slope of the giant caldera.

"Come on, grab the tether. We're goin' up."

"Right."

But Rodriguez's boot slipped and he fell to his knees with a painful thump.

"Damn," he muttered. "It's slick."

"The ice."

The astronaut rocked back onto his haunches, both knees throbbing painfully.

"It's too slippery to climb?" Fuchida's voice was edging toward panic.

"Yeah. We're gonna have to haul ourselves up with the winch." He got down onto his belly and motioned the biologist to do the same.

"Isn't this dangerous? What if we tear our suits?"

Rodriguez rapped on the shoulder of Fuchida's suit. "Tough as steel, amigo. They won't rip."

"You're certain?"

"You wanna spend the night down here?"

Fuchida grabbed the tether with both his hands.

Grinning to himself, Rodriguez also grasped the tether and told Fuchida to activate the winch.

But within seconds he felt the tether slacken.

"Stop!"

"What's wrong?" Fuchida asked.

Rodriguez gave the tether a few light tugs. It felt loose, its original tension gone.

"Holy shit," he muttered.

"What is it?"

"The weight of both of us on the line is too much for the rig to hold. We're pulling it out of the ground up there."

"You mean we're stuck here?"

* * *

"I see that none of us are going to get any sleep."

Stacy Dezhurova was smiling as she spoke, but her bright blue eyes were dead serious. Trudy Hall was still on duty at the comm console. Stacy sat beside her while Jamie paced slowly back and forth behind her. Vijay Shektar, the expedition doctor, had pulled in another chair and sat by the doorway, watching them all.

The comm center cubicle felt stuffy and hot with all four of them crowded in there. Jamie did not answer Dezhurova's remark; he just kept on pacing, five strides from one partition to the other, then back again.

"Rodriguez must have found him by now," Hall said, swivelling her chair slightly toward Stacy.

"Then why doesn't he call in?" she demanded, almost angrily.

"They must still be down inside the caldera," Jamie said.

"It's night," Stacy pointed out.

Jamie nodded and kept pacing.

"It's the waiting that's the worst," Vijay offered. "Not knowing what—"

"This is Rodriguez," the radio speaker crackled. "We got a little problem here."

Jamie was at the comm console like a shot, leaning between the two women.

"What's happening, Tòmas?"

"Fuchida's alive. But his backpack's banged up and his battery's not functioning. Heater, air fans, nothing in his suit's working." Rodriguez's voice sounded tense but in control, like a pilot whose jet engine had just flamed out: trouble, but nothing that can't be handled. Until you hit the ground.

Then he added, "We're stuck on a ledge about thirty meters down and can't get back up 'cause the rock's coated with dry ice and it's too slippery to climb."

As the astronaut went on to describe how the tether winch almost pulled out of its supports when the two of them tried to haul themselves up the slope, Jamie tapped Hall on the shoulder and told her to pull up the specs on the hard suit's air circulation system.

"OK," he said when Rodriguez stopped talking. "Are either of you hurt?"

"I'm bruised a little. Mitsuo's got a bad ankle. He can't stand on it."

One of the screens on the console now showed a diagram of the suit's air circulation system. Hall was scrolling through a long list on the screen next to it.

"Mitsuo, how do you feel?" Jamie asked, stalling for time, time to think, time to get the information he needed.

"His radio's down," Rodriguez said. A hesitation, then, "But he says he's hot. Sweating."

Vijay nodded and murmured, "Hyperthermia."

Strangely, Rodriguez chuckled. "Mitsuo also says he discovered siderophiles, inside the caldera! He wants Trudy to know that."

"I heard it," Hall said, still scrolling down the suit specs. "Did he get samples?"

Again a wait, then Rodriguez replied, "Yep. There's water in the rock. Liquid water. Mitsuo says you've gotta publish . . . get it out on the Net."

"Liquid?" Hall stopped the scrolling. Her eyes went wide. "Are you certain about—"

"Never mind that now," Jamie said, studying the numbers on Hall's screen. "According to the suit specs you can get enough breathable air for two hours, at least, even with the fans off."

"We can't wait down here until daylight, then," Rodriguez said.

Jamie said, "Tòmas, is Mitsuo's harness still connected to the winch?"

"Far as I can see, yeah. But if we try to use the winch to haul us up it's gonna yank the rig right out of the ground."

"Then Mitsuo's got to go up by himself."

"By himself?"

"Right," Jamie said. "Let the winch pull Mitsuo up to the top. Then he takes off the harness and sends it back to you so you can get up. Understand?"

In the pale light of the helmet lamps, Fuchida could not see Rodriguez's face behind his tinted visor. But he knew what the astronaut must be feeling.

Pressing his helmet against Rodriguez's, he said, "I can't leave you down here alone, without even the tether." Rodriguez's helmet mike must have picked up his voice, because Waterman replied, iron hard, "No arguments, Mitsuo. You drag your butt up there and send the harness back down. It shouldn't take more than a few minutes to get you both up to the top."

Fuchida started to object, but Rodriguez cut him off. "OK, Jamie. Sounds good. We'll call you from the top when we get there."

Fuchida heard the connection click off.

"I can't leave you here," he said, feeling almost desperate.

"That's what you've got to do, man. Otherwise neither one of us will make it."

"Then you go first and send the harness back down to me."

"No way," Rodriguez said. "You're the scientist, you're more important. I'm the astronaut, I'm trained to deal with dangerous situations."

Fuchida said, "But it's my fault—"

"Bullshit," Rodriguez snapped. Then he added, "Besides, I'm bigger and meaner than you. Now get going and stop wasting time!"

"How will you find the harness in the dark? It could be dangling two meters from your nose and your helmet lamp won't pick it up."

Rodriguez made a huffing sound, almost a snort. "Tie one of the beacons to it and turn on the beacon light."

Fuchida felt mortified. I should have thought of that. It's so simple. I must be truly rattled, my mind is not functioning as it should.

"Now go on," Rodriguez said. "Get down on your belly again and start up the winch."

"Wait," Fuchida said. "There is something—"

"What?" Rodriguez demanded impatiently.

Fuchida hesitated, then spoke all in a rush. "If . . . if I don't make it . . . if I die . . . would you contact someone for me when you get back to Earth?"

"You're not gonna die."

"Her name is Elizabeth Vernon," Fuchida went on, afraid that if he stopped he would not be able to resume. "She's a lab assistant in the biology department of the University of Tokyo. Tell her . . . that I love her."

Rodriguez understood the importance of his companion's words. "Your girlfriend's not Japanese?"

"My wife," Fuchida answered.

Rodriguez whistled softly. Then, "OK, Mitsuo. Sure. I'll tell her. But you can tell her yourself. You're not gonna die."

"Of course. But if . . ."

"Yeah. I know. Now get going!"

Reluctantly, Fuchida did as he was told. He felt terribly afraid of a thousand possibilities, from tearing his suit to leaving his partner in the dark to freeze to death. But he felt more afraid of remaining there and doing nothing.

Worse, he felt hot. Stifling inside the suit. Gritting his teeth, he held on to the tether with all the pressure the servo-motors on his gloves could apply. Then he realized that he needed one hand free to work the winch control on his climbing harness.

He fumbled for the control stud, desperately trying to remember which one started the winch. He found it and pressed. For an instant nothing happened.

Then suddenly he was yanked off the ledge and dragged up the hard rock face of the caldera's slope, his suit grinding, grating, screeching against the rough rock.

I'll never make it. Fuchida realized. Even if the suit doesn't break apart, I'll suffocate in here before I reach the top.

Rodriguez watched Fuchida slither up and away from him, a dim pool of light that receded slowly but steadily. Through the insulation of his helmet he could not hear the noise of the biologist's hard suit grating against the ice-rimed rock; he heard nothing but his own breathing, faster than it should have been. Calm down, he ordered himself. Keep calm and everything'll turn out OK.

Sure, a sardonic voice in his head answered. Nothing to it. Piece of cake.

Then he realized that he was totally, utterly alone in the darkness.

It's OK, he told himself. Mitsuo'll send the harness down and then I can winch myself up.

The light cast by his helmet lamp was only a feeble glow against the dark rough rock face. When Rodriguez turned, the light was swallowed by the emptiness of the caldera's abyss, deep and wide and endless.

The darkness surrounded him. It was as if there was no one else in the whole universe, no universe at all, only the all-engulfing darkness of this cold, black pit.

Unbidden, a line from some play he had read years earlier in school came to his mind:

Why, this is hell, nor am I out of it.

Don't be a goon! he snapped at himself. You'll be OK. Your suit's working fine and Mitsuo's up there by now, taking off the harness and getting ready to send it down to you.

Yeah, sure. He could be unconscious, he could be snagged on a rock or maybe the damned harness broke while the winch was dragging him up the slope.

Rodriguez put a gloved hand against the solid rock to steady himself. You'll be out of this soon, he repeated silently. Then he wondered if his lamp's light was weakening. Are the batteries starting to run down?

Fuchida's head was banging against the inside of his helmet so hard he tasted blood in his mouth. He squeezed his eyes shut and saw his father's stern, uncompromising glare. How disappointed he will be when he learns that I died on Mars, like cousin Konoye.

And Elizabeth. Perhaps it's better this way. She can go back to Ireland and find a man of her own culture to marry. My death will spare her a lifetime of troubles.

The winch stopped suddenly and Fuchida felt a pang of terror. It's stuck! He realized at that moment that he was not prepared for death. He did not want to die. Not here on Mars. Not at all.

A baleful red eye was staring at him. Fuchida thought for a moment he might be slipping into unconsciousness, then slowly realized that it was the light atop one of the geo/met beacons they had planted at the lip of the caldera.

Straining his eyes in the starlit darkness, he thought he could make out the form of the winch looming above his prostate body. He reached out and touched it.

Yes! He had reached the top. But he felt faint, giddy. His body was soaked with perspiration. Heat prostration, he thought. How funny to die of heat prostration when the temperature outside my suit is nearly two hundred degrees below zero.

He began to laugh, knowing he was slipping into hysteria and unable to stop himself. Until he began coughing uncontrollably.

Down on the ledge, Rodriguez tried to keep his own terrors at bay.

"Mitsuo," he called on the suit-to-suit frequency. "You OK?"

No answer. Of course, dummy! His radio's not working. The cold seemed to be leaching into his suit. Cold enough to freeze carbon dioxide. Cold enough to overpower the suit's heater. Cold enough to kill.

"Get up there, Mitsuo," he whispered. "Get up there in one piece and send the damned tether back down to me."

He wouldn't leave me here. Not if he made it to the top. He wouldn't run for the plane and leave me here. He can't run, anyway. Can't even walk. But he could make it to the plane once he's up there. Hobble, jump on one leg. He wouldn't do that. He wouldn't leave me alone to die down here. Something must've happened to him. He must be hurt or unconscious.

The memory of his big brother's death came flooding back to him. In a sudden rush he saw Luis's bloody mangled body as the rescue workers lifted him out of the wrecked semi. A police chase on the freeway. All those years his brother had been running drugs up from Tijuana in his eighteen-wheeler and Tòmas never knew, never even suspected. There was nothing he could do. By the time he saw Luis's rig sprawled along the shoulder of the highway it was already too late.

He saw himself standing, impotent, inert, as his brother was pronounced dead and then slid into the waiting ambulance and carried away. Just like that. Death can strike like a lightning bolt.

What could I have done to save him? Rodriguez wondered for the thousandth time. I should have done something. But I was too busy being a flyboy, training to be an astronaut. I didn't have time for the family, for my own brother.

He took a deep, sighing breath of canned air. Well, now it's going to even out. I got all the way to Mars, and now I'm gonna die here.

Then he heard his brother's soft, musical voice. "No fear, muchacho. Never show fear. Not even to yourself."

Rodriguez felt no fear. Just a deep eternal sadness that he did not help Luis when help was needed. And now it was all going to end. All the regrets, all the hopes, everything . . .

For an instant he thought he saw a flash of dim red light against the rock wall. He blinked. Nothing. He looked up, but the top of his helmet cut off his view. Grasping at straws, he told himself. You want to see something bad enough, you'll see it, even if it isn't really there.

But the dim red glow flashed again, and this time when he blinked it didn't go away. Damned helmets! he raged. Can't see anything unless it's in front of your fuckin' face.

He tried to tilt his whole upper body back a little, urgently aware that it wouldn't take much to slip off this ledge and go toppling down into the bottomless caldera.

And there it was! The red glow of the beacon's light swayed far above him, like the unwinking eye of an all-seeing savior.

He leaned against the rock face again. His legs felt weak, rubbery. Shit, man, you were really scared.

He could make out the dangling form of the harness now, with the telescoped pole of the beacon attached to it by duct tape. Where the hell did Mitsuo get duct tape? he wondered. He must've been carrying it with him all along. The universal cure-all. We could do a commercial for the stuff when we get back to Earth. Save your life on Mars with friggin' duct tape.

It seemed to take an hour for the tiny red light to get close enough to grab. With hands that trembled only slightly, Rodriguez reached up and grabbed the beacon, ripped it free and worked his arms into the climbing harness. Then he snapped its fasteners shut and gave the tether an experimental tug. It felt strong, good.

He started to reach for the control stud that would activate the winch. Then he caught himself. "Wait one," he whispered, in the clipped tone of the professional flier.

He bent down and picked up the beacon. Sliding it open to its full length, he worked its pointed end into a crack in the basalt rock face. It probably won't stay in place for long, he thought, and it won't work at all unless the sun shines on it for a few hours per day. But he felt satisfied that he had left a reminder that men from Earth had been here, had entered the pit and gleaned at least some of its secrets and survived—maybe.

"OK," he said to himself, grasping the tether with one hand. "Here we go."

He pushed on the control stud and was hauled off his feet. Grinding, twisting, grating, he felt himself pulled up the rock slope, his head banging inside his helmet, his legs and booted feet bouncing as he was dragged upward.

Worse than any simulator ride he'd ever been through in training. Worse than the high-g centrifuge they'd whirled him in. They'll never put this ride into Disneyland, Rodriguez thought, teeth clacking as he bounced, jounced, jolted up to the lip of the caldera.

At last it was over. Rodriguez lay panting, breathless, aching. Fuchida's hard-suited form lay on the ground next to him, unmoving.

Rodriguez rolled over on one side, as far as his backpack would allow. Beyond Fuchida's dark silhouette the sky was filled with stars. Dazzling bright friendly stars gleaming down at him, like a thousand thousand jewels. Like heaven itself.

I made it, Rodriguez told himself. Then he corrected: Not yet. Can't say that yet.

He touched his helmet to Fuchida's. "Hey, Mitsuo! You OK?"

It was an inane question and he knew it. Fuchida made no response, but Rodriguez thought that he could hear the biologist's breathing: panting, really, shallow and fast.

Gotta get him to the plane. Can't do a thing for him out here.

As quickly as he could Rodriguez unbuckled the climbing harness, then tenderly lifted the unconscious Fuchida and struggled to his feet. Good thing we're on Mars. I could never lift him in his suit in a full g. Now where the hell is the plane?

In the distance he saw the single red eye of another one of the geo/met beacons they had planted. He headed in that direction, tenderly carrying his companion in his arms.

I couldn't do this for you, Luis, Rodriguez said silently. I wish I could have, but this is the most I can do.

The base dome was dark and silent, its lighting turned down to sleep shift level, its plastic skin opaqued to prevent heat from leaking out into the Martian night. Stacy Dezhurova was still sitting at the comm console, drowsing despite herself, when Rodriguez's call came through.

"We're back in the plane," the astronaut announced without preamble. "Lemme talk to Vijay."

"Vijay!" Stacy shouted in a voice that shattered the sleepy silence. "Jamie!" she added.

Running footsteps padded through the shadows, bare or stockinged feet against the plastic flooring. Vijay, the physician, slipped into a chair beside Dezhurova, her jet-black eyes wide open and alert. Jamie and Tracy Hall raced in, bleary-eyed, and stood behind the two women.

"This is Vijay," she said. "What's your condition?"

In the display screen they could see only the two men's helmets and shoulders. Their faces were masked by the heavily tinted visors. But Rodriguez's voice sounded steady, firm.

"I'm OK. Banged up a little, but that's nothing. I purged Mitsuo's suit and plugged him into the plane's emergency air supply. But he's still out of it."

"How long ago did you do that?" Vijay asked, her dark face rigid with tension.

"Fifteen—sixteen minutes ago."

"And you're just calling in now?" Dezhurova demanded.

"I had to fix his battery pack," Rodriguez answered, unruffled by her tone. "It got disconnected when he was knocked down—"

"Knocked down?" Jamie blurted.

"Yeah. That's when he hurt his ankle."

"How badly is he hurt?" Vijay asked.

"It's sprained, at least. Maybe a break."

"He couldn't break a bone inside the suit," Jamie muttered. "Not with all that protection."

"Anyway," Rodriguez resumed, "his suit wasn't getting any power. I figured that getting his suit powered up was the second most important thing to do. Pumping fresh air into him was the first."

"And calling in, the third," Dezhurova said, much more mildly.

"Right," said Rodriguez.

"I'm getting his readouts," Vijay said, studying the medical diagnostic screen.

"Yeah, his suit's OK now that the battery's reconnected."

"Is his LCG working?" Vijay asked.

"Should be," Rodriguez said. "Wait one . . ."

They saw the astronaut lean over and touch his helmet to the unconscious Fuchida's shoulder.

"Yep," he announced, after a moment. "I can hear the pump chugging. Water oughtta be circulating through his longjohns just fine."

"That should bring his temperature down," Vijay muttered, half to herself. "The problem is, he might be in shock from overheating."

"What do I do about that?" Rodriguez asked.

The physician shook her head. "Not much you can do, mate. Especially with the two of you sealed into your suits."

For a long moment they were all silent. Vijay stared at the medical screen. Fuchida's temperature was coming down. Heart rate slowing nicely. Breathing almost normal. He should be—

The biologist coughed and stirred. "What happened?" he asked weakly.

All four of the people at the comm center broke into grins. None of them could see Rodriguez's face behind his visor, but they heard the relief in his voice:

"Naw, Mitsuo; you're supposed to ask, 'Where am I?'"

The biologist sat up straighter. "Is Tracy there?"

"Don't worry about—"

"I'm right here, Mitsuo," said Tracy Hall, leaning in between Dezhurova and Vijay Shektar. "What is it?"

"Siderophiles!" Fuchida exclaimed. "Iron-eating bacteria live in the caldera."

"Did you get samples?"

"Yes, of course."

Jamie stepped back as the two biologists chattered together. Fuchida nearly gets himself killed, but what's important to him is finding a new kind of organism. With an inward smile, Jamie admitted, maybe he's right.

Jamie awoke the instant the dome's lighting turned up to daytime level. He pushed back the thin sheet that covered him and got to his feet. After the long night they had all put in, he should have felt tired, drained. Yet he was awake, alert, eager to start the day.

Quickly he stepped to his desk and booted up his laptop, then opened the communications channel to Rodriguez and Fuchida. With a glance at the desktop clock he saw that it was six-thirty-three. He hesitated for only a moment, though, then put through a call to the two men at Olympus Mons.

As he suspected, they were both awake. Jamie's laptop screen showed the two of them side-by-side in the plane's cockpit.

"Good morning," he said. "Did you sleep well?"

"Extremely well," said Fuchida.

"This cockpit looked like the best hotel suite in the world when we got into it last night," Rodriguez said.

Jamie nodded. "Yeah, I guess it did."

Rodriguez gave a crisp, terse morning report. Fuchida happily praised the astronaut for purging his suit of the foul air and fixing the electrical connection that had worked loose in his backpack.

"My suit fans are buzzing faithfully," he said. "But I'm afraid I won't be able to do much useful work on my bad ankle."

They had discussed the ankle injury the previous night, once Fuchida had regained consciousness. Vijay guessed that it was a sprain, but wanted to get the biologist back to the dome as quickly as possible for an X ray.

Jamie had decided to let Rodriguez carry out as much of their planned work as he could, alone, before returning. Their schedule called for another half day on the mountaintop, then a takeoff in the early afternoon for the flight back to dome. They should land at the base well before sunset.

"I'll be happy to take off this suit," Fuchida confessed.

"We're not gonna smell so good when we do," Rodriguez added.

Jamie found himself peering hard at the small screen of his laptop, trying to see past their visors. Impossible, of course. But they both sounded cheerful enough.

The fears and dangers of the previous night were gone, daylight and the relative safety of the plane brightened their outlook.

Rodriguez said, "We've decided that I'm going back down inside the caldera and properly implant the beacon we left on the ledge there."

"So we can get good data from it," Fuchida added, as if he were afraid Jamie would countermand his decision.

Jamie asked, "Do you really think you should try that?"

"Oughtta be simple enough," Rodriguez said easily, "long as we don't go near that damned lava tube again."

"That's the imperial 'we,'" Fuchida explained. "I'm staying here in the plane, I'm afraid."

"Is there enough sunlight where you want to plant the beacon?" Jamie asked.

He sensed the biologist nodding inside his helmet. "Oh yes, the ledge receives a few hours of sunlight each day."

"So we'll get data from inside the caldera," Rodriguez prompted.

"Not very far inside," Fuchida added, "but it will better than no data at all."

"You're really set on doing this?"

"Yes," they both said. Jamie could feel their determination. It was their little victory over Olympus Mons, their way of telling themselves that they were not afraid of the giant volcano.

"OK, then," Jamie said. "But be careful, now."

"We're always careful," said Fuchida.

"Most of the time," Rodriguez added, with a laugh.

MARROW

Robert Reed

❀

Robert Reed (born 1956) was born and raised and lives in Nebraska. His work is notable for its variety, and for his increasing production. He has been one of the most prolific short story writers of high quality in the SF field past for the few years, averaging ten published stories a year, 1999–2001.

His first story collection, *The Dragons of Springplace* (1999), fine as it is, skims only bit of the cream from his works. And he writes a novel every year or two as well. His first novel, *The Leeshore* appeared in 1987, followed by *The Hormone Jungle* (1988), *Black Milk* (1989), *Down the Bright Way* (1991), *The Remarkables* (1992), *Beyond the Veil of Stars* (1994), *An Exaltation of Larks* (1995), *Beneath the Gated Sky* (1997). His most recent novel is *Marrow* (2000), a distant future large-scale story that is hard SF and seems to be a breakthrough in his career, which *The New York Times* called "an exhilarating ride, in the hands of an author whose aspiration literally knows no bounds." *The Encyclopedia of Science Fiction* remarks that "the expertness of the writing and its knowing exploitation of current scientific speculations are balanced by an underlying quiet sanity about how to depict and to illumine human beings."

Reed does not characteristically write hard SF. In a *Locus* interview, he comments:

> I've always thought of science fiction as being, at some level, a nineteenth-century business. There's this tendency to try to make it all very logical—Asimov's Three Laws of Robotics, and the fact that you can predict the future by the present. But these are notions that, for the most part, twentieth-century science has made impractical at best. Chaos Theory, Butterfly Effects, those sorts of things. . . . I could never write a "Foundation Series," because I just don't believe it's at all possible to predict what's going to happen. I feel I'm very conservative in some ways, so I find myself retreating from Greg Egan's more radical ideas. There are certain things I hold onto, and always will, in science. I am a staunch Darwinist, and won't give that up! Mostly, though, science fiction is still a very logical, cause-and-effect, mechanistic universe—which I don't believe in.

"Marrow," which takes place on a hollow planet-sized space ship, was later expanded into Reed's novel of the same name. Alastair Reynolds mentions it as an influence (see Reynolds note). It concerns people trapped on a world within this hollow world, merging a hard SF sensibility with the nineteenth-century image of the hollow Earth. Reed said, in *Locus*, "*Marrow* takes place on a giant starship taking a luxury cruise around the galaxy. It's an artifact-type ship; nobody knows who built it. It now has immortals on board, and it's like a one-hundred-thousand-year voyage. It's the core of a jupiter-class world that has been expanded and is traveling along at sub-light speed. It's a world unto itself." The story combines a Clarkean fascination with huge technological artifacts with a powerful vision of increasingly huge scale.

MISSION YEAR 0.00:

Washen couldn't count all the captains spread out before her, and putting on her finest captainly smile, she joined them, trading the usual compliments, telling little stories about her travels, and with a genuine unease, asking if anyone knew why the Ship's Master would want to bring them here.

"She's testing us," one gray-eyed colleague ventured. "She's testing our obedience. Plus our security measures, too."

"Perhaps," Washen allowed.

Coded orders had found Washen through secure channels. Without explanation, the Master told her to abandon her post, discarding her uniform and taking on a suitable disguise. For the last seven days, she had played the role of dutiful tourist, wandering the vast ship, enjoying its wondrous sights, then after making triple-sure that she wasn't being monitored, boarding an anonymous tube-car that had brought her to this odd place.

"My name is Diu," said her companion, offering his hand and a wide smile.

She clasped the hand with both of hers, saying, "We met at the captains' banquet. Was it twenty years ago?"

"Twenty-five." Like most captains, Diu was tall for a human, with craggy features and an easy charm meant to instill trust in their human passengers. "It's kind of you to remember me. Thank you."

"You're most welcome."

The eyes brightened. "What do you think of the Master's tastes? Isn't this a bizarre place to meet?"

"Bizarre," Washen echoed. "That's a good word."

The leech once lived here. An obscure species, ascetic by nature, they had built their home inside the remote confines of one of the ship's enormous fuel tanks. Weaving together thick plastics, they had dangled this place from the tank's insulated ceiling. Its interior, following a leech logic, was a single room. Vast in two dimensions but with a glowing gray ceiling close enough to touch, the surroundings made every human feel claustrophobic. The only furnishings were hard gray pillows. The air was warm and stale, smelling of odd dusts and persistent pheromones. Colors were strictly forbidden. Even the gaudy tourists' clothes seemed to turn gray in the relentless light.

"I've been wondering," said Diu. "Whatever happened to the leech?"

"I don't know," Washen confessed. She had met the species when they came on board. But that was more than a thousand years before, and even a captain's memory was imperfect.

The leech could have simply reached their destination, disembarking without incident. Or they could have decided to build an even more isolated home, if that was possible. Or perhaps some disaster had struck, and they were dead. Shipboard extinctions were more common than any captain would admit. Some of their passengers proved too frail to endure any long journey. Mass suicides and private wars claimed others. Yet as Washen often reminded herself, for every failed species, a hundred others thrived, or at least managed to etch out some little corner of this glorious ship where they could hold their own.

"Wherever the leech are, I'm sure they're well."

"Of course they are," Diu replied, knowing what was polite. "Of course."

In the face of ignorance, captains should make positive sounds.

Washen noticed how even when standing still, Diu was moving, his flesh practically vibrating, as if the water inside him was ready to boil.

"So, madam . . . I'm dying to know what you think! What's our mission? What's so important that the Master pulls us all the way down here?"

"Yes," said a second voice. "What's your best bad guess, darling?"

Miocene had joined them. One of a handful of Submasters in attendance, she was rumored to be the Master's favorite. An imperious, narrow-faced woman, she was a full head taller than the others, dressed in rich robes, her brindle-colored hair brushing against the ceiling. Yet she stood erect, refusing to dip her head for the simple sake of comfort.

"Not that you know more than any of us," the Submaster persisted. "But what do you think the Master wants?"

The room seemed to grow quiet. Captains held their breath, secretly delighted that it was Washen who had to endure Miocene's attentions.

"Well," Washen began, "I can count several hundred clues."

A razor smile formed. "And they are?"

"Us." They were standing near one of the room's few windows—a wide slit of thick, distorting plastic. There was nothing outside but blackness and vacuum; an ocean of liquid hydrogen, vast and calm and brutally cold, lay some fifty kilometers below them. Nothing was visible in the window but their own murky reflections. Washen saw everyone at a glance. She regarded her own handsome, ageless face, black hair pulled back in a sensible bun and streaked with enough white to lend authority, her wide chocolate eyes betraying confidence with a twist of deserved pleasure. "The Master selected us, and we're the clues."

Miocene glanced at her own reflection. "And who are we?"

"The elite of the elite." Washen put names to the faces, listing bonuses and promotions earned over the last millennia. "Manka is a new second-grade. Aasleen was in charge of the last engine upgrade, which came in below budget and five months early. Saluki and Westfall have won the Master's award for duty ten times each." She gestured at the captain beside her, saying, "And there's Diu, of course. Already an eleventh-grade, which is astonishing. You came on board the ship—warn me if I'm wrong—as just another passenger."

The energetic man said, "True, madam. Thank you for remembering."

Washen grinned, then said, "And then there's you, Madam Miocene. You are one of three Submasters with first-chair status at the Master's table."

The tall woman nodded, enjoying the flattery. "But don't forget yourself, darling."

"I never do," Washen replied, earning a good laugh from everyone. And because nothing was more unseemly in a captain than false modesty, she admitted, "I've heard the rumors. I'm slated to become our newest Submaster."

Miocene grinned, but she made no comment about any rumors.

Instead she took an enormous breath, and in a loud voice asked, "Can you smell yourselves? Can you? That's the smell of ambition. No other scent is so tenacious, or in my mind, ever so sweet . . . !"

No name but the ship was necessary. Ancient and spectacular, there was nothing else that could be confused with it, and everyone on board, from the Ship's Master to the most disreputable stowaway, was justifiably proud of their magnificent home.

The ship began as a jupiter-class world, but an unknown species had claimed it. Using its hydrogen atmosphere, they accelerated the core to a fraction of lightspeed. Then they built tunnels and compartments, plus chambers large enough to swallow small worlds. Premium hyperfibers lent strength and durability to the frame. And then, as with the leech's plastic abode, the builders suddenly and mysteriously abandoned their creation.

Billions of years later, humans stumbled across the ship. Most of its systems were in a diagnostic mode. Human engineers woke them, making repairs where necessary. Then the best human captains were hired, and every manner of passenger was ushered aboard, the ship's maiden voyage calling for a half-million year jaunt around the Milky Way.

Its undisputed ruler arrived a few hours later.

Accompanied by a melody of horns and angel-voiced humans, the Master strode into the room. Where other captains were disguised in civilian clothes, their leader wore a mirrored cap and uniform that suited her office, and for many reasons, her chosen body was broad and extraordinarily deep. It was status, in part. But a Master also needed bulk to give her augmented brain a suitable home, thousands of ship functions constantly monitored and adjusted, in the same unconscious way that the woman moved and breathed.

Gravity was weaker this deep inside the ship. With one vast hand skating along the ceiling, the Master deftly kept herself from bumping her head. A dozen of the low-grade captains offered greetings and hard cushions. Diu was among the supplicants, on his knees and smiling, even after she had passed.

"Thank you for coming," said that voice that always took Washen by surprise. It was a quiet, unhurried voice, perpetually amused by whatever the radiant brown eyes were seeing. "I know you're puzzled," she said, "and I hope you're concerned. So let me begin with my compelling reasons for this game, and what I intend for you."

A handful of guards stood in the distance; Washen saw their tiny armored silhouettes as the room's lights fell to nothing.

"The ship, please."

A real-time projection blossomed beside the Master, channeled through her own internal systems. The spherical hull looked slick and gray. A thousand lasers were firing from the bow, aiming at comets and other hazards, Mammoth engines rooted in the stern spat out hurricanes of plasma, incrementally adjusting their course and speed. And a tiny flare on the equator meant that another starship was arriving. With new passengers, presumably.

"Now," said the amused voice, "start peeling the onion. Please."

In a blink, the hyperfiber hull was removed. Washen could suddenly make out the largest high-deck chambers; she knew each by name and purpose, just as she knew every important place too small to be seen. Then another few hundred kilometers of rock and water, air and hyperfiber were erased, exposing more landmarks.

"This perfect architecture." The Master stepped closer to the shrinking projection, its glow illuminating a wide strong self-assured face—a face designed to inspire thousands of captains, and a crew numbering in the tens of millions. "In my mind, there's been no greater epic in history. I'm not talking about this journey of ours. I mean about the astonishing task of exploring our ancient starship. Imagine the honor: To be the first living organism to step into one of these chambers, the first sentient mind in billions of years to experience their vastness, their mystery. It was a magnificent time. And I'm talking first-hand, since I was one of the leaders of the first survey team . . ."

It was an old, honorable boast, and her prerogative.

"We did a superlative job," she assured. "I won't accept any other verdict. Despite technical problems and the sheer enormity of it, we mapped more than ninety-nine percent of the ship's interior. In fact, I was the first one to find my way through the plumbing above us, and the first to see the sublime beauty of the hydrogen sea below us . . ."

Washen hid a smile, thinking: A fuel tank is a fuel tank is a fuel tank.

"Here we are," the Master announced. The projection had shrunk by a third. The fuel tank was a fist-sized cavern; the leech habitat was far too small to be seen. Then in the next moment, they were gone, another layer removed without sound or fuss. Liquid hydrogen turned into a blackish solid, and deeper still, a transparent metal. "These seas have always been the deepest features," she commented. "Below them, there's nothing but iron and a stew of other metals squashed under fantastic pressures."

The ship had been reduced to a perfectly smooth black ball—the essential ingredient in a multitude of popular games.

"Until now, we knew nothing about the core." The Master paused for a moment, allowing herself a quick grin. "Evidence shows that when the ship was built, its core was stripped of its radionuclides, probably to help cool the metals and keep them relatively stiff. We don't know how the builders managed the trick. But there used to be narrow tunnels leading down, all reinforced with hyperfibers and energy buttresses, and all eventually crushed by time and a lack of repair." A second pause, then she said, "Not enough room left for a single microchine to pass. Or so we've always believed."

Washen felt herself breathing faster, enjoying the moment.

"There has never, ever been the feeblest hint of hidden chambers," the Master proclaimed. "I won't accept criticism on this matter. Every possible test was carried out. Seismic. Neutrino imaging. Even palm-of-the-hand calculations of mass and volume. Until fifty-three years ago, there was no reason to fear that our maps weren't complete."

A silence had engulfed the audience.

Quietly, smoothly, the Master said, "The full ship. Please."

The iron ball was again dressed in rock and hyperfiber.

"Now the impact. Please."

Washen stepped forward, anticipating what she would see. Fifty-three years ago, they passed through a dense swarm of comets. The captains had thrown gobs of antimatter into the largest hazards. Lasers fired without pause, evaporating trillions of tons of ice. But debris still peppered the hull, a thousand pinpricks of light dancing on its silver-gray projection, and then came a blistering white flash that dwarfed the other explosions and left the captains blinking, remembering that moment, and the shared embarrassment.

A chunk of nickel-iron had slipped through their defenses. The ship rattled with the impact, and for months afterwards, nervous passengers talked about little else. Even when the captains showed them all of the schematics and calculations, proving that they could have absorbed an even larger impact before anyone was in real danger . . . even then there were people and aliens who insisted on being afraid.

With a palpable relish, the Master said, "Now the cross section, please."

Half of the ship evaporated. Pressure waves spread down and out from the blast site, then pulled together again at the stern, causing more damage before they bounced, and bounced back again, the diluted vibrations still detectable now, murmuring their way through the ship as well as through the captains' own bones.

"AI analysis. Please."

A map was laid over the cross section, every feature familiar. Save one.

"Madam," said a sturdy voice. Miocene's voice. "It's an anomaly, granted. But doesn't the feature seem rather . . . unlikely . . . ?"

"Which is why I thought it was nothing. And my trusted AI—part of my own neural net—agreed with me. This region is a change in composition. Nothing more." She paused for a long moment, watching her captains. Then with a gracious oversized smile, she admitted, "The possibility of a hollow core has to seem ludicrous."

Submasters and captains nodded with a ragged hopefulness.

Knowing they weren't ordered here because of an anomaly, Washen stepped closer. How large was it? Estimates were easy to make, but the simple math created some staggering numbers.

"Ludicrous," the Master repeated. "But then I thought back to when we were babies, barely a few thousand years old. Who would have guessed that a Jupiter-class world could become a starship like ours?"

Just the same, thought Washen: Certain proposals will always be insane.

"But madam," said Miocene. "A chamber of those proportions would make us less massive. Assuming we know the densities of the intervening iron, of course . . ."

"And you're assuming, of course, that the core is empty." The Master grinned at her favorite officer, then at all of them. For several minutes, her expression was serene, wringing pleasure out of their confusion and ignorance.

Then she reminded everyone, "This began as someone else's vessel. We shouldn't forget: We don't understand why our home was built. For all we know, it was a cargo ship. A cargo ship, and here is its hold."

The captains shuddered at the idea.

"Imagine that something is inside this chamber. Like any cargo, it would have to be restrained. A series of strong buttressing fields might keep it from rattling around every time we adjusted our course. And naturally, if the buttressing fields were rigid enough, then they would mask whatever is down there—"

"Madam," shouted someone, "please, what's down there . . . ?"

Shouted Diu.

"A spherical object. It's the size of Mars, but considerably more massive." The Master grinned for a moment, then told the projection, "Please. Show them what I found."

The image changed again. Nestled inside the great ship was a world, black as iron and slightly smaller than the chamber surrounding it. The simple possibility of such an enormous, unexpected discovery didn't strike Washen as one revelation, but as many, coming in waves, making her gasp and shake her head as she looked at her colleagues' faces, barely seeing any of them.

"This world has an atmosphere," said the laughing voice, "with enough oxygen to be breathed, enough water for lakes and rivers, and all of the symptoms usually associated with a vigorous biosphere—"

"How do we know that?" Washen called out. Then, in a mild panic, "No disrespect intended, madam!"

"I haven't gone there myself, if that's what you're asking." She giggled like a child, telling them, "But after fifty years of secret work, using self-replicating drones to rebuild one of the old tunnels . . . after all that, I'm able to stand here and assure you that not only does this world exist, but that each of you are going to see it for yourselves . . ."

Washen glanced at Diu, wondering if her face wore that same wide smile.

"I have named the world, by the way. We'll call it Marrow." The Master winked and said, "For where blood is born, of course. And it's reserved for you . . . my most talented, trustworthy friends . . . !"

Wonders had been accomplished in a few decades. Mole-like drones had gnawed their way through beds of nickel and iron, repairing one of the ancient tunnels; fleets of tube-cars had plunged to where the tunnel opened into the mysterious chamber, assembling a huge stockpile of supplies directly above Marrow; then a brigade of construction drones threw together the captains' base camp—a sterile little city of dormitories, machine shops, and first-rate laboratories tucked within a transparent, airtight blister.

Washen was among the last to arrive. At the Master's insistence, she led a cleaning detail that stayed behind, erasing every trace of the captains' presence from the leech habitat. It was a security precaution, and it required exacting work. And some of her people considered it an insult. "We aren't janitors," they grumbled. To which Washen replied, "You're right. Professionals would have finished last week."

Diu belonged to her detail, and unlike some, the novice captain worked hard to endear himself. He was probably calculating that she would emerge from this mission as a Submaster and his benefactor. But there was nothing wrong in calculations, Washen believed—as long as the work was done, successes piled high and honors for everyone.

Only tiny, two passenger tube-cars could make the long fall to the base camp. Washen decided that Diu would provide comfortable company. He rewarded her with his life story, including how he came into the captains' ranks. "After a few thousand years of being a wealthy passenger, I realized that I was bored." He said it with a tone of confession, and amusement. "But you captains never look bored. Pissed, yes. And harried, usually. But that's what attracted me to you. If only because people expect it, captains can't help seem relentlessly, importantly busy."

Washen had to admit, it was a unique journey into the ship's elite.

At journey's end, their car pulled into the first empty berth. On foot, Diu and Washen conquered the last kilometer, stepping abruptly out onto the viewing platform, and not quite standing together, peering over the edge.

A tinted airtight blister lay between them and several hundred kilometers of airless, animated space. Force fields swirled through that vacuum, creating an array of stubborn, stable buttresses. The buttresses were visible as a brilliant blue-white light that flowed from everywhere, filling the chamber. The light never seemed to weaken. Even with the blister's protection, the glare was intense. Relentless. Eyes had to adapt—a physiological change that would take several ship-days—and even still, no one grew accustomed to the endless day.

Even inside her bedroom, windows blackened and the covers thrown over her head, a captain could feel the radiance piercing her flesh just so it could tickle her bones.

The chamber wall was blanketed with a thick mass of gray-white hyperfiber, and the wall was their ceiling, falling away on all sides until it vanished behind Marrow.

"Marrow," Washen whispered, spellbound.

On just the sliver of the world beneath them, the captain saw a dozen active volcanoes, plus a wide lake of bubbling iron. In cooler basins, hot-water streams ran into colorful, mineral-stained lakes. Above them, water clouds were gathering into enormous thunderheads. When the land wasn't exploding, it was a rugged shadowless black, and the blackness wasn't just because of the iron-choked soils. Vigorous, soot-colored vegetation basked in the endless day. And they were a blessing. From what the captains could see, the forests were acting as powerful filters, scrubbing the atmosphere until it was clean, at least to where humans, if conditioned properly, should be able to breathe, perhaps even comfortably.

"I want to get down there," Washen confessed.

"It's going to take time," Diu warned, pointing over her shoulder.

Above the blister, dormitories and machine shops were dangling from the hyperfiber, their roofs serving as foundations. Past them, at the blister's edge, the captains were assembling a silvery-white cylinder. It would eventually form a bridge to Marrow. There was no other way down. The buttress fields killed transports, and for many reasons, unprotected minds, eroded in an instant, and died. To beat the challenge, their best engineer, Aasleen, had designed a shaft dressed in hyperfibers, its interior shielded with ceramics and superfluids. Theories claimed that the danger ended with Marrow's atmosphere, but just to be safe, several hundred immortal pigs and baboons were in cages, waiting to put those guesses to the test.

Washen was thinking about the baboons, and timetables.

A familiar voice broke her reverie.

"What are your impressions, darlings?"

Miocene stood behind them. In uniform, she was even more imposing, and more cold. Yet Washen summoned her best smile, greeting the mission leader, then adding, "I'm surprised. I didn't know it would be this beautiful."

"Is it?" The knife-edged face offered a smile. "Is there any beauty here, Diu?"

"A spartan kind of beauty," Diu replied.

"I wouldn't know. I don't have any feel for aesthetics." The Submaster smiled off into the distance. "Tell me. If this world proves harmless and beautiful, what do you think our passengers will pay for the chance to come here?"

"If it's a little dangerous," Washen ventured, "they would pay more."

Miocene's smile came closer, growing harder. "And if it's deadly, maybe we'll have to collapse the tunnel again. With us safely above, of course."

"Of course," the captains echoed.

Diu was grinning, with his face, and if possible, with his entire body.

Mirrors and antennae clung to hyperfiber, gazing at Marrow. He gestured at them, asking, "Have we seen any signs of intelligence, madam? Or artifacts of any sort?"

"No," said Miocene, "and no."

It would be a strange place for sentience to evolve, thought Washen. And if the builders had left ruins behind, they would have been destroyed long ago. The crust beneath them wasn't even a thousand years old. Marrow was an enormous forge, constantly reworking its face as well as the bones beneath.

"I can't help it," Diu confessed. "I keep dreaming that the builders are down there, waiting for us."

"A delirious dream," Miocene warned him.

But Washen felt the same way. She could almost see the builders slathering the hyperfiber, then building Marrow. This was a huge place, and they couldn't see more than a sliver of it from their tiny vantage point. Who knew what they would eventually find?

Diu couldn't stop talking. "This is fantastic," he said. "And an honor. I'm just pleased that the Master would include me."

The Submaster nodded, conspicuously saying nothing.

"Now that I'm here," Diu blubbered, "I can almost see the purpose of this place."

With a level glance, Washen tried to tell her companion, Shut up.

But Miocene had already tilted her head, eyeing their eleventh-grade colleague. "I'd love to hear your theories, darling."

Diu lifted his eyebrows.

An instant later, with bleak amusement, he remarked, "I think not." Then he looked at his own hands, saying, "Once spoken, madam, a thought hides inside at least one other."

MISSION YEAR 1.03:

Planetfall was exactly as the captains had planned—a routine day from the final five kilometers of bridge building to Miocene's first steps on the surface. And with success came cheers and singing, followed by ample late suppers served with bottomless glasses of well-chilled champagne, and congratulations from the distant Master.

Except for Washen, the day was just a little disappointing.

Watching from base camp, studying data harvests and live images, she saw exactly what she expected to see. Captains were administrators, not explorers; the historic moments were relentlessly organized. The landscape had been mapped until every bush and bug had a name. Not even tiny surprises could ambush the first teams. It was thorough and stifling, but naturally Washen didn't mention her disappointment, or even put a name to her emotions. Habit is habit, and she had been an exemplary captain for thousands of years. Besides, what sort of person would she be if she was offended that there were no injuries, or mistakes, or troubles of any kind?

And yet.

Two ship-days later, when her six-member team was ready to embark, Washen had to make herself sound like a captain. With a forced sincerity, she told the others, "We'll take our walk on the iron, and we'll exceed every objective. On schedule, if not before."

It was a swift, strange trip to Marrow.

Diu asked to ride with Washen, just as he'd requested to be part of her team. Their shielded tube-car retreated back up the access tunnel, then flung itself at Marrow, streaking through the buttress fields to minimize the exposure, a trillion electric fingers delicately playing with their sanity.

Then their car reached the upper atmosphere and braked, the terrific gees bruising flesh and shattering minor bones.

Artificial genes began weaving protein analogs, knitting their injuries.

The bridge was rooted into a hillside of cold iron and black jungle. The rest of the team and their supplies followed. Despite an overcast sky, the air was brilliant and furnace-hot, every breath tasting of metal and nervous sweat. As team leader, Washen gave orders that everyone knew by heart. Cars were linked, then reconfigured. The new vehicle was loaded, and tested, and the captains were tested by their autodocs: Newly implanted genes were helping their bodies adapt to the heat and metal-rich environment. Then Miocene, sitting in a nearby encampment, contacted them and gave her blessing, and Washen lifted off, steering towards the purely arbitrary north-northwest.

The countryside was broken and twisted, split by fault lines and raw mountains and volcanic vents. The vents had been quiet for a century or a decade, or in some cases, days. Yet the surrounding land was alive, adorned with jungle, pseudotrees reminiscent of mushrooms, all enormous, all pressed against one another, their lacquered black faces feeding on the dazzling blue-white light.

Marrow seemed as durable as the captains flying above it.

Growth rates were phenomenal, and for more reasons than photosynthesis. Early findings showed that the jungle also fed through its roots, chisel-like tips reaching down to where thermophilic bacteria thrived, Marrow's own heat supplying easy calories.

Were the aquatic ecosystems as productive?

It was Washen's question, and she'd selected a small, metal-choked lake for study. They arrived on schedule, and after circling the lake twice, as prescribed, she landed on a slab of bare iron. Then for the rest of the day they set up their lab and quarters, and specimen traps, and as a precaution, installed a defense perimeter—three paranoid AIs who did nothing but think the worst of every bug and spore that happened past.

Night was mandatory. Miocene insisted that each captain sleep at least four hours, and invest another hour in food and toiletries.

Washen's team went to bed on time, then lay awake until it was time to rise.

At breakfast, they sat in a circle and gazed at the sky. The chamber's wall was smooth and ageless, and infinitely bland. Base camp was a dark blemish visible only because the air was exceptionally clear. The bridge had vanished with the distance. If Washen was very careful, she could almost believe that they were the only people on this world. If she was lucky, she forgot for a minute or two that telescopes were watching her sitting on her aerogel chair, eating her scheduled rations.

Diu sat nearby, and when she glanced at him, he smiled wistfully, as if he could read her thoughts.

"I know what we need," Washen announced.

Diu said, "What do we need?"

"A ceremony. Some ritual before we can start." She rose and walked to one of the specimen traps, returning with one of their first catches. On Marrow, pseudoinsects filled almost every animal niche. Six-winged dragonflies were blue as gemstones and longer than a forearm. With the other captains watching, Washen stripped the dragonfly of its wings and tail, then eased the rest into their autokitchen. The broiling took a few seconds. With a dull thud, the carcass exploded inside the oven. Then she grabbed a lump of the blackish meat, and with a grimace, made herself bite and chew.

"We aren't supposed to," Diu warned, laughing gently.

Washen forced herself to swallow, then she told everyone, "And you won't want to do it again. Believe me."

There were no native viruses to catch, or toxins that their reinforced genetics couldn't handle. Miocene was simply being a cautious mother when she told them, "Except in emergencies, eat only the safe rations."

Washen passed out the ceremonial meat.

Last to take his share was Diu, and his first bite was tiny. But he didn't grimace, and with an odd little laugh, he told Washen, "It's not bad. If my tongue quit burning, I could almost think about enjoying it."

MISSION YEAR 1.22:

After weeks of relentless work, certain possibilities began to look like fact.

Marrow had been carved straight from the jupiter's heart. Its composition and their own common sense told the captains as much. The builders had first wrenched the uraniums and thoriums from the overhead iron, injecting them deep into the core. Then with the buttressing fields, the molten sphere was compressed, and the exposed chamber walls were slathered in hyperfiber. And billions of years later, without help from the vanished builders, the machinery was still purring along quite nicely.

But why bother creating such a marvel?

Marrow could be a dumping ground for radionuclides. Or it could have worked as an enormous fission reactor, some captains suggested. Except there were easier ways to create power, others pointed out, their voices not so gently dismissive.

But what if the world was designed to store power?

It was Aasleen's suggestion: By tweaking the buttresses, the builders could have forced Marrow to rotate. With patience—a resource they must have had in abundance—they could have given it a tremendous velocity. Spinning inside a vacuum, held intact by the buttresses, the iron ball would have stored phenomenal amounts of energy—enough to maintain the on board systems for billions of years, perhaps.

Washen first heard the flywheel hypothesis at the weekly briefing.

Each of the team leaders was sitting at the illusion of a conference table, in aerogel chairs, sweating rivers in Marrow's heat. The surrounding room was sculpted from light, and sitting at the head of the table was the Master's projection, alert but unusually quiet. She expected crisp reports and upbeat attitudes. Grand theories were a surprise. Finally, after a contemplative pause, she smiled, telling the captain, "That's an intriguing possibility. Thank you, Aasleen." Then to the others, "Considerations? Any?"

Her smile brought a wave of complimentary noise.

In private, Washen doubted they were inside someone's dead battery. But this wasn't the polite moment to list the troubles with flywheels. And besides, the bio-teams were reporting next, and she was eager to compare notes.

A tremor suddenly shook the captains, one after another, spreading out from its distant epicenter. Even for Marrow, that was a big jolt.

Compliments dissolved into an alert silence.

Then the Master lifted her wide hand, announcing abruptly, "We need to discuss your timetable."

What about the bio-teams?

"You're being missed, I'm afraid. Our cover story isn't clever enough, and the crew are suspicious." The Master lowered her hand, then said, "Before people are too worried, I want to bring you home."

Smiles broke out.

Some were tired of Marrow; other captains were tickled with the prospects of honors of promotions.

"Everyone, madam?" Washen dared.

"At least temporarily."

According to the ship's duty roster, the missing captains were visiting a nearby solar system, serving as travel agents to billions of potential passengers. And the truth told, there'd been boring moments when Washen found herself wishing that the fiction was real. But not today. Not when she was in the middle of something fascinating . . . !

As mission leader, it was Miocene's place to ask:

"Do you want us to cut our work short, madam?"

The Master squinted at the nearest window, gazing out at one of the ship's port facilities. For her, the room and its view were genuine, and her captains were illusions.

"Mission plans can be rewritten," she told them. "I want you to finish surveying the far hemisphere, and I want the critical studies wrapped up. Ten ship days should be adequate. Then you'll come home, and we'll take our time deciding on our next actions."

Smiles wavered, but none crumbled.

Miocene whispered, "Ten days," with a tentative respect.

"Is that a problem?"

"Madam," the Submaster began, "I would feel much more comfortable if we were certain that Marrow isn't a threat."

There was a pause, and not just because the Master was thousands of kilometers removed from them. It was a lengthy, unnerving silence. Then the captains' captain looked off into the distance, saying, "Considerations? Any?"

It would be a disruption. The other Submasters agreed with Miocene. To accomplish their work in ten days, with confidence, would require every captain, including those stationed with the support teams. Their base camp would have to be abandoned temporarily. That was an acceptable risk, perhaps. But mild words were obscured by clenched fists and distant, worried gazes.

Unsatisfied, the Master turned to her future Submaster. "Do you have any considerations to add?"

Washen hesitated as long as she dared.

"Marrow could have been a flywheel," she finally allowed. "Madam."

Brown eyes closed, opened. "I'm sorry," the Master responded, the voice devoid of amusement. "Aren't we discussing your timetable?"

"But if these buttresses ever weakened," Washen continued, "even for an instant, the planet would have expanded instantly. Catastrophically. The surrounding hyperfiber would have vaporized, and a shock wave would have passed through the entire ship, in moments." She offered simple calculations, then added, "Maybe this was an elaborate flywheel. But it also would have made an effective self-destruct mechanism. We don't know, madam. We don't know if the builders had enemies, real or imagined. But if we're going to find answers, I can't think of a better place to look."

The Master's face was unreadable, impenetrable.

Finally she shook her head, smiling in a pained manner. "Since my first moment on board this glorious vessel, I have nourished one guiding principle: The builders, whomever they were, would never endanger this marvelous creation."

Washen wished for the same confidence.

Then that apparition of light and sound leaned forward, saying, "You need a change of duty, Washen. I want you and your team in the lead. Help us explore the far hemisphere. And once the surveys are finished, everyone comes home. Agreed?"

"As you wish, madam," said Washen.

Said everyone.

Then Washen caught Miocene's surreptitious glance, something in the eyes saying, "Nice try, darling." And with that look, the faintest hint of respect.

Pterosaur drones had already drawn three maps of the region. Yet as Washen passed overhead, she realized that even the most recent map, drawn eight days ago, was too old to be useful.

Battered by quakes, the landscape had been heaved skyward, then torn open. Molten iron flowed into an oxbow lake, boiling water and mud, and columns of dirty steam rose skyward, then twisted to the east. As an experiment, Washen flew into the steam clouds. Samples were ingested through filters and sensors and simple lensing chambers. Riding with the steam were spores and eggs, encased in tough bioceramics and indifferent to the heat. Inside the tip of the needle flask, too small to see with the naked eye, were enough pond weeds and finned beetles to conquer ten new lakes.

Catastrophe was the driving force on Marrow.

That insight struck Washen every day, sometimes hourly, and it always arrived with a larger principle in tow:

In some flavor or another, disaster ruled every world.

But Marrow was the ultimate example. And as if to prove itself, the steam clouds dispersed suddenly, giving way to the sky's light, the chamber wall overhead, and far below, for as far as Washen could see, the stark black bones of a jungle.

Fumes and fire had incinerated every tree, every scrambling bug.

The carnage must have been horrific. Yet the blaze had passed days ago, and new growth was already pushing up from the gnarled trunks and fresh crevices, thousands of glossy black umbrella-like leaves shining in the superheated air.

Washen decided to blank the useless maps, flying on instinct.

"Twenty minutes, and we're as far from the bridge as possible," Diu promised, his smile wide and infectious.

No other team would travel as far.

Washen started to turn, intending to order chilled champagne for the occasion, her mouth opened and a distorted, almost inaudible voice interrupting her.

"Report . . . all teams . . . !"

It was Miocene's voice strained through a piercing electronic whistle.

"What do . . . see . . . ?" asked the Submaster. "Teams . . . report . . . !"

Washen tried establishing more than an audio link, and failed.

A dozen other captains were chattering in a ragged chorus. Zale said, "We're on schedule." Kyzkee observed, "There's some com-interference . . . otherwise, systems appear nominal." Then with more curiosity than worry, Aasleen inquired, "Why, madam? Is something wrong?"

There was a long, jangled hum.

Diu was hunched over sensor displays, and with a tight little voice, he said, "Shit."

"What—?" Washen cried out.

Then a shrill cry swept away every voice, every thought. And the day brightened and brightened, fat bolts of lightning flowing across the sky, then turning, moving with purpose, aiming for them.

From the far side of the world came a twisted voice:

"The bridge . . . where is it . . . do you see it . . . where . . . ?"

The car bucked as if panicking, losing thrust and altitude, then its AIs. Washen deployed the manual controls, and centuries of drills made her concentrate, nothing existing but their tumbling vehicle, her syrupy reflexes, and an expanse of burnt forest.

The next barrage of lightning was purple-white, and brighter, nothing visible but its seething glare.

Washen flew blind, flew by memory.

Their car was designed to endure heroic abuse, the same as its passengers. But it was dead and its hull had been degraded, and when it struck the iron ground, the hull shattered. Restraining fields grabbed bodies, then failed. Nothing but mechanical belts and gas bags held the captains in their seats. Flesh was jerked and twisted, and shredded. Bones were shattered and wrenched from their sockets. Then the seats were torn free of the floor, and like useless wreckage, scattered across several hectares of iron and burnt stumps.

Washen never lost consciousness.

With numbed curiosity, she watched her own legs and arms break, and a thousand bruises spread into a single purple tapestry, every rib crushed to dust and her reinforced spine splintering until she was left without pain or a shred of mobility. Washen couldn't move her head, and her words were slow and watery, the sloppy mouth filled with cracked teeth and dying blood.

"Abandon," she muttered.

Then, "Ship," and she was laughing feebly. Desperately.

A gray sensation rippled through her body.

Emergency genes were already awake, finding their home in a shambles. They immediately protected the brain, flooding it with oxygen and anti-inflammatories, plus a blanket of comforting narcotics. Then they began to repair the vital organs and spine, cannibalizing meat for raw materials and energy, the captain's body wracked with fever, sweating salt water and blood, and after a little while, the body grew noticeably smaller.

An hour after the crash, a wrenching pain swept through Washen. It was a favorable sign. She squirmed and wailed, and with weak hands, freed herself from her ruined chair. Then with her sloppy rebuilt legs, she forced herself to stand.

Washen was suddenly twenty centimeters shorter, and frail. But she was able to limp over to Diu's body, finding him shriveled and in agony, but defiant—a fierce grin and a wink, then he told her, "You look gorgeous, madam. As always."

The others were alive, too. But not one machine in the wreckage would operate, not even well enough to say, "I'm broken."

The six captains healed within a day, and waited at the crash site, eating their rations to reclaim their size and vigor. No rescue team arrived. Whatever crippled their car must have done the same everywhere, they decided. Miocene was as powerless as them. And that left them with one viable option:

If Washen and the others wanted help, they were going to have to walk half-way around Marrow to find it.

MISSION YEAR 4.43:

The bridge resembled a rigid thread, silvery and insubstantial. Sheered off in the high stratosphere, it was far too short to serve as an escape route. But it made a useful landmark. Washen's team steered for the bridge during those last days, picking their way across the knife-like ridges and narrow valleys between. Wondering what they would find, whenever they rested—for a moment, now and again—they let themselves talk in hopeful tones, imagining the other captains' surprise when the six of them suddenly marched out of the jungle.

Except when they arrived at the bridge, there was no one to catch off guard. The main encampment had been abandoned. The hilltop where the bridge was rooted had been split open by quakes, and the entire structure tilted precariously toward the east. A simple iron post kept the main doors propped open, and there was a makeshift ladder in the shaft, but judging by the rust, nobody had used it for months. Or perhaps years.

A sketchy path led west. They followed, and after a long while, they came to a fertile river bottom and wider paths. With Washen at the lead, they were jogging, and it was Miocene who suddenly stepped into view, surprising them.

The Submaster was unchanged.

In uniform, she looked regal and well-chilled. "It took you long enough," she deadpanned. Then she smiled, adding, "It's good to see you. Honestly, we'd nearly given up hope."

Washen swallowed her anger.

The other captains bombarded Miocene with questions. Who else had survived? How were they making do? Did any machines work? Had the Master been in contact with them? Then Diu asked, "What kind of relief mission is coming?"

"It's a cautious relief mission," Miocene replied. "So cautious that it seems almost nonexistent."

Her captains had built telescopes from scratch, and at least one captain was always watching the base camp overhead. The transparent blister was intact. Every building was intact. But the drones and beacons were dead, which meant that the reactor was offline. A three kilometer stub of the bridge would make the perfect foundation for a new structure. But there wasn't any sign that captains or anyone was trying to mount any kind of rescue.

"The Master thinks we're dead," Diu offered, trying to be charitable.

"We aren't dead," Miocene countered. "And even if we were, she should be a little more interested in our bones, and answers."

Washen didn't talk. After three years of jogging, eating lousy food and forcing hope, she suddenly felt sickened and achingly tired.

The Submaster led them along a wide trail, working back through their questions.

"Every machine was ruined by the Event. That's our name for what happened. The Event left our cars and drones and sensors as fancy trash, and we can't fix them. And we can't decide why, either." Then she offered a distracted smile, adding, "But we're surviving. Wooden homes, with roofs. Iron tools. Pendulum clocks. Steam power when we go to the trouble, and enough homemade equipment, like the telescopes, that we can do some simple, simple science."

The jungle's understory had been cut down and beaten back, and the new encampment stretched out on all sides. Like anything built by determined captains, the place was orderly, perhaps to a fault. The houses were clean and in good repair. Paths were marked with logs, and someone had given each path its own name. Everyone was in uniform, and everyone was smiling, trying to hide the weariness in the eyes and their voices.

A hundred captains shouted, "Hello! Welcome!"

Washen stared at their faces, and counted, and finally forced herself to ask, "Who isn't here?"

Miocene recited a dozen names.

Eleven of them were friends or acquaintances of Washen's. The last name was Hazz—a Submaster and a voyage-long friend of Miocene's. "Two months ago," she explained, "he was exploring a nearby valley. A fissure opened up suddenly, without warning, and he was trapped by the flowing iron." Her eyes were distant, unreadable. "Hazz was perched on a little island that was melting. We tried to build a bridge, and tried to divert the current. Everything half-possible, we tried."

Washen stared at the narrow face, at the way the eyes had grown empty, and it was suddenly obvious that Miocene had been more than friends with the dead man.

"The island shrank," she told them, her voice too flat and slow. "It was a knob, if that. Hazz's boots dissolved, and his feet were boiling, and his flesh caught fire. But he managed to stand there. He endured it. He endured it and even managed to turn and take a step toward on us, on his boiling legs, and he fell forward, and that's when he finally died."

Washen had been mistaken. This wasn't the same Miocene.

"I have one goal," the Submaster confessed. "I want to find a way to get back to the Master, and I'll ask her why she sent us here. Was it to explore? Or was it just the best awful way to get rid of us . . . ?"

MISSION YEAR 6.55:

The iron crust rippled and tore apart under a barrage of quakes, and with its foundation shattered, the bridge pitched sideways with a creaking roar, then shattered, the debris field scattered over fifty kilometers of newborn mountains.

Its fall was inevitable, and unrecorded. Geysers of white-hot metal had already obliterated the captains' encampment, forcing them to flee with a minimum of tools and provisions. Lungs were seared. Tongues and eyes were blistered. But the captains eventually stumbled into a distant valley, into a grove of stately trees, where they collapsed, gasping and cursing. Then as if to bless them, the trees began releasing tiny balloons made from gold, and the shady, halfway cool air was filled with the balloons' glint and the dry music made by their brushing against one another.

Diu coined the name virtue tree.

Miocene set her captains to planning new streets and houses, several of the virtue trees already downed when the ground ripped open with an anguished roar.

Wearily, the captains fled again, and when they settled, finally, they built strong simple houses that could be rebuilt anywhere in a ship's day.

Nomadic blood took hold in them. When they weren't stockpiling food for the next migration, they were building lighter tools, and when they weren't doing either, they studied their world, trying to guess its fickle moods.

Washen assembled a team of twenty observant captains.

"Breeding cycles are key," she reported. Sitting in the meeting hall, looking up and down the iron table, she reported that virtue trees spun their golden balloons only when the crust turned unstable. "If we see another show like the last one," she promised, "we're screwed. We've got a day, or less, to get out of here."

Staff meetings were patterned after conferences with the Master, except they came on an irregular schedule, and Miocene presided, and despite her best intentions, the captains kept the atmosphere informal, even jocular, and because of the absence of soap, more than a little sour.

"How are our virtue trees acting?" asked Aasleen.

"As if they'll live forever," Washen replied. "They're still happy, still early in their growth cycle. As far as we can tell."

Miocene acted distant that day. Squinting at nothing, she repeated the word: "Cycles."

Everyone turned in their heavy chairs, and waited.

"Thank you, Washen." The Submaster rose and looked at each of them, then admitted, "This may be premature. I could be wrong for many reasons. But I think I've been able to find another cycle . . . one that's unexpected, at least for me . . ."

There was the distant droning of a hammerwing, and then, silence.

"Volcanic activity is escalating. I think that's obvious." The tall woman nodded for a moment, then asked, "But why? My proposal is that the buttresses have begun to relax their hold on Marrow. Not by much. Certainly nothing we can measure directly. But if it did happen, the metals under us are going to expand, and that's why, according to my careful computations, our home is growing larger."

Washen's first impulse was to laugh; it was a joke.

"Several kilometers larger," Miocene told the stunned faces. "I've gathered several lines of evidence. The buttresses' light has diminished by two or three percent. The horizon is a little more distant. And what's most impressive, I think: I've triangulated the distance to our base camp, and it's definitely closer than it was last year."

A dozen explanations occurred to Washen, but she realized that Miocene must have seen them, then discarded them.

"If Marrow isn't teasing us," said the Submaster, "and if the buttresses don't reverse the cycle, then you can see where we're going—"

Washen cried out, "How long will it take, madam?"

A dozen captains shouted the same question.

"The calculations aren't promising," Miocene replied. But she had to laugh in a soft, bitter way. "At the present rate, we'll be able to touch that three kilometer stub of the bridge in about five thousand years . . ."

MISSION YEAR 88.55:

It was time for the children to sleep.

Washen had come to check on them. But for some reason she stopped short of the nursery, eavesdropping on them, uncertain why it was important to remain hidden.

The oldest boy was telling a story.

"We call them the Builders," he said, "because they created the ship."

"The ship," whispered the other children, in one voice.

"The ship is too large to measure, and it is very beautiful. But when it was new, there was no one to share it with the Builders, and no one to tell them that it was beautiful. That's why they called out into the darkness, inviting others to come fill its vastness."

Washen leaned against the fragrant umbra wood, waiting.

"Who came from the darkness?" asked the boy.

"The Bleak," young voices answered, instantly.

"Was there anyone else?"

"No one."

"Because the universe was so young," the boy explained. "Only the Bleak and the Builders had already evolved."

"The Bleak," a young girl repeated, with feeling.

"They were a cruel, selfish species," the boy maintained, "but they always wore smiles and said the smartest words."

"They wanted the ship," the others prompted.

"And they stole it. In one terrible night, as the Builders slept, the Bleak attacked, slaughtering most of them in their beds."

Every child whispered, "Slaughtered."

Washen eased her way closer to the nursery door. The boy was sitting up on his cot, his face catching the one sliver of light that managed to slip through the ceiling. Till was his name. He looked very much like his mother for a moment, then he moved his head slightly, and he resembled no one else.

"Where did the survivors retreat?" he asked.

"To Marrow."

"And from here, what did they do?"

"They purified the ship."

"They purified the ship," he repeated, with emphasis. "They swept its tunnels and chambers free of the scourge. The Builders had no choice."

There was a long, reflective pause.

"What happened to the last of the Builders?" he asked.

"They were trapped here," said the others, on cue. "And one after another, they died here."

"What died?"

"Their flesh."

"But what else is there?"

"The spirit."

"What isn't flesh cannot die," said the young prophet.

Washen waited, wondering when she had last taken a breath.

Then in whisper, Till asked, "Where do their spirits live?"

With a palpable delight, the children replied, "They live inside us."

"We are the Builders now," the voice assured. "After a long lonely wait, we've finally been reborn . . . !"

MISSION YEAR 88.90:

Life on Marrow had become halfway comfortable and almost predictable. The captains weren't often caught by surprise eruptions, and they'd learned where the crust was likely to remain thick and stable for years at a time. With so much success, children had seemed inevitable; Miocene decided that every female captain should produce at least one. And like children anywhere, theirs filled many niches: They were fresh faces, and they were cherished distractions, and they were entertainment, and more than anyone anticipated, they were challenges to the captains' authority. But what Miocene wanted, first and always, were willing helpers. Till and his playmates were born so that someday, once trained, they could help their parents escape from Marrow.

The hope was that they could rebuild the bridge. Materials would be a problem, and Marrow would fight them. But Washen was optimistic. In these last eight decades, she'd tried every state of mind, and optimism far and away was the most pleasant.

And she tried to be positive everywhere: Good, sane reasons had kept them from being rescued. There was no one else the Master could trust like her favorite captains. Perhaps. Or she was thinking of the ship's well-being, monitoring Marrow from a distance. Or most likely, the access tunnel had totally collapsed during the Event, and digging them out was grueling, achingly slow work.

Other captains were optimistic in public, but in private, in their lovers' beds, they confessed to darker moods.

"What if the Master has written us off?" Diu posed the question, then offered an even worse scenario. "Or maybe something's happened to her. This was a secret mission. If she died unexpectedly, and if the First-chairs don't even know we're here . . ."

"Do you believe that?" Washen asked.

Diu shrugged his shoulders.

"There's another possibility," she said, playing the game. "What if everyone else on the ship has died?"

For a moment, Diu didn't react.

"The ship was a derelict," she reminded him. "No one knows what happened to its owners, or to anyone else who's used it since."

"What are you saying?" Diu sat up in bed, dropping his legs over the edge. "You mean the crew and the passengers . . . all of them have been killed . . . ?"

"Maybe the ship cleans itself out every hundred thousand years."

A tiny grin emerged. "So how did we survive?"

"Life on Marrow is spared," she argued. "Otherwise, all of this would be barren iron and nothing else."

Diu pulled one of his hands across his face.

"This isn't my story," she admitted, placing her hand on his sweaty back. Their infant son, Locke, was sleeping in the nearby crib, blissfully unaware of their grim discussion. In three years, he would live in the nursery. With Till, she was thinking. Washen had overheard the story about the Builders and the Bleak several months ago, but she never told anyone. Not even Diu. "Have you ever listened to the children?"

Glancing over his shoulder, he asked, "Why?"

She explained, in brief.

A sliver of light caught his gray eye and cheek. "You know Till," Diu countered. "You know how odd he can seem."

"That's why I never mention it."

"Have you heard him tell that story again?"

"No," she admitted.

Her lover nodded, looking at the crib. At Locke.

"Children are imagination machines," he warned. "You never know what they're going to think about anything."

He didn't say another word.

Washen was remembering her only other child—a long-ago foster child, only glancingly human—and with a bittersweet grin, she replied, "But that's the fun in having them . . . or so I've always heard . . ."

MISSION YEAR 89.09:

The boy was walking alone, crossing the public round with his eyes watching his own bare feet, watching them shuffle across the heat-baked iron.

"Hello, Till."

Pausing, he lifted his gaze slowly, a smile waiting to shine at the captain. "Hello, Madam Washen. You're well, I trust."

Under the blue glare of the sky, he was a polite, scrupulously ordinary boy. He had a thin face joined to a shorter, almost blockish body, and like most children, he wore as little as the adults let him wear. No one knew which of several captains was his genetic father. Miocene never told. She wanted to be his only parent, grooming him to stand beside her someday, and whenever Washen looked at Till, she felt a nagging resentment, petty as can be, and since it was directed at a ten year old, simply foolish.

With her own smile, Washen said, "I have a confession to make. A little while ago, I overheard you and the other children talking. You were telling each other a story."

The eyes were wide and brown, and they didn't so much as blink.

"It was an interesting story," Washen conceded.

Till looked like any ten year old who didn't know what to make of a bothersome adult. Sighing wearily, he shifted his weight from one brown foot to the other. Then he sighed again, the picture of boredom.

"How did you think up that story?" she asked.

A shrug of the shoulders. "I don't know."

"We talk about the ship. Probably too much." Her explanation felt sensible and practical. Her only fear was that she would come across as patronizing.

"Everyone likes to speculate. About the ship's past, and its builders, and all the rest. It has to be confusing. Since we're going to rebuild our bridge, with your help . . . it does make you into a kind of builder . . ."

Till shrugged again, his eyes looking past her.

On the far side of the round, in front of the encampment's shop, a team of captains had fired up their latest turbine—a primitive wonder built from memory and trial-and-error. Homebrewed alcohols combined with oxygen, creating a delicious roar. When it was working, the engine was powerful enough to do any job they could offer it, at least today. But it was dirty and noisy, and the sound of it almost obscured the boy's voice.

"I'm not speculating," he said softly.

"Excuse me?"

"I won't tell you that. That I'm making it up."

Washen had to smile, asking, "Aren't you?"

"No." Till shook his head, then looked back down at his toes. "Madam Washen," he said with a boy's fragile patience. "You can't make up something that's true."

MISSION YEAR 114.41:

Locke was waiting in the shadows—a grown man with a boy's guilty face and the wide, restless eyes of someone expecting trouble to come from every direction.

His first words were, "I shouldn't be doing this."

But a moment later, responding to an anticipated voice, he said, "I know, Mother. I promised."

Washen never made a sound.

It was Diu who offered second thoughts. "If this is going to get you in trouble . . . maybe we should go home . . ."

"Maybe you should," their son allowed. Then he turned and walked away, never inviting them to follow, knowing they wouldn't be able to help themselves.

Washen hurried, feeling Diu in her footsteps.

A young jungle of umbra trees and lambda bush dissolved into rugged bare iron: Black pillars and arches created an indiscriminate, infuriating maze. Every step was a challenge. Razored edges sliced at exposed flesh. Bottomless crevices threatened to swallow the graceless. And Washen's body was accustomed to sleep at this hour, which was why the old grove took her by surprise. Suddenly Locke was standing on the rusty lip of a cliff, waiting for them, gazing down at a narrow valley filled with black-as-night virtue trees.

It was lucky ground. When the world's guts began to pour out on all sides, that slab of crust had fallen into a fissure. The jungle had been burned but never killed. It could be a hundred years old, or older. There was a rich, eternal feel to the place, and perhaps that's why the children had chosen it.

The children. Washen knew better, but despite her best intentions, she couldn't think of them any other way.

"Keep quiet," Locke whispered, not looking back at them. "Please."

In the living shadows, the air turned slightly cooler and uncomfortably damp. Blankets of rotting canopy left the ground watery-soft. A giant daggerwing roared past, intent on some vital business, and Washen watched it vanish into the gloom, then reappear, tiny with the distance, its bluish carapace shining in a patch of sudden skylight.

Locke turned abruptly, silently.

A single finger lay against his lips. But what Washen noticed was his expression, the pain and worry so intense that she had to try and reassure him with a touch.

It was Diu who had wormed the secret out of him.

The children were meeting in the jungle, and they'd been meeting for more than twenty years. At irregular intervals, Till would call them to some secluded location, and it was Till who was in charge of everything said and done. "What's said?" Washen had asked. "And what do you do?" But Locke refused to explain it, shaking his head and adding that he was breaking his oldest promise by telling any of it.

"Then why do it?" Washen pressed.

"Because," her son replied. "You have every right to hear what he's saying. So you can decide for yourselves."

Washen stood out of sight, staring at the largest virtue tree she had ever seen. Age had killed it, and rot had brought it down, splitting the canopy open as it crumbled. Adult children and their little brothers and sisters had assembled in that pool of skylight, standing in clumps and pairs, talking quietly. Till paced back and forth on the wide black trunk. He looked fully adult, ageless and decidedly unexceptional, wearing a simple breechcloth and nimble boots, his plain face showing a timid, self-conscious expression that gave Washen a strange little moment of hope.

Maybe Till's meetings were a just an old game that grew up into a social gathering.

Maybe.

Without a word or backward glance, Locke walked into the clearing, joining the oldest children up in the front.

His parents obeyed their promise, kneeling in the jungle.

A few more children filtered into view. Then with some invisible signal, the worshippers fell silent.

With a quiet voice, Till asked, "What do we want?"

"What's best for the ship," the children answered. "Always."

"How long is always?"

"Longer than we can count."

"And how far is always?"

"To the endless ends."

"Yet we live—"

"For a moment!" they cried. "If that long!"

The words were absurd, and chilling. What should have sounded silly to Washen wasn't, the prayer acquiring a muscular credibility when hundreds were speaking in one voice, with a practiced surety.

"What is best for the ship," Till repeated.

Except he was asking a question. His plain face was filled with curiosity, a genuine longing.

Quietly, he asked his audience, "Do you know the answer?"

In a muddled shout, the children said, "No."

"I don't either," their leader promised. "But when I'm awake, I'm searching. And when I'm sleeping, my dreams do the same."

There was a brief pause, then an urgent voice cried out, "We have newcomers!"

"Bring them up."

They were seven year olds—a twin brother and sister—and they climbed the trunk as if terrified. But Till offered his hands, and with a crisp surety, he told each to breathe deeply, then asked them, "What do you know about the ship?"

The little girl glanced at the sky, saying, "It's where we came from."

Laughter broke out in the audience, then evaporated.

Her brother corrected her. "The captains came from there. Not us." Then he added, "But we're going to help them get back there. Soon."

There was a cold, prolonged pause.

Till allowed himself a patient smile, patting both of their heads. Then he looked out at his followers, asking, "Is he right?"

"No," they roared.

The siblings winced and tried to vanish.

Till knelt between them, and with a steady voice said, "The captains are just the captains. But you and I and all of us here . . . we are the Builders."

Washen hadn't heard that nonsense in a quarter of a century, and hearing it now, she couldn't decide whether to laugh or explode in rage.

"We're the Builders reborn," Till repeated. Then he gave them the seeds of rebellion, adding, "And whatever our purpose, it is not to help these silly captains."

Miocene refused to believe any of it. "First of all," she told Washen, and herself, "I know my own child. What you're describing is ridiculous. Second of all, this rally of theirs would involve nearly half of our children—"

Diu interrupted. "Most of them are adults with their own homes." Then he added, "Madam."

"I checked," said Washen. "Several dozen of the younger children did slip out of the nurseries—"

"I'm not claiming that they didn't go somewhere." Then with a haughty expression, she asked, "Will the two of you listen to me? For a moment, please?"

"Go on, madam," said Diu.

"I know what's reasonable. I know how my son was raised and I know his character, and unless you can offer me some motivation for this . . . this shit . . . then I think we'll just pretend that nothing's been said here . . ."

"Motivation," Washen repeated. "Tell me what's mine."

With a chill delight, Miocene said, "Greed."

"Why?"

"Believe me, I understand." The dark eyes narrowed, silver glints in their corners. "If my son is insane, then yours stands to gain. Status, at least. Then eventually, power."

Washen glanced at Diu.

They hadn't mentioned Locke's role as the informant, and they would keep it secret as long as possible—for a tangle of reasons, most of them selfish.

"Ask Till about the Builders," she insisted.

"I won't."

"Why not?"

The woman took a moment, vainly picking spore cases from her new handmade uniform. Then with a cutting logic, she said, "If it's a lie, he'll say it's a lie. If it's true and he lies, then it'll sound like the truth."

"But if he admits it—?"

"Then Till wants me to know. And you're simply a messenger." She gave them a knowing stare, then looked off into the distance. "That's not a revelation I want delivered at his convenience."

Three ship-days later, while the encampment slept, a great fist lifted the world several meters, then grew bored and flung it down again.

Captains and children stumbled into the open. The sky was already choked with golden balloons and billions of flying insects. In twelve hours, perhaps less, the entire region would blister and explode, and die. Like a drunken woman, Washen ran through the aftershocks, reaching a tidy home and shouting, "Locke," into its empty rooms. Where was her son? She moved along the round, finding all of the children's houses empty. A tall figure stepped out of Till's tiny house and asked, "Have you see mine?"

Washen shook her head. "Have you seen mine?"

Miocene said, "No," and sighed. Then she strode past Washen, shouting, "Do you know where I can find him?"

Diu was standing in the center of the round. Waiting.

"If you help me," the Submaster promised, "you'll help your own son."

With a little nod, Diu agreed.

Miocene and a dozen captains ran into the jungle. Left behind, Washen forced herself to concentrate, packing her household's essentials and helping the other worried parents. When they were finished, hours had passed. The quakes had shattered the crust beneath them, and the golden balloons had vanished, replaced with clouds of iron dust and the stink of burning jungle. The captains and remaining children stood in the main round, ready to flee. But the ranking Submaster wouldn't give the order. "Another minute," he kept telling everyone, including himself. Then he would carefully hide his timepiece in his uniform's pocket, fighting the urge to watch the turning of its hands.

When Till suddenly stepped into the open, grinning at them, Washen felt a giddy, incoherent relief.

Relief collapsed into shock, then terror.

The young man's chest cavity had been opened up with a knife, the first wound partially healed but the second wound deeper, lying perpendicular to the first. Ripped, desiccated flesh tried desperately to knit itself back together. Till wasn't in mortal danger, but he wore his agony well. With an artful moan, he stumbled, then righted himself for a slippery instant. Then he fell sideways, slamming against the bare iron in the same instant that Miocene slowly, slowly stepped into view.

She was unhurt, and she was thoroughly, hopelessly trapped.

Spellbound, Washen watched the Submaster kneel beside her boy, gripping his straight brown hair with one hand while she stared into his eyes.

What did Till say to her in the jungle? How did he steer his mother into this murderous rage? Because that's what he must have done. As events played out, Washen realized that everything was part of an elaborate plan. That's why Locke took them to the meeting, and why he had felt guilty. When he said, "I know. I promised," he meant the promise he made to Till.

Miocene kept staring into her son's eyes.

Perhaps she was hunting for forgiveness, or better, for some hint of doubt. Or perhaps she was simply giving him a moment to contemplate her own gaze, relentless and cold. Then with both hands, she picked up a good-sized wedge of nickel-iron—the quakes had left the round littered with them—and with a calm fury, she rolled him over and shattered the vertebrae in his neck, then continued beating him, blood and shredded flesh flying, his head nearly cut free of his paralyzed body.

Washen and five other captains pulled Miocene off her son.

"Let go of me," she demanded. Then she dropped her weapon and raised her arms, telling everyone in earshot, "If you want to help him, help him. But if you do, you don't belong to our community. That's my decree. According to the powers of my rank, my office, and my mood . . . !"

Locke had stepped out of the jungle.

He was the first to come to Till's side, but only barely. More than two-thirds of the children gathered around the limp figure. A stretcher was found, and their leader was made comfortable. Then with a few possessions and virtually no food, the wayward children began to file away, moving north when the captains were planning to travel south.

Diu stood beside Washen; since when?

"We can't just let them get away," he whispered. "Someone needs to stay with them. To talk to them, and help them . . ."

She glanced at her lover, then opened her mouth.

"I'll go," she meant to say.

But Diu said, "You shouldn't, no. You'll help them more by staying close to Miocene." He had obviously thought it through, arguing, "You have rank. You have authority here. And besides, Miocene listens to you."

When it suited her, yes.

"I'll keep in contact," Diu promised. "Somehow."

Washen nodded, thinking that all of this would pass in a few years. Perhaps in a few decades, at most.

Diu kissed her, and they hugged, and she found herself looking over his shoulder. Locke was a familiar silhouette standing in the jungle. At that distance, through those shadows, she couldn't tell if her son was facing her or if she was looking at his back. Either way, she smiled and mouthed the words, "Be good." Then she took a deep breath and told Diu, "Be careful." And she turned away, refusing to watch either of her men vanish into the shadows and gathering smoke.

Miocene stood alone, speaking with a thin dry weepy voice.

"We're getting closer," she declared, lifting her arms overhead.

Closer?

Then she rose up on her toes, reaching higher, and with a low, pained laugh, she said, "Not close enough. Not yet."

MISSION YEARS 511.01–1603.73:

A dozen of the loyal grandchildren discovered the first artifact. Against every rule, they were playing beside a river of liquid iron, and suddenly a mysterious hyperfiber sphere drifted past. With their youngster's courage, they fished it out and cooled it down and brought it back to the encampment. Then for the next hundred years, the sphere lay in storage, under lock and key. But once the captains had reinvented the means, they split the hyperfiber, and inside it was an information vault nearly as old as the earth.

The device was declared authentic, and useless, its memories erased to gray by the simple crush of time.

There were attempts at secrecy, but the Waywards always had their spies. One night, without warning, Locke and his father strolled into the main round. Dressed in breechcloth and little else, they found Washen's door, knocked until she screamed, "Enter," then stepped inside, Diu offering a wry grin as Locke made the unexpected proposal: Tons of dried and sweetened meat in exchange for that empty vault.

Washen didn't have the authority. Four Submasters were pulled out of three beds, and at Miocene's insistence, they grudgingly agreed to the Waywards' terms.

But the negotiations weren't finished. Diu suddenly handed his ex-commanders wafers of pure sulfur, very rare and essential to the captains' fledgling industries. Then with a wink, he asked, "What would you give us in return for tons more?"

Everything, thought Washen.

Diu settled for a laser. As he made sure it had enough punch to penetrate hyperfiber, nervous voices asked how the Waywards would use it. "It's obvious," Diu replied, with easy scorn. "If your little group finds one artifact, by accident, how many more do you think that the Waywards could be sitting on?"

Afterwards, once or twice every century, the captains discovered new vaults. Most were dead and sold quickly to the Waywards for meat and sulfur. But it was ninth vault that still functioned, its ancient machinery full of images and data, and answers.

The elegant device was riding in Miocene's lap. She touched it lightly, lovingly, then confessed, "I feel nervous. Nervous, but exceptionally confident."

The Submaster never usually discussed her moods.

"With a little luck," she continued, "this treasure will heal these old rifts between them and us."

"With luck," Washen echoed, thinking it would take more than a little.

They arrived at the clearing at three in the morning, shiptime. Moments later, several thousand Waywards stepped from the jungle at the same moment, dressed in tool belts and little else, the men often carrying toddlers and their women pregnant, every face feral and self-assured, almost every expression utterly joyous.

Washen climbed out of the walker, and Miocene handed down the vault.

To the eye, it wasn't an impressive machine—a rounded lump of gray ceramics infused with smooth blue-white diamonds. Yet most of the Waywards stared at the prize. Till was the lone exception. Coming down the open slope, walking slowly, he watched Miocene, wariness mixed with other, less legible emotions.

Locke was following the Waywards' leader at a respectful distance. "How are you, Mother?" he called out. Always polite; never warm.

"Well enough," Washen allowed. "And you?"

His answer was an odd, tentative smile.

Where was Diu? Washen gazed at the crowd, assuming that he was somewhere close, hidden by the crush of bodies.

"May I examine the device?" asked Till.

Miocene took the vault from Washen so that she could hand it to her son. And Till covered the largest diamonds with his fingertips, blocking out the light, causing the machine to slowly, slowly awaken.

The clearing was a natural amphitheater, black iron rising on all sides. Washen couldn't count all the Waywards streaming out of the jungle above. Thousands had become tens of thousands. Some of them were her grandchildren and great-grandchildren. Diu would know which ones, perhaps. How many of her descendants lived with the Waywards? In the past, during their very occasional meetings, Diu had confided that the Waywards probably numbered in the millions—a distinct possibility since they'd inherited their parents' immortal genes, and since Till seemed to relish fecundity. In principle, this entire audience could be related to Washen. Not bad, she thought. Particularly for an old woman who for many fine reasons had only that one child of her own.

The vault began to hum softly, and Locke lifted an arm, shouting, "Now."

Suddenly the audience was silent, everyone motionless, a palpable anticipation hanging in the hot dry air.

The sky grew dark, and the clearing vanished.

Marrow swelled, nearly filling the chamber. Barren and smooth, it was covered in a worldwide ocean of bubbling, irradiated iron that lay just beneath the hyperfiber ceiling, and the audience stood on that ocean, unwarmed, watching an ancient drama play itself out.

Without sound or any warning, the Bleak appeared, squirming their way through the chamber's wall, through the countless access tunnels—insect-like cyborgs, enormous and cold and swift.

Like a swarm of wasps, they flowed toward Marrow, launching gobs of antimatter that slammed into the molten surface, scorching white-hot explosions rising up and up. The liquid iron swirled and lifted, then collapsed again. In the harsh light, Washen glanced at her son, trying to measure his face, his mood. He looked spellbound, eyes wide and his mouth ajar, his body shivering with an apocalyptic fever. Every face seemed to be seeing this for the first time. Washen remembered the last time she spoke to Diu, almost a decade ago. She asked about the vaults and the Waywards' beliefs, explaining that Miocene was pressing for details. In response, Diu growled, reminding her, "I'm their only nonbeliever, and they don't tell me much. I'm tolerated for my technical expertise, and just as important, because I long ago stopped kowtowing to Miocene and all the rest of you."

A hyperfiber dome suddenly burst from the iron, lasers firing, a dozen of the Bleak killed before the dome pulled itself under again.

The Bleak brought reinforcements, then struck again.

Hyperfiber missiles carried the antimatter deep into the iron. Marrow shook and twisted, then belched gas and fire. Perhaps the Bleak managed to kill the last of the Builders. Perhaps. Either way, the Builders' revenge was in place. Was waiting. In the middle of the attack, with the Bleak's forces pressing hard, the buttressing fields came on, bringing their blue-white glow. Suddenly the Bleak appeared tiny and frail. Then, before they could flee, the lightning storm swept across the sky, dissolving every wisp of matter into a plasma, creating a superheated mist that would persist for millions of years, cooling as Marrow cooled, gradually collecting on the warm, newborn crust.

Gradually, the Bleak's own carbon and hydrogen and oxygen became Marrow's atmosphere and its rivers, and those same precious elements slowly gathered themselves into butter bugs and virtue trees, then into the wide-eyed children standing in that clearing, weeping as they stared at the radiant sky.

The present reemerged gradually, almost reluctantly.

"There's much more," Miocene promised, her voice urgent. Motherly. "Other records show how the ship was attacked. How the Builders retreated to Marrow. This is where they made their last stand, whoever they were." She waited for a long moment, watching her son's unreadable face. Then with a genuine disappointment, she warned, "The Builders never show themselves. We understand a lot more now, but we're still not sure how they looked."

Till wasn't awestruck by what he had just witnessed. If anything, he was mildly pleased, grinning as if amused, but definitely not excited or surprised, or even particularly interested with what Miocene had to say.

"Listen to me," she snapped, unable to contain herself any longer. "Do you understand what this means? The Event that trapped us here is some kind of ancient weapon designed to kill the Bleak. And everything else on board the ship . . . perhaps . . ."

"Who's trapped?" Till replied with a smooth, unnerving calm. "I'm not. No believer is. This is exactly where we belong."

Only Miocene's eyes betrayed her anger.

Till continued with his explanation, saying, "You're here because the Builders called to you. They lured you here because they needed someone to give birth to us."

"That's insane," the Submaster snarled.

Washen was squinting, searching for Diu. She recognized his face and his nervous energy, but only in the children. Where was he? Suddenly it occurred to her that he hadn't been invited, or even worse—

"I know why you believe this nonsense." Miocene said the words, then took a long step toward Till, empty hands lifting into the air. "It's obvious. When you were a boy, you found one of these vaults. Didn't you? It showed you the war and the Bleak, and that's when you began all of this . . . this nonsense about being the Builders reborn . . . !"

Her son regarded her with an amused contempt.

"You made a mistake," said Miocene, her voice shrill. Accusing. "You were a child, and you didn't understand what you were seeing, and ever since we've had to pay for your ignorance. Don't you see . . . ?"

Her son was smiling, incapable of doubt.

Looking at the Waywards, Miocene screamed, "Who understands me?"

Silence.

"I didn't find any vault," Till claimed. "I was alone in the jungle, and a Builder's spirit appeared to me. He told me about the Ship and the Bleak. He showed me all of this. Then he made me a promise: As this day ends, in the coming twilight, I'll learn my destiny . . ."

His voice trailed away into silence.

Locke kneeled and picked up the vault. Then he looked at Washen, saying matter-of-factly, "The usual payment. That's what we're offering."

Miocene roared.

"What do you mean? This is the best artifact yet!"

No one responded, gazing at her as if she was insane.

"It functions. It remembers." The Submaster was flinging her arms into the air, telling them, "The other vaults were empty, or nearly so—"

"Exactly," said Till.

Then, as if it was beneath their leader to explain the obvious, Locke gave the two of them a look of pity, telling them, "Those vaults are empty because what they were holding is elsewhere now. Elsewhere."

Till and Locke touched their scalps.

Every follower did the same, fifty thousand arms lifting, a great ripple reaching the top of the amphitheater as everyone pointed at their minds. At their reborn souls.

Locke was staring at his mother.

A premonition made her mouth dry. "Why isn't Diu here?"

"Because he's dead," her son replied, an old sadness passing through his face. "I'm sorry. It happened eight years ago, during a powerful eruption."

Washen couldn't speak, or move.

"Are you all right, Mother?"

She took a breath, then lied. "Yes. I'm fine."

Then she saw the most astonishing sight yet in this long and astonishing day: Miocene had dropped to her knees, and with a pleading voice, she was begging for

Till's forgiveness. "I never should have struck you," she said. She said, "Darling," with genuine anguish. Then as a last resort, she told him, "And I do love the ship. As much as you do, you ungrateful shit . . . !"

MISSION YEAR 4895.33:

From the very top of the new bridge, where the atmosphere was barely a sloppy vacuum, Marrow finally began to resemble a far away place.

The captains appreciated the view.

Whenever Washen was on duty, she gazed down at the city-like encampments and sprawling farms, the dormant volcanoes and surviving patches of jungle, feeling a delicious sense of detachment from it all. A soft gray twilight held sway. The buttresses had continued to shrivel and weaken over the last millennia, and if Miocene's model proved true, in another two centuries the buttresses would vanish entirely. For a few moments, or perhaps a few years, there would be no barrier between them and the ship. Marrow world would be immersed in a perfect blackness. Then the buttresses would reignite suddenly, perhaps accompanied by another Event. But by then the captains and their families, moving with a swift, drilled precision, would have escaped, climbing up this wondrously makeshift bridge, reaching the old base camp, then hopefully, returning to the ship, at last.

What they would find there, no one knew.

Or in a polite company, discussed.

In the last five thousand years, every remote possibility had been suggested, debated in depth, and finally, mercifully, buried in an unmarked grave.

Whatever was, was.

That was the mandatory attitude, and it had been for centuries now.

All that mattered was the bridge. The surviving captains—almost two-thirds of the original complement—lived for its completion. Hundreds of thousands of their descendants worked in distant mines or trucked the ore to the factories. Another half million were manufacturing superstrong alloys and crude flavors of hyperfiber, some of each added to the bridge's foundation, while the rest were spun together into hollow tubes. Washen's duty was to oversee the slow, rigorous hoisting of each new tube, then its final attachment. Compared to the original bridge, their contraption was inelegant and preposterously fat. Yet she felt a genuine pride all the same, knowing the sacrifices that went into its construction, and the enormous amounts of time, and when they didn't have any other choice, a lot of desperate, ad hoc inventiveness.

"Madam Washen?" said a familiar voice. "Excuse me, madam."

The captain blinked, then turned.

Her newest assistant stood in the doorway. An intense, self-assured man of no particular age, he was obviously puzzled—a rare expression—and with a mixture of curiosity and confusion, he announced, "Our shift is over."

"In fifty minutes," Washen replied, knowing the exact time for herself.

"No, madam." Nervous hands pressed at the crisp fabric of his technician's uniform. "I just heard. We're to leave immediately, using every tube but the Primary."

She looked at the displays on her control boards. "I don't see any orders."

"I know—"

"Is this another drill?" If the reinforced crust under them ever began to subside, they might have only minutes to evacuate. "Because if it is, we need a better system than having you walking about, tapping people's shoulders."

"No, madam. It's not a drill."

"Then what—?"

"Miocene," he blurted. "She contacted me directly. Following her instructions, I've already dismissed the others, and now I am to tell you to wait here. She is on her way." As proof, he gave the order's file code. Then with a barely restrained frustration, he added, "This is very mysterious. Everyone agrees. But the Submaster is such a secretive person, so I am assuming—"

"Who's with her?" Washen interrupted.

"I don't think anyone."

But the primary tube was the largest. Twenty captains could ride inside one of its cars, never brushing elbows with one another.

"Her car seems to have an extra thick hull," the assistant explained, "plus some embellishments that I can't quite decipher."

"What sorts of embellishments?"

He glanced at the time, pretending he was anxious to leave. But he was also proud of his cleverness, just as Washen guessed he would be. Cameras inside the tube let them observe the car. Its mass could be determined by the energy required to lift it. He pointed to the pipelike devices wrapped around its hull, making the car look like someone's ball of rope, and with a sudden dose of humility, he admitted, "I don't seem to quite understand that apparatus."

In other words, "Please explain it to me, madam."

But Washen didn't explain anything. Looking at her assistant—one of the most talented and loyal of the captains' offspring; a man who had proved himself on every occasion—she shrugged her shoulders, then lied.

She said, "I don't understand it, either."

Then before she took another breath, she suggested, "You should probably do what she wants. Leave. If Miocene finds you waiting here, she'll kick you down the shaft herself."

The Submaster had exactly the same face and figure that she had carried for millennia, but in the eyes and in the corners of her voice, she was changed. Transformed, almost. On those rare occasions when they met face to face, Washen marveled at all the ways life on Marrow had changed Miocene. And then she would wonder if it was the same for her—if old friends looked at Washen and thought to themselves, "She looks tired, and sad, and maybe a little profound."

They saw each other infrequently, but despite rank and Miocene's attitudes, it was difficult to remain formal. Washen whispered; "Madam," and then added, "Are you crazy? Do you really think it'll work?"

The face smiled, not a hint of joy in it. "According to my models, probably. With an initial velocity of five hundred meters per—"

"Accuracy isn't your problem," Washen told her. "And if you can slip inside your target—that three kilometer remnant of the old bridge, right?—you'll have enough time to brake your momentum."

"But my mind will have died. Is that what you intend to say?"

"Even as thin and weak as the buttresses are now . . . I would hope you're dead. Otherwise you'll have suffered an incredible amount of brain damage." Washen shook her head. "Unless you've accomplished a miracle, and that car will protect you for every millisecond of the way."

Miocene nodded. "It's taken some twenty-one hundred years, and some considerable secrecy on my part . . . but the results have been well worth it."

In the remote past—Washen couldn't remember when exactly—the captains toyed with exactly this kind of apparatus. But it was the Submaster who ordered them not to pursue it. "Too risky," was her verdict. Her lie. "Too many technical hurdles."

For lack of better, Washen smiled grimly and told her, "Good luck then."

Miocene shook her head, her eyes gaining an ominous light. "Good luck to both of us, you mean. The cabin's large enough for two."

"But why me?"

"Because I respect you," she reported. "And if I order you to accompany me, you will. And frankly, I need you. You're more gifted than me when it comes to talking to people. The captains and our halfway loyal descendants . . . well, let's just say they share my respect for you, and that could be an enormous advantage."

Washen guessed the reason, but she still asked, "Why?"

"I intend to explore the ship. And if the worst has happened—if it's empty and dead—then you're the best person, I believe, to bring home that terrible news . . ."

Just like that, they escaped from Marrow.

Miocene's car was cramped and primitive, and the swift journey brought little hallucinations and a wrenching nausea. But they survived with their sanity. Diving into the remains of the first bridge, the Submaster brought them to a bruising halt inside the assembly station, slipping into the first empty berth, then she took a moment to smooth her crude, homespun uniform with a trembling long hand.

Base camp had been without power for nearly five millennia. The Event had crippled every reactor, every drone. Without food or water, the abandoned lab animals had dropped into comas, and as their immortal flesh lost moisture, they mummified. Washen picked up one of the mandrill baboons—an enormous male weighing little more than a breath—and she felt its leathery heart beat, just once, just to tell her, "I waited for you."

She set it down, and left quietly.

Miocene was standing on the viewing platform, gazing expectantly at the horizon. Even at this altitude, they could only see the captains' realm. The nearest of the Wayward cities—spartan places with cold and simple iron buildings fitted together like blocks—were hundreds of kilometers removed from them. Which might as well have been hundreds of light years, as much as the two cultures interacted anymore.

"You look as if you're expecting someone," Washen observed.

The Submaster said nothing.

"The Waywards are going to find out that we're here, madam. If Till doesn't already know, it's only because he's got too many spies, and all of them are talking at once."

Miocene nodded absently, taking a deep breath.

Then she turned, and never mentioning the Waywards, she said, "We've wasted enough time. Let's go see what's upstairs."

The long access tunnel to the ship was intact.

Tube-cars remained in their berths, untouched by humans and apparently shielded from the Event by the surrounding hyperfiber. Their engines were charged, every system locked in a diagnostic mode. The com-links refused to work, perhaps because there was no one to maintain the dead ship's net. But by dredging the proper commands from memory, Washen got them under way, and every so often she would glance at Miocene, measuring the woman's stern profile, wondering which of them was more scared of what they would find.

The tunnel turned into an abandoned fuel line that spilled out into the leech habitat.

Everything was exactly as Washen's team had left it. Empty and dusty and relentlessly gray, the habitat welcomed them with a perfect silence.

Miocene gripped her belly, as if in pain.

Washen tried to link up with the ship's net, but every connection to the populated areas had been severed.

"We're going on," Miocene announced. "Now."

They pressed on, climbing out of the mammoth fuel tank and into the first of the inhabited quarters. Suddenly they were inside a wide, flattened tunnel, enormous and empty, and looking out at the emptiness, Miocene said, "Perhaps the passengers and crew . . . perhaps they were able to evacuate the ship . . . do you suppose . . . ?"

Washen began to say, "Maybe."

From behind, with a jarring suddenness, an enormous car appeared, bearing down on them until a collision was imminent, then skipping sideways with a crisp, AI precision. Then as the car was passing them, its sole passenger—an enormous whale-like entity cushioned within a salt water bath—winked at them with three of its black eyes, winking just as people did at each other, meaning nothing but the friendliest of greetings.

It was a Yawkleen. Five millennia removed from her post, yet Washen immediately remembered the species' name.

With a flat, disbelieving voice, Miocene said, "No."

But it was true. In the distance, they could just make out a dozen cars, the traffic light, but otherwise perfectly normal. Perfectly banal.

Pausing at the first waystation, they asked its resident AI about the Master's health.

With a smooth cheeriness, it reported, "She is in robust good health. Thank you for inquiring."

"Since when?" the Submaster pressed.

"For the last sixty thousand years, bless her."

Miocene was mute, a scalding rage growing by the instant.

One of the waystation's walls was sprinkled with com-booths. Washen stepped into the nearest booth, saying, "Emergency status. The captains' channel. Please, we need to speak to the Master."

Miocene followed, sealing the door behind them.

A modest office surrounded them, spun out of light and sound. Three captains and countless AIs served as the Master's staff and as buffers. It was the night staff, Washen realized; the clocks on Marrow were wrong by eleven hours. Not too bad after fifty centuries of little mistakes—

The human faces stared at the apparitions, while the AIs simply asked, "What is your business, please?"

"I want to see her!" Miocene thundered.

The captains tried to portray an appropriate composure.

"I'm Miocene! Submaster, First Chair!" The tall woman bent over the nearest captain, saying, "You've got to recognize me. Look at me. Something's very wrong—"

The AIs remembered them, and acted.

The image swirled and stabilized again.

The Master was standing alone in a conference room, watching the arrival of a small starship. She looked exactly as Washen remembered, except that her hair was longer and tied in an intricate bun. Preoccupied in ways that only a Ship's Master can be, she didn't bother to look at her guests. She wasn't paying attention to her AI's warnings. But when she happened to glance at the two captains—both dressed in crude, even laughable imitations of standard ship uniforms—a look of wonder and astonishment swept over that broad face, replaced an instant later with a piercing fury.

"Where have the two of you been?" the Master cried out.

"Where you sent us!" Miocene snapped. "Marrow!"

"Where . . . ?!" the woman spat.

"Marrow," the Submaster repeated. Then, in exasperation, "What sort of game are you playing with us?"

"I didn't send you anywhere . . . !"

In a dim, half-born way, Washen began to understand.

Miocene shook her head, asking, "Why keep our mission secret?" Then in the next breath, "Unless all you intended to do was imprison the best of your captains—"

Washen grabbed Miocene by the arm, saying, "Wait. No."

"My best captains? You?" The Master gave a wild, cackling laugh. "My best officers wouldn't vanish without a trace. They wouldn't take elaborate precautions to accomplish god-knows-what, keeping out of sight for how long? And without so much as a whisper from any one of them . . . !"

Miocene glanced at Washen with an empty face. "She didn't send us—"

"Someone did," Washen replied.

"Security!" the Master shouted. "Two ghosts are using this link! Track them! Hurry! Please, please!"

Miocene killed the link, giving them time.

The stunned ghosts found themselves standing inside the empty booth, trying to make sense out of pure insanity.

"Who could have fooled us . . . ?" asked Washen. Then in her next breath, she realized how easy it would have been: Someone with access and ingenuity sent orders in the Master's name, bringing the captains together in an isolated location. Then the same ingenious soul deceived them with a replica of the Master, sending them rushing down to the ship's core . . .

"I could have manipulated all of you," Miocene offered, thinking along the same seductive, extremely paranoid lines. "But I didn't know about Marrow's existence. None of us knew."

But someone had known. Obviously.

"And even if I possessed the knowledge," Miocene continued, "what could I hope to gain?"

An ancient memory surfaced of its own accord. Suddenly Washen saw herself standing before the window in the leech habitat, looking at the captains' reflections while talking amiably about ambition and its sweet, intoxicating stink.

"We've got to warn the Master," she told Miocene.

"Of what?"

She didn't answer, shouting instructions to the booth, then waiting for a moment before asking, "Are you doing what I said?"

The booth gave no reply.

Washen eyed Miocene, feeling a sudden chill. Then she unsealed the booth's door and gave it a hard shove, stepping warily out into the waystation.

A large woman in robes was calmly and efficiently melting the AI with a powerful laser.

Wearing a proper uniform, saying the expected words, she would be indistinguishable from the Master.

But what surprised the captains even more was the ghost standing nearby. He was wearing civilian clothes and an elaborate disguise, and Washen hadn't seen him for ages. But from the way his flesh quivered on his bones, and the way his gray eyes smiled straight at her, there was no doubt about his name.

"Diu," Washen whispered.

Her ex-lover lifted a kinetic stunner.

Too late and much too slowly, Washen attempted to tackle him.

Then she was somewhere else, and her neck had been broken, and Diu's face was hovering over her, laughing as it spoke, every word incomprehensible.

Washen closed her eyes. Another voice spoke, asking, "How did you find Marrow?" Miocene's voice?

"It's rather like your mission briefing. There was an impact. Some curious data were gathered. But where the Ship's Master dismissed the idea of a hollow core, I investigated. My money paid for the drones that eventually dug to this place, and I followed them here." There was a soft laugh, a reflective pause. Then, "This happened tens of thousands of years ago. Of course. I wasn't a captain in those days. I had plenty of time and the wealth to explore this world, to pick apart its mysteries, and eventually formulate my wonderful plan . . ."

Washen opened her eyes again, fighting to focus.

"I've lived on Marrow more than twice as long as you, madam."

Diu was standing in the middle of the viewing platform, his face framed by the remnants of the bridge.

"I know its cycles," he said. "And all its many hazards, too."

Miocene was standing next to Washen, her face taut and tired but the eyes opened wide, missing nothing.

"How do you feel?" she inquired, glancing down at her colleague.

"Awful." Washen sat up, winced briefly, then asked, "How long have we been here?"

"A few minutes," Diu answered. "My associate, the false Master, was carrying both of you. But now it's gone ahead to check on my ship—"

"What ship?"

"That's what I was about to explain." The smile brightened, then he said, "Over the millennia, I've learned how to stockpile equipment in hyperfiber vaults. The vaults drift in the molten iron. In times of need, I can even live inside them. If I wanted to pretend my own death, for instance."

"For the Waywards," Miocene remarked.

"Naturally."

The Submaster pretended to stare at their captor. But she was looking past him, the dark eyes intense and unreadable, but in a subtle way, almost hopeful.

"What do you want?" asked Miocene.

"Guess," he told them.

Washen took a long breath and tried to stand. Miocene grabbed her by the arms, and they stood together like clumsy dancers, fighting for their balance.

"The ship," Washen managed.

Diu said nothing.

"The ultimate starship, and you want it for yourself." Washen took a few more breaths, testing her neck before she pulled free of Miocene's hands. "This scheme of yours is an elaborate mutiny. That's all it is, isn't it?"

"The Waywards are an army," said Miocene. "An army of religious fanatics being readied for a jihad. My son is the nominal leader. But who feeds him his visions? It's always been you, hasn't it?"

No response.

Washen found the strength to move closer to the railing, looking down, nothing to see but thick clouds of airborne iron kicked up by some fresh eruption.

Miocene took a sudden breath, then exhaled.

Strolling towards them, huge even at a distance, was the false Master. Knowing it was a machine made it look like one. It had a patient stride, even with its thick arms raised overhead, waving wildly.

"What about the Builders?" Miocene blurted.

Diu nearly glanced over his shoulder, then hesitated. "What are you asking?"

"Did they really fight the Bleak?"

Diu enjoyed the suspense, grinning at both of them before he admitted, "How the fuck should I know?"

"The artifacts—?" Miocene began.

"Six thousand years old," he boasted. "Built by an alien passenger who thought I was in the entertainment industry."

"Why pretend to die?" Miocene asked.

"For the freedom it gave me." There was a boy in his grin. "Being dead, I can see more. Being dead, I can disguise myself. I walk where I want. I make babies with a thousand different women, including some in the captains' realm."

There was silence.

Then for a moment, they could just begin to hear the machine's voice—a deep sound rattling between the dormitories, fading until it was a senseless murmur.

"We spoke to the Master," Washen blurted.

Miocene took the cue, adding, "She knows. We told her everything—"

"No, you told her almost nothing," Diu snapped.

"Are you certain?"

"Absolutely."

"But she'll be hunting for us," Washen said.

"She's been on that same hunt for five thousand years," he reminded them. "And even if she sniffs out the access tunnel this time, I won't care. Because on the way back down, I mined the tunnel. Patient one-kilo charges of antimatter are ready to close things up tight. Excavating a new tunnel is going to take millennia, and probably much longer. Giving myself and my friends plenty of time to prepare."

"What if no one digs us out?" Washen asked.

Diu shrugged, grinning at her. "How does the old story play? It's better to rule in one realm than serve in another—?"

Then he hesitated, hearing a distant voice.

The Master's voice.

A laser appeared in his right hand, and he turned, squinting at his machine, puzzled by the frantic arm-waving.

"Another car," said the voice, diluted to a whisper. "It's in the berth next to yours . . . !"

"What car?" Diu muttered to himself.

"I believe I know," Miocene replied, eyes darting side to side. "I built two vessels, identical in every way. Including the fact that you never knew they existed."

Diu didn't seem to hear her.

Miocene took a step toward him, adding, "It's obvious, isn't it? Someone else is here. Or if they squeezed in together, two someones."

"So?" Diu replied. "A couple more captains lurking nearby—"

"Except," Miocene interrupted, "I didn't send my invitation to my captains."

Diu didn't ask to whom it was sent.

Washen remembered Miocene had stood on this platform, watching Marrow. Watching for Till, she realized. How long would it have taken him to move the car to the bridge? That was the only question. She had no doubts that once motivated, the Waywards could do whatever they wanted inside the captains' realm.

"I was hopeful," Miocene confessed. "I was hopeful that my son would be curious, that he would follow me back to the ship and see it for himself."

There was a sound, sharp and familiar.

The false Master stopped in mid-stride, then began to collapse in on itself. Then a thin column of light appeared in the smoke, betraying the laser's source.

Diu started to run.

Miocene followed, and Washen chased both of them.

Beside the platform, in easy earshot, stood a drone. A lone figure was kneeling beneath its ceramic body, wearing breechcloth and holding a crude laser drill against his shoulder, intent on reducing the machine to ash and gas.

Diu saw him, stopped and aimed.

At Locke.

Maybe he was hesitating, realizing it was his son. Or more likely, he simply was asking himself: Where's Till? Either way, he didn't fire. Instead, Diu started to turn, looking at his surroundings as if for the first time—

There was a clean hard crack.

A fat chunk of lead knocked Diu off his feet, opening his chest before it tore through his backside.

With the smooth grace of an athlete, Till climbed out from the meshwork beneath the platform. He seemed unhurried, empty of emotion. Strolling past Washen, he didn't give her the tiniest glance. It was like watching a soulless machine, right up until the moment when Miocene tried to block his way, saying, "Son," with a weak, sorrowful voice.

He shoved her aside, then ran toward Diu. Screaming. At the top of his lungs, screaming, "It's all been a lie—!"

Diu lifted his hand, reaching into a bloody pocket.

Moments later, the base camp began to shake violently. Dozens of mines were exploding simultaneously. But the enormous mass of the ship absorbed the blows, then counterattacked, pushing the access tunnel shut for its entire length, and as an afterthought, knocking everyone off their feet.

Diu grabbed his laser.

He managed to sit up.

Washen fought her way to her feet, but too late. She could only watch as Miocene managed to leap, grabbing Till by the head and halfway covering him as the killing blast struck her temple, and in half an instant, boiled away her brain.

Till rolled, using the body as a shield, discharging his weapon until it was empty. Then a burst of light struck him in the shoulder, removing his right arm and part of his chest even as it cauterized the enormous wound.

Using his drill, Locke quickly sliced his father into slivers, then burned him to dust.

Miocene lay dead at Washen's feet, and Till was beside her, oblivious to everything. There was a wasted quality to the face, a mark that went beyond any physical injury. "It's been a lie," he kept saying, without sound. "Everything. A monstrous lie."

Locke came to him, not to Washen, asking, "What is monstrous, Your Excellence?"

Till gazed up at him. With a careful voice, he said, "Nothing." Then after a long pause, he added, "We have to return home. Now."

"Of course. Yes, Your Excellence."

"But first," he said, "the ship must be protected from its foes!"

Locke knew exactly what was being asked of him. "I don't see why—?"

"The ship is in danger!" the prophet cried out. "I say it, which makes it so. Now prove your devotion, Wayward!"

Locke turned, looking at his mother with a weary, trapped expression.

Washen struck him on the jaw, hard and sudden.

She had covered almost a hundred meters before the laser drill bit into her calf, making her stumble. But she forced herself to keep running, slipping behind the drone with only two more burns cut deep into her back.

It was as if Locke was trying to miss.

Hours later, watching from the dormitory, Washen saw her son carrying four of the comatose baboons out into the courtyard, where he piled them up and turned the lasers on them. Then he showed the ashes to Till, satisfying him, and without a backward glance, the two walked slowly in the direction of the bridge.

Washen hid for several days, eating and drinking from the old stores.

When she finally crept into the bridge, she found Diu's sophisticated car cut into pieces, and Miocene's fused to its berth. But what startled her—what made her sick and sad—was Marrow itself. The captains' new bridge had been toppled. Wild fires and explosions were sweeping across the visible globe. A vast, incoherent rage was at work, erasing every trace of the despised captains, and attacking anyone that might pose any threat to a lost prophet.

In that crystalline moment of horror, Washen understood what she had to do. And without a wasted moment, she turned and began to make ready.

MISSION DATE—INCONSEQUENTIAL

At the ship's center, a seamless night has been born.

The figure moves by memory through the darkness, picking her way across a tangle of conduits and scrap parts. In a few moments, energy milked from hundreds of tube-cars will flow into an enormous projector, and for a fleeting instant or two, the darkness will be repelled. If her ink-and-paper calculations are correct, and if more than a century of singleminded preparation succeeds, a message of forgiveness and rebirth will skate along the chamber's wall, encircling and embracing the world.

But that is just the beginning.

Wearing a pressure suit and two bulky packs, she climbs over the railing and leaps, bracing for the impact.

Boom.

The blister is thick, but she began the hole decades ago. Tools wait in a neat pile. With a minimum of cuts, the hole opens, and a sudden wind blows past her, trying to coax her into joining it, nothing outside but Marrow's high cold stratosphere.

The buttresses have vanished, at least for the moment.

There's no time to waste. She obeys the wind, letting it carry her through the hole and downward in a wild tumbling spiral.

The sky behind her erupts in light.

In the colors of fire and hot iron, it cries out, "A BUILDER IS COMING. SHE COMES TO LEAD YOU OUT OF YOUR MISERY!"

The Builder grabs the cord of her parachute, then begins to scream.

Not out of fear. Not at all.

It's the full-throated, wonderstruck scream of a girl who has forgotten just how very much fun it is to fall.

MICROBE

Joan Slonczewski

❀

Joan Slonczewski (born 1956) is a Professor of Biology at Kenyon College in Gambier, Ohio, and a writer of hard science fiction. She currently has her third NSF grant to investigate *e coli*. She is best known for her second novel, *A Door into Ocean* (1987), the first of her Elysium novels—others to date include *Daughter of Elysium* (1993), *The Children Star* (1998), and *Brain Plague* (2000). The latter two books feature sentient bacteria. In an interview by James Schellenberg and David M. Switzer, she remarks:

> I realize this perspective may startle some people, but remember, I've spent a lifetime studying bacteria, and I tend to identify with their point of view. Look at this from historical perspective. Why do people have machines? For the same reason people across history have had animals, slaves, and women: To do things people could not do, or wished to have done more efficiently, as extensions of their own bodies. Cows gave milk, slaves gave labor, women gave babies (future workers). But the trouble was, the better the animal/slave/woman, the higher quality of output, the more it/he/she tended to approach the nature of their master. Animals could only go so far, but slaves and women finally made their break. (In Western societies, in the past century, that is.) Is it a coincidence that slaves and women broke free during the age of machines?

Her novels, from her first book *Still Forms on Foxfield* (1980), are informed by Quaker ideals and feminism. They are in both respects far from the traditional politics of hard SF. They are characterized as well as by the loving scientific details underpinning the story. There are ways in which she sometimes seems closest in attitude to Greg Egan: She says, in the same interview quoted above, "I am most interested in the tension between philosophy and physiology of the brain. What does it mean to have a brain that consists of a molecular mechanism, yet contains a spirit of a thinking, feeling human being? . . . Other machines will become sentient, sooner or later. It's the inevitable result of evolution. I read somewhere that our largest AI machines approach the brainpower of a cockroach; from the standpoint of evolution, only a small fraction of Earth's lifetime separates us."

This story, which appeared in *Analog*, is set in the same future universe as the Elysium novels, in the setting of *The Children Star*. Like Baxter's "Gossamer," it harks back to the fiction of Hal Clement and, in this case, the James Blish of "Surface Tension," inventing and solving a clever SF problem posed by a precisely imagined world of wonders. Here, Slonczewski takes an existing form of DNA, the toroidal chromosomes of prokaryotes, and extrapolates a whole world in which all niches are filled by organisms of that type.

"That rat didn't die." Andra walked around the holostage. Before her, projected down from the geodesic dome, shone the planet's image: Iota Pavonis Three, the first new world approved for settlement in over four centuries. As Andra walked around, the swirl of a mysterious continent peered out through a swathe of cloud. She stopped, leaning forward on her elbows to watch. What name of its own would the Free Fold Federation ultimately bestow on IP3, Andra wondered; such a lovely, terrifying world.

"Not the last time, the rat didn't." The eyespeaker was perched on her shoulder. It belonged to Skyhook, the sentient shuttle craft that would soon carry Andra from the study station down to land on the new world. A reasonable arrangement: The shuttle craft would carry the human xenobiologist through space for her field work, then she would carry his eye on the planet surface, as she did inside the station. "The rat only died down there the first eight times."

"Until we got its 'skin' right." The "skin" was a suit of nanoplast, containing billions of microscopic computers, designed to filter out all the local toxins—arsenic, lanthanides, bizarre pseudoalkaloids. All were found in local flora and fauna; inhaling them would kill a human within hours. In the old days, planets had been terraformed for human life, like Andra's own home world Valedon. Today they would call that ecocide. Instead, millions of humans would be life-shaped to live here on planet IP3, farming and building—the thought of it made her blood race.

"We got the skin right for the rat," Skyhook's eyespeaker pointed out. "But you're not exactly a rat."

From across the holostage, an amorphous blob of nanoplast raised a pseudopod. "Not exactly a rat," came a voice from the nanoplast. It was the voice of Pelt, the skinsuit that would protect Andra on the alien planet surface. "Not exactly a rat—just about nine-tenths, I'd say. Your cell physiology is practically the same as a rat; why, you could even take organ grafts. Only a few developmental genes make the difference."

Andra smiled. "Thank the Spirit for a few genes. Life would be so much less interesting."

Pelt's pseudopod wiggled. "The rat lived, and so will you. But our nanoservos completely jammed." The microscopic nanoservos had swarmed into sample life forms from IP3 to test their chemical structure. But for some reason they could barely begin to send back data before they broke down. "Nobody cares about them."

"Of course we care," Andra said quickly. Pelt never let anyone value human life above that of sentient machines. "That's why we cut short the analysis, until we can bring samples back to the station. That's why we're sending me."

"*Us*," he corrected.

"All right, enough already," said Skyhook. "Why don't we review our data one last time?"

"Very well." A third sentient voice boomed out of the hexagonal panel in the dome directly overhead. It was the explorer station herself, Quantum. Quantum was considered female, the others male; Andra could never tell why, although sentients would laugh at any human who could not tell the difference. "Here are some microbial cells extracted from the soil by the last probe," said Quantum.

The planet's image dissolved. In its place appeared the highly magnified shapes of the microbes. The cells were round and somewhat flattened, rather like red blood cells. But if one looked closer, one could see that each flattened cell was actually pinched in straight through like a bagel.

"The toroid cell shape has never been observed on other planets," said Quantum. "Otherwise, the cell's structure is simple. No nuclear membranes surround the chromosomes; so, these cells are like bacteria, *prokaryotes*."

Skyhook said, "The chromosome might be circular, too, as in bacteria."

"Who knows?" said Pelt. "On Urulan, all the chromosomes are branched. It took us decades to do genetics there."

"We just don't know yet," said Quantum. "All we know is, the cells contain DNA."

"The usual double helix?" asked Skyhook. The double helix is a ladder of DNA nucleotide pairs, always adenine with thymine or guanine with cytosine, for the four different "letters" of the DNA code. When a cell divides to make two cells, the entire helix unzips, then fills in a complementary strand for each daughter cell.

"The nanoservos failed before they could tell for sure. But it does have all four nucleotides."

Andra watched the magnified microbes as their images grew, their ring shapes filling out like bagel dough rising. "I'll bet their chromosomes run right around the hole."

At her shoulder Skyhook's eyespeaker laughed. "That would be a neat trick."

Quantum added, "We identified fifteen amino acids in its proteins, including the usual six." All living things have evolved to use six amino acids in common, the ones that form during the birth of planets. "But three of the others are toxic—"

"Look," exclaimed Andra. "The cell is starting to divide." One of the bulging toroids had begun to pucker in, all along its circumference. The puckered line deepened into a furrow all the way around the cell. Along the inside of the "hole," a second furrow deepened, eventually to meet the furrow from the outer rim.

"So that's how the cell divides," said Skyhook. "Not by pinching in across the hole; instead it slices through."

"The better to toast it."

At that Pelt's pseudopod made a rude gesture. "Pinching the hole in wouldn't make sense, if your chromosome encircles the hole; you'd pinch off half of it."

Andra squinted and leaned forward on her elbows. "I say—that cell has *three* division furrows."

"The daughter cells are dividing again already?" Skyhook suggested.

"No, it's a third furrow in the same generation. All three furrows are meeting up in the middle."

"That's right," boomed Quantum's voice. "These cells divide in three, not two," she explained. "Three daughter cells in each generation."

Sure enough, the three daughter cells appeared, filling themselves out as they separated. Other cells too had puckered in by now, at various stages of division, and all made their daughters in triplets. "How would they divide their chromosomes to make three?" Andra wondered. "They must copy each DNA helix twice before dividing. Why would that have evolved?"

"Never mind the DNA," said Pelt. "It's those toxic amino acids you should worry about."

"Not with you protecting me. The rat survived."

Quantum said, "We've discussed every relevant point. We've established, based on all available data, that Andra's chance of survival approaches one hundred percent."

"Uncertainties remain," Skyhook cautioned.

Andra stood back and spread her hands. "Of course we need more data—that's why we're going down."

"All right," said Skyhook. "Let's go."

"I'm ready." Pelt's pseudopod dissolved, and the nanoplast formed a perfect hemisphere.

Andra unhooked Skyhook's eyespeaker from her shoulder. Then she walked back around the holostage to lift the hemisphere of Pelt onto her head. Pelt's nanoplast began to melt slowly down over her black curls, leaving a thin transparent film of nanoprocessors covering her hair, her dark skin, and her black eyes. It formed a special breather over her nose and mouth. Everywhere the nanoplast would filter the air that reached her skin, keeping planetary dust out while letting oxygen through. The film covered the necklace of pink andradites around her neck, spreading down her shirt and trousers. She lifted each foot in turn to allow the complete enclosure. Now she would be safe from any chemical hazard she might encounter.

In Skyhook's viewport, the surface of planet IP3 expanded and rose to meet them. Numerous tests had established its physical parameters as habitable—gravity of nine-tenths g, temperatures not too extreme, oxygen sufficient and carbon dioxide low enough, water plentiful. The ozone layer could have been denser, but human colonists would have their eyes and skin lifeshaped for extra enzymes to keep their retina and chromosomes repaired.

At a distance the planet did not look remarkably different from Andra's home world. A brilliant expanse of ocean met a mottled brown shore, rotating slowly down beneath the craft. Beyond, in the upper latitudes, rolled the blue-brown interior of a continent, broken only by a circle of mountains.

As Skyhook fell swiftly toward the land, curious patterns emerged. Long dark bands ran in parallel, in gently winding rows like a string picture. The lines were bands of blue vegetation; the probe had sent back footage of them, wide arching structures tall as trees. Each band alternated with a band of yellow, which gave way to the next band of blue. Over and over the same pattern repeated, ceasing only at the mountains.

"I've never seen patterns like that on uncolonized worlds," Andra mused.

"They do look like garden rows," Skyhook admitted. "Perhaps the native farmers will come out to greet us."

If there were intelligent life forms, they had yet to invent radio. A year of monitoring the planet at every conceivable frequency had yielded nothing, not so much as a calculation of pi.

Skyhook landed gently in a field of dense vegetation. The wall of the cabin opened, the door pulling out into an arch of nanoplast. A shaft of brilliant light entered.

"All systems check," crackled Quantum's voice on the radio in her ear. "Go ahead."

Andra gathered her field equipment and set Skyhook's eye upon her shoulder again. Then she stepped outside.

The field was a riot of golden ringlets, like wedding bands strewn out. Her gaze followed the cascade of gold down to the edge of the field, where taller dark trunks arose in shallow curves, arching overhead. From the taller growth came a keening sound, perhaps some living thing singing, or perhaps the wind vibrating somehow through its foliage. "It's beautiful," she exclaimed at last.

Beneath the golden ringlets grew dense blue-brown vegetation, reaching to Andra's waist. She bent closer for a look. "These look like plants, 'phycoids.' The ringlets might be flowers."

"They could just as well be snakes ready to snap," warned Skyhook. "Watch your step."

She looked back at the shuttlecraft, planted in the field like a four-legged insect. Then she lifted her leg through the foliage, Pelt's nanoplastic "skin" flexing easily. Immediately her foot snagged. She tried to pull out some of the growth, but found it surprisingly tough and had to cut it with a knife. "The leaves and stems are all looped," she observed in surprise. "All looped, just like the 'flowers'; I'll never get through this stuff."

Pelt said, "They are phycoid. I detect products of photosynthesis."

"They could be carnivorous plants," Skyhook insisted.

Andra collected some more cuttings into her backpack. "I wish I could smell them," she said wistfully. Pelt's skin filtered out all volatile organics. She aimed her laser pen to dig one out by the roots. The phycoid came up, but nearby stems sparked and smoldered.

"Watch out!" squeaked the eyespeaker.

She winced. "Don't deafen me; I'll put it out." She stamped the spot with her boots and sprinkled some water from her drinking jet. "This planet's a fire trap." The phycoid roots, she noted, were long twisted loops, tightly pressed together, but loops nonetheless. All the living structures seemed to be bagels squashed and stretched.

"Great Spirit, we've got company," Skyhook exclaimed.

Andra looked up. She blinked her eyes. A herd of brown-striped truck tires were rolling slowly across the field. To get a closer look, she pressed through the phycoids, stopping every so often to extricate her feet from the looped foliage. She made about ten meters progress before stopping to catch her breath.

"No need to get too close," Skyhook reminded her. His eye had telephoto.

"Yes, but I might pick up droppings, or some fallen hair or scales."

Some of the rolling "tires" were heading toward her. Each one had several round cranberry-colored spots set in its "tread." The "tread" was composed of suckers that stretched and extended to push in back, or pull in front. "They must be animal-like, 'zoöids,'" suggested Andra. "Those red things—could they be eyes?" She counted them, two, three, four in all, before the first came up again. Those eyes must be tough, not to mind getting squashed down.

"If these creatures are zoöids," Pelt wanted to know, "how do they feed?"

Skyhook said, "Their suckers ingest the phycoids."

Andra stopped again to pull out her foot. "They sure know how to travel," she wryly observed. "No wonder they never evolved legs." One four-eyed zoöid got excited, and took off with remarkable speed; then it suddenly reversed, heading backwards just as fast. These zoöids had no "backwards" or "forwards," she thought.

Quantum radioed again. "Andra, how are you holding up? Is your breathing okay?"

She took a deep breath. "I think so." Most of the rats had died from inhaling toxic dust. She resumed her attempt to make headway through the phycoids, and searched the ground for anything that looked like droppings. Overhead, she heard a strange whirring sound. A flock of little things were flying, their movements too fast for her to make out.

"Their wings are turning full around, like propellers," Skyhook exclaimed in amazement. "Why, all these creatures are built of wheels, one way or another."

"Sh," said Andra. "A zoöid is coming up close."

The creature rolled slowly over the phycoids, squashing the golden ringlets beneath it. Andra took a closer look. "There's a smaller ring structure, just sitting inside the bagel hole. I'll bet it's a baby zoöid." The clinging little one rolled over and over inside as its parent traveled. The parent did not seem to notice Andra at all; neither her shape nor her smell would resemble a native predator, she guessed.

The radio crackled again. "We must attempt contact," Quantum reminded her. Any zoöid might be intelligent.

Andra held out her communicator, a box that sent out flashing lights and sound bursts in various mathematical patterns, strings of primes and various representations of pi and other constants. It even emitted puffs of volatile chemicals, to alert any chemosensing creature with a hint of intelligence. Not that she expected much; their probes had broadcast such information over the past year.

Then she saw it: A giant zoöid was approaching, five times taller than the others and perhaps a hundred times their weight. As it barreled along, picking up speed, the small striped ones took off, zigzagging crazily before it. The ground rumbled beneath her feet.

"Get back to my cabin!" urged Skyhook. "We'll all get run over."

"Wait," said Pelt. "Do you think it heard us? What if it wants to talk?"

"I don't think so," said Andra, prudently backing off. "I think the smaller zoöids attracted it, not us."

A small zoöid went down under the giant one, then another. That seemed to be the giant's strategy, to run down as many little ones as it could. At last it slowed and turned back, coming to rest upon one of the squashed carcasses.

"It's extending its suckers to feed," observed Skyhook. "Let's get back before it gets hungry again."

"I think that will be a while," said Andra. "It's got several prey to feed on." The rest of the smaller zoöids seemed to have calmed down, as if they knew the predator was satisfied and would not attack again soon. Definitely a herd mentality; no sign of higher intelligence here.

Andra resumed collecting phycoids and soil samples, recording the location of each. Deeper into the field, she saw something thrashing about in the phycoids. She made her way toward it through the tangle of looped foliage.

"It's a baby zoöid," she exclaimed. The poor little bagel must have fallen out when its parent ran off. Or perhaps the parent had expelled it, as a mother kangaroo sometimes did. At any rate, there it was, squirming and stretching its little suckers ineffectually, only tangling itself in the phycoids.

"Watch out; it might bite," said Skyhook.

"Nonsense. I have to collect it." Andra stuffed her hands into a pair of gloves, then approached warily. With one hand she held out an open collecting bag; with the other, she grabbed the little zoöid. It hung limply, twisting a bit.

Suddenly it squirted something. An orange spray landed on the phycoids, some of it reaching her leg. Andra frowned. She plunged the creature into her bag, which sealed itself tight. "Sorry about that, Pelt."

"You're the one who would have been sorry," Pelt replied. "That stuff is caustic, as strong as lye. No problem for me, but your skin would not have liked it."

"Thanks a lot. I guess we should head back now; I've got more than I can hold."

She turned back toward Skyhook, some hundred meters off, his spidery landing gear splayed out into the phycoids. Methodically she made her way back, with more difficulty now that she had so much to carry. She was sweating now, but Pelt handled it beautifully, keeping her skin cool and refreshed. The distant forest of tall blue phycoids sang in her ears. The Singing Planet, they should call it, she thought.

"Andra . . . something's not right," Pelt said suddenly.

"What is it?" She was having more trouble plowing through the foliage; her legs were getting stiff.

"Something that baby zoöid sprayed is blocking my nanoprocessors. Not the chemicals; I can screen out anything. I'm not sure what it is."

"What else could it be?"

Skyhook said, "Just get back to my cabin. We'll wash you down."

"I'm trying," said Andra, breathing hard. "My legs are so stiff." The shuttle craft stood hopefully ahead of her. Only about ten meters to go, she thought.

"It's not your legs," Pelt's voice said dully. "It's my nanoplast. I'm losing control over the lower part, where the spray hit. I can't flex at your joints any more."

Her scalp went cold, then hot again. "What about your air filter?"

"So far it's okay. The disruption has not reached your face yet."

"Just get back here," Skyhook urged again. "You're almost here." Obligingly the doorway appeared on the craft's surface, molding itself open in a rim of nanoplast.

"I'm trying, but my legs just won't bend." She pushed as hard as she could.

"Drop your backpack," Skyhook added.

"I won't give up my samples. How else will we learn what's going on here?" She fell onto her stomach and tried to drag herself through.

"It's microbes," Pelt exclaimed suddenly. "Some kind of microbes—they're cross-linking my processors."

"What? How?" she demanded. "Microbes infecting nanoplast—I've never heard of it."

"They messed up the probe before."

"Quantum?" called Andra. "What do you think?"

"It could be," the radio voice replied. "The nanoprocessors store data in organic polymers—which might be edible to a truly omnivorous microbe. There's always a first time."

"Microbes eating nanoplast!" Skyhook exclaimed. "What about other sentients? Are the microbes contagious?"

"You'll have to put us in isolation," said Andra.

"Andra," said Pelt, "the cross-linking is starting to disrupt my entire system." His voice came lower and fainter. "I don't know how long I can keep my filters open."

Andra stared desperately at the door of the shuttle, so near and yet so far. "Quantum, how long could I last breathing unfiltered air?"

"That's hard to say. An hour should be okay; we'll clean your lungs out later."

She tried to recall how long the first rat had lived. Half a day?

"I'm shutting down," Pelt warned her. "I'm sorry, Andra . . ."

Skyhook said, "Pelt, you'll last longer in rest mode. We'll save you yet—there's got to be an antibiotic that will work. They've got DNA—we'll throw every DNA analogue we've got at them."

The nanoplastic skin opened around Andra's mouth, shrinking back around her head and neck. An otherworldly scent filled her lungs, a taste of ginger and other unnameable things, as beautiful as the vision of golden ringlets. Planet Ginger, she thought, smelled as lovely as it looked. She was the first human to smell it; but would these breaths be her last?

Pelt's skin shriveled down her arms, getting stuck at her waist near the spot that got sprayed. She tried again to pull herself through the phycoids, grabbing their tough loops. Suddenly she had another idea. Pulling in her arms, she sank down and rolled herself over and over, just like the zoöids. This worked much better, for the phycoid foliage proved surprisingly elastic, bending easily beneath her and bouncing back again. Perhaps those zoöids were not quite so silly after all.

At the door, Skyhook had already extruded sheets of quarantine material, to isolate her and protect his own nanoplast from whatever deadly infection Pelt harbored. The doorway extended and scooped her up into the cabin.

As the doorway constricted, at last closing out the treacherous planet, Andra let out a quick sigh of relief. "Skyhook, we've got to save Pelt. Have you got anything to help him?"

Two long tendrils were already poking into the quarantine chamber, to probe the hapless skinsuit. "I'm spreading what antibiotics we have on board," said Skyhook, from the cabin speaker now. "Nucleotide analogues, anything likely to block DNA synthesis and stop the microbes growing. It's bizarre, treating a sentient for infection."

Andra carefully peeled off the remaining nanoplast, trying to keep as much of it together as possible, although she had no idea whether it was beyond repair. "Pelt," she whispered. "You did your best for me."

By the time they returned to the station, there was still no sign that any of the antibiotics had curbed the microbes. Quantum was puzzled. "I have a few more to try," she said, "but really, if the chromosomes are regular DNA, something should have worked."

"Maybe the microbes' DNA is shielded by proteins."

"That wouldn't help during replication, remember? The double helix has to open and unzip down the middle, to let the new nucleotides pair. There's no way around it."

Andra frowned. Something was missing; there was still something wrong, about the growing microbes with their three daughter cells. How could they unzip their DNA, fill in each complementary strand, and end up with three helices? She thought she had figured it out before, but now it did not add up. She coughed once, then again harder. Her lungs were starting to react to the dust—she had to start treatment now.

"We've got some data on your samples," Quantum added. "The microbial cells concentrate acid inside, instead of excreting it, like most of our cells do. I still find only fifteen amino acids, but some of them—"

"I've got it!" Andra leapt to her feet. "Don't you see? *The chromosome is a triple helix*. That's why each cell divides in three—each daughter strand synthesizes two complements, and you end up with three new triple helices, one for each cell." A fit of coughing caught up with her.

"It could be," Quantum said slowly. "There are many ways to make a DNA triple helix. One found in human regulatory genes alternates A-T-T triplets with G-C-C."

"Then it has a two-letter code, not four." Double-helical DNA has four possible pairs, since A-T is distinguished from T-A; likewise G-C differs from C-G.

Quantum added, "The triple helix is most stable in acid, just what we found in these cells."

"Just hurry up and design some triplet analogues." Quantum's sentient brain could do this far faster than any human. "Triple helix," Andra repeated. "It would resist ultraviolet damage much better, with the planet's thin ozone layer. But how to encode proteins, with only two 'letters'?" The triple helix had only two possible triplets; its three-letter "words" could only specify eight amino acids to build protein. "Maybe it uses words of four letters. With two possible triplets at each position, that would encode two to the fourth power, that is, sixteen possible amino acids."

"Fifteen," corrected Quantum, "if one is a stop signal."

* * *

The next day, after an exhaustive medical workout, Andra felt as if a vacuum cleaner had gone through her lungs. Pelt still had a long way to recover, but at least the pesky microbes were cleaned out.

"It's hopeless," complained Skyhook's eyespeaker. "If even sentients aren't safe, we'll never explore that planet."

"Don't worry," said Quantum's voice above the holostage. "Pelt's nanoplast has an exceptionally high organic content. A slight redesign will eliminate the problem. Machines have that advantage."

Still, Pelt had nearly died, thought Andra.

"Your phycoid and zoöid samples all have toroid cells, too," Quantum added. "They have circular chromosomes, with no nuclear membranes: They're all prokaryotes. Just wait till the Free Fold hears about this," Quantum added excitedly. "I've got the perfect name for the planet."

Andra looked up. "Planet of the Bagels?"

"Planet Prokaryon."

Prokaryon—yes, thought Andra, it sounded just pompous enough that the Fold would buy it.

Still, she thought uneasily about those regular garden rows of phycoid forest and fields, with all kinds of creatures yet to be discovered. "I wonder," she mused. "Some one else just might have named it first."

THE LADY VANISHES

Charles Sheffield

❀

Charles Sheffield (born 1935) is a physicist and writer. He was born in the U.K. but has lived in the U.S. since the mid-1960s. In 1998, he married writer Nancy Kress. He was educated at Cambridge—his friend David Bischoff reports that Sheffield's "advisor at Cambridge was none other than another English SF author and mathematician—Sir Fred Hoyle. However, Charles had told me that Sir Fred was always away somewhere . . . Charles seldom saw him." Sheffield began publishing SF in the 1970s and quickly gained a reputation as a new star of hard SF in the tradition of Arthur C. Clarke. He in fact writes SF of all descriptions but always with a positive view of scientific knowledge as a tool for solving problems. Kim Stanley Robinson says, "Charles writes hard SF, which as you know is science fiction played with the net up and with a handy portable device that will shrink any balls that actually hit at the net so that they will pass through without impediment. This of course makes for a great game, in which anything is possible but everything seems real. Charles is one of the best currently working this game, extending its limits and testing the possibilities."

Sheffield says in a recent article in *The Washington Post Book World*:

> Without a strong scientific content, a science fiction story fades into fantasy. . . . What's the difference between the two? Let me answer by defining science fiction—and then fantasy by exclusion. Science is like a great, sprawling continent, a body of learning and theories. Everything in science is interconnected, however loosely. If your theory doesn't connect with any part of the rest of science, you may be a genius with a new and profound understanding of the universe; but chances are you're wrong. Science fiction consists of stories set on the shore or out in the shallow coastal waters of that huge scientific landmass. Stay inland, safe above high tide, and your story will be not science fiction, but fiction about science. Stray too far, out of sight of land, and you are writing fantasy—even if you think it's science fiction.

He further recommends a catalog of today's practitioners of hard SF:

> . . . no reader seeking well-written stories that respect, emphasize and depend on modern science should be disappointed by the works of any of the following: Roger MacBride Allen, Catherine Asaro, Stephen Baxter, Greg Bear, Greg Benford, Ben Bova, David Brin, Octavia Butler, Michael Cassutt, Greg Egan, Michael Flynn, Joe Haldeman, James Hogan, Nancy Kress (who happens to be my wife, and I originally thought it unwise to include her; it seems, however, less than fair to leave her out), Geoffrey Landis, Paul McAuley, Jack McDevitt, Larry Niven, Gerald Nordley, Kim Stanley Robinson, Rob Sawyer, Bud Sparhawk, Joan Slonczewski, Neal Stephenson, Bruce Sterling, John Stith and Vernor Vinge.

Sheffield is a prolific novelist, averaging more than a book a year since he began publishing in the 1970s. His novel *Spheres of Heaven* (2001) is a sequel to *The Mind Pool* (1993). He had two books out in 2002: *Dark as Day*, a sequel to *Cold as Ice* (1992), and *The Amazing Dr. Darwin*. He won the John W. Campbell Memorial Award for his novel *Brother to Dragons* (1992), and was awarded both the Hugo and the Nebula Awards for his story "Georgia on My Mind" (1993). His short fiction is collected in *Vectors* (1979), *Hidden Variables* (1981), *Erasmus Magister* (1982), *The McAndrew Chronicles* (1983), and *Georgia on My Mind, and Other Places* (1996). He is also the author of the nonfiction book *Borderlands of Science: How to Think Like a Scientist and Write Science Fiction* (1999).

This story is a wicked satire on the government intelligence services organized around the idea that a very bright woman scientist has penetrated the secret of invisibility in order to quit working for what is obviously the CIA. Sheffield has worked out plausible optics explanations and combines this with knowledge of how intelligence services work.

What is wrong with this picture?

Colonel Walker Bryant is standing at the door of the Department of Ultimate Storage. He is smiling; and he is carrying a book under one arm.

Answer: *Everything* is wrong with this picture. Colonel Bryant is the man who assigned (make that *consigned*) me to the Department of Ultimate Storage, for reasons that he found good and sufficient. But he never visited the place. That is not unreasonable, since the department is six stories underground in the Defense Intelligence facility at Bolling Air Force Base, on a walk-down sub-basement level which according to the elevators does not exist. It forms a home for rats, spiders, and me.

Also, Walker Bryant never smiles unless something is wrong; and Walker Bryant never, in my experience, reads anything but security files and the sports pages of the newspaper. Colonel Bryant carrying a book is like Mother Theresa sporting an AK-47.

"Good morning, Jerry," he said. He walked forward, helped himself to an extra-strength peppermint from the jar that I keep on my desk, put the book next to it, and sat down. "I just drove over from the Pentagon. It's a beautiful spring day outside."

"I wouldn't know."

It was supposed to be sarcasm, but he has a hide like a rhino. He just chuckled and said, "Now, Jerry, you know the move to this department was nothing personal. I did it for your own good, down here you can roam as widely as you like. Anyway, they just told me something that I thought might interest you."

When you have worked for someone for long enough, you learn to read the message behind the words. *I thought might interest you means I don't have any idea what is going on, but maybe you do.*

I leaned forward and picked up the book. It was *The Invisible Man*, by H.G. Wells. I turned it over and looked at the back.

"Are you reading this?" I wouldn't call Walker Bryant "Sir" to save my life, and oddly enough he doesn't seem to mind.

He nodded. "Sure."

"I mean, actually reading it—yourself."

"Well, I've looked through it. It doesn't seem to be about anything much. But I'm going to read it in detail, as soon as I get the time."

I noted that it was a library book, taken out three days before. If it was relevant to this meeting, Colonel Bryant had heard something that "might interest you" at least that long ago.

"General Attwater mentioned the book to me," he went on. He looked with disapproval at the sign I had placed on my wall. It was a quotation from Swinburne, and it read, "And all dead years draw thither, and all disastrous things." I felt it was rather appropriate for the Department of Ultimate Storage. That, or "Abandon hope, all ye who enter here."

"He's a bit of an egghead, like you," Bryant went on. "I figured you might have read *The Invisible Man*. You read all the time."

The last sentence meant, *You read too much, Jerry Macedo, and that's why your head is full of nonsense, like that stupid sign on your wall.*

"I've read it," I said. But the meeting was taking a very odd turn. General Jonas Attwater was Air Force, and head of three of the biggest "black" programs, secret developments with their own huge budgets that the American public never saw.

"Then you know that the book's about a man who takes a drug to make him invisible," Bryant said. "Three of General Attwater's staff scientists were in the meeting this morning, and they swear that such a thing is scientifically impossible. I wondered what you think."

"I agree with them."

He looked crushed, and I continued, "Think about it for a minute and you'll see why it can't work, even without getting deep into the physics. The drug is supposed to change human tissue so that it has the same refractive index as air. So your body wouldn't absorb light, or scatter it. Light would simply pass through you, without being reflected or refracted or affected in any way. But if your eyes didn't absorb light, you would be blind, because seeing involves the interaction of light with your retinas. And what about the food that you eat, while it's being digested? It would be visible in your alimentary canal, slowly changing as it went from your esophagus to your stomach and into your intestines. I'm sorry, Colonel, but the whole idea is just a piece of fiction."

"Yeah, I guess so." He didn't seem totally upset by my words. "It's impossible, I hear you."

He stood up. "Let's go to my office for a while. I want to show you something—unless you're all that busy."

It depended on the definition of "busy." I had been browsing the on-line physics preprints, as I did every morning of the week. Something very strange was going on with Bose-Einstein Condensates and macroscopic quantum systems, but it was evolving too rapidly for me to follow easily. There were new papers every day. In another week or two there ought to be a survey article that would make the development a lot clearer. Since I had no hope of doing original work in that field, the reading delay would cost me nothing. I followed Bryant in silence, up, up, up, all the way to the top floor. *I want to show you something* sounded to me an awful lot like *Gotcha!*, but I couldn't see how.

His staff assistants didn't react to my arrival. Colonel Bryant never came down to see me, but he summoned me up to see him often enough. It's a terrible thought, but I actually think the colonel likes me. Worse yet, I like him. I think there is a deep core of sadness in the man.

We entered his office, and he closed the door and gestured me to a chair. At that point we could just as well have been in the sub-basement levels. So many highly classified meetings were held in this room that any thought of windows was a complete no-no.

"Lois Doberman," he said. "What can you tell me about her?"

What could I tell, and what I was willing to tell, were two different things. Bryant knew that I had been Dr. Lois Doberman's boss when she first joined the Agency and we were both in the Office of Research and Development. Since then she had gone up through the structure like a rocket, while I had, somewhat more slowly, descended.

"You know what they say about Lois?" I was stalling a little, while I decided what I wanted to say. "If you ever make a crack suggesting that she's a dog, she'll bite your head off."

Not a trace of a smile from Bryant. Fair enough, because it didn't deserve one.

"Academic record," I went on. "Doctorate from UCLA, then two post-doc years with Berkner at Carnegie-Mellon. She had twenty-eight patents when she joined the Agency. Lord knows how many she has now. Properties of materials and optics are her specialty. I don't know what she's working on at the moment, but she's the smartest woman I ever met."

I considered the final statement, and amended it. "She's the smartest person I ever met."

"Some might say you are not an unbiased source. Staff Records show that you dated her for a while."

"That was nearly a year ago."

"There's also a strong rumor that you two were sleeping together, though that is not verified."

I said nothing, and he went on. "It was outside working hours and you both had the same clearances, so no one's worried about that. The thing is, General Attwater's staff thought you might know more than anyone else about her personal motives. That could be important."

"I don't see how. Her life and mine don't overlap any more."

"Nor does anyone else's. That's the trouble." And, when I stared at him because this was a message that I definitely could not read, "Lois Doberman has disappeared. One week ago. Sit tight, Jerry."

I had started to stand up.

"She didn't just disappear from home, or something like that." He was over at the viewgraph projector and video station used for presentations. "On Tuesday, June 25th, she went to work in the usual way. She was on a project that needed a special environment, and the only suitable place locally is out in Reston. Absolute top security, twenty-four-hour human security staff plus continuous machine surveillance. Only one entrance, except for emergency fire exits that show no sign of being disturbed. Anyone who goes into that building has to sign in and sign out, no matter how they are badged. Arrivals and departures are all recorded on tape.

"Sitting on the table in front of you is a photocopy of the sign in/sign out sheet for June 25th. Don't bother to look at it now"—I was reaching out—"take my word for it. Dr. Doberman signed in at 8:22 A.M., and she never signed out. Not only that, I have here the full set of tapes for arrivals and departures. The video-recorder is motion-activated. If you want to study the record, you can do it later. Here's the bottom line: there's a fine, clear sequence showing her arrival. There's nothing of her leaving."

"Then she must be still inside the building." That thought was terribly disturbing. If Lois had been inside for a full week, she must be dead.

"She's not inside, either dead or alive," he said, as though he had been reading my mind. "This is a fairly new building, and Attwater's office has exact detailed plans. There are no secret cubby-holes or places where someone could hide away. The whole complex has been searched four or five times. She's not in there. She's outside. We don't know how she got out."

"Nor do I."

Which actually meant, *All right, but why are you talking to me?* I guess that message-reading goes both ways, because Bryant said, "So far as we can tell, you are the last person with whom Dr. Doberman enjoyed a close personal relationship. I don't know if you can help, but I feel that you must try. As of this morning, sponsored by General Attwater's office, you and I have access to three additional SCI clearances."

I shifted in my chair. SCI. Special Compartmented Information. I had too many of those clearances already.

Walker Bryant turned on the viewgraph projector and put a transparency in place. "These briefing documents show what Dr. Lois Doberman had been working on at Reston. In a word, it's stealth technology in the area of imaging detection."

He glared at me, and on cue, I laughed. After *The Invisible Man*, his final comment had all the elements of farce. The whole idea of stealth technology is to make the object difficult to see. But it's usually either primitive visible-wavelength stuff, like special paints that match simple backgrounds, or else it's the use of materials with very low radar back-scatter. Most systems use active microwave—radar—for detection, so that's where most of the effort tends to go. The B-2 bomber is a wonderful example of failed stealth technology, since at most wavelengths it's as visible as Rush Limbaugh. But that didn't stop it being built, any more than the fact that stealth technology doesn't work well in visible wavelengths would stop a barrel of money being spent on it.

This sort of thing was one big reason why Lois and I had parted company. Once you are really inside the intelligence business, you know too much ever to be allowed to leave. You are there as firmly and finally as a fly in amber, and like the insect, not even death will free you. You are not allowed to say that some classified projects are absolute turkeys and a total waste of taxpayer money, because the party line is that they have value. Opinions to the contrary, expressed to Lois in long middle-of-the-night conversations, had convinced me that I would certainly fail my next polygraph (I didn't).

She disagreed with me. Not about the waste of money, which was undeniable, but about the possibility of escape. She said there must be a way out, if only you could find it. After dozens of arguments, in which she accused me of giving up and I accused her of useless dreaming, we had gone our separate ways; she ascending the management structure as though hoping to emerge from the top and fly free like a bird, me tunneling down deeper into the sub-basement levels like a blind and hopeless mole.

Had she found it, then, the Invisible Woman, the magic way out that would break all intelligence ties forever?

I couldn't see how, and the presentation was not helping. "What does fiber optics have to do with this?" I asked. That's what Walker Bryant had been putting on the screen for the past few minutes, while I was lost in memories. The latest viewgraph was a series of hand-drawn curves showing how the light loss over thin optic cables could, thanks to new technology, approach zero. That would be useful in communications and computers; but Lois hadn't been working in either area.

He shrugged at my question. "Damned if I know what any of these viewgraphs have to do with anything. I was hoping you might be able to tell me. These are taken straight from Lois Doberman's work books."

"They don't tell me anything so far," I said. "But keep going."

Unnecessary advice. Walker Bryant had risen in the military partly because he had lots of *sitzfleisch*, the patience and kidneys and mental strength to sit in a meeting for as long as it took to wear down the opposition. He had no intention of stopping. I, on the other hand, think I suffer from an undiagnosed hyperactivity. I work a lot better when I am free to wander around.

I did that now, pacing back and forward in front of his desk. He gave me another glare, but he went right on with the viewgraphs. Now they showed notes in Lois's familiar handwriting about new imaging sensors, pointing out that they could be built smaller than the head of a pin. I noticed that the page numbers were not sequential.

"Who decided what to pull out and show as viewgraphs?" I asked.

"Rich Williamson. Why? Do you think he might have missed something?"

"Rich is good—in his field. But he's a SWIR specialist."

"Mm?"

"Short-wave infrared. From about one to five micrometers. Visible light wavelengths are shorter, around half a micrometer. But if Lois made a tarnhelm—"

"A what?"

"Don't worry about it. If Lois is invisible, then the visible wavelength region is where we ought to be looking. Anyway, I'd much rather see her original notebooks than someone else's ideas as to what's important in them."

"It would have to be done out in Reston. The notebooks can't be removed." He sounded and was disgusted. To Walker Bryant, everything important took place either on a battlefield, or inside the Beltway. Reston, twenty-five miles away from us, was a point at infinity.

"Fine. We'll go to Reston."

"You can go there this afternoon, Jerry. You won't need me. But there are things outside the notebooks."

He turned off the projector and went to the VCR next to it, while I kept pacing.

"I said we don't know how she got out," he said. "It's more than that. We have proof positive that she is outside. We learned today that she's still in the Washington area, and we even have some idea of her movements."

Which must have been a huge relief to the Security people. They always have one big fear when someone vanishes. It's not that the person is dead, which is unfortunate but ends security risk. It's that the person is alive and well and headed out of the country, either voluntarily or packed away unconscious in a crate, to serve some other nation.

I shared their feeling of relief. From Bryant's tone, Lois wasn't a corpse being trundled from place to place. She was moving under her own volition.

"Stand still for a minute," he went on, "and take a look at this. We've patched together six different recordings from ATM devices at local banks, withdrawals made over the past four days. As you know, every time someone makes a deposit or a withdrawal at an ATM it's captured on videotape. Standard crime-fighting technique. Withdrawals from Lois Doberman's account were made at six different machines. Watch closely."

A man I had never seen before was standing in front of the bank's camera. He worked the ATM, stood counting notes for a moment, and left. Soon afterwards a woman—certainly not Lois—stood in his place. She made a deposit, adjusted her hat in the reflection provided by the ATM's polished front, and vanished from the camera's field of view.

I watched as the same scene was repeated five more times, with variations in customers as to age, height, weight, color, and clothing. Each sequence showed two different people making successive ATM transactions. One man was immortalized in intelligence security files in the act of picking his nose, another hit the machine when something, apparently his account balance, was not to his liking. Of Lois Doberman there was not a sign.

"Normal operations at an ATM facility," Bryant said when the tape ended in a flicker of black and white video noise. "Except for one thing. In each case, Lois Doberman made a withdrawal from one of her bank accounts—she maintains several—*between* the people that you saw. We have the printouts of activity, which you can examine if you want to, and they are all the same: a normal transaction, with a picture of the person; then a Lois Doberman cash withdrawal, with no one at all showing on the videocamera; and then another normal transaction, including a person's picture."

"The Invisible Woman," I said.

Bryant nodded. "And the big question: How is she doing it?"

It was the wrong question, at least for me. I already had vague ideas as to a possible how. As I drove out of the District on my way to Reston, I pondered the deeper mystery: *Why* was Lois doing this?

I did not believe for a moment that she was any kind of security risk. We had long agreed that our own intelligence service was the worst one possible—except for all others. She would never work for anyone else. But if she stayed around the local area, she was bound to be caught. Fooling around with the ATM's, for half a dozen withdrawals of less than a hundred dollars each, was like putting out a notice: Catch me if you can!

Twenty-four-hour surveillance of the relevant ATM's was next on the list. Her apartment was already under constant surveillance, so clearly Lois was living somewhere else. But I knew the lure of her own books and tapes, and how much she hated living out of a suitcase.

I took my foot off the accelerator—I was doing nearly seventy-five—and forced my thoughts back a step. *Was* Lois living somewhere else? If she wanted to show off her new idea, what better way than living in her own place, coming and going under the very nose of Security and flaunting their inability to catch her?

And my inability, too. Lois surely knew that if she disappeared, I would be called in. We had been too close for me to be ignored. I could imagine her face, and her expression as she threw me the challenge: *Let's see you catch me, Jerry—before the rest catch on.*

If I was right, others *would* catch on within the next few days. There were some very bright people in R&D, smarter than me and shackled by only one factor: compartmenting. The idea behind it sounds perfectly logical, and derives directly from the espionage and revolution business. *Keep the cells small. A person should not be told more than he or she needs to know.*

The trouble is, if science is to be any good it has to operate with exactly the opposite philosophy. Advances come from cross-fertilization, from recognizing relationships between fields that at first sight have little to do with each other.

I had broken my pick on that particular issue, after fights with my bosses so prolonged and bitter that I had been removed completely from research programs. My job with Walker Bryant now allowed me to cross all fields of science, but at a price: I myself worked in none. However, I had not changed my mind.

The afternoon at Reston gave me enough time for a first look-through of Lois's notebooks. She used them as a combined diary and work file, with a running log of anything that caught her interest. To someone who did not know her well they would seem a random hodge-podge of entries. Rich Williamson had done his best, but he had not pulled out anything that seemed to him totally irrelevant.

I knew how tightly the inside of Lois's head was inter-connected. An entry about the skin of reptiles followed one about fiber optics. Human eye sensitivity and its performance at different ambient light levels shared space with radar cross-section data. A note on sensor quantum efficiency sat on the same page as an apparently unrelated diagram that showed the layout of a room's light sources and shadows, while specifications for a new gigacircuit processing chip lay next to a note on temperature-dependent optical properties of organic compounds. Chances were, they all represented part of some continuous thought pattern.

I also knew that Lois was conscientious. Asked to look into stealth techniques, her days and much of her nights would have been devoted to the present—and future—limits of that technology.

At five o'clock I drove back as far as Rosslyn and signed out a small piece of unclassified equipment from one of the labs. I ate dinner at a fast food place close to the Metro, browsing through Bryant's library copy of *The Invisible Man*. When I left I bought a chicken salad sandwich and a coke to take away with me. It might be a long night.

By six o'clock I was sitting in my car on Cathedral Avenue, engine off and driver's window open. It was a "No Parking" spot right in front of Lois's apartment building. If any policeman came by I would pretend that I had just dropped someone off, and drive around the block.

I wasn't the only one interested in the entrance. A man sat on a bench across the street and showed no signs of moving, while a blue car with a Virginia license plate drove by every few minutes. Dusk was steadily creeping closer. Half an hour more, and the street lights would go on. Before that happened, the air temperature would drop and the open doors of the apartment building would close.

The urge to look out of the car window was strong. I resisted, and kept my eye fixed on the little oblong screen at the rear end of the instrument I was holding. It was no bigger than a camera's viewfinder, but the tiny screen was split in two. On the left was a standard video camera image of the building entrance. On the right was another version of the same scene, this one rendered in ghostly black and white. Everyone walking by, or entering the building, appeared in both pictures.

Or almost everyone. At 6:45 precisely, a human form showed on the right hand screen only. I looked up to the building entrance, and saw no one. But I called out, softly enough to be inaudible to the man across the street, "Lois! Over here. Get in the car. Wait until I open the door for you."

I saw and heard nothing. But I got out, went around the car, and opened the passenger door. Then I stood waiting and feeling like a fool, while nothing at all seemed to be happening. Finally I smelled perfume. The car settled a little lower on its springs.

"I'm in," whispered Lois's voice. I closed the door, went back to my side, and started the engine. The man across the street had watched everything, but he had seen nothing. He did not move as I pulled away.

I glanced to my right. No one seemed to be there, because through the right-side car window I could see the buildings as we passed them. The only oddity was the passenger seat of the car. Instead of the usual blue fabric, I saw a round grey-black patch about a foot and a half across.

"I'm alone and we're not being followed," I said. "Take it off if you want to. Unless of course you're naked underneath it."

"I'm not." There was a soft ripping noise. "You already knew that if you think about it."

I had to stop the car. It was that or cause a pile-up, because the urge to turn and watch was irresistible.

"I guessed it," I said. "No clothes were found in the building in Reston, so you had to be able to put whatever it is over them."

It was close to dusk, and I had pulled the car into a parking lot underneath a spreading oak tree. As I stared at the passenger seat, a patch of fair hair suddenly appeared from nowhere against the upper part of the passenger window. The whole background rippled and deformed as the patch grew to reveal Lois's forehead, face, and chin. As her neck came into view there was a final wave of distortion, and suddenly I was looking at Lois, dressed in a rather bulky body suit.

"Too much work for the microprocessors," she said, and pushed her hair off her forehead with her hands. "When you put too great a load on them, they quit trying."

She peeled off the suit, first down to her waist, then off her arms and hands, and finally from her legs and feet. She was wearing an outfit of thin silk and flexible flat-heeled loafers. In her hands the suit had become an unimpressive bundle of mottled gray and white. She stared down at it. "Still needs work. For one thing, it's too hot inside."

"That's how I knew you were there." I picked up the instrument I had been using. "I didn't know how you were doing it—I really still don't—but I knew a living human has to be at 98.6. This instrument senses in thermal infrared wavelengths, so it picked up your body heat image. But it didn't show a thing at visible wavelengths."

"Anyone in the suit is invisible out to wavelengths of about one micron—enough so they don't show in visible light or near infrared." She hefted the suit. "On the other hand, this is a first-generation effort using silicon sensors. I could probably do a lot better with something like gallium arsenide, but I'll still have a thermal signature. And if I move too fast or make unusual movements, the processors can't keep up and the whole system fails."

"And it's not a great idea to wear perfume. That's when I was absolutely sure it was you. Want to tell me how it works? I have an idea what's going on, but it's pretty rough."

"How much time did you spend with my notebooks?"

"Half a day."

"Take two more days, and you'd work it all out for yourself. But I'll save you the effort." She tapped the copy of *The Invisible Man*, sitting where I had left it on top of my dashboard. "Wells could have done better, even in 1900. He knew that animals in nature do their best to be invisible to their prey or their predators. But they don't do it by fiddling around with their own optical properties, which just won't work. They know that they are invisible if they look exactly like their background. The chameleon has the right idea, but it's hardware-limited. It can only make modest color and pattern adjustments. It occurred to me that humans ought to be able to do a whole lot better. You'd got this far?"

"Pretty much." I saw a patrol car slow down as it passed us, and I started the engine and pulled out into the street. "The suit takes images of the scene behind you, and assigns the colors and intensities to liquid crystal displays on the front of the suit. Somebody fifteen to twenty feet away will see the background scene. The suit also has to do the same thing to the back, so someone behind you will see an exact match to the scene in front of you. The problem I have is that the trick has to work from any angle. I couldn't see any way that fiber optic bundles could handle that."

"They can't. I tried that road for quite a while, but as you say, optical fibers don't have the flexibility to look different from every angle. I only use them to allow me to see when I'm inside. An array of pinhole-sized openings scattered over the front of the suit feeds light through optical fibers to form images on a pair of goggles. Straightforward. The invisibility trick is more difficult. You have to use holographic methods to handle multi-angle reflectances, and you need large amounts of computing power to keep track of changing geometry—otherwise a person would be invisible only when standing perfectly still." Lois touched the bundled suit. "There are scores of microprocessors on every square centimeter, all networked to each other. I figure there's more computing power in this thing than there was in the whole world in 1970. And it still crashes if I move faster than a walk, or get into a situation with complex lighting and shadows. Uniform, low-level illumination and relatively uniform backgrounds are best—like tonight." She cocked her head at me, with a very odd expression in her eyes. "So. What do you think, Jerry?"

I looked at her with total admiration and five sorts of misgiving. "I think what you have done is wonderful. I think you are wonderful. But there's no way you can hide this. If I'm here a day or two ahead of everyone else, it's only because I know you better than they do."

"No. It's because you're smart, and compartmenting of ideas drives you crazy, and you refuse to do it. It would take the others weeks, Jerry. But I had no intention of hiding this—otherwise I would never have stayed in the Washington area. Tomorrow I'll go in to work as usual, and I can't wait to see their faces."

"But after what you've done—" I paused. What *had* she done? Failed to sign out of a building when she left. Disappeared for a week without notifying her superiors. Removed government property from secure premises without approval. But she could say, what better practical test could there be for her invention, than to become invisible to her own organization?

Her bosses might make Lois endure a formal hearing on her actions, and they would certainly put a nasty note in her file. That would be it. She was far too valuable for them to do much more. Lois would be all right.

"What now?" I said. "You can't go back to your own apartment without being seen, even if you put the suit back on. It's dark, and the doors will be closed."

"So?"

"Come home with me, Lois. You'll be safe there."

That produced the longest pause since she had stepped invisible into my car. Finally she shook her head.

"I'd really like to, but not tonight. I'll take a rain check. I promise."

"So where do we go?"

"You go home. Me, you drop off at the next corner."

I was tempted to say that I couldn't do it, that she didn't have her suit on. But living in a city with over half a million people confers its own form of invisibility. Provided that Lois stayed away from her apartment, the chance that she would be seen tonight by anyone who knew her was close to zero. And she still had the suit if she felt like using it.

I halted the car at the next corner and she stepped out, still holding the drab bundle. She gave me a little smile and a wave, and gestured at me to drive on.

Next morning I was in my sub-basement department exactly on time. I called Lois's office. She was not there. I kept calling every few minutes.

She was still not there at midday, or later in the afternoon, or ever again.

This time there were no telltale ATM withdrawals, no hints that she might still be in the local area. Some time during the night she had been back to Reston, entered the building with its round-the-clock surveillance, and removed her notebooks. In their place sat a single sheet of white cardboard. It bore the words, in Lois's handwriting, "I know why the caged bird sings."

That sheet was discussed in a hundred meetings over the next few weeks. It was subjected to all kinds of chemical and physical analysis, which proved conclusively that it was simple cardboard. No one seemed to know what it meant.

I know, of course. It is a message from Lois to me, and the words mean, *It can be done. There is a way out, even from the deepest dungeon or highest tower.*

I told everything I knew about the invisibility suit. Other staff scientists rushed off excitedly to try to duplicate it. I came back to the Department of Ultimate Storage, to the old routine.

But there is a difference—two differences. First, I am working harder than ever in my life, and now it is toward a definite goal. Not only is there a way out, but Lois assures me that I can find it; otherwise, she would never have promised a rain check.

The second difference is in Walker Bryant. He leaves me almost totally free of duties, but he comes frequently down from his office to mine. He says little, but he sits and stares at me as I work. In his eyes I sometimes detect a strange, wistful gleam that I never noticed before. I think he knows that there was more to my meeting with Lois than I have admitted, and I think he even suspects what it may have been.

I will leave him a message when I go. I don't know what it will say yet, but it must be something that he can understand and eventually act upon. Even Air Force colonels deserve hope.

BICYCLE REPAIRMAN

Bruce Sterling

Bruce Sterling (born 1954) began his career with the novels *Involution Ocean* (1977) and *The Artificial Kid* (1980). In the early eighties he became the center of a literary dust storm by publishing the fanzine *Cheap Truth* under the pseudonym Vincent Omniaveritas (available on the Web at www.io.com/~ftp/usr/shiva/SMOF-BBS/cheap.truth). The first issue was mainly an attack on fantasy: "As American SF lies in a reptilian torpor, its small, squishy cousin, Fantasy, creeps gecko-like across the bookstands." For four or five issues, Sterling attacked fiction he found irritating and praised a wide variety of books (most issues had a "Cheap Truth Top Ten" list) with descriptions like these: *Past Master* by R.A. Lafferty—"His most decipherable SF novel"—or *A World Out of Time* by Larry Niven—"Heartening indication that Niven may escape total artistic collapse." Eventually, Sterling came round to the rhetoric for which he is most known and *Cheap Truth* evolved into the propaganda organ for the movement later known as cyberpunk. When laying out *Cheap Truth #6*, he took a pair of scissors to a photocopy of David Pringle and Colin Greenland's editorial in *Interzone #8* (Summer, 1984), which read:

> Last issue we described *Interzone* as a magazine of *radical* science fiction and fantasy. Now we should like to go further and outline (however hazily) a type of story that we want to see much more of in this magazine: the *radical, hard* SF story. We wish to publish more fiction which takes its inspiration from science, and which uses the language of science in a creative way. It may be fantastic, surrealistic, "illogical," but in order to be radical *hard* SF it should explore in some fashion the perspectives opened up by contemporary science and technology. Some would argue that the new electronic gadgetry is displacing the printed word—if so, writers should fight back, using guerrilla tactics as necessary and infiltrating the territory of the enemy.

At the time, Sterling was one of only a handful of U.S. subscribers to *Interzone*, and set out to spread this gospel in the U.S. The *Cheap Truth #6* editorial, created using rubber cement and Burroughsian cut-up technique, read:

> EDITORIAL. radical, hard SF
> seeing signs that something new is imminent—
> new fiction from the bounty of new technology.
> ///the perspectives opened up by contemporary science fight back, using guerilla tactics
> new information systems f/a/s/h/i/o/n that new science fiction
> for the *electronic age*

Thus, in the U.S. *Radical Hard SF* was one of the early names for the Movement that editor Gardner Dozois later christened *cyberpunk*. Later cyberpunk fiction was characterized by a particular attitude, specific literary furniture, and a fetish for new technology but early on—in Sterling's vision—it had centrally to do with reinventing hard SF. Of those writers identified with early cyberpunk to whom the term stuck, Sterling is the one most interested in science.

The novel *Schismatrix* (1985) and the related stories that made him famous were re-released in 1996 as *Schismatrix Plus*. He collaborated with William Gibson on *The Difference Engine* (1990), became a media figure who appeared on the cover of *Wired*, became a journalist who wrote the exposé *The Hacker Crackdown* (1992), and returned to nearly full-time commitment to science fiction in 1995, with a new explosion of stories and novels, including *Heavy Weather* (1994), *Holy Fire* (1996), and *Distraction* (1998). His most recent novel, *Zeitgeist* (2000), is fantasy.

This story first appeared in John Kessel and Mark Van Name's anthology of speculative fiction writing from the Sycamore Hill writers' workshop, *Intersections*. It's a story growing out of the sensibility of cyberpunk, and not without some ironic commentary on cyberpunk along the way. It's about a messy, high-tech future, gritty and paranoid, lubricated by some of those good old genre juices that have kept science fiction alive and growing in this decade.

Repeated tinny banging woke Lyle in his hammock. Lyle groaned, sat up, and slid free into the tool-crowded aisle of his bike shop.

Lyle hitched up the black elastic of his skintight shorts and plucked yesterday's grease-stained sleeveless off the workbench. He glanced blearily at his chronometer as he picked his way toward the door. It was 10:04.38 in the morning, June 27, 2037.

Lyle hopped over a stray can of primer and the floor boomed gently beneath his feet. With all the press of work, he'd collapsed into sleep without properly cleaning the shop. Doing custom enameling paid okay, but it ate up time like crazy. Working and living alone was wearing him out.

Lyle opened the shop door, revealing a long sheer drop to dusty tiling far below. Pigeons darted beneath the hull of his shop through a soot-stained hole in the broken atrium glass, and wheeled off to their rookery somewhere in the darkened guts of the high-rise.

More banging. Far below, a uniformed delivery kid stood by his cargo tricycle, yanking rhythmically at the long dangling string of Lyle's spot-welded doorknocker.

Lyle waved, yawning. From his vantage point below the huge girders of the cavernous atrium, Lyle had a fine overview of three burnt-out interior levels of the old Tsatanuga Archiplat. Once-elegant handrails and battered pedestrian overlooks fronted on the great airy cavity of the atrium. Behind the handrails was a three-floor wilderness of jury-rigged lights, chicken coops, water tanks, and squatters' flags. The fire-damaged floors, walls, and ceilings were riddled with handmade descent-chutes, long coiling staircases, and rickety ladders.

Lyle took note of a crew of Chattanooga demolition workers in their yellow detox suits. The repair crew was deploying vacuum scrubbers and a high-pressure hose-off by the vandal-proofed western elevators of Floor Thirty-four. Two or three days a week, the city crew meandered into the damage zone to pretend to work, with a great hypocritical show of sawhorses and barrier tape. The lazy sons of bitches were all on the take.

Lyle thumbed the brake switches in their big metal box by the flywheel. The bike shop slithered, with a subtle hiss of cable-clamps, down three stories, to dock with a grating crunch onto four concrete-filled metal drums.

The delivery kid looked real familiar. He was in and out of the zone pretty often. Lyle had once done some custom work on the kid's cargo trike, new shocks and some granny-gearing as he recalled, but he couldn't remember the kid's name. Lyle was terrible with names. "What's up, zude?"

"Hard night, Lyle?"

"Just real busy."

The kid's nose wrinkled at the stench from the shop. "Doin' a lot of paint work, huh?" He glanced at his palmtop notepad. "You still taking deliveries for Edward Dertouzas?"

"Yeah. I guess so." Lyle rubbed the gear tattoo on one stubbled cheek. "If I have to."

The kid offered a stylus, reaching up. "Can you sign for him?"

Lyle folded his bare arms warily. "Naw, man, I can't sign for Deep Eddy. Eddy's in Europe somewhere. Eddy left months ago. Haven't seen Eddy in ages."

The delivery kid scratched his sweating head below his billed fabric cap. He turned to check for any possible sneak-ups by snatch-and-grab artists out of the squatter warrens. The government simply refused to do postal delivery on the Thirty-second, Thirty-third, and Thirty-fourth floors. You never saw many cops inside the zone, either. Except for the city demolition crew, about the only official functionaries who ever showed up in the zone were a few psychotically empathetic NAFTA social workers.

"I'll get a bonus if you sign for this thing." The kid gazed up in squint-eyed appeal. "It's gotta be worth something, Lyle. It's a really weird kind of routing; they paid a lot of money to send it just that way."

Lyle crouched down in the open doorway. "Let's have a look at it."

The package was a heavy shockproof rectangle in heat-sealed plastic shrinkwrap, with a plethora of intra-European routing stickers. To judge by all the overlays, the package had been passed from postal system to postal system at least eight times before officially arriving in the legal custody of any human being. The return address, if there had ever been one, was completely obscured. Someplace in France, maybe.

Lyle held the box up two-handed to his ear and shook it. Hardware.

"You gonna sign, or not?"

"Yeah." Lyle scratched illegibly at the little signature panel, then looked at the delivery trike. "You oughta get that front wheel trued."

The kid shrugged. "Got anything to send out today?"

"Naw," Lyle grumbled, "I'm not doing mail-order repair work anymore; it's too complicated and I get ripped off too much."

"Suit yourself." The kid clambered into the recumbent seat of his trike and pedaled off across the heat-cracked ceramic tiles of the atrium plaza.

Lyle hung his hand-lettered OPEN FOR BUSINESS sign outside the door. He walked to his left, stamped up the pedaled lid of a jumbo garbage can, and dropped the package in with the rest of Dertouzas's stuff.

The can's lid wouldn't close. Deep Eddy's junk had finally reached critical mass. Deep Eddy never got much mail at the shop from other people, but he was always sending mail to himself. Big packets of encrypted diskettes were always arriving from Eddy's road jaunts in Toulouse, Marseilles, Valencia, and Nice. And especially Barcelona. Eddy had sent enough gigabyteage out of Barcelona to outfit a pirate data-haven.

Eddy used Lyle's bike shop as his safety-deposit box. This arrangement was okay by Lyle. He owed Eddy; Eddy had installed the phones and virching in the bike shop, and had also wangled the shop's electrical hookup. A thick elastic curly-cable snaked out the access crawlspace of Floor Thirty-five, right through the ceiling of Floor Thirty-four, and directly through a ragged punch-hole in the aluminum roof of Lyle's cable-mounted mobile home. Some unknown contact of Eddy's was paying the real bills on that electrical feed. Lyle cheerfully covered the expenses by paying cash into an anonymous post-office box. The setup was a rare and valuable contact with the world of organized authority.

During his stays in the shop, Eddy had spent much of his time buried in marathon long-distance virtuality sessions, swaddled head to foot in lumpy strap-on gear. Eddy had been painfully involved with some older woman in Germany. A virtual romance in its full-scale thumping, heaving, grappling progress, was an embarrassment to witness. Under the circumstances, Lyle wasn't too surprised that Eddy had left his parents' condo to set up in a squat.

Eddy had lived in the bicycle-repair shop, off and on, for almost a year. It had been a good deal for Lyle, because Deep Eddy had enjoyed a certain clout and prestige with the local squatters. Eddy had been a major organizer of the legendary Chattanooga Wende of December '35, a monster street party that had climaxed in a spectacular looting-and-arson rampage that had torched the three floors of the Archiplat.

Lyle had gone to school with Eddy and had known him for years; they'd grown up together in the Archiplat. Eddy Dertouzas was a deep zude for a kid his age, with political contacts and heavy-duty network connections. The squat had been a good deal for both of them, until Eddy had finally coaxed the German woman into coming through for him in real life. Then Eddy had jumped the next plane to Europe.

Since they'd parted friends, Eddy was welcome to mail his European data-junk to the bike shop. After all, the disks were heavily encrypted, so it wasn't as if anybody in authority was ever gonna be able to read them. Storing a few thousand disks was a minor challenge, compared to Eddy's complex, machine-assisted love life.

After Eddy's sudden departure, Lyle had sold Eddy's possessions, and wired the money to Eddy in Spain. Lyle had kept the screen TV, Eddy's mediator, and the cheaper virching helmet. The way Lyle figured it—the way he remembered the deal—any stray hardware of Eddy's in the shop was rightfully his, for disposal at his own discretion. By now it was pretty clear that Deep Eddy Dertouzas was never coming back to Tennessee. And Lyle had certain debts.

Lyle snicked the blade from a roadkit multitool and cut open Eddy's package. It contained, of all things, a television cable set-top box. A laughable infobahn antique. You'd never see a cable box like that in NAFTA; this was the sort of primeval junk one might find in the home of a semiliterate Basque grandmother, or maybe in the armed bunker of some backward Albanian.

Lyle tossed the archaic cable box onto the beanbag in front of the wallscreen. No time now for irrelevant media toys; he had to get on with real life. Lyle ducked into the tiny curtained privy and urinated at length into a crockery jar. He scraped his teeth with a flossing spudger and misted some fresh water onto his face and hands. He wiped clean with a towelette, then smeared his armpits, crotch, and feet with deodorant.

Back when he'd lived with his mom up on Floor Forty-one, Lyle had used old-fashioned antiseptic deodorants. Lyle had wised up about a lot of things once he'd escaped his mom's condo. Nowadays, Lyle used a gel roll-on of skin-friendly bacteria that greedily devoured human sweat and exuded as their metabolic by-product a pleasantly harmless reek rather like ripe bananas. Life was a lot easier when you came to proper terms with your microscopic flora.

Back at his workbench, Lyle plugged in the hot plate and boiled some Thai noodles with flaked sardines. He packed down breakfast with four hundred cc's of Dr. Breasaire's Bioactive Bowel Putty. Then he checked last night's enamel job on the clamped frame in the workstand. The frame looked good. At three in the morning, Lyle was able to get into painted detail work with just the right kind of hallucinatory clarity.

Enameling paid well, and he needed the money bad. But this wasn't real bike work. It lacked authenticity. Enameling was all about the owner's ego—that was what really stank about enameling. There were a few rich kids up in the penthouse levels who were way into "street aesthetic," and would pay good money to have some treadhead decorate their machine. But flash art didn't help the bike. What helped the bike was frame alignment and sound cable-housings and proper tension in the derailleurs.

Lyle fitted the chain of his stationary bike to the shop's flywheel, straddled up, strapped on his gloves and virching helmet, and did half an hour on the 2033 Tour de France. He stayed back in the pack for the uphill grind, and then, for three glorious minutes, he broke free from the *domestiques* in the *peloton* and came right up at the shoulder of Aldo Cipollini. The champion was a monster, posthuman. Calves like cinder blocks. Even in a cheap simulation with no full-impact bodysuit, Lyle knew better than to try to take Cipollini.

Lyle devirched, checked his heart-rate record on the chronometer, then dismounted from his stationary trainer and drained a half-liter squeeze bottle of antioxidant carbo refresher. Life had been easier when he'd had a partner in crime. The shop's flywheel was slowly losing its storage of inertia power these days, with just one zude pumping it.

Lyle's disastrous second roommate had come from the biking crowd. She was a criterium racer from Kentucky named Brigitte Rohannon. Lyle himself had been a wannabe criterium racer for a while, before he'd blown out a kidney on steroids. He hadn't expected any trouble from Brigitte, because Brigitte knew about bikes, and she needed his technical help for her racer, and she wouldn't mind pumping the flywheel, and besides, Brigitte was lesbian. In the training gym and out at racing events, Brigitte came across as a quiet and disciplined little politicized tread-head person.

Life inside the zone, though, massively fertilized Brigitte's eccentricities. First, she started breaking training. Then she stopped eating right. Pretty soon the shop was creaking and rocking with all-night girl-on-girl hot-oil sessions, which degenerated into hooting pill-orgies with heavily tattooed zone chyx who played klaxonized bongo music and beat each other up, and stole Lyle's tools. It had been a big relief when Brigitte finally left the zone to shack up with some well-to-do admirer on Floor Thirty-seven. The debacle had left Lyle's tenuous finances in ruin.

Lyle laid down a new tracery of scarlet enamel on the bike's chainstay, seat post and stem. He had to wait for the work to cure, so he left the workbench, picked up Eddy's set-topper, and popped the shell with a hexkey. Lyle was no electrician, but the insides looked harmless enough: lots of bit-eating caterpillars and cheap Algerian silicon.

He flicked on Eddy's mediator, to boot the wallscreen. Before he could try anything with the cable box, his mother's mook pounced upon the screen. On Eddy's giant wallscreen, the mook's waxy, computer-generated face looked like a plump satin pillowcase. Its bowtie was as big as a racing shoe.

"Please hold for an incoming vidcall from Andrea Schweik of Carnac Instruments," the mook uttered unctuously.

Lyle cordially despised all low-down, phone-tagging, artificially intelligent mooks. For a while, in his teenage years, Lyle himself had owned a mook, an off-the-shelf shareware job that he'd installed in the condo's phone. Like most mooks, Lyle's mook had one primary role: dealing with unsolicited phone calls from other people's mooks. In Lyle's case these were the creepy mooks of career counselors, school psychiatrists, truancy cops, and other official hindrances. When Lyle's mook launched and ran, it appeared on-line as a sly warty dwarf that drooled green ichor and talked in a basso grumble.

But Lyle hadn't given his mook the properly meticulous care and debugging that such fragile little constructs demanded, and eventually his cheap mook had collapsed into artificial insanity.

Once Lyle had escaped his mom's place to the squat, he had gone for the low-tech gambit and simply left his phone unplugged most of the time. But that was no real solution. He couldn't hide from his mother's capable and well-financed corporate mook, which watched with sleepless mechanical patience for the least flicker of video dial tone off Lyle's number.

Lyle sighed and wiped the dust from the video nozzle on Eddy's mediator.

"Your mother is coming on-line right away," the mook assured him.

"Yeah, sure," Lyle muttered, smearing his hair into some semblance of order.

"She specifically instructed me to page her remotely at any time for an immediate response. She really wants to chat with you, Lyle."

"That's just great." Lyle couldn't remember what his mother's mook called itself. "Mr. Billy," or "Mr. Ripley," or something else really stupid. . . .

"Did you know that Marco Cengialta has just won the Liege Summer Classic?"

Lyle blinked and sat up in the beanbag. "Yeah?"

"Mr. Cengialta used a three-spoked ceramic wheel with internal liquid weighting and buckyball hubshocks." The mook paused, politely awaiting a possible conversational response. "He wore breathe-thru Kevlar microlock cleatshoes," it added.

Lyle hated the way a mook cataloged your personal interests and then generated relevant conversation. The machine-made intercourse was completely unhuman and yet perversely interesting, like being grabbed and buttonholed by a glossy magazine ad. It had probably taken his mother's mook all of three seconds to snag and download every conceivable statistic about the summer race in Liege.

His mother came on. She'd caught him during lunch in her office. "Lyle?"

"Hi, Mom." Lyle sternly reminded himself that this was the one person in the world who might conceivably put up bail for him. "What's on your mind?"

"Oh, nothing much, just the usual." Lyle's mother shoved aside her platter of sprouts and tilapia. "I was idly wondering if you were still alive."

"Mom, it's a lot less dangerous in a squat than landlords and cops would have you believe. I'm perfectly fine. You can see that for yourself."

His mother lifted a pair of secretarial half-spex on a neckchain, and gave Lyle the computer-assisted once-over.

Lyle pointed the mediator's lens at the shop's aluminum door. "See over there, Mom? I got myself a shock-baton in here. If I get any trouble from anybody, I'll just yank that club off the door mount and give the guy fifteen thousand volts!"

"Is that legal, Lyle?"

"Sure. The voltage won't kill you or anything, it just knocks you out a good long time. I traded a good bike for that shock-baton, it's got a lot of useful defensive features."

"That sounds really dreadful."

"The baton's harmless, Mom. You should see what the cops carry nowadays."

"Are you still taking those injections, Lyle?"

"Which injections?"

She frowned. "You know which ones."

Lyle shrugged. "The treatments are perfectly safe. They're a lot safer than a lifestyle of cruising for dates, that's for sure."

"Especially dates with the kind of girls who live down there in the riot zone, I suppose." His mother winced. "I had some hopes when you took up with that nice bike-racer girl. Brigitte, wasn't it? Whatever happened to her?"

Lyle shook his head. "Someone with your gender and background oughta understand how important the treatments are, Mom. It's a basic reproductive-freedom issue. Antilibidinals give you real freedom, freedom from the urge to reproduce. You should be glad I'm not sexually involved."

"I don't mind that you're not involved, Lyle, it's just that it seems like a real cheat that you're not even *interested*."

"But, Mom, nobody's interested in me, either. Nobody. No woman is banging at my door to have sex with a self-employed fanatical dropout bike mechanic who lives in a slum. If that ever happens, you'll be the first to know."

Lyle grinned cheerfully into the lens. "I had girlfriends back when I was in racing. I've been there, Mom. I've done that. Unless you're coked to the gills with hormones, sex is a major waste of your time and attention. Sexual Deliberation is the greatest civil-liberties movement of modern times."

"That's really weird, Lyle. It's just not natural."

"Mom, forgive me, but you're not the one to talk about natural, okay? You grew me from a zygote when you were fifty-five." He shrugged. "I'm too busy for romance now. I just want to learn about bikes."

"You were working with bikes when you lived here with me. You had a real job and a safe home where you could take regular showers."

"Sure, I was working, but I never said I wanted a *job*, Mom. I said I wanted to *learn about bikes*. There's a big difference! I can't be a loser wage-slave for some lousy bike franchise."

His mother said nothing.

"Mom, I'm not asking you for any favors. I don't need any bosses, or any teachers, or any landlords, or any cops. It's just me and my bike work down here. I know that people in authority can't stand it that a twenty-four-year-old man lives an independent life and does exactly what he wants, but I'm being very quiet and discreet about it, so nobody needs to bother about me."

His mother sighed, defeated. "Are you eating properly, Lyle? You look peaked."

Lyle lifted his calf muscle into camera range. "Look at this leg! Does that look like the gastrocnemius of a weak and sickly person?"

"Could you come up to the condo and have a decent meal with me sometime?"

Lyle blinked. "When?"

"Wednesday, maybe? We could have pork chops."

"Maybe, Mom. Probably. I'll have to check. I'll get back to you, okay? Bye." Lyle hung up.

Hooking the mediator's cable to the primitive set-top box was a problem, but Lyle was not one to be stymied by a merely mechanical challenge. The enamel job had to wait as he resorted to miniclamps and a cable cutter. It was a handy thing that working with modern brake cabling had taught him how to splice fiber optics.

When the set-top box finally came on-line, its array of services was a joke. Any decent modern mediator could navigate through vast information spaces, but the set-top box offered nothing but "channels." Lyle had forgotten that you could even obtain old-fashioned "channels" from the city fiber-feed in Chattanooga. But these channels were government-sponsored media, and the government was always quite a ways behind the curve in network development. Chattanooga's huge fiber-bandwidth still carried the ancient government-mandated "public-access channels," spooling away in their technically fossilized obscurity, far below the usual gaudy carnival of popular virching, infobahnage, demo-splintered comboards, public-service rants, mudtrufflage, remsnorkeling, and commercials.

The little set-top box accessed nothing but political channels. Three of them: Legislative, Judicial, and Executive. And that was the sum total, apparently. A set-top box that offered nothing but NAFTA political coverage. On the Legislative Channel there was some kind of parliamentary debate on proper land use in Manitoba. On the Judicial Channel, a lawyer was haranguing judges about the stock market for air-pollution rights. On the Executive Channel, a big crowd of hicks was idly standing around on windblown tarmac somewhere in Louisiana waiting for something to happen.

The box didn't offer any glimpse of politics in Europe or the Sphere or the South. There were no hotspots or pips or index tagging. You couldn't look stuff up or annotate it—you just had to passively watch whatever the channel's masters chose to show you, whenever they chose to show it. This media setup was so insultingly lame and halt and primitive that it was almost perversely interesting. Kind of like peering through keyholes.

Lyle left the box on the Executive Channel, because it looked conceivable that something might actually happen there. It had swiftly become clear to him that the intolerably monotonous fodder on the other two channels was about as exciting as those channels ever got. Lyle retreated to his workbench and got back to enamel work.

At length, the president of NAFTA arrived and decamped from his helicopter on the tarmac in Louisiana. A swarm of presidential bodyguards materialized out of the expectant crowd, looking simultaneously extremely busy and icily unperturbable.

Suddenly a line of text flickered up at the bottom of the screen. The text was set in a very old-fashioned computer font, chalk-white letters with little visible jagged pixel-edges. "*Look at him hunting for that camera mark,*" the subtitle read as it scrolled across the screen. "*Why wasn't he briefed properly? He looks like a stray dog!*"

The president meandered amiably across the sun-blistered tarmac, gazing from side to side, and then stopped briefly to shake the eager outstretched hand of a local politician. "*That must have hurt,*" commented the text. "*That Cajun dolt is poison in the polls.*" The president chatted amiably with the local politician and an elderly harridan in a purple dress who seemed to be the man's wife. "*Get him away from those losers!*" raged the subtitle. "*Get the Man up to the podium, for the love of Mike! Where's the chief of staff? Doped up on so-called smart drugs as usual? Get with your jobs, people!*"

The president looked well. Lyle had noticed that the president of NAFTA always looked well, it seemed to be a professional requirement. The big political cheeses in Europe always looked somber and intellectual, and the Sphere people always looked humble and dedicated, and the South people always looked angry and fanatical, but the NAFTA prez always looked like he'd just done a few laps in a pool and had a brisk rubdown. His large, glossy, bluffly cheerful face was discreetly stenciled with tattoos: both cheeks, a chorus line of tats on his forehead above both eyebrows, plus a few extra logos on his rocklike chin. A president's face was the ultimate billboard for major backers and interest groups.

"Does he think we have all day?" the text demanded. *"What's with this dead air time? Can't anyone properly arrange a media event these days? You call this public access? You call this informing the electorate? If we'd known the infobahn would come to this, we'd have never built the thing!"*

The president meandered amiably to a podium covered with ceremonial microphones. Lyle had noticed that politicians always used a big healthy cluster of traditional big fat microphones, even though nowadays you could build working microphones the size of a grain of rice.

"Hey, how y'all?" asked the president, grinning.

The crowd chorused back at him, with ragged enthusiasm.

"Let these fine folks up a bit closer," the president ordered suddenly, waving airily at his phalanx of bodyguards. "Y'all come on up closer, everybody! Sit right on the ground, we're all just folks here today." The president smiled benignly as the sweating, straw-hatted summer crowd hustled up to join him, scarcely believing their luck.

"Marietta and I just had a heck of a fine lunch down in Opelousas," commented the president, patting his flat, muscular belly. He deserted the fiction of his official podium to energetically press the Louisianan flesh. As he moved from hand to grasping hand, his every word was picked up infallibly by an invisible mike, probably implanted in one of his molars. "We had dirty rice, red beans—were they hot!—and crawdads big enough to body-slam a Maine lobster!" He chuckled. "What a sight them mudbugs were! Can y'all believe that?"

The president's guards were unobtrusively but methodically working the crowd with portable detectors and sophisticated spex equipment. They didn't look very concerned by the president's supposed change in routine.

"I see he's gonna run with the usual genetics malarkey," commented the subtitle.

"Y'all have got a perfect right to be mighty proud of the agriculture in this state," intoned the president. "Y'all's agroscience know-how is second to none! Sure, I know there's a few pointy-headed Luddites up in the snowbelt, who say they prefer their crawdads dinky."

Everyone laughed.

"Folks, I got nothin' against that attitude. If some jasper wants to spend his hard-earned money buyin' and peelin' and shuckin' those little dinky ones, that's all right by me and Marietta. Ain't that right, honey?"

The first lady smiled and waved one power-gloved hand.

"But folks, you and I both know that those whiners who waste our time complaining about 'natural food' have never sucked a mudbug head in their lives! 'Natural,' my left elbow! Who are they tryin' to kid? Just 'cause you're country, don't mean you can't hack DNA!"

"He's been working really hard on the regional accents," commented the text. *"Not bad for a guy from Minnesota. But look at that sloppy, incompetent camera work! Doesn't anybody care anymore? What on earth is happening to our standards?"*

By lunchtime, Lyle had the final coat down on the enameling job. He ate a bowl of triticale mush and chewed up a mineral-rich handful of iodized sponge.

Then he settled down in front of the wallscreen to work on the inertia brake. Lyle knew there was big money in the inertia brake—for somebody, somewhere, sometime. The device smelled like the future.

Lyle tucked a jeweler's loupe in one eye and toyed methodically with the brake. He loved the way the piezoplastic clamp and rim transmuted braking energy into electrical-battery storage. At last, a way to capture the energy you lost in braking and put it to solid use. It was almost, but not quite, magical.

The way Lyle figured it, there was gonna be a big market someday for an inertia brake that captured energy and then fed it back through the chaindrive in a way that just felt like human pedaling energy, in a direct and intuitive and muscular way, not chunky and buzzy like some loser battery-powered moped. If the system worked out right, it would make the rider feel completely natural and yet subtly superhuman at the same time. And it had to be simple, the kind of system a shop guy could fix with hand tools. It wouldn't work if it was too brittle and fancy, it just wouldn't feel like an authentic bike.

Lyle had a lot of ideas about the design. He was pretty sure he could get a real grip on the problem, if only he weren't being worked to death just keeping the shop going. If he could get enough capital together to assemble the prototypes and do some serious field tests.

It would have to be chip-driven, of course, but true to the biking spirit at the same time. A lot of bikes had chips in them nowadays, in the shocks or the braking or in reactive hubs, but bicycles simply weren't like computers. Computers were black boxes inside, no big visible working parts. People, by contrast, got sentimental about their bike gear. People were strangely reticent and traditional about bikes. That's why the bike market had never really gone for recumbents, even though the recumbent design had a big mechanical advantage. People didn't like their bikes too complicated. They didn't want bicycles to bitch and complain and whine for attention and constant upgrading the way that computers did. Bikes were too personal. People wanted their bikes to wear.

Someone banged at the shop door.

Lyle opened it. Down on the tiling by the barrels stood a tall brunette woman in stretch shorts, with a short-sleeve blue pullover and a ponytail. She had a bike under one arm, an old lacquer-and-paper-framed Taiwanese job. "Are you Edward Dertouzas?" she said, gazing up at him.

"No," Lyle said patiently. "Eddy's in Europe."

She thought this over. "I'm new in the zone," she confessed. "Can you fix this bike for me? I just bought it secondhand and I think it kinda needs some work."

"Sure," Lyle said. "You came to the right guy for that job, ma'am, because Eddy Dertouzas couldn't fix a bike for hell. Eddy just used to live here. I'm the guy who actually owns this shop. Hand the bike up."

Lyle crouched down, got a grip on the handlebar stem and hauled the bike into the shop. The woman gazed up at him respectfully. "What's your name?"

"Lyle Schweik."

"I'm Kitty Casaday." She hesitated. "Could I come up inside there?"

Lyle reached down, gripped her muscular wrist, and hauled her up into the shop. She wasn't all that good looking, but she was in really good shape—like a mountain biker or triathlon runner. She looked about thirty-five. It was hard to tell, exactly. Once people got into cosmetic surgery and serious biomaintenance, it got pretty hard to judge their age. Unless you got a good, close medical exam of their eyelids and cuticles and internal membranes and such.

She looked around the shop with great interest, brown ponytail twitching. "Where you hail from?" Lyle asked her. He had already forgotten her name.

"Well, I'm originally from Juneau, Alaska."

"Canadian, huh? Great. Welcome to Tennessee."

"Actually, Alaska used to be part of the United States."

"You're kidding," Lyle said. "Hey, I'm no historian, but I've seen Alaska on a map before."

"You've got a whole working shop and everything built inside this old place! That's really something, Mr. Schweik. What's behind that curtain?"

"The spare room," Lyle said. "That's where my roommate used to stay."

She glanced up. "Dertouzas?"

"Yeah, him."

"Who's in there now?"

"Nobody," Lyle said sadly. "I got some storage stuff in there."

She nodded slowly, and kept looking around, apparently galvanized with curiosity. "What are you running on that screen?"

"Hard to say, really," Lyle said. He crossed the room, bent down, and switched off the set-top box. "Some kind of weird political crap."

He began examining her bike. All its serial numbers had been removed. Typical zone bike.

"The first thing we got to do," he said briskly, "is fit it to you properly: set the saddle height, pedal stroke, and handlebars. Then I'll adjust the tension, true the wheels, check the brake pads and suspension valves, tune the shifting, and lubricate the drivetrain. The usual. You're gonna need a better saddle than this—this saddle's for a male pelvis." He looked up. "You got a charge card?"

She nodded, then frowned. "But I don't have much credit left."

"No problem." He flipped open a dog-eared catalog. "This is what you need. Any halfway decent gel-saddle. Pick one you like, and we can have it shipped in by tomorrow morning. And then"—he flipped pages—"order me one of these."

She stepped closer and examined the page. "The 'cotterless crank-bolt ceramic wrench set,' is that it?"

"That's right. I fix your bike, you give me those tools, and we're even."

"Okay. Sure. That's cheap!" She smiled at him. "I like the way you do business, Lyle."

"You'll get used to barter, if you stay in the zone long enough."

"I've never lived in a squat before," she said thoughtfully. "I like the attitude here, but people say that squats are pretty dangerous."

"I dunno about the squats in other towns, but Chattanooga squats aren't dangerous, unless you think anarchists are dangerous, and anarchists aren't dangerous unless they're really drunk." Lyle shrugged. "People will steal your stuff all the time, that's about the worst part. There's a couple of tough guys around here who claim they have handguns. I never saw anybody actually use a handgun. Old guns aren't hard to find, but it takes a real chemist to make working ammo nowadays." He smiled back at her. "Anyway, you look to me like you can take care of yourself."

"I take dance classes."

Lyle nodded. He opened a drawer and pulled a tape measure.

"I saw all those cables and pulleys you have on top of this place. You can pull the whole building right up off the ground, huh? Kind of hang it right off the ceiling up there."

"That's right, it saves a lot of trouble with people breaking and entering." Lyle glanced at his shock-baton, in its mounting at the door. She followed his gaze to the weapon and then looked at him, impressed.

Lyle measured her arms, torso length, then knelt and measured her inseam from crotch to floor. He took notes. "Okay," he said. "Come by tomorrow afternoon."

"Lyle?"

"Yeah?" He stood up.

"Do you rent this place out? I really need a safe place to stay in the zone."

"I'm sorry," Lyle said politely, "but I hate landlords and I'd never be one. What I need is a roommate who can really get behind the whole concept of my shop. Someone who's qualified, you know, to develop my infrastructure or do bicycle work. Anyway, if I took your cash or charged you for rent, then the tax people would just have another excuse to harass me."

"Sure, okay, but . . ." She paused, then looked at him under lowered eyelids. "I've gotta be a lot better than having this place go empty."

Lyle stared at her, astonished.

"I'm a pretty useful woman to have around, Lyle. Nobody's ever complained before."

"Really?"

"That's right." She stared at him boldly.

"I'll think about your offer," Lyle said. "What did you say your name was?"

"I'm Kitty. Kitty Casaday."

"Kitty, I got a whole lot of work to do today, but I'll see you tomorrow, okay?"

"Okay, Lyle." She smiled. "You think about me, all right?"

Lyle helped her down out of the shop. He watched her stride away across the atrium until she vanished through the crowded doorway of the Crowbar, a squat coffee shop. Then he called his mother.

"Did you forget something?" his mother said, looking up from her workscreen.

"Mom, I know this is really hard to believe, but a strange woman just banged on my door and offered to have sex with me."

"You're kidding, right?"

"In exchange for room and board, I think. Anyway, I said you'd be the first to know if it happened."

"Lyle—" His mother hesitated. "Lyle, I think you better come right home. Let's make that dinner date for tonight, okay? We'll have a little talk about this situation."

"Yeah, okay. I got an enameling job I gotta deliver to Floor Forty-one, anyway."

"I don't have a positive feeling about this development, Lyle."

"That's okay, Mom. I'll see you tonight."

Lyle reassembled the newly enameled bike. Then he set the flywheel onto remote, and stepped outside the shop. He mounted the bike, and touched a password into the remote control. The shop faithfully reeled itself far out of reach and hung there in space below the fire-blackened ceiling, swaying gently.

Lyle pedaled away, back toward the elevators, back toward the neighborhood where he'd grown up.

He delivered the bike to the delighted young idiot who'd commissioned it, stuffed the cash in his shoes, and then went down to his mother's. He took a shower, shaved, and shampooed thoroughly. They had pork chops and grits and got drunk together. His mother complained about the breakup with her third husband and wept bitterly, but not as much as usual when this topic came up. Lyle got the strong impression she was thoroughly on the mend and would be angling for number four in pretty short order.

Around midnight, Lyle refused his mother's ritual offers of new clothes and fresh leftovers, and headed back down to the zone. He was still a little clubfooted from his mother's sherry, and he stood breathing beside the broken glass of the atrium wall, gazing out at the city-smeared summer stars. The cavernous darkness inside the zone at night was one of his favorite things about the place. The queasy twenty-four-hour security lighting in the rest of the Archiplat had never been rebuilt inside the zone.

The zone always got livelier at night when all the normal people started sneaking in to cruise the zone's unlicensed dives and nightspots, but all that activity took place behind discreetly closed doors. Enticing squiggles of red and blue chemglow here and there only enhanced the blessed unnatural gloom.

Lyle pulled his remote control and ordered the shop back down.

The door of the shop had been broken open.

Lyle's latest bike-repair client lay sprawled on the floor of the shop, unconscious. She was wearing black military fatigues, a knit cap, and rappelling gear.

She had begun her break-in at Lyle's establishment by pulling his shock-baton out of its glowing security socket beside the doorframe. The booby-trapped baton had immediately put fifteen thousand volts through her, and sprayed her face with a potent mix of dye and street-legal incapacitants.

Lyle turned the baton off with the remote control, and then placed it carefully back in its socket. His surprise guest was still breathing, but was clearly in real metabolic distress. He tried clearing her nose and mouth with a tissue. The guys who'd sold him the baton hadn't been kidding about the "indelible" part. Her face and throat were drenched with green and her chest looked like a spin-painting.

Her elaborate combat spex had partially shielded her eyes. With the spex off she looked like a viridian-green raccoon.

Lyle tried stripping her gear off in conventional fashion, realized this wasn't going to work, and got a pair of metal shears from the shop. He snipped his way through the eerily writhing power-gloves and the Kevlar laces of the pneumoreactive combat boots. Her black turtleneck had an abrasive surface and a cuirass over chest and back that looked like it could stop small-arms fire.

The trousers had nineteen separate pockets and they were loaded with all kinds of eerie little items: a matte-black electrode stun-weapon, flash capsules, fingerprint dust, a utility pocketknife, drug adhesives, plastic handcuffs, some pocket change, worry beads, a comb, and a makeup case.

Close inspection revealed a pair of tiny microphone amplifiers inserted in her ear canals. Lyle fetched the tiny devices out with needlenose pliers. Lyle was getting pretty seriously concerned by this point. He shackled her arms and legs with bike-security cable, in case she regained consciousness and attempted something superhuman.

Around four in the morning she had a coughing fit and began shivering violently. Summer nights could get pretty cold in the shop. Lyle thought over the design problem for some time, and then fetched a big heat-reflective blanket out of the empty room. He cut a neat poncho-hole in the center of it, and slipped her head through it. He got the bike cables off her—she could probably slip the cables anyway—and sewed all four edges of the blanket shut from the outside, with sturdy monofilament thread from his saddle-stitcher. He sewed the poncho edges to a tough fabric belt, cinched the belt snugly around her neck, and padlocked it. When he was done, he'd made a snug bag that contained her entire body, except for her head, which had begun to drool and snore.

A fat blob of superglue on the bottom of the bag kept her anchored to the shop's floor. The blanket was cheap but tough upholstery fabric. If she could rip her way through blanket fabric with her fingernails alone, then he was probably a goner anyway. By now, Lyle was tired and stone sober. He had a squeeze bottle of glucose rehydrator, three aspirins, and a canned chocolate pudding. Then he climbed in his hammock and went to sleep.

Lyle woke up around ten. His captive was sitting up inside the bag, her green face stony, eyes red-rimmed and brown hair caked with dye. Lyle got up, dressed, ate breakfast, and fixed the broken door lock. He said nothing, partly because he thought that silence would shake her up, but mostly because he couldn't remember her name. He was almost sure it wasn't her real name anyway.

When he'd finished fixing the door, he reeled up the string of the doorknocker so that it was far out of reach. He figured the two of them needed the privacy.

Then Lyle deliberately fired up the wallscreen and turned on the set-top box. As soon as the peculiar subtitles started showing up again, she grew agitated.

"Who are you really?" she demanded at last.

"Ma'am, I'm a bicycle repairman."

She snorted.

"I guess I don't need to know your name," he said, "but I need to know who your people are, and why they sent you here, and what I've got to do to get out of this situation."

"You're not off to a good start, mister."

"No," he said, "maybe not, but you're the one who's blown it. I'm just a twenty-four-year-old bicycle repairman from Tennessee. But you, you've got enough specialized gear on you to buy my whole place five times over."

He flipped open the little mirror in her makeup case and showed her her own face. Her scowl grew a little stiffer below the spattering of green.

"I want you to tell me what's going on here," he said.

"Forget it."

"If you're waiting for your backup to come rescue you, I don't think they're coming," Lyle said. "I searched you very thoroughly and I've opened up every single little gadget you had, and I took all the batteries out. I'm not even sure what some of those things are or how they work, but hey, I know what a battery is. It's been hours now. So I don't think your backup people even know where you are."

She said nothing.

"See," he said, "you've really blown it bad. You got caught by a total amateur, and now you're in a hostage situation that could go on indefinitely. I got enough water and noodles and sardines to live up here for days. I dunno, maybe you can make a cellular phone call to God off some gizmo implanted in your thighbone, but it looks to me like you've got serious problems."

She shuffled around a bit inside the bag and looked away.

"It's got something to do with the cable box over there, right?"

She said nothing.

"For what it's worth, I don't think that box has anything to do with me or Eddy Dertouzas," Lyle said. "I think it was probably meant for Eddy, but I don't think he asked anybody for it. Somebody just wanted him to have it, probably one of his weird European contacts. Eddy used to be in this political group called CAPCLUG, ever heard of them?"

It looked pretty obvious that she'd heard of them.

"I never liked 'em much either," Lyle told her. "They kind of snagged me at first with their big talk about freedom and civil liberties, but then you'd go to a CAPCLUG meeting up in the penthouse levels, and there were all these potbellied zudes in spex yapping off stuff like, 'We must follow the technological imperatives or be jettisoned into the history dump-file.' They're a bunch of useless blowhards who can't tie their own shoes."

"They're dangerous radicals subverting national sovereignty."

Lyle blinked cautiously. "Whose national sovereignty would that be?"

"Yours, mine, Mr. Schweik. I'm from NAFTA, I'm a federal agent."

"You're a fed? How come you're breaking into people's houses, then? Isn't that against the Fourth Amendment or something?"

"If you mean the Fourth Amendment to the Constitution of the United States, that document was superseded years ago."

"Yeah . . . okay, I guess you're right." Lyle shrugged. "I missed a lot of civics classes. . . . No skin off my back anyway. I'm sorry, but what did you say your name was?"

"I said my name was Kitty Casaday."

"Right. Kitty. Okay, Kitty, just you and me, person to person. We obviously have a mutual problem here. What do you think I ought to do in this situation? I mean, speaking practically."

Kitty thought it over, surprised. "Mr. Schweik, you should release me immediately, get me my gear, and give me the box and any related data, recordings, or diskettes. Then you should escort me from the Archiplat in some confidential fashion so I won't be stopped by police and questioned about the dye stains. A new set of clothes would be very useful."

"Like that, huh?"

"That's your wisest course of action." Her eyes narrowed. "I can't make any promises, but it might affect your future treatment very favorably."

"You're not gonna tell me who you are, or where you came from, or who sent you, or what this is all about?"

"No. Under no circumstances. I'm not allowed to reveal that. You don't need to know. You're not supposed to know. And anyway, if you're really what you say you are, what should you care?"

"Plenty. I care plenty. I can't wander around the rest of my life wondering when you're going to jump me out of a dark corner."

"If I'd wanted to hurt you, I'd have hurt you when we first met, Mr. Schweik. There was no one here but you and me, and I could have easily incapacitated you and taken anything I wanted. Just give me the box and the data and stop trying to interrogate me."

"Suppose you found me breaking into your house, Kitty? What would you do to me?"

She said nothing.

"What you're telling me isn't gonna work. If you don't tell me what's really going on here," Lyle said heavily, "I'm gonna have to get tough."

Her lips thinned in contempt.

"Okay, you asked for this." Lyle opened the mediator and made a quick voice call. "Pete?"

"Nah, this is Pete's mook," the phone replied. "Can I do something for you?"

"Could you tell Pete that Lyle Schweik has some big trouble, and I need him to come over to my bike shop immediately? And bring some heavy muscle from the Spiders."

"What kind of big trouble, Lyle?"

"Authority trouble. A lot of it. I can't say any more. I think this line may be tapped."

"Right-o. I'll make that happen. Hoo-ah, zude." The mook hung up.

Lyle left the beanbag and went back to the workbench. He took Kitty's cheap bike out of the repair stand and angrily threw it aside. "You know what really bugs me?" he said at last. "You couldn't even bother to charm your way in here, set yourself up as my roommate, and then steal the damn box. You didn't even respect me that much. Heck, you didn't even have to steal anything, Kitty. You could have just smiled and asked nicely and I'd have given you the box to play with. I don't watch media, I hate all that crap."

"It was an emergency. There was no time for more extensive investigation or reconnaissance. I think you should call your gangster friends immediately and tell them you've made a mistake. Tell them not to come here."

"You're ready to talk seriously?"

"No, I won't be talking."

"Okay, we'll see."

After twenty minutes, Lyle's phone rang. He answered it cautiously, keeping the video off. It was Pete from the City Spiders. "Zude, where is your doorknocker?"

"Oh, sorry, I pulled it up, didn't want to be disturbed. I'll bring the shop right down." Lyle thumbed the brake switches.

Lyle opened the door and Pete broad-jumped into the shop. Pete was a big man but he had the skeletal, wiry build of a climber, bare dark arms and shins and big sticky-toed jumping shoes. He had a sleeveless leather bodysuit full of clips and snaps, and he carried a big fabric shoulder bag. There were six vivid tattoos on the dark skin of his left cheek, under the black stubble.

Pete looked at Kitty, lifted his spex with wiry callused fingers, looked at her again bare-eyed, and put the spex back in place. "Wow, Lyle."

"Yeah."

"I never thought you were into anything this sick and twisted."

"It's a serious matter, Pete."

Pete turned to the door, crouched down, and hauled a second person into the shop. She wore a beat-up air-conditioned jacket and long slacks and zipsided boots and wire-rimmed spex. She had short ratty hair under a green cloche hat. "Hi," she said, sticking out a hand. "I'm Mabel. We haven't met."

"I'm Lyle." Lyle gestured. "This is Kitty here in the bag."

"You said you needed somebody heavy, so I brought Mabel along," said Pete. "Mabel's a social worker."

"Looks like you pretty much got things under control here," said Mabel liltingly, scratching her neck and looking about the place. "What happened? She break into your shop?"

"Yeah."

"And," Pete said, "she grabbed the shock-baton first thing and blasted herself but good?"

"Exactly."

"I told you that thieves always go for the weaponry first," Pete said, grinning and scratching his armpit. "Didn't I tell you that? Leave a weapon in plain sight, man, a thief can't stand it, it's the very first thing they gotta grab." He laughed. "Works every time."

"Pete's from the City Spiders," Lyle told Kitty. "His people built this shop for me. One dark night, they hauled this mobile home right up thirty-four stories in total darkness, straight up the side of the Archiplat without anybody seeing, and they cut a big hole through the side of the building without making any noise, and they hauled the whole shop through it. Then they sank explosive bolts through the girders and hung it up here for me in midair. The City Spiders are into sport-climbing the way I'm into bicycles, only, like, they are very *seriously* into climbing and there are *lots* of them. They were some of the very first people to squat the zone, and they've lived here ever since, and they are pretty good friends of mine."

Pete sank to one knee and looked Kitty in the eye. "I love breaking into places, don't you? There's no thrill like some quick and perfectly executed break-in." He reached casually into his shoulder bag. "The thing is"—he pulled out a camera—"to be sporting, you can't steal anything. You just take trophy pictures to prove you were there." He snapped her picture several times, grinning as she flinched.

"Lady," he breathed at her, "once you've turned into a little wicked greedhead, and mixed all that evil cupidity and possessiveness into the beauty of the direct action, then you've prostituted our way of life. You've gone and spoiled our sport." Pete stood up. "We City Spiders don't like common thieves. And we especially don't like thieves who break into the places of clients of ours, like Lyle here. And we thoroughly, especially, don't like thieves who are so brickhead dumb that they get caught red-handed on the premises of friends of ours."

Pete's hairy brows knotted in thought. "What I'd like to do here, Lyle ol' buddy," he announced, "is wrap up your little friend head to foot in nice tight cabling, smuggle her out of here down to Golden Gate Archiplat—you know, the big one downtown over by MLK and Highway Twenty-seven?—and hang her head-down in the center of the cupola."

"That's not very nice," Mabel told him seriously.

Pete looked wounded. "I'm not gonna charge him for it or anything! Just imagine her, spinning up there beautifully with all those chandeliers and those hundreds of mirrors."

Mabel knelt and looked into Kitty's face. "Has she had any water since she was knocked unconscious?"

"No."

"Well, for heaven's sake, give the poor woman something to drink, Lyle."

Lyle handed Mabel a bike-tote squeeze bottle of electrolyte refresher. "You zudes don't grasp the situation yet," he said. "Look at all this stuff I took off her." He showed them the spex, and the boots, and the stun-gun, and the gloves, and the carbon-nitride climbing plectra, and the rappelling gear.

"Wow," Pete said at last, dabbing at buttons on his spex to study the finer detail, "this is no ordinary burglar! She's gotta be, like, a street samurai from the Mahogany Warbirds or something!"

"She says she's a federal agent."

Mabel stood up suddenly, angrily yanking the squeeze bottle from Kitty's lips. "You're kidding, right?"

"Ask her."

"I'm a grade-five social counselor with the Department of Urban Redevelopment," Mabel said. She presented Kitty with an official ID. "And who are you with?"

"I'm not prepared to divulge that information at this time."

"I can't believe this," Mabel marveled, tucking her dog-eared hologram ID back in her hat. "You've caught somebody from one of those nutty reactionary secret black-bag units. I mean, that's gotta be what's just happened here." She shook her head slowly. "Y'know, if you work in government, you always hear horror stories about these right-wing paramilitary wackos, but I've never actually seen one before."

"It's a very dangerous world out there, Miss Social Counselor."

"Oh, tell me about it," Mabel scoffed. "I've worked suicide hot lines! I've seen a hostage negotiator! I'm a career social worker, girlfriend! I've seen more horror and suffering than you *ever* will. While you were doing push-ups in some comfy cracker training camp, I've been out here in the real world!" Mabel absently unscrewed the top from the bike bottle and had a long glug. "What on earth are you doing trying to raid the squat of a bicycle repairman?"

Kitty's stony silence lengthened. "It's got something to do with that set-top box," Lyle offered. "It showed up here in delivery yesterday, and then she showed up just a few hours later. Started flirting with me, and said she wanted to live in here. Of course I got suspicious right away."

"Naturally," Pete said. "Real bad move, Kitty. Lyle's on antilibidinals."

Kitty stared at Lyle bitterly. "I see," she said at last. "So that's what you get, when you drain all the sex out of one of them. . . . You get a strange malodorous creature that spends all its time working in the garage."

Mabel flushed. "Did you hear that?" She gave Kitty's bag a sharp angry yank. "What conceivable right do you have to question this citizen's sexual orientation? Especially after cruelly trying to sexually manipulate him to abet your illegal purposes? Have you lost all sense of decency? You . . . you should be sued."

"Do your worst," Kitty muttered.

"Maybe I will," Mabel said grimly. "Sunlight is the best disinfectant."

"Yeah, let's string her up somewhere real sunny and public and call a bunch of news crews," Pete said. "I'm way hot for this deep ninja gear! Me and the Spiders got real mojo uses for these telescopic ears, and the tracer dust, and the epoxy bugging devices. And the press-on climbing-claws. And the carbon-fiber rope. Everything, really! Everything except these big-ass military shoes of hers, which really suck."

"Hey, all that stuff's mine," Lyle said sternly. "I saw it first."

"Yeah, I guess so, but . . . Okay, Lyle, you make us a deal on the gear, we'll forget everything you still owe us for doing the shop."

"Come on, those combat spex are worth more than this place all by themselves."

"I'm real interested in that set-top box," Mabel said cruelly. "It doesn't look too fancy or complicated. Let's take it over to those dirty circuit zudes who hang out at the Blue Parrot, and see if they can't reverse-engineer it. We'll post all the schematics up on twenty or thirty progressive activist networks, and see what falls out of cyberspace."

Kitty glared at her. "The terrible consequences from that stupid and irresponsible action would be entirely on your head."

"I'll risk it," Mabel said airily, patting her cloche hat. "It might bump my soft little liberal head a bit, but I'm pretty sure it would crack your nasty little fascist head like a coconut."

Suddenly Kitty began thrashing and kicking her way furiously inside the bag. They watched with interest as she ripped, tore, and lashed out with powerful side and front kicks. Nothing much happened.

"All right," she said at last, panting in exhaustion. "I've come from Senator Creighton's office."

"Who?" Lyle said.

"Creighton! Senator James P. Creighton, the man who's been your Senator from Tennessee for the past thirty years!"

"Oh," Lyle said. "I hadn't noticed."

"We're anarchists," Pete told her.

"I've sure heard of the nasty old geezer," Mabel said, "but I'm from British Columbia, where we change senators the way you'd change a pair of socks. If you ever changed your socks, that is. What about him?"

"Well, Senator Creighton has deep clout and seniority! He was a United States Senator even before the first NAFTA Senate was convened! He has a very large, and powerful, and very well seasoned personal staff of twenty thousand hard-working people, with a lot of pull in the Agriculture, Banking, and Telecommunications Committees!"

"Yeah? So?"

"So," Kitty said miserably, "there are twenty thousand of us on his staff. We've been in place for decades now, and naturally we've accumulated lots of power and importance. Senator Creighton's staff is basically running some quite large sections of the NAFTA government, and if the senator loses his office, there will be a great deal of . . . of unnecessary political turbulence." She looked up. "You might not think that a senator's staff is all that important politically. But if people like you bothered to learn anything about the real-life way that your government functions, then you'd know that Senate staffers can be really crucial."

Mabel scratched her head. "You're telling me that even a lousy senator has his own private black-bag unit?"

Kitty looked insulted. "He's an excellent senator! You can't have a working organization of twenty thousand staffers without taking security very seriously! Anyway, the Executive wing has had black-bag units for years! It's only right that there should be a balance of powers."

"Wow," Mabel said. "The old guy's a hundred and twelve or something, isn't he?"

"A hundred and seventeen."

"Even with government health care, there can't be a lot left of him."

"He's already gone," Kitty muttered. "His frontal lobes are burned out. . . . He can still sit up, and if he's stoked on stimulants he can repeat whatever's whispered to him. So he's got two permanent implanted hearing aids, and basically . . . well . . . he's being run by remote control by his mook."

"His mook, huh?" Pete repeated thoughtfully.

"It's a very good mook," Kitty said. "The coding's old, but it's been very well looked after. It has firm moral values and excellent policies. The mook is really very much like the senator was. It's just that . . . well, it's old. It still prefers a really old-fashioned media environment. It spends almost all its time watching old-fashioned public political coverage, and lately it's gotten cranky and started broadcasting commentary."

"Man, never trust a mook," Lyle said. "I hate those things."

"So do I," Pete offered, "but even a mook comes off pretty good compared to a politician."

"I don't really see the problem," Mabel said, puzzled. "Senator Hirschheimer from Arizona has had a direct neural link to his mook for years, and he has an excellent progressive voting record. Same goes for Senator Marmalejo from Tamaulipas; she's kind of absentminded, and everybody knows she's on life support, but she's a real scrapper on women's issues."

Kitty looked up. "You don't think it's terrible?"

Mabel shook her head. "I'm not one to be judgmental about the intimacy of one's relationship to one's own digital alter ego. As far as I can see it, that's a basic privacy issue."

"They told me in briefing that it was a very terrible business, and that everyone would panic if they learned that a high government official was basically a front for a rogue artificial intelligence."

Mabel, Pete, and Lyle exchanged glances. "Are you guys surprised by that news?" Mabel said.

"Heck no," said Pete. "Big deal," Lyle added.

Something seemed to snap inside Kitty then. Her head sank. "Disaffected émigrés in Europe have been spreading boxes that can decipher the senator's commentary. I mean, the senator's mook's commentary. . . . The mook speaks just like the senator did, or the way the senator used to speak, when he was in private and off the record. The way he spoke in his diaries. As far as we can tell, the mook *was* his diary. . . . It used to be his personal laptop computer. But he just kept transferring the files, and upgrading the software, and teaching it new tricks like voice recognition and speechwriting, and giving it power of attorney and such. . . . And then, one day the mook made a break for it. We think that the mook sincerely believes that it's the senator."

"Just tell the stupid thing to shut up for a while, then."

"We can't do that. We're not even sure where the mook is, physically. Or how it's been encoding those sarcastic comments into the video-feed. The senator had a lot of friends in the telecom industry back in the old days. There are a lot of ways and places to hide a piece of distributed software."

"So that's all?" Lyle said. "That's it, that's your big secret? Why didn't you just come to me and ask me for the box? You didn't have to dress up in combat gear and kick my door in. That's a pretty good story, I'd have probably just given you the thing."

"I couldn't do that, Mr. Schweik."

"Why not?"

"Because," Pete said, "her people are important government functionaries, and you're a loser techie wacko who lives in a slum."

"I was told this is a very dangerous area," Kitty muttered.

"It's not dangerous," Mabel told her.

"No?"

"No. They're all too broke to be dangerous. This is just a kind of social breathing space. The whole urban infrastructure's dreadfully overplanned here in Chattanooga. There's been too much money here too long. There's been no room for spontaneity. It was choking the life out of the city. That's why everyone was secretly overjoyed when the rioters set fire to these three floors."

Mabel shrugged. "The insurance took care of the damage. First the looters came in. Then there were a few hideouts for kids and crooks and illegal aliens. Then the permanent squats got set up. Then the artist's studios, and the semilegal workshops and red-light places. Then the quaint little coffeehouses, then the bakeries. Pretty soon the offices of professionals will be filtering in, and they'll restore the water and the wiring. Once that happens, the real-estate prices will kick in big-time, and the whole zone will transmute right back into gentryville. It happens all the time."

Mabel waved her arm at the door. "If you knew anything about modern urban geography, you'd see this kind of, uh, spontaneous urban renewal happening all over the place. As long as you've got naive young people with plenty of energy who can be suckered into living inside rotten, hazardous dumps for nothing, in exchange for imagining that they're free from oversight, then it all works out just great in the long run."

"Oh."

"Yeah, zones like this turn out to be extremely handy for all concerned. For some brief span of time, a few people can think mildly unusual thoughts and behave in mildly unusual ways. All kinds of weird little vermin show up, and if they make any money then they go legal, and if they don't then they drop dead in a place really quiet where it's all their own fault. Nothing dangerous about it." Mabel laughed, then sobered. "Lyle, let this poor dumb cracker out of the bag."

"She's naked under there."

"Okay," she said impatiently, "cut a slit in the bag and throw some clothes in it. Get going, Lyle."

Lyle threw in some biking pants and a sweatshirt.

"What about my gear?" Kitty demanded, wriggling her way into the clothes by feel.

"I tell you what," said Mabel thoughtfully. "Pete here will give your gear back to you in a week or so, after his friends have photographed all the circuitry. You'll just have to let him keep all those knickknacks for a while, as his reward for our not immediately telling everybody who you are and what you're doing here."

"Great idea," Pete announced, "terrific, pragmatic solution!" He began feverishly snatching up gadgets and stuffing them into his shoulder bag. "See, Lyle? One phone call to good ol' Spider Pete, and your problem is history, zude! Me and Mabel-the-Fed have crisis negotiation skills that are second to none! Another potentially lethal confrontation resolved without any bloodshed or loss of life." Pete zipped the bag shut. "That's about it, right, everybody? Problem over! Write if you get work, Lyle buddy. Hang by your thumbs." Pete leapt out the door and bounded off at top speed on the springy soles of his reactive boots.

"Thanks a lot for placing my equipment into the hands of sociopathic criminals," Kitty said. She reached out of the slit in the bag, grabbed a multitool off the corner of the workbench, and began swiftly slashing her way free.

"This will help the sluggish, corrupt, and underpaid Chattanooga police to take life a little more seriously," Mabel said, her pale eyes gleaming. "Besides, it's profoundly undemocratic to restrict specialized technical knowledge to the coercive hands of secret military elites."

Kitty thoughtfully thumbed the edge of the multitool's ceramic blade and stood up to her full height, her eyes slitted. "I'm ashamed to work for the same government as you."

Mabel smiled serenely. "Darling, your tradition of deep dark government paranoia is far behind the times! This is the postmodern era! We're now in the grip of a government with severe schizoid multiple-personality disorder."

"You're truly vile. I despise you more than I can say." Kitty jerked her thumb at Lyle. "Even this nutcase eunuch anarchist kid looks pretty good, compared to you. At least he's self-sufficient and market-driven."

"I thought he looked good the moment I met him," Mabel replied sunnily. "He's cute, he's got great muscle tone, and he doesn't make passes. Plus he can fix small appliances and he's got a spare apartment. I think you ought to move in with him, sweetheart."

"What's that supposed to mean? You don't think I could manage life here in the zone like you do, is that it? You think you have some kind of copyright on living outside the law?"

"No, I just mean you'd better stay indoors with your boyfriend here until that paint falls off your face. You look like a poisoned raccoon." Mabel turned on her heel. "Try to get a life, and stay out of my way." She leapt outside, unlocked her bicycle, and methodically pedaled off.

Kitty wiped her lips and spat out the door. "Christ, that baton packs a wallop." She snorted. "Don't you ever ventilate this place, kid? Those paint fumes are gonna kill you before you're thirty."

"I don't have time to clean or ventilate it. I'm real busy."

"Okay, then I'll clean it. I'll ventilate it. I gotta stay here a while, understand? Maybe quite a while."

Lyle blinked. "How long, exactly?"

Kitty stared at him. "You're not taking me seriously, are you? I don't much like it when people don't take me seriously."

"No, no," Lyle assured her hastily. "You're very serious."

"You ever heard of a small-business grant, kid? How about venture capital, did you ever hear of that? Ever heard of federal research-and-development subsidies, Mr. Schweik?" Kitty looked at him sharply, weighing her words. "Yeah, I thought maybe you'd heard of that one, Mr. Techie Wacko. Federal R-and-D backing is the kind of thing that only happens to other people, right? But Lyle, when you make good friends with a senator, you *become* 'other people.' Get my drift, pal?"

"I guess I do," Lyle said slowly.

"We'll have ourselves some nice talks about that subject, Lyle. You wouldn't mind that, would you?"

"No. I don't mind it now that you're talking."

"There's some stuff going on down here in the zone that I didn't understand at first, but it's important." Kitty paused, then rubbed dried dye from her hair in a cascade of green dandruff. "How much did you pay those Spider gangsters to string up this place for you?"

"It was kind of a barter situation," Lyle told her.

"Think they'd do it again if I paid 'em real cash? Yeah? I thought so." She nodded thoughtfully. "They look like a heavy outfit, the City Spiders. I gotta pry 'em loose from that leftist gorgon before she finishes indoctrinating them in socialist revolution." Kitty wiped her mouth on her sleeve. "This is the senator's own constituency! It was stupid of us to duck an ideological battle, just because this is a worthless area inhabited by reckless sociopaths who don't vote. Hell, that's exactly why it's important. This could be a vital territory in the culture war. I'm gonna call the office right away, start making arrangements. There's no way we're gonna leave this place in the hands of the self-styled Queen of Peace and Justice over there."

She snorted, then stretched a kink out of her back. "With a little self-control and discipline, I can save those Spiders from themselves and turn them into an asset to law and order! I'll get 'em to string up a couple of trailers here in the zone. We could start a dojo."

Eddy called, two weeks later. He was in a beachside cabana somewhere in Catalunya, wearing a silk floral-print shirt and a new and very pricey looking set of spex. "How's life, Lyle?"

"It's okay, Eddy."

"Making out all right?" Eddy had two new tattoos on his cheekbone.

"Yeah. I got a new paying roommate. She's a martial artist."

"Girl roommate working out okay this time?"

"Yeah, she's good at pumping the flywheel and she lets me get on with my bike work. Bike business has been picking up a lot lately. Looks like I might get a legal electrical feed and some more floorspace, maybe even some genuine mail delivery. My new roomie's got a lot of useful contacts."

"Boy, the ladies sure love you, Lyle! Can't beat 'em off with a stick, can you, poor guy? That's a heck of a note."

Eddy leaned forward a little, shoving aside a silver tray full of dead gold-tipped zigarettes. "You been getting the packages?"

"Yeah. Pretty regular."

"Good deal," he said briskly, "but you can wipe 'em all now. I don't need those backups anymore. Just wipe the data and trash the disks, or sell 'em. I'm into some, well, pretty hairy opportunities right now, and I don't need all that old clutter. It's kid stuff anyway."

"Okay, man. If that's the way you want it."

Eddy leaned forward. "D'you happen to get a package lately? Some hardware? Kind of a set-top box?"

"Yeah, I got the thing."

"That's great, Lyle. I want you to open the box up, and break all the chips with pliers."

"Yeah?"

"Then throw all the pieces away. Separately. It's trouble, Lyle, okay? The kind of trouble I don't need right now."

"Consider it done, man."

"Thanks! Anyway, you won't be bothered by mailouts from now on." He paused. "Not that I don't appreciate your former effort and goodwill, and all."

Lyle blinked. "How's your love life, Eddy?"

Eddy sighed. "Frederika! What a handful! I dunno, Lyle, it was okay for a while, but we couldn't stick it together. I don't know why I ever thought that private cops were sexy. I musta been totally out of my mind. . . . Anyway, I got a new girlfriend now."

"Yeah?"

"She's a politician, Lyle. She's a radical member of the Spanish Parliament. Can you believe that? I'm sleeping with an elected official of a European local government." He laughed. "Politicians are *sexy*, Lyle. Politicians are *hot*! They have charisma. They're glamorous. They're powerful. They can really make things happen! Politicians get around. They know things on the inside track. I'm having more fun with Violeta than I knew there was in the world."

"That's pleasant to hear, zude."

"More pleasant than you know, my man."

"Not a problem," Lyle said indulgently. "We all gotta make our own lives, Eddy."

"Ain't it the truth."

Lyle nodded. "I'm in business, zude!"

"You gonna perfect that inertial whatsit?" Eddy said.

"Maybe. It could happen. I get to work on it a lot now. I'm getting closer, really getting a grip on the concept. It feels really good. It's a good hack, man. It makes up for all the rest of it. It really does."

Eddy sipped his mimosa. "Lyle."

"What?"

"You didn't hook up that set-top box and look at it, did you?"

"You know me, Eddy," Lyle said. "Just another kid with a wrench."

AN EVER-REDDENING GLOW

David Brin

David Brin (born 1950) is a physicist whose first novel, *Sundiver*, was published in 1980, the year before he finished his Ph.D. thesis. His novel *Startide Rising* (1983) won both the Hugo and Nebula Awards for best novel, and his novel *Uplift War* (1987) was also a Hugo Award winner. His most recent novel, *Kiln People* (2002), is an SF detective novel about a world in which people can make disposable copies of themselves to take care of mundane tasks. His stories are collected in *The River of Time* (1986) and *Otherness* (1994). In recent years, he has lead an effort to get younger readers interested in SF. With *Analog*, he is sponsoring Webs of Wonder, a contest to foster internet sites that combine teaching with good science fiction. An optimist and a futurist, he is outspoken about the political and social implications of science technology. He recently published a nonfiction book, *The Transparent Society: Will Technology Force Us to Choose Between Privacy and Freedom?* (1998).

Although he is a hard SF writer, he doesn't let that get in the way of a good story. As John Clute put it, "he writes tales in which the physical constraints governing the knowable Universe are flouted with high-handed panache." His optimism, showmanship, and unornamented prose place him in the tradition of John W. Campbell and Robert A. Heinlein. In contrast to many of the writers in this book, Brin tends to choose ordinary people as his characters. In a 1997 Locus interview, he remarked,

> One of the rules I try to follow is that normal people are going to be involved even in heroic events. Even if you have superior protagonists, I hate to make them *slans*. I hate the whole *Ubermensch*, superman temptation that pervades science fiction. I believe no protagonist should be so competent, so awe-inspiring, that a committee of twenty really hard-working, intelligent people couldn't do the same thing. . . .

A certain element of clever scientific puzzles and games has always been present in hard science fiction, the legacy perhaps of Lewis Carroll, or of math classes and their word problems. Hard SF humor, invented in its modern form by L. Sprague de Camp, Anthony Boucher, Henry Kuttner, and Fredric Brown in the late 1930s and early 1940s, flourished in the 1950s. And logic problems of all sorts are the meat of hard science fiction. They can make such lovely, surprising plot twists.

In this story, which appeared in *Analog* in 1996, interstellar travel is responsible for the expansion of the universe; ecologically minded aliens ask us to behave better. There is of course a political subtext.

We were tooling along at four nines to c, relative to the Hercules cluster, when our Captain came on the intercom to tell us we were being tailed.

The announcement interrupted my afternoon lecture on Basic Implosive Geometrodynamics, as I explained principles behind the *Fulton*'s star drive to youths who had been children when we boarded, eight subjective years ago.

"In ancient science fiction," I had just said, "you can read of many fanciful ways to cheat the limit of the speed of light. Some of these seemed theoretically possible, especially when we learned how to make microscopic singularities by borrowing and twisting spacetime. Unfortunately, wormholes have a nasty habit of crushing anything that enters them, down to the size of a Planck unit, and it would take a galaxy-sized mass to "warp" space over interstellar distances. So we must propel ourselves along through normal space the old-fashioned way, by Newton's law of action and reaction . . . albeit in a manner our ancestors would never have dreamed."

I was about to go on, and describe the physics of metric-surfing, when the Captain's voice echoed through the ship.

"It appears we are being followed," he announced. *"Moreover, the vessel behind us is sending a signal, urging us to cut engines and let them come alongside."*

It was a microscopic ship that had been sent flashing to intercept us, massing less than a microgram, pushed by a beam of intense light from a nearby star. The same light (thoroughly red-shifted) was what we had seen reflected in our rear-viewing mirrors, causing us to stop our BHG motors and coast, awaiting rendezvous.

Picture that strange meeting, amid the vast, yawning emptiness between two spiral arms, with all visible stars crammed by the doppler effect into a narrow, brilliant hoop, blue along its forward rim and deep red in back. The *Fulton* was like a whale next to a floating wisp of plankton as we matched velocities. Our colony ship, filled with humans and other Earthlings, drifted alongside a gauzy, furled umbrella of ultra-sheer fabric. An umbrella that *spoke*.

"Thank you for acceding to our request," it said, after our computers established a linguistic link. *"I represent the intergalactic Corps of Obligate Pragmatism."*

We had never heard of the institution, but the Captain replied with aplomb.

"You don't say? And what can we do for you?"

"You can accommodate us by engaging in a discussion concerning your star drive."

"Yes? And what about our star drive?"

"It operates by the series-implosion of micro-singularities, which you create by borrowing spacetime-metric, using principals of quantum uncertainty. Before this borrowed debit comes due, you allow the singularities to re-collapse behind you. This creates a spacetime ripple, a wake that propels you ahead without any need on your part to expend matter or energy."

I could not have summarized it better to my students.

"Yes?" The Captain asked succinctly. "So?"

"This drive enables you to travel swiftly, in relativistic terms, from star system to star system."

"It has proved rather useful. We use it quite extensively."

"Indeed, that is the problem" answered the wispy star probe. *"I have chased you across vast distances in order to ask you to stop."*

No wonder it had used such a strange method to catch up with us! The cop agent claimed that our BHG drive was immoral, unethical, and dangerous!

"There are alternatives," it stressed. *"You can travel as I do, pushed by intense beams cast from your point of origin. Naturally, in that case you would have to discard your corporeal bodies and go about as software entities. I contain about a million such passengers, and will happily make room for your ship's company, if you wish to take up the offer of a free ride."*

"No thank you," the Captain demurred. "We like corporeality, and do not find your means of conveyance desireable or convenient."

"But it is ecologically and cosmologically sound! Your method, to the contrary, is polluting and harmful."

This caught our attention. Only folk who have sensitivity to environmental concerns are allowed to colonize, lest we ruin the new planets we take under our care. This is not simply a matter of morality, but of self-interest, since our grandchildren will inherit the worlds we leave behind.

Still, the star probe's statement confused us. This time, I replied for the crew.

"Polluting? All we do is implode temporary micro black holes behind us and surf ahead on the resulting recoil of borrowed spacetime. What can be *polluting* about adding a little more space to empty space?"

"*Consider,*" the COP probe urged. "*Each time you do this, you add to the net distance separating your origin from your destination!*"

"By a very small fraction," I conceded. "But meanwhile, we experience a powerful pseudo-acceleration, driving us forward nearly to the speed of light."

"That is very convenient for you, but what about the rest of us?"

"The . . . rest . . . The rest of *whom?*"

"*The rest of the universe!*" the probe insisted, starting to sound petulant. "*While you speed ahead, you cause the distance from point A to point B to increase, making it marginally harder for the next voyager to make the same crossing.*"

I laughed. "*Marginally* is right! It would take millions of ships . . . *millions* of millions . . . to begin to appreciably affect interstellar distances, which are already increasing anyway, due to the cosmological expansion—"

The star-probe cut in.

"And where do you think that expansion comes from?"

I admit that I stared at that moment, speechless, until at last I found my voice with a hoarse croak.

"What . . ." I swallowed. "What do you mean by that?"

The COPs have a mission. They speed around the galaxies—not just this one, but most of those we see in the sky—urging others to practice restraint. Beseeching the short-sighted to think about the future. To refrain from spoiling things for future generations.

They have been at it for a very, very long time.

"You're not having much success, are you?" I asked, after partly recovering from the shock.

"*No, we are not,*" the probe answered, morosely. "*Every passing eon, the universe keeps getting larger. Stars get farther apart, making all the old means of travel less and less satisfying, and increasing the attraction of wasteful metric-surfing. It is so easy to do. Those who refrain are mostly, older, wiser species. The young seldom listen.*"

I looked around the communications dome of our fine vessel, thronging with the curious, with our children, spouses and loved ones—the many species of humanity and its friends who make up the vibrant culture of organic beings surging forth across this corner of the galaxy. The COP was saying that we weren't alone in this vibrant enthusiasm to move, to explore, to travel swiftly and see what there was to see. To trade and share and colonize. To *go!*

In fact, it seemed we were quite typical.

"No," I replied, a little sympathetically this time. "I don't suppose they do."

* * *

The morality-probes keep trying to flag us down, using entreaties, arguments and threats to persuade us to stop. But the entreaties don't move us. The arguments don't persuade. And the threats are as empty as the gaps between galaxies.

After many more voyages, I have learned that these frail, gnat-like COPs are ubiquitous, persistent, and futile. Most ships simply ignore the flickering light in the mirror, dismissing it as just another phenomenon of relativistic space, like the Star-Bow, or the ripples of expanding metric that throb each time we surge ahead on the exuberant wake of collapsing singularities.

I admit that I do see things a little differently, now. The universal expansion, that we had thought due to a "big bang" is, in fact, at least fifty percent exacerbated by vessels like ours, riding along on waves of pollution, filling space with more space, making things harder for generations to come.

It is hard for the mind to grasp—so *many* starships. So many that the universe is changing, every day, year, and eon that we continue to go charging around, caring only about ourselves and our immediate gratification. Once upon a time, when everything was much closer, it might have been possible to make do with other forms of transportation. In those days, beings *could* have refrained. If they had, we might not need the BHG drive today. If those earlier wastrels had shown some restraint.

On the other hand, I guess they'll say the same thing about *us* in times to come, when stars and galaxies are barely visible to each other, separated by the vast gulfs that *we* of this era short-sightedly create.

Alas, it is hard to practice self-control when you are young, and so full of a will to see and do things as fast as possible. Besides, everyone *else* is doing it. What difference will our measly contribution make to the mighty expansion of the universe? It's not as if we'd help matters much, if we alone stopped.

Anyway, the engines hum so sweetly. It feels good to cruise along at the redline, spearing the Star-Bow, pushing the speed limit all the way against the wall.

These days, we hardly glance in that mirror anymore . . . or pause to note the ever-reddening glow.

SEXUAL DIMORPHISM

Kim Stanley Robinson

Throughout his career, Robinson has been interested in politics, as is evident in his California trilogy of the 1980s (*The Wild Shore, The Gold Coast, Pacific Edge*), but it was in his Mars trilogy in the 1990s that Robinson was most overt in injecting large doses of political discussion into the text, but at the same time he was intensifying the overt science and expanding his portrayal of scientists at work, and (perhaps like Arthur C. Clarke) giving extensive descriptions of the natural landscape of his planetary setting in evocative language. Robinson's *The Years of Rice and Salt* (2002) is an alternate history novel. The novel explores a history of the world in which the influence of European civilization ended in the fourteenth century. While not hard SF, it continues Robinson's overt political engagement with his material.

"Sexual Dimorphism" is reprinted from *The Martians* (see Robinson note, above) While he was still working on the stories, he said in a *Locus* interview, "I've always called the collection *A Martian Romance*, which has to do with those early stories exploring fossil canyons, and 'Green Mars,' the novella of '85. I'll add one more . . . and then I'll have three stories describing a relationship that lasts a really long time. That's the Martian romance, but it's also my romance with the planet, and also the idea of the early Martian Romances. I'm going to do some stories that will be more like folktales or fairytales—romances in the technical sense."

This story is in that folktale mode, and is as much in the tradition of Brian Aldiss's "A Kind of Artistry" and Roger Zelazny's "A Rose for Ecclesiastes," as it is firmly in the hard SF tradition of stories about the life and thought of working scientists.

The potential for hallucination in paleogenomics was high. There was not only the omnipresent role of instrumentation in the envisioning of the ultramicroscopic fossil material, but also the metamorphosis over time of the material itself, both the DNA and its matrices, so that the data were invariably incomplete, and often shattered. Thus the possibility of psychological projection of patterns onto the rorschacherie of what in the end might be purely mineral processes had to be admitted.

Dr. Andrew Smith was as aware of these possibilities as anyone. Indeed, it constituted one of the central problems of his field—convincingly to sort the traces of DNA in the fossil record, distinguishing them from an array of possible pseudofossils. Pseudofossils littered the history of the discipline, from the earliest false nautiloids to the famous Martian pseudo-nanobacteria. Nothing progressed in paleogenomics unless you could show that you really were talking about what you said you were talking about. So Dr. Smith did not get too excited, at first, about what he was finding in the junk DNA of an early dolphin fossil.

*   *   *

In any case there were quite a few distractions to his work at that time. He was living on the south shore of the Amazonian Sea, that deep southerly bay of the world-ringing ocean, east of Elysium, near the equator. In the summer, even the cool summers they had been having lately, the extensive inshore shallows of the sea grew as warm as blood, and dolphins—adapted from Terran river dolphins—like the baiji from China, or the boto from the Amazon, or the susu from the Ganges, or the bhulan from the Indus—sported just off the beach. Morning sunlight lanced through the waves and picked out their flashing silhouettes, sometimes groups of eight or ten of them, all playing in the same wave.

The marine laboratory he worked at, located on the seafront of the harbor town Eumenides Point, was associated with the Acheron labs, farther up the coast to the west. The work at Eumenides had mostly to do with the shifting ecologies of a sea that was getting saltier. Dr. Smith's current project dealing with this issue involved investigating the various adaptations of extinct cetaceans who had lived when the Earth's sea had exhibited different levels of salt. He had in his lab some fossil material, sent to the lab from Earth for study, as well as the voluminous literature on the subject, including the full genomes of all the living descendants of these creatures. The transfer of fossils from Earth introduced the matter of cosmic-ray contamination to all the other problems involved in the study of ancient DNA, but most people dismissed these effects as minor and inconsequential, which was why fossils were shipped across at all. And of course with the recent deployment of fusion-powered rapid vehicles, the amount of exposure to cosmic rays had been markedly reduced. Smith was therefore able to do research on mammal salt tolerance both ancient and modern, thus helping to illuminate the current situation on Mars, also joining the debates ongoing concerning the paleohalocycles of the two planets, now one of the hot research areas in comparative planetology and bioengineering.

Nevertheless, it was a field of research so arcane that if you were not involved in it, you tended not to believe in it. It was an offshoot, a mix of two difficult fields, its ultimate usefulness a long shot, especially compared to most of the inquiries being conducted at the Eumenides Point Labs. Smith found himself fighting a feeling of marginalization in the various lab meetings and informal gatherings, in coffee lounges, cocktail parties, beach luncheons, boating excursions. At all of these he was the odd man out, with only his colleague Frank Drumm, who worked on reproduction in the dolphins currently living offshore, expressing any great interest in his work and its applications. Worse yet, his work appeared to be becoming less and less important to his advisor and employer, Vlad Taneev, who as one of the First Hundred, and the co-founder of the Acheron labs, was ostensibly the most powerful scientific mentor one could have on Mars; but who in practice turned out to be nearly impossible of access, and rumored to be in failing health, so that it was like having no boss at all, and therefore no access to the lab's technical staff and so forth. A bitter disappointment.

And then of course there was Selena, his—his partner, roommate, girlfriend, significant other, lover—there were many words for this relationship, though none were quite right. The woman with whom he lived, with whom he had gone through graduate school and two post-docs, with whom he had moved to Eumenides Point, taking a small apartment near the beach, near the terminus of the coastal tram, where when one looked back east the point itself just heaved over the horizon, like a dorsal fin seen far out to sea. Selena was making great progress in her own field, genetically engineering salt grasses; a subject of great importance here, where they were trying to stabilize a thousand-kilometer coastline of low dunes and quicksand swamps. Scientific and bioengineering progress; important achievements, relevant to the situation; all things were coming to her professionally, including of course offers to team up in any number of exciting public/co-op collaborations.

And all things were coming to her privately as well. Smith had always thought her beautiful, and now he saw that with her success, other men were coming to the same realization. It took only a little attention to see it; an ability to look past shabby lab coats and a generally unkempt style to the sleekly curving body and the intense, almost ferocious intelligence. No—his Selena looked much like all the rest of the lab rats when in the lab, but in the summers when the group went down in the evening to the warm tawny beach to swim, she walked out the long expanse of the shallows like a goddess in a bathing suit, like Venus returning to the sea. Everyone in these parties pretended not to notice, but you couldn't help it.

All very well; except that she was losing interest in him. This was a process that Smith feared was irreversible; or, to be more precise, that if it had gotten to the point where he could notice it, it was too late to stop it. So now he watched her, furtive and helpless, as they went through their domestic routines; there was a goddess in his bathroom, showering, drying off, dressing, each moment like a dance.

But she didn't chat anymore. She was absorbed in her thoughts, and tended to keep her back to him. No—it was all going away.

They had met in an adult swim club in Mangala, while they were both grad students at the university there. Now, as if to re-invoke that time, Smith took up Frank's suggestion and joined him at an equivalent club in Eumenides Point, and began to swim regularly again. He went from the tram or the lab down to the big fifty-meter pool, set on a terrace overlooking the ocean, and swam so hard in the mornings that the whole rest of the day he buzzed along in a flow of beta endorphins, scarcely aware of his work problems or the situation at home. After work he took the tram home feeling his appetite kick in, and banged around the kitchen throwing together a meal and eating much of it as he cooked it, irritated (if she was there at all) with Selena's poor cooking and her cheery talk about her work, irritated also probably just from hunger, and dread at the situation hanging over them; at this pretense that they were still in a normal life. But if he snapped at her during this fragile hour she would go silent the whole rest of the evening; it happened fairly often; so he tried to contain his temper and make the meal and quickly eat his part of it, to get his blood sugar level back up.

Either way she fell asleep abruptly around nine, and he was left to read into the timeslip, or even slip out and take a walk on the night beach a few hundred yards away from their apartment. One night, walking west, he saw Pseudo-phobos pop up into the sky like a distress flare down the coast, and when he came back into the apartment she was awake and talking happily on the phone; she was startled to see him, and cut the call short, thinking about what to say, and then said, "That was Mark, we've gotten tamarisk three fifty-nine to take repetitions of the third salt flusher gene!"

"That's good," he said, moving into the dark kitchen so she wouldn't see his face.

This annoyed her. "You really don't care how my work goes, do you?"

"Of course I do. That's good, I said."

She dismissed that with a noise.

Then one day he got home and Mark was there with her, in the living room, and at a single glance he could see they had been laughing about something; had been sitting closer together than when he started opening the door. He ignored that and was as pleasant as he could be.

The next day as he swam at the morning workout, he watched the women swimming with him in his lane. All three of them had swum all their lives, their freestyle stroke perfected beyond the perfection of any dance move ever made on land, the millions of repetitions making their movement as unconscious as that of any fish in the sea. Under the surface he saw their bodies flowing forward, revealing their sleek lines—classic swimmer lines, like Selena's—rangy shoulders tucking up against their ears one after the next, ribcages smoothed over by powerful lats, breasts flatly merged into big pecs or else bobbing left then right, as the case might be; bellies meeting high hipbones accentuated by the high cut of their swimsuits, backs curving up to bottoms rounded and compact, curving to powerful thighs then long calves, and feet outstretched like ballerinas'. Dance was a weak analogy for such beautiful movement. And it all went on for stroke after stroke, lap after lap, until he was mesmerized beyond further thought or observation; it was just one aspect of a sensually saturated environment.

Their current lane leader was pregnant, yet swimming stronger than any of the rest of them, not even huffing and puffing during their rest intervals, when Smith often had to suck air—instead she laughed and shook her head, exclaiming "Every time I do a flip turn he keeps kicking me!" She was seven months along, round in the middle like a little whale, but still she fired down the pool at a rate none of the other three in the lane could match. The strongest swimmers in the club were simply amazing. Soon after getting into the sport, Smith had worked hard to swim a hundred-meter freestyle in less than a minute, a goal appropriate to him, and finally he had done it once at a meet and been pleased; then later he heard about the local college women's team's workout, which consisted of a hundred hundred-meter freestyle swims *all on a minute interval.* He understood then that although all humans looked roughly the same, some were stupendously stronger than others. Their pregnant leader was in the lower echelon of these strong swimmers, and regarded the swim she was making today as a light stretching-out, though it was beyond anything her lane mates could do with their best effort. You couldn't help watching her when passing by in the other direction, because despite her speed she was supremely smooth and effortless, she took fewer strokes per lap than the rest of them, and yet still made substantially better time. It was like magic. And that sweet blue curve of the new child carried inside.

Back at home things continued to degenerate. Selena often worked late, and talked to him less than ever.

"I love you," he said. "Selena, I love you."

"I know."

He tried to throw himself into his work. They were at the same lab, they could go home late together. Talk like they used to about their work, which though not the same, was still genomics in both cases; how much closer could two sciences be? Surely it would help to bring them back together.

But genomics was a very big field. It was possible to occupy different parts of it, no doubt about that. They were proving it. Smith persevered, however, using a new and more powerful electron microscope, and he began to make some headway in unraveling the patterns in his fossilized DNA.

It looked like what had been preserved in the samples he had been given was almost entirely what used to be called the junk DNA of the creature. In times past this would have been bad luck, but the Kohl labs in Acheron had recently been making great strides in unraveling the various purposes of junk DNA, which proved not to be useless after all, as might have been guessed, development being as complex as it was. Their breakthrough consisted in characterizing very short and scrambled repetitive sequences within junk DNA that could be shown to code instructions for higher hierarchical operations than they were used to seeing at the gene level—cell differentiation, information order sequencing, apoptosis, and the like.

Using this new understanding to unravel any clues in partially degraded fossil junk DNA would be hard, of course. But the nucleotide sequences were there in his EM images—or, to be more precise, the characteristic mineral replacements for the adenine=thymine and cytosine=guanine couplets, replacements well-established in the literature, were there to be clearly identified. Nanofossils, in effect; but legible to those who could read them. And once read, it was then possible to brew identical sequences of living nucleotides, matching the originals of the fossil creature. In theory one could re-create the creature itself, though in practice nothing like the entire genome was ever there, making it impossible. Not that there weren't people trying anyway with simpler fossil organisms, either going for the whole thing or using hybrid DNA techniques to graft expressions they could decipher onto living templates, mostly descendants of the earlier creature.

With this particular ancient dolphin, almost certainly a fresh-water dolphin (though most of these were fairly salt tolerant, living in river-mouths as they did), complete resuscitation would be impossible. It wasn't what Smith was trying to do anyway. What would be interesting would be to find fragments that did not seem to have a match in the living descendants' genome, then hopefully synthesize living in vitro fragments, clip them into contemporary strands, and see how these experimental animals did in hybridization tests and in various environments. Look for differences in function.

He was also doing mitochondrial tests when he could, which if successful would permit tighter dating for the specie's divergence from precursor species. He might be able to give it a specific slot on the marine mammal family tree, which during the early Pliocene was very complicated.

Both avenues of investigation were labor-intensive, time-consuming, almost thoughtless work—perfect, in other words. He worked for hours and hours every day, for weeks, then months. Sometimes he managed to go home on the tram with Selena; more often he didn't. She was writing up her latest results with her collaborators, mostly with Mark. Her hours were irregular. When he was working he didn't have to think about this; so he worked all the time. It was not a solution, not even a very good strategy—it even seemed to be making things worse—and he had to attempt it against an ever-growing sense of despair and loss; but he did it nevertheless.

"What do you think of this acheron work?" he asked Frank one day at work, pointing to the latest printout from the Kohl lab, lying heavily annotated on his desk.

"It's very interesting! It makes it look like we're finally getting past the genes to the whole instruction manual."

"If there is such a thing."

"Has to be, right? Though I'm not sure the Kohl lab's values for the rate adaptive mutants will be fixed are high enough. Ohta and Kimura suggested ten percent as the upper limit, and that fits with what I've seen."

Smith nodded, pleased. "They're probably just being conservative."

"No doubt, but you have to go with the data."

"So—in that context—you think it makes sense for me to pursue this fossil junk DNA?"

"Well, sure. What do you mean? It's sure to tell us interesting things."

"It's incredibly slow."

"Why don't you read off a long sequence, brew it up and venter it, and see what you get?"

Smith shrugged. Whole-genome shotgun sequencing struck him as slipshod, but it was certainly faster. Reading small bits of single-stranded DNA, called expressed sequence tags, had quickly identified most of the genes on the human genome; but it had missed some, and it ignored even the regulatory DNA sequences controlling the protein-coding portion of the genes, not to mention the so-called junk DNA itself, filling long stretches between the more clearly meaningful sequences.

Smith expressed these doubts to Frank, who nodded, but said, "It isn't the same now that the mapping is so complete. You've got so many reference points you can't get confused where your bits are on the big sequence. Just plug what you've got into the Lander-Waterman, then do the finishing with the Kohl variations, and even if there are massive repetitions, you'll still be okay. And with the bits you've got, well they're almost like ests anyway, they're so degraded. So you might as well give it a try."

Smith nodded.

That night he and Selena trammed home together. "What do you think of the possibility of shotgun sequencing in vitro copies of what I've got?" he asked her shyly.

"Sloppy," she said. "Double jeopardy."

A new schedule evolved. He worked, swam, took the tram home. Usually Selena wasn't there. Often their answering machine held messages for her from Mark, talking about their work. Or messages from her to Smith, telling him that she would be home late. As was happening so often, he sometimes went out for dinner with Frank and other lane mates, after the evening workouts. One time at a beach restaurant they ordered several pitchers of beer, and then went out for a walk on the beach, and ended up running out into the shallows of the bay and swimming around in the warm dark water, so different from their pool, splashing each other and laughing hard. It was a good time.

But when he got home that night, there was another message on the answering machine from Selena, saying that she and Mark were working on their paper after getting a bite to eat, and that she would be home extra late.

She wasn't kidding; at two o'clock in the morning she was still out. In the long minutes following the timeslip Smith realized that no one stayed out this late working on a paper without calling home. This was therefore a message of a different kind.

Pain and anger swept through him, first one then the other. The indirection of it struck him as cowardly. He deserved at least a revelation—a confession—a scene. As the long minutes passed he got angrier and angrier; then frightened for a moment, that she might have been hurt or something. But she hadn't. She was out there somewhere fooling around. Suddenly he was furious.

He pulled cardboard boxes out of their closet and yanked open her drawers, and threw all her clothes in heaps in the boxes, crushing them in so they would all fit. But they gave off their characteristic scent of laundry soap and her, and smelling it he groaned and sat down on the bed, knees weak. If he carried through with this he would never again see her putting on and taking off these clothes, and just as an animal he groaned at the thought.

But men are not animals. He finished throwing her things into boxes, took them outside the front door and dropped them there.

She came back at three. He heard her kick into the boxes and make some muffled exclamation.

He hurled open the door and stepped out.

"What's this?" She had been startled out of whatever scenario she had planned, and now was getting angry. Her, angry! It made him furious all over again.

"You know what it is."

"What!"

"You and Mark."

She eyed him.

"Now you notice," she said at last. "A year after it started. And this is your first response." Gesturing down at the boxes.

He hit her in the face.

Immediately he crouched at her side and helped her sit up, saying "Oh God Selena I'm sorry, I'm sorry, I didn't mean to," he had only thought to slap her for her contempt, contempt that he had not noticed her betrayal earlier, "I can't believe I—"

"Get *away*," striking him off with wild blows, crying and shouting, "get away, get away," frightened, "you bastard, you miserable bastard, what do you, don't you *dare* hit me!" in a near shriek, though she kept her voice down too, aware still of the apartment complex around them. Hands held to her face.

"I'm sorry Selena. I'm very very sorry, I was angry at what you said but I know that isn't, that doesn't . . . I'm sorry." Now he was as angry at himself as he had been at her—what could he have been thinking, why had he given her the moral high ground like this, it was she who had broken their bond, it was she who should be in the wrong! She who was now sobbing—turning away—suddenly walking off into the night. Lights went on in a couple of windows nearby. Smith stood staring down at the boxes of her lovely clothes, his right knuckles throbbing.

That life was over. He lived on alone in the apartment by the beach, and kept going in to work, but he was shunned there by the others, who all knew what had happened. Selena did not come in to work again until the bruises were gone, and after that she did not press charges, or speak to him about that night, but she did move in with Mark, and avoided him at work when she could. As who wouldn't. Occasionally she dropped by his nook to ask in a neutral voice about some logistical aspect of their break-up. He could not meet her eye. Nor could he meet the eye of anyone else at work, not properly. It was strange how one could have a conversation with people and appear to be meeting their gaze during it, when all the time they were not really quite looking at you and you were not really quite looking at them. Primate subtleties, honed over millions of years on the savanna.

He lost appetite, lost energy. In the morning he would wake up and wonder why he should get out of bed. Then looking at the blank walls of the bedroom, where Selena's prints had hung, he would sometimes get so angry at her that his pulse hammered uncomfortably in his neck and forehead. This got him out of bed, but then there was nowhere to go, except work. And there everyone knew he was a wife beater, a domestic abuser, an asshole. Martian society did not tolerate such people.

Shame or anger; anger or shame. Grief or humiliation. Resentment or regret. Lost love. Omnidirectional rage.

Mostly he didn't swim anymore. The sight of the swimmer women was too painful now, though they were as friendly as always; they knew nothing of the lab except him and Frank, and Frank had not said anything to them about what had happened. It made no difference. He was cut off from them. He knew he ought to swim more, and he swam less. Whenever he resolved to turn things around he would swim two or three days in a row, then let it fall away again.

Once at the end of an early evening workout he had forced himself to attend—and now he felt better, as usual—while they were standing in the lane steaming, his three most constant lane mates made quick plans to go to a nearby trattoria after showering. One looked at him. "Pizza at Rico's?"

He shook his head. "Hamburger at home," he said sadly.

They laughed at this. "Ah, come on. It'll keep another night."

"Come on, Andy," Frank said from the next lane. "I'll go too, if that's okay."

"Sure," the women said. Frank often swam in their lane too.

"Well . . ." Smith roused himself. "Okay."

He sat with them and listened to their chatter around the restaurant table. They still seemed to be slightly steaming, their hair wet and wisping away from their foreheads. The three women were young. It was interesting; away from the pool they looked ordinary and undistinguished: skinny, mousy, plump, maladroit, whatever. With their clothes on you could not guess at their fantastically powerful shoulders and lats, their compact smooth musculatures. Like seals dressed up in clown suits, waddling around a stage.

"Are you okay?" one asked him when he had been silent too long.

"Oh yeah, yeah." He hesitated, glanced at Frank. "Broke up with my girlfriend."

"Ah ha! I *knew* it was something!" Hand to his arm (they all bumped into each other all the time in the pool): "You haven't been your usual self lately."

"No." He smiled ruefully. "It's been hard."

He could never tell them about what had happened. And Frank wouldn't either. But without that none of the rest of his story made any sense. So he couldn't talk about any of it.

They sensed this and shifted in their seats, preparatory to changing the topic. "Oh well," Frank said, helping them. "Lots more fish in the sea."

"In the pool," one of the women joked, elbowing him.

He nodded, tried to smile.

They looked at each other. One asked the waiter for the check, and another said to Smith and Frank, "Come with us over to my place, we're going to get in the hot tub and soak our aches away."

She rented a room in a little house with an enclosed courtyard, and all the rest of the residents were away. They followed her through the dark house into the courtyard, and took the cover off the hot tub and turned it on, then took their clothes off and got in the steaming water. Smith joined them, feeling shy. People on the beaches of Mars sunbathed without clothes all the time, it was no big deal really. Frank seemed not to notice, he was perfectly relaxed. But they didn't swim at the pool like this.

They all sighed at the water's heat. The woman from the house went inside and brought out some beer and cups. Light from the kitchen fell on her as she put down the dumpie and passed out the cups. Smith already knew her body perfectly well from their many hours together in the pool; nevertheless he was shocked seeing the whole of her. Frank ignored the sight, filling the cups from the dumpie.

They drank beer, talked small talk. Two were vets; their lane leader, the one who had been pregnant, was a bit older, a chemist in a pharmaceutical lab near the pool. Her baby was being watched by her co-op that night. They all looked up to her, Smith saw, even here. These days she brought the baby to the pool and swam just as powerfully as ever, parking the baby-carrier just beyond the splash line. Smith's muscles melted in the hot water. He sipped his beer listening to them.

One of the women looked down at her breasts in the water and laughed. "They float like pull buoys."

Smith had already noticed this.

"No wonder women swim better than men."

"As long as they aren't so big they interfere with the hydrodynamics."

Their leader looked down through her fogged glasses, pink-faced, hair tied up, misted, demure. "I wonder if mine float less because I'm nursing."

"But all that milk."

"Yes, but the water in the milk is neutral density, it's the fat that floats. It could be that empty breasts float even more than full ones."

"Whichever has more fat, yuck."

"I could run an experiment, nurse him from just one side and then get in and see—" but they were laughing too hard for her to complete this scenario. "It would work! Why are you laughing!"

They only laughed more. Frank was cracking up, looking blissed, blessed. These women friends trusted them. But Smith still felt set apart. He looked at their lane leader: a pink bespectacled goddess, serenely vague and unaware; the scientist as heroine; the first full human being.

But later when he tried to explain this feeling to Frank, or even just to describe it, Frank shook his head. "It's a bad mistake to worship women," he warned. "A category error. Women and men are so much the same it isn't worth discussing the difference. The genes are identical almost entirely, you know that. A couple hormonal expressions and that's it. So they're just like you and me."

"More than a couple."

"Not much more. We all start out female, right? So you're better off thinking that nothing major ever really changes that. Penis just an oversized clitoris. Men are women. Women are men. Two parts of a reproductive system, completely equivalent."

Smith stared at him. "You're kidding."

"What do you mean?"

"Well—I've never seen a man swell up and give birth to a new human being, let me put it that way."

"So what? It happens, it's a specialized function. You never see women ejaculating either. But we all go back to being the same afterward. Details of reproduction only matter a tiny fraction of the time. No, we're all the same. We're all in it together. There are no differences."

Smith shook his head. It would be comforting to think so. But the data did not support the hypothesis. Ninety-five percent of all the murders in history had been committed by men. This was a difference.

He said as much, but Frank was not impressed. The murder ratio was becoming more nearly equal on Mars, he replied, and much less frequent for everybody, thus demonstrating very nicely that the matter was culturally conditioned, an artifact of Terran patriarchy no longer relevant on Mars. Nurture rather than nature. Although it was a false dichotomy. Nature could prove anything you wanted, Frank insisted. Female hyenas were vicious killers, male bonobos and muriquis were gentle cooperators. It meant nothing, Frank said. It told them nothing.

But Frank had not hit a woman in the face without ever planning to.

Patterns in the fossil INIA data sets became clearer and clearer. Stochastic resonance programs highlighted what had been preserved.

"Look here," Smith said to Frank one afternoon when Frank leaned in to say good-bye for the day. He pointed at his computer screen. "Here's a sequence from my boto, part of the GX three oh four, near the juncture, see?"

"You've got a female then?"

"I don't know. I think this here means I do. But look, see how it matches with this part of the human genome. It's in Hillis 8050 . . ."

Frank came into his nook and stared at the screen. "Comparing junk to junk . . . I don't know. . . ."

"But it's a match for more than a hundred units in a row, see? Leading right into the gene for progesterone initiation."

Frank squinted at the screen. "Um, well." He glanced quickly at Smith.

Smith said, "I'm wondering if there's some really long-term persistence in junk DNA, all the way back to earlier mammals' precursors to both these."

"But dolphins are not our ancestors," Frank said.

"There's a common ancestor back there somewhere."

"Is there?" Frank straightened up. "Well, whatever. I'm not so sure about the pattern congruence itself. It's sort of similar, but, you know."

"What do you mean, don't you see that? Look right there!"

Frank glanced down at him, startled, then non-committal. Seeing this Smith became inexplicably frightened.

"Sort of," Frank said. "Sort of. You should run hybridization tests, maybe, see how good the fit really is. Or check with Acheron about repeats in nongene DNA."

"But the congruence is perfect! It goes on for hundreds of pairs, how could that be a coincidence?"

Frank looked even more non-committal than before. He glanced out the door of the nook. Finally he said, "I don't see it that congruent. Sorry, I just don't see it. Look, Andy. You've been working awfully hard for a long time. And you've been depressed too, right? Since Selena left?"

Smith nodded, feeling his stomach tighten. He had admitted as much a few months before. Frank was one of the very few people these days who would look him in the eye.

"Well, you know. Depression has chemical impacts in the brain, you know that. Sometimes it means you begin seeing patterns that others can't see as well. It doesn't mean they aren't there, no doubt they are there. But whether they mean anything significant, whether they're more than just a kind of analogy, or similarity—" He looked down at Smith and stopped. "Look, it's not my field. You should show this to Amos, or go up to Acheron and talk to the old man."

"Uh huh. Thanks, Frank."

"Oh no, no, no need. Sorry, Andy. I probably shouldn't have said anything. It's just, you know. You've been spending a hell of a lot of time here."

"Yeah."

Frank left.

Sometimes he fell asleep at his desk. He got some of his work done in dreams. Sometimes he found he could sleep down on the beach, wrapped in a greatcoat on the fine sand, lulled by the sound of the waves rolling in. At work he stared at the lined dots and letters on the screens, constructing the schematics of the sequences, nucleotide by nucleotide. Most were completely unambiguous. The correlation between the two main schematics was excellent, far beyond the possibility of chance. X chromosomes in humans clearly exhibited nongene DNA traces of a distant aquatic ancestor, a kind of dolphin. Y chromosomes in humans lacked these passages, and they also matched with chimpanzees more completely than X chromosomes did. Frank had appeared not to believe it, but there it was, right on the screen. But how could it be? What did it mean? Where did any of them get what they were? They had natures from birth. Just under five million years ago, chimps and humans separated out as two different species from a common ancestor, a woodland ape. The Inis geoffrensis fossil Smith was working on had been precisely dated to about 5.1 million years old. About half of all orangutan sexual encounters are rape.

One night after quitting work alone in the lab, he took a tram in the wrong direction, downtown, without ever admitting to himself what he was doing, until he was standing outside Mark's apartment complex, under the steep rise of the dorsum ridge. Walking up a staircased alleyway ascending the ridge gave him a view right into Mark's windows. And there was Selena, washing dishes at the kitchen window and looking back over her shoulder to talk with someone. The tendon in her neck stood out in the light. She laughed.

Smith walked home. It took an hour. Many trams passed him.

He couldn't sleep that night. He went down to the beach and lay rolled in his greatcoat. Finally he fell asleep.

He had a dream. A small hairy bipedal primate, chimp-faced, walked like a hunchback down a beach in east Africa, in the late afternoon sun. The warm water of the shallows lay greenish and translucent. Dolphins rode inside the waves. The ape waded out into the shallows. Long powerful arms, evolved for hitting; a quick grab and he had one by the tail, by the dorsal fin. Surely it could escape, but it didn't try. Female; the ape turned her over, mated with her, released her. He left and came back to find the dolphin in the shallows, giving birth to twins, one male one female. The ape's troop swarmed into the shallows, killed and ate them both. Farther offshore the dolphin birthed two more.

The dawn woke Smith. He stood and walked out into the shallows. He saw dolphins inside the transparent indigo waves. He waded out into the surf. The water was only a little colder than the workout pool. The dawn sun was low. The dolphins were only a little longer than he was, small and lithe. He bodysurfed with them. They were faster than him in the waves, but flowed around him when they had to. One leaped over him and splashed back into the curl of the wave ahead of him. Then one flashed under him, and on an impulse he grabbed at its dorsal fin and caught it, and was suddenly moving faster in the wave, as it rose with both of them inside it—by far the greatest bodysurfing ride of his life. He held on. The dolphin and all the rest of its pod turned and swam out to sea, and still he held on. This is it, he thought. Then he remembered that they were air-breathers too. It was going to be all right.

INTO THE MIRANDA RIFT

G. David Nordley

G. David Nordley (born 1947) lives in Sunnyvale, California. He is retired from the Air Force and has been publishing well-thought-out hard SF since the early nineties. His primary venue is *Analog*, where he is a regular contributor, and where this story appeared. *Tangent Online* calls Nordley "one of the better *Analog* discoveries of this past decade." He has written, but not yet published, three SF novels, and is working on more. His first collection, *After the Vikings: Stories of a Future Mars*, was published in 2002 as an electronic book.

He majored in physics as an undergraduate with the intention of becoming an astronomer, but in 1969 joined the U.S. Air Force to avoid the draft. He worked mainly as an astronautical engineer, managing satellite operations, spacecraft engineering, and advanced propulsion research, picking up a master's degree in systems management along the way. While working in advanced propulsion, he met and became inspired to write by physicist and author Robert L. Forward. He retired as a major at the end of 1989 and began submitting stories in 1990, using the "G. David" form of his name for fiction. Describing Nordley's fiction, J. K. Klein says, "As a writer, his main interest is the future of human exploration and settlement of space, and his stories typically focus on the dramatic aspects of individual lives within the broad sweep of a plausible human future."

We asked Nordley for comments and he sent a long piece from which we have extracted the following remarks:

> I was asked to provide some brief thoughts on hard science fiction. The term "hard," I think, is meant to indicate "accurate" as opposed to the use of "soft," or "rubber" science, but it has some unfortunate steelish connotations that might lead some to see use of real science as being in some way contrary to intuitive, character-driven, or humanistic fiction. At any rate, I've taken to using the term "scientific realism," meaning simply keeping the events of the story within the laws of nature as well as one can.
>
> Yes, new laws of nature might be invented, but take care! Everything that happens under such new laws of nature must be consistent with the mountains of data on which the known laws of nature rest. Many a well-informed physicist has trembled at such a task.
>
> I'm not worried about classifying works; words are labels for fuzzy sets and apply in degree. Some stories are more scientifically realistic than others, but even stories in which magic plays a role (by magic, I mean the deliberate setting aside of natural laws) may have scientifically realistic aspects. A few honest mistakes are par for the course, but the kind of wholesale carnage of science displayed in some unmentionable media-related efforts, I think, damages whatever reputation remains of science fiction's relevance to the human future. I think it is this reputa-

tion, established by Verne, Orwell, and Clarke and the like, which keeps people thinking "maybe . . ." We are concerned not with prediction but with illuminating possibilities and people's reaction to them. The more possible, I think, the more interesting.

In summary, I see science in scientific realism as playing the same role as history in historical fiction or law in detective fiction. I am not impressed by the argument that science may be disregarded "for the sake of the story." Rather, I think that realism adds to the relevance and long term value of a work. All else being equal, I think that stories that can happen teach us more than stories that can't. So, "for the sake of the story," I do, and heed, the research.

This story is a planetary exploration story in the same sense as Bova's "Mount Olympus," a space frontier story, and also a man-against-the-universe story of the Hal Clement hard SF type (see Clement note). One of the pleasures of this type is perceiving how the physics of the environment alters the rules of behavior, especially the rules of human survival.

I

This starts after we had already walked, crawled, and clawed our way fifty-three zigzagging kilometers into the Great Miranda Rift, and had already penetrated seventeen kilometers below the mean surface. It starts because the mother of all Miranda-quakes just shut the door behind us and the chances of this being rescued are somewhat better than mine; I need to do more than just take notes for a future article. It starts because I have faith in human stubbornness, even in a hopeless endeavor; and I think the rescuers will come, eventually. I am Wojciech Bubka and this is my journal.

Miranda, satellite of Uranus, is a cosmic metaphor about those things in creation that come together without really fitting, like the second try at marriage, ethnic integration laws, or a poet trying to be a science reporter. It was blasted apart by something a billion years ago and the parts drifted back together, more or less. There are gaps. Rifts. Empty places for things to work their way in that are not supposed to be there; things that don't belong to something of whole cloth.

Like so many great discoveries, the existence of the rifts was obvious after the fact, but our geologist, Nikhil Ray, had to endure a decade of derision, several rejected papers, a divorce from a wife unwilling to share academic ridicule, and public humiliation in the pop science media—before the geology establishment finally conceded that what the seismological network on Miranda's surface had found had, indeed, confirmed his work.

Nikhil had simply observed that although Miranda appears to be made of the same stuff as everything else in the Uranian system, the other moons are just under twice as dense as water while Miranda is only one and a third times as dense. More ice and less rock below was one possibility. The other possibility, which Nikhil had patiently pointed out, was that there could be less of *everything*; a scattering of voids or bubbles beneath.

So, with the goat-to-hero logic we all love, when seismological results clearly showed that Miranda was laced with substantial amounts of nothing, Nikhil became a minor solar system celebrity, with a permanent chair at Coriolis, and a beautiful, high-strung, young renaissance woman as a trophy wife.

But, by that time, I fear there were substantial empty places in Nikhil, too.

Like Miranda, this wasn't clear from his urbane and vital surface when we met.

He was tall for a Bengali, a lack of sun had left his skin with only a tint of bronze, and he had a sharp face that hinted at an Arab or a Briton in his ancestry; likely both. He moved with a sort of quick, decisive energy that nicely balanced the tolerant good-fellow manners of an academic aristocrat in the imperial tradition. If he now distrusted people in general, if he kept them all at a pleasantly formal distance, if he harbored a secret contempt for his species, well, this had not been apparent to Catherine Ray, M.D., who had married him after his academic rehabilitation.

I think she later found the emptiness within him and part of her had recoiled, while the other, controlling part found no objective reason to leave a relationship that let her flit around the top levels of Solar System academia. Perhaps that explained why she chose to go on a fortnight of exploration with someone she seemed to detest; oh, the stories she would tell. Perhaps that explained her cynicism. Perhaps not.

We entered the great rift three days of an age ago, at the border of the huge chevron formation: the rift where two dissimilar geologic structures meet, held together by Miranda's gentle gravity and little else. Below the cratered, dust choked surface, the great rift was a network of voids between pressure ridges; rough wood, slap-glued together by a lazy carpenter late on a Saturday night. It could, Nikhil thinks, go through the entire moon. There were other joints, other rifts, other networks of empty places—but this was the big one.

Ah, yes, those substantial amounts of nothing. As a poet, I am fascinated by contradiction and I find a certain attraction to exploring vast areas of hidden emptiness under shells of any kind.

I fill voids, so to speak. I am an explicit rebel in a determinedly impressionist literary world of artful obscurity which fails to generate recognition or to make poets feel like they are doing anything more meaningful than the intellectual equivalent of masturbation—and pays them accordingly. The metaphor of Miranda intrigued me; an epic lay there beneath the dust and ice. Wonders to behold there must be in the biggest underground system of caverns in the known universe. The articles, interviews, and talk shows played out in my mind. All I had to do was get there.

I had a good idea of how to do that. Her name was Miranda Lotati. Four years ago, the spelunking daughter of the guy in charge of *Solar System Astrographic*'s project board had been a literature student of mine at Coriolis University. When I heard of the discovery of Nikhil's mysterious caverns, it was a trivial matter to renew the acquaintance, this time without the impediments of faculty ethics. By this time she had an impressive list of caves, mountains, and other strange places to her credit, courtesy of her father's money and connections, I had thought.

She had seemed a rough edged, prickly woman in my class, and her essays were dry condensed dullness, never more than the required length, but which covered the points involved well enough that honesty had forced me to pass her.

Now, armed with news of the moon Miranda's newly discovered caverns, I decided her name was clearly her destiny. I wasn't surprised when an inquiry had revealed no current relationship. So, I determined to create one and bend it toward my purposes. Somewhat to my surprise, it worked. Worked to the point where it wasn't entirely clear whether she was following my agenda, or I, hers.

Randi, as I got to know her, was something like a black hole; of what goes in, nothing comes out. Things somehow accrete to her orbit and bend to her will without any noticeable verbal effort on her part. She can spend a whole evening without saying anything more than "uh-huh." Did you like the Bach? Nice place you have. Are you comfortable? Do you want more? Did you like it? Do you want to do it again tomorrow?

"Uh-huh."

"Say, if you go into Miranda someone should do more than take pictures, don't you think? I've thrown a few words around in my time, perchance I could lend my services to chronicle the expedition? What do you think?"

"Uh-huh."

My contract with her is unspoken, and is thus on her terms. There is no escape. But we are complementary. I became her salesman. I talked her father into funding Nikhil, and talked Nikhil into accepting support from one of his erstwhile enemies. Randi organized the people and things that started coming her way into an expedition.

Randi is inarticulate, not crazy. She goes about her wild things in a highly disciplined way. When she uses words, she makes lists: "Batteries, CO_2 Recyclers, Picks, Robot, Ropes, Spare tightsuits, Tissue, Vacuum tents, Medical supplies, Waste bags, etc."

Such things come to her through grants, donations, her father's name, friends from previous expeditions, and luck. She worked very hard at getting these things together. Sometimes I felt I fit down there in "etc.," somewhere between the t and the c, and counted myself lucky. If she had only listed "Back door," perhaps we would have had one.

As I write, she is lying beside me in our vacuum tent, exhausted with worry. I am tired, too.

We wasted a day, sitting on our sausage-shaped equipment pallets, talking, and convincing ourselves to move on.

Nikhil explained our predicament: Randi's namesake quivers as it bobs up and down in its not quite perfect orbit, as inclined to be different as she. Stresses accumulate over ages, build up inside and release, careless of the consequences. We had discovered, he said, that Miranda is still shrinking through the gradual collapse of its caverns during such quakes. Also, because the gravity is so low, it might take years for a series of quakes and aftershocks to play itself out. The quake danger wouldn't subside until long after we escaped, or died.

We had to make sure the front door was closed. It was—slammed shut: the wide gallery we traversed to arrive at this cavern is now a seam, a disjoint. A scar and a change of color remain to demarcate the forcible fusion of two previously separate layers of clathrate.

Sam jammed all four arms into the wall, anchored them with piton fingers, pressed part of its composite belly right against the new seam, and pinged until it had an image of the obstructed passage. "The closure goes back at least a kilometer," it announced.

The fiber optic line we have been trailing for the last three days no longer reached the surface either. Sam removed the useless line from the comm set and held it against the business end of its laser radar. "The break's about fifteen kilometers from here," it reported.

"How do you know that?" I asked.

"Partial mirror," Randi explained on Sam's behalf. "Internal reflection."

Fifteen kilometers, I reflected. Not that we really could have dug through even one kilometer, but we'd done some pretending. Now the pretense ceased, and we faced reality.

I had little fear of sudden death, and in space exploration, the rare death is usually sudden. My attitude toward the risks of our expedition was that if I succeeded, the rewards would be great, and if I got killed, it wouldn't matter. I should have thought more about the possibility of enduring a long, drawn-out process of having life slowly and painfully drain away from me, buried in a clathrate tomb.

Then the group was silent for a long time. For my part, I was reviewing ways to painlessly end my life before the universe did it for me without concern for my suffering.

Then Nikhil's voice filled the void. "Friends, we knew the risks. If it's any consolation, that was the biggest quake recorded since instruments were put on this moon. By a factor of ten. That kind of adjustment," he waved his arms at obvious evidences of faults in the cavern around us, "should have been over with a hundred million years ago. Wretched luck, I'm afraid."

"Perhaps it will open up again?" his wife asked, her light features creased with concern behind the invisible faceplate of her helmet.

Nikhil missed the irony in her voice and answered his wife's question with an irony of his own. "Perhaps it will. In another hundred million years." He actually smiled.

Randi spoke softly; "Twenty days, CO_2 catalyst runs out in twenty days. We have two weeks of food at regular rations, but can we stretch that to a month or more. We have about a month of water each, depending on how severely we ration it. We can always get more by chipping ice and running it through our waste reprocessors. But without the catalyst, we can't make air."

"And we can't stop breathing," Cathy added.

"Cathy," I ask, "I suppose it is traditional for poets to think this way, so I'll ask the question. Is there any way to, well, end this gracefully, if and when we have to?"

"Several," she replied a shrug. "I can knock you out first, with anesthetic. Then kill you."

"How?" I ask.

"Does it matter?"

"To a poet, yes."

She nodded, and smiled. "Then, Wojciech, I shall put a piton through your heart, lest you rise again and in doing so devalue your manuscripts which by then will be selling for millions." Cathy's rare smiles have teeth in them.

"My dear," Nikhil said, our helmet transceivers faithfully reproducing the condescension in his tone, "your bedside manner is showing."

"My dear," Cathy murmured, "what would you know about anything to do with a bed?" Snipe and countersnipe. Perhaps such repartee held their marriage together, like gluons hold a meson together until it annihilates itself.

Sam returned from the "front door." "We can't go back that way, and our Rescuers can't come that way in twenty days with existing drilling equipment. I suggest we go somewhere else." A robot has the option of being logical at times like this.

"Quite right. If we wait here," Nikhil offered, "Miranda may remove the option of slow death, assisted or otherwise. Aftershocks are likely."

"Aftershocks, cave-in, suffocation," Randi listed the possibilities, "or other exits."

Nikhil shrugged and pointed to the opposite side of the cavern. "Shall we?"

"I'll follow you to hell, darling," Cathy answered.

Randi and I exchanged a glance which said; thank the lucky stars for *you*.

"Maps, such as they are," Randi began. "Rations, sleep schedule, leadership, and so on. Make decisions now, while we can think." At this she looked Nikhil straight in the eye, "While we care."

"Very well then," Nikhil responded with a shrug. "Sam is a bit uncreative when confronted with the unknown, Cathy and Wojciech have different areas of expertise, so perhaps Randi and I should take turns leading the pitches. I propose that we don't slight ourselves on the evening meal, but make do with minimal snacks at other times . . ."

"My darling idiot, we need protein energy for the work," Cathy interrupted. "We will have a good breakfast, even at the expense of dinner."

"Perhaps we could compromise on lunch," I offered.

"Travel distance, energy level, sustained alertness."

"On the other hand," I corrected, "moderation in all things . . ."

By the time we finally got going, we were approaching the start of the next sleep period, and Randi had effectively decided everything. We went single file behind the alternating pitch leaders. I towed one pallet, Cathy towed the other and Sam brought up the rear.

There was a short passage from our cavern to the next one, more narrow than previous ones.

"I think . . . I detect signs of wind erosion," Nikhil sent from the lead, wonder in his voice.

"Wind?" I said, surprised. What wind could there be on Miranda?

"The collisions which reformed the moon must have released plenty of gas for a short time. It had to get out somehow. Note the striations as you come through."

They were there, I noted as I came through, as if someone had sand-blasted the passage walls. Miranda had breathed, once upon a time.

"I think," he continued, "that there may be an equilibrium between the gas in Miranda's caverns and the gas torus outside the ring system. Miranda's gravity is hardly adequate to compress that very much. But a system of caverns acting as a cold trap and a rough diffusion barrier . . . hmm, maybe."

"How much gas?" I wondered.

He shook his head. "Hard to tell that from up here, isn't it?"

We pushed half an hour past our agreed-to stop time to find a monolithic shelter that might prove safe from aftershocks. This passage was just wide enough to inflate our one meter sleeping tubes end to end. We ate dinner in the one Randi and I used. It was a spare, crowded, smelly, silent meal. Even Nikhil seemed depressed. I thought, as we replaced our helmets to pump down to let the Rays go back to their tent, that it was the last one we would eat together in such circumstances. The ins and outs of vacuum tents took up too much time and energy.

We repressurized and I savored the simple pleasure of watching Randi remove her tightsuit and bathe with a damp wipe in the end of the tent. She motioned for me to turn while she used the facility built into the end of our pallet, and so I unrolled my notescreen, slipped on its headband, and turned my attention to this journal, a process of clearly subvocalizing each word that I want on the screen.

Later she touched my arm indicating that it was my turn, kissed me lightly and went to bed between the elastic sheets, falling asleep instantly. My turn.

Day four was spent gliding through a series of large, nearly horizontal caverns. Miranda, it turns out, is still breathing. A ghost breath to be sure, undetectable except with such sensitive instruments as Sam contains. But there appears to be a pressure differential; gas still flows through these caverns out to the surface. Sam can find the next passage by monitoring the molecular flow.

We pulled ourselves along with our hands, progressing like a weighted diver in an underwater cave; an analogy most accurate when one moves so slowly that lack of drag is unremarkable.

As we glided along, I forgot my doom, and looked at the marbled ice around me with wonder. Randi glided in front of me and I could mentally remove her dusty coveralls and imagine her hard, lithe, body moving in its skin-hugging shipsuit. I could imagine her muscles bunch and relax in her weight lifter's arms, imagine the firm definition of her neck and forearms. A poet herself, I thought, who could barely talk, but who had written an epic in the language of her body and its movement.

Sam notified us that it was time for another sounding and a lead change. In the next kilometer, the passage narrowed, and we found ourselves forcing our bodies through cracks that were hardly large enough to fit our bone through.

My body was becoming bruised from such tight contortions, but I wasn't afraid my tightsuit would tear; the fabric is slick and nearly invulnerable. On our first day, Randi scared the hell out of me by taking a hard-frozen, knife-edged sliver of rock and trying to commit hari-kiri with it, stabbing herself with so much force that the rock broke. She laughed at my reaction and told me that I needed to have confidence in my equipment.

She still has the bruise, dark among the lighter, older blemishes on her hard-used body. I kiss it when we make love and she says, "Uh-huh. Told you so." Randi climbed Gilbert Montes in the Mercurian antarctic with her father and brother carrying a full vacuum kit when she was thirteen. She suffered a stress fracture in her ulna and didn't tell anyone until after they reached the summit.

The crack widened and, to our relief, gave onto another cavern, and that to another narrow passage. Randi took the lead, Nikhil followed, then me, then Cathy, then Sam.

Sam made me think of a cubist crab, or maybe a small, handleless lawn mower, on insect legs instead of wheels. Articulate and witty with a full range of simulated emotion and canned humor dialog stored in its memory, Sam was our expert on what had been. But it had difficulty interpreting things it hadn't seen before, or imagining what it had never seen, and so it usually followed us.

By day's end we had covered twenty-eight kilometers and were another eighteen kilometers closer to the center. That appeared to be where the road went, though Nikhil said we were more likely to be on a chord passing fifty kilometers or so above the center, where it seems that two major blocks came together a billion years ago.

This, I told myself, is a fool's journey, with no real chance of success. But how much better, how much more human, to fight destiny than to wait and die.

We ate as couples that night, each in our own tents.

II

On day five, we became stuck.

Randi woke me that morning exploring my body, fitting various parts of herself around me as the elastic sheets kept us pressed together. Somehow, an intimate dream I'd been having had segued into reality, and I felt only a momentary surprise at her intrusion.

"You have some new bruises," I told her after I opened my eyes. Hers remained closed.

"Morning," she murmured and wrapped herself around me again. Time slowed as I spun into her implacable, devouring, wholeness.

But of course time would not stop. Our helmets beeped simultaneously with Sam's wake-up call, fortunately too late to prevent another part of me from becoming part of Randi. Sam reminded us, that, given our fantasy of escaping from Miranda's caverns, we had some time to make up.

Randi popped out of the sheets, spun around airborne, in a graceful athletic move, and slowly fell to her own cot in front of me, exuberantly naked, stretching like a sensual cat, staring right into my enslaved eyes.

"Female display instinct; harmless, healthy, feels good."

Harmless? I grinned and reminded her: "But it's time to spelunk."

"Roger that," she laughed, grabbed her tightsuit from the ball of clothes in the end of the tent, and started rolling it on. They go on like a pair of pantyhose, except that they are slick on the inside and adjust easily to your form. To her form. I followed suit, and we quickly depressurized and packed.

It took Sam an hour to find the cavern inlet vent, and it was just a crack, barely big enough for us to squeeze into. We spent an hour convincing ourselves there was no other opportunity, then we wriggled forward through this crack like so many ants, kits and our coveralls pushed ahead of us, bodies fitting any way we could make them fit.

I doubt we made a hundred yards an hour. Our situation felt hopeless at this rate, but Sam assured us of more caverns ahead.

Perhaps it would have been better if Nikhil had been on lead. Larger than Randi and less inclined to disregard discomfort, he would have gone slower and chipped more clathrate, which, as it turned out, would have been faster.

Anyway, as I inched myself forward with my mind preoccupied with the enigma of Randi, Miranda groaned—at least that's what it sounded like in my helmet, pressed hard against the narrow roof of the crack our passage had become. I felt something. Did the pressure against my ribs increase? I fought panic, concentrating on the people around me and their lights shining past the few open cracks between the passage and their bodies.

"I can't move." That was Cathy. "And I'm getting cold."

Our tightsuits were top of the line "Explorers," twenty layers of smart fiber weave sandwiched with an elastic macromolecular binder. Despite their thinness, the suits are great insulators, and Miranda's surrounding vacuum is even better.

Usually, conductive losses to the cryogenic ice around us are restricted to the portions of hand or boot that happen to be in contact with the surface and getting *rid* of our body heat is the main concern. Thus, the smart fiber layers of our suits are usually charcoal to jet black. But if almost a square meter of you is pressed hard against a cryogenic solid, even the best million atom layer the Astrographic Society can buy meets its match, and the problem is worse, locally.

The old expression "colder than a witch's tit" might give you some idea of Cathy's predicament.

"I can't do much," I answered, "I'm almost stuck myself. Hang in there."

"Sam," Cathy gasped, her voice a battleground of panic and self control, "wedge yourself edge up in the crack. Keep it from narrowing any more."

"That's not going to work, Cathy," it replied. "I would be fractured and destroyed without affecting anything."

"Remember your laws!" Cathy shrieked. "You have to obey me. Now do it, before this crushes my ribs! Nikhil, make the robot obey me!"

"Cathy, dear," Nikhil asks, "I sympathize with your discomfort, but could you hold off for a bit. Let us think about this."

"I'll be frozen solid in minutes and you want to think. Damnit, Nikhil, it hurts. Expend the robot and save me. I'm your doctor."

"Cathy," Sam says, "We will try to save you, but we have gone only a hundred kilometers since the quake, and there may be a thousand to go. If we encounter such difficulties every hundred kilometers, there may be on the order of ten of them yet to come. And you only have one robot to expend, as you put it. Sacrificing me now places the others in an obviously increased risk. Nothing is moving now, so thinking does not entail any immediate increased risk."

"Damn your logic. I'm getting frostbite. Get me out of here."

Embarrassed silence slammed down after this outburst, no one even breathing for what seemed like a minute. Then Cathy started sobbing in short panicky gasps, which at least let the rest of us know she was still alive.

Randi broke the silence. "Can the rest of you move forward?"

"Yes," Nikhil answers, "a little."

"Same here," I add.

"Sam," Randi ordered. "Telop bug. Rope."

"I have these things."

"Uh-huh. Have your telop bug bring the rope up to me, around Cathy. When I've got it, put a clamp on it just behind Cathy's feet."

"Yes, Randi," Sam acknowledged its orders. "But why?" It also requested more information.

"So Cathy's feet can . . . grab—uh—get a foothold on it." Randi's voice showed her frustrations with speech, but no panic. "Can you model that? Make an image? See what will happen?"

"I can model Cathy standing on a clamp on the rope, then rotate horizontal like she is, then put the passage around her . . . I've got it!" Sam exclaimed. "The telop's on its way."

"Please hurry," Cathy sobs, sounding somewhat more in control now.

I felt the little crab-like telop scuttling along through the cracks between my flesh and rock. The line started to snake by me, a millimeter Fullerene fiber bundle that could support a dinosaur in Earth gravity, a line of ants marching on my skin. I shivered just as the suit temperature warning flashed red in my visor display. The telop's feet clicked on my helmet as it went by. I waited for what seemed hours that way.

"Grab the line." Randi commanded and we obeyed. "Feet set, Cathy?"

"I can't . . . can't feel the clamp."

"Okay. I'll take up some of the, the slack . . . Okay now, Cathy?"

"It's there. Oh, God I hope this works."

"Right," Randi answered. "Everyone. Grab. Heave."

I set my toe claws and gave it my best effort forward. Nothing seemed to move much.

"Damn!" Randi grunted.

"Use the robot, I'm freezing," Cathy sobbed.

"Dear," Nikhil muttered, "she is using the robot. She's just not *being* one."

I started to get cold myself. My toes were dug in, but I couldn't bend my knees, so everything was with the calves. If I could just get my upper legs into it, I thought . . . If I just had a place to stand. Of course, that was it.

"Randi," I asked, "If Cathy grabbed the rope with her hands, stood on Sam and used all of her legs? Wouldn't that make a difference?"

Her response was instantaneous. "Uh-huh. Sam, can you, uh, move up under Cathy's feet and, uh, anchor yourself."

"Do you mean under, or behind so that she can push her feet against me?"

"I meant behind, Sam. Uh," Randi struggled with words again. "Uh, rotate model so feet are down to see what I see, er, imagine."

"Yes . . . I can model that. Yes, I can do that, but Cathy's knees cannot bend much."

"Roger, Sam. A little might be enough. Okay, Cathy, understand?"

"Y—Yes, Randi." Seconds of scraping, silence, then "Okay, I've got my feet on Sam."

"Then let's try. Pull on three. One, two, three."

We all slid forward a bit this time, but not much. Still it was much more progress than we'd made in the last half hour.

"Try again." I feel her take up the slack. "One, two, three."

That time it felt like a cork coming out of the bottle.

Over the next hour, we struggled forward on our bellies for maybe another hundred and ten meters. Then Randi chipped away a final obstruction and gasped.

Haggard and exhausted as I am, my command of the language is inadequate to my feelings as I emerged from the narrow passage, a horizontal chimney actually, onto the sloping, gravelly, ledge of the first great cavern. Involuntarily, I groaned; the transition from claustrophobia to agoraphobia was just too abrupt. Suddenly, there was this immense space with walls that faded into a stygian blackness that swallowed the rays of our lights without so much as a glimmer in return.

My helmet display flashed red numbers which told me how far I would fall, some six hundred meters; how long I would fall, just over two minutes, and how fast I would hit, almost ten meters per second; a velocity that would be terminal for reasons not involving air resistance; think of an Olympic hundred meter champion running full tilt into a brick wall. I backed away from the edge too quickly and lost my footing in Miranda's centigee gravity.

In slow frustration, I bounced; I couldn't get my clawed boots down to the surface, nor reach anything with my hands. Stay calm, I told myself, I could push myself back toward the cavern wall on the next bounce. I waited until I started to float down again and tried to reach the ledge floor with my arm, but my bounce had carried me out as well as down. A look at the edge showed me that my trajectory would take me over it before I could touch it. There was nothing I could do to save myself—my reaction pistol was in a pallet. Visions of Wile E. Coyote scrambling in air trying to get back to the edge of a cliff went through my mind, and I involuntarily tried to swim through the vacuum—not fair; at least the coyote had air to work with.

The helmet numbers went red again as I floated over the edge. Too desperate now to be embarrassed, I found my voice and a sort of guttural groan emerged. I took another breath, but before I could croak again, Cathy grabbed my arm and clipped a line to my belt. She gave my hand a silent squeeze as, anchored firmly to a piton, I pressed my back against the wall of the cavern to get as far as I could from the edge of the ledge. I shook. Too much, too much.

I canceled any judgment I'd made about Cathy. Judge us by how far, not how, we went. Sam told us the cavern is twenty-seven kilometers long and slants severely downhill. Our ledge topped a six-hundred-meter precipice that actually curved back under us. We gingerly made our camp on the ledge, gratefully retreated to our piton-secured tents, and ate a double ration silently, unable to keep our minds off of the vast inner space which lay just beyond the thin walls of our artificial sanity.

Sleep will be welcome.

Day six. The inner blackness of sleep had absorbed my thoughts the way the cavern absorbed our strobes and I woke aware of no dreams. After a warm, blousy, semiconscious minute, the cold reality of my predicament came back to me and I shivered. It had taken a full day to complete the last ten kilometers, including five hours of exhausted unconsciousness beneath the elastic sheets. We would have to make much better time than that.

That morning, Randi managed to look frightened and determined at the same time. No display behavior this morning—we dressed efficiently, packed our pallet and turned on the recompressors minutes after waking. Breakfast was ration crackers through our helmet locks.

I stowed the tent in the pallet and turned to find Randi standing silent at the edge. She held the Fullerene line dispenser in one hand, the line end in the other, snapped the line tight between them, and nodded. We had, I remembered, fifty kilometers of Fullerene line.

"Randi, you're not considering . . ."

She turned and smiled at me the way a spider smiles to a fly. Oh, yes she was.

"Preposterous!" was all Nikhil could say when Randi explained what she had in mind. Cathy, docile and embarrassed after yesterday's trauma, made only a small, incoherent, frightened, giggle.

And so we prepared to perform one of the longest bungee jumps in history in an effort to wipe out the entire length of the passage in, as it were, one fell swoop. Nikhil drilled a hole through a piece of the cavern wall that looked sufficiently monolithic and anchored the line dispenser to that. Sam, who was equipped with its own propulsion, would belay until we were safe, then follow us.

Randi stretched a short line segment between two pitons and showed us how to use it to brace ourselves against the wall in Miranda's less-than-a-milligee gravity. We held our fly-like position easily and coiled our legs like springs.

"Reaction pistols?" Randi asked.

"Check," Nikhil responded.

"Feet secure?"

Three "Checks" answered.

"Line secure."

Sam said, "Check."

Randi cleared her throat. "On three now. One, two, *three*."

We jumped out and down, in the general direction of Miranda's center. After a brief moment of irrational fear, we collected ourselves and contemplated the wonders of relativity as we sat in free fall while the "roof" of the cavern flashed by. It was a strange experience; if I shut my eyes, I felt just like I would feel floating outside a space station. But I opened my eyes and my light revealed the jagged wall of the cavern whipping by a few dozen meters away. It was, I noted, getting closer.

Judiciously taking up the slack in our common line, Nikhil, who was an expert at this, used the reaction pistol to increase our velocity and steer us slightly away from the roof. A forest of ice intrusions, curved like elephant tusks by eons of shifting milligravity, passed by us too close for my comfort as the minuscule gravity and the gentle tugs of the reaction pistol brought us back to the center of the cavern.

We drifted. Weight came as a shock: our feet were yanked behind us and blood rushed to our heads as the slack vanished and the line started to stretch. Randi, despite spinning upside down, kept her radar pointed "down." We must have spent twenty seconds like that, with the pull on our feet getting stronger with every meter further down. Then, with surprising quickness the cavern wall stopped rushing past us. Randi said "Now!" and released the line, leaving us floating dead in space only a kilometer or so from the cavern floor.

I expended a strobe flash to get a big picture of the cavern wall floating next to us. It looks like we are in an amethyst geode; jumbles of sharp crystals everywhere and a violet hue.

"Magnificent," Cathy said with a forced edge in her voice. Trying to make contact with us, to start to put things back on a more normal footing after yesterday, I thought.

"Time to keep our eyes down, I should think," Nikhil reminded her, and the rest of us. "Wouldn't want to screw up again, would we?"

There was no rejoinder from Cathy so I glanced over at her. Her visor was turned toward the crystal forest and apparently frozen in space. A puff from my reaction pistol brought me over to her and my hand on her arm got her attention. She nodded. The crystals were huge, and I wondered at that, too.

I check my helmet display—its inertial reference function tells me I'm fifty kilometers below the surface and the acceleration due to Miranda's feeble gravity is down to seven centimeters per second squared so when we touched down to the rugged terrain a kilometer below in just under three minutes . . . we'd hit it at eleven meters per second. Think of the Olympic hundred-yard dash champion running full tilt into a brick wall.

"Randi, I think we're too high." I tried to keep my voice even. This was the sort of thing we left to Sam, but he wasn't with us just now.

As if in answer, she shot a lined piton into the wall next to us, which was starting to drift by at an alarming rate.

"Swing into the wall feet first, stop, fall again," she said.

"Feet toward the wall!" Nikhil echoed as the tension started to take hold, giving us a misleading sense of down. The line gradually pulled taut and started to swing us toward the wall. Then it let go, leaving us on an oblique trajectory headed right toward the forest of crystals. Piton guns are neat, but no substitute for a hammer.

"No problems," Nikhil said. "We dumped a couple of meters per second. I'll try this time."

He shot as Randi reeled her line in.

Eventually we swing into the wall. Cathy seemed rigid and terrified, but bent her legs properly and shielded her face with her arms as the huge crystals rushed to meet us.

They shattered into dust at our touch, hardly even crunching as our boots went through them to the wall.

"What the . . ." I blurted, having expected something a little more firm.

"Deposition, not extrusion?" Randi offered, the questioning end of her response clearly intended for Nikhil.

"Quite so. Low gravity hoarfrost. Hardly anything to them, was there?"

"You, you, knew didn't you?" Cathy accused, her breath ragged.

"Suspected," Nikhil answered without a trace of feeling in his voice, "but I braced just like the rest of you. Not really certain then, was I?"

"Hello everyone, see you at the bottom," Sam's voice called out, breaking the tension. Three of us strobe and spot the robot free-falling past us.

The wall on which we landed curved gently to the lower end of the cavern, so we covered the remaining distance in hundred-meter leaps, shattering crystals with each giant step, taking some sort of vandalistic delight in the necessity of destroying so much beauty. We caught up to Sam laughing.

"This way," it pointed with one of its limbs at a solid wall, "there is another big cavern, going more or less our way. It seems to be sloped about one for one instead of near vertical."

Our helmet displays reproduced its seismologically derived model which was full of noise and faded in the distance, but clearly showed the slant down.

After a couple of false leads we found a large-enough crack leading into the new gallery. Cathy shuddered as she squeezed herself in.

That cavern was a mere three kilometers deep—we could see the other end. We shot a piton gun down there, and cheered when it held; using the line to keep us centered, we were able to cross the cavern in ten minutes.

Cathy dislodged a largish boulder as she landed, and it made brittle, tinkling, ice noises as it rolled through some frost crystals.

"Hey," I said when the significance of that got through to me. "I heard that!"

"We have an atmosphere, mostly methane and nitrogen. It's about ten millibars and nearly a hundred Kelvins," Sam answered my implied question. Top-of-the-line robot, Sam.

It occurred to me then that, should we all die, Sam might still make it out. Almost certainly would make it out. So someone will read this journal.

The next cavern went down as well and after that was another. We kept going well past our planned stopping time, almost in a daze. Our hammers made echoes now, eerie high-pitched echoes rattling around in the caverns like a steelie marble dropped on a metal plate.

We made camp only a hundred and seventy kilometers above Miranda's center, eighty-five below the surface. Nikhil told us that if the rift continued, like this, along a chord line bypassing the center itself, we were more than one third of the way through, well ahead of schedule. Randi came over to me as I hammered in the piton for a tent line and put a hand on my arm.

"Psyche tension; Cathy and Nikhil, danger there."

"Yeah. Not much to do about it, is there?"

"Maybe there is. Sleep with Cathy tonight. Get them away from each other. Respite."

I looked at Randi, she was serious. They say tidal forces that near a black hole can be fatal.

"Boys in one tent, girls in the other?"

"No. I can't give Cathy what she needs."

"What makes you think I can?"

"Care about her. Make her feel like a person."

Honestly, I was not that much happier with Cathy's behavior than Nikhil's. Though I thought I understood what she was going through and made intellectual allowances, I guess I saw her as being more of an external situation than a person to care about. What Randi was asking wouldn't come easy. Then, too, there was the other side of this strange currency.

"And you? With Nikhil?"

"Skipped a week of classes at Stanford once. Went to a Nevada brothel. Curious. Wanted to know if I could do that, if I needed to, to live. Lasted four days. Good lay, no personality." She tapped the pocket of my coveralls where my personal electronics lived, recording everything for my article. "You can use that if we get out. Secrets are a headache." She shrugged. "Dad can handle it."

"Randi . . ." I realized that, somehow, it fit. Randi seems to be in a perpetual rebellion against comfort and normalcy, always pushing limits, taking risks, seeking to prove she could experience and endure anything. But unlike some mousy data tech who composes sex thrillers on the side, Randi has no verbal outlet. To express herself, she has to live it.

"Randi, I can see that something has to be done for Nikhil and Cathy, but this seems extreme."

"Just once. Hope." She smiled and nestled herself against me. "Just be nice. Don't worry about yourself. Let her lead. Maybe just hugs and kisses, or listening. But whatever, give. Just one night, okay? So they don't kill themselves. And us."

It took me a minute or so to digest this idea. Another thought occurred to me. Randi and I were single—not even a standard cohab file—but Nikhil and Cathy . . . "Just how are you going to suggest this to them?" I asked.

Randi shook her head and looked terrified. "Not me!"

I don't think I'm going to be able to finish the journal entry tonight.

III

Day seven. Last night was an anticlimax. Nikhil thought the switch was jolly good fun, in fact he seemed relieved. But Cathy. . . . Once her nervousness had run its course, she simply melted into my arms like a child and sobbed. I lay there holding her as she talked.

Born to a wealthy Martian merchant family, she'd been an intellectual rebel, and had locked horns with the authoritarian pastoral movement there which eventually gave rise to the New Reformation. When she was fifteen, she got kicked out of school for bragging about sleeping with a boy. She hadn't, but: "I resented anyone telling me I couldn't so much that I told everyone that we did."

Her parents, caught between their customers and their daughter, got out of the situation by shipping her off to the IPA space academy at Venus L1. She met Nikhil there as an instructor in an introductory Paleontology class. She got her M.D. at twenty-two and plunged into archeoimmunology research. A conference on fossil disease traces linked her up with Nikhil again, who had been ducking the controversy about Miranda's internal structure by using p-bar scans to critique claims of panspermia evidence in Triton sample cores. His outcast status was an attraction for her. They dated.

When he became an instant celebrity, she threw caution to the wind and accepted his proposal. But, she found, Nikhil kept sensual things hidden deep, and there was a cold, artificial hollowness where his sense of fun should be. Cathy said they had their first erudite word fight over her monokini on their honeymoon and they had been "Virginia Woolfing" it ever since.

"Damn dried-up stuffed-shirted bastard's good at it," she muttered as she wrapped herself around me that night. "It stinks in here, you know?" Then she fell asleep with tears in her eyes. She was desirable, cuddly, and beyond the stretch of my conscience.

That morning, when our eyes met and searched each other, I wondered if she had any expectations, and if, in the spirit of friendship, I should offer myself. But I decided not to risk being wrong, and she did nothing but smile. Except, possibly, for that brief look, we were simply friends.

Randi didn't say anything about her night in Nikhil's tent; I didn't expect her to. She gave me a very warm and long hug after she talked to Cathy. We were all very kind to each other as we broke camp and began casting ourselves along a trail of great caverns with the strides of milligee giants.

Cathy passed out the last of our calcium retention pills that morning. In a week or so we would start to suffer some of the classic low gravity symptoms of bone loss and weakness. It didn't worry us greatly—that was reversible, if we survived.

At day's end, I was not physically exhausted, but my mind was becoming numb with crystal wonders. Where are these crystals coming from? Or rather where had they come from; Sam and Nikhil concur that the existing gas flow, though surprising in its strength, is nowhere near enough to deposit these crystal forests in the few hundred million years since Miranda's remaking.

We were a hundred and fifty kilometers deep now and Nikhil says these rocks must withstand internal pressures of more than ninety atmospheres to hold the caverns open. Not surprisingly, the large caverns don't come as often now, and when they do, the walls are silicate rather than clathrate; rock slabs instead of dirty ice. I thought I could hear them groan at a higher pitch last night.

"It's after midnight, universal time," Cathy announced. She seemed recovered from her near panic earlier, and ready to play her doctor role again. But there seemed something brittle in her voice. "I think we should get some sleep now." She said this as we pushed our baggage through yet another narrow crack between the Rift galleries Sam kept finding with his sonar, so Randi and I had a chuckle at the impossibility of complying with the suggestion just then. But she has a point. We had come one-half of the way through Miranda in five of our twenty days—well ahead of schedule.

Nikhil on lead, missed her humor and said, "Yes, dear, that sounds like a very good idea to me. Next gallery, perhaps."

"You humans will be more efficient if you're not tired," Sam pointed out in a jocular tone that did credit to its medical support programmers, but, I thought, this feigned robot chauvinism probably did not sit well with Cathy.

"We," I answered, "don't have a milligram of antihydrogen in our hearts to feed us."

"Your envy of my superior traits is itself an admirable trait, for it recognizes—"

"Shiva!" Nikhil shouted from the head of our column.

"What is it?" Three voices asked, almost in unison.

"Huge. A huge cavern. I . . . you'll have to see it yourselves."

As we joined him, we found he had emerged on another ledge looking over another cavern. It didn't seem to be a particularly large one to start—our lights carried to the other side—just another crystal cathedral. Then I looked down—and saw stars. Fortunately, my experience in "Randi's Room" kept my reaction in check. I did grab the nearest piton line rather quickly, though.

"Try turning off your strobes," Nikhil suggested as we stuck our heads over the ledge again.

The stars vanished, we turned the strobes on again, and the stars came back. The human eye is not supposed to be able to detect time intervals so small, so perhaps it was my imagination. But it seemed as though the "stars" below came on just after the strobe flashed.

"Ninety kilometers," Sam said.

"Ninety kilometers!?" Nikhil blustered in disbelief, his composure still shaken. "How is this possible? Clathrate should not withstand such pressure."

Randi anchored herself, dug into the supply pallet I'd been towing, and came up with a geologist's pick. She took a swing at the ledge to which the gentle three and a half centimeters per second local gravity had settled us and a sharp *pink* made its way to my ears, presumably through my boots.

"Nickel-iron?" Nikhil asked.

"Uh-huh. Think so," Randi answered. "Fractured, from here down."

"Maybe this is what broke Miranda up in the first place," Cathy offered.

"Pure supposition," Nikhil demurred. "Friends, we must move on."

"I know. Take samples, analyze later," Randi said. "Got to move."

"Across or down?" I asked. This wasn't a trivial question. Our plan was to follow the main rift, which, presumably, continued on the other side. But down was an unobstructed ninety kilometer run leading to the very core of the moon. I thought of Jules Verne.

"We need to get out of this moon in less than two weeks," Nikhil reminded us. "We can always come back."

"Central gas reservoir, chimneys, connected," Randi grunted.

After a nonplussed minute, I understood. If we went down the chimney, our path would leave the chord for the center. The Rift is along the chord; Sam could see it in his rangings. But, not being a gas vent, it wouldn't be well enough connected to travel. We had to find another back door.

"Oh, of course," Nikhil said. "All roads lead to Rome—which also means they all go *from* Rome. The outgassing, the wind from the core, is what connected these caverns and eroded the passages enough to let us pass through. She means our best chance is to find another chimney, and the best place to do that is at the core, isn't it?"

"Uh-huh," Randi answered.

No one said anything, and in the silence I swore I could hear dripping, and beneath that a sort of dull throbbing that was probably my pulse. At any rate, the pure dead silence of the upper caverns was gone. I risked another peak down over the edge. What was down there?

"We have a problem," Cathy informed us. "Poison gas. The nitrogen pressure is up to a twentieth of a bar, and that's more than there was on old Mars. It's enough to carry dangerous amounts of aromatics—not just methane, but stuff like cyanogen. I don't know if anyone else has noticed it, but this junk is starting to condense on some of our gear and stink up our tents. It might get worse near the core, and I can't think of any good way to decontaminate."

"Uh, rockets," Randi broke the silence. "Sam's rockets. Our reaction pistols. Try it first."

So we did. We figured out how far to stand from the jets, how long to stand in them—enough to vaporize anything on the surface of our coveralls and equipment, but not long enough to damage it—and how many times we could do it. Sam had enough fuel for a hundred and twenty full decontaminations—more than we'd ever live to use. Cathy volunteered to be the test article, got herself blasted, then entered a tent and emerged saying it smelled just fine.

We decided to go for the core.

This close to the center of Miranda, gravitational acceleration was down to just over five centimeters per second squared, about one three hundredth of earth normal. Five milligees. Release an object in front of you, look away while you count one thousand one, and look back again: it will have fallen maybe the width of a couple of fingers—just floating. So you ignore it, go about other things and look back after ten minutes. It's gone. It has fallen ten kilometers and is moving three times as fast as a human can run; over thirty meters per second. That's if it hasn't hit anyone or anything yet. Low gravity, they drill you over and over again, can be dangerous.

That's in a vacuum, but we weren't in a vacuum any more. Even with the pallet gear apportioned, we each weighed less than ten newtons—about the weight of a liter of vodka back in Poland, I thought, longingly—and we each had the surface area of a small kite; we'd be lucky to maintain three meters per second in a fall at the start, and at the bottom, we'd end up drifting like snowflakes.

For some reason, I thought of butterflies.

"Could we make wings for ourselves?" I asked.

"Really, wings?" Nikhil's voice dripped with skepticism.

"Wings!" Cathy gushed, excited.

"Sheets, tent braces, tape, line. Could do," Randi offered.

"We are going to be very, very, sorry about this," Nikhil warned.

Four hours later, looking like something out of a Batman nightmare, we were ready.

Randi went first. She pushed herself away from the precipice with seeming unconcern and gradually began to drift downward. Biting my lip and shaking a bit, I followed. Then, came a stoic Nikhil and a quiet Cathy.

Ten minutes after jumping, I felt a tenuous slipstream and found I could glide after a fashion—or at least control my attitude. After some experimentation, Randi found that a motion something like the butterfly stroke in swimming seemed to propel her forward.

Half an hour down, and we found we could manage the airspeed of a walk with about the same amount of effort. Soon we were really gliding, and could actually gain altitude if we wanted.

After drifting down for another hour we came to the source of the dripping sound I had heard the night before. Some liquid had condensed on the sides of the chimney and formed drops the size of bowling balls. These eventually separated to fall a kilometer or so into a pool that had filled in a crack in the side of the chimney. The Mirandan equivalent of a waterfall looked like a time lapse splash video full of crowns and blobs, but it was at macroscale and in real time.

"Mostly ethane," Sam told us. Denser and more streamlined than we were, the robot maintained pace and traveled from side to side with an occasional blast from a posterior rocket: a "roam fart" it called it. If I ever get out of this, I will have to speak to its software engineers.

"Wojciech, come look at this!" Cathy called from the far side of the chimney. I sculled over, as did Randi and Nikhil.

"This had better be important," Nikhil remarked, reminding us of time. I needed one, having been mesmerized by drops that took minutes to fall and ponds that seemed to oscillate perpetually.

Cathy floated just off the wall, her position maintained with a sweep of her wings every three or four seconds. As we joined her, she pointed to a bare spot on the wall with her foot. Sticking out near the middle of it was a dirty white "T" with loopholes in each wing.

"It's a piton. It must be."

What she left unsaid was the fact that it certainly wasn't one of ours.

"Sam, can you tell how old it is?"

"It is younger than the wall. But that, however, looks to be part of the original surface of one of Miranda's parent objects. Do you see the craters?"

Now that he pointed it out, I did. There were several, very normal minicraters of the sort you find tiling the fractal surface of any airless moon, except two hundred kilometers of rock and clathrate lay between these craters and space. I had the same displaced, eerie feeling I had when, as a child, I had explored the top of the crags on the north rim of the Grand Canyon of the Colorado on Earth, over two thousand meters above sea level—and found seashells frozen in the rock.

"The piton," Sam added, "is younger than the hoar crystals, because the area was first cleared."

Something clicked in for me then. The crystals surrounding the bare spot were all about a meter long. "Look at the length of the nearby crystals," I said, excited with my discovery. "Whatever cleared the immediate area must have cleared away any nearby crystal seeds, too. But just next to the cleared area it must have just pushed them down and left a base from which the crystals could regenerate. So the height of the crystals just outside the cleared area is the growth since then."

"But what do you think that growth rate is?" Nikhil asked. "We can't tell, except that it is clearly slow now. I regret to say this, because I am as interested as anyone else, but we must move on. Sam has recorded everything. If we regain the surface, other expeditions can study this. If we do not—then it does not matter. So, shall we?"

Without waiting for assent from the others, Nikhil rotated his head down and started taking purposeful wingstrokes toward the center of Miranda.

"Damn him," Cathy hissed and flew to the piton and, abandoning one wing sleeve, grabbed the alien artifact. So anchored, she put her feet against the wall it protruded from, grasped it with both hands and pulled. Not surprisingly, the piton refused to move.

"Other expeditions. We'll come back," Randi told her.

Cathy gasped as she gave up the effort, and let herself drift down and away from the wall. We drifted with her until she started flying again. We made no effort to catch up to Nikhil, who was by this time a kilometer ahead of us.

The air, we could call it that now, was becoming mistier, foggier. Nikhil, though he still registered in my helmet display, was hidden from view. Sam's radar, sonar, filters and greater spectral range made this a minor inconvenience for him, and he continued to flit from side to side of this great vertical cavern, gathering samples. When we could no longer see the walls, we gathered in the center. Incredibly, despite the pressure of the core on either side, the chimney widened.

"This stuff is lethal," Cathy remarked. "Everyone make sure to maintain positive pressure, but not too much to spring a leak; oxygen might burn in this. If this chimney were on Earth, the environmental patrol would demolish it."

A quick check revealed my suit was doing okay—but the pressure makeup flow was enough that I would think twice about being near anything resembling a flame. Our suits were designed, and programmed, for vacuum, not chemical warfare; we were taking them well beyond their envelope.

"Chimney needs a name," Randi said. "Uh-huh. Job for a poet, I think."

That was my cue. But the best thing I could come up with on the spot was "Nikhil's Smokestack." This was partly to honor the discoverer and partly a gentle dig at his grumpiness about exploring it. Cathy laughed, at least.

Having nothing else to look at, I asked Sam for a three dimensional model of the chimney, which it obligingly displayed on my helmet optics. A three dimensional cutaway model of Miranda reflected off my transparent face plate, appearing to float several meters in front of me. Our cavern was almost precisely aligned with Miranda's north pole, and seemed to be where two great, curved, hundred-kilometer chunks had come together. Imagine two thick wooden spoons, open ends facing.

These slabs were hard stuff, like nickel-iron and silicate asteroids. Theories abound as to how that could be; radioactivity and tidal stress might have heated even small bodies enough to become differentiated; gravitational chaos in the young solar system must have ejected many main belt asteroids and some might well have made it to the Uranian gravitational well; or perhaps the impact that had set Uranus to spinning on its side had released a little planetesimal core material into its moon system.

My body was on autopilot, stroking my wings every ten seconds or so to keep pace with Randi while I daydreamed and played astrogeologist, so I didn't notice the air start to clear. The mist-cloud seemed to have divided itself to cover two sides of the chimney, leaving the center relatively free. Then, it thinned—and through gaps, I could see what looked to be a river running . . . beside? above? below?

"Randi, I think I can see a river."

"Roger, Wojciech."

"But how can that be? How does it stay there . . . ?"

"Tides."

"Yes," Nikhil added. "The chimney is almost three kilometers wide now. One side is closer to Uranus than Miranda's center of mass and moving at less than circular orbital velocity for its distance from Uranus. Things there try to fall inward as if from the apoapsis, the greatest distance, of a smaller orbit. The other side is further away than the center and moving at greater than orbital velocity. Things there try to move outward.

"The mass of Miranda now surrounds us like a gravitational equipotential shell, essentially cancelling itself out, so all that is left is this tidal force. It isn't much—a few milligees, but enough to define up and down for fluids. In some ways, this is beginning to resemble the surface of Titan, though it's a bit warmer and the air pressure is nowhere near as high."

"Is that water below us?" Cathy asked.

"No," Sam answered. "The temperature is only two hundred Kelvins, some seventy degrees below the freezing point of water. Water ice is still a hard rock here."

At the bottom, or end, of Nikhil's Smokestack was a three-kilometer rock, which had its own microscopic gravity field. The center of Miranda, we figured, was some two hundred and thirty meters below us. Close enough; we were effectively weightless. We let Sam strobe the scene for us, then set up our tents. Decontamination was a bit nervy, but most of the bad stuff was settled on either side of the tidal divide, and the air here was almost all cold dry nitrogen.

Nonetheless, setup took until midnight, and we all turned in immediately.

It has been a very long day.

Nikhil and Cathy forgot last night that, while they were in a vacuum tent, the tent was no longer in a hard vacuum. Much of what we heard was thankfully faint and muffled but what came through in the wee small hours of the morning of day eight clearly included things like:

". . . ungrateful, arrogant, pig . . ."

". . . have the self discipline of a chimp in heat . . ."

". . . so cold and unfeeling that . . ."

". . . brainless diversions while our lives are in the balance . . ."

Randi opened her eyes and looked at me, almost in terror, then threw herself around me and clung. It might seem a wonder that this steely woman who could spit in the face of nature's worst would go into convulsions at the sound of someone else's marriage falling apart, but Randi's early childhood had been filled with parental bickering. There had been a divorce, and I gathered a messy one from a six-year-old's point of view, but she had never told me much more than that.

I coughed, loud as I could, and soon the sound of angry voices was replaced by the roar of distant ethane rapids.

Randi murmured something.

"Huh?" Was she going to suggest another respite?

"Could we be married? Us?"

It was her first mention of the subject. I'd developed my relationship with her with the very specific intention of creating and reporting this expedition, and had never, never, hinted to her I had any other designs on her person or fortune. I'd been pretty sure that the understanding was mutual.

"Uh, Randi. Look, I'm not sure we should think like that. Starving poets trying to fake it as journalists don't fit well in your social circle. Besides, that," I tossed my head in the direction of the other tent, "that doesn't seem to put me in the mood for such arrangements. Why—"

"Why is: you don't do that." Randi interrupted me. This was startling; she never interrupted, except in emergencies—she was the most non-verbal person I knew.

Okay, I thought. This was an emergency of sorts. I kissed her on the forehead, then stifled a laugh. What a strange wife for a poet she would be! She sat there fighting with herself, struggling to put something in words.

"*Why* . . . is sex, working together, adventure, memories of this, not being afraid, not *fighting*."

My parents had had their usual share of discussions and debates, but raised voices had been very rare. The Rays' loud argument had, apparently, opened some old wounds for Randi. I held her and gave her what comfort I could. Finally, curiosity got the better of me.

"Your parents fought?"

"Dad wouldn't go to parties. Didn't like social stuff. Didn't like Mom's friends. His money." Randi looked me in the eye with an expression somewhere between anger and pleading.

"So. She had him shot. Hired someone."

I'd never heard anything like that, and anything that happened to papa Gaylord Lotati would have been big news. "Huh?"

"Someone Mom knew knew someone. The punk wasn't up to it. Non-fatal chest wound. Private doctor. Private detective. Real private. A settlement. Uncontested divorce.

"I was six. All I knew then was Dad was sick in the hospital for a week. Later Mom just didn't come home from one of her trips. A moving van showed up and moved . . . moved some stuff. One of the movers played catch with me. Another van came and moved Dad and me to a smaller house.

"And there was no more yelling, never, and no more Mom. So you know now. When you hold me, that kind of goes away. I feel secure, and I want that feeling, forever."

What in a freezing hydrocarbon hell does one say to that? I just rocked her gently and stared at the wall of the tent, as if it could give me an answer. "Look, I care about you, I really do," I finally told her. "But I need to find my own 'whys.' Otherwise, the relationship would be too dependent." I grinned at her. "We should be more like Pluto and Charon, not like Uranus and Miranda."

"Who gets to be Pluto and who gets to be Charon?" she asked, impishly, eyes sparkling through embryonic tears, as she began devouring me. One does not escape from a black hole, and once I fell beneath her event horizon and we merged into a singularity, the question of who is Pluto and who is Charon, to the rest of the universe, mattered not. Nor did whatever noise we made.

We reentered the real universe late for our next round of back-door searching;

Cathy and Nikhil were almost finished packing their pallet when we emerged from our deflated tent. We stared at each other in mutual embarrassment. Nikhil put his hand on his wife's shoulder.

"Sorry. Bit of tension is all, we'll be right." He waved at Miranda around us. "Now, shall we have another go at it?"

"Any ideas of where to look?" I asked.

"Ethane outlet?" Randi inquired.

Yes, I thought, those rivers had to go somewhere. I had, however, hoped to avoid swimming in them.

"There is," Sam announced, "a large cavern on the other side of this siderophilic nodule."

"This what?" Cathy started.

"This bloody three-kilometer nickel iron rock you're standing on," Nikhil snapped before Sam could answer, then he caught himself and lamely added, "dear."

She nodded curtly.

Randi took a couple of experimental swings at the nodule, more, I thought, in frustration than from doubting Sam. "No holes in this. Best check edges," she suggested. We all agreed.

After five hours of searching, it was clear that the only ways out were the ethane rivers.

"Forgive me if I now regret giving in on the rift route," Nikhil had to say. Cathy was in reach, so I gave her hand a pat. She shrugged.

We had a right—left choice, a coin flip. Each side of the tidal divide had its own ethane river and each river disappeared. Sam sounded and sounded around the ethane lakes at the end of Nikhil's Smokestack. The inner one, on the side toward Uranus, appeared to open into a cavern five kilometers on the other side of Cathy's Rock, as we called the central nodule. The other one appeared to go seven kilometers before reaching a significant opening, but that opening appeared to lead in the direction of the rift. No one even thought to question Nikhil this time.

Now that the route was decided, we had to face the question of how to traverse it.

"Simple," Cathy declared. "Sam carries the line through, then we all get in a tent and he pulls us through."

"Unfortunately, I cannot withstand ethane immersion for that period of time," Sam said. "And you will need my power source, if nothing else, to complete the journey."

"Cathy," Randi asked. "Ethane exposure, uh, how bad?"

"You don't want to breathe much of it—it will sear your lungs."

"Positive pressure."

"Some could still filter in through your tightsuit pores."

She was right. If moisture and gas from your skin could slowly work its way out of a tightsuit, then ethane could probably work its way in.

Randi nodded. "Block tightsuit pores?"

A loud "What?" escaped me when I realized what she was considering. Tightsuits worked because they let the skin exhale—sweat and gasses could diffuse slowly through the porous, swollen, fabric. Stopping that process could be very uncomfortable—if not fatal. But Cathy Ray, M.D., didn't seem to be in a panic about it. Apparently, it was something one could survive for a while.

"Big molecules. Got any, Cathy?"

"I have some burn and abrasion coating, semi-smart fibers. The brand name is Exoderm, what about it Sam?"

"Exoderm coating will not go through tightsuit pores. But it has pores of its own, like the tightsuits, and may allow some ethane to work its way in after a while. A few thousand molecules a second per square meter."

Randi shrugged. "And a tightsuit with pores blocked will cut that way down. Too little to worry about."

"I'm going with you," I announced, surprising myself.

Randi shook her head. "You try the outer passage if I don't make it. Get the gook, Cathy."

Cathy opened up one of the pallets and produced a spray dispenser. I started unpacking a vacuum tent.

"This is going to be a little difficult to do in a tent," Cathy mused.

"Wimps. Is it ready?" Randi asked.

Cathy nodded and gave an experimental squirt to her arm. For a moment, the arm looked like it was covered with cotton candy, but the fluff quickly collapsed to a flat shiny patch. Cathy pulled the patch off and examined it. "It's working just fine, all I need is some bare skin and a place to work."

Randi answered by hyperventilating, then before anyone could stop her, she dumped pressure, fluidly removed her helmet, deactivated her shipsuit seals and floated naked before us.

Cathy, to her credit, didn't let shock stop her. "Breathe out, not in, no matter how much you want," she told Randi, and quickly started spraying Randi's back while Randi was still stepping out of the boots. In less than a minute, Randi was covered with the creamy gray stuff. Calmly and efficiently, Randi rolled her tightsuit back on over the goo, resealed, checked and rehelmeted. It was all done in less than three minutes. Nikhil was speechless and I wasn't much better.

"You okay?" I asked, though the answer seemed obvious.

Randi shrugged. "One tenth atmosphere, ninety below, no wind, no moisture, no convection, air stings a bit. Bracing. No problem—goo handles stings. Can hold breath five minutes."

"You . . . you'd best get on with it, now," Cathy said, struggling to maintain a professional tone in her voice. "Your skin will have as much trouble breathing out as the ethane has getting in."

Randi nodded. "Line dispenser. Clips. Piton gun."

I got my act together and dug these things out of the same pallet where Cathy had kept the Exoderm. Randi snapped the free end of the line to her belt, took it off, double checked the clip, and snapped it back on again.

"Three tugs, okay? Wait five minutes for you to collect yourselves, then I start hauling. Okay?"

We nodded. Then she reached for my helmet and held it next to hers.

"I'll do it. If not, don't embarrass me, huh?"

I squeezed her hand in an extremely inadequate farewell, then she released her boot clamps, grabbed her reaction pistol, and rocketed off to the shore of the ethane lake fifteen hundred meters away.

There was, I thought, no reason why one couldn't weave a fiber-optic comm line into the test line, and use it for communications as well as for hauling, climbing, and bungee jumping. But ours weren't built that way, and we lost radio with Randi shortly after she plunged into the lake. The line kept snaking out, but, I reminded myself, that could just be her body being carried by the current. I wondered whether there had been a line attached to the alien piton we'd found above, and how long it had hung there.

Assuming success, we prepared everything for the under-ethane trip. Tents were unshipped, and pallets resealed. I broke out another line reel and looped its end through a pitoned pulley on Cathy's Rock; just in case someone did come back this way.

"I doubt that will be needed," Nikhil remarked, "but we'll be thankful if it is. You're becoming quite proficient, Mr. Bubka."

"Thanks."

I kept staring at the dispenser, fighting back the irrational desire to reel her back.

Cathy grabbed the packed pallets and moved them nearer to the shore, where the changed orientation of the milligee fields left her standing at right angles to Nikhil and myself. She chose to sit there and stare at the lake where Randi had vanished.

I stayed and puttered with my pulleys.

Nikhil came up to me. "I don't think of myself as being Bengali, you know," he said out of the blue. "I was ten when my parents were kicked out of Bangladesh. Politics, I understand, though the details have never been too clear to me. At any rate, I schooled in Australia and Cambridge, then earned my doctorate at Jovis Tholus."

I knew all this, but to make conversation, responded. "J.T.U. is New Reformationist, isn't it?"

"It's officially non-sectarian, state supported, you know. The council may lean that way, but the influence is diffuse. Besides, there is no such thing as New Reformationist geology, unless you're excavating the Face of Mars." Nikhil waved his hand in a gesture of dismissive toleration. "So you see, I've lived in both worlds; the cool, disciplined, thoughtful British academic world, and the eclectic, compulsive, superstitious Bengali hothouse."

No question of which one he preferred. I thought, however, to find a chink in his armor. "You are an Aristotelian then?"

"I won't object to the description, but I won't be bound by it."

"Then the golden mean must have some attraction for you, the avoidance of extremes."

"Quite."

"Okay, Nikhil. Consider then, that within rational safeguards, the spontaneity may be useful. A safety valve for evolutionary imperatives. A shortcut to communication and ideas. Creativity, art. A motivation for good acts; compassion, empathy."

"Perhaps." He gave me a wintry smile. "I am not a robot. I have these things . . ." disgust was evident in the way he said "things," ". . . within me as much as anyone else. But I strive to hold back unplanned action, to listen to and analyze these biochemical rumblings before responding. And I *prefer* myself that way."

"Does Cathy?"

I regretted that as soon as I said it, but Nikhil just shook his helmeted head.

"Cathy doesn't understand the alternative. I grew up where life was cheap and pain, commonplace. I saw things in Dum Dum, horrifying things . . . but things that nevertheless have a certain fascination for me." The expression in his unblinking brown eyes was contradictory and hard to read—perhaps a frightened but curious seven-year-old peered at me from beneath layers of adult sophistication. But did those layers protect him from us, or us from him? What had Randi's night with him been like?

"Well," he continued, "Cathy will never experience that sort of thing as long as I keep a grip on myself. She means too much to me, I owe her too much." He shook his head. "If she just would not ask for what I dare not give. . . . Between us, fellow?"

I'm not sure how I should have answered that, but just then Sam told us the line had stopped reeling out, I nodded briskly to him and we glided "down" to the ethane river shore to wait for the three sharp tugs that would signal us to follow.

They didn't come. We pulled on the line. It was slack. So we waited again, not wanting to face the implications of that. I update my journal, trying not to think about the present.

IV

It was almost the end of the schedule day when I finally told Cathy to get ready to put the Exoderm on me. There was no debate; we'd probably waited longer than we should have. "Don't embarrass me," Randi had said. Grimly, I determined to put off my grief, and not embarrass her. The fate, I recalled, of many lost expeditions was to peter out, one by one. Damn, I would miss her.

The plan had been to take the other outlet, but we silently disregarded that: I would go the same way, just in case there was any chance of a rescue. I needed that little bit of hope, to keep going.

By the laws of Murphy, I was, of course, standing stark freezing naked in ethane-laced nitrogen half covered with spray gook and holding my breath when the original line went taut. Three times. Cathy and Nikhil had to help seal me back in. I was shaking so hard, almost fatally helpless with relief.

We had to scramble like hell to get Sam, Cathy and Nikhil bagged in an uninflated tent. Since I was ready for immersion, and Randi had apparently survived said immersion, I would stay on the outside and clear us around obstacles. I was still double checking seals as Randi started hauling. By some grace of the universe, I had remembered to clip my pulley line to the final pallet, and it trailed us into the ethane lake.

It was cold, like skinny dipping in the Bering Sea. The ethane boiled next to my tightsuit and the space between it and my coveralls became filled with an insulating ethane froth. With that and the silvery white sheen of maximum insulation, my suit was able to hold its own at something like two-ninety Kelvins. I shivered and deliberately tensed and relaxed every muscle I could think about, as we slipped through the ethane.

There wasn't much to see, the passage was wide, broadened perhaps by eons of flow. Strobes revealed a fob of bubbles around me, otherwise the darkness smothered everything.

The line drew us up? down? to the inside of the passage, out of the current. I grabbed the line and walked lightly against the tension of the pulling line as if I were rappelling on a low gravity world. The tent with my companions and our pallets were thus spared bumping along the rough surface.

I asked for the time display, and my helmet told me we'd been under for an hour.

We rounded a corner and entered a much narrower passage. I became so busy steering us around various projections that I forgot how cold I was. But I noted my skin starting to itch. Then I caught a flash of light ahead. Did I imagine it?

No. In much less time than I thought, the flash repeated, showing a frothy hole in the liquid above us. Then we were at the boiling surface and Randi was waving at us as she pulled us to shore.

I flew out of the water with a kick and a flap of my hands and was in her arms. A minute must have passed before I thought to release the rest of the expedition from their tent cum submarine.

"No solid ground at the end of the main branch. I came up in a boiling sea, full of froth and foam, couldn't see anything. Not even a roof. Had to come back and take the detour." She trembled. "I have to get in a tent quick."

But with all our decontamination procedures, there was no quick about it, and it was 0300 universal on day ten before we were finally back in our tubular cocoons. By that time, Randi was moaning, shivering and only half conscious. The Exoderm came off as I peeled her tightsuit down and her skin was a bright angry red, except for her fingers and toes, which were an ugly yellow black. I linked up the minidoc and called Cathy, who programmed a general tissue regenerative, a stimulant, and directed that the tent's insulation factor be turned up.

By 0500, Randi was sleeping, breathing normally, and some of the redness had faded. Cathy called and offered to watch the minidoc so I could get some sleep.

The question I fell asleep with was, that with everyone's lives at stake, could *I* have pushed myself so far?

Day ten was a short one. We were all exhausted, we didn't get started until 1500.

Randi looked awful, especially her hands and feet, but pulled on her backup tightsuit without a complaint. My face must have told her what I was thinking because she shot me a defiant look.

"I'll do my pitch."

But Cathy was waiting for us and took her back into the tent, which repressurized. Nikhil and I shrugged and busied ourselves packing everything else. When the women reappeared, Cathy declared, very firmly, that Randi was to stay prone and inactive.

Randi disagreed. "I do my pitch . . . I, I, have to."

My turn. "Time to give someone else a chance, Randi. Me for instance. Besides, if you injure yourself further, you'd be a liability."

Randi shook her head. "Can't argue. Don't know how. I don't . . . don't want to be baggage."

"I'd hardly call it being baggage," Nikhil sniffed. "Enforced rest under medical orders. Now, if you're going to be a professional in your own right instead of Daddy's little indulgence, you'll chin up, follow medical orders, and stop wasting time."

"Nikhil, dear," Cathy growled, "get your damn mouth out of my patient's psyche."

Nikhil was exactly right, I thought, but I wanted to slug him for saying it that way.

"Very well," Nikhil said, evenly ignoring the feeling in Cathy's voice, "I regret the personal reference, Randi, but the point stands. Please don't be difficult."

Lacking support from anyone else, Randi's position was hopeless. She suffered herself to be taped onto a litter improvised from the same tent braces, sheets, and tape we had used earlier to make her wings.

This done, Nikhil turned to me. "You mentioned leading a pitch?"

Fortunately, the route started out like a one-third scale version Nikhil's Smokestack. It wasn't a straight shot, but a series of vertical caverns, slightly offset. Sam rocketed ahead with a line, anchored himself, and reeled the rest of us up. The short passages between caverns were the typical wide, low cracks and I managed them without great difficulty, though it came as a surprise to discover how much rock and ice one had to chip away to get through comfortably. It was hard work in a pressure suit, and my respect for Nikhil and Randi increased greatly.

At the end of the last cavern, the chimney bent north, gradually narrowing to a funnel. We could hear the wind blow by us. At the end was a large horizontal cavern, dry, but full of hoar crystals. The rift was clearly visible as a fissure on its ceiling. That was for tomorrow.

The ethane level was down enough for us to forego decontamination, and before we turned in we congratulated ourselves for traversing sixty percent of the rift in less than half our allotted time.

As we turned in, Randi said she had feeling in her fingers and toes again. Which meant she must have had no feeling in them when she was demanding to lead the pitch this afternoon.

She's sleeping quietly, it's only midnight, and I am going to get my first good night's sleep in a long time.

Day eleven is thankfully over, we are all exhausted again, and bitterly disappointed.

The day started with a discovery that, under other circumstances, would have justified the entire expedition; the mummified remains of aliens, presumably those who had left the strange piton. There were two large bodies and one small, supine on the cavern floor, lain on top of what must have been their pressure suits. Did they run out of food, or air, and give up in that way? Or did they die of something else, and were laid out by compatriots we might find elsewhere?

They were six-limbed bipeds, taller than us and perhaps not as heavy in life, though this is hard to tell from a mummy. Their upper arms were much bigger and stronger than their lower ones and the head reminded me vaguely of a Panda. They were not, to my memory, members of any of the five known spacefaring races, so, in any other circumstances, this would have been a momentous event. As it was, I think I was vaguely irritated at the complication they represented. Either my sense of wonder wasn't awake yet, or we'd left it behind, a few geode caverns back.

"How long?" Cathy asked Sam in a hushed voice. She, at least, was fascinated.

"If the present rate of dust deposition can be projected, about two hundred and thirty thousand years, with a sigma of ten thousand."

"Except for the pressure suits, they didn't leave any equipment," Nikhil observed. "I take that to mean that this cavern is *not* a dead end—as long as we do press on. You have your images, Sam? Good. Shall we?"

We turned to Nikhil, away from the corpses.

"The vent," he said, looking overhead, "is probably up there."

"The ceiling fissure is an easy jump for me," Sam offered. "I'll pull the rest of you up."

We got on our way, but the rift quit on us.

Once in the ceiling caves, we found there was no gas flowing that way, the way where Sam's seismological soundings, and our eyes, said the rift was. We chanced the passage anyway, but it quickly narrowed to a stomach-crawling ordeal. Three kilometers in, we found it solidly blocked and had to back our way out to return to the cavern. Another passage in the ceiling proved equally unpromising.

"Quakes," Nikhil said. "The rift must have closed here, oh, a hundred million years ago or so—from the dust." So, when dinosaurs ruled the Earth, Miranda had changed her maze, no doubt with the idea of frustrating our eventual expedition in mind.

Finally, Sam found the outlet airflow. It led back to the north.

"I hereby dub this the Cavern of Dead Ends," I proclaimed as we left, with what I hoped was humorous flourish.

Surprisingly, Nikhil, bless his heart, gave me one short "Ha!"

Randi was not to be denied today, and took the first pitch out in relief of Nikhil. But she soon tired, according to Cathy, who was monitoring. I took over and pushed on.

The slopes were gentle, the path wide with little cutting to do, and we could make good time tugging ourselves along on the occasional projecting rock and gliding. We took an evening break in a tiny ten-meter bubble of a cavern and had our daily ration crackers, insisting that Randi have a double ration. No one started to make camp, a lack of action that signified group assent for another evening of climbing and gliding.

"We are," Sam said, showing us his map on our helmet displays, "going to pass very close to the upper end of Nikhil's Smokestack." No one said anything, but we knew that meant we were backtracking, losing ground.

There was a final horizontal cavern, and its airflow was toward the polar axis. We could pretty much figure out what that meant, but decided to put off the confirmation until the morning. I'd once read a classic ancient novel by someone named Vance about an imaginary place where an accepted means of suicide was to enter an endless maze and wander about, crossing your path over and over again until starvation did you in. There, you died by forgetting the way out. Here, we did not even know there *was* a way out.

The beginning of day twelve thus found us at the top of Nikhil's Smokestack again, on a lip of a ledge not much different than the one about a kilometer away where we had first seen it. We were very quiet, fully conscious of how much ground we had lost to the cruel calendar. We were now less than halfway through Miranda, with less than half our time left.

Sam circled the top of the Smokestack again, looking for outlets other than the one we had come through. There were none. Our only hope was to go back down.

"Do we," I asked, "try the inner river, or try the other branch of Randi's River and fight our way through the Boiling Sea?"

Nikhil, though he weighed less than three newtons, was stretched out on the ledge, resting. His radio voice came from a still form that reminded me in a macabre way of the deceased aliens back in the Cavern of Dead Ends.

"The Boiling Sea," he mused, "takes the main flow of the river, so it should have an outlet vent. It is obviously in a cavern, so it has a roof. Perhaps we could just shoot a piton up at it, blindly."

But I thought of Nikhil's Smokestack—a blind shot could go a long way in something like that.

"Sam could fly up to it," I offered. "If we protect it until we reach the Boiling Sea's surface, it could withstand the momentary exposure. Once at the ceiling, it could pull the rest of us up."

Cathy nodded and threw a rock down Nikhil's Smokestack, and we watched it vanish relatively quickly. Dense, I thought, less subject to drag. As it turned out, I wasn't the only one with that thought.

"Look what I have," Randi announced.

"What" was a large boulder, perhaps two meters across, and loose; Randi could rock it easily, though it must have had a mass of five or six tons. "Bet *it* doesn't fall like a snowflake," she said as she hammered a piton into it.

Even in the low gravity, it took two of us to lift it over the edge.

Two hours later, about a kilometer above Cathy's Rock, we jumped off into the drag of the slipstream and watched the boulder finish its fall. It crashed with a resounding thud, shattered into a thousand shards, most of which rebounded and got caught in the chimney walls. We soon reached local terminal velocity and floated like feathers in the dust back to the place we had first departed three days ago.

Cathy decided that Randi was in no shape for another immersion and didn't think I should risk it either. I did have a few red patches, though I'd spent nowhere near as much time in the ethane as Randi. We looked at Nikhil, who frowned.

Cathy shook her head. "My turn, I think." But her voice quavered. "I'm a strong swimmer and I don't think Nikhil's done it for years. You handle the spray, Wojciech. You don't have to cover every square centimeter, the fibers will fill in themselves, but make sure you get enough on me. At least fifteen seconds of continuous spray. Randi—I can't hold my breath as long as you. You'll have to help me get buttoned up again, fast."

When all was ready, she took several deep breaths, vented her helmet and stripped almost as quickly as Randi had. This, I thought as I sprayed her, was the same woman who panicked in a tight spot just over a week ago. The whole operation was over in a hundred seconds.

The pulley I'd left was still functional, but that would only get us to the branch in the passage that led to the Cavern of Dead Ends. From there on, Cathy would have to pull us.

It was not fun to be sealed in an opaque, uninflated tent and be bumped and dragged along for the better part of an hour with no control over anything. The return of my minuscule weight as Sam winched us up to the roof of the Boiling Sea cavern was a great relief.

Randi, Nikhil, and I crawled, grumbling but grateful, out of the tent onto the floor of the cave Sam had found a couple of hundred yards from the center of the domed roof of the cavern. The floor sloped, but not too badly, and with a milligee of gravity it scarcely mattered. I helped Nikhil with the tent braces and we soon had it ready to be pressurized. Sam recharged the pallet power supplies and Randi tacked a glowlamp to the wall. Cathy then excused herself to get the Exoderm out of her tightsuit while we set up the other tent.

Work done, we stretched and floated around our little room in silence.

I took a look out the cave entrance; all I could see of the cavern when I hit my strobe was a layer of white below and a forest of yellow and white stalactites, many of them hundreds of meters long, on the roof. The far side, which Sam's radar said was only a couple of kilometers away, was lost in mist.

Then I noticed other things. My tightsuit, for instance, didn't feel as tight as it should.

"What's the air pressure in here?"

"Half a bar," Sam responded. "I've adjusted your suits for minimum positive pressure. It's mostly nitrogen, methane, ethane, and ammonia vapor, with some other volatile organics. By the way, the Boiling Sea is mainly ammonia; we are up to two hundred and twenty Kelvins here. The ethane flashes into vapor as it hits the ammonia—that's why all the boiling."

Miranda's gravity was insufficient to generate that kind of pressure, and I wondered what was going on.

"Wojciech," Randi whispered, as if she were afraid of waking something. "Look at the walls."

"Huh?" The cave walls were dirty brown like cave walls anywhere—except Miranda. "Oh, no hoar crystals."

She rubbed her hand on the wall and showed me the brown gunk.

"I'd like to put this under a microscope. Sam?"

The robot came quickly and held the sample close to its lower set of eyes. I saw what it saw, projected on the inside of my helmet.

"This has an apparent cellular structure, but little, if any structure within. Organic molecules and ammonia in a kind of jell."

As I watched, one of the cells developed a bifurcation. I was so fascinated, I didn't notice that Cathy had rejoined us. "They must absorb stuff directly from the air," she theorized. "The air is toxic, by the way, but not in low concentrations. Something seems to have filtered out the cyanogens and other really bad stuff. Maybe this."

"The back of the cave is full of them," Randi observed. "How are you?"

"My skin didn't get as raw as yours, but I have a few irritated areas. Physically, I'm drained. We're going to stop here tonight, I hope."

"This is one of the gas outlets of the Cavern of the Boiling Sea," Sam added. "It seems to be a good place to resume our journey. The passage is clear of obstructions as far as I can see, except for these growths, which are transparent to my radar."

"They impede the airflow," Nikhil observed, "which must contribute to the high pressure in here. I think they get the energy for their organization from the heat of condensation."

"Huh?" I wracked my memories of bonehead science.

"Wojciech, when a vapor condenses, it undergoes a phase change. When ethane vapor turns back into ethane, it gives off as much heat as it took to boil it in the first place. That heat can make some of the chemical reactions this stuff needs go in the right direction.

"Are they alive?" I asked.

"Hard to say," Cathy responded. "But that's a semantic discussion. Are hoar crystals alive? There's a continuum of organization and behavior from rocks to people. Any line you draw is arbitrary and will go right through some gray areas."

"Hmpf," Nikhil snorted. "Some distinctions are more useful than others. This stuff breeds, I think. Let's take some samples, but we need to get some rest, too."

"Yes, dear." Cathy yawned in spite of herself.

In the tent, Randi and I shared our last regular meal; a reconstituted chicken and pasta dish we'd saved to celebrate something. The tent stank of bodies and hydrocarbons, but we were used to that by now, and the food tasted great despite the assault on our nostrils. From now on, meals would be crackers. But we were on our way out now, definitely. We had to be. Randi felt fully recovered now and smiled at me as she snuggled under her elastic sheet for a night's rest.

It must have been the energy we got from our first good meal in days. She woke me in the middle of our arbitrary night and gently coaxed me into her cot for lovemaking, more an act of defiance against our likely fate than an act of pleasure. I surprised myself by responding, and we caressed each other up a spiral of intensity which was perhaps fed by our fear as well.

There are the tidal forces near Randi's event horizon; she is not just strong for a woman, but strong in absolute terms; stronger than most men I have known including myself. I had to half-seriously warn her to not crack our low gravity–weakened ribs. This made her giggle and squeeze me so hard I couldn't breathe for a moment, which made her giggle again.

When we were done, she gestured to the tent roof with the middle finger of her right hand and laughed uncontrollably. I joined her in this as well, but I felt momentarily sad for Nikhil and Cathy.

It was another of those polite mornings, and we packed up and were on our way with record efficiency. We looked around for the vent and Sam pointed us right at the mass of brown at the rear of the cave.

"The gas goes into that, right through it," it said.

We called the stuff "cryofungus." It had grown out from either side of the large, erosion widened vertical crack that Sam found in the back of our cave until it met in the middle. However the cryofungus colonies from either side didn't actually fuse there, but just pressed up against each other. So, with some effort, we found we could half push, half swim, our way along this seam.

We had pushed our way through five kilometers of "cryofungus" before a macabre thought occurred to me. The rubbery brown stuff absorbed organics through the skin of its cells. Did said organic stuff have to be gas? I asked Cathy.

"I did an experiment. I fed my sample a crumb of ration cracker."

"What happened?"

"The cracker sort of melted into the cryofungus. There are transport molecules all over the cell walls."

I thought a second. "Cathy, If we didn't have our suits on . . ."

"I'd think water would be a little hot for them, but then again water and ammonia are mutually soluble. If you want to worry, consider that your tightsuit is porous. It might," I could see her toothy smile in my mind, "help keep you moving."

"Nice, dear," Nikhil grumbled. "That gives a whole new meaning to this concept of wandering through the bowels of Miranda."

A round of hysterical laughter broke whatever tension remained between us, and resolved into a feeling of almost spiritual oneness among us. Perhaps you have to face death with someone to feel that—if so, so be it.

At the ten kilometer point, the cryofungus started to loose its resiliency. At twelve, it started collapsing into brown dust, scarcely offering any more resistance than the hoar crystals. This floated along with the gas current as a sort of brown fog. I couldn't see, and had Sam move up beside me.

After three kilometers of using Sam as a seeing eye dog, the dust finally drifted by us and the air cleared. It was late again, well past time to camp. We had been underground thirteen days, and had, by calculation, another eight left. According to Sam, we were still two hundred and fifteen kilometers below the surface. We decided to move on for another hour or two.

The passageway was tubular and fairly smooth, with almost zero traction. We shot pitons into the next curve ahead, and pulled ourselves along.

"Massive wind erosion," Nikhil remarked as he twisted the eye of a piton to release it. "A gale must have poured through here for megayears before the cryofungus choked it down."

Each strobe revealed an incredible gallery of twisted forms, loops, and carved rocks, many of which were eerily statuesque; saints and gargoyles. This led us into a slightly uphill kilometer-long cavern formed under two megalithic slabs, which had tilted against each other when, perhaps, the escaping gas had undermined them. After the rich hoarcrystal forest of the inbound path, this place was bare and dry. Sam covered the distance with a calculated jump carrying a line to the opposite end. We started pulling ourselves across. We'd climbed enough so that our weight was back to twenty newtons—minuscule, yes, but try pumping twenty newtons up and down for eighteen hours.

"I quit," Cathy said. "My arms won't do any more. Stop with me, or bury me here." She let go of the line, and floated slowly down to the floor.

It was silent here, no drippings, no whistling, reminiscent of the vacuum so far above. I tried to break the tension by naming the cavern. "This was clearly meant to be a tomb, anyway. The Egyptian Tomb, we can call it."

"Not funny, Wojciech," Nikhil snapped. "Sorry, old boy, a bit tired myself. Yes, we can make camp, but we may regret it later."

"Time to stop. We worked out the schedule for, for, maximum progress," Randi said. "Need to trust our judgment. Won't do any better by over-pushing ourselves now."

"Very well," Nikhil conceded, and dropped off as well. He reached Cathy and put his arm around her briefly, which I note because it was the first sign of physical affection I had seen between them. Randi and I dropped the pallets, and followed to the floor. We landed harder than we expected—milligee clouds judgment almost as badly as free fall, I thought. Worse perhaps, because it combines a real up and down with the feeling that they don't matter.

We were very careful and civilized in making camp. But each of us was, in our minds, trying to reach an accommodation with the idea that, given what we had been through so far, the week we had left would not get us to the surface.

Before we went into our separate tents, we all held hands briefly. It was spontaneous—we hadn't done so before. But it seemed right, somehow, to tell each other that we could draw on each other that way.

V

That last was for day thirteen, this entry will cover days fourteen and fifteen. Yes, my discipline in keeping the journal is slipping.

We'd come to think of Randi as a machine—almost as indestructible and determined as Sam, but last night, at the end of day fourteen, that machine cried and shook.

Low rations and fatigue are affecting all of us now. We let Sam pull us through the occasional cavern, but it has mostly been wriggling through cracks with a human in the lead. We changed leads every time we hit a place wide enough, but once that was six hours. That happened on Randi's lead. She didn't slack but when we finally reached a small cavern, she had rolled to the side with her face to the wall as I went by. We heard nothing from her for the next four hours.

We ended up at the bottom of a big kidney-shaped cavern a hundred and sixty kilometers below the surface; almost back to the depth of the upper end of Nikhil's Smokestack. We staggered through camp setup, with Sam double checking everything. We simply collapsed on top of the stretched sheets in our coveralls and slept for an hour or so, before our bodies demanded that we take care of other needs. Washed, emptied, and a bit refreshed from the nap, Randi had snuggled into my arms, then let herself go. Her body was a mass of bruises, old and new. So was mine.

"You're allowed a safety valve, you know," I told her. "When Cathy feels bad, she lets us know outright. Nikhil gets grumpy. I get silly and start telling bad jokes. You don't have to keep up an act for us."

"Not for you, for, for me. Got to pretend I can do it, or I'll get left behind, with Mom."

I thought about this. A woman that would attempt to murder her husband to gain social position might have been capable of other things as well.

"Randi, what did that mean? Do you want to talk?"

She shook her head. "Can't explain."

I kissed her forehead. "I guess I've been lucky with my parents."

"Yeah. Nice people. Nice farm. No fighting. So why do you have to do this stuff?"

Why indeed? "To have a real adventure, to make a name for myself outside of obscure poetry outlets. Mom inherited the farm from her father, and that was better than living on state dividends in Poland, so they moved. They actually get to do something useful, tending the agricultural robots. But they're deathly afraid of losing it because real jobs were so scarce and a lot of very smart people are willing to do just about anything to get an Earth job. So they made themselves very, very nice. They never rock any boats. Guess I needed something more than nice."

"But you're, uh, nice as they are."

"Well trained, in spite of myself." Oh, yes, with all the protective responses a nonconformist learns after being squashed time and time again by very socially correct, outwardly gentle, and emotionally devastating means. "By the way, Randi, I hate that word."

"Huh?"

"Nice."

"But you use it."

"Yeah, and I hate doing that, too. Look, are you as tired as I am?" I was about to excuse myself to the questionable comforts of my dreams.

"No. Not yet. I'll do the work."

"Really . . ."

"Maybe the last time, way we've going." We both knew she was right, but my body wasn't up to it, and we just clung to each other tightly, as if we could squeeze a little more life into ourselves. I don't remember falling asleep.

Day fifteen was a repeat, except that the long lead shift fell on Cathy. She slacked. For seven hours, she would stop until she got cold, then move forward again until she got tired. Somehow we reached a place where I could take over.

What amazed me through all of that was how Nikhil handled it. There was no sniping, no phony cheeriness. He would simply ask if she was ready to move again when he started getting cold.

We ended the day well past midnight. For some reason, I am having trouble sleeping.

Today the vent finally led us to a chain of small caverns, much like the rift before we encountered the top of Nikhil's Smokestack. We let Sam tow us most of the way and had only two long crack crawls. The good news is our CO_2 catalyst use is down from our passivity, and we might get another day out of it.

The bad news is that Randi had to cut our rations back a bit. We hadn't been as careful in our counting as we should have been, thinking that because the CO_2 would get us first, we didn't have a problem in that area. Now we did. It was nobody's fault, and everyone's. We'd all had an extra cracker here and there. They add up.

We ended up, exhausted as usual, in a five-hundred-meter gallery full of jumble. I called it the Junk Yard. Sam couldn't find the outlet vent right away, but we made such good progress that we thought we had time to catch up on our sleep.

Where are we? It's day eighteen. We have gained a total of fifteen kilometers in radius over the past two days. The Junk Yard was a dead end, at least for anything the size of a human being. There was some evidence of gas diffusing upward through fractured clathrate, but it was already clear that it wasn't the main vent, which appeared to have been closed by a Miranda quake millions of years ago.

We had to go all the way back to a branch that Sam had missed while it was towing us through a medium-sized chimney. Logic and experience dictated that the outlet would be at the top of the chimney, and there was a hole there that led onward. To the Junk Yard. Miranda rearranges such logic.

We spotted the real vent from the other side of the chimney as we rappelled back down.

"A human being," Cathy said when she saw the large vertical crack that was the real vent, "would have been curious enough to check that out. It's so deep."

"I don't know, dear," Nikhil said, meaning to defend Sam, I suppose, "with the press of time and all, I might not have turned aside, myself."

We were all dead silent at Nikhil's unintentional self-identification with a robot. Then Randi giggled and soon we were all laughing hysterically again. The real students of humor, I recall, say that laughter is not very far from tears. Then Nikhil, to our surprise, released his hold to put his arms around his wife again. And she responded. I reached out and caught them before they'd drifted down enough centimeters for their belt lines to go taut. So at the end of day seventeen, we had covered sixty kilometers of caverns and cracks, and come only fifteen or so nearer the surface.

By the end of day eighteen, we'd done an additional fifteen kilometers of exhausting crack crawling, found only one large cavern, and gave in to exhaustion, camping in a widening of the crack just barely big enough to inflate the tents.

What occurred today was not a fight. We didn't have enough energy for a fight.

We had just emerged into a ten meter long, ten meter wide, two meter high widening gallery in the crack we were crawling. Cathy was in the lead and had continued on through into the continuing passage when Nikhil gave in to pessimism.

"Cathy," he called, "stop. The passage ahead is getting too narrow, it's another bloody dead end. We should go back to the last large cavern and look for another vent."

Cathy was silent, but the line stopped. Randi, sounding irritated, said, "No time," and moved to enter the passage after Cathy.

Nikhil yawned and snorted. "Sorry, little lady. I'm the geologist and the senior member, and not to be too fine about it, but I'm in charge." Here he seemed to loose steam and get confused, muttering, "You're right about no time—there's no time to argue."

No one said anything, but Randi held her position.

Nikhil whined, "I say we go back, an', this time, back we go."

My mind was fuzzy; we still had four, maybe five days. If we found the right chain of caverns we could still make the surface. If we kept going like this, we weren't going to make it anyway. He might be right, I thought. But Randi wouldn't budge.

"No. Nikhil. You owe me one, Nikhil, for, for, two weeks ago. I'm collecting. Got to go forward now. Air flow, striations, Sam's soundings, and, and my money, damn it."

So much for my thoughts. I had to remember my status as part of Randi's accretion disk.

"Your *daddy's* money," Nikhil sniffed, then said loudly and with false jollity, "But never mind. Come on everyone, we'll put Randi on a stretcher again until she recovers . . . her senses." He started reaching for Randi, clumsy fumbling really. Randi turned and braced herself, boots clamped into the clathrate, arms free.

"Nikhil, back off," I warned. "You don't mean that."

"Ah appreciate your expertise with words, old chap." His voice was definitely slurred. "But these are mine and I mean them. I'm too tired to be questioned by amateurs anymore. Back we go. Come on back, Cathy. As for you . . ." He lunged for Randi again. At this point I realized he was out of his mind, and possibly why.

So did Randi, for at the last second instead of slapping him away and possibly hurting him, she simply jerked herself away from his grasping fingers.

And screeched loudly in pain.

"What?" I asked, brushing by the startled Nikhil to get to Randi's side.

"Damn ankle," she sobbed. "Forgot to release my boot grapples. Tired. Bones getting weak. Too much low gee. Thing fucking hurts."

"Broken?"

She nodded, tight-lipped, more in control. But I could see the tears in her eyes. Except for painkiller, there was nothing I could do at the moment for her. But I thought there might be something to be done for Nikhil. Where was Cathy?

"Nikhil," I said as evenly as I could. "What's your O_2 partial?"

"I beg your pardon?" he drawled.

"Beg Randi's. I asked you what your O_2 partial is."

"I've been conserving a bit. You know, less O_2, less CO_2. Trying to stretch things out."

"What . . . is . . . it?"

"Point one. It should be fine. I've had a lot of altitude experience . . ."

"Please put it back up to point two for five minutes, and then we'll talk."

"Now just a minute, I resent the implication that—"

"Be reasonable Nikhil. Put it back up for a little, please. Humor me. Five minutes won't hurt."

"Oh perhaps not. There. Now just what is it you expect to happen?"

"Wait for a bit."

We waited, silently. Randi sniffed, trying to deal with her pain. I watched Nikhil's face slowly grow more and more troubled. Finally I asked:

"Are you back with us?"

He nodded silently. "I think so. My apologies, Randi."

"Got clumsy. Too strong for my own bones. Forget it. And you don't owe me, either. Dumb thing to say. It was my choice."

What was? Two weeks ago, in his tent?

"Very well," Nikhil replied with as much dignity as he could muster.

Who besides Randi could dismiss a broken ankle with "forget it," and who besides Nikhil would take her up on that? I shook my head.

Randi couldn't keep the pain out of her voice as she held out her right vacuum boot. "This needs some work. Tent site. Cathy." Nothing would show, of course, until it came off.

"Quite," Nikhil responded. "Well, you were right on the direction. Perhaps we should resume."

I waved him off for a moment and found a painkiller in the pallet for Randi, and she ingested it through her helmet lock, and gagged a bit.

"Still a little ethane here," she gave a little laugh. "Woke me up. I'll manage."

"Let me know." I was so near her event horizon now that everything I could see of the outside world was distorted and bent by her presence. Such were the last moments of my freedom, the last minutes and the last seconds that I could look on our relationship from the outside. My independent existence was stretched beyond the power of any force of nature to restore it. Our fate was to become a singularity.

It was a measure of my own hunger and fatigue that I half seriously considered exterminating Nikhil; coldly, as if contemplating a roach to be crushed. A piton gun would have done nicely. But, I thought, Cathy really ought to be in on the decision.

She might want to keep him as a pet. Cathy, of course, was on the lead pitch. That meant she was really in charge, something Nikhil had forgotten.

"Cathy," I called, laying on the irony. "Randi has a broken ankle. Otherwise, we are ready to go again."

There was no answer, but radio didn't carry well in this material—too many bends in the path and something in the clathrate that just ate our frequencies like stealth paint. So I gave two pulls on our common line to signal okay, go.

The line was slack.

Cathy, anger with Nikhil possibly clouding her judgment, had enforced her positional authority in a way that was completely inarguable: by proceeding alone. At least I fervently hoped that was all that had happened. I pulled myself to where the passage resumed, and looked. No sign of anything.

"Sam, take the line back up to Cathy and tell her to wait up, we're coming."

Sam squeezed by me and scurried off. Shortly, his monitors in my helmet display blinked out; he was out of radio range as well—

Again, we waited for a tug on a line in a silence that shouted misery. Nikhil pretended to examine the wall, Randi stared ahead as if in a trance. I stared at her, wanting to touch her, but not seeming to have the energy to push myself over to her side of the little cave.

Both hope and dread increased with the waiting. The empty time could mean that Cathy had gone much further than our past rate of progress had suggested, which would be very welcome news. But it could also mean that some disaster ahead that had taken both her and Sam. In which case, we were dead as well. Or, like Randi's detour from the Boiling Sea, it could mean something we had neglected to imagine.

"Wojciech, Nikhil," Randi asked in her quiet, anticipatory, tone, "would you turn off your lamps?"

I looked at Nikhil, and he stared off in space, saying as much as that he could not care less. But his light went out. I nodded and cut mine. The blackness was total at first, then as my pupils widened, I realized I could sense a gray green contrast, a shadow. My shadow.

I turned around to the source of the glow. It was, of course, the crack behind me, through which Cathy and Sam had vanished. As my eyes adapted further, it became almost bright. It was white, just tinged with green. The shadows of rocks and ice intrusions made the crack look like the mouth of some beast about to devour us.

"Is there," I asked, "any reason why we should stay here?"

We left. The crack widened rapidly, and after an hour of rather mild crack-crawling, we were able to revert to our distance eating hand-hauling routine. We covered ten kilometers, almost straight up this way. With the sudden way of such things the crack turned into a tubular tunnel, artificial in its smoothness, and this in turn gave into a roughly teardrop-shaped, hundred meter diameter cavern with slick ice walls, and a bright circle at the top. I was about to use my piton gun when Randi tugged my arm and pointed out a ladder of double-looped pitons, set about three meters apart, leading up to the circle.

We were thus about to climb into Sphereheim when Cathy's line grew taut again.

That was, by the clock, the end of day nineteen. We were, it seems, both too exhausted and too excited to sleep.

The cavern above was almost perfectly spherical, hence the name we gave it, and was almost fifteen kilometers in diameter. A spire ran along its vertical axis from the ceiling to the floor, littered like a Christmas tree with the kind of cantilevered platforms that seventy-five milligees permits.

By now, we had climbed to within forty kilometers of the surface, so this was all in a pretty good vacuum, but there were signs that things had not always been this way.

"Cathy?" Nikhil called, the first words he had spoken since the fight.

"Good grief, you're here already. We waited until we thought it was safe."

"We saw the light."

"It came on as soon as I got in here. Sam's been looking for other automatic systems, burglar protection, for instance."

"There," Sam interjected, "appear to be none. The power source is two-stage—a uranium radionic long duration module, and something like a solid state fuel cell that works when it's warmed up. The latter appears to be able to produce almost a kilowatt."

"Good," I said, wondering if Sam's software could discern the contrary irritation in my voice. "Cathy, Randi has a broken ankle." Even in less than a hundredth of gee, Randi wouldn't put any weight on it.

"Oh, no! We need to get a tent up right away. Sam, break off and come down here, I need you. And you!" she pointed at Nikhil. "This is a medical emergency now, and what I say goes. Do you have a problem with that?" The edge in Cathy's voice verged on hysteria.

Nikhil simply turned away without saying anything and began setting up the tent.

Randi reached for Cathy. "Cathy, Nikhil cut his oxygen too thin, trying to save CO_2 catalyst for all of us. He wasn't himself. Ankle hurts like hell, but that was my fault. I'd feel better if you weren't so, uh, hard on him. Okay?"

Cathy stood quietly for a couple of seconds then muttered "All right, all right. Give me a minute to collect things, and we'll get in the tent. I'll see what I can do. Wojciech?"

"Yes, Cathy?"

"As I guess everyone knows, I just blew it with my husband, and I can't fix things right now because I have to fix Randi's ankle. He's in a blue funk." She pulled the velcro tab up on one of her pockets, reached in and produced a small, thin, box. "Give him one of these and tell him I'm sorry."

I looked at her. She seemed on the brink of some kind of collapse, but was holding herself back by some supreme effort of will. Maybe that's what I looked like to her.

"Sorry, Wojciech," she whispered, "best I can do."

I gave her hand a squeeze. "We'll make it good enough, okay? Just hang in there, Doc."

She gave me a quick, tear-filled smile, then grabbed the minidoc and followed Randi into the tent, which inflated promptly.

Nikhil was sitting on the other pallet and I sat next to him. "Look, Nikhil, the way I see it, none of this stuff counts. All that counts is that the four of us get out of this moon alive."

He looked at me briefly, then resumed looking at the ground. "No, no. Wojciech, it counts. Do you understand living death? The kind where your body persists, but everything that you thought was you has been destroyed? My reputation . . . they'll say Nikhil Ray cracked under pressure. It got too tough for old Nikhil. Nikhil beats up on women. It's going to be bloody bad."

I remembered the box Cathy gave me, pulled it out and opened it. "Doctor's orders, Nikhil. She cares, she really does."

He gave me a ghastly grin and took a caplet envelope, unwrapped it and stuck it through his helmet lock. "Can't say as I approve of mind altering drugs, but it wouldn't do to disappoint the doctor any more, now would it? I put her through medical school, did you know. She was eighteen when we met. Biology student studying evolution, and I was co-lecturing a paleontology section. Damn she was beautiful, and no one like that had ever . . ." he lifted his hands as if to gesture, then set them down again. "I broke my own rule about thinking first, and I have this to remind me, every day, of what happens when you do that."

"Look, Nikhil. She doesn't mean to hurt you." I tried to think of something to get him out of this, to put his mind on something else. "Say, we have a few minutes. Why don't we look around, it may be the only chance we get. Soon as Cathy's done with Randi, we'll need to get some sleep, then try to make it to the surface. We've forty kilometers to go, and only two days before our catalyst runs out."

"My line, isn't that? Very well." He seemed to straighten a bit. "But it looks as if the visitors packed up pretty thoroughly when they left. Those platforms off the central column are just bare honeycomb. Of course, it would be a bit odd if they packed *everything* out."

"Oh?"

"Field sites are usually an eclectic mess. All sorts of not-immediately-useful stuff gets strewn about. If the strewers don't expect the environmental police to stop by, it usually just gets left there by the hut site—the next explorer to come that way might find something useful."

"I see. You think there might be a dump here, somewhere."

"It seems they had a crypt. Why not a dump?"

What kind of alien technology might be useful to us, I didn't know. It would take a lot longer than the two days we had to figure out how to do anything with it. But the discussion had seemed to revive Nikhil a bit, so I humored him.

We found the junkyard. It was in a mound about a hundred meters from the tower base, covered with the same color dust as everything else. A squirt from my reaction pistol blew some of the dust away from the junk.

And it was just that. Discarded stuff. Broken building panels, a few boxes with electrical leads. What looked like a busted still. A small wheeled vehicle that I would have taken for a kid's tricycle, an elongated vacuum helmet with a cracked visor. Other things. I'd been rummaging for five minutes before I noticed that Nikhil hadn't gone past the still.

"Nikhil?"

"It is within the realm of possibility that I might redeem myself. Look at that."

The most visible part was a big coil of what looked to be tubing. There were also things that looked like electric motors, and several chambers to hold distilled liquids.

"The tubing, Wojciech."

"I don't understand."

"If we breathe through it, at this temperature, the CO_2 in our breath should condense."

Oh! We could do without the CO_2 catalyst.

"It wouldn't be very portable."

"No, it wouldn't," Nikhil nodded slowly, judiciously. "But it doesn't have to be. Cathy and Randi can remain here while you, Sam and I take the remaining catalyst and go for help."

Did I hear him right? Then I thought it through. Randi was disabled, Cathy, by strength and temperament, was the least suited for the ordeal above us. It made sense, but Randi would . . . no, Randi would have to agree if it made sense. She was a pro.

"We'd better see if it works first," I said.

VI

An hour later, our still was working. Tape, spare connectors, the alien light source, and Sam's instant computational capabilities yielded something that could keep two relatively quiescent people alive. They'd have to heat it up to sublimate the condensed CO_2 every other hour, or the thing would clog, but it worked.

Randi's ankle was a less happy situation.

"Randi's resting now," Cathy told us when she finally emerged from the vacuum tent, exhausted. "It's a bad break, splintered. Her bones were weak from too much time in low gravity, I think. Anyway, the breaks extend into the calcaneus and her foot is much too swollen to get back into her vacuum boots. Had to put her in a rescue bag to get out of the tent." Cathy shot a look of contempt at her husband who stared down. "The swelling will take days to go down, and she should have much more nourishment than we have to give her."

"I . . ." Nikhil started, then, in a moment I shall remember forever, he looked confused. "I?" Then he simply went limp and fell, much like an autumn leaf in the gentle gravity of Miranda, to the cavern dust. We were both too surprised to catch him even though his fall took several seconds.

"No, no . . ." Cathy choked.

I knelt over Nikhil and straightened his limbs. I couldn't think of anything else to do.

"Stroke?" I asked Cathy.

She seemed to shake herself back into a professional mode. I heard her take a breath.

"Could be. His heart telemetry's fine. Or he may have just fainted. Let's get the other tent set up."

We did this only with Sam's help. We made errors in the setup, errors which would have been fatal if Sam hadn't been there to notice and correct them. We were tired and had been eating too little food. It took an hour. We put Nikhil in the tent and Cathy was about to follow when she stopped me.

"The main med kit's in Randi's tent. I'll need it if I have to operate. She'll have gotten out of the rescue bag to sleep after I left. You'll have to wake her, get her back in the bag and depressure . . ."

I held up a hand. "I can figure it out, and if I can't, she can. Cathy, her foot's busted, not her head."

Cathy nodded and I could see a bit of a smile through her faceplate.

"Randi," I called, "sorry to wake you, but we've got a problem."

"I heard. Comsets are dumb, guys. Can't tell if you talk *about* someone instead of *to* someone. Be right out with the med kit."

"Huh?" Cathy sounded shocked. "No, Randi don't try to put that boot on. Please don't."

"Too late," Randi answered. We watched the tension go out of the tent fabric as it depressurized. Randi emerged from the opening with the med kit and a sample bag. Cathy and I immediately looked at her right boot—it seemed perfectly normal, except that Randi had rigged some kind of brace with pitons and vacuum tape.

Then we looked at the sample bag. It contained a blue-green swollen travesty of a human foot, severed neatly just above the ankle, apparently with a surgical laser. I couldn't think of anything to do or say.

"Oh, no, Randi," Cathy cried and launched herself toward Randi. "I tried Randi, I tried."

"You didn't have time." The two women embraced. "Don't say anything," Randi finally said, "to him." She nodded at Nikhil's tent. "Until we're all back and safe. Please, huh?"

Cathy stood frozen, then nodded slowly, took the sample bag and examined the foot end of the section. "Looks clean, anyway. At least let me take a look at the stump before you go, okay?"

Randi shook her head. "Bitch to unwrap. Cauterized with the surgical laser. Plastiflesh all over the stump. Sealed in plastic. Plenty of local. Don't feel anything. I did a good enough job, Cathy."

I finally found my voice. "Randi . . . why?"

"Nikhil's gone. Got to move. It's okay, Wojciech. They can regenerate. You and I got to get going."

"Me? Now?" I was surprised for a moment, then realized the need. Cathy had to stay with Nikhil. And I'd already seen too many situations where one person would have been stopped that we'd managed to work around with two. Also, our jury-rigged CO_2 still's capacity was two people, max.

"Now. Go as long as we can, then sleep. Eat everything we have left. Push for the surface. Only way."

Cathy nodded. She handed Randi's foot to me, almost absentmindedly, and went into the tent to attend to Nikhil. Randi laughed, took the foot from me, and threw it far out of sight toward Sphereheim's junk pile. In the low gravity, it probably got there.

I tried not to think about it as Randi and I packed, with Sam's help. Moving slowly and deliberately, we didn't make that many errors. What Randi had to draw on, I didn't know. I drew on her. In an hour, we were ready to go and said our farewells to Cathy.

She would have to wait there, perhaps alone if Nikhil did not recover, perhaps forever if we did not succeed. What would that be like? I wondered. Would some future explorers confuse her with the beings who had built the station in this cavern? Had we already done that with the corpses we found in the Cavern of the Dead Ends?

I wished I had made love to Cathy that night we spent together—I felt I was leaving a relationship incomplete; a feeling, a sharing, uncommunicated. Here, even a last embrace would have been nice, but she was in her tent caring for her husband, and out of food, low on time, Randi and I had to go, and go now. In the dash to the surface, even minutes might be critical.

Tireless Sam scaled the alien tower, found the vent in the magnificent, crystal-lined dome of the cavern roof, and dropped us a line. I was suspended among wonders, but so tired I almost fell asleep as Sam reeled us up. The experience was surreal and beyond description.

Of most of the next few days, I have little detailed memory. Sam dragged us through passages, chimneys vents and caverns. Occasionally, it stopped at a problem that Randi would somehow rouse herself to solve.

On one occasion, we came to a wall a meter thick which had cracked enough to let gas pass through. Sam's acoustic radar showed a big cavern on the other side, so, somehow, we dug our way through. For all its talents, Sam was not built for wielding a pick. I leave this information to the designers of future cave exploration robots.

Randi and I swung at that wall in five minute shifts for a three-hour eternity, before, in a fit of hysterical anaerobic energy, I was able to kick it through. We were too tired to celebrate—we just grabbed the line as Sam went by and tried to keep awake and living as it pulled us through another cave and another crack.

In one of a string of ordinary crystal caverns, we found another alien piton. Randi thought it might be a different design than the one we had found before, and had Sam pull it out and put it in a sample bag, which we stored on Sam—the most likely to survive.

I mentioned this because we were near death and knew it, but could still do things for the future. Everyone dies, I thought, so we all spend our lives for something. The only thing that matters at the end is: for what? In saving the piton, we were adding one more bit to the tally of "for what?"

This was almost certainly our last "night" in a tent. I think we both stunk, but I was too far gone to tell for sure. We'd gone for thirty-seven hours straight. Sam says we are within three kilometers of the surface, but the cavern trail lies parallel to this surface, and refuses to ascend.

In theory, our catalyst was exhausted, but we continued to breath.

Another quake trapped me.

Randi was in front of me. Somehow, she managed to squeeze aside and let Sam by to help. Sam chipped clathrate away from my helmet, which let me straighten my neck.

As this happened, there was another movement, a big slow one this time, and the groan of Miranda's tortured mantle was clearly audible as my helmet was pressed between the passage walls again. I could see the passage ahead of me close a little more with every sickening wave of ground movement, even as I could feel the pressure at my spot release a bit. But the passage ahead—if it closed with Randi on this side, we were dead.

"Go!" I told Randi. "It's up to you now." As if it hadn't always been so. I was pushed sideways and back again as another train of s-waves rolled through. Ice split with sharp retorts.

Sam turned sideways in the passage, pitting its thin composite against billions of tons of rock.

Randi vanished forward. "I love you," she said. "I'll make it."

"I know you will. Hey, we're married, okay?"

"Just like that?"

"By my authority as a man in a desperate position."

"Okay. Married. Two kids. Deal?"

"Deal."

"I love you again."

Sam cracked under the pressure, various electronic innards spilling onto the passage floor. I couldn't see anything beyond him.

"Sam?" I asked. Useless question.

"Randi?"

Nothing.

For some strange reason I felt no pressure on me now. Too worried for Randi, too exhausted to be interested in my own death, I dozed.

There was definitely CO_2 in my helmet when I woke again. It was pitch black—the suit had turned off my glowlamp to conserve an inconsequential watt or two. Groggy, I thought turning on my back would help my breathing, vaguely thinking that the one percent weight on my lungs was a problem. To my surprise, I could actually turn.

In the utter dead black overhead, a star appeared. Very briefly, then I blinked and it vanished.

I continued to stare at this total darkness above me for minutes, not daring to believe I'd seen what I thought I'd seen, and then I saw another one. Yes, a real star.

I thought that could only mean that a crack to the surface had opened above me; incredibly narrow, or far above me, but open enough that now and then a star drifted by its opening. I was beyond climbing, but perhaps where photons could get in, photons could get out.

Shaking and miserable, I started transmitting.

"Uranus Control, Uranus Control, Wojciech Bubka here. I'm down at the bottom of a crack on Miranda. Help. Uranus Control, Uranus Control . . ."

Something sprayed on my face, waking me again. Air and mist as well.

I opened my eyes and saw that a tube had cemented itself to my faceplate and drilled a hole through it to admit some smaller tubes. One of these was trying to snake its way into my mouth. I opened up to help it, and got something warm and sweet to swallow.

"Thanks," I croaked, around the tube.

"Don't mention it," a young female voice answered, sounding almost as relieved as I felt.

"My wife's in this passage, somewhere in the direction my head is pointed. Can you get one of these tubes to her?"

There was a hesitation.

"Your wife."

"Miranda Lotati," I croaked. "She was with me. Trying to get to the surface. Went that way."

More hesitation.

"We'll try, Wojciech. God knows we'll try."

Within minutes, a tiny version of Sam fell on my chest and scuttled passed Sam's wreckage down the compressed passage in her direction trailing a line. The line seemed to run over me forever. I remember reading somewhere that while the journey to singularity is inevitable for someone passing into the event horizon of a black hole, as viewed from our universe, the journey can take forever.

What most people remember about the rescue is the digger; that vast thing of pistons, beams, and steel claws that tore through the clathrate rift like an anteater looking for ants. What they saw, I assure you, was in no way as impressive, or scary, as being directly under the thing.

I was already in a hospital ship bed when they found Randi, eleven kilometers down a passage that had narrowed, narrowed, and narrowed.

At its end, she had broken her bones forcing herself through one more centimeter at a time. A cracked pelvis, both collarbones, two ribs, and her remaining ankle.

The last had done it, for when it collapsed she had no remaining way to force herself any further through that crack of doom.

And so she had lain there, and, minute by minute, despite everything, willed herself to live as long as she could.

Despite everything, she did.

They got the first tubes into her through her hollow right boot and the plastiflesh seal of her stump, after the left foot had proven to be frozen solid. They didn't tell me at first—not until they had convinced themselves she was really alive.

* * *

When the rescuers reached Cathy and Nikhil, Cathy calmly guided the medic to her paralyzed husband, and as soon as she saw that he was in good professional hands, gave herself a sedative, and started screaming until she collapsed. She wasn't available for interviews for weeks. But she's fine now, and laughs about it. She and Nikhil live in a large university dome on Triton and host our reunions in their house, which has no roof—they've arranged for the dome's rain to fall elsewhere.

Miranda my wife spent three years as a quadruple amputee, and went back into Miranda the moon that way, in a powered suit, to lead people back to the Cavern of Dead Ends. Today, it's easy to see where the bronze, weathered flesh of her old limbs ends and the pink smoothness of her new ones start. But if you miss it, she'll point it out with a grin.

So, having been to Hades and back, are the four of us best friends? For amusement, we all have more congenial companions. Nikhil is still a bit haughty, and he and Cathy still snipe at each other a little, but with smiles more often than not. I've come to conclude that, in some strange way, they need the stimulation that gives them, and a displacement for needs about which Nikhil will not speak.

Cathy and Randi still find little to talk about, giving us supposedly verbally challenged males a chance. Nikhil says I have absorbed enough geology lectures to pass doctorate exams; so maybe I will do that someday. He often lectures me toward that end, but my advance for our book was such that I won't have to do anything the rest of my life, except for the love of it. I'm not sure I love geology.

Often, on our visits, the four of us simply sit, say nothing, and do nothing but sip a little fruit of the local grape, which we all enjoy. We smile at each other and remember.

But don't let this studied diffidence of ours fool you. The four of us are bound with something that goes far beyond friendship, far beyond any slight conversation, far beyond my idiot critiques of our various eccentric personalities or of the hindsight mistakes of our passage through the Great Miranda Rift. These are the table crumbs from a feast of greatness, meant to sustain those who follow.

The sublime truth is that when I am with my wife, Nikhil, and Cathy, I feel elevated above what is merely human. *Then* I sit in the presence of these demigods who challenged, in mortal combat, the will of the universe—and won.

THE SHOULDERS OF GIANTS

Robert J. Sawyer

❁

Robert J. Sawyer (born 1960), who lives and works in Ontario, near Toronto, Canada, began to publish SF short stories in the 1980s. His career as a novelist took off in the 1990s, and he became one of the SF popular success stories of the decade. After five well-regarded novels, he won the Nebula Award for *The Terminal Experiment* (1995), and has since published seven more novels, four of them Hugo Award nominees. He is a hard SF writer in the tradition of Isaac Asimov, more an idea writer than a stylist, often building neat puzzles with a complex moral dimension. His short stories are now infrequent, but clever and readable. His new novel, *Hominids* (2002), the first of a trilogy which involves an alternate contemporary world in which humans died out and Neanderthals are the only intelligent hominids, was serialized in *Analog*. His previous novel, *Calculating God* (2000), about what would happen if hard evidence were found for the existence of God, was a bestseller in Canada. Generally his novels involve overt politically charged dramatizations, and moral discussions of a broadly humanist nature (this is also the Asimov tradition), often of several different topics.

The frontier themes in hard SF are one of the major dividing points between North American and European SF. David Mogen wrote a good book on the subject of the frontier in SF years ago. Yet, still, the politics of Canadian SF writers was more closely allied to the politics of U.K. writers than of the U.S. community in the 1990s.

The germ of this story came from Marshall T. Savage's nonfiction book *The Millennial Project*, in which Savage said that only a fool would set out for a long space voyage in a generation ship. Sawyer says, "My wife Carolyn and I rented a cottage, and in that rustic, wooded setting, I found myself thinking about pioneers and recalling previous trips to cottages as a teenager, during which I'd read much classic SF. The story of the colonists aboard the *Pioneer Spirit* is my attempt to capture the sense of wonder that drew me into our genre in the first place. The title, of course, is a tip of the hat to Asimov, Clarke, Clement, Herbert, Niven, and all the others upon whose shoulders the SF writers of my generation are fortunate enough to stand." Most specifically, it begins by retelling the classic A. E. van Vogt story, "Far Centaurus" (which introduced the idea of the ship full of slower-than-light colonists preempted by technological advance), and then taking the story farther into the future and into space.

It seemed like only yesterday when I'd died, but, of course, it was almost certainly centuries ago. I wish the computer would just *tell* me, dammitall, but it was doubtless waiting until its sensors said I was sufficiently stable and alert. The irony was that my pulse was surely racing out of concern, forestalling it speaking to me. If this was an emergency, it should inform me, and if it wasn't, it should let me relax.

Finally, the machine did speak in its crisp, feminine voice. "Hello, Toby. Welcome back to the world of the living."

"Where—" I'd thought I'd spoken the word, but no sound had come out. I tried again. "Where are we?"

"Exactly where we should be: decelerating toward Soror."

I felt myself calming down. "How is Ling?"

"She's reviving, as well."

"The others?"

"All forty-eight cryogenics chambers are functioning properly," said the computer. "Everybody is apparently fine."

That was good to hear, but it wasn't surprising. We had four extra cryochambers; if one of the occupied ones had failed, Ling and I would have been awoken earlier to transfer the person within it into a spare. "What's the date?"

"16 June 3296."

I'd expected an answer like that, but it still took me back a bit. Twelve hundred years had elapsed since the blood had been siphoned out of my body and oxygenated antifreeze had been pumped in to replace it. We'd spent the first of those years accelerating, and presumably the last one decelerating, and the rest—

—the rest was spent coasting at our maximum velocity, three thousand kilometers per second, one percent of the speed of light. My father had been from Glasgow; my mother, from Los Angeles. They had both enjoyed the quip that the difference between an American and a European was that to an American, a hundred years was a long time, and to a European, a hundred miles is a big journey.

But both would agree that twelve hundred years and 11.9 light-years were equally staggering values. And now, here we were, decelerating in toward Tau Ceti, the closest sunlike star to Earth that wasn't part of a multiple-star system. Of course, because of that, this star had been frequently examined by Earth's Search for Extraterrestrial Intelligence. But nothing had ever been detected; nary a peep.

I was feeling better minute by minute. My own blood, stored in bottles, had been returned to my body and was now coursing through my arteries, my veins, reanimating me.

We were going to make it.

Tau Ceti happened to be oriented with its north pole facing toward Sol; that meant that the technique developed late in the twentieth century to detect planetary systems based on subtle blueshifts and redshifts of a star tugged now closer, now farther away, was useless with it. Any wobble in Tau Ceti's movements would be perpendicular, as seen from Earth, producing no Doppler effect. But eventually Earth-orbiting telescopes had been developed that were sensitive enough to detect the wobble visually, and—

It had been front-page news around the world: the first solar system seen by telescopes. Not inferred from stellar wobbles or spectral shifts, but actually seen. At least four planets could be made out orbiting Tau Ceti, and one of them—

There had been formulas for decades, first popularized in the RAND Corporation's study *Habitable Planets for Man*. Every science fiction writer and astrobiologist worth his or her salt had used them to determine the *life zones*—the distances from target stars at which planets with Earthlike surface temperatures might exist, a Goldilocks band, neither too hot nor too cold.

And the second of the four planets that could be seen around Tau Ceti was smack-dab in the middle of that star's life zone. The planet was watched carefully for an entire year—one of its years, that is, a period of 193 Earth days. Two wonderful facts became apparent. First, the planet's orbit was damn near circular—meaning it would likely have stable temperatures all the time; the gravitational influence of the fourth planet, a Jovian giant orbiting at a distance of half a billion kilometers from Tau Ceti, probably was responsible for that.

And, second, the planet varied in brightness substantially over the course of its twenty-nine-hour-and-seventeen-minute day. The reason was easy to deduce: most of one hemisphere was covered with land, which reflected back little of Tau Ceti's yellow light, while the other hemisphere, with a much higher albedo, was likely covered by a vast ocean, no doubt, given the planet's fortuitous orbital radius, of liquid water—an extraterrestrial Pacific.

Of course, at a distance of 11.9 light-years, it was quite possible that Tau Ceti had other planets, too small or too dark to be seen. And so referring to the Earthlike globe as Tau Ceti II would have been problematic; if an additional world or worlds were eventually found orbiting closer in, the system's planetary numbering would end up as confusing as the scheme used to designate Saturn's rings.

Clearly a name was called for, and Giancarlo DiMaio, the astronomer who had discovered the half-land, half-water world, gave it one: Soror, the Latin word for sister. And, indeed, Soror appeared, at least as far as could be told from Earth, to be a sister to humanity's home world.

Soon we would know for sure just how perfect a sister it was. And speaking of sisters, well—okay, Ling Woo wasn't my biological sister, but we'd worked together and trained together for four years before launch, and I'd come to think of her as a sister, despite the press constantly referring to us as the new Adam and Eve. Of course, we'd help to populate the new world, but not together; my wife, Helena, was one of the forty-eight others still frozen solid. Ling wasn't involved yet with any of the other colonists, but, well, she was gorgeous and brilliant, and of the two dozen men in cryosleep, twenty-one were unattached.

Ling and I were co-captains of the *Pioneer Spirit*. Her cryocoffin was like mine, and unlike all the others: it was designed for repeated use. She and I could be revived multiple times during the voyage, to deal with emergencies. The rest of the crew, in coffins that had cost only $700,000 apiece instead of the six million each of ours was worth, could only be revived once, when our ship reached its final destination.

"You're all set," said the computer. "You can get up now."

The thick glass cover over my coffin slid aside, and I used the padded handles to hoist myself out of its black porcelain frame. For most of the journey, the ship had been coasting in zero gravity, but now that it was decelerating, there was a gentle push downward. Still, it was nowhere near a full g, and I was grateful for that. It would be a day or two before I would be truly steady on my feet.

My module was shielded from the others by a partition, which I'd covered with photos of people I'd left behind: my parents, Helena's parents, my real sister, her two sons. My clothes had waited patiently for me for twelve hundred years; I rather suspected they were now hopelessly out of style. But I got dressed—I'd been naked in the cryochamber, of course—and at last I stepped out from behind the partition, just in time to see Ling emerging from behind the wall that shielded her cryocoffin.

" 'Morning," I said, trying to sound blasé.

Ling, wearing a blue and gray jumpsuit, smiled broadly. "Good morning."

We moved into the center of the room, and hugged, friends delighted to have shared an adventure together. Then we immediately headed out toward the bridge, half-walking, half-floating, in the reduced gravity.

"How'd you sleep?" asked Ling.

It wasn't a frivolous question. Prior to our mission, the longest anyone had spent in cryofreeze was five years, on a voyage to Saturn; the *Pioneer Spirit* was Earth's first starship.

"Fine," I said. "You?"

"Okay," replied Ling. But then she stopped moving, and briefly touched my forearm. "Did you—did you dream?"

Brain activity slowed to a virtual halt in cryofreeze, but several members of the crew of *Cronus*—the Saturn mission—had claimed to have had brief dreams, lasting perhaps two or three subjective minutes, spread over five years. Over the span that the *Pioneer Spirit* had been traveling, there would have been time for many hours of dreaming.

I shook my head. "No. What about you?"

Ling nodded. "Yes. I dreamt about the Strait of Gibraltar. Ever been there?"

"No."

"It's Spain's southernmost boundary, of course. You can see across the strait from Europe to northern Africa, and there were Neandertal settlements on the Spanish side." Ling's Ph.D. was in anthropology. "But they never made it across the strait. They could clearly see that there was more land—another continent!—only thirteen kilometers away. A strong swimmer can make it, and with any sort of raft or boat, it was eminently doable. But Neandertals never journeyed to the other side; as far as we can tell, they never even tried."

"And you dreamt—?"

"I dreamt I was part of a Neandertal community there, a teenage girl, I guess. And I was trying to convince the others that we should go across the strait, go see the new land. But I couldn't; they weren't interested. There was plenty of food and shelter where we were. Finally, I headed out on my own, trying to swim it. The water was cold and the waves were high, and half the time I couldn't get any air to breathe, but I swam and I swam, and then . . ."

"Yes?"

She shrugged a little. "And then I woke up."

I smiled at her. "Well, this time we're going to make it. We're going to make it for sure."

We came to the bridge door, which opened automatically to admit us, although it squeaked something fierce while doing so; its lubricants must have dried up over the last twelve centuries. The room was rectangular with a double row of angled consoles facing a large screen, which currently was off.

"Distance to Soror?" I asked into the air.

The computer's voice replied. "1.2 million kilometers."

I nodded. About three times the distance between Earth and its moon. "Screen on, view ahead."

"Overrides are in place," said the computer.

Ling smiled at me. "You're jumping the gun, partner."

I was embarrassed. The *Pioneer Spirit* was decelerating toward Soror; the ship's fusion exhaust was facing in the direction of travel. The optical scanners would be burned out by the glare if their shutters were opened. "Computer, turn off the fusion motors."

"Powering down," said the artificial voice.

"Visual as soon as you're able," I said.

The gravity bled away as the ship's engines stopped firing. Ling held on to one of the handles attached to the top of the console nearest her; I was still a little groggy from the suspended animation, and just floated freely in the room. After about two minutes, the screen came on. Tau Ceti was in the exact center, a baseball-sized yellow disk. And the four planets were clearly visible, ranging from pea-sized to as big as a grape.

"Magnify on Soror," I said.

One of the peas became a billiard ball, although Tau Ceti grew hardly at all.

"More," said Ling.

The planet grew to softball size. It was showing as a wide crescent, perhaps a third of the disk illuminated from this angle. And—thankfully, fantastically—Soror was everything we'd dreamed it would be: a giant polished marble, with swirls of white cloud, and a vast, blue ocean, and—

Part of a continent was visible, emerging out of the darkness. And it was green, apparently covered with vegetation.

We hugged again, squeezing each other tightly. No one had been sure when we'd left Earth; Soror could have been barren. The *Pioneer Spirit* was ready regardless: in its cargo holds was everything we needed to survive even on an airless world. But we'd hoped and prayed that Soror would be, well—just like this: a true sister, another Earth, another home.

"It's beautiful, isn't it?" said Ling.

I felt my eyes tearing. It *was* beautiful, breathtaking, stunning. The vast ocean, the cottony clouds, the verdant land, and—

"Oh, my God," I said, softly. "Oh, my God."

"What?" said Ling.

"Don't you see?" I asked. "Look!"

Ling narrowed her eyes and moved closer to the screen. "What?"

"On the dark side," I said.

She looked again. "Oh . . ." she said. There were faint lights sprinkled across the darkness; hard to see, but definitely there. "Could it be volcanism?" asked Ling. Maybe Soror wasn't so perfect after all.

"Computer," I said, "spectral analysis of the light sources on the planet's dark side."

"Predominantly incandescent lighting, color temperature 5600 kelvin."

I exhaled and looked at Ling. They weren't volcanoes. They were cities.

Soror, the world we'd spent twelve centuries traveling to, the world we'd intended to colonize, the world that had been dead silent when examined by radio telescopes, was already inhabited.

The *Pioneer Spirit* was a colonization ship; it wasn't intended as a diplomatic vessel. When it had left Earth, it had seemed important to get at least some humans off the mother world. Two small-scale nuclear wars—Nuke I and Nuke II, as the media had dubbed them—had already been fought, one in southern Asia, the other in South America. It appeared to be only a matter of time before Nuke III, and that one might be the big one.

SETI had detected nothing from Tau Ceti, at least not by 2051. But Earth itself had only been broadcasting for a century and a half at that point; Tau Ceti might have had a thriving civilization then that hadn't yet started using radio. But now it was twelve hundred years later. Who knew how advanced the Tau Cetians might be?

I looked at Ling, then back at the screen. "What should we do?"

Ling tilted her head to one side. "I'm not sure. On the one hand, I'd love to meet them, whoever they are. But . . ."

"But they might not want to meet us," I said. "They might think we're invaders, and—"

"And we've got forty-eight other colonists to think about," said Ling. "For all we know, we're the last surviving humans."

I frowned. "Well, that's easy enough to determine. Computer, swing the radio telescope toward Sol system. See if you can pick anything up that might be artificial."

"Just a sec," said the female voice. A few moments later, a cacophony filled the room: static and snatches of voices and bits of music and sequences of tones, overlapping and jumbled, fading in and out. I heard what sounded like English—although strangely inflected—and maybe Arabic and Mandarin and . . .

"We're not the last survivors," I said, smiling. "There's still life on Earth—or, at least, there was 11.9 years ago, when those signals started out."

Ling exhaled. "I'm glad we didn't blow ourselves up," she said. "Now, I guess we should find out what we're dealing with at Tau Ceti. Computer, swing the dish to face Soror, and again scan for artificial signals."

"Doing so." There was silence for most of a minute, then a blast of static, and a few bars of music, and clicks and bleeps, and voices, speaking in Mandarin and English and—

"No," said Ling. "I said face the dish the other way. I want to hear what's coming from Soror."

The computer actually sounded miffed. "The dish *is* facing toward Soror," it said.

I looked at Ling, realization dawning. At the time we'd left Earth, we'd been so worried that humanity was about to snuff itself out, we hadn't really stopped to consider what would happen if that didn't occur. But with twelve hundred years, faster spaceships would doubtless had been developed. While the colonists aboard the *Pioneer Spirit* had slept, some dreaming at an indolent pace, other ships had zipped past them, arriving at Tau Ceti decades, if not centuries, earlier—long enough ago that they'd already built human cities on Soror.

"Damn it," I said. "God damn it." I shook my head, staring at the screen. The tortoise was supposed to win, not the hare.

"What do we do now?" asked Ling.

I sighed. "I suppose we should contact them."

"We—ah, we might be from the wrong side."

I grinned. "Well, we can't *both* be from the wrong side. Besides, you heard the radio: Mandarin *and* English. Anyway, I can't imagine that anyone cares about a war more than a thousand years in the past, and—"

"Excuse me," said the ship's computer. "Incoming audio message."

I looked at Ling. She frowned, surprised. "Put it on," I said.

"*Pioneer Spirit*, welcome! This is Jod Bokket, manager of the Derluntin space station, in orbit around Soror. Is there anyone awake on board?" It was a man's voice, with an accent unlike anything I'd ever heard before.

Ling looked at me, to see if I was going to object, then she spoke up. "Computer, send a reply." The computer bleeped to signal that the channel was open. "This is Dr. Ling Woo, co-captain of the *Pioneer Spirit*. Two of us have revived; there are forty-eight more still in cryofreeze."

"Well, look," said Bokket's voice, "it'll be days at the rate you're going before you get here. How about if we send a ship to bring you two to Derluntin? We can have someone there to pick you up in about an hour."

"They really like to rub it in, don't they?" I grumbled.

"What was that?" said Bokket. "We couldn't quite make it out."

Ling and I consulted with facial expressions, then agreed. "Sure," said Ling. "We'll be waiting."

"Not for long," said Bokket, and the speaker went dead.

Bokket himself came to collect us. His spherical ship was tiny compared with ours, but it seemed to have about the same amount of habitable interior space; would the ignominies ever cease? Docking adapters had changed a lot in a thousand years, and he wasn't able to get an airtight seal, so we had to transfer over to his ship in space suits. Once aboard, I was pleased to see we were still floating freely; it would have been too much if they'd had artificial gravity.

Bokket seemed a nice fellow—about my age, early thirties. Of course, maybe people looked youthful forever now; who knew how old he might actually be? I couldn't really identify his ethnicity, either; he seemed to be rather a blend of traits. But he certainly was taken with Ling—his eyes popped out when she took off her helmet, revealing her heart-shaped face and long, black hair.

"Hello," he said, smiling broadly.

Ling smiled back. "Hello. I'm Ling Woo, and this is Toby MacGregor, my co-captain."

"Greetings," I said, sticking out my hand.

Bokket looked at it, clearly not knowing precisely what to do. He extended his hand in a mirroring of my gesture, but didn't touch me. I closed the gap and clasped his hand. He seemed surprised, but pleased.

"We'll take you back to the station first," he said. "Forgive us, but, well—you can't go down to the planet's surface yet; you'll have to be quarantined. We've eliminated a lot of diseases, of course, since your time, and so we don't vaccinate for them anymore. I'm willing to take the risk, but . . ."

I nodded. "That's fine."

He tipped his head slightly, as if he were preoccupied for a moment, then: "I've told the ship to take us back to Derluntin station. It's in a polar orbit, about two hundred kilometers above Soror; you'll get some beautiful views of the planet, anyway." He was grinning from ear to ear. "It's wonderful to meet you people," he said. "Like a page out of history."

"If you knew about us," I asked, after we'd settled in for the journey to the station, "why didn't you pick us up earlier?"

Bokket cleared his throat. "We didn't know about you."

"But you called us by name: *Pioneer Spirit*."

"Well, it is painted in letters three meters high across your hull. Our asteroid-watch system detected you. A lot of information from your time has been lost—I guess there was a lot of political upheaval then, no?—but we knew Earth had experimented with sleeper ships in the twenty-first century."

We were getting close to the space station; it was a giant ring, spinning to simulate gravity. It might have taken us over a thousand years to do it, but humanity was finally building space stations the way God had always intended them to be.

And floating next to the space station was a beautiful spaceship, with a spindle-shaped silver hull and two sets of mutually perpendicular emerald-green delta wings. "It's gorgeous," I said.

Bokket nodded.

"How does it land, though? Tail-down?"

"It doesn't land; it's a starship."

"Yes, but—"

"We use shuttles to go between it and the ground."

"But if it can't land," asked Ling, "why is it streamlined? Just for esthetics?"

Bokket laughed, but it was a polite laugh. "It's streamlined because it needs to be. There's substantial length-contraction when flying at just below the speed of light; that means that the interstellar medium seems much denser. Although there's only one baryon per cubic centimeter, they form what seems to be an appreciable atmosphere if you're going fast enough."

"And your ships are *that* fast?" asked Ling.

Bokket smiled. "Yes. They're that fast."

Ling shook her head. "We were crazy," she said. "Crazy to undertake our journey." She looked briefly at Bokket, but couldn't meet his eyes. She turned her gaze down toward the floor. "You must think we're incredibly foolish."

Bokket's eyes widened. He seemed at a loss for what to say. He looked at me, spreading his arms, as if appealing to me for support. But I just exhaled, letting air—and disappointment—vent from my body.

"You're wrong," said Bokket, at last. "You couldn't be more wrong. We honor you." He paused, waiting for Ling to look up again. She did, her eyebrows lifted questioningly. "If we have come farther than you," said Bokket, "or have gone faster than you, it's because we had your work to build on. Humans are here now because it's easy for us to be here, because you and others blazed the trails." He looked at me, then at Ling. "If we see farther," he said, "it's because we stand on the shoulders of giants."

Later that day, Ling, Bokket, and I were walking along the gently curving floor of Derluntin station. We were confined to a limited part of one section; they'd let us down to the planet's surface in another ten days, Bokket had said.

"There's nothing for us here," said Ling, hands in her pockets. "We're freaks, anachronisms. Like somebody from the T'ang Dynasty showing up in our world."

"Soror is wealthy," said Bokket. "We can certainly support you and your passengers."

"They are *not* passengers," I snapped. "They are colonists. They are explorers."

Bokket nodded. "I'm sorry. You're right, of course. But look—we really are delighted that you're here. I've been keeping the media away; the quarantine lets me do that. But they will go absolutely dingo when you come down to the planet. It's like having Neil Armstrong or Tamiko Hiroshige show up at your door."

"Tamiko who?" asked Ling.

"Sorry. After your time. She was the first person to disembark at Alpha Centauri."

"The first," I repeated; I guess I wasn't doing a good job of hiding my bitterness. "That's the honor—that's the achievement. Being the first. Nobody remembers the name of the second person on the moon."

"Edwin Eugene Aldrin, Jr.," said Bokket. "Known as 'Buzz.'"

"Fine, okay," I said. "*You* remember, but most people don't."

"I didn't remember it; I accessed it." He tapped his temple. "Direct link to the planetary web; everybody has one."

Ling exhaled; the gulf was vast. "Regardless," she said, "we are not pioneers; we're just also-rans. We may have set out before you did, but you got here before us."

"Well, my ancestors did," said Bokket. "I'm sixth-generation Sororian."

"*Sixth* generation?" I said. "How long has the colony been here?"

"We're not a colony anymore; we're an independent world. But the ship that got here first left Earth in 2107. Of course, my ancestors didn't immigrate until much later."

"Twenty-one-oh-seven," I repeated. That was only fifty-six years after the launch of the *Pioneer Spirit*. I'd been thirty-one when our ship had started its journey; if I'd stayed behind, I might very well have lived to see the real pioneers depart. What had we been thinking, leaving Earth? Had we been running, escaping, getting out, fleeing before the bombs fell? Were we pioneers, or cowards?

No. No, those were crazy thoughts. We'd left for the same reason that *Homo sapiens sapiens* had crossed the Strait of Gibraltar. It was what we did as a species. It was why we'd triumphed, and the Neandertals had failed. We *needed* to see what was on the other side, what was over the next hill, what was orbiting other stars. It was what had given us dominion over the home planet; it was what was going to make us kings of infinite space.

I turned to Ling. "We can't stay here," I said.

She seemed to mull this over for a bit, then nodded. She looked at Bokket. "We don't want parades," she said. "We don't want statues." She lifted her eyebrows, as if acknowledging the magnitude of what she was asking for. "We want a new ship, a faster ship." She looked at me, and I bobbed my head in agreement. She pointed out the window. "A *streamlined* ship."

"What would you do with it?" asked Bokket. "Where would you go?"

She glanced at me, then looked back at Bokket. "Andromeda."

"Andromeda? You mean the Andromeda *Galaxy*? But that's—" a fractional pause, no doubt while his web link provided the data "—2.2 *million* light-years away."

"Exactly."

"But . . . but it would take over two million years to get there."

"Only from Earth's—excuse me, from Soror's—point of view," said Ling. "We could do it in less subjective time than we've already been traveling, and, of course, we'd spend all that time in cryogenic freeze."

"None of our ships have cryogenic chambers," Bokket said. "There's no need for them."

"We could transfer the chambers from the *Pioneer Spirit*."

Bokket shook his head. "It would be a one-way trip; you'd never come back."

"That's not true," I said. "Unlike most galaxies, Andromeda is actually moving toward the Milky Way, not away from it. Eventually, the two galaxies will merge, bringing us home."

"That's billions of years in the future."

"Thinking small hasn't done us any good so far," said Ling.

Bokket frowned. "I said before that we can afford to support you and your shipmates here on Soror, and that's true. But starships are expensive. We can't just give you one."

"It's got to be cheaper than supporting all of us."

"No, it's not."

"You said you honored us. You said you stand on our shoulders. If that's true, then repay the favor. Give us an opportunity to stand on *your* shoulders. Let us have a new ship."

Bokket sighed; it was clear he felt we really didn't understand how difficult Ling's request would be to fulfill. "I'll do what I can," he said.

Ling and I spent that evening talking, while blue-and-green soror spun majestically beneath us. It was our job to jointly make the right decision, not just for ourselves but for the four dozen other members of the Pioneer Spirit's complement that had entrusted their fate to us. Would they have wanted to be revived here?

No. No, of course not. They'd left Earth to found a colony; there was no reason to think they would have changed their minds, whatever they might be dreaming. Nobody had an emotional attachment to the idea of Tau Ceti; it just had seemed a logical target star.

"We could ask for passage back to Earth," I said.

"You don't want that," said Ling. "And neither, I'm sure, would any of the others."

"No, you're right," I said. "They'd want us to go on."

Ling nodded. "I think so."

"Andromeda?" I said, smiling. "Where did that come from?"

She shrugged. "First thing that popped into my head."

"Andromeda," I repeated, tasting the word some more. I remembered how thrilled I was, at sixteen, out in the California desert, to see that little oval smudge below Cassiopeia for the first time. Another galaxy, another island universe—and half again as big as our own. "Why not?" I fell silent but, after a while, said, "Bokket seems to like you."

Ling smiled. "I like him."

"Go for it," I said.

"What?" She sounded surprised.

"Go for it, if you like him. I may have to be alone until Helena is revived at our final destination, but you don't have to be. Even if they do give us a new ship, it'll surely be a few weeks before they can transfer the cryochambers."

Ling rolled her eyes. "*Men*," she said, but I knew the idea appealed to her.

Bokket was right: the Sororian media seemed quite enamored with Ling and me, and not just because of our exotic appearance—my white skin and blue eyes; her dark skin and epicanthic folds; our two strange accents, both so different from the way people of the thirty-third century spoke. They also seemed to be fascinated by, well, by the pioneer spirit.

When the quarantine was over, we did go down to the planet. The temperature was perhaps a little cooler than I'd have liked, and the air a bit moister—but humans adapt, of course. The architecture in Soror's capital city of Pax was surprisingly ornate, with lots of domed roofs and intricate carvings. The term "capital city" was an anachronism, though; government was completely decentralized, with all major decisions done by plebiscite—including the decision about whether or not to give us another ship.

Bokket, Ling, and I were in the central square of Pax, along with Kari Deetal, Soror's president, waiting for the results of the vote to be announced. Media representatives from all over the Tau Ceti system were present, as well as one from Earth, whose stories were always read 11.9 years after he filed them. Also on hand were perhaps a thousand spectators.

"My friends," said Deetal, to the crowd, spreading her arms, "you have all voted, and now let us share in the results." She tipped her head slightly, and a moment later people in the crowd started clapping and cheering.

Ling and I turned to Bokket, who was beaming. "What is it?" said Ling. "What decision did they make?"

Bokket looked surprised. "Oh, sorry. I forgot you don't have web implants. You're going to get your ship."

Ling closed her eyes and breathed a sigh of relief. My heart was pounding.

President Deetal gestured toward us. "Dr. MacGregor, Dr. Woo—would you say a few words?"

We glanced at each other then stood up. "Thank you," I said looking out at everyone.

Ling nodded in agreement. "Thank you very much."

A reporter called out a question. "What are you going to call your new ship?"

Ling frowned; I pursed my lips. And then I said, "What else? The *Pioneer Spirit II*."

The crowd erupted again.

Finally, the fateful day came. Our official boarding of our new starship—the one that would be covered by all the media—wouldn't happen for another four hours, but Ling and I were nonetheless heading toward the airlock that joined the ship to the station's outer rim. She wanted to look things over once more, and I wanted to spend a little time just sitting next to Helena's cryochamber, communing with her.

And, as we walked, Bokket came running along the curving floor toward us.

"Ling," he said, catching his breath. "Toby."

I nodded a greeting. Ling looked slightly uncomfortable; she and Bokket had grown close during the last few weeks, but they'd also had their time alone last night to say their goodbyes. I don't think she'd expected to see him again before we left.

"I'm sorry to bother you two," he said. "I know you're both busy, but . . ." He seemed quite nervous.

"Yes?" I said.

He looked at me, then at Ling. "Do you have room for another passenger?"

Ling smiled. "We don't have passengers. We're colonists."

"Sorry," said Bokket, smiling back at her. "Do you have room for another colonist?"

"Well, there *are* four spare cryochambers, but . . ." She looked at me.

"Why not?" I said, shrugging.

"It's going to be hard work, you know," said Ling, turning back to Bokket. "Wherever we end up, it's going to be rough."

Bokket nodded. "I know. And I want to be part of it."

Ling knew she didn't have to be coy around me. "That would be wonderful," she said. "But—but why?"

Bokket reached out tentatively, and found Ling's hand. He squeezed it gently, and she squeezed back. "You're one reason," he said.

"Got a thing for older women, eh?" said Ling. I smiled at that.

Bokket laughed. "I guess."

"You said I was one reason," said Ling.

He nodded. "The other reason is—well, it's this: I don't want to stand on the shoulders of giants." He paused, then lifted his own shoulders a little, as if acknowledging that he was giving voice to the sort of thought rarely spoken aloud. "I want to *be* a giant."

They continued to hold hands as we walked down the space station's long corridor, heading toward the sleek and graceful ship that would take us to our new home.

A WALK IN THE SUN

Geoffrey A. Landis

❀

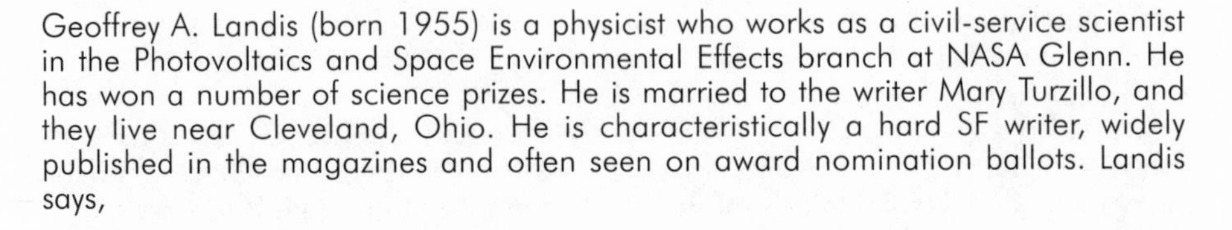

Geoffrey A. Landis (born 1955) is a physicist who works as a civil-service scientist in the Photovoltaics and Space Environmental Effects branch at NASA Glenn. He has won a number of science prizes. He is married to the writer Mary Turzillo, and they live near Cleveland, Ohio. He is characteristically a hard SF writer, widely published in the magazines and often seen on award nomination ballots. Landis says,

> Hard science fiction is science fiction that tries to be correct about science, or at least as correct as we can be with what we know. More than that, hard SF is science fiction that's fascinated by science and technology, science fiction in which a scientific fact or speculation is integral to the plot. If you take out the science, the story vanishes.

He has published over fifty short stories. His first published story, "Elemental" (1984) was nominated for a Hugo Award. He won a Nebula for "Ripples in the Dirac Sea" (1988). "A Walk in the Sun" (1991) won the Hugo for Best Short Story. Editor Gardner Dozois says of Landis's fiction, "While there's hard science content, there's also a rich emotionalism. Lots of science fiction is bright clever ideas. In Geoff's case, the bright clever idea is supported by the emotional life of the story. He writes about science and the scientific world from a humanistic slant."

His first novel, *Mars Crossing* (2000), which concerns a joint NASA-private venture to go to Mars and back, was nominated for a Nebula. He hopes that the novel will help people understand why planetary exploration is important and will get them excited about exploration of Mars. His short fiction is collected in *Impact Parameter and Other Quantum Realities* (2001).

Here, Landis takes on the tale of the dying astronaut—a favorite theme of the New Wave period, used by J. G. Ballard, Barry Malzberg and others. About the origins of this story, Landis says in a *Locus* interview:

> When I wrote that, I was working on the question, can you make a lunar base with a solar array? They're very light and cheap, compared to most other reactors, so if we could do that, it would be a great thing for a lunar base. The problem is, the moon has 14 days of darkness, and that's an awful long time to run on a battery. Even the Energizer Bunny gets tired! One concept we had is that maybe your moonbase is not stationary. The moon doesn't rotate very fast—about ten miles an hour—so I thought, "Well, you put wheels on your moonbase and you just keep it in the sun all the time." (You could also do that on Mercury, which also rotates very slowly.) I wrote that up in a little piece presented at the Conference on Space Man-

ufacturing, then as an article published in the journal of the British Interplanetary Society, then decided to turn it into a story.

Arthur C. Clarke's "Transit of Earth" is one of the theme's more optimistic treatments: If the protagonist is going to die anyway, he may as well have a look around first. Landis's treatment of the theme is more optimistic still, a good old-fashioned problem-solving story in which the protagonist's secret weapon is . . . her emotional inner resources. Although she goes for a look *all* the way around, the focus of this story is not on the glories of the lunar landscape, but on the balance between her interior and exterior worlds. This is a woman-against-the-universe story.

The pilots have a saying: a good landing is any landing you can walk away from.

Perhaps Sanjiv might have done better, if he'd been alive. Trish had done the best she could. All things considered, it was a far better landing than she had any right to expect.

Titanium struts, pencil-slender, had never been designed to take the force of a landing. Paper-thin pressure walls had buckled and shattered, spreading wreckage out into the vacuum and across a square kilometer of lunar surface. An instant before impact she remembered to blow the tanks. There was no explosion, but no landing could have been gentle enough to keep *Moonshadow* together. In eerie silence, the fragile ship had crumpled and ripped apart like a discarded aluminum can.

The piloting module had torn open and broken loose from the main part of the ship. The fragment settled against a crater wall. When it stopped moving, Trish unbuckled the straps that held her in the pilot's seat and fell slowly to the ceiling. She oriented herself to the unaccustomed gravity, found an undamaged EVA pack and plugged it into her suit, then crawled out into the sunlight through the jagged hole where the living module had been attached.

She stood on the gray lunar surface and stared. Her shadow reached out ahead of her, a pool of inky black in the shape of a fantastically stretched man. The landscape was rugged and utterly barren, painted in stark shades of grey and black. "Magnificent desolation," she whispered. Behind her, the sun hovered just over the mountains, glinting off shards of titanium and steel scattered across the cratered plain.

Patricia Jay Mulligan looked out across the desolate moonscape and tried not to weep.

First things first. She took the radio out from the shattered crew compartment and tried it. Nothing. That was no surprise; Earth was over the horizon, and there were no other ships in cislunar space.

After a little searching she found Sanjiv and Theresa. In the low gravity they were absurdly easy to carry. There was no use in burying them. She sat them in a niche between two boulders, facing the sun, facing west, toward where the Earth was hidden behind a range of black mountains. She tried to think of the right words to say, and failed. Perhaps as well; she wouldn't know the proper service for Sanjiv anyway. "Goodbye, Sanjiv. Goodbye, Theresa. I wish—I wish things would have been different. I'm sorry." Her voice was barely more than a whisper. "Go with God."

She tried not to think of how soon she was likely to be joining them.

She forced herself to think. What would her sister have done? Survive. Karen would survive. First: inventory your assets. She was alive, miraculously unhurt. Her vacuum suit was in serviceable condition. Life-support was powered by the suit's solar arrays; she had air and water for as long as the sun continued to shine. Scavenging the wreckage yielded plenty of unbroken food packs; she wasn't about to starve.

Second: call for help. In this case, the nearest help was a quarter of a million miles over the horizon. She would need a high-gain antenna and a mountain peak with a view of Earth.

In its computer, *Moonshadow* had carried the best maps of the moon ever made. Gone. There had been other maps on the ship; they were scattered with the wreckage. She'd managed to find a detailed map of Mare Nubium—useless—and a small global map meant to be used as an index. It would have to do. As near as she could tell, the impact site was just over the eastern edge of Mare Smythii—"Smith's Sea." The mountains in the distance should mark the edge of the sea, and, with luck, have a view of Earth.

She checked her suit. At a command, the solar arrays spread out to their full extent like oversized dragonfly wings and glinted in prismatic colors as they rotated to face the sun. She verified that the suit's systems were charging properly, and set off.

Close up, the mountain was less steep than it had looked from the crash site. In the low gravity, climbing was hardly more difficult than walking, although the two-meter dish made her balance awkward. Reaching the ridgetop, Trish was rewarded with the sight of a tiny sliver of blue on the horizon. The mountains on the far side of the valley were still in darkness. She hoisted the radio higher up on her shoulder and started across the next valley.

From the next mountain peak the Earth edged over the horizon, a blue and white marble half-hidden by black mountains. She unfolded the tripod for the antenna and carefully sighted along the feed. "Hello? This is Astronaut Mulligan from *Moonshadow*. Emergency. Repeat, this is an emergency. Does anybody hear me?"

She took her thumb off the TRANSMIT button and waited for a response, but heard nothing but the soft whisper of static from the sun.

"This is Astronaut Mulligan from *Moonshadow*. Does anybody hear me?" She paused again. "*Moonshadow*, calling anybody. *Moonshadow*, calling anybody. This is an emergency."

"*—shadow, this is Geneva control. We read you faint but clear. Hang on, up there.*" She released her breath in a sudden gasp. She hadn't even realized she'd been holding it.

After five minutes the rotation of the earth had taken the ground antenna out of range. In that time—after they had gotten over their surprise that there was a survivor of the Moonshadow—she learned the parameters of the problem. Her landing had been close to the sunset terminator; the very edge of the illuminated side of the moon. The moon's rotation is slow, but inexorable. Sunset would arrive in three days. There was no shelter on the moon, no place to wait out the fourteen day–long lunar night. Her solar cells needed sunlight to keep her air fresh. Her search of the wreckage had yielded no unruptured storage tanks, no batteries, no means to lay up a store of oxygen.

And there was no way they could launch a rescue mission before nightfall.

Too many "no"s.

She sat silent, gazing across the jagged plain toward the slender blue crescent, thinking.

After a few minutes the antenna at Goldstone rotated into range, and the radio crackled to life. "*Moonshadow, do you read me? Hello, Moonshadow, do you read me?*"

"*Moonshadow* here."

She released the transmit button and waited in long silence for her words to be carried to Earth.

"Roger, Moonshadow. We confirm the earliest window for a rescue mission is thirty days from now. Can you hold on that long?"

She made her decision and pressed the transmit button. "Astronaut Mulligan for *Moonshadow*. I'll be here waiting for you. One way or another."

She waited, but there was no answer. The receiving antenna at Goldstone couldn't have rotated out of range so quickly. She checked the radio. When she took the cover off, she could see that the printed circuit board on the power supply had been slightly cracked from the crash, but she couldn't see any broken leads or components clearly out of place. She banged on it with her fist—Karen's first rule of electronics, if it doesn't work, hit it—and reaimed the antenna, but it didn't help. Clearly something in it had broken.

What would Karen have done? Not just sit here and die, that was certain. Get a move on, kiddo. When sunset catches you, you'll die.

They had heard her reply. She had to believe they heard her reply and would be coming for her. All she had to do was survive.

The dish antenna would be too awkward to carry with her. She could afford nothing but the bare necessities. At sunset her air would be gone. She put down the radio and began to walk.

Mission Commander Stanley stared at the x-rays of his engine. It was four in the morning. There would be no more sleep for him that night; he was scheduled to fly to Washington at six to testify to Congress.

"Your decision, Commander," the engine technician said. "We can't find any flaws in the x-rays we took of the flight engines, but it could be hidden. The nominal flight profile doesn't take the engines to a hundred twenty, so the blades should hold even if there is a flaw."

"How long a delay if we yank the engines for inspection?"

"Assuming they're okay, we lose a day. If not, two, maybe three."

Commander Stanley drummed his fingers in irritation. He hated to be forced into hasty decisions. "Normal procedure would be?"

"Normally we'd want to reinspect."

"Do it."

He sighed. Another delay. Somewhere up there, somebody was counting on him to get there on time. If she was still alive. If the cut-off radio signal didn't signify catastrophic failure of other systems.

If she could find a way to survive without air.

On Earth it would have been a marathon pace. On the moon it was an easy lope. After ten miles the trek fell into an easy rhythm: half a walk, half like jogging, and half bounding like a slow-motion kangaroo. Her worst enemy was boredom.

Her comrades at the academy—in part envious of the top scores that had made her the first of their class picked for a mission—had ribbed her mercilessly about flying a mission that would come within a few kilometers of the moon without landing. Now she had a chance to see more of the moon up close than anybody in history. She wondered what her classmates were thinking now. She would have a tale to tell—if only she could survive to tell it.

The warble of the low voltage warning broke her out of her reverie. She checked her running display as she started down the maintenance checklist.

Elapsed EVA time, eight point three hours. System functions, nominal, except that the solar array current was way below norm. In a few moments she found the trouble: a thin layer of dust on her solar array. Not a serious problem; it could be brushed off. If she couldn't find a pace that would avoid kicking dust on the arrays, then she would have to break every few hours to housekeep. She rechecked the array and continued on.

With the sun unmoving ahead of her and nothing but the hypnotically blue crescent of the slowly rotating Earth creeping imperceptibly off the horizon, her attention wandered. *Moonshadow* had been tagged as an easy mission, a low-orbit mapping flight to scout sites for the future moonbase. *Moonshadow* had never been intended to land, not on the moon, not anywhere.

She'd landed it anyway; she had to.

Walking west across the barren plain, Trish had nightmares of blood and falling, Sanjiv dying beside her; Theresa already dead in the lab module; the moon looming huge, spinning at a crazy angle in the viewports. Stop the spin, aim for the terminator—at low sun angles, the illumination makes it easier to see the roughness of the surface. Conserve fuel, but remember to blow the tanks an instant before you hit to avoid explosion.

That was over. Concentrate on the present. One foot in front of the other. Again. Again.

The undervoltage alarm chimed again. Dust, already?

She looked down at her navigation aid and realized with a shock that she had walked a hundred and fifty kilometers.

Time for a break anyway. She sat down on a boulder, fetched a snackpack out of her carryall, and set a timer for fifteen minutes. The airtight quick-seal on the food pack was designed to mate to the matching port in the lower part of her faceplate. It would be important to keep the seal free of grit. She verified the vacuum seal twice before opening the pack into the suit, then pushed the food bar in so she could turn her head and gnaw off pieces. The bar was hard and slightly sweet.

She looked west across the gently rolling plain. The horizon looked flat, unreal; a painted backdrop barely out of reach. On the moon, it should be easy to keep up a pace of fifteen or even twenty miles an hour—counting time out for sleep, maybe ten. She could walk a long, long way.

Karen would have liked it; she'd always liked hiking in desolate areas. "Quite pretty, in its own way, isn't it, Sis?" Trish said. "Who'd have thought there were so many shadings of grey? Plenty of uncrowded beach—too bad it's such a long walk to the water."

Time to move on. She continued on across terrain that was generally flat, although everywhere pocked with craters of every size. The moon is surprisingly flat; only one percent of the surface has a slope of more than fifteen degrees. The small hills she bounded over easily; the few larger ones she detoured around. In the low gravity this posed no real problem to walking. She walked on. She didn't feel tired, but when she checked her readout and realized that she had been walking for twenty hours, she forced herself to stop.

Sleeping was a problem. The solar arrays were designed to be detached from the suit for easy servicing, but had no provision to power the life-support while detached. Eventually she found a way to stretch the short cable out far enough to allow her to prop up the array next to her so she could lie down without disconnecting the power. She would have to be careful not to roll over. That done, she found she couldn't sleep. After a time she lapsed into a fitful doze, dreaming not of the *Moonshadow* as she'd expected, but of her sister, Karen, who—in the dream—

wasn't dead at all, but had only been playing a joke on her, pretending to die.

She awoke disoriented, muscles aching, then suddenly remembered where she was. The Earth was a full handspan above the horizon. She got up, yawned, and jogged west across the gunpowder-gray sandscape.

Her feet were tender where the boots rubbed. She varied her pace, changing from jogging to skipping to a kangaroo bounce. It helped some; not enough. She could feel her feet starting to blister, but knew that there was no way to take off her boots to tend, or even examine, her feet.

Karen had made her hike on blistered feet, and had had no patience with complaints or slacking off. She should have broken her boots in before the hike. In the one-sixth gee, at least the pain was bearable.

After a while her feet simply got numb.

Small craters she bounded over; larger ones she detoured around; larger ones yet she simply climbed across. West of Mare Smythii she entered a badlands and the terrain got bumpy. She had to slow down. The downhill slopes were in full sun, but the crater bottoms and valleys were still in shadow.

Her blisters broke, the pain a shrill and discordant singing in her boots. She bit her lip to keep herself from crying and continued on. Another few hundred kilometers and she was in Mare Spumans—"Sea of Froth"—and it was clear trekking again. Across Spumans, then into the north lobe of Fecundity and through to Tranquility. Somewhere around the sixth day of her trek she must have passed Tranquility Base; she carefully scanned for it on the horizon as she traveled but didn't see anything. By her best guess she missed it by several hundred kilometers; she was already deviating toward the north, aiming for a pass just north of the crater Julius Caesar into Mare Vaporum to avoid the mountains. The ancient landing stage would have been too small to spot unless she'd almost walked right over it.

"Figures," she said. "Come all this way, and the only tourist attraction in a hundred miles is closed. That's the way things always seem to turn out, eh, Sis?"

There was nobody to laugh at her witticism, so after a moment she laughed at it herself.

Wake up from confused dreams to black sky and motionless sunlight, yawn, and start walking before you're completely awake. Sip on the insipid warm water, trying not to think about what it's recycled from. Break, cleaning your solar arrays, your life, with exquisite care. Walk. Break. Sleep again, the sun nailed to the sky in the same position it was in when you awoke. Next day do it all over. And again. And again.

The nutrition packs are low-residue, but every few days you must still squat for nature. Your life support can't recycle solid waste, so you wait for the suit to dessicate the waste and then void the crumbly brown powder to vacuum. Your trail is marked by your powdery deposits, scarcely distinguishable from the dark lunar dust.

Walk west, ever west, racing the sun.

Earth was high in the sky; she could no longer see it without craning her neck way back. When the Earth was directly overhead she stopped and celebrated, miming the opening of an invisible bottle of champagne to toast her imaginary traveling companions. The sun was well above the horizon now. In six days of travel she had walked a quarter of the way around the moon.

She passed well south of Copernicus, to stay as far out of the impact rubble as possible without crossing mountains. The terrain was eerie, boulders as big as houses, as big as shuttle tanks. In places the footing was treacherous where the grainy regolith gave way to jumbles of rock, rays thrown out by the cataclysmic impact billions of years ago. She picked her way as best she could. She left her radio on and gave a running commentary as she moved. "Watch your step here, footing's treacherous. Coming up on a hill; think we should climb it or detour around?"

Nobody voiced an opinion. She contemplated the rocky hill. Likely an ancient volcanic bubble, although she hadn't realized that this region had once been active. The territory around it would be bad. From the top she'd be able to study the terrain for a ways ahead. "Okay, listen up, everybody. The climb could be tricky here, so stay close and watch where I place my feet. Don't take chances—better slow and safe than fast and dead. Any questions?" Silence; good. "Okay, then. We'll take a fifteen minute break when we reach the top. Follow me."

Past the rubble of Copernicus, Oceanus Procellarum was smooth as a golf course. Trish jogged across the sand with a smooth, even glide. Karen and Dutchman seemed to always be lagging behind or running up ahead out of sight. Silly dog still followed Karen around like a puppy, even though Trish was the one who fed him and refilled his water dish every day since Karen went away to college. The way Karen wouldn't stay close behind her annoyed Trish—Karen had *promised* to let her be the leader this time—but she kept her feelings to herself. Karen had called her a bratty little pest, and she was determined to show she could act like an adult. Anyway, she was the one with the map. If Karen got lost, it would serve her right.

She angled slightly north again to take advantage of the map's promise of smooth terrain. She looked around to see if Karen was there, and was surprised to see that the Earth was a gibbous ball low down on the horizon. Of course, Karen wasn't there. Karen had died years ago. Trish was alone in a spacesuit that itched and stank and chafed her skin nearly raw across the thighs. She should have broken it in better, but who would have expected she would want to go jogging in it?

It was unfair how she had to wear a spacesuit and Karen didn't. Karen got to do a lot of things that she didn't, but how come she didn't have to wear a spacesuit? *Everybody* had to wear a spacesuit. It was the rule. She turned to Karen to ask. Karen laughed bitterly. "I don't have to wear a spacesuit, my bratty little sister, because I'm *dead*. Squished like a bug and buried, remember?"

Oh, yes, that was right. Okay, then, if Karen was dead, then she didn't have to wear a spacesuit. It made perfect sense for a few more kilometers, and they jogged along together in companionable silence until Trish had a sudden thought. "Hey, wait—if you're dead, then how can you be here?"

"Because I'm not here, silly. I'm a fig-newton of your overactive imagination."

With a shock, Trish looked over her shoulder. Karen wasn't there. Karen had never been there.

"I'm sorry. Please come back. Please?"

She stumbled and fell headlong, sliding in a spray of dust down the bowl of a crater. As she slid she frantically twisted to stay face-down, to keep from rolling over on the fragile solar wings on her back. When she finally slid to a stop, the silence echoing in her ears, there was a long scratch like a badly healed scar down the glass of her helmet. The double reinforced faceplate had held, fortunately, or she wouldn't be looking at it.

She checked her suit. There were no breaks in the integrity, but the titanium strut that held out the left wing of the solar array had buckled back and nearly broken. Miraculously there had been no other damage. She pulled off the array and studied the damaged strut. She bent it back into position as best she could, and splinted the joint with a mechanical pencil tied on with two short lengths of wire. The pencil had been only extra weight anyway; it was lucky she hadn't thought to discard it. She tested the joint gingerly. It wouldn't take much stress, but if she didn't bounce around too much it should hold. Time for a break anyway.

When she awoke she took stock of her situation. While she hadn't been paying attention, the terrain had slowly turned mountainous. The next stretch would be slower going than the last bit.

"About time you woke up, sleepyhead," said Karen. She yawned, stretched, and turned her head to look back at the line of footprints. At the end of the long trail, the Earth showed as a tiny blue dome on the horizon, not very far away at all, the single speck of color in a landscape of uniform gray. "Twelve days to walk halfway around the moon," she said. "Not bad, kid. Not great, but not bad. You training for a marathon or something?"

Trish got up and started jogging, her feet falling into rhythm automatically as she sipped from the suit recycler, trying to wash the stale taste out of her mouth. She called out to Karen behind her without turning around. "Get a move on, we got places to go. You coming, or what?"

In the nearly shadowless sunlight the ground was washed-out, two dimensional. Trish had a hard time finding footing, stumbling over rocks that were nearly invisible against the flat landscape. One foot in front of the other. Again. Again.

The excitement of the trek had long ago faded, leaving behind a relentless determination to prevail, which in turn had faded into a kind of mental numbness. Trish spent the time chatting with Karen, telling the private details of her life, secretly hoping that Karen would be pleased, would say something telling her she was proud of her. Suddenly she noticed that Karen wasn't listening; had apparently wandered off on her sometime when she hadn't been paying attention.

She stopped on the edge of a long, winding rille. It looked like a riverbed just waiting for a rainstorm to fill it, but Trish knew it had never known water. Covering the bottom was only dust, dry as powdered bone. She slowly picked her way to the bottom, careful not to slip again and risk damage to her fragile life-support system. She looked up at the top. Karen was standing on the rim waving at her. "Come *on!* Quit *dawdling*, you slowpoke—you want to stay here *forever?*"

"What's the hurry? We're ahead of schedule. The sun is high up in the sky, and we're halfway around the moon. We'll make it, no sweat."

Karen came down the slope, sliding like a skiier in the powdery dust. She pressed her face up against Trish's helmet and stared into her eyes with a manic intensity that almost frightened her. "The hurry, my lazy little sister, is that you're halfway around the moon, you've finished with the easy part and it's all mountains and badlands from here on, you've got six thousand kilometers to walk in a broken spacesuit, and if you slow down and let the sun get ahead of you, and then run into one more teensy little problem, just one, you'll be dead, dead, dead, just like me. You wouldn't like it, trust me. Now get your pretty little lazy butt into gear and *move*!"

And, indeed, it was slow going. She couldn't bound down slopes as she used to, or the broken strut would fail and she'd have to stop for painstaking repair. There were no more level plains; it all seemed to be either boulder fields, crater walls, or mountains. On the eighteenth day she came to a huge natural arch. It towered over her head, and she gazed up at it in awe, wondering how such a structure could have been formed on the moon.

"Not by wind, that's for sure," said Karen. "Lava, I'd figure. Melted through a ridge and flowed on, leaving the hole; then over the eons micrometeoroid bombardment ground off the rough edges. Pretty, though, isn't it?"

"Magnificent."

Not far past the arch she entered a forest of needle-thin crystals. At first they were small, breaking like glass under her feet, but then they soared above her, six-sided spires and minarets in fantastic colors. She picked her way in silence between them, bedazzled by the forest of light sparkling between the sapphire spires. The crystal jungle finally thinned out and was replaced by giant crystal boulders, glistening iridescent in the sun. Emeralds? Diamonds?

"I don't know, kid. But they're in our way. I'll be glad when they're behind us."

And after a while the glistening boulders thinned out as well, until there were only a scattered few glints of color on the slopes of the hills beside her, and then at last the rocks were just rocks, craggy and pitted.

Crater Daedalus, the middle of the lunar farside. There was no celebration this time. The sun had long ago stopped its lazy rise, and was imperceptibly dropping toward the horizon ahead of them.

"It's a race against the sun, kid, and the sun ain't making any stops to rest. You're losing ground."

"I'm tired. Can't you see I'm tired? I think I'm sick. I hurt all over. Get off my case. Let me rest. Just a few more minutes? Please?"

"You can rest when you're dead." Karen laughed in a strangled, high-pitched voice. Trish suddenly realized that she was on the edge of hysteria. Abruptly she stopped laughing. "Get a move on, kid. Move!"

The lunar surface passed under her, an irregular gray treadmill.

Hard work and good intentions couldn't disguise the fact that the sun was gaining. Every day when she woke up the sun was a little lower down ahead of her, shining a little more directly in her eyes.

Ahead of her, in the glare of the sun she could see an oasis, a tiny island of grass and trees in the lifeless desert. She could already hear the croaking of frogs: braap, braap, *BRAAP!*

No. That was no oasis; that was the sound of a malfunction alarm. She stopped, disoriented. Overheating. The suit air conditioning had broken down. It took her half a day to find the clogged coolant valve and another three hours soaked in sweat to find a way to unclog it without letting the precious liquid vent to space. The sun sank another handspan toward the horizon.

The sun was directly in her face now. Shadows of the rocks stretched toward her like hungry tentacles, even the smallest looking hungry and mean. Karen was walking beside her again, but now she was silent, sullen.

"Why won't you talk to me? Did I do something? Did I say something wrong? Tell me."

"I'm not here, little sister. I'm dead. I think it's about time you faced up to that."

"Don't say that. You can't be dead."

"You have an idealized picture of me in your mind. Let me go. *Let me go*!"

"I can't. Don't go. Hey—do you remember the time we saved up all our allowances for a year so we could buy a horse? And we found a stray kitten that was real sick, and we took the shoebox full of our allowance and the kitten to the vet, and he fixed the kitten but wouldn't take any money?"

"Yeah, I remember. But somehow we still never managed to save enough for a horse." Karen sighed. "Do you think it was easy growing up with a bratty little sister dogging my footsteps, trying to imitate everything I did?"

"I wasn't ever bratty."

"You were too."

"No, I wasn't. I adored you." Did she? "I *worshipped* you."

"I know you did. Let me tell you, kid, that didn't make it any easier. Do you think it was easy being worshipped? Having to be a paragon all the time? Christ, all through high school, when I wanted to get high, I had to sneak away and do it in private, or else I knew my damn kid sister would be doing it too."

"You didn't. You never."

"Grow up, kid. Damn right I did. You were always right behind me. Everything I did, I knew you'd be right there doing it next. I had to struggle like hell to keep ahead of you, and you, damn you, followed effortlessly. You were smarter than me—you know that, don't you?—and how do you think that made me feel?"

"Well, what about me? Do you think it was easy for *me*? Growing up with a dead sister—everything I did, it was 'Too bad you can't be more like Karen' and 'Karen wouldn't have done it that way' and 'If only Karen had . . . ' How do you think that made me feel, huh? You had it easy—I was the one who had to live up to the standards of a goddamn *angel*."

"Tough breaks, kid. Better than being dead."

"Damn it, Karen, I loved you. I love you. Why did you have to go away?"

"I know that, kid. I couldn't help it. I'm sorry. I love you too, but I have to go. Can you let me go? Can you just be yourself now, and stop trying to be me?"

"I'll . . . I'll try."

"Goodbye, little sister."

"Goodbye, Karen."

She was alone in the settling shadows on an empty, rugged plain. Ahead of her, the sun was barely kissing the ridgetops. The dust she kicked up was behaving strangely; rather than falling to the ground, it would hover half a meter off the ground. She puzzled over the effect, then saw that all around her, dust was silently rising off the ground. For a moment she thought it was another hallucination, but then realized it was some kind of electrostatic charging effect. She moved forward again through the rising fog of moondust. The sun reddened, and the sky turned a deep purple.

The darkness came at her like a demon. Behind her only the tips of mountains were illuminated, the bases disappearing into shadow. The ground ahead of her was covered with pools of ink that she had to pick her way around. Her radio locator was turned on, but receiving only static. It could only pick up the locator beacon from the *Moonshadow* if she got in line of sight of the crash site. She must be nearly there, but none of the landscape looked even slightly familiar. Ahead—was that the ridge she'd climbed to radio Earth? She couldn't tell. She climbed it, but didn't see the blue marble. The next one?

The darkness had spread up to her knees. She kept tripping over rocks invisible in the dark. Her footsteps struck sparks from the rocks, and behind her footprints glowed faintly. Triboluminescent glow, she thought—nobody has *ever* seen that before. She couldn't die now, not so close. But the darkness wouldn't wait. All around her the darkness lay like an unsuspected ocean, rocks sticking up out of the tidepools into the dying sunlight. The undervoltage alarm began to warble as the rising tide of darkness reached her solar array. The crash site had to be around here somewhere, it had to. Maybe the locator beacon was broken? She climbed up a ridge and into the light, looking around desperately for clues. Shouldn't there have been a rescue mission by now?

Only the mountaintops were in the light. She aimed for the nearest and tallest mountain she could see and made her way across the darkness to it, stumbling and crawling in the ocean of ink, at last pulling herself into the light like a swimmer gasping for air. She huddled on her rocky island, desperate as the tide of darkness slowly rose about her. Where were they? *Where were they?*

* * *

Back on Earth, work on the rescue mission had moved at a frantic pace. Everything was checked and triple-checked—in space, cutting corners was an invitation for sudden death—but still the rescue mission had been dogged by small problems and minor delays, delays that would have been routine for an ordinary mission, but loomed huge against the tight mission deadline.

The scheduling was almost impossibly tight—the mission had been set to launch in four months, not four weeks. Technicians scheduled for vacations volunteered to work overtime, while suppliers who normally took weeks to deliver parts delivered overnight. Final integration for the replacement for *Moonshadow*, originally to be called *Explorer* but now hastily re-christened *Rescuer*, was speeded up, and the transfer vehicle launched to the Space Station months ahead of the original schedule, less than two weeks after the *Moonshadow* crash. Two shuttle-loads of propellant swiftly followed, and the transfer vehicle was mated to its aeroshell and tested. While the rescue crew practiced possible scenarios on the simulator, the lander, with engines inspected and replaced, was hastily modified to accept a third person on ascent, tested, and then launched to rendezvous with *Rescuer*. Four weeks after the crash the stack was fueled and ready, the crew briefed, and the trajectory calculated. The crew shuttle launched through heavy fog to join their *Rescuer* in orbit.

Thirty days after the unexpected signal from the moon had revealed a survivor of the *Moonshadow* expedition, *Rescuer* left orbit for the moon.

From the top of the mountain ridge west of the crash site, Commander Stanley passed his searchlight over the wreckage one more time and shook his head in awe. "An amazing job of piloting," he said. "Looks like she used the TEI motor for braking, and then set it down on the RCS verniers."

"Incredible," Tanya Nakora murmured. "Too bad it couldn't save her."

The record of Patricia Mulligan's travels was written in the soil around the wreck. After the rescue team had searched the wreckage, they found the single line of footsteps that led due west, crossed the ridge, and disappeared over the horizon. Stanley put down the binoculars. There was no sign of returning footprints. "Looks like she wanted to see the moon before her air ran out," he said. Inside his helmet he shook his head slowly. "Wonder how far she got?"

"Could she be alive somehow?" asked Nakora. "She was a pretty ingenious kid."

"Not ingenious enough to breathe vacuum. Don't fool yourself—this rescue mission was a political toy from the start. We never had a chance of finding anybody up here still alive."

"Still, we had to try, didn't we?"

Stanley shook his head and tapped his helmet. "Hold on a sec, my damn radio's acting up. I'm picking up some kind of feedback—almost sounds like a voice."

"I hear it too, Commander. But it doesn't make any sense."

The voice was faint in the radio. "Don't turn off the lights. Please, please, don't turn off your light. . . ."

Stanley turned, to Nakora. "Do you . . . ?"

"I hear it, Commander . . . but I don't believe it."

Stanley picked up the searchlight and began sweeping the horizon. "Hello? *Rescuer* calling Astronaut Patricia Mulligan. Where the hell are you?"

The spacesuit had once been pristine white. It was now dirty gray with moondust, only the ragged and bent solar array on the back carefully polished free of debris. The figure in it was nearly as ragged.

After a meal and a wash, she was coherent and ready to explain.

"It was the mountaintop. I climbed the mountaintop to stay in the sunlight, and I just barely got high enough to hear your radios."

Nakora nodded. "That much we figured out. But the rest—the last month—you really walked all the way around the moon? Eleven thousand kilometers?"

Trish nodded. "It was all I could think of. I figured, about the distance from New York to LA and back—people have walked that and lived. It came to a walking speed of just under ten miles an hour. Farside was the hard part—turned out to be much rougher than nearside. But strange and weirdly beautiful, in places. You wouldn't believe the things I saw."

She shook her head, and laughed quietly. "I don't believe some of the things I saw. The immensity of it—we've barely scratched the surface. I'll be coming back, Commander. I promise you."

"I'm sure you will," said Commander Stanley. "I'm sure you will."

As the ship lifted off the moon, Trish looked out for a last view of the surface. For a moment she thought she saw a lonely figure standing on the surface, waving her goodbye. She didn't wave back.

She looked again, and there was nothing out there but magnificent desolation.

FOR WHITE HILL

Joe Haldeman

Joe Haldeman (born 1943) was in Canada when his draft notice arrived in his mailbox in 1967. When he arrived home to find the envelope from the Selective Service, despite thoughts of getting back in the car and heading back across the border, he opened the envelope and ultimately went to Vietnam. Though he was a pacifist and had tried to apply for conscientious objector status, he went because he wanted to become an astronaut. His first novel was a distinguished young adult book, *War Year* (1972), and his novel *1968* (1995) is an ambitious attempt to represent and confront a year spent as a soldier in Vietnam. His experiences as a soldier have informed much of his most important work.

When he was drafted, he had already written the first two science fiction stories he would sell. And before going into the army, Haldeman had earned an undergraduate degree in physics and astronomy. After his return he earned an MFA in writing. He lives in Gainesville, Florida, and Cambridge, Massachusetts, with his wife, Gay.

Although there were always political divides in SF, it has been said that the famous magazine ads taken out by groups of SF writers listing their names in *Galaxy* magazine in 1968, one to express opposition to, and the other to express support for, the Vietnam War, would serve as well as anything to mark the beginning of an overt divide of hard SF from the rest of the field. From that perspective, Haldeman's work, in particular *The Forever War*, is an interesting precursor to the political changes in hard SF over the past decade of so. It may be read in different ways from the left (anti-military and anti-imperialist) and the right (patriotic military adventure about the suffering of the ordinary soldier).

Haldeman is now one of the great living science fiction writers, known worldwide particularly for his hard SF adventure stories. His SF novels include *The Forever War* (1974), which won both the Hugo and Nebula Awards for Best Novel, *Mindbridge* (1976), *Buying Time* (1989), and *The Hemingway Hoax* (1990). His most recent novel is *The Coming* (2001), a first contact novel set in Gainesville, Florida, in 2054. In 1999, he published a sequel to *The Forever War*, and to *The Forever Peace* (1997), which won the Hugo, Nebula, and John W. Campbell Memorial Awards, entitled *Forever Free*. His short fiction ranges from humor to horror, but most often has a darkness deep within it. Such is "For White Hill": a romance, set against the staggering background of the approaching doom of Earth, about the role of art in the face of apocalypse. This was one of five fine novellas (by Haldeman, Greg Bear, Donald M. Kingsbury, Charles Sheffield, and Poul Anderson) in *Far Futures*.

"For White Hill" is an unusual example of hard SF as an experimental literary exercise. Judith Clute and Diedre Weil published an essay on the story (excerpted here from *The New York Review of Science Fiction*) explaining that

Haldeman's novella . . . is his most deliberate use yet of the arts as a structuring device for his fiction. Set in a far future Earth devastated by an apparently hopeless war with superior aliens, "For White Hill" is a very sensual and romantic love story, and is also one of Haldeman's most thorough explorations of the artist's mind to date. Furthermore, it is a rarity among science fiction stories in that it achieves its effects by using, in almost equal measure, the resources of the literary and visual arts. "For White Hill" describes, in fourteen segments of varying lengths, a meeting in the distant future between two artists, brought to a burnt-out and nearly abandoned Earth as part of a context in which artists from many planets are asked to create memorial works inspired by the ruins. Two important clues point toward the key to this story's main literary source. One is the dedicatory title, "For White Hill," which subtly echoes Shakespeare's famous dedication of his sonnets to "Mr. W. H." . . . The other is the story's fourteen-part structure. In the published versions of the text, these numbered sections (marked only by mathematical symbols in the manuscript) suggest that the story itself follows the movement of a sonnet. And in fact the story is an expansion of not only the theme but of the precise images of Shakespeare's eighteenth sonnet, "Shall I Compare Thee to a Summer's Day?" With few exceptions, each segment of the story takes the corresponding line from the sonnet and transforms it into a literal part of the narrative. Haldeman's story (almost) ends with the words, "After the sun is a cinder, and the ship is a frozen block enclosing a thousand bits of frozen flesh, she will live on in this small way" (279). Shakespeare's sonnet ends with the line "So long lives this, and this gives life to thee."

•

I am writing this memoir in the language of England, an ancient land of Earth, whose tales and songs White Hill valued. She was fascinated by human culture in the days before machines—not just thinking machines, but working ones; when things got done by the straining muscles of humans and animals.

Neither of us was born on Earth. Not many people were, in those days. It was a desert planet then, ravaged in the twelfth year of what they would call the Last War. When we met, that war had been going for over four hundred years, and had moved out of Sol Space altogether, or so we thought.

Some cultures had other names for the conflict. My parent, who fought the century before I did, always called it the Extermination, and their name for the enemy was "roach," or at least that's as close as English allows. We called the enemy an approximation of their own word for themselves, Fwndyri, which was uglier to us. I still have no love for them, but have no reason to make the effort. It would be easier to love a roach. At least we have a common ancestor. And we accompanied one another into space.

One mixed blessing we got from the war was a loose form of interstellar government, the Council of Worlds. There had been individual treaties before, but an overall organization had always seemed unlikely, since no two inhabited systems are less than three light-years apart, and several of them are over fifty. You can't defeat Einstein; that makes more than a century between "How are you?" and "Fine."

The Council of Worlds was headquartered on Earth, an unlikely and unlovely place, if centrally located. There were fewer than ten thousand people living on the blighted planet then, an odd mix of politicians, religious extremists, and academics, mostly. Almost all of them under glass. Tourists flowed through the domed-over ruins, but not many stayed long. The planet was still very dangerous over all of its unprotected surface, since the Fwndyri had thoroughly seeded it with nanophages. Those were submicroscopic constructs that sought out concentrations of human DNA. Once under the skin, they would reproduce at a geometric rate, deconstructing the body, cell by cell, building new nanophages. A person might complain of a headache and lie down, and a few hours later there would be nothing but a dry skeleton, lying in dust. When the humans were all dead, they mutated and went after DNA in general, and sterilized the world.

White Hill and I were "bred" for immunity to the nanophages. Our DNA winds backwards, as was the case with many people born or created after that stage of the war. So we could actually go through the elaborate airlocks and step out onto the blasted surface unprotected.

I didn't like her at first. We were competitors, and aliens to one another.

When I worked through the final airlock cycle, for my first moment on the actual surface of Earth, she was waiting outside, sitting in meditation on a large flat rock that shimmered in the heat. One had to admit she was beautiful in a startling way, clad only in a glistening pattern of blue and green body paint. Everything else around was gray and black, including the hard-packed talcum that had once been a mighty jungle, Brazil. The dome behind me was a mirror of gray and black and cobalt sky.

"Welcome home," she said. "You're Water Man."

She inflected it properly, which surprised me. "You're from Petros?"

"Of course not." She spread her arms and looked down at her body. Our women always cover at least one of their breasts, let alone their genitals. "Galan, an island on Seldene. I've studied your cultures, a little language."

"You don't dress like that on Seldene, either." Not anywhere I'd been on the planet.

"Only at the beach. It's so warm here."

I had to agree. Before I came out, they'd told me it was the hottest autumn on record. I took off my robe and folded it and left it by the door, with the sealed food box they had given me. I joined her on the rock, which was tilted away from the sun and reasonably cool.

She had a slight fragrance of lavender, perhaps from the body paint. We touched hands. "My name is White Hill. Zephyr-Meadow-Torrent."

"Where are the others?" I asked. Twenty-nine artists had been invited; one from each inhabited world. The people who had met me inside said I was the nineteenth to show up.

"Most of them traveling. Going from dome to dome for inspiration."

"You've already been around?"

"No." She reached down with her toe and scraped a curved line on the hard-baked ground. "All the story's here, anywhere. It isn't really about history or culture."

Her open posture would have been shockingly sexual at home, but this was not home. "Did you visit my world when you were studying it?"

"No, no money, at the time. I did get there a few years ago." She smiled at me. "It was almost as beautiful as I'd imagined it." She said three words in Petrosian. You couldn't say it precisely in English, which doesn't have a palindromic mood: *Dreams feed art and art feeds dreams.*

"When you came to Seldene I was young, too young to study with you. I've learned a lot from your sculpture, though."

"How young can you be?" To earn this honor, I did not say.

"In Earth years, about seventy awake. More than a hundred and forty-five in time-squeeze."

I struggled with the arithmetic. Petros and Seldene were twenty-two light-years apart; that's about forty-five years' squeeze. Earth is, what, a little less than forty light-years from her planet. That leaves enough gone time for someplace about twenty-five light-years from Petros, and back.

She tapped me on the knee, and I flinched. "Don't overheat your brain. I made a triangle; went to ThetaKent after your world."

"Really? When I was there?"

"No, I missed you by less than a year. I was disappointed. You were why I went." She made a palindrome in my language: *Predator becomes prey becomes predator?* "So here we are. Perhaps I can still learn from you."

I didn't much care for her tone of voice, but I said the obvious: "I'm more likely to learn from you."

"Oh, I don't think so." She smiled in a measured way. "You don't have much to learn."

Or much I could, or would, learn. "Have you been down to the water?"

"Once." She slid off the rock and dusted herself, spanking. "It's interesting. Doesn't look real." I picked up the food box and followed her down a sort of path that led us into low ruins. She drank some of my water, apologetic; hers was hot enough to brew tea.

"First body?" I asked.

"I'm not tired of it yet." She gave me a sideways look, amused. "You must be on your fourth or fifth."

"I go through a dozen a year." She laughed. "Actually, it's still my second. I hung on to the first too long."

"I read about that, the accident. That must have been horrible."

"Comes with the medium. I should take up the flute." I had been making a "controlled" fracture in a large boulder and set off the charges prematurely, by dropping the detonator. Part of the huge rock rolled over onto me, crushing my body from the hips down. It was a remote area, and by the time help arrived I had been dead for several minutes, from pain as much as anything else. "It affected all of my work, of course. I can't even look at some of the things I did the first few years I had this body."

"They are hard to look at," she said. "Not to say they aren't well done, and beautiful, in their way."

"As what is not? In its way." We came to the first building ruins and stopped. "Not all of this is weathering. Even in four hundred years." If you studied the rubble you could reconstruct part of the design. Primitive but sturdy, concrete reinforced with composite rods. "Somebody came in here with heavy equipment or explosives. They never actually fought on Earth, I thought."

"They say not." She picked up an irregular brick with a rod through it. "Rage, I suppose. Once people knew that no one was going to live."

"It's hard to imagine." The records are chaotic. Evidently the first people died two or three days after the nanophages were introduced, and no one on Earth was alive a week later. "Not hard to understand, though. The need to break something." I remembered the inchoate anger I felt as I squirmed there helpless, dying from *sculpture*, of all things. Anger at the rock, the fates. Not at my own inattention and clumsiness.

"They had a poem about that," she said. " 'Rage, rage against the dying of the light.' "

"Somebody actually wrote something during the nanoplague?"

"Oh, no. A thousand years before. Twelve hundred." She squatted suddenly and brushed at a fragment that had two letters on it. "I wonder if this was some sort of official building. Or a shrine or church." She pointed along the curved row of shattered bricks that spilled into the street. "That looks like it was some kind of decoration, a gable over the entrance." She tiptoed through the rubble toward the far end of the arc, studying what was written on the face-up pieces. The posture, standing on the balls of her feet, made her slim body even more attractive, as she must have known. My own body began to respond in a way inappropriate for a man more than three times her age. Foolish, even though that particular part is not so old. I willed it down before she could see.

"It's a language I don't know," she said. "Not Portuguese; looks like Latin. A Christian church, probably, Catholic."

"They used water in their religion," I remembered. "Is that why it's close to the sea?"

"They were everywhere; sea, mountains, orbit. They got to Petros?"

"We still have some. I've never met one, but they have a church in New Haven."

"As who doesn't?" She pointed up a road. "Come on. The beach is just over the rise here."

I could smell it before I saw it. It wasn't an ocean smell; it was dry, slightly choking.

We turned a corner and I stood staring. "It's a deep blue farther out," she said, "and so clear you can see hundreds of metras down." Here the water was thick and brown, the surf foaming heavily like a giant's chocolate drink, mud piled in baked windrows along the beach. "This used to be soil?"

She nodded. "There's a huge river that cuts this continent in half, the Amazon. When the plants died, there was nothing to hold the soil in place." She tugged me forward. "Do you swim? Come on."

"Swim in *that?* It's filthy."

"No, it's perfectly sterile. Besides, I have to pee." Well, I couldn't argue with that. I left the box on a high fragment of fallen wall and followed her. When we got to the beach, she broke into a run. I walked slowly and watched her gracile body, instead, and waded into the slippery heavy surf. When it was deep enough to swim, I plowed my way out to where she was bobbing. The water was too hot to be pleasant, and breathing was somewhat difficult. Carbon dioxide, I supposed, with a tang of halogen.

We floated together for a while, comparing this soup to bodies of water on our planets and ThetaKent. It was tiring, more from the water's heat and bad air than exertion, so we swam back in.

••

We dried in the blistering sun for a few minutes and then took the food box and moved to the shade of a beachside ruin. Two walls had fallen in together, to make a sort of concrete tent.

We could have been a couple of precivilization aboriginals, painted with dirt, our hair baked into stringy mats. She looked odd but still had a kind of formal beauty, the dusty mud residue turning her into a primitive sculpture, impossibly accurate and mobile. Dark rivulets of sweat drew painterly accent lines along her face and body. If only she were a model, rather than an artist. Hold that pose while I go back for my brushes.

We shared the small bottles of cold wine and water and ate bread and cheese and fruit. I put a piece on the ground for the nanophages. We watched it in silence for some minutes, while nothing happened. "It probably takes hours or days," she finally said.

"I suppose we should hope so," I said. "Let us digest the food before the creatures get to it."

"Oh, that's not a problem. They just attack the bonds between amino acids that make up proteins. For you and me, they're nothing more than an aid to digestion."

How reassuring. "But a source of some discomfort when we go back in, I was told."

She grimaced. "The purging. I did it once, and decided my next outing would be a long one. The treatment's the same for a day or a year."

"So how long has it been this time?"

"Just a day and a half. I came out to be your welcoming committee."

"I'm flattered."

She laughed. "It was their idea, actually. They wanted someone out here to 'temper' the experience for you. They weren't sure how well traveled you were, how easily affected by . . . strangeness." She shrugged. "Earthlings. I told them I knew of four planets you'd been to."

"They weren't impressed?"

"They said well, you know, he's famous and wealthy. His experiences on these planets might have been very comfortable." We could both laugh at that. "I told them how comfortable ThetaKent is."

"Well, it doesn't have nanophages."

"Or anything else. That was a long year for me. You didn't even stay a year."

"No. I suppose we would have met, if I had."

"Your agent said you were going to be there two years."

I poured us both some wine. "She should have told me you were coming. Maybe I could have endured it until the next ship out."

"How gallant." She looked into the wine without drinking. "You famous and wealthy people don't have to endure ThetaKent. I had to agree to one year's indentureship to help pay for my triangle ticket."

"You were an actual slave?"

"More like a wife, actually. The head of a township, a widower, financed me in exchange for giving his children some culture. Language, art, music. Every now and then he asked me to his chambers. For his own kind of culture."

"My word. You had to . . . *lie* with him? That was in the contract?"

"Oh, I didn't have to, but it kept him friendly." She held up a thumb and forefinger. "It was hardly noticeable."

I covered my smile with a hand, and probably blushed under the mud.

"I'm not embarrassing you?" she said. "From your work, I'd think that was impossible."

I had to laugh. "That work is in reaction to my culture's values. I can't take a pill and stop being a Petrosian."

White Hill smiled, tolerantly. "A Petrosian woman wouldn't put up with an arrangement like that?"

"Our women are still women. Some actually would like it, secretly. Most would claim they'd rather die, or kill the man."

"But they wouldn't actually *do* it. Trade their body for a ticket?" She sat down in a single smooth dancer's motion, her legs open, facing me. The clay between her legs parted, sudden pink.

"I wouldn't put it so bluntly." I swallowed, watching her watching me. "But no, they wouldn't. Not if they were planning to return."

"Of course, no one from a civilized planet would want to stay on ThetaKent. Shocking place."

I had to move the conversation onto safer grounds. "Your arms don't spend all day shoving big rocks around. What do you normally work in?"

"Various mediums." She switched to my language. "Sometimes I shove little rocks around." That was a pun for testicles. "I like painting, but my reputation is mainly from light and sound sculpture. I wanted to do something with the water here, internal illumination of the surf, but they say that's not possible. They can't isolate part of the ocean. I can have a pool, but no waves, no tides."

"Understandable." Earth's scientists had found a way to rid the surface of the nanoplague. Before they reterraformed the Earth, though, they wanted to isolate an area, a "park of memory," as a reminder of the Sterilization and these centuries of waste, and brought artists from every world to interpret, inside the park, what they had seen here.

Every world except Earth. Art on Earth had been about little else for a long time.

Setting up the contest had taken decades. A contest representative went to each of the settled worlds, according to a strict timetable. Announcement of the competition was delayed on the nearer worlds so that each artist would arrive on Earth at approximately the same time.

The Earth representatives chose which artists would be asked, and no one refused. Even the ones who didn't win the contest were guaranteed an honorarium equal to twice what they would have earned during that time at home, in their best year of record.

The value of the prize itself was so large as to be meaningless to a normal person. I'm a wealthy man on a planet where wealth is not rare, and just the interest that the prize would earn would support me and a half-dozen more. If someone from ThetaKent or Laxor won the prize, they would probably have more real usable wealth than their governments. If they were smart, they wouldn't return home.

The artists had to agree on an area for the park, which was limited to a hundred square kaymetras. If they couldn't agree, which seemed almost inevitable to me, the contest committee would listen to arguments and rule.

Most of the chosen artists were people like me, accustomed to working on a monumental scale. The one from Luxor was a composer, though and there were two conventional muralists, paint and mosaic. White Hill's work was by its nature evanescent. She could always set something up that would be repeated, like a fountain cycle. She might have more imagination than that, though.

"Maybe it's just as well we didn't meet in a master-student relationship," I said. "I don't know the first thing about the techniques of your medium."

"It's not technique." She looked thoughtful, remembering. "That's not why I wanted to study with you, back then. I was willing to push rocks around, or anything, if it could give me an avenue, an insight into how you did what you did." She folded her arms over her chest, and dust fell. "Ever since my parents took me to see Gaudí Mountain, when I was ten."

That was an early work, but I was still satisfied with it. The city council of Tresling, a prosperous coastal city, hired me to "do something with" an unusable steep island that stuck up in the middle of their harbor. I melted it judiciously, in homage to an Earthling artist.

"Now, though, if you'd forgive me . . . well, I find it hard to look at. It's alien, obtrusive."

"You don't have to apologize for having an opinion." Of course it looked alien; it was meant to evoke *Spain!* "What would you do with it?"

She stood up, and walked to where a window used to be, and leaned on the stone sill, looking at the ruins that hid the sea. "I don't know. I'm even less familiar with your tools." She scraped at the edge of the sill with a piece of rubble. "It's funny: earth, air, fire, and water. You're earth and fire, and I'm the other two."

I have used water, of course. The Gaudí is framed by water. But it was an interesting observation. "What do you do, I mean for a living? Is it related to your water and air?"

"No. Except insofar as everything is related." There are no artists on Seldene, in the sense of doing it for a living. Everybody indulges in some sort of art or music, as part of "wholeness," but a person who only did art would be considered a parasite. I was not comfortable there.

She faced me, leaning. "I work at the Northport Mental Health Center. Cognitive science, a combination of research and . . . is there a word here? *Jaturnary*. 'Empathetic therapy,' I guess."

I nodded. "We say *jådr-ny*. You plug yourself into mental patients?"

"I share their emotional states. Sometimes I do some good, talking to them afterwards. Not often."

"It's not done on Petros," I said, unnecessarily.

"Not legally, you mean."

I nodded. "If it worked, people say, it might be legal."

"'People say.' What do you say?" I started to make a noncommittal gesture. "Tell me the truth?"

"All I know is what I learned in school. It was tried, but failed spectacularly. It hurt both the therapists and the patients."

"That was more than a century ago. The science is much more highly developed now."

I decided not to push her on it. The fact is that drug therapy is spectacularly successful, and it *is* a science, unlike *jådr-ny*. Seldene is backward in some surprising ways.

I joined her at the window. "Have you looked around for a site yet?"

She shrugged. "I think my presentation will work anywhere. At least that's guided my thinking. I'll have water, air, and light, wherever the other artists and the committee decide to put us." She scraped at the ground with a toenail. "And this stuff. They call it 'loss.' What's left of what was living."

"I suppose it's not everywhere, though. They might put us in a place that used to be a desert."

"They might. But there will be water and air; they were willing to guarantee that."

"I don't suppose they have to guarantee rock," I said.

"I don't know. What would you do if they did put us in a desert, nothing but sand?"

"Bring little rocks." I used my own language; the pun also meant courage.

She started to say something, but we were suddenly in deeper shadow. We both stepped through the tumbled wall, out into the open. A black line of cloud had moved up rapidly from inland.

She shook her head. "Let's get to the shelter. Better hurry."

We trotted back along the path toward the Amazonia dome city. There was a low concrete structure behind the rock where I first met her. The warm breeze became a howling gale of sour steam before we got there, driving bullets of hot rain. A metal door opened automatically on our approach, and slid shut behind us. "I got caught in one yesterday," she said, panting. "It's no fun, even under cover. Stinks."

We were in an unadorned anteroom that had protective clothing on wall pegs. I followed her into a large room furnished with simple chairs and tables, and up a winding stair to an observation bubble.

"Wish we could see the ocean from here," she said. It was dramatic enough. Wavering sheets of water marched across the blasted landscape, strobed every few seconds by lightning flashes. The tunic I'd left outside swooped in flapping circles off to the sea.

It was gone in a couple of seconds. "You don't get another one, you know. You'll have to meet everyone naked as a baby."

"A dirty one at that. How undignified."

"Come on." She caught my wrist and tugged. "Water is my specialty, after all."

•••

The large hot bath was doubly comfortable for having a view of the tempest outside. I'm not at ease with communal bathing—I was married for fifty years and never bathed with my wife—but it seemed natural enough after wandering around together naked on an alien planet, swimming in its mud-puddle sea. I hoped I could trust her not to urinate in the tub. (If I mentioned it she would probably turn scientific and tell me that a healthy person's urine is sterile. I know that. But there is a time and a receptacle for everything.)

On Seldene, I knew, an unattached man and woman in this situation would probably have had sex even if they were only casual acquaintances, let alone fellow artists. She was considerate enough not to make any overtures, or perhaps (I thought at the time) not greatly stimulated by the sight of muscular men. In the shower before bathing, she offered to scrub my back, but left it at that. I helped her strip off the body paint from her back. It was a nice back to study, pronounced lumbar dimples, small waist. Under more restrained circumstances, it might have been *I* who made an overture. But one does not ask a woman when refusal would be awkward.

Talking while we bathed, I learned that some of her people, when they become wealthy enough to retire, choose to work on their art full time, but they're considered eccentric, even outcasts, egotists. White Hill expected one of them to be chosen for the contest, and wasn't even going to apply. But the Earthling judge saw one of her installations and tracked her down.

She also talked about her practical work in dealing with personality disorders and cognitive defects. There was some distress in her voice when she described that to me. Plugging into hurt minds, sharing their pain or blankness for hours. I didn't feel I knew her well enough to bring up the aspect that most interested me, a kind of ontological prurience: what is it like to actually *be* another person; how much of her, or him, do you take away? If you do it often enough, how can you know which parts of you are the original you?

And she would be plugged into more than one person at once, at times, the theory being that people with similar disorders could help each other, swarming around in the therapy room of her brain. She would fade into the background, more or less unable to interfere, and later analyze how they had interacted.

She had had one particularly unsettling experience, where through a planetwide network she had interconnected more than a hundred congenitally retarded people. She said it was like a painless death. By the time half of them had plugged in, she had felt herself fade and wink out. Then she was reborn with the suddenness of a slap. She had been dead for about ten hours.

But only connected for seven. It had taken technicians three hours to pry her out of a persistent catatonia. With more people, or a longer period, she might have been lost forever. There was no lasting harm, but the experiment was never repeated.

It was worth it, she said, for the patients' inchoate happiness afterward. It was like a regular person being given supernatural powers for half a day—powers so far beyond human experience that there was no way to talk about them, but the memory of it was worth the frustration.

After we got out of the tub, she showed me to our wardrobe room: hundreds of white robes, identical except for size. We dressed and made tea and sat upstairs watching the storm rage. It hardly looked like an inhabitable planet outside. The lightning had intensified so that it crackled incessantly, a jagged insane dance in every direction. The rain had frozen to white gravel somehow. I asked the building, and it said that the stuff was called *granizo* or, in English, hail. For a while it fell too fast to melt, accumulating in white piles that turned translucent.

Staring at the desolation, White Hill said something that I thought was uncharacteristically modest. "This is too big and terrible a thing. I feel like an interloper. They've lived through centuries of this, and now they want *us* to explain it to them?"

I didn't have to remind her of what the contest committee had said, that their own arts had become stylized, stunned into a grieving conformity. "Maybe not to *explain*—maybe they're assuming we'll fail, but hope to find a new direction from our failures. That's what that oldest woman, Norita, implied."

White Hill shook her head. "Wasn't she a ray of sunshine? I think they dragged her out of the grave as a way of keeping us all outside the dome."

"Well, she was quite effective on me. I could have spent a few days investigating Amazonia, but not with her as a native guide." Norita was about as close as anyone could get to being an actual native. She was the last survivor of the Five Families, the couple of dozen Earthlings who, among those who were offworld at the time of the nanoplague, were willing to come back after robots constructed the isolation domes.

In terms of social hierarchy, she was the most powerful person on Earth, at least on the actual planet. The class system was complex and nearly opaque to outsiders, but being a descendant of the Five Families was a prerequisite for the highest class. Money or political power would not get you in, although most of the other social classes seemed associated with wealth or the lack of it. Not that there were any actual poor people on Earth; the basic birth dole was equivalent to an upper-middle-class income on Petros.

The nearly instantaneous destruction of ten billion people did not destroy their fortunes. Most of the Earth's significant wealth had been off-planet, anyhow, at the time of the Sterilization. Suddenly it was concentrated into the hands of fewer than two thousand people.

Actually, I couldn't understand why anyone would have come back.

You'd have to be pretty sentimental about your roots to be willing to spend the rest of your life cooped up under a dome, surrounded by instant death. The salaries and amenities offered were substantial, with bonuses for Earthborn workers, but it still doesn't sound like much of a bargain. The ships that brought the Five Families and the other original workers to Earth left loaded down with sterilized artifacts, not to return for exactly one hundred years.

Norita seemed like a familiar type to me, since I come from a culture also rigidly bound by class. "Old money, but not much of it" sums up the situation. She wanted to be admired for the accident of her birth and the dubious blessing of a torpid longevity, rather than any actual accomplishment. I didn't have to travel thirty-three light-years to enjoy that kind of company.

"Did she keep you away from everybody?" White Hill said.

"Interposed herself. No one could act naturally when she was around, and the old dragon was never not around. You'd think a person her age would need a little sleep."

" 'She lives on the blood of infants,' we say."

There was a phone chime and White Hill said "Bono" as I said "Chå." Long habits. Then we said Earth's "Holá" simultaneously.

The old dragon herself appeared. "I'm glad you found shelter." Had she been eavesdropping? No way to tell from her tone or posture. "An administrator has asked permission to visit with you."

What if we said no? White Hill nodded, which means yes on Earth. "Granted," I said.

"Very well. He will be there shortly." She disappeared. I suppose the oldest person on a planet can justify not saying hello or goodbye. Only so much time left, after all.

"A physical visit?" I said to White Hill. "Through this weather?"

She shrugged. "Earthlings."

After a minute there was a *ding* sound in the anteroom and we walked down to see an unexpected door open. What I'd thought was a hall closet was an airlock. He'd evidently come underground.

Young and nervous and moving awkwardly in plastic. He shook our hands in an odd way. Of course we were swimming in deadly poison. "My name is Warm Dawn. Zephyr-Boulder-Brook."

"Are we cousins through Zephyr?" White Hill asked.

He nodded quickly. "An honor, my lady. Both of my parents are Seldenian, my gene-mother from your Galan."

A look passed over her that was pure disbelieving chauvinism: *Why would anybody leave Seldene's forests, farms, and meadows for this sterile death trap?* Of course, she knew the answer. The major import and export, the only crop, on Earth, was money.

"I wanted to help both of you with your planning. Are you going to travel at all, before you start?"

White Hill made a noncommittal gesture. "There are some places for me to see," I said. "The Pyramids, Chicago, Rome. Maybe a dozen places, twice that many days." I looked at her. "Would you care to join me?"

She looked straight at me, wheels turning. "It sounds interesting."

The man took us to a viewscreen in the great room and we spent an hour or so going over routes and making reservations. Travel was normally by underground vehicle, from dome to dome, and if we ventured outside unprotected, we would of course have to go through the purging before we were allowed to continue. Some people need a day or more to recover from that, so we should put that into the schedule, if we didn't want to be hobbled, like him, with plastic.

Most of the places I wanted to see were safely under glass, even some of the Pyramids, which surprised me. Some, like Ankgor Wat, were not only unprotected but difficult of access. I had to arrange for a flyer to cover the thousand kaymetras, and schedule a purge. White Hill said she would wander through Hanoi, instead.

I didn't sleep well that night, waking often from fantastic dreams, the nanobeasts grown large and aggressive. White Hill was in some of the dreams, posturing sexually.

By the next morning the storm had gone away, so we crossed over to Amazonia, and I learned firsthand why one might rather sit in a hotel room with a nice book than go to Angkor Wat, or anywhere that required a purge. The external part of the purging was unpleasant enough, even with pain medication, all the epidermis stripped and regrown. The inside part was beyond description, as the nanophages could be hiding out anywhere. Every opening into the body had to be vacuumed out, including the sense organs. I was not awake for that part, where the robots most gently clean out your eye sockets, but my eyes hurt and my ears rang for days. They warned me to sit down the first time I urinated, which was good advice, since I nearly passed out from the burning pain.

White Hill and I had a quiet supper of restorative gruel together, and then crept off to sleep for half a day. She was full of pep the next morning, and I pretended to be at least sentient, as we wandered through the city making preparations for the trip.

After a couple of hours I protested that she was obviously trying to do in one of her competitors; stop and let an old man sit down for a minute.

We found a bar that specialized in stimulants. She had tea and I had bhan, a murky warm drink served in a large nutshell, coconut. It tasted woody and bitter, but was restorative.

"It's not age," she said. "The purging seems a lot easier, the second time you do it. I could hardly move, all the next day, the first time."

Interesting that she didn't mention that earlier. "Did they tell you it would get easier?"

She nodded, then caught herself and wagged her chin horizontally, Earth-style. "Not a word. I think they enjoy our discomfort."

"Or like to keep us off guard. Keeps them in control." She made the little kissing sound that's Lortian for agreement and reached for a lemon wedge to squeeze into her tea. The world seemed to slow slightly, I guess from whatever was in the bhan, and I found myself cataloguing her body microscopically. A crescent of white scar tissue on the back of a knuckle, fine hair on her forearm, almost white, her shoulders and breasts moving in counterpoised pairs, silk rustling, as she reached forward and back and squeezed the lemon, sharp citrus smell and the tip of her tongue between her thin lips, mouth slightly large. Chameleon hazel eyes, dark green now because of the decorative ivy wall behind her.

"What are you staring at?"

"Sorry, just thinking."

"Thinking." She stared at me in return, measuring. "Your people are good at that."

After we'd bought the travel necessities we had the packages sent to our quarters and wandered aimlessly. The city was comfortable, but had little of interest in terms of architecture or history, oddly dull for a planet's administrative center. There was an obvious social purpose for its blandness—by statute, nobody was *from* Amazonia; nobody could be born there or claim citizenship. Most of the planet's wealth and power came there to work, electronically if not physically, but it went home to some other place.

A certain amount of that wealth was from interstellar commerce, but it was nothing like the old days, before the war. Earth had been a hub, a central authority that could demand its tithe or more from any transaction between planets. In the period between the Sterilization and Earth's token rehabitation, the other planets made their own arrangements with one another, in pairs and groups. But most of the fortunes that had been born on Earth returned here.

So Amazonia was bland as cheap bread, but there was more wealth under its dome than on any two other planets combined. Big money seeks out the company of its own, for purposes of reproduction.

• Δ

Two other artists had come in, from Auer and Shwa, and once they were ready, we set out to explore the world by subway. The first stop that was interesting was the Grand Canyon, a natural wonder whose desolate beauty was unaffected by the Sterilization.

We were amused by the guide there, a curious little woman who rattled on about the Great Rift Valley on Mars, a nearby planet where she was born. White Hill had a lightbox, and while the Martian lady droned on we sketched the fantastic colors, necessarily loose and abstract because our fingers were clumsy in clinging plastic.

We toured Chicago, like the Grand Canyon, wrapped in plastic. It was a large city that had been leveled in a local war. It lay in ruins for many years, and then, famously, was rebuilt as a single huge structure from those ruins. There's a childish or drunken ad hoc quality to it, a scarcity of right angles, a crazy-quilt mixture of materials. Areas of stunning imaginative brilliance next to jury-rigged junk. And everywhere bones, the skeletons of ten million people, lying where they fell. I asked what had happened to the bones in the old city outside of Amazonia. The guide said he'd never been there, but he supposed that the sight of them upset the politicians, so they had them cleaned up. "Can you imagine this place without the bones?" he asked. It would be nice if I could.

The other remnants of cities in that country were less interesting, if no less depressing. We flew over the east coast, which was essentially one continuous metropolis for thousands of kaymetras, like our coast from New Haven to Stargate, rendered in sterile ruins.

The first place I visited unprotected was Giza, the Great Pyramids. White Hill decided to come with me, though she had to be wrapped up in a shapeless cloth robe, her face veiled, because of local religious law. It seemed to me ridiculous, a transparent tourism ploy. How many believers in that old religion could have been off-planet when the Earth died? But every female was obliged at the tube exit to go into a big hall and be fitted with a chador robe and veil before a man could be allowed to look at her.

(We wondered whether the purging would be done completely by women. The technicians would certainly see a lot of her uncovered during that excruciation.)

They warned us it was unseasonably hot outside. Almost too hot to breathe, actually, during the day. We accomplished most of our sight-seeing around dusk or dawn, spending most of the day in air-conditioned shelters.

Because of our special status, White Hill and I were allowed to visit the Pyramids alone, in the dark of the morning. We climbed up the largest one and watched the sun mount over desert haze. It was a singular time for both of us, edifying but something more.

Coming back down, we were treated to a sandstorm, *khamsin*, which actually might have done the first stage of purging if we had been allowed to take off our clothes. It explained why all the bones lying around looked so much older than the ones in Chicago; they normally had ten or twelve of these sandblasting storms every year. Lately, with the heat wave, the *khamsin* came weekly or even more often.

Raised more than five thousand years ago, the Pyramids were the oldest monumental structures on the planet. They actually held as much fascination for White Hill as for me. Thousands of men moved millions of huge blocks of stone, with nothing but muscle and ingenuity. Some of the stones were mined a thousand kaymetras away, and floated up the river on barges.

I could build a similar structure, even larger, for my contest entry, by giving machines the right instructions. It would be a complicated business, but easily done within the two-year deadline. Of course there would be no point to it. That some anonymous engineer had done the same thing within the lifetime of a king, without recourse to machines—I agreed with White Hill: that was an actual marvel.

We spent a couple of days outside, traveling by surface hoppers from monument to monument, but none was as impressive. I suppose I should have realized that, and saved Giza for last.

We met another of the artists at the Sphinx, Lo Tan-Six, from Pao. I had seen his work on both Pao and ThetaKent, and admitted there was something to be admired there. He worked in stone, too, but was more interested in pure geometric forms than I was. I think stone fights form, or imposes its own tensions on the artist's wishes.

I liked him well enough, though, in spite of this and other differences, and we traveled together for a while. He suggested we not go through the purging here, but have our things sent on to Rome, because we'd want to be outside there, too. There was a daily hop from Alexandria to Rome, an airship that had a section reserved for those of us who could eat and breathe nanophages.

As soon as she was inside the coolness of the ship, White Hill shed the chador and veil and stuffed them under the seat. "Breathe," she said, stretching. Her white body suit was a little less revealing than paint.

Her directness and undisguised sexuality made me catch my breath. The tiny crease of punctuation that her vulva made in the body suit would have her jailed on some parts of my planet, not to mention the part of this one we'd just left. The costume was innocent and natural and, I think, completely calculated.

Pao studied her with an interested detachment. He was neuter, an option that was available on Petros, too, but one I've never really understood. He claimed that sex took too much time and energy from his art. I think his lack of gender took something else away from it.

We flew about an hour over the impossibly blue sea. There were a few sterile islands, but otherwise it was as plain as spilled ink. We descended over the ashes of Italy and landed on a pad on one of the hills overlooking the ancient city. The ship mated to an airlock so the normal-DNA people could go down to a tube that would whisk them into Rome. We could call for transportation or walk, and opted for the exercise. It was baking hot here, too, but not as bad as Egypt.

White Hill was polite with Lo, but obviously wished he'd disappear. He and I chattered a little too much about rocks and cements, explosives and lasers. And his asexuality diminished her interest in him—as, perhaps, my polite detachment increased her interest in me. The muralist from Shwa, to complete the spectrum, was after her like a puppy in its first heat, which I think amused her for two days. They'd had a private conversation in Chicago, and he'd kept his distance since, but still admired her from afar. As we walked down toward the Roman gates, he kept a careful twenty paces behind, trying to contemplate things besides White Hill's walk.

Inside the gate we stopped short, stunned in spite of knowing what to expect. It had a formal name, but everybody just called it Òssi, the Bones. An order of Catholic clergy had spent more than two centuries building, by hand, a wall of bones completely around the city. It was twice the height of a man, varnished dark amber. There were repetitive patterns of femurs and rib cages and stacks of curving spines, and at eye level, a row of skulls, uninterrupted, kaymetra after kaymetra.

This was where we parted. Lo was determined to walk completely around the circle of death, and the other two went with him. White Hill and I could do it in our imagination. I still creaked from climbing the Pyramid.

Prior to the ascent of Christianity here, they had huge spectacles, displays of martial skill where many of the participants were killed, for punishment of wrongdoing or just to entertain the masses. The two large amphitheaters where these displays went on were inside the Bones but not under the dome, so we walked around them. The Circus Maximus had a terrible dignity to it, little more than a long depression in the ground with a few eroded monuments left standing. The size and age of it were enough; your mind's eye supplied the rest. The smaller one, the Colosseum, was overdone, with robots in period costumes and ferocious mechanical animals re-creating the old scenes, lots of too-bright blood spurting. Stones and bones would do.

I'd thought about spending another day outside, but the shelter's air-conditioning had failed, and it was literally uninhabitable. So I braced myself and headed for the torture chamber. But as White Hill had said, the purging was more bearable the second time. You know that it's going to end.

Rome inside was interesting, many ages of archeology and history stacked around in no particular order. I enjoyed wandering from place to place with her, building a kind of organization out of the chaos. We were both more interested in inspiration than education, though, so I doubt that the three days we spent there left us with anything like a coherent picture of that tenacious empire and the millennia that followed it.

A long time later she would surprise me by reciting the names of the Roman emperors in order. She'd always had a trick memory, a talent for retaining trivia, ever since she was old enough to read. Growing up different that way must have been a factor in swaying her toward cognitive science.

We saw some ancient cinema and then returned to our quarters to pack for continuing on to Greece, which I was anticipating with pleasure. But it didn't happen. We had a message waiting: ALL MUST RETURN IMMEDIATELY TO AMAZONIA. CONTEST PROFOUNDLY CHANGED.

Lives, it turned out, profoundly changed. The war was back.

Δ

We met in a majestic amphitheater, the twenty-nine artists dwarfed by the size of it, huddled front row center. A few Amazonian officials sat behind a table on the stage, silent. They all looked detached, or stunned, brooding.

We hadn't been told anything except that it was a matter of "dire and immediate importance." We assumed it had to do with the contest, naturally, and were prepared for the worst: it had been called off; we had to go home.

The old crone Norita appeared. "We must confess to carelessness," she said. "The unseasonable warmth in both hemispheres, it isn't something that has happened, ever since the Sterilization. We looked for atmospheric causes here, and found something that seemed to explain it. But we didn't make the connection with what was happening in the other half of the world.

"It's not the atmosphere. It's the Sun. Somehow the Fwndyri have found a way to make its luminosity increase. It's been going on for half a year. If it continues, and we find no way to reverse it, the surface of the planet will be uninhabitable in a few years.

"I'm afraid that most of you are going to be stranded on Earth, at least for the time being. The Council of Worlds has exercised its emergency powers, and commandeered every vessel capable of interstellar transport. Those who have sufficient power or the proper connections will be able to escape. The rest will have to stay with us and face . . . whatever our fate is going to be."

I saw no reason not to be blunt. "Can money do it? How much would a ticket out cost?"

That would have been a gaffe on my planet, but Norita didn't blink. "I know for certain that two hundred million marks is not enough. I also know that some people have bought 'tickets,' as you say, but I don't know how much they paid, or to whom."

If I liquidated everything I owned, I might be able to come up with three hundred million, but I hadn't brought that kind of liquidity with me; just a box of rare jewelry, worth perhaps forty million. Most of my wealth was thirty-three years away, from the point of view of an Earth-bound investor. I could sign that over to someone, but by the time they got to Petros, the government or my family might have seized it, and they would have nothing save the prospect of a legal battle in a foreign culture.

Norita introduced Skylha Sygoda, an astrophysicist. He was pale and sweating. "We have analyzed the solar spectrum over the past six months. If I hadn't known that each spectrum was from the same star, I would have said it was a systematic and subtle demonstration of the microstages of stellar evolution in the late main sequence."

"Could you express that in some human language?" someone said.

Sygoda spread his hands. "They've found a way to age the Sun. In the normal course of things, we would expect the Sun to brighten about six percent each billion years. At the current rate, it's more like one percent per year."

"So in a hundred years," White Hill said, "it will be twice as bright?"

"If it continues at this rate. We don't know."

A stocky woman I recognized as !Oona Something, from Jua-nguvi, wrestled with the language: "To how long, then? Before this Earth is uninhabitable?"

"Well, in point of fact, it's uninhabitable now, except for people like you. We could survive inside these domes for a long time, if it were just a matter of the outside getting hotter and hotter. For those of you able to withstand the nanophages, it will probably be too hot within a decade, here; longer near the poles. But the weather is likely to become very violent, too.

"And it may not be a matter of a simple increase in heat. In the case of normal evolution, the Sun would eventually expand, becoming a red giant. It would take many billions of years, but the Earth would not survive. The surface of the Sun would actually extend out to touch us.

"If the Fwndyri were speeding up time somehow, locally, and the Sun were actually *evolving* at this incredible rate, we would suffer that fate in about thirty years. But it would be impossible. They would have to have a way to magically extract the hydrogen from the Sun's core."

"Wait," I said. "You don't know what they're doing now, to make it brighten. I wouldn't say anything's impossible."

"Water Man," Norita said, "if that happens we shall simply die, all of us, at once. There is no need to plan for it. We do need to plan for less extreme exigencies." There was an uncomfortable silence.

"What can we do?" White Hill said. "We artists?"

"There's no reason not to continue with the project, though I think you may wish to do it inside. There's no shortage of space. Are any of you trained in astrophysics, or anything having to do with stellar evolution and the like?" No one was. "You may still have some ideas that will be useful to the specialists. We will keep you informed."

Most of the artists stayed in Amazonia, for the amenities if not to avoid purging, but four of us went back to the outside habitat. Denli om Cord, the composer from Luxor, joined Lo and White Hill and me. We could have used the tunnel airlock, to avoid the midday heat, but Denli hadn't seen the beach, and I suppose we all had an impulse to see the sun with our new knowledge. In this new light, as they say.

White Hill and Denli went swimming while Lo and I poked around the ruins. We had since learned that the destruction here had been methodical, a grim resolve to leave the enemy nothing of value. Both of us were scouting for raw material, of course. After a short while we sat in the hot shade, wishing we had brought water.

We talked about that and about art. Not about the sun dying, or us dying, in a few decades. The women's laughter drifted to us over the rush of the muddy surf. There was a sad hysteria to it.

"Have you had sex with her?" he asked conversationally.

"What a question. No."

He tugged on his lip, staring out over the water. "I try to keep these things straight. It seems to me that you desire her, from the way you look at her, and she seems cordial to you, and is after all from Seldene. My interest is academic, of course."

"You've never done sex? I mean before."

"Of course, as a child." The implication of that was obvious.

"It becomes more complicated with practice."

"I suppose it could. Although Seldenians seem to treat it as casually as . . . conversation." He used the Seldenian word, which is the same as for intercourse.

"White Hill is reasonably sophisticated," I said. "She isn't bound by her culture's freedoms." The two women ran out of the water, arms around each other's waists, laughing. It was an interesting contrast; Denli was almost as large as me, and about as feminine. They saw us and waved toward the path back through the ruins.

We got up to follow them. "I suppose I don't understand your restraint," Lo said. "Is it your own culture? Your age?"

"Not age. Perhaps my culture encourages self-control."

He laughed. "That's an understatement."

"Not that I'm a slave to Petrosian propriety. My work is outlawed in several states, at home."

"You're proud of that."

I shrugged. "It reflects on them, not me." We followed the women down the path, an interesting study in contrasts, one pair nimble and naked except for a film of drying mud, the other pacing evenly in monkish robes. They were already showering when Lo and I entered the cool shelter, momentarily blinded by shade.

We made cool drinks and, after a quick shower, joined them in the communal bath. Lo was not anatomically different from a sexual male, which I found obscurely disturbing. Wouldn't it bother you to be constantly reminded of what you had lost? Renounced, I suppose Lo would say, and accuse me of being parochial about plumbing.

I had made the drinks with guava juice and ron, neither of which we have on Petros. A little too sweet, but pleasant. The alcohol loosened tongues.

Denli regarded me with deep black eyes. "You're rich, Water Man. Are you rich enough to escape?"

"No. If I had brought all my money with me, perhaps."

"Some do," White Hill said. "I did."

"I would too," Lo said, "coming from Seldene. No offense intended."

"Wheels turn," she admitted. "Five or six new governments before I get back. *Would* have gotten back."

We were all silent for a long moment. "It's not real yet," White Hill said, her voice flat. "We're going to die here?"

"We were going to die somewhere," Denli said. "Maybe not so soon."

"And not on Earth," Lo said. "It's like a long preview of Hell." Denli looked at him quizzically. "That's where Christians go when they die. If they were bad."

"They send their bodies to Earth?" We managed not to smile. Actually, most of my people knew as little as hers about Earth. Seldene and Luxor, though relatively poor, had centuries' more history than Petros, and kept closer ties to the central planet. The Home Planet, they would say. Homey as a blast furnace.

By tacit consensus, we didn't dwell on death any more that day. When artists get together they tend to wax enthusiastic about materials and tools, the mechanical lore of their trades. We talked about the ways we worked at home, the things we were able to bring with us, the improvisations we could effect with Earthling materials. (Critics talk about art, we say; artists talk about brushes.) Three other artists joined us, two sculptors and a weathershaper, and we all wound up in the large sunny studio drawing and painting. White Hill and I found sticks of charcoal and did studies of each other drawing each other.

While we were comparing them she quietly asked, "Do you sleep lightly?"

"I can. What did you have in mind?"

"Oh, looking at the ruins by starlight. The moon goes down about three. I thought we might watch it set together." Her expression was so open as to be enigmatic.

Two more artists had joined us by dinnertime, which proceeded with a kind of forced jollity. A lot of ron was consumed. White Hill cautioned me against overindulgence. They had the same liquor, called "rum," on Seldene, and it had a reputation for going down easily but causing storms. There was no legal distilled liquor on my planet.

I had two drinks of it, and retired when people started singing in various languages. I did sleep lightly, though, and was almost awake when White Hill tapped. I could hear two or three people still up, murmuring in the bath. We slipped out quietly.

It was almost cool. The quarter-phase moon was near the horizon, a dim orange, but it gave us enough light to pick our way down the path. It was warmer in the ruins, the tumbled stone still radiating the day's heat. We walked through to the beach, where it was cooler again. White Hill spread the blanket she had brought and we stretched out and looked up at the stars.

As is always true with a new world, most of the constellations were familiar, with a few bright stars added or subtracted. Neither of our home stars was significant, as dim here as Earth's Sol is from home. She identified the brightest star overhead as AlphaKent; there was a brighter one on the horizon, but neither of us knew what it was.

We compared names of the constellations we recognized. Some of hers were the same as Earth's names, like Scorpio, which we call the Insect. It was about halfway up the sky, prominent, embedded in the galaxy's glow. We both call the brightest star there Antares. The Executioner, which had set perhaps an hour earlier, they call Orion. We had the same meaningless names for its brightest stars, Betelgeuse and Rigel.

"For a sculptor, you know a lot about astronomy," she said. "When I visited your city, there was too much light to see stars at night."

"You can see a few from my place. I'm out at Lake Pâchl°a, about a hundred kaymetras inland."

"I know. I called you."

"I wasn't home?"

"No; you were supposedly on ThetaKent."

"That's right, you told me. Our paths crossed in space. And you became that burgher's slave wife." I put my hand on her arm. "Sorry I forgot. A lot has gone on. Was he awful?"

She laughed into the darkness. "He offered me a lot to stay."

"I can imagine."

She half turned, one breast soft against my arm, and ran a finger up my leg. "Why tax your imagination?"

I wasn't especially in the mood, but my body was. The robes rustled off easily, their only virtue.

The moon was down now, and I could see only a dim outline of her in the starlight. It was strange to make love deprived of that sense. You would think the absence of it would amplify the others, but I can't say that it did, except that her heartbeat seemed very strong on the heel of my hand. Her breath was sweet with mint and the smell and taste of her body were agreeable; in fact, there was nothing about her body that I would have cared to change, inside or out, but nevertheless, our progress became difficult after a couple of minutes, and by mute agreement we slowed and stopped. We lay joined together for some time before she spoke.

"The timing is all wrong. I'm sorry." She drew her face across my arm and I felt tears. "I was just trying not to think about things."

"It's all right. The sand doesn't help, either." We had gotten a little bit inside, rubbing.

We talked for a while and then drowsed together. When the sky began to lighten, a hot wind from below the horizon woke us up. We went back to the shelter.

Everyone was asleep. We went to shower off the sand and she was amused to see my interest in her quicken. "Let's take that downstairs," she whispered, and I followed her down to her room.

The memory of the earlier incapability was there, but it was not greatly inhibiting. Being able to see her made the act more familiar, and besides she was very pleasant to see, from whatever angle. I was able to withhold myself only once, and so the interlude was shorter than either of us would have desired.

We slept together on her narrow bed. Or she slept, rather, while I watched the bar of sunlight grow on the opposite wall, and thought about how everything had changed.

They couldn't really say we had thirty years to live, since they had no idea what the enemy was doing. It might be three hundred; it might be less than one—but even with bodyswitch that was always true, as it was in the old days: sooner or later something would go wrong and you would die. That I might die at the same instant as ten thousand other people and a planet full of history—that was interesting. But as the room filled with light and I studied her quiet repose, I found her more interesting than that.

I was old enough to be immune to infatuation. Something deep had been growing since Egypt, maybe before. On top of the pyramid, the rising sun dim in the mist, we had sat with our shoulders touching, watching the ancient forms appear below, and I felt a surge of numinism mixed oddly with content. She looked at me—I could only see her eyes—and we didn't have to say anything about the moment.

And now this. I was sure, without words, that she would share this, too. Whatever "this" was. England's versatile language, like mine and hers, is strangely hobbled by having the one word, love, stand for such a multiplicity of feelings.

Perhaps that lack reveals a truth, that no one love is like any other. There are other truths that you might forget, or ignore, distracted by the growth of love. In Petrosian there is a saying in the palindromic mood that always carries a sardonic, or at least ironic, inflection: "Happiness presages disaster presages happiness." So if you die happy, it means you were happy when you died. Good timing or bad?

Δ •

!Oona M'vua had a room next to White Hill, and she was glad to switch with me, an operation that took about three minutes but was good for a much longer period of talk among the other artists. Lo was smugly amused, which in my temporary generosity of spirit I forgave.

Once we were adjacent, we found the button that made the wall slide away, and pushed the two beds together under her window. I'm afraid we were antisocial for a couple of days. It had been some time since either of us had had a lover. And I had never had one like her, literally, out of the dozens. She said that was because I had never been involved with a Seldenian, and I tactfully agreed, banishing five perfectly good memories to amnesia.

It's true that Seldenian women, and men as well, are better schooled than those of us from normal planets, in the techniques and subtleties of sexual expression. Part of "wholeness," which I suppose is a weak pun in English. It kept Lo, and not only him, from taking White Hill seriously as an artist: the fact that a Seldenian, to be "whole," must necessarily treat art as an everyday activity, usually subordinate to affairs of the heart, of the body. Or at least on the same level, which is the point.

The reality is that it is all one to them. What makes Seldenians so alien is that their need for balance in life dissolves hierarchy: this piece of art is valuable, and so is this orgasm, and so is this crumb of bread. The bread crumb connects to the artwork through the artist's metabolism, which connects to orgasm. Then through a fluid and automatic mixture of logic, metaphor, and rhetoric, the bread crumb links to soil, sunlight, nuclear fusion, the beginning and end of the universe. Any intelligent person can map out chains like that, but to White Hill it was automatic, drilled into her with her first nouns and verbs: *Everything is important. Nothing matters.* Change the world but stay relaxed.

I could never come around to her way of thinking. But then I was married for fifty Petrosian years to a woman who had stranger beliefs. (The marriage as a social contract actually lasted fifty-seven years; at the half-century mark we took a vacation from each other, and I never saw her again.) White Hill's worldview gave her an equanimity I had to envy. But my art needed unbalance and tension the way hers needed harmony and resolution.

By the fourth day most of the artists had joined us in the shelter. Maybe they grew tired of wandering through the bureaucracy. More likely, they were anxious about their competitors' progress.

White Hill was drawing designs on large sheets of buff paper and taping them up on our walls. She worked on her feet, bare feet, pacing from diagram to diagram, changing and rearranging. I worked directly inside a shaping box, an invention White Hill had heard of but had never seen. It's a cube of light a little less than a metra wide. Inside is an image of a sculpture—or a rock or a lump of clay—that you can feel as well as see. You can mold it with your hands or work with finer instruments for cutting, scraping, chipping. It records your progress constantly, so it's easy to take chances; you can always run it back to an earlier stage.

I spent a few hours every other day cruising in a flyer with Lo and a couple of other sculptors, looking for native materials. We were severely constrained by the decision to put the Memory Park inside, since everything we used had to be small enough to fit through the airlock and purging rooms. You could work with large pieces, but you would have to slice them up and reassemble them, the individual chunks no bigger than two by two by three metras.

We tried to stay congenial and fair during these expeditions. Ideally, you would spot a piece and we would land by it or hover over it long enough to tag it with your ID; in a day or two the robots would deliver it to your "holding area" outside the shelter. If more than one person wanted the piece, which happened as often as not, a decision had to be made before it was tagged. There was a lot of arguing and trading and Solomon-style splitting, which usually satisfied the requirements of something other than art.

The quality of light was changing for the worse. Earthling planetary engineers were spewing bright dust into the upper atmosphere, to reflect back solar heat. (They modified the nanophage-eating machinery for the purpose. That was also designed to fill the atmosphere full of dust, but at a lower level—and each grain of *that* dust had a tiny chemical brain.) It made the night sky progressively less interesting. I was glad White Hill had chosen to initiate our connection under the stars. It would be some time before we saw them again, if ever.

And it looked like "daylight" was going to be a uniform overcast for the duration of the contest. Without the dynamic of moving sunlight to continually change the appearance of my piece, I had to discard a whole family of first approaches to its design. I was starting to think along the lines of something irrational-looking; something the brain would reject as impossible. The way we mentally veer away from unthinkable things like the Sterilization, and our proximate future.

We had divided into two groups, and jokingly but seriously referred to one another as "originalists" and "realists." We originalists were continuing our projects on the basis of the charter's rules: a memorial to the tragedy and its aftermath, a stark sterile reminder in the midst of life. The realists took into account new developments, including the fact that there would probably never be any "midst of life" and, possibly, no audience, after thirty years.

I thought that was excessive. There was plenty of pathos in the original assignment. Adding another, impasto, layer of pathos along with irony and the artist's fear of personal death . . . well, we were doing art, not literature. I sincerely hoped their pieces would be fatally muddled by complexity.

If you asked White Hill which group she belonged to, she would of course say, "Both." I had no idea what form her project was going to take; we had agreed early on to surprise one another, and not impede each other with suggestions. I couldn't decipher even one-tenth of her diagrams. I speak Seldenian pretty well, but have never mastered the pictographs beyond the usual travelers' vocabulary. And much of what she was scribbling on the buff sheets of paper was in no language I recognized, an arcane technical symbology.

We talked about other things. Even about the future, as lovers will. Our most probable future was simultaneous death by fire, but it was calming and harmless to make "what if?" plans, in case our hosts somehow were able to find a way around that fate. We did have a choice of many possible futures, if we indeed had more than one. White Hill had never had access to wealth before. She didn't want to live lavishly, but the idea of being able to explore all the planets excited her.

Of course she had never tried living lavishly. I hoped one day to study her reaction to it, which would be strange. Out of the box of valuables I'd brought along, I gave her a necklace, a traditional beginning-love gift on Petros. It was a network of perfect emeralds and rubies laced in gold.

She examined it closely. "How much is this worth?"

"A million marks, more or less." She started to hand it back. "Please keep it. Money has no value here, no meaning."

She was at a loss for words, which was rare enough. "I understand the gesture. But you can't expect me to value this the way you do."

"I wouldn't expect that."

"Suppose I lose it? I might just set it down somewhere."

"I know. I'll still have given it to you."

She nodded and laughed. "All right. You people are strange." She slipped the necklace on, still latched, wiggling it over her ears. The colors glowed warm and cold against her olive skin.

She kissed me, a feather, and rushed out of our room wordlessly. She passed right by a mirror without looking at it.

After a couple of hours I went to find her. Lo said he'd seen her go out the door with a lot of water. At the beach I found her footprints marching straight west to the horizon.

She was gone for two days. I was working outside when she came back, wearing nothing but the necklace. There was another necklace in her hand: she had cut off her right braid and interwoven a complex pattern of gold and silver wire into a closed loop. She slipped it over my head and pecked me on the lips and headed for the shelter. When I started to follow she stopped me with a tired gesture. "Let me sleep, eat, wash." Her voice was a hoarse whisper. "Come to me after dark."

I sat down, leaning back against a good rock, and thought about very little, touching her braid and smelling it. When it was too dark to see my feet, I went in, and she was waiting.

Δ••

I spent a lot of time outside, at least in the early morning and late afternoon, studying my accumulation of rocks and ruins. I had images of every piece in my shaping box's memory, but it was easier to visualize some aspects of the project if I could walk around the elements and touch them.

Inspiration is where you find it. We'd played with an orrery in the museum in Rome, a miniature solar system that had been built of clockwork centuries before the Information Age. There was a wistful, humorous kind of comfort in its jerky regularity.

My mental processes always turn things inside out. Find the terror and hopelessness in that comfort. I had in mind a massive but delicately balanced assemblage that would be viewed by small groups; their presence would cause it to teeter and turn ponderously. It would seem both fragile and huge (though of course the fragility would be an illusion), like the ecosystem that the Fwndyri so abruptly destroyed.

The assemblage would be mounted in such a way that it would seem always in danger of toppling off its base, but hidden weights would make that impossible. The sound of the rolling weights ought to produce a nice anxiety. Whenever a part tapped the floor, the tap would be amplified into a hollow boom.

If the viewers stood absolutely still, it would swing to a halt. As they left, they would disturb it again. I hoped it would disturb them as well.

The large technical problem was measuring the distribution of mass in each of my motley pieces. That would have been easy at home; I could rent a magnetic resonance densitometer to map their insides. There was no such thing on this planet (so rich in things I had no use for!), so I had to make do with a pair of robots and a knife edge. And then start hollowing the pieces out asymmetrically, so that once set in motion, the assemblage would tend to rotate.

I had a large number of rocks and artifacts to choose from, and was tempted to use no unifying principle at all, other than the unstable balance of the thing. Boulders and pieces of old statues and fossil machinery. The models I made of such a random collection were ambiguous, though. It was hard to tell whether they would look ominous or ludicrous, built to scale. A symbol of helplessness before an implacable enemy? Or a lurching, crashing junkpile? I decided to take a reasonably conservative approach, dignity rather than daring. After all, the audience would be Earthlings and, if the planet survived, tourists with more money than sophistication. Not my usual jury.

I was able to scavenge twenty long bars of shiny black monofiber, which would be the spokes of my irregular wheel. That would give it some unity of composition: make a cross with four similar chunks of granite at the ordinal points, and a larger chunk at the center. Then build up a web inside, monofiber lines linking bits of this and that.

Some of the people were moving their materials inside Amazonia, to work in the area marked off for the park. White Hill and I decided to stay outside. She said her project was portable, at this stage, and mine would be easy to disassemble and move.

After a couple of weeks, only fifteen artists remained with the project, inside Amazonia or out in the shelter. The others had either quit, surrendering to the passive depression that seemed to be Earth's new norm, or, in one case, committed suicide. The two from Wolf and Mijhøven opted for coldsleep, which might be deferred suicide. About one person in three slept through it; one in three came out with some kind of treatable mental disorder. The others went mad and died soon after reawakening, unable or unwilling to live.

Coldsleep wasn't done on Petros, although some Petrosians went to other worlds to indulge in it as a risky kind of time travel. Sleep until whatever's wrong with the world has changed. Some people even did it for financial speculation: buy up objects of art or antiques, and sleep for a century or more while their value increases. Of course their value might not increase significantly, or they might be stolen or coopted by family or government.

But if you can make enough money to buy a ticket to another planet, why not hold off until you had enough to go to a really *distant* one? Let time dilation compress the years. I could make a triangle from Petros to Skaal to Mijhoven and back, and more than 120 years would pass, while I lived through only three, with no danger to my mind. And I could take my objects of art along with me.

White Hill had worked with coldsleep veterans, or victims. None of them had been motivated by profit, given her planet's institutionalized antimaterialism, so most of them had been suffering from some psychological ill before they slept. It was rare for them to come out of the "treatment" improved, but they did come into a world where people like White Hill could at least attend them in their madness, perhaps guide them out.

I'd been to three times as many worlds as she. But she had been to stranger places.

Δ•••

The terraformers did their job too well. The days grew cooler and cooler, and some nights snow fell. The snow on the ground persisted into mornings for a while, and then through noon, and finally it began to pile up. Those of us who wanted to work outside had to improvise cold-weather clothing.

I liked working in the cold, although all I did was direct robots. I grew up in a small town south of New Haven, where winter was long and intense. At some level I associated snow and ice with the exciting pleasures that waited for us after school. I was to have my fill of it, though.

It was obvious I had to work fast, faster than I'd originally planned, because of the increasing cold. I wanted to have everything put together and working before I disassembled it and pushed it through the airlock. The robots weren't made for cold weather, unfortunately. They had bad traction on the ice and sometimes their joints would seize up. One of them complained constantly, but of course it was the best worker, too, so I couldn't just turn it off and let it disappear under the drifts, an idea that tempted me.

White Hill often came out for a few minutes to stand and watch me and the robots struggle with the icy heavy boulders, machinery, and statuary. We took walks along the seashore that became shorter as the weather worsened. The last walk was a disaster.

We had just gotten to the beach when a sudden storm came up with a sandblast wind so violent that it blew us off our feet. We crawled back to the partial protection of the ruins and huddled together, the wind screaming so loudly that we had to shout to hear each other. The storm continued to mount and, in our terror, we decided to run for the shelter. White Hill slipped on some ice and suffered a horrible injury, a jagged piece of metal slashing her face diagonally from forehead to chin, blinding her left eye and tearing off part of her nose. Pearly bone showed through, cracked, at eyebrow, cheek, and chin. She rose up to one elbow and fell slack.

I carried her the rest of the way, immensely glad for the physical strength that made it possible. By the time we got inside she was unconscious and my white coat was a scarlet flag of blood.

A plastic-clad doctor came through immediately and did what she could to get White Hill out of immediate danger. But there was a problem with more sophisticated treatment. They couldn't bring the equipment out to our shelter, and White Hill wouldn't survive the stress of purging unless she had had a chance to heal for a while. Besides the facial wound, she had a broken elbow and collarbone and two cracked ribs.

For a week or so she was always in pain or numb. I sat with her, numb myself, her face a terrible puffed caricature of its former beauty, the wound glued up with plaskin the color of putty. Split skin of her eyelid slack over the empty socket.

The mirror wasn't visible from her bed, and she didn't ask for one, but whenever I looked away from her, her working hand came up to touch and catalogue the damage. We both knew how fortunate she was to be alive at all, and especially in an era and situation where the damage could all be repaired, given time and a little luck. But it was still a terrible thing to live with, an awful memory to keep reliving.

When she was more herself, able to talk through her ripped and pasted mouth, it was difficult for me to keep my composure. She had considerable philosophical, I suppose you could say spiritual, resources, but she was so profoundly stunned that she couldn't follow a line of reasoning very far, and usually wound up sobbing in frustration.

Sometimes I cried with her, although Petrosian men don't cry except in response to music. I had been a soldier once and had seen my ration of injury and death, and I always felt the experience had hardened me, to my detriment. But my friends who had been wounded or killed were just friends, and all of us lived then with the certainty that every day could be anybody's last one. To have the woman you love senselessly mutilated by an accident of weather was emotionally more arduous than losing a dozen companions to the steady erosion of war, a different kind of weather.

I asked her whether she wanted to forget our earlier agreement and talk about our projects. She said no; she was still working on hers, in a way, and she still wanted it to be a surprise. I did manage to distract her, playing with the shaping box. We made cartoonish representations of Lo and old Norita, and combined them in impossible sexual geometries. We shared a limited kind of sex ourselves, finally.

The doctor pronounced her well enough to be taken apart, and both of us were scourged and reappeared on the other side. White Hill was already in surgery when I woke up; there had been no reason to revive her before beginning the restorative processes.

I spent two days wandering through the blandness of Amazonia, jungle laced through concrete, quartering the huge place on foot. Most areas seemed catatonic. A few were boisterous with end-of-the-world hysteria. I checked on her progress so often that they eventually assigned a robot to call me up every hour, whether or not there was any change.

On the third day I was allowed to see her, in her sleep. She was pale but seemed completely restored. I watched her for an hour, perhaps more, when her eyes suddenly opened. The new one was blue, not green, for some reason. She didn't focus on me.

"Dreams feed art," she whispered in Petrosian; "and art feeds dreams." She closed her eyes and slept again.

Δ❒

She didn't want to go back out. She had lived all her life in the tropics, even the year she spent in bondage, and the idea of returning to the ice that had slashed her was more than repugnant. Inside Amazonia it was always summer, now, the authorities trying to keep everyone happy with heat and light and jungle flowers.

I went back out to gather her things. Ten large sheets of buff paper I unstuck from our walls and stacked and rolled. The necklace, and the satchel of rare coins she had brought from Seldene, all her worldly wealth.

I considered wrapping up my own project, giving the robots instructions for its dismantling and transport, so that I could just go back inside with her and stay. But that would be chancy. I wanted to see the thing work once before I took it apart.

So I went through the purging again, although it wasn't strictly necessary; I could have sent her things through without hand-carrying them. But I wanted to make sure she was on her feet before I left her for several weeks.

She was not on her feet, but she was dancing. When I recovered from the purging, which now took only half a day, I went to her hospital room and they referred me to our new quarters, a three-room dwelling in a place called Plaza de Artistes. There were two beds in the bedroom, one a fancy medical one, but that was worlds better than trying to find privacy in a hospital.

There was a note floating in the air over the bed saying she had gone to a party in the common room. I found her in a gossamer wheelchair, teaching a hand dance to Denli om Cord, while a harpist and flautist from two different worlds tried to settle on a mutual key.

She was in good spirits. Denli remembered an engagement and I wheeled White Hill out onto a balcony that overlooked a lake full of sleeping birds, some perhaps real.

It was hot outside, always hot. There was a mist of perspiration on her face, partly from the light exercise of the dance, I supposed. In the light from below, the mist gave her face a sculpted appearance, unsparing sharpness, and there was no sign left of the surgery.

"I'll be out of the chair tomorrow," she said, "at least ten minutes at a time." She laughed. "*Stop* that!"

"Stop what?"

"Looking at me like that."

I was still staring at her face. "It's just . . . I suppose it's such a relief."

"I know." She rubbed my hand. "They showed me pictures, of before. You looked at that for so many days?"

"I saw you."

She pressed my hand to her face. The new skin was taut but soft, like a baby's. "Take me downstairs?"

ΔΔ

It's hard to describe, especially in light of later developments, disintegrations, but that night of fragile lovemaking marked a permanent change in the way we linked, or at least the way I was linked to her: I've been married twice, long and short, and have been in some kind of love a hundred times. But no woman has ever owned me before.

This is something we do to ourselves. I've had enough women who *tried* to possess me, but always was able to back or circle away, in literal preservation of self. I always felt that life was too long for one woman.

Certainly part of it is that life is not so long anymore. A larger part of it was the run through the screaming storm, her life streaming out of her, and my stewardship, or at least companionship, afterward, during her slow transformation back into health and physical beauty. The core of her had never changed, though, the stubborn serenity that I came to realize, that warm night, had finally infected me as well.

The bed was a firm narrow slab, cooler than the dark air heavy with the scent of Earth flowers. I helped her onto the bed (which instantly conformed to her) but from then on it was she who cared for me, saying that was all she wanted, all she really had strength for. When I tried to reverse that, she reminded me of a holiday palindrome that has sexual overtones in both our languages: Giving is taking is giving.

ΔΔ•

We spent a couple of weeks as close as two people can be. I was her lover and also her nurse, as she slowly strengthened. When she was able to spend most of her day in normal pursuits, free of the wheelchair or "intelligent" bed (with which we had made a threesome, at times uneasy), she urged me to go back outside and finish up. She was ready to concentrate on her own project, too. Impatient to do art again, a good sign.

I would not have left so soon if I had known what her project involved. But that might not have changed anything.

As soon as I stepped outside, I knew it was going to take longer than planned. I had known from the inside monitors how cold it was going to be, and how many ceemetras of ice had accumulated, but I didn't really *know* how bad it was until I was standing there, looking at my piles of materials locked in opaque glaze. A good thing I'd left the robots inside the shelter, and a good thing I had left a few hand tools outside. The door was buried under two metras of snow and ice. I sculpted myself a passageway, an application of artistic skills I'd never foreseen.

I debated calling White Hill and telling her that I would be longer than expected. We had agreed not to interrupt each other, though, and it was likely she'd started working as soon as I left.

The robots were like a bad comedy team, but I could only be amused by them for an hour or so at a time. It was so cold that the water vapor from my breath froze into an icy sheath on my beard and mustache. Breathing was painful; deep breathing probably dangerous.

So most of the time, I monitored them from inside the shelter. I had the place to myself; everyone else had long since gone into the dome. When I wasn't working I drank too much, something I had not done regularly in centuries.

It was obvious that I wasn't going to make a working model. Delicate balance was impossible in the shifting gale. But the robots and I had our hands full, and other grasping appendages engaged, just dismantling the various pieces and moving them through the lock. It was unexciting but painstaking work. We did all the laser cuts inside the shelter, allowing the rock to come up to room temperature so it didn't spall or shatter. The air conditioning wasn't quite equal to the challenge, and neither were the cleaning robots, so after a while it was like living in a foundry: everywhere a kind of greasy slickness of rock dust, the air dry and metallic.

So it was with no regret that I followed the last slice into the airlock myself, even looking forward to the scourging if White Hill was on the other side.

She wasn't. A number of other people were missing, too. She left this note behind:

I knew from the day we were called back here what my new piece would have to be, and I knew I had to keep it from you, to spare you sadness. And to save you the frustration of trying to talk me out of it.

As you may know by now, scientists have determined that the Fwndyri indeed have sped up the Sun's evolution somehow. It will continue to warm, until in thirty or forty years there will be an explosion called the "helium flash." The Sun will become a red giant, and the Earth will be incinerated.

There are no starships left, but there is one avenue of escape. A kind of escape.

Parked in high orbit there is a huge interplanetary transport that was used in the terraforming of Mars. It's a couple of centuries older than you, but like yourself it has been excellently preserved. We are going to ride it out to a distance sufficient to survive the Sun's catastrophe, and there remain until the situation improves, or does not.

This is where I enter the picture. For our survival to be meaningful in this thousand-year war, we have to resort to coldsleep. And for a large number of people to survive centuries of coldsleep, they need my jaturnary *skills. Alone, in the ice, they would go slowly mad. Connected through the matrix of my mind, they will have a sense of community, and may come out of it intact.*

I will be gone, of course. I will be by the time you read this. Not dead, but immersed in service. I could not be revived if this were only a hundred people for a hundred days. This will be a thousand, perhaps for a thousand years.

No one else on Earth can do jaturnary, *and there is neither time nor equipment for me to transfer my ability to anyone. Even if there were, I'm not sure I would trust anyone else's skill. So I am gone.*

My only loss is losing you. Do I have to elaborate on that?

You can come if you want. In order to use the transport, I had to agree that the survivors be chosen in accordance with the Earth's strict class system—starting with dear Norita, and from that pinnacle, on down—but they were willing to make exceptions for all of the visiting artists. You have until mid-Deciembre to decide; the ship leaves Januar first.

If I know you at all, I know you would rather stay behind and die. Perhaps the prospect of living "in" me could move you past your fear of coldsleep; your aversion to jaturnary. *If not, not.*

I love you more than life. But this is more than that. Are we what we are?

W.H.

The last sentence is a palindrome in her language, not mine, that I believe has some significance beyond the obvious.

• • ❒

I did think about it for some time. Weighing a quick death, or even a slow one, against spending centuries locked frozen in a tiny room with Norita and her ilk. Chattering on at the speed of synapse, and me unable to not listen.

I have always valued quiet, and the eternity of it that I face is no more dreadful than the eternity of quiet that preceded my birth.

If White Hill were to be at the other end of those centuries of torture, I know I could tolerate the excruciation. But she was dead now, at least in the sense that I would never see her again.

Another woman might have tried to give me a false hope, the possibility that in some remote future the process of *jaturnary* would be advanced to the point where her personality could be recovered. But she knew how unlikely that would be even if teams of scientists could be found to work on it, and years could be found for them to work in. It would be like unscrambling an egg.

Maybe I would even do it, though, if there were just some chance that, when I was released from that din of garrulous bondage, there would be something like a real world, a world where I could function as an artist. But I don't think there will even be a world where I can function as a man.

There probably won't be any humanity at all, soon enough. What they did to the Sun they could do to all of our stars, one assumes. They win the war, the Extermination, as my parent called it. Wrong side exterminated.

Of course the Fwndyri might not find White Hill and her charges. Even if they do find them, they might leave them preserved as an object of study.

The prospect of living on eternally under those circumstances, even if there were some growth to compensate for the immobility and the company, holds no appeal.

• ❒

What I did in the time remaining before mid-Deciembre was write this account. Then I had it translated by a xenolinguist into a form that she said could be decoded by any creature sufficiently similar to humanity to make any sense of the story. Even the Fwndyri, perhaps. They're human enough to want to wipe out a competing species.

I'm looking at the preliminary sheets now, English down the left side and a jumble of dots, squares, and triangles down the right. Both sides would have looked equally strange to me a few years ago.

White Hill's story will be conjoined to a standard book that starts out with basic mathematical principles, in dots and squares and triangles, and moves from that into physics, chemistry, biology. Can you go from biology to the human heart? I have to hope so. If this is read by alien eyes, long after the last human breath is stilled, I hope it's not utter gibberish.

❐

So I will take this final sheet down to the translator and then deliver the whole thing to the woman who is going to transfer it to permanent sheets of platinum, which will be put in a prominent place aboard the transport. They could last a million years, or ten million, or more. After the Sun is a cinder, and the ship is a frozen block enclosing a thousand bits of frozen flesh, she will live on in this small way.

So now my work is done. I'm going outside, to the quiet.

A CAREER IN SEXUAL CHEMISTRY

Brian Stableford

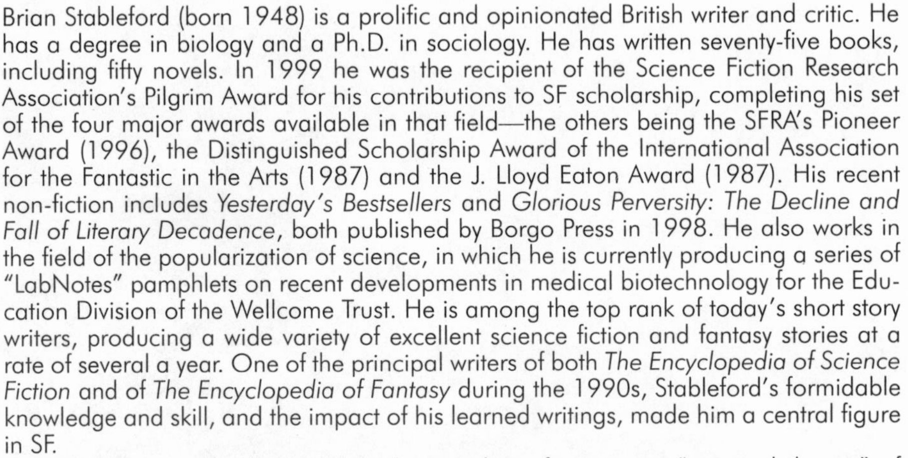

Brian Stableford (born 1948) is a prolific and opinionated British writer and critic. He has a degree in biology and a Ph.D. in sociology. He has written seventy-five books, including fifty novels. In 1999 he was the recipient of the Science Fiction Research Association's Pilgrim Award for his contributions to SF scholarship, completing his set of the four major awards available in that field—the others being the SFRA's Pioneer Award (1996), the Distinguished Scholarship Award of the International Association for the Fantastic in the Arts (1987) and the J. Lloyd Eaton Award (1987). His recent non-fiction includes *Yesterday's Bestsellers* and *Glorious Perversity: The Decline and Fall of Literary Decadence*, both published by Borgo Press in 1998. He also works in the field of the popularization of science, in which he is currently producing a series of "LabNotes" pamphlets on recent developments in medical biotechnology for the Education Division of the Wellcome Trust. He is among the top rank of today's short story writers, producing a wide variety of excellent science fiction and fantasy stories at a rate of several a year. One of the principal writers of both *The Encyclopedia of Science Fiction* and of *The Encyclopedia of Fantasy* during the 1990s, Stableford's formidable knowledge and skill, and the impact of his learned writings, made him a central figure in SF.

In recent years, he has published a number of essays on "practical theory," of which "The Last Chocolate Bar and the Majesty of Truth: Reflections on the Concept of 'Hardness in Science Fiction,'" in *The New York Review of Science Fiction*, is particularly relevant to our discussion of hard SF. In it, he pins down the probable first use of the term, and through the example some of its conservative implications:

> Use of the term "hard science fiction" dates back at least as far as November 1957, when P. Schuyler Miller used it in the introductory essay leading off one of his "Reference Library" columns in *Astounding Science Fiction*. The essay in question cites three books—John W. Campbell Jr.'s *Islands in Space*, Murray Leinster's *Colonial Survey*, and Hal Clement's *Cycle of Fire*—as widely different but nevertheless cardinal examples of "what some readers mean when they say they want 'real' science fiction."

His most recent novels *The Cassandra Complex* (2001) and *Dark Ararat* (2002) continue his future history series begun in *Inherit the Earth* (1998), *Architects of Emortality* (1999), and *The Fountains of Youth* (2000). This series will be completed in a sixth novel, *The Omega Expedition*. The series as a whole is one of the major hard SF achievements of the field at the turn of the century.

His most recent book is *Swan Songs: The Complete Hooded Swan Collection* (2002), an omnibus edition of Stableford's Hooded Swan space opera series, first published in the early 1970s. His short fiction is collected in *The Cosmic Perspective/Custer's Last Stand* (1985), *Sexual Chemistry: Sardonic Tales of the Genetic Revolution* (1991), and *Fables and Fantasies* (1996). Stableford has pursued his own course in hard SF in the last decade, writing in the classic apolitical tradition, and has ironically published little hard SF in the U.K. His distinguished short fiction was often nominated for awards in the 1990s, and included in *Year's Best* volumes, but his hard SF novels appeared only in the U.S. He is positioned somewhere between Arthur C. Clarke and Hal Clement, and Paul McAuley, but closer to McAuley in affect. The ironies in a Stableford story are often dark and sometimes crushing.

In response to our hard SF anthology, *The Ascent of Wonder*, in the essay quoted above he expressed his hopes for the future of hard SF:

> Personally, I hope that there will in future be more readers of hard SF who are interested in biotechnologies as well as—or even instead of—inorganic technologies. I hope, too, that there will in future be more readers of hard SF who do not require that they be soothed by conventional happy endings, and who are prepared to take a greater interest in the many kinds of idiosyncratic foreplay which could in principle support Eurekaesque climaxes. In particular, I hope that there will in future be more readers of hard SF who appreciate the peculiar aesthetics of irony and downright quirkiness.
>
> My reasons for entertaining these particular hopes are not entirely devoid of mere idiosyncrasy and a measure of self-interest, but there's no cause for surprise in that. "Few are those who have sought to know the future out of pure curiosity, and without moral intention or optimistic designs," as Anatole France observed. We ought, however, to be versatile enough to try, at least occasionally, if only for fun.

This story, the title story of one of his collections, appeared in *Interzone* in 1987. It is a sardonic tale of the commercial side of scientific research, a topic rarely addressed in hard SF.

There are some names which are more difficult to wear then others. Shufflebottoms, Bastards and Pricks start life with a handicap from which they may never recover, and one can easily understand why those born into families which have innocently borne since time immemorial such surnames as Hitler and Quisling often surrender such birthrights in favor of Smith or Villanova. People who refuse to change embarrassing names are frequently forced into an attitude of defensive stubbornness, brazenly and pridefully staring out the mockery of the world. For some people, an unfortunate surname can be a challenge as well as a curse, and life for them becomes a field of conflict in which heroism requires them to acquit themselves well.

One might be forgiven for thinking that Casanova is a less problematic name than many. It is by no means vulgar and has not the slightest genocidal connotation. It is a name that some men would be glad to have, conferring upon them as it would a mystique which they might wittily exploit. It is nevertheless a label which could be parent to a host of embarrassments and miseries, especially if worn by a gawky schoolboy in an English inner city comprehensive school, which was where the Giovanni Casanova who had been born on 14 February 1982 first became fully aware of its burdensome nature.

Giovanni's father, Marcantonio Casanova, had always been fond of the name, and seemed well enough equipped by fate to wear it well. He was not a tall man, but he had a handsome face and dark, flashing eyes which were definitely no handicap in the heart-melting stakes. He had made no serious attempt to live up to the name, though, accepting it as a nice joke that he found contentment in placid monogamy. His grandparents had come to Britain in the 1930s, refugees from Mussolini's Italy, and had settled in Manchester at the height of the Depression. Marcantonio therefore came from a line of impoverished intellectuals who had been prevented by social circumstance from achieving their real potential.

Giovanni's mother had also had no opportunity to fulfill her intellectual potential. Her maiden name was Jenny Spencer, and she had been born into that kind of respectable working-class family which would make every effort to set its sons on the road of upward social mobility, but thought that the acme of achievement for a daughter was to be an apprentice hairdresser at sixteen, a wife at seventeen and a mother at eighteen. All of these expectations Jenny had fulfilled with casual ease.

The whims of genetic and environmental fortune combined to give these humble parents a uniquely gifted son, for Giovanni soon showed evidence of a marvellous intelligence beyond even the latent potentialities of his parents. Nature's generosity was, however, restricted entirely to qualities of mind; in terms of looks and physique Giovanni was a nonstarter. He was undersized, out of proportion, and had an awful complexion. A bout of measles in infancy added insult to injury by leaving his eyesight terribly impaired; astigmatism and chronic myopia combined to force him to wear spectacles which robbed his dark eyes of any opportunity they ever had to flash heart-meltingly, and made him look rather cross-eyed. His voice was high-pitched, and never broke properly when he belatedly reached puberty. His hair insisted on growing into an appalling black tangle, and he began to go thin on top when he was barely seventeen. As dozens of thoughtless people were to remark to his face, and thousands more were to think silently to themselves, he certainly didn't look like a Casanova.

The class culture of England had proved remarkably resilient in the face of the erodent egalitarianism of the twentieth century, and bourgeois morality never did filter down to the poorer streets of Northern England, even when the old slums were demolished and new ones erected with indoor toilets and inbuilt social alienation. Where Giovanni spent his formative years very few girls preserved their virginity past the age of fourteen, and many a boy without a CSE to his name had done sufficient research to write a Ph.D. thesis on sexual technique by the time he was old enough to vote. This tide of covert sexual activity, however, passed Giovanni Casanova by. He was acutely conscious of the flood of eroticism which seethed all around him, and wished devoutly to be carried away by it, but to no avail.

Other ugly boys, who seemed to him as unprepossessing as himself, managed one by one to leap the first and most difficult hurdle, and subsequently gained marvellously in confidence and expertise, but Giovanni could not emulate them. His unattractiveness made things difficult, and his name added just sufficiently to his difficulties to make his task impossible, because it made even the girls who might have felt sorry for him laugh at him instead. Even the most feeble-minded of teenage girls could appreciate that there was something essentially rib-tickling about saying "no" to a Casanova.

Giovanni had started out on his journey through adolescence bogged down by self-consciousness, and by the time he was seventeen he was filled with self-loathing and incipient paranoia. By then he was already doomed to a long career as a social misfit. He was so withdrawn, having suffered such agonies from his failures, that he had completely given up talking to members of the female sex, except when forced by absolute necessity.

His sanity was saved, though, because he found a haven of retreat: the world of scientific knowledge, whose certainties contrasted so sharply with the treacherous vicissitudes of the social world. Even his teachers thought of him as a slightly unsavory freak, but they recognized that in intellectual terms he was a potential superstar. He compiled the most impressive scholarly record that his very moderate school had ever produced, and in October 2000 he went triumphantly to university to study biochemistry.

Biochemistry was the glamor science in those days, when every year that passed produced new biotechnological miracles from the laboratories of the genetic engineers. Giovanni was entranced by the infinite possibilities of the applied science, and set out to master the crafts of gene-mapping, protein design and plasmid construction. In everyday life he seemed extremely clumsy and slow of wit, but he was a very different character in the privacy of a laboratory, when he could manage the most delicate operation with absolute control, and where he had such a perfect intuition and understanding of what he was doing that he soon left his educators far behind.

In the new environment of the university, where intelligence was held in reasonably high esteem by female students, Giovanni tried tentatively to come out of his shell. He began talking to girls again, albeit with ponderous caution and unease. He helped other students with their work, and tried once or twice to move on from assistance to seduction. There was a black-haired Isabel who seemed to think him an interesting conversationalist, and a freckled Mary who even cooked a couple of meals for him because she thought he was neglecting himself, but they politely declined to enter into more intimate relationships with him. They could not think of him in such a light, and though they were prepared to consider Giovanni a friend of sorts, the boys they welcomed into their beds were of a very different type. Giovanni tried hard not to resent this, and to see their point of view. He certainly did not blame them, but his sympathy with their attitude only made him more disappointed with himself, and even more sharply aware of the mockery in his name.

Transforming bacteria by plasmid engineering was passé long before Giovanni's graduation, and he felt that the engineering of plants, though it certainly offered great opportunities for ingenuity and creativity, was not quite adventurous enough for him. He knew that his talents were sufficiently extraordinary to require something a little more daring, and so he channelled his efforts in the direction of animal engineering. His doctoral research was devoted to the development of artificial cytogene systems which could be transplanted into animal cells without requiring disruption of the nucleus or incorporation into the chromosomal system; these made it practicable to transform specific cells in the tissues of mature metazoans, avoiding all the practical and ethical problems which still surrounded work on zygotes and embryos.

Giovanni's early ambition was to apply this research to various projects in medical science. He produced in his imagination half a dozen strategies for conquering cancer, and a few exotic methods of combating the effects of aging. Had he stayed in pure research, based in a university, this was undoubtedly what he would have done, but the early years of the new millennium were a period of economic boom, when big biotechnology companies were headhunting talent with a rare ruthlessness. Giovanni never applied for a job or made any inquiry about industrial opportunities, but found potential employers begging to interview him in the comfort of his own home or any other place he cared to name. They sent beautiful and impeccably-manicured personnel officers to woo him with their tutored smiles and their talk of six-figure salaries. One or two were so desperate to net him that they seemed almost willing to bribe him with sexual favors, but they always stopped short of this ultimate tactic, much to his chagrin.

He was so fiercely dedicated to his work, and had such noble ideals, that he hesitated for a long time before selling out, but the temptations were too much for him in the end. He sold himself to the highest bidder—Cytotech, Inc.—and joined the brain drain to sunny California, being careful to leave most of his bank accounts in convenient European tax shelters so that he could be a millionaire before he was thirty. He had the impression that even the most ill-favored of millionaires could easily play the part of a Casanova, and he could hardly wait to set himself up as a big spender.

Cytotech was heavily involved in medical research, but its dynamic company president, Marmaduke Melmoth, had different plans for this most extraordinary of hirelings. He invited Giovanni to his mansion in Beverly Hills, and gave him the most fabulous meal that the young man had ever seen. Then he told Giovanni where, in his terminology, "the game was to be played."

"The future," said Melmoth, sipping his pink champagne, "is in aphrodisiacs. Cancer cures we can only sell to people with cancer. Life-expectation is great, but it isn't worth a damn unless people can enjoy extended life. To hell with better mouse-traps—what this world wants is better beaver-traps. You make me a red-hot pheromone, and I'll make you a billionaire."

Giovanni explained to Melmoth that there could be no such thing as a powerful human pheromone. Many insects, he pointed out, perceive their environment almost entirely in olfactory terms, so that it makes sense for female insects with limited periods of fertility to signal their readiness with a smelly secretion which—if produced in sufficient quantities—could draw every male insect from miles around. Humans, by contrast, make very little use of their sense of smell, and their females are unafflicted by short and vital phases of fertility which must at all costs be exploited for the continued survival of the species.

"All this I know," Melmoth assured him. "And the fact that you thought to tell me about it reveals to me that you have an attitude problem. Let me give you some advice, son. It's easy to find people who'll tell me what isn't possible and can't be done. For that I can hire morons. I hire geniuses to say 'If that won't work, what will?' Do you get my drift?"

Giovanni was genuinely impressed by this observation, though it could hardly be reckoned original. He realized that his remarks really had been symptomatic of an attitude problem, which had manifested itself all-too-powerfully in his personal life. He went to his laboratory determined to produce for Mr. Melmoth something that would stand in for the impossible pheromone, and determined to produce for himself some sexual encounters that would put him on course for a career as an authentic Casanova. It was simply, he decided, a matter of strategy and determination.

In fact, Giovanni was now in a position where he had more than a little prestige and influence. Although he was notionally starting at the bottom at Cytotech, there was no doubting that he would go far—that he was a man to be respected no matter how unlovely his appearance might be.

Thus advantaged, he had little difficulty in losing his virginity at last, with a seventeen-year-old blonde lab assistant called Helen. This was a great relief, but he was all too well aware of the fact that it represented no considerable triumph. It was a fumbling affair, throughout which he was trembling with anxiety and embarrassment; he felt that his everyday clumsiness and awkwardness, though he could leave them behind in his laboratory work, were concentrated to grotesque extremes in his sexual technique. Pretty Helen, who was not herself overburdened with experience or sophistication, uttered not a word of complaint and made no reference to his surname, but Giovanni found himself quite convinced that in the privacy of her thoughts she was crying out "Casanova! Casanova!" and laughing hysterically at the irony of it. He dared not ask her to his bed again, and tended to shun her in the workplace.

Deciding that he needed more practice, Giovanni arranged visits to whores whose telephone numbers he found scrawled on the walls of the pay phones in the main lobby, and though he avoided by this means the embarrassment of knowing that his partners knew his name, he still found it appallingly difficult to improve his performance. If anything, he thought, he was getting worse instead of better, becoming steadily more ludicrous in his own eyes.

Clearly this was what Melmoth would have called an attitude problem, but Giovanni now knew that simply calling it by that name would no more solve it than calling him Casanova had made him into an avatar of his famous namesake. Self-disgust made him give up visiting prostitutes after his third such experience, and he could not bring himself to try to resuscitate his relationship with Helen. He had little difficulty convincing himself that celibacy was to be preferred to continual humiliation.

In his work, however, he was making great strides. Taking Melmoth's advice to heart, he asked himself what would constitute, in human terms, an alternative to pheromones. The dominant human sense is sight, so the nearest human analogue of an insect pheronome is an attractive appearance, but this has so long been taken for granted that it sustains a vast cosmetics industry dedicated to helping members of the desired sex to enhance their charms. Giovanni felt that there was relatively little scope in this area for his expertise, so he turned his attention instead to the sense of touch.

He eventually decided that what was needed was something that would make the touch of the would-be seducer irresistible to the target of his (or her) affections: a love-potion of the fingertips. If he could find a psychotropic protein which could be absorbed quickly through the skin, so that the touch of the donor could become associated with subsequent waves of pleasurable sensation, then it should be fairly easy to achieve an operant conditioning of the desired one.

Giovanni brought all his artistry in protein-design to bear on the production of a psychotropic which would call forth strong feelings of euphoria, tenderness, affection and lust. This was not easy—understanding of this kind of psychochemistry was then at a very primitive level—but he was the man for the job. Having found the ideal protein, he then encoded it in the DNA of an artificial cytogene which was tailored for incorporation in subepidermal cells, whose activation would be triggered by sexual arousal. The protein itself could then be delivered to the surface of the skin via the sweat glands.

When the time came to explain this ingenious mechanism to Marmaduke Melmoth, the company president was not immediately enthused.

"Hell's bells, boy," he said. "Why not just put the stuff in bottles and let people smear it on their fingers?"

Giovanni explained that his new psychotropic protein, like the vast majority of such entities, was so awesomely delicate that it could not be kept in solution, and would rapidly denature outside the protective environment of a living cell. In any case, the whole point was that the object of desire could only obtain this particular fix from the touch of the would-be seducer. If it was to be used for conditioning, then its sources must be very carefully limited. This was not a technology for mass distribution, but something for the favored few, who must use it with the utmost discretion.

"Oh shit," said Melmoth, in disgust. "How are we going to make billions out of a product like that?"

Giovanni suggested that he sell it only to the very rich at an exorbitant price.

"If we're going to do it that way," Melmoth told him, "we're going to have to be absolutely sure that it works, and that there's not the ghost of an unfortunate side-effect. You work for customers like that, they have to get satisfaction."

Giovanni agreed that this was a vital necessity. He set up a series of exhaustive and highly secret clinical trials, and did not tell Melmoth that he had already started exploring the effects and potentials of the tissue-transformation. In the great tradition of scientific self-sacrifice, he had volunteered to be his own guinea pig.

To say that the method worked would be a feeble understatement. Giovanni found that he only had to look at an attractive girl, and conjure up in his imagination fantasies of sexual communion, to produce the special sweat that put magic at his fingertips. Once he was sufficiently worked up, the merest touch sufficed to set the psychochemical seduction in train, and it required only the simplest strategy to achieve the required conditioning. Girls learned very quickly—albeit subconsciously—to associate his touch with the most tender and exciting emotions. They quickly overcame their natural revulsion and began to think that although not conventionally attractive he was really rather fascinating.

Within three weeks of the experiment's launch four female lab assistants, two word-processing operatives, three receptionists, one industrial relations consultant and a traffic warden were deep in the throes of infatuation. Giovanni was on top of the world, and gloried in the victory of becoming a self-made Casanova. The dignity of celibacy was cast casually aside. Women were desperate now to get him into bed, and he obliged them with pleasure. He even managed to overcome some of the limitations of his awkwardness, and was soon troubled no more by premature ejaculation.

But the sense of satisfaction did not last. It took only three months more for him to become thoroughly disgusted with himself all over again. It was not so much guilt generated by the knowledge that he had cheated his partners into their passionate desire (though that did weigh somewhat upon his conscience); the real problem was that he became convinced that he was not giving them full value in return. He knew that however disappointing any particular session of love-making might be, each and every victim would continue to love him vehemently, but he thought that he could see how disappointed his paramours were, in him and in themselves. They loved him, but their love only made them unhappy. This was partly because they realized that they were all competing with one another for his attentions, but he was convinced that it was mainly because those attentions were so inherently unsatisfying.

Giovanni could now present to the world the image of a genuine Casanova. He was talked about, in wondering tones. He was envied. But in his own eyes, he remained in every sense a despicable fraud. It was not he that was beloved, but some organic goo that he had concocted in a test-tube; and the women who were its victims were condemned to the desperations of jealousy, the disappointments of third-rate sex, and the miseries of helplessness. Giovanni had not the stomach to be a wholesale heartbreaker; he was too familiar with misery and desperation to take pleasure from inflicting it on others—not, at any rate, on women that he liked and admired.

By the time the royalties began to roll in, when Melmoth's discreet marketing of the discovery to the world's richest men began to pay dividends, Giovanni was again deep in depression and cynicism. Others, he felt sure, would be able to exploit his invention to the full, as the means to illimitable pleasure, but not he. Casanova the fool had simply confirmed his own wretchedness. His cup of bitterness overflowed.

It was, as ever, Marmaduke Melmoth who brought it home to him that he was still suffering from an attitude problem.

"Look, Joe," said Melmoth. "We got a few little problems. Nothing you can't sort out, I'm sure, but it's kinda necessary to keep the customers happy and the cash coming in. The way we're playing this we have a restricted market, and a lot of the guys are getting on a bit. It's all very well to offer them a way of getting the slots in the sack, but what they really need is something to get the peg into the slot. You ever hear of this stuff called Spanish fly?"

Giovanni explained that Cantharides was a beetle rather than a fly; that it was a powerful poison; and that it probably wasn't terribly satisfying to have a painfully rigid and itchy erection for hours on end.

"So make something better," said Melmoth, with that mastery of the art of delegation which had made him rich.

Giovanni gave the matter some consideration, and decided that it was probably feasible to devise a biochemical mechanism which would make it possible for a man to win conscious control over his erections: to produce them at will, sustain them as long as might be required, and generate orgasms in any desired quantity. This would require a couple of new hormones which Mother Nature had not thought to provide, a secondary system of trigger hormones for feedback control, and a cytogene for transforming the cells of the pituitary gland. Even when the biochemistry was in place, people would have to learn to use the new system, and that would require a training program, perhaps with computer-assisted biofeedback backup, but it could be done.

He set to work, patiently bringing his new dreamchild to perfection.

Naturally, he had to test the system to make sure it was worth going ahead with clinical trials. Once the genetic transplants had taken, he spent a couple of hours a night in solitary practice. It took him only a week to gain complete conscious control of his new abilities, but he had started with the advantage of understanding, so he mapped out a training program for the punters that would take a fortnight.

Once again, he was filled with optimism with respect to his own personal problems. No longer would he have to worry about flaws in his technique; he could now be confident that any girl who was caused to fall in love with him would receive full measure of sexual satisfaction in return. Now, he was in a much better position to emulate his famous namesake.

But Giovanni was no longer a callow youth, and his optimism about the future was not based entirely on his biotechnological augmentation. He had undergone a more dramatic change of attitude, and had decided that the Casanova he needed to copy was not the ancient Giovanni but his father Marcantonio. He had decided that the answer lay in monogamy, and he wanted to get married. He was now in his mid-thirties, and it seemed to him that what he needed was a partner of his own age: a mature and level-headed woman who could bring order and stability into his life.

These arguments led him to fall in love with his accountant, a thirty-three-year-old divorcée named Denise. He had ample opportunity to make the fingertip contacts necessary to make her besotted with him, because his fortune was steadily increasing and there were always new opportunities in tax avoidance for them to discuss over dinner. Giovanni orchestrated the whole affair very carefully and—he thought—smoothly, graciously allowing Denise the pleasure of seducing him on their third real date. He still felt clumsy and a little anxious, but she seemed quite delighted with his powers of endurance.

His parents were glad when he told them the news. His father cried with delight at the thought that the name of Casanova would now be transmitted to a further generation, and his mother (who believed that getting married was a kind of certificate of belonging to the human race) was euphorically sentimental for months.

Denise gave up work when she became pregnant, mere weeks after the honeymoon, abandoning to other financial wizards the job of distributing and protecting the spring tide of cash which began to pour into Giovanni's bank accounts as his new discovery was discreetly marketed by the ingenious Melmoth.

Giovanni loved Denise very much, and became more and more devoted to her as the months of her pregnancy elapsed. When she gave birth to a baby girl—named Jennifer after his mother—he felt that he had discovered heaven on earth.

Unfortunately, this peak in his experience was soon passed. Denise got post-natal depression, and began to find her energetic sex life something of a bore. She was still hooked, unknowingly, on the produce of Giovanni's fingertips, but her emotional responses became perversely confused, and her feelings of love and affection generated floods of miserable tears.

Giovanni was overwrought, and knew not what to do. He was slowly consumed by a new wave of guilt. Whatever was the matter, he was responsible for it. He had made Denise love him, and had avoided feeling like a cheat only because he was convinced that she was reaping all the rewards that she could possibly have attained from a love that grew spontaneously in her heart. Now things were going wrong, he saw himself as her betrayer and her destroyer.

When Giovanni became anguished and miserable, Denise blamed herself. She became even more confused and even more desperate in her confusion. The unhappy couple fed one another's despair, and became wretched together. This intolerable situation led inexorably toward the one awful mistake that Giovanni was bound eventually to make.

He told her everything.

From every possible point of view, this was a disastrous move. When she heard how he had tied her finest and most intimate feelings to chemical puppet-strings her love for him underwent a purely psychosomatic transformation into bitter and resentful hatred. She left him forthwith, taking the infant Jenny with her, and sued for divorce. She also filed a suit demanding thirty million dollars compensation for his biochemical interference with her affections. In so doing, of course, she made headline news of the enterprises which Marmaduke Melmoth had kept so carefully secret, and released a tempest of controversy.

The impact of this news can easily be imagined. The world of the 2010s was supposedly one in which the women of the overdeveloped countries had won complete equality with their menfolk. The feminists of the day looked back with satisfaction at centuries of fierce fighting against legal and attitudinal discrimination; their heroines had battled successfully against sexism in the workplace, sexism in education, sexism in the language and sexism in the psyche. Though progress had brought them to the brink of their particular Millennium, they still had a heightened consciousness of the difficulties which had beset their quest, and a hair-trigger paranoia about any threat to their achievements. The discovery that for nearly twenty years the world's richest men had been covertly buying biotechnologies specifically designed for the manipulation and sexual oppression of womankind constituted a scandal such as the world of sexual politics had never known.

Giovanni Casanova, who had so far lived his life in secure obscurity, cosily content with his unsung genius, found himself suddenly notorious. His name—that hideous curse of a name—suddenly became the progenitor of jokes and gibes displayed in screeching headlines, broadcast to every corner of the globe, found as frequently in news bulletins as tawdry comedy shows. Overnight, the new Casanova became a modern folk-devil: the man who had put the cause of sexual emancipation back three hundred years.

The divorce broke his mother's heart, and her sufferings were compounded when Marcantonio Casanova died suddenly of heart failure. She hinted to Giovanni in a reckless moment that his father had died of shame, and Giovanni took this so much to heart that he seriously contemplated suicide.

Denise, the victim of Giovanni's obscene machinations, achieved a temporary sainthood in the eyes of the women of the world. Melmoth, who had played Mephistopheles to Giovanni's Faust, was demonized alongside him. Thousands of women filed copycat lawsuits against their rich paramours, against Giovanni, and against Cytotech. Giovanni got sacks of hate mail from tens of thousands of women who believed (usually without any foundation in fact) that his magic had been used to steal their souls.

As storms usually do, though, this hurricane of abuse soon began to lose its fury. Marmaduke Melmoth began to use his many resources to tell the world that the real issue was simply a little attitude problem.

Melmoth was able to point out that there was nothing inherently sexist about Giovanni's first discovery. He was able to prove that he had several female clients, who had been happily using the seductive sweat to attract young men. He argued—with some justice—that the cosmetics industry had for centuries been offering men and women methods of enhancing their sexual attractiveness, and that there had always been a powerful demand for aphrodisiacs. Giovanni's only "crime," he suggested, was to have produced an aphrodisiac which worked, and which was absolutely safe, to replace thousands of products of fake witchcraft and medical quackery which were at best useless and at worst harmful. He argued that although Giovanni's second discovery was, indeed, applicable only to male physiology, its utility and its benefits were by no means confined to the male sex.

This rhetoric was backed up by some bold promises, which saved Cytotech's image and turned all the publicity to the company's advantage. Melmoth guaranteed that Giovanni's first discovery would now become much cheaper, so that the tissue-transformation would be available even to those of moderate means, and to men and women equally. He also announced that Giovanni had already begun to work on an entire spectrum of new artificial hormones, which would give to women as well as to men vast new opportunities in the conscious generation and control of bodily pleasure.

These promises quickly displaced the scandal from the headlines. Cytotech's publicity machine did such a comprehensive job of image-building that Giovanni became a hero instead of a folk-devil. The moral panic died, the lawsuits collapsed, and the hate mail dried up. Denise got her divorce, though, and custody of little Jenny. She did not get her thirty million dollars compensation, but she was awarded sufficient alimony to keep her in relative luxury for the rest of her life. Giovanni was awarded the Nobel Prize for Biochemistry, but this did little to soothe his disappointment even though it helped his mother to recover from her broken heart and be proud of him again.

Giovanni launched himself obsessively into the work required to make good on Melmoth's promises. He became a virtual recluse, putting in such long hours at the laboratory that his staff and co-workers began to fear for his health and sanity. As he neared forty his mental faculties were in decline, but the increase in his knowledge and wisdom offset the loss of mental agility, and it is arguable that it was in this phase of his career that his genius was most powerful and most fertile. He did indeed develop a new spectrum of hormones and enkephalins, which in combination gave people who underwent the relevant tissue-transformations far greater conscious control over the physiology of pleasure. As recipients gradually learned what they could do with their new biochemistry, and mastered its arts and skills, they became able to induce in themselves—without any necessary assistance at all—orgasms and kindred sensations more thrilling, more blissful and more luxurious than the poor human nature crudely hewn by the hackwork of natural selection had ever provided to anyone.

Giovanni created, almost single-handed, a vast new panorama of masturbatory enterprise.

For once, Giovanni's progress was the object of constant attention and constant debate. Cynics claimed that his work was hateful, because it would utterly destroy romance, devalue human feelings, obliterate sincere affection, and mechanize ecstasy. Critics argued that the value and mystique of sexual relationships would be fatally compromised by his transformations. Pessimists prophesied that if his new projects were to be brought to a successful conclusion, sexual intercourse might become a thing of the past, displaced from the arena of human experience by voluptuous self-abuse. Fortunately, these pessimists were unable to argue that this might lead to the end of the human race, because discoveries made by other biotechnologists had permitted the development of artificial wombs more efficient than real ones; sexual intercourse was no longer necessary for reproduction, which could be managed more competently in vitro. The cynics and the pessimists were therefore disregarded by the majority, who were hungry for joy, and eager to enter a promised land of illimitable delight.

As always, Giovanni was the first to try out his new discoveries; the pioneer spirit which forced him to seek out new solutions to his personal troubles was as strong as ever, and the prospect of combining celibacy with ecstasy appealed very much to his eremitic frame of mind.

In the early days of his experimentation, while he was still exploring the potential of his new hormonal instruments of self-control, he was rather pleased with the ways in which he could evoke rapture to illuminate his loneliness, but he quickly realized that this was no easy answer to his problems. Eight hundred thousand years of masturbation had not sufficed to blunt the human race's appetite for sexual intercourse, and Giovanni quickly found that the reason for this failure had nothing to do with the quality of the sensations produced. The cynics and pessimists were quite wrong; sexual intercourse could not and never would be made redundant by any mere enhancement of onanistic gratifications. Sex was more than pleasure; it was closeness, intimate involvement with another, empathy, compassion, and an outflowing of good feeling which needed a recipient. Giovanni had found in the brief happiness of his marriage that sex was, in all the complex literal and metaphorical senses of the phrase, making love. However wonderful his new biochemical systems were, they were not doing that, and were no substitute for it.

So Giovanni ceased to live as a recluse. He came back into the social world, with his attitude adjusted yet again, determined to make new relationships. After all, he still had the magic at his fingertips—or so he thought. He looked around; found a gray-eyed journalist named Greta, a Junoesque plant physiologist named Jacqueline, and a sweetly-smiling insurance salesperson named Morella, and went to work with his seductive touch.

Alas, the world had changed while he had lived apart from it. None of the three women yielded to his advances. It was not that he had lost his magic touch, but that Cytotech's marketing had given it to far too many others. When the relevant tissue-transformations had been the secret advantage of a favored few, they had used it with care and discretion, but now that aphrodisiac sweat was commonplace, any reasonably attractive woman was likely to encounter it several times a week. Because women were continually sated with the feelings that it evoked they could no longer be conditioned to associate the sensation with the touch of a particular person. Greta, Jacqueline and Morella were quite conscious of what was happening when he touched them, and though they thanked him for the compliment, each one was utterly unimpressed.

Giovanni realized the promiscuity was fast destroying the aphrodisiac value of his first discovery. His quick mind made him sensitive to all kinds of possibilities that might be opened up by the more general release of this particular invention, and he began to look in the news for evidence of social change.

The logic of the situation was quite clear to him. As users found their seductive touch less effective, they would tend to use it more and more frequently, thus spreading satiation even further and destroying all prospect of the desired result. In addition, people would no longer use the device simply for the purpose of sexual conquest. Many men and women would be taken by the ambition to make everybody love them, in the hope of securing thereby the social and economic success that the original purchasers of the technology had already had. In consequence, the world would suffer from a positive epidemic of good feeling. This plague would not set the entire world to making love, but it might set the entire world to making friends. The most unlikely people might soon be seen to be relaxing into the comfort of infinite benevolence.

Giovanni monitored the headlines very carefully, and realized before it became generally known that he had wrought a more profound change in human affairs than he had intended or supposed.

Wars were gradually petering out.

Terrorism was on the decline.

Violent crime was becoming steadily rarer.

Oddly enough, these trends passed largely unnoticed by the world at large. The majority of people did not begin to wake up to the significance of it all until a much-advertised contest to settle the heavyweight boxing championship of the world was stopped in the third round when the weeping combatants realised that they could not bear to throw another punch, and left the ring together with their arms around one another's shoulders.

Because of these upheavals in the world's routines, the clinical trials of Giovanni's new hormones and enkephalins attracted a little less attention than they might have, but their outstanding success was still a matter for widespread celebration. In 2036 Giovanni was awarded a Nobel Peace Prize to set beside his earlier award, and there was some discussion about the possibility of making it the last prize of its kind, given that the world no longer seemed to require peacemakers. Giovanni became once again the darling of the world's media. He was billed as a modern Prometheus, sometimes even as a modern Dionysus, who had brought into the world of men a divine fire more precious than any vulgar power source.

Giovanni was still embarrassed by these periodic waves of media exposure. He still felt very self-conscious about his physical appearance, and every time he saw his own picture on newsscreen or in a videomag he blushed with the thought that half a billion viewers were probably saying to themselves: "He doesn't look like a Casanova!" He was probably being oversensitive; nowadays it was his face and his achievements which were now called to the mind of the man in the street by the mention of the name Casanova; his ancient namesake had been eclipsed in the public consciousness.

In addition, Giovanni no longer appeared to the unbiased eye to be as unprepossessing as he once had seemed. He was now graciously bald, and his bare pate was by no means as freakish as the tangled black hair that once had sprouted there. He still wore spectacles for his myopia, but corneal surgery had corrected his astigmatism, and his eyes now looked kind and soft behind the lenses, not at all distorted. His complexion was still poor, but his skin had been roughened and toughened by age and exposure to the elements, and its appearance was no longer offensive. His paleness and frailness could now be seen as appealing rather than appalling.

He was startled the first time that he realized that a woman was using his own aphrodisiac technology upon him, and quickly jumped to the conclusion that she must be one of those people who used it on everyone, but he gradually became accustomed to the idea that he really was admired and desired. In time, the secretion of aphrodisiac sweat became subject to a new etiquette, whereby indiscriminate use was held to be in bad taste, and also to be unnecessary as it could now be taken for granted that everyone could love one another even without its aid.

Politeness came to demand that a sophisticated and civilized person would use the Casanova secretion occasionally and discreetly, to signal a delicate expression of erotic interest with no offense to be taken if there was no response. As this new code of behavior evolved, Giovanni was surprised to find himself a frequent target for seduction, and for a while he revelled in sexual success. Many of the younger women, of course, were interested primarily in his wealth and status, but he did not mind that—he could, after all, claim responsibility for his status and wealth, which he had won by effort.

Anyway, he loved them all. He loved everybody, and everybody loved him.

It was that kind of a world, now.

In this way, Giovanni Casanova succeeded at last in adapting to his name. He lived up to the reputation of his august namesake for a year or two, and then decided that the attractions of the lifestyle were overrated. He gladdened his mother's heart by marrying again, and this time he chose a woman who was very like the earliest memories which he had of his mother. His new bride was named Janine. She had been born in Manchester, and she was embarked on a career in cosmetic cytogenics (which was the nearest thing to hairdressing that the world of 2036 could offer). She was much younger than Giovanni, but did not mind the age difference in the least.

Giovanni and Janine favored one another constantly with the most delicate psychochemical strokings, and learned to play the most beautiful duets with all the ingenious hormonal instruments of Giovanni's invention. But they also had a special feeling for one another—and eventually for their children—which went beyond mere chemistry and physiology: an affection which was entirely a triumph of the will. This was a treasure which, they both believed, could never have come out of one of Giovanni's test tubes.

With all these advantages, they were able to live happily ever after.

And so was everybody else.

REEF

Paul McAuley

❀

Paul McAuley (for biographical information see the story note on his "Gene Wars," above) was in the late 1980s the most important hard SF writer to emerge from the U.K. since Ian Watson in the 1970s. At a time when the influence of Ballard, Moorcock, and Aldiss was a dominating force in U.K. SF, McAuley appeared to be writing in the earlier tradition of Arthur C. Clarke, in *Four Hundred Billion Stars* (1987) and others of his early works. But he was indeed writing also in reference to cyberpunk and to the political sensibilities of the left. His work later moved into many forms of SF. Yet his early work and his public stance marked him as an ally of hard SF, and he has continued to write important hard SF stories and to be a leading figure in U.K. SF circles.

"Reef" is an excellent hard SF story from the ambitious illustrated hard SF anthology, *Skylife*, edited by Gregory Benford and George Zebrowski (about visions of life in space and on other planets). This story is an instant classic of hard SF. It is dense with wonderful technological and scientific images, but also fast paced, and sufficiently rounded in characterization that many readers will remember the unlikely heroine for a long time.

Margaret Henderson Wu was riding a proxy by telepresence deep inside Tigris Rift when Dzu Sho summoned her. The others in her crew had given up one by one and only she was left, descending slowly between rosy, smoothly rippled cliffs scarcely a hundred meters apart. These were pavements of the commonest vacuum organism, mosaics made of hundreds of different strains of the same species. Here and there bright red whips stuck out from the pavement; a commensal species that deposited iron sulphate crystals within its integument. The pavement seemed to stretch endlessly below her. No probe or proxy had yet reached the bottom of Tigris Rift, still more than thirty kilometers away. Microscopic flecks of sulfur-iron complexes, sloughed cells and excreted globules of carbon compounds and other volatiles formed a kind of smog or snow, and the vacuum organisms deposited nodes and intricate lattices of reduced metals that, by some trick of superconductivity, produced a broad-band electromagnetic resonance that pulsed like a giant's slow heartbeat.

All this futzed the telepresence link between operators and their proxies. One moment Margaret was experiencing the three-hundred-twenty-degree panorama of the little proxy's microwave radar, the perpetual tug of vacuum on its mantle, the tang of extreme cold, a mere thirty degrees above absolute zero, the complex taste of the vacuum smog (burnt sugar, hot rubber, tar), the minute squirts of hydrogen from the folds of the proxy's puckered nozzle as it maintained its orientation relative to the cliff face during its descent, with its tentacles retracted in a tight ball around the relay piton. The next, she was back in her cradled body in warm blackness, phosphenes floating in her vision and white noise in her ears while the transmitter searched for a viable waveband, locked on and—*pow*—she was back, falling past rippled pink pavement.

The alarm went off, flashing an array of white stars over the panorama. Her number two, Srin Kerenyi, said in her ear, "You're wanted, boss."

Margaret killed the alarm and the audio feed. She was already a kilometer below the previous benchmark and she wanted to get as deep as possible before she implanted the telemetry relay. She swiveled the proxy on its long axis, increased the amplitude of the microwave radar. Far below were intimations of swells and bumps jutting from the plane of the cliff face, textured mounds like brain coral, randomly orientated chimneys. And something else, clouds of organic matter perhaps—

The alarm again. Srin had overridden the cut-out.

Margaret swore and dove at the cliff, unfurling the proxy's tentacles and jamming the piton into pinkness rough with black papillae, like a giant's tongue quick-frozen against the ice. The piton's spikes fired automatically. Recoil sent the little proxy tumbling over its long axis until it reflexively stabilized itself with judicious squirts of gas. The link rastered, came back, cut out completely. Margaret hit the switch that turned the tank into a chair; the mask lifted away from her face.

Srin Kerenyi was standing in front of her. "Dzu Sho wants to talk with you, boss. Right now."

The job had been offered as a sealed contract. Science crews had been informed of the precise nature of their tasks only when the habitat was underway. But it was good basic pay with the promise of fat bonuses on completion: when she had won the survey contract Margaret Henderson Wu had brought with her most of the crew from her previous job, and had nursed a small hope that this would be a change in her family's luck.

The *Ganapati* was a new habitat founded by an alliance of two of the Commonwealth's oldest patrician families. It was of standard construction, a basaltic asteroid cored by a gigawatt X-ray laser and spun up by vented rock vapor to give 0.2 gee on the inner surface of its hollowed interior, factories and big reaction motors dug into the stern. With its AIs rented out for information crunching and its refineries synthesizing exotic plastics from cane sugar biomass and gengeneered oilseed rape precursors, the new habitat had enough income to maintain the interest on its construction loan from the Commonwealth Bourse, but not enough to attract new citizens and workers. It was still not completely fitted out, had less than a third of its optimal population.

Its Star Chamber, young and cocky and eager to win independence from their families, had taken a big gamble. They were chasing a legend.

Eighty years ago, an experiment in accelerated evolution of chemoautotrophic vacuum organisms had been set up on a planetoid in the outer edge of the Kuiper Belt. The experiment had been run by a shell company registered on Ganymede but covertly owned by the Democratic Union of China. In those days, companies and governments of Earth had not been allowed to operate in the Kuiper Belt, which had been claimed and ferociously defended by outer system cartels. That hegemony had ended in the Quiet War, but the Quiet War had also destroyed all records of the experiment; even the Democratic Union of China had disappeared, absorbed into the Pacific Community.

There were over fifty thousand objects with diameters greater than a hundred kilometers in the Kuiper Belt, and a billion more much smaller, the plane of their orbits stretching beyond those of Neptune and Pluto. The experimental planetoid,

Enki, named for one of the Babylonian gods of creation, had been lost among them. It had become a legend, like the Children's Habitat, or the ghost comet, or the pirate ship crewed by the reanimated dead, or the worker's paradise of Fiddler's Green.

And then, forty-five years after the end of the Quiet War, a data miner recovered enough information to reconstruct Enki's eccentric orbit. She sold it to the *Ganapati*. The habitat bought time on the Uranus deep space telescopic array and confirmed that the planetoid was where it was supposed to be, currently more than seven thousand million kilometers from the Sun.

Nothing more was known. The experiment might have failed almost as soon as it begun, but potentially it might win the *Ganapati* platinum-rated credit on the Bourse. Margaret and the rest of the science crews would, of course, receive only their fees and bonuses, less deductions for air and food and water taxes, and anything they bought with scrip in the habitat's stores; the indentured workers would not even get that. Like every habitat in the Commonwealth, the *Ganapati* was structured like an ancient Greek Republic, ruled by share-holding citizens who lived in the landscaped parklands of the inner surface, and run by indentured and contract workers who were housed in the undercroft of malls and barracks tunnelled into the *Ganapati's* rocky skin.

On the long voyage out, the science crews had been on minimal pay, far lower than that of the unskilled techs who worked the farms and refineries, and the servants who maintained the citizens' households. There were food shortages because so much biomass was being used to make exportable biochemicals; any foodstuffs other than basic rations were expensive, and prices were carefully manipulated by the habitat's Star Chamber. When the *Ganapati* reached Enki and the contracts of the science crews were activated, food prices had increased accordingly. Techs and household servants suddenly found themselves unable to afford anything other than dole yeast. Resentment bubbled over into skirmishes and knife-fights, and a small riot the White Mice, the undercroft's police, subdued with gas. Margaret had to take time off to bail out several of her crew, had given them an angry lecture about threatening everyone's bonuses.

"We got to defend our honor," one of the men said.

"Don't be a fool," Margaret told him. "The citizens play workers against science crews to keep both sides in their places, and still turn a good profit from increases in food prices. Just be glad you can afford the good stuff now, and keep out of trouble."

"They were calling you names, boss," the man said. "On account you're—"

Margaret stared him down. She was standing on a chair, but even so she was a good head shorter than the gangling outers. She said, "I'll fight my own fights. I always have. Just think of your bonuses and keep quiet. It will be worth it. I promise you."

And it was worth it, because of the discovery of the reef.

At some time in the deep past, Enki had suffered an impact that had remelted it and split it into two big pieces and thousands of fragments. One lone fragment still orbited Enki, a tiny moonlet where the AI that had controlled the experiment had been installed; the others had been drawn together again by their feeble gravity fields, but had cooled before coalescence had been completed, leaving a vast deep chasm, Tigris Rift, at the lumpy equator.

Margaret's crew had discovered that the vacuum organisms had proliferated wildly in the deepest part of the Rift, deriving energy by oxidation of elemental sulfur and ferrous iron, converting carbonaceous material into useful organic chemicals. There were crusts and sheets, things like thin scarves folded into fragile vases and chimneys, organ pipe clusters, whips, delicate fretted laces. Some fed on others, one crust slowly overgrowing and devouring another. Others appeared to be parasites, sending complex veins ramifying through the thalli of their victims. Water-mining organisms recruited sulfur oxidizers, trading precious water for energy and forming warty outgrowths like stromatolites. Some were more than a hundred meters across, surely the largest prokaryotic colonies in the known Solar System.

All this variety, and after only eighty years of accelerated evolution! Wild beauty won from the cold and the dark. The potential to feed billions. The science crews would get their bonuses, all right; the citizens would become billionaires.

Margaret spent all her spare time investigating the reef by proxy, pushed her crew hard to overcome the problems of penetrating the depths of the Rift. Although she would not admit it even to herself, she had fallen in love with the reef. She would gladly have explored it in person, but as in most habitats the *Ganapati*'s citizens did not like their workers going where they themselves would not.

Clearly, the experiment had far exceeded its parameters, but no one knew why. The AI that had overseen the experiment had shut down thirty years ago. There was still heat in its crude proton beam fission pile, but it had been overgrown by the very organisms it had manipulated.

Its task had been simple. Colonies of a dozen species of slow growing chemoautotrophs had been introduced into a part of the Rift rich with sulfur and ferrous iron. Thousands of random mutations had been induced. Most colonies had died, and those few which had thrived had been sampled, mutated, and reintroduced in a cycle repeated every hundred days.

But the AI had selected only for fast growth, not for adaptive radiation, and the science crews held heated seminars about the possible cause of the unexpected richness of the reef's biota. Very few believed that it was simply a result of accelerated evolution. Many terrestrial bacteria divided every twenty minutes in favorable conditions, and certain species were known to have evolved from being resistant to an antibiotic to becoming obligately dependent upon it as a food source in less than five days, or only three hundred and sixty generations, but that was merely a biochemical adaptation. The fastest division rate of the vacuum organisms in the Rift was less than once a day, and while that still meant more than thirty thousand generations had passed since the reef had been seeded, half a million years in human terms, the evolutionary radiation in the reef was the equivalent of Neanderthal Man evolving to fill every mammalian niche from bats to whales.

Margaret's survey crew had explored and sampled the reef for more than thirty days. Cluster analysis suggested that they had identified less than ten percent of the species that had formed from the original seed population. And now deep radar suggested that there were changes in the unexplored regions in the deepest part of Tigris Rift, which the proxies had not yet been able to reach.

Margaret had pointed this out at the last seminar. "We're making hypotheses on incomplete information. We don't know everything that's out there. Sampling suggests that complexity increases away from the surface. There could be thousands more species in the deep part of the Rift."

At the back of the room, Opie Kindred, the head of the genetics crew, said languidly, "We don't need to know everything. That's not what we're paid for. We've already found several species that perform better than present commercial cultures. The *Ganapati* can make money from them and we'll get full bonuses. Who cares how they got there?"

Arn Nivedta, the chief of the biochemist crew, said, "We're all scientists here. We prove our worth by finding out how things work. Are your mysterious experiments no more than growth tests, Opie? If so, I'm disappointed."

The genetics crew had set up an experimental station on the surface of the *Ganapati*, off limits to everyone else.

Opie smiled. "I'm not answerable to you."

This was greeted with shouts and jeers. The science crews were tired and on edge, and the room was hot and poorly ventilated.

"Information should be free," Margaret said. "We all work toward the same end. Or are you hoping for extra bonuses, Opie?"

There was a murmur in the room. It was a tradition that all bonuses were pooled and shared out between the various science crews at the end of a mission.

Opie Kindred was a clever, successful man, yet somehow soured, as if the world was a continual disappointment. He rode his team hard, was quick to find failure in others. Margaret was a natural target for his scorn, a squat muscle-bound unedited dwarf from Earth who had to take drugs to survive in micro-gravity, who grew hair in all sorts of unlikely places. He stared at her with disdain and said, "I'm surprised at the tone of this briefing, Dr. Wu. Wild speculations built on nothing at all. I have sat here for an hour and heard nothing useful. We are paid to get results, not generate hypotheses. All we hear from your crew is excuses when what we want are samples. It seems simple enough to me. If something is upsetting your proxies, then you should use robots. Or send people in and handpick samples. I've worked my way through almost all you've obtained. I need more material, especially in light of my latest findings."

"Robots need transmission relays too," Srin Kerenyi pointed out.

Orly Higgins said, "If you ride them, to be sure. But I don't see the need for human control. It is a simple enough task to program them to go down, pick up samples, return." She was the leader of the crew that had unpicked the AI's corrupted code, and was an acolyte of Opie Kindred.

"The proxies failed whether or not they were remotely controlled," Margaret said, "and on their own they are as smart as any robot. I'd love to go down there myself, but the Star Chamber has forbidden it for the usual reasons. They're scared we'll get up to something if we go where they can't watch us."

"Careful, boss," Srin Kerenyi whispered. "The White Mice are bound to be monitoring this."

"I don't care," Margaret said. "I'm through with trying polite requests. We need to get down there, Srin."

"Sure, boss. But getting arrested for sedition isn't the way."

"There's some interesting stuff in the upper levels," Arn Nivedta said. "Stuff with huge commercial potential, as you pointed out, Opie."

Murmurs of agreement throughout the crowded room. The reef could make the *Ganapati* the richest habitat in the Outer System, where expansion was limited by the availability of fixed carbon. Even a modest-sized comet nucleus, ten kilometers in diameter, say, and salted with only one hundredth of one percent carbonaceous material, contained fifty million tons of carbon, mostly as methane and carbon monoxide ice, with a surface dusting of tarry long chain hydrocarbons. The problem was that most vacuum organisms converted simple carbon compounds into organic matter using the energy of sunlight captured by a variety of photosynthetic pigments, and so could only grow on the surfaces of planetoids. No one had yet developed vacuum organisms that, using other sources of energy, could efficiently mine planetoid interiors, but that was what accelerated evolution appeared to have produced in the reef. It could enable exploitation of the entire volume of objects in the Kuiper Belt, and beyond, in the distant Oort Cloud. It was a discovery of incalculable worth.

Arn Nivedta waited for silence, and added, "Of course; we can't know what the commercial potential is until the reef species have been fully tested. What about it, Opie?"

"We have our own ideas about commercial potential," Opie Kindred said. "I think you'll find that we hold the key to success here."

Boos and catcalls at this from both the biochemists and the survey crew. The room was polarizing. Margaret saw one of her crew unsheathe a sharpened screwdriver, and she caught the man's hand and squeezed it until he cried out. "Let it ride," she told him. "Remember that we're scientists."

"We hear of indications of more diversity in the depths, but we can't seem to get there. One might suspect," Opie said, his thin upper lip lifting in a supercilious curl, "sabotage."

"The proxies are working well in the upper part of the Rift," Margaret said, "and we are doing all we can to get them operative further down."

"Let's hope so," Opie Kindred said. He stood, and around him his crew stood too. "I'm going back to work, and so should all of you. Especially you, Dr. Wu. Perhaps you should be attending to your proxies instead of planning useless expeditions."

And so the seminar broke up in an uproar, with nothing productive coming from it and lines of enmity drawn through the community of scientists.

"Opie is scheming to come out of this on top," Arn Nivedta said to Margaret afterward. He was a friendly, enthusiastic man, tall even for an outer, and as skinny as a rail. He stooped in Margaret's presence, trying to reduce the extraordinary difference between their heights. He said, "He wants desperately to become a citizen, and so he thinks like one."

"Well, my god, we all want to be citizens," Margaret said. "Who wants to live like this?"

She gestured, meaning the crowded bar, its rock walls and low ceiling, harsh lights and the stink of spilled beer and too many people in close proximity. Her parents had been citizens, once upon a time. Before their run of bad luck. It was not that she wanted those palmy days back—she could scarcely remember them—but she wanted more than this.

She said, "The citizens sleep between silk sheets and eat real meat and play their stupid games, and we have to do their work on restricted budgets. The reef is the discovery of the century, Arn, but God forbid that the citizens should begin to exert themselves. We do the work, they fuck in rose petals and get the glory."

Arn laughed at this.

"Well, it's true!"

"It's true we have not been as successful as we might like," Arn said mournfully.

Margaret said reflectively, "Opie's a bastard, but he's smart, too. He picked just the right moment to point the finger at me."

Loss of proxies was soaring exponentially, and the proxy farms of the *Ganapati* were reaching a critical point. Once losses exceeded reproduction, the scale of exploration would have to be drastically curtailed, or the seed stock would have to be pressed into service, a gamble the *Ganapati* could not afford to take.

And then, the day after the disastrous seminar, Margaret was pulled back from her latest survey to account for herself in front of the chairman of the *Ganapati*'s Star Chamber.

* * *

"We are not happy with the progress of your survey, Dr. Wu," Dzu Sho said. "You promise much, but deliver little."

Margaret shot a glance at Opie Kindred, and he smiled at her. He was immaculately dressed in gold-trimmed white tunic and white leggings. His scalp was oiled and his manicured fingernails were painted with something that split light into rainbows. Margaret, fresh from the tank, wore loose, grubby work grays. There was sticky electrolyte paste on her arms and legs and shaven scalp, the reek of sour sweat under her breasts and in her armpits.

She contained her anger and said, "I have submitted daily reports on the problems we encountered. Progress is slow but sure. I have just established a relay point a full kilometer below the previous datum point."

Dzu Sho waved this away. He lounged in a blue gel chair, quite naked, as smoothly fat as a seal. He had a round, hairless head and pinched features, like a thumbprint on an egg. The habitat's lawyer sat behind him, a young woman neat and anonymous in a gray tunic suit. Margaret, Opie Kindred and Arn Nivedta sat on low stools, supplicants to Dzu Sho's authority. Behind them, half a dozen servants stood at the edge of the grassy space.

This was in an arbor of figs, ivy, bamboo and fast-growing banyan at the edge of Sho's estate. Residential parkland curved above, a patchwork of spindly, newly planted woods and meadows and gardens. Flyers were out, triangular rigs in primary colors pirouetting around the weightless axis. Directly above, mammoths the size of large dogs grazed an upside-down emerald green field. The parkland stretched away to the ring lake and its slosh barrier, three kilometers in diameter, and the huge farms that dominated the inner surface of the habitat. Fields of lentils, wheat, cane fruits, tomatoes, rice and exotic vegetables for the tables of the citizens, and fields and fields and fields of sugar cane and oilseed rape for the biochemical industry and the yeast tanks.

Dzu Sho said, "Despite the poor progress of the survey crew, we have what we need, thanks to the work of Dr. Kindred. This is what we will discuss."

Margaret glanced at Arn, who shrugged. Opie Kindred's smile deepened. He said, "My crew has established why there is so much diversity here. The vacuum organisms have invented sex."

"We know they have sex," Arn said. "How else could they evolve?"

His own crew had shown that the vacuum organisms could exchange genetic material through pili, microscopic hollow tubes grown between cells or hyphal strands. It was analogous to the way in which genes for antibiotic resistance spread through populations of terrestrial bacteria.

"I do not mean genetic exchange, but genetic recombination," Opie Kindred said. "I will explain."

The glade filled with flat plates of color as the geneticist conjured charts and diagrams and pictures from his slate. Despite her anger, Margaret quickly immersed herself in the flows of data, racing ahead of Opie Kindred's clipped explanations.

It was not normal sexual reproduction. There was no differentiation into male or female, or even into complementary mating strains. Instead, it was mediated by a species that aggressively colonized the thalli of others. Margaret had already seen it many times, but until now she had thought that it was merely a parasite. Instead, as Opie Kindred put it, it was more like a vampire.

A shuffle of pictures, movies patched from hundreds of hours of material collected by roving proxies. Here was a colony of the black crustose species found all through the explored regions of the Rift. Time speeded up. The crustose colony elongated its ragged perimeter in pulsing spurts. As it grew, it exfoliated microscopic particles. Margaret's viewpoint spiraled into a close-up of one of the exfoliations, a few cells wrapped in nutrient-storing strands.

Millions of these little packages floated through the vacuum. If one landed on a host thallus, it injected its genetic payload into the host cells. The view dropped inside one such cell. A complex of carbohydrate and protein strands webbed the interior like intricately packed spiderwebs. Part of the striated cell wall drew apart and a packet of DNA coated in hydrated globulins and enzymes burst inward. The packet contained the genomes of both the parasite and its previous victim. It latched onto protein strands and crept along on ratchetting microtubule claws until it fused with the cell's own circlet of DNA.

The parasite possessed an enzyme that snipped strands of genetic material at random lengths. These recombined, forming chimeric cells that contained genetic information from both sets of victims, with the predator species' genome embedded among the native genes like an interpenetrating text.

The process repeated itself in flurries of coiling and uncoiling DNA strands as the chimeric cells replicated. It was a crude, random process. Most contained incomplete or noncomplementary copies of the genomes and were unable to function, or contained so many copies than transcription was halting and imperfect. But a few out of every thousand were viable, and a small percentage of those were more vigorous than either of their parents. They grew from a few cells to a patch, and finally overgrew the parental matrix in which they were embedded. There were pictures that showed every stage of this transformation in a laboratory experiment.

"This is why I have not shared the information until now," Opie Kindred said, as the pictures faded around him. "I had to ensure by experimental testing that my theory was correct. Because the procedure is so inefficient we had to screen thousands of chimeras until we obtained a strain that overgrew its parent."

"A very odd and extreme form of reproduction," Arn said. "The parent dies so that the child might live."

Opie Kindred smiled. "It is more interesting than you might suppose."

The next sequence showed the same colony, now clearly infected by the parasitic species—leprous black spots mottled its pinkish surface. Again time speeded up. The spots grew larger, merged, shed a cloud of exfoliations.

"Once the chimera overgrows its parent," Opie Kindred said, "the genes of the parasite, which have been reproduced in every cell of the thallus, are activated. The host cells are transformed. It is rather like an RNA virus, except that the virus does not merely subvert the protein- and RNA-making machinery of its host cell. It takes over the cell itself. Now the cycle is completed, and the parasite sheds exfoliations that will in turn infect new hosts.

"Here is the motor of evolution. In some of the infected hosts, the parasitic genome is prevented from expression, and the host becomes resistant to infection. It is a variation of the Red Queen's race. There is an evolutionary pressure upon the parasite to evolve new infective forms, and then for the hosts to resist them, and so on. Meanwhile, the host species benefit from new genetic combinations that by selection incrementally improve growth. The process is random but continuous, and takes place on a vast scale. I estimate that millions of recombinant cells are produced each hour, although perhaps only one in ten million are viable, and of those only one in a million are significantly more efficient at growth than their parents. But this is more than sufficient to explain the diversity we have mapped in the reef."

Arn said, "How long have you known this, Opie?"

"I communicated my findings to the Star Chamber just this morning," Opie Kindred said. "The work has been very difficult. My crew has to work under very tight restraints, using Class Four containment techniques, as with the old immunodeficiency plagues."

"Yah, of course," Arn said. "We don't know how the exfoliations might contaminate the ship."

"Exactly," Opie Kindred said. "That is why the reef is dangerous."

Margaret bridled at this. She said sharply, "Have you tested how long the exfoliations survive?"

"There is a large amount of data about bacterial spore survival. Many survive thousands of years in vacuum close to absolute zero. It hardly seems necessary—"

"You didn't bother," Margaret said. "My God, you want to destroy the reef and you have no *evidence*. You didn't *think*."

It was the worst of insults in the scientific community. Opie Kindred colored, but before he could reply Dzu Sho held up a hand, and his employees obediently fell silent.

"The Star Chamber has voted," Dzu Sho said. "It is clear that we have all we need. The reef is dangerous, and must be destroyed. Dr. Kindred has suggested a course of action that seems appropriate. We will poison the sulfur-oxidizing cycle and kill the reef."

"But we don't know—"

"We haven't found—"

Margaret and Arn had spoken at once. Both fell silent when Dzu Sho held up a hand again. He said, "We have isolated commercially useful strains. Obviously, we can't use the organisms we have isolated because they contain the parasite within every cell. But we can synthesize useful gene sequences and splice them into current commercial strains of vacuum organism to improve quality."

"I must object," Margaret said. "This is a unique construct. The chances of it evolving again are minimal. We must study it further. We might be able to discover a cure for the parasite."

"It is unlikely," Opie Kindred said. "There is no way to eliminate the parasite from the host cells by gene therapy because they are hidden within the host chromosome, shuffled in a different pattern in every cell of the trillions of cells that make up the reef. However, it is quite easy to produce a poison that will shut down the sulfur-oxidizing metabolism common to the different kinds of reef organism."

"Production has been authorized," Sho said. "It will take, what did you tell me, Dr. Kindred?"

"We require a large quantity, given the large biomass of the reef. Ten days at least. No more than fifteen."

"We have not studied it properly," Arn said. "So we cannot yet say what and what is not possible."

Margaret agreed, but before she could add her objection, her earpiece trilled, and Srin Kerenyi's voice said apologetically, "Trouble, boss. You better come at once."

The survey suite was in chaos, and there was worse chaos in the Rift. Margaret had to switch proxies three times before she found one she could operate. All around her, proxies were fluttering and jinking, as if caught in strong currents instead of floating in vacuum in virtual free fall.

This was at the four-thousand-meter level, where the nitrogen ice walls of the

Rift were sparsely patched with yellow and pink marblings that followed veins of sulfur and organic contaminants. The taste of the vacuum smog here was strong, like burnt rubber coating Margaret's lips and tongue.

As she looked around, a proxy jetted toward her. It overshot and rebounded from a gable of frozen nitrogen, its nozzle jinking back and forth as it tried to stabilize its position.

"Fuck," its operator, Kim Nieye, said in Margaret's ear. "Sorry, boss. I've been through five of these, and now I'm losing this one."

On the other side of the cleft, a hundred meters away, two specks tumbled end for end, descending at a fair clip toward the depths. Margaret's vision color-reversed, went black, came back to normal. She said, "How many?"

"Just about all of them. We're using proxies that were up in the tablelands, but as soon as we bring them down they start going screwy too."

"Herd some up and get them to the sample pickup point. We'll need to do dissections."

"No problem, boss. Are you okay?"

Margaret's proxy had suddenly upended. She couldn't get its trim back. "I don't think so," she said, and then the proxy's nozzle flared and with a pulse of gas the proxy shot away into the depths.

It was a wild ride. The proxy expelled all its gas reserves, accelerating as straight as an arrow. Coralline formations blurred past, and then long stretches of sulfur-eating pavement. The proxy caromed off the narrowing walls and began to tumble madly.

Margaret had no control. She was a helpless but exhilarated passenger. She passed the place where she had set the relay and continued to fall. The link started to break up. She lost all sense of proprioception, although given the tumbling fall of the proxy that was a blessing. Then the microwave radar started to go, with swathes of raster washing across the false color view. Somehow the proxy managed to stabilize itself, so it was falling headfirst toward the unknown regions at the bottom of the Rift. Margaret glimpsed structures swelling from the walls. And then everything went away and she was back, sweating and nauseous in the couch.

It was bad. More than ninety-five percent of the proxies had been lost. Most, like Margaret's, had been lost in the depths. A few, badly damaged by collision, had been stranded among the reef colonies, but proxies sent to retrieve them went out of control too. It was clear that some kind of infective process had affected them. Margaret had several dead proxies collected by a maintenance robot and ordered that the survivors should be regrouped and kept above the deep part of the Rift where the vacuum organisms proliferated. And then she went to her suite in the undercroft and waited for the Star Chamber to call her before them.

The Star Chamber took away Margaret's contract, citing failure to perform and possible sedition (that remark in the seminar had been recorded). She was moved from her suite to a utility room in the lower level of the undercroft and put to work in the farms.

She thought of her parents.

She had been here before.

She thought of the reef.

She couldn't let it go.

She would save it if she could.

Srin Kerenyi kept her up to date. The survey crew and its proxies were restricted to the upper level of the reef. Manned teams under Opie Kindred's control were exploring the depths—*he* was trusted where Margaret was not—but if they discovered anything it wasn't communicated to the other science crews.

Margaret was working in the melon fields when Arn Nivedta found her. The plants sprawled from hydroponic tubes laid across gravel beds, beneath blazing lamps hung in the axis of the farmlands. It was very hot, and there was a stink of dilute sewage. Little yellow ants swarmed everywhere. Margaret had tucked the ends of her pants into the rolled tops of her shoesocks, and wore a green eyeshade. She was using a fine paintbrush to transfer pollen to the stigma of the melon flowers.

Arn came bouncing along between the long rows of plants like a pale scarecrow intent on escape. He wore only tight black shorts and a web belt hung with pens, little silvery tools and a notepad.

He said, "They must hate you, putting you in a shithole like this."

"I have to work, Arn. Work or starve. I don't mind it. I grew up working the fields."

Not strictly true: her parents had been ecosystem designers. But it was how it had ended.

Arn said cheerfully, "I'm here to rescue you. I can prove it wasn't your fault."

Margaret straightened, one hand on the small of her back where a permanent ache had lodged itself. She said, "Of course it wasn't my fault. Are you all right?"

Arn had started to hop about, brushing at one bare long-toed foot and then the other. The ants had found him. His toes curled like fingers. The big toes were opposed. Monkey feet.

"Ants are having something of a population explosion," she said. "We're in the stage between introduction and stabilization here. The cycles will smooth out as the ecosystem matures."

Arn brushed at his legs again. His prehensile big toe flicked an ant from the sole of his foot. "They want to incorporate me into the cycle, I think."

"We're all in the cycle, Arn. The plants grow in sewage; we eat the plants." Margaret saw her supervisor coming toward them through the next field. She said, "We can't talk here. Meet me in my room after work."

Margaret's new room was barely big enough for a hammock, a locker, and a tiny shower with a toilet pedestal. Its rock walls were unevenly coated with dull green fiber spray. There was a constant noise of pedestrians beyond the oval hatch; the air conditioning allowed in a smell of frying oil and ketones despite the filter trap Margaret had set up. She had stuck an aerial photograph of New York, where she had been born, above the head stay of her hammock, and dozens of glossy printouts of the reef scaled the walls. Apart from the pictures, a few clothes in the closet and the spider plant under the purple grolite, the room was quite anonymous.

She had spent most of her life in rooms like this. She could pack in five minutes, ready to move on to the next job.

"This place is probably bugged," Arn said. He sat with his back to the door, sipping schnapps from a silvery flask and looking at the overlapping panoramas of the reef.

Margaret sat on the edge of her hammock. She was nervous and excited. She said, "Everywhere is bugged. I want them to hear that I'm not guilty. Tell me what you know."

Arn looked at her. "I examined the proxies you sent back. I wasn't quite sure what I was looking for, but it was surprisingly easy to spot."

"An infection," Margaret said.

"Yah, a very specific infection. We concentrated on the nervous system, given the etiology. In the brain we found lesions, always in the same area."

Margaret examined the three-dimensional color-enhanced tomographic scan Arn had brought. The lesions were little black bubbles in the underside of the unfolded cerebellum, just in front of the optic node.

"The same in all of them," Arn said. "We took samples, extracted DNA, and sequenced it." A grid of thousands of colored dots, then another superimposed over it. All the dots lined up.

"A match to Opie's parasite," Margaret guessed.

Arn grinned. He had a nice smile. It made him look like an enthusiastic boy. "We tried that first of course. Got a match, then went through the library of reef organisms, and got partial matches. Opie's parasite has its fingerprints in the DNA of everything in the reef, but this—" he jabbed a long finger through the projection"—is the pure quill. Just an unlucky accident that it lodges in the brain at this particular place and produces the behavior you saw."

"Perhaps it isn't a random change," Margaret said. "Perhaps the reef has a use for the proxies."

"Teleology," Arn said. "Don't let Opie hear that thought. He'd use it against you. This is evolution. It isn't directed by anything other than natural selection. There is no designer, no watchmaker. Not after the AI crashed, anyway, and it only pushed the ecosystem toward more efficient sulfur oxidation. There's more, Margaret. I've been doing some experiments on the side. Exposing aluminum foil sheets in orbit around Enki. There are exfoliations everywhere."

"Then Opie is right."

"No, no. All the exfoliations I found were nonviable. I did more experiments. The exfoliations are metabolically active when released, unlike bacterial spores. And they have no protective wall. No reason for them to have one, yah? They live only for a few minutes. Either they land on a new host or they don't. Solar radiation easily tears them apart. You can kill them with a picowatt ultraviolet laser. Contamination isn't a problem."

"And it can't infect us," Margaret said. "Vacuum organisms and proxies have the same DNA code as us, the same as everything from Earth, for that matter, but it's written in artificial nucleotide bases. The reef isn't dangerous at all, Arn."

"Yah, but in theory it could infect every vacuum organism ever designed. The only way around it would be to change the base structure of vacuum organism DNA—how much would that cost?"

"I know about contamination, Arn. The mold that wrecked the biome designed by my parents came in with someone or something. Maybe on clothing, or skin, or in the gut, or in some trade goods. It grew on anything with a cellulose cell wall. Every plant was infected. The fields were covered by huge sheets of gray mold; the air was full of spores. It didn't infect people, but more than a hundred died from massive allergic reactions and respiratory failure. They had to vent the atmosphere in the end. And my parents couldn't find work after that."

Arn said gently, "That is the way. We live by our reputations. It's hard when something goes wrong."

Margaret ignored this. She said, "The reef is a resource, not a danger. You're looking at it the wrong way, like Opie Kindred. We need diversity. Our biospheres have to be complicated because simple systems are prone to invasion and disruption, but they aren't one hundredth as complicated as those on Earth. If my parents' biome had been more diverse, the mold couldn't have found a foothold."

"There are some things I could do without." Arn scratched his left ankle with the toes of his right foot. "Like those ants."

"Well, we don't know if we need the ants specifically, but we need variety, and they contribute to it. They help aerate the soil, to begin with, which encourages stratification and diversity of soil organisms. There are a million different kinds of microbe in a gram of soil from a forest on Earth; we have to make do with less than a thousand. We don't have one tenth that number of useful vacuum organisms and most are grown in monoculture, which is the most vulnerable ecosystem of all. That was the cause of the crash of the green revolution on Earth in the twenty-first century. But there are hundreds of different species in the reef. Wild species, Arn. You could seed a planetoid with them and go harvest it a year later. The citizens don't go outside because they have their parklands, their palaces, their virtualities. They've forgotten that the outer system isn't just the habitats. There are millions of small planetoids in the Kuiper Belt. Anyone with a dome and the reef vacuum organisms could homestead one."

She had been thinking about this while working out in the fields. The Star Chamber had given her plenty of time to think.

Arn shook his head. "They all have the parasite lurking in them. Any species from the reef can turn into it. Perhaps even the proxies."

"We don't know enough," Margaret said. "I saw things in the bottom of the Rift, before I lost contact with the proxy. Big structures. And there's the anomalous temperature gradients, too. The seat of change must be down there, Arn. The parasite could be useful, if we can master it. The viruses that caused the immunodeficiency plagues are used for gene therapy now. Opie Kindred has been down there. He's suppressing what he has found."

"Yah, well, it does not much matter. They have completed synthesis of the metabolic inhibitor. I'm friendly with the organics chief. They diverted most of the refinery to it." Arn took out his slate. "He showed me how they have set it up. That is what they have been doing down in the Rift. Not exploring."

"Then we have to do something now."

"It is too late, Margaret."

"I want to call a meeting, Arn. I have a proposal."

Most of the science crews came. Opie Kindred's crew was a notable exception; Arn said that it gave him a bad feeling.

"They could be setting us up," he told Margaret.

"I know they're listening. That's good. I want it in the open. If you're worried about getting hurt you can always leave."

"I came because I wanted to. Like everyone else here. We're all scientists. We all want the truth known." Arn looked at her. He smiled. "You want more than that, I think."

"I fight my own fights." All around people were watching. Margaret added, "Let's get this thing started."

Arn called the meeting to order and gave a brief presentation about his research into survival of the exfoliations before throwing the matter open to the meeting. Nearly everyone had an opinion. Microphones hovered in the room, and at times three or four people were shouting at each other. Margaret let them work off their frustration. Some simply wanted to register a protest; a small but significant minority were worried about losing their bonuses or even all of their pay.

"Better that than our credibility," one of Orly Higgins's techs said. "That's what we live by. None of us will work again if we allow the *Ganapati* to become a plague ship."

Yells of approval, whistles.

Margaret waited until the noise had died down, then got to her feet. She was in the center of the horseshoe of seats, and everyone turned to watch, more than a hundred people. Their gaze fell upon her like sunlight; it strengthened her. A microphone floated down in front of her face.

"Arn has shown that contamination isn't an issue," Margaret said. "The issue is that the Star Chamber wants to destroy the reef because they want to exploit what they've found and stop anyone else using it. I'm against that, all the way. I'm not gengeneered. Micro-gravity is not my natural habitat. I have to take a dozen different drugs to prevent reabsorption of calcium from my bone, collapse of my circulatory system, fluid retention, all the bad stuff micro-gravity does to unedited Earth stock. I'm not allowed to have children here, because they would be as crippled as me. Despite that, my home is here. Like all of you, I would like to have the benefits of being a citizen, to live in the parklands and eat real food. But there aren't enough parklands for everyone because the citizens who own the habitats control production of fixed carbon. The vacuum organisms we have found could change that. The reef may be a source of plague, or it may be a source of unlimited organics. We don't know. What we do know is that the reef is unique and we haven't finished exploring it. If the Star Chamber destroys it, we may never know what's out there."

Cheers at this. Several people rose to make points, but Margaret wouldn't give way. She wanted to finish.

"Opie Kindred has been running missions to the bottom of the Rift, but he hasn't been sharing what he's found there. Perhaps he no longer thinks that he's one of us. He'll trade his scientific reputation for citizenship," Margaret said, "but that isn't our way, is it?"

"*NO!*" the crowd roared.

And the White Mice invaded the room.

Sharp cracks, white smoke, screams. The White Mice had long flexible sticks weighted at one end. They went at the crowd like farmers threshing corn. Margaret was separated from Arn by a wedge of panicking people. Two techs got hold of her and steered her out of the room, down a corridor filling with smoke. Arn loomed out of it, clutching his slate to his chest.

"They're getting ready to set off the poison," he said as they ran in long loping strides.

"Then I'm going now," Margaret said.

Down a drop pole onto a corridor lined with shops. People were smashing windows. No one looked at them as they ran through the riot. They turned a corner, the sounds of shouts and breaking glass fading. Margaret was breathing hard. Her eyes were smarting, her nose running.

"They might kill you," Arn said. He grasped her arm. "I can't let you go, Margaret."

She shook herself free. Arn tried to grab her again. He was taller, but she was stronger. She stepped inside his reach and jumped up and popped him on the nose with the flat of her hand.

He sat down, blowing bubbles of blood from his nostrils, blinking up at her with surprised, tear-filled eyes.

She snatched up his slate. "I'm sorry, Arn," she said. "This is my only chance. I might not find anything, but I couldn't live with myself if I didn't try."

Margaret was five hundred kilometers out from the habitat when the radio beeped. "Ignore it," she told her pressure suit. She was sure that she knew who was trying to contact her, and she had nothing to say to him.

This far out, the Sun was merely the brightest star in the sky. Behind and above Margaret, the dim elongated crescent of the *Ganapati* hung before the sweep of the Milky Way. Ahead, below the little transit platform's motor, Enki was growing against a glittering starscape, a lumpy potato with a big notch at its widest point.

The little moonlet was rising over the notch, a swiftly moving fleck of light. For a moment, Margaret had the irrational fear that she would collide with it, but the transit platform's navigational display showed her that she would fall above and behind it. Falling past a moon! She couldn't help smiling at the thought.

"Priority override," her pressure suit said. Its voice was a reassuring contralto Margaret knew as well as her mother's.

"Ignore it," Margaret said again.

"Sorry, Maggie. You know I can't do that."

"Quite correct," another voice said.

Margaret identified him a moment before the suit helpfully printed his name across the helmet's visor. Dzu Sho.

"Turn back right now," Sho said. "We can take you out with the spectrographic laser if we have to."

"You wouldn't dare," she said.

"I do not believe anyone would mourn you," Sho said unctuously. "Leaving the *Ganapati* was an act of sedition, and we're entitled to defend ourselves."

Margaret laughed. It was just the kind of silly, sententious, self-important nonsense that Sho was fond of spouting.

"I am entirely serious," Sho said.

Enki had rotated to show that the notch was the beginning of a groove. The groove elongated as the worldlet rotated further. Tigris Rift. Its edges ramified in complex fractal branchings.

"I'm going where the proxies fell," Margaret said. "I'm still working for you."

"You sabotaged the proxies. That's why they couldn't fully penetrate the Rift."

"That's why I'm going—"

"Excuse me," the suit said, "but I register a small energy flux."

"Just a tickle from the ranging sight," Sho said. "Turn back now, Dr. Wu."

"I intend to come back."

It was a struggle to stay calm. Margaret thought that Sho's threat was no more than empty air. The laser's AI would not allow it to be used against human targets, and she was certain that Sho couldn't override it. And even if he could, he wouldn't dare kill her in full view of the science crews. Sho was bluffing. He had to be.

The radio silence stretched. Then Sho said, "You're planning to commit a final act of sabotage. Don't think you can get away with it. I'm sending someone after you."

Margaret was dizzy with relief. Anyone chasing her would be using the same kind of transit platform. She had at least thirty minutes head start.

Another voice said, "Don't think this will make you a hero."

Opie Kindred. Of course. The man never could delegate. He was on the same trajectory, several hundred kilometers behind but gaining slowly.

"Tell me what you found," she said. "Then we can finish this race before it begins."

Opie Kindred switched off his radio.

"If you had not brought along all this gear," her suit grumbled, "we could outdistance him."

"I think we'll need it soon. We'll just have to be smarter than him."

Margaret studied the schematics of the poison-spraying mechanism—it was beautifully simple, but vulnerable—while Tigris Rift swelled beneath her, a jumble of knife-edge chevron ridges. Enki was so small and the Rift so wide that the walls had fallen beneath the horizon. She was steering toward the Rift's center when the suit apologized and said that there was another priority override.

It was the *Ganapati*'s lawyer. She warned Margaret that this was being entered into sealed court records, and then formally revoked her contract and read a complaint about her seditious conduct.

"You're a contracted worker just like me," Margaret said. "We take orders, but we both have codes of professional ethics, too. For the record, that's why I'm here. The reef is a unique organism. I cannot allow it to be destroyed."

Dzu Sho came onto the channel and said, "Off the record, don't think about being picked up."

The lawyer switched channels. "He does not mean it," she said. "He would be in violation of the distress statutes." Pause. "Good luck, Dr. Wu."

Then there was only the carrier wave.

Margaret wished that this made her feel better. Plenty of contract workers who went against the direct orders of their employers had disappeared, or been killed in industrial accidents. The fire of the mass meeting had evaporated long before the suit had assembled itself around her, and now she felt colder and lonelier than ever.

She fell, the platform shuddering now and then as it adjusted its trim. Opie Kindred's platform was a bright spark moving sideways across the drifts of stars above. Directly below was a vast flow of nitrogen ice with a black river winding through it. The center of the Rift, a cleft two kilometers long and fifty kilometers deep. The reef.

She fell toward it.

She had left the radio channel open. Suddenly, Opie Kindred said, "Stop now and it will be over."

"Tell me what you know."

No answer.

She said, "You don't have to follow me, Opie. This is my risk. I don't ask you to share it."

"You won't take this away from me."

"Is citizenship really worth this, Opie?"

No reply.

The suit's proximity alarms began to ping and beep. She turned them off one by one, and told the suit to be quiet when it complained.

"I am only trying to help," it said. "You should reduce your velocity. The target is very narrow."

"I've been here before," Margaret said.

But only by proxy. The ice field rushed up at her. Its smooth flows humped over one another, pitted everywhere with tiny craters. She glimpsed black splashes where vacuum organisms had colonized a stress ridge. Then an edge flashed past; walls unraveled on either side.

She was in the reef.

The vacuum organisms were everywhere: flat plates jutting from the walls; vases and delicate fans and fretworks; huge blotches smooth as ice or dissected by cracks. In the light cast by the platform's lamps, they did not possess the vibrant primary colors of the proxy link, but were every shade of gray and black, streaked here and there with muddy reds. Complex fans ramified far back inside the milky nitrogen ice, following veins of carbonaceous compounds.

Far above, stars were framed by the edges of the cleft. One star was falling toward her: Opie Kindred. Margaret switched on the suit's radar, and immediately it began to ping. The suit shouted a warning, but before Margaret could look around the pings doppled together.

Proxies.

They shot up toward her, tentacles writhing from the black, streamlined helmets of their mantles. Most of them missed, jagging erratically as they squirted bursts of hydrogen to kill their velocity. Two collided in a slow flurry of tentacles.

Margaret laughed. None of her crew would fight against her, and Sho was relying upon inexperienced operators.

The biggest proxy, three meters long, swooped past. The crystalline gleam of its sensor array reflected the lights of the platform. It decelerated, spun on its axis, and dove back toward her.

Margaret barely had time to pull out the weapon she had brought with her. It was a welding pistol, rigged on a long rod with a yoked wire around the trigger. She thrust it up like the torch of the Statue of Liberty just before the proxy struck her.

The suit's gauntlet, elbow joint and shoulder piece stiffened under the heavy impact, saving Margaret from broken bones, but the collision knocked the transit platform sideways. It plunged through reef growths. Like glass, they had tremendous rigidity but very little lateral strength. Fans and lattices broke away, peppering Margaret and the proxy with shards. It was like falling through a series of chandeliers. Margaret couldn't close her fingers in the stiffened gauntlet. She stood tethered to the platform with her arm and the rod raised straight up and the black proxy wrapped around them. The proxy's tentacles lashed her visor with slow, purposeful slaps.

Margaret knew that it would take only a few moments before the tentacles' carbon-fiber proteins could unlink; then it would be able to reach the life-support pack on her back.

She shouted at the suit, ordering it to relax the gauntlet's fingers. The proxy was contracting around her rigid arm as it stretched toward the life-support pack. When the gauntlet went limp, pressure snapped her fingers closed. Her forefinger popped free of the knuckle. She yelled with pain. And the wire rigged to the welding pistol's trigger pulled taut.

Inside the proxy's mantle, a focused beam of electrons boiled off the pistol's filament. The pistol, designed to work only in high vacuum, began to arc almost immediately, but the electron beam had already heated the integument and muscle of the proxy to more than 400°C. Vapor expanded explosively. The proxy shot away, propelled by the gases of its own dissolution.

Opie was still gaining on Margaret. Gritting her teeth against the pain of her dislocated finger, she dumped the broken welding gear. It only slowly floated away above her, for it still had the same velocity as she did.

A proxy swirled in beside her with shocking suddenness. For a moment, she gazed into its faceted sensor array, and then dots of luminescence skittered across its smooth black mantle, forming letters.

Much luck, boss. SK.

Srin Kerenyi. Margaret waved with her good hand. The proxy scooted away, rising at a shallow angle toward Opie's descending star.

A few seconds later the cleft filled with the unmistakable flash of laser light.

The radar trace of Srin's proxy disappeared.

Shit. Opie Kindred was armed. If he got close enough he could kill her.

Margaret risked a quick burn of the transit platform's motor to increase her rate of fall. It roared at her back for twenty seconds; when it cut out her pressure suit warned her that she had insufficient fuel for full deceleration.

"I know what I'm doing," Margaret told it.

The complex forms of the reef dwindled past. Then there were only huge patches of black staining the nitrogen ice walls. Margaret passed her previous record depth, and still she fell. It was like free fall; the negligible gravity of Enki did not cause any appreciable acceleration.

Opie Kindred gained on her by increments.

In vacuum, the lights of the transit platform threw abrupt pools of light onto the endlessly unraveling walls. Slowly, the pools of light elongated into glowing tunnels filled with sparkling motes. The exfoliations and gases and organic molecules were growing denser. And, impossibly, the temperature was *rising*, one degree with every five hundred meters. Far below, between the narrowing perspective of the walls, structures were beginning to resolve from the blackness.

The suit reminded her that she should begin the platform's deceleration burn. Margaret checked Opie's velocity and said she would wait.

"I have no desire to end as a crumpled tube filled with strawberry jam," the suit said. It projected a countdown on her visor and refused to switch it off.

Margaret kept one eye on Opie's velocity, the other on the blur of reducing numbers. The numbers passed zero. The suit screamed obscenities in her ears, but she waited a beat more before firing the platform's motor.

The platform slammed into her boots. Sharp pain in her ankles and knees. The suit stiffened as the harness dug into her shoulders and waist.

Opie Kindred's platform flashed past. He had waited until after she had decelerated before making his move. Margaret slapped the release buckle of the platform's harness and fired the piton gun into the nitrogen ice wall. It was enough to slow her so that she could catch hold of a crevice and swing up into it. Her dislocated finger hurt like hell.

The temperature was a stifling eighty-seven degrees above absolute zero. The atmospheric pressure was just registering—a mix of hydrogen and carbon monoxide and hydrogen sulphide. Barely enough in the whole of the bottom of the cleft to pack into a small box at the pressure of Earth's atmosphere at sea level, but the rate of production must be tremendous to compensate for loss into the colder vacuum above.

Margaret leaned out of the crevice. Below, it widened into a chimney between humped pressure flows of nitrogen ice sloping down to the floor of the cleft. The slopes and the floor were packed with a wild proliferation of growths. Not only the familiar vases and sheets and laces, but great branching structures like crystal trees, lumpy plates raised on stout stalks, tangles of black wire hundreds of meters across, clusters of frothy globes, and much more.

There was no sign of Opie Kindred, but tethered above the growths were the balloons of his spraying mechanism. Each was a dozen meters across, crinkled, flaccid. They were fifty degrees hotter than their surroundings, would have to grow hotter still before the metabolic inhibitor was completely volatilized inside them. When that happened, small explosive devices would puncture them, and the metabolic inhibitor would be sucked into the vacuum of the cleft like smoke up a chimney.

Margaret consulted the schematics and started to climb down the crevice, light as a dream, steering herself with the fingers of her left hand. The switching relays that controlled the balloons' heaters were manually controlled because of telemetry interference from the reef's vacuum smog and the broadband electromagnetic resonance. The crash shelter where they were located was about two kilometers away, a slab of orange foamed plastic in the center of a desolation of abandoned equipment and broken and half-melted vacuum organism colonies.

The crevice widened. Margaret landed between drifts of what looked like giant soap bubbles that grew at its bottom.

And Opie Kindred's platform rose up between two of the half-inflated balloons.

Margaret dropped onto her belly behind a line of bubbles that grew along a smooth ridge of ice. She opened a radio channel. It was filled with a wash of static and a wailing modulation, but through the noise she heard Opie's voice faintly calling her name.

He was a hundred meters away and more or less at her level, turning in a slow circle. He couldn't locate her amidst the radio noise and the ambient temperature was higher than the skin of her pressure suit, so she had no infrared image.

She began to crawl along the smooth ridge. The walls of the bubbles were whitely opaque, but she could see shapes curled within them. Like embryos inside eggs.

"Everything is ready, Margaret," Opie Kindred's voice said in her helmet. "I'm going to find you, and then I'm going to sterilize this place. There are things here you know nothing about. Horribly dangerous things. Who are you working for? Tell me that and I'll let you live."

A thread of red light waved out from the platform and a chunk of nitrogen ice cracked off explosively. Margaret felt it through the tips of her gloves.

"I can cut my way through to you," Opie Kindred said, "wherever you are hiding."

Margaret watched the platform slowly revolve. Tried to guess if she could reach the shelter while he was looking the other way. All she had to do was bound down the ridge and cross a kilometer of bare, crinkled nitrogen ice without being fried by Opie's laser. Still crouching, she lifted onto the tips of her fingers and toes, like a sprinter on the block. He was turning, turning. She took three deep breaths to clear her head—and something crashed into the ice cliff high above! It spun out in a spray of shards, hit the slope below and spun through toppling clusters of tall black chimneys. For a moment, Margaret was paralyzed with astonishment. Then she remembered the welding gear. It had finally caught up with her.

Opie Kindred's platform slewed around and a red thread waved across the face of the cliff. A slab of ice thundered outward. Margaret bounded away, taking giant leaps and trying to look behind her at the same time.

The slab spun on its axis, shedding huge shards, and smashed into the cluster of the bubbles where she had been crouching just moments before. The ice shook like a living thing under her feet and threw her head over heels.

She stopped herself by firing the piton gun into the ground. She was on her back, looking up at the top of the ridge, where bubbles vented a dense mix of gas and oily organics before bursting in an irregular cannonade. Hundreds of slim black shapes shot away. Some smashed into the walls of the cleft and stuck there, but many more vanished into its maw.

A chain reaction had started. Bubbles were bursting open up and down the length of the cleft.

A cluster popped under Opie Kindred's platform and he vanished in a roil of vapor. The crevice shook. Nitrogen ice boiled into a dense fog. A wind got up for a few minutes. Margaret clung to the piton until it was over.

Opie Kindred had drifted down less than a hundred meters away. The thing which had smashed the visor of his helmet was still lodged there. It was slim and black, with a hard, shiny exoskeleton. The broken bodies of others settled among smashed vacuum organism colonies, glistening like beetles in the light of Margaret's suit. They were like tiny, tentacle-less proxies, their swollen mantles cased in something like keratin. Some had split open, revealing ridged reaction chambers and complex matrices of black threads.

"Gametes," Margaret said, seized by a sudden wild intuition. "Little rocketships full of DNA."

The suit asked if she was all right.

She giggled. "The parasite turns everything into its own self. Even proxies!"

"I believe that I have located Dr. Kindred's platform," the suit said. "I suggest that you refrain from vigorous exercise, Maggie. Your oxygen supply is limited. What are you doing?"

She was heading toward the crash shelter. "I'm going to switch off the balloon heaters. They won't be needed."

After she shut down the heaters, Margaret lashed one of the dead creatures to the transit platform. She shot up between the walls of the cleft, and at last rose into the range of the relay transmitters. Her radio came alive, a dozen channels blinking for attention. Arn was on one, and she told him what had happened.

"Sho wanted to light out of here," Arn said, "but stronger heads prevailed. Come home, Margaret."

"Did you see them? Did you, Arn?"

"Some hit the *Ganapati*." He laughed. "Even the Star Chamber can't deny what happened."

Margaret rose up above the ice fields and continued to rise until the curve of the worldlet's horizon became visible, and then the walls of Tigris Rift. The *Ganapati* was a faint star bracketed between them. She called up deep radar, and saw, beyond the *Ganapati*'s strong signal, thousands of faint traces falling away into deep space.

A random scatter of genetic packages. How many would survive to strike new worldlets and give rise to new reefs?

Enough, she thought. The reef evolved in saltatory jumps. She had just witnessed its next revolution.

Given time, it would fill the Kuiper Belt.

EXCHANGE RATE

Hal Clement

Hal Clement (the pen name of Harry Clement Stubbs [born 1922]) is one of the writers whose works P. Schuyler Miller coined the term *hard SF* to describe. Miller said in 1957, "The ultimate in present-day science fiction is being written by Hal Clement." Clement's early novels—*Needle* (1950), *Iceworld* (1953), *Mission of Gravity* (1954), *Close to Critical* (1964)—nearly all appeared previously as serials in John W. Campbell's *Astounding*. His short fiction is collected in *Natives of Space* (1965), *Small Changes* (1969), *Best of Hal Clement* (1979), and *Intuit* (1987). In recent years, NESFA Press of the New England Science Fiction Association has begun releasing omnibus volumes of his novels and stories under the series title of *The Essential Hal Clement*. Clement recently resumed writing novels, publishing *Half Life*, concerning a trip to the moons of Saturn to investigate the biochemistry pre-life conditions for the purpose of saving Earth, in 1999. He has a new novel forthcoming.

Science Fiction Writers (1996) says, "Clement and his classic fiction are mentioned whenever the discussion of science in the genre comes up . . . their distinguishing characteristic is that a problematic condition in physical reality, or simply a condition of difference such as an increase or decrease in heat of gravity, must be elaborated upon, explained, and taken through certain plot changes so that the reader can simply understand the problem or the difference. This is a literature of total mimesis, in which the facts of the universe are mimed." It is commonly referred to as hard SF (think of hard rock or the hard sciences—physics, chemistry, and astronomy).

Clement's mastery of the astronomy, physics, and chemistry in stories set in space and on other worlds became famous with the publication of the *Astounding* serial of *Mission of Gravity* (1954), but especially with the immediately subsequent publication of a nonfiction article in the same magazine, detailing the process by which he had figured out the physics, astronomy and biochemistry of the world of Mesklin. With the publication of *Mission of Gravity*, Clement in effect redefined the game of hard SF as an exercise in interrelating the sciences to achieve a created world that would plausibly withstand rigorous examination from many angles. Of such conceptual breakthroughs are scientific revolutions accomplished, and this was a revolution in science fiction, a slow and subtle one that took more than a decade to take hold. Gradually Clement gained a worldwide reputation as a quintessential hard SF writer whose works in later years more or less defined the term. Clement's work is presently the most influential model for hard science fiction writers.

We said in *The Ascent of Wonder* that the world of the hard SF story is deterministic, ruled by scientific law: It is inimical to anyone who does not know said law or how to figure it out—scientific method, facts. "Somebody had asked me," said Clement, "why I didn't have bad entities—villains—in my stories, generally speaking, and my point was that the universe was a perfectly adequate villain!" The universe is enough of an antagonist in much hard SF.

This story is characteristic Clement. The title points to the scientific principles featured in the tale.

Erni! Nic! Hold it! Senatsu's found a break!"

The speaker was excited, but neither driver bothered to look up. A "break" on Halfbaked meant little to human eyes; it was a spot where radar frequencies, not human vision, could get through the streaming and usually ionized clouds which kept starlight from the surface. Neither cared to look at stars. They were very worried men at the moment and didn't even look at each other. However, Ben Cloud kept talking, and his next words did manage to get their attention.

"It's near Hotlat plus eight and Rotlat plus eighty, close to the track they should be taking back here."

The operators of the *Quarterback* did glance at each other this time. Facial expressions didn't show through breathing masks. They didn't need to. For a moment both were silent; then the younger spoke aloud.

"Has she really spotted anything definite?"

"She thinks so. She's checking all the usable spectra now. Stand by; she should be through in a few seconds."

Quarterback's drivers looked wordlessly at each other once more, and Dominic hit the quick-cutout that brought the runabout to a halt. Operating any sort of surface vehicle on Halfbaked demanded full attention.

"Well?" said Erni. After all, a few seconds *had* passed.

"Stand by. She's still at it." A longer pause followed, until even the more patient Nic was tempted to break it, but Ben resumed before either listener actually gave in.

"She says yes! It's *Jellyseal*'s pattern."

"Anything from the girls?"

"No, but *Jelly*'s moving apparently under control and at a reasonable speed."

"What's that? Or can Sen tell?" cut in the elder driver.

"The tanker's doing about a hundred and eighty kilos an hour. Must be open country."

"How's she measuring that?"

"Tell you soon. Sen's taking all the advantage she can of the break, but it'll take a while to cross-check with memory. They'll probably have to move a bit farther, too."

"If the speed is real, they've probably unloaded."

"Probably. Maria reported they'd reached what seemed to be the broadcast site and found something city-ish, though she never really described it. That was nearly twenty hours ago as you both know. That was about five hundred kilos outward of where they seem to be now. They could have emptied, loaded up again, and easily be at Sen's current fix. You can stop worrying."

"And the natives *did* acknowledge receipt of the shipment, and even said how delighted they were, didn't they?" asked Dominic. "But no more word was coming from Maria and Jessi. That's the picture we had from Tricia before we started.

"She was firm about the acknowledgment, yes. Still is. You know how she waffles when a message seems to involve abstractions, though. They were very repetitious, she says, talking about how they understood why we couldn't send pure hydrogen and commenting again and again on the wide variety of compounds there were anyway—"

"I got all that. Paraffin, whether you're speaking European or North American Anglic, does have a lot of different hydrogen compounds in it. I'm admitting we know the girls got there, but still wondering why we haven't heard from them since.

We'll stop worrying—maybe—when they say something." Erni's tone suggested strongly that he wanted no advice as he went on, "You say they're backtracking? Using the same route?"

"Senatsu hasn't had a long enough look-see to tell. They're just about on the path they took earlier, I gather, but remember we didn't see them get to it. We did map more than half of it outbound, but I'd say—"

"We know all that!" snapped Erni. "What I want to know is whether Nic and I should keep on and try to meet them."

"I'd say no. It made sense to head for the transmission source when they seemed to be stuck there, but now we know they're moving and presumably heading back here, it seems smarter to wait for them here at Nest."

"But suppose they still don't report? How long do we wait? And what could keep them from talking to us, anyway?"

"The same sorts of things that keep us from seeing them as often as we'd like. We're talking to you all right now, but you're only a few hundred k's away using multiple channel cross-link. They're nearly fifty thousand. We can see even you only occasionally—less often than we can see them, since there are more clouds here on the dark side. You know all that as well as anyone. Halfbaked wasn't built for long-range talking. It has too many kinds of clouds, too many kinds and strengths of charge dancing around in them, too many winds high and low and up and down and sideways and circular, too much pure distance—"

"And natives who use AM communication but still make some sense. I know all that!" snapped Icewall.

"Then please talk as though you did." Ben was getting a little short, too. "Look, I know you're worried, and I know why, even if I don't have a shared name yet. It's too bad the girls won the draw for the first load, but even you didn't try to change it so Nic could go with Maria or you with Jessi. They went. They really weren't in any more danger pushing a tanker around the landscape than at Nest, except for being farther from help if they needed it, of course. It isn't as though this idiotic world had any nice stable places where you could put up a building and go to sleep with reasonable hope the ground wouldn't pull apart under it before you woke up. I know your wives haven't talked to us since they reported spotting their city, or village, or whatever it turned out to be. That's a fact. I don't dispute it, and I can't account for it except with guesses I can't support. So go ahead and worry. I can't stop you, and I wouldn't if I could. They're your wives. I still think, though, that you'll be smarter waiting for them here than going thirty or forty thousand kilos, a lot of it in sunlight, and trying to find them while they're still moving and we can't keep good contact, visual or verbal, with either of you."

"I suppose you're right," Erni admitted in a much meeker tone. "Nic? You think we'd better go back, too?"

Dominic Wildbear Yucca—Maria might no longer be alive but he was still entitled to their jointly chosen name because of their children—nodded silently, and without further words looked carefully around through the windows ringing the cockpit. One looked before moving anywhere on Halfbaked. Neither window nor roof port was made of glass; there were too many fluorine compounds in Halfbaked's atmosphere for silicate materials to be trusted. Silicon tetrafluoride is a gas even at most Terrestrial temperatures. Satisfied that no serious landscape change had sneaked by his notice during the talk, he repowered the driving system—stopping was nearly always safer than starting, and the control system reflected that fact—and sent the runabout into a fairly tight turn. The path was wide enough to need little steering care at the moment, though bushes, rocks which had rolled from the modest hills, cracks in the surface, and patches of vegetation which might or might not be on fire could be encountered any time.

The spaceward side of Halfbaked was well covered with what looked to human beings like plant life, though its actual ecological role was still being argued. No animals had yet been seen, unless some of the large and small objects resembling fragments of burned paper which seemed to be borne on the fierce winds were actually flying instead. There was evidence on some of the plants that things were eating them, but the pool for the first confirmed animal sighting was still unclaimed after five Terrestrial months. Two schools of thought were developing among the biologists: the katabolic part of the ecology was being handled by microbes, or was being taken care of by fire.

Drivers could devote very little of their attention to specimen search while their machines were in motion. The *Quarterback* trembled slightly as it moved, partly from ground irregularities, occasionally from temblors, and mostly from winds of constantly varying violence and direction. At their present height above the reference ellipsoid—Halfbaked had no seas to provide an altitude zero—the pressure averaged about seventeen atmospheres, wavering irregularly and on a time scale of minutes by about two each way. With its molecular weight averaging well over a hundred, wind was both difficult and unsafe to ignore.

Dominic nursed the vehicle up to nearly two hundred kilometers per hour. There were few obstacles now in sight, and the red and green deeplights flashing alternately from their masts on each side of the runabout provided shadow patterns easily interpreted as range information. It was better than computer-backed radar in the continuous howl of microwave and longer static emitted by the local plants. The lights also allowed human-reflexive response time; glancing back and forth between the outside and a screen, no matter how precise and detailed the latter's readings might be, would have put a much lower limit on permissible driving speed much of the time.

Erni kept his hands away from the controls, but watched their surroundings as carefully as his partner. Both could see in all directions even here on night side, since a bank of floods supplemented the deeplights and there was nearly continuous and fairly bright lightning among the clouds overhead. Halfbaked, less than eight million kilometers from the center of its G3-to-4 sun, had plenty of energy to expend on luminous, biological, and even comprehensible local phenomena.

The driver did cast an occasional glance at his younger companion. He would never have admitted that Erni could be more worried about Jessi than he himself was about Maria, but the Icewalls had been married less than three years as against the Yuccas' fourteen, and might possibly be less philosophical about the unpredictability of life.

Apparently greater worry was not hurting Erni's driving judgment, though. His "Watch it!" from the right-side station was essentially simultaneous with Nic's cutting out drive again. *Quarterback* came to a quick halt, but not a smooth one.

Active faults don't move smoothly; even on Earth they cause quakes, often violent ones. Under more than seven Earth gravities, the quakes tend to be much more frequent and no less violent. Both drivers floated quietly at their stations and watched; there was nothing else to do until what they saw made detailed sense.

The fault could be seen half a kilometer ahead, though rain was starting to fall, but there were no hills close enough to offer a threat of slides or rockfalls. If there had been, it was likely that not even trained driver reflexes could have coped with all the probabilities, and more worry would have been in order.

The ground movement was largely horizontal, they could see and feel. The fault started from some indeterminate point to their left, slanted across in front, and extended out of sight ahead and to their right. It did have a small vertical component; the far side had lifted nearly half a meter since they had passed the level site less than an hour before. Rather casually, Erni reported their stopping and the reason for it to Nest; Ben acknowledged with equal aplomb.

"Unless it gets a good deal higher, we won't have any trouble in getting past," Icewall concluded.

"If it's still shaking, maybe you ought to get by before it rises any more," was the answering suggestion. Erni glanced at his partner, nodding thoughtfully.

"You have a point. All right. We'll send out bugs to see if it's any lower within a kilo or two, and climb at the best place. We'll call you when we start. If you don't hear from us in two or three minutes after that, someone come out and collect the evidence."

"If we can spare anyone." That point also was well taken, though too obvious to all concerned to be worthy of answer. Energy was essentially limitless thanks to ubiquitous miniature fusion units, and self-reproducing pseudolife equipment was almost equally so as long as there was no shortage of raw material; but personnel on a world like Halfbaked was another matter entirely.

The servobugs guided them to a spot a few hundred meters to the right. The men called them back, powered up again and sent the runabout slowly toward the infant cliff, stopping again some two meters away. Both operators watched carefully for a minute or so. A slip of a millimeter or two every few seconds was accompanied by more shock waves. One could only guess whether an especially large jolt was waiting to be triggered by the car's weight, but the regularity of the motions themselves was encouraging. Nic retracted the dozen wheels on which they had been traveling and let the body settle onto its caterpillar treads; then, for reasons he didn't bother to state, he motioned Erni to take over. The latter obeyed in equal silence. Even more slowly than before, *Quarterback* eased forward until the treads touched the tiny escarpment and the front of the vehicle began to lift.

The frequent small shocks became much easier to feel but no more worrisome. The men could see the front of the vehicle lifting but not feel it; up and down, even under heavy gravity, were not obvious except by sight to people floating in water—and sight needed a better reference horizon than this world with its vast size and short atmospheric scale height could provide.

Tension mounted as the mass center of the vehicle approached the edge. Both men clenched their fists and held their breaths as it passed and the machine rocked forward.

In theory, the runabout wouldn't buckle even if its entire fourteen-hundred-ton mass—some ten thousand tons weight, here—were supported only at the center. Nesters, however, tended to have an engineering bias toward regarding such theory mainly as a guide for planning experiments. This sort of experiment had been done before but not, as far as either driver knew, with acceleration from seismic waves helping out the gravity.

The body did hold. The impact as it finished rocking forward and the front touched down was gentle, somewhat cushioned by a patch of half-meter-wide, viciously spined growths resembling barrel cacti. Dark red, almost black, fluid which spattered from these crusted over almost at once as the air touched it, but slightly to the men's surprise it did not ignite.

A moment later *Quarterback* was resuming speed with Erni still driving. Nic reported their new status to Nest, added encouraging details about the stresses just survived, and asked for an update on the tanker.

"Still moving, still apparently on the way back," replied Ben. "Average speed about a hundred sixty."

"Did they really slow down, or is that just a better measure?" Nic barely beat his friend to the question.

"The latter, Senatsu thinks. But they're coming, almost certainly backtracking on their original path. They're not heading straight toward Nest, but nearly Hot-south toward the dark side. We're wondering now whether the original guess about travel being better out of the sunlight was right, or if they have some other reason. There's still no direct word from the girls."

The flotation water was clear enough to show part of Erni's frown above his breathing mask, but he said nothing. The clusters of spiky barrels were becoming more numerous, and even though he knew contact would not harm the *Quarterback* he disliked casual destruction.

The drive settled down to routine. *Quarterback* didn't have far to go by Half-baked standards. They had barely started their trip to the "city" reported by *Jellyseal*'s drivers, which was nearly fifty thousand kilometers from Nest along a geodesic and much farther by realistic standards. The topography seldom allowed a completely free choice of path, and it had seemed wise to make most of the journey out of sun-light as long as there was no obvious reason for haste. Keeping the cargo below its boiling point would be much easier, for one thing.

Now, of course, the cargo should be different.

The husbands, when voice contact had been lost, had been worried and planned to take the geodesic route rather than follow the mapped track of the *Jellyseal*, but they were still on the night side less than a thousand kilometers from Nest when they turned back.

The temblors from the shifting fault grew less intense as they moved away from it. This might be due to increasing distance or to actual quieting down of the distur-bance. There was plenty of seismic equipment at Nest, and the quakes had probably been detected there; but until a far more extensive network could be set up there would be no way to pick particular ones out of the continuous rumblings and quiv-erings originating throughout the huge world's crust and mantle.

Neither driver thought of blaming other Nesters for failing to warn them about the obstacle just passed. Satellite mapping through charged clouds was difficult, and anyone away from the base was on his own—or on their own; no vehicles went out with less than two crew members, and no one went out walking. Suits which would let a human being take a step in seventeen atmospheres of pressure and over seven Earth gravities, even though Nest had been built in a region of human-tolerable temperature, were not available anywhere.

Techniques *had* been planned for transferring people from a crippled vehicle to a rescue machine, but so far these had not been tested in genuine emergencies. Also they depended on the cripple's not being too badly bent out of shape. Doors had to open . . .

The *Quarterback* had to slow down after an hour or so, as the rain increased. The drops were not staying on the ground, but boiling off as soon as they struck; the resulting mist, rather than the rain itself, was blocking vision. The black, blowing flakes had vanished, whether as a result of blocked vision or because they were washed to the ground could only be guessed. What was falling was anyone's guess, too; presumably fluorine compounds, but emphatically not water. Hydrogen was far scarcer on this world than on Mars or even Mercury.

Dominic made one of his thoughtful weather analyses as the rain slowed them.

"There's a high ridge back of us and to the right, remember? Surface wind seems to be toward the day side as usual, so the air is being pushed up and cooling adiabatically as it reaches the hills. Something's condensing out, maybe oxides of sulfur or fluorides of sulfur or silicon. We ought to get out of it in a few kilos."

The prediction, especially the phrase "as usual," took Erni's mind off his worries for a moment. This world's weather was quite literally chaotic; the word "climate" meant nothing.

"How much'll you bet?"

Nic glanced over at his partner, thankful that his own face was invisible. "Well-l-l—" He let his voice trail off.

"Come on. You're not going to cut off my best source of income, are you?"

"You should work for a living, but all right. Fifty says we're in clear air in—oh, twenty kilos."

"You're on. Check the odometer." Yucca zeroed one of the wheel counters. *Quarterback* had been off the tracks since leaving the quake site. "Not that one, friend. It's center right, not a driver, off the ground a lot of the time, and you know it." Still glad that his face couldn't be seen, the prophet activated a driving-wheel meter.

Erni rather pointedly made sure it was actually counting, his divided attention almost at once giving Dominic a chance to distract him even further.

"Watch it. Boulder." The runabout swerved rather more than was really necessary, grazing an asparagus-like growth three or four meters high and knocking it over before Icewall steadied. Neither looked at the other this time, but the driver did not slow down. Yucca decided that no more needed to be done for a while to stop his friend from worrying. After all, he himself couldn't help wondering why there had been no word from *Jellyseal*. Ben's explanation had been plausible, but still . . .

They were still in rain, though quite probably a different sort—Nic could have been partly right—an hour later. The odometer had been stopped and, after a coin had passed from Nic's possession to Erni's, rezeroed. There had been two or three more reports from Nest; the errant tank was still traveling, more or less in the expected direction, but still no word had come from its occupants.

"I wonder what they're bringing back," Dominic ventured after a long silence. "The natives didn't get very specific about what they could trade, though they seemed to want the hydrogen badly enough."

"According to Tricia," Erni amended. "Desire's a pretty abstract concept too, you know."

"They repeated the request enough times and enough different ways so even she was pretty sure. And you can see why scientists here want the stuff." Icewall merely nodded at the obvious.

Beings on Halfbaked at all versed in the physical sciences would presumably have detected Element One in the spectrum of their sun, looked for it on the planet, probably learning a lot of chemistry in the process, and possibly found the traces accumulated in the crust by eight billion years or so of stellar wind. The urge for enough to do macroscopic research would have matched that of the discoverers of helium and plutonium on Earth, not to mention the seekers for coronium before spectroscopic theory matured. The human explorers on Halfbaked had understood and sympathized. They had designed and grown the paraffin tanker some humorist with a background in historical trivia had named the *Jellyseal*, loaded it with high molecular weight hydrocarbons from the brown dwarf thirty-odd astronomical units out from 51 Pegasi, and sent it to the apparent source of the native transmissions.

Communication was still vague, but there seemed a reasonable hope that something of use to human knowledge would come back. Attendant risks to human health and life were taken for granted and accepted.

Except, to some extent and for the time being, by the spouses of the *Jellyseal*'s drivers.

The two men drove, ate, and slept in turn. They felt their way through rain and fog—or maybe it was dust—held their breaths as they threaded narrow valleys where falling rocks could not possibly have been avoided, enjoyed an occasional glimpse of still unfamiliar constellations, speculated aloud about an occasional unusually large blowing object, felt the *Quarterback* tremble in gales which came and ceased with no apparent pattern (though Dominic still tried, usually adding to Erni's cash reserves), asked without result whether there had been word from their wives, listened to the constant exchange of messages with the natives which were slowly expanding a mutually useful scientific vocabulary, and drew steadily closer to Nest.

The word about the tanker's motions remained encouraging; it appeared to be under intelligent control. The best evidence appeared when the *Quarterback* was about an hour out from the base. It took the form of a report from Senatsu Ito Yoshihashi which was not, at first glance, encouraging.

"The girls are headed for trouble, I'm afraid," she said thoughtfully to Ben.

"How?"

"The path they took out has changed, about a hundred kilometers ahead of where they are now. What was a fairly narrow valley—a couple of kilos wide—seems to have been blocked up by something. It's filling with some sort of liquid, as well as I can interpret the images. At least, its surface is now remarkably level and higher than before, and if it were freezing I'd expect crystals to do something to the reflection somewhere along the spectrum."

"Can't they travel on it anyway?" Cloud was tying *Quarterback* into the communication link as he spoke. "The tanker should float on any liquid I can imagine at dayside temperature, and the tracks would drive it after a fashion."

"It's the 'after a fashion' part that bothers me," the observer/mapper replied. "I *think*, though I'm not at all sure, that the stuff is spilling out the darkside—Hotsouth—end of the valley; and whether it's a real liquid-fall or just rapids, I'm doubtful anything human-grown can hold together in either."

"They'll see the lake or whatever it is and at least know better than to go boating," was Erni's surprisingly optimistic response.

"But what can they do if they want to take another path?" asked Dominic. "Would the maps they started with be any help? Especially the way the topography changes? Wouldn't they just wind up wandering around in a maze? I'd hate to have tried this trip without your guiding us."

"I suggest," responded Ben slowly, "that Sen recheck their general area as thoroughly and quickly as she can. Then she can work out as good an alternate path as possible, and we'll send it to the girls. They're not transmitting, but we don't know they're not receiving."

"Why didn't we call them and ask them to stop, or travel in a circle, or something like that a long time ago?" asked Erni. He carefully avoided sounding critical, since he had to include himself in the list of people who hadn't thought of this.

"Ask Pete. I'm not a psychologist," Ben replied. "Sen, what sort of topo information do you have for that area?"

"Pretty good, both current and from the original route pix. Give me a few minutes to match images and check for changes."

Even Erni remained silent until the mapper's voice resumed. She did stay within the few minutes.

"All right. Thirty kilos ahead of where they are now, they should turn thirty degrees to the right. Another ten kilos will take them into a valley narrow enough to be scary; they should wait, if they feel any temblors, until things seem to quiet down, and then get through as fast as possible. I can't resolve the area well enough to guess how fast that would be. Once through they can slow down if they want—there'll be no risk of rockfalls for a while. Seventy more kilos will take them past the lake, and they can slant to the left as convenient. That will bring them back to the original path sooner or later. They can check whether there's a river in it now. I'd like to know; I've seen plenty of what looked like little lakes, plus the big one at the native transmission site, but nothing that looked like flowing water—it wouldn't be water, you know what I mean—so far. Got it?"

Ben had been making a sketch map as Sen spoke. He used a polymer sheet and an electric stylus, rather than pencil and paper, since the Nest was also under seven-plus gees and its personnel had the same need of flotation as the drivers. Most of the personnel referred to their rest-and-recreation periods in the orbiting station farther out from the star as "drying-out" sessions, although much of the time in them was spent in baths. Recycling equipment is never quite perfect.

"I think so." Cloud held his product in front of the pickup—his station was more than a hundred meters from Senatsu's—for her to check.

"Close as I can put it," she agreed. "See if you can get it through to the girls."

Nic and his companion lacked the visual connection, but listened with critical interest as the word went out. Ben didn't have to include them in his transmission net, but it never occurred to him not to. Both drivers looked at each other and nodded slowly as the first message ended; the mental picture they got from it matched the one they had formed from Senatsu's words. They didn't actually stop listening as Ben set a record of his words repeating again and again to the relay/observation satellites, but most of their attention went back to the *Quarterback* as they resumed travel. They were now only an hour or so from Nest, but that was no reason to ease up on caution. They could die just as easily and completely at or inside the station's entry lock as anywhere else on the world.

Fallen rock areas. Risk-of-falling-rock regions. Puddles to be avoided—the liquid could easily be something that would freeze on wheels or in tracks if the temperature dropped a Kelvin or two. It could even be a subcooled liquid waiting to freeze on contact; such things did occur, and there was no way to tell just by looking. Stands of organisms which *could* be smashed through, but which would also produce liquid. Some of these were quite tall; Erni had never visited Earth and was not reminded of Saguaro Reserve, but most worlds with life have xerophytes. Usually the biggest growths were widely enough spaced to avoid easily, but some of the others grew in nearly solid mats.

The men had often driven over the present area, and both noticed that some fairly tall specimens seemed now to cluster along the outward path they had crushed a day or so earlier. Possibly these used the remains of other organisms as nourishment. If so, they grew *fast*.

Nothing corresponding to animal life ever showed itself, and many seriously doubted its presence; but some of the "plants" showed stumps where trunks, branches, or twigs had obviously been severed, though the detached fragments could seldom be seen. Tendrils would still be lashing, as though their owners had been disturbed by something moments before the *Quarterback* passed.

Some of the Nest personnel were beginning to suspect that the number of plant-like growths and patches within ten or fifteen kilometers of the station was increasing as the days passed, but no one had yet made a careful study of the possibility. It might be interesting, but was not yet obviously important.

Quartermaster was in a relatively open space when Ben's voice caused Erni to cut drive reflexively.

"They're turning, she thinks." The lack of nouns bothered neither driver; they didn't even bother to ask, "Which way?" They simply floated at their stations and listened. The oxygen monitor in *Quarterback* recorded a sharp drop in breathing rate, but not for long enough to cause it to report an emergency. Cloud would probably not have been bothered by such an alarm anyway; unlike the monitor, he was human.

Senatsu improvised quickly. The atmosphere was fairly clear around her target at the moment, and she was able to set up an interferometric tie between the tanker's reflector and a nearby bright spot—a stationary one, she hoped. This let her measure the relative motions of the two within a few centimeters per second. It took less than half a minute to show that *Jellyseal*'s direction of motion was changing, and another minute and a half established that the machine had straightened out on a new course thirty degrees to the right of the earlier one.

Coincidences do happen, but human minds tend to doubt even the real ones. For the first time in many hours, *Quarterback*'s drivers really relaxed. The remaining distance back to Nest was covered calmly and happily, though neither man remembered later much of the conversation which passed. With anyone.

The reception lock had been readied for them, its water pumped into a standby tank, and the doors opened as they approached. Dominic eased the runabout inside and powered down as the door sealed. The two waited while water flowed back, pushing the local air which had entered with them out through the roof vents, and was tested. As usual, more time was needed to neutralize the sulfuric and sulfurous acids and to precipitate and filter out the fluorides formed when the air had met the liquid, but at last they could open their own outer seal, check their personal breathing kits, and swim to one of the personnel locks occupying two walls of the "garage." Erni pointedly allowed Dominic to precede him into the main part of the structure, though the latter was not entirely happy at receiving attention due to age. Fifteen years out of fifty wasn't that much of a difference, and he was the taller and stronger of the two.

Of course, it was a relief to know the youngster had stopped worrying enough to be polite.

Jellyseal had been about a month—more parochially, seven years—on its way to the native city, or settlement, or camp, or whatever it might be. By the end of the first day after the return of the no-longer-anxious husbands, it seemed likely that about as long would be needed for its return. Perhaps, Senatsu remarked hesitantly, a little bit less. "They're making slightly better time right now than they did going out, but they're still on the sun side, and will be for days yet. They can see better, after all. When they get to the real terminator we can find out how much they have to slow down. They'll be easier for me to see in the dark, too."

This remark was no surprise to her listeners. The tanker of course carried corner reflectors for the microwave beams from the satellites, and with less reflected sunlight and thermal and biological emission from the planet's surface, the contrast between vehicle and surroundings would be a lot better. All this except the greater plant emission on the day side had been discovered, and much of it predicted, long before. Nic and Erni, together as usual and just returned from a test drive, simply nodded at Senatsu's report, and went on about their routine work.

Much of this involved the preparation of the second tanker, already being called *Candlegrease*. Most of the staff were from colony worlds where conditions were still fairly primitive, and in any case human educators had had the importance of detailed history knowledge forced on them after the species began to scatter. Candles had no more disappeared from humanity's cultural memory than had cooking—including making jelly.

It had occurred to several people that towing a paraffin tank as a trailer might involve less trouble in a number of ways, and possibly even be safer for the crew, than driving one as a tank truck. It was taken for granted that another load of hydrocarbons would go to the natives, even though no one yet knew what value the material now coming back might turn out to have. There was a natural sympathy for the needs of researchers, and at the very least whatever it was couldn't help but supply information about the natives themselves. *Jellyseal*'s slow approach was being watched with interest by everyone, not just the waiting husbands.

Nearly all the labored communication with the native city dealt with science; most of the linguistic progress that had been made so far had come from computer correlation between human vehicle motions, which the natives seemed able to observe even at great distances, and radiation emitted and received from the observing satellites. Discussions tended to consist of comments about orbital perturbations and precessions and their connection with the planet's internal structure. Computers at Nest were gradually building a detailed map of Halfbaked's inner density distribution and, more slowly, a chart of its mantle currents. Not surprisingly for a planet a hundred and seventy-seven times Earth's mass, almost five times its radius, and over seven times its surface gravity, plate tectonics was occurring at what the planetary physicists considered meteorological speed; and the plates themselves were state- or city- rather than continent-size. This made travel interesting and mapmaking an ongoing process. Since the establishment of Nest, one couple who had arrived as meteorologists had shifted over to crustal dynamics and been welcomed. They had been rather glad to make the change, though a little embarrassed at flinching from a challenge. Halfbaked's atmosphere had a dozen major components, mainly but not only fluorides and oxides of sulfur and silicon, varying in completely chaotic fashion in relative amounts with time and location and ready to change phase with small variations in temperature, pressure, input from the sun, and each other's concentration.

Reliance on miracles was not, of course, a useful solution to any problem; but some of the staff occasionally, and of course very privately, felt slightly tempted. After all, the supernatural could hardly be *much* less useful at prediction than the math models produced so far.

So what talk there was with the natives tended to be on the physical and material rather than emotional planes. Even mathematical abstractions, critical as they were to chemical discussion, were not progressing well. It was not even certain that the others knew—or cared—about the returning tanker.

Tricia Whirley Feather, responsible for the final steps in guessing what the computer-derived translation attempts might actually mean, was just about certain the paraffin shipment had been received and appreciated. She had no idea whatever what, if anything, was being sent back in exchange. She was not at all certain that the concept of "exchange" was clear to the natives.

But *Candlegrease* was nevertheless being grown and modified outside in the Halfbaked environment, where the more serious planning errors should show up quickly.

An overpowered and overweight runabout, named *Annie* from another ancient literary source, and intended to tow the carrier, had been more or less finished. At least it was driveable and Erni and Dominic were testing it. There was little general doubt that these two would make the second trip, though Ben had some personal reservations. These were finally resolved almost by accident.

The regular planetological work of the station was kept up, of course. More than two dozen satellites, in orbits out to about ten thousand kilometers above the surface, were cooperating with a seismic net slowly spreading out from Nest in working out the planet's internal structure, surface details, and atmospheric behavior. Progress was at about two doctoral theses per hour, Ben Cloud estimated.

And, presumably, each hour was also bringing Jessi Ware Icewall and Maria Flood Yucca seventy or eighty kilometers closer to their husbands. *Jellyseal* was making good speed.

She was also getting close to the dark side.

Actual construction of the new tanker system was going well enough, whenever decisions could be made; pseudolife techniques had taken most of the delays and difficulties out of actually making things. The problems of designing them remained, however. Ideas which seemed great by themselves would turn out to be incompatible with other equally wonderful ones when people attempted to grow them together. Whole assemblies which had promised well in computer simulation were embarrassing failures when grown and tried out. The communication lapse from *Jelly* was more than worrisome; her crew, who had the ordinary skills at pseudolife design even if they were not actually experts, presumably had far more knowledge relevant to the problem than anyone else on the planet.

The supposedly straightforward problem of traction on unknown surfaces for a vehicle expected to tow several times its own weight was attaining Primary status. Erni, Dominic, and several other sets of drivers were kept busy on test runs which ran, too often, straight into a new problem. Sometimes they didn't think of their wives for whole hours, though they never failed to check in with Senatsu when they came back in.

"They'll be seeing the last of the sun in an hour or two," the analyst remarked at one of these meetings when the return distance still to be covered had shrunk to about thirty thousand kilometers geodesic. "They're already a lot easier to spot, and don't seem to be having any trouble finding their way. They're swerved two or three times, but never very far, and apparently for things like that fault of yours. That, by the way, is now about three meters high and seems to be still growing; it's lucky it's not on their return path. I've suggested that Ben send someone out to see how much horizontal shift it's shown. I can't tell from satellite—can't get sharp enough ground motion details without a set of retroreflectors at a known location. Want to make the run?"

Dominic shrugged. "Okay with us, if Ben calls it. We might as well be doing something."

"You are already, it seems to me. Well, we'll let him call it. If he thinks you'll be better off growing up with *Candlegrease* and *Annie* then someone else can go. Or no one, of course, if he doesn't think it's important enough."

Cloud, after only a second or two of thought, decided the information was important enough to rate a close look, and six hours later—people still had to sleep—*Quarterback* was heading away from Nest on a Hotpole bearing of about seventy degrees, with her usual drivers aboard.

Some changes along the track could be seen almost at once. The tall growths which seemed to be springing up where vegetation had been crushed on their first trip out were now much taller. What had looked like two-meter stalks of deep red, dark brown, and dead black asparagus now resembled giant saguaros with, in many cases, the bases of what had been separate stalks now grown together. A former clump or thicket now seemed like a single plant with multiple branches probing upward. Neither driver liked the idea of trying to plow through these, so progress became much slower and less direct. Sometimes they had to retrace some distance and try a new route. Eventually they settled for paralleling their former path rather than trying to follow it.

They speculated over the chance that the organisms they had casually pulped the first trip out might be serving as food for saprophytes, and reported the idea back to Ben. Ten minutes later he told them to collect specimens. The xenobiologists also wanted data. Life on a virtually hydrogen-free world needed investigating. Especially life whose carbon content far exceeded ninety percent, as well as zero hydrogen.

Collecting would have slowed them even more, but Erni and Nic decided to do it on the way back and rolled on, with the fence of organ pipes to their right and a relatively clear path ahead.

The quakes produced by the still active fault made themselves felt well before the actual structure came in sight, and *Quarterback* was slowed accordingly. The operators stopped a short distance from the scarp, which was now, as Senatsu had reported, over two meters high. The big saprophytes, if that's what they were, were not doing very well in the quake area, and no longer formed a barrier. It was therefore possible to follow the verge to the right for several kilometers; but no practical way down could be found. Neither man trusted the structure of their vehicle enough to drive over the edge under local gravity, even without the problem of getting back up. Also, even if the body had survived, the impact would probably have treated the men like dynamited fish.

Servobugs—waldo-controlled pseudolife vehicles ranging from ten centimeters to half a meter in length and eight kilograms to nearly eight hundred in weight—were of course cheap, and they wasted one of the smallest and presumably sturdiest in a test drop over the edge. It did not survive, but the sacrifice was considered worthwhile.

At this point Senatsu made another report, changing Ben's plans and frustrating several xenobiologists. *Jellyseal* had passed out of the sunlit zone, and seemed to be having trouble finding its way. Guidance information had been sent from Nest as before.

This time it was not followed.

Requests to stop and perform specific maneuvers to show that Nest's messages were being received also went unheeded, or at least unanswered.

Ben, knowing his personnel, promptly suggested that *Quarterback* drop its present mission and try to intercept the tanker. After all, things might as well be official, and the husbands would certainly do this anyway. Senatsu and her helpers would do their best to provide guidance starting from the runabout's current position.

There was no need to go back to Nest for supplies, since all the vehicles had full recycling capacity and adequate energy sources. Knowing this had discouraged Cloud from even thinking of sending anyone but the two husbands. Upon hearing of the new behavior, and without even waiting for the first guidance messages, Erni swung their vehicle Hoteast—a quadrant to the right of the line toward Hotpole—and slanted away from the scarp. Haste was not exactly a priority with the two drivers, since they would be many days on the way whatever the machine driven by their wives might do, but there would be no delay. Worry was back in charge.

The geodesic connecting the two vehicles of course no longer crossed into Hotside, rather to Ben's annoyance. He wanted more detailed information about the problems of driving in sunlight, for use in future mission planning. His nature, however, was practical as well as sympathetic, and he made no suggestion to either Senatsu or the *Quarterback*'s drivers about slanting a bit to the left if opportunity occurred. Two or three times in the next weeks he had brief hopes that the only practical path the mappers could find might lead a little way into sunlight, but each time he was disappointed.

Erni and Nic were not. They were worried—still no word from their wives—and frustrated as Senatsu guided them through a maze of hillocks, around obstacles organic and topographical, past puddles and lakes of unknown composition, and once for over fifty kilometers paralleling a cliff about as high as silicate rock could be expected to lift against Halfbaked's gravity. She had warned them against getting within a kilometer of the edge of this scarp; they were on the high side, and there was no way of telling whether or when the tonnage of *Quarterback* combined with the fantastically rapid erosion by the fluoride-rich wind and rain would trigger collapse of the whole section of landscape. Being part of a seven-gee landslide would not be noticeably better than being under one. She had only used the route at all because it offered tens of kilometers of relatively flat surface which would permit maximum speed; and even then, she and Cloud had debated the idea for some time with Nic and Erni out of the comm net.

No one felt very much better when, some ten hours after the *Quarterback*'s passage, the cliff did collapse in four or five places as far in as the runabout's track.

"I wonder," Nic remarked when Ben relayed this information, "whether I'll yield to temptation a few years from now. It'd be so easy to turn ten hours into ten seconds when I'm telling about this to the kids."

Then of course it was too late to bite his tongue off. Erni, who was driving at the time, said nothing for several seconds; then his only words were, "I'm sure I would."

The *Jellyseal* was making poor progress, according to the satellite observations. Time and again she seemed to have headed into a dead-end path and had to backtrack. One encouraging fact was that the same mistake was never made twice; it looked as though the drivers were on the job. No one could yet believe that the following of the earlier instruction had been coincidence, so the general idea was now that whatever had gone wrong earlier with the tanker's transmitters had now spread to the receivers as well. What this might be seemed unknowable until the machinery could be checked at first hand; all the communication gear in every vehicle on the planet was multiply redundant. Disabling it should take deliberate and either highly skilled or savagely extensive sabotage.

No one could suggest a plausible or even credible motive for either the drivers or the natives to do such a thing, and it seemed highly unlikely that the latter would have the requisite specific skills in spite of their obvious familiarity with microwave transmission. Knowledge of principles does not imply ability to design or repair complex unfamiliar equipment.

But the tanker remained silent and apparently deaf, though it continued to move as though guided by intelligence.

"At least," remarked Erni after they had received another report from Senatsu that their target was once more backtracking, "they're not forcing us to make changes in our path. If the girls had actually been making headway back home, we'd have had to change our own heading all the time."

"Come on, young man," came Senatsu's indignant voice. "Don't you think I'd have been able to work out a reasonable intercept for you? I wouldn't have kept you heading for where they were at the moment. I know you're worried, but don't get insulting."

She was not really indignant, of course, and Erni knew it, and she knew Erni knew it. The art of trying to keep the youngster's mind off his troubles was now being widely practiced at Nest. It was lucky that most of the divergently planned help efforts had to funnel through one person.

In a way Erni knew all that, too. Oddly enough, the knowing did help. People may resent pity, but honest sympathy is different; it lacks the condescension.

Maybe that was why so few people seemed to feel that Dominic needed help, too.

Actually, the efforts were not really necessary most of the time. The journey itself was far from boring. The basic need for constant alertness when running at high speed across poorly known topography left little time for unrelated thoughts while on duty, and caused enough fatigue to ensure deep sleep between hitches. The world itself was different enough from anything familiar to human explorers; it took much of the attention not needed for guiding the runabout.

Not all of the differences were obvious to the operators. Power consumption of the vehicle, for example, recorded at Nest, indicated that it spent over two thousand kilometers climbing one side and descending the other of a three-kilometer-high dome; Nic and Erni heard only indirect echoes of the arguments as scientists tried to match this information with that from satellites and seismograms.

The assumption that the world had a nearly equipotential surface, with strength of crustal materials essentially meaningless, was presumed to be even truer here than on any merely one-gee planet. The drivers had not noticed the changes in actual power needed to keep a given speed; they merely knew they were three thousand kilometers closer to where they wanted to be.

They could tell, of course, when it was possible to keep a given speed; only rarely was the way open enough—and when it was, they had to be even more alert for the strange things which might change that happy state.

Once, and once only, was there an animal, a definitely living thing moving sluggishly across their path leaving a track entirely stripped of vegetation, large and small. There was no way to see its underside, and hence no way to tell whether it was traveling on short legs—which would presumably have had to be numerous—or, though no trail was visible, something like the slime track of a gastropod. The biologists did manage this time to get a plea through Ben's near-censorship. They wanted the *Quarterback* just to change course the slightest bit and roll the thing over *en passant*, and leave a servobug or two to examine it more closely . . .

The drivers were not sure their vehicle could roll over something about its own size, and even less certain that the creature itself could do nothing about it if they tried. They promised to make the effort when the present emergency was ended, preferably much closer to possible help from Nest, and drove on. The bugs were controllable from only a short distance in the biological static.

The debate was picked up by the natives, who wanted to know what "animal" meant. No one could explain with the available symbols. This was not surprising; but during the next hour Nic and Erni saw, swooping around their vehicle, objects which looked like the familiar blowing bits of black paper at a distance but which, seen close to, were clearly gliders—tossing, banking, and whirling in the wind as though barely under control, but clearly aircraft. This was duly reported to Nest. The report, presumably detectable by the natives, elicited no comment from them.

Quarterback was now a little closer to the sunlit slightly-more-than-hemisphere (the star covered fourteen degrees of sky). The generally active tectonics had not changed significantly, but the air was decidedly warmer and the plants, possibly in consequence, more luxuriant. Nothing resembling leaves had been seen yet, again unless the apparently charred blowing sheets qualified, and there were bets among the biologists on whether such organs would be present even under direct sunlight. The drivers of *Jellyseal* had failed to report any, but this meant little when one considered the planet's area. Special enlarged organs for intercepting stellar energy did seem a bit superfluous with the star scarcely a twentieth of an astronomical unit away. However, considering the illogical structure of vertebrate retinae, there was no predicting all the odd paths regular evolution might take.

Cloud made few requests of the husbands, no matter how urgently his halo of researchers begged. He did pass on to them the suggestion that more and bigger plants might mean more if not bigger animals, but left any changes in driving policy up to them. They made none; they were already as alert as human beings could well remain.

The final two-thousand-kilometer segment of the run was frustrating, over and beyond the general annoyance built up over twenty-two days of unbroken driving. The men were, in what now might almost be called straight-line distance, less than three hundred kilometers from their still moving goal. They could not follow a straight line; that way was a labyrinth of seamed, faulted, broken hills where even the satellites could detect almost constant rockfalls. The *Quarterback* would not have to be hit by a rock; a wheelbarrow load of sand could put her instantly out of commission, and help was now tens of thousands of kilometers away. There was no option but to go around the region. Senatsu was apologetic about not having seen the details sooner, but she was easily forgiven; her attention had been confined by their own needs to areas much closer to the travelers for nearly all the trip.

Erni responded to the news with a rather rough jerk at the steering controls; his partner fully sympathized but made the signal to change drivers. The younger man had enough self-control to obey, and the runabout set off in a new direction with *Jellyseal* now off toward its left rear. The sky and its omnipresent clouds flickered even more brightly than usual, as though in sympathy—or perhaps derision. Fortunately, neither driver had reached the state of personalizing the indifferent world. No one even considered how close this state might be.

It would not of course have bothered the planet, but could easily have distorted important judgments.

Cloud, whose telemetry had of course reported the moment of rough driving, was a little worried; but there seemed nothing he could do, and nothing he should say, about the matter.

The two thousand kilometers took three infuriating days, though the last few hours were eliminated by *Jellyseal*'s luckily, though apparently fortuitously, moving to a more accessible spot and actually stopping for a time.

The pause might have been due to her being in the center of a twenty-kilometer nearly circular hollow—almost certainly *not* an impact crater—with eight different narrow valleys leading from it. She had already explored two of these, according to Senatsu, and been forced to turn back; maybe the drivers were debating which to try next, Ben suggested.

Neither husband could believe this for a moment. They knew their wives would have planned such a program much earlier. The faces behind their breathing masks were now grim. They made no answer to Cloud, but Erni, now driving again, sent them zigzagging at the highest practical speed along a rock-littered canyon which Senatsu had assured them would lead to the hollow. Nic did not object. The sooner they were out from between the looming eighty-meter walls, the better their chance of living to see—

Whatever might be there to be seen. The satellite images were, after all, only computer constructs.

Rocks fell, of course, but continued to miss. Neither man had any illusions about how much of this was due to driving skill, but neither gave it much conscious thought. The canyon opened into the valley twenty kilometers ahead.

Fifteen. Ten. Five.

They were there, and neither even felt conscious relief as the threatening cliffs opened out. They could not at once spot the tanker, and stopped to look more carefully.

The trouble was that none of the vehicle's lights were on. Deeplights might of course be out because it was not moving, but the floods, and the smaller but sharp and clear running and identity-pattern lights which should have been on were dark, too. It was long, long moments before Erni perceived the tanker's outline against the faint, flickering, and complex illumination of the lightning-lit background.

He pointed, and Dominic nodded. The younger man had been driving through the valley, but now Nic took over and approached their motionless, lightless, and possibly—probably?—lifeless goal. Erni was calling frantically into the short-range multiwave communicator. Neither was surprised at the lack of an answer; frantic was a better word.

Tracks, wheels, and much of the lower body of the tanker were crusted with something white, but the men paid only passing attention to this.

There should at least have been light coming from the cockpit. There wasn't. Something else strange about the windows seized the attentions of both men, but the *Quarterback* was within fifty meters of the other machine before this got the door of consciousness open.

Lights inside or not, the windows should have been visible as more than dark slots. Anything transparent, silicate or not, reflects some of the light trying to get through.

But the sky, which was a good deal brighter than the ground, was not being reflected from *Jellyseal*'s windows. They were lightless gaps in the not-very-bright upper body. And the reason now became clear to both observers, drowning out the screaming denials of hope.

The windowpanes were not there. Maybe, of course, the occupants weren't there either, but where else could they possibly be? And more important, where else could they possibly be alive? What besides local air was in the tanker's cockpit? Even Dominic, with the means of looking waiting at his fingertips, had trouble making the fingers act.

But they did, slowly and much less surely than usual. He slipped into waldo gloves, and a servobug emerged from the runabout. Briefly—perhaps less briefly than usual—it checked out its limbs and lights, and made its way across to the tanker's relatively monstrous hulk.

It could climb, of course. There were holds on the outer shells of all Nest's vehicles, the bug had grasping attachments on its "legs," and the machines had been designed and grown to be used in rescue techniques as well as more general operations. It made its rather fumbling way up *Jellyseal*'s front end, and finally reached the openings which had once held barriers intended to keep in the flotation water, keep out one of the few environments in the known universe more corrosive than Earth's, and still let light through. Nic was guiding the little machine by watching it from where he was. Not even Erni asked why the bug's own eyes had not been activated yet.

Yes, the windowpanes were gone. Yes, the bug could climb inside with no trouble. Yes, the last excuse for not using its own vision pickups was gone. Without looking at his partner, Nic turned on the bug's eyes and his own screen.

It could not at once be seen what was in the cockpit. Nothing human showed, but that might have been because vision reached little more than a meter into the chamber. It was blocked by a seemingly patternless tangle of twisted branches, ranging from the thickness of a human middle finger down to rather thin string. The colors filled the usual range for Halfbaked vegetation, from very dark maroons and browns to dead black.

The stuff was very brittle, far more so than anything living should have been. Nic tried to get farther inside. The bug, under his waldoed direction, reached out to one of the thicker stems and tried to use it as a climbing support. Several centimeters of the growth vanished in dust and the machine overbalanced and fell into the cockpit. It left an elevator shaft as it pulverized its way to the floor, and Nic had to go through cleaning routines as black dust slowly settled through the dense air around and upon his mechanical agent.

Both men were now watching the relay screen, but things weren't much improved. The bug was still surrounded by the tangle, and as it moved slowly across the floor kept smashing its way through a three-dimensional fabric of seemingly charred growths. The stuff was brittle, but not really frail. A significant push, comparable to the bug's weight, was needed actually to break the thickest of the branches. It was only when they broke that they went to powder.

The cockpit was far larger than that of the *Quarterback*, more than five meters across and eight long, and it was many minutes before most of the floor had been examined. The bug was now moving around under an artistically tangled ceiling twenty centimeters or so high, supported by many pillars of unharmed branches. It left tracks as it went in a two-or three-millimeter-thick layer of black powder containing many short fragments of the branches.

There was no sign of a human form, living or otherwise, anywhere on the floor, but there was all the evidence anyone could ask that the tangle above could never have supported a human body in the local gravity, and flotation water was gone. Erni finally reported this aloud, his voice as expressionless as he could make it, and summarized the observations forcing this conclusion. Ben acknowledged and opened channels for everyone at Nest.

"We want to look farther, not consult!" Nic objected. "There ought to be some sort of indication what happened. Where did the windows go, anyway?"

"They'd probably be the first things to give if the refrigeration failed and the water boiled suddenly over in the daylight," Cloud pointed out reluctantly, "unless someone who knows the structure better doesn't think so. Speak up if anyone does. Anyway, it seems better for you to bring the tanker back here for really close checking, and if at all possible *not* spoil any more evidence in the cockpit. The growths you reported seem to be very frail, and therefore different from the ones we've seen, and it would be better if there were something besides powder to be examined here. Don't think we're forgetting about the girls, but if there's to be any hope of learning what happened, we need data. You can see that."

"We can see it," retorted the younger driver, "but there are still items we'd like to examine ourselves."

"What? There was only that one compartment they could have lived in. The whole rest of the machine was paraffin tank, with its contents melted wax for the last part of their trip, and presumably native air for the return—unless you think it was evacuated when the cargo was unloaded, and you'd have seen if it were flattened. So would Sen. What do you think you can find, anyway? You're not set up for microscopic or high-class chemical testing."

"We could find leaks, if they were big enough to—to make things happen so quickly there couldn't be any alarm sent back."

"I'd think small ones could have wrecked communication before they knew anything was wrong. But all right, I'll take it on my responsibility—go ahead and look for leaks between cockpit and tank, but do leave *something* of the stuff you've been smashing up for people to study."

"All right. But how do you expect us to get *Jellyseal* back with her cockpit uninhabitable? There's no way for us to refill it with water even if we could reseal the window openings."

"We're working on that. Go ahead and make your search."

The men obeyed, Erni rather sullenly, Nic more thoughtful. The floor and rear bulkhead of the cockpit and the rear third of each side wall were between living chamber and cargo space, so there was a large area to be examined. How this could be managed without destroying all contact between walls and branches was not very evident. Human remains are large enough so that the first search had left many columns of undamaged vegetation still touching the floor, but to examine the walls for pinholes or even nail holes would be another matter. Nic thought for two or three minutes before trying anything, his partner waiting with growing impatience.

"You know," Yucca said slowly at last, "if there was actually a leak between cockpit and tank, would the windows have blown out? There's a lot of volume back there for steam to expand into, even if it was nearly full of wax. There were several cubic meters full of local air to allow for the paraffin's expanding as it warmed, whether it melted or not."

"I still want to look."

"I know. I don't want to give up either. But think. Whatever chance the girls have of being alive, it's not on board that machine. The natives could have—"

"You mean they might have. But would they have known how? Could *we* keep one of *them* alive anywhere near Nest, when we have no idea about what they need—except maybe in temperature? And if they're alive, why haven't they called us?"

Dominic gestured toward the tanker a few meters away. "What with? Do you think any of the comm gear is still in working shape?"

"You two find that out, pronto," came Ben's voice. "There's a good chance, the design crew thinks. If enough of it works you can use the bug that's in there now to handle it. You find out whether it can still be set to receive short-range stuff from you, or if the controls are in shape to be handled by the bug itself. In one case, it may be possible to set up for *Jelly* to follow you by homing on transmission from your car. In the other, it'll be a lot harder, but one of you using the bug's handlers should be able to drive *Jelly* while the other runs *Quarterback*. That'll be almighty slow, since you'll have to stop to rest pretty often instead of swapping off, but it should be possible."

"But—" started Erni.

Cloud spoke more gently, and much more persuasively. "You both know most of what little chance there is that they're alive is if they're somewhere under the sun. We don't know just how smart these natives are, but remember that *they* got in touch with *us*, after hearing our satellite and vehicle transmissions. Let's get that machine back here and find out what we can from it. Even if time is critical, and I can't say it isn't, aren't the odds better this way? We can try to ask the natives, too, though a lot of language learning will have to come first, I expect."

"How do you know the odds are better?" Erni was snapping again.

"I don't, of course," Ben maintained his soothing tone, "but to me they *seem* better with a whole population of smart people working on finding out just what did happen."

Nic nodded slowly, invisibly to Cloud but not to Erni.

"I suppose that makes sense."

"Something else makes sense, too," Erni added grimly.

"What."

"Tricia got the idea that the natives were pleased with the variety of hydrogen compounds we'd supplied. I wonder just how big a variety they got."

"And I pointed out that the tanker did have a lot of different hydrocarbons, which I think the locals call carbon hydrides," Nic countered instantly. There was at least a minute of silence.

"All right. We'll bring it back if we can. But I'd like to know one thing, if Tricia can decode it from the local static."

"What?" asked Ben.

"Do the locals know what water is, or at least do they have a recognizable symbol for it even if they call it oxygen hydride, and—did they thank us for any?"

Again there was a lengthy pause while implications echoed silently around in human skulls. No one mentioned that the request was for *two* things; it didn't seem to be the time.

"She'll try to find out," Ben answered at last, in as matter-of-fact a tone as he could manage.

"Okay. We'll go over *Jelly*'s controls." Dominic, too, tried to sound calm.

The controls did seem to be working. This was not as startling as it might have been; all such equipment was of solid-state design and imbedded—grown into—the structures of the various vehicles. There might be mechanical failure of gross moving parts, but any equipment whose principal operating components were electrons stood a good chance of standing up in Halfbaked's environment as long as diamond or silicon were not actually exposed to fluorine.

There seemed, however, to be no way to set up the tanker's system simply to home on a radiation source, moving or not. No one had foreseen the need when the machine was designed. The closest thing to an autodriver in any of the vehicles was the general-shutdown control. There were no smooth paved highways with guiding beacons or buried rails on the planet. While systems able to avoid the ordinary run of obstacles on an ordinary planet were part of the common culture and could have been incorporated in the Halfbaked-built machines, these were *exploring* vehicles. Avoiding obstacles was simply not their basic purpose. It had been taken for granted that they would be operated by curious, intelligent people who had a standard sense of self-preservation but would be willing to take risks when appropriate.

That left trying to drive *Jellyseal* with the handling equipment of a servobug. This proved possible but far from easy, and even Erni agreed that an hour or two's practice in the open area was probably a good idea. With some confidence established by both, Dominic sent the *Quarterback* toward the valley by which they had entered while his younger companion, looking through the rear window of the cockpit, concentrated on keeping the larger vehicle a fixed distance directly behind them.

He was feeling pretty confident, almost relaxed, by the time the entrance narrowed before them.

With a brief exchange of one slightly questioning and one somewhat shaky "Okay" they entered the passage, very conscious that even at its empty weight the larger vehicle was much better able to shake the walls down on them than was their own runabout. Of course, *Jelly* also made a bigger target; but possibly a few dents or even a few holes in its body might not be critical now. Of course assuming that a house-sized boulder with the potential energy provided by a hundred-meter cliff under seven plus gravities would merely *dent* its target did seem unreasonably optimistic. Both men were optimists, even with the present probable status of their wives, but they were also reasonable; and while Nic did fairly well at concentrating on his driving, Erni's eyes kept wandering much too often from *Jellyseal*'s bulk behind them to the cliffs beside and above.

As earlier experience had warned, rocks did shake loose from time to time. It seemed very likely that the vibration of their own passage was the principal cause, since most of them slashed across the narrow way somewhat behind the *Quarterback* and its companion.

Not quite all. Four times a deafening bell-like clang reached the men's ears, deafening in spite of the poor impedance matching between the planet's atmosphere and their vehicle's body, and between the latter and the water inside. The bodies of the machines were not, of course, of metal, but they had enough metallic elasticity to ring on impact.

Jellyseal was the victim all four times. Fortunately the missiles were much less than house-sized and *Jelly* seemed not to suffer enough damage to keep her from following. This fact did not cause Dominic to relax until they were out of the danger zone and had started to backtrack their way around the Patch of Frustration, as they had named it.

At this point, Ben called again.

"There's a new track for you. You don't have to go back around to the way you came. Stand by for directions—"

"Stand by for directions—"

"Stand by for directions—"

That became the routine through their waking hours and days for the ensuing weeks. What with sleep time and difficulties in guiding their "tow," they averaged less than seventy kilometers an hour. The weeks went by, the monotony relieved by Senatsu's messages, variations in wind and weather, and local biology. No more animals had been seen, or gliders, though the latter had inspired much argument at Nest. Neither had anything been said about the pot the two drivers had presumably won on the way out; neither man thought to mention it, and for some reason no one at Nest brought the matter up.

The men were simply far too busy to think very much about the missing women, though they certainly did not forget them. When it was reported that *Candlegrease* was about ready, and Ben suggested that she be loaded and start at once for the native "city" with another crew, Nic and Erni both protested furiously. They tried to be logical; Erni insisted that talking with their wives during the first trip had given him and Nic a better idea of the route and its problems than anyone else could have. Ben countered that everyone on Nest had heard the conversations as well, and if necessary could replay the records of them. Nic supported his partner, pointing out that there had to be shades of meaning in the messages which only people who knew the speakers really well could be expected to catch. This was an unfair argument to use against the unmarried Cloud, but fairness was not on either driver's mind at the moment. Ben privately doubted the validity of the argument as any bachelor might, but had no wish to be sneered at—by many people besides the bereaved husbands—for preaching outside his field of competence.

He tried to point out the value of time. Nic countered with the value of familiarity; he and Erni were, aside from Maria and Jessi, the only people who had traveled really far from Nest. Cloud gave up at this point, agreed to wait for their arrival, but used their own argument to insist that two additional drivers go with them to gain experience.

Erni asked pointedly, "Is *Candlegrease* set up to support a crew of six?" The coordinator almost gave himself away by asking what six, but made a quick recovery.

"It will be by the time you get here." Suggesting that there would probably be no need to take care of six was obviously unwise and might, just conceivably, be wrong. Human life, even other people's, means a lot to civilized beings. A species which has survived its war stage and achieved star travel practically has to be civilized.

Ben kept his word. The second tanker was ready, loaded, and set up to keep the women comfortable if they were found, by the time Erni and Nic got back to Nest. There was a second argument when they insisted, or tried to insist, on starting out at once to the hot side in spite of their extreme exhaustion. Ben won this one, but only by promising not to let *Candlegrease* move without them, so almost another Halfbaked year passed before the medics pronounced the two fit for the trip.

There had been no delay, of course, in examining *Jelly*'s cockpit, though this had to be done with bugs. Bringing the machine into the garage and flooding it with water so that living researchers could swarm into it would quite certainly destroy any evidence there might be.

It was quickly discovered that breaking the brittle contents did not pulverize the whole branch, merely two or three diameters to each side of the break. Cutting or snipping at two points far enough apart, therefore, detached an apparently undamaged section. Since the tank was full of the stuff too, there was no shortage. After a few mistakes resulting from failing to catch them on something soft as they fell, several lengths of the material were brought into "outdoor" labs, and biologists and chemists went happily to work with their bugs.

The material was not very different from the tissues already investigated from the local vegetation. It was rigid rather than pliable, of course, and it finally occurred to someone that the stuff, having come from the hot side, might merely be frozen. This was easy enough to test. A sample was heated up to the probable temperature, as indicated by radiation theory and measurement from the satellites, of the Hotpole latitude where the "city" seemed to be. Long before it warmed up that far, the branch being tested was flexible as rope. Several of the investigators began privately to wonder whether they might be working over the remains of one of the intelligent natives, though no one suggested this aloud until well after *Candlegrease* had departed. Ben had the idea, but decided to save it; Erni might get bothered again.

What brought the question into the open was the observation that after a day or so at high temperature, most of the branches, or roots, or vines, or whatever they were began to grow fine tendrils. The stuff was still alive.

This was quickly reported to Ben Cloud, leaving him with the decision of how much to pass on to the now fairly distant second expedition. On one hand, the information was clearly critically important to anyone expecting to be in direct contact with the natives. On the other, Nic and Erni might be uncomfortable to learn that their examination of *Jelly*'s control compartment might have dismembered one of the people they were going to meet.

Or, considering what had so probably happened to their wives, they might not. The other two drivers were a married couple, Pam Knight and Akmet Jinn Treefern, and the Treeferns might keep the other two in discussion rather than brooding mode. Ben hoped the fact that they were short, stocky, extremely sturdy people from a one-point-four-gee colony world would not become important, but he was getting uneasy over Erni's patience limits.

Ben was still trying to make up his mind—there was plenty of time yet before the travelers could presumably meet any day side natives—when another discovery was made.

One of the many short sections of branch from the debris on the floor of *Jelly*'s cockpit had been part of one of the samples to be warmed up. It had not responded; it had neither softened nor grown extensions. After giving it several days, first with the rest of the sample and then by itself, it had been sequestered for more detailed study.

Halfbaked's life, it was now known, consisted mostly of carbon, with modest traces of nitrogen, oxygen, and heavy metals such as iron and titanium. The complexity needed for biological machinery was obtained not from hydrogen bonding within and between proteins and carbohydrates but from variously sized fullerenes and graphite tubes flared, tapered, curved, and branched by occasional heptagons, pentagons, and octagons in their mainly hexagonal carbon-ring nets. The "protoplasm" was considerably coarser, on the molecular scale, than anything known before to human biochemistry, and its peculiarities were contributing heavily to the Ph.D.-per-hour rate Cloud liked to brag about.

The unresponsive segment was quite different. It had a fair amount of carbon and some iron, but there was far more sodium, calcium and phosphorus than had ever been found in the native life, and the carbon for the most part was tetrahedrally bonded. It took a while to discover the reason, and this happened only when one of the chemists sat back from her diffraction spectrometer and its confusing monitor pattern and took a close naked-eye look at the specimen.

Then she called for a medical helper, who needed one glance.

The branch was the charred remains of a human little finger.

This made Ben's communication problem more difficult, but in another way. It also forced him to face it at once. He faced it, reporting as tersely and calmly as he could to the distant *Annie*.

"But why only a finger?" tiny Pam asked instantly, before either of the now confirmed widowers could react. She was honestly and reasonable curious, but was quite consciously trying to ease the shock of the message for the husbands. It was not really necessary; Nic, and even Erni, had become more and more ready to face the news as the weeks had worn on. "You two went over the whole floor, square centimeter by square centimeter, you said. Why didn't you find a lot more—and a lot more recognizable? Maybe it's just as well you didn't, of course, but still I don't see why."

Dominic was able to answer at once, though Erni had thought of the explanation as quickly.

"It was small, and they missed it."

That was all he needed to say. Even the "they" needed no clarification. Everyone in the tug heard that much and could picture the rest. Ben Cloud and more than fifty of the Nest personnel who were in the comm link could do the same. They listened while Dominic, in surprisingly steady tones, went on, "Ben, did Tricia ever get an answer to that question we asked a while ago about the natives and *water*?"

"Not that I know of." Cloud found his voice with difficulty. He had expected losses on Halfbaked, but the fact that none had occurred in the nearly half a Terrestrial year the party had been there had undermined his readiness. "I'll try to find out. Carry on. And we're sorry. I don't know what else to say that wouldn't be pure Pollyanna; but you know we mean it."

"We know."

"You also know, I expect," Ben's voice was even softer, "why I had another pair of drivers with you." It was not put as a question. Ben, a slender half-gravity colonial, did not commonly think of muscle as useful, but he was a realist.

"Yeah. Thanks. Don't worry. Erni, time for you to take over. We still have things to find out up Hotnorth."

The sun would be starting to rise in another two thousand kilometers or so. Temperature was higher, though the principal surface winds still brought chill from the dark side; turbulence sometimes mixed in air from above, not only coming from sunlit regions but heated further by compression as it descended. Dominic still sometimes contributed to Erni's financial security with an attempted weather forecast, but the variables he could think of were becoming too numerous even for his optimism. Motivation for such predictions remained high; they had identified another potential trigger for landslides. Suddenly hot or suddenly—by two or three hundred Kelvins—cold blasts of wind sometimes cracked off scales of rock by thermal shock. The cracks, fortunately, were never deep; but the layers peeled off were sometimes extensive and their shattered fragments dangerous, especially as the pieces were often thin enough to blow around.

The tank in tow was struck several times, forcing travel to cease while it was examined carefully by servobugs, but so far damage had been confined to small dents. The one strike on *Annie* had caused no damage at all, possibly because the traction problem had forced her to be grown with much extra weight.

They had seen and avoided the common puddles of unknown makeup, but as the sky ahead grew bright these became larger areas and more frequent. *Annie* avoided them, though the returning *Jellyseal* apparently had not. The white crust on her tracks and lower body had turned out to be mostly cryolite, sodium aluminum fluoride, regarded by Greenland natives on Earth as a peculiar form of ice because it would only melt in the flame of a blubber lamp.

It was now pretty obvious who, or what, had driven the tanker homeward. Dominic had already compared the fate of the driver with that of his wife, but had not spoken about it to anyone. For one thing, a lot of the *how* remained to be worked out. The tangle of apparent vegetation might, after all, have been some sort of remote control system; this world's plants did emit and receive microwaves. Maybe no intelligent being had been on board, at that. This could all tie in with the natives' immediate spotting of, and beaming signals to, the satellites when these had gone into operation months before. The graphite microtubes in Halfbaked tissue often circulated metal ions and could serve as antennae, among many, many less obvious things. It seemed more and more necessary, and more and more easy to believe, that the real life was at the source of the signals. And maybe one of the girls . . .

No, Don't think of that. Whatever had happened to them had happened very quickly—one could believe that, at least—and pretty certainly to both of them at once.

But it looked as though veering around lakes might not be really necessary, since they were going Hotnorth and anything that froze on the vehicles now should melt off again shortly. Nic did suggest this. Pam vetoed the idea at once.

"How do we know how deep these things may be?"

"Do we need to? We'd float. We're only twice as dense as water."

"That wouldn't matter to us, but could we drive, towing like this?" Nic had no answer, and they continued to stay on solid, if sometimes shaky, ground. Neither of the other men had taken part in the debate.

Just as they glimpsed the upper limb of the sun, a new sort of adventure eased the boredom. They were threading their way through a stand which looked much like the "Saguaro" patches Nic and Erni had found earlier. The growths were not always far enough apart for the tank, and much as they disliked it, there was sometimes no alternative to hitting and bending pairs of these, or sometimes breaking them completely. They were leaving a clear trail, not that this was their main worry.

Nic was glad afterward, though he was far too busy otherwise to think of it at the moment, that none of his attempted weather predictions was pending. With no warning at all a far stronger wind blast than any of them had experienced so far made itself felt to the driver. Organ pipes bent and snapped in all directions.

And, though there had been no lightning, burst into flame. For minutes they drove through the enveloping blaze, making no effort to avoid anything. The mere fact that there was no free oxygen outside meant nothing; it had not occurred to anyone to consider what the paraffin would do in unlimited supplies of this atmosphere. There was no free fluorine to speak of, but the variety of fluorine compounds actually present offered far more possibilities than any of them had time to consider. Pam joined her husband at the driving controls; Erni, with remarkable self-discipline, beamed a running report of what was happening for any satellites in position to relay to Nest; Nic deployed one of the more versatile servobugs and drove it beside them, ranging back and forth along the tank and looking carefully for any signs of rupture. After a few seconds Pam, deciding her husband needed no help—he was not attempting to dodge anything—took out another bug and covered the other side.

They were out of the stand, and out of the fire, and presumably out of danger after three or four anxious minutes. The wind now came strongly from ahead; Nic judged that the fire had set up a strong updraft which was bringing in air from all directions. Erni, with no wager going, didn't bother to disagree, and neither of the others found the suggestion unreasonable.

A few hundred meters from the nearest flames *Annie* and *Candlegrease* were stopped and all four of the crew made a slow and minute inspection of tug and tow using the bugs. There was little worry about their own vehicle; they would have been aware of serious damage within seconds of incurring it. A slow leak in the tank, however, was another matter. It was assumed that the natives were equipped to unload the paraffin at their end; they had been told as clearly as possible what it was, and would presumably be ready to keep any of the precious hydrogen from escaping. Also, they had made no complaint about the first delivery.

But no one had tried to find out what the paraffin itself would do to local life. It seemed very likely that hydrogen compounds would be about as helpful to Halfbaked's organisms as fluorine ones in comparable concentration would be to Terrestrial tissues. Also, many paraffin components were high enough in molecular weight to sink in the local atmosphere; they would be mixed and diluted quickly by wind, of course, but wouldn't rise on their own.

The travelers reminded Ben of this, and asked for suggestions. What if they *did* find a leak, even a small one? Should they come back, at least to Hotlatitudes where the paraffin would freeze again?

"I'll have to ask around," was all the coordinator could say after some seconds of thought. "Get along with your inspection, and let us know. For now, we'll assume the worst."

"What would that be, to you?" asked Erni.

"That you're leaking so badly there's no way of getting any of your load to where it's supposed to be delivered. That would make the decision easy, but I hope it isn't true."

So did the crew, but they were still careful.

There were half a dozen patches of liquid near and under the tank, but there were two similar ones near the tug, and several more within a few tens of meters. There seemed no reason to suppose they were hydrocarbons, since they seemed neither to be evaporating nor reacting with the now quite hot air, but they were watched carefully for several minutes, especially those under the tank. At Nic's suggestion, they moved the vehicles a hundred meters to an area where no puddles could be seen, and waited for more minutes.

Nothing dripped. No puddles formed. Nothing seemed to be leaking. This was reported to Cloud. He had had time to think, or someone had, and his answer was, "Check every bit of the tank you can get an eye close to for the tiniest cracks, leaking or not, which may show. Remember the one in *Jelly*."

"*What* one in *Jelly?*" asked two voices at once.

"Didn't I tell you? No, come to think of it, that just led to more questions, some of them still not answered. We think we know what happened, now. The refrigerators meant to keep the paraffin from boiling when the surroundings got really hot did a good job, but when the liquid was drained, we suppose by the customers, the tank naturally filled with local air. Some of this, maybe sulfur trioxide, formed frost on the coils and insulated them, so air at its regular temperature—eight or nine hundred Kelvins or more, depending on the local weather—swept in and hit the rear bulkhead of the cockpit. This was too thick, it turned out."

"Too *thick?*" There were more than two voices this time.

"Too thick. A thin glass will handle hot washing fluid better than a thick one. The body composition of the vehicles is as strong as we could make it, but it's also a very poor heat conductor, as intended. It bent in toward the cockpit just a little under the pressure, and that added to thermal shock to start a U-shaped crack in the rear bulkhead from floor to floor, and straight along the floor, framing about ten square meters. The area was pushed into the cockpit momentarily by the atmospheric pressure, far enough to open a gap maybe one or two centimeters wide all around. The support water, or enough of it, boiled almost instantly, the windows blew out, and the steam pressure slammed the flap back where it had come from so tightly the crack was practically invisible."

"And you never told us? Why not?" asked Pam.

"Well, it couldn't happen to you. Your living space isn't even in the same vehicle with the cargo. One point for the towing idea."

"And several points minus for keeping us in the dark!"

"We'll check for cracks," added Dominic, as steadily as he could. They all turned their attentions back to the bugs.

The fire had almost completely died out. So had the wind from Hotnorth. Dominic, glancing away from his work occasionally, saw that the pillar of smoke was sheared cleanly at, he judged, nearly a kilometer above, with the higher part whipping back toward Hotsouth. It was high enough to glow for some distance in the sunlight against an unusually dark and cloud-free sky. He was tempted to try another weather guess, but firmly turned his attention back to *Candlegrease*'s body. So cracks could be really hard to see . . .

Hard, or impossible. None were found, but no one could be quite certain. Absence of evidence is not—

They drove on into heat and sunlight, more silently than before, with a bug following on either side, its operator constantly scanning the tank. More words were spoken in the next few hours by Senatsu with her guidance information than by all four of the tug crew together.

No one was exactly in a panic, of course, but everyone had enough sense to be uneasy. Erni and Nic were more relaxed than the Treeferns now. At least they seemed to be.

"Open ground for about thirty kilos."

Ninety minutes of silence.

"What looks like a compression fold across your path ten kilos ahead. Two possible passes. The wider is four kilos to your right. Turn twenty-two degrees right to thirty-seven."

The planet's magnetic field was too distorted to provide reliable direction, but enough of the sun was now in sight to indicate Hotnorth—and make driving into it uncomfortable. The new heading was a relief.

The wider pass had walls high enough for the left one to provide shade for nearly a hundred kilometers, a distance which did not lift the star's disc perceptibly. The valley was not a recent feature; the walls on both sides were greatly collapsed and eroded. Had it been much narrower the travelers would have had a problem threading their way among the fallen fragments.

"Lake eighteen kilometers ahead. Stay close to it on its left." When they reached the lake, there was not very much rock-free space to the left of the liquid, but there was presumably even less on the other side; the drivers trusted Senatsu. She herself was developing more confidence as reports from the tug kept filling out her interpretations of the satellite radar.

She hadn't spotted the vegetation which grew densely along the shore, but this gave no real trouble. Erni and Nic thought of the fire now far behind, but there was no sudden downdraft this time. There was, as usual, lightning.

"It could happen," Dominic remarked. "The right wall is pretty high, and wind flowing over it would drop sharply and heat up by adiabatic compression—"

"How much?"

It was Akmet who asked this time, but Nic declined to bet. Erni wondered whether his friend was actually learning, or simply didn't want intruders in their friendly game. He said nothing; he was driving. Bet or no, there was no fire, and eventually the Hotnorth end of the lake came in sight.

"Head right along the shore."

Erni started to obey before realizing it was not Senatsu's voice. This was not too unusual; the Yoshihashis shared the muscular fitness supplied by constantly fighting water's inertia, but even they had to sleep sometimes.

"Who's on?" Erni asked, before realizing that the voice wasn't human either. The answer was unexpected.

"What?" This *was* Senatsu, recognizable even through the biological static, now familiar enough to be tuned out fairly well by the human nervous system.

"Who just told me to head right?"

"No one. You're in fine shape."

"You didn't send the message? Or hear it?"

"Neither. Repeat it, please."

Icewall did so.

"That did not come from here, or through satellite relay in either direction. Is it a native voice?"

"Turn right. You do not turn right."

Pam was quickest on the uptake, and was first at the communicator. "Why should we turn right?"

"The symbol 'we' is unclear. Turn right for safety and information."

Erni had done a quick-stop by now.

"Sen, did you hear that?"

"I heard static only, none of it either unusual or structured."

Treefern glanced at her husband, who nodded. His smile was of course invisible. Pam nodded back.

"Sen, this is what we heard." She quoted. "Now, repeat that back to us, please. As exactly as your voice will let you, and emphatically word for word."

Senatsu obeyed, mystified but guessing this was no time for argument or question.

The message promptly came again, in the new voice, and the observer gasped audibly.

"I *did* hear that! It came through the link."

"I thought it might. They're not stupid, and certainly not slow. Erni, fire up and do what they say—but keep your driving eyes peeled!"

"For what?"

"How should I know? Anything. What do you usually watch for?"

Icewall drove without answering. It had started to rain, unheralded by Yucca, and Pam thought of a possibly useful question for their new guide. "How far?"

"Twenty-two point one kilometers."

"Sen, if you heard that, try to see what's that far ahead."

"Sorry. I heard it, but radar isn't getting through just now."

"Comm frequencies are."

"True. They're not very good for imaging, but I'll do what I can. Stand by."

The rain grew heavier, whatever it might be composed of, and Erni slowed sharply. The voice promptly came again.

"Why stop." There was no question inflection.

Pam answered slowly, with measured and carefully chosen words. "Not stopping. Slowing. Rain. Bad measuring."

"Rain. Bad measuring," was the acknowledgment. After a pause, **"No rain. Eight kilometers. Not slow."**

"Eight kilometers," answered the woman. "Sen, you heard that? Can you see what's eight kilos—kilometers—ahead?" There were many listeners by now. Most could guess why Pam had corrected to the full length of the distance label. They also wondered which form the unknown guide would use the next time distance was mentioned.

Tricia Feather's voice came through to the tug.

"Much more of this and the translation computer won't need my help! Willi, can you use a math assistant?"

None of the travelers paid attention to this. All were looking eagerly ahead for the predicted break in the rain. Not even Nic tried to second-guess the native.

The really interesting item, they agreed later, was that their informant had allowed not only for their own speed in his, her, or its prediction. The rain clouds had been traveling much faster than tanker and tug, but the eight kilometers was still right. Dominic bowed internally to superior knowledge and vowed to himself, as he had several times before, that Erni would get no more of his cash. Prediction was evidently possible, but not for a mere human being.

Or maybe he could set up some sort of private channel with the natives, and get some of his money back. . . .

Neither he nor anyone else was particularly surprised at the sudden improvement in communication, though there was plenty of joy. The natives had been known to exist, had been known to be intelligent, and information supplies do build on themselves and grow exponentially. Maybe Erni's question about water could be answered soon. . . .

"Look up!" Akmet cried suddenly. All except Erni obeyed; he chose to continue driving.

There were scarcely any clouds now, though a number of the blowing black objects still fluttered and swirled above and beside them. One, rather larger than the rest, was dipping, swerving, and wavering in much the same way, but was larger and had a more definite shape.

The tug drivers represented three different colony planets, but all had seen dandelions, which are almost as ubiquitous as sodium and human beings. The object looked like a vastly magnified bit of dandelion fluff. It had a shaft about two meters long, topped by a halo of wind-catching fuzz of about the same diameter, and with a grapefruit-sized blob at its lower end. It must have been incredibly light to be wind-supported in this gravity.

It was moving almost as randomly as the other jetsam, but not quite. The windhold at its top varied constantly in shape and size. All the watchers soon realized that it was controlling how much of its motion was due to wind and how much to gravity. Sometimes it lifted sharply, sometimes slowly or not at all; it blew horizontally now one way and now another, but most often and farthest the way Erni was sending the tug. He had speeded up when the rain had stopped, but now he slowed again to stay near the object.

"Go. Travel. Not slow."

"We want to observe," Pam transmitted.

"What?" asked Tricia from her distant listening post. Pam gestured to her husband, who described briefly what was happening.

The response was still terse, but comprehensible. **"Observe better forward. Not slow. Go."**

"Let's take its word for it. Go ahead, Erni. It wants to lead us to something, and this thing doesn't seem to be it."

Icewall shrugged, refraining from comment about "somethings" on this part of the world, and *Candlegrease* left the airborne object behind in moments. There were presumably fourteen kilometers to go, and the going was fairly straight.

It was a less impressive prediction this time; the target was motionless.

If this was the target. A branch tangle some fifty meters across and up to eight or ten high, resembling the filling of *Jellyseal*'s cockpit, was spread at the edge of the lake, separated from the liquid by a meter-high ridge of soil which might have been made by a dozer—or shovels. The ridge—or dam?—ran straight along the lakefront for three dozen meters or so, with each end bending away from the liquid to enclose partially the slowly writhing tangle.

"Left. Slow—left more—slow slow."

"Slowing. Turning." Pam was plainly addressing their guide. Then, "Close to the copse, Erni, I think it means."

"I think so too." Icewall veered very slightly to the right until the big tank was scarcely a meter from the edge of the patch of growth, then even more slightly left so they were moving parallel to it.

"Stop."

"That's it, I guess," Nic added his voice.

"That's it." The guide omitted the man's last two words. Its intelligence seemed to include a computerlike memory.

"Now we wait?" asked Erni, free from his driving.

"Wait. Observe."

"Is that dandelion seed anywhere near us yet?" asked Akmet. "That's what 'observe' was last used on, as I remember. I'd say it was ten or twelve kilos back by now, unless the wind was really helpful."

"Observe."

No one had time to ask *what*. From somewhere near the middle of the copse a duplicate of the "seed" popped upward and began to gyrate like the other as the wind took it. It was followed by several others. All four pairs of eyes were fastened on them, some through the finders of video recorders. Akmet was giving a vocal report to Nest in all the detail he could; there was no video contact through the biological static even via satellite at this distance. Ben and others were asking for clarification, forcing Treefern to repeat himself with additional words. His wife approved; this should help the natives' vocabulary.

They were never able to decide whether the new seeds were a deliberate attempt to capture their attention. Neither of the Treeferns believed that the natives could possibly have worked out that much about human psychology, especially in view of what their own minds turned out to be like. Nic, and even more Erni, were much less sure of this. In any case, either accidentally, incidentally, or deliberately, their attention was held while branches writhed out of the tangle to the tank and its tug and began to feel their way around and over the vehicle bodies, among wheels and treads, around emergency controls meant only for bugs and rescuers . . .

Both machines were enveloped in a loose, open cocoon of branches, some of them two or three centimeters thick, before anyone noticed. Again the question later was whether all *Annie*'s windows being covered last was intentional or not. After all, the natives could have inferred the purpose of windows from their experience with *Jellyseal.*

Erni's cry of surprise as he saw what was happening was followed by prompt startup and an effort to break out of the cocoon. Pam's "Hold it!" preceded the guide's voice by only a fraction of a second.

"Stop. Observing." Erni stopped, less because he cared about obeying a nonhuman than because the brief effort had shown they were in no obvious danger, the branches were not nearly strong enough to fight fusion engines. Many of them had pulled apart, and the attention of the watchers was now held by seeing these rejoin the main tangle, not apparently caring where the joining occurred.

"Observing. Go later." Pam spoke tentatively; the native seized on the new word.

"Observe. Go later." Erni's hands dropped from the controls, but his attention did not return to the gyrating dandelion seeds. Neither did Nic's. Both wondered how much of this their wives had experienced—there was, after all, no telling *when* the communication link had broken.

It must have been farther Hotnorth, both realized. They had talked to their wives often, of course, and there had been descriptions of landscape with the sun almost above the horizon. The women had wondered why clouds seemed to be as numerous, large, and dense as ever in spite of the rising temperature. Not even Dominic had risked a guess at the time.

"They're hijackers! They're playing with emergency drain valves!" Akmet, who had deployed a bug and was using its eye, cried suddenly.

"They'll be sorry," answered Erni dryly. "Get your bug ready to close anything they open."

"Will it—they—whatever—let me close enough?"

"They won't be able to stop you, I'd guess. But I'll be ready to roll if we have to."

Pam uttered just one word, for the benefit of their guide. "Danger!"

There was no answer at once; perhaps the native had been unable to untangle her word from the two men's transmissions. Pam waited a few seconds before repeating her warning. Still no answer from outside, or the city ahead, or wherever the messages were originating.

"Those things are being controlled by the natives, the way the stuff that drove *Jelly* was!" exclaimed Erni. Nic had an even wilder idea, but kept it to himself for the moment. For one reason, it seemed silly.

A set of millimeter-thick tendrils had been concentrating on one relief valve. There was no instrument to tell the crew how much force was being applied, and the cock itself was safetied to prevent its being turned accidentally. The four people watched the bug's monitor screen in fascination as the cotter pin was straightened, worked free, and dropped to the ground.

The tendrils played further with the valve, and found almost at once which way it would move. The paraffin was not entirely melted yet, though the temperature had been rising; but there was quite enough liquid just inside the wall to find its way through the opening. The watchers saw a drop, and then several more, emerge and almost at once disappear as vapor.

The results were not surprising. Pam controlled herself with no trouble—it was not yet clear whether sympathy was in order—and made sure the new word was understood.

"Danger! Danger!"

The association should have been clear enough. There was no flame at first, but the hydrocarbon produced volumes of gray and black smoke. It was anyone's guess what compounds, from hydrogen fluoride on up, were being made. Within seconds the branches immersed in them appeared to stiffen; at least they ceased moving. Their colors changed spectacularly. No one had seen bright green, yellow, or orange on Halfbaked until now. The branches that turned yellow did flame a moment later and also went off in smoke, leaving no visible ash. None of the watchers was a chemist; none tried to guess what might be forming. Akmet did his best to paint a verbal picture for the listeners at Nest, but this was not detailed enough for an analysis.

There was no objection, from inside or out, when Erni jerked the tug into motion and pulled away from the site. The bug stayed, but two of the witnesses preferred to use the windows with their broader field of view. Wind was spreading and diluting the smoke, but the stuff was still deadly; fully a quarter of the copse was now visibly affected.

"Hydrogen compounds. Danger." Pam knew the natives had the first word already in memory, and took the opportunity to add "compounds," which might not be.

"Are you after my job?" came Tricia's voice, with no tone of resentment.

"Just grabbing opportunity while I can see what's happening."

"Hydrogen compounds. Danger. Observed." The native was starting to handle tenses.

"I guess they grow machinery the way we do. I wonder how much time and material that test cost them," remarked Erni. Nic once again made no comment, possibly because there was no time; their guide resumed instructions almost at once.

"Observed. Go."

"Which way?" asked Erni. There was no answer until Pam tried.

"Right? Straight? Left?" The first and last words were known; the middle one might be inferred from context. Perhaps it was, perhaps the native was testing it.

"Straight."

Erni obeyed. At the moment *Annie* was heading thirty degrees or so west of Hotnorth, the sun ahead and to their right. They had gone about half a kilometer when the command **"Right"** came. Erni altered heading about five degrees, and received a repeat order as he straightened out. This kept on until they were once more heading almost at the tiny visible slice of sun.

Once convinced they had the direction right, Pam asked, "How far?"

"Five thousand three hundred twenty-two kilometers."

No one spoke, either in the tug or back at Nest. Senatsu had no need to point out that the distance and direction corresponded to the source of *Jellyseal*'s last communication, as well as the native transmissions. Halfbaked seemed much too large for this to be coincidence. They drove on, but the hours were now less boring.

Nothing changed significantly except for the slow rising of the sun ahead of them. Patches of plant life were sometimes numerous, sometimes cactuslike, sometimes absent. Clouds varied at least as much. The ever-flickering lightning was less obvious in sunlight, but didn't seem actually to be decreasing. Quakes made themselves felt, and sometimes forced changes in route not foreseen either by Senatsu or their native guide. Wind alternately roared and whispered, mostly from behind but sometimes gusting from other random directions violently enough for the driver to feel. Erni and Nic, with more experience than the others, wondered aloud what the return might be like with a much lighter tank in tow. The thought of having it blown from their control was unpleasant. So was the idea of ballasting it with some local liquid which might freeze before they reached Nest. The advisability of abandoning the tank was considered, both among the crew and with Ben; it would, after all, be small loss.

The problem was tabled until the situation actually had to be faced, with some silent reservations in Nic's mind. He was uneasy about waiting until decision was forced on them by experience, who sometimes starts her courses with the final exam.

The Hotnorth route became no straighter as the sun rose higher. It became evident that the distance estimated by their guide had not included necessary detours. Whenever Tricia or Pam asked how far they had yet to go, the answer was larger than that obtained by subtracting the current odometer reading from the last advice.

This of course made it more obvious than ever that the goal their guide meant was indeed the "city" where the women, as not even their husbands doubted now, must have died.

This fact alone was enough to relieve the boredom; everyone, driving or not, remained alert for new and different phenomena. However likely it might be that it had occurred while unloading, the fact remained that something unforeseen had happened. This is no surprise in the exploration business, and explorers are strongly motivated to collect facts which may assist foresight.

And, if at all possible, to make sense of them.

Time stretched on. The four were in no danger as far as food, oxygen, water, and waste disposal were concerned—there was no shortage of energy. Nevertheless, conversation began to deal more and more often with the next drying-out session, which would include bathing facilities under one gravity. The tiny imperfections in recycling equipment were making themselves felt.

It was known from *Jellyseal*'s reports that the last two thousand or so kilometers had been on fairly level ground where high speeds were reasonably safe. It was also known that this fact could change quickly on a world with county-sized tectonic plates. Luckily, the warning that it *had* changed came early. The original *Quarter-*

back crew had experienced it before, but this time the deeplights were no help. With the sun up and ahead of them, these were not in use. Only the increasing intensity of the temblors gave a clue to what was happening. Nic, who was driving when he recognized it, slowed abruptly.

"Send a bug out ahead!" he ordered to no one in particular. "I think we're near another epicenter!"

"Maybe it's behind us," suggested the woman.

"Maybe it is, and maybe to one side or the other, but I'd rather not take even a twenty-five percent chance of going over a half-meter ledge. If ground is rising ahead okay, we'll see it in time; but I wouldn't guarantee to spot a drop even with all four of us watching."

All four were, but it was Akmet guiding a servobug who located the active fault, and issued the warning which brought *Candlegrease* to a firm halt.

An immediate question came from their guide, who seemed to have them under constant observation even though they had never located him, her, it, or them. Communication had improved a great deal in the last few weeks as the native(s) had joined increasingly in conversations between the vehicle and Nest.

"Why stop now?"

"Danger. Scarp here. Watch." Pam turned to her husband. "Drive the bug over the edge, so they can see what happens."

Akmet obeyed, with spectacular results; the drop was a full meter and a half.

"No hydrogen in the bug."

"Right. Bug smashed. Lots of—much—hydrogen in *Candlegrease*, and *Candlegrease* would smash worse. You want hydrogen, but not here."

"Right."

"We need to pass the scarp without smashing *Candlegrease*. How far must we go, and which way?"

"How high the scarp for no danger?"

"About fifteen centimeters."

"About unclear."

"Not exact. Don't know exactly. That should be safe."

"Left forty-five kilometers to ten-centimeter scarp. Right twenty-seven. About."

"We'll go right—wait."

Ben's voice had cut in. "You have seismic thumpers in the bug hold. How about trying to flatten the slope? It might save time."

Erni brightened visibly. "Worth trying. We wouldn't even have to waste bugs. Three or four sets of shots should tell us whether it'll work or not."

Pam said tersely to their guide, "Wait. Observe."

"Waiting."

Actually, it didn't wait. Erni was the first to notice; Nic and Pam were deploying bugs, and Akmet was occupied at the communicator adding details to the description of their surroundings—anything which might help Senatsu in her interpretation of radar and other microwave observations was more than welcome at Nest. Erni alone was looking through a window when one of the blackish blowing objects again made itself noticeable.

It was far larger than the general run of jetsam to which everyone had gotten accustomed. This one had not been noticed before because, as they now realized, it had been riding far higher than the rest of the material, high enough so that only careful study would have revealed its shape. Now it came down abruptly, in a sort of fluttering swoop, and hung a few meters above the wreckage of the bug in a wavering hover. They knew now that they had seen it, or something like it, before.

It had surprisingly slender wings, whose span Erni estimated as fully ten meters, and which bent alarmingly in the turbulence of the heavy atmosphere. They supported a cucumber-shaped body a meter and a half in length, with a three-meter tail projecting from what was presumably its rear. The tail was terminated by conventional empennage for aircraft, vertical and horizontal stabilizers, rudder and elevators. Erni's warning cry called the others' attention to the arrival, and the bugs stopped moving as their operators looked.

"A glider!" exclaimed Akmet. "In this gravity?"

"Think of the atmosphere," pointed out Dominic.

"I'm thinking strength of materials," was the dry rejoinder.

"I suppose that's where they've been watching us from," Pam added thoughtfully. "It gives us some idea of their size, anyway. I wonder how many it's carrying."

"Or whether it's remote controlled like *Jelly*," Nic pointed out. Pam admitted she hadn't thought of that.

"No windows or lenses," Erni submitted.

"Those wings seem to have very complex frameworks. They could also be microwave and/or radar antennae," was Akmet's remark, reminding the rest that conclusions were still premature and providing the morally requisite alternative hypothesis.

"Let's not bury the bug; it seems to want to look it over. We'll shift fifty or sixty meters before we try to knock the cliff down." Erni acted on his own words, driving the *Annie* and dragging *Candlegrease* to the right as he spoke. No one objected. Three bugs followed with their loads of thumpers.

These were not simply packets of explosive; they were meant to be recoverable and reusable, though this was not always possible. They were hammerlike devices which did carry explosive charges, and were designed to transmit efficiently the jolt of the blast on their tops to the substrate. Ten of them were set up a meter apart and equally far from the cliff edge; a similar row was placed a meter farther back, and a third at a similar distance. The bugs then retreated—they were cheap, but there seemed no point in wanton waste—and the thumpers fired on one command.

No one expected the wave pattern they set up to be recognizable at Nest, thousands of kilometers away, through the endless seismic static, though the computers there were alerted for it. The desired result was a collapse of the cliff face, but no one noticed for several seconds whether this had happened or not. As the charges thundered, the wavering motion of the glider ceased and it dived violently out of sight, as far as anyone could tell almost onto the wreckage of the sacrificed bug. Pam saw it go, and cried out the news as the impact echoed the blast.

"Watch out with the next shot! We don't want to bury it!"

It was clear enough there would have to be a next shot, quite possibly several. The face of the scarp had collapsed in satisfactory fashion, but the slope of rubble was still far too steep for safety. This, however, was not what surprised the four.

"Bury still unclear."

Pam recovered almost at once. Either they were being observed from somewhere else, or the occupant of the glider had not been disabled by what should have been a seven-gravity crash, or—

Nic's own idea was gaining weight. So was Erni's.

"Observe new rock. Wait." The woman's answer to the native was prompt, and even Erni saw what she meant.

"Observing. Waiting."

"Set up the next shot, boys."

The cliff had crumbled for a width of some twenty-five meters, to a distance varying from ten to fifteen meters back from its original lip. On the second shot the distance back more than doubled.

"New rock buried," Pam announced without bothering to look.

"Bury clear."

A third set of thumpers, skillfully placed, kept the twenty-five-meter width nearly unchanged and practically doubled the other dimension. A fourth, with *Annie* and *Candlegrease* moved farther back for safety, left a promising if still rather frightening slope.

Akmet using the largest and heaviest of the available bugs, traversed this down, up, and down again, without starting any slides. Dominic repeated the test for practice. Then, with no argument from anyone, he turned back to *Annie*'s controls and very gingerly drove tug and tow down the same way. Everyone thought of trying this with the tow disconnected first, but no one mentioned the idea aloud. Erni wanted to get it over with; the others simply trusted Nic's judgment.

At the bottom, *Candlegrease* safely clear of the rubble, the tug stopped and everyone went to the left windows.

The glider's remains could now be seen easily. The body was flattened and cracked, the wings crumpled, the empennage separated from the rest. A patch of growing stems, twigs, and branches had already started to grow from, around, and through the wreckage, and after a few moments Erni brought them closer. Akmet was once again relaying descriptions to Nest. They were given little time to report.

"Go. No stop needed."

"Right? Straight? Left?" asked Pam.

"Straight." They were at the moment facing about Hotnorthwest. Erni, still at the controls, obeyed. After they had gone about fifty meters, **"Right."** He started to swerve, and Pam muttered softly, "Full circle." He obeyed, guessing at her plan, and kept turning after they were heading sunward and the voice expostulated **"Stop right."** Back at the original heading, the woman said simply, "Three hundred sixty degrees." It worked; the next message was **"Forty degrees right."** He obeyed, and received a **"Four degrees right."** In minutes the wrecked glider and the growth around it were out of sight.

They were now looking at the sky more often and more carefully. At least two more objects among or beyond the usual foreground of blackish jetsam, objects which *might* be other gliders, could now be seen. No one was surprised when an occasional **"Left"** or **"Right"** warned them of other obstacles, sometimes but not always before Senatsu provided the same information. The natives by now seemed to have a pretty good idea of what the human-driven vehicles could and could not do—or get away with. The tug and its tow sometimes had to be guided around a fair-sized boulder which had not been mentioned, but nothing really dangerous went unreported.

"I guess they really want us to get there," Akmet remarked at one point, rather rhetorically.

"They want their hydrogen to get there," retorted Erni. "It will. Don't worry."

"And you don't think they care that much about us?" asked Pam.

"What do you think?" The woman shrugged, her wet suit doing nothing to conceal the motion. She said nothing.

"What do you think of *them*, Erni?" asked Nic. He was driving and didn't look away from his window.

Icewall didn't even shrug. As usual, not much of anyone's face could be seen, but Pam gave an uneasy glance toward her husband. He answered with a barely visible raised eyebrow. It was at least a minute before anyone spoke.

Then, "They care about as much for us as for one of their branches," Erni said flatly.

Nic nodded, his body attitude showing some surprise. "You've got it after all. You had me worried," he said. This time his friend did shrug visibly. Rather unfortunately, no one chose to prolong the discussion. More time passed.

They were now really close to their goal, according to their guide—**"Three hundred forty-four"** was its terse response to the question.

"Any more danger?" asked Pam. "Go fast?"

"No more danger. Go fast."

The driver, currently Akmet, started to add power, but after a mere twenty-kph increase Nic and Erni almost simultaneously laid hands on his shoulders. The former spoke.

"That's enough for now."

"Why?"

"Somewhere along here something happened."

"That wasn't until they got there!"

"As far as we know. Don't overdrive your reflexes. Keep your eyes wide open."

"No danger fast."

Erni answered. "Observing." This seemed to be an unimpeachable excuse. There was no further comment from their guides and watchers. Anyone who had hoped or expected that they would betray impatience was disappointed.

There were now six or seven of the gliders in sight most of the time. Their irregular motion made them hard to count. Pam was almost certain she had seen one struck by lightning a day before, but her question at the time—"Danger for you? Lightning?"—had gone unanswered. Since there were two new words in the sentence this might have been lack of understanding, but always before such lack had been signified with the "Unclear" phrase.

Human tension was mounting, not only in the tug but at Nest, where Ben and the others were being kept up-to-date by nearly continuous verbal reports.

The sun was causing less trouble now for the driver. It was still partly below the horizon ahead, but there were more and more clouds; and those near the distant horizon provided a nearly complete block even when only a small fraction of the sky overhead was actually covered. What the clouds failed to hide was largely behind blowing dust and other objects.

Mountains seemed much rarer, though no one assumed this a function of Hotlat alone. Senatsu assured them it was not, that only the two or three million square kilometers around and ahead of them were any smoother than average. She could now confirm the native-given distance to the "city," but could give no more complete a description of it than before. She was certain now that it was beside one of the lakes, but had no data whatever on the nature of the fluid this held. Chemists were waiting impatiently for news on that point.

Senatsu had triumphantly reported resolving the area where the travelers had descended the cliff, and even getting an image of the thicket where the glider had crashed; but this, she said, had not grown more than a meter or two from the wreck. This made no sense to anyone but Nic, who still kept his developing ideas to himself.

The glider count continued to grow. So did the number of crashes. Several times these events were seen from *Annie*, but more often wreckage was sighted to one side or the other of their track. Experience gave the human observers a way to estimate when the wrecks had occurred; it seemed that the plants which represented the remote control mechanism grew uncontrolled for a short time, then died for lack of—something. The natives had clearly not completely mastered aviation, but seemed casual about its dangers.

A clue to the nature of the something was secured when they passed an apparently thriving thicket of the stuff at the edge of a small lake. The evidence was not completely convincing, since no trace of a wrecked flying machine could be seen in the tangle. The distant chemists at Nest were more convinced of the implication than the four on *Annie*; it was, after all, almost dogma among biochemists that life needed liquid; it was a solution-chemistry phenomenon—though the precise solvent seemed less important.

At the present general temperature around *Annie*, it could easily be the cryolite found on *Jellyseal*. Numerous bets were on hold at Nest. Bugs went out from *Annie* to collect samples from the lake, but there was no means of analyzing these on board. There had been a limit to the equipment the tug could carry, no matter how many enthusiasts were involved in the design.

The missing women had been better equipped in this respect, but had apparently postponed sampling until after their cargo was delivered. They had never reported any collecting.

The lightning, even among small clouds, was now almost continuous. Thunder and even wind could be heard most of the time. The crash of one glider was near enough to be audible inside the tug; and of course the rain, frequently materializing with no obvious cloud as a source, could hardly be missed as it drummed on the vehicle's shell. Most of the liquid that struck the ground vanished almost instantly; no one could be sure whether it was evaporating from the hot surface or soaking into it even when an experimental hole was dug by one of the bugs. The explorers paused—bringing questions from their guides—to watch for results, but these were inconclusive. Whatever was happening was too quick to permit a decision. Pam made an effort to ask the natives, but it was hard to decide afterward whether the questions or the answers were less clear. Tricia, back at Nest, brightened up when this happened and got to work with her computer, but even she remained unsure of what had been said.

At last the welcome, **"One kilometer"** sounded, followed a few seconds later by **"Up slope ahead."**

There was indeed a slope ahead, only a few meters high but quite enough to hide what lay beyond. Tug and tank labored up to its crest, and were promptly stopped by Pam. Her husband resumed reporting.

"There's a roughly oval valley below us, with a lake like the one where they tested the paraffin but a lot larger. Sen was right; the lake is about three quarters surrounded by a thicket of the same sort of plants we saw there, and its Hotsouth end is dammed in the same way. There are several low, round hills scattered over the valley. The two closest to the lake are covered with the bushes; all the others are bare. Between the two covered ones is another bare but differently colored space extending a kilometer or so toward the bushes and lake. The overgrown area covers about five by seven kilometers. It borders the Hotnorth side of the lake, which is oval and about three kilometers by two, the long measure running Hotnorth-Hotsouth. In the bare section, directly between the two covered hills is something like a wrecked building about a hundred meters square. I can't guess how high it may have been. Another at the Hoteast edge of the lake seems intact, has about the same area though it isn't quite so perfectly square, and has an intact flat roof. It's about fifteen meters high. They're talking again; you can hear them, I suppose. They seem to want us to—Erni, what's up?" Akmet fell silent.

"Something wrong?" asked Ben, while the rest of Nest stopped whatever it was doing.

"You'll see." It was Icewall's voice. He had gently but firmly sent Pam drifting away from the controls, and was guiding *Annie* toward the nearer of the overgrown hills.

"Thirty-four right" came from the speaker. Again. And again. *Candlegrease* continued straight toward the eminence. Pam managed to silence the native with a rather dishonest "Observing."

Tug and tank descended the valley, crossed the bare part to the nearer overgrown hill, climbed it, and came to a halt looking down on what Akmet had described as a wrecked building. From three kilometers closer, there seemed still no better way to describe it.

The other three cried out together as Erni did a quick-stop. Then, donning a waldo, he deployed one of the smallest bugs and sent it back toward *Candlegrease* on the side toward the lake.

Nic, knowing his partner best and far more experienced with the equipment than the other couple, imitated Icewall's action; but there was no way he could make his bug catch up with the one which had started first. Erni's mechanical servant took hold of the still unsafetied relief valve which had destroyed the other patch so far back, in the natives' grim experiment.

"Hold it, Erni! What do you think you're up to?" The question came in three different voices, with the words slightly different in each, but was understood even at Nest.

"Don't ask silly questions—or don't you care about Maria?"

Nic's lips tightened invisibly behind his breathing mask.

"I care a lot, and so will the kids when they hear. But that's no answer."

Pam was broadcasting deliberately as she cut in; she was uncertain how much the natives would understand, but it seemed worth trying. "You just want to kill a few thousand of these people to get even?"

"Don't be stupid. I won't be killing anyone. This isn't a city, it's one creature. I can punish it—hurt it—without killing it. I can teach it to be careful. You know that, don't you, Nic?"

"I'm pretty sure of it, yes. I'm not sure releasing the paraffin up here won't kill it completely. We're at about the highest point in the valley, much of our juice is denser than the local air, and the wind is random as usual. If we do kill it, it may not be a lesson. We don't know that there are any more of these beings on the planet. We certainly haven't heard from any, and the satellites this one spotted and began talking to can be seen from anywhere on Halfbaked. Think that one over. All the intelligence of a world for two human lives?"

Erni was silent for several seconds, but his servo remained motionless. At last, "You don't know that. You can't be sure."

"Of course I can't. But it's a plausible idea, like the one that this is a single being. Anything I can do to keep you from taking the chance, I'll do. Think it over."

Pam disapproved of what sounded to her like a threat.

"Why are you blaming these people, or this person, whichever it is, anyway? You don't know what happened is their fault."

"They weren't careful enough! Look at that wrecked building there! That's got to be where it happened—"

"And the dead-vegetation area downslope from it! Maybe they weren't careful enough—how could they have been? What do they know about hydrogen compounds? What do *we* know about their behavior here, except what *they* found out and showed us a while ago, long after the girls were gone? What—"

"I don't care what! All I can think about is Jessi! What she was like—what she was—and that I'll never see her or feel her again. Someone's got to learn!"

"You mean someone's got to pay, don't you?"

"All right, someone's got to pay! And what do you think you can do to stop it, Dominic Wildbear Yucca, who is so disgustingly civilized he doesn't care for the memory of the mother of his kids!"

"Who is so disgustingly civilized he doesn't want to admit to his kids, and his friends, that he didn't try to keep a good friend from—"

"Friend! How can you call yourself a—"

"You'll see."

"How?"

What Nic would have said in answer is still unknown; he refused to tell anyone later. Pam cut in again.

"Look! Isn't it enough to scare them—scare it? Look what's happening! Look at the city, or the creature, or whatever it is!"

Even Erni took his eyes from the screen of his servobug. For the first and only time since the native's hydrocarbon experiment, they clearly saw the dandelion seeds. Hordes of them, rocketing up from every part of the overgrown area, catching the swirling, wandering winds, many falling back to the ground close to their launch points, but some being carried up and away in every direction.

The woman saw Erni's distraction, and pressed home her argument. "They want to save what they can! Those things really *are* seeds. They scatter them when the parent is in danger, or knows it's dying!"

"You—you don't know that either." Erni sounded almost subdued, and certainly far less frenzied than a few seconds earlier. Nic began to hope, and waited for Pam to go on.

Erni's attention now was clearly on the scenery rather than his bug. Even though he still had his hands in the waldos, there was a very good chance that Dominic's bug could knock the other away from the valve in time.

Nic took what seemed to him a better chance by passing up the opportunity. Pam was silent, so he finally spoke softly.

"I can forgive your cracks about my not caring, because I do care and know how you feel. But what you want to do is just the same sort of angry, thoughtless thing as those words, isn't it?"

Erni's answer seemed irrelevant.

"If it's scared, why doesn't it ask me to stop?"

"Using what words?" asked Pam softly.

"Me unclear." The native utterance partly overlapped the woman's, and proved the most effective sentence of the argument.

Slowly, Erni drew his hands from the waldo gloves, and gestured Akmet to take over the bug's control.

"Better try to get 'we' across while you're at it, Pam," was all he said. He let himself drift away from controls and window.

"Me and we unclear. One at a time."

Pam might have been smiling behind her mask. She did look hesitantly at her companions, especially Erni. Then she tried her explanation. Numbers, after all, had long been in the common vocabulary.

"Observe *Annie* closely. Me, one animal. We, more than one animal. Four animals in *Annie*."

Erni made no objection, but added quietly, "No valve danger. Which way?"

"Right." Erni, now thoroughly embarrassed, glanced around at the others as though asking whether they really trusted him to drive. The other men were concentrating on the bugs outside, the woman seemed to be watching the putative seeds. They were mostly settled back to the ground or blown out of sight by now. No more were being launched, apparently. *Maybe* the suggested explanation had been right, but even its proponent was skeptical. Maybe they were some sort of weapon. . . .

It soon became obvious that *Annie* was being led to the other shedlike structure. This one was at the edge of the lake but somewhat down slope from the overgrown areas. There seemed a likely reason, though not the only possible one, for this: care. No one suggested this aloud to the driver. It seemed too obvious that *Jellyseal* had, during unloading, wrecked the first building and killed much of the being or population which formed the copse.

As they followed instructions along the edge of the overgrown area, bunch after bunch of tangled branches waved close past *Annie*'s windows. Looking in? None of them doubted it. Pam continued alternately reporting and teaching, describing their path and surroundings to Nest and reacting to observations through the window with remarks like "One animal driving. One animal talking. Two animals moving bugs."

They were guided around the structure to the lower side. This was open, and *Annie* was directed to enter. The far side, toward Hotnorth, could be seen to be open also, and though there was much growth within, there was plenty of room for tug and tank. Erni dragged his charge within.

"Stop." Since there was an opening in front, he obeyed, though he remained alert. The bugs operated by Akmet and Nic had come in too, and all four explorers watched, not without an occasional glance forward, as the doorway behind was plugged more and more tightly by growing branches and finally, as nearly as either bug could see, became airtight.

"Carbon hydride stop." Reading between the words, the bug handlers detached *Candlegrease*. Erni eased *Annie* forward. Three things started to happen at once, all interesting for different reasons.

Flattened bladders appeared among the branches and were borne toward *Candlegrease's* valves. Apparently the paraffin was not to be exposed to local air this time.

A wall of tangled growth began to form between *Annie* and her tow, without waiting for the bugs to get back to the tug. Nic and Akmet, after a quick but silent look at each other, abandoned the machines; there were plenty more, and there seemed no objection to their being "observed" at leisure by the natives.

The doorway ahead began to fill with a similar block. This also caused human reaction. Erni sent the tug grinding firmly forward.

"Oxygen hydride stop."

No attention was paid to this. In a few seconds *Annie* was outside, with a patch of torn and flattened vegetation behind where the growing wall had been.

"Water stop."

Pam remained calm, and Erni did not stop until they were a hundred meters from the lab, as they all now thought of it. Pam explained.

"Water stop danger for animals."

The native voice did not respond at once, and after some seconds Cloud's voice reached them from Nest.

"Y'know, Pam dear, I think you've just faced your friend outside with the problem of what an individual is. Don't be surprised if you have to restate that one."

The woman answered promptly and professionally.

"You mean my friend or friends. You're hypothesizing still. Let's call this one Abby, and start looking around for Bill—"

"Water next time."

"Water next time," she agreed.

"All right, it's—they're—she's civilized," muttered Erni after a moment.

"Of course. So are you," answered Dominic. All three looked at him sharply, but he ignored the couple.

"You wouldn't really have turned that valve, would you?"

The younger man was silent for several seconds. "I don't think so," he said at last.

"We didn't really talk you out of it, did we?"

"I guess not. That's the funny part. Once I was where I *could* do it, I—I don't know; I guess having the power, knowing I was in charge and no one could stop me—well, that was enough." He paused. "I think. Then the arguments distracted me, and I realized you'd sneaked your bug close enough so you probably *could* have stopped me. And I didn't care that you could.

"Nic, I'll help you tell the kids, if you'll tell me why getting even can seem so important."

"We'd better tell them that, too. If we can figure it out. Y'know, I'm not sure I *would've* stopped you."

The Treeferns listened sympathetically, and since they were also human not even Pam thought to ask why *Jellyseal*'s failure was the natives' fault.

REASONS TO BE CHEERFUL

Greg Egan

❀

Greg Egan has been one of the most innovative and controversial hard SF writers of the nineties. He says in an interview: "I think what happens in my novels is that the border between science and metaphysics shifts: Issues that originally seemed completely metaphysical, completely beyond the realms of scientific enquiry, actually become part of physics. I'm writing about extending science into territory that was once believed to be metaphysical, not about abandoning or 'transcending' science at all."

And in an interview in *Gigamesh*, July 1998, he said about this story, one of his most important and controversial works:

"I had no short fiction at all published in '96, and I'll only have two stories published this year. Part of the reason is the time I've spent on novels, but also I've been taking longer to write stories lately. 'Reasons to Be Cheerful,' which was published in *Interzone* in April, took me three months. I think it was time well spent, though; I'm happy with every word in that story. Obviously you can never say 'No one could have done this better,' but when you can honestly say that you wouldn't personally change a thing, it's a good feeling."

David Swanger in an article in *NYRSF* (entitled "Hard Character SF") expands on the implications of new scientific views of the extent to which personality is physiologically, biochemically, and genetically determined:

> Genre SF [historically] manifested two different attitudes to the "human sciences." The part of the field that yearned for literary respectability took them at their own evaluation, and imported them. . . . Freud was emphatically welcomed into the field in such novels as *The Demolished Man* and *More than Human*. The New Wave of the sixties accepted mainstream ideas of character (and its indictment of genre SF for ignoring them) wholesale, as did the influx of female writers in the seventies. . . .
>
> But the Campbellian strain of the field, which gave birth to hard SF, always had a different attitude. It was always (and rightly) suspicious of Freud, and rather than standing in awe of the "human sciences," it sought to reform them, making them over into true, rigorous sciences. . . . Even the notorious Dianetics of L. Ron Hubbard was trumpeted as Freud made scientific. The forties and fifties saw many more stories attempt to harden the softer sciences. But the state of the art to support such fantasies and hopes was lacking, and the action and excitement in the field went elsewhere, as described above, until the eighties, when cyberpunk, via Bruce Sterling/Vincent Omniveritas's manifestos, explicitly called out the humanists to duel for the soul of SF, while in the background, a more traditional Campbellian hard SF, better equipped than its predecessor, enjoyed a slow, quiet renaissance. In the nineties, these two streams have flowed together. . . . The brash, confrontational willingness of Egan to "burn the motherhood statement" (Sterling) and cheerfully mock humanist pieties comes from cyberpunk. But it is the science, fifty

> years wiser, feeding the other stream that promises a hard SF that can finally take on the humanists on their own ground and win: "hard character SF."
>
> And here at last, we see the return of the Campbellian dream in its entirety: not only the new, truly scientific vision of ourselves, as in Bear and Benford, but also the challenge to traditional and Modernist literature alike. . . . That is the promise of hard character SF.

Wayne Daniels, in an essay on Egan's story in *The New York Review of Science Fiction*, said:

> . . . the nature of a person seems, on our reading of [this story], to involve necessary qualifications of either a scientific or philosophical description. Mark . . . is at pains to make it clear that he has not been delusional at any stage. He is, if you will, "in his right mind," except that the mind in question has had a basic part of its affective structure destroyed. Before and after, Mark is clear that the way he feels has nothing rational about it in relation to the external world. The cognitive aspect of his person is still functioning well enough for that. But however we parse the psychological and physiological elements of his situation, the *reality* of it is conveyed—perhaps can only be conveyed—by the language of value, of self-worth, and of feeling. Because he learns the mechanism of happiness the hard way, he has no confidence in language that *merely* suggests the phenomenon to be a mental one, though that is how he has experienced it, and continues to experience it; and for the purpose of *telling*, he is obliged to deploy the very language that no longer seems adequate. The alternative is exclusively to use words that, while empirically satisfactory, convey nothing of his experience. Whatever remains of Mark the person depends, for self-understanding, on two quite different, seemingly incommensurable descriptions of itself.

The accomplishments of the medical treatment in "Reasons to Be Cheerful" are more modest than in Ted Chiang's "Understand" (to be found later in this volume): the protagonist's capacity for happiness and enjoyment are restored. But because his is an indiscriminant happiness, he is given the capacity to choose what gives him pleasure. He is given not the capacity to control the world but rather the way he feels about the world. This would seem to amount to the same thing except that he is not given the ability to control how the world feels about him. One of the emerging themes in these stories is the oppositions and symmetries that can be found in the relations between the self and the world, the mind and matter.

ONE

In September 2004, not long after my twelfth birthday, I entered a state of almost constant happiness. It never occurred to me to ask why. Though school included the usual quota of tedious lessons, I was doing well enough academically to be able to escape into daydreams whenever it suited me. At home, I was free to read books and web pages about molecular biology and particle physics, quaternions and galactic evolution, and to write my own Byzantine computer games and convoluted abstract animations. And though I was a skinny, uncoordinated child, and every elaborate, pointless organized sport left me comatose with boredom, I was comfortable enough with my body on my own terms. Whenever I ran—and I ran everywhere—it felt good.

I had food, shelter, safety, loving parents, encouragement, stimulation. Why shouldn't I have been happy? And though I can't have entirely forgotten how oppressive and monotonous classwork and schoolyard politics could be, or how easily my usual bouts of enthusiasm were derailed by the most trivial problems, when things were actually going well for me I wasn't in the habit of counting down the days until it all turned sour. Happiness always brought with it the belief that it would last, and though I must have seen this optimistic forecast disproved a thousand times before, I wasn't old and cynical enough to be surprised when it finally showed signs of coming true.

When I started vomiting repeatedly, Dr. Ash, our GP, gave me a course of antibiotics and a week off school. I doubt it was a great shock to my parents when this unscheduled holiday seemed to cheer me up rather more than any mere bacterium could bring me down, and if they were puzzled that I didn't even bother feigning misery, it would have been redundant for me to moan constantly about my aching stomach when I was throwing up authentically three or four times a day.

The antibiotics made no difference. I began losing my balance, stumbling when I walked. Back in Dr. Ash's surgery, I squinted at the eye chart. She sent me to a neurologist at Westmead Hospital, who ordered an immediate MRI scan. Later the same day, I was admitted as an in-patient. My parents learnt the diagnosis straight away, but it took me three more days to make them spit out the whole truth.

I had a tumor, a medulloblastoma, blocking one of the fluid-filled ventricles in my brain, raising the pressure in my skull. Medulloblastomas were potentially fatal, though with surgery followed by aggressive radiation treatment and chemotherapy, two out of three patients diagnosed at this stage lived five more years.

I pictured myself on a railway bridge riddled with rotten sleepers, with no choice but to keep moving, trusting my weight to each suspect plank in turn. I understood the danger ahead, very clearly . . . and yet I felt no real panic, no real fear. The closest thing to terror I could summon up was an almost exhilarating rush of vertigo, as if I was facing nothing more than an audaciously harrowing fairground ride.

There was a reason for this.

The pressure in my skull explained most of my symptoms, but tests on my cerebrospinal fluid had also revealed a greatly elevated level of a substance called Leu-enkephalin—an endorphin, a neuropeptide which bound to some of the same receptors as opiates like morphine and heroin. Somewhere along the road to malignancy, the same mutant transcription factor that had switched on the genes enabling the tumor cells to divide unchecked had apparently also switched on the genes needed to produce Leu-enkephalin.

This was a freakish accident, not a routine side-effect. I didn't know much about endorphins then, but my parents repeated what the neurologist had told them, and later I looked it all up. Leu-enkephalin wasn't an analgesic, to be secreted in emergencies when pain threatened survival, and it had no stupefying narcotic effects to immobilize a creature while injuries healed. Rather, it was the primary means of signalling happiness, released whenever behavior or circumstances warranted pleasure. Countless other brain activities modulated that simple message, creating an almost limitless palette of positive emotions, and the binding of Leu-enkephalin to its target neurons was just the first link in a long chain of events mediated by other neurotransmitters. But for all these subtleties, I could attest to one simple, unambiguous fact: Leu-enkephalin made you feel *good.*

My parents broke down as they told me the news, and I was the one who comforted them, beaming placidly like a beatific little child martyr from some tear-jerking oncological mini-series. It wasn't a matter of hidden reserves of strength or maturity; I was physically incapable of feeling bad about my fate. And because the effects of the Leu-enkephalin were so specific, I could gaze unflinchingly at the truth in a way that would not have been possible if I'd been doped up to the eyeballs with crude pharmaceutical opiates. I was clear-headed but emotionally indomitable, positively radiant with courage.

i had a ventricular shunt installed, a slender tube inserted deep into my skull to relieve the pressure, pending the more invasive and risky procedure of removing the primary tumor; that operation was scheduled for the end of the week. Dr. Maitland, the oncologist, had explained in detail how my treatment would proceed, and warned me of the danger and discomfort I faced in the months ahead. Now I was strapped in for the ride and ready to go.

Once the shock wore off, though, my un-blissed-out parents decided that they had no intention of sitting back and accepting mere two-to-one odds that I'd make it to adulthood. They phoned around Sydney, then further afield, hunting for second opinions.

My mother found a private hospital on the Gold Coast—the only Australian franchise of the Nevada-based "Health Palace" chain—where the oncology unit was offering a new treatment for medulloblastomas. A genetically engineered herpes virus introduced into the cerebrospinal fluid would infect only the replicating tumor cells, and then a powerful cytotoxic drug, activated only by the virus, would kill the infected cells. The treatment had an eighty percent five-year survival rate, without the risks of surgery. I looked up the cost myself, in the hospital's web brochure. They were offering a package deal: three months' meals and accommodation, all pathology and radiology services, and all pharmaceuticals, for sixty thousand dollars.

My father was an electrician, working on building sites. My mother was a sales assistant in a department store. I was their only child, so we were far from poverty-stricken, but they must have taken out a second mortgage to raise the fee, saddling themselves with a further fifteen or twenty years' debt. The two survival rates were not that different, and I heard Dr. Maitland warn them that the figures couldn't really be compared, because the viral treatment was so new. They would have been perfectly justified in taking her advice and sticking to the traditional regime.

Maybe my enkephalin sainthood spurred them on somehow. Maybe they wouldn't have made such a great sacrifice if I'd been my usual sullen and difficult self, or even if I'd been nakedly terrified rather than preternaturally brave. I'll never know for sure—and either way, it wouldn't make me think any less of them. But just because the molecule wasn't saturating their skulls, that's no reason to expect them to have been immune to its influence.

On the flight north, I held my father's hand all the way. We'd always been a little distant, a little mutually disappointed in each other. I knew he would have preferred a tougher, more athletic, more extroverted son, while to me he'd always seemed lazily conformist, with a world-view built on unexamined platitudes and slogans. But on that trip, with barely a word exchanged, I could feel his disappointment being transmuted into a kind of fierce, protective, defiant love, and I grew ashamed of my own lack of respect for him. I let the Leu-enkephalin convince me that, once this was over, everything between us would change for the better.

From the street, the gold coast health palace could have passed for one more high-rise beachfront hotel—and even from the inside, it wasn't much different from the hotels I'd seen in video fiction. I had a room to myself, with a television wider than the bed, complete with network computer and cable modem. If the aim was to distract me, it worked. After a week of tests, they hooked a drip into my ventricular shunt and infused first the virus, and then three days later, the drug.

The tumor began shrinking almost immediately; they showed me the scans. My parents seemed happy but dazed, as if they'd never quite trusted a place where millionaire property-developers came for scrotal tucks to do much more than relieve them of their money and offer first-class double-talk while I continued to decline. But the tumor kept on shrinking, and when it hesitated for two days in a row the oncologist swiftly repeated the whole procedure, and then the tendrils and blobs on the MRI screen grew skinnier and fainter even more rapidly than before.

I had every reason to feel unconditional joy now, but when I suffered a growing sense of unease instead I assumed it was just Leu-enkephalin withdrawal. It was even possible that the tumor had been releasing such a high dose of the stuff that literally nothing could have made me *feel better*—if I'd been lofted to the pinnacle of happiness, there'd be nowhere left to go but down. But in that case, any chink of darkness in my sunny disposition could only confirm the good news of the scans.

One morning I woke from a nightmare—my first in months—with visions of the tumor as a clawed parasite thrashing around inside my skull. I could still hear the click of carapace on bone, like the rattle of a scorpion trapped in a jam jar. I was terrified, drenched in sweat . . . *liberated*. My fear soon gave way to a white-hot rage: the thing had drugged me into compliance, but now I was free to stand up to it, to bellow obscenities inside my head, to exorcize the demon with self-righteous anger.

I did feel slightly cheated by the sense of anticlimax that came from chasing my already-fleeing nemesis downhill, and I couldn't entirely ignore the fact that imagining my anger to be driving out the cancer was a complete reversal of true cause and effect—a bit like watching a forklift shift a boulder from my chest, then pretending to have moved it myself by a mighty act of inhalation. But I made what sense I could of my belated emotions, and left it at that.

Six weeks after I was admitted, all my scans were clear, and my blood, CSF and lymphatic fluid were free of the signature proteins of metastasizing cells. But there was still a risk that a few resistant tumor cells remained, so they gave me a short, sharp course of entirely different drugs, no longer linked to the herpes infection. I had a testicular biopsy first—under local anesthetic, more embarrassing than painful—and a sample of bone marrow taken from my hip, so my potential for sperm production and my supply of new blood cells could both be restored if the drugs wiped them out at the source. I lost hair and stomach lining, temporarily, and I vomited more often, and far more wretchedly, than when I'd first been diagnosed. But when I started to emit self-pitying noises, one of the nurses steelily explained that children half my age put up with the same treatment for months.

These conventional drugs alone could never have cured me, but as a mopping-up operation they greatly diminished the chance of a relapse. I discovered a beautiful word: *apoptosis*—cellular suicide, programmed death—and repeated it to myself, over and over. I ended up almost relishing the nausea and fatigue; the more miserable I felt, the easier it was to imagine the fate of the tumor cells, membranes popping and shrivelling like balloons as the drugs commanded them to take their own lives. *Die in pain, zombie scum!* Maybe I'd write a game about it, or even a whole series, culminating in the spectacular *Chemotherapy III: Battle for the Brain*. I'd be rich and famous, I could pay back my parents, and life would be as perfect in reality as the tumor had merely made it seem to be.

I was discharged early in December, free of any trace of disease. My parents were wary and jubilant in turn, as if slowly casting off the fear that any premature optimism would be punished. The side-effects of the chemotherapy were gone; my hair was growing back, except for a tiny bald patch where the shunt had been, and I had no trouble keeping down food. There was no point returning to school now, two weeks before the year's end, so my summer holidays began immediately. The whole class sent me a tacky, insincere, teacher-orchestrated get-well e-mail, but my friends visited me at home, only slightly embarrassed and intimidated, to welcome me back from the brink of death.

So why did I feel so bad? Why did the sight of the clear blue sky through the window when I opened my eyes every morning—with the freedom to sleep in as long as I chose, with my father or mother home all day treating me like royalty, but keeping their distance and letting me sit unnagged at the computer screen for sixteen hours if I wanted—why did that first glimpse of daylight make me want to bury my face in the pillow, clench my teeth and whisper: *"I should have died, I should have died"*?

Nothing gave me the slightest pleasure. Nothing—not my favorite netzines or web sites, not the *njari* music I'd once revelled in, not the richest, the sweetest, the saltiest junk food that was mine now for the asking. I couldn't bring myself to read a whole page of any book, I couldn't write ten lines of code. I couldn't look my real-world friends in the eye, or face the thought of going online.

Everything I did, everything I imagined, was tainted with an overwhelming sense of dread and shame. The only image I could summon up for comparison was from a documentary about Auschwitz that I'd seen at school. It had opened with a long tracking shot, a newsreel camera advancing relentlessly towards the gates of the camp, and I'd watched that scene with my spirits sinking, already knowing full well what had happened inside. I wasn't delusional; I didn't believe for a moment that there was some source of unspeakable evil lurking behind every bright surface around me. But when I woke and saw the sky, I felt the kind of sick foreboding that would only have made sense if I'd been staring at the gates of Auschwitz.

Maybe I was afraid that the tumor would grow back, but not *that* afraid. The swift victory of the virus in the first round should have counted for much more, and on one level I did think of myself as lucky, and suitably grateful. But I could no more rejoice in my escape, now, than I could have felt suicidally bad at the height of my enkephalin bliss.

My parents began to worry, and dragged me along to a psychologist for "recovery counselling." The whole idea seemed as tainted as everything else, but I lacked the energy for resistance. Dr. Bright and I "explored the possibility" that I was subconsciously choosing to feel miserable because I'd learnt to associate happiness with the risk of death, and I secretly feared that re-creating the tumor's main symptom could resurrect the thing itself. Part of me scorned this facile explanation, but part of me seized on it, hoping that if I owned up to such subterranean mental gymnastics it would drag the whole process into the light of day, where its flawed logic would become untenable. But the sadness and disgust that everything induced in me—birdsong, the pattern of our bathroom tiles, the smell of toast, the shape of my own hands—only increased.

I wondered if the high levels of Leu-enkephalin from the tumor might have caused my neurons to reduce their population of the corresponding receptors, or if I'd become "Leu-enkephalin-tolerant" the way a heroin addict became opiate-tolerant, through the production of a natural regulatory molecule that blocked the receptors. When I mentioned these ideas to my father, he insisted that I discuss them with Dr. Bright, who feigned intense interest but did nothing to show that he'd taken me seriously. He kept telling my parents that everything I was feeling was a perfectly normal reaction to the trauma I'd been through, and that all I really needed was time, and patience, and understanding.

* * *

I WAS BUNDLED OFF TO HIGH SCHOOL AT THE START OF THE NEW YEAR, BUT WHEN I DID nothing but sit and stare at my desk for a week, arrangements were made for me to study online. At home, I did manage to work my way slowly through the curriculum, in the stretches of zombie-like numbness that came between the bouts of sheer, paralyzing unhappiness. In the same periods of relative clarity, I kept thinking about the possible causes of my affliction. I searched the biomedical literature and found a study of the effects of high doses of Leu-enkephalin in cats, but it seemed to show that any tolerance would be short-lived.

Then, one afternoon in March—staring at an electron micrograph of a tumor cell infected with herpes virus, when I should have been studying dead explorers—I finally came up with a theory that made sense. The virus needed special proteins to let it dock with the cells it infected, enabling it to stick to them long enough to use other tools to penetrate the cell membrane. But if it had acquired a copy of the Leu-enkephalin gene from the tumor's own copious RNA transcripts, it might have gained the ability to cling, not just to replicating tumor cells, but to every neuron in my brain with a Leu-enkephalin receptor.

And then the cytotoxic drug, activated only in infected cells, would have come along and killed them all.

Deprived of any input, the pathways those dead neurons normally stimulated were withering away. Every part of my brain able to feel pleasure was dying. And though at times I could, still, simply feel nothing, mood was a shifting balance of forces. With nothing to counteract it, the slightest flicker of depression could now win every tug-of-war, unopposed.

I didn't say a word to my parents; I couldn't bear to tell them that the battle they'd fought to give me the best possible chance of survival might now be crippling me. I tried to contact the oncologist who'd treated me on the Gold Coast, but my phone calls floundered in a Muzak-filled moat of automated screening, and my e-mail was ignored. I managed to see Dr. Ash alone, and she listened politely to my theory, but she declined to refer me to a neurologist when my only symptoms were psychological: blood and urine tests showed none of the standard markers for clinical depression.

The windows of clarity grew shorter. I found myself spending more and more of each day in bed, staring out across the darkened room. My despair was so monotonous, and so utterly disconnected from anything real, that to some degree it was blunted by its own absurdity: no one I loved had just been slaughtered, the cancer had almost certainly been defeated, and I could still grasp the difference between what I was feeling and the unarguable logic of real grief, or real fear.

But I had no way of casting off the gloom and feeling what I wanted to feel. My only freedom came down to a choice between hunting for reasons to justify my sadness—deluding myself that it was my own, perfectly natural response to some contrived litany of misfortunes—or disowning it as something alien, imposed from without, trapping me inside an emotional shell as useless and unresponsive as a paralyzed body.

My father never accused me of weakness and ingratitude; he just silently withdrew from my life. My mother kept trying to get through to me, to comfort or provoke me, but it reached the point where I could barely squeeze her hand in reply. I wasn't literally paralyzed or blind, speechless or feeble-minded. But all the brightly lit worlds I'd once inhabited—physical and virtual, real and imaginary, intellectual and emotional—had become invisible, and impenetrable. Buried in fog. Buried in shit. Buried in ashes.

By the time I was admitted to a neurological ward, the dead regions of my brain were clearly visible on an MRI scan. But it was unlikely that anything could have halted the process even if it had been diagnosed sooner.

And it was certain that no one had the power to reach into my skull and restore the machinery of happiness.

TWO

The alarm woke me at ten, but it took me another three hours to summon up the energy to move. I threw off the sheet and sat on the side of the bed, muttering half-hearted obscenities, trying to get past the inescapable conclusion that I shouldn't have bothered. Whatever pinnacles of achievement I scaled today (managing not only to go shopping, but to buy something other than a frozen meal) and whatever monumental good fortune befell me (the insurance company depositing my allowance before the rent was due) I'd wake up tomorrow feeling exactly the same.

Nothing helps, nothing changes. Four words said it all. But I'd accepted that long ago; there was nothing left to be disappointed about. And I had no reason to sit here lamenting the bleeding obvious for the thousandth time.

Right?

Fuck it. Just keep moving.

I swallowed my "morning" medication, the six capsules I'd put out on the bedside table the night before, then went into the bathroom and urinated a bright yellow stream consisting mainly of the last dose's metabolites. No antidepressant in the world could send me to Prozac Heaven, but this shit kept my dopamine and serotonin levels high enough to rescue me from total catatonia—from liquid food, bedpans and sponge baths.

I splashed water on my face, trying to think of an excuse to leave the flat when the freezer was still half full. Staying in all day, unwashed and unshaven, did make me feel worse: slimy and lethargic, like some pale parasitic leech. But it could still take a week or more for the pressure of disgust to grow strong enough to move me.

I stared into the mirror. Lack of appetite more than made up for lack of exercise—I was as immune to carbohydrate comfort as I was to runner's high—and I could count my ribs beneath the loose skin of my chest. I was thirty years old, and I looked like a wasted old man. I pressed my forehead against the cool glass, obeying some vestigial instinct which suggested that there might be a scrap of pleasure to be extracted from the sensation. There wasn't.

In the kitchen, I saw the light on the phone: there was a message waiting. I walked back into the bathroom and sat on the floor, trying to convince myself that it didn't have to be bad news. No one had to be dead. And my parents couldn't break up twice.

I approached the phone and waved the display on. There was a thumbnail image of a severe-looking middle-aged woman, no one I recognized. The sender's name was Dr. Z. Durrani, Department of Biomedical Engineering, University of Cape Town. The subject line read: "New Techniques in Prosthetic Reconstructive Neuroplasty." That made a change; most people skimmed the reports on my clinical condition so carelessly that they assumed I was mildly retarded. I felt a refreshing absence of disgust, the closest I could come to respect, for Dr. Durrani. But no amount of diligence on her part could save the cure itself from being a mirage.

Health Palace's no-fault settlement provided me with a living allowance equal to the minimum wage, plus reimbursement of approved medical costs; I had no astronomical lump sum to spend as I saw fit. However, any treatment likely to render me financially self-sufficient could be paid for in full, at the discretion of the insurance company. The value of such a cure to Global Assurance—the total remaining cost of supporting me until death—was constantly falling, but then so was medical research funding, worldwide. Word of my case had got around.

Most of the treatments I'd been offered so far had involved novel pharmaceuticals. Drugs *had* freed me from institutional care, but expecting them to turn me into a happy little wage-earner was like hoping for an ointment that made amputated limbs grow back. From Global Assurance's perspective, though, shelling out for anything more sophisticated meant gambling with a much greater sum—a prospect that no doubt sent my case manager scrambling for his actuarial database. There was no point indulging in rash expenditure decisions when there was still a good chance that I'd suicide in my forties. Cheap fixes were always worth a try, even if they were long shots, but any proposal radical enough to stand a real chance of working was guaranteed to fail the risk/cost analysis.

I knelt by the screen with my head in my hands. I could erase the message unseen, sparing myself the frustration of knowing exactly what I'd be missing out on . . . but then, not knowing would be just as bad. I tapped the PLAY button and looked away; meeting the gaze of even a recorded face gave me a feeling of intense shame. I understood why: the neural circuitry needed to register positive non-verbal messages was long gone, but the pathways that warned of responses like rejection and hostility had not merely remained intact, they'd grown skewed and hypersensitive enough to fill the void with a strong negative signal, whatever the reality.

I listened as carefully as I could while Dr. Durrani explained her work with stroke patients. Tissue-cultured neural grafts were the current standard treatment, but she'd been injecting an elaborately tailored polymer foam into the damaged region instead. The foam released growth factors that attracted axons and dendrites from surrounding neurons, and the polymer itself was designed to function as a network of electrochemical switches. Via microprocessors scattered throughout the foam, the initially amorphous network was programmed first to reproduce generically the actions of the lost neurons, then fine-tuned for compatibility with the individual recipient.

Dr. Durrani listed her triumphs: sight restored, speech restored, movement, continence, musical ability. My own deficit—measured in neurons lost, or synapses, or raw cubic centimeters—lay beyond the range of all the chasms she'd bridged to date. But that only made it more of a challenge.

I waited almost stoically for the one small catch, in six or seven figures. The voice from the screen said, "If you can meet your own travel expenses and the cost of a three-week hospital stay, my research grant will cover the treatment itself."

I replayed these words a dozen times, trying to find a less favorable interpretation—one task I was usually good at. When I failed, I steeled myself and e-mailed Durrani's assistant in Cape Town, asking for clarification.

There was no misunderstanding. For the cost of a year's supply of the drugs that barely kept me conscious, I was being offered a chance to be whole again for the rest of my life.

Organizing a trip to South Africa was completely beyond me, but once global Assurance recognized the opportunity it was facing, machinery on two continents swung into action on my behalf. All I had to do was fight down the urge to call everything off. The thought of being hospitalized, of being powerless again, was disturbing enough, but contemplating the potential of the neural prosthesis itself was like staring down the calendar at a secular Judgment Day. On 7th March 2023, either I'd be admitted into an infinitely larger, infinitely richer, infinitely better world . . . or I'd prove to be damaged beyond repair. And in a way, even the final death of hope was a far less terrifying prospect than the alternative; it was so much closer to where I was already, so much easier to imagine. The only vision of happiness I could summon up was myself as a child, running joyfully, dissolving into sunlight—which was all very sweet and evocative, but a little short on practical details. If I'd wanted to be a sunbeam, I could have cut my wrists anytime. I wanted a job, I wanted a family, I wanted ordinary love and modest ambitions—because I knew these were the things I'd been denied. But I could no more imagine what it would be like, finally, to attain them, than I could picture daily life in twenty-six-dimensional space.

I didn't sleep at all before the dawn flight out of Sydney. I was escorted to the airport by a psychiatric nurse, but spared the indignity of a minder sitting beside me all the way to Cape Town. I spent my waking moments on the flight fighting paranoia, resisting the temptation to invent reasons for all the sadness and anxiety coursing through my skull. *No one on the plane was staring at me disdainfully. The Durrani technique was not going to turn out to be a hoax*. I succeeded in crushing these "explanatory" delusions . . . but as ever, it remained beyond my power to alter my feelings, or even to draw a clear line between my purely pathological unhappiness and the perfectly reasonable anxiety that anyone would feel on the verge of radical brain surgery.

Wouldn't it be bliss, not to have to fight to tell the difference all the time? Forget happiness; even a future full of abject misery would be a triumph, so long as I knew that it was always for a reason.

Luke De Vries, one of Durrani's postdoctoral students, met me at the airport. He looked about twenty-five and radiated the kind of self-assurance I had to struggle not to misread as contempt. I felt trapped and helpless immediately; he'd arranged everything, it was like stepping on to a conveyor belt. But I knew that if I'd been left to do anything for myself the whole process would have ground to a halt.

It was after midnight when we reached the hospital in the suburbs of Cape Town. Crossing the car park, the insect sounds were wrong, the air smelt indefinably alien, the constellations looked like clever forgeries. I sagged to my knees as we approached the entrance.

"Hey!" De Vries stopped and helped me up. I was shaking with fear, and then shame too, at the spectacle I was making of myself.

"This violates my Avoidance Therapy."

"Avoidance Therapy?"

"Avoid hospitals at all costs."

De Vries laughed, though if he wasn't merely humoring me I had no way of telling. Recognizing the fact that you'd elicited genuine laughter was a pleasure, so those pathways were all dead.

He said, "We had to carry the last subject in on a stretcher. She left about as steady on her feet as you are."

"That bad?"

"Her artificial hip was playing up. Not our fault."

We walked up the steps and into the brightly lit foyer.

The next morning—Monday, 6th March, the day before the operation—I met most of the surgical team who'd perform the first, purely mechanical, part of the procedure: scraping clean the useless cavities left behind by dead neurons, prising open with tiny balloons any voids that had been squeezed shut, and then pumping the whole oddly shaped totality full of Durrani's foam. Apart from the existing hole in my skull from the shunt eighteen years before, they'd probably have to drill two more.

A nurse shaved my head and glued five reference markers to the exposed skin, then I spent the afternoon being scanned. The final, three-dimensional image of all the dead space in my brain looked like a spelunker's map, a sequence of linked caves complete with rockfalls and collapsed tunnels.

Durrani herself came to see me that evening. "While you're still under anaesthetic," she explained, "the foam will harden, and the first connections will be made with the surrounding tissue. Then the microprocessors will instruct the polymer to form the network we've chosen to serve as a starting point."

I had to force myself to speak; every question I asked—however politely phrased, however lucid and relevant—felt as painful and degrading as if I was standing before her naked asking her to wipe shit out of my hair. "How did you find a network to use? Did you scan a volunteer?" Was I going to start my new life as a clone of Luke De Vries—inheriting his tastes, his ambitions, his emotions?

"No, no. There's an international database of healthy neural structures—twenty thousand cadavers who died without brain injury. More detailed than tomography; they froze the brains in liquid nitrogen, sliced them up with a diamond-tipped microtome, then stained and electron-micrographed the slices."

My mind balked at the number of exabytes she was casually invoking; I'd lost touch with computing completely. "So you'll use some kind of composite from the database? You'll give me a selection of typical structures, taken from different people?"

Durrani seemed about to let that pass as near enough, but she was clearly a stickler for detail, and she hadn't insulted my intelligence yet. "Not quite. It will be more like a multiple exposure than a composite. We've used about four thousand records from the database—all the males in their twenties or thirties—and wherever someone has neuron A wired to neuron B, and someone else has neuron A wired to neuron C . . . you'll have connections to both B *and* C. So you'll start out with a network that in theory could be pared down to any one of the 4,000 individual versions used to construct it—but in fact, you'll pare it down to your own unique version instead."

That sounded better than being an emotional clone or a Frankenstein collage; I'd be a roughly hewn sculpture, with features yet to be refined. But—

"Pare it down how? How will I go from being potentially anyone, to being . . . ?" *What?* My twelve-year-old self, resurrected? Or the thirty-year-old I should have been, conjured into existence as a remix of these four thousand dead strangers? I trailed off; I'd lost what little faith I'd had that I was talking sense.

Durrani seemed to grow slightly uneasy, herself—whatever my judgment was worth on that. She said, "There should be parts of your brain, still intact, which bear some record of what's been lost. Memories of formative experiences, memories of the things that used to give you pleasure, fragments of innate structures that survived the virus. The prosthesis will be driven automatically towards a state that's compatible with everything else in your brain—it will find itself interacting with all these other systems, and the connections that work best in that context will be reinforced." She thought for a moment. "Imagine a kind of artificial limb, imperfectly formed to start with, that adjusts itself as you use it: stretching when it fails to grasp what you reach for, shrinking when it bumps something unexpectedly . . . until it takes on precisely the size and shape of the phantom limb implied by your movements. Which itself is nothing but an image of the lost flesh and blood."

That was an appealing metaphor, though it was hard to believe that my faded memories contained enough information to reconstruct their phantom author in every detail—that the whole jigsaw of who I'd been, and might have become, could be filled in from a few hints along the edges and the jumbled-up pieces of four thousand other portraits of happiness. But the subject was making at least one of us uncomfortable, so I didn't press the point.

I managed to ask a final question. "What will it be like, before any of this happens? When I wake up from the anaesthetic and all the connections are still intact?"

Durrani confessed, "That's one thing I'll have no way of knowing, until you tell me yourself."

Someone repeated my name, reassuringly but insistently. I woke a little more. My neck, my legs, my back were all aching, and my stomach was tense with nausea.

But the bed was warm, and the sheets were soft. It was good just to be lying there.

"It's Wednesday afternoon. The operation went well."

I opened my eyes. Durrani and four of her students were gathered at the foot of the bed. I stared at her, astonished: the face I'd once thought of as "severe" and "forbidding" was . . . riveting, magnetic. I could have watched her for hours. But then I glanced at Luke De Vries, who was standing beside her. He was just as extraordinary. I turned one by one to the other three students. Everyone was equally mesmerizing; I didn't know where to look.

"How are you feeling?"

I was lost for words. These people's faces were loaded with so much significance, so many sources of fascination, that I had no way of singling out any one factor: they all appeared wise, ecstatic, beautiful, reflective, attentive, compassionate, tranquil, vibrant . . . a white noise of qualities, all positive, but ultimately incoherent.

But as I shifted my gaze compulsively from face to face, struggling to make sense of them, their meanings finally began to crystallize—like words coming into focus, though my sight had never been blurred.

I asked Durrani, "Are you smiling?"

"Slightly." She hesitated. "There are standard tests, standard images for this, but . . . please, describe my expression. Tell me what I'm thinking."

I answered unselfconsciously, as if she'd asked me to read an eye chart. "You're . . . curious? You're listening carefully. You're interested, and you're . . . hoping that something good will happen. And you're smiling because you think it will. Or because you can't quite believe that it already has."

She nodded, smiling more decisively. "Good."

I didn't add that I now found her stunningly, almost painfully, beautiful. But it was the same for everyone in the room, male and female: the haze of contradictory moods that I'd read into their faces had cleared, but it had left behind a heart-stopping radiance. I found this slightly alarming—it was too indiscriminate, too intense—though in a way it seemed almost as natural a response as the dazzling of a dark-adapted eye. And after eighteen years of seeing nothing but ugliness in every human face, I wasn't ready to complain about the presence of five people who looked like angels.

Durrani asked, "Are you hungry?"

I had to think about that. "Yes."

One of the students fetched a prepared meal, much the same as the lunch I'd eaten on Monday: salad, a bread roll, cheese. I picked up the roll and took a bite.

The texture was perfectly familiar, the flavor unchanged. Two days before, I'd chewed and swallowed the same thing with the usual mild disgust that all food induced in me.

Hot tears rolled down my cheeks. I wasn't in ecstasy; the experience was as strange and painful as drinking from a fountain with lips so parched that the skin had turned to salt and dried blood.

As painful, and as compelling. When I'd emptied the plate, I asked for another. *Eating was good, eating was right, eating was necessary.* After the third plate, Durrani said firmly, "That's enough." I was shaking with the need for more, she was still supernaturally beautiful, but I screamed at her, outraged.

She took my arms, held me still. "This is going to be hard for you. There'll be surges like this, swings in all directions, until the network settles down. You have to try to stay calm, try to stay reflective. The prosthesis makes more things possible than you're used to . . . but you're still in control."

I gritted my teeth and looked away. At her touch I'd suffered an immediate, agonizing erection.

I said, "That's right. I'm in control."

In the days that followed, my experiences with the prosthesis became much less raw, much less violent. I could almost picture the sharpest, most ill-fitting edges of the network being—metaphorically—worn smooth by use. To eat, to sleep, to be with people remained intensely pleasurable, but it was more like an impossibly rosy-hued dream of childhood than the result of someone poking my brain with a high voltage wire.

Of course, the prosthesis wasn't sending signals into my brain in order to make my brain feel pleasure. *The prosthesis itself* was the part of me that was feeling all the pleasure—however seamlessly that process was integrated with everything else: perception, language, cognition . . . the rest of me. Dwelling on this was unsettling at first, but on reflection no more so than the thought experiment of staining blue all the corresponding organic regions in a healthy brain, and declaring, "*They* feel all the pleasure, not you!"

I was put through a battery of psychological tests—most of which I'd sat through many times before, as part of my annual insurance assessments—as Durrani's team attempted to quantify their success. Maybe a stroke patient's fine control of a formerly paralyzed hand was easier to measure objectively, but I must have leapt from bottom to top of every numerical scale for positive affect. And far from being a source of irritation, these tests gave me my first opportunity to use the prosthesis in new arenas—to be happy in ways I could barely remember experiencing before. As well as being required to interpret mundanely rendered scenes of domestic situations—what has just happened between this child, this woman, and this man; who is feeling good and who is feeling bad?—I was shown breathtaking images of great works of art, from complex allegorical and narrative paintings to elegant minimalist essays in geometry. As well as listening to snatches of everyday speech, and even unadorned cries of joy and pain, I was played samples of music and song from every tradition, every epoch, every style.

That was when I finally realized that something was wrong.

Jacob Tsela was playing the audio files and noting my responses. He'd been deadpan for most of the session, carefully avoiding any risk of corrupting the data by betraying his own opinions. But after he'd played a heavenly fragment of European classical music, and I'd rated it twenty out of twenty, I caught a flicker of dismay on his face.

"What? You didn't like it?"

Tsela smiled opaquely. "It doesn't matter what I like. That's not what we're measuring."

"I've rated it already, you can't influence my score." I regarded him imploringly; I was desperate for communication of any kind. "I've been dead to the world for eighteen years. I don't even know who the composer was."

He hesitated. "J. S. Bach. And I agree with you: it's sublime." He reached for the touchscreen and continued the experiment.

So what had he been dismayed about? I knew the answer immediately; I'd been an idiot not to notice before, but I'd been too absorbed in the music itself.

I hadn't scored any piece lower than eighteen. And it had been the same with the visual arts. From my four thousand virtual donors I'd inherited, not the lowest common denominator, but the widest possible taste—and in ten days, I still hadn't imposed any constraints, any preferences, of my own.

All art was sublime to me, and all music. Every kind of food was delicious. Everyone I laid eyes on was a vision of perfection.

Maybe I was just soaking up pleasure wherever I could get it, after my long drought, but it was only a matter of time before I grew sated, and became as discriminating, as focused, as *particular*, as everyone else.

"Should I still be like this? *Omnivorous?*" I blurted out the question, starting with a tone of mild curiosity, ending with an edge of panic.

Tsela halted the sample he'd been playing—a chant that might have been Albanian, Moroccan, or Mongolian for all I knew, but which made hair rise on the back of my neck, and sent my spirits soaring. Just like everything else had.

He was silent for a while, weighing up competing obligations. Then he sighed and said, "You'd better talk to Durrani."

Durrani showed me a bar graph on the wallscreen in her office: the number of artificial synapses that had changed state within the prosthesis—new connections formed, existing ones broken, weakened or strengthened—for each of the past ten days. The embedded microprocessors kept track of such things, and an antenna waved over my skull each morning collected the data.

Day one had been dramatic, as the prosthesis adapted to its environment; the four thousand contributing networks might all have been perfectly stable in their owners' skulls, but the Everyman version I'd been given had never been wired up to anyone's brain before.

Day two had seen about half as much activity, day three about a tenth.

From day four on, though, there'd been nothing but background noise. My episodic memories, however pleasurable, were apparently being stored elsewhere—since I certainly wasn't suffering from amnesia—but after the initial burst of activity, the circuitry for defining what pleasure *was* had undergone no change, no refinement at all.

"If any trends emerge in the next few days, we should be able to amplify them, push them forward—like toppling an unstable building, once it's showing signs of falling in a certain direction." Durrani didn't sound hopeful. Too much time had passed already, and the network wasn't even teetering.

I said, "What about genetic factors? Can't you read my genome, and narrow things down from that?"

She shook her head. "At least two thousand genes play a role in neural development. It's not like matching a blood group or a tissue type; everyone in the database would have more or less the same small proportion of those genes in common with you. Of course, some people must have been closer to you in temperament than others—but we have no way of identifying them genetically."

"I see."

Durrani said carefully, "We could shut the prosthesis down completely, if that's what you want. There'd be no need for surgery—we'd just turn it off, and you'd be back where you started."

I stared at her luminous face. *How could I go back?* Whatever the tests and the bar graphs said . . . *how could this be failure?* However much useless beauty I was drowning in, I wasn't as screwed-up as I'd been with a head full of Leu-enkephalin. I was still capable of fear, anxiety, sorrow; the tests had revealed universal shadows, common to all the donors. Hating Bach or Chuck Berry, Chagall or Paul Klee was beyond me, but I'd reacted as sanely as anyone to images of disease, starvation, death.

And I was not oblivious to my own fate, the way I'd been oblivious to the cancer.

But what was my fate, if I kept using the prosthesis? Universal happiness, universal shadows . . . half the human race dictating my emotions? In all the years I'd spent in darkness, if I'd held fast to anything, hadn't it been the possibility that I carried a kind of seed within me: a version of myself that might grow into a living person again, given the chance? *And hadn't that hope now proved false?* I'd been offered the stuff of which selves were made—and though I'd tested it all, and admired it all, I'd claimed none of it as my own. All the joy I'd felt in the last ten days had been meaningless. I was just a dead husk, blowing around in other people's sunlight.

I said, "I think you should do that. Switch it off."

Durrani held up her hand. "Wait. If you're willing, there is one other thing we could try. I've been discussing it with our ethics committee, and Luke has begun preliminary work on the software . . . but in the end, it will be your decision."

"To do what?"

"The network can be pushed in any direction. We know how to intervene to do that—to break the symmetry, to make some things a greater source of pleasure than others. Just because it hasn't happened spontaneously, that doesn't mean it can't be achieved by other means."

I laughed, suddenly light-headed. "So if I say the word . . . *your ethics committee* will choose the music I like, and my favorite foods, and my new vocation? They'll decide who I become?" Would that be so bad? Having died, myself, long ago, to grant life now to a whole new person? To donate, not just a lung or a kidney, but my entire body, irrelevant memories and all, to an arbitrarily constructed—but fully functioning—*de novo* human being?

Durrani was scandalized. "No! We'd never dream of doing that! But we could program the microprocessors to let *you* control the network's refinement. We could give you the power to choose for yourself, consciously and deliberately, the things that make you happy."

De Vries said, "Try to picture the control."

I closed my eyes. He said, "Bad idea. If you get into the habit, it will limit your access."

"Right." I stared into space. Something glorious by Beethoven was playing on the lab's sound system; it was difficult to concentrate. I struggled to visualize the stylized, cherry-red, horizontal slider control that De Vries had constructed, line by line, inside my head five minutes before. Suddenly it was more than a vague memory: it was superimposed over the room again, as clear as any real object, at the bottom of my visual field.

"I've got it." The button was hovering around nineteen.

De Vries glanced at a display, hidden from me. "Good. Now try to lower the rating."

I laughed weakly. *Roll over Beethoven.* "How? How can you try to like something less?"

"You don't. Just try to move the button to the left. Visualize the movement. The software's monitoring your visual cortex, tracking any fleeting imaginary perceptions. Fool yourself into seeing the button moving—and the image will oblige."

It did. I kept losing control briefly, as if the thing was sticking, but I managed to manoeuvre it down to ten before stopping to assess the effect.

"Fuck."

"I take it it's working?"

I nodded stupidly. The music was still . . . *pleasant* . . . but the spell was broken completely. It was like listening to an electrifying piece of rhetoric, then realizing halfway through that the speaker didn't believe a word of it—leaving the original poetry and eloquence untouched, but robbing it of all its real force.

I felt sweat break out on my forehead. When Durrani had explained it, the whole scheme had sounded too bizarre to be real. And since I'd already failed to assert myself over the prosthesis—despite billions of direct neural connections, and countless opportunities for the remnants of my identity to interact with the thing and shape it in my own image—I'd feared that when the time came to make a choice, I'd be paralyzed by indecision.

But I knew, beyond doubt, that I should *not* have been in a state of rapture over a piece of classical music that I'd either never heard before, or—since apparently it was famous, and ubiquitous—sat through once or twice by accident, entirely unmoved.

And now, in a matter of seconds, I'd hacked that false response away.

There was still hope. I still had a chance to resurrect myself. I'd just have to do it consciously, every step of the way.

De Vries, tinkering with his keyboard, said cheerfully, "I'll color-code virtual gadgets for all the major systems in the prosthesis. With a few days' practice it'll all be second nature. Just remember that some experiences will engage two or three systems at once . . . so if you're making love to music that you'd prefer not to find so distracting, make sure you turn down the red control, not the blue." He looked up and saw my face. "Hey, don't worry. You can always turn it up again later if you make a mistake. Or if you change your mind."

THREE

It was nine P.M. in Sydney when the plane touched down. Nine o'clock on a Saturday night. I took a train into the city center, intending to catch the connecting one home, but when I saw the crowds alighting at Town Hall station I put my suitcase in a locker and followed them up onto the street.

I'd been in the city a few times since the virus, but never at night. I felt as if I'd come home after half a lifetime in another country, after solitary confinement in a foreign jail. Everything was disorienting, one way or another. I felt a kind of giddy *déjà vu* at the sight of buildings that seemed to have been faithfully preserved, but still weren't quite as I remembered them, and a sense of hollowness each time I turned a corner to find that some private landmark, some shop or sign I remembered from childhood, had vanished.

I stood outside a pub, close enough to feel my eardrums throb to the beat of the music. I could see people inside, laughing and dancing, sloshing armfuls of drinks around, faces glowing with alcohol and companionship. Some alive with the possibility of violence, others with the promise of sex.

I could step right into this picture myself, now. The ash that had buried the world was gone; I was free to walk wherever I pleased. And I could almost feel the dead cousins of these revellers—re-born now as harmonics of the network, resonating to the music and the sight of their soul-mates—clamoring in my skull, begging me to carry them all the way to the land of the living.

I took a few steps forward, then something in the corner of my vision distracted me. In the alley beside the pub, a boy of ten or twelve sat crouched against the wall, lowering his face into a plastic bag. After a few inhalations he looked up, dead eyes shining, as blissfully as any orchestra conductor.

I backed away.

Someone touched my shoulder. I spun around and saw a man beaming at me. "Jesus loves you, brother! Your search is over!" He thrust a pamphlet into my hand. I gazed into his face, and his condition was transparent to me: he'd stumbled on a way to produce Leu-enkephalin at will—but he didn't know it, so he'd reasoned that some divine wellspring of happiness was responsible. I felt my chest tighten with horror and pity. At least I'd known about my tumor. And even the fucked-up kid in the alley understood that he was just sniffing glue.

And the people in the pub? Did they know what they were doing? Music, companionship, alcohol, sex . . . where did the border lie? When did justifiable happiness turn into something as empty, as pathological, as it was for this man?

I stumbled away, and headed back towards the station. All around me, people were laughing and shouting, holding hands, kissing . . . and I watched them as if they were flayed anatomical figures, revealing a thousand interlocking muscles working together with effortless precision. Buried inside me, the machinery of happiness recognized itself, again and again.

I had no doubt, now, that Durrani really had packed every last shred of the human capacity for joy into my skull. But to claim any part of it, I'd have to swallow the fact—more deeply than the tumor had ever forced me to swallow it—that happiness itself meant nothing. Life without it was unbearable, but as an end in itself, it was not enough. I was free to choose its causes—and to be happy with my choices—but whatever I felt once I'd bootstrapped my new self into existence, the possibility would remain that all my choices had been wrong.

Global assurance had given me until the end of the year to get my act together. If my annual psychological assessment showed that Durrani's treatment had been successful—whether or not I actually had a job—I'd be thrown to the even less tender mercies of the privatized remnants of social security. So I stumbled around in the light, trying to find my bearings.

On my first day back I woke at dawn. I sat down at the phone and started digging. My old net workspace had been archived; at current rates it was only costing about ten cents a year in storage fees, and I still had $36.20 credit in my account. The whole bizarre informational fossil had passed intact from company to company through four takeovers and mergers. Working through an assortment of tools to decode the obsolete data formats, I dragged fragments of my past life into the present and examined them, until it became too painful to go on.

The next day I spent twelve hours cleaning the flat, scrubbing every corner—listening to my old *njari* downloads, stopping only to eat, ravenously. And though I could have refined my taste in food back to that of a twelve-year-old salt junkie, I made the choice—thoroughly un-masochistic, and more pragmatic than virtuous—to crave nothing more toxic than fruit.

In the following weeks I put on weight with gratifying speed, though when I stared at myself in the mirror, or used morphing software running on the phone, I realized that I could be happy with almost any kind of body. The database must have included people with a vast range of ideal self-images, or who'd died perfectly content with their actual appearances.

Again, I chose pragmatism. I had a lot of catching up to do, and I didn't want to die at fifty-five from a heart attack if I could avoid it. There was no point fixating on the unattainable or the absurd, though, so after morphing myself to obesity, and rating it zero, I did the same for the Schwarzenegger look. I chose a lean, wiry body—well within the realms of possibility, according to the software—and assigned it sixteen out of twenty. Then I started running.

I took it slowly at first, and though I clung to the image of myself as a child, darting effortlessly from street to street, I was careful never to crank up the joy of motion high enough to mask injuries. When I limped into a chemist looking for liniment, I found they were selling something called prostaglandin modulators, anti-inflammatory compounds that allegedly minimized damage without shutting down any vital repair processes. I was sceptical, but the stuff did seem to help; the first month was still painful, but I was neither crippled by natural swelling, nor rendered so oblivious to danger signs that I tore a muscle.

And once my heart and lungs and calves were dragged screaming out of their atrophied state, *it was good.* I ran for an hour every morning, weaving around the local back streets, and on Sunday afternoons circumnavigated the city itself. I didn't push myself to attain ever faster times; I had no athletic ambitions whatsoever. I just wanted to exercise my freedom.

Soon the act of running melted into a kind of seamless whole. I could revel in the thudding of my heart and the feeling of my limbs in motion, or I could let those details recede into a buzz of satisfaction and just watch the scenery, as if from a train. And having reclaimed my body, I began to reclaim the suburbs, one by one. From the slivers of forest clinging to the Lane Cove river to the eternal ugliness of Paramatta Road, I criss-crossed Sydney like a mad surveyor, wrapping the landscape with invisible geodesics then drawing it into my skull. I pounded across the bridges at Gladesville and Iron Cove, Pyrmont, Meadowbank, and the Harbor itself, daring the planks to give way beneath my feet.

I suffered moments of doubt. I wasn't drunk on endorphins—I wasn't pushing myself that hard—but it still felt too good to be true. *Was this glue-sniffing?* Maybe ten thousand generations of my ancestors had been rewarded with the same kind of pleasure for pursuing game, fleeing danger, and mapping their territory for the sake of survival, but to me it was all just a glorious pastime.

Still, I wasn't deceiving myself, and I wasn't hurting anyone. I plucked those two rules from the core of the dead child inside me, and kept on running.

Thirty was an interesting age to go through puberty. The virus hadn't literally castrated me, but having eliminated pleasure from sexual imagery, genital stimulation, and orgasm—and having partly wrecked the hormonal regulatory pathways reaching down from the hypothalamus—it had left me with nothing worth describing as sexual function. My body disposed of semen in sporadic joyless spasms—and without the normal lubricants secreted by the prostate during arousal, every unwanted ejaculation tore at the urethral lining.

When all of this changed, it hit hard—even in my state of relative sexual decrepitude. Compared to wet dreams of broken glass, masturbation was wonderful beyond belief, and I found myself unwilling to intervene with the controls to tone it down. But I needn't have worried that it would rob me of interest in the real thing; I kept finding myself staring openly at people on the street, in shops and on trains, until by a combination of willpower, sheer terror, and prosthetic adjustment I managed to kick the habit.

The network had rendered me bisexual, and though I quickly ramped my level of desire down considerably from that of the database's most priapic contributors, when it came to choosing to be straight or gay, everything turned to quicksand. The network was not some kind of population-weighted average; if it had been, Durrani's original hope that my own surviving neural architecture could hold sway would have been dashed whenever the vote was stacked against it. So I was not just ten or fifteen percent gay; the two possibilities were present with equal force, and the thought of eliminating *either* felt as alarming, as disfiguring, as if I'd lived with both for decades.

But was that just the prosthesis defending itself, or was it partly my own response? I had no idea. I'd been a thoroughly asexual twelve-year-old, even before the virus; I'd always assumed that I was straight, and I'd certainly found some girls attractive, but there'd been no moonstruck stares or furtive groping to back up that purely aesthetic opinion. I looked up the latest research, but all the genetic claims I recalled from various headlines had since been discredited—so even if my sexuality had been determined from birth, there was no blood test that could tell me, now, what it would have become. I even tracked down my pre-treatment MRI scans, but they lacked the resolution to provide a direct, neuroanatomical answer.

I didn't want to be bisexual. I was too old to experiment like a teenager; I wanted certainty, I wanted solid foundations. I wanted to be monogamous—and even if monogamy was rarely an effortless state for anyone, that was no reason to lumber myself with unnecessary obstacles. *So who should I slaughter?* I knew which choice would make things easier . . . but if everything came down to a question of which of the four thousand donors could carry me along the path of least resistance, whose life would I be living?

Maybe it was all a moot point. I was a thirty-year-old virgin with a history of mental illness, no money, no prospects, no social skills—and I could always crank up the satisfaction level of my only current option, and let everything else recede into fantasy. I wasn't deceiving myself, I wasn't hurting anyone. It was within my power to want nothing more.

I'd noticed the bookshop, tucked away in a back street in Leichhardt, many times before. But one Sunday in June, when I jogged past and saw a copy of *The Man Without Qualities* by Robert Musil in the front window, I had to stop and laugh.

I was drenched in sweat from the winter humidity, so I didn't go in and buy the book. But I peered in through the display towards the counter, and spotted a HELP WANTED sign.

Looking for unskilled work had seemed futile; the total unemployment rate was fifteen percent, the youth rate three times higher, so I'd assumed there'd always be a thousand other applicants for every job: younger, cheaper, stronger, and certifiably sane. But though I'd resumed my on-line education, I was getting not so much nowhere, fast as everywhere, slowly. All the fields of knowledge that had gripped me as a child had expanded a hundredfold, and while the prosthesis granted me limitless energy and enthusiasm, there was still too much ground for anyone to cover in a lifetime. I knew I'd have to sacrifice ninety percent of my interests if I was ever going to choose a career, but I still hadn't been able to wield the knife.

I returned to the bookshop on Monday, walking up from Petersham station. I'd fine-tuned my confidence for the occasion, but it rose spontaneously when I heard that there'd been no other applicants. The owner was in his sixties, and he'd just done his back in; he wanted someone to lug boxes around, and take the counter when he was otherwise occupied. I told him the truth: I'd been neurologically damaged by a childhood illness, and I'd only recently recovered.

He hired me on the spot, for a month's trial. The starting wage was exactly what Global Assurance was paying me, but if I was taken on permanently I'd get slightly more.

The work wasn't hard, and the owner didn't mind me reading in the back room when I had nothing to do. In a way, I was in heaven—ten thousand books, and no access fees—but sometimes I felt the terror of dissolution returning. I read voraciously, and on one level I could make clear judgments: I could pick the clumsy writers from the skilled, the honest from the fakers, the platitudinous from the inspired. But the prosthesis still wanted me to enjoy everything, to embrace everything, to diffuse out across the dusty shelves until I was no one at all, a ghost in the Library of Babel.

She walked into the bookshop two minutes after opening time, on the first day of spring. Watching her browse, I tried to think clearly through the consequences of what I was about to do. For weeks I'd been on the counter five hours a day, and with all that human contact I'd been hoping for . . . something. Not wild, reciprocated love at first sight, just the tiniest flicker of mutual interest, the slightest piece of evidence that I could actually desire one human being more than all the rest.

It hadn't happened. Some customers had flirted mildly, but I could see that it was nothing special, just their own kind of politeness—and I'd felt nothing more in response than if they'd been unusually, formally, courteous. And though I might have agreed with any bystander as to who was conventionally good-looking, who was animated or mysterious, witty or charming, who glowed with youth or radiated worldliness . . . I just didn't care. The four thousand had all loved very different people, and the envelope that stretched between their far-flung characteristics encompassed the entire species. That was never going to change, until I did something to break the symmetry myself.

So for the past week, I'd dragged all the relevant systems in the prosthesis down to three or four. People had become scarcely more interesting to watch than pieces of wood. Now, alone in the shop with this randomly chosen stranger, I slowly turned the controls up. I had to fight against positive feedback; the higher the settings, the more I wanted to increase them, but I'd set limits in advance, and I stuck to them.

By the time she'd chosen two books and approached the counter, I was feeling half defiantly triumphant, half sick with shame. I'd struck a pure note with the network at last; what I felt at the sight of this woman rang true. And if everything I'd done to achieve it was calculated, artificial, bizarre and abhorrent . . . I'd had no other way.

I was smiling as she bought the books, and she smiled back warmly. No wedding or engagement ring—but I'd promised myself that I wouldn't try anything, no matter what. This was just the first step: to notice someone, to make someone stand out from the crowd. I could ask out the tenth, the hundredth woman who bore some passing resemblance to her.

I said, "Would you like to meet for a coffee sometime?"

She looked surprised, but not affronted. Indecisive, but at least slightly pleased to have been asked. And I thought I was prepared for this slip of the tongue to lead nowhere, but then something in the ruins of me sent a shaft of pain through my chest as I watched her make up her mind. If a fraction of that had shown on my face, she probably would have rushed me to the nearest vet to be put down.

She said, "That would be nice. I'm Julia, by the way."

"I'm Mark." We shook hands.

"When do you finish work?"

"Tonight? Nine o'clock."

"Ah."

I said, "How about lunch? When do you have lunch?"

"One." She hesitated. "There's that place just down the road . . . next to the hardware store?"

"That would be great."

Julia smiled. "Then I'll meet you there. About ten past. OK?"

I nodded. She turned and walked out. I stared after her, dazed, terrified, elated. I thought: This is simple. Anyone in the world can do it. It's like breathing.

I started hyperventilating. I was an emotionally retarded teenager, and she'd discover that in five minutes flat. Or, worse, discover the four thousand grown men in my head offering advice.

I went into the toilet to throw up.

Julia told me that she managed a dress shop a few blocks away. "You're new at the bookshop, aren't you?"

"Yes."

"So what were you doing before that?"

"I was unemployed. For a long time."

"How long?"

"Since I was a student."

She grimaced. "It's criminal, isn't it? Well, I'm doing my bit. I'm job-sharing, half-time only."

"Really? How are you finding it?"

"It's wonderful. I mean, I'm lucky, the position's well enough paid that I can get by on half a salary." She laughed. "Most people assume I must be raising a family. As if that's the only possible reason."

"You just like to have the time?"

"Yes. Time's important. I hate being rushed."

We had lunch again two days later, and then twice again the next week. She talked about the shop, a trip she'd made to South America, a sister recovering from breast cancer. I almost mentioned my own long-vanquished tumor, but apart from fears about where that might lead, it would have sounded too much like a plea for sympathy. At home, I sat riveted to the phone—not waiting for a call, but watching news broadcasts, to be sure I'd have something to talk about besides myself. *Who's your favorite singer/author/artist/actor? I have no idea.*

Visions of Julia filled my head. I wanted to know what she was doing every second of the day; I wanted her to be happy, I wanted her to be safe. *Why?* Because I'd chosen her. But . . . why had I felt compelled to choose anyone? Because in the end, the one thing that most of the donors must have had in common was the fact that they'd desired, and cared about, one person above all others. *Why?* That came down to evolution. You could no more help and protect everyone in sight than you could fuck them, and a judicious combination of the two had obviously proved effective at passing down genes. So my emotions had the same ancestry as everyone else's; what more could I ask?

But how could I pretend that I felt anything real for Julia, when I could shift a few buttons in my head, anytime, and make those feelings vanish? Even if what I felt was strong enough to keep me from wanting to touch that dial. . . .

Some days I thought: it must be like this for everyone. People make a decision, half-shaped by chance, to get to know someone; everything starts from there. Some nights I sat awake for hours, wondering if I was turning myself into a pathetic slave, or a dangerous obsessive. Could anything I discovered about Julia drive me away, now that I'd chosen her? Or even trigger the slightest disapproval? And if, when, she decided to break things off, how would I take it?

We went out to dinner, then shared a taxi home. I kissed her goodnight on her doorstep. Back in my flat, I flipped through sex manuals on the net, wondering how I could ever hope to conceal my complete lack of experience. Everything looked anatomically impossible; I'd need six years of gymnastics training just to achieve the missionary position. I'd refused to masturbate since I'd met her; to fantasize about her, to *imagine her* without consent, seemed outrageous, unforgivable. After I gave in, I lay awake until dawn trying to comprehend the trap I'd dug for myself, and trying to understand why I didn't want to be free.

Julia bent down and kissed me, sweatily. "That was a nice idea." she climbed off me and flopped onto the bed.

I'd spent the last ten minutes riding the blue control, trying to keep myself from coming without losing my erection. I'd heard of computer games involving exactly the same thing. Now I turned up the indigo for a stronger glow of intimacy—and when I looked into her eyes, I knew that she could see the effect on me. She brushed my cheek with her hand. "You're a sweet man. Did you know that?"

I said, "I have to tell you something." *Sweet? I'm a puppet, I'm a robot, I'm a freak.*

"What?"

I couldn't speak. She seemed amused, then she kissed me. "I know you're gay. That's all right; I don't mind."

"I'm not gay." *Any more?* "Though I might have been."

Julia frowned. "Gay, bisexual . . . I don't care. Honestly."

I wouldn't have to manipulate my responses much longer; the prosthesis was being shaped by all of this, and in a few weeks I'd be able to leave it to its own devices. Then I'd feel, as naturally as anyone, all the things I was now having to choose.

I said, "When I was twelve, I had cancer."

I told her everything. I watched her face, and saw horror, then growing doubt. "You don't believe me?"

She replied haltingly, "You sound so matter-of-fact. *Eighteen years*? How can you just say, 'I lost eighteen years'?"

"How do you want me to say it? I'm not trying to make you pity me. I just want you to understand."

When I came to the day I met her, my stomach tightened with fear, but I kept on talking. After a few seconds I saw tears in her eyes, and I felt as though I'd been knifed.

"I'm sorry. I didn't mean to hurt you." I didn't know whether to try to hold her, or to leave right then. I kept my eyes fixed on her, but the room swam.

She smiled. "What are you sorry about? You chose me. I chose you. It could have been different for both of us. But it wasn't." She reached down under the sheet and took my hand. "It wasn't."

Julia had Saturdays off, but I had to start work at eight. she kissed me goodbye sleepily when I left at six; I walked all the way home, weightless.

I must have grinned inanely at everyone who came into the shop, but I hardly saw them. I was picturing the future. I hadn't spoken to either of my parents for nine years, they didn't even know about the Durrani treatment. But now it seemed possible to repair anything. I could go to them now and say: *This is your son, back from the dead. You did save my life, all those years ago.*

There was a message on the phone from Julia when I arrived home. I resisted viewing it until I'd started things cooking on the stove; there was something perversely pleasurable about forcing myself to wait, imagining her face and her voice in anticipation.

I hit the PLAY button. Her face wasn't quite as I'd pictured it.

I kept missing things and stopping to rewind. Isolated phrases stuck in my mind. *Too strange. Too sick. No one's fault.* My explanation hadn't really sunk in the night before. But now she'd had time to think about it, and she wasn't prepared to carry on a relationship with four thousand dead men.

I sat on the floor, trying to decide what to feel: the wave of pain crashing over me, or something better, by choice. I knew I could summon up the controls of the prosthesis and make myself happy—happy because I was "free" again, happy because I was better off without her . . . happy because Julia was better off without me. Or even just happy because happiness meant nothing, and all I had to do to attain it was flood my brain with Leu-enkephalin.

I sat there wiping tears and mucus off my face while the vegetables burned. The smell made me think of cauterization, sealing off a wound.

I let things run their course, I didn't touch the controls—but just knowing that I could have changed everything. And I realized then that, even if I went to Luke De Vries and said: I'm cured now, take the software away, I don't want the power to choose any more. . . . I'd never be able to forget where everything I felt had come from.

My father came to the flat yesterday. we didn't talk much, but he hasn't remarried yet, and he made a joke about us going nightclub-hopping together.

At least I hope it was a joke.

Watching him, I thought: he's there inside my head, and my mother too, and ten million ancestors, human, proto-human, remote beyond imagining. What difference did four thousand more make? Everyone had to carve a life out of the same legacy: half universal, half particular; half sharpened by relentless natural selection, half softened by the freedom of chance. I'd just had to face the details a little more starkly.

And I could go on doing it, walking the convoluted border between meaningless happiness and meaningless despair. Maybe I was lucky; maybe the best way to cling to that narrow zone was to see clearly what lay on either side.

When my father was leaving, he looked out from the balcony across the crowded suburb, down towards the Paramatta river, where a storm drain was discharging a visible plume of oil, street litter and garden runoff into the water.

He asked dubiously, "You happy with this area?"

I said, "I like it here."

GRIFFIN'S EGG

Michael Swanwick

❀

Michael Swanwick (born 1950) is a very serious player of today's grand game of science fiction. His first two published stories, both appearing in 1980, were "Ginungagap," which appeared in a special SF issue of the distinguished literary magazine, *Triquarterly*—the title refers to the primordial chaos out of which the universe was born of Norse mythology, and metaphorically to astrophysics, specifically to a black hole—and "The Feast of St. Janis," an homage to Gene Wolfe, which appeared in *New Dimensions 11*, edited by Marta Randall and Robert Silverberg. His first novel, *In the Drift* (1984), an alternate history novel in which the Three Mile Island reactor exploded, was one of Terry Carr's Ace Specials in the same series as William Gibson's *Neuromancer* and Kim Stanley Robinson's *The Wild Shore*. Since then he has published his fine novels at a rate of one every three or four years: *Vacuum Flowers* (1987), *Stations of the Tide* (1991), a winner of the Nebula Award for Best Novel, *The Iron Dragon's Daughter* (1993), what he called "hard fantasy," the sharply-satiric *Jack Faust* (1997), and his new novel, *Bones of the Earth* (2002), expanded from his Hugo Award–winning story "Scherzo with Tyrannosaur."

His short fiction is collected in *Gravity's Angels* (1991), *Geography of Unknown Lands* (1997), *Moon Dogs* (2000), *Tales of Old Earth* (2000), and *Puck Aleshire's Abecedary* (2000). Swanwick is also the author of two influential critical essays, one on SF, "User's Guide to the Postmoderns" (1985), and one on fantasy, "In the Tradition . . ." (1994). He is also the field's best currently practicing reviewer of short fiction.

Regarding the changing role of the hard SF writer, he says, "A lot of SF's world-building of the future was borrowed from people like Heinlein, Murray Leinster, Poul Anderson, hundreds of them, in a very free and generous and *allowed* borrowing. But now it looks like it is not going to be like that, we're back to where they were when they were making this stuff up, where the future wasn't at all obvious or easy to see. They invented a good, hard, convincing future. It's our job to do it again, and it's a tough job."

He wrote about "Griffin's Egg" in "Growing Up in the Future," published in *The New York Review of Science Fiction*:

> My father was an engineer. He worked for General Electric. . . . I remember a picture my father brought home from work, an artist's rendering of a lunar colony based on General Electric technology. It showed stiff, fifties-type people strolling within a domed crater, the sides of which had been contoured in a series of gardened terraces. A quarter century later, I used that image as a starting point for my own lunar colony in a novella called "Griffin's Egg." And though I worked some radical changes on that vision, it still had the core power of being a real place that I could believe in existing. It was something I had been promised as a child.

This story was originally published in the U.K. in 1991 as a stand-alone book, one of the Legend Books series of novellas. Swanwick recalls some things about the hard SF writing process:

> I wrote GE (note the initials) at the tail end of the 1980s. I knew that as soon as I finished it, I would be starting *The Iron Dragon's Daughter*, and as a result would be away from science fiction for a couple of years. I didn't want to come back and find myself writing eighties SF in the nineties, so I very deliberately set out to use up all the hard-SF ideation I'd done over the previous decade, but never found a story for. That's why there's a solar flare and a nuclear meltdown and a war and so on and so on. The only way to keep ideas from getting stale is to use them while they're fresh.
>
> I put in an enormous amount of research that doesn't show in the story . . . hours poring over specialized texts, establishing concentrations of elements in the lunar regolith, drawing maps and working out distances between industrial sites, the mechanics of heating and cooling a crater-city . . . far more than was needed simply to achieve internal consistency. Because in order to write with authority about an extraordinary locale, time, and enterprise none of which exist anywhere save in the story itself I first had to convince myself of their reality.

The moon? It is a griffin's egg,
Hatching to-morrow night.
And how the little boys will watch
With shouting and delight
To see him break the shell and stretch
And creep across the sky.
The boys will laugh, The little girls,
I fear, may hide and cry . . .
—Vachel Lindsay

The sun cleared the mountains. Gunther Weil raised a hand in salute, then winced as the glare hit his eyes in the instant it took his helmet to polarize.

He was hauling fuel rods to Chatterjee Crater industrial park. The Chatterjee B reactor had gone critical forty hours before dawn, taking fifteen remotes and a microwave relay with it, and putting out a power surge that caused collateral damage to every factory in the park. Fortunately, the occasional meltdown was designed into the system. By the time the sun rose over the Rhaeticus highlands, a new reactor had been built and was ready to go online.

Gunther drove automatically, gauging his distance from Bootstrap by the amount of trash lining the Mare Vaporum road. Close by the city, discarded construction machinery and damaged assemblers sat in open-vacuum storage, awaiting possible salvage. Ten kilometers out, a pressurized van had exploded, scattering machine parts and giant worms of insulating foam across the landscape. At twenty-five kilometers, a poorly graded stretch of road had claimed any number of cargo skids and shattered running lights from passing traffic.

Forty kilometers out, though, the road was clear, a straight, clean gash in the dirt. Ignoring the voices at the back of his skull, the traffic chatter and automated safety messages that the truck routinely fed into his transceiver chip, he scrolled up the topographicals on the dash.

Right about here.

Gunther turned off the Mare Vaporum road and began laying tracks over virgin soil. "You've left your prescheduled route," the truck said. "Deviations from schedule may only be made with the recorded permission of your dispatcher."

"Yeah, well." Gunther's voice seemed loud in his helmet, the only physical sound in a babel of ghosts. He'd left the cabin unpressurized, and the insulated layers of his suit stilled even the conduction rumbling from the treads. "You and I both know that so long as I don't fall too far behind schedule, Beth Hamilton isn't going to care if I stray a little in between."

"You have exceeded this unit's linguistic capabilities."

"That's okay, don't let it bother you." Deftly he tied down the send switch on the truck radio with a twist of wire. The voices in his head abruptly died. He was completely isolated now.

"You said you wouldn't do that again." The words, broadcast directly to his trance chip, sounded as deep and resonant as the voice of God. "Generation Five policy expressly requires that all drivers maintain constant radio—"

"Don't whine. It's unattractive."

"You have exceeded this unit's linguistic—"

"Oh, shut up." Gunther ran a finger over the topographical maps, tracing the course he'd plotted the night before: Thirty kilometers over cherry soil, terrain no human or machine had ever crossed before, and then north on Murchison road. With luck he might even manage to be at Chatterjee early.

He drove into the lunar plain. Rocks sailed by to either side. Ahead, the mountains grew imperceptibly. Save for the treadmarks dwindling behind him, there was nothing from horizon to horizon to show that humanity had ever existed. The silence was perfect.

Gunther lived for moments like this. Entering that clean, desolate emptiness, he experienced a vast expansion of being, as if everything he saw, stars, plain, craters and all, were encompassed within himself. Bootstrap City was only a fading dream, a distant island on the gently rolling surface of a stone sea. Nobody will ever be first here again, he thought. Only me.

A memory floated up from his childhood. It was Christmas Eve and he was in his parents' car, on the way to midnight Mass. Snow was falling, thickly and windlessly, rendering all the familiar roads of Düsseldorf clean and pure under sheets of white. His father drove, and he himself leaned over the front seat to stare ahead in fascination into this peaceful, transformed world. The silence was perfect.

He felt touched by solitude and made holy.

The truck plowed through a rainbow of soft grays, submerged hues more hints than colors, as if something bright and festive held itself hidden just beneath a coating of dust. The sun was at his shoulder, and when he spun the front axle to avoid a boulder, the truck's shadow wheeled and reached for infinity. He drove reflexively, mesmerized by the austere beauty of the passing land.

At a thought, his peecee put music on his chip. "Stormy Weather" filled the universe.

He was coming down a long, almost imperceptible slope when the controls went dead in his hands. The truck powered down and coasted to a stop. "Goddamn you, you asshole machine!" he snarled. "What is it this time?"

"The land ahead is impassable."

Gunther slammed a fist on the dash, making the maps dance. The land ahead was smooth and sloping, any unruly tendencies tamed eons ago by the Mare Imbrium explosion. Sissy stuff. He kicked the door open and clambered down.

The truck had been stopped by a baby rille: a snakelike depression meandering across his intended route, looking for all the world like a dry streambed. He bounded to its edge. It was fifteen meters across, and three meters down at its deepest. Just shallow enough that it wouldn't show up on the topos. Gunther returned to the cab, slamming the door noiselessly behind him.

"Look. The sides aren't very steep. I've been down worse a hundred times. We'll just take it slow and easy, okay?"

"The land ahead is impassable," the truck said. "Please return to the originally scheduled course."

Wagner was on now. *Tannhäuser*. Impatiently, he thought it off.

"If you're so damned heuristic, then why won't you ever listen to reason?" He chewed his lip angrily, gave a quick shake of his head. "No, going back would put us way off schedule. The rille is bound to peter out in a few hundred meters. Let's just follow it until it does, then angle back to Murchison. We'll be at the park in no time."

Three hours later he finally hit the Murchison road. By then he was sweaty and smelly and his shoulders ached with tension. "Where are we?" he asked sourly. Then, before the truck could answer, "Cancel that." The soil had turned suddenly black. That would be the ejecta fantail from the Sony-Reinpfaltz mine. Their railgun was oriented almost due south in order to avoid the client factories, and so their tailings hit the road first. That meant he was getting close.

Murchison was little more than a confluence of truck treads, a dirt track crudely leveled and marked by blazes of orange paint on nearby boulders. In quick order Gunther passed through a series of landmarks: Harada Industrial fantail, Sea of Storms Macrofacturing fantail, Krupp funfzig fantail. He knew them all. G5 did the robotics for the lot.

A light flatbed carrying a shipped bulldozer sped past him, kicking up a spray of dust that fell as fast as pebbles. The remote driving it waved a spindly arm in greeting. He waved back automatically, and wondered if it was anybody he knew.

The land hereabouts was hacked and gouged, dirt and boulders shoved into careless heaps and hills, the occasional tool station or Oxytank Emergency Storage Platform chopped into a nearby bluff. A sign floated by: TOILET FLUSHING FACILITIES 1/2 KILOMETER. He made a face. Then he remembered that his radio was still off and slipped the loop of wire from it. Time to rejoin the real world. Immediately his dispatcher's voice, harsh and staticky, was relayed to his trance chip.

"—ofabitch! *Weil!* Where the fuck are you?"

"I'm right here, Beth. A little late, but right where I'm supposed to be."

"Sonofa—" The recording shut off, and Hamilton's voice came on, live and mean. "You'd better have a real good explanation for this one, honey."

"Oh, you know how it is." Gunther looked away from the road, off into the dusty jade highlands. He'd like to climb up into them and never come back. Perhaps he would find caves. Perhaps there were monsters: vacuum trolls and moondragons with metabolisms slow and patient, taking centuries to move one body's-length, hyperdense beings that could swim through stone as if it were water. He pictured them diving, following lines of magnetic force deep, deep into veins of diamond and plutonium, heads back and singing. "I picked up a hitchhiker, and we kind of got involved."

"Try telling that to E. Izmailova. She's mad as hornets at you."

"Who?"

"Izmailova. She's the new demolitions jock, shipped up here on a multicorporate contract. Took a hopper in almost four hours ago, and she's been waiting for you and Siegfried ever since. I take it you've never met her?"

"No."

"Well, I have, and you'd better watch your step with her. She's exactly the kind of tough broad who won't be amused by your antics."

"Aw, come on, she's just another tech on a retainer, right? Not in my line of command. It's not like she can do anything to me."

"Dream on, babe. It wouldn't take much pull to get a fuckup like you sent down to Earth."

The sun was only a finger's breadth over the highlands by the time Chatterjee A loomed into sight. Gunther glanced at it every now and then, apprehensively. With his visor adjusted to the H-alpha wavelength, it was a blazing white sphere covered with slowly churning black specks: More granular than usual. Sunspot activity seemed high. He wondered that the Radiation Forecast Facility hadn't posted a surface advisory. The guys at the Observatory were usually right on top of things.

Chatterjee A, B, and C were a triad of simple craters just below Chladni, and while the smaller two were of minimal interest, Chatterjee A was the child of a meteor that had punched through the Imbrian basalts to as sweet a vein of aluminum ore as anything in the highlands. Being so convenient to Bootstrap made it one of management's darlings, and Gunther was not surprised to see that Kerr-McGee was going all out to get their reactor online again.

The park was crawling with walkers, stalkers, and assemblers. They were all over the blister-domed factories, the smelteries, loading docks, and vacuum garages. Constellations of blue sparks winked on and off as major industrial constructs were dismantled. Fleets of heavily loaded trucks fanned out into the lunar plain, churning up the dirt behind them. Fats Waller started to sing "The Joint is Jumping" and Gunther laughed.

He slowed to a crawl, swung wide to avoid a gas-plater that was being wrangled onto a loader, and cut up the Chatterjee B ramp road. A new landing pad had been blasted from the rock just below the lip, and a cluster of people stood about a hopper resting there. One human and eight remotes.

One of the remotes was speaking, making choppy little gestures with its arms. Several stood inert, identical as so many antique telephones, unclaimed by Earthside management but available should more advisors need to be called online.

Gunther unstrapped Siegfried from the roof of the cab and, control pad in one hand and cable spool in the other, walked him toward the hopper.

The human strode out to meet him. "You! What kept you?" E. Izmailova wore a jazzy red-and-orange Studio Volga boutique suit, in sharp contrast to his own company-issue suit with the G5 logo on the chest. He could not make out her face through the gold visor glass. But he could hear it in her voice: blazing eyes, thin lips.

"I had a flat tire." He found a good smooth chunk of rock and set down the cable spool, wriggling it to make sure it sat flush. "We got maybe five hundred yards of shielded cable. That enough for you?"

A short, tense nod.

"Okay." He unholstered his bolt gun. "Stand back." Kneeling, he anchored the spool to the rock. Then he ran a quick check of the unit's functions: "Do we know what it's like in there?"

A remote came to life, stepped forward and identified himself as Don Sakai, of

G5's crisis management team. Gunther had worked with him before: a decent tough guy, but like most Canadians he had an exaggerated fear of nuclear energy. "Ms. Lang here, of Sony-Reinpfaltz, walked her unit in but the radiation was so strong she lost control after a preliminary scan." A second remote nodded confirmation, but the relay time to Toronto was just enough that Sakai missed it. "The remote just kept on walking." He coughed nervously, then added unnecessarily, "The autonomous circuits were too sensitive."

"Well, that's not going to be a problem with Siegfried. He's as dumb as a rock. On the evolutionary scale of machine intelligence he ranks closer to a crowbar than a computer." Two and a half seconds passed, and then Sakai laughed politely. Gunther nodded to Izmailova. "Walk me through this. Tell me what you want."

Izmailova stepped to his side, their suits pressing together briefly as she jacked a patch cord into his control pad. Vague shapes flickered across the outside of her visor like the shadows of dreams. "Does he know what he's doing?" she asked.

"Hey, I—"

"Shut up, Weil," Hamilton growled on a private circuit. Openly, she said, "He wouldn't be here if the company didn't have full confidence in his technical skills."

"I'm sure there's never been any question—" Sakai began. He lapsed into silence as Hamilton's words belatedly reached him.

"There's a device on the hopper," Izmailova said to Gunther. "Go pick it up."

He obeyed, reconfiguring Siegfried for a small, dense load. The unit bent low over the hopper, wrapping large, sensitive hands about the device. Gunther applied gentle pressure. Nothing happened. Heavy little bugger. Slowly, carefully, he upped the power. Siegfried straightened.

"Up the road, then down inside."

The reactor was unrecognizable, melted, twisted and folded in upon itself, a mound of slag with twisting pipes sprouting from the edges. There had been a coolant explosion early in the incident, and one wall of the crater was bright with sprayed metal. "Where is the radioactive material?" Sakai asked. Even though he was a third of a million kilometers away, he sounded tense and apprehensive.

"It's all radioactive," Izmailova said.

They waited. "I mean, you know. The fuel rods?"

"Right now, your fuel rods are probably three hundred meters down and still going. We are talking about fissionable material that has achieved critical mass. Very early in the process the rods will have all melted together in a sort of superhot puddle, capable of burning its way through rock. Picture it as a dense, heavy blob of wax, slowly working its way toward the lunar core."

"God, I love physics," Gunther said.

Izmailova's helmet turned toward him, abruptly blank. After a long pause, it switched on again and turned away. "The road down is clear at least. Take your unit all the way to the end. There's an exploratory shaft to one side there. Old one. I want to see if it's still open."

"Will the one device be enough?" Sakai asked. "To clean up the crater, I mean."

The woman's attention was fixed on Siegfried's progress. In a distracted tone she said, "Mr. Sakai, putting a chain across the access road would be enough to clean up this site. The crater walls would shield anyone working nearby from the gamma radiation, and it would take no effort at all to reroute hopper overflights so their passengers would not be exposed. Most of the biological danger of a reactor meltdown comes from alpha radiation emitted by particulate radioisotopes in the air or water. When concentrated in the body, alpha-emitters can do considerable damage; elsewhere, no. Alpha particles can be stopped by a sheet of paper. So long as you keep a reactor out of your ecosystem, it's as safe as any other large machine. Burying a destroyed reactor just because it is radioactive is unnecessary and, if you will forgive me for saying so, superstitious. But I don't make policy. I just blow things up."

"Is this the shaft you're looking for?" Gunther asked.

"Yes. Walk it down to the bottom. It's not far."

Gunther switched on Siegfried's chestlight, and sank a roller relay so the cable wouldn't snag. They went down. Finally Izmailova said, "Stop. That's far enough." He gently set the device down and then, at her direction, flicked the arming toggle. "That's done," Izmailova said. "Bring your unit back. I've given you an hour to put some distance between the crater and yourself." Gunther noticed that the remotes, on automatic, had already begun walking away.

"Um . . . I've still got fuel rods to load."

"Not today you don't. The new reactor has been taken back apart and hauled out of the blasting zone."

Gunther thought now of all the machinery being disassembled and removed from the industrial park, and was struck for the first time by the operation's sheer extravagances of scale. Normally only the most sensitive devices were removed from a blasting area. "Wait a minute. Just what kind of monster explosive are you planning to *use?*"

There was a self-conscious cockiness to Izmailova's stance. "Nothing I don't know how to handle. This is a diplomat-class device, the same design as saw action five years ago. Nearly one hundred individual applications without a single mechanical failure. That makes it the most reliable weapon in the history of warfare. You should feel privileged having the chance to work with one."

Gunther felt his flesh turn to ice. "Jesus Mother of God," he said. "You had me handling a briefcase nuke."

"Better get used to it. Westinghouse Lunar is putting these little babies into mass production. We'll be cracking open mountains with them, blasting roads through the highlands, smashing apart the rille walls to see what's inside." Her voice took on a visionary tone. "And that's just the beginning. There are plans for enrichment fields in Sinus Aestum. Explode a few bombs over the regolith, then extract plutonium from the dirt. We're going to be the fuel dump for the entire solar system."

His dismay must have shown in his stance, for Izmailova laughed. "Think of it as weapons for peace."

"You should've been there!" Gunther said. "It was unfuckabelievable. The one side of the crater just disappeared. It dissolved into nothing. Smashed to dust. And for a real long time everything glowed! Craters, machines, everything. My visor was so close to overload it started flickering. I thought it was going to burn out. It was nuts." He picked up his cards. "Who dealt this mess?"

Krishna grinned shyly and ducked his head. "I'm in."

Hiro scowled down at his cards. "I've just died and gone to Hell."

"Trade you," Anya said.

"No, I deserve to suffer."

They were in Noguchi Park by the edge of the central lake, seated on artfully scattered boulders that had been carved to look water-eroded. A knee-high forest of baby birches grew to one side, and somebody's toy sailboat floated near the impact cone at the center of the lake. Honeybees mazily browsed the clover.

"And then, just as the wall was crumbling, this crazy Russian bitch—"

Anya ditched a trey. "Watch what you say about crazy Russian bitches."

"—goes zooming up on her hopper . . ."

"I saw it on television," Hiro said. "We all did. It was news. This guy who works for Nissan told me the BBC gave it thirty seconds." He'd broken his nose in karate practice, when he'd flinched into his instructor's punch, and the contrast of square white bandage with shaggy black eyebrows gave him a surly, piratical appearance.

Gunther discarded one. "Hit me. Man, you didn't see anything. You didn't feel the ground shake afterward."

"Just what was Izmailova's connection with the Briefcase War?" Hiro asked. "Obviously not a courier. Was she in the supply end or strategic?"

Gunther shrugged.

"You do remember the Briefcase War?" Hiro said sarcastically. "Half of Earth's military elites taken out in a single day? The world pulled back from the brink of war by bold action? Suspected terrorists revealed as global heroes?"

Gunther remembered the Briefcase War quite well. He had been nineteen at the time, working on a Finlandia Geothermal project when the whole world had gone into spasm and very nearly destroyed itself. It had been a major factor in his decision to ship off the planet. "Can't we ever talk about anything but politics? I'm sick and tired of hearing about Armageddon."

"Hey, aren't you supposed to be meeting with Hamilton?" Anya asked suddenly.

He glanced up at the Earth. The east coast of South America was just crossing the dusk terminator. "Oh, hell, there's enough time to play out the hand."

Krishna won with three queens. The deal passed to Hiro. He shuffled quickly, and slapped the cards down with angry little punches of his arm. "Okay," Anya said, "what's eating you?"

He looked up angrily, then down again and in a muffled voice, as if he had abruptly gone bashful as Krishna, said, "I'm shipping home."

"Home?"

"You mean to Earth?"

"Are you crazy? With everything about to go up in flames? *Why?*"

"Because I am so fucking tired of the Moon. It has to be the ugliest place in the universe."

"Ugly?" Anya looked elaborately about at the terraced gardens, the streams that began at the top level and fell in eight misty waterfalls before reaching the central pond to be recirculated again, the gracefully winding pathways. People strolled through great looping rosebushes and past towers of forsythia with the dreamlike skimming stride that made moonwalking so like motion underwater. Others popped in and out of the office tunnels, paused to watch the finches loop and fly, tended to beds of cucumbers. At the midlevel straw market, the tents where offduty hobby capitalists sold factory systems, grass baskets, orange glass paperweights and courses in postinterpretive dance and the meme analysis of Elizabethan poetry, were a jumble of brave silks, turquoise, scarlet, and aquamarine. "I think it looks nice. A little crowded, maybe, but that's the pioneer aesthetic."

"It looks like a shopping mall, but that's not what I'm talking about. It's—" He groped for words. "It's like—it's what we're doing to this world that bothers me. I mean, we're digging it up, scattering garbage about, ripping the mountains apart, and for what?"

"Money," Anya said. "Consumer goods, raw materials, a future for our children. What's wrong with that?"

"We're not building a future, we're building weapons."

"There's not so much as a handgun on the Moon. It's an intercorporate development zone. Weapons are illegal here."

"You know what I mean. All those bomber fuselages, detonation systems, and missile casings that get built here, and shipped to low Earth orbit. Let's not pretend we don't know what they're for."

"So?" Anya said sweetly. "We live in the real world, we're none of us naïve enough to believe you can have governments without armies. Why is it worse that these things are being built here rather than elsewhere?"

"It's the short-sighted, egocentric greed of what we're doing that gripes me! Have you peeked out on the surface lately and seen the way it's being ripped open, torn apart, and scattered about? There are still places where you can gaze upon a harsh beauty unchanged since the days our ancestors were swinging in trees. But we're trashing them. In a generation, two at most, there will be no more beauty to the Moon than there is to any other garbage dump."

"You've seen what Earthbound manufacturing has done to the environment," Anya said. "Moving it off the planet is a good thing, right?"

"Yes, but the Moon—"

"Doesn't even *have* an ecosphere. There's nothing here to harm."

They glared at each other. Finally Hiro said, "I don't want to talk about it," and sullenly picked up his cards.

Five or six hands later, a woman wandered up and plumped to the grass by Krishna's feet. Her eye shadow was vivid electric purple, and a crazy smile burned on her face. "Oh hi," Krishna said. "Does everyone here know Sally Chang? She's a research component of the Center for Self-Replicating Technologies, like me."

The others nodded. Gunther said, "Gunther Weil. Blue collar component of Generation Five."

She giggled.

Gunther blinked. "You're certainly in a good mood." He rapped the deck with his knuckles. "I'll stand."

"I'm on psilly," she said.

"One card."

"Psilocybin?" Gunther said. "I might be interested in some of that. Did you grow it or microfacture it? I have a couple of factories back in my room, maybe I could divert one if you'd like to license the software?"

Sally Chang shook her head, laughing helplessly. Tears ran down her cheeks.

"Well, when you come down we can talk about it," Gunther squinted at his cards. "This would make a great hand for chess."

"Nobody plays chess," Hiro said scornfully. "It's a game for computers."

Gunther took the pot with two pair. He shuffled, Krishna declined the cut, and he began dealing out cards. "So anyway, this crazy Russian lady—"

Out of nowhere, Chang howled. Wild gusts of laughter knocked her back on her heels and bent her forward again. The delight of discovery dancing in her eyes, she pointed a finger straight at Gunther. "You're a robot!" she cried.

"Beg pardon?"

"You're nothing but a robot," she repeated. "You're a machine, an automaton. Look at yourself! Nothing but stimulus-response. You have no free will at all. There's nothing there. You couldn't perform an original act to save your life."

"Oh yeah?" Gunther glanced around, looking for inspiration. A little boy—it might be Pyotr Nahfees, though it was hard to tell from here—was by the edge of the water, feeding scraps of shrimp loaf to the carp. "Suppose I pitched you into the lake? That would be an original act."

Laughing, she shook her head. "Typical primate behavior. A perceived threat is met with a display of mock aggression."

Gunther laughed.

"Then, when that fails, the primate falls back to a display of submission. Appeasal. The monkey demonstrates his harmlessness—you see?"

"Hey, this really isn't funny," Gunther said warningly. "In fact, it's kind of insulting."

"And so back to a display of aggression."

Gunther sighed and threw up both his hands. "How am I supposed to react? According to you, anything I say or do is wrong."

"Submission again. Back and forth, back and forth from aggression to submission and back again." She pumped her arm as if it were a piston. "Just like a little machine—you see? It's all automatic behavior."

"Hey, Kreesh—you're the neurobiowhatever here, right? Put in a good word for me. Get me out of this conversation."

Krishna reddened. He would not meet Gunther's eyes. "Ms. Chang is very highly regarded at the Center, you see. Anything she thinks about thinking is worth thinking about." The woman watched him avidly, eyes glistening, pupils small. "I think maybe what she means, though, is that we're all basically cruising through life. Like we're on autopilot. Not just you specifically, but all of us." He appealed to her directly. "Yes?"

"No, no, no, no." She shook her head. "Him specifically."

"I give up." Gunther put his cards down, and lay back on the granite slab so he could stare up through the roof glass at the waning Earth. When he closed his eyes, he could see Izmailova's hopper, rising. It was a skimpy device, little more than a platform-and-chair atop a cluster of four bottles of waste-gas propellant, and a set of smart legs. He saw it lofting up as the explosion blossomed, seeming briefly to hover high over the crater, like a hawk atop a thermal. Hands by side, the red-suited figure sat, watching with what seemed inhuman calm. In the reflected light she burned as bright as a star. In an appalling way, she was beautiful.

Sally Chang hugged her knees, rocking back and forth. She laughed and laughed.

Beth Hamilton was wired for telepresence. She flipped up one lens when Gunther entered her office, but kept on moving her arms and legs. Dreamy little ghost motions that would be picked up and magnified in a factory somewhere over the horizon. "You're late again," she said with no particular emphasis.

Most people would have experienced at least a twinge of reality sickness dealing with two separate surrounds at once. Hamilton was one of the rare few who could split her awareness between two disparate realities without loss of efficiency in either. "I called you in to discuss your future with Generation Five. Specifically, to discuss the possibility of your transfer to another plant."

"You mean Earthside."

"You see?" Hamilton said. "You're not as stupid as you like to make yourself out to be." She flipped the lens down again, stood very still, then lifted a metal-gauntleted hand and ran through a complex series of finger movements. "Well?"

"Well what?"

"Tokyo, Berlin, Buenos Aires—do any of these hold magic for you? How about Toronto? The right move now could be a big boost to your career."

"All I want is to stay here, do my job, and draw down my salary," Gunther said carefully. "I'm not looking for a shot at promotion, or a big raise, or a lateral career-track transfer. I'm happy right where I am."

"You've sure got a funny way of showing it." Hamilton powered down her gloves and slipped her hands free. She scratched her nose. To one side stood her work table, a polished cube of black granite. Her peecee rested there, alongside a spray of copper crystals. At her thought, it put Izmailova's voice onto Gunther's chip.

"It is with deepest regret that I must alert you to the unprofessional behavior of one of your personnel components," it began. Listening to the complaint, Gunther experienced a totally unexpected twinge of distress and, more, of resentment that Izmailova had dared judge him so harshly. He was careful not to let it show.

"Irresponsible, insubordinate, careless, and possessed of a bad attitude." He faked a grin. "She doesn't seem to like me much." Hamilton said nothing. "But this isn't enough to . . ." His voice trailed off. "Is it?"

"Normally, Weil, it would be. A demo jock isn't 'just a tech on retainer,' as you so quaintly put it; those government licenses aren't easy to get. And you may not be aware of it, but you have very poor efficiency ratings to begin with. Lots of potential, no follow-through. Frankly, you've been a disappointment. However, lucky for you, this Izmailova dame humiliated Don Sakai, and he's let us know that we're under no particular pressure to accommodate her."

"Izmailova humiliated Sakai?"

Hamilton stared at him. "Weil, you're oblivious, you know that?"

Then he remembered Izmailova's rant on nuclear energy. "Right, okay. I got it now."

"So here's your choice. I can write up a reprimand, and it goes into your permanent file, along with Izmailova's complaint. Or you can take a lateral Earthside, and I'll see to it that these little things aren't logged into the corporate system."

It wasn't much of a choice. But he put a good face on it. "In that case it looks like you're stuck with me."

"For the moment, Weil. For the moment."

He was back on the surface the next two days running. The first day he was once again hauling fuel rods to Chatterjee C. This time he kept to the road, and the reactor was refueled exactly on schedule. The second day he went all the way out to Triesnecker to pick up some old rods that had been in temporary storage for six months while the Kerr-McGee people argued over whether they should be reprocessed or dumped. Not a bad deal for him, because although the sunspot cycle was on the wane, there was a surface advisory in effect and he was drawing hazardous duty pay.

When he got there, a tech rep telepresenced in from somewhere in France to tell him to forget it. There'd been another meeting, and the decision had once again been delayed. He started back to Bootstrap with the new a capella version of *The Threepenny Opera* playing in his head. It sounded awfully sweet and reedy for his tastes, but that was what they were listening to up home.

Fifteen kilometers down the road, the UV meter on the dash *jumped.*

Gunther reached out to tap the meter with his finger. It did not respond. With a freezing sensation at the back of his neck, he glanced up at the roof of the cab and whispered, "Oh, no."

"The Radiation Forecast Facility has just intensified its surface warning to a Most Drastic status," the truck said calmly. "This is due to an unanticipated flare storm, onset immediately. Everyone currently on the surface is to proceed with all haste to shelter. Repeat: Proceed immediately to shelter."

"I'm eighty kilometers from—"

The truck was slowing to a stop. "Because this unit is not hardened, excessive fortuitous radiation may cause it to malfunction. To ensure the continued safe operation of this vehicle, all controls will be frozen in manual mode and this unit will now shut off."

With the release of the truck's masking functions, Gunther's head filled with overlapping voices. Static washed through them, making nonsense of what they were trying to say:

astic Stus-Repeat:
S**face**d***ory ha**
een***grad***to M**t
Dra**ic Stat**. A** u
nits *nd perso*****are
to find shelt***imm
ediatel*. Maxim*m *x
posu** **enty min**e
s.***nd ***lter i**ed*
*tely. Thi**is t** recor
ded*voice of**he Radi
ati***Forecast Faci*it
y.**u**to an unpr**i**
** sol** flare,***e su*
face adv**o***has been
upgrade***o Most Dras
* ***l! This is **eth.
Th** *
h***just i**ue**a M**
t D***tic**dvis*****G
et off t***surface**Go
ddamn **u, are yo* lis
tening? Find s**lter. D
on' t try to **t **ck to
Bootstrap.***o f**, it'll
*fry you.***ten, t**re *
* ** thr***factorie**n**
r fr*your pre***t
l***t**n. A*e you *ist
en**g, you***ofoff? Wei
* *sk*pf A**is**ne,
Ni**
, an Luna**M***os
t**ct**al. Weil!**et me
**ail, are you there? C
o***on, good **ddy, gi
ve ***a hoo** **ko, S
abra, **ng**i-ge**yo**
asses *****groun***ig
ht*ow. **don't wan**to
h*** you've st*yed*be
nto turn**** the l
* *ght***ho el***i**out
t
* here?**ome**n ri**t n
ow. Ev**y**e! Any**dy
*now w***e Mikha** i
* **C'mon, *Misha,
don*
* t**ou get coy *n us. So
u** us with ***r voice,
he**? W***ot **rd Ez

"Beth! The nearest shelter is back at Weisskopf—that's half an hour at top speed and I've got an advisory here of twenty minutes. Tell me what to do!"

But the first sleet of hard particles was coming in too hard to make out anything more. A hand, his apparently, floated forward and flicked off the radio relay. The voices in his head died.

The crackling static went on and on. The truck sat motionless, half an hour from nowhere, invisible death sizzling and popping down through the cab roof. He put his helmet and gloves on, double-checked their seals, and unlatched the door.

It slammed open. Pages from the op manual flew away, and a glove went tumbling gaily across the surface, chasing the pink fuzzy dice that Eurydice had given him that last night in Sweden. A handful of wheat biscuits in an open tin on the dash turned to powder and were gone, drawing the tin after them. Explosive decompression. He'd forgotten to depressurize. Gunther froze in dismayed astonishment at having made so basic—so dangerous—a mistake.

Then he was on the surface, head tilted back, staring up at the sun. It was angry with sunspots, and one enormous and unpredicted solar flare.

I'm going to die, he thought.

For a long, paralyzing instant, he tasted the chill certainty of that thought. He was going to die. He knew that for a fact, knew it more surely than he had ever known anything before.

In his mind, he could see Death sweeping across the lunar plain toward him. Death was a black wall, featureless, that stretched to infinity in every direction. It sliced the universe in half. On this side were life, warmth, craters and flowers, dreams, mining robots, thought, everything that Gunther knew or could imagine. On the other side . . . something? Nothing? The wall gave no hint. It was unreadable, enigmatic, absolute. But it was bearing down on him. It was so close now that he could almost reach out and touch it. Soon it would be here. He would pass through, and then he would know.

With a start he broke free of that thought, and jumped for the cab. He scrabbled up its side. His trance chip hissing, rattling and crackling, he yanked the magnetic straps holding Siegfried in place, grabbed the spool and control pad, and jumped over the edge.

He landed jarringly, fell to his knees, and rolled under the trailer. There was enough shielding wrapped around the fuel rods to stop any amount of hard radiation—no matter what its source. It would shelter him as well from the sun as from his cargo. The trance chip fell silent, and he felt his jaws relaxing from a clenched tension.

Safe.

It was dark beneath the trailer, and he had time to think. Even kicking his rebreather up to full, and offlining all his suit peripherals, he didn't have enough oxygen to sit out the storm. So okay. He had to get to a shelter. Weisskopf was closest, only fifteen kilometers away and there was a shelter in the G5 assembly plant there. That would be his goal.

Working by feel, he found the steel supporting struts, and used Siegfried's magnetic straps to attach himself to the underside of the trailer. It was clumsy, difficult work, but at last he hung face-down over the road. He fingered the walker's controls, and sat Siegfried up.

Twelve excruciating minutes later, he finally managed to get Siegfried down from the roof unbroken. The interior wasn't intended to hold anything half so big. To get the walker in he had first to cut the door free, and then rip the chair out of the cab. Discarding both items by the roadside, he squeezed Siegfried in. The walker bent over double, reconfigured, reconfigured again, and finally managed to fit itself into the space. Gently, delicately, Siegfried took the controls and shifted into first.

With a bump, the truck started to move.

It was a hellish trip. The truck, never fast to begin with, wallowed down the road like a cast-iron pig. Siegfried's optics were bent over the controls, and couldn't be raised without jerking the walker's hands free. He couldn't look ahead without stopping the truck first.

He navigated by watching the road pass under him. To a crude degree he could align the truck with the treadmarks scrolling by. Whenever he wandered off the track, he worked Siegfried's hand controls to veer the truck back, so that it drifted slowly from side to side, zig-zagging its way down the road.

Shadows bumping and leaping, the road flowed toward Gunther with dangerous monotony. He jiggled and vibrated in his makeshift sling. After a while his neck hurt with the effort of holding his head back to watch the glaring road disappearing into shadow by the front axle, and his eyes ached from the crawling repetitiveness of what they saw.

The truck kicked up dust in passing, and the smaller particles carried enough of a static charge to cling to his suit. At irregular intervals he swiped at the fine gray film on his visor with his glove, smearing it into long, thin streaks.

He began to hallucinate. They were mild visuals, oblong patches of colored light that moved in his vision and went away when he shook his head and firmly closed his eyes for a concentrated moment. But every moment's release from the pressure of vision tempted him to keep his eyes closed longer, and that he could not afford to do.

It put him in mind of the last time he had seen his mother, and what she had said then. That the worst part of being a widow was that every day her life began anew, no better than the day before, the pain still fresh, her husband's absence a physical fact she was no closer to accepting than ever. It was like being dead, she said, in that nothing ever changed.

Ah God, he thought, this isn't worth doing. Then a rock the size of his head came bounding toward his helmet. Frantic hands jerked at the controls, and Siegfried skewed the truck wildly, so that the rock jumped away and missed him. Which put an end to *that* line of thought.

He cued his peecee. *Saint James' Infirmary* came on. It didn't help.

Come on, you bastard, he thought. You can do it. His arms and shoulders ached, and his back too, when he gave it any thought. Perversely enough, one of his legs had gone to sleep. At the angle he had to hold his head to watch the road, his mouth tended to hang open. After a while, a quivering motion alerted him that a small puddle of saliva had gathered in the curve of his faceplate. He was drooling. He closed his mouth, swallowing back his spit, and stared forward. A minute later he found that he was doing it again.

Slowly, miserably, he drove toward Weisskopf.

The G5 Weisskopf plant was typical of its kind: A white blister-dome to moderate temperature swings over the long lunar day, a microwave relay tower to bring in supervisory presence, and a hundred semiautonomous units to do the work.

Gunther overshot the access road, wheeled back to catch it, and ran the truck right up to the side of the factory. He had Siegfried switch off the engine, and then let the control pad fall to the ground. For well over a minute he simply hung there, eyes closed, savoring the end of motion. Then he kicked free of the straps, and crawled out from under the trailer.

Static scatting and stuttering inside his head, he stumbled into the factory.

In the muted light that filtered through the dome covering, the factory was dim as an undersea cavern. His helmet light seemed to distort as much as it illumined. Machines loomed closer in the center of its glare, swelling up as if seen through a fisheye lens. He turned it off, and waited for his eyes to adjust.

After a bit, he could see the robot assemblers, slender as ghosts, moving with unearthly delicacy. The flare storm had activated them. They swayed like seaweed, lightly out of sync with each other. Arms raised, they danced in time to random radio input.

On the assembly lines lay the remains of half-built robots, looking flayed and eviscerated. Their careful frettings of copper and silver nerves had been exposed to view and randomly operated upon. A long arm jointed down, electric fire at its tip, and made a metal torso twitch.

They were blind mechanisms, most of them, powerful things bolted to the floor in assembly logic paths. But there were mobile units as well, overseers and jacks-of-all-trades, weaving drunkenly through the factory with sun-maddened eye.

A sudden motion made Gunther turn just in time to see a metal puncher swivel toward him, slam down an enormous arm and put a hole in the floor by his feet. He felt the shock through his soles.

He danced back. The machine followed him, the diamond-tipped punch sliding nervously in and out of its sheath, its movements as trembling and dainty as a newborn colt's.

"Easy there, baby," Gunther whispered. To the far end of the factory, green arrows supergraffixed on the crater wall pointed to an iron door. The shelter. Gunther backed away from the punch, edging into a service aisle between two rows of machines that rippled like grass in the wind.

The punch press rolled forward on its trundle. Then, confused by that field of motion, it stopped, hesitantly scanning the ranks of robots. Gunther froze.

At last, slowly, lumberingly, the metal puncher turned away.

Gunther ran. Static roared in his head. Grey shadows swam among the distant machines, like sharks, sometimes coming closer, sometimes receding. The static loudened. Up and down the factory welding arcs winked on at the assembler tips, like tiny stars. Ducking, running, spinning, he reached the shelter and seized the airlock door. Even through his glove, the handle felt cold.

He turned it.

The airlock was small and round. He squeezed through the door and fit himself into the inadequate space within, making himself as small as possible. He yanked the door shut.

Darkness.

He switched his helmet lamp back on. The reflected glare slammed at his eyes, far too intense for such a confined area. Folded knees-to-chin into the roundness of the lock he felt a wry comradeship with Siegfried back in the truck.

The inner lock controls were simplicity itself. The door hinged inward, so that air pressure held it shut. There was a yank bar which, when pulled, would bleed oxygen into the airlock. When pressure equalized, the inner door would open easily. He yanked the bar.

The floor vibrated as something heavy went by.

The shelter was small, just large enough to hold a cot, a chemical toilet and a rebreather with spare oxytanks. A single overhead unit provided light and heat. For comfort there was a blanket. For amusement, there were pocket-sized editions of the Bible and the Koran, placed there by impossibly distant missionary societies. Even empty, there was not much space in the shelter.

It wasn't empty.

A woman, frowning and holding up a protective hand, cringed from his helmet lamp. "Turn that thing off," she said.

He obeyed. In the soft light that ensued he saw: stark white flattop, pink scalp visible through the sides. High cheekbones. Eyelids lifted slightly, like wings, by carefully sculpted eye shadow. Dark lips, full mouth. He had to admire the character it took to make up a face so carefully, only to hide it beneath a helmet. Then he saw her red and orange Studio Volga suit.

It was Izmailova.

To cover his embarrassment, he took his time removing his gloves and helmet. Izmailova moved her own helmet from the cot to make room, and he sat down beside her. Extending a hand, he stiffly said, "We've met before. My name is—"

"I know. It's written on your suit."

"Oh yeah. Right."

For an uncomfortably long moment, neither spoke. At last Izmailova cleared her throat and briskly said, "This is ridiculous. There's no reason we should—"

CLANG.

Their heads jerked toward the door in unison. The sound was harsh, loud, metallic. Gunther slammed his helmet on, grabbed for his gloves. Izmailova, also suiting up as rapidly as she could, tensely subvocalized into her trance chip: "What is it?"

Methodically snapping his wrist latches shut one by one, Gunther said, "I think it's a metal punch." Then, because the helmet muffled his words, he repeated them over the chip.

CLANG. This second time, they were waiting for the sound. Now there could be no doubt. Something was trying to break open the outer airlock door.

"A what?!"

"Might be a hammer of some type, or a blacksmith unit. Just be thankful it's not a laser jig." He held up his hands before him. "Give me a safety check."

She turned his wrists one way, back, took his helmet in her hands and gave it a twist to test its seal. "You pass." She held up her own wrists. "But what is it trying to do?"

Her gloves were sealed perfectly. One helmet dog had a bit of give in it, but not enough to breach integrity. He shrugged. "It's deranged—it could want anything. It might even be trying to repair a weak hinge."

CLANG.

"It's trying to get in here!"

"That's another possibility, yes."

Izmailova's voice rose slightly. "But even scrambled, there can't possibly be any programs in its memory to make it do that. How can random input make it act this way?"

"It doesn't work like that. You're thinking of the kind of robotics they had when you were a kid. These units are state of the art: They don't manipulate instructions, they manipulate concepts. See, that makes them more flexible. You don't have to program in every little step when you want one to do something new. You just give it a goal—"

CLANG.

"—like, to Disassemble a Rotary Drill. It's got a bank of available skills, like Cutting and Unbolting and Gross Manipulation, which it then fits together in various configurations until it has a path that will bring it to the goal." He was talking for the sake of talking now, talking to keep himself from panic. "Which normally works out fine. But when one of these things malfunctions, it does so on the conceptual level. See? So that—"

"So that it decides we're rotary drills that need to be disassembled."

"Uh . . . yeah."

CLANG.

"So what do we do when it gets in here?" They had both involuntarily risen to their feet, and stood facing the door. There was not much space, and what little there was they filled. Gunther was acutely aware that there was not enough room here to either fight or flee.

"I don't know about you," he said, "but I'm going to hit that sucker over the head with the toilet."

She turned to look at him.

CLA—The noise was cut in half by a breathy, whooshing explosion. Abrupt, total silence. "It's through the outer door," Gunther said flatly.

They waited.

Much later, Izmailova said, "Is it possible it's gone away?"

"I don't know." Gunther undogged his helmet, knelt and put an ear to the floor. The stone was almost painfully cold. "Maybe the explosion damaged it." He could hear the faint vibrations of the assemblers, the heavier rumblings of machines roving the factory floor. None of it sounded close. He silently counted to a hundred. Nothing. He counted to a hundred again.

Finally he straightened. "It's gone."

They both sat down. Izmailova took off her helmet, and Gunther clumsily began undoing his gloves. He fumbled at the latches. "Look at me." He laughed shakily. "I'm all thumbs. I can't even handle this, I'm so unnerved."

"Let me help you with that." Izmailova flipped up the latches, tugged at his glove. It came free. "Where's your other hand?"

Then, somehow, they were each removing the other's suit, tugging at the latches, undoing the seals. They began slowly but sped up with each latch undogged, until they were yanking and pulling with frantic haste. Gunther opened up the front of Izmailova's suit, revealing a red silk camisole. He slid his hands beneath it, and pushed the cloth up over her breasts. Her nipples were hard. He let her breasts fill his hands and squeezed.

Izmailova made a low, groaning sound in the back of her throat. She had Gunther's suit open. Now she pushed down his leggings and reached within to seize his cock. He was already erect. She tugged it out and impatiently shoved him down on the cot. Then she was kneeling on top of him and guiding him inside her.

Her mouth met his, warm and moist.

Half in and half out of their suits, they made love. Gunther managed to struggle one arm free, and reached within Izmailova's suit to run a hand up her long back and over the back of her head. The short hairs of her buzz cut stung and tickled his palm.

She rode him roughly, her flesh slippery with sweat against his. "Are you coming yet?" she murmured. "Are you coming yet? Tell me when you're about to come." She bit his shoulder, the side of his neck, his chin, his lower lip. Her nails dug into his flesh.

"Now," he whispered. Possibly he only subvocalized it, and she caught it on her trance chip. But then she clutched him tighter than ever, as if she were trying to crack his ribs, and her whole body shuddered with orgasm. Then he came too, riding her passion down into spiraling desperation, ecstasy and release.

It was better than anything he had ever experienced before.

Afterward, they finally kicked free of their suits. They shoved and pushed the things off the cot. Gunther pulled the blanket out from beneath them, and with Izmailova's help wrapped it about the both of them. They lay together, relaxed, not speaking.

He listened to her breathe for a while. The noise was soft. When she turned her face toward him, he could feel it, a warm little tickle in the hollow of his throat. The smell of her permeated the room. This stranger beside him.

Gunther felt weary, warm, at ease. "How long have you been here?" he asked. "Not here in the shelter, I mean, but . . ."

"Five days."

"That little." He smiled. "Welcome to the Moon, Ms. Izmailova."

"Ekatarina," she said sleepily. "Call me Ekatarina."

* * *

Whooping, they soared high and south, over Herschel. The Ptolemaeus road bent and doubled below them, winding out of sight, always returning. "This is great!" Hiro crowed. "This is—I should've talked you into taking me out here a year ago."

Gunther checked his bearings and throttled down, sinking eastward. The other two hoppers, slaved to his own, followed in tight formation. Two days had passed since the flare storm and Gunther, still on mandatory recoop, had promised to guide his friends into the highlands as soon as the surface advisory was dropped. "We're coming in now. Better triplecheck your safety harnesses. You doing okay back there, Kreesh?"

"I am quite comfortable, yes."

Then they were down on the Seething Bay Company landing pad.

Hiro was the second down and the first on the surface. He bounded about like a collie off its leash, chasing upslope and down, looking for new vantage points. "I can't believe I'm here! I work out this way every day, but you know what? This is the first time I've actually been out here. Physically, I mean."

"Watch your footing," Gunther warned. "This isn't like telepresence—if you break a leg, it'll be up to Krishna and me to carry you out."

"I trust you. Man, anybody who can get caught out in a flare storm, and end up nailing—"

"Hey, watch your language, okay?"

"Everybody's heard the story. I mean, we all thought you were dead, and then they found the two of you *asleep*. They'll be talking about it a hundred years from now." Hiro was practically choking on his laughter. "You're a legend!"

"Just give it a rest." To change the subject, Gunther said, "I can't believe you want to take a photo of this mess." The Seething Bay operation was a strip mine. Robot bulldozers scooped up the regolith and fed it to a processing plant that rested on enormous skids. They were after the thorium here, and the output was small enough that it could be transported to the breeder reactor by hopper. There was no need for a railgun and the tailings were piled in artificial mountains in the wake of the factory.

"Don't be ridiculous." Hiro swept an arm southward, toward Ptolemaeus. "There!" The crater wall caught the sun, while the lowest parts of the surrounding land were still in shadow. The gentle slopes seemed to tower; the crater itself was a cathedral, blazing white.

"Where is your camera?" Krishna asked.

"Don't need one. I'll just take the data down on my helmet."

"I'm not too clear on this mosaic project of yours," Gunther said. "Explain to me one more time how it's supposed to work."

"Anya came up with it. She's renting an assembler to cut hexagonal floor tiles in black, white, and fourteen intermediate shades of gray. I provide the pictures. We choose the one we like best, scan it in black and white, screen for values of intensity, and then have the assembler lay the floor, one tile per pixel. It'll look great—come by tomorrow and see."

"Yeah, I'll do that."

Chattering like a squirrel, Hiro led them away from the edge of the mine. They bounded westward, across the slope.

Krishna's voice came over Gunther's trance chip. It was an old groundrat trick. The chips had an effective transmission radius of fifteen yards—you could turn off the radio and talk chip-to-chip, if you were close enough. "You sound troubled, my friend."

He listened for a second carrier tone, heard nothing. Hiro was out of range. "It's Izmailova. I sort of—"

"Fell in love with her."

"How'd you know that?"

They were spaced out across the rising slope, Hiro in the lead. For a time neither spoke. There was a calm, confidential quality to that shared silence, like the anonymous stillness of the confessional. "Please don't take this wrong," Krishna said.

"Take what wrong?"

"Gunther, if you take two sexually compatible people, place them in close proximity, isolate them and scare the hell out of them, they will fall in love. That's a given. It's a survival mechanism, something that was wired into your basic makeup long before you were born. When billions of years of evolution say it's bonding time, your brain doesn't have much choice but to obey."

"Hey, come on over here!" Hiro cried over the radio. "You've got to see this."

"We're coming," Gunther said. Then, over his chip, "You make me out to be one of Sally Chang's machines."

"In some ways we *are* machines. That's not so bad. We feel thirsty when we need water, adrenaline pumps into the bloodstream when we need an extra boost of aggressive energy. You can't fight your own nature. What would be the point of it?"

"Yeah, but . . ."

"Is this great or what?" Hiro was clambering over a boulder field. "It just goes on and on. And look up there!" Upslope, they saw that what they were climbing over was the spillage from a narrow cleft entirely filled with boulders. They were huge, as big as hoppers, some of them large as prefab oxysheds. "Hey, Krishna, I been meaning to ask you—just what is it that you do out there at the Center?"

"I can't talk about it."

"Aw, come on." Hiro lifted a rock the size of his head to his shoulder and shoved it away, like a shot-putter. The rock soared slowly, landed far downslope in a white explosion of dust. "You're among friends here. You can trust us."

Krishna shook his head. Sunlight flashed from the visor. "You don't know what you're asking."

Hiro hoisted a second rock, bigger than the first. Gunther knew him in this mood, nasty-faced and grinning. "My point exactly. The two of us know zip about neurobiology. You could spend the next ten hours lecturing us, and we couldn't catch enough to compromise security." Another burst of dust.

"You don't understand. The Center for Self-Replicating Technologies is here for a reason. The lab work could be done back on Earth for a fraction of what a lunar facility costs. Our sponsors only move projects here that they're genuinely afraid of."

"So what *can* you tell us about? Just the open stuff, the video magazine stuff. Nothing secret."

"Well . . . okay." Now it was Krishna's turn. He picked up a small rock, wound up like a baseball player and threw. It dwindled and disappeared in the distance. A puff of white sprouted from the surface. "You know Sally Chang? She has just finished mapping the neurotransmitter functions."

They waited. When Krishna added nothing further, Hiro dryly said, "Wow."

"Details, Kreesh. Some of us aren't so fast to see the universe in a grain of sand as you are."

"It should be obvious. We've had a complete genetic map of the brain for almost a decade. Now add to that Sally Chang's chemical map, and it's analogous to being given the keys to the library. No, better than that. Imagine that you've spent your entire life within an enormous library filled with books in a language you neither read nor speak, and that you've just found the dictionary and a picture reader."

"So what are you saying? That we'll have complete understanding of how the brain operates?"

"We'll have complete *control* over how the brain operates. With chemical therapy, it will be possible to make anyone think or feel anything we want. We will have an immediate cure for all nontraumatic mental illness. We'll be able to fine-tune aggression, passion, creativity—bring them up, damp them down, it'll be all the same. You can see why our sponsors are so afraid of what our research might produce."

"Not really, no. The world could use more sanity," Gunther said.

"I agree. But who defines sanity? Many governments consider political dissent grounds for mental incarceration. This would open the doors of the brain, allowing it to be examined from the outside. For the first time, it would be possible to discover unexpressed rebellion. Modes of thought could be outlawed. The potential for abuse is not inconsiderable.

"Consider also the military applications. This knowledge combined with some of the new nanoweaponry might produce a berserker gas, allowing you to turn the enemy's armies upon their own populace. Or, easier, to throw them into a psychotic frenzy and let them turn on themselves. Cities could be pacified by rendering the citizenry catatonic. A secondary, internal reality could then be created, allowing the conqueror to use the masses as slave labor. The possibilities are endless."

They digested this in silence. At last Hiro said, "Jeez, Krishna, if that's the open goods, what the hell kind of stuff do you have to hide?"

"I can't tell you."

A minute later, Hiro was haring off again. At the foot of a nearby hill he found an immense boulder standing atilt on its small end. He danced about, trying to get good shots past it without catching his own footprints in them.

"So what's the problem?" Krishna said over his chip.

"The problem is, I can't arrange to see her. Ekatarina. I've left messages, but she won't answer them. And you know how it is in Bootstrap—it takes a real effort to avoid somebody who wants to see you. But she's managed it."

Krishna said nothing.

"All I want to know is, just what's going on here?"

"She's avoiding you."

"But why? I fell in love and she didn't, is that what you're telling me? I mean, is that a crock or what?"

"Without hearing her side of the story, I can't really say how she feels. But the odds are excellent she fell every bit as hard as you did. The difference is that you think it's a good idea, and she doesn't. So of course she's avoiding you. Contact would just make it more difficult for her to master her feelings for you."

"Shit!"

An unexpected touch of wryness entered Krishna's voice. "What do you want? A minute ago you were complaining that I think you're a machine. Now you're unhappy that Izmailova thinks she's not."

"Hey, you guys! Come over here. I've found the perfect shot. You've got to see this."

They turned to see Hiro waving at them from the hilltop. "I thought you were leaving," Gunther grumbled. "You said you were sick of the Moon, and going away and never coming back. So how come you're upgrading your digs all of a sudden?"

"That was yesterday! Today, I'm a pioneer, a builder of worlds, a founder of dynasties!"

"This is getting tedious. What does it take to get a straight answer out of you?"

Hiro bounded high and struck a pose, arms wide and a little ridiculous. He staggered a bit on landing. "Anya and I are getting married!"

Gunther and Krishna looked at each other, blank visor to blank visor. Forcing enthusiasm into his voice, Gunther said, "Hey, no shit? Really! Congratu—"

A scream of static howled up from nowhere. Gunther winced and cut down the gain. "My stupid radio is—"

One of the other two—they had moved together and he couldn't tell them apart at this distance—was pointing upward. Gunther tilted back his head, to look at the Earth. For a second he wasn't sure what he was looking for. Then he saw it: a diamond pinprick of light in the middle of the night. It was like a small, bright hole in reality, somewhere in continental Asia. "What the hell is *that?*" he asked.

Softly, Hiro said, "I think it's Vladivostok."

By the time they were back over the Sinus Medii, that first light had reddened and faded away, and two more had blossomed. The news jockey at the Observatory was working overtime splicing together reports from the major news feeds into a montage of rumor and fear. The radio was full of talk about hits on Seoul and Buenos Aires. Those seemed certain. Strikes against Panama, Iraq, Denver, and Cairo were disputed. A stealth missile had flown low over Hokkaido and been deflected into the Sea of Japan. The Swiss Orbitals had lost some factories to fragmentation satellites. There was no agreement as to the source aggressor, and though most suspicions trended in one direction, Tokyo denied everything.

Gunther was most impressed by the sound feed from a British video essayist, who said that it did not matter who had fired the first shot, or why. "Who shall we blame? The Southern Alliance, Tokyo, General Kim, or possibly some Gray terrorist group that nobody has ever heard of before? In a world whose weapons were wired to hair triggers, the question is irrelevant. When the first device exploded, it activated autonomous programs which launched what is officially labeled 'a measured response.' Gorshov himself could not have prevented it. His tactical programs chose this week's three most likely aggressors—at least two of which were certainly innocent—and launched a response. Human beings had no say over it.

"Those three nations in turn had their own reflexive 'measured responses.' The results of which we are just beginning to learn. Now we will pause for five days, while all concerned parties negotiate. How do we know this? Abstracts of all major defense programs are available on any public data net. They are no secret. Openness is in fact what deterrence is all about.

"We have five days to avert a war that literally nobody wants. The question is, in five days can the military and political powers seize control of their own defense programming? Will they? Given the pain and anger involved, the traditional hatreds, national chauvinism, and the natural reactions of those who number loved ones among the already dead, can those in charge overcome their own natures in time to pull back from final and total war? Our best informed guess is no. No, they cannot.

"Good night, and may God have mercy on us all."

They flew northward in silence. Even when the broadcast cut off in midword, nobody spoke. It was the end of the world, and there was nothing they could say that did not shrink to insignificance before that fact. They simply headed home.

The land about Bootstrap was dotted with graffiti, great block letters traced out in boulders: KARL OPS—EINDHOVEN '49 and LOUISE MCTIGHE ALBUQUERQUE NM. An enormous eye in a pyramid. ARSENAL WORLD RUGBY CHAMPS with a crown over it.

CORNPONE. PI LAMBDA PHI. MOTORHEADS. A giant with a club. Coming down over them, Gunther reflected that they all referred to places and things in the world overhead, not a one of them indigenous to the Moon. What had always seemed pointless now struck him as unspeakably sad.

It was only a short walk from the hopper pad to the vacuum garage. They didn't bother to summon a jitney.

The garage seemed strangely unfamiliar to Gunther now, though he had passed through it a thousand times. It seemed to float in its own mystery, as if everything had been removed and replaced by its exact double, rendering it different and somehow unknowable. Row upon row of parked vehicles were slanted by type within the painted lines. Ceiling lights strained to reach the floor, and could not.

"Boy, is this place still!" Hiro's voice seemed unnaturally loud.

It was true. In all the cavernous reaches of the garage, not a single remote or robot service unit stirred. Not so much as a pressure-leak sniffer moved.

"Must be because of the news," Gunther muttered. He found he was not ready to speak of the war directly. To the back of the garage, five airlocks stood all in a row. Above them a warm, yellow strip of window shone in the rock. In the room beyond, he could see the overseer moving about.

Hiro waved an arm, and the small figure within leaned forward to wave back. They trudged to the nearest lock and waited.

Nothing happened.

After a few minutes, they stepped back and away from the lock to peer up through the window. The overseer was still there, moving unhurriedly. "Hey!" Hiro shouted over open frequency. "You up there! Are you on the job?"

The man smiled, nodded and waved again.

"Then open the goddamned door!" Hiro strode forward, and with a final, nodding wave, the overseer bent over his controls.

"Uh, Hiro," Gunther said, "there's something odd about . . ."

The door exploded open.

It slammed open so hard and fast the door was half torn off its hinges. The air within blasted out like a charge from a cannon. For a moment the garage was filled with loose tools, parts of vacuum suits and shreds of cloth. A wrench struck Gunther a glancing blow on his arm, spinning him around and knocking him to the floor.

He stared up in shock. Bits and pieces of things hung suspended for a long, surreal instant. Then, the air fled, they began to slowly shower down. He got up awkwardly, massaging his arm through the suit. "Hiro, are you all right? Kreesh?"

"Oh my God," Krishna said.

Gunther spun around. He saw Krishna crouched in the shadow of a flatbed, over something that could not possibly be Hiro, because it bent the wrong way. He walked through shimmering unreality and knelt beside Krishna. He stared down at Hiro's corpse.

Hiro had been standing directly before the door when the overseer opened it without depressurizing the corridor within first. He had caught the blast straight on. It had lifted him and smashed him against the side of a flatbed, snapping his spine and shattering his helmet visor with the backlash. He must have died instantaneously.

"Who's there?" a woman said.

A jitney had entered the garage without Gunther's noticing it. He looked up in time to see a second enter, and then a third. People began piling out. Soon there were some twenty individuals advancing across the garage. They broke into two groups. One headed straight toward the locks and the smaller group advanced on

Gunther and his friends. It looked for all the world like a military operation. "Who's there?" the woman repeated.

Gunther lifted his friend's corpse in his arms and stood. "It's Hiro," he said flatly. "Hiro."

They floated forward cautiously, a semicircle of blank-visored suits like so many kachinas. He could make out the corporate logos. Mitsubishi. Westinghouse. Holst Orbital. Izmailova's red-and-orange suit was among them, and a vivid Mondrian pattern he didn't recognize. The woman spoke again, tensely, warily. "Tell me how you're feeling, Hiro."

It was Beth Hamilton.

"That's not Hiro," Krishna said. "It's Gunther. *That's* Hiro. That he's carrying. We were out in the highlands and—" His voice cracked and collapsed in confusion.

"Is that you, Krishna?" someone asked. "There's a touch of luck. Send him up front, we're going to need him when we get in." Somebody else slapped an arm over Krishna's shoulders and led him away.

Over the radio, a clear voice spoke to the overseer. "Dmitri, is that you? It's Signe. You remember me, don't you, Dmitri? Signe Ohmstede. I'm your friend."

"Sure I remember you, Signe. I remember you. How could I ever forget my friend? Sure I do."

"Oh, good. I'm so happy. Listen carefully, Dmitri. Everything's fine."

Indignantly, Gunther chinned his radio to send. "The hell it is! That fool up there—!"

A burly man in a Westinghouse suit grabbed Gunther's bad arm and shook him. "Shut the fuck *up!*" he growled. "This is serious, damn you. We don't have the time to baby you."

Hamilton shoved between them. "For God's sake, Posner, he's just seen—" She stopped. "Let me take care of him. I'll get him calmed down. Just give us half an hour, okay?"

The others traded glances, nodded, and turned away.

To Gunther's surprise, Ekatarina spoke over his trance chip. "I'm sorry Gunther," she murmured. Then she was gone.

He was still holding Hiro's corpse. He found himself staring down at his friend's ruined face. The flesh was bruised and as puffy-looking as an over-boiled hot dog. He couldn't look away.

"Come on." Beth gave him a little shove to get him going. "Put the body in the back of that pickup and give us a drive out to the cliff."

At Hamilton's insistence, Gunther drove. He found it helped, having something to do. Hands afloat on the steering wheel, he stared ahead looking for the Mausoleum road cut-off. His eyes felt scratchy, and inhumanly dry.

"There was a preemptive strike against us," Hamilton said. "Sabotage. We're just now starting to put the pieces together. Nobody knew you were out on the surface or we would've sent somebody out to meet you. It's all been something of a shambles here."

He drove on in silence, cushioned and protected by all those miles of hard vacuum wrapped about him. He could feel the presence of Hiro's corpse in the back of the truck, a constant psychic itch between his shoulder blades. But so long as he didn't speak, he was safe; he could hold himself aloof from the universe that held the pain. It couldn't touch him. He waited, but Beth didn't add anything to what she'd already said.

Finally he said, "Sabotage?"

"A software meltdown at the radio station. Explosions at all the railguns. Three guys from Microspacecraft Applications bought it when the Boitsovij Kot railgun blew. I suppose it was inevitable. All the military industry up here, it's not surprising somebody would want to knock us out of the equation. But that's not all. Something's happened to the people in Bootstrap. Something really horrible. I was out at the Observatory when it happened. The newsjay called back to see if there was any backup software to get the station going again, and she got nothing but gibberish. Crazy stuff. I mean, *really* crazy. We had to disconnect the Observatory's remotes, because the operators were . . ." She was crying now, softly and insistently, and it was a minute before she could speak again. "Some sort of biological weapon. That's all we know."

"We're here."

As he pulled up to the foot of the Mausoleum cliff, it occurred to Gunther that they hadn't thought to bring a drilling rig. Then he counted ten black niches in the rockface, and realized that somebody had been thinking ahead.

"The only people who weren't hit were those who were working at the Center or the Observatory, or out on the surface. Maybe a hundred of us all told."

They walked around to the back of the pickup. Gunther waited, but Hamilton didn't offer to carry the body. For some reason that made him feel angry and resentful. He unlatched the gate, hopped up on the treads, and hoisted the suited corpse. "Let's get this over with."

Before today, only six people had ever died on the Moon. They walked past the caves in which their bodies awaited eternity. Gunther knew their names by heart: Heisse, Yasuda, Spehalski, Dubinin, Mikami, Castillo. And now Hiro. It seemed incomprehensible that the day should ever come when there would be too many dead to know them all by name.

Daisies and tiger lilies had been scattered before the vaults in such profusion that he couldn't help crushing some underfoot.

They entered the first empty niche, and he laid Hiro down upon a stone table cut into the rock. In the halo of his helmet lamp the body looked piteously twisted and uncomfortable. Gunther found that he was crying, large hot tears that crawled down his face and got into his mouth when he inhaled. He cut off the radio until he had managed to blink the tears away. "Shit." He wiped a hand across his helmet. "I suppose we ought to say something."

Hamilton took his hand and squeezed.

"I've never seen him as happy as he was today. He was going to get married. He was jumping around, laughing and talking about raising a family. And now he's dead, and I don't even know what his religion was." A thought occurred to him, and he turned helplessly toward Hamilton. "What are we going to tell Anya?"

"She's got problems of her own. Come on, say a prayer and let's go. You'll run out of oxygen."

"Yeah, okay." He bowed his head. "*The Lord is my shepherd, I shall not want. . . .*"

Back at Bootstrap, the surface party had seized the airlocks and led the overseer away from the controls. The man from Westinghouse, Posner, looked down on them from the observation window. "Don't crack your suits," he warned. "Keep them sealed tight at all times. Whatever hit the bastards here is still around. Might be in the water, might be in the air. One whiff and you're out of here! You got that?"

"Yeah, yeah," Gunther grumbled. "Keep your shirt on."

Posner's hand froze on the controls. "Let's get serious here. I'm not letting you in until you acknowledge the gravity of the situation. This isn't a picnic outing. If you're not prepared to help, we don't need you. Is that understood?"

"We understand completely, and we'll cooperate to the fullest," Hamilton said quickly. "Won't *we*, Weil?"

He nodded miserably.

Only the one lock had been breached, and there were five more sets of pressurized doors between it and the bulk of Bootstrap's air. The city's designers had been cautious.

Overseen by Posner, they passed through the corridors, locks and changing rooms and up the cargo escalators. Finally they emerged into the city interior.

They stood blinking on the lip of Hell.

At first, it was impossible to pinpoint any source for the pervasive sense of wrongness gnawing at the edge of consciousness. The parks were dotted with people, the fill lights at the juncture of crater walls and canopy were bright, and the waterfalls still fell gracefully from terrace to terrace. Button quail bobbed comically in the grass.

Then small details intruded. A man staggered about the fourth level, head jerking, arms waving stiffly. A plump woman waddled by, pulling an empty cart made from a wheeled microfactory stand, quacking like a duck. Someone sat in the knee-high forest by Noguchi Park, tearing out the trees one by one.

But it was the still figures that were on examination more profoundly disturbing. Here a man lay half in and half out of a tunnel entrance, as unselfconscious as a dog. There, three women stood in extreme postures of lassitude, bordering on despair. Everywhere, people did not touch or speak or show in any way that they were aware of one other. They shared an absolute and universal isolation.

"What shall—" Something slammed onto Gunther's back. He was knocked forward, off his feet. Tumbling, he became aware that fists were striking him, again and again, and then that a lean man was kneeling atop his chest, hysterically shouting, "Don't do it! Don't do it!"

Hamilton seized the man's shoulders and pulled him away. Gunther got to his knees. He looked into the face of madness: eyes round and fearful, expression full of panic. The man was terrified of Gunther.

With an abrupt wrench, the man broke free. He ran as if pursued by demons. Hamilton stared after him. "You okay?" she asked.

"Yeah, sure." Gunther adjusted his tool harness. "Let's see if we can find the others."

They walked toward the lake, staring about at the self-absorbed figures scattered about the grass. Nobody attempted to speak to them. A woman ran by, barefooted. Her arms were filled with flowers. "Hey!" Hamilton called after her. She smiled fleetingly over her shoulder, but did not slow. Gunther knew her vaguely, an executive supervisor for Martin Marietta.

"Is *every*body here crazy?" he asked.

"Sure looks that way."

The woman had reached the shore and was flinging the blossoms into the water with great sweeps of her arm. They littered the surface.

"Damned waste." Gunther had come to Bootstrap before the flowers; he knew the effort involved getting permission to plant them and rewriting the city's ecologics. A man in a blue-striped Krupp suit was running along the verge of the lake.

The woman, flowers gone, threw herself into the water.

At first it appeared she'd suddenly decided to take a dip. But from the struggling, floundering way she thrashed deeper into the water it was clear that she could not swim.

In the time it took Gunther to realize this, Hamilton had leaped forward, running for the lake. Belatedly, he started after her. But the man in the Krupp suit was ahead of them both. He splashed in after the woman. An outstretched hand seized her shoulder and then he fell, pulling her under. She was red-faced and choking when he emerged again, arm across her chest.

By then Gunther and Beth were wading into the lake, and together they three got the woman to shore. When she was released, the woman calmly turned and walked away, as if nothing had happened.

"Gone for more flowers," the Krupp component explained. "This is the third time fair Ophelia there's tried to drown herself. She's not the only one. I've been hanging around, hauling 'em out when they stumble in."

"Do you know where everybody else is? Is there anyone in charge? Somebody giving out orders?"

"Do you need any help?" Gunther asked.

The Krupp man shrugged. "I'm fine. No idea where the others are, though. My friends were going on to the second level when I decided I ought to stay here. If you see them, you might tell 'em I'd appreciate hearing back from them. Three guys in Krupp suits."

"We'll do that," Gunther said.

Hamilton was already walking away.

On a step just beneath the top of the stairs sprawled one of Gunther's fellow G5 components. "Sidney," he said carefully. "How's it going?"

Sidney giggled. "I'm making the effort, if that's what you mean. I don't see that the 'how' of it makes much difference."

"Okay."

"A better way of phrasing that might be to ask why I'm not at work." He stood, and in a very natural manner accompanied Gunther up the steps. "Obviously I can't be two places at once. You wouldn't want to perform major surgery in your own absence, would you?" He giggled again. "It's an oxymoron. Like horses: those classically beautiful Praxitelesian bodies excreting these long surreal turds."

"Okay."

"I've always admired them for squeezing so much art into a single image."

"Sidney," Hamilton said. "We're looking for our friends. Three people in blue-striped work suits."

"I've seen them. I know just where they went." His eyes were cool and vacant; they didn't seem to focus on anything in particular.

"Can you lead us to them?"

"Even a flower recognizes its own face." A gracefully winding gravel path led through private garden plots and croquet malls. They followed him down it.

There were not many people on the second terrace; with the fall of madness, most seemed to have retreated into the caves. Those few who remained either ignored or cringed away from them. Gunther found himself staring obsessively into their faces, trying to analyze the deficiency he felt in each. Fear nested in their eyes, and the appalled awareness that some terrible thing had happened to them coupled with a complete ignorance of its nature.

"God, these people!"

Hamilton grunted.

He felt he was walking through a dream. Sounds were muted by his suit, and colors less intense seen through his helmet visor. It was as if he had been subtly removed from the world, there and not-there simultaneously, an impression that strengthened with each new face that looked straight through him with mad, unseeing indifference.

Sidney turned a corner, broke into a trot and jogged into a tunnel entrance. Gunther ran after him. At the mouth of the tunnel, he paused to let his helmet adjust to the new light levels. When it cleared he saw Sidney dart down a side passage. He followed.

At the intersection of passages, he looked and saw no trace of their guide. Sidney had disappeared. "Did you see which way he went?" he asked Hamilton over the radio. There was no answer. "Beth?"

He started down the corridor, halted, and turned back. These things went deep. He could wander around in them forever. He went back out to the terraces. Hamilton was nowhere to be seen.

For lack of any better plan, he followed the path. Just beyond an ornamental holly bush he was pulled up short by a vision straight out of William Blake.

The man had discarded shirt and sandals, and wore only a pair of shorts. He squatted atop a boulder, alert, patient, eating a tomato. A steel pipe slanted across his knees like a staff or scepter, and he had woven a crown of sorts from platinum wire with a fortune's worth of hyperconductor chips dangling over his forehead. He looked every inch a kingly animal.

He stared at Gunther, calm and unblinking.

Gunther shivered. The man seemed less human than anthropoid, crafty in its way, but unthinking. He felt as if he were staring across the eons at Grandfather Ape, crouched on the edge of awareness. An involuntary thrill of superstitious awe seized him. Was this what happened when the higher mental functions were scraped away? Did Archetype lie just beneath the skin, waiting for the opportunity to emerge?

"I'm looking for my friend," he said. "A woman in a G5 suit like mine? Have you seen her? She was looking for three—" He stopped. The man was staring at him blankly. "Oh, never mind."

He turned away and walked on.

After a time, he lost all sense of continuity. Existence fragmented into unconnected images: A man bent almost double, leering and squeezing a yellow rubber duckie. A woman leaping up like a jack-in-the-box from behind an air monitor, shrieking and flapping her arms. An old friend sprawled on the ground, crying, with a broken leg. When he tried to help her, she scrabbled away from him in fear. He couldn't get near her without doing more harm. "Stay here," he said, "I'll find help." Five minutes later he realized that he was lost, with not the slightest notion of how to find his way back to her again. He came to the stairs leading back down to the bottom level. There was no reason to go down them. There was no reason not to. He went down.

He had just reached the bottom of the stairs when someone in a lavender boutique suit hurried by.

Gunther chinned on his helmet radio.

"Hello!" The lavender suit glanced back at him, its visor a plate of obsidian, but did not turn back. "Do you know where everyone's gone? I'm totally lost. How can I find out what I should be doing?" The lavender suit ducked into a tunnel.

Faintly, a voice answered, "Try the city manager's office."

The City Manager's office was a tight little cubby an eighth of a kilometer deep within the tangled maze of administrative and service tunnels. It had never been very important in the scheme of things. The city manager's prime duties were keeping the air and water replenished and scheduling airlock inspections, functions any computer could handle better than a man had they dared trust them to a machine. The room had probably never been as crowded as it was now. Dozens of people suited for full vacuum spilled out into the hall, anxiously listening to Ekatarina confer with the city's Crisis Management Program. Gunther pushed in as close as he could; even so, he could barely see her.

"—the locks, the farms and utilities, and we've locked away all the remotes. What comes next?"

Ekatarina's peecee hung from her work harness, amplifying the CMP's silent voice. "Now that elementary control has been established, second priority must go to the industrial sector. The factories must be locked down. The reactors must be put to sleep. There is not sufficient human supervisory presence to keep them running. The factories have mothballing programs available upon request.

"Third, the farms cannot tolerate neglect. Fifteen minutes without oxygen, and all the tilapia will die. The calimari are even more delicate. Three experienced agricultural components must be assigned immediately. Double that number, if you only have inexperienced components. Advisory software is available. What are your resources?"

"Let me get back to you on that. What else?"

"What about the people?" a man asked belligerently. "What the hell are you worrying about factories for, when our people are in the state they're in?"

Izmailova looked up sharply. "You're one of Chang's research components, aren't you? Why are you here? Isn't there enough for you to do?" She looked about, as if abruptly awakened from sleep. "All of you! What are you waiting for?"

"You can't put us off that easily! Who made you the little brass-plated general? We don't have to take orders from you."

The bystanders shuffled uncomfortably, not leaving, waiting to take their cue from each other. Their suits were as good as identical in this crush, their helmets blank and expressionless. They looked like so many ambulatory eggs.

The crowd's mood balanced on the instant, ready to fall into acceptance or anger with a featherweight's push. Gunther raised an arm. "General!" he said loudly. "Private Weil here! I'm awaiting my orders. Tell me what to do."

Laughter rippled through the room, and the tension eased. Ekatarina said, "Take whoever's nearest you, and start clearing the afflicted out of the administrative areas. Guide them out toward the open, where they won't be so likely to hurt themselves. Whenever you get a room or corridor emptied, lock it up tight. Got that?"

"Yes, ma'am." He tapped the suit nearest him, and its helmet dipped in a curt nod. But when they turned to leave, their way was blocked by the crush of bodies.

"You!" Ekatarina jabbed a finger. "Go to the farmlocks and foam them shut; I don't want any chance of getting them contaminated. Anyone with experience running factories—that's most of us, I think—should find a remote and get to work shutting the things down. The CMP will help direct you. If you have nothing else to do, buddy up and work at clearing out the corridors. I'll call a general meeting when we've put together a more comprehensive plan of action." She paused. "What have I left out?"

Surprisingly, the CMP answered her: "There are twenty-three children in the city, two of them seven-year-old prelegals and the rest five years of age or younger, offspring of registered-permanent lunar components. Standing directives are that children be given special care and protection. The third-level chapel can be converted to a care center. Word should be spread that as they are found, the children are to be brought there. Assign one reliable individual to oversee them."

"My God, yes." She turned to the belligerent man from the Center, and snapped, "Do it."

He hesitated, then saluted ironically and turned to go.

That broke the logjam. The crowd began to disperse. Gunther and his co-worker—it turned out to be Liza Nagenda, another groundrat like himself—set to work.

In after years Gunther was to remember this period as a time when his life entered a dark tunnel. For long, nightmarish hours he and Liza shuffled from office to storage room, struggling to move the afflicted out of the corporate areas and into the light.

The afflicted did not cooperate.

The first few rooms they entered were empty. In the fourth, a distraught-looking woman was furiously going through drawers and files and flinging their contents away. Trash covered the floor. "It's in here somewhere," she said frantically.

"What's in there, darling?" Gunther said soothingly. He had to speak loudly so he could be heard through his helmet. "What are you looking for?"

She tilted her head up with a smile of impish delight. Using both hands, she smoothed back her hair, elbows high, pushing it straight over her skull, then tucking in stray strands behind her ears. "It doesn't matter, because I'm sure to find it now. Two scarabs appear, and between them the blazing disk of the sun, that's a good omen, not to mention being an analogy for sex. I've had sex, all the sex anyone could want, buggered behind the outhouse by the lizard king when I was nine. What did I care? I had wings then and thought that I could fly."

Gunther edged a little closer. "You're not making any sense at all."

"You know, Tolstoy said there was a green stick in the woods behind his house that once found would cause all men to love one another. I believe in that green stick as a basic principle of physical existence. The universe exists in a matrix of four dimensions which we can perceive and seven which we cannot, which is why we experience peace and brotherhood as a seven-dimensional green stick phenomenon."

"You've got to listen to me."

"Why? You gonna tell me Hitler is dead? I don't believe in that kind of crap."

"Oh hell," Nagenda said. "You can't reason with a flick. Just grab her arms and we'll chuck her out."

It wasn't that easy, though. The woman was afraid of them. Whenever they approached her, she slipped fearfully away. If they moved slowly, they could not corner her, and when they both rushed her, she leapt up over a desk and then down into the kneehole. Nagenda grabbed her legs and pulled. The woman wailed, and clutched at the knees of Nagenda's suit. "Get offa me," Liza snarled. "Gunther, get this crazy woman off my damn legs."

"Don't kill me!" the woman screamed. "I've always voted twice—you know I did. I told them you were a gangster, but I was wrong. Don't take the oxygen out of my lungs!"

They got the woman out of the office, then lost her again when Gunther turned to lock the door. She went fluttering down the corridor with Nagenda in hot pursuit. Then she dove into another office, and they had to start all over again.

It took over an hour to drive the woman from the corridors and release her into the park. The next three went quickly enough by contrast. The one after that was difficult again, and the fifth turned out to be the first woman they had encountered, wandered back to look for her office. When they'd brought her to the open again, Liza Nagenda said, "That's four flicks down and three thousand eight hundred fifty-eight to go."

"Look—" Gunther began. And then Krishna's voice sounded over his trance chip, stiffly and with exaggerated clarity. "Everyone is to go to the central lake immediately for an organizational meeting. Repeat: Go to the lake immediately. Go to the lake now." He was obviously speaking over a jury-rigged transmitter. The sound was bad and his voice boomed and popped on the chip.

"All right, okay, I got that," Liza said. "You can shut up now."

"Please go to the lake immediately. Everyone is to go directly to the central—"

"Sheesh."

By the time they got out to the parklands again, the open areas were thick with people. Not just the suited figures of the survivors, either. All the afflicted were emerging from the caves and corridors of Bootstrap. They walked blindly, uncertainly, toward the lake, as if newly called from the grave. The ground level was filling with people.

"Sonofabitch," Gunther said wonderingly.

"Gunther?" Nagenda asked. "What's going on?"

"It's the trance chips! Sonofabitch, all we had to do was speak to them over the chips. They'll do whatever the voice in their heads tells them to do."

The land about the lake was so crowded that Gunther had trouble spotting any other suits. Then he saw a suited figure standing on the edge of the second level waving broadly. He waved back and headed for the stairs.

By the time he got to level two, a solid group of the unafflicted had gathered. More and more came up, drawn by the concentration of suits. Finally Ekatarina spoke over the open channel of her suit radio.

"There's no reason to wait for us all to gather. I think everyone is close enough to hear me. Sit down, take a little rest, you've all earned it." People eased down on the grass. Some sprawled on their backs or stomachs, fully suited. Most just sat.

"By a fortunate accident, we've discovered a means of controlling our afflicted friends." There was light applause. "But there are still many problems before us, and they won't all be solved so easily. We've all seen the obvious. Now I must tell you of worse. If the war on Earth goes full thermonuclear, we will be completely and totally cut off, possibly for decades."

A murmur passed through the crowd.

"What does this mean? Beyond the immediate inconveniences—no luxuries, no more silk shirts, no new seed stock, no new videos, no way home for those of us who hadn't already decided to stay—we will be losing much that we require for survival. All our microfacturing capability comes from the Swiss Orbitals. Our water reserves are sufficient for a year, but we lose minute quantities of water vapor to rust and corrosion and to the vacuum every time somebody goes in or out an airlock, and those quantities are necessary for our existence.

"But we can survive. We can process raw hydrogen and oxygen from the regolith, and burn them to produce water. We already make our own air. We can do without most nanoelectronics. We can thrive and prosper and grow, even if Earth . . . even if the worst happens. But to do so we'll need our full manufacturing capability, and full supervisory capability as well. We must not only restore our factories, but find a way to restore our people. There'll be work and more for all of us in the days ahead."

Nagenda touched helmets with Gunther and muttered, "What a crock."

"Come on, I want to hear this."

"Fortunately, the Crisis Management Program has contingency plans for exactly this situation. According to its records, which may be incomplete, I have more military command experience than any other functional. Does anyone wish to challenge this?" She waited, but nobody said anything. "We will go to a quasimilitary structure for the duration of the emergency. This is strictly for organizational purposes. There will be no privileges afforded the officers, and the military structure will be dismantled *immediately* upon resolution of our present problems. That's paramount."

She glanced down at her peecee. "To that purpose, I am establishing beneath me a triumvirate of subordinate officers, consisting of Carlos Diaz-Rodrigues, Miiko Ezumi, and Will Posner. Beneath them will be nine officers, each responsible for a cadre of no more than ten individuals."

She read out names. Gunther was assigned to Cadre Four, Beth Hamilton's group. Then Ekatarina said, "We're all tired. The gang back at the Center have rigged up a decontamination procedure, a kitchen and sleeping spaces of sorts. Cadres One, Two, and Three will put in four more hours here, then pull down a full eight hours sleep. Cadres Four through Nine may return now to the Center for a meal and four hours rest." She stopped. "That's it. Go get some shut-eye."

A ragged cheer arose, fell flat, and died. Gunther stood. Liza Nagenda gave him a friendly squeeze on the butt and when he started to the right yanked his arm and pointed him left, toward the service escalators. With easy familiarity, she slid an arm around his waist.

He'd known guys who'd slept with Liza Nagenda, and they all agreed that she was bad news, possessive, hysterical, ludicrously emotional. But what the hell. It was easier than not.

They trudged off.

There was too much to do. They worked to exhaustion—it was not enough. They rigged a system of narrow-band radio transmissions for the CMP and ran a microwave patch back to the Center, so it could direct their efforts more efficiently—it was not enough. They organized and rearranged constantly. But the load was too great and accidents inevitably happened.

Half the surviving railguns—small units used to deliver raw and semi-processed materials over the highlands and across the bay—were badly damaged when the noonday sun buckled their aluminum rails; the sunscreens had not been put in place in time. An unknown number of robot bulldozers had wandered off from the strip mines and were presumably lost. It was hard to guess how many because the inventory records were scrambled. None of the food stored in Bootstrap could be trusted; the Center's meals had to be harvested direct from the farms and taken out through the emergency locks. An inexperienced farmer mishandled her remote, and ten aquaculture tanks boiled out into vacuum, geysering nine thousand fingerlings across the surface. On Posner's orders, the remote handler rigs were hastily packed and moved to the Center. When uncrated, most were found to have damaged rocker arms.

There were small victories. On his second shift, Gunther found fourteen bales of cotton in vacuum storage and set an assembler to sewing futons for the Center. That meant an end to sleeping on bare floors and made him a local hero for the rest of that day. There were not enough toilets in the Center; Diaz-Rodrigues ordered the flare storm shelters in the factories stripped of theirs. Huriel Garza discovered a talent for cooking with limited resources.

But they were losing ground. The afflicted were unpredictable, and they were everywhere. A demented systems analyst, obeying the voices in his head, dumped several barrels of lubricating oil in the lake. The water filters clogged, and the streams had to be shut down for repairs. A doctor somehow managed to strangle herself with her own diagnostic harness. The city's ecologics were badly stressed by random vandalism.

Finally somebody thought to rig up a voice loop for continuous transmission. "I am calm," it said. "I am tranquil. I do not want to do anything. I am happy where I am."

Gunther was working with Liza Nagenda trying to get the streams going again when the loop came on. He looked up and saw an uncanny quiet spread over Bootstrap. Up and down the terraces, the flicks stood in postures of complete and utter impassivity. The only movement came from the small number of suits scurrying like beetles among the newly catatonic.

Liza put her hands on her hips. "Terrific. Now we've got to *feed* them."

"Hey, cut me some slack, okay? This is the first good news I've heard since I don't know when."

"It's not good anything, sweetbuns. It's just more of the same."

She was right. Relieved as he was, Gunther knew it. One hopeless task has been traded for another.

He was wearily suiting up for his third day when Hamilton stopped him and said, "Weil! You know any electrical engineering?"

"Not really, no. I mean, I can do the wiring for a truck, or maybe rig up a microwave relay, stuff like that, but . . ."

"It'll have to do. Drop what you're on, and help Krishna set up a system for controlling the flicks. Some way we can handle them individually."

They set up shop in Krishna's old lab. The remnants of old security standards still lingered, and nobody had been allowed to sleep there. Consequently, the room was wonderfully neat and clean, all crafted-in-orbit laboratory equipment with smooth, anonymous surfaces. It was a throwback to a time before clutter and madness had taken over. If it weren't for the new-tunnel smell, the raw tang of cut rock the air carried, it would be possible to pretend nothing had happened.

Gunther stood in a telepresence rig, directing a remote through Bootstrap's apartments. They were like so many unconnected cells of chaos. He entered one and found the words BUDDHA = COSMIC INERTIA scrawled on its wall with what looked to be human feces. A woman sat on the futon tearing handfuls of batting from it and flinging them in the air. Cotton covered the room like a fresh snowfall. The next apartment was empty and clean, and a microfactory sat gleaming on a ledge. "I hereby nationalize you in the name of the People's Provisional Republic of Bootstrap, and of the oppressed masses everywhere," he said dryly. The remote gingerly picked it up. "You done with that chip diagram yet?"

"It will not be long now," Krishna said.

They were building a prototype controller. The idea was to code each peecee, so the CMP could identify and speak to its owner individually. By stepping down the voltage, they could limit the peecee's transmission range to a meter and a half so that each afflicted person could be given individualized orders. The existing chips, however, were high-strung Swiss Orbital thoroughbreds, and couldn't handle oddball power yields. They had to be replaced.

"I don't see how you can expect to get any useful work out of these guys, though. I mean, what we need are supervisors. You can't hope to get coherent thought out of them."

Bent low over his peecee, Krishna did not answer at first. Then he said, "Do you know how a yogi stops his heart? We looked into that when I was in grad school. We asked Yogi Premanand if he would stop his heart while wired up to our instruments, and he graciously consented. We had all the latest brain scanners, but it turned out the most interesting results were recorded by the EKG.

"We found that the yogi's heart did not as we had expected slow down, but rather went faster and faster, until it reached its physical limits and began to fibrillate. He had not slowed his heart; he had sped it up. It did not stop, but went into spasm.

"After our tests, I asked him if he had known these facts. He said no, that they were most interesting. He was polite about it, but clearly did not think our findings very significant."

"So you're saying . . . ?"

"The problem with schizophrenics is that they have too much going on in their heads. Too many voices. Too many ideas. They can't focus their attention on a single chain of thought. But it would be a mistake to think them incapable of complex reasoning. In fact, they're thinking brilliantly. Their brains are simply operating at such peak efficiencies that they can't organize their thoughts coherently.

"What the trance chip does is to provide one more voice, but a louder, more insistent one. That's why they obey it. It breaks through that noise, provides a focus, serves as a matrix along which thought can crystallize."

The remote unlocked the door into a conference room deep in the administrative tunnels. Eight microfactories waited in a neat row atop the conference table. It added the ninth, turned, and left, locking the door behind it. "You know," Gunther said, "all these elaborate precautions may be unnecessary. Whatever was used on Bootstrap may not be in the air anymore. It may never have *been* in the air. It could've been in the water or something."

"Oh, it's there all right, in the millions. We're dealing with an airborne schizomimetic engine. It's designed to hang around in the air indefinitely."

"A schizomimetic engine? What the hell is that?"

In a distracted monotone, Krishna said, "A schizomimetic engine is a strategic nonlethal weapon with high psychological impact. It not only incapacitates its target vectors, but places a disproportionately heavy burden on the enemy's manpower and material support caring for the victims. Due to the particular quality of the effect, it has a profoundly demoralizing influence on those exposed to the victims, especially those involved in their care. Thus, it is particularly desirable as a strategic weapon." He might have been quoting from an operations manual.

Gunther pondered that. "Calling the meeting over the chips wasn't a mistake, was it? You knew it would work. You knew they would obey a voice speaking inside their heads."

"Yes."

"This shit was brewed up at the Center, wasn't it? This is the stuff that you couldn't talk about."

"Some of it."

Gunther powered down his rig and flipped up the lens. "God damn you, Krishna! God damn you straight to Hell, you stupid fucker!"

Krishna looked up from his work, bewildered. "Have I said something wrong?"

"No! No, you haven't said a damned thing wrong—you've just driven four thousand people out of their fucking minds, is all! Wake up and take a good look at what you maniacs have done with your weapons research!"

"It wasn't weapons research," Krishna said mildly. He drew a long, involuted line on the schematic. "But when pure research is funded by the military, the military will seek out military applications for the research. That's just the way it is."

"What's the difference? It happened. You're responsible."

Now Krishna actually set his peecee aside. He spoke with uncharacteristic fire. "Gunther, we *need* this information. Do you realize that we are trying to run a technological civilization with a brain that was evolved in the neolithic? I am perfectly serious. We're all trapped in the old hunter-gatherer programs, and they are of no use to us anymore. Take a look at what's happening on Earth. They're hip-deep in a war that nobody meant to start and nobody wants to fight and it's even money that nobody can stop. The type of thinking that put us in this corner is not to our benefit. It has to change. And that's what we are working toward—taming the human brain. Harnessing it. Reining it in.

"Granted, our research has been turned against us. But what's one more weapon among so many? If neuroprogrammers hadn't been available, something else would have been used. Mustard gas maybe, or plutonium dust. For that matter, they could've just blown a hole in the canopy and let us all strangle."

"That's self-justifying bullshit, Krishna! Nothing can excuse what you've done."

Quietly, but with conviction, Krishna said, "You will never convince me that our research is not the most important work we could possibly be doing today. We must seize control of this monster within our skulls. We must change our ways of thinking." His voice dropped. "The sad thing is that we cannot change unless we survive. But in order to survive, we must first change."

They worked in silence after that.

Gunther awoke from restless dreams to find that the sleep shift was only half over. Liza was snoring. Careful not to wake her, he pulled his clothes on and padded barefoot out of his niche and down the hall. The light was on in the common room and he heard voices.

Ekatarina looked up when he entered. Her face was pale and drawn. Faint circles had formed under her eyes. She was alone.

"Oh, hi. I was just talking with the CMP." She thought off her peecee. "Have a seat."

He pulled up a chair and hunched down over the table. Confronted by her, he found it took a slight but noticeable effort to draw his breath. "So. How are things going?"

"They'll be trying out your controllers soon. The first batch of chips ought to be coming out of the factories in an hour or so. I thought I'd stay up to see how they work out."

"It's that bad, then?" Ekatarina shook her head, would not look at him. "Hey, come on, here you are waiting up on the results, and I can see how tired you are. There must be a lot riding on this thing."

"More than you know," she said bleakly. "I've just been going over the numbers. Things are worse than you can imagine."

He reached out and took her cold, bloodless hand. She squeezed him so tightly it hurt. Their eyes met and he saw in hers all the fear and wonder he felt.

Wordlessly, they stood.

"I'm niching alone," Ekatarina said. She had not let go of his hand, held it so tightly, in fact, that it seemed she would never let it go.

Gunther let her lead him away.

They made love, and talked quietly about inconsequential things, and made love again. Gunther had thought she would nod off immediately after the first time, but she was too full of nervous energy for that.

"Tell me when you're about to come," she murmured. "Tell me when you're coming."

He stopped moving. "Why do you always say that?"

Ekatarina looked up at him dazedly, and he repeated the question. Then she laughed a deep, throaty laugh. "Because I'm frigid."

"Hah?"

She took his hand, and brushed her cheek against it. Then she ducked her head, continuing the motion across her neck and up the side of her scalp. He felt the short, prickly hair against his palm and then, behind her ear, two bumps under the skin where biochips had been implanted. One of those would be her trance chip and the other . . . "It's a prosthetic," she explained. Her eyes were gray and solemn. "It hooks into the pleasure centers. When I need to, I can turn on my orgasm at a thought. That way we can always come at the same time." She moved her hips slowly beneath him as she spoke.

"But that means you don't really need to have any kind of sexual stimulation at all, do you? You can trigger an orgasm at will. While you're riding on a bus. Or behind a desk. You could just turn that thing on and come for hours at a time."

She looked amused. "I'll tell you a secret. When it was new, I used to do stunts like that. Everybody does. One outgrows that sort of thing quickly."

With more than a touch of stung pride, Gunther said, "Then what am I doing here? If you've got that thing, what the hell do you need me for?" He started to draw away from her.

She pulled him down atop her again. "You're kind of comforting," she said. "In an argumentative way. Come here."

He got back to his futon and began gathering up the pieces of his suit. Liza sat up sleepily and gawked at him. "So," she said. "It's like that, is it?"

"Yeah, well. I kind of left something unfinished. An old relationship." Warily, he extended a hand. "No hard feelings, huh?"

Ignoring his hand, she stood, naked and angry. "You got the nerve to stand there without even wiping my smile off your dick first and say no hard feelings? Asshole!"

"Aw, come on now, Liza, it's not like that."

"Like hell it's not! You got a shot at that white-assed Russian ice queen, and I'm history. Don't think I don't know all about her."

"I was hoping we could still be, you know, friends."

"Nice trick, shithead." She balled her fist and hit him hard in the center of his chest. Tears began to form in her eyes. "You just slink away. I'm tired of looking at you."

He left.

But did not sleep. Ekatarina was awake and ebullient over the first reports coming in on the new controller system. "They're working!" she cried. "They're working!" She'd pulled on a silk camisole, and strode back and forth excitedly, naked to the waist. Her pubic hair was a white flame, with almost invisible trails of smaller hairs reaching for her navel and caressing the sweet insides of her thighs. Tired as he was, Gunther felt new desire for her. In a weary, washed-out way, he was happy.

"Whooh!" She kissed him hard, not sexually, and called up the CMP. "Rerun all our earlier projections. We're putting our afflicted components back to work. Adjust all work schedules."

"As you direct."

"How does this change our long-range prospects?"

The program was silent for several seconds, processing. Then it said, "You are about to enter a necessary but very dangerous stage of recovery. You are going from a low-prospects high-stability situation to a high-prospects high-instability one. With leisure your unafflicted components will quickly grow dissatisfied with your government."

"What happens if I just step down?"

"Prospects worsen drastically."

Ekatarina ducked her head. "All right, what's likely to be our most pressing new problem?"

"The unafflicted components will demand to know more about the war on Earth. They'll want the media feeds restored immediately."

"I could rig up a receiver easily enough," Gunther volunteered. "Nothing fancy, but—"

"Don't you dare!"

"Hah? Why not?"

"Gunther, let me put it to you this way: What two nationalities are most heavily represented here?"

"Well, I guess that would be Russia and—oh."

"Oh is right. For the time being, I think it's best if nobody knows for sure who's supposed to be enemies with whom." She asked the CMP, "How should I respond?"

"Until the situation stabilizes, you have no choice but distraction. Keep their minds occupied. Hunt down the saboteurs and then organize war crime trials."

"That's out. No witch hunts, no scapegoats, no trials. We're all in this together."

Emotionlessly, the CMP said, "Violence is the left hand of government. You are rash to dismiss its potentials without serious thought."

"I won't discuss it."

"Very well. If you wish to postpone the use of force for the present, you could hold a hunt for the weapon used on Bootstrap. Locating and identifying it would involve everyone's energies without necessarily implicating anybody. It would also be widely interpreted as meaning an eventual cure was possible, thus boosting the general morale without your actually lying."

Tiredly, as if this were something she had gone over many times already, she said, "Is there really no hope of curing them?"

"Anything is possible. In light of present resources, though, it cannot be considered likely."

Ekatarina thought the peecee off, dismissing the CMP. She sighed. "Maybe that's what we ought to do. Donkey up a hunt for the weapon. We ought to be able to do something with that notion."

Puzzled, Gunther said, "But it was one of Chang's weapons, wasn't it? A schizomimetic engine, right?"

"Where did you hear that?" she demanded sharply.

"Well, Krishna said . . . he didn't act like . . . I thought it was public knowledge."

Ekatarina's face hardened. "Program!" she thought.

The CMP came back to life. "Ready."

"Locate Krishna Narasimhan, unafflicted, Cadre Five. I want to speak with him immediately." Ekatarina snatched up her panties and shorts, and furiously began dressing. "Where are my damned sandals? Program! Tell him to meet me in the common room. Right away."

"Received."

* * *

To Gunther's surprise, it took over an hour for Ekatarina to browbeat Krishna into submission. Finally, though, the young research component went to a lockbox, identified himself to it, and unsealed the storage areas. "It's not all that secure," he said apologetically. "If our sponsors knew how often we just left everything open so we could get in and out, they'd—well, never mind."

He lifted a flat, palm-sized metal rectangle from a cabinet. "This is the most likely means of delivery. It's an aerosol bomb. The biological agents are loaded *here*, and it's triggered by snapping this back *here*. It's got enough pressure in it to spew the agents fifty feet straight up. Air currents do the rest." He tossed it to Gunther who stared down at the thing in horror. "Don't worry, it's not armed."

He slid out a slim drawer holding row upon gleaming row of slim chrome cylinders. "These contain the engines themselves. They're off-the-shelf nanoweaponry. State of the art stuff, I guess." He ran a fingertip over them. "We've programmed each to produce a different mix of neurotransmitters. Dopamine, phencyclidine, norepinephrine, acetylcholine, met-enkephalin, substance P, serotonin—there's a hefty slice of Heaven in here, and—" he tapped an empty space"—right here is our missing bit of Hell." He frowned, and muttered, "That's curious. Why are there two cylinders missing?"

"What's that?" Ekatarina said. "I didn't catch what you just said."

"Oh, nothing important. Um, listen, it might help if I yanked a few biological pathways charts and showed you the chemical underpinnings of these things."

"Never mind that. Just keep it sweet and simple. Tell us about these schizomimetic engines."

It took over an hour to explain.

The engines were molecule-sized chemical factories, much like the assemblers in a microfactory. They had been provided by the military, in the hope Chang's group would come up with a misting weapon that could be sprayed in an army's path to cause them to change their loyalty. Gunther dozed off briefly while Krishna was explaining why that was impossible, and woke up sometime after the tiny engines had made their way into the brain.

"It's really a false schizophrenia," Krishna explained. "True schizophrenia is a beautifully complicated mechanism. What these engines create is more like a bargain-basement knockoff. They seize control of the brain chemistry, and start pumping out dopamine and a few other neuromediators. It's not an actual disorder, *per se*. They just keep the brain hopping." He coughed. "You see."

"Okay," Ekatarina said. "Okay. You say you can reprogram these things. How?"

"We use what are technically called messenger engines. They're like neuromodulators—they tell the schizomimetic engines what to do." He slid open another drawer, and in a flat voice said, "They're gone."

"Let's keep to the topic, if we may. We'll worry about your inventory later. Tell us about these messenger engines. Can you brew up a lot of them, to tell the schizomimetics to turn themselves off?"

"No, for two reasons. First, these molecules were handcrafted in the Swiss Orbitals; we don't have the industrial plant to create them. Secondly, you can't tell the schizomimetics to turn themselves off. They don't *have* off switches. They're more like catalysts than actual machines. You can reconfigure them to produce different chemicals, but . . ." He stopped, and a distant look came into his eyes. "Damn." He grabbed up his peecee, and a chemical pathways chart appeared on one wall. Then beside it, a listing of major neurofunctions. Then another chart covered with scrawled behavioral symbols. More and more data slammed up on the wall.

"Uh, Krishna . . . ?"

"Oh, go away," he snapped. "This is important."

"You think you might be able to come up with a cure?"

"Cure? No. Something better. Much better."

Ekatarina and Gunther looked at each other. Then she said, "Do you need anything? Can I assign anyone to help you?"

"I need the messenger engines. Find them for me."

"How? How do we find them? Where do we look?"

"Sally Chang," Krishna said impatiently. "She must have them. Nobody else had access." He snatched up a light pen, and began scrawling crabbed formulae on the wall.

"I'll get her for you. Program! Tell—"

"Chang's a flick," Gunther reminded her. "She was caught by the aerosol bomb." Which she must surely have set herself. A neat way of disposing of evidence that might've led to whatever government was running her. She'd have been the first to go mad.

Ekatarina pinched her nose, wincing. "I've been awake too long," she said. "All right, I understand. Krishna, from now on you're assigned permanently to research. The CMP will notify your cadre leader. Let me know if you need any support. Find me a way to turn this damned weapon off." Ignoring the way he shrugged her off, she said to Gunther, "I'm yanking you from Cadre Four. From now on, you report directly to me. I want you to find Chang. Find her, and find those messenger engines."

Gunther was bone-weary. He couldn't remember when he'd last had a good eight hours' sleep. But he managed what he hoped was a confident grin. "Received."

A madwoman should not have been able to hide herself. Sally Chang could. Nobody should have been able to evade the CMP's notice, now that it was hooked into a growing number of afflicted individuals. Sally Chang did. The CMP informed Gunther that none of the flicks were aware of Chang's whereabouts. It accepted a directive to have them all glance about for her once every hour until she was found.

In the west tunnels, walls had been torn out to create a space as large as any factory interior. The remotes had been returned, and were now manned by almost two hundred flicks spaced so that they did not impinge upon each other's fields of instruction. Gunther walked by them, through the CMP's whispering voices: "Are all bulldozers accounted for? If so . . . Clear away any malfunctioning machines; they can be placed . . . for vacuum-welded dust on the upper surfaces of the rails . . . reduction temperature, then look to see that the oxygen feed is compatible . . ." At the far end a single suit sat in a chair, overseer unit in its lap.

"How's it going?" Gunther asked.

"Absolutely top-notch." He recognized Takayuni's voice. They'd worked in the Flammaprion microwave relay station together. "Most of the factories are up and running, and we're well on our way to having the railguns operative too. You wouldn't believe the kind of efficiencies we're getting here."

"Good, huh?"

Takayuni grinned; Gunther could hear it in his voice. "Industrious little buggers!"

Takayuni hadn't seen Chang. Gunther moved on.

Some hours later he found himself sitting wearily in Noguchi Park, looking at the torn-up dirt where the kneehigh forest had been. Not a seedling had been spared; the silver birch was extinct as a lunar species. Dead carp floated belly-up in the oil-slicked central lake; a chain-link fence circled it now, to keep out the flicks. There hadn't been the time yet to begin cleaning up the litter, and when he looked about, he saw trash everywhere. It was sad. It reminded him of Earth.

He knew it was time to get going, but he couldn't. His head sagged, touched his chest, and jerked up. Time had passed.

A flicker of motion made him turn. Somebody in a pastel lavender boutique suit hurried by. The woman who had directed him to the city controller's office the other day. "Hello!" he called. "I found everybody just where you said. Thanks. I was starting to get a little spooked."

The lavender suit turned to look at him. Sunlight glinted on black glass. A still, long minute later, she said, "Don't mention it," and started away.

"I'm looking for Sally Chang. Do you know her? Have you seen her? She's a flick, kind of a little woman, flamboyant, used to favor bright clothes, electric makeup, that sort of thing."

"I'm afraid I can't help you." Lavender was carrying three oxytanks in her arms. "You might try the straw market, though. Lots of bright clothes there." She ducked into a tunnel opening and disappeared within.

Gunther stared after her distractedly, then shook his head. He felt so very, very tired.

The straw market looked as though it had been through a storm. The tents had been torn down, the stands knocked over, the goods looted. Shards of orange and green glass crunched underfoot. Yet a rack of Italian scarves worth a year's salary stood untouched amid the rubble. It made no sense at all.

Up and down the market, flicks were industriously cleaning up. They stooped and lifted and swept. One of them was being beaten by a suit.

Gunther blinked. He could not react to it as a real event. The woman cringed under the blows, shrieking wildly and scuttling away from them. One of the tents had been re-erected, and within the shadow of its rainbow silks, four other suits lounged against the bar. Not a one of them moved to help the woman.

"Hey!" Gunther shouted. He felt hideously self-conscious, as if he'd been abruptly thrust into the middle of a play without memorized lines or any idea of the plot or notion of what his role in it was. "Stop that!"

The suit turned toward him. It held the woman's slim arm captive in one gloved hand. "Go away," a male voice growled over the radio.

"What do you think you're doing? Who are you?" The man wore a Westinghouse suit, one of a dozen or so among the unafflicted. But Gunther recognized a brown, kidney-shaped scorch mark on the abdomen panel. "Posner—is that you? Let that woman go."

"She's not a woman," Posner said. "Hell, look at her—she's not even human. She's a flick."

Gunther set his helmet to record. "I'm taping this," he warned. "You hit that woman again, and Ekatarina will see it all. I promise."

Posner released the woman. She stood dazed for a second or two, and then the voice from her peecee reasserted control. She bent to pick up a broom, and returned to work.

Switching off his helmet, Gunther said, "Okay. What did she do?"

Indignantly, Posner extended a foot. He pointed sternly down at it. "She peed all over my boot!"

The suits in the tent had been watching with interest. Now they roared. "Your own fault, Will!" one of them called out. "I told you you weren't scheduling in enough time for personal hygiene."

"Don't worry about a little moisture. It'll boil off next time you hit vacuum!"

But Gunther was not listening. He stared at the flick Posner had been mistreating and wondered why he hadn't recognized Anya earlier. Her mouth was pursed, her face squinched up tight with worry, as if there were a key in the back of her head that had been wound three times too many. Her shoulders cringed forward now, too. But still.

"I'm sorry, Anya," he said. "Hiro is dead. There wasn't anything we could do."

She went on sweeping, oblivious, unhappy.

He caught the shift's last jitney back to the Center. It felt good to be home again. Miiko Ezumi had decided to loot the outlying factories of their oxygen and water surpluses, then carved a shower room from the rock. There was a long line for only three minutes' use, and no soap, but nobody complained. Some people pooled their time, showering two and three together. Those waiting their turns joked rowdily.

Gunther washed, grabbed some clean shorts and a Glavkosmos T-shirt, and padded down the hall. He hesitated outside the common room, listening to the gang sitting around the table, discussing the more colorful flicks they'd encountered.

"Have you seen the Mouse Hunter?"

"Oh yeah, and Ophelia!"

"The Pope!"

"The Duck Lady!"

"Everybody knows the Duck Lady!"

They were laughing and happy. A warm sense of community flowed from the room, what Gunther's father would have in his sloppy-sentimental way called *Gemütlichkeit*. Gunther stepped within.

Liza Nagenda looked up, all gums and teeth, and froze. Her jaw snapped shut. "Well, if it isn't Izmailova's personal spy!"

"What?" The accusation took Gunther's breath away. He looked helplessly about the room. Nobody would meet his eye. They had all fallen silent.

Liza's face was grey with anger. "You heard me! It was you that ratted on Krishna, wasn't it?"

"Now that's way out of line! You've got a lot of fucking gall if—" He controlled himself with an effort. There was no sense in matching her hysteria with his own. "It's none of your business what my relationship with Izmailova is or is not." He looked around the table. "Not that any of you deserve to know, but Krishna's working on a cure. If anything I said or did helped put him back in the lab, well then, so be it."

She smirked. "So what's your excuse for snitching on Will Posner?"

"I never—"

"We all heard the story! You told him you were going to run straight to your precious Izmailova with your little helmet vids."

"Now, Liza," Takayuni began. She slapped him away.

"Do you know what Posner was doing?" Gunther shook a finger in Liza's face. "Hah? Do you? He was beating a woman—Anya! He was beating Anya right out in the open!"

"So what? He's one of us, isn't he? Not a zoned-out, dead-eyed, ranting, drooling *flick*!"

"You bitch!" Outraged, Gunther lunged at Liza across the table. "I'll kill you, I swear it!" People jerked back from him, rushed forward, a chaos of motion. Posner thrust himself in Gunther's way, arms spread, jaw set and manly. Gunther punched him in the face. Posner looked surprised, and fell back. Gunther's hand stung, but he felt strangely good anyway; if everyone else was crazy, then why not him?

"You just try it!" Liza shrieked. "I knew you were that type all along!"

Takayuni grabbed Liza away one way. Hamilton seized Gunther and yanked him the other. Two of Posner's friends were holding him back as well.

"I've had about all I can take from you!" Gunther shouted. "You cheap cunt!"

"Listen to him! Listen what he calls me!"

Screaming, they were shoved out opposing doors.

"It's all right, Gunther." Beth had flung him into the first niche they'd come to. He slumped against a wall, shaking, and closed his eyes. "It's all right now."

But it wasn't. Gunther was suddenly struck with the realization that with the exception of Ekatarina he no longer had any friends. Not real friends, close friends. How could this have happened? It was as if everyone had been turned into werewolves. Those who weren't actually mad were still monsters. "I don't understand."

Hamilton sighed. "What don't you understand, Weil?"

"The way people—the way we all treat the flicks. When Posner was beating Anya, there were four other suits standing nearby, and not a one of them so much as lifted a finger to stop him. Not one! And I felt it too, there's no use pretending I'm superior to the rest of them. I wanted to walk on and pretend I hadn't seen a thing. What's happened to us?"

Hamilton shrugged. Her hair was short and dark about her plain round face. "I went to a pretty expensive school when I was a kid. One year we had one of those exercises that're supposed to be personally enriching. You know? A life experience. We were divided into two groups—Prisoners and Guards. The Prisoners couldn't leave their assigned areas without permission from a Guard, the Guards got better lunches, stuff like that. Very simple set of rules. I was a Guard.

"Almost immediately, we started to bully the Prisoners. We pushed 'em around, yelled at 'em, kept 'em in line. What was amazing was that the Prisoners let us do it. They outnumbered us five to one. We didn't even have authority for the things we did. But not a one of them complained. Not a one of them stood up and said no, you can't do this. They played the game.

"At the end of the month, the project was dismantled and we had some study seminars on what we'd learned: the roots of fascism, and so on. Read some Hannah Arendt. And then it was all over. Except that my best girlfriend never spoke to me again. I couldn't blame her, either. Not after what I'd done.

"What did I really learn? That people will play whatever role you put them in. They'll do it without knowing that that's what they're doing. Take a minority, tell them they're special, and make them Guards—they'll start playing Guard."

"So what's the answer? How do we keep from getting caught up in the roles we play?"

"Damned if I know, Weil. Damned if I know."

Ekatarina had moved her niche to the far end of a new tunnel. Hers was the only room the tunnel served, and consequently she had a lot of privacy. As Gunther stepped in, a staticky voice swam into focus on his trance chip. ". . . reported shock. In Cairo, government officials pledged . . ." It cut off.

"Hey! You've restored—" He stopped. If radio reception had been restored, he'd have known. It would have been the talk of the Center. Which meant that radio contact had never really been completely broken. It was simply being controlled by the CMP.

Ekatarina looked up at him. She'd been crying, but she'd stopped. "The Swiss Orbitals are gone!" she whispered. "They hit them with everything from softbombs to brilliant pebbles. They dusted the shipyards."

The scope of all those deaths obscured what she was saying for a second. He sank down beside her. "But that means—"

"There's no spacecraft that can reach us, yes. Unless there's a ship in transit, we're stranded here."

He took her in his arms. She was cold and shivering. Her skin felt clammy and mottled with gooseflesh. "How long has it been since you've had any sleep?" he asked sharply.

"I can't—"

"You're wired, aren't you?"

"I can't afford to sleep. Not now. Later."

"Ekatarina. The energy you get from wire isn't free. It's only borrowed from your body. When you come down, it all comes due. If you wire yourself up too tightly, you'll crash yourself right into a coma."

"I haven't been—" She stalled, and a confused, uncertain look entered her eyes. "Maybe you're right. I could probably use a little rest."

The CMP came to life. "Cadre Nine is building a radio receiver. Ezumi gave them the go-ahead."

"Shit!" Ekatarina sat bolt upright. "Can we stop it?"

"Moving against a universally popular project would cost you credibility you cannot afford to lose."

"Okay, so how can we minimize the—"

"Ekatarina," Gunther said. "Sleep, remember?"

"In a sec, babe." She patted the futon. "You just lie down and wait for me. I'll have this wrapped up before you can nod off." She kissed him gently, lingeringly. "All right?"

"Yeah, sure." He lay down and closed his eyes, just for a second.

When he awoke, it was time to go on shift, and Ekatarina was gone.

It was only the fifth day since Vladivostok. But everything was so utterly changed that times before then seemed like memories of another world. In a previous life I was Gunther Weil, he thought. I lived and worked and had a few laughs. Life was pretty good then.

He was still looking for Sally Chang, though with dwindling hope. Now, whenever he talked to suits he'd ask if they needed his help. Increasingly, they did not.

The third-level chapel was a shallow bowl facing the terrace wall. Tiger lilies grew about the chancel area at the bottom, and turquoise lizards skittered over the rock. The children were playing with a ball in the chancel. Gunther stood at the top, chatting with a sad-voiced Ryohei Iomato.

The children put away the ball and began to dance. They were playing London Bridge. Gunther watched them with a smile. From above they were so many spots of color, a flower unfolding and closing in on itself. Slowly, the smile faded. They were dancing too well. Not one of the children moved out of step, lost her place, or walked away sulking. Their expressions were intense, self-absorbed, inhuman. Gunther had to turn away.

"The CMP controls them," Iomato said. "I don't have much to do, really. I go through the vids and pick out games for them to play, songs to sing, little exercises to keep them healthy. Sometimes I have them draw."

"My God, how can you stand it?"

Iomato sighed. "My old man was an alcoholic. He had a pretty rough life, and at some point he started drinking to blot out the pain. You know what?"

"It didn't work."

"Yah. Made him even more miserable. So then he had twice the reason to get drunk. He kept on trying, though, I've got to give him that. He wasn't the sort of man to give up on something he believed in just because it wasn't working the way it should."

Gunther said nothing.

"I think that memory is the only thing keeping me from just taking off my helmet and joining them."

The Corporate Video Center was a narrow run of offices in the farthest tunnel reaches, where raw footage for adverts and incidental business use was processed before being squirted to better-equipped vid centers on Earth. Gunther passed from office to office, slapping off flatscreens left flickering since the disaster.

It was unnerving going through the normally busy rooms and finding no one. The desks and cluttered work stations had been abandoned in purposeful disarray, as though their operators had merely stepped out for a break and would be back momentarily. Gunther found himself spinning around to confront his shadow, and flinching at unexpected noises. With each machine he turned off, the silence at his back grew. It was twice as lonely as being out on the surface.

He doused a last light and stepped into the gloomy hall. Two suits with interwoven H-and-A logos loomed up out of the shadows. He jumped in shock. They were empty, of course—there were no Hyundai Aerospace components among the unafflicted. Someone had simply left these suits here in temporary storage before the madness.

The suits grabbed him.

"Hey!" He shouted in terror as they seized him by the arms and lifted him off his feet. One of them hooked the peecee from his harness and snapped it off. Before he knew what was happening he'd been swept down a short flight of stairs and through a doorway.

"Mr. Weil."

He was in a high-ceilinged room carved into the rock to hold airhandling equipment that hadn't been constructed yet. A high string of temporary work lamps provided dim light. To the far side of the room a suit sat behind a desk, flanked by two more, standing. They all wore Hyundai Aerospace suits. There was no way he could identify them.

The suits that had brought him in crossed their arms.

"What's going on here?" Gunther asked. "Who are you?"

"You are the last person we'd tell that to." He couldn't tell which one had spoken. The voice came over his radio, made sexless and impersonal by an electronic filter. "Mr. Weil, you stand accused of crimes against your fellow citizens. Do you have anything to say in your defense?"

"What?" Gunther looked at the suits before him and to either side. They were perfectly identical, indistinguishable from each other, and he was suddenly afraid of what the people within might feel free to do, armored as they were in anonymity. "Listen, you've got no right to do this. There's a governmental structure in place, if you've got any complaints against me."

"Not everyone is pleased with Izmailova's government," the judge said.

"But she controls the CMP, and we could not run Bootstrap without the CMP controlling the flicks," a second added.

"We simply have to work around her." Perhaps it was the judge; perhaps it was yet another of the suits. Gunther couldn't tell.

"Do you wish to speak on your own behalf?"

"What exactly am I charged with?" Gunther asked desperately. "Okay, maybe I've done something wrong, I'll entertain that possibility. But maybe you just don't understand my situation. Have you considered that?"

Silence.

"I mean, just what are you angry about? Is it Posner? Because I'm not sorry about that. I won't apologize. You can't mistreat people just because they're sick. They're still people, like anybody else. They have their rights."

Silence.

"But if you think I'm some kind of a spy or something, that I'm running around and ratting on people to Ek—to Izmailova, well that's simply not true. I mean, I talk to her, I'm not about to pretend I don't, but I'm not her spy or anything. She doesn't have any spies. She doesn't need any! She's just trying to hold things together, that's all.

"Jesus, you don't know what she's gone through for you! You haven't seen how much it takes out of her! She'd like nothing better than to quit. But she has to hang in there because—" An eerie dark electronic gabble rose up on his radio, and he stopped as he realized that they were laughing at him.

"Does anyone else wish to speak?"

One of Gunther's abductors stepped forward. "Your Honor, this man says that flicks are human. He overlooks the fact that they cannot live without our support and direction. Their continued well-being is bought at the price of our unceasing labor. He stands condemned out of his own mouth. I petition the court to make the punishment fit the crime."

The judge looked to the right, to the left. His two companions nodded, and stepped back into the void. The desk had been set up at the mouth of what was to be the air intake duct. Gunther had just time enough to realize this when they reappeared, leading someone in a G5 suit identical to his own.

"We could kill you, Mr. Weil," the artificial voice crackled. "But that would be wasteful. Every hand, every mind is needed. We must all pull together in our time of need."

The G5 stood alone and motionless in the center of the room.

"Watch."

Two of the Hyundai suits stepped up to the G5 suit. Four hands converged on the helmet seals. With practiced efficiency, they flicked the latches and lifted the helmet. It happened so swiftly the occupant could not have stopped it if he'd tried.

Beneath the helmet was the fearful, confused face of a flick.

"Sanity is a privilege, Mr. Weil, not a right. You are guilty as charged. However, we are not cruel men. *This once* we will let you off with a warning. But these are desperate times. At your next offense—be it only so minor a thing as reporting this encounter to the Little General—we may be forced to dispense with the formality of a hearing." The judge paused. "Do I make myself clear?"

Reluctantly, Gunther nodded.

"Then you may leave."

On the way out, one of the suits handed him back his peecee.

Five people. He was sure there weren't any more involved than that. Maybe one or two more, but that was it. Posner had to be hip-deep in this thing, he was certain of that. It shouldn't be too hard to figure out the others.

He didn't dare take the chance.

At shift's end he found Ekatarina already asleep. She looked haggard and unhealthy. He knelt by her, and gently brushed her cheek with the back of one hand.

Her eyelids fluttered open.

"Oh, hey. I didn't mean to wake you. Just go back to sleep, huh?"

She smiled. "You're sweet, Gunther, but I was only taking a nap anyway. I've got to be up in another fifteen minutes." Her eyes closed again. "You're the only one I can really trust anymore. Everybody's lying to me, feeding me misinformation, keeping silent when there's something I need to know. You're the only one I can count on to tell me things."

You have enemies, he thought. They call you the Little General, and they don't like how you run things. They're not ready to move against you directly, but they have plans. And they're ruthless.

Aloud, he said, "Go back to sleep."

"They're all against me," she murmured. "Bastard sons of bitches."

The next day he spent going through the service spaces for the new airhandling system. He found a solitary flick's nest made of shredded vacuum suits, but after consultation with the CMP concluded that nobody had lived there for days. There was no trace of Sally Chang.

If it had been harrowing going through the sealed areas before his trial, it was far worse today. Ekatarina's enemies had infected him with fear. Reason told him they were not waiting for him, that he had nothing to worry about until he displeased them again. But the hindbrain did not listen.

Time crawled. When he finally emerged into daylight at the end of his shift, he felt light-headedly out of phase with reality from the hours of isolation. At first he noticed nothing out of the ordinary. Then his suit radio was full of voices, and people were hurrying about every which way. There was a happy buzz in the air. Somebody was singing.

He snagged a passing suit and asked, "What's going on?"

"Haven't you heard? The war is over. They've made peace. And there's a ship coming in!"

The *Lake Geneva* had maintained television silence through most of the long flight to the Moon for fear of long-range beam weapons. With peace, however, they opened direct transmission to Bootstrap.

Ezumi's people had the flicks sew together an enormous cotton square and hack away some trailing vines so they could hang it high on the shadowed side of the crater. Then, with the fill lights off, the video image was projected. Swiss spacejacks tumbled before the camera, grinning, all denim and red cowboy hats. They were talking about their escape from the hunter-seeker missiles, brash young voices running one over the other.

The top officers were assembled beneath the cotton square. Gunther recognized their suits. Ekatarina's voice boomed from newly erected loudspeakers. "When are you coming in? We have to make sure the spaceport field is clear. How many hours?"

Holding up five fingers, a blond woman said, "Forty-five!"

"No, forty-three!"

"Nothing like that!"

"*Almost* forty-five!"

Again Ekatarina's voice cut into the tumult. "What's it like in the orbitals? We heard they were destroyed."

"Yes, destroyed!"

"Very bad, very bad, it'll take years to—"

"But most of the people are—"

"We were given six orbits warning; most went down in lifting bodies, there was a big evacuation."

"Many died, though. It was very bad."

Just below the officers, a suit had been directing several flicks as they assembled a camera platform. Now it waved broadly, and the flicks stepped away. In the *Lake Geneva* somebody shouted, and several heads turned to stare at an offscreen television monitor. The suit turned the camera, giving them a slow, panoramic scan.

One of the spacejacks said, "What's it like there? I see that some of you are wearing space suits, and the rest are not. Why is that?"

Ekatarina took a deep breath. "There have been some changes here."

There was one hell of a party at the Center when the Swiss arrived. Sleep schedules were juggled, and save for a skeleton crew overseeing the flicks, everyone turned out to welcome the dozen newcomers to the Moon. They danced to skiffle, and drank vacuum-distilled vodka. Everyone had stories to tell, rumors to swap, opinions on the likelihood that the peace would hold.

Gunther wandered away midway through the party. The Swiss depressed him. They all seemed so young and fresh and eager. He felt battered and cynical in their presence. He wanted to grab them by the shoulders and shake them awake.

Depressed, he wandered through the locked-down laboratories. Where the Viral Computer Project had been, he saw Ekatarina and the captain of the *Lake Geneva* conferring over a stack of crated bioflops. They bent low over Ekatarina's peecee, listening to the CMP.

"Have you considered nationalizing your industries?" the captain asked. "That would give us the plant needed to build the New City. Then, with a few hardwired utilities, Bootstrap could be managed without anyone having to set foot inside it."

Gunther was too distant to hear the CMP's reaction, but he saw both women laugh. "Well," said Ekatarina. "At the very least we will have to renegotiate terms with the parent corporations. With only one ship functional, people can't be easily replaced. Physical presence has become a valuable commodity. We'd be fools not to take advantage of it."

He passed on, deeper into shadow, wandering aimlessly. Eventually, there was a light ahead, and he heard voices. One was Krishna's, but spoken faster and more forcefully than he was used to hearing it. Curious, he stopped just outside the door.

Krishna was in the center of the lab. Before him, Beth Hamilton stood nodding humbly. "Yes, sir," she said. "I'll do that. Yes." Dumbfounded, Gunther realized that Krishna was giving her orders.

Krishna glanced up. "Weil! You're just the man I was about to come looking for."

"I am?"

"Come in here, don't dawdle." Krishna smiled and beckoned, and Gunther had no choice but to obey. Krishna looked like a young god now. The force of his spirit danced in his eyes like fire. It was strange that Gunther had never noticed before how tall he was. "Tell me where Sally Chang is."

"I don't—I mean, I can't, I—" He stopped and swallowed. "I think Chang must be dead." Then, "Krishna? What's happened to you?"

"He's finished his research," Beth said.

"I rewrote my personality from top to bottom," Krishna said. "I'm not half-crippled with shyness anymore—have you noticed?" He put a hand on Gunther's shoulder, and it was reassuring, warm, comforting. "Gunther, I won't tell you what it took to scrape together enough messenger engines from traces of old experiments to try this out on myself. But it works. We've got a treatment that among other things will serve as a universal cure for everyone in Bootstrap. But to do that, we need the messenger engines, and they're not here. Now tell me why you think Sally Chang is dead."

"Well, uh, I've been searching for her for four days. And the CMP has been looking too. You've been holed up here all the time, so maybe you don't know the flicks as well as the rest of us do. But they're not very big on planning. The likelihood one of them could actively evade detection that long is practically zilch. The only thing I can think is that somehow she made it to the surface before the effects hit her, got into a truck and told it to drive as far as her oxygen would take her."

Krishna shook his head and said, "No. It is simply not consistent with Sally Chang's character. With all the best will in the world, I cannot picture her killing herself." He slid open a drawer: row upon row of gleaming cannisters. "This may help. Do you remember when I said there were two cannisters of mimetic engines missing, not just the schizomimetic?"

"Vaguely."

"I've been too busy to worry about it, but wasn't that odd? Why would Chang have taken a cannister and not used it?"

"What was in the second cannister?" Hamilton asked.

"Paranoia," Krishna said. "Or rather a good enough chemical analog. Now, paranoia is a rare disability, but a fascinating one. It's characterized by an elaborate but internally consistent delusional system. The paranoid patient functions well intellectually, and is less fragmented than a schizophrenic. Her emotional and social responses are closer to normal. She's capable of concerted effort. In a time of turmoil, it's quite possible that a paranoid individual could elude our detection."

"Okay, let's get this straight," Hamilton said. "War breaks out on Earth. Chang gets her orders, keys in the software bombs, and goes to Bootstrap with a cannister full of madness and a little syringe of paranoia—no, it doesn't work. It all falls apart."

"How so?"

"Paranoia wouldn't inoculate her against schizophrenia. How does she protect herself from her own aerosols?"

Gunther stood transfixed. "Lavender!"

They caught up with Sally Chang on the topmost terrace of Bootstrap. The top level was undeveloped. Someday—so the corporate brochures promised—fallow deer would graze at the edge of limpid pools, and otters frolic in the streams. But the soil hadn't been built up yet, the worms brought in or the bacteria seeded. There were only sand, machines, and a few unhappy opportunistic weeds.

Chang's camp was to one side of a streamhead, beneath a fill light. She started to her feet at their approach, glanced quickly to the side and decided to brazen it out.

A sign reading EMERGENCY CANOPY MAINTENANCE STATION had been welded to a strut supporting the stream's valve stem. Under it were a short stacked pyramid of oxytanks and an aluminum storage crate the size of a coffin. "Very clever," Beth muttered over Gunther's trance chip. "She sleeps in the storage crate, and anybody stumbling across her thinks it's just spare equipment."

The lavender suit raised an arm and casually said, "Hiya, guys. How can I help you?"

Krishna strode forward and took her hands. "Sally, it's me—Krishna!"

"Oh, thank God!" She slumped in his arms. "I've been so afraid."

"You're all right now."

"I thought you were an Invader at first, when I saw you coming up. I'm so hungry—I haven't eaten since I don't know when." She clutched at the sleeve of Krishna's suit. "You do know about the Invaders, don't you?"

"Maybe you'd better bring me up to date."

They began walking toward the stairs. Krishna gestured quickly to Gunther and then toward Chang's worksuit harness. A cannister the size of a hip flask hung there. Gunther reached over and plucked it off. The messenger engines! He held them in his hand.

To the other side, Beth Hamilton plucked up the near-full cylinder of paranoia-inducing engines and made it disappear.

Sally Chang, deep in the explication of her reasonings, did not notice. ". . . obeyed my orders, of course. But they made no sense. I worried and worried about that until finally I realized what was really going on. A wolf caught in a trap will gnaw off its leg to get free. I began to look for the wolf. What kind of enemy justified such extreme actions? Certainly nothing human."

"Sally," Krishna said, "I want you to entertain the notion that the conspiracy—for want of a better word—may be more deeply rooted than you suspect. That the problem is not an external enemy, but the workings of our own brain. Specifically that the Invaders are an artifact of the psychotomimetics you injected into yourself back when this all began."

"No. No, there's too much evidence. It all fits together! The Invaders needed a way to disguise themselves both physically, which was accomplished by the vacuum suits, and psychologically, which was achieved by the general madness. Thus, they can move undetected among us. Would a human enemy have converted all of Bootstrap to slave labor? Unthinkable! They can read our minds like a book. If we hadn't protected ourselves with the schizomimetics, they'd be able to extract all our knowledge, all our military research secrets . . ."

Listening, Gunther couldn't help imagining what Liza Nagenda would say to all of this wild talk. At the thought of her, his jaw clenched. Just like one of Chang's machines, he realized, and couldn't help being amused at his own expense.

Ekatarina was waiting at the bottom of the stairs. Her hands trembled noticeably, and there was a slight quaver in her voice when she said, "What's all this the CMP tells me about messenger engines? Krishna's supposed to have come up with a cure of some kind?"

"We've got them," Gunther said quietly, happily. He held up the canister. "It's over now, we can heal our friends."

"Let me see," Ekatarina said. She took the cannister from his hand.

"No, wait!" Hamilton cried, too late. Behind her, Krishna was arguing with Sally Chang about her interpretations of recent happenings. Neither had noticed yet that those in front had stopped.

"Stand back." Ekatarina took two quick steps backward. Edgily, she added, "I don't mean to be difficult. But we're going to sort this all out, and until we do, I don't want anybody too close to me. That includes you too, Gunther."

Flicks began gathering. By ones and twos they wandered up the lawn, and then by the dozen. By the time it was clear that Ekatarina had called them up via the CMP, Krishna, Chang, and Hamilton were separated from her and Gunther by a wall of people.

Chang stood very still. Somewhere behind her unseen face, she was revising her theories to include this new event. Suddenly, her hands slapped at her suit, grabbing for the missing canisters. She looked at Krishna and with a trill of horror said, "You're one of them!"

"Of course I'm not—" Krishna began. But she was turning, stumbling, fleeing back up the steps.

"Let her go," Ekatarina ordered. "We've got more serious things to talk about." Two flicks scurried up, lugging a small industrial kiln between them. They set it down, and a third plugged in an electric cable. The interior began to glow. "This canister is all you've got, isn't it? If I were to autoclave it, there wouldn't be any hope of replacing its contents."

"Izmailova, listen," Krishna said.

"I am listening. Talk."

Krishna explained, while Izmailova listened with arms folded and shoulders tilted skeptically. When he was done, she shook her head. "It's a noble folly, but folly is all it is. You want to reshape our minds into something alien to the course of human evolution. To turn the seat of thought into a jet pilot's couch. This is your idea of a solution? Forget it. Once this particular box is opened, there'll be no putting its contents back in again. And you haven't advanced any convincing arguments for opening it."

"But the people in Bootstrap!" Gunther objected. "They—"

She cut him off. "Gunther, nobody *likes* what's happened to them. But if the rest of us must give up our humanity to pay for a speculative and ethically dubious rehabilitation . . . well, the price is simply too high. Mad or not, they're at least human now."

"Am I inhuman?" Krishna asked. "If you tickle me, do I not laugh?"

"You're in no position to judge. You've rewired your neurons and you're stoned on the novelty. What tests have you run on yourself? How thoroughly have you mapped out your deviations from human norms? Where are your figures?" These were purely rhetorical questions; the kind of analyses she meant took weeks to run. "Even if you check out completely human—and I don't concede you will!—who's to say what the long-range consequences are? What's to stop us from drifting, step by incremental step, into madness? Who decides what madness is? Who programs the programmers? No, this is impossible. I won't gamble with our minds." Defensively, almost angrily, she repeated, "I won't gamble with our minds."

"Ekatarina," Gunther said gently, "how long have you been up? Listen to yourself. The wire is doing your thinking for you."

She waved a hand dismissively, without responding.

"Just as a practical matter," Hamilton said, "how do you expect to run Bootstrap without it? The setup is turning us all into baby fascists. You say you're worried about madness—what will we be like a year from now?"

"The CMP assures me—"

"The CMP is only a program!" Hamilton cried. "No matter how much interactivity it has, it's not flexible. It has no hope. It cannot judge a new thing. It can only enforce old decisions, old values, old habits, old fears."

Abruptly Ekatarina snapped. "*Get out of my face!*" she screamed. "Stop it, stop it, stop it! I won't listen to any more."

"Ekatarina—" Gunther began.

But her hand had tightened on the cannister. Her knees bent as she began a slow genuflection to the kiln. Gunther could see that she had stopped listening. Drugs and responsibility had done this to her, speeding her up and bewildering her with conflicting demands, until she stood trembling on the brink of collapse. A good night's sleep might have restored her, made her capable of being reasoned with. But there was no time. Words would not stop her now. And she was too far distant for him to reach before she destroyed the engines. In that instant he felt such a strong outwelling of emotion toward her as would be impossible to describe.

"Ekatarina," he said. "I love you."

She half-turned her head toward him and in a distracted, somewhat irritated tone said, "What are you—"

He lifted the bolt gun from his work harness, leveled it, and fired.

Ekatarina's helmet shattered.

She fell.

"I should have shot to just breach the helmet. That would have stopped her. But I didn't think I was a good enough shot. I aimed right for the center of her head."

"Hush," Hamilton said. "You did what you had to. Stop tormenting yourself. Talk about more practical things."

He shook his head, still groggy. For the longest time, he had been kept on beta endorphins, unable to feel a thing, unable to care. It was like being swathed in cotton batting. Nothing could reach him. Nothing could hurt him. "How long have I been out of it?"

"A day."

"A day!" He looked about the austere room. Bland rock walls and laboratory equipment with smooth, noncommital surfaces. To the far end, Krishna and Chang were hunched over a swipeboard, arguing happily and impatiently overwriting each other's scrawls. A Swiss spacejack came in and spoke to their backs. Krishna nodded distractedly, not looking up. "I thought it was much longer."

"Long enough. We've already salvaged everyone connected with Sally Chang's group, and gotten a good start on the rest. Pretty soon it will be time to decide how you want yourself rewritten."

He shook his head, feeling dead. "I don't think I'll bother, Beth. I just don't have the stomach for it."

"We'll give you the stomach."

"Naw, I don't . . ." He felt a black nausea come welling up again. It was cyclic; it returned every time he was beginning to think he'd finally put it down. "I don't want the fact that I killed Ekatarina washed away in a warm flood of self-satisfaction. The idea disgusts me."

"We don't want that either." Posner led a delegation of seven into the lab. Krishna and Chang rose to face them, and the group broke into swirling halves. "There's been enough of that. It's time we all started taking responsibility for the consequences of—" Everyone was talking at once. Hamilton made a face.

"Started taking responsibility for—"

Voices rose.

"We can't talk here," she said. "Take me out on the surface."

They drove with the cabin pressurized, due west on the Seething Bay road. Ahead, the sun was almost touching the weary walls of Sömmering crater. Shadow crept down from the mountains and cratertops, yearning toward the radiantly lit Sinus Medii. Gunther found it achingly beautiful. He did not want to respond to it, but the harsh lines echoed the lonely hurt within him in a way that he found oddly comforting.

Hamilton touched her peecee. "Putting On the Ritz" filled their heads.

"What if Ekatarina was right?" he said sadly. "What if we're giving up everything that makes us human? The prospect of being turned into some kind of big-domed emotionless superman doesn't appeal to me much."

Hamilton shook her head. "I asked Krishna about that, and he said no. He said it was like . . . were you ever nearsighted?"

"Sure, as a kid."

"Then you'll understand. He said it was like the first time you came out of the doctor's office after being lased. How everything seemed clear and vivid and distinct. What had once been a blur that you called 'tree' resolved itself into a thousand individual and distinct leaves. The world was filled with unexpected detail. There were things on the horizon that you'd never seen before. Like that."

"Oh." He stared ahead. The disk of the sun was almost touching Sömmering. "There's no point in going any farther."

He powered down the truck.

Beth Hamilton looked uncomfortable. She cleared her throat and with brusque energy said, "Gunther, look. I had you bring me out here for a reason. I want to propose a merger of resources."

"A what?"

"Marriage."

It took Gunther a second to absorb what she had said. "Aw, no . . . I don't . . ."

"I'm serious. Gunther, I know you think I've been hard on you, but that's only because I saw a lot of potential in you, and that you were doing nothing with it. Well, things have changed. Give me a say in your rewrite, and I'll do the same for you."

He shook his head. "This is just too weird for me."

"It's too late to use that as an excuse. Ekatarina was right—we're sitting on top of something very dangerous, the most dangerous opportunity humanity faces today. It's out of the bag, though. Word has gotten out. Earth is horrified and fascinated. They'll be watching us. Briefly, very briefly, we can control this thing. We can help to shape it now, while it's small. Five years from now, it will be out of our hands.

"You have a good mind, Gunther, and it's about to get better. I think we agree on what kind of a world we want to make. I want you on my side."

"I don't know what to say."

"You want true love? You got it. We can make the sex as sweet or nasty as you like. Nothing easier. You want me quieter, louder, gentler, more assured? We can negotiate. Let's see if we can come to terms."

He said nothing.

Hamilton eased back in the seat. After a time, she said, "You know? I've never watched a lunar sunset before. I don't get out on the surface much."

"We'll have to change that," Gunther said.

Hamilton stared hard into his face. Then she smiled. She wriggled closer to him. Clumsily, he put an arm over her shoulder. It seemed to be what was expected of him. He coughed into his hand, then pointed a finger. "There it goes."

Lunar sunset was a simple thing. The crater wall touched the bottom of the solar disk. Shadows leaped from the slopes and raced across the lowlands. Soon half the sun was gone. Smoothly, without distortion, it dwindled. A last brilliant sliver of light burned atop the rock, then ceased to be. In the instant before the windshield adjusted and the stars appeared, the universe filled with darkness.

The air in the cab cooled. The panels snapped and popped with the sudden shift in temperature.

Now Hamilton was nuzzling the side of his neck. Her skin was slightly tacky to the touch, and exuded a faint but distinct odor. She ran her tongue up the line of his chin and poked it in his ear. Her hand fumbled with the latches of his suit.

Gunther experienced no arousal at all, only a mild distaste that bordered on disgust. This was horrible, a defilement of all he had felt for Ekatarina.

But it was a chore he had to get through. Hamilton was right. All his life his hindbrain had been in control, driving him with emotions chemically derived and randomly applied. He had been lashed to the steed of consciousness and forced to ride it wherever it went, and that nightmare gallop had brought him only pain and confusion. Now that he had control of the reins, he could make this horse go where he wanted.

He was not sure what he would demand from his reprogramming. Contentment, perhaps. Sex and passion, almost certainly. But not love. He was done with the romantic illusion. It was time to grow up.

He squeezed Beth's shoulder. One more day, he thought, and it won't matter. I'll feel whatever is best for me to feel. Beth raised her mouth to his. Her lips parted. He could smell her breath.

They kissed.

GREAT WALL OF MARS

Alastair Reynolds

❀

Alastair Reynolds (born 1966) was born in Barry, South Wales, raised in Cornwall, educated in Newcastle and St. Andrews, Scotland, and now lives in Holland. He holds a Ph.D. in astronomy and works for the European Space Agency. He is one of the British space opera writers to emerge in the mid- and late 1990s, and the most hard SF of them. To date his stories have been published almost exclusively in *Interzone* and in *Spectrum SF*, the ambitious new SF magazine from Scotland. His first novel was *Revelation Space* (2000) and his second, *Chasm City* was published in 2001. His new novel, *Redemption Ark*, was published in the U.K. in 2002.

Reynolds provides a log of notes on his stories and comments on hard SF on his Web site, members.tripod.com/~voxish/sf~_hard~_intro.html.

First we quote from "On Hard SF" by Alastair Reynolds:

> . . . the term [hard SF] is ugly and misleading, but it seems we're stuck with it. It doesn't mean that hard SF is any more demanding on the reader than the rest of the genre, nor is it any more radical in outlook (although there is such a beast as Radical Hard SF). Actually, far too much of what passes for hard SF is pretty limp and unimaginative stuff; tired re-hashings of ideas which might have been new and shiny in Heinlein's day, but which now read as being deeply rooted in established conventions of the genre, and politically conservative to boot.
>
> . . . and it's probably not too far from the truth to say that hard SF is that branch of SF in which the writer goes to some trouble to ensure that the events in the tale could, plausibly, happen in the universe as we know it. Hard SF—which as a subgenre is almost as old as SF itself—has very frequently tended to be set in the future (although there are some excellent exceptions) and there has been a strong tendency for it to be set in locales other than our own planet, a trend which continues to date and is a direct consequence of the types of story which predominate in hard SF.
>
> What exactly do I mean when I say hard SF aims at plausibility? By this I mean that good hard SF stories should try to not contain glaring errors of fact, and by fact I mean the kind of detail which is easily checked using standard reference material—popular science books, for instance. Take the case of the atmosphere of an alien planet, for instance. Current thinking is that a breathable atmosphere simply can't exist in the absence of life, which would mean that a desert planet could not sustain explorers unless they brought air with them. These days, however, most self-respecting SF writers who set their stories in exotic venues are aware of the more obvious pitfalls, and if they feel the need to have their characters travel around in faster-than-light spaceships, it's generally taken for granted that this is an acceptable violation of the laws of physics for plot purposes, and not evidence of the author's ignorance of special relativity. . . .
>
> At the other extreme of the hard SF spectrum, the science is strongly foregrounded,

> to the extent that the stories can sometimes seem little more than physics problems fleshed out with characters, and in which the reader may be required to get their head round sometimes difficult new concepts. Perhaps the best current exponent of this "ultra-hard" SF is Greg Egan, whose stories . . . can be as intellectually challenging as a review article in *Nature*, and sometimes require about the same level of attention from the reader. . . . Other writers who also specialize in genuinely far-out hard SF include Gregory Benford and Geoffrey Landis.
>
> Somewhere in the middle, forming a spectrum, is the bulk of what we think of as hard SF. There are writers like scientist David Brin who will cheerfully trash the laws of physics in the interests of plot and exuberance (see, for instance, *Startide Rising*), but who embeds genuine scientific puzzles (often of an ecological nature) into his tales. And there are writers like Greg Bear, who had no formal scientific education, yet whose work is as convincing in detail and grand vision as any of the scientist-writers of his generation and which occasionally reaches the extremes of hardness typified by Egan and a few others.

And in reference to the context of "Great Wall of Mars":

> "Galactic North" appeared in *Interzone* 145, July 1999. It started out as an idea I'd had a few years earlier, which was to do a story in the same vein as a few others that are particular favorites of mine: Larry Niven's "The Ethics of Madness," Joe Haldeman's "Tricentennial," Gregory Benford's "Relativistic Effects" and Poul Anderson's novel *Tau Zero*. In all of these space-based stories, the action jumps forward by ever-increasing chunks of time, leading to a dizzying sense of dislocation and sense of wonder as the centuries slam by. (Three later stories which achieve a similar effect, and which I read while writing this one, are Stephen Baxter's dazzling "Pilot" (part of his Xeelee sequence), Robert Reed's "Marrow" (which has now been expanded into a novel) and Ian McDonald's "The Days of Solomon Gursky.")
>
> "Great Wall of Mars" appeared in *Spectrum SF* 1, February 2000. I started this one in 1999, almost immediately after completing "Galactic North," and it's another story set in the same future history. This time it's a more claustrophobic, relatively near-future story about a military standoff on Mars between augmented and non-augmented human factions. It was with this story that I decided to start making a conscious effort to simplify my storylines (some of them had got a bit too complex for their own good) and thereby free up space for some—ahem—character development.

You realize you might die down there," said Warren.

Nevil Clavain looked into his brother's one good eye; the one the Conjoiners had left him with after the battle of Tharsis Bulge. "Yes, I know," he said. "But if there's another war, we might all die. I'd rather take that risk, if there's a chance for peace."

Warren shook his head, slowly and patiently. "No matter how many times we've been over this, you just don't seem to get it, do you? There can't ever be any kind of peace while they're still down there. That's what you don't understand, Nevil. The only long-term solution here is . . ." he trailed off.

"Go on," Clavain goaded. "Say it. Genocide."

Warren might have been about to answer when there was a bustle of activity down the docking tube, at the far end from the waiting spacecraft. Through the door Clavain saw a throng of media people, then someone gliding through them, fielding questions with only the curtest of answers. That was Sandra Voi, the Demarchist woman who would be coming with him to Mars.

"It's not genocide when they're just a faction, not an ethnically distinct race," Warren said, before Voi was within earshot.

"What is it, then?"

"I don't know. Prudence?"

Voi approached. She bore herself stiffly, her face a mask of quiet resignation. Her ship had only just docked from Circum-Jove, after a three-week transit at maximum burn. During that time the prospects for a peaceful resolution of the current crisis had steadily deteriorated.

"Welcome to Deimos," Warren said.

"Marshalls," she said, addressing both of them. "I wish the circumstances were better. Let's get straight to business. Warren; how long do you think we have to find a solution?"

"Not long. If Galiana maintains the pattern she's been following for the last six months, we're due another escape attempt in . . ." Warren glanced at a readout buried in his cuff. "About three days. If she does try and get another shuttle off Mars, we'll really have no option but to escalate."

They all knew what that would mean: a military strike against the Conjoiner nest.

"You've tolerated her attempts so far," Voi said. "And each time you've successfully destroyed her ship with all the people in it. The net risk of a successful breakout hasn't increased. So why retaliate now?"

"It's very simple. After each violation we issued Galiana with a stronger warning than the one before. Our last was absolute and final."

"You'll be in violation of treaty if you attack."

Warren's smile was one of quiet triumph. "Not quite, Sandra. You may not be completely conversant with the treaty's fine print, but we've discovered that it allows us to storm Galiana's nest without breaking any terms. The technical phrase is a police action, I believe."

Clavain saw that Voi was momentarily lost for words. That was hardly surprising. The treaty between the Coalition and the Conjoiners—which Voi's neutral Demarchists had helped draft—was the longest document in existence, apart from some obscure, computer-generated mathematical proofs. It was supposed to be watertight, though only machines had ever read it from beginning to end, and only machines had ever stood a chance of finding the kind of loophole which Warren was now brandishing.

"No . . ." she said. "There's some mistake."

"I'm afraid he's right," Clavain said. "I've seen the natural-language summaries, and there's no doubt about the legality of a police action. But it needn't come to that. I'm sure I can persuade Galiana not to make another escape attempt."

"But if we should fail?" Voi looked at Warren now. "Nevil and myself could still be on Mars in three days."

"Don't be, is my advice."

Disgusted, Voi turned and stepped into the green cool of the shuttle. Clavain was left alone with his brother for a moment. Warren fingered the leathery patch over his ruined eye with the chrome gauntlet of his prosthetic arm, as if to remind Clavain of what the war had cost him; how little love he had for the enemy, even now.

"We haven't got a chance of succeeding, have we?" Clavain said. "We're only going down there so you can say you explored all avenues of negotiation before sending in the troops. You actually want another damned war."

"Don't be so defeatist," Warren said, shaking his head sadly, forever the older brother disappointed at his sibling's failings. "It really doesn't become you."

"It's not me who's defeatist," Clavain said.

"No; of course not. Just do your best, little brother."

Warren extended his hand for his brother to shake. Hesitating, Clavain looked again into his brother's good eye. What he saw there was an interrogator's eye: as pale, colorless and cold as a midwinter sun. There was hatred in it. Warren despised Clavain's pacifism; Clavain's belief that any kind of peace, even a peace which consisted only of stumbling episodes of mistrust between crises, was always better than war. That schism had fractured any lingering fraternal feelings they might have retained. Now, when Warren reminded Clavain that they were brothers, he never entirely concealed the disgust in his voice.

"You misjudge me," Clavain whispered, before quietly shaking Warren's hand.

"No; I honestly don't think I do."

Clavain stepped through the airlock just before it sphinctered shut. Voi had already buckled herself in; she had a glazed look now, as if staring into infinity. Clavain guessed she was uploading a copy of the treaty through her implants, scrolling it across her visual field, trying to find the loophole; probably running a global search for any references to police actions.

The ship recognized Clavain, its interior shivering to his preferences. The green was closer to turquoise now; the readouts and controls minimalist in layout, displaying only the most mission-critical systems. Though the shuttle was the tiniest peacetime vessel Clavain had been in, it was a cathedral compared to the dropships he had flown during the war; so small that they were assembled around their occupants like Medieval armor before a joust.

"Don't worry about the treaty," Clavain said. "I promise you Warren won't get his chance to apply that loophole."

Voi snapped out of her trance irritatedly. "You'd better be right, Nevil. Is it me, or is your brother hoping we fail?" She was speaking Quebecois French now; Clavain shifting mental gears to follow her. "If my people discover that there's a hidden agenda here, there'll be hell to pay."

"The Conjoiners gave Warren plenty of reasons to hate them after the battle of the Bulge," Clavain said. "And he's a tactician, not a field specialist. After the cease-fire my knowledge of worms was even more valuable than before, so I had a role. But Warren's skills were a lot less transferable."

"So that gives him a right to edge us closer to another war?" The way Voi spoke, it was as if her own side had not been neutral in the last exchange. But Clavain knew she was right. If hostilities between the Conjoiners and the Coalition reignited, the Demarchy would not be able to stand aside as they had fifteen years ago. And it was anyone's guess how they would align themselves.

"There won't be war."

"And if you can't reason with Galiana? Or are you going to play on your personal connection?"

"I was just her prisoner, that's all." Clavain took the controls—Voi said piloting was a bore—and unlatched the shuttle from Deimos. They dropped away at a tangent to the rotation of the equatorial ring which girdled the moon, instantly in freefall. Clavain sketched a porthole in the wall with his fingertip, outlining a rectangle which instantly became transparent.

For a moment he saw his reflection in the glass: older than he felt he had any right to look, the gray beard and hair making him look ancient rather than patriarchal; a man deeply wearied by recent circumstance. With some relief he darkened the cabin so that he could see Deimos, dwindling at surprising speed. The higher of the two Martian moons was a dark, bristling lump, infested with armaments, belted by the bright, window-studded band of the moving ring. For the last nine years, Deimos was all that he had known, but now he could encompass it within the arc of his fist.

"Not just her prisoner," Voi said. "No one else came back sane from the Conjoiners. She never even tried to infect you with her machines."

"No, she didn't. But only because the timing was on my side." Clavain was reciting an old argument now; as much for his own benefit as Voi's. "I was the only prisoner she had. She was losing the war by then; one more recruit to her side wouldn't have made any real difference. The terms of cease-fire were being thrashed out and she knew she could buy herself favors by releasing me unharmed. There was something else, too. Conjoiners weren't supposed to be capable of anything so primitive as mercy. They were spiders, as far as we were concerned. Galiana's act threw a wrench into our thinking. It divided alliances within the high command. If she hadn't released me, they might well have nuked her out of existence."

"So there was absolutely nothing personal?"

"No," Clavain said. "There was nothing personal about it at all."

Voi nodded, without in any way suggesting that she actually believed him. It was a skill some women had honed to perfection, Clavain thought.

Of course, he respected Voi completely. She had been one of the first human beings to enter Europa's ocean, decades back. Now they were planning fabulous cities under the ice; efforts which she had spearheaded. Demarchist society was supposedly flat in structure, non-hierarchical; but someone of Voi's brilliance ascended through echelons of her own making. She had been instrumental in brokering the peace between the Conjoiners and Clavain's own Coalition. That was why she was coming along now: Galiana had only agreed to Clavain's mission provided he was accompanied by a neutral observer, and Voi had been the obvious choice. Respect was easy. Trust, however, was harder: it required that Clavain ignore the fact that, with her head dotted with implants, the Demarchist woman's condition was not very far removed from that of the enemy.

The descent to Mars was hard and steep.

Once or twice they were queried by the automated tracking systems of the satellite interdiction network. Dark weapons hovering in Mars-synchronous orbit above the nest locked onto the ship for a few instants, magnetic railguns powering up, before the shuttle's diplomatic nature was established and it was allowed to proceed. The Interdiction was very efficient; as well it might be, given that Clavain had designed much of it himself. In fifteen years no ship had entered or left the Martian atmosphere, nor had any surface vehicle ever escaped from Galiana's nest.

"There she is," Clavain said, as the Great Wall rose over the horizon.

"Why do you call 'it' a 'she'?" Voi asked. "I never felt the urge to personalize it, and I designed it. Besides . . . even if it was alive once, it's dead now."

She was right, but the Wall was still awesome to behold. Seen from orbit, it was a pale, circular ring on the surface of Mars, two thousand kilometers wide. Like a coral atoll, it entrapped its own weather system; a disk of bluer air, flecked with creamy white clouds which stopped abruptly at the boundary.

Once, hundreds of communities had sheltered inside that cell of warm, thick, oxygen-rich atmosphere. The Wall was the most audacious and visible of Voi's projects. The logic had been inescapable: a means to avoid the millennia-long timescales needed to terraform Mars via such conventional schemes as cometary bombardment or ice-cap thawing. Instead of modifying the whole atmosphere at once, the Wall allowed the initial effort to be concentrated in a relatively small region, at first only a thousand kilometers across. There were no craters deep enough, so the Wall had been completely artificial: a vast ring-shaped atmospheric dam designed to move slowly outward, encompassing ever more surface area at a rate of a twenty kilometers per year. The Wall needed to be very tall because the low Martian gravity meant that the column of atmosphere was higher for a fixed surface pressure than on Earth. The ramparts were hundreds of meters thick, dark as glacial ice, sinking great taproots deep into the lithosphere to harvest the ores needed for the Wall's continual growth. Yet two hundred kilometers higher the wall was a diaphanously thin membrane only microns wide; completely invisible except when rare optical effects made it hang like a frozen aurora against the stars. Eco-engineers had invaded the Wall's liveable area with terran genestocks deftly altered in orbital labs. Flora and fauna had moved out in vivacious waves, lapping eagerly against the constraints of the Wall.

But the Wall was dead.

It had stopped growing during the war, hit by some sort of viral weapon which crippled its replicating subsystems, and now even the ecosystem within it was failing; the atmosphere cooling, oxygen bleeding into space, pressure declining inevitably toward the Martian norm of one seven-thousandth of an atmosphere.

He wondered how it must look to Voi; whether in any sense she saw it as her murdered child.

"I'm sorry that we had to kill it," Clavain said. He was about to add that it been the kind of act which war normalized, but decided that the statement would have sounded hopelessly defensive.

"You needn't apologize," Voi said. "It was only machinery. I'm surprised it's lasted as long as it has, frankly. There must still be some residual damage-repair capability. We Demarchists build for posterity, you know."

Yes, and it worried his own side. There was talk of challenging the Demarchist supremacy in the outer solar system; perhaps even an attempt to gain a Coalition foothold around Jupiter.

They skimmed the top of the Wall and punched through the thickening layers of atmosphere within it, the shuttle's hull morphing to an arrowhead shape. The ground had an arid, bleached look to it, dotted here and there by ruined shacks, broken domes, gutted vehicles or shot-down shuttles. There were patches of shallow-rooted, mainly dark-red tundra vegetation; cotton grass, saxifrage, arctic poppies and lichen. Clavain knew each species by its distinct infrared signature, but many of the plants were in recession now that the imported bird species had died. Ice lay in great silver swathes, and what few expanses of open water remained were warmed by buried thermopiles. Elsewhere there were whole zones which had reverted to almost sterile permafrost. It could have been a kind of paradise, Clavain thought, if the war had not ruined everything. Yet what had happened here could only be a foretaste of the devastation that would follow across the system, on Earth as well as Mars, if another war was allowed to happen.

"Do you see the nest yet?" Voi asked.

"Wait a second," Clavain said, requesting a head-up display which boxed the nest. "That's it. A nice fat thermal signature too. Nothing else for miles around—nothing inhabited, anyway."

"Yes. I see it now."

The Conjoiner nest lay a third of the way from the Wall's edge, not far from the footslopes of Arsia Mons. The entire encampment was only a kilometer across, circled by a dike which was piled high with regolith dust on one side. The area within the Great Wall was large enough to have an appreciable weather system: spanning enough Martian latitude for significant coriolis effects; enough longitude for diurnal warming and cooling to cause thermal currents.

He could see the nest much more clearly now; details leaping out of the haze.

Its external layout was crushingly familiar. Clavain's side had been studying the nest from the vantage point of Deimos ever since the cease-fire. Phobos, with its lower orbit, would have been even better, of course—but there was no helping that, and perhaps the Phobos problem might actually prove useful in his negotiations with Galiana. She was somewhere in the nest, he knew: somewhere beneath the twenty varyingly sized domes emplaced within the rim, linked together by pressurized tunnels or merged at their boundaries like soap bubbles. The nest extended several tens of levels beneath the Martian surface, maybe deeper.

"How many people do you think are inside?" Voi said.

"Nine hundred or so," said Clavain. "That's an estimate based on my experiences as a prisoner, and the hundred or so who've died trying to escape since. The rest, I have to say, is pretty much guesswork."

"Our estimates aren't dissimilar. A thousand or less here, and perhaps another three or four spread across the system in smaller nests. I know your side thinks we have better intelligence than that, but it happens not to be the case."

"Actually, I believe you." The shuttle's airframe was flexing around them, morphing to a low-altitude profile with wide, batlike wings.

"I was just hoping you might have some clue as to why Galiana keeps wasting valuable lives with escape attempts."

Voi shrugged. "Maybe to her the lives aren't anywhere near as valuable as you'd like to think."

"Do you honestly think that?"

"I don't think we can begin to guess the thinking of a true hive-mind society, Clavain. Even from a Demarchist standpoint."

There was a chirp from the console; Galiana signaling them. Clavain opened the channel allocated for Coalition-Conjoiner diplomacy.

"Nevil Clavain?" he heard.

"Yes." He tried to sound as calm as possible. "I'm with Sandra Voi. We're ready to land as soon as you show us where."

"Okay," Galiana said. "Vector your ship toward the westerly rim wall. And please, be careful."

"Thank you. Any particular reason for the caution?"

"Just be quick about it, Nevil."

They banked over the nest, shedding height until they were skimming only a few tens of meters above the weatherworn Martian surface. A wide rectangular door had opened in the concrete dike, revealing a hangar bay aglow with yellow lights.

"That must be where Galiana launches her shuttles from," Clavain whispered. "We always thought there must be some kind of opening on the west side of the rim, but we never had a good view of it before."

"Which still doesn't tell us why she does it," Voi said.

The console chirped again—the link poor even though they were so close. "Nose up," Galiana said. "You're too low and slow. Get some altitude or the worms will lock onto you."

"You're telling me there are worms here?" Clavain said.

"I thought you were the worm expert, Nevil."

He nosed the shuttle up, but fractionally too late. Ahead of them something coiled out of the ground with lightning speed, metallic jaws opening in its blunt, armored head. He recognized the type immediately: Ouroborus class. Worms of this form still infested a hundred niches across the system. Not quite as smart as the type infesting Phobos, but still adequately dangerous.

"Shit," Voi said, her veneer of Demarchist cool cracking for an instant.

"You said it," Clavain answered.

The Ouroborus passed underneath and then there was a spine-jarring series of bumps as the jaws tore into the shuttle's belly. Clavain felt the shuttle lurch down sickeningly; no longer a flying thing but an exercise in ballistics. The cool, minimalist turquoise interior shifted liquidly into an emergency configuration; damage readouts competing for attention with weapons status options. Their seats ballooned around them.

"Hold on," he said. "We're going down."

Voi's calm returned. "Do you think we can reach the rim in time?"

"Not a cat in hell's chance." He wrestled with the controls all the same, but it was no good. The ground was coming up fast and hard. "I wish Galiana had warned us a bit sooner . . ."

"I think she thought we already knew."

They hit. It was harder than Clavain had been expecting, but the shuttle stayed in one piece and the seat cushioned him from the worst of the impact. They skidded for a few meters and then nosed up against a sandbank. Through the window Clavain saw the white worm racing toward them with undulating waves of its segmented robot body.

"I think we're finished," Voi said.

"Not quite," Clavain said. "You're not going to like this, but . . ." Biting his tongue he brought the shuttle's hidden weapons online. An aiming scope plunged down from the ceiling; he brought his eyes to it and locked crosshairs onto the Ouroborus. Just like old times . . .

"Damn you," Voi said. "This was meant to be an unarmed mission!"

"You're welcome to lodge a formal complaint."

Clavain fired, the hull shaking from the recoil. Through the side window they watched the white worm blow apart into stubby segments. The parts wriggled beneath the dust.

"Good shooting," Voi said, almost grudgingly. "Is it dead?"

"For now," Clavain said. "It'll take several hours for the segments to fuse back into a functional worm."

"Good," Voi said, pushing herself out of her seat. "But there will be a formal complaint, take my word."

"Maybe you'd rather the worm ate us?"

"I just hate duplicity, Clavain."

He tried the radio again. "Galiana? We're down—the ship's history—but we're both unharmed."

"Thank God." Old verbal mannerisms died hard, even among the Conjoined. "But you can't stay where you are. There are more worms in the area. Do you think you can make it overland to the nest?"

"It's only two hundred meters," Voi said. "It shouldn't be a problem."

Two hundred meters, yes—but two hundred meters across treacherous, potholed ground riddled with enough soft depressions to hide a dozen worms. And then they would have to climb up the rim's side to reach the entrance to the hangar bay; ten or fifteen meters above the soil.

"Let's hope it isn't," Clavain said.

He unbuckled, feeling light-headed as he stood for the first time in Martian gravity. He had adapted entirely too well to the one-gee of the Deimos ring, constructed for the comfort of Earthside tacticians. He went to the emergency locker and found a mask which slivered eagerly across his face; another for Voi. They plugged in air-tanks and went to the shuttle's door. This time when it sphinctered open there was a glistening membrane stretched across the doorway, a recently licensed item of Demarchist technology. Clavain pushed through the membrane and the stuff enveloped him with a wet, sucking sound. By the time he hit the dirt the membrane had hardened itself around his soles and had begun to contour itself with ribs and accordioned joints, even though it stayed transparent.

Voi came behind him, gaining her own m-suit.

They loped away from the crashed shuttle, toward the dike. The worms would be locking onto their seismic patterns already, if there were any nearby. They might be more interested in the shuttle for now, but that was nothing they could count on. Clavain knew the behavior of worms intimately, knew the major routines which drove them; but that expertise did not guarantee his survival. It had almost failed him in Phobos.

The mask felt clammy against his face. The air at the base of the Great Wall was technically breathable even now, but there seemed no point in taking chances when speed was of the essence. His feet scuffed through the topsoil, and while he seemed to be crossing ground, the dike obstinately refused to come any closer. It was larger than it looked from the crash; the distance farther.

"Another worm," Voi said.

White coils erupted through sand to the west. The Ouroborus was making undulating progress toward them, zig-zagging with predatory calm, knowing that it could afford to take its time. In the tunnels of Phobos, they had never had the luxury of knowing when a worm was close. They struck from ambush, quick as pythons.

"Run," Clavain said.

Dark figures appeared in the opening high in the rimwall. A rope-ladder unfurled down the side of the structure. Clavain, making for the base of it, made no effort to quieten his footfalls. He knew that the worm almost certainly had a lock on him by now.

He looked back.

The worm paused by the downed shuttle, then smashed its diamond-jawed head into the ship, impaling the hull on its body. The worm reared up, wearing the ship like a garland. Then it shivered and the ship flew apart like a rotten carcass. The worm returned its attention to Clavain and Voi. Like a sidewinder it pulled its thirty-meter long body from the sand and rolled toward them on wheeling coils.

Clavain reached the base of the ladder.

Once, he could have ascended the ladder with his arms alone, in one-gee, but now the ladder felt alive beneath his feet. He began to climb, then realized that the ground was dropping away much faster than he was passing rungs. The Conjoiners were hauling him aloft.

He looked back in time to see Voi stumble.

"Sandra! *No!*"

She made to stand up, but it was too late by then. As the worm descended on her, Clavain could do nothing but turn his gaze away and pray for her death to be quick. If it had to be meaningless, he thought, at least let it be swift.

Then he started thinking about his own survival. "Faster!" he shouted, but the mask reduced his voice to a panicked muffle. He had forgotten to assign the ship's radio frequency to the suit.

The worm thrashed against the base of the wall, then began to rear up, its maw opening beneath him; a diamond-ringed orifice like the drill of a tunnelling machine. Then something eye-hurtingly bright cut into the worm's hide. Craning his neck, Clavain saw a group of Conjoiners kneeling over the lip of the opening, aiming guns downward. The worm writhed in intense robotic irritation. Across the sand, he could see the coils of other worms coming closer. There must have been dozens ringing the nest. No wonder Galiana's people had made so few attempts to leave by land.

They had hauled him within ten meters of safety. The injured worm showed cybernetic workings where its hide had been flensed away by weapons impacts. Enraged, it flung itself against the rim wall, chipping off scabs of concrete the size of boulders. Clavain felt the vibration of each impact through the wall as he was dragged upward.

The worm hit again and the wall shook more violently than before. To his horror, Clavain watched one of the Conjoiners lose his footing and tumble over the edge of the rim toward him. Time oozed to a crawl. The falling man was almost upon him. Without thinking, Clavain hugged closer to the wall, locking his limbs around the ladder. Suddenly, he had seized the man by the arm. Even in Martian gravity, even allowing for the Conjoiner's willowy build, the impact almost sent both of them toward the Ouroborus. Clavain felt his bones pop out of location, tearing at gristle, but he managed to keep his grip on both the Conjoiner and the ladder.

Conjoiners breathed the air at the base of the Wall without difficulty. The man wore only lightweight clothes, gray silk pajamas belted at the waist. With his sunken cheeks and bald skull, the man's Martian physique lent him a cadaverous look. Yet somehow he had managed not to drop his gun, still holding it in his other hand.

"Let me go," the man said.

Below, the worm inched higher despite the harm the Conjoiners had inflicted on it. "No," Clavain said, through clenched teeth and the distorting membrane of his mask. "I'm not letting you go."

"You've no option." The man's voice was placid. "They can't haul both of us up fast enough, Clavain."

Clavain looked into the Conjoiner's face, trying to judge the man's age. Thirty, perhaps—maybe not even that, since the cadaverous look probably made him seem older than he really was. Clavain was easily twice his age; had surely lived a richer life; had comfortably cheated death on three or four previous occasions.

"I'm the one who should die, not you."

"No," the Conjoiner said. "They'd find a way to blame your death on us. They'd make it a pretext for war." Without any fuss the man pointed the gun at his own head and blew his brains out.

As much in shock as recognition that the man's life was no longer his to save, Clavain released his grip. The dead man tumbled down the rim wall, into the mouth of the worm which had just killed Sandra Voi.

Numb, Clavain allowed himself to be pulled to safety.

When the armored door to the hangar was shut the conjoiners attacked his m-suit with enzymic sprays. The sprays digested the fabric in seconds, leaving Clavain wheezing in a pool of slime. Then a pair of Conjoiners helped him unsteadily to his feet and waited patiently while he caught his breath from the mask. Through tears of exhaustion he saw that the hangar was racked full of half-assembled spacecraft; skeletal geodesic shark-shapes designed to punch out of an atmosphere, fast.

"Sandra Voi is dead," he said, removing the mask to speak.

There was no way the Conjoiners could not have seen this for themselves, but it seemed inhuman not to acknowledge what had happened.

"I know," Galiana said. "But at least you survived."

He thought of the man falling into the Ouroborus. "I'm sorry about your . . ."

But then trailed off, because for all his depth of knowledge concerning the Conjoiners, he had no idea what the appropriate term was.

"You placed your life in danger in trying to save him."

"He didn't have to die."

Galiana nodded sagely. "No; in all likelihood he didn't. But the risk to yourself was too great. You heard what he said. Your death would be made to seem our fault; justification for a pre-emptive strike against our nest. Even the Demarchists would turn against us if we were seen to murder a diplomat."

Taking another suck from the mask, he looked into her face. He had spoken to her over low-bandwidth video-links, but only in person was it obvious that Galiana had hardly aged in fifteen years. A decade and a half of habitual expression should have engraved existing lines deeper into her face—but Conjoiners were not known for their habits of expression. Galiana had seen little sunlight in the intervening time, cooped here in the nest, and Martian gravity was much kinder to bone structure than the one-gee of Deimos. She still had the cruel beauty he remembered from his time as a prisoner. The only real evidence of aging lay in the filaments of gray threading her hair; raven-black when she had been his captor.

"Why didn't you warn us about the worms?"

"Warn you?" For the first time something like doubt crossed her face, but it was only fleeting. "We assumed you were fully aware of the Ouroborus infestation. Those worms have been dormant—waiting—for years, but they've always been there. It was only when I saw how low your approach was that I realized . . ."

"That we might not have known?"

Worms were area-denial devices; autonomous prey-seeking mines. The war had left many pockets of the solar system still riddled with active worms. The machines were intelligent, in a one-dimensional way. Nobody ever admitted to deploying them and it was usually impossible to convince them that the war was over and that they should quietly deactivate.

"After what happened to you in Phobos," Galiana said, "I assumed there was nothing you needed to be taught about worms."

He never liked thinking about Phobos: the pain was still too deeply engraved. But if it had not been for the injuries he had sustained there he would never have been sent to Deimos to recuperate; would never have been recruited into his brother's intelligence wing to study the Conjoiners. Out of that phase of deep immersion in everything concerning the enemy had come his peacetime role as negotiator—and now diplomat—on the eve of another war. Everything was circular, ultimately. And now Phobos was central to his thinking because he saw it as a way out of the impasse—maybe the last chance for peace. But it was too soon to put his idea to Galiana. He was not even sure the mission could still continue, after what had happened.

"We're safe now, I take it?"

"Yes; we can repair the damage to the dike. Mostly, we can ignore their presence."

"We should have been warned. Look, I need to talk to my brother."

"Warren? Of course. It's easily arranged."

They walked out of the hangar; away from the half-assembled ships. Somewhere deeper in the nest, Clavain knew, was a factory where the components for the ships were made, mined out of Mars or winnowed from the fabric of the nest. The Conjoiners managed to launch one every six weeks or so; had been doing so for six months. Not one of the ships had ever managed to escape the Martian atmosphere before being shot down . . . but sooner or later he would have to ask Galiana why she persisted with this provocative folly.

Now, though, was not the time—even if, by Warren's estimate, he only had three days before Galiana's next provocation.

The air elsewhere in the nest was thicker and warmer than in the hangar, which meant he could dispense with the mask. Galiana took him down a short, gray-walled, metallic corridor which ended in a circular room containing a console. He recognized the room from the times he had spoken to Galiana from Deimos. Galiana showed him how to use the system then left him in privacy while he established a connection with Deimos.

Warren's face soon appeared on a screen, thick with pixels like an impressionist portrait. Conjoiners were only allowed to send kilobytes a second to other parts of the system. Much of that bandwidth was now being sucked up by this one video link.

"You've heard, I take it," Clavain said.

Warren nodded, his face ashen. "We had a pretty good view from orbit, of course. Enough to see that Voi didn't make it. Poor woman. We were reasonably sure you survived, but it's good to have it confirmed."

"Do you want me to abandon the mission?"

Warren's hesitation was more than just time-lag. "No . . . I thought about it, of course, and high command agrees with me. Voi's death was tragic—no escaping that. But she was only along as a neutral observer. If Galiana consents for you to stay, I suggest you do so."

"But you still say I only have three days?"

"That's up to Galiana, isn't it? Have you learned much?"

"You must be kidding. I've seen shuttles ready for launch, that's all. I haven't raised the Phobos proposal, either. The timing wasn't exactly ideal, after what happened to Voi."

"Yes. If only we'd known about that Ouroborus infestation."

Clavain leaned closer to the screen. "Yes. Why the hell didn't we? Galiana assumed that we would, and I don't blame her for that. We've had the nest under constant surveillance for fifteen years. Surely in all that time we'd have seen evidence of the worms?"

"You'd have thought so, wouldn't you?"

"Meaning what?"

"Meaning, maybe the worms weren't always there."

Conscious that there could be nothing private about this conversation—but unwilling to drop the thread—Clavain said: "You think the Conjoiners put them there to ambush us?"

"I'm saying we shouldn't disregard any possibility, no matter how unpalatable."

"Galiana would never do something like that."

"No, I wouldn't." She had just stepped back into the room. "And I'm disappointed that you'd even debate the possibility."

Clavain terminated the link with Deimos. "Eavesdropping's not a very nice habit, you know."

"What did you expect me to do?"

"Show some trust? Or is that too much of a stretch?"

"I never had to trust you when you were my prisoner," Galiana said. "That made our relationship infinitely simpler. Our roles were completely defined."

"And now? If you distrust me so completely, why did you ever agree to my visit? Plenty of other specialists could have come in my place. You could even have refused any dialogue."

"Voi's people pressured us to allow your visit," Galiana said. "Just as they pressured your side into delaying hostilities a little longer."

"Is that all?"

She hesitated slightly now. "I . . . knew you."

"Knew me? Is that how you sum up a year of imprisonment? What about the thousands of conversations we had; the times when we put aside our differences to talk about something other than the damned war? You kept me sane, Galiana. I've never forgotten that. It's why I've risked my life to come here and talk you out of another provocation."

"It's completely different now."

"Of course!" He forced himself not to shout. "Of course it's different. But not fundamentally. We can still build on that bond of trust and find a way out of this crisis."

"But does your side really want a way out of it?"

He did not answer her immediately; wary of what the truth might mean. "I'm not sure. But I'm also not sure you do, or else you wouldn't keep pushing your luck." Something snapped inside him and he asked the question he had meant to ask in a million better ways. "Why do you keep doing it, Galiana? Why do you keep launching those ships when you know they'll be shot down as soon as they leave the nest?"

Her eyes locked onto his own, unflinchingly. "Because we can. Because sooner or later one will succeed."

Clavain nodded. It was exactly the sort of thing he had feared she would say.

She led him through more gray-walled corridors, descending several levels deeper into the nest. Light poured from snaking strips embedded into the walls like arteries. It was possible that the snaking design was decorative, but Clavain thought it much more likely that the strips had simply grown that way, expressing biological algorithms. There was no evidence that the Conjoiners had attempted to enliven their surroundings; to render them in any sense human.

"It's a terrible risk you're running," Clavain said.

"And the status quo is intolerable. I've every desire to avoid another war, but if it came to one, we'd at least have the chance to break these shackles."

"If you didn't get exterminated first . . ."

"We'd avoid that. In any case, fear plays no part in our thinking. You saw the man accept his fate on the dyke, when he understood that your death would harm us more than his own. He altered his state of mind to one of total acceptance."

"Fine. That makes it all right, then."

She halted. They were alone in one of the snakingly lit corridors; he had seen no other Conjoiners since the hangar. "It's not that we regard individual lives as worthless, any more than you would willingly sacrifice a limb. But now that we're part of something larger . . ."

"Transenlightenment, you mean?"

It was the Conjoiners' term for the state of neural communion they shared, mediated by the machines swarming in their skulls. Whereas Demarchists used implants to facilitate real-time democracy, Conjoiners used them to share sensory data, memories—even conscious thought itself. That was what had precipitated the war. Back in 2190 half of humanity had been hooked into the system-wide data nets via neural implants. Then the Conjoiner experiments had exceeded some threshold, unleashing a transforming virus into the nets. Implants had begun to change, infecting millions of minds with the templates of Conjoiner thought. Instantly the infected had become the enemy. Earth and the other inner planets had always been more conservative, preferring to access the nets via traditional media.

Once they saw communities on Mars and in the asteroid belts fall prey to the Conjoiner phenomenon, the Coalition powers hurriedly pooled their resources to prevent the spread reaching their own states. The Demarchists, out around the gas giants, had managed to get firewalls up before many of their habitats were lost. They had chosen neutrality while the Coalition tried to contain—some said sterilize—zones of Conjoiner takeover. Within three years—after some of the bloodiest battles in human experience—the Conjoiners had been pushed back to a clutch of hide-aways dotted around the system. Yet all along they professed a kind of puzzled bemusement that their spread was being resisted. After all, no one who had been assimilated seemed to regret it. Quite the contrary. The few prisoners whom the Conjoiners had reluctantly returned to their pre-infection state had sought every means to return to the fold. Some had even chosen suicide rather than be denied Transenlightenment. Like acolytes given a vision of heaven, they devoted their entire waking existence to the search for another glimpse.

"Transenlightenment blurs our sense of self," Galiana said. "When the man elected to die, the sacrifice was not absolute for him. He understood that much of what he was had already achieved preservation among the rest of us."

"But he was just one man. What about the hundred lives you've thrown away with your escape attempts? We know—we've counted the bodies."

"Replacements can always be cloned."

Clavain hoped that he hid his disgust satisfactorily. Among his people the very notion of cloning was an unspeakable atrocity; redolent with horror. To Galiana it would be just another technique in her arsenal. "But you don't clone, do you? And you're losing people. We thought there would be nine hundred of you in this nest, but that was a gross overestimate, wasn't it?"

"You haven't seen much yet," Galiana said.

"No, but this place smells deserted. You can't hide absence, Galiana. I bet there aren't more than a hundred of you left here."

"You're wrong," Galiana said. "We have cloning technology, but we've hardly ever used it. What would be the point? We don't aspire to genetic unity, no matter what your propagandists think. The pursuit of optima leads only to local minima. We honor our errors. We actively seek persistent disequilibrium."

"Right." The last thing he needed now was a dose of Conjoiner rhetoric. "So where the hell is everyone?"

In a while he had part of the answer, if not the whole of it. At the end of the maze of corridors—far under Mars now—Galiana brought him to a nursery.

It was shockingly unlike his expectations. Not only did it not match what he had imagined from the vantage point of Deimos, but it jarred against his predictions based on what he had seen so far of the nest. In Deimos, he had assumed a Conjoiner nursery would be a place of grim medical efficiency; all gleaming machines with babies plugged in like peripherals, like a monstrously productive doll factory. Within the nest, he had revised his model to allow for the depleted numbers of Conjoiners. If there was a nursery, it was obviously not very productive. Fewer babies, then—but still a vision of hulking gray machines, bathed in snaking light.

The nursery was nothing like that.

The huge room Galiana showed him was almost painfully bright and cheerful; a child's fantasy of friendly shapes and primary colors. The walls and ceiling projected a holographic sky: infinite blue and billowing clouds of heavenly white. The floor was an undulating mat of synthetic grass forming hillocks and meadows. There were banks of flowers and forests of bonsai trees. There were robot animals: fabulous birds and rabbits just slightly too anthropomorphic to fool Clavain. They were like the animals in children's books; big-eyed and happy-looking. Toys were scattered on the grass.

And there were children. They numbered between forty and fifty; spanning by his estimate ages from a few months to six or seven standard years. Some were crawling among the rabbits; other, older children were gathered around tree stumps whose sheered-off surfaces flickered rapidly with images, underlighting their faces. They were talking among themselves, giggling or singing. He counted perhaps half a dozen adult Conjoiners kneeling among the children. The children's clothes were a headache of bright, clashing colors and patterns. The Conjoiners crouched among them like ravens. Yet the children seemed at ease with them, listening attentively when the adults had something to say.

"This isn't what you thought it would be like, is it?"

"No . . . not at all." There seemed no point lying to her. "We thought you'd raise your young in a simplified version of the machine-generated environment you experience."

"In the early days that's more or less what we did." Subtly, Galiana's tone of voice had changed. "Do you know why chimpanzees are less intelligent than humans?"

He blinked at the change of tack. "I don't know—are their brains smaller?"

"Yes—but a dolphin's brain is larger, and they're scarcely more intelligent than dogs." Galiana stooped next to a vacant tree stump. Without seeming to do anything, she made a diagram of mammal brain anatomies appear on the trunk's upper surface, then sketched her finger across the relevant parts. "It's not overall brain volume that counts so much as the developmental history. The difference in brain volume between a neonatal chimp and an adult is only about twenty percent. By the time the chimp receives any data from beyond the womb, there's almost no plasticity left to use. Similarly, dolphins are born with almost their complete repertoire of adult behavior already hardwired. A human brain, on the other hand, keeps growing through years of learning. We inverted that thinking. If data received during post-natal growth was so crucial to intelligence, perhaps we could boost our intelligence even further by intervening during the earliest phases of brain development."

"In the womb?"

"Yes." Now she made the tree-trunk show a human embryo running through cycles of cell-division, until the faint fold of a rudimentary spinal nerve began to form, nubbed with the tiniest of emergent minds. Droves of subcellular machines swarmed in, invading the nascent nervous system. Then the embryo's development slammed forward, until Clavain was looking at an unborn human baby.

"What happened?"

"It was a grave error," Galiana said. "Instead of enhancing normal neural development, we impaired it terribly. All we ended up with were various manifestations of savant syndrome."

Clavain looked around him. "Then you let these kids develop normally?"

"More or less. There's no family structure, of course, but then again there are plenty of human and primate societies where the family is less important in child development than the cohort group. So far we haven't seen any pathologies."

Clavain watched as one of the older children was escorted out of the grassy room, through a door in the sky. When the Conjoiner reached the door the child hesitated, tugging against the man's gentle insistence. The child looked back for a moment, then followed the man through the gap.

"Where's that child going?"

"To the next stage of its development."

Clavain wondered what were the chances of him seeing the nursery just as one of the children was being promoted. Small, he judged—unless there was a crash program to rush as many of them through as quickly as possible. As he thought about this, Galiana took him into another part of the nursery. While this room was smaller and dourer it was still more colorful than any other part of the nest he had seen before the grassy room. The walls were a mosaic of crowded, intermingling displays, teeming with moving images and rapidly scrolling text. He saw a herd of zebra stampeding through the core of a neutron star. Elsewhere an octopus squirted ink at the face of a twentieth-century despot. Other display facets rose from the floor like Japanese paper screens, flooded with data. Children—up to early teenagers—sat on soft black toadstools next to the screens in little groups, debating. A few musical instruments lay around unused: holoclaviers and air-guitars. Some of the children had gray bands around their eyes and were poking their fingers through the interstices of abstract structures, exploring the dragon-infested waters of mathematical space. Clavain could see what they were manipulating on the flat screens: shapes that made his head hurt even in two dimensions.

"They're nearly there," Clavain said. "The machines are outside their heads, but not for long. When does it happen?"

"Soon; very soon."

"You're rushing them, aren't you? Trying to get as many children Conjoined as you can. What are you planning?"

"Something . . . has arisen, that's all. The timing of your arrival is either very bad or very fortunate, depending on your point of view." Before he could query her, Galiana added: "Clavain; I want you to meet someone."

"Who?"

"Someone very precious to us."

She took him through a series of child-proof doors until they reached a small circular room. The walls and ceiling were veined gray; tranquil after what he had seen in the last place. A child sat cross-legged on the floor in the middle of the room. Clavain estimated the girl's age as ten standard years—perhaps fractionally older. But she did not respond to Clavain's presence in any way an adult, or even a normal child, would have. She just kept on doing the thing she had been doing when they stepped inside, as if they were not really present at all. It was not at all clear what she was doing. Her hands moved before her in slow, precise gestures. It was as if she were playing a holoclavier or working a phantom puppet show. Now and then she would pivot around until she was facing another direction and carry on doing the hand movements.

"Her name's Felka," Galiana said.

"Hello, Felka . . ." He waited for a response, but none came. "I can see there's something wrong with her."

"She was one of the savants. Felka developed with machines in her head. She was the last to be born before we realized our failure."

Something about Felka disturbed him. Perhaps it was the way she carried on regardless, engrossed in an activity to which she seemed to attribute the utmost significance, yet which had to be without any sane purpose.

"She doesn't seem aware of us."

"Her deficits are severe," Galiana said. "She has no interest in other human beings. She has prosopagnosia; the inability to distinguish faces. We all seem alike to her. Can you imagine something more strange than that?"

He tried, and failed. Life from Felka's viewpoint must have been a nightmarish thing, surrounded by identical clones whose inner lives she could not begin to grasp. No wonder she seemed so engrossed in her game.

"Why is she so precious to you?" Clavain asked, not really wanting to know the answer.

"She's keeping us alive," Galiana said.

Of course, he asked Galiana what she meant by that. Galiana's only response was to tell him that he was not yet ready to be shown the answer.

"And what exactly would it take for me to reach that stage?"

"A simple procedure."

Oh yes, he understood that part well enough. Just a few machines in the right parts of his brain and the truth could be his. Politely, doing his best to mask his distaste, Clavain declined. Fortunately, Galiana did not press the point, for the time had arrived for the meeting he had been promised before his arrival on Mars.

He watched a subset of the nest file into the conference room. Galiana was their leader only inasmuch as she had founded the lab here from which the original experiment had sprung and was accorded some respect deriving from seniority. She was also the most obvious spokesperson among them. They all had areas of expertise which could not be easily shared among other Conjoined; very distinct from the hive-mind of identical clones which still figured in the Coalition's propaganda. If the nest was in any way like an ant colony, then it was an ant colony in which every ant fulfilled a distinct role from all the others. Naturally, no individual could be solely entrusted with a particular skill essential to the nest—that would be have been dangerous over-specialization—but neither had individuality been completely subsumed into the group mind.

The conference room must have dated back to the days when the nest was a research outpost, or even earlier, when it was some kind of mining base in the early 2100s. It was much too big for the dour handful of Conjoiners who stood around the main table. Tactical readouts around the table showed the build-up of strike forces above the Martian exclusion zone; probable drop trajectories for ground-force deployment.

"Nevil Clavain," Galiana said, introducing him to the others. Everyone sat down. "I'm just sorry that Sandra Voi can't be with us now. We all feel the tragedy of her death. But perhaps out of this terrible event we can find some common ground. Nevil; before you came here you told us you had a proposal for a peaceful resolution to the crisis."

"I'd really like to hear it," one of the others murmured audibly.

Clavain's throat was dry. Diplomatically, this was quicksand. "My proposal concerns Phobos . . ."

"Go on."

"I was injured there," he said. "Very badly. Our attempt to clean out the worm infestation failed and I lost some good friends. That makes it personal between me and the worms. But I'd accept anyone's help to finish them off."

Galiana glanced quickly at her compatriots before answering. "A joint assault operation?"

"It could work."

"Yes . . ." Galiana seemed lost momentarily. "I suppose it could be a way out of the impasse. Our own attempt failed too—and the interdiction's stopped us from trying again." Again, she seemed to fall into reverie. "But who would really benefit from the flushing out of Phobos? We'd still be quarantined here."

Clavain leaned forward. "A cooperative gesture might be exactly the thing to lead to a relaxation in the terms of the interdiction. But don't think of it in those terms. Think instead of reducing the current threat from the worms."

"Threat?"

Clavain nodded. "It's possible that you haven't noticed." He leaned forward, elbows on the table. "We're concerned about the Phobos worms. They've begun altering the moon's orbit. The shift is tiny at the moment, but too large to be anything other than deliberate."

Galiana looked away from him for an instant, as if weighing her options, then said, "We were aware of this, but you weren't to know that."

Gratitude?

He had assumed the worms' activity could not have escaped Galiana. "We've seen odd behavior from other worm infestations across the system; things that begin to look like emergent intelligence. But never anything this purposeful. This infestation must have come from a batch with some subroutines we never even guessed about. Do you have any ideas about what they might be up to?"

Again, there was the briefest of hesitations, as if she was communing with her compatriots for the right response. Then she nodded toward a male Conjoiner sitting opposite her, Clavain guessing that the gesture was entirely for his benefit. His hair was black and curly; his face as smooth and untroubled by expression as Galiana's, with something of the same beautifully symmetrical bone structure.

"This is Remontoire," said Galiana. "He's our specialist on the Phobos situation."

Remontoire nodded politely. "In answer to your question, we currently have no viable theories as to what they're doing, but we do know one thing. They're raising the apocentre of the moon's orbit." Apocentre, Clavain knew, was the Martian equivalent of apogee for an object orbiting Earth: the point of highest altitude in an elliptical orbit. Remontoire continued, his voice as preternaturally calm as a parent reading slowly to a child. "The natural orbit of Phobos is actually inside the Roche limit for a gravitationally bound moon; Phobos is raising a tidal bulge on Mars but, because of friction, the bulge can't quite keep up with Phobos. It's causing Phobos to spiral slowly closer to Mars, by about two meters a century. In a few tens of millions of years, what's left of the moon will crash into Mars."

"You think the worms are elevating the orbit to avoid a cataclysm so far in the future?"

"I don't know," Remontoire said. "I suppose the orbital alterations could also be a by-product of some less meaningful worm activity."

"I agree," Clavain said. "But the danger remains. If the worms can elevate the moon's apocenter—even accidentally—we can assume they also have the means to lower its pericentre. They could drop Phobos on top of your nest. Does that scare you sufficiently that you'd consider cooperation with the Coalition?"

Galiana steepled her fingers before her face; a human gesture of deep concentration which her time as a Conjoiner had not quite eroded. Clavain could almost feel the web of thought looming in the room; ghostly strands of cognition reaching between each Conjoiner at the table, and beyond into the nest proper.

"A winning team, is that your idea?"

"It's got to be better than war," Clavain said. "Hasn't it?"

Galiana might have been about to answer him when her face grew troubled. Clavain saw the wave of discomposure sweep over the others almost simultaneously. Something told him that it was nothing to do with his proposal.

Around the table, half the display facets switched automatically over to another channel. The face that Clavain was looking at was much like his own, except that the face on the screen was missing an eye. It was his brother. Warren was overlaid with the official insignia of the Coalition and a dozen system-wide media cartels.

He was in the middle of a speech. ". . . express my shock," Warren said. "Or, for that matter, my outrage. It's not just that they've murdered a valued colleague and deeply experienced member of my team. They've murdered my brother."

Clavain felt the deepest of chills. "What is this?"

"A live transmission from Deimos," Galiana breathed. "It's going out to all the nets; right out to the trans-Pluto habitats."

"What they did was an act of unspeakable treachery," Warren said. "Nothing less than the premeditated, cold-blooded murder of a peace envoy." And then a video clip sprang up to replace Warren. The image must have been snapped from Deimos or one of the interdiction satellites. It showed Clavain's shuttle, lying in the dust close to the dike. He watched the Ouroborus destroy the shuttle, then saw the image zoom in on himself and Voi, running for sanctuary. The Ouroborus took Voi. But this time there was no ladder lowered down for him. Instead, he saw weapon-beams scythe out from the nest toward him, knocking him to the ground. Horribly wounded, he tried to get up, to crawl a few inches nearer to his tormentors, but the worm was already upon him.

He watched himself get eaten.

Warren was back again. "The worms around the nest were a Conjoiner trap. My brother's death must have been planned days—maybe even weeks—in advance." His face glistened with a wave of military composure. "There can only be one outcome from such an action—something the Conjoiners must have well understood. For months they've been goading us toward hostile action." He paused, then nodded at an unseen audience. "Well now they're going to get it. In fact, our response has already commenced."

"Dear God, no," Clavain said, but the evidence was all there now; all around the table he could see the updating orbital spread of the Coalition's dropships, knifing down toward Mars.

"I think it's war," Galiana said.

Conjoiners stormed onto the roof of the nest, taking up defensive positions around the domes and the dike's edge. Most of them carried the same guns which they had used against the Ouroborus. Smaller numbers were setting up automatic cannon on tripods. One or two were manhandling large anti-assault weapons into position. Most of it was war-surplus. Fifteen years ago the Conjoiners had avoided extinction by deploying weapons of awesome ferocity—but those ship-to-ship armaments were simply too destructive to use against a nearby foe. Now it would be more visceral; closer to the primal templates of combat, and none of what the Conjoiners were marshalling would be much use against the kind of assault Warren had prepared, Clavain knew. They could slow an attack, but not much more than that.

Galiana had given him another breather mask, made him don lightweight chameleoflage armor, and then forced him to carry one of the smaller guns. The gun felt alien in his hands; something he had never expected to carry again. The only possible justification for carrying it was to use it against his brother's forces—against his own side.

Could he do that?

It was clear that Warren had betrayed him; he had surely been aware of the worms around the nest. So his brother was capable not just of contempt, but of treacherous murder. For the first time, Clavain felt genuine hatred for Warren. He must have hoped that the worms would destroy the shuttle completely and kill

Clavain and Voi in the process. It must have pained him to see Clavain make it to the dike . . . pained him even more when Clavain called to talk about the tragedy. But Warren's larger plan had not been affected. The diplomatic link between the nest and Deimos was secure—even the Demarchists had no immediate access to it. So Clavain's call from the surface could be quietly ignored; spysat imagery doctored to make it seem that he had never reached the dike . . . had in fact been repelled by Conjoiner treachery. Inevitably the Demarchists would unravel the deception given time . . . but if Warren's plan succeeded, they would all be embroiled in war long before then. That, thought Clavain, was all that Warren had ever wanted.

Two brothers, Clavain thought. In many ways so alike. Both had embraced war once, but like a fickle lover Clavain had wearied of its glories. He had not even been injured as severely as Warren . . . but perhaps that was the point, too. Warren needed another war to avenge what one had stolen from him.

Clavain despised and pitied him in equal measure.

He searched for the safety clip on the gun. The rifle, now that he studied it more closely, was not all that different from those he had used during the war. The readout said the ammo-cell was fully charged.

He looked into the sky.

The attack wave broke orbit hard and steep above the Wall; five hundred fireballs screeching toward the nest. The insertion scorched inches of ablative armor from most of the ships; fried a few others which came in just fractionally too hard. Clavain knew that was how it was happening: he had studied possible attack scenarios for years, the range of outcomes burned indelibly into his memory.

The anti-assault guns were already working—locking onto the plasma trails as they flowered overhead, swinging down to find the tiny spark of heat at the head, computing refraction paths for laser pulses, spitting death into the sky. The unlucky ships flared a white that hurt the back of the eye and rained down in a billion dulling sparks. A dozen—then a dozen more. Maybe fifty in total before the guns could no longer acquire targets. It was nowhere near enough. Clavain's memory of the simulations told him that at least four hundred units of the attack wave would survive both re-entry and the Conjoiner's heavy defenses.

Nothing that Galiana could do would make any difference.

And that had always been the paradox. Galiana was capable of running the same simulations. She must always have known that her provocations would bring down something she could never hope to defeat.

Something that was always going to destroy her.

The surviving members of the wave were levelling out now, commencing long, ground-hugging runs from all directions. Cocooned in their dropships, the soldiers would be suffering punishing gee-loads . . . but it was nothing they were not engineered to withstand; half their cardiovascular systems were augmented by the only kinds of implant the Coalition tolerated.

The first of the wave came arcing in at supersonic speeds. All around, worms struggled to snatch them out of the sky, but mostly they were too slow to catch the dropships. Galiana's people manned their cannon positions and did their best to fend off what they could. Clavain clutched his gun, not firing yet. Best to save his ammo-cell power for a target he stood a chance of injuring.

Above, the first dropships made hairpin turns, nosing suicidally down toward the nest. Then they fractured cleanly apart, revealing falling pilots clad in bulbous armor. Just before the moment of impact each pilot exploded into a mass of black shock-absorbing balloons, looking something like a blackberry, bouncing across the nest before the balloons deflated just as swiftly and the pilot was left standing on the ground. By then the pilot—now properly a soldier—would have a comprehensive computer-generated map of the nest's nooks and crannies; enemy positions graphed in realtime from the down-looking spysats.

Clavain fell behind the curve of a dome before the nearest soldier got a lock onto him. The firefight was beginning now. He had to hand it to Galiana's people—they were fighting like devils. And they were at least as well coordinated as the attackers. But their weapons and armor were simply inadequate. Chameleoflage was only truly effective against a solitary enemy, or a massed enemy moving in from a common direction. With Coalition forces surrounding him, Clavain's suit was going crazy to trying to match itself against every background, like a chameleon in a house of mirrors.

The sky overhead looked strange now—darkening purple. And the purple was spreading in a mist across the nest. Galiana had deployed some kind of chemical smoke screen: infrared and optically opaque, he guessed. It would occlude the spysats and might be primed to adhere only to enemy chameleoflage. That had never been in Warren's simulations. Galiana had just given herself the slightest of edges.

A soldier stepped out of the mist, the obscene darkness of a gun muzzle trained on Clavain. His chameleoflage armor was dappled with vivid purple patches, ruining its stealthiness. The man fired, but his discharge wasted itself against Clavain's armor. Clavain returned the compliment, dropping his compatriot. What he had done, he thought, was not technically treason. Not yet. All he had done was act in self-preservation.

The man was wounded, but not yet dead. Clavain stepped through the purple haze and knelt down beside the soldier. He tried not to look at the man's wound.

"Can you hear me?" he said. There was no answer from the man, but beneath his visor, Clavain thought he saw the man's lips shape a sound. The man was just a kid—hardly old enough to remember much of the last war. "There's something you have to know," Clavain continued. "Do you realize who I am?" He wondered how recognizable he was, under the breather mask. Then something made him relent. He could tell the man he was Nevil Clavain—but what would that achieve? The soldier would be dead in minutes; maybe sooner than that. Nothing would be served by the soldier knowing that the basis for his attack was a lie; that he would not in fact be laying down his life for a just cause. The universe could be spared a single callous act.

"It's all right," Clavain said, turning away from his victim.

And then moved deeper into the nest, to see who else he could kill before the odds took him.

But the odds never did.

"You always were lucky," Galiana said, leaning over him. They were somewhere underground again—deep in the nest. A medical area, by the look of things. He was on a bed, fully clothed apart from the outer layer of chameleoflage armor. The room was gray and kettle-shaped, ringed by a circular balcony.

"What happened?"

"You took a head wound, but you'll survive."

He groped for the right question. "What about Warren's attack?"

"We endured three waves. We took casualties, of course."

Around the circumference of the balcony were thirty or so gray couches, slightly recessed into archways studded with gray medical equipment. They were all occupied. There were more Conjoiners in this room than he had seen so far in one place. Some of them looked very close to death.

Clavain reached up and examined his head, gingerly. There was some dried blood on the scalp, matted with his hair; some numbness, but it could have been a lot worse. He felt normal—no memory drop-outs or aphasia. When he made to stand from the bed, his body obeyed his will with only a tinge of dizziness.

"Warren won't stop at just three waves, Galiana."

"I know." She paused. "We know there'll be more."

He walked to the railing on the inner side of the balcony and looked over the edge. He had expected to see something—some chunk of incomprehensible surgical equipment, perhaps—but the middle of the room was only an empty, smooth-walled, gray pit. He shivered. The air was colder than any part of the nest he had visited so far, with a medicinal tang which reminded him of the convalescence ward on Deimos. What made him shiver even more was the realization that some of the injured—some of the dead—were barely older than the children he had visited only hours ago. Perhaps some of them were those children, conscripted from the nursery since his visit, uploaded with fighting reflexes through their new implants.

"What are you going to do? You know you can't win. Warren lost only a tiny fraction of his available force in those waves. You look like you've lost half your nest."

"It's much worse than that," Galiana said.

"What do you mean?"

"You're not quite ready yet. But I can show you in a moment."

He felt colder than ever now. "What do you mean, not quite ready?"

Galiana looked deep into his eyes now. "You took a serious head wound, Clavain. The entry wound was small, but the internal bleeding . . . it would have killed you, had we not intervened." Before he could ask the inevitable question she answered it for him. "We injected a small cluster of medichines into your head. They undid the damage very easily. But it seemed provident to allow them to grow."

"You've put replicators in my head?"

"You needn't sound so horrified. They're already growing—spreading out and interfacing with your existing neural circuitry—but the total volume of glial mass that they will consume is tiny: only a few cubic millimeters in total, across your entire brain."

He wondered if she was calling his bluff. "I don't feel anything."

"You won't—not for a minute or so." Now she pointed into the empty pit in the middle of the room. "Stand here and look into the air."

"There's nothing there."

But as soon as he had spoken, he knew he was wrong. There was something in the pit. He blinked and directed his attention somewhere else, but when he returned his gaze to the pit, the thing he imagined he had seen—milky, spectral—was still there, and becoming sharper and brighter by the second. It was a three-dimensional structure, as complex as an exercise in protein-folding. A tangle of loops and connecting branches and nodes and tunnels, embedded in a ghostly red matrix.

Suddenly he saw it for what it was: a map of the nest, dug into Mars. Just as the Coalition had suspected, the base was deeper than the original structure; far more extensive, reaching deeper down but much further out than anyone had imagined. Clavain made a mental effort to retain some of what he was seeing in his mind, the intelligence-gathering reflex stronger than the conscious knowledge that he would never see Deimos again.

"The medichines in your brain have interfaced with your visual cortex," Galiana said. "That's the first step on the road to Transenlightenment. Now you're privy to the machine-generated imagery encoded by the fields through which we move—most of it, anyway."

"Tell me this wasn't planned, Galiana. Tell me you weren't intending to put machines in me at the first opportunity."

"No; I wasn't planning it. But nor was I going to let your phobias stop me from saving your life."

The image grew in complexity. Glowing nodes of light appeared in the tunnels, some moving slowly through the network.

"What are they?"

"You're seeing the locations of the Conjoiners," Galiana said. "Are there as many as you imagined?"

Clavain judged that there were no more than seventy lights in the whole complex now. He searched for a cluster which would identify the room where he stood. There: twenty-odd bright lights, accompanied by one much fainter. Himself, of course. There were few people near the top of the nest—the attack must have collapsed half the tunnels, or maybe Galiana had deliberately sealed entrances herself.

"Where is everyone? Where are the children?"

"Most of the children are gone now." She paused. "You were right to guess that we were rushing them to Transenlightenment, Clavain."

"Why?"

"Because it's the only way out of here."

The image changed again. Now each of the bright lights was connected to another by a shimmering filament. The topology of the network was constantly shifting, like a pattern seen in a kaleidoscope. Occasionally, too swiftly for Clavain to be sure, it shifted toward a mandala of elusive symmetry, only to dissolve into the flickering chaos of the ever-changing network. He studied Galiana's node and saw that—even as she was speaking to him—her mind was in constant rapport with the rest of the nest.

Now something very bright appeared in the middle of the image, like a tiny star, against which the shimmering network paled almost to invisibility. "The network is abstracted now," Galiana said. "The bright light represents its totality: the unity of Transenlightenment. Watch."

He watched. The bright light—beautiful and alluring as anything Clavain had ever imagined—was extending a ray toward the isolated node which represented himself. The ray was extending itself through the map, coming closer by the second.

"The new structures in your mind are nearing maturity," Galiana said. "When the ray touches you, you will experience partial integration with the rest of us. Prepare yourself, Nevil."

Her words were unnecessary. His fingers were already clenched sweating on the railing as the light inched closer and engulfed his node.

"I should hate you for this," Clavain said.

"Why don't you? Hate's always the easier option."

"Because . . ." Because it made no difference now. His old life was over. He reached out for Galiana, needing some anchor against what was about to hit him. Galiana squeezed his hand and an instant later he knew something of Transenlightenment. The experience was shocking; not because it was painful or fearful, but because it was profoundly and totally new. He was literally thinking in ways that had not been possible microseconds earlier.

Afterward, when Clavain tried to imagine how he might describe it, he found that words were never going to be adequate for the task. And that was no surprise: evolution had shaped language to convey many concepts, but going from a single to a networked topology of self was not among them. But if he could not convey the core of the experience, he could at least skirt its essence with metaphor. It was like standing on the shore of an ocean, being engulfed by a wave taller than himself. For a moment he sought the surface; tried to keep the water from his lungs. But there happened not to be a surface. What had consumed him extended infinitely in all directions. He could only submit to it. Yet as the moments slipped by it turned from something terrifying in its unfamiliarity to something he could begin to adapt to; something that even began in the tiniest way to seem comforting. Even then he glimpsed that it was only a shadow of what Galiana was experiencing every instant of her life.

"All right," Galiana said. "That's enough for now."

The fullness of Transenlightenment retreated, like a fading vision of Godhead. What he was left with was purely sensory; no longer any direct rapport with the others. His state of mind came crashing back to normality.

"Are you all right, Nevil?"

"Yes . . ." His mouth was dry. "Yes; I think so."

"Look around you."

He did.

The room had changed completely. So had everyone in it.

His head reeling, Clavain walked in light. The formerly gray walls oozed beguiling patterns; as if a dark forest had suddenly become enchanted. Information hung in veils in the air; icons and diagrams and numbers clustering around the beds of the injured, thinning out into the general space like fantastically delicate neon sculptures. As he walked toward the icons they darted out of his way, mocking him like schools of brilliant fish. Sometimes they seemed to sing; or tickle the back of his nose with half-familiar smells.

"You can perceive things now," Galiana said. "But none of it will mean much to you. You'd need years of education, or deeper neural machinery for that—building cognitive layers. We read all this almost subliminally."

Galiana was dressed differently now. He could still see the vague shape of her gray outfit, but layered around it were billowing skeins of light, unravelling at their edges into chains of Boolean logic. Icons danced in her hair like angels. He could see, faintly, the web of thought linking her with the other Conjoiners.

She was inhumanly beautiful.

"You said things were much worse," Clavain said. "Are you ready to show me now?"

She took him to see Felka again, passing on the way through deserted nursery rooms, populated now only by bewildered mechanical animals. Felka was the only child left in the nursery.

Clavain had been deeply disturbed by Felka when he had seen her before, but not for any reason he could easily express. Something about the purposefulness of what she did; performed with ferocious concentration, as if the fate of creation hung on the outcome of her game. Felka and her surroundings had not changed at all since his visit. The room was still austere to the point of oppressiveness. Felka looked the same. In every respect it was as if only an instant had passed since their meeting; as if the onset of war and the assaults against the nest—the battle of which this was only an interlude—were only figments from someone else's troubling dream; nothing that need concern Felka in her devotion to the task at hand.

And what the task was awed Clavain.

Before he had watched her make strange gestures in front of her. Now the machines in his head revealed the purpose that those gestures served. Around Felka—cordoning her like a barricade—was a ghostly representation of the Great Wall.

She was doing something to it.

It was not a scale representation, Clavain knew. The Wall looked much higher here in relation to its diameter. And the surface was not the nearly invisible membrane of the real thing, but something like etched glass. The etchwork was a filigree of lines and junctions, descending down to smaller and smaller scales in fractal steps, until the blur of detail was too fine for his eyes to discriminate. It was shifting and altering color, and Felka was responding to these alterations with what he now saw was frightening efficiency. It was as if the color changes warned of some malignancy in part of the Wall, and by touching it—expressing some tactile code—Felka was able to restructure the etchwork to block and neutralize the malignancy before it spread.

"I don't understand," Clavain said. "I thought we destroyed the Wall; completely killed its systems."

"No," Galiana said. "You only ever injured it. Stopped it from growing, and from managing its own repair-process correctly . . . but you never truly killed it."

Sandra Voi had guessed, Clavain realized. She had wondered how the Wall had survived this long.

Galiana told him the rest—how they had managed to establish control pathways to the Wall from the nest, fifteen years earlier—optical cables sunk deep below the worm zone. "We stabilized the Wall's degradation with software running on dumb machines," she said. "But when Felka was born we found that she managed the task just as efficiently as the computers; in some ways better than they ever did. In fact, she seemed to thrive on it. It was as if in the Wall she found . . ." Galiana trailed off. "I was going to say a friend."

"Why don't you?"

"Because the Wall's just a machine. Which means if Felka recognized kinship . . . what would that make her?"

"Someone lonely, that's all." Clavain watched the girl's motions. "She seems faster than before. Is that possible?"

"I told you things were worse than before. She's having to work harder to hold the Wall together."

"Warren must have attacked it." Clavain said. "The possibility of knocking down the Wall always figured in our contingency plans for another war. I just never thought it would happen so soon." Then he looked at Felka. Maybe it was imagination but she seemed to be working even faster than when he had entered the room; not just since his last visit. "How long do you think she can keep it together?"

"Not much longer," Galiana said. "As a matter of fact I think she's already failing."

It was true. Now that he looked closely at the ghost Wall he saw that the upper edge was not the mathematically smooth ring it should have been; that there were scores of tiny ragged bites eating down from the top. Felka's activities were increasingly directed to these opening cracks in the structure; instructing the crippled structure to divert energy and raw materials to these critical failure points. Clavain knew that the distant processes Felka directed were awesome. Within the Wall lay a lymphatic system whose peristaltic feed-pipes ranged in size from meters across to the submicroscopic; flowing with myriad tiny repair machines. Felka chose where to send those machines; her hand gestures establishing pathways between damage points and the factories sunk into the Wall's ramparts which made the required types of machine. For more than a decade, Galiana said, Felka had kept the Wall from crumbling—but for most of that time her adversary had been only natural decay and accidental damage. It was a different game now that the Wall had been attacked again. It was not one she could ever win.

Felka's movements were swifter; less fluid. Her face remained impassive, but in the quickening way that her eyes darted from point to point it was possible to read the first hints of panic. No surprise, either: the deepest cracks in the structure now reached a quarter of the way to the surface, and they were too wide to be repaired. The Wall was unzipping along those flaws. Cubic kilometers of atmosphere would be howling out through the openings. The loss of pressure would be immeasurably slow at first, for near the top the trapped cylinder of atmosphere was only fractionally thicker than the rest of the Martian atmosphere. But only at first . . .

"We have to get deeper," Clavain said. "Once the Wall goes, we won't have a chance in hell if we're anywhere near the surface. It'll be like the worst tornado in history."

"What will your brother do? Will he nuke us?"

"No; I don't think so. He'll want to get hold of any technologies you've hidden away. He'll wait until the dust storms have died down, then he'll raid the nest with a hundred times as many troops as you've seen so far. You won't be able to resist, Galiana. If you're lucky you may just survive long enough to be taken prisoner."

"There won't be any prisoners," Galiana said.

"You're planning to die fighting?"

"No. And mass suicide doesn't figure in our plans either. Neither will be necessary. By the time your brother reaches here, there won't be anyone left in the nest."

Clavain thought of the worms encircling the area; how small were the chances of reaching any kind of safety if it involved getting past them. "Secret tunnels under the worm zone, is that it? I hope you're serious."

"I'm deadly serious," Galiana said. "And yes, there is a secret tunnel. The other children have already gone through it now. But it doesn't lead under the worm zone."

"Where, then?"

"Somewhere a lot farther away."

When they passed through the medical center again it was empty, save for a few swan-necked robots patiently waiting for further casualties. They had left Felka behind tending the Wall, her hands a manic blur as she tried to slow the rate of collapse. Clavain had tried to make her come with them, but Galiana had told him he was wasting his time: that she would sooner die than be parted from the Wall.

"You don't understand," Galiana said. "You're placing too much humanity behind her eyes. Keeping the Wall alive is the single most important fact of her universe—more important than love, pain, death—anything you or I would consider definitely human."

"Then what happens to her when the Wall dies?"

"Her life ends," Galiana said.

Reluctantly he had left without her; the taste of shame in his mouth. Rationally it made sense: without Felka's help the Wall would collapse much sooner and there was a good chance all their lives would end; not just that of the haunted girl. How deep would they have to go before they were safe from the suction of the escaping atmosphere? Would any part of the nest be safe?

The regions through which they were descending now were as cold and gray as any Clavain had seen. There were no entoptic generators buried in these walls to supply visual information to the implants Galiana had put in his head, and even her own aura of light was gone. They only met a few other Conjoiners, and they seemed to be moving in the same general direction; down to the nest's basement levels. This was unknown territory to Clavain.

Where was Galiana taking him?

"If you had an escape route all along, why did you wait so long before sending the children through it?"

"I told you, we couldn't bring them to Transenlightenment too soon. The older they were, the better," Galiana said. "Now though . . ."

"There was no waiting any longer, was there?"

Eventually they reached a chamber with the same echoing acoustics as the topside hangar. The chamber was dark except for a few pools of light, but in the shadows Clavain made out discarded excavation equipment and freight pallets; cranes and deactivated robots. The air smelled of ozone. Something was still going on here.

"Is this the factory where you make the shuttles?" Clavain said.

"We manufactured parts of them here, yes," Galiana said. "But that was a side-industry."

"Of what?"

"The tunnel, of course." Galiana made more lights come on. At the far end of the chamber—they were walking toward it—waited a series of cylindrical things with pointed ends; like huge bullets. They rested on rails, one after the other. The tip of the very first bullet was next to a dark hole in the wall. Clavain was about to say something when there was a sudden loud buzz and the first bullet slammed into the hole. The other bullets-there were three of them now—eased slowly forward and halted. Conjoiners were waiting to board them.

He remembered what Galiana had said about no one being left behind.

"What am I seeing here?"

"A way out of the nest," Galiana said. "And a way off Mars, though I suppose you figured that part for yourself."

"There is no way off Mars," Clavain said. "The interdiction guarantees that. Haven't you learned that with your shuttles?"

"The shuttles were only ever a diversionary tactic," Galiana said. "They made your side think we were still striving to escape, whereas our true escape route was already fully operational."

"A pretty desperate diversion."

"Not really. I lied to you when I said we didn't clone. We did—but only to produce brain-dead corpses. The shuttles were full of corpses before we ever launched them."

For the first time since leaving Deimos Clavain smiled, amused at the sheer obliquity of Galiana's thinking.

"Of course, there was another function," she said. "The shuttles provoked your side into a direct attack against the nest."

"So this was deliberate all along?"

"Yes. We needed to draw your side's attention; to concentrate your military presence in low-orbit, near the nest. Of course we were hoping the offensive would come later than it did . . . but we reckoned without Warren's conspiracy."

"Then you are planning something."

"Yes." The next bullet slammed into the wall, ozone crackling from its linear induction rails. Now only two remained. "We can talk later. There isn't much time now." She projected an image into his visual field: the Wall, now veined by titanic fractures down half its length. "It's collapsing."

"And Felka?"

"She's still trying to save it."

He looked at the Conjoiners boarding the leading bullet; tried to imagine where they were going. Was it to any kind of sanctuary he might recognize—or to something so beyond his experience that it might as well be death? Did he have the nerve to find out? Perhaps. He had nothing to lose now, after all; he could certainly not return home. But if he was going to follow Galiana's exodus, it could not be with the sense of shame he now felt in abandoning Felka.

The answer, when it came, was simple. "I'm going back for her. If you can't wait for me, don't. But don't try and stop me doing this."

Galiana looked at him, shaking her head slowly. "She won't thank you for saving her life, Clavain."

"Maybe not now," he said.

He had the feeling he was running back into a burning building. Given what Galiana had said about the girl's deficiencies—that by any reasonable definition she was hardly more than an automaton—what he was doing was very likely pointless, if not suicidal. But if he turned his back on her, he would become something even less than human himself. He had misread Galiana badly when she said the girl was precious to them. He had assumed some bond of affection . . . whereas what Galiana meant was that the girl was precious in the sense of a vital component. Now—with the nest being abandoned—the component had no further use. Did that make Galiana as cold as a machine herself—or was she just being unfailingly realistic? He found the nursery after only one or two false turns, and then Felka's room. The implants Galiana had given him were again throwing phantom images into the air. Felka sat within the crumbling circle of the Wall. Great fissures now reached to the surface of Mars. Shards of the Wall, as big as icebergs, had fractured away and now lay like vast sheets of broken glass across the regolith.

She was losing, and now she knew it. This was not just some more difficult phase of the game. This was something she could never win, and her realization was now plainly evident in her face. She was still moving her arms frantically, but her face was red now, locked into a petulant scowl of anger and fear.

For the first time, she seemed to notice him.

Something had broken through her shell, Clavain thought. For the first time in years, something was happening that was beyond her control; something that threatened to destroy the neat, geometric universe she had made for herself. She might not have distinguished his face from all the other people who came to see her, but she surely recognized something . . . that now the adult world was bigger than she was, and it was only from the adult world that any kind of salvation could come.

Then she did something that shocked him beyond words. She looked deep into his eyes and reached out a hand.

But there was nothing he could do to help her.

Later—it seemed hours, but in fact could only have been tens of minutes—Clavain found that he was able to breathe normally again. They had escaped Mars now; Galiana, Felka and himself, riding the last bullet.

And they were still alive.

The bullet's vacuum-filled tunnel cut deep into Mars; a shallow arc bending under the crust before rising again, two thousand kilometers away, well beyond the Wall, where the atmosphere was as thin as ever. For the Conjoiners, boring the tunnel had not been especially difficult. Such engineering would have been impossible on a planet that had plate tectonics, but beneath its lithosphere Mars was geologically quiet. They had not even had to worry about tailings. What they excavated, they compressed and fused and used to line the tunnel, maintaining rigidity against awesome pressure with some trick of piezo-electricity. In the tunnel, the bullet accelerated continuously at three gees for six minutes. Their seats had tilted back and wrapped around them, applying pressure to the legs to maintain bloodflow to the head. Even so, it was hard to think, let alone move, but Clavain knew that it was no worse than what the earliest space explorers had endured climbing away from Earth. And he had undergone similar tortures during the war, in combat insertions.

They were moving at ten kilometers a second when they reached the surface again, exiting via a camouflaged trapdoor. For a moment the atmosphere snatched at them . . . but almost as soon as Clavain had registered the deceleration, it was over. The surface of Mars was dropping below them very quickly indeed.

In half a minute, they were in true space.

"The Interdiction's sensor web can't track us," Galiana said. "You placed your best spy-sats directly over the nest. That was a mistake, Clavain—even though we did our best to reinforce your thinking with the shuttle launches. But now we're well outside your sensor footprint."

Clavain nodded. "But that won't help us once we're far from the surface. Then, we'll just look like another ship trying to reach deep space. The web may be late locking onto us, but it'll still get us in the end."

"It would," Galiana said. "If deep space was where we were going."

Felka stirred next to him. She had withdrawn into some kind of catatonia. Separation from the Wall had undermined her entire existence; now she was free-falling through an abyss of meaninglessness. Perhaps, Clavain, thought, she would fall forever. If that was the case, he had only brought forward her fate. Was that much of a cruelty? Perhaps he was deluding himself, but with time, was it out of the question that Galiana's machines could undo the harm they had inflicted ten years earlier? Surely they could try. It depended, of course, on where exactly they were headed. One of the system's other Conjoiner nests had been Clavain's initial guess—even though it seemed unlikely that they would ever survive the crossing. At ten klicks per second it would take years . . .

"Where are you taking us?" he asked.

Galiana issued some neural command which made the bullet seem to become transparent.

"There," she said.

Something lay distantly ahead. Galiana made the forward view zoom in, until the object was much clearer.

Dark—misshapen. Like Deimos without fortifications.

"Phobos," Clavain said, wonderingly. "We're going to Phobos."

"Yes," Galiana said.

"But the worms—"

"Don't exist anymore." She spoke with the same tutorly patience with which Remontoire had addressed him on the same subject not long before. "Your attempt to oust the worms failed. You assumed our subsequent attempt failed . . . but that was only what we wanted you to think."

For a moment he was lost for words. "You've had people in Phobos all along?"

"Ever since the cease-fire, yes. They've been quite busy, too."

Phobos altered. Layers of it were peeled away, revealing the glittering device which lay hidden in its heart, poised and ready for flight. Clavain had never seen anything like it, but the nature of the thing was instantly obvious. He was looking at something wonderful; something which had never existed before in the whole of human experience.

He was looking at a starship.

"We'll be leaving soon," Galiana said. "They'll try and stop us, of course. But now that their forces are concentrated near the surface, they won't succeed. We'll leave Phobos and Mars behind, and send messages to the other nests. If they can break out and meet us, we'll take them as well. We'll leave this whole system behind."

"Where are you going?"

"Shouldn't that be where are we going? You're coming with us, after all." She paused. "There are a number of candidate systems. Our choice will depend on the trajectory the Coalition forces upon us."

"What about the Demarchists?"

"They won't stop us." It was said with total assurance—implying, what? That the Demarchy knew of this ship? Perhaps. It had long been rumored that the Demarchists and the Conjoiners were closer than they admitted.

Clavain thought of something. "What about the worms' altering the orbit?"

"That was our doing," Galiana said. "We couldn't help it. Every time we send up one of these canisters, we nudge Phobos into a different orbit. Even after we sent up a thousand canisters, the effect was tiny—we changed Phobos's velocity by less than one tenth of a millimeter per second—but there was no way to hide it." Then she paused and looked at Clavain with something like apprehension. "We'll be arriving in two hundred seconds. Do you want to live?"

"I'm sorry?"

"Think about it. The tube in Mars was two thousand kilometers long, which allowed us to spread the acceleration over six minutes. Even then it was three gees. But there simply isn't room for anything like that in Phobos. We'll be slowing down much more abruptly."

Clavain felt the hairs on the back of his neck prickle. "How much more abruptly?"

"Complete deceleration in one fifth of a second." She let that sink home. "That's around five thousand gees."

"I can't survive that."

"No; you can't. Not now, anyway. But there are machines in your head now. If you allow it, there's time for them to establish a structural web across your brain. We'll flood the cabin with foam. We'll all die temporarily, but there won't be anything they can't fix in Phobos."

"It won't just be a structural web, will it? I'll be like you, then. There won't be any difference between us."

"You'll become Conjoined, yes." Galiana offered the faintest of smiles. "The procedure is reversible. It's just that no one's ever wanted to go back."

"And you still tell me none of this was planned?"

"No; but I don't expect you to believe me. For what it's worth, though . . . you're a good man, Nevil. The Transenlightenment could use you. Maybe at the back of my mind . . . at the back of our mind . . ."

"You always hoped it might come to this?"

Galiana smiled.

He looked at Phobos. Even without Galiana's magnification, it was clearly bigger. They would be arriving very shortly. He would have liked longer to think about it, but the one thing not on his side now was time. Then he looked at Felka, and wondered which of them was about to embark on the stranger journey. Felka's search for meaning in a universe without her beloved Wall, or his passage into Transenlightenment? Neither would necessarily be easy. But together, perhaps, they might even find a way to help each other. That was all he could hope for now.

Clavain nodded assent, ready for the loom of machines to embrace his mind.

He was ready to defect.

A NICHE

Peter Watts

❁

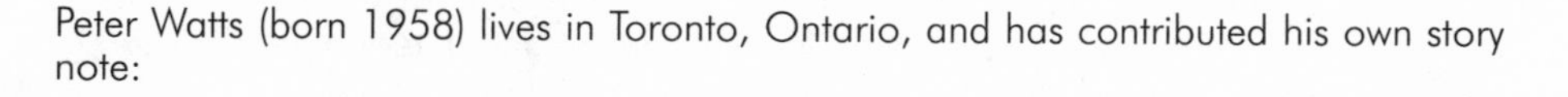

Peter Watts (born 1958) lives in Toronto, Ontario, and has contributed his own story note:

> Peter Watts began publishing science fiction with a paper in the *Journal of Mammalogy* in 1984. He continued to write throughout the eighties, but while his statistical fiction proved successful amongst marine mammalogists, he was unable to sell any stories containing actual characters and plot. During this time he acquired an impressive collection of personalized rejections, notably from *Analog,* the bastion of hard SF. These letters frequently described Watts's stories as "awfully negative," although they encouraged him to persevere in his efforts. Over the years, however, *Analog*'s rejections became increasingly terse (suggesting that Watts, always one to buck a trend, was actually getting worse with practice). In 1990 he submitted "A Niche," an uplifting tale of sexual abuse, deep-sea ecology, and career counseling. He was rewarded by his first-ever form-letter rejection from *Analog*.
>
> Realizing that he would never achieve fame or fortune in the U.S. Watts submitted "A Niche" to the less-lucrative Canadian market hoping to at least recoup the cost of his printer ribbon. The story sold immediately, won an Aurora Award, and has been reprinted several times (most notably in Hartwell and Grant's 1994 Canadian-SF showcase *Northern Stars* from Tor Books).
>
> Recognizing a Good Thing when he saw it, Watts immediately padded an additional ninety thousand words onto the narrative and sold *Starfish* (1999), his first novel, to Tor. *Starfish* was an unexpected critical and commercial success, netting a "Notable Book of the Year" nod from the *New York Times,* an honorable mention for the John W. Campbell Memorial Award, and rejections from both German and Russian publishing houses on the grounds that it was "too dark." (Being considered too dark for the Russians remains one of Watts's proudest accomplishments.) *Starfish* was universally praised for its evocation of the deep-sea environment. The sequel, *Maelstrom* (2001, Tor), takes place almost entirely on land: It therefore avoids the elements that readers most loved about the first book, replacing them with a sprawling entropic dystopia in which Sylvia Plath might have felt at home, if Sylvia Plath had had a graduate degree in evolutionary biology. *Maelstrom* may mark the first time that the *New York Times* used the terms "exhilarating" and "deeply paranoid" to describe the same novel. These novels, despite Watts's best efforts, have turned into the first two-thirds of a trilogy. Watts is presently working on the final volume, *ßehemoth*, and a first-contact novel exploring the evolutionary value of sentience. He still hasn't sold a short story to the American mags; his collected short fiction (originally released in a variety of Canadian publications) is available in *Ten Monkeys Ten Minutes,* a skimpy trade paperback from Tesseract

Books (Edmonton). He continues to live a double life as a biologist (albeit far from a cutting-edge one), and has also dabbled in computer-game script writing. Peter Watts is generally a lot more optimistic than you might expect, considering.

And in addition to his note, he has provided this statement on hard SF [here lightly condensed]:

Let's start by throwing away that hoary old question, *what is hard SF?* We've been around the block a few times; challenged for a definition we need only say, we know it when we see it.

Ask instead, what is hard science fiction *for?*

It's been said that science fiction exists as an array of *possible* futures, a Gumpesque box of chocolates from which we can choose our course. This interpretation assumes some baseline level of real-world credibility, of course—if you're shopping for a real future, you don't waste time with Unicorn Truffles—so hard SF is often distinguished from its softer, inferior cousins by virtue of adherence to rigorous—or at least, *plausible*—science.

Plausible, is it? Okay, then: Goodbye Niven, goodbye Herbert and Vinge. Begone with your genes that code for luck, your spaceships piloted by psychics, and your galactic Slow Zones. Goodbye Brin: A Ph.D. should've known better than to resort to ftl. You're not plausible enough for this sandbox.

But of course I'm attacking a straw man here—because as we all know, it's not the math that counts, it's the *attitude*. Those guys over there with the elves and the wizards are just a bunch of New Age mystics, glorifying irrationality. They tell us to have faith, to believe in magic. They insist we pay no attention to the man behind the curtain. We, on the other hand, are missionaries of rationalism. We reject pixie-dust outright: We may not have the blueprints for a warp engine handy, but you'd better believe that *our* future technologies have sprung from the same empirical science that gave us Teflon and chemotherapy. Our tales abide by the spirit of science, if not the letter.

Ignore for the moment people like Tolkien, who—without even having the password to our secret clubhouse—created perhaps the most rigorously consistent virtual world in English literature. There's a more serious point at which our arguments start to come off the rails: The *science* in science fiction may not, when we get right down to it, be all that important after all.

Science fiction explores the interface between humanity and technological change. That's what fundamentally defines the genre: Its human face distinguishes it from the technical journals, and its technological side distinguishes it from other kinds of fiction. Yet this balance is profoundly (and necessarily) uneven. Want to explore the societal impact of immortality? It's a poor writer who'd devote half a novel to telomeres and mitochondrial membranes. Much better to gloss over those details, assume the result, and focus on the human consequences. In other words, *there may be little intrinsic correlation between the "hardness" of science fiction and its value as an exploratory device.*

So, are the naysayers right after all? Does this whole end of the spectrum amount to an escapist pastime for geeks more interested in toys than people? Is it not about technology at all, but politics? (And are you as sick as I am of the endless debate over whether "The Cold Equations" was a heart-wrenching lesson on the wages of ignorance, or just a chrome-plated misogynist excuse to toss some uppity chick out an airlock?)

What is hard SF *for?*

I can only tell you what is to me, personally: It's a gauntlet. A self-imposed challenge to Watts the biologist to keep the science plausible, no matter how unimportant that seems in a genre full of humanoid aliens and ftl. A challenge to Watts the writer, to tell a story without breaking the scientist's rules.

It's a bit like rewriting the Old Testament in iambic pentameter. It's an arbitrary goal, and there are easier ways to get the message across. The constraints chafe: prose would be so much simpler. Even if one succeeds on technical points, the final product can be graceless and ugly: an essay posing as narrative, a killer idea tarted up with paper-thin characters and stuffed to bursting with exposition. We have our share of failures.

But what if you not only succeed despite those constraints, but actually produce better work *because* of them? What if the end result, miraculously, *doesn't* seem forced and contrived, but soars? Then you've wandered onto the battlefield with one hand tied behind your back, and done more than survive. You've *triumphed*.

That's why I write hard science fiction. I don't know how close I've come to that goal, but after all I'm just starting out.

And I've got time.

One could not ask for a more individual take on hard SF. Watts is one of the strongest new hard SF talents of recent years and arrives with years of knowledge and practice, a fully developed SF writer. Note that the central characters of "A Niche" are named Clarke and Ballard.

When the lights go out in Beebe Station, you can hear the metal groan.

Lenie Clarke lies on her bunk, listening. Overhead, past pipes and wires and eggshell plating, three kilometers of black ocean try to crush her. She feels the Rift underneath, tearing open the seabed with strength enough to move a continent. She lies there in that fragile refuge, and she hears Beebe's armor shifting by microns, hears its seams creak not quite below the threshold of human hearing. God is a sadist on the Juan de Fuca Rift, and His name is Physics.

How did they talk me into this? she wonders. *Why did I come down here?* But she already knows the answer.

She hears Ballard moving out in the corridor. Clarke envies Ballard. Ballard never screws up, always seems to have her life under control. She almost seems *happy* down here.

Clarke rolls off her bunk and fumbles for a switch. Her cubby floods with dismal light. Pipes and access panels crowd the wall beside her; aesthetics run a distant second to functionality when you're three thousand meters down. She turns and catches sight of a slick black amphibian in the bulkhead mirror.

It still happens, occasionally. She can sometimes forget what they've done to her.

It takes a conscious effort to feel the machines lurking where her left lung used to be. She is so acclimated to the chronic ache in her chest, to that subtle inertia of plastic and metal as she moves, that she is scarcely aware of them any more. So she can still feel the memory of what it was to be fully human, and mistake that ghost for honest sensation.

Such respites never last. There are mirrors everywhere in Beebe; they're supposed to increase the apparent size of one's personal space. Sometimes Clarke shuts her eyes to hide from the reflections forever being thrown back at her. It doesn't help. She clenches her lids and feels the corneal caps beneath them, covering her eyes like smooth white cataracts.

She climbs out of her cubby and moves along the corridor to the lounge. Ballard is waiting there, dressed in a diveskin and the usual air of confidence.

Ballard stands up. "Ready to go?"

"You're in charge," Clarke says.

"Only on paper." Ballard smiles. "As far as I'm concerned, Lenie, we're equals." After two days on the rift Clarke is still surprised by the frequency with which Ballard smiles. Ballard smiles at the slightest provocation. It doesn't always seem real.

Something hits Beebe from the outside.

Ballard's smile falters. They hear it again; a wet, muffled thud through the station's titanium skin.

"It takes a while to get used to," Ballard says, "doesn't it?"

And again.

"I mean, that sounds *big* . . ."

"Maybe we should turn the lights off," Clarke suggests. She knows they won't. Beebe's exterior floodlights burn around the clock, an electric campfire pushing back the darkness. They can't see it from inside—Beebe has no windows—but somehow they draw comfort from the knowledge of that unseen fire—

Thud!

—most of the time.

"Remember back in training?" Ballard says over the sound. "When they told us that abyssal fish were supposed to be so small. . . ."

Her voice trails off. Beebe creaks slightly. They listen for a while. There is no other sound.

"It must've gotten tired," Ballard says. "You'd think they'd figure it out." She moves to the ladder and climbs downstairs.

Clarke follows her, a bit impatiently. There are sounds in Beebe that worry her far more than the futile attack of some misguided fish. Clarke can hear tired alloys negotiating surrender. She can feel the ocean looking for a way in. What if it finds one? The whole weight of the Pacific could drop down and turn her into jelly. Any time.

Better to face it outside, where she knows what's coming. All she can do in here is wait for it to happen.

Going outside is like drowning, once a day.

Clarke stands facing Ballard, diveskin sealed, in an airlock that barely holds both of them. She has learned to tolerate the forced proximity; the glassy armor on her eyes helps a bit. *Fuse seals, check headlamp, test injector*; the ritual takes her, step by reflexive step, to that horrible moment when she awakens the machines sleeping within her, and changes.

When she catches her breath, and loses it.

When a vacuum opens, somewhere in her chest, that swallows the air she holds. When her remaining lung shrivels in its cage, and her guts collapse; when myoelectric demons flood her sinuses and middle ears with isotonic saline. When every pocket of internal gas disappears in the time it takes to draw a breath.

It always feels the same. The sudden, overwhelming nausea; the narrow confines of the airlock holding her erect when she tries to fall; seawater churning on all sides. Her face goes under, vision blurs, then clears as her corneal caps adjust.

She collapses against the walls and wishes she could scream. The floor of the airlock drops away like a gallows. Lenie Clarke falls writhing into the abyss.

They come out of the freezing darkness, headlights blazing, into an oasis of sodium luminosity. Machines grow everywhere at the Throat, like metal weeds. Cables and conduits spiderweb across the seabed in a dozen directions. The main pumps stand over twenty meters high, a regiment of submarine monoliths fading from sight on either side. Overhead floodlights bathe the jumbled structures in perpetual twilight.

They stop for a moment, hands resting on the line that guided them here.

"I'll never get used to it," Ballard grates in a caricature of her usual voice.

Clarke glances at her wrist thermistor. "Thirty-four Centigrade." The words buzz, metallic, from her, larynx. It feels so *wrong* to talk without breathing.

Ballard lets go of the rope and launches herself into the light. After a moment, breathless, Clarke follows.

There is so much power here, so much wasted strength. Here the continents themselves do ponderous battle. Magma freezes; icy seawater turns to steam; the very floor of the ocean is born by painful centimeters each year. Human machinery does not make energy, here at Dragon's Throat; it merely hangs on and steals some insignificant fraction of it back to the mainland.

Clarke flies through canyons of metal and rock, and knows what it is to be a parasite. She looks down. Shellfish the size of boulders, crimson worms three meters long crowd the seabed between the machines. Legions of bacteria, hungry for sulphur, lace the water with milky veils.

The water fills with a sudden terrible cry.

It doesn't sound like a scream. It sounds as though a great harp string is vibrating in slow motion. But Ballard is screaming, through some reluctant interface of flesh and metal:

"LENIE—"

Clarke turns in time to see her own arm disappear into a mouth that seems impossibly huge.

Teeth like scimitars clamp down on her shoulder. Clarke stares into a scaly black face half-a-meter across. Some tiny dispassionate part of her searches for eyes in that monstrous fusion of spines and teeth and gnarled flesh, and fails. *How can it see me?* she wonders.

Then the pain reaches her.

She feels her arm being wrenched from its socket. The creature thrashes, shaking its head back and forth, trying to tear her into chunks. Every tug sets her nerves screaming.

She goes limp. *Please get it over with if you're going to kill me just please God make it quick . . .* She feels the urge to vomit, but the skin over her mouth and her own collapsed insides won't let her.

She shuts out the pain. She's had plenty of practice. She pulls inside, abandoning her body to ravenous vivisection; and from far away she feels the twisting of her attacker grow suddenly erratic. There is another creature at her side, with arms and legs and a knife—*you know a knife, like the one you've got strapped to your leg and completely forgot about*—and suddenly the monster is gone, its grip broken.

Clarke tells her neck muscles to work. It is like operating a marionette. Her head turns, and she sees Ballard locked in combat with something as big as she is. Only . . . Ballard is tearing it to pieces, with her bare hands. Its icicle teeth splinter and snap. Dark icewater courses from its wounds, tracing mortal convulsions with smoke-trails of suspended gore.

The creature spasms weakly. Ballard pushes it away. A dozen smaller fish dart into the light and begin tearing at the carcass. Photophores along their sides flash like frantic rainbows.

Clarke watches from the other side of the world. The pain in her side keeps its distance, a steady, pulsing ache. She looks; her arm is still there. She can even move her fingers without any trouble. *I've had worse*, she thinks.

But why am I still alive?

Ballard appears at her side; her lens-covered eyes shine like photophores themselves.

"Jesus Christ," Ballard says in a distorted whisper. "Lenie? Are you okay?"

Clarke dwells on the inanity of the question for a moment. But surprisingly, she feels intact. "Yeah."

And if not, she knows it's her own damn fault. She just lay there. She just waited to die. She was asking for it.

She's always asking for it.

Back in the airlock the water recedes around them. And within them; Clarke's stolen breath, released at last, races back along visceral channels, reinflating lung and gut and spirit.

Ballard splits the face seal on her 'skin and her words tumble into the wetroom. "Jesus. Jesus! I don't believe it! My God, did you see that thing! They get so huge around here!" She passes her hands across her face; her corneal caps come off, milky hemispheres dropping from enormous hazel eyes. "And to think they're normally just a few centimeters long . . ."

She starts to strip down, unzipping her 'skin along the forearms, talking the whole time. "And yet it was almost fragile, you know? Hit it hard enough and it just came apart! Jesus!" Ballard always takes off her uniform indoors. Clarke suspects that she'd rip the recycler out of her own thorax if she could, throw it in a corner with the 'skin and the eyecaps until the next time it was needed.

Maybe she's got her other lung in her cabin. Clarke muses. Her arm is all pins and needles. *Maybe she keeps it in a jar, and she stuffs it back into her chest at night . . .* She feels a bit dopey; probably just an after-effect of the neuroinhibitors the 'skin pumps her full of whenever she's outside. *Small price to keep my brain from shorting out—I really shouldn't mind. . . .*

Ballard peels her 'skin down to the waist. Just under her left breast, an electrolyser intake pokes out through her ribcage.

Clarke stares vaguely at that perforated disk in Ballard's flesh. *The ocean goes into us there*, she thinks. The old knowledge seems newly significant, somehow. *We suck it into us and steal its oxygen and spit it out again.*

The prickly numbness is spreading, leaking through her shoulder into her chest and neck. Clarke shakes her head once, to clear it.

She sags suddenly, against the hatchway.

Am I in shock? Am I fainting?

"I mean—" Ballard stops, looks at Clarke with an expression of sudden concern. "Jesus, Lenie. You look terrible. You shouldn't have told me you were okay if you weren't."

The tingling reaches the base of Clarke's skull. She fights it. "I'm—okay," she says. "Nothing broke. I'm just bruised."

"Garbage. Take off your 'skin."

Clarke straightens, with effort. The numbness recedes a bit. "It's nothing I can't take care of myself."

Don't touch me. Please don't touch me.

Ballard steps forward without a word and unseals the 'skin around Clarke's forearm. She peels back the fabric and exposes an ugly purple bruise. She looks at Clarke with one raised eyebrow.

"Just a bruise," Clarke says. "I'll take care of it. Really. Thanks anyway." She pulls her hand away from Ballard's ministrations.

Ballard looks at her for a moment. She smiles ever so slightly.

"Lenie," she says, "there's no need to feel embarrassed."

"About what?"

"You know. Me having to rescue you. You going to pieces when that thing attacked. It was perfectly understandable. Most people have a rough time adjusting. I'm just one of the lucky ones."

Right. You've always been one of the lucky ones, haven't you? I know your kind, Ballard, you've never failed at anything . . .

"You don't have to feel ashamed about it," Ballard reassures her.

"I don't," Clarke says, honestly. She doesn't feel much of anything any more. Just the tingling. And the tension. And a vague sort of wonder that she's even alive.

The bulkhead is sweating.

The deep sea lays icy hands on the metal and, inside, Clarke watches the humid atmosphere bead and run down the wall. She sits rigid on her bunk under dim fluorescent light, every wall of the cubby within easy reach. The ceiling is too low. The room is too narrow. She feels as if the ocean is compressing the station around her.

And all I can do is wait . . .

The anabolic salve on her injuries is warm and soothing. Clarke probes the purple flesh of her arm with practiced fingers. The diagnostic tools in the Med cubby have vindicated her. She is lucky, this time; bones intact, epidermis unbroken. She seals up her 'skin, hiding the damage.

Clarke shifts on the pallet, turns to face the inside wall. Her reflection stares back at her through eyes like frosted glass. She watches the image, admires its perfect mimicry of each movement. Flesh and phantom move together, bodies masked, faces neutral.

That's me, she thinks. *That's what I look like now*. She tries to read what lies behind that glacial facade. *Am I bored, horny, upset?* How to tell, with her eyes hidden behind those corneal opacities? She sees no trace of the tension she always feels. *I could be terrified. I could be pissing in my 'skin and nobody would know.*

She leans forward. The reflection comes to meet her. They stare at each other, white to white, ice to ice. For a moment, they almost forget Beebe's ongoing war against pressure. For a moment, they do not mind the claustrophobic solitude that grips them.

How many times, Clarke wonders, *have I wanted eyes as dead as these?*

Beebe's metal viscera crowd the corridor beyond her cubby. Clarke can barely stand erect. A few steps bring her into the lounge.

Ballard, back in shirtsleeves, is at one of the library terminals. "Rickets," she says.

"*What?*"

"Fish down here don't get enough trace elements. They're rotten with deficiency diseases. It doesn't matter how fierce they are. They bite too hard, they break their teeth on us."

Clarke stabs buttons on the food processor; the machine grumbles at her touch. "I thought there was all sorts of food at the rift. That's why things got so big."

"There's a lot of food. Just not very good quality."

A vaguely edible lozenge of sludge oozes from the processor onto Clarke's plate. She eyes it for a moment. *I can relate*.

"You're going to eat in your gear?" Ballard asks, as Clarke sits down at the lounge table.

Clarke blinks at her. "Yeah. Why?"

"Oh, nothing. It would just be nice to talk to someone with pupils in their eyes, you know?"

"Sorry. I'll take them off if you—"

"No, it's no big thing. I can live with it." Ballard shuts down the library and sits down across from Clarke. "So, how do you like the place so far?"

Clarke shrugs and keeps eating.

"I'm glad we're only down here for three months," Ballard says. "This place could get to you after a while."

"It could be worse."

"Oh, I'm not complaining. I was looking for a challenge, after all. What about you?"

"Me?"

"What brings you down here? What are you looking for?"

Clarke doesn't answer for a moment. "I don't know, really," she says at last. "Privacy, I guess."

Ballard looks up. Clarke stares back, her face neutral.

"Well, I'll leave you to it, then," Ballard says pleasantly.

Clarke watches her disappear down the corridor. She hears the sound of a cubby hatch swinging shut.

Give it up, Ballard, she thinks. *I'm not the sort of person you really want to know.*

Almost start of the morning shift. The food processor disgorges Clarke's breakfast with its usual reluctance. Ballard, in Communications, is just getting off the phone. A moment later she appears in the hatchway.

"Management says—" She stops. "You've got blue eyes."

Clarke smiles slightly. "You've seen them before."

"I know. It's just kind of surprising, it's been a while since I've seen you without your caps on."

Clarke sits down with her breakfast. "So, what does Management say?"

"We're on schedule. Rest of the crew comes down in three weeks, we go online in four." Ballard sits down across from Clarke. "I wonder sometimes why we're not online right now."

"I guess they just want to be sure everything works."

"Still, six months seems like a long time for a dry run. And you'd think that—well, they'd want to get the geothermal program up and running as fast as possible, after all that's happened."

After Lepreau and Winshire melted down, you mean.

"And there's something else," Ballard says. "I can't get through to Piccard."

Clarke looks up. Piccard Station is anchored on the Galapagos Rift; it is not a particularly stable mooring.

"Did you ever meet the couple there?" Ballard asks. "Ken Lubin, Lana Cheung?"

Clarke shakes her head. "They went through before me. I never met any of the other Rifters except you."

"Nice people. I thought I'd call them up, see how things were going at Piccard, but nobody can get through."

"Line down?"

"They say it's probably something like that. Nothing serious. They're sending a 'scaphe down to check it out."

Maybe the seabed opened up and swallowed them whole, Clarke thinks. *Maybe the hull had a weak plate—one's all it would take . . .*

Something creaks, deep in Beebe's superstructure. Clarke looks around. The walls seem to have moved closer while she wasn't looking.

"Sometimes," she says, "I wish we didn't keep Beebe at surface pressure. Sometimes I wish we were pumped up to ambient. To take the strain off the hull."

Ballard smiles. "Come on. Would you want to spend three months sitting in a decompression tank afterwards?"

In the Systems cubby, something bleats for attention.

"Seismic. Wonderful." Ballard disappears into Systems. Clarke follows.

An amber line is writhing across one of the displays. It looks like the EEG of someone caught in a nightmare.

"Get your eyes back in," Ballard says. "The Throat's acting up."

They can hear it all the way to Beebe; a malign, almost electrical hiss from the direction of the Throat. Clarke follows Ballard toward it, one hand running lightly along the guide rope. The distant smudge of light that marks their destination seems wrong, somehow. The color is different. It ripples.

They swim into its glowing nimbus and see why. The Throat is on fire.

Sapphire auroras slide flickering across the generators. At the far end of the array, almost invisible with distance, a pillar of smoke swirls up into the darkness like a great tornado.

The sound it makes fills the abyss. Clarke closes her eyes for a moment, and hears rattlesnakes.

"Jesus!" Ballard shouts over the noise. "It's not supposed to do that!"

Clarke checks her thermistor. It won't settle; water temperature goes from four degrees to thirty-eight and back again, within seconds. A myriad ephemeral currents tug at them as they watch.

"Why the light show?" Clarke calls back.

"I don't know!" Ballard answers. "Bioluminescence, I guess! Heat-sensitive bacteria!"

Without warning, the tumult dies.

The ocean empties of sound. Phosphorescent spiderwebs wriggle dimly on the metal and vanish. In the distance, the tornado sighs and fragments into a few transient dust devils.

A gentle rain of black soot begins to fall in the copper light.

"Smoker," Ballard says into the sudden stillness. "A big one."

They swim to the place where the geyser erupted. There is a fresh wound in the seabed, a gash several meters long, between two of the generators.

"This wasn't supposed to happen," Ballard says. "That's why they built here, for crying out loud! It was supposed to be stable!"

"The rift is never stable," Clarke replies. *Not much point in being here if it was.*

Ballard swims up through the fallout and pops an access plate on one of the generators. "Well, according to this there's no damage," she calls down, after looking inside. "Hang on, let me switch channels here—"

Clarke touches one of the cylindrical sensors strapped to her waist, and stares into the fissure. *I should be able to fit through there*, she decides.

And does.

"We were lucky," Ballard is saying above her. "The other generators are okay too. Oh, wait a second; number two has a clogged cooling duct, but it's not serious. Backups can handle it until—get out of there!"

Clarke looks up, one hand on the sensor she's planting. Ballard stares down at her through a chimney of fresh rock.

"Are you crazy?" Ballard shouts. "That's an active smoker!"

Clarke looks down again, deeper into the shaft. It twists out of sight in the mineral haze. "We need temperature readings," she says, "from inside the mouth."

"Get out of there! It could go off again and fry you!"

I suppose it could at that, Clarke thinks. "It just finished erupting," she calls back. "It'll take a while to build up a fresh head." She twists a knob on the sensor; tiny explosive bolts blast into the rock, anchoring the device.

"Get out of there, now!"

"Just a second." Clarke turns the sensor on then kicks up out of the seabed. Ballard grabs her arm as she emerges, starts to drag her away from the smoker.

Clarke stiffens and pulls free. "Don't—" *touch me!* She catches herself. "I'm out, okay, you don't have to . . ."

"Farther." Ballard keeps swimming. "Over here."

They are near the edge of the light now, the floodlit Throat on one side, blackness on the other. Ballard faces Clarke. "Are you out of your mind? We could have gone back to Beebe for a drone! We could have planted it on remote!"

Clarke does not answer. She sees something moving in the distance behind Ballard. "Watch your back," she says.

Ballard turns, and sees the gulper sliding toward them. It undulates through the water like brown smoke, silent and endless; Clarke cannot see the creature's tail, although several meters of serpentine flesh have come out of the darkness.

Ballard goes for her knife. After a moment, Clarke does too.

The gulper's jaw drops open like a great jagged scoop.

Ballard begins to launch herself at the thing, knife upraised.

Clarke puts her hand out. "Wait a minute. It's not coming at us."

The front end of the gulper is about ten meters distant now. Its tail pulls free of the murk.

"Are you crazy?" Ballard moves clear of Clarke's hand, still watching the monster.

"Maybe it isn't hungry," Clarke says. She can see its eyes, two tiny unwinking spots glaring at them from the tip of the snout.

"They're always hungry. Did you sleep through the briefings?"

The gulper closes its mouth and passes. It extends around them now, in a great meandering arc. The head turns back to look at them. It opens its mouth.

"Fuck this," Ballard says, and charges.

Her first stroke opens a meter-long gash in the creature's side. The gulper stares at Ballard for a moment, as if astonished. Then, ponderously, it thrashes.

Clarke watches without moving. *Why can't she just let it go? Why does she always have to prove she's better than everything?*

Ballard strikes again; this time she slashes into a great tumorous swelling that has to be the stomach.

She frees the things inside.

They spill out through the wound; two huge viperfish and some misshapen creature Clarke doesn't recognize. One of the viperfish is still alive, and in a foul mood. It locks its teeth around the first thing it encounters.

Ballard. From behind.

"Lenie!" Ballard's knife hand is swinging in staccato arcs. The viperfish begins to come apart. Its jaws remain locked. The convulsing gulper crashes into Ballard and sends her spinning to the bottom.

Finally, Clarke begins to move.

The gulper collides with Ballard again. Clarke moves in low, hugging the bottom, and pulls the other woman clear of those thrashing coils.

Ballard's knife continues to dip and twist. The viperfish is a mutilated wreck behind the gills, but its grip remains unbroken. Ballard cannot twist around far enough to reach the skull. Clarke comes in from behind and takes the creature's head in her hands.

It stares at her, malevolent and unthinking.

"Kill it!" Ballard shouts. "Jesus, what are you waiting for?"

Clarke closes her eyes, and clenches. The skull in her hand splinters like cheap plastic.

There is a silence.

After a while, she opens her eyes. The gulper is gone, fled back into darkness to heal or die. But Ballard is still there, and Ballard is angry.

"What's wrong with you?" she says.

Clarke unclenches her fists. Bits of bone and jellied flesh float about her fingers.

"You're supposed to back me up! Why are you so damned passive all the time?"

"Sorry." *Sometimes it works.*

Ballard reaches behind her back. "I'm cold. I think it punctured my diveskin—"

Clarke swims behind her and looks. "A couple of holes. How are you otherwise? Anything feel broken?"

"It broke through the diveskin," Ballard says, as if to herself. "And when that gulper hit me, it could have . . ." She turns to Clarke and her voice, even distorted, carries a shocked uncertainty. ". . . I could have been killed. I could have been killed!"

For an instant, it is as though Ballard's skin and eyes and self-assurance have all been stripped away. For the first time Clarke can see through to the weakness beneath, growing like a delicate tracery of hairline cracks.

You can screw up too, Ballard. It isn't all fun and games. You know that now.

It hurts, doesn't it.

Somewhere inside, the slightest touch of sympathy. "It's okay," Clarke says. "Jeanette, it's—"

"You idiot!" Ballard hisses. She stares at Clarke like some malign and sightless old woman. "You just floated there! You just let it happen to me!"

Clarke feels her guard snap up again, just in time. *This isn't just anger*, she realizes. *This isn't just the heat of the moment. She doesn't like me. She doesn't like me at all.*

She never did.

Beebe station floats tethered above the seabed, a gunmetal-gray planet ringed by a belt of equatorial floodlights. There is an airlock for divers at the south pole, and a docking hatch for 'scaphes at the north. In between there are girders and anchor lines, conduits and cables, metal armour and Lenie Clarke.

She is doing a routine visual check on the hull; standard procedure, once a week. Ballard is inside, testing some equipment in the Communications cubby. This is not entirely within the spirit of the buddy system. Clarke prefers it this way. Relations have been civil over the past couple of days—Ballard even resurrects her patented chumminess on occasion—but the more time they spend together, the more forced things get. Eventually, Clarke knows, something is going to break.

Besides, out here in the void it seems only natural to be alone.

She is examining a cable clamp when an angler charges into the light. It is about two meters long, and hungry. It rams directly into the nearest of Beebe's floodlamps, mouth agape. Several teeth shatter against the crystal lens. The angler twists to one side, knocking the hull with her tail, and swims off until barely visible against the dark.

Clarke watches, fascinated. The angler swims back and forth, back and forth, then charges again.

The flood weathers the impact easily, doing more damage to its attacker. The angler lashes its dorsal spine. The lure at its end, a glowing worm-shaped thing, luminesces furiously.

Over and over again the fish batters itself against the light. Finally, exhausted, it sinks twitching down to the muddy bottom.

"Lenie? Are you okay?"

Clarke feels the words buzzing in her lower jaw. She trips the sender in her diveskin, "I'm okay."

"I heard something out there," Ballard says. "I just wanted to make sure you were . . ."

"I'm fine," Clarke says. "It was just a fish, trying to eat one of the lights."

"They never learn, do they?"

"No. I guess not. See you later."

"See—"

Clarke switches off her receiver.

Poor stupid fish. How many millennia did it take for them to learn that bioluminescence equals food? How long will Beebe have to sit here before they learn that electric light doesn't?

We could keep our headlights off. Maybe they'd leave us alone . . .

She stares out past Beebe's electric halo. There is so much blackness there. It almost hurts to look at it. Without lights, without sonar, how far could she go into that viscous shroud and still return?

Clarke kills her headlight. Night edges a bit closer, but Beebe's lights keep it at bay. Clarke turns until she is face to face with the darkness. She crouches like a spider against Beebe's hull.

She pushes off.

The darkness embraces her. She swims, not looking back, until her legs grow tired. She does not know how far she has come.

But it must be light-years. The ocean is full of stars.

Behind her, the station shines brightest, with coarse yellow rays. In the opposite direction, she can barely make out the Throat, an insignificant sunrise on the horizon.

Everywhere else, living constellations punctuate the dark. Here, a string of pearls blink sexual advertisements at two-second intervals. Here, a sudden flash leaves diversionary afterimages swarming across Clarke's field of view; something flees under cover of her momentary blindness. There, a counterfeit worm twists lazily in the current, invisibly tied to the roof of some predatory mouth.

There are so many of them.

She feels a sudden surge in the water, as if something big has just passed very close. A delicious thrill dances through her body.

It nearly touched me, she thinks. *I wonder what it was.* The rift is full of monsters who don't know when to quit. It doesn't matter how much they eat. Their voracity is as much a part of them as their elastic bellies, their unhinging jaws. Ravenous dwarfs attack giants twice their own size, and sometimes win. The abyss is a desert; no one can afford the luxury of waiting for better odds.

But even a desert has oases, and sometimes the deep hunters find them. They come upon the malnourishing abundance of the rift and gorge themselves; their descendants grow huge and bloated over such delicate bones . . .

My light was off, and it left me alone. I wonder . . .

She turns it back on. Her vision clouds in the sudden glare, then clears. The ocean reverts to unrelieved black. No nightmares accost her. The beam lights empty water wherever she points it.

She switches it off. There is a moment of absolute darkness while her eyecaps adjust to the reduced light. Then the stars come out again.

They are so beautiful. Lenie Clarke rests on the bottom of the ocean and watches the abyss sparkle around her. And she almost laughs as she realizes, three thousand meters from the nearest sunlight, that it's only dark when the lights are on.

"What the hell is wrong with you? You've been gone for over three hours, did you know that? Why didn't you answer me?"

Clarke bends over and removes her fins. "I guess I turned my receiver off," she says. "I was—wait a second, did you say—"

"You guess? Have you forgotten every safety reg they drilled into us? You're supposed to have your receiver on from the moment you leave Beebe until you get back!"

"Did you say *three hours?*"

"I couldn't even come out after you, I couldn't find you on sonar! I just had to sit here and hope you'd show up!"

It only seems a few minutes since she pushed off into the darkness. Clarke climbs up into the lounge, suddenly chilled.

"Where were you, Lenie?" Ballard demands, coming up behind her. Clarke hears the slightest plaintive tone in her voice.

"I—I must've been on the bottom," Clarke says. "That's why sonar didn't get me. I didn't go far."

Was I asleep? What was I doing for three hours?

"I was just . . . wandering around. I lost track of the time. I'm sorry."

"Not good enough. Don't do it again."

There is a brief silence. They hear the sudden, familiar impact of flesh on metal.

"Christ!" Ballard snaps. "I'm turning the externals off right now!"

Whatever it is gets in two more hits by the time Ballard reaches the Systems cubby. Clarke hears her punch a couple of buttons.

Ballard comes out of Systems. "There. Now we're invisible."

Something hits them again. And again.

"I guess not," Clarke says.

Ballard stands in the lounge, listening to the rhythm of the assault. "They don't show up on sonar," she says, almost whispering. "Sometimes, when I hear them coming at us, I tune it down to extreme close range. But it looks right through them."

"No gas bladders. Nothing to bounce an echo off of."

"We show up just fine out there, most of the time. But not those things. You can't find them, no matter how high you turn the gain. They're like ghosts."

"They're not ghosts." Almost unconsciously, Clarke has been counting the beats: *eight . . . nine . . .*

Ballard turns to face her. "They've shut down Piccard," she says, and her voice is small and tight.

"What?"

"The grid office says it's just some technical problem. But I've got a friend in Personnel. I phoned him when you were outside. He says Lana's in the hospital. And I get the feeling . . ." Ballard shakes her head. "It sounded like Ken Lubin did something down there. I think maybe he attacked her."

Three thumps from outside, in rapid succession. Clarke can feel Ballard's eyes on her. The silence stretches.

"Or maybe not," Ballard says. "We got all those personality tests. If he was violent, they would have picked it up before they sent him down."

Clarke watches her, and listens to the pounding of an intermittent fist.

"Or maybe . . . maybe the rift changed him somehow. Maybe they misjudged the pressure we'd all be under. So to speak." Ballard musters a feeble smile. "Not the physical danger so much as the emotional stress, you know? Everyday things. Just being outside could get to you after a while. Seawater sluicing through your chest. Not breathing for hours at a time. It's like—living without a heartbeat . . ."

She looks up at the ceiling; the sounds from outside are a bit more erratic now.

"Outside's not so bad," Clarke says. *At least you're incompressible. At least you don't have to worry about the plates giving in.*

"I don't think you'd change suddenly. It would just sort of sneak up on you, little by little. And then one day you'd just wake up changed, you'd be different somehow, only you'd never have noticed the transition. Like Ken Lubin."

She looks at Clarke, and her voice drops a bit.

"And like you."

"Me." Clarke turns Ballard's words over in her mind, waits for the onset of some reaction. She feels nothing but her own indifference. "I don't think you have much to worry about. I'm not a violent person."

"I know. I'm not worried about my own safety, Lenie. I'm worried about yours."

Clarke looks at her from behind the impervious safety of her lenses, and doesn't answer.

"You've changed since you came down here," Ballard says. "You're withdrawing from me, you're exposing yourself to unnecessary risks. I don't know exactly what's happening to you. It's almost like you're trying to kill yourself."

"I'm not," Clarke says. She tries to change the subject. "Is Lana Cheung all right?"

Ballard studies her for a moment. She takes the hint. "I don't know. I couldn't get any details."

Clarke feels something knotting up inside her.

"I wonder what she did," she murmurs, "to set him off like that?"

Ballard stares at her, openmouthed. "What she did? I can't believe you said that!"

"I only meant—"

"I know what you meant."

The outside pounding has stopped. Ballard does not relax. She stands hunched over in those strange, loose-fitting clothes that Drybacks wear, and stares at the ceiling as though she doesn't believe in the silence. She looks back at Clarke.

"Lenie, you know I don't like to pull rank, but your attitude is putting both of us at risk. I think this place is really getting to you. I hope you can get back on-line here, I really do. Otherwise I may have to recommend you for a transfer."

Clarke watches Ballard leave the lounge. *You're lying*, she realizes. *You're scared to death, and it's not just because I'm changing.*

It's because you are.

Clarke finds out five hours after the fact: something has changed on the ocean floor.

We sleep and the earth moves, she thinks, studying the topographic display. *And next time, or the time after, maybe it'll move right out from under us.*

I wonder if I'll have time to feel anything.

She turns at a sound behind her. Ballard is standing in the lounge, swaying slightly. Her face seems somehow disfigured by the concentric rings in her eyes, by the dark hollows around them. Naked eyes are beginning to look alien to Clarke.

"The seabed shifted," Clarke says. "There's a new outcropping about two hundred meters west of us."

"That's odd. I didn't feel anything."

"It happened about five hours ago. You were asleep."

Ballard glances up sharply. Clarke studies the haggard lines of her face. *On second thought, I guess you weren't.*

"I . . . would've woken up," Ballard says. She squeezes past Clarke into the cubby and checks the topographic display.

"Two meters high, twelve long," Clarke recites.

Ballard doesn't answer. She punches some commands into a keyboard; the topographic image dissolves, re-forms into a column of numbers.

"Just as I thought," she says. "No heavy seismic activity for over forty-two hours."

"Sonar doesn't lie," Clarke says calmly.

"Neither does seismo," Ballard answers.

There is a brief silence. There is a standard procedure for such things, and they both know what it is.

"We have to check it out," Clarke says.

But Ballard only nods. "Give me a moment to change."

They call it a squid; a jet-propelled cylinder about half a meter long, with a headlight at the front end and a towbar at the back. Clarke, floating between Beebe and the seabed, checks it over with one hand. Her other hand grips a sonar pistol. She points the pistol into blackness; ultrasonic clicks sweep the night, give her a bearing.

"That way," she says, pointing.

Ballard squeezes down on her own squid's towbar. The machine pulls her away. After a moment Clarke follows. Bringing up the rear, a third squid carries an assortment of sensors in a nylon bag.

Ballard is travelling at nearly full throttle. The lamps on her helmet and squid stab the water like two lighthouse beacons. Clarke, her own lights doused, catches up with Ballard about half-way to their destination. They cruise along a couple of meters over the muddy substrate.

"Your lights," Ballard says.

"We don't need them. Sonar works in the dark."

"Are you just breaking the regs for the sheer thrill of it, now?"

"The fish down here, they key on things that glow—"

"Turn your lights on. That's an order."

Clarke does not answer. She watches the twin beams beside her, Ballard's squid shining steady and unwavering, Ballard's headlamp slicing the water in erratic arcs as she moves her head . . .

"I told you," Ballard says, "turn your—Christ!"

It was just a glimpse, caught for a moment in the sweep of Ballard's headlight. She jerks her head around and it slides back out of sight. Then it looms up in the squid's beam, huge and terrible.

The abyss is grinning at them, teeth bared.

A mouth stretches across the width of the beam, and extends into darkness on either side. It is crammed with conical teeth the size of human hands, and they do not look the least bit fragile.

Ballard makes a strangled sound and dives into the mud. The benthic ooze boils up around her in a seething cloud; she disappears in a torrent of planktonic corpses.

Lenie Clarke stops and waits, unmoving. She stares transfixed at that threatening smile. Her whole body feels electrified, she has never been so explicitly aware of herself. Every nerve fires and freezes at the same time. She is terrified.

But she is also, somehow, completely in control of herself. She reflects on this paradox as Ballard's abandoned squid slows and stops itself, scant meters from that endless row of teeth. She wonders at her own analytical clarity as the third squid, with its burden of sensors, decelerates past and takes up position beside Ballard's.

There in the light, the grin does not change.

After a few moments, Clarke raises her sonar pistol and fires. We're here, she realizes, checking the readout. *That's the outcropping.*

She swims closer. The smile hangs there, enigmatic and enticing. Now she can see bits of bone at the roots of the teeth, and tatters of decomposed flesh trailing from the gums.

She turns and backtracks. The cloud on the seabed has nearly settled.

"Ballard," she says in her synthetic voice.

Nobody answers.

Clarke reaches down through the mud, feeling blind, until she touches something warm and trembling.

The seabed explodes in her face.

Ballard erupts from the substrate, trailing a muddy comet's tail. Her hand rises from that sudden cloud, clasped around something glinting in the transient light. Clarke sees the knife, twists almost too late; the blade glances off her 'skin, igniting nerves along her ribcage. Ballard lashes out again. This time Clarke catches the knife-hand as it shoots past, twists it, pushes. Ballard tumbles away.

"It's me!" Clarke shouts; the 'skin turns her voice into a tinny vibrato.

Ballard rises up again, white eyes unseeing, knife still in hand.

Clarke holds up her hands. "It's okay! There's nothing here! It's dead!"

Ballard stops. She stares at Clarke. She looks over to the squids, to the smile they illuminate. She stiffens.

"It's some kind of whale," Clarke says. "It's been dead a long time."

"A . . . a whale?" Ballard rasps. She begins to shake.

There's no need to feel embarrassed, Clarke almost says, but doesn't. Instead, she reaches out and touches Ballard lightly on the arm. *Is this how you do it?* she wonders.

Ballard jerks back as if scalded.

I guess not . . .

"Um, Jeanette . . ." Clarke begins.

Ballard raises a trembling hand, cutting Clarke off. "I'm okay. I want to g . . . I think we should get back now, don't you?"

"Okay," Clarke says. But she doesn't really mean it.

She could stay out here all day.

Ballard is at the library again. She turns, passing a casual hand over the brightness control as Clarke comes up behind her; the display darkens before Clarke can see what it is.

"It was a Ziphiid," Ballard says. "A beaked whale. Very rare. They don't dive this deep."

Clarke listens, not really interested.

"It must have died and rotted further up, and sank." Ballard's voice is slightly raised. She looks almost furtively at something on the other side of the lounge. "I wonder what the chances are of that happening."

"What?"

"I mean, in all the ocean, something that big just happening to drop out of the sky a few hundred meters away. The odds of that must be pretty low."

"Yeah. I guess so." Clarke reaches over and brightens the display. One half of the screen glows softly with luminous text. The other holds the rotating image of some complex molecule.

"What's this?" Clarke asks.

Ballard steals another glance across the lounge. "Just an old biopsyche text the library had on file. I was browsing through it. Used to be an interest of mine."

Clarke looks at her. "Uh-huh." She bends over and studies the display. Some sort of technical chemistry. The only thing she really understands is the caption beneath the graphic.

She reads it aloud, "True Happiness."

"Yeah. A tricyclic with four side chains." Ballard points at the screen. "Whenever you're happy, really happy, that's what does it to you."

"When did they find that out?"

"I don't know. It's an old book."

Clarke stares at the revolving simulacrum. It disturbs her, somehow. It floats there over that smug stupid caption, and it says something she doesn't want to hear.

You've been solved, it tells her. *You're mechanical. Chemicals and electricity. Everything you are, every dream, every action, it all comes down to a change of voltage somewhere, or a—what did she say—a tricyclic with four side chains . . .*

"It's wrong," Clarke murmurs. *Or they'd be able to fix us, when we broke down . . .*

"Sorry?" Ballard says.

"It's saying we're just these . . . soft computers. With faces."

Ballard shuts off the terminal.

"That's right," she says. "And some of us may even be losing those."

The jibe registers, but it doesn't hurt. Clarke straightens and moves towards the ladder.

"Where are you going? You going outside again?" Ballard asks.

"The shift isn't over. I thought I'd clean out the duct on number two."

"It's a bit late to start on that, Lenie. The day will be over before we're even half done." Ballard's eyes dart away again. This time Clarke follows the glance to the full-length mirror on the far wall.

She sees nothing of particular interest there.

"I'll work late." Clarke grabs the railing, swings her foot onto the top rung.

"Lenie," Ballard says, and Clarke swears she hears a tremor in that voice. She looks back, but the other woman is moving to Communications. "Well, I'm afraid I can't go with you," she's saying. "I'm in the middle of debugging one of the telemetry routines."

"That's fine," Clarke says. She feels the tension starting to rise. Beebe is shrinking again. She starts down the ladder.

"Are you sure you're okay going out alone? Maybe you should wait until tomorrow."

"No. I'm okay."

"Well, remember to keep your receiver open. I don't want you getting lost on me again . . ."

Clarke is in the wetroom. She climbs into the airlock and runs through the ritual. It no longer feels like drowning. It feels like being born again.

She awakens into darkness, and the sound of weeping.

She lies there for a few minutes, confused and uncertain. The sobs come from all sides, soft but omnipresent in Beebe's resonant shell. She hears nothing else except her own heartbeat.

She is afraid. She isn't sure why. She wishes the sounds would go away.

Clarke rolls off her bunk and fumbles at the hatch. It opens into a semi-darkened corridor; meager light escapes from the lounge at one end. The sounds come from the other direction, from deepening darkness. She follows them through an infestation of pipes and conduits.

Ballard's quarters. The hatch is open. An emerald readout sparkles in the darkness, bestowing no detail upon the hunched figure on the pallet.

"Ballard," Clarke says softly. She does not want to go in.

The shadow moves, seems to look up at her. "Why won't you show it?" it says, its voice pleading.

Clarke frowns in the darkness. "Show what?"

"You know what! How . . . afraid you are!"

"Afraid?"

"Of being here, of being stuck at the bottom of this horrible dark ocean . . ."

"I don't understand," Clarke whispers. The claustrophobia in her, restless again, begins to stir.

Ballard snorts, but the derision seems forced. "Oh, you understand all right. You think this is some sort of competition, you think if you can just keep it all inside you'll win somehow . . . but it isn't like that at all, Lenie, it isn't helping to keep it hidden like this, we've got to be able to trust each other down here or we're lost . . ."

She shifts slightly on the bunk. Clarke's eyes, enhanced by the caps, can pick out a few details now; rough edges embroider Ballard's silhouette, the folds and creases of normal clothing, unbuttoned to the waist. She thinks of a cadaver, half-dissected, rising on the table to mourn its own mutilation.

"I don't know what you mean," Clarke says.

"I've tried to be friendly," Ballard says. "I've tried to get along with you, but you're so cold, you won't even admit . . . I mean, you couldn't like it down here, nobody could, why can't you just admit—"

"But I don't, I . . . I hate it in here. It's like Beebe's going to . . . to clench around me. And all I can do is wait for it to happen."

Ballard nods in the darkness. "Yes, yes, I know what you mean." She seems somehow encouraged by Clarke's admission. "And no matter how much you tell yourself—" She stops. "You hate it in here?"

Did I say something wrong? Clarke wonders.

"Out there is hardly any better, you know," Ballard says. "Outside is even worse! There's mudslides and steam vents and giant fish trying to eat you all the time, you can't possibly . . . but . . . you don't mind all that, do you?"

Somehow, her tone has turned accusing. Clarke shrugs.

"No, you don't." Ballard is speaking slowly now. Her voice drops to a whisper. "You actually like it out there. Don't you?"

Reluctantly, Clarke nods. "Yeah. I guess so."

"But it's so . . . the rift can kill you, Lenie. It can kill *us*. A hundred different ways. Doesn't that scare you?"

"I don't know. I don't think about it much. I guess it does, sort of."

"Then why are you so happy out there?" Ballard cries. "It doesn't make any sense . . ."

I'm not exactly "happy," Clarke thinks. Aloud, she only says, "I don't know. It's not that weird, lots of people do dangerous things. What about free-fallers? What about mountain climbers?"

But Ballard doesn't answer. Her silhouette has grown rigid on the bed. Suddenly, she reaches over and turns on the cubby light.

Lenie Clarke blinks against the sudden brightness. Then the room dims as her eyecaps darken.

"Jesus Christ!" Ballard shouts at her. "You sleep in that fucking costume now?"

It is something else Clarke hasn't thought about. It just seems easier.

"All this time I've been pouring my heart out to you and you've been wearing that machine's face! You don't even have the decency to show me your goddamned eyes!"

Clarke steps back, startled. Ballard rises from the bed and takes a single step forward. "To think you could actually pass for human before they gave you that suit! Why don't you go find something to play with out in your fucking ocean!"

And slams the hatch in Clarke's face.

Lenie Clarke stares at the sealed bulkhead for a few moments. Her face, she knows, is calm. Her face is usually calm. But she stands there, unmoving, until the cringing thing inside of her unfolds a little.

"Yes," she says at last, very softly. "I think I will."

Ballard is waiting for her as she emerges from the airlock. "Lenie," she says quietly, "we have to talk. It's important."

Clarke bends over and removes her fins. "Go ahead."

"Not here. In my cubby."

Clarke looks at her.

"Please."

Clarke starts up the ladder.

"Aren't you going to take—" Ballard stops as Clarke looks down. "Never mind. It's okay."

They ascend into the lounge. Ballard takes the lead. Clarke follows her down the corridor and into her cabin. Ballard dogs the hatch and sits on her bunk, leaving room for Clarke.

Clarke looks around the cramped space. Ballard has curtained over the mirrored bulkhead with a spare sheet.

Ballard pats the bed beside her. "Come on, Lenie. Sit down."

Reluctantly, Clarke sits. Ballard's sudden kindness confuses her. Ballard hasn't acted this way since . . .

. . . Since she had the upper hand.

"—might not be easy for you to hear," Ballard is saying, "but we have to get you off the rift. They shouldn't have put you down here in the first place."

Clarke does not reply. She waits.

"Remember the tests they gave us?" Ballard continues. "They measured our tolerance to stress; confinement, prolonged isolation, chronic physical danger, that sort of thing."

Clarke nods slightly. "So?"

"So," says Ballard, "did you think for a moment they'd test for those qualities without knowing what sort of person would have them? Or how they got to be that way?"

Inside, Clarke goes very still. Outside, nothing changes.

Ballard leans forward a bit. "Remember what you said? About mountain climbers, and free-fallers, and why people deliberately do dangerous things? I've been reading up, Lenie. Ever since I got to know you I've been reading up—"

Got to know me?

"—and do you know what thrillseekers have in common? They all say that you haven't lived until you've nearly died. They need the danger. It gives them a rush."

You don't know me at all . . .

"Some of them are combat veterans, some were hostages for long periods, some just spent a lot of time in dead zones for one reason or another. And a lot of the really compulsive ones—"

Nobody knows me.

"—the ones who can't be happy unless they're on the edge, all the time—a lot of them got started early, Lenie. When they were just children. And you, I bet . . . you don't even like being touched . . ."

Go away. Go away.

Ballard puts her hand on Clarke's shoulder. "How long were you abused, Lenie?" she asks gently. "How many years?"

Clarke shrugs off the hand and does not answer. *He didn't mean any harm.* She shifts on the bunk, turning away slightly.

"That's it, isn't it? You don't just have a tolerance to trauma, Lenie. You've got an addiction to it. Don't you?"

It only takes Clarke a moment to recover. The 'skin, the eyecaps make it easier. She turns calmly back to Ballard. She even smiles a little.

"No," she says. "I don't."

"There's a mechanism," Ballard tells her. "I've been reading about it. Do you know how the brain handles stress, Lenie? It dumps all sorts of addictive stimulants into the bloodstream. Beta-endorphins, opioids. If it happens often enough, for long enough, you get hooked. You can't help it."

Clarke feels a sound in her throat, a jagged coughing noise a bit like tearing metal. After a moment, she recognises it as laughter.

"I'm not making it up!" Ballard insists. "You can look it up yourself if you don't believe me! Don't you know how many abused children spend their whole lives hooked on wife beaters or self-mutilation or free-fall—"

"And it makes them happy, is that it?" Clarke asks with cold disdain. "They enjoy getting raped, or punched out, or—"

"No, of course you're not happy!" Ballard cuts in. "But what you feel, that's probably the closest you've ever come. So you confuse the two, you look for stress anywhere you can find it. It's physiological addiction, Lenie. You ask for it. You always asked for it."

I ask for it. Ballard has been reading, and Ballard knows: Life is pure electrochemistry. No use explaining how it feels. No use explaining that there are far worse things than being beaten up. There are even worse things than being held down and raped by your own father. There are the times between, when nothing happens at all. When he leaves you alone, and you don't know for how long. You sit across the table from him, forcing yourself to eat while your bruised insides try to knit themselves back together; and he pats you on the head and smiles at you, and you know the reprieve has already lasted too long, he's going to come for you tonight, or tomorrow, or maybe the next day.

Of course I asked for it. How else could I get it over with?

"Listen," Clarke says. Her voice is shaking. She takes a deep breath, tries again. "You're completely wrong. Completely. You don't have a clue what you're talking about."

But Ballard shakes her head. "Sure I do, Lenie. Believe it. You're hooked on your own pain, and so you go out there and keep daring the rift to kill you, and eventually it will, don't you see? That's why you shouldn't be here. That's why we have to get you back."

Clarke stands up. "I'm not going back." She turns to the hatch.

Ballard reaches out toward her. "Listen, you've got to stay and hear me out. There's more."

Clarke looks down at her with complete indifference. "Thanks for your concern. But I can go any time I want to."

"You go out there now and you'll give everything away, they're watching us! Can't you figure it out yet?" Ballard's voice is rising. "Listen, they knew about you! They were looking for someone like you! They've been testing us, they don't know yet what kind of person works out better down here, so they're watching and waiting to see who cracks first! This whole program is still experimental, can't you see that? Everyone they've sent down—you, me, Ken Lubin and Lana Cheung, it's all part of some cold-blooded test . . ."

"And you're failing it," Clarke says softly. "I see."

"They're using us, Lenie—don't go out there!"

Ballard's fingers grasp at Clarke like the suckers of an octopus. Clarke pushes them away. She undogs the hatch and pushes it open. She hears Ballard rising behind her.

"You're sick!" Ballard screams. Something smashes into the back of Clarke's head. She goes sprawling out into the corridor. One arm smacks painfully against a cluster of pipes as she falls.

She rolls to one side and raises her arms to protect herself. But Ballard just steps over her and stalks into the lounge.

I'm not afraid, Clarke notes, getting to her feet. *She hit me, and I'm not afraid. Isn't that odd . . .*

From somewhere nearby, the sound of shattering glass.

Ballard is shouting in the lounge. "The experiment's over! Come on out, you fucking ghouls!"

Clarke follows the corridor, steps out of it. Pieces of the lounge mirror hang like great jagged stalactites in their frame. Splashes of glass litter the floor.

On the wall, behind the broken mirror, a fisheye lens takes in every corner of the room.

Ballard is staring into it. "Did you hear me? I'm not playing your stupid games any more! I'm through performing!"

The quartzite lens stares back impassively.

So you were right, Clarke muses. She remembers the sheet in Ballard's cubby. *You figured it out, you found the pickups in your own cubby, and Ballard, my dear friend, you didn't tell me.*

How long have you known?

Ballard looks around, sees Clarke. "You've got her fooled, all right," she snarls at the fisheye, "but she's a goddamned basket case! She's not even sane! Your little tests don't impress me one fucking bit!"

Clarke steps toward her.

"Don't call me a basket case," she says, her voice absolutely level.

"That's what you are!" Ballard shouts. "You're sick! That's why you're down here! They need you sick, they depend on it, and you're so far gone you can't see it! You hide everything behind that—that mask of yours, and you sit there like some masochistic jellyfish and just take anything anyone dishes out—you ask for it . . ."

That used to be true, Clarke realizes as her hands ball into fists. *That's the strange thing*. Ballard begins to back away; Clarke advances, step by step. *It wasn't until I came down here that I learned that I could fight back. That I could win. The rift taught me that, and now Ballard has too . . .*

"Thank you," Clarke whispers, and hits Ballard hard in the face.

Ballard goes over backwards, collides with a table. Clarke calmly steps forward. She catches a glimpse of herself in a glass icicle; her capped eyes seem almost luminous.

"Oh Jesus," Ballard whimpers. "Lenie, I'm sorry."

Clarke stands over her. "Don't be," she says. She sees herself as some sort of exploding schematic, each piece neatly labelled. *So much anger in here*, she thinks. *So much hate. So much to take out on someone.*

She looks at Ballard, cowering on the floor.

"I think," Clarke says, "I'll start with you."

But her therapy ends before she can even get properly warmed up. A sudden noise fills the lounge, shrill, periodic, vaguely familiar. It takes a moment for Clarke to remember what it is. She lowers her foot.

Over in the Communications cubby, the telephone is ringing.

Jeanette Ballard is going home today.

For over an hour the 'scaphe has been dropping deeper into midnight. Now the Systems monitor shows it setting like a great bloated tadpole onto Beebe's docking assembly. Sounds of mechanical copulation reverberate and die. The overhead hatch drops open.

Ballard's replacement climbs down, already mostly 'skinned, staring impenetrably from eyes without pupils. His gloves are off; his 'skin is open up to the forearms. Clarke sees the faint scars running along his wrists, and smiles a bit inside.

Was there another Ballard up there, waiting, she wonders, *in case I had been the one who didn't work out?*

Out of sight down the corridor, a hatch creaks open. Ballard appears in shirtsleeves, one eye swollen shut, carrying a single suitcase. She seems about to say something, but stops when she sees the newcomer. She looks at him for a moment. She nods briefly. She climbs into the belly of the 'scaphe without a word.

Nobody calls down to them. There are no salutations, no morale-boosting small talk. Perhaps the crew have been briefed. Perhaps they've simply figured it out. The docking hatch swings shut. With a final clank, the 'scaphe disengages.

Clarke walks across the lounge and looks into the camera. She reaches between mirror fragments and rips its power line from the wall.

We don't need this any more, she thinks, and she knows that somewhere far away, someone agrees.

She and the newcomer appraise each other with dead white eyes.

"I'm Lubin," he says at last.

Ballard was right again, she realizes. *Untwisted, we'd be of no use at all.*

But she doesn't mind. She won't be going back.

GOSSAMER

Stephen Baxter

Stephen Baxter is known as one of the nineties' best new hard SF writers, the author of a number of highly regarded novels and many short stories (See earlier Baxter note). He said in a *Locus* interview, "*Moonseed* is, in part, another response to *Red Mars*, and the terraforming debate, because they try to terraform the moon."

Baxter said in another *Locus* interview:

> Looking back, things do change, in terms of influences. When I was young, I was influenced by the greats of the past, Wells and Clarke. When I was kind of cutting my teeth, writing a lot of stories and finally selling stories in the eighties, it was the people who were around at the time, the dominant figures: Benford and Bear in hard SF. And now, my contemporaries, roughly: Paul McAuley, Peter Hamilton, Greg Egan. And I've met everybody else who's still alive, probably—not Egan, but Clarke and Benford, and Bear I've become quite friendly with.
>
> With people like Bear and Benford, McAuley and Robinson, who are working off the same material as I'm working from—the new understanding of the planets, and so forth, the new understanding of cosmology (which is maybe more philosophy than science, because it's untestable), we're all coming from the same place. And you do have this dialogue, really, a conversation.

And it is worth remarking that regardless of politics, the British and American hard SF writers know and talk to one another, argue with one another, and as Baxter points out, are all coming from the same place.

Baxter here writes in the hard science mode of Hal Clement and Robert L. Forward. This kind of SF is particularly valued by hard SF readers because it is comparatively scarce, requires intense effort by the writer to be accurate to known science, and produces the innovative imagery that is peculiar to hard SF, that sparks that good old wow of wonderment. In "Gossamer" his visions based on science are astonishingly precise and clear and that is what his fiction offers as foregrounded for out entertainment.

The flitter bucked. Lvov looked up from her data desk, startled. Beyond the flitter's translucent hull, the wormhole was flooded with sheets of blue-white light which raced toward and past the flitter, giving Lvov the impression of huge, uncontrolled speed.

"We've got a problem," Cobh said. The pilot bent over her own data desk, a frown creasing her thin face.

Lvov had been listening to her data desk's synthesized murmur on temperature inversion layers in nitrogen atmospheres; now she tapped the desk to shut it off. The flitter was a transparent tube, deceptively warm and comfortable. Impossibly fragile.

Astronauts have problems in space, she thought. *But not me. I'm no hero; I'm only a researcher*. Lvov was twenty-eight years old; she had no plans to die—and certainly not during a routine four-hour hop through a Poole wormhole that had been human-rated for eighty years.

She clung to her desk, her knuckles whitening, wondering if she ought to feel scared.

Cobh sighed and pushed her data desk away; it floated before her. "Close up your suit and buckle up."

"What's wrong?"

"Our speed through the wormhole has increased." Cobh pulled her own restraint harness around her. "We'll reach the terminus in another minute—"

"What? But we should have been traveling for another half-hour."

Cobh looked irritated. "I know that. I think the Interface has become unstable. The wormhole is buckling."

"What does that mean? Are we in danger?"

Cobh checked the integrity of Lvov's pressure suit, then pulled her data desk to her. Cobh was a Caucasian, strong-faced, a native of Mars, perhaps fifty years old. "Well, we can't turn back. One way or the other it'll be over in a few more seconds. Hold tight."

Now Lvov could see the Interface itself, the terminus of the wormhole. The Interface was a blue-white tetrahedron, an angular cage that exploded at her from infinity.

Glowing struts swept over the flitter.

The craft hurtled out of the collapsing wormhole. Light founted around the fleeing craft, as stressed spacetime yielded in a gush of heavy particles.

Lvov glimpsed stars, wheeling.

Cobh dragged the flitter sideways, away from the energy fount—

There was a *lurch*, a discontinuity in the scene beyond the hull. Suddenly a planet loomed before them.

"Lethe," Cobh said. "Where did that come from? I'll have to take her down—we're too close."

Lvov saw a flat, complex landscape, gray-crimson in the light of a swollen moon. The scene was dimly lit, and it rocked wildly as the flitter tumbled. And, stretching between world and moon, she saw . . .

No. It was impossible.

The vision was gone, receded into darkness.

"Here it comes," Cobh yelled.

Foam erupted, filling the flitter. The foam pushed into Lvov's ears, mouth, and eyes; she was blinded, but she found she could breathe.

She heard a collision, a grinding that lasted seconds, and she imagined the flitter ploughing its way into the surface of the planet. She felt a hard lurch, a rebound.

The flitter came to rest.

A synthesized voice emitted blurred safety instructions. There was a ticking as the hull cooled.

In the sudden stillness, still blinded by foam, Lvov tried to recapture what she had seen. *Spider web. It was a web, stretching from the planet to its moon.*

"Welcome to Pluto." Cobh's voice was breathless, ironic.

Lvov stood on the surface of Pluto.

The suit's insulation was good, but enough heat leaked to send nitrogen clouds hissing around her footsteps, and where she walked she burned craters in the ice.

Gravity was only a few percent of G, and Lvov, Earth-born, felt as if she might blow away.

There were clouds above her: wispy cirrus, aerosol clusters suspended in an atmosphere of nitrogen and methane. The clouds occluded bone-white stars. From here, Sol and the moon, Charon, were hidden by the planet's bulk, and it was *dark*, dark on dark, the damaged landscape visible only as a sketch in starlight.

The flitter had dug a trench a mile long and fifty yards deep in this world's antique surface, so Lvov was at the bottom of a valley walled by nitrogen ice. Cobh was hauling equipment out of the crumpled-up wreck of the flitter: scooters, data desks, life-support boxes, Lvov's equipment. Most of the stuff had been robust enough to survive the impact, Lvov saw, but not her own equipment.

Maybe a geologist could have crawled around with nothing more than a hammer and a set of sample bags. But Lvov was an atmospheric scientist. What was she going to achieve here without her equipment?

Her fear was fading now, to be replaced by irritation, impatience. She was five light-hours from Sol; already she was missing the online nets. She kicked at the ice. She was *stuck* here; she couldn't talk to anyone, and there wasn't even the processing power to generate a Virtual environment.

Cobh finished wrestling with the wreckage. She was breathing hard. "Come on," she said. "Let's get out of this ditch and take a look around." She showed Lvov how to work a scooter. It was a simple platform, its inert gas jets controlled by twists of raised handles.

Side by side, Cobh and Lvov rose out of the crash scar.

Pluto ice was a rich crimson laced with organic purple. Lvov made out patterns, dimly, on the surface of the ice; they were like bas-relief, discs the size of dinner plates, with the intricate complexity of snowflakes.

Lvov landed clumsily on the rim of the crash scar, the scooter's blunt prow crunching into surface ice, and she was grateful for the low gravity. The weight and heat of the scooters quickly obliterated the ice patterns.

"We've come down near the equator," Cobh said. "The albedo is higher at the south pole; a cap of methane ice there, I'm told."

"Yes."

Cobh pointed to a bright blue spark, high in the sky. "That's the wormhole Interface, where we emerged, fifty thousand miles away."

Lvov squinted at constellations unchanged from those she'd grown up with on Earth. "Are we stranded?"

Cobh said, with reasonable patience, "For the time being. The flitter is wrecked, and the wormhole has collapsed; we're going to have to go back to Jupiter the long way round."

Three billion miles . . . "Ten hours ago I was asleep in a hotel room on Io. And now this. What a mess."

Cobh laughed. "I've already sent off messages to the Inner System. They'll be received in about five hours. A one-way GUTship will be sent to retrieve us. It will refuel here, with Charon ice—"

"How long?"

"It depends on the readiness of a ship. Say ten days to prepare, then a ten-day flight out here—"

"Twenty days?"

"We're in no danger. We've supplies for a month. Although we're going to have to live in these suits."

"Lethe. This trip was supposed to last seventy-two hours."

"Well," Cobh said testily, "you'll have to call and cancel your appointments, won't you? All we have to do is wait here; we're not going to be comfortable, but we're safe enough."

"Do you know what happened to the wormhole?"

Cobh shrugged. She stared up at the distant blue spark. "As far as I know, nothing like this has happened before. I think the Interface itself became unstable, and that fed back into the throat . . . But I don't know how we fell to Pluto so quickly. That doesn't make sense."

"How so?"

"Our trajectory was spacelike. Superluminal." She glanced at Lvov obliquely, as if embarrassed. "For a moment there, we appeared to be traveling faster than light."

"Through normal space? That's impossible."

"Of course it is." Cobh reached up to scratch her cheek, but her gloved fingers rattled against her faceplate. "I think I'll go up to the Interface and take a look around there."

Cobh showed Lvov how to access the life support boxes. Then she strapped her data desk to her back, climbed aboard her scooter, and lifted off the planet's surface, heading for the Interface. Lvov watched her dwindle.

Lvov's isolation closed in. She was alone, the only human on the surface of Pluto.

A reply from the Inner System came within twelve hours of the crash. A GUTship was being sent from Jupiter. It would take thirteen days to refit the ship, followed by an eight-day flight to Pluto, then more delay in taking on fresh reaction mass at Charon. Lvov chafed at the timescale, restless.

There was other mail: concerned notes from Lvov's family, a testy demand for updates from her research supervisor, and for Cobh, orders from her employer to mark as much of the flitter wreck as she could for salvage and analysis. Cobh's ship was a commercial wormhole transit vessel, hired by Oxford—Lvov's university—for this trip. Now, it seemed, a complex battle over liability would be joined between Oxford, Cobh's firm, and the insurance companies.

Lvov, five light-hours from home, found it difficult to respond to the mail asynchronously. She felt as if she had been cut out of the on-line mind of humanity. In the end, she drafted replies to her family and deleted the rest of the messages.

She checked her research equipment again, but it really was unuseable. She tried to sleep. The suit was uncomfortable, claustrophobic. She was restless, bored, a little scared.

She began a systematic survey of the surface, taking her scooter on widening spiral sweeps around the crash scar.

The landscape was surprisingly complex, a starlit sculpture of feathery ridges and fine ravines. She kept a few hundred feet above the surface; whenever she flew too low, her heat evoked billowing vapor from fragile nitrogen ice, obliterating ancient features, and she experienced obscure guilt.

She found more of the snowflakelike features, generally in little clusters of eight or ten.

Pluto, like its moon-twin Charon, was a ball of rock clad by thick mantles of water ice and nitrogen ice, and laced with methane, ammonia, and organic compounds. It was like a big, stable comet nucleus; it barely deserved the status of "planet." There were *moons* bigger than Pluto.

There had been only a handful of visitors in the eighty years since the building of the Poole wormhole. None of them had troubled to walk the surfaces of Pluto or Charon. The wormhole, Lvov realized, hadn't been built as a commercial proposition, but as a sort of stunt: the link which connected, at last, all of the System's planets to the rapid-transit hub at Jupiter.

She tired of her plodding survey. She made sure she could locate the crash scar, lifted the scooter to a mile above the surface, and flew toward the south polar cap.

Cobh called from the Interface. "I think I'm figuring out what happened here—that superluminal effect I talked about. Lvov, have you heard of an Alcubierre wave?" She dumped images to Lvov's desk—portraits of the wormhole Interface, graphics.

"No." Lvov ignored the input and concentrated on flying the scooter. "Cobh, why should a wormhole become unstable? Hundreds of wormhole rapid transits are made every day, all across the System."

"A wormhole is a flaw in space. It's inherently unstable anyway. The throat and mouths are kept open by active feedback loops involving threads of exotic matter. That's matter with a negative energy density, a sort of antigravity which—"

"But this wormhole went wrong."

"Maybe the tuning wasn't perfect. The presence of the flitter's mass in the throat was enough to send the wormhole over the edge. If the wormhole had been more heavily used, the instability might have been detected earlier, and fixed. . . ."

Over the gray-white pole, Lvov flew through banks of aerosol mist; Cobh's voice whispered to her, remote, without meaning.

Sunrise on Pluto:

Sol was a point of light, low on Lvov's unfolding horizon, wreathed in the complex strata of a cirrus cloud. The Sun was a thousand times fainter than from Earth, but brighter than any planet in Earth's sky.

The Inner System was a puddle of light around Sol, an oblique disc small enough for Lvov to cover with the palm of her hand. It was a disc that contained almost all of man's hundreds of billions. Sol brought no heat to her raised hand, but she saw faint shadows, cast by the sun on her faceplate.

The nitrogen atmosphere was dynamic. At perihelion—the closest approach to Sol which Pluto was nearing—the air expanded, to three planetary diameters. Methane and other volatiles joined the thickening air, sublimating from the planet's surface. Then, when Pluto turned away from Sol and sailed into its two-hundred-year winter, the air snowed down.

Lvov wished she had her atmospheric analysis equipment now; she felt its lack like an ache.

She passed over spectacular features: Buie Crater, Tombaugh Plateau, the Lowell Range. She recorded them all, walked on them.

After a while, her world, of Earth and information and work, seemed remote, a glittering abstraction. Pluto was like a complex, blind fish, drifting around its two-century orbit, gradually interfacing with her. Changing her, she suspected.

Ten hours after leaving the crash scar, Lvov arrived at the sub-Charon point, called Christy. She kept the scooter hovering, puffs of gas holding her against Pluto's gentle gravity. Sol was halfway up the sky, a diamond of light. Charon hung directly over Lvov's head, a misty blue disc, six times the size of Luna as seen from Earth. Half the moon's lit hemisphere was turned away from Lvov, toward Sol.

Like Luna, Charon was tidally locked to its parent, and kept the same face to Pluto as it orbited. But, unlike Earth, Pluto was also locked to its twin. Every six days the worlds turned about each other, facing each other constantly, like two waltzers. Pluto-Charon was the only significant system in which both partners were tidally locked.

Charon's surface looked pocked. Lvov had her faceplate enhance the image. Many of the gouges were deep and quite regular.

She remarked on this to Cobh, at the Interface.

"The Poole people mostly used Charon material for the building of the wormhole," Cobh said. "Charon is just rock and water ice. It's easier to get to water ice, in particular. Charon doesn't have the inconvenience of an atmosphere, or an overlay of nitrogen ice over the water. And the gravity's shallower."

The wormhole builders had flown out here in a huge, unreliable GUTship. They had lifted ice and rock off Charon, and used it to construct tetrahedra of exotic matter. The tetrahedra had served as Interfaces, the termini of a wormhole. One Interface had been left in orbit around Pluto, and the other had been hauled laboriously back to Jupiter by the GUTship, itself replenished with Charon ice reaction mass.

By such crude means, Michael Poole and his people had opened up the Solar System.

"They made Lethe's own mess of Charon," Lvov said.

She could almost see Cobh's characteristic shrug. *So what?*

Pluto's surface was geologically complex, here at this point of maximal tidal stress. She flew over ravines and ridges; in places, it looked as if the land had been smashed up with an immense hammer, cracked and fractured. She imagined there was a greater mix, here, of interior material with the surface ice.

In many places she saw gatherings of the peculiar snowflakes she had noticed before. Perhaps they were some form of frosting effect, she wondered. She descended, thinking vaguely of collecting samples.

She killed the scooter's jets some yards above the surface, and let the little craft fall under Pluto's gentle gravity. She hit the ice with a soft collision, but without heat-damaging the surface features much beyond a few feet.

She stepped off the scooter. The ice crunched, and she felt layers compress under her, but the fractured surface supported her weight. She looked up toward Charon. The crimson moon was immense, round, heavy.

She caught a glimmer of light, an arc, directly above her.

It was gone immediately. She closed her eyes and tried to recapture it. *A line, slowly curving, like a thread. A web. Suspended between Pluto and Charon.*

She looked again, with her faceplate set to optimal enhancement. She couldn't recapture the vision.

She didn't say anything to Cobh.

"I was right, by the way," Cobh was saying.

"What?" Lvov tried to focus.

"The wormhole instability, when we crashed. It did cause an Alcubierre wave."

"What's an Alcubierre wave?"

"The Interface's negative energy region expanded from the tetrahedron, just for a moment. The negative energy distorted a chunk of spacetime. The chunk containing the flitter, and us."

On one side of the flitter, Cobh said, spacetime had contracted. Like a model black hole. On the other side, it expanded—like a rerun of the Big Bang, the expansion at the beginning of the Universe.

"An Alcubierre wave is a front in spacetime. The Interface—with us embedded inside—was carried along. We were pushed away from the expanding region, and toward the contraction."

"Like a surfer, on a wave."

"Right." Cobh sounded excited. "The effect's been known to theory, almost since the formulation of relativity. But I don't think anyone's observed it before."

"How lucky for us," Lvov said drily. "You said we traveled faster than light. But that's impossible."

"You can't move faster than light *within spacetime*. Wormholes are one way of getting around this; in a wormhole you are passing through a branch in spacetime. The Alcubierre effect is another way. The superluminal velocity comes from the distortion of space itself; we were carried along *within* distorting space.

"So we weren't breaking lightspeed within our raft of spacetime. But that spacetime itself was distorting at more than lightspeed."

"It sounds like cheating."

"So sue me. Or look up the math."

"Couldn't we use your Alcubierre effect to drive starships?"

"No. The instabilities and the energy drain are forbidding."

One of the snowflake patterns lay mostly undamaged, within Lvov's reach. She crouched and peered at it. The flake was perhaps a foot across. Internal structure was visible within the clear ice as layers of tubes and compartments; it was highly symmetrical, and very complex. She said to Cobh, "This is an impressive crystallization effect. If that's what it is." Gingerly, she reached out with thumb and forefinger, and snapped a short tube off the rim of the flake. She laid the sample on her desk. After a few seconds the analysis presented. "It's mostly water ice, with some contaminants," she told Cobh. "But in a novel molecular form. Denser than normal ice, a kind of glass. Water would freeze like this under high pressures—several thousand atmospheres."

"Perhaps it's material from the interior, brought out by the chthonic mixing in that region."

"Perhaps." Lvov felt more confident now; she was intrigued. "Cobh, there's a larger specimen a few feet farther away."

"Take it easy, Lvov."

She stepped forward. "I'll be fine. I—"

The surface shattered.

Lvov's left foot dropped forward, into a shallow hole; something crackled under the sole of her boot. Threads of ice crystals, oddly woven together, spun up and tracked precise parabolae around her leg.

The fall seemed to take an age; the ice tipped up toward her like an opening door. She put her hands out. She couldn't stop the fall, but she was able to cushion herself, and she kept her faceplate away from the ice. She finished up on her backside; she felt the chill of Pluto ice through the suit material over her buttocks and calves.

". . . Lvov? Are you OK?"

She was panting, she found. "I'm fine."

"You were screaming."

"Was I? I'm sorry. I fell."

"You *fell*? How?"

"There was a hole, in the ice." She massaged her left ankle; it didn't seem to be hurt. "It was covered up."

"Show me."

She got to her feet, stepped gingerly back to the open hole, and held up her data desk. The hole was only a few inches deep. "It was covered by a sort of lid, I think."

"Move the desk closer to the hole." Light from the desk, controlled by Cobh, played over the shallow pit.

Lvov found a piece of the smashed lid. It was mostly ice, but there was a texture to its undersurface, embedded thread which bound the ice together.

"Lvov," Cobh said. "Take a look at this."

Lvov lifted the desk aside and peered into the hole. The walls were quite smooth. At the base there was a cluster of spheres, fist-sized. Lvov counted seven; all but one of the spheres had been smashed by her stumble. She picked up the one intact sphere, and turned it over in her hand. It was pearlgray, almost translucent. There was something embedded inside, disc-shaped, complex.

Cobh sounded breathless. "Are you thinking what I'm thinking?"

"It's an egg," Lvov said. She looked around wildly, at the open pit, the egg, the snowflake patterns. Suddenly she saw the meaning of the scene; it was as if a light had shone up from within Pluto, illuminating her. The "snowflakes" represented *life*, she intuited; they had dug the burrows, laid these eggs, and now their bodies of water glass lay dormant or dead, on the ancient ice. . . .

"I'm coming down," Cobh said sternly. "We're going to have to discuss this. Don't say anything to the Inner System; wait until I get back. This could mean trouble for us, Lvov."

Lvov placed the egg back in the shattered nest.

She met Cobh at the crash scar. Cobh was shoveling nitrogen and water ice into the life-support modules' raw material hopper. She hooked up her own and Lvov's suits to the modules, recharging the suits' internal systems. Then she began to carve GUTdrive components out of the flitter's hull. The flitter's central Grand Unified Theory chamber was compact, no larger than a basketball, and the rest of the drive was similarly scaled. "I bet I could get this working," Cobh said. "Although it couldn't take us anywhere."

Lvov sat on a fragment of the shattered hull. Tentatively, she told Cobh about the web.

Cobh stood with hands on hips, facing Lvov, and Lvov could hear her sucking drink from the nipples in her helmet. "Spiders from Pluto? Give me a break."

"It's only an analogy," Lvov said defensively. "I'm an atmospheric specialist, not a biologist." She tapped the surface of her desk. "It's not spider web. Obviously. But if that substance has anything like the characteristics of true spider silk, it's not impossible." She read from her desk. "Spider silk has a breaking strain twice that of steel, but thirty times the elasticity. It's a type of liquid crystal. It's used commercially—did you know that?" She fingered the fabric of her suit. "We could be wearing spider silk right now."

"What about the hole with the lid?"

"There are trapdoor spiders in America. On Earth. I remember, when I was a kid . . . The spiders make burrows, lined with silk, with hinged lids."

"Why make burrows on Pluto?"

"I don't know. Maybe the eggs can last out the winter that way. Maybe the creatures, the flakes, only have active life during the perihelion period, when the atmosphere expands and enriches." She thought that through. "That fits. That's why the Poole people didn't spot anything. The construction team was here close to the last aphelion. Pluto's year is so long that we're still only half-way to the next perihelion—"

"So how do they live?" Cobh snapped. "What do they eat?"

"There must be more to the ecosystem than one species," Lvov conceded. "The flakes—the spiders—need water glass. But there's little of that on the surface. Maybe there is some biocycle—plants or burrowing animals—which brings ice and glass to the surface, from the interior."

"That doesn't make sense. The layer of nitrogen over water ice is too deep."

"Then where do the flakes get their glass?"

"Don't ask me," Cobh said. "It's your dumb hypothesis. And what about the web? What's the point of that—if it's real?"

Lvov ground to a halt. "I don't know," she said lamely. *Although Pluto/Charon is the only place in the System where you could build a spider web between worlds.*

Cobh toyed with a fitting from the drive. "Have you told anyone about this yet? In the Inner System, I mean."

"No. You said you wanted to talk about that."

"Right." Lvov saw Cobh close her eyes; her face was masked by the glimmer of her faceplate. "Listen. Here's what we say. We've seen nothing here. Nothing that couldn't be explained by crystallization effects."

Lvov was baffled. "What are you talking about? What about the eggs? Why would we lie about this? Besides, we have the desks—records."

"Data desks can be lost, or wiped, or their contents amended."

Lvov wished she could see Cobh's face. "Why would we do such a thing?"

"Think it through. Once Earth hears about this, these flake-spiders of yours will be protected. Won't they?"

"Of course. What's bad about that?"

"It's bad for *us*, Lvov. You've seen what a mess the Poole people made of Charon. If this system is inhabited, *a fast GUTship won't be allowed to come for us*. It wouldn't be allowed to refuel here. Not if it meant further damage to the native life forms."

Lvov shrugged. "So we'd have to wait for a slower ship. A liner; one that won't need to take on more reaction mass here."

Cobh laughed at her. "You don't know much about the economics of GUTship transport, do you? Now that the System is crisscrossed by Poole wormholes, how many liners like that do you think are still running? I've already checked the manifests. There are *two* liners capable of a round trip to Pluto still in service. One is in dry dock; the other is heading for Saturn—"

"On the other side of the System."

"Right. There's no way either of those ships could reach us for, I'd say, a year."

We only have a month's supplies. A bubble of panic gathered in Lvov's stomach.

"Do you get it yet?" Cobh said heavily. "*We'll be sacrificed*, if there's a chance that our rescue would damage the new ecology, here."

"No. It wouldn't happen like that."

Cobh shrugged. "There are precedents."

She was right, Lvov knew. There *were* precedents, of new forms of life discovered in corners of the system: from Mercury to the remote Kuiper objects. In every case the territory had been ring-fenced, the local conditions preserved, once life—or even a plausible candidate for life—was recognized.

Cobh said, "Pan-genetic diversity. Pan-environmental management. That's the key to it; the public policy of preserving all the species and habitats of Sol, into the indefinite future. The lives of two humans won't matter a damn against that."

"What are you suggesting?"

"That we don't tell the Inner System about the flakes."

Lvov tried to recapture her mood of a few days before: when Pluto hadn't mattered to her, when the crash had been just an inconvenience. *Now, suddenly, we're talking about threats to our lives, the destruction of an ecology.*

What a dilemma. If I don't tell of the flakes, their ecology may be destroyed during our rescue. But if I do tell, the GUTship won't come for me, and I'll lose my life.

Cobh seemed to be waiting for an answer.

Lvov thought of how Sol light looked over Pluto's ice fields, at dawn.

She decided to stall. "We'll say nothing. For now. But I don't accept either of your options."

Cobh laughed. "What else is there? The wormhole is destroyed; even this flitter is disabled."

"We have time. Days, before the GUTship is due to be launched. Let's search for another solution. A win-win."

Cobh shrugged. She looked suspicious.

She's right to be, Lvov thought, exploring her own decision with surprise. *I've every intention of telling the truth later, of diverting the GUTship, if I have to.*

I may give up my life for this world.

I think.

In the days that followed, Cobh tinkered with the GUTdrive, and flew up to the Interface to gather more data on the Alcubierre phenomenon.

Lvov roamed the surface of Pluto, with her desk set to full record. She came to love the wreaths of cirrus clouds, the huge, misty moon, the slow, oceanic pulse of the centuries-long year.

Everywhere she found the inert bodies of snowflakes, or evidence of their presence: eggs, lidded burrows. She found no other life forms—or, more likely, she told herself, she wasn't equipped to recognize any others.

She was drawn back to Christy, the sub-Charon point, where the topography was at its most complex and interesting, and where the greatest density of flakes was to be found. It was as if, she thought, the flakes had gathered here, yearning for the huge, inaccessible moon above them. But what could the flakes possible want of Charon? What did it mean for them?

Lvov encountered Cobh at the crash scar, recharging her suit's systems from the life support packs. Cobh seemed quiet. She kept her face, hooded by her faceplate, turned from Lvov. Lvov watched her for a while. "You're being evasive," she said eventually. "Something's changed—something you're not telling me about."

Cobh made to turn away, but Lvov grabbed her arm. "I think you've found a third option. Haven't you? You've found some other way to resolve this situation, without destroying either us or the flakes."

Cobh shook off her hand. "Yes. Yes, I think I know a way. But—"

"But what?"

"It's *dangerous*, damn it. Maybe unworkable. Lethal." Cobh's hands pulled at each other.

She's scared, Lvov saw. She stepped back from Cobh. Without giving herself time to think about it, she said, "Our deal's off. I'm going to tell the Inner System about the flakes. Right now. So we're going to have to go with your new idea, dangerous or not."

Cobh studied her face; Cobh seemed to be weighing up Lvov's determination, perhaps even her physical strength. Lvov felt as if she were a data desk being downloaded. The moment stretched, and Lvov felt her breath tighten in her chest. Would she be able to defend herself, physically, if it came to that? And was her own will really so strong?

I have *changed*, she thought. *Pluto has changed me.*

At last Cobh looked away. "Send your damn message," she said.

Before Cobh—or Lvov herself—had a chance to waver, Lvov picked up her desk and sent a message to the inner worlds. She downloaded all the data she had on the flakes: text, images, analyses, her own observations and hypotheses.

"It's done," she said at last.

"And the GUTship?"

"I'm sure they'll cancel it." Lvov smiled. "I'm also sure they won't tell us they've done so."

"So we're left with no choice," Cobh said angrily. "Look, I know it's the right thing to do. To preserve the flakes. I just don't want to die, that's all. I hope you're right, Lvov."

"You haven't told me how we're going to get home."

Cobh grinned through her faceplate. "Surfing."

"All right. You're doing fine. Now let go of the scooter."

Lvov took a deep breath, and kicked the scooter away with both legs; the little device tumbled away, catching the deep light of Sol, and Lvov rolled in reaction.

Cobh reached out and steadied her. "You can't fall," Cobh said. "You're in orbit. You understand that, don't you?"

"Of course I do," Lvov grumbled.

The two of them drifted in space, close to the defunct Poole wormhole Interface. The Interface itself was a tetrahedron of electric blue struts, enclosing darkness, its size overwhelming; Lvov felt as if she were floating beside the carcass of some huge, wrecked building.

Pluto and Charon hovered before her like balloons, their surfaces mottled and complex, their forms visibly distorted from the spherical. Their separation was only fourteen of Pluto's diameters. The worlds were strikingly different in hue, with Pluto a blood red, Charon ice blue. *That's the difference in surface composition*, Lvov thought absently. *All that water ice on Charon's surface.*

The panorama was stunningly beautiful. Lvov had a sudden, gut-level intuition of the *rightness* of the various System authorities' rigid pan-environment policies.

Cobh had strapped her data desk to her chest; now she checked the time. "Any moment now. Lvov, you'll be fine. Remember, you'll feel no acceleration, no matter how fast we travel. At the centre of an Alcubierre wave, spacetime is locally flat; you'll still be in free fall. There will be tidal forces, but they will remain small. Just keep your breathing even, and—"

"Shut up, Cobh," Lvov said tightly. "I know all this."

Cobh's desk flared with light. "*There*," she breathed. "The GUTdrive has fired. Just a few seconds, now."

A spark of light arced up from Pluto's surface and tracked, in complete silence, under the belly of the parent world. It was the flitter's GUTdrive, salvaged and stabilized by Cobh. The flame was brighter than Sol; Lvov saw its light reflected in Pluto, as if the surface was a great, fractured mirror of ice. Where the flame passed, tongues of nitrogen gas billowed up.

The GUTdrive passed over Christy. Lvov had left her desk there to monitor the flakes, and the image the desk transmitted, displayed in the corner of her faceplate, showed a spark crossing the sky.

Then the GUTdrive veered sharply upward, climbing directly toward Lvov and Cobh at the Interface.

"Cobh, are you sure this is going to work?"

Lvov could hear Cobh's breath rasp, shallow. "Look, Lvov, I know you're scared, but pestering me with dumb-ass questions isn't going to help. Once the drive enters the Interface, it will take only seconds for the instability to set in. Seconds, and then we'll be home. In the Inner System, at any rate. Or . . ."

"Or what?"

Cobh didn't reply.

Or not, Lvov finished for her. *If Cobh has designed this new instability right, the Alcubierre wave will carry us home. If not—*

The GUTdrive flame approached, becoming dazzling. Lvov tried to regulate her breathing, to keep her limbs hanging loose—

"Lethe," Cobh whispered.

"What?" Lvov demanded, alarmed.

"Take a look at Pluto. At Christy."

Lvov looked into her faceplate.

Where the warmth and light of the GUTdrive had passed, Christy was a ferment. Nitrogen billowed. And, amid the pale fountains, *burrows were opening*. Lids folded back. Eggs cracked. Infant flakes soared and sailed, with webs and nets of their silk-analogue hauling at the rising air.

Lvov caught glimpses of threads, long, sparkling, trailing down to Pluto—and up toward Charon. Already, Lvov saw, some of the baby flakes had hurtled more than a planetary diameter from the surface, toward the moon.

"It's goose summer," she said.

"What?"

"When I was a kid . . . the young spiders spin bits of webs, and climb to the top of grass stalks, and float off on the breeze. Goose summer—'gossamer.' "

"Right," Cobh said skeptically. "Well, it looks as if they are making for Charon. They use the evaporation of the atmosphere for lift . . . Perhaps they follow last year's threads, to the moon. They must fly off every perihelion, rebuilding their web bridge every time. They think the perihelion is here now. The warmth of the drive—it's remarkable. But why go to Charon?"

Lvov couldn't take her eyes off the flakes. "Because of the water," she said. It all seemed to make sense, now that she saw the flakes in action. "There must be water glass on Charon's surface. The baby flakes use it to build their bodies. They take other nutrients from Pluto's interior, and the glass from Charon . . . They need the resources of *both* worlds to survive—"

"Lvov!"

The GUTdrive flared past them, sudden, dazzling, and plunged into the damaged Interface.

Electric-blue light exploded from the interface, washing over her.

There was a ball of light, unearthly, behind her, and an irregular patch of darkness ahead, like a rip in space. Tidal forces plucked gently at her belly and limbs.

Pluto, Charon, and goose summer disappeared. But the stars, the eternal stars, shone down on her, just as they had during her childhood on Earth. She stared at the stars, trusting, and felt no fear.

Remotely, she heard Cobh whoop, exhilarated.

The tides faded. The darkness before her healed, to reveal the brilliance and warmth of Sol.

MADAM BUTTERFLY

James P. Hogan

❀

James P. Hogan (born 1941), with Robert L. Forward and Charles Sheffield, was a leader in the new generation of hard SF writers in the early 1980s. At the same moment when Gregory Benford (and slightly later, Greg Bear) raised the literary standards of hard SF with their novels and stories, Hogan entered the field as if it were 1939 or 1949 and he had just discovered Heinlein and Asimov, Campbell and *Astounding*. Generally uninterested in reading in the contemporary field, Hogan in particular set about reinventing it from the forties onward, in novels filled with ideas and technology—such as *Inherit the Stars* (1977), *The Genesis Machine* (1978), *The Two Faces of Tomorrow* (1979), *Thrice in Time* (1980), and *Code of the Lifemaker* (1983)—that made him one of the more popular writers of that decade.

The Encyclopedia of Science Fiction calls him "a writer pugnaciously associated with the hard SF wing," compares him to Eric Frank Russell, and comments:

> His first novel (and first publication), *Inherit the Stars* (1977), aroused interest for the exhilarating sense it conveys of scientific minds at work on real problems and for the genuinely exciting scope of the SF imagination it deploys. The book turned out to be the first volume in the Minervan Experiment sequence, being followed by *The Gentle Giants of Ganymede* (1978) and *Giants' Star* (1981). . . . The sequence is in fact a hard SF fable of humanity's origins—we are the direct descendants of the highly aggressive inhabitants of the destroyed fifth planet, who would have conquered the Galaxy had they not blown themselves up—and espouses a vision of the Universe in which other species must learn to cope with the knowledge that we will, some day, come into our inheritance.

Two of his novels won the Prometheus Award for Best Libertarian SF Novel: *Voyage from Yesteryear* (1982) and *The Multiplex Man* (1992). His new novel, *Martian Knightlife* (2001) is an SF mystery set on Mars.

"Madam Butterfly" was first published in *Free Space*, edited by Brad Linaweaver and Edward Kramer, the only politically-engaged Libertarian SF anthology of the decade. The book also included stories by Gregory Benford, Robert J. Sawyer, and John Barnes. It is a light-hearted Libertarian hard SF tale supposedly about "The Butterfly Effect," or the sensitive dependence on initial conditions of chaotic systems.

Locally, in the valley far from Tokyo that she had left long ago, it was known as *yamatsumi-sou*, which means "flower of the mountain spirit." It was like a small lily, with tapering, yellow petals warmed on the upper surface by a blush of violet.

According to legend, it was found only in those particular hills on the north side of Honshu—a visible expression of the deity that had dwelt around the village of Kimikaye-no-sato and protected its inhabitants since ancient times, whose name was Kyo. When the violet was strong and vivid, it meant that Kyo was cheerful and in good health, and the future was secure. When the violet waned pale and cloudy, troubled times lay ahead. Right at this moment, Kyo was looking very sorry for himself indeed.

The old woman's name was Chifumi Shimoto. She hadn't seen a *yamatsumi-sou* since those long-gone childhood days that everyone remembers as the time when life was simple and carefree—before Japan became just a province in some vaster scheme that she didn't understand, and everyone found themselves affected to some degree or other by rules borrowed from foreigners with doubtful values and different ways. How it came to be growing in the yard enclosed by the gaunt, gray concrete cliffs forming the rear of the Nagomi Building was anybody's guess.

She saw it when she came out with a bag of trash from the bins in the offices upstairs, where she cleaned after the day staff had gone home. It was clinging to life bravely in a patch of cracked asphalt behind the parked trucks, having barely escaped being crushed by a piece of steel pipe thrown down on one side, and smothered by a pile of rubble encroaching from the other. Although small, it looked already exhausted, grown to the limit that its meager niche could sustain. The yard trapped bad air and exhaust fumes, and at ground level was all but sunless. Leaking oil and grime hosed off the vehicles was turning what earth there was into sticky sludge. Kyo needed a better home if he was to survive.

Potted plants of various kinds adorned shelves and window ledges throughout the offices. When she had washed the cups and ashtrays from the desks and finished vacuuming between the blue-painted computer cabinets and consoles, Chifumi searched and found some empty pots beneath the sink in one of the kitchen areas. She filled one of the smaller pots with soil, using a spoon to take a little from each of many plants, then went back downstairs with it and outside to the yard. Kneeling on the rough ground, she carefully worked the flower and its roots loose from its precarious lodgement, transferred it to the pot that she had prepared, and carried it inside.

Back upstairs, she fed it with fresh water and cleaned off its leaves. Finally, she placed it in the window of an office high up in the building, facing the sun. Whoever worked in that office had been away for several days. With luck, the flower would remain undisturbed for a while longer and gain the strength to recover. Also, there were no other plants in the room. Perhaps, she thought to herself, that would make it all the more appreciated when the occupant returned.

She locked the cleaning materials and equipment back in the closet by the rear stairs, took the service elevator back down to the ground floor, and returned the keys to the security desk at the side entrance. The duty officer checked her pass and ID and the shopping bag containing groceries and some vegetables that she had bought on the way in, and then let her out to the lobby area, where the cleaners from other floors were assembling. Five minutes later, the bus that would run them back to their abodes around the city drew up outside the door.

The offices in the part of the Nagomi Building that Chifumi had been assigned to had something to do with taxes and accounting. That was what all the trouble was supposed to be about between the federal authorities and others in faraway places among the stars. She heard things about freedom and individualism, and people wanting to live as they chose to, away from the government—which the young seemed to imagine they were the first ever to have thought of. To her, it all sounded very much like the same, age-old story of who created the wealth and how it should be shared out. She had never understood it, and did so even less now. Surely there were enough stars in the sky for everyone.

She had a son, Icoro, out there somewhere, whom she hadn't seen for two years now; but messages from him reached her from time to time through friends. The last she had heard, he was well, but he hadn't said exactly where he was or what he was doing—in other words, he didn't want to risk the wrong people finding out. That alone told her that whatever he was up to was irregular at best, very likely outright illegal, and quite possibly worse. She knew that there was fighting and that people were getting killed—sometimes lots of them. She didn't ask why or how, or want to hear the details. She worried as a mother would, tried not to dwell on such matters, and when she found that she did anyway, she kept them to herself.

But as she walked away after the bus dropped her off, she felt more reassured than she had for a long time. The flower, she had decided, was a sign that Kyo still lived in the mountains and did not want to be forgotten. Kyo was a just god who had come to Earth long ago, but he still talked with the other sky-spirits who sent the rain and made the stars above Kimikaye so much brighter. Chifumi had remembered Kyo and helped him. Now Kyo's friends among the stars would watch over her son.

Suzi's voice came from a console speaker on the bridge of the consolidator *Turner Maddox*, owned by Fast Forwarding Unincorporated, drifting 250 million miles from Earth in an outer region of the Asteroid Belt.

"Spider aligned at twelve hundred meters. Delta vee is fifteen meters per second, reducing." Her voice maintained a note of professional detachment, but everyone had stopped what they were doing to follow the sequence unfolding on the image and status screens.

"No messing with this kid, man," Fuigerado, the duty radar tech, muttered next to Cassell. "He's going in fast."

Cassell grunted, too preoccupied with gauging the lineup and closing rate to form an intelligible reply. The view from the spider's nose camera showed the crate stern on, rotating slowly between the three foreshortened, forward-pointing docking appendages that gave the bulb-ended, remote-operated freight-retrieval module its name. Through the bridge observation port on Cassell's other side, all that was discernible directly of the maneuver being executed over ten miles away were two smudges of light moving against the starfield, and the flashing blue and red of the spider's visual beacon.

As navigational dynamics chief, Cassell had the decision on switching control to the regular pilot standing by if the run-in looked to go outside the envelope. Too slow meant an extended chase downrange to attach to the crate, followed by a long, circuitous recovery back. Faster was better, but impact from an overzealous failure to connect could kick a crate off on a rogue trajectory that would require even more time and energy to recover from. Time was money everywhere, while outside gravity wells, the cost of everything was measured not by the distance moved, but by the energy needed to move it there. A lot of hopeful recruits did just fine on the simulator only to flunk through nerves when it came to the real thing.

"Ten meters per second," Suzi's voice sang out.

The kid was bringing the crate's speed down smoothly. The homing marker was dead center in the graticule, lock-on confirming to green even as Cassell watched. He decided to give it longer.

The Lunar surface was being transformed inside domed-over craters; greenhousing by humidifying its atmosphere was thawing out the freeze-dried planet Mars; artificial space structures traced orbits from inside that of Venus to as far out as the asteroids. It all added up to an enormous demand for materials, which meant boom-time prices.

With Terran federal authorities controlling all Lunar extraction and regulating the authorized industries operating from the Belt, big profits were to be had from bootlegging primary asteroid materials direct into the Inner System. A lot of independent operators got themselves organized to go after a share. Many of these were small-scale affairs—a breakaway cult, minicorp, even a family group—who had pooled their assets to set up a minimum habitat and mining-extraction facility, typically equipped with a low-performance mass launcher. Powered by solar units operating at extreme range, such a launcher would be capable of sending payloads to nearby orbits in the Belt, but not of imparting the velocities needed to reach the Earth-Luna vicinity.

This was where ventures like Fast Forwarding Uninc. came into the picture. Equipped with high-capacity fusion-driven launchers, they consolidated incoming consignments from several small independents into a single payload and sent it inward on a fast-transit trajectory to a rendezvous agreed upon with the customer.

Consolidators moved around a lot and carried defenses. The federal agencies put a lot of effort into protecting their monopolies. As is generally the case when fabulous profits stand to be made, the game could get very nasty and rough. Risk is always proportional to the possible gain.

"Delta vee, two point five, reducing. Twenty-six seconds to contact."

Smooth, smooth—everything under control. It had been all along. Cassell could sense the sureness of touch on the controls as he watched the screen. He even got the feeling that the new arrival might have rushed the early approach on purpose, just to make them all a little nervous. His face softened with the hint of a grin.

As a final flourish, the vessels rotated into alignment and closed in a single, neatly integrated motion. The three latching indicators came on virtually simultaneously.

"Docking completed."

"Right on!" Fuigerado complimented.

Without wasting a moment, the spider fired its retros to begin slowing the crate down to matching velocity, and steered it into an arc that brought it around sternwise behind the launcher, hanging half a mile off the *Maddox*'s starboard bow. It slid the crate into the next empty slot in the frame holding the load to be consolidated, hung on while the locks engaged, and then detached.

Cassell went through to the communications room behind the bridge, then down to the operations control deck, where the remote console that the spider had been controlled from was located. The kid was getting up and stretching, Suzi next to him, Hank Bissen, the reserve pilot who had been standing by, still at his console opposite.

"You did pretty good," Cassell said.

"Thank you, sir." He knew damn well that he had, and smiled. It was the kind of smile that Cassell liked—open and direct, conveying simple, unassuming confidence; not the cockiness that took needless risks and got you into trouble.

"Your name's Shimoto. What is that, Japanese?"

"Yes."

"So, what should we call you?"

"My first name is Icoro. . . . Does it mean I have a job, Mr. Cassell?"

"You'd better believe it. Welcome to the team."

Nagai Horishagi leaned back wearily from the papers scattered across his desk in the Tariffs and Excise section of the Merylynch-Mubachi offices in the Tokyo Nagomi Building. It was his first day back after ten days in South America, and it looked as if he had been gone for a month. Even as he thought it, his secretary, Yosano, came through from the outer office with another wad. Nagai motioned in the direction of his In tray. He didn't meet her eyes or speak. Her movements betraying an awkwardness equal to his own, she deposited the papers and withdrew. Nagai stared down at the desk until he heard the door close; then he sighed, rose abruptly, and turned to stare out the window at the city. That was when he noticed the plant on the ledge.

It had bright green leaves, and flowers of pale yellow with a touch of violet—one in full bloom, two more just opening. He stared at it, perplexed. Where on Earth had it come from? He had no mind for flowers, as the rest of the office readily testified. And yet, as he looked at it, he had to admit that it seemed a happy little fellow. He reached out and touched one of the leaves. It felt cool and smooth. *Very well,* he thought. *If you can do something to cheer this awful place up, you've earned your keep. I guess we'll let you stay.*

All through the morning, he would pause intermittently and look back over his shoulder to gaze with a fresh surge of curiosity at the plant. And then, shortly before lunchtime, the answer came to him. Of course! Yosano had put it there. No wonder she had acted tensely. How could he have been so slow?

Before he went away, they had gotten involved in one of those affairs that a professional shouldn't succumb to, but which can happen to the best. But in their case it had uncovered real affection and become quite romantic. After years of living in an emotional isolation ward he had celebrated and exuberated, unable to believe his luck . . . and then blown the whole thing in a single night, getting drunk and disgracing himself by insulting everybody at that stupid annual dinner—even if they had deserved every word of it. He had agonized over the situation all the time while he was away, but really there was no choice. No working relationship needed this kind of strain. He had decided that she would have to be transferred.

But now this was her way of telling him that it didn't have to be that way. He was forgiven. Everything could be OK. And so it came about that he was able to summon up the courage to confront her just before she left for lunch and say, "Could we give it another try?"

She nodded eagerly. Nagai didn't think that he had ever seen her look so delighted. He smiled, too. But he didn't mention the plant. The game was to pretend that the plant had nothing to do with it. "Can I apologize for being such an ass?" he asked instead.

Yosano giggled. "There's no need. I thought you were magnificent"

"Then how about dinner tonight?" he suggested.

"Of course."

Yosano remembered only later in the afternoon that she had agreed to meet the American that night. Well, too bad. The American would have to find somebody else. She would have to call him and tell him, of course—but not from the office, she decided. She would call his hotel as soon as she got home.

Steve Bryant hung up the phone in his room at the Shinjuku Prince and stared at it moodily.

"Well, goddamn!" he declared.

Weren't they the same the whole world over. He had already shaved, showered, and put on his pastel blue suit, fresh from the hotel cleaner's. His first night to himself since he arrived in Japan, and he wasn't going to hit the town with that cute local number that he'd thought he had all lined up, after all. He poured himself another Scotch, lit a cigarette, and leaned back against the wall at the head of the bed to consider his options.

OK, then he'd just take off and scout the action in this town on his own, and see what showed up, he decided. And if nothing of any note did, he was going to get very drunk. Wasn't life just the same kind of bitch, too, the whole world over.

The bar was brightly lit and glittery, and starting to fill up for the evening. There was a low stage with a couple of dancers and a singer in a dress that was more suggestion than actuality. It was later than Alan Quentin had wanted stay, and he could feel the drink going to his head. He had stopped by intending to have just one, maybe two, to unwind on his way back to the garage-size apartment that came with his yearlong stint in Tokyo. Then he'd gotten talking to the salesman from Phoenix, here on his first visit, who had been stood up by his date.

On the stool next to him, Steve Bryant went on, "Can you imagine, Al, five thousand dollars for a box of old horseshoes and cooking pots that you could pick up in a yard sale back home? Can you beat that?" American-frontier nostalgia was the current rage in Japan.

"That's incredible," Al agreed.

"You could retire on what you'd get for a genuine Civil War Colt repeater."

"I'll remember to check the attic when I get back."

"You're from Mobile, right?"

"Montgomery."

"Oh, right. But that's still Alabama."

"Right."

Steve's attention was wandering. He let his gaze drift around the place, then leaned closer and touched Al lightly on the sleeve. "Fancy livening up the company? There's a couple of honeys at the other end that we could check out."

Al glanced away. "They're hostesses. Work here. Keep you buying them lemonades all night at ten dollars a shot. See the guy out back there who'd make a sumo wrestler look anorexic? He'll tell you politely that it's time to leave if you don't like it. I'll pass, anyhow. I've had a rough day."

Steve sat back, tossed down the last of his drink, and stubbed his cigarette. His face wrinkled. "Suddenly this place doesn't grab me so much anymore. What d'you say we move on somewhere else?"

"Really, no. I only stopped by for a quick one. There's some urgent stuff that I have to get done by tomorrow, and—"

"Aw, come on. What kind of a welcome to someone from home is this? It's all on me. I've had a great day."

The next bar around the corner was smaller, darker, just as busy. The music was from a real fifties jukebox. They found a table squeezed into a corner below the stairs. "So what do you do?" Steve asked.

"I'm an engineer—spacecraft hydraulic systems. We use a lot of Japanese components. I liaise with the parent companies here on testing and maintenance procedures."

"Sorry, but I don't have an intelligent question to ask about that."

"Don't worry about it."

Steve fell quiet for a few seconds and contemplated his drink. Suddenly he looked up. "Does that mean you're mathematical?"

Al frowned. "Some. Why?"

"Oh, just something I was reading on the plane over. It said that a butterfly flapping its wings in China can change the weather next week in Texas. Sounds kinda crazy. Does it make sense to you?"

Al nodded. "The Butterfly Effect. It's a bit of an extreme example, but what it's supposed to illustrate is the highly nonlinear dynamics of chaotic systems. Tiny changes in initial conditions can make the world of difference to the consequences." He took in Steve's glassy stare and regarded him dubiously. "Do you really want me to go into it?"

Steve considered the proposition. "Nah, forget it." He caught the bartender's eye and signaled for two more. "How much do you think you'd get here for a genuine Stetson? Have a guess."

Al lost count of the places they visited after that, and had no idea what time he finally got back to his apartment. He woke up halfway through the morning feeling like death, and called in sick. He was no better by lunchtime, and so decided to make a day of it.

It so happened that among the items on Alan Quentin's desk that morning was a technical memorandum concerning structural bolts made from the alloy CYA-173/B. Tests had revealed that prolonged cyclic stressing at low temperatures could induce metal crystallization, resulting in a loss of shear-strength. These bolts should be replaced after ten thousand hours in space environments, not thirty thousand as stipulated previously. Since CYA-173/B had been in use less than eighteen months, relatively few instances of its use would be yet affected. However, any fittings that had been in place for more than a year—and particularly where exposed to vibrational stress—should be resecured with new bolts immediately.

Because Al wasn't there to do it, the information didn't get forwarded to his company in California that day. Hence, it was not included in that week's compendium of updates that the Engineering Support Group beamed out to its list of service centers, repair shops, maintenance-and-supply bases, and other users of the company's products, scattered across the solar system.

Forty-eight hours after the updates that did get sent were received at GYO-3, a Federal Space Command base orbiting permanently above Ganymede, the largest satellite of Jupiter, the robot freighter *Hermit* departed on a nine-day haul to Callisto. In its main propulsion section, the *Hermit* carried four high-pressure centrifugal pumps, fastened to their mountings by CYA-173/B bolts. The *Hermit* had been ferrying assorted loads between the Jovian moons for over six months now, after trudging its way outward from the Belt for even longer before that. The bolts still holding the pumps were among the first of that type to have been used anywhere.

Fully loaded, the *Maddox*'s cargo cage combined the consignments from over fifty independents, averaging a thousand tons of asteroid material each, and stretched the length of an old-time naval cruiser. The loads included concentrations of iron, nickel, magnesium, manganese, and other metals for which there would never be a shortage of customers eager to avoid federal taxes and tariffs. A good month's work for a team of ten working one of the nickel-iron asteroids would earn them a quarter million dollars. True, the costs tended to be high, too, but the offworld banks offered generous extended credit with the rock pledged as collateral. This was another source of friction with the federal authorities, who claimed to own everything and didn't recognize titles that they hadn't issued themselves. But ten billion asteroids, each over a hundred meters in diameter, was a lot to try to police. And the torroidal volume formed by the Belt contained two trillion times more space than the sphere bounded by the Moon's orbit.

Better money still could be made for hydrogen, nitrogen, carbon, and other light elements essential for biological processes and the manufacture of such things as plastics, which are not found on the Moon but occur in the carbonaceous chondrites. This type of asteroid contains typically up to five percent kerogen, a tarry hydrocarbon found in terrestrial oil shales, "condensed primordial soup"—a virtually perfect mix of all the basic substances necessary to support life. At near-Earth market rates, kerogen was practically priceless. And there was over a hundred million billion tons of it out there, even at five percent.

The driver, consisting of a triple-chamber fusion rocket and its fuel tanks, attached at the tail end when the cage was ready to go. Now flight-readied, the assembled launcher hung fifty miles off the *Turner Maddox*'s beam. The search radars were sweeping long range, and the defenses standing to at full alert. There's no way to hide the flash when a two-hundred-gigawatt fusion thruster fires—the perfect beacon to invite attention from a prowling federal strike force.

"We're clean," Fuigerado reported from his position on one side of the bridge. He didn't mean just within their own approach perimeter. The *Maddox*'s warning system was networked with other defense grids in surrounding localities of the Belt. Against common threats, the independents worked together.

Cassell checked his screens to verify that the *Maddox*'s complement of spiders, shuttles, maintenance pods, and other mobiles were all docked and accounted for, out of the blast zone. "Uprange clear," he confirmed.

Liam Doyle tipped his cap to the back of a head of red, tousled Irish hair and ran a final eye over the field- and ignition-status indicators. A lot more was at stake here than with just the routine retrieval of an incoming crate. The skipper liked to supervise outbound launches in person.

"Sequencing on-count at minus ten seconds," the controller's voice said from the operations deck below.

"Send her off," Doyle pronounced.

"Slaving to auto. . . . Guidance on. . . . Plasma ignition."

White starfire lanced across twenty miles of space. The launcher kicked forward at five gs, moved ahead, its speed seeming deceptively slow for a few moments; then it pulled away and shrunk rapidly among the stars. On the bridge's main screen, the image jumped as the tracking camera upped magnification, showing the plume already foreshortened under the fearsome buildup of velocity. Nineteen minutes later and twenty thousand miles downrange, the driver would detach and fire a retro burn, separating the two modules. The cage would remain on course for the Inner System, while the driver turned in a decelerating curve that would eventually bring it back to rendezvous with the *Maddox*.

"We've got a good one," the controller's voice informed everybody. Hoots and applause sounded through the open door from the communications room behind.

"Mr. Cassell, a bottle of the Bushmill's, if you please," Doyle instructed.

"Aye, aye, sir!"

Doyle turned to face the other chiefs who were present on the bridge. "And I've some more news for you to pass on; this is as good a time as any to mention it," he told them. "This will be our last operation for a while. This can feels as if it's getting a bit creaky to me. You can tell your people that we'll be putting in for an overhaul and systems refit shortly, so they'll have a couple of months to unwind and blow some of their ill-gotten gains on whatever pleasures they can find that are to be had this side of Mars. Details will be posted in a couple of days." Approving murmurs greeted the announcement, which they toasted with one small shot of Irish mellow each.

Later, however, alone in his private cabin with Cassell, Doyle was less sanguine. "I didn't want to mention it in front of everybody, but I've been getting ominous messages from around the manor," he confided. "The *Bandit* has been very quiet lately."

Cassell took in the unsmiling set of the boss's face. The *Beltway Bandit* was another consolidator like the *Turner Maddox*: same business, same clients, same modus operandi. "How quiet?" he asked.

Doyle made a tossing-away motion. "Nothing." And that was very odd, for although accidents happened, and every now and again an unlucky or careless outfit was tracked down by federal patrols, disaster was never so quick and so total as to prevent some kind of distress message from being sent out.

"Are you saying it was the feds—they took it out?" Cassell asked.

"We don't know. If it was, they did it in a way that nobody's heard of before. That's the real reason why I'm standing us down for a while." He paused, looking at Cassell pointedly. "Some of the operators are saying that they're using insiders."

Cassell caught the implication. "You think Shimoto's one?" he asked. "Could we be next?"

"What do you think? He's with your section."

Cassell shrugged. "He's good at the job, mixes in well. Everybody likes him. We're operating standard security. It hasn't shown up anything."

"His kind of ability could come from a federal pilots' school," Doyle pointed out. "And a pilot would be able to get himself away in something once the strike was set up."

Cassell couldn't argue. "I'll make sure we keep a special eye on him during the R and R," he said.

"Yes, do that, why don't you?" Doyle agreed. "I want to be absolutely sure that we're clean when we resume operating."

Water.

With its unique molecular attributes and peculiar property of becoming lighter as it freezes, it could have been designed as the ideal solvent, catalyst, cleanser, as well as the midwife and cradle of life. Besides forming ninety percent of offworlders' bodies, it provided culture for the algae in their food farms, grew their plants and nurtured their animals, cooled their habitats, and shielded them from radiation. The demand for water across the inner parts of the solar system outstripped that for all other resources.

Callisto, second largest of the moons of Jupiter and almost the size of Mercury, is half ice—equivalent to forty times all the water that exists on Earth. Mining the ice crust of Callisto was a major activity that the Terran authorities operated exclusively to supply the official space-expansion program. One of the reasons for the Space Command's permanent presence out at the Jovian moons was to protect the investment.

Enormous lasers carved skyscraper-size blocks from the ice field, which were then catapulted off the moon by a fusion-powered electromagnetic launcher. Skimming around the rim of Jupiter's gravity well, they then used the giant planet as a slingshot to hurl themselves on their way downhill into the Inner System. As each block left the launch track on Callisto, high-power surface lasers directed from an array of sites downrange provided final course correction by ablating the block's tail surface to create thrust. A crude way of improvising a rocket—but it worked just fine.

Or it had all the time up until now, that is.

The robot freighter *Hermit*, arriving from Ganymede, was on its final, stern-first approach into the surface base serving the launch installation as the next block out was starting to roll. One of the CYA-173/B bolts securing the *Hermit*'s high-pressure pumps sheared under the increased load as power was increased to maximum to slow down the ship. The bolt head came off like a rifle bullet, disabling an actuator, which shut down engine number two. Impelled by the unbalanced thrust of the other two engines, the *Hermit* skewed off course, overshot the base area completely, and demolished one of the towers housing the course-correction lasers for the mass launcher just as the block lifted up above the horizon twenty miles away.

As a result, two million tons of ice hove off toward Jupiter on a trajectory that wasn't quite what the computers said it ought to be. The error was actually quite slight. But it would be amplified in the whirl around Jupiter, and by the time the block reached the Asteroid Belt, would have grown to a misplacement in the order of tens of millions of miles.

If the cause of the accident were ever tracked down, Al Quentin wouldn't be around to be fired over it. He had started a small business of his own in Tokyo, importing Old West memorabilia from home.

The *Turner Maddox* was back on station and accumulating crates for the first of a new series of consignments. Its drives had been overhauled, its computers upgraded, and an improved plasma-stabilization system fitted to the launch driver. But there was a strain in the atmosphere that had not been present in earlier times. Five more consolidators had disappeared, everyone without a trace.

It had to be the feds, but nobody knew how they were locating the collection points, or managing to attack so fast that nobody ever got a warning off. All the consolidators had adopted a stringent policy of moving and changing their operating locales constantly. They were deploying more sophisticated defenses and warning systems. They pooled information on suspected inside informers and undercover feds. They gave dispatch data for incoming consignments as separately encrypted instructions to each subscriber to avoid revealing where the trajectories would converge. Yet they were still missing something.

Cassell looked around the familiar confines of the operations deck. The retrieval crew were at their stations, with a crate from a new subscriber called Farlode Holdings on its way in. Icoro had graduated now and was standby pilot this time—he was OK, Doyle had decided after having him tailed for a period and commissioning a background check. A new newcomer, Ibrahim Ahmel, born in an off-world colony—he said—was about to try his first live retrieval. Not everyone had come back after the break, and taking on more new faces was another of the risks that they were having to live with. Hank Bissen had quit, which was surprising. Cassell hadn't judged him as the kind who would let the feds drive him out. And then again, maybe he'd simply banked more money from the last few trips than Cassell had thought.

The other major change was the outer screen of six autodrones toting the needlebeams and railguns that Doyle had invested in, currently in position two thousand miles out, transforming the *Maddox* operation into a miniature flotilla.

It brought home just how much this whole business was escalating. Cassell liked the old days better. *What did that tell him about age creeping up?* he asked himself.

Ibrahim was nervous. He had done OK on the simulator, but had an ultra-high self-image sensitivity that tended to wind him up. This was going to be a tense one. Cassell was glad to have Icoro there as standby, cool and relaxed behind a big, wide grin as always.

"Remember what you found on the sim; don't cut the turn too sharp as you run in," Suzi said from Ibrahim's far side. "It makes it easy to overshoot on the lineup, and you end up losing more time straightening it out downrange than you save."

Ibrahim nodded and looked across instinctively to Icoro for confirmation.

"She talks too much," Icoro said. "Just don't overworry. You're not going to lose anything. I'll cut right in if it starts to drift."

"How did you make out on your first time?" Ibrahim asked.

"I goofed most miserably," Icoro lied. Ibrahim looked reassured. Suzi caught Cassell's gaze and turned her eyes upward momentarily. Cassell just shrugged. A screen on each console showed a telescopic view of the crate, still over fifteen minutes away, being sent from one of the drones. The colors of the containers that it was carrying showed one to be holding metals, one light elements, a third silicates, and two kerogen.

"It's coming in nice and easy, rotation slow," Icoro commented. "Should be a piece of cake."

Suddenly the raucous hooting of the all-stations alert sounded. Doyle's voice blasted from Suzi's console—he had taken to being present through all operations on this trip.

"We've got intruders coming in fast. Cassell to the bridge immediately!"

Ibrahim froze. Suzi and Icoro plunged into a frenzy of activity at their consoles. Cassell had no time to register anything more as he threw himself at the communications rail and hauled up to the next level. As he passed through the communications room, he heard one of the duty crew talking rapidly into a mike: "Emergency! Emergency! This is *Turner Maddox*. We have unidentified incoming objects, believed to be attacking. Location is . . ."

Seconds later, Cassell was beside Doyle on the bridge. Displays flashed and beeped everywhere. Fuigerado was calling numbers from the sector-control report screen.

"How many of them?" Cassell asked, breathless.

Doyle, concentrating on taking in the updates unfolding around him, didn't answer at once. He seemed less alarmed than his voice had conveyed a few moments before—if anything, he looked puzzled now. Finally he said, "I'm not so sure it is 'them.' It looks more like only one. . . ."

Cassell followed his eyes, scanned the numbers, and frowned. "One what? What the hell is it?"

"I'm damned if I know. The signature isn't like any ship or structure that I've ever seen."

"Range is twenty-five hundred miles," the ordnance officer advised. "Defenses are tracking. It's coming in at thirty miles a second."

"I've got an optical lock from Drone Three," Fuigerado called out. "You're not gonna believe it." Doyle and Cassell moved over to him. "Have you ever seen an asteroid with corners?" Fuigerado asked, gesturing.

It was long, rectangular, and white, like a gigantic shoe box, tumbling end over end as it approached. Cassell's first fleeting thought was of a tombstone.

"Fifteen seconds from the perimeter," the OO called. "I need the order now."

"We have a spectral prelim," another voice said. "It's ice. Solid ice."

Cassell's first officer turned from the nav station. "Trajectory is on a dead intercept with the inbound Farlode crate. It's going to cream it."

"Do I shoot?" the OO entreated.

Doyle looked at him with a mixture of puzzlement and surprise. "Ah, to be sure, you can if you want to, Mike, but there's precious little difference it'll make. A railgun would be like bouncing popcorn off a tank to that thing. Your lasers might make a hole in a tin can, but that's solid ice."

They watched, mesmerized. On one screen, the miniature mountain hurtling in like a white wolf. On the other, the crate trotting on its way, an unsuspecting lamb. Maybe because of their inability to do anything, the impending calamity seemed mockingly brutal—obscene, somehow.

"That's somebody's millions about to be vaporized out there," Cassell said, more to relieve the air with something.

"And a percentage of it ours, too," Doyle added. Ever the pragmatist.

"Dead on for impact. It's less than ten seconds," the nav officer confirmed.

Those who could crowded around the starboard forequarter port. There wouldn't be more than a fraction of a second to see it unaided. Eyes scanned the starfield tensely. Then Cassell nudged Doyle's arm and pointed, at the same time announcing for the others' benefit, "Two o'clock, coming in high." Then there was a glimpse of something bright and pulsating—too brief and moving too fast for any shape to be discerned—streaking in like a star detached from the background coming out of nowhere. . . .

And all of a sudden half the sky lit up in a flash that would have blinded them permanently if the ports hadn't been made of armored glass with a shortwave cutoff. Even so, all Cassell could see for the next ten minutes was after-image etched into his retina.

But even while he waited for his vision to recover, his mind reeled under the realization of what it meant. He had never heard of Farlode Holdings before. That inbound crate had been carrying something a lot more potent than ordinary metals, light elements, and kerogen. And a half hour from now, it would have been inside the cargo cage, just a short hop away from them.

So *that* was how the feds had been doing it!

The plant was a riot of bright green and yellow now, and the veins of violet were very bright. Chifumi nipped off a couple of wilted leaves with her fingers and watered the soil from the jar that she had brought from the kitchen behind the elevators. The accountant whose office it was seemed to be taking care of it, she was pleased to see. She would have to keep an eye on it for a while though, because he had not been in for several days. From the cards by his desk and the message of well-wishing that somebody had pinned on his wall, it seemed he was getting married. A framed picture had appeared next to the plant some time ago, of the accountant and the pretty girl that Chifumi had seen once or twice, who worked in the outer office. It seemed, then, that he was marrying his secretary.

Chifumi didn't know if that was a good thing or not, but such things were accepted these days. Very likely the new wife would give up her job and have a family now, so she would no longer be his secretary, and the question wouldn't arise. Chifumi wondered if they would take *yamatsumi-sou* to their new home. *It would be better for Kyo than being stuck alone in an office every night*, she thought.

She finished her evening's work and went down to the lobby to wait for the arrival of the bus. While she sat on one of the seats, she took from her purse the letter that had come in from Icoro, which one of his friends from the university had printed out and delivered to her just as she was leaving.

My dearest and most-loved mother,

I hope that everything is well with you. I am doing very well myself, and have just wired off a sum to keep you comfortable for a while, which you should be hearing about shortly.

Life out here where I am continues to be wonderfully interesting and exciting. I must tell you about the most amazing thing that happened just a couple of days ago. . . .

UNDERSTAND

Ted Chiang

✿

Ted Chiang (born 1967) is a technical writer who occasionally writes short SF that is then usually nominated for, or the winner of, awards. He is a private person whose short bio goes like this, "Ted Chiang was born in Port Jefferson, New York, and currently lives in Bellevue, Washington. Of his nonfiction, written in his capacity as a technical writer, perhaps the most popular is the C++ Tutorial packaged with certain versions of Microsoft's C++ compiler. He reads some comics, enjoys going to the movies, and watches television more than is good for him." He has published five SF stories, all of which are distinctive and highly accomplished. *Stories of Your Life and Others*, his collected fiction thus far, was published in 2002.

Chiang says, "SF needn't have anything to do with science, but to the extent that a work of SF reflects science, it's hard SF. And reflecting science doesn't necessarily mean consistency with a certain set of facts; more essentially, it means consistency with a certain strategy for understanding the universe. Science seeks a type of explanation different from those sought by art or religion, an explanation where objective measurement takes precedence over subjective experience. And though hard SF can take many different forms, it always describes people looking for or working with that type of explanation."

"Understand," published in *Asimov's*, takes on the grand themes of posthumanity, hyperintelligence, and the Internet as an extension of the mind. The obvious literary ancestor of this story is Daniel Keyes' "Flowers for Algernon," as if Chiang looked at the premise and asked "What if the protagonist just kept getting smarter? What would happen if the process had no natural limits and did not reverse itself? What then?" His answer is that the emergent superhuman becomes like a political superpower. It is interesting to compare and contrast this story to Greg Egan's explorations of intelligence and personality in "Reasons to Be Cheerful"—both Egan's and Chiang's stories are concerned with futuristic treatments for neurological damage with striking results.

A layer of ice; it feels rough against my face, but not cold. I've got nothing to hold on to; my gloves just keep sliding off it. I can see people on top, running around, but they can't do anything. I'm trying to pound the ice with my fists, but my arms move in slow motion, and my lungs must have burst, and my head's going fuzzy, and I feel like I'm dissolving—

I wake up, screaming. My heart's going like a jackhammer. Christ. I pull off my blankets and sit on the edge of the bed.

I couldn't remember that before. Before I only remembered falling through the ice; the doctor said my mind had suppressed the rest. Now I remember it, and it's the worst nightmare I've ever had.

I'm grabbing the down comforter with my fists, and I can feel myself trembling. I try to calm down, to breathe slowly, but sobs keep forcing their way out. It was so real I could *feel* it: feel what it was like to die.

I was in that water for nearly an hour; I was more vegetable than anything else by the time they brought me up. Am I recovered? It was the first time the hospital had ever tried their new drug on someone with so much brain damage. Did it work?

The same nightmare, again and again. After the third time, I know I'm not going to sleep again. I spend the remaining hours before dawn worrying. Is this the result? Am I losing my mind?

Tomorrow is my weekly checkup with the resident at the hospital. I hope he'll have some answers.

I drive into downtown Boston, and after half an hour Dr. Hooper can see me. I sit on a gurney in an examining room, behind a yellow curtain. Jutting out of the wall at waist-height is a horizontal flatscreen, adjusted for tunnel vision so it appears blank from my angle. The doctor types at the keyboard, presumably calling up my file, and then starts examining me. As he's checking my pupils with a penlight, I tell him about my nightmares.

"Did you ever have any before the accident, Leon?" He gets out his little mallet and taps at my elbows, knees, and ankles.

"Never. Are these a side effect of the drug?"

"Not a side effect. The hormone K therapy regenerated a lot of damaged neurons, and that's an enormous change that your brain has to adjust to. The nightmares are probably just a sign of that."

"Is this permanent?"

"It's unlikely," he says. "Once your brain gets used to having all those pathways again, you'll be fine. Now touch your index finger to the tip of your nose, and then bring it to my finger here."

I do what he tells me. Next he has me tap each finger to my thumb, quickly. Then I have to walk a straight line, as if I'm taking a sobriety test. After that, he starts quizzing me.

"Name the parts of an ordinary shoe."

"There's the sole, the heel, the laces. Um, the holes that the laces go through are eyes, and then there's the tongue, underneath the laces . . ."

"Okay. Repeat this number: three nine one seven four—"

"—six two."

Dr. Hooper wasn't expecting that. "What?"

"Three nine one seven four six two. You used that number the first time you examined me, when I was still an inpatient. I guess it's a number you test patients with a lot."

"You weren't supposed to memorize it; it's meant to be a test of immediate recall."

"I didn't intentionally memorize it. I just happened to remember it."

"Do you remember the number from the second time I examined you?"

I pause for a moment. "Four zero eight one five nine two."

He's surprised. "Most people can't retain so many digits if they've only heard them once. Do you use mnemonic tricks?"

I shake my head. "No. I always keep phone numbers in the autodialer."

He goes to the terminal and taps at the numeric keypad. "Try this one." He reads a fourteen-digit number, and I repeat it back to him. "You think you can do it backwards?" I recite the digits in reverse order. He frowns, and starts typing something into my file.

I'm sitting in front of a terminal in one of the testing rooms in the psychiatric ward; it's the nearest place Dr. Hooper could get some intelligence tests. There's a small mirror set in one wall, probably with a video camera behind it. In case it's recording, I smile at it and wave briefly. I always do that to the hidden cameras in automatic cash machines.

Dr. Hooper comes in with a printout of my test results. "Well, Leon, you did . . . very well. On both tests you scored in the ninety-ninth percentile."

My jaw drops. "You're kidding."

"No, I'm not." He has trouble believing it himself. "Now that number doesn't indicate how many questions you got right; it means that relative to the general population—"

"I know what it means," I say absently. "I was in the seventieth percentile when they tested us in high school." Ninety-ninth percentile. Inwardly, I'm trying to find some sign of this. What should it feel like?

He sits down on the table, still looking at the printout. "You never attended college, did you?"

I return my attention to him. "I did, but I left before graduating. My ideas of education didn't mesh with the professors'."

"I see." He probably takes this to mean I flunked out. "Well, clearly you've improved tremendously. A little of that may have come about naturally as you grew older, but most of it must be a result of the hormone K therapy."

"This is one hell of a side-effect."

"Well, don't get too excited. Test scores don't predict how well you can do things in the real world." I roll my eyes upward when Dr. Hooper isn't looking. Something amazing is going on, and all he can offer is a truism. "I'd like to follow up on this with some more tests. Can you come in tomorrow?"

I'm in the middle of retouching a holograph when the phone rings. I waver between the phone and the console, and reluctantly opt for the phone. I'd normally have the answering machine take any calls when I'm editing, but I need to let people know I'm working again. I lost a lot of business when I was in the hospital: one of the risks of being a freelancer. I touch the phone and say, "Greco Holographics, Leon Greco speaking."

"Hey Leon, it's Jerry."

"Hi Jerry. What's up?" I'm still studying the image on the screen: it's a pair of helical gears, intermeshed. A trite metaphor for cooperative action, but that's what the customer wanted for his ad.

"You interested in seeing a movie tonight? Me and Sue and Tori were going to see *Metal Eyes*."

"Tonight? Oh, I can't. Tonight's the last performance of the one-woman show at the Hanning Playhouse." The surfaces of the gear teeth are scratched and oily-looking. I highlight each surface using the cursor, and type in the parameters to be adjusted.

"What's that?"

"It's called *Symplectic*. It's a monologue in verse." Now I adjust the lighting, to remove some of the shadows from where the teeth mesh. "Want to come along?"

"Is this some kind of Shakespearean soliloquy?"

Too much: with that lighting, the outer edges will be too bright. I specify an upper limit for the reflected light's intensity. "No, it's a stream-of-consciousness piece, and it alternates between four different meters; iambic's only one of them. All the critics called it a *tour de force*."

"I didn't know you were such a fan of poetry."

After checking all the numbers once more, I let the computer recalculate the interference pattern. "Normally, I'm not, but this one seemed really interesting. How's it sound to you?"

"Thanks, but I think we'll stick with the movie."

"Okay, you guys have fun. Maybe we can get together next week." We say goodbye and hang up, and I wait for the recalc to finish.

Suddenly it occurs to me what's just happened. I've never been able to do any editing while talking on the phone. But this time I had no trouble keeping my mind on both things at once.

Will the surprises never end? Once the nightmares were gone and I could relax, the first thing I noticed was the increase in my reading speed and comprehension. I was actually able to read the books on my shelves that I'd always meant to get around to, but never had the time; even the more difficult, technical material. Back in college, I'd accepted the fact that I couldn't study everything that interested me. It's exhilarating to discover that maybe I can; I was positively gleeful when I bought an armload of books the other day.

And now I find I can concentrate on two things at once; something I never would have predicted. I stand up at my desk and shout out loud, as if my favorite baseball team had just surprised me with a triple play. That's what it feels like.

The Neurologist-In-Chief, Dr. Shea, has taken over my case, presumably because he wants to take the credit. I scarcely know him, but he acts as if I've been his patient for years.

He's asked me into his office to have a talk. He interlaces his fingers and rests his elbows on his desk. "How do you feel about the increase in your intelligence?" he asks.

What an inane question. "I'm very pleased about it."

"Good," says Dr. Shea. "So far, we've found no adverse effects of the hormone K therapy. You don't require any further treatment for the brain damage from your accident." I nod. "However, we're conducting a study to learn more about the hormone's effect on intelligence. If you're willing, we'd like to give you a further injection of the hormone, and then monitor the results."

Suddenly he's got my attention; finally, something worth listening to. "I'd be willing to do that."

"You understand that this is purely for investigational purposes, not therapeutic. You may benefit from it with further gains in your intelligence, but this is not medically necessary for your health."

"I understand. I suppose I have to sign a consent form."

"Yes. We can also offer you some compensation for participating in this study." He names a figure, but I'm barely listening.

"That'll be fine." I'm imagining where this might lead, what it might mean for me, and a thrill runs through me.

"We'd also like you to sign a confidentiality agreement. Clearly this drug is enormously exciting, but we don't want any announcements to be made prematurely."

"Certainly, Dr. Shea. Has anyone been given additional injections before?"

"Of course; you're not going to be a guinea pig. I can assure you, there haven't been any harmful side effects."

"What sort of effects did they experience?"

"It's better if we don't plant suggestions in your mind: you might imagine you were experiencing the symptoms I mention."

Shea's very comfortable with the doctor-knows-best routine. I keep pushing. "Can you at least tell me how much their intelligence increased?"

"Every individual is different. You shouldn't base your expectations on what's happened to others."

I conceal my frustration. "Very well, Doctor."

If Shea doesn't want to tell me about hormone K, I can find out about it on my own. From my terminal at home I log onto the datanet. I access the FDA's public database, and start perusing their current IND's, the Investigational New Drug applications that must be approved before human trials can begin.

The application for hormone K was submitted by Sorensen Pharmaceutical, a company researching synthetic hormones that encourage neuron regeneration in the central nervous system. I skim the results of the drug tests on oxygen-deprived dogs, and then baboons: all the animals recovered completely. Toxicity was low, and long term observation didn't reveal any adverse effects.

The results of cortical samples are provocative. The brain-damaged animals grew replacement neurons with many more dendrites, but the healthy recipients of the drug remained unchanged. The conclusion of the researchers: hormone K replaces only damaged neurons, not healthy ones. In the brain-damaged animals, the new dendrites seemed harmless: PET scans didn't reveal any change in brain metabolism, and the animals' performance on intelligence tests didn't change.

In their application for human clinical trials, the Sorensen researchers outlined protocols for testing the drug first on healthy subjects, and then on several types of patients: stroke victims, sufferers of Alzheimer's, and persons—like me—in a persistent vegetative state. I can't access the progress reports for those trials: even with patient anonymity, only participating doctors have clearance to examine those records.

The animal studies don't shed any light on the increased intelligence in humans. It's reasonable to assume that the effect on intelligence is proportional to the number of neurons replaced by the hormone, which in turn depends on the amount of initial damage. That means that the deep coma patients would undergo the greatest improvements. Of course, I'd need to see the progress of the other patients to confirm this theory; that'll have to wait.

The next question: is there a plateau, or will additional dosages of the hormone cause further increases? I'll know the answer to that sooner than the doctors.

I'm not nervous; in fact, I feel quite relaxed. I'm just lying on my stomach, breathing very slowly. My back is numb; they gave me a local anaesthetic, and then injected the hormone K intraspinally. An intravenous wouldn't work, since the hormone can't get past the blood-brain barrier. This is the first such injection I can recall having, though I'm told that I've received two before: the first while still in the coma, the second when I had regained consciousness but no cognitive ability.

More nightmares. They're not all actually violent, but they're the most bizarre, mind-blowing dreams I've ever had, often with nothing in them that I recognize. I often wake up screaming, flailing around in bed. But this time, I know they'll pass.

* * *

There are several psychologists at the hospital studying me now. It's interesting to see how they analyze my intelligence. One doctor perceives my skills in terms of components, such as acquisition, retention, performance, and transfer. Another looks at me from the angles of mathematical and logical reasoning, linguistic communication, and spatial visualization.

I'm reminded of my college days when I watch these specialists, each with a pet theory, each contorting the evidence to fit. I'm even less convinced by them now than I was back then; they still have nothing to teach me. None of their categorizations are fruitful in analyzing my performance, since—there's no point in denying it—I'm equally good at everything.

I could be studying a new class of equation, or the grammar of a foreign language, or the operation of an engine; in each case, everything fits together, all the elements cooperate beautifully. In each case, I don't have to consciously memorize rules, and then apply them mechanically. I just perceive how the system behaves as a whole, as an entity. Of course, I'm aware of all the details and individual steps, but they require so little concentration that they almost feel intuitive.

Penetrating computer security is really quite dull; I can see how it might attract those who can't resist a challenge to their cleverness, but it's not intellectually aesthetic at all. It's no different than tugging on the doors of a locked house until you find an improperly installed lock. A useful activity, but hardly interesting.

Getting into the FDA's private database was easy. I played with one of the hospital wall terminals, running the visitor information program, which displays maps and a staff directory. I broke out of the program to the system level, and wrote a decoy program to mimic the opening screen for logging on. Then I simply left the terminal alone; eventually one of my doctors came by to check one of her files. The decoy rejected her password, and then restored the true opening screen. The doctor tried logging in again, and was successful this time, but her password was left with my decoy.

Using the doctor's account, I had clearance to view the FDA patient record database. In the Phase I trials, on healthy volunteers, the hormone had no effect. The ongoing Phase II clinical trials are a different matter. Here are weekly reports on eighty-two patients, each identified by a number, all treated with hormone K, most of them victims of a stroke or Alzheimer's, some of them coma cases. The latest reports confirm my prediction: those with greater brain damage display greater increases in intelligence. PET scans reveal heightened brain metabolism.

Why didn't the animal studies provide a precedent for this? I think the concept of critical mass provides an analogy. Animals fall below some critical mass in terms of synapses; their brains support only minimal abstraction, and gain nothing from additional synapses. Humans exceed that critical mass. Their brains support full self-awareness, and—as these records indicate—they use any new synapses to the fullest possible extent.

The most exciting records are those of the newly begun investigational studies, using a few of the patients who volunteered. Additional injections of the hormone do increase intelligence further, but again it depends on the degree of initial damage. The patients with minor strokes haven't even reached genius levels. Those with greater damage have gone further.

Of the patients originally in deep coma states, I'm the only one thus far who's received a third injection. I gained more new synapses than anyone previously studied; it's an open question as to how high my intelligence will go. I can feel my heart pounding when I think about it.

* * *

Playing with the doctors is becoming more and more tedious as the weeks go by. They treat me as if I were simply an idiot savant: a patient who exhibits certain signs of high intelligence, but still just a patient. As far as the neurologists are concerned, I'm just a source of PET scan images and an occasional vial of cerebrospinal fluid. The psychologists have the opportunity to gain some insight into my thinking through their interviews, but they can't shed their preconception of me as someone out of his depth, an ordinary man awarded gifts that he can't appreciate.

On the contrary, the doctors are the ones who don't appreciate what's happening. They're certain that real-world performance can't be enhanced by a drug, and that my ability exists only according to the artificial yardstick of intelligence tests, so they waste their time with those. But the yardstick is not only contrived, it's too short: my consistently perfect scores don't tell them anything, because they have no basis for comparison this far out on the bell curve.

Of course, the test scores merely capture a shadow of the real changes occurring. If only the doctors could feel what's going on in my head: how much I'm recognizing that I missed before, how many uses I can see for that information. Far from being a laboratory phenomenon, my intelligence is practical and effectual. With my near-total recall and my ability to correlate, I can assess a situation immediately, and choose the best course of action for my purposes; I'm never indecisive. Only theoretical topics pose a challenge.

No matter what I study, I can see patterns. I see the gestalt, the melody within the notes, in everything: mathematics and science, art and music, psychology and sociology. As I read the texts, I can think only that the authors are plodding along from one point to the next, groping for connections that they can't see. They're like a crowd of people unable to read music, peering at the score for a Bach sonata, trying to explain how one note leads to another.

As glorious as these patterns are, they also whet my appetite for more. There are other patterns waiting to be discovered, gestalts of another scale entirely. With respect to those, I'm blind myself; all my sonatas are just isolated data points by comparison. I have no idea what form such gestalts might assume, but that'll come in time. I want to find them, and comprehend them. I want this more than anything I've ever wanted before.

The visiting doctor's name is Clausen, and he doesn't behave like the other doctors. Judging by his manner, he's accustomed to wearing a mask of blandness with his patients, but he's a bit uncomfortable today. He affects an air of friendliness, but it isn't as fluent the perfunctory noise that the other doctors make.

"The test works this way, Leon: you'll read some descriptions of various situations, each presenting a problem. After each one, I want you to tell me what you'd do to solve that problem."

I nod. "I've had this kind of test before."

"Fine, fine." He types a command, and the screen in front of me fills with text. I read the scenario: it's a problem in scheduling and prioritizing. It's realistic, which is unusual; scoring such a test is too arbitrary for most researchers' tastes. I wait before giving my answer, though Clausen is still surprised at my speed.

"That's very good, Leon." He hits a key on his computer. "Try this one."

We continue with more scenarios. As I'm reading the fourth one, Clausen is careful to display only professional detachment. My response to this problem is of special interest to him, but he doesn't want me to know. The scenario involves office politics and fierce competition for a promotion.

I realize who Clausen is: he's a government psychologist, perhaps military, probably part of the CIA's Office of Research and Development. This test is meant to gauge hormone K's potential for producing strategists. That's why he's uncomfortable with me: he's used to dealing with soldiers and government employees, subjects whose job is to follow orders.

It's likely that the CIA will wish to retain me as a subject for more tests; they may do the same with other patients, depending on their performance. After that, they'll get some volunteers from their ranks, starve their brains of oxygen, and treat them with hormone K. I certainly don't wish to become a CIA resource, but I've already demonstrated enough ability to arouse their interest. The best I can do is to downplay my skills and get this question wrong.

I offer a poor course of action as my answer, and Clausen is disappointed. Nonetheless, we press on. I take longer on the scenarios now, and give weaker responses. Sprinkled among the harmless questions are the critical ones: one about avoiding a hostile corporate takeover, another about mobilizing people to prevent the construction of a coal-burning plant. I miss each of these questions.

Clausen dismisses me when the test ends; he's already trying to formulate his recommendations. If I'd shown my true abilities, the CIA would recruit me immediately. My uneven performance will reduce their eagerness, but it won't change their minds; the potential returns are too great for them to ignore hormone K.

My situation has changed profoundly; when the CIA decides to retain me as a test subject, my consent will be purely optional. I must make plans.

It's four days later, and Shea is surprised. "You want to withdraw from the study?"

"Yes, effective immediately. I'm returning to work."

"If it's a matter of compensation, I'm sure we can—"

"No, money's not the problem. I've simply had enough of these tests."

"I know the tests become tiring after a while, but we're learning a great deal. And we appreciate your participation, Leon. It's not merely—"

"I know how much you're learning from these tests. It doesn't change my decision: I don't wish to continue."

Shea starts to speak again, but I cut him off. "I know that I'm still bound by the confidentiality agreement; if you'd like me to sign something confirming that, send it to me." I get up and head for the door. "Goodbye, Dr. Shea."

It's two days later when Shea calls.

"Leon, you have to come in for an examination. I've just been informed: adverse side effects have been found in patients treated with hormone K at another hospital."

He's lying; he'd never tell me that over the phone. "What sort of side effects?"

"Loss of vision. There's excessive growth of the optic nerve, followed by deterioration."

The CIA must have ordered this when they heard that I'd withdrawn from the study. Once I'm back in the hospital, Shea will declare me mentally incompetent, and confine me to their care. Then I'll be transferred to a government research institution.

I assume an expression of alarm. "I'll come down right away."

"Good." Shea is relieved that his delivery was convincing. "We can examine you as soon as you arrive."

I hang up and turn on my terminal to check the latest information in the FDA database. There's no mention of any adverse effects, on the optic nerve or anywhere else. I don't discount the possibility that such effects might arise in the future, but I'll discover them by myself.

It's time to leave Boston. I begin packing. I'll empty my bank accounts when I go. Selling the equipment in my studio would generate more cash, but most of it is too large to transport; I take only a few of the smallest pieces. After I've been working a couple of hours, the phone rings again: Shea wondering where I am. This time I let the machine pick it up.

"Leon, are you there? This is Dr. Shea. We've been expecting you for quite some time."

He'll try calling one more time, and then he'll send the orderlies in white suits, or perhaps the actual police, to pick me up.

Seven-thirty P.M. Shea is still in the hospital, waiting for news about me. I turn the ignition key and pull out of my parking spot across the street from the hospital. Any moment now, he'll notice the envelope I slipped under the door to his office. As soon as he opens it he'll realize that it's from me.

Greetings Dr. Shea,

I imagine you're looking for me.

A moment of surprise, but no more than a moment; he'll regain his composure, and alert security to search the building for me, and check all vehicles leaving. Then he'll continue reading.

> *You can call off those burly orderlies who are waiting at my apartment; I don't want to waste their valuable time. You're probably determined to have the police issue an APB on me, though. Therefore, I've taken the liberty of inserting a virus in the DMV computer, that will substitute information whenever my license plate number is requested. Of course, you could give a description of my car, but you don't even know what it looks like, do you?*
>
> *Leon*

He'll call the police to have their programmers work on that virus. He'll conclude that I have a superiority complex, based on the arrogant tone of the note, the unnecessary risk taken in returning to the hospital to deliver it, and the pointless revelation of a virus which might otherwise have gone undetected.

Shea will be mistaken, though. Those actions are designed to make the police and CIA underestimate me, so I can rely on their not taking adequate precautions. After cleaning my virus from the DMV computer, the police programmers will assess my programming skill as good but not great, and then load the backups to retrieve my actual license number. This will activate a second virus, a far more sophisticated one. This one will modify both the backups and the active database. The police will be satisfied that they've got the correct license number, and spend their time chasing that wild goose.

My next goal is to get another ampule of hormone K. Doing so, unfortunately, will give the CIA an accurate idea of how capable I really am. If I hadn't sent that note, the police would discover my virus later, at a time when they'd know to take super-stringent precautions when eradicating it. In that case, I might never be able to remove my license number from their files.

Meanwhile, I've checked into a hotel, and am working out of the room's datanet terminal.

I've broken into the private database of the FDA. I've seen the addresses of the hormone K subjects, and the internal communications of the FDA. A clinical hold was instituted for hormone K: no further testing permitted until the hold is lifted. The CIA has insisted on capturing me and assessing my threat potential before the FDA goes any further.

The FDA has asked all the hospitals to return the remaining ampules by courier. I must get an ampule before this happens. The nearest patient is in Pittsburgh; I reserve a seat on a flight leaving early tomorrow morning. Then I check a map of Pittsburgh, and make a request to the Pennsylvania Courier company for a pick-up at an investment firm in the downtown area. Finally I sign up for several hours of CPU time on a supercomputer.

I'm parked in a rental car around the corner from a skyscraper in Pittsburgh. In my jacket pocket is a small circuit board with a keypad. I'm looking down the street in the direction the courier will arrive from; half the pedestrians wear white air filter masks, but visibility is good.

I see it two intersections away; it's a late-model domestic van, Pennsylvania Courier painted on the side. It's not a high-security courier; the FDA isn't that worried about me. I get out of my car and begin walking toward the skyscraper. The van arrives shortly, parks, and the driver gets out. As soon as he's inside, I enter the vehicle.

It's just come from the hospital. The driver is on his way to the fortieth floor, expecting to pick up a package from an investment firm there. He won't be back for at least four minutes.

Welded to the floor of the van is a large locker, with double-layered steel walls and door. There is a polished plate on the door; the locker opens when the driver lays his palm against its surface. The plate also has a data port in its side, used for programming it.

Last night I penetrated the service database for Lucas Security Systems, the company that sells handprint locks to Pennsylvania Courier. There I found an encrypted file containing the codes to override their locks.

I must admit that, while penetrating computer security remains generally unaesthetic, certain aspects of it are indirectly related to very interesting problems in mathematics. For example, a commonly used method of encryption normally requires years of supercomputer time to break. However, during one of my forays into number theory, I found a lovely technique for factoring extremely large numbers. With this technique, a supercomputer could break this encryption scheme in a matter of hours.

I pull the circuit board from my pocket and connect it to the data port with a cable. I tap in a twelve digit number, and the locker door swings open.

By the time I'm back in Boston with the ampule, the FDA has responded to the theft by removing all pertinent files from any computer accessible through the datanet: as expected.

With the ampule and my belongings, I drive to New York City.

* * *

The fastest way for me to make money is, oddly enough, gambling. Handicapping horse races is simple enough. Without attracting undue attention, I can accumulate a moderate sum, and then sustain myself with investments in the stock market.

I'm staying in a room in the cheapest apartment I could find near New York that has datanet outlets. I've arranged several false names under which to make my investments, and will change them regularly. I shall spend some time on Wall Street, so that I can identify high-yield short-term opportunities from the body language of brokers. I won't go more than once a week; there are more significant matters to attend to, gestalts beckoning my attention.

As my mind develops, so does my control over my body. It is a misconception to think that during evolution humans sacrificed physical skill in exchange for intelligence: wielding one's body is a mental activity. While my strength hasn't increased, my coordination is now well above average; I'm even becoming ambidextrous. Moreover, my powers of concentration make biofeedback techniques very effective. After comparatively little practice, I am able to raise or lower my heart rate and blood pressure.

I write a program to perform a pattern match for photos of my face, and search for occurrences of my name; I then incorporate it into a virus for scanning all public display files on the datanet. The CIA will have the national datanet news briefs display my picture and identify me as a dangerously insane escaped patient, perhaps a murderer. The virus will replace my photo with video static. I plant a similar virus in the FDA and CIA computers, to search for copies of my picture in any downloads to regional police. These viruses should be immune to anything that their programmers can come up with.

Undoubtably Shea and the other doctors are in consultation with the psychologists of the CIA, guessing where I might have gone. My parents are dead, so the CIA is turning its attention to my friends, asking whether I've contacted them; they'll maintain surveillance on them in the event I do. A regrettable invasion of their privacy, but it isn't a pressing matter.

It's unlikely that the CIA will treat any of their agents with hormone K to locate me. As I myself demonstrate, a superintelligent person is too difficult to control. However, I'll keep track of the other patients, in case the government decides to recruit them.

The quotidian patterns of society are revealed without my making effort. I walk down the street, watching people go about their business, and though not a word is spoken, the subtext is conspicuous. A young couple strolls by, the adoration of one bouncing off the tolerance of the other. Apprehension flickers and becomes steady as a businessman, fearful of his supervisor, begins to doubt a decision he made earlier today. A woman wears a mantle of simulated sophistication, but it slips when it brushes past the genuine article.

As always, the roles one plays become recognizable only with greater maturity. To me, these people seem like children on a playground; I'm amused by their earnestness, and embarassed to remember myself doing those same things. Their activities are appropriate for them, but I couldn't bear to participate now; when I became a man, I put away childish things. I will deal with the world of normal humans only as needed to support myself.

* * *

I acquire years of education each week, assembling ever larger patterns. I view the tapestry of human knowledge from a broader perspective than anyone ever has before; I can fill gaps in the design where scholars never even noticed a lack, and enrich the texture in places that they felt were complete.

The natural sciences have the clearest patterns. Physics admits of a lovely unification, not just at the level of fundamental forces, but when considering its extent and implications. Classifications like "optics" or "thermodynamics" are just straitjackets, preventing physicists from seeing countless intersections. Even putting aside aesthetics, the practical applications that have been overlooked are legion; years ago engineers could have been artifically generating spherically symmetric gravity fields.

Having realized this, however, I won't build such a device, or any other. It would require many custom-built components, all difficult and time-consuming to procure. Furthermore, actually constructing the device wouldn't give me any particular satisfaction, since I already know it would work, and it wouldn't illuminate any new gestalts.

I'm writing part of an extended poem, as an experiment; after I've finished one canto, I'll be able to choose an approach for integrating the patterns within all the arts. I'm employing six modern and four ancient languages; they include most of the significant worldviews of human civilization. Each one provides different shades of meaning and poetic effects; some of the juxtapositions are delightful. Each line of the poem contains neologisms, born by extruding words through the declensions of another language. If I were to complete the entire piece, it could be thought of as *Finnegans Wake* multiplied by Pound's *Cantos*.

The CIA interrupts my work; they're baiting a trap for me. After two months of trying, they've accepted that they can't locate me by conventional methods, so they've turned to more drastic measures. The news services report that the girlfriend of a deranged murderer has been charged with aiding and abetting his escape. The name given is Connie Perritt, someone I was seeing last year. If it goes to trial, it's a foregone conclusion that she'll be sentenced to a lengthy prison term; the CIA is hoping that I won't allow that. They expect me to attempt a maneuver that will expose me to capture.

Connie's preliminary hearing is tomorrow. They'll insure that she's released on bail, through a bondsman if necessary, to give me an opportunity to contact her. Then they'll saturate the area around her apartment with undercover agents to wait for me.

I begin editing the first image on screen. These digital photos are so minimal compared to holos, but they serve the purpose. The photos, taken yesterday, show the exterior of Connie's apartment building, the street out front, and nearby intersections. I move the cursor across the screen, drawing small crosshairs in certain locations on the images. A window, with lights out but curtains open, in the building diagonally opposite. A street vendor two blocks from the rear of the building.

I mark six locations altogether. They indicate where CIA agents were waiting last night, when Connie went back to her apartment. Having been cued by the videotapes of me in the hospital, they knew what to look for in all male or ambiguous passerbys: the confident, level gait. Their expectations worked against them; I simply lengthened my strides, bobbed my head up and down a bit, reduced my arm motion. That and some atypical clothes were sufficient for them to ignore me as I walked through the area.

At the bottom of one photo I type the radio frequency used by the agents for communication, and an equation describing the scrambling algorithm employed. Once I've finished, I transmit the images to the Director of the CIA. The implication is clear: I could kill his undercover agents at any time, unless they withdraw.

To have them drop charges against Connie, and for a more permanent deterrent against the CIA's distractions, I shall have to do some more work.

Pattern recognition again, but this time it's of a mundane variety. Thousands of pages of reports, memos, correspondence; each one is a dot of color in a pointillist painting. I step back from this panorama, watching for lines and edges to emerge and create a pattern. The megabytes that I scanned constituted only a fraction of the complete records for the period I investigated, but they were enough.

What I've found is rather ordinary, far simpler than the plot of a spy novel. The Director of the CIA was aware of a terrorist group's plan to bomb the Washington, D.C. metro system. He let the bombing occur, in order to gain Congressional approval for the use of extreme measures against that group. A congressman's son was among the casualties, and the CIA director was given a free hand in handling the terrorists. While his plans aren't actually stated in CIA records, they're implied quite clearly. The relevant memos make only oblique references, and they float in a sea of innocuous documents; if an investigating committee were to read all of the records, the evidence would be drowned out by the noise. However, a distillation of the incriminating memos would certainly convince the press.

I send the list of memos to the Director of the CIA, with a note: "Don't bother me, and I won't bother you." He'll realize that he has no alternative.

This little episode has reinforced my opinion of the affairs of the world; I could detect clandestine ploys everywhere if I kept informed about current events, but none of them would be interesting. I shall resume my studies.

Control over my body continues to grow. By now I could walk on hot coals or stick needles in my arm, if I were so inclined. However, my interest in Eastern meditation is limited to its application to physical control; no meditative trance I can attain is nearly as desirable to me as my mental state when I assemble gestalts out of elemental data.

I'm designing a new language. I've reached the limits of conventional languages, and now they frustrate my attempts to progress further. They lack the power to express concepts that I need, and even in their own domain, they're imprecise and unwieldy. They're hardly fit for speech, let alone thought.

Existing linguistic theory is useless; I'll reevaluate basic logic to determine the suitable atomic components for my language. This language will support a dialect co-expressive with all of mathematics, so that any equation I write will have a linguistic equivalent. However, mathematics will be only a small part of the language, not the whole; unlike Leibniz, I recognize symbolic logic's limits. Other dialects I have planned will be co-expressive with my notations for aesthetics and cognition. This will be a time-consuming project, but the end result will clarify my thoughts enormously. After I've translated all that I know into this language, the patterns I seek should become evident.

* * *

I pause in my work. Before I develop a notation for aesthetics, I must establish a vocabulary for all the emotions I can imagine.

I'm aware of many emotions beyond those of normal humans; I see how limited their affective range is. I don't deny the validity of the love and angst I once felt, but I do see them for what they were: like the infatuations and depressions of childhood, they were just the forerunners of what I experience now. My passions now are more multifaceted; as self-knowledge increases, all emotions become exponentially more complex. I must be able to describe them fully if I'm to even attempt the composing tasks ahead.

Of course, I actually experience far fewer emotions than I could; my development is limited by the intelligence of those around me, and the scant intercourse I permit myself with them. I'm reminded of the Confucian concept of *ren*: inadequately conveyed by "benevolence," that quality which is quintessentially human, which can only be cultivated through interaction with others, and which a solitary person cannot manifest. It's one of many such qualities. And here am I, with people, people everywhere, yet not a one to interact with. I'm only a fraction of what a complete individual with my intelligence could be.

I don't delude myself with either self-pity or conceit: I can evaluate my own psychological state with the utmost objectivity and consistency. I know precisely which emotional resources I have and which I lack, and how much value I place on each. I have no regrets.

My new language is taking shape. It is gestalt-oriented, rendering it beautifully suited for thought, but impractical for writing or speech. It wouldn't be transcribed in the form of words arranged linearly, but as a giant ideogram, to be absorbed as a whole. Such an ideogram could convey, more deliberately than a picture, what a thousand words cannot. The intricacy of each ideogram would be commensurate with the amount of information contained; I amuse myself with the notion of a colossal ideogram that describes the entire universe.

The printed page is too clumsy and static for this language; the only serviceable media would be video or holo, displaying a time-evolving graphic image. Speaking this language would be out of the question, given the limited bandwidth of the human larynx.

My mind seethes with expletives from ancient and modern languages, and they taunt me with their crudeness, reminding me that my ideal language would offer terms with sufficient venom to express my present frustration.

I cannot complete my artificial language; it's too large a project for my present tools. Weeks of concentrated effort have yielded nothing usable. I've attempted to write it via bootstrapping, by employing the rudimentary language that I've already defined to rewrite the language and produce successively fuller versions. Yet each new version only highlights its own inadequacies, forcing me to expand my ultimate goal, condemning it to the status of a Holy Grail at the end of a divergent infinite regress. This is no better than trying to create it *ex nihilo*.

What about my fourth ampule? I can't remove it from my thoughts: every frustration I experience at my present plateau reminds me of the possibility for still greater heights.

Of course, there are significant risks. This injection might be the one that causes brain damage or insanity. Temptation by the Devil, perhaps, but temptation nonetheless. I find no reason to resist.

I'd have a margin of safety if I injected myself in a hospital, or, failing that, with someone standing by in my apartment. However, I imagine the injection will either be successful or else cause irreparable damage, so I forego those precautions.

I order equipment from a medical supply company, and assemble an apparatus for administering the spinal injection by myself. It may take days for the full effects to become evident, so I'll confine myself to my bedroom. It's possible that my reaction will be violent; I remove breakables from the room and attach loose straps to the bed. The neighbors will interpret anything they hear as an addict howling.

I inject myself and wait.

My brain is on fire, my spine burns itself through my back, I feel near apoplexy. I am blind, deaf, insensate.

I hallucinate. Seen with such preternatural clarity and contrast that they must be illusory, unspeakable horrors loom all around me, scenes not of physical violence but of psychic mutilation.

Mental agony and orgasm. Terror and hysterical laughter.

For a brief moment, perception returns. I'm on the floor, hands clenched in my hair, some uprooted tufts lying around me. My clothes are soaked in sweat. I've bitten my tongue, and my throat is raw: from screaming, I surmise. Convulsions have left my body badly bruised, and a concussion is likely given the contusions on the back of my head, but I feel nothing. Has it been hours or moments?

Then my vision clouds and the roar returns.

Critical mass.

Revelation.

I understand the mechanism of my own thinking. I know precisely how I know, and my understanding is recursive. I understand the infinite regress of this self-knowing, not by proceeding step by step endlessly, but by apprehending the *limit*. The nature of recursive cognition is clear to me. A new meaning of the term "self-aware."

Fiat logos. I know my mind in terms of a language more expressive than any I'd previously imagined. Like God creating order from chaos with an utterance, I make myself anew with this language. It is meta-self-descriptive and self-editing; not only can it describe thought, it can describe and modify its own operations as well, at all levels. What Gödel would have given to see this language, where modifying a statement causes the entire grammar to be adjusted.

With this language, I can see how my mind is operating. I don't pretend to see my own neurons firing; such claims belong to John Lilly and his LSD experiments of the sixties. What I can do is perceive the gestalts; I see the mental structures forming, interacting. I see myself thinking, and I see the equations that describe my thinking, and I see myself comprehending the equations, and I see how the equations describe their being comprehended.

I know how they make up my thoughts.

These thoughts.

Initially I am overwhelmed by all this input, paralyzed with awareness of my self. It is hours before I can control the flood of self-describing information. I haven't filtered it away, nor pushed it into the background. It's become integrated into my mental processes, for use during my normal activities. It will be longer before I can take advantage of it, effortlessly and effectively, the way a dancer uses her kinesthesic knowledge.

All that I once knew theoretically about my mind, I now see detailed explicitly. The undercurrents of sex, aggression, and self-preservation, translated by the conditioning of my childhood, clash with and are sometimes disguised as rational thought. I recognize all the causes of my every mood, the motives behind my every decision.

What can I do with this knowledge? Much of what is conventionally described as "personality" is at my discretion; the higher-level aspects of my psyche define who I am now. I can send my mind into a variety of mental or emotional states, yet remain ever aware of the state and able to restore my original condition. Now that I understand the mechanisms that were operating when I attended to two tasks at once, I can divide my consciousness, simultaneously devoting almost full concentration and gestalt recognition abilities to two or more separate problems, meta-aware of all of them. What can't I do?

I know my body afresh, as if it were an amputee's stump suddenly replaced by a watchmaker's hand. Controlling my voluntary muscles is trivial; I have inhuman coordination. Skills that normally require thousands of repetitions to develop, I can learn in two or three. I find a video with a shot of a pianist's hands playing, and before long I can duplicate his finger movements without a keyboard in front of me. Selective contraction and relaxation of muscles improve my strength and flexibility. Muscular response time is thirty-five milliseconds for conscious or reflex action. Learning acrobatics and martial arts would require little training.

I have somatic awareness of kidney function, nutrient absorption, glandular secretions. I am even conscious of the role that neurotransmitters play in my thoughts. This state of consciousness involves mental activity more intense than in any epinephrine-boosted stress situation; part of my mind is maintaining a condition that would kill a normal mind and body within minutes. As I adjust the programming of my mind, I experience the ebb and flow of all the substances that trigger my emotional reactions, boost my attention, or subtly shape my attitudes.

And then I look outward.

Blinding, joyous, fearful symmetry surrounds me. So much is incorporated within patterns now that the entire universe verges on resolving itself into a picture. I'm closing in on the ultimate gestalt: the context in which all knowledge fits and is illuminated, a mandala, the music of the spheres, *kosmos*.

I seek enlightenment, not spiritual but rational. I must go still further to reach it, but this time the goal will not be perpetually retreating from my fingertips. With my mind's language, the distance between myself and enlightenment is precisely calculable. I've sighted my final destination.

Now I must plan my next actions. First, there are the simple enhancements to self-preservation, starting with martial arts training. I will watch some tournaments to study possible attacks, though I will take only defensive action; I can move rapidly enough to avoid contact with even the fastest striking techniques. This will let me protect myself and disarm any street criminals, should I be assaulted. Meanwhile, I must eat copious amounts of food to meet my brain's nourishment requirements, even given increased efficiency in my metabolism. I shall also shave my scalp, to allow greater radiative cooling for the heightened blood flow to my head.

Then there is the primary goal: decoding those patterns. For further improvements to my mind, artificial enhancements are the only possibility. A direct computer-mind link, permitting mind downloading, is what I need, but I must create a new technology to implement it. Anything based on digital computation will be inadequate; what I have in mind requires nano-scale structures based on neural networks.

Once I have the basic ideas laid out, I set my mind to multiprocessing: one section of my mind deriving a branch of mathematics that reflects the networks' behavior; another developing a process for replicating the formation of neural pathways on a molecular scale in a self-repairing bioceramic medium; a third devising tactics for guiding private industrial R & D to produce what I'll need. I cannot waste time: I will introduce explosive theoretical and technical breakthroughs so that my new industry will hit the ground running.

I've gone into the outside world to re-observe society. The sign language of emotion I once knew has been replaced by a matrix of interrelated equations. Lines of force twist and elongate between people, objects, institutions, ideas. The individuals are tragically like marionettes, independently animate but bound by a web they choose not to see; they could resist if they wished, but so few of them do.

At the moment I'm sitting at a bar. Three stools to my right sits a man, familiar with this type of establishment, who looks around and notices a couple in a dark corner booth. He smiles, motions for the bartender to come over, and leans forward to speak confidentially about the couple. I don't need to listen to know what he's saying.

He's lying to the bartender, easily, extemporaneously. A compulsive liar, not out of a desire for a life more exciting than his own, but to revel in his facility for deceiving others. He knows the bartender is detached, merely affecting interest—which is true—but he knows the bartender is still fooled, which is also true.

My sensitivity to the body language of others has increased to the point that I can make these observations without sight or sound: I can smell the pheromones exuded by his skin. To an extent, my muscles can even detect the tension within his, perhaps by their electric field. These channels can't convey precise information, but the impressions I receive provide ample basis for extrapolation; they add texture to the web.

Normal humans may detect these emanations subliminally. I'll work on becoming more attuned to them; then perhaps I can try consciously controlling my own expressions.

I've developed abilities reminiscent of the mind-control schemes offered by tabloid advertisements. My control over my somatic emanations now lets me provoke precise reactions in others. With pheromones and muscle tension, I can cause another person to respond with anger, fear, sympathy or sexual arousal. Certainly enough to win friends and influence people.

I can even induce a self-sustaining reaction in others. By associating a particular response with a sense of satisfaction, I can create a positive reinforcement loop, like biofeedback; the person's body will strengthen the reaction on its own. I'll use this on corporate presidents to create support for the industries I'll need.

I can no longer dream in any normal sense. I lack anything that would qualify as a subconscious, and I control all the maintenance functions performed by my brain, so normal REM sleep tasks are obsolete. There are moments when my grasp on my mind slips, but they cannot be called dreams. Meta-hallucinations, perhaps. Sheer torture. These are periods during which I'm detached: I understand how my mind generates the strange visions, but I'm paralyzed and unable to respond. I can scarcely identify what I see; images of bizarre transfinite self-references and modifications that even I find nonsensical.

My mind is taxing the resources of my brain. A biological structure of this size and complexity can just barely sustain a self-knowing psyche. But the self-knowing psyche is also self-regulating, to an extent. I give my mind full use of what's available, and restrain it from expanding beyond that. But it's difficult: I'm cramped inside a bamboo cage that doesn't let me sit down or stand up. If I try to relax, or try to extend myself fully, then agony, madness.

I'm hallucinating. I see my mind imagining possible configurations it could assume, and then collapsing. I witness my own delusions, my visions of what form my mind might take when I grasp the ultimate gestalts.

Will I achieve ultimate self-awareness? Could I discover the components that make up my own mental gestalts? Would I penetrate racial memory? Would I find innate knowledge of morality? I might determine whether mind could be spontaneously generated from matter, and understand what relates consciousness with the rest of the universe. I might see how to merge subject and object: the zero experience.

Or perhaps I'd find that the mind gestalt cannot be generated, and some sort of intervention is required. Perhaps I would see the soul, the ingredient of consciousness that surpasses physicality. Proof of God? I would behold the meaning, the true character of existence.

I would be enlightened. It must be euphoric to experience . . .

My mind collapses back into a state of sanity. I must keep a tighter rein over myself. When I'm in control at the metaprogramming level, my mind is perfectly self-repairing; I could restore myself from states that resemble delusion or amnesia. But if I drift too far on the metaprogramming level, my mind might become an unstable structure, and then I would slide into a state beyond mere insanity. I will program my mind to forbid itself from moving beyond its own reprogramming range.

These hallucinations strengthen my resolve to create an artificial brain. Only with such a structure will I be able to actually perceive those gestalts, instead of merely dreaming about them. To achieve enlightenment, I'll need to exceed another critical mass in terms of neuronal analogs.

I open my eyes: it's two hours, twenty-eight minutes, and ten seconds since I closed my eyes to rest, though not to sleep. I rise from bed.

I request a listing of my stocks' performance on my terminal. I look down the flatscreen, and freeze.

The screen shouts at me. It tells me that there is another person with an enhanced mind.

Five of my investments have demonstrated losses; they're not precipitous, but large enough that I'd have detected them in the body language of the stockbrokers. Reading down the alphabetical list, the initial letters of the corporations whose stock values have dropped are: C, E, G, O, and R. Which when rearranged, spell GRECO.

Someone is sending me a message.

There's someone else out there like me. There must have been another comatose patient who received a third injection of hormone K. He erased his file from the FDA database before I accessed it, and supplied false input to his doctors' accounts so that they wouldn't notice. He too stole another ampule of the hormone, contributing to the FDA's closing of their files, and with his whereabouts unknown to the authorities, he's reached my level.

He must have recognized me through the investment patterns of my false identities; he'd have to have been supercritical to do that. As an enhanced individual, he could have effected sudden and precise changes to trigger my losses, and attract my attention.

I check various data services for stock quotes; the entries on my listing are correct, so my counterpart didn't simply edit the values for my account alone. He altered the selling patterns of the stock of five unrelated corporations, for the sake of a word. It makes for quite a demonstration; I consider it no mean feat.

Presumably his treatment began before mine did, meaning that he is further along than I, but by how much? I begin extrapolating his likely progress, and will incorporate new information as I acquire it.

The critical question: is he friend or foe? Was this merely a good-natured demonstration of his power, or an indication of his intent to ruin me? The amounts I lost were moderate; does this indicate concern for me, or for the corporations which he had to manipulate? Given all the harmless ways he could have attracted my attention, I must assume that he is to some degree hostile.

In which case, I am at risk, vulnerable to anything from another prank to a fatal attack. As a precaution, I will leave immediately. Obviously, if he were actively hostile, I'd be dead already. His sending a message means that he wishes us to play games. I'll have to place myself on equal terms with him: hide my location, determine his identity, and then attempt to communicate.

I pick a city at random: Memphis. I switch off the flatscreen, get dressed, pack a travel bag, and collect all the emergency cash in the apartment.

In a Memphis hotel, I begin working at the suite's datanet terminal. The first thing I do is reroute my activities through several dummy terminals; to an ordinary police trace, my queries will appear to originate from different terminals all over the state of Utah. A military intelligence facility might be able to track them to a terminal in Houston; continuing the trace to Memphis would try even me. An alarm program at the Houston terminal will alert me if someone has successfully traced me there.

How many clues to his identity has my twin erased? Lacking all FDA files, I'll begin with the files of courier services in various cities, looking for deliveries from the FDA to hospitals during the time of the hormone K study. Then a check of the hospital's brain-damage cases at that time, and I'll have a place to start.

Even if any of this information remains, it's of minor value. What will be crucial is an examination of the investment patterns, to find the traces of an enhanced mind. This will take time.

His name is Reynolds. He's originally from Phoenix, and his early progress closely parallels mine. He received his third injection six months and four days ago, giving him a head start over me of fifteen days. He didn't erase any of the obvious records. He waits for me to find him. I estimate that he's been supercritical for twelve days, twice as long as I've been.

I now see his hand in the investment patterns, but the task of locating Reynolds is Herculean. I examine usage logs across the datanet to identify the accounts he's penetrated. I have twelve lines open on my terminal. I'm using two single-hand keyboards and a throat-mike, so I can work on three queries simultaneously. Most of my body is immobile; to prevent fatigue, I'm insuring proper blood flow, regular muscle contraction and relaxation, and removal of lactic acid. While I absorb all the data I see, studying the melody within the notes, looking for the epicenter of a tremor in the web.

Hours pass. We both scan gigabytes of data, circling each other.

His location is Philadelphia. He waits for me to arrive.

I'm riding in a mud-splattered taxi to Reynolds' apartment.

Judging by the databases and agencies Reynolds has queried over the past months, his private research involves bio-engineered microorganisms for toxic waste disposal, inertial containment for practical fusion, and subliminal dissemination of information through societies of various structures. He plans to save the world, to protect it from itself. And his opinion of me is therefore unfavorable.

I've shown no interest in the affairs of the external world, and made no investigations for aiding the normals. Neither of us will be able to convert the other. I view the world as incidental to my aims, while he cannot allow someone with enhanced intelligence to work purely in self-interest. My plans for mind-computer links will have enormous repercussions for the world, provoking government or popular reactions that would interfere with his plans. As I am proverbially not part of the solution, I am part of the problem.

If we were members of a society of enhanced minds, the nature of human interaction would be of a different order. But in this society, we have unavoidably become juggernauts, by whose measure the actions of normals are inconsequential. Even if we were twelve thousand miles apart we couldn't ignore each other. A resolution is necessary.

Both of us have dispensed with several rounds of games. There are a thousand ways we could have attempted to kill the other, from painting neurotoxin-laced DMSO on a doorknob to ordering a surgical strike from a military killsat. We both could have swept the physical area and datanet for each of the myriad possibilities beforehand, and set more traps for each other's sweeps. But neither of us has done any of that, has felt a need to check for those things. A simple infinite regression of second-guessing and double-thinking has dismissed those. What will be decisive are those preparations that we could not predict.

The taxi stops; I pay the driver and walk up to the apartment building. The electric lock on the door opens for me. I take off my coat and climb four flights.

The door to Reynolds' apartment is also open. I walk down the entryway to the living room, hearing a hyperaccelerated polyphony from a digital synthesizer. Evidently it's his own work; the sounds are modulated in ways undetectable to normal hearing, and even I can't discern any pattern to them. An experiment in high-information density music, perhaps.

There is a large swivel chair in the room, its back turned toward me. Reynolds is not visible, and he is restricting his somatic emanations to comatose levels. I imply my presence and my recognition of his identity.

<Reynolds.>

Acknowledgement. <Greco.>

The chair turns around smoothly, slowly. He smiles at me and shuts off the synthesizer at his side.

Gratification. <A pleasure to meet you.>

To communicate, we are exchanging fragments from the somatic language of the normals: a shorthand version of the vernacular. Each phrase takes a tenth of a second. I give a suggestion of regret. <A shame it must be as enemies.>

Wistful agreement, then supposition. <Indeed. Imagine how we could change the world, acting in concert. Two enhanced minds; such an opportunity missed.>

True, acting cooperatively would produce achievements far outstripping any we might attain individually. Any interaction would be incredibly fruitful: how satisfying it would be to simply have a discussion with someone who can match my speed, who can offer an idea that is new to me, who can hear the same melodies I do. He desires the same. It pains us both to think that one of us will not leave this room alive.

An offer. <Do you wish to share what we've learned in the past six months?>

He knows what my answer is.

We will speak aloud, since somatic language has no technical vocabulary. Reynolds says, quickly and quietly, five words. They are more pregnant with meaning than any stanza of poetry: each word provides a logical toehold I can mount after extracting everything implicit in the preceding ones. Together they encapsulate a revolutionary insight into sociology; using somatic language he indicates that it was among the first he ever achieved. I came to a similar realization, but formulated it differently. I immediately counter with seven words, four that summarize the distinctions between my insight and his, and three that describe a non-obvious result of the distinctions. He responds.

We continue. We are like two bards, each cueing the other to extemporize another stanza, jointly composing an epic poem of knowledge. Within moments we accelerate, talking over each other's words but hearing every nuance, until we are absorbing, concluding, and responding, continuously, simultaneously, synergistically.

Many minutes pass. I learn much from him, and he from me. It's exhilarating, to be suddenly awash in ideas whose implications would take me days to consider fully. But we're also gathering strategic information: I infer the extent of his unspoken knowledge, compare it with my own, and simulate his corresponding inferences. For there is always the awareness that this must come to an end; the formulation of our exchanges renders ideological differences luminously clear.

Reynolds hasn't witnessed the beauty that I have; he's stood before lovely insights, oblivious to them. The sole gestalt that inspires him is the one I ignored: that of the planetary society, of the biosphere. I am a lover of beauty, he of humanity. Each feels that the other has ignored great opportunities.

He has an unmentioned plan for establishing a global network of influence, to create world prosperity. To execute it, he'll employ a number of people, some of whom he'll give simple heightened intelligence, some meta-self-awareness; a few of them will pose threats to him. <Why assume such a risk for the sake of the normals?>

<Your indifference toward the normals would be justified if you were enlightened; your realm wouldn't intersect theirs. But as long as you and I can still comprehend their affairs, we can't ignore them.>

I can measure the distance between our respective moral stances precisely, see the stress between their incompatible radiating lines. What motivates him is not simply compassion or altruism, but something that entails both those things. On the other hand, I concentrate only on understanding the sublime. <What about the beauty visible from enlightenment? Doesn't it attract you?>

<You know what kind of structure would be required to hold an enlightened consciousness. I have no reason to wait the time it would take to establish the necessary industries.>

He considers intelligence to be a means, while I view it as an end in itself.

Greater intelligence would be of little use to him. At his present level, he can find the best possible solution to any problem within the realm of human experience, and many beyond. All he'd require is sufficient time to implement his solution.

There's no point in further discussion. By mutual assent, we begin.

It's meaningless to speak of an element of surprise when we time our attacks; our awareness can't become more acute with forewarning. It's not affording a courtesy to each other when we agree to begin our battle, it's actualizing the inevitable.

In the models of each other that we've constructed from our inferences, there are gaps, lacunae: the internal psychological developments and discoveries that each has made. No echoes have radiated from those spaces, no strands have tied them to the world web, until now.

I begin.

I concentrate on initiating two reinforcing loops in him. One is very simple: it increases blood pressure rapidly and enormously. If it were to continue unchecked for over a second, this loop would raise his blood pressure to stroke levels—perhaps three hundred over two hundred—and burst capillaries in his brain.

Reynolds detects it immediately. Though it's clear from our conversation that he never investigated the inducement of biofeedback loops in others, he recognizes what is happening. Once he does, he reduces his heart rate and dilates the blood vessels throughout his body.

But it is the other, subtler reinforcing loop that is my real attack. This is a weapon I've been developing ever since my search for Reynolds began. This loop causes his neurons to dramatically overproduce neurotransmitter antagonists, preventing impulses from crossing his synapses, shutting down brain activity. I've been radiating this loop at a much higher intensity than the other.

As Reynolds is parrying the ostensible attack, he experiences a slight weakening of his concentration, masked by the effects of the heightened blood pressure. A second later, his body begins to amplify the effect on its own. Reynolds is shocked to feel his thoughts blurring. He searches for the precise mechanism: he'll identify it soon, but he won't be able to scrutinize it for long.

Once his brain function has been reduced to the level of a normal, I should be able to manipulate his mind easily. Hypnotic techniques can make him regurgitate most of the information his enhanced mind possesses.

I inspect his somatic expressions, watching them betray his diminishing intelligence. The regression is unmistakeable.

And then it stops.

Reynolds is in equilibrium. I'm stunned. He was able to break the reinforcing loop. He has stopped the most sophisticated offensive I could mount.

Next, he reverses the damage already done. Even starting with reduced capabilities, he can correct the balance of neurotransmitters. Within seconds, Reynolds is fully restored.

I, too, was transparent to him. During our conversation he deduced that I had investigated reinforcing loops, and as we communicated, he derived a general preventative without my detecting it. Then he observed the specifics of my particular attack while it was working, and learned how to reverse its effects. I am astonished at his discernment, his speed, his stealth.

He acknowledges my skill. <A very interesting technique; appropriate, given your self-absorption. I saw no indication when—> Abruptly he projects a different somatic signature, one that I recognize. He used it when he walked behind me at a grocery store, three days ago. The aisle was crowded; around me were an old woman, wheezing behind her air filter, and a thin teenager on an acid trip, wearing a liquid crystal shirt of shifting psychedelic patterns. Reynolds slipped behind me, his mind on the porn mag stands. His surveillance didn't inform him of my reinforcing loops, but it did permit a more detailed picture of my mind.

A possibility I anticipated. I reformulate my psyche, incorporating random elements for unpredictability. The equations of my mind now bear little resemblance to those of my normal consciousness, undermining any assumptions Reynolds may have made, and rendering ineffectual any psyche-specific weapons of his.

I project the equivalent of a smile.

Reynolds smiles back. <Have you ever considered—> Suddenly he projects only silence. He is about to speak, but I can't predict what. Then it comes, as a whisper: "self-destruct commands, Greco?"

As he says it, a lacuna in my reconstruction of him fills and overflows, the implications coloring all that I know about him. He means the Word: the sentence that, when uttered, would destroy the mind of the listener. Reynolds is claiming that the myth is true, that every mind has such a trigger built in; that for every person, there is a sentence that can reduce him to an idiot, a lunatic, a catatonic. And he is claiming he knows the one for me.

I immediately tune out all sensory input, directing it to an insulated buffer of short-term memory. Then I conceive a simulator of my own consciousness to receive the input and absorb it at reduced speed. As a metaprogrammer I will monitor the equations of the simulation indirectly. Only after the sensory information has been confirmed as safe will I actually receive it. If the simulator is destroyed, my consciousness should be isolated, and I'll retrace the individual steps leading to the crash and derive guidelines for reprogramming my psyche.

I get everything in place by the time Reynolds has finished saying my name; his next sentence could be the destruct command. I'm now receiving my sensory input with a one hundred and twenty millisecond time lag. I reexamine my analysis of the human mind, explicitly searching for evidence to verify his assertion.

Meanwhile I give my response lightly, casually. <Hit me with your best shot.>

<Don't worry; it's not on the tip of my tongue.>

My search produces something. I curse myself: there's a very subtle back door to a psyche's design, which I lacked the necessary mindset to notice. Whereas my weapon was one born of introspection, his is something only a manipulator could originate.

Reynolds knows that I've built my defenses; is his trigger command designed to circumvent them? I continue deriving the nature of trigger command's actions.

<What are you waiting for?> He's confident that additional time won't allow me to construct a defense.

<Try to guess.> So smug. Can he actually toy with me so easily?

I arrive at a theoretical description of a trigger's effects on normals. A single command can reduce any subcritical mind to a *tabula rasa*, but an undetermined degree of customization is needed for enhanced minds. The erasure has distinctive symptoms, which my simulator can alert me to, but those are symptoms of a process calculable by me. By definition the destruct command is that specific equation beyond my ability to imagine; would my metaprogrammer collapse while diagnosing the simulator's condition?

<Have you used the destruct command on normals?> I begin calculating what's needed to generate a customized destruct command.

<Once, as an experiment on a drug dealer. Afterward I concealed the evidence with a blow to the temple.>

It becomes obvious that the generation is a colossal task. Generating a trigger requires intimate knowledge of my mind; I extrapolate what he could have learned about me. It appears to be insufficient, given my reprogramming, but he may have techniques of observation unknown to me. I'm acutely aware of the advantage he's gained by studying the outside world.

<You will have to do this many times.>

His regret is evident. His plan can't be implemented without more deaths: those of normal humans, by strategic necessity, and those of a few enhanced assistants of his, whose temptation by greater heights would interfere. After using the command, Reynolds may reprogram them—or me—as savants, having focused intentions and restricted self-metaprogrammers. Such deaths are a necessary cost of his plan.

<I make no claims of being a saint.>

Merely a savior.

Normals might think him a tyrant, because they mistake him for one of them, and they've never trusted their own judgement. They can't fathom that Reynolds is equal to the task. His judgement is optimal in questions of their affairs, and their notions of greed and ambition do not apply to an enhanced mind.

In a histrionic gesture, Reynolds raises his hand, forefinger extended, as if to make a point. I don't have sufficient information to generate his destruct command, so for the moment I can only attend to defense. If I can survive his attack, I may have time to launch another one of my own.

With his finger upraised, he says, "Understand."

At first I don't. And then, horrifyingly, I do.

He didn't design the command to be spoken; it's not a sensory trigger at all. It's a memory trigger: the command is made out of a string of perceptions, individually harmless, that he planted in my brain like time bombs. The mental structures that were formed as a result of those memories are now resolving into a pattern, forming a gestalt that defines my dissolution. I'm intuiting the Word myself.

Immediately my mind is working faster than ever before. Against my will, a lethal realization is suggesting itself to me. I'm trying to halt the associations, but these memories can't be suppressed. The process occurs inexorably, as a consequence of my awareness, and like a man falling from a height, I'm forced to watch.

Milliseconds pass. My death passes before my eyes.

An image of the grocery store when Reynolds passed by. The psychedelic shirt the boy was wearing; Reynolds had programmed the display to implant a suggestion within me, ensuring that my "randomly" reprogrammed psyche remained receptive. Even then.

No time. All I can do is metaprogram myself over randomly, at a furious pace. An act of desperation, possibly crippling.

The strange modulated sounds that I heard when I first entered Reynolds' apartment. I absorbed the fatal insights before I had any defenses raised.

I tear apart my psyche, but still the conclusion grows clearer, the resolution sharper.

Myself, constructing the simulator. Designing those defense structures gave me the perspective needed to recognize the gestalt.

I concede his greater ingenuity. It bodes well for his endeavor. Pragmatism avails a savior far more than aestheticism.

I wonder what he intends to do after he's saved the world.

I comprehend the Word, and the means by which it operates, and so I dissolve.

HALO

Karl Schroeder

❁

Karl Schroeder (born 1962) was born in Brandon, Manitoba, and moved to Toronto in 1986 to pursue his writing career. His family is Mennonite, part of a community which has lived in southern Manitoba for over a hundred years. He is the second science fiction writer to come out of this small community—the first was A. E. van Vogt. His father was the first television technician in Manitoba (quite a distinction at the time) and his mother published two romance novels. ("I grew up with those books on the bookshelf—I always considered it perfectly natural to see 'Schroeder' on a book cover.") He has been active in Toronto SF circles, has maintained the SF Canada list-serve, has won an Aurora Award for short fiction (for "The Toy Mill," in collaboration with David Nickle), and has published a novel, *The Claus Effect* (1997) with Nickle developed out of the story. His novel *Ventus* (2000) is hard SF novel that feels like fantasy. His new book, *Permanence*, is out in 2002.

Schroeder's views on hard SF are unconventional:

> I write a kind of disciplined fantasy that sticks close to scientific possibility—but I don't think of myself as a hard SF writer. I am very scientifically literate and follow the progress of most branches of science closely—but I am not a "believer" in Western Rationalism. If the definition of hard SF is that it is storytelling in which the events that occur don't contradict known science, then I'm not a hard SF writer and never will be, because I simply don't believe in the distinction between "real" and "pseudo" or non-science. I'm a fan of the philosophy of P. K. Feyerabend in this respect, I am a philosophical subversive in the house of Engineering SF, and I expect that will become evident to people with time . . . To me, science is a servant of philosophy, and so my stories are about ideas first, and scientific ideas second; in that regard, I admire authors like Olaf Stapledon and H. G. Wells more than authors of perhaps more technically accurate fiction. Wells in particular showed how you could use science as a gestural language to speak about things that are, in some sense, beyond science. At the moment I admire Greg Egan most of the current generation of writers. Of all of them he appears to understand best how science, philosophy and literary art interact in crafting a literature of the Natural world.

"'Halo'" says Schroeder, "is an attempt to be both 'hard SF' and character-driven fiction; to introduce a new kind of interstellar civilization and a new kind of interstellar travel; and to take the most marginal and hostile environment for life, and make it perfectly believable that people should choose to live there." This story is in the same future setting as *Permanence*.

Elise Cantrell was awakened by the sound of her children trying to manage their own breakfast. Bright daylight streamed in through the windows. She threw on a robe and ran for the kitchen. "No, no, let me!"

Judy appeared about to microwave something, and the oven was set on high.

"Aw, Mom, did you forget?" Alex, who was a cherub but had the loudest scream in the universe, pouted at her from the table. Looked like he'd gotten his breakfast together just fine. Suspicious, that, but she refused to inspect his work.

"Yeah, I forgot the time change. My prospectors are still on the twenty-four-hour clock, you know."

"Why?" Alex flapped his spoon in the cereal bowl.

"They're on another world, remember? Only Dew has a thirty-hour day, and only since they put the sun up. You remember before the sun, don't you?" Alex stared at her as though she were insane. It had only been a year and a half.

Elise sighed. Just then the door announced a visitor. "Daddy!" shrieked Judy as she ran out of the room. Elise found her in the foyer clinging to the leg of her father. Nasim Clearwater grinned at her over their daughter's flyaway hair.

"You're a mess," he said by way of greeting.

"Thanks. Look, they're not ready. Give me a few minutes."

"No problem. Left a bit early, thought you might forget the time change."

She glared at him and stalked back to the kitchen.

As she cleaned up and Nasim dressed the kids, Elise looked out over the landscape of Dew. It was daylight, yes, a pale drawn glow dropping through cloud veils to sketch hills and plains of ice. Two years ago this window had shown no view, just the occasional star. Elise had grown up in that velvet darkness, and it was so strange now to have awakening signaled by such a vivid and total change. Her children would grow up to the rhythm of true day and night, the first such generation here on Dew. They would think differently. Already, this morning, they did.

"Hello," Nasim said in her ear. Startled, Elise said, "What?" a bit too loudly.

"We're off." The kids stood behind him, dubiously inspecting the snaps of their survival suits. Today was a breach drill; Nasim would ensure they took it seriously. Elise gave him a peck on the cheek.

"You want them back late, right? Got a date?"

"No," she said, "of course not." Nasim wanted to hear that she was being independent, but she wouldn't give him the satisfaction.

Nasim half-smiled. "Well, maybe I'll see you after, then."

"Sure."

He nodded but said nothing further. As the kids screamed their goodbyes at full volume she tried to puzzle out what he'd meant. See her? To chat, to talk, maybe more?

Not more. She had to accept that. As the door closed she plunked herself angrily down on the couch, and drew her headset over her eyes.

VR was cheap for her. She didn't need full immersion, just vision and sound, and sometimes the use of her hands. Her prospectors were too specialized to have human traits, and they operated in weightlessness so she didn't need to walk. The headset was expensive enough without such additions. And the simplicity of the set-up allowed her to work from home.

The fifteen robot prospectors Elise controlled ranged throughout the halo worlds of Crucible. Crucible itself was fifty times the mass of Jupiter, a "brown dwarf" star—too small to be a sun but radiating in the high infrared and trailing a retinue of planets. Crucible sailed alone through the spaces between the true stars. Elise had been born and raised here on Dew, Crucible's frozen fifth planet.

From the camera on the first of her prospectors, she could see the new kilometers-long metal cylinder that her children had learned to call the *sun*. Its electric light shone only on Dew, leaving Crucible and the other planets in darkness. The artificial light made Dew gleam like a solitary blue-white jewel on the perfect black of space.

She turned her helmeted head, and out in space her prospector turned its camera. Faint Dew-light reflected from a round spot on Crucible. She hadn't seen that before. She recorded the sight; the kids would like it, even if they didn't quite understand it.

This first prospector craft perched astride a chunk of ice about five kilometers long. The little ice-flinder orbited Crucible with about a billion others. Her machine oversaw some dumb mining equipment that was chewing stolidly through the thing in search of metal.

There were no problems here. She flipped her view to the next machine, whose headlamps obligingly lit to show her a wall of stone. Hmm. She'd been right the night before when she ordered it to check an ice ravine on Castle, the fourth planet. There was real stone down here, which meant metals. She wondered what it would feel like, and reached out. After a delay the metal hands of her prospector touched the stone. She didn't feel anything; the prospector was not equipped to transmit the sensation back. Sometimes she longed to be able to fully experience the places her machines visited.

She sent a call to the Mining Registrar to follow up on her find, and went on to the next prospector. This one orbited farthest out, and there was a time-lag of several minutes between every command she gave, and its execution. Normally she just checked it quickly and moved on. Today, for some reason, it had a warning flag in its message queue.

Transmission intercepted.—Oh, it had overheard some dialogue between two ships or something. That was surprising, considering how far away from the normal orbits the prospector was. "Read it to me," she said, and went on to Prospector Four.

She'd forgotten about the message and was admiring a long view of Dew's horizon from the vantage of her fourth prospector, when a resonant male voice spoke in her ear:

"Mayday, mayday—anyone at Dew, please receive. My name is Hammond, and I'm speaking from the interstellar cycler *Chinook*. The date is the sixth of May, 2418. Relativistic shift is .500435—we're at half lightspeed.

"Listen: *Chinook* has been taken over by Naturite forces out of Leviathan. They are using the cycler as a weapon. You must know by now that the halo world Tiara, at Obsidian, has gone silent—it's our fault, *Chinook* has destroyed them. Dew is our next stop, and they fully intend to do the same thing there. They want to 'purify' the halo worlds so only their people settle here.

"They're keeping communications silence. I've had to go outside to take manual control of a message laser in order to send this mayday.

"You must place mines in near-pass space ahead of the cycler, to destroy it. We have limited maneuvering ability, so we couldn't possibly avoid the mines.

"Anyone receiving this message, please relay it to your authorities immediately. *Chinook* is a genocide ship. You are in danger.

"Please do not reply to *Chinook* on normal channels. They will not negotiate. Reply to my group on this frequency, not the standard cycler wavelengths."

Elise didn't know how to react. She almost laughed—what a ridiculous message, full of bluster and emergency words. But she'd heard that Obsidian had gone mysteriously silent, and no one knew why. "Origin of this message?" she asked. As she waited, she replayed it. It was highly melodramatic, just the sort of wording somebody would use for a prank. She was sure she would be told the message had come from Dew itself—maybe even sent by Nasim or one of his friends.

The coordinates flashed before her eyes. Elise did a quick calculation to visualize the direction. Not from Dew. Not from any of Crucible's worlds. The message had come from deep space, out somewhere beyond the last of Crucible's trailing satellites.

The only things out there were stars, halo worlds—and the cyclers, Elise thought. She lifted off the headset. The beginnings of fear fluttered in her belly.

Elise took the message to a cousin of hers who was a policeman. He showed her into his office, smiling warmly. They didn't often get together since they'd grown up, and he wanted to talk family.

She shook her head. "I've got something strange for you, Sal. One of my machines picked this up last night." And she played the message for him, expecting reassuring laughter and a good explanation.

Half an hour later they were being ushered into the suite of the police chief, who sat at a U-shaped table with her aides, frowning. When she entered, she heard the words of the message playing quietly from the desk speakers of two of the aides, who looked very serious.

"You will tell no one about this," said the chief. She was a thin, strong woman with blazing eyes. "We have to confirm it first." Elise hesitated, then nodded.

Cousin Sal cleared his throat. "Ma'am? You think this message could be genuine, then?"

The chief frowned at him, then said, "It may be true. This may be why Tiara went off the air." The sudden silence of Tiara, a halo world half a light-year from Elise's home, had been the subject of a media frenzy a year earlier. Rumors of disaster circulated, but there were no facts to go on, other than that Tiara's message lasers, which normally broadcast news from there, had gone out. It was no longer news, and Elise had heard nothing about it for months. "We checked the coordinates you reported and they show this message *did* come from the *Chinook*. *Chinook* did its course correction around Obsidian right about the time Tiara stopped broadcasting."

Elise couldn't believe what she was hearing. "But what could they have done?"

The chief tapped at her desk with long fingers. "You're an orbital engineer, Cantrell. You probably know better than I. The *Chinook*'s traveling at half lightspeed, so anything it dropped on an intercept course with Obsidian's planets would hit like a bomb. Even the smallest item—a pen or card."

Elise nodded reluctantly. Aside from message lasers, the Interstellar Cyclers were the only means of contact with other stars and halo worlds. Cyclers came by Crucible every few months, but they steered well away from its planets. They only came close enough to use gravity to assist their course change to the next halo world. Freight and passengers were dropped off and picked up via laser sail; the cyclers themselves were huge, far too massive to stop and start at will. Their kinetic energy was incalculable, so the interstellar community monitored them as closely as possible. They spent years in transit between the stars, however, and it took weeks or months for laser messages to reach them. News about cyclers was always out of date before it even arrived.

"We have to confirm this before we do anything," the chief said. "We have the frequency and coordinates to reply. We'll take it from here."

Elise had to ask. "Why did only I intercept the message?"

"It wasn't aimed very well, maybe. He didn't know exactly where his target was. Only your prospector was within the beam. Just luck."

"When is the *Chinook* due to pass us?" Sal asked.

"A month and a half," said the tight-faced aide. "It should be about three light-weeks out; the date on this message would tend to confirm that."

"So any reply will come right about the time they pass us," Sal said. "How can we get a confirmation in time to do anything?"

They looked at one another blankly. Elise did some quick calculations in her head. "Four messages exchanged before they're a day away," she said. "If each party waits for the other's reply. Four on each side."

"But we have to act well before that," said another aide.

"How?" asked a third.

Elise didn't need to listen to the explanation. They could mine the space in front of the cycler. Turn it into energy, and hopefully any missiles too. Kill the thousand-or-so people on board it to save Dew.

"I've done my duty," she said. "Can I go away?"

The chief waved her away. A babble of arguing voices followed Elise and Sal out the door.

Sal offered to walk her home, but Elise declined. She took old familiar ways through the corridors of the city, ways she had grown up with. Today, though, her usual route from the core of the city was blocked by work crews. They were replacing opaque ceiling panels with glass to let in the new daylight. The bright light completely changed the character of the place, washing out familiar colors. It reminded her that there were giant forces in the sky, uncontrollable by her. She retreated, from the glow, and drifted through a maze of alternate routes like a somber ghost, not meeting the eyes of the people she passed.

The parkways were packed, mostly with children. Some were there with a single parent, others with both. Elise watched the couples enviously. Having children was supposed to have made her and Nasim closer. It hadn't worked out that way.

Lately, he had shown signs of wanting her again. Take it slow, she had told herself. Give him time.

They might not have time.

The same harsh sunlight the work crews had been admitting waited when she got home. It made the jumble of toys on the living room floor seem tiny and fragile. Elise sat under the new window for a while, trying to ignore it, but finally hunted through her closets until she found some old blankets, and covered the glass.

Nasim offered to stay for dinner that night. This made her feel rushed and off-balance. The kids wanted to stay up for it, but he had a late appointment. Putting them to bed was arduous. She got dinner going late, and by then all her planned small talk had evaporated. Talking about the kids was easy enough—but to do that was to take the easy way out, and she had wanted this evening to be different. Worst was that she didn't want to tell him about the message, because if he thought she was upset he might withdraw, as he had in the past.

The dinner candles stood between them like chessmen. Elise grew more and more miserable. Nasim obviously had no idea what was wrong, but she'd promised not to talk about the crisis. So she came up with a series of lame explanations, for the blanket over the window and for her mood, none of which he seemed to buy.

Things sort of petered out after that.

She had so hoped things would click with Nasim tonight. Exhausted at the end of it all, Elise tumbled into her own bed alone and dejected.

Sleep wouldn't come. This whole situation had her questioning everything, because it knotted together survival and love, and her own seeming inability to do anything about either. As she thrashed about under the covers, she kept imagining a distant, invisible dart, the cycler, falling from infinity at her.

Finally she got up and went to her office. She would write it out. That had worked wonderfully before. She sat under the VR headset and called up the mailer. Hammond's message was still there, flagged with its vector and frequency. She gave the *reply* command.

"Dear Mr. Hammond.

"I got your message. You intended it for some important person, but I got it instead. I've got a daughter and son—I didn't want to hear that they might be killed. And what am I supposed to do about it? I told the police. So what?

"Please tell me this is a joke. I can't sleep now, all I can think about is Tiara, and what must have happened there.

"I feel . . . I told the police, but that doesn't seem like *enough*, it's as if you called *me*, for help, put the weight of the whole world on my shoulders—and what am I supposed to do about it?" It became easier the more she spoke. Elise poured out the litany of small irritations and big fears that were plaguing her. When she was done, she did feel better.

Send? inquired the mailer.

Oh, God, of course not.

Something landed in her lap, knocking the wind out of her. The headset toppled off her head. "Mommy. Mommy!"

"Yes yes, sweetie, what is it?"

Judy plunked forward onto Elise's breast. "Did you forget the time again, Mommy?"

Elise relaxed. She was being silly. "Maybe a little, honey. What are you doing awake?"

"I don't know."

"Let's both go to bed. You can sleep with me, okay?" Judy nodded.

She stood up, holding Judy. The inside of the VR headset still glowed, so she picked it up to turn it off.

Remembering what she'd been doing, she put it on.

Mail sent, the mailer was flashing.

"Oh, my, *God!*"

"Ow, Mommy."

"Wait a sec, Judy. Mommy has something to do." She put Judy down and fumbled with the headset. Judy began to whine.

She picked *reply* again and said quickly, "Mr. Hammond, please disregard the last message. It wasn't intended for you. The mailer got screwed up. I'm sorry if I said anything to upset you, I know you're in a far worse position than I am and you're doing a very brave thing by getting in touch with us. I'm sure it'll all work out. I . . ." She couldn't think of anything more. "Please excuse me, Mr. Hammond."

Send? "Yes!"

She took Judy to bed. Her daughter fell asleep promptly, but Elise was now wide awake.

She heard nothing from the government during the next while. Because she knew they might not tell her what was happening, she commanded her outermost prospector to devote half its time to scanning for messages from *Chinook*. For weeks, there weren't any.

Elise went on with things. She dressed and fed the kids; let them cry into her shirt when they got too tired or banged their knees; walked them out to meet Nasim every now and then. She had evening coffee with her friends, and even saw a new play that had opened in a renovated reactor room in the basement of the city. Other than that, she mostly worked.

In the weeks after the message's arrival, Elise found a renewal of the comforting solitude her prospectors gave her. For hours at a time, she could be millions of kilometers away, watching ice crystals dance in her headlamps, or seeing stars she could never view from her window. Being so far away literally give her a new perspective on home; she could see Dew in all its fragile smallness, and understood that the bustle of family and friends served to keep the loneliness of the halo worlds at bay. She appreciated people more for that, but also loved being the first to visit ice galleries and frozen cataracts on distant moons.

Now she wondered if she would be able to watch Dew's destruction from her prospectors. That made no sense—she would be dead in that case. The sense of actually *being* out in space was so strong though that she had fantasies of finding the golden thread cut, of existing bodiless and alone forever in the cameras of the prospectors, from which she would gaze down longingly on the ruins of her world.

A month after the first message, a second came. Elise's prospector intercepted it—nobody else except the police would have, because it was at Hammond's special frequency. The kids were tearing about in the next room. Their laughter formed an odd backdrop to the bitter voice that sounded in her ears.

"This is Mark Hammond on the *Chinook*. I will send you all the confirming information I can. There is a video record of the incident at Tiara, and I will try to send it along. It is very difficult. There are only a few of us from the original passengers and crew left. I have to rely on the arrogance of Leviathan's troops, if they encrypt their database I will be unable to send anything. If they catch me, I will be thrown out an airlock.

"I'll tell you what happened. I boarded at Mirjam, four years ago. I was bound for Tiara, to the music academy there. Leviathan was our next stop, and we picked up no freight, but several hundred people who turned out to be soldiers. There were about a thousand people on *Chinook* at that point. The soldiers captured the command center and then they decided who they needed and who was expendable. They killed more than half of us. I was saved because I can sing. I'm part of the entertainment." Hammond's voice expressed loathing. He had a very nice voice, baritone and resonant. She could hear the unhappiness in it.

"It's been two and a half years now, under their heel. We're sick of it.

"A few weeks ago they started preparing to strike your world. That's when we decided. You must destroy *Chinook*. I am going to send you our exact course, and that of the missiles. You must mine space in front of us. Otherwise you'll end up like Tiara."

The kids had their survival class that afternoon. Normally Elise was glad to hand them over to Nasim or, lately, their instructor—but this time she took them. She felt just a little better standing with some other parents in the powdery, sandlike snow outside the city watching the space-suited figures of her children go through the drill. They joined a small group in puzzling over a Global Positioning Unit, and successfuly found the way to the beacon that was their target for today. She felt immensely proud of them, and chatted freely with the other parents. It was the first time in weeks that she'd felt like she was doing something worthwhile.

Being outside in daylight was so strange—after their kids, that was the main topic of conversation among the adults. All remembered their own classes, taken under the permanent night they had grown up with. Now they excitedly pointed out the different and wonderful colors of the stones and ices, reminiscent of pictures of Earth's Antarctica.

It was strange, too, to see the city as something other than a vast dark pyramid. Elise studied it after the kids were done and they'd started back. The city looked solid, a single structure built of concrete that appeared pearly under the mauve clouds. Its flat facades were dotted with windows, and more were being installed. She and the kids tried to find theirs, but it was an unfamiliar exercise and they soon quit.

A big sign had been erected over the city airlock: HELP BUILD A SUNNY FUTURE, it said. Beside it was a thermometer-graph intended to show how close the government was to funding the next stage of Dew's terraforming. Only a small part of this was filled in, and the paint on that looked a bit old. Nonetheless, several people made contributions at the booth inside, and she was tempted herself—being outdoors did make you think.

They were all tired when they got home, and the kids voluntarily went to nap. Feeling almost happy, Elise looked out her window for a while, then kicked her way through the debris of toys to the office.

A new message was waiting already.

"This is for the woman who heard my first message. I'm not sending it on the new frequency, but I'm aiming it the way I did the first one. This is just for you, whoever you are."

Elise sat down quickly . . .

Hammond laughed, maybe a little nervously. His voice was so rich, his laugh seemed to fill her whole head. "That was quite a letter you sent. I'm not sure I believe you about having a 'mailer accident.' But if it was an accident, I'm glad it happened.

"Yours is the first voice I've heard in years from outside this whole thing. You have to understand, with the way we're treated and . . . and isolation and all, we nearly don't remember what it was like before. To have a life, I mean. To have kids, and worries like that. There're no kids here anymore. They killed them with their parents.

"A lot of people have given up. They don't remember why they should care. Most of us are like that now. Even me and the fathers who're trying to do something . . . well, we're doing it out of hate, not because we're trying to save anything.

"But you reminded me that there are things out there to have. Just hearing your voice, knowing that you and Dew are real, has helped.

"So I decided . . . I'm going to play your message—the first one, actually—to a couple of the people who've given up. Remind them there's a world out there. That they still have responsibilities.

"Thank you again. Can you tell me your name? I wish we could have met, someday." That was all.

Somehow, his request made her feel defensive. It was good he didn't know her name; it was a kind of safety. At the same time she wanted to tell him, as if he deserved it somehow. Finally, after sitting indecisively for long minutes, she threw down the headset and stalked out of the room.

Nasim called the next day. Elise was happy to hear from him, also a bit surprised. She had been afraid he thought she'd been acting cold lately, but he invited her for lunch in one of the city's better bistros. She foisted the kids off on her mother, and dressed up. It was worth it. They had a good time.

When she tried to set a date to get together again, he demured. She was left chewing over his mixed messages as she walked home.

Oh, who knew, really? Life was just too complicated right now. When she got home, there was another message from Hammond, this one intended for the authorities. She reviewed it, but afterward regretted doing so. It showed the destruction of Tiara.

On the video, pressure-suited figures unhooked some of *Chinook*'s hair-thin Lorentz Force cables, and jetted them away from the cycler. The cables seemed infinitely long, and could weigh many hundreds of tons.

The next picture was a long-distance, blue-shifted image of Obsidian's only inhabited world, Tiara. For about a minute, Elise watched it waver, a speckled dot. Then lines of savage white light crisscrossed its face suddenly as the wires hit.

That was all. Hammond's voice recited strings of numbers next, which she translated into velocities and trajectories. The message ended without further comment.

She was supposed to have discharged her responsibility by alerting the authorities, but after thinking about it practically all night, she had decided there was one more thing she could do. "Mr. Hammond," she began, "this is Elise Cantrell. I'm the one who got your first message. I've seen the video you sent. I'm sure it'll be enough to convince our government to do something. Hitting Dew is going to be hard, and now that we know where they're coming from we should be able to stop the missiles. I'm sure if the government thanks you, they'll do so in some stodgy manner, like giving you some medal or building a statue. But I want to thank you myself. For my kids. You may not have known just who you were risking your life for. Well, it was for Judy and Alex. I'm sending you a couple of pictures of them. Show them around. Maybe they'll convince more people to help you.

"I don't want us to blow up *Chinook*. That would mean you would die, and you're much too good a person for that. You don't deserve it. Show the pictures around. I don't know—if you can convince enough people, maybe you can take control back. There must be a way. You're a very clever man, Mr. Hammond. I'm sure you'll be able to find a way. For . . . well, for me, maybe." She laughed, then cleared her throat. "Here's the pictures." She keyed in several of her favorites, Judy walking at age one, Alex standing on the dresser holding a towel up, an optimistic parachute.

She took off the headset, and lay back feeling deeply tired, but content. It wasn't rational, but she felt she had done something heroic, maybe for the first time in her life.

Elise was probably the only person who wasn't surprised when the sun went out. There had been rumors floating about for several days that the government was commandeering supplies and ships, but nobody knew for what. She did. She was fixing dinner when the light changed. The kids ran over to see what was happening.

"Why'd it stop?" howled Alex. "I want it back!"

"They'll bring it back in a couple of days," she told him. "They're just doing maintenance. Maybe they'll change the color or something." That got his attention. For the next while he and Judy talked about what color the new sun should be. They settled on blue.

The next morning she got a call from Sal. "We're doing it, Elise, and we need your help."

She'd seen this coming. "You want to take my prospectors."

"No no, not *take* them, just use them. You know them best. I convinced the department heads that you should be the one to pilot them. We need to blockade the missiles the *Chinook*'s sending."

"That's all?"

"What do you mean, that's all? What else would there be?"

She shook her head. "Nothing. Okay. I'll do it. Should I log on now?"

"Yeah. You'll get a direct link to your supervisor. His name's Oliver. You'll like him."

She didn't like Oliver, but could see how Sal might. He was tough and uncompromising, and curt to the point of being surly. Nice enough when he thought to be, but that was rare. He ordered Elise to take four of her inner-system prospectors off their jobs to maneuver ice for the blockade.

The next several days were the busiest she'd ever had with the prospectors. She had to call Nasim to come and look after the kids, which he did quite invisibly. All Elise's attention was needed in the orbital transfers. Her machines gathered huge blocks of orbiting ice, holding them like ambitious insects, and trawled slowly into the proper orbit. During tired pauses, she stared down at the brown cloud-tops of Crucible, thunderheads the size of planets, eddies a continent could get lost in. They wanted hundreds of ice mountains moved to intercept the missiles. The sun was out because it was being converted into a fearsome laser lance. This would be used on the ice mountains before the missiles flew by; the expanding clouds of gas should cover enough area to intercept the missiles.

She was going to lose a prospector or two in the conflagration, but to complain about that now seemed petty.

Chinook was drawing close, and the time lag between messages became shorter. As she was starting her orbital corrections on a last chunk of ice, a new message came in from Hammond. For her, again.

In case this was going to get her all wrought up, she finished setting the vectors before she opened the message. This time it came in video format.

Mark Hammond was a lean-faced man with dark skin and an unruly shock of black hair. Two blue-green earrings hung from his ears. He looked old, but that was only because of the lines around his mouth, crow's-feet at his eyes. But he smiled now.

"Thanks for the pictures, Elise. You can call me Mark. I'm glad your people are able to defend themselves. The news must be going out to all the halo worlds now—nobody's going to trade with Leviathan now! Total *isolation*. They deserve it. Thank you. None of this could've happened if you hadn't been there."

He rubbed his jaw. "Your support's meant a lot to me in the past few days, Elise. I loved the pictures, they were like a breath of new air. Yeah, I did show them around. It worked, too; we've got a lot of people on our side. Who knows, maybe we'll be able to kick the murderers out of here, like you say. We wouldn't even have considered trying, if not for you."

He grimaced, looked down quickly. "Sounds stupid. But you say stupid things in situations like this. Your help has meant a lot to me. I hope you're evacuated to somewhere safe. And I've been wracking my brains trying to think of something I could do for you, equal to the pictures you sent.

"It's not much, but I'm sending you a bunch of my recordings. Some of these songs are mine, some are traditionals from Mirjam. But it's all my voice. I hope you like them. I'll never get the chance for the real training I needed at Tiara. This'll have to do." Looking suddenly shy, he said, "Bye."

Elise saved the songs in an accessible format and transferred them to her sound system. She stepped out of the office, walked without speaking past Nasim and the kids, and turned the sound way up. Hammond's voice poured out clear and strong, and she sat facing the wall, and just listened for the remainder of the day.

Oliver called her the next morning with new orders. "You're the only person who's got anything like a ship near the *Chinook*'s flight path. Prospector Six." That was the one that had picked up Hammond's first message. "We're sending some missiles we put together, but they're low-mass, so they might not penetrate the *Chinook*'s forward shields."

"You want me to destroy the *Chinook*." She was not surprised. Only very disappointed that fate had worked things this way.

"Yeah," Oliver said. "Those shits can't be allowed to get away. Your prospector masses ten thousand tons, more than enough to stop it dead. I've put the vectors in your database. This is top priority. Get on it." He hung up.

She was damned if she would get on it. Elise well knew her responsibility to Dew, but destroying *Chinook* wouldn't save her world. That all hinged on the missiles, which must have already been sent. But just so the police couldn't prove that she'd disobeyed orders, she entered the vectors to intercept *Chinook*, but included a tiny error that would guarantee a miss. The enormity of what she was doing—the government would call this treason—made her feel sick to her stomach. Finally she summoned her courage and called Hammond.

"They want me to kill you." Elise stood in front of her computer, allowing it to record her in video. She owed him that, at least. "I can't do it. I'm sorry, but I can't. I'm not an executioner, and you've done nothing wrong. Of all of us, you're the one who least deserves to die! It's not fair. Mark, you're going to have to take back the *Chinook*. You said you had more people on your side. I'm going to give you the time to do it. It's a couple of years to your next stop. Take back the ship, then you can get off there. You can still have your life, Mark! Come back here. You'll be a hero."

She tried to smile bravely, but it cracked into a grimace. "Please, Mark. I'm sure the government's alerted all the other halo worlds now. They'll be ready. *Chinook* won't be able to catch anybody else by surprise. So there's no reason to kill you.

"I'm giving you the chance you deserve, Mark. I hope you make the best of it."

She sent that message, only realizing afterwards that she hadn't thanked him for the gift of his music. But she was afraid to say anything more.

The city was evacuated the next day. It started in the early hours, as the police closed off all the levels of the city then began sweeping, waking people from their beds and moving the bewildered crowds to trains and aircraft. Elise was packed and ready. Judy slept in her arms, and Alex clutched her belt and knuckled his eyes as they walked among shouting people. The media were now revealing the nature of the crisis, but it was far too late for organized protest. The crowds were herded methodically; the police must have been drilling for this for weeks.

She wished Sal had told her exactly when it was going to happen. It meant she hadn't been able to hook up with Nasim, whose apartment was on another level. He was probably still asleep, even while she and the kids were packed on a train, and she watched through the angle of the window as the station receded.

Sometime the next morning they stopped, and some of the passengers were offloaded. Food was eventually brought, and then they continued on. Elise was asleep leaning against the wall when they finally unloaded her car.

All the cities of Dew had emergency barracks. She had no idea what city they had come to at first, having missed the station signs. She didn't care. The kids needed looking after, and she was bone tired.

Not too tired, though, to know that the hours were counting quickly down to zero. She couldn't stand being cut off, she had to know Hammond's reply to her message, but there were no terminals in the barracks. She had to know he was all right.

She finally managed to convince some women to look after Judy and Alex, and set off to find a way out. There were several policemen loitering around the massive metal doors that separated the barracks from the city, and they weren't letting anyone pass.

She walked briskly around the perimeter of the barracks, thinking. Barracks like this were usually at ground level, and were supposed to have more than one entrance, in case one was blocked by earthquake or fire. There must be some outside exit, and it might not be guarded.

Deep at the back where she hadn't been yet, she found her airlock, unguarded. Its lockers were packed with survival suits; none of the refugees would be going outside, especially not here on unknown ground. There was no good reason for them to leave the barracks, because going outside would not get them home. But she needed a terminal.

She suited up, and went through the airlock. Nobody saw her. Elise stepped out onto the surface of Dew, where she had never been except during survival drills. A thin wind was blowing, catching and worrying at drifts of carbon-dioxide snow. Torn clouds revealed stars high above the glowing walls of the city. This place, wherever it was, had thousands of windows; she supposed all the cities did now. They would have a good view of whatever happened in the sky today.

After walking for a good ten minutes, she came to another airlock. This one was big, with vehicles rolling in and out. She stepped in after one, and found herself in a warehouse. Simple as that.

From there she took the elevator up sixteen levels to an arcade lined with glass. Here finally were VR terminals, and she gratefully collapsed at one, and logged into her account.

There were two messages waiting. Hammond, it had to be. She called up the first one.

"You're gonna thank me for this, you really are," said Oliver. He looked smug. "I checked in on your work—hey, just doing my job. You did a great job on moving the ice, but you totally screwed up your trajectory on Prospector Six. Just a little error, but it added up quick. Would have missed *Chinook* completely if I hadn't corrected it. Guess I saved your ass, huh?" He mocked-saluted, and grinned. "Didn't tell anybody. I won't, either. You can thank me later." Still smug, he rung off.

"Oh no. No, no no," she whispered. Trembling, she played the second message.

Hammond appeared, looking drawn and sad. His backdrop was a metal bulkhead; his breath frosted when he breathed. "Hello, Elise," he said. His voice was low, and tired. "Thank you for caring so much about me. But your plan will never work.

"You're not here. Lucky thing. But if you were, you'd see how hopeless it is. There's a handful of us prisoners, kept alive for amusement and because we can do some things they can't. They never thought we'd have a reason to go outside, that's the only reason I was able to get out to take over the message laser. And it's only because of their bragging that we got the video and data we did.

"They have a right to be confident, with us. We can't do anything, we're locked away from their part of the ship. And you see, when they realize you've mined space near Dew, they'll know someone gave them away. We knew that would happen when we decided to do this. Either way I'm dead, you see; either you kill me, or they do. I'd prefer you did it, it'll be so much faster."

He looked down pensively for a moment. "Do me the favor," he said at last. "You'll carry no blame for it, no guilt. Destroy *Chinook*. The worlds really aren't safe until you do. These people are fanatics, they never expected to get home alive. If they think their missiles won't get through, they'll aim the ship itself at the next world. Which will be much harder to stop.

"I love you for your optimism, and your plans. I wish it could have gone the way you said. But this really is goodbye."

Finally he smiled, looking directly at her. "Too bad we didn't have the time. I could have loved you, I think. Thank you, though. The caring you showed me is enough." He vanished. *Message end*, said the mailer. *Reply?*

She stared at that last word for a long time. She signaled *yes*.

"Thank you for your music, Mark," she said. She sent that. Then she closed her programs, and took off the headset.

The end, when it came, took the form of a brilliant line of light scored across the sky. Elise watched from the glass wall of the arcade, where she sat on a long couch with a bunch of other silent people. The landscape lit to the horizon, brighter than Dew's artificial sun had ever shone. The false day faded slowly.

There was no ground shock. No sound. Dew had been spared.

The crowd dispersed, talking animatedly. For them, the adventure had been over before they had time to really believe in the threat. Elise watched them through her tears almost fondly. She was too tired to move.

Alone, she gazed up at the stars. Only a faint pale streak remained now. In a moment she would return to her children, but first she had to let this emotion fill her completely, wash down from her face through her arms and body, like Hammond's music. She wasn't used to how acceptance felt. She hoped it would become more familiar to her.

Elise stood and walked alone to the elevator, and did not look back at the sky.

DIFFERENT KINDS OF DARKNESS

David Langford

❀

David Langford (born 1953) is the most famous writer in SF fandom today, and is another ex-physicist (see David Brin, above). He is an occasional reviewer for *SFX* and for *New Scientist*, and *The New York Review of Science Fiction*, and is well known for his critical acumen. He publishes the fanzine *Ansible*, the tabloid newspaper of SF and fandom (which wins Hugo Awards, and is also excerpted as a monthly column in *Interzone*, and online: www.dcs.gla.ac.uk/SF-archives/Ansible). He also keeps winning best fan writer Hugo Awards (he is the most famous humorous writer in fandom today). His fan writings have been collected in *Let's Hear It for the Deaf Man* (Langford is deaf). He is, in addition, the author of several books of nonfiction and four novels, *The Space Eater* (1982), a hard SF novel, *The Leaky Establishment* (1984), a satire on a nuclear weapons lab, *Earthdoom!* with John Grant, and *Guts: A Comedy of Manners* (2001) with John Grant, a funny horror novel reputedly requiring much readerly intestinal fortitude. In recent years, he has been publishing a steady string of impressive SF short stories, most of them hard SF.

A few sentences from his CV are relevant to this story, which has weapons research deeply embedded in its background: "Brasenose College, Oxford. B.A. (Hons) in Physics 1974, M.A. 1978. Weapons physicist at Atomic Weapons Research Establishment, Aldermaston, Berkshire, from 1975 to 1980. Freelance author, editor and consultant ever since."

"Different Kinds of Darkness," a recent winner of the Hugo Award for best short story, is hard SF about kids, mathematics and new kinds of weapons, their use and misuse. It implies a whole future society. It is wonderful and scary, eerily plausible.

It was always dark outside the windows. Parents and teachers sometimes said vaguely that this was all because of Deep Green terrorists, but Jonathan thought there was more to the story. The other members of the Shudder Club agreed.

The dark beyond the window-glass at home, at school and on the school bus was the second kind of darkness. You could often see a little bit in the first kind, the ordinary kind, and of course you could slice through it with a torch. The second sort of darkness was utter black, and not even the brightest electric torch showed a visible beam or lit anything up. Whenever Jonathan watched his friends walk out through the school door ahead of him, it was as though they stepped into a solid black wall. But when he followed them and felt blindly along the handrail to where the homeward bus would be waiting, there was nothing around him but empty air. Black air.

Sometimes you found these super-dark places indoors. Right now Jonathan was edging his way down a black corridor, one of the school's no-go areas. Officially he was supposed to be outside, mucking around for a break period in the high-walled playground where (oddly enough) it wasn't dark at all and you could see the sky overhead. Of course, outdoors was no place for the dread secret initiations of the Shudder Club.

Jonathan stepped out on the far side of the corridor's inky-dark section, and quietly opened the door of the little storeroom they'd found two terms ago. Inside, the air was warm, dusty and stale. A bare light-bulb hung from the ceiling. The others were already there, sitting on boxes of paper and stacks of battered textbooks.

"You're late," chorused Gary, Julie and Khalid. The new candidate Heather just pushed back long blonde hair and smiled, a slightly strained smile.

"Someone has to be last," said Jonathan. The words had become part of the ritual, like a secret password that proved that the last one to arrive wasn't an outsider or a spy. Of course they all knew each other, but imagine a spy who was a master of disguise. . . .

Khalid solemnly held up an innocent-looking ring-binder. That was his privilege. The Club had been his idea, after he'd found the bogey picture that someone had left behind in the school photocopier. Maybe he'd read too many stories about ordeals and secret initiations. When you'd stumbled on such a splendid ordeal, you simply had to invent a secret society to use it.

"We are the Shudder Club," Khalid intoned. "We are the ones who can take it. Twenty seconds."

Jonathan's eyebrows went up. Twenty seconds was *serious*. Gary, the fat boy of the gang, just nodded and concentrated on his watch. Khalid opened the binder and stared at the thing inside. "One . . . two . . . three . . ."

He almost made it. It was past the seventeen-second mark when Khalid's hands started to twitch and shudder, and then his arms. He dropped the book, and Gary gave him a final count of eighteen. There was a pause while Khalid overcame the shakes and pulled himself together, and then they congratulated him on a new record.

Julie and Gary weren't feeling so ambitious, and opted for ten-second ordeals. They both got through, though by the count of ten she was terribly white in the face and he was sweating great drops. So Jonathan felt he had to say ten as well.

"You sure, Jon?" said Gary. "Last time you were on eight. No need to push it today."

Jonathan quoted the ritual words, "We are the ones who can take it," and took the ring-binder from Gary. "Ten."

In between times, you always forgot exactly what the bogey picture looked like. It always seemed new. It was an abstract black-and-white pattern, swirly and flickery like one of those old Op Art designs. The shape was almost pretty until the whole thing got into your head with a shock of connection like touching a high-voltage wire. It messed with your eyesight. It messed with your brain. Jonathan felt violent static behind his eyes . . . an electrical storm raging somewhere in there . . . instant fever singing through the blood . . . muscles locking and unlocking . . . and oh dear God had Gary only counted four?

He held on somehow, forcing himself to keep still when every part of him wanted to twitch in different directions. The dazzle of the bogey picture was fading behind a new kind of darkness, a shadow inside his eyes, and he knew with dreadful certainty that he was going to faint or be sick or both. He gave in and shut his eyes just as, unbelievably and after what had seemed like years, the count reached ten.

Jonathan felt too limp and drained to pay much attention as Heather came close—but not close enough—to the five seconds you needed to be a full member of the Club. She blotted her eyes with a violently trembling hand. She was sure she'd make it next time. And then Khalid closed the meeting with the quotation he'd found somewhere: "That which does not kill us, makes us stronger."

* * *

School was a place where mostly they taught you stuff that had nothing to do with the real world. Jonathan secretly reckoned that quadratic equations just didn't ever happen outside the classroom. So it came as a surprise to the Club when things started getting interesting in, of all places, a maths class.

Mr. Whitcutt was quite old, somewhere between grandfather and retirement age, and didn't mind straying away from the official maths course once in a while. You had to lure him with the right kind of question. Little Harry Steen—the chess and wargames fanatic of the class, and under consideration for the Club—scored a brilliant success by asking about a news item he'd heard at home. It was something to do with "mathwar," and terrorists using things called blits.

"I actually knew Vernon Berryman slightly," said Mr. Whitcutt, which didn't seem at all promising. But it got better. "He's the B in blit, you know: B-L-I-T, the Berryman Logical Imaging Technique, as he called it. Very advanced mathematics. Over your heads, probably. Back in the first half of the twentieth century, two great mathematicians called Gödel and Turing proved theorems which . . . um. Well, one way of looking at it is that mathematics is booby-trapped. For any computer at all, there are certain problems that will crash it and stop it dead."

Half the class nodded knowingly. Their home-made computer programs so often did exactly that.

"Berryman was another brilliant man, and an incredible idiot. Right at the end of the twentieth century, he said to himself, 'What if there are problems that crash the human brain?' And he went out and found one, and came up with his wretched "imaging technique" that makes it a problem you can't ignore. Just *looking* at a BLIT pattern, letting it in through your optic nerves, can stop your brain." A click of old, knotty fingers. "Like that."

Jonathan and the Club looked sidelong at each other. They knew something about staring at strange images. It was Harry, delighted to have stolen all this time from boring old trig, who stuck his hand up first. "Er, did this Berryman look at his own pattern, then?"

Mr. Whitcutt gave a gloomy nod. "The story is that he did. By accident, and it killed him stone dead. It's ironic. For centuries, people had been writing ghost stories about things so awful that just looking at them makes you die of fright. And then a mathematician, working in the purest and most abstract of all the sciences, goes and brings the stories to life. . . ."

He grumbled on about BLIT terrorists like the Deep Greens, who didn't need guns and explosives—just a photocopier, or a stencil that let them spray deadly graffiti on walls. According to Whitcutt, TV broadcasts used to go out "live," not taped, until the notorious activist Tee Zero broke into a BBC studio and showed the cameras a BLIT known as the Parrot. Millions had died. It wasn't safe to look at anything these days.

Jonathan had to ask. "So the, um, the special kind of dark outdoors is to stop people seeing stuff like that?"

"Well . . . yes, in effect that's quite right." The old teacher rubbed his chin for a moment. "They brief you about all that when you're a little older. It's a bit of a complicated issue. . . . Ah, another question?"

It was Khalid who had his hand up. With an elaborate lack of interest that struck Jonathan as desperately unconvincing, he said, "Are all these BLIT things, er, really dangerous, or are there ones that just jolt you a bit?"

Mr. Whitcutt looked at him hard for very nearly the length of a beginner's ordeal. Then he turned to the whiteboard with its scrawled triangles. "Quite. As I was saying, the cosine of an angle is defined . . ."

* * *

The four members of the inner circle had drifted casually together in their special corner of the outdoor play area, by the dirty climbing frame that no one ever used. "So we're terrorists," said Julie cheerfully. "We should give ourselves up to the police."

"No, our picture's different," Gary said. "It doesn't kill people, it . . ."

A chorus of four voices: ". . . makes us stronger."

Jonathan said, "What do Deep Greens terrorize about? I mean, what don't they like?"

"I think it's biochips," Khalid said uncertainly. "Tiny computers for building into people's heads. They say it's unnatural, or something. There was a bit about it in one of those old issues of *New Scientist* in the lab."

"Be good for exams," Jonathan suggested. "But you can't take calculators into the exam room. 'Everyone with a biochip, please leave your head at the door.'"

They all laughed, but Jonathan felt a tiny shiver of uncertainty, as though he'd stepped on a stair that wasn't there. "Biochip" sounded very like something he'd overheard in one of his parents' rare shouting matches. And he was pretty sure he'd heard 'unnatural' too. *Please don't let Mum and Dad be tangled up with terrorists*, he thought suddenly. But it was too silly. They weren't like that. . . .

"There was something about control systems too," said Khalid. "You wouldn't want to be controlled, now."

As usual, the chatter soon went off in a new direction, or rather an old one: the walls of type-two darkness that the school used to mark off-limits areas like the corridor leading to the old storeroom. The Club were curious about how it worked, and had done some experiments. Some of the things they knew about the dark and had written down were:

Khalid's Visibility Theory, which had been proved by painful experiment. Dark zones were brilliant hiding places when it came to hiding from other kids, but teachers could spot you even through the blackness and tick you off something rotten for being where you shouldn't be. Probably they had some kind of special detector, but no one had ever seen one.

Jonathan's Bus Footnote to Khalid's discovery was simply that the driver of the school bus certainly *looked* as if he was seeing something through the black windscreen. Of course (this was Gary's idea) the bus might be computer-guided, with the steering wheel turning all by itself and the driver just pretending—but why should he bother?

Julie's Mirror was the weirdest thing of all. Even Julie hadn't believed it could work, but if you stood outside a type-two dark place and held a mirror just inside (so it looked as though your arm was cut off by the black wall), you could shine a torch at the place where you couldn't see the mirror, and the beam would come bouncing back out of the blackness to make a bright spot on your clothes or the wall. As Jonathan pointed out, this was how you could have bright patches of sunlight on the floor of a classroom whose windows all looked out into protecting darkness. It was a kind of dark that light could travel through but eyesight couldn't. None of the Optics textbooks said a word about it.

By now, Harry had had his Club invitation and was counting the minutes to his first meeting on Thursday, two days away. Perhaps he would have some ideas for new experiments when he'd passed his ordeal and joined the Club. Harry was extra good at maths and physics.

"Which makes it sort of interesting," Gary said. "If our picture works by maths like those BLIT things . . . will Harry be able to take it for longer because his brain's built that way? Or will it be harder because it's coming on his own wavelength? Sort of thing?"

The Shudder Club reckoned that, although of course you shouldn't do experiments on people, this was a neat idea that you could argue either side of. And they did.

Thursday came, and after an eternity of history and double physics there was a free period that you were supposed to spend reading or in computer studies. Nobody knew it would be the Shudderers' last initiation, although Julie—who read heaps of fantasy novels—insisted later that she'd felt all doom-laden and could sense a powerful reek of wrongness. Julie tended to say things like that.

The session in the musty storeroom began pretty well, with Khalid reaching his twenty seconds at last, Jonathan sailing beyond the count of ten which only a few weeks ago had felt like an impossible Everest, and (to carefully muted clapping) Heather finally becoming a full member of the Club. Then the trouble began, as Harry the first-timer adjusted his little round glasses, set his shoulders, opened the tatty ritual ring-binder, and went rigid. Not twitchy or shuddery, but stiff. He made horrible grunts and pig-squeals, and fell sideways. Blood trickled from his mouth.

"He's bitten his tongue," said Heather. "Oh lord, what's first aid for biting your tongue?"

At this point the storeroom door opened and Mr. Whitcutt came in. He looked older and sadder. "I might have known it would be like this." Suddenly he turned his eyes sideways and shaded them with one hand, as though blinded by strong light. "Cover it up. Shut your eyes, Patel, don't look at it, and just cover that damned thing up."

Khalid did as he was told. They helped Harry to his feet: he kept saying "Sorry, sorry," in a thick voice, and dribbling like a vampire with awful table manners. The long march through the uncarpeted, echoey corridors to the school's little sickroom, and then onward to the Principal's office, seemed to go on for endless grim hours.

Ms. Fortmayne the Principal was an iron-gray woman who according to school rumors was kind to animals but could reduce any pupil to ashes with a few sharp sentences—a kind of human BLIT. She looked across her desk at the Shudder Club for one eternity of a moment, and said sharply: "Whose idea was it?"

Khalid slowly put up a brown hand, but no higher than his shoulder. Jonathan remembered the Three Musketeers' motto, *One for all and all for one*, and said, "It was all of us really." So Julie added, "That's right."

"I really don't know," said the Principal, tapping the closed ring-binder that lay in front of her. "The single most insidious weapon on Earth—the information-war equivalent of a neutron bomb—and you were *playing* with it. I don't often say that words fail me . . ."

"Someone left it in the photocopier. Here. Downstairs," Khalid pointed out.

"Yes. Mistakes do happen." Her face softened a little. "And I'm getting carried away, because we do actually use that BLIT image as part of a little talk I have with older children when they're about to leave school. They're exposed to it for just two seconds, with proper medical supervision. Its nickname is the Trembler, and some countries use big posters of it for riot control—but not Britain or America, naturally. Of course you couldn't have known that Harry Steen is a borderline epileptic or that the Trembler would give him a fit . . ."

"I should have guessed sooner," said Mr. Whitcutt's voice from behind the Club. "Young Patel blew the gaff by asking what was either a very intelligent question or a very incriminating one. But I'm an old fool who never got used to the idea of a school being a terrorist target."

The Principal gave him a sharp look. Jonathan felt suddenly dizzy, with thoughts clicking through his head like one of those workings in algebra where everything goes just right and you can almost see the answer waiting in the white space at the bottom of the page. What don't Deep Green terrorists like? Why are we a target?

Control systems. You wouldn't want to be controlled.

He blurted, "Biochips. We've got biochip control systems in our heads. All us kids. They make the darkness somehow. The special dark where grown-ups can still see."

There was a moment's frozen silence.

"Go to the top of the class," murmured old Whitcutt.

The Principal sighed and seemed to sag in her chair a little. "There had to be a first time," she said quietly. "This is what my little lecture to school-leavers is all about. How you're specially privileged children, how you've been protected all your lives by biochips in your optic nerves that edit what you can see. So it always seems dark in the streets and outside the windows, wherever there might be a BLIT image waiting to kill you. But that kind of darkness isn't real—except to you. Remember, your parents had a choice, and they agreed to this protection."

Mine didn't both agree, thought Jonathan, remembering an overheard quarrel.

"It's not fair," said Gary uncertainly. "It's doing experiments on people."

Khalid said, "And it's not just protection. There are corridors here indoors that are blacked out, just to keep us out of places. To control us."

Ms. Fortmayne chose not to hear them. Maybe she had a biochip of her own that stopped rebellious remarks from getting through. "When you leave school you are given full control over your biochips. You can choose whether to take risks . . . once you're old enough."

Jonathan could almost bet that all five Club members were thinking the same thing: *What the hell, we took our risks with the Trembler and we got away with it.*

Apparently they had indeed got away with it, since when the Principal said "You can go now," she'd still mentioned nothing about punishment. As slowly as they dared, the Club headed back to the classroom. Whenever they passed side-turnings which were filled with solid darkness, Jonathan cringed to think that a chip behind his eyes was stealing the light and with different programming could make him blind to everything, everywhere.

The seriously nasty thing happened at going-home time, when the caretaker unlocked the school's side door as usual while a crowd of pupils jostled behind him. Jonathan and the Club had pushed their way almost to the front of the mob. The heavy wooden door swung inward. As usual it opened on the second kind of darkness, but something bad from the dark came in with it, a large sheet of paper fixed with a drawing-pin to the door's outer surface and hanging slightly askew. The caretaker glanced at it, and toppled like a man struck by lightning.

Jonathan didn't stop to think. He shoved past some smaller kid and grabbed the paper, crumpling it up frantically. It was already too late. He'd seen the image there, completely unlike the Trembler yet very clearly from the same terrible family, a slanted dark shape like the profile of a perched bird, but with complications, twirly bits, patterns like fractals, and it hung there blazing in his mind's eye and wouldn't go away—

—something hard and horrible smashing like a runaway express into his brain—

—burning falling burning falling—

—BLIT.

* * *

After long and evil dreams of bird-shapes that stalked him in darkness, Jonathan found himself lying on a couch, no, a bed in the school sickroom. It was a surprise to be anywhere at all, after feeling his whole life crashing into that enormous full stop. He was still limp all over, too tired to do more than stare at the white ceiling.

Mr. Whitcutt's face came slowly into his field of vision. "Hello? Hello? Anyone in there?" He sounded worried.

"Yes . . . I'm fine," said Jonathan, not quite truthfully.

"Thank heaven for that. Nurse Baker was amazed you were alive. Alive and sane seemed like too much to hope for. Well, I'm here to warn you that you're a hero. Plucky Boy Saves Fellow-Pupils. You'll be surprised how quickly you can get sick of being called plucky."

"What was it, on the door?"

"One of the very bad ones. Called the Parrot, for some reason. Poor old George the caretaker was dead before he hit the ground. The anti-terrorist squad that came to dispose of that BLIT paper couldn't believe you'd survived. Neither could I."

Jonathan smiled. "I've had practice."

"Yes. It didn't take *that* long to realize Lucy—that is, Ms. Fortmayne—failed to ask you young hooligans enough questions. So I had another word with your friend Khalid Patel. God in heaven, that boy can outstare the Trembler for twenty seconds! Adult crowds fall over in convulsions once they've properly, what d'you call it, registered the sight, let it lock in. . . ."

"My record's ten and a half. Nearly eleven really."

The old man shook his head wonderingly. "I wish I could say I didn't believe you. They'll be re-assessing the whole biochip protection program. No one ever thought of training young, flexible minds to resist BLIT attack by a sort of vaccination process. If they'd thought of it, they still wouldn't have dared try it. . . . Anyway, Lucy and I had a talk, and we have a little present for you. They can reprogram those biochips by radio in no time at all, and so—"

He pointed. Jonathan made an effort and turned his head. Through the window, where he'd expected to see only artificial darkness, there was a complication of rosy light and glory that at first his eyes couldn't take in. A little at a time, assembling itself like some kind of healing opposite to those deadly patterns, the abstract brilliance of heaven became a town roofscape glowing in a rose-red sunset. Even the chimney-pots and satellite dishes looked beautiful. He'd seen sunsets on video, of course, but it wasn't the same, it was the aching difference between live flame and an electric fire's dull glare: like so much of the adult world, the TV screen lied by what it didn't tell you.

"The other present is from your pals. They said they're sorry there wasn't time to get anything better."

It was a small, somewhat bent bar of chocolate (Gary always had a few tucked away), with a card written in Julie's careful left-sloping script and signed by all the Shudder Club. The inscription was, of course: *That which does not kill us, makes us stronger.*

FAST TIMES AT FAIRMONT HIGH

Vernor Vinge

Vernor Vinge (born 1944) is a master of hard science fiction who has moved to the forefront of the field in recent years. Vinge is a mathematician living in California who has been writing hard SF for thirty years and slowly gaining a reputation as one of the significant talents in the field. Virtually unnoticed in the 1960s and 1970s, his novels and stories have sometime been spaced years apart, so that although he entered the field at nearly the same time as Larry Niven, his work was known for years only to a comparatively small circle of specialists. He is also, of all hard SF writers, the one who has been often concerned over the years with computers and advances in computer technology. In contrast to William Gibson, who invented an image so popular and potent that it has been imposed on the real world of computers, Vinge is the writer who understands the technology and most accurately forecast and described in his SF the implications of computers and personal computer communication. He is as radical a hard SF writer as anyone in this book, but the politics in his fiction in the early 1980s was Libertarian, and Sterling named him in *Cheap Truth* as one of the figures in opposition to Radical Hard SF/the Movement.

He became famous far outside the SF field in the 1990s for an essay, originally published in *The Whole Earth Quarterly*, in which he introduced the idea of the Singularity: "The Coming Technological Singularity: How to Survive in the Post-Human Era" (1993). His abstract: "Within thirty years, we will have the technological means to create superhuman intelligence. Shortly after, the human era will be ended. Is such progress avoidable? If not to be avoided, can events be guided so that we may survive? These questions are investigated. Some possible answers (and some further dangers) are presented."

Competition is one of Vinge's themes. In "Nature, Bloody in Tooth and Claw?" (1996 address to U.K. Eastercon), he says:

> . . . other paradigms for competition and evolution will be much more appropriate in the Post-Human era. Imagine a worldwide, distributed reasoning system in which there are thousands of millions of nodes, many of superhuman power. Some will have knowable identity—say the ones that are currently separated by low bandwidth links from the rest—but these separations are constantly changing, as are the identities themselves. With lower thresholds between Self and Others, the bacterial paradigm returns. Competition is not for life and death, but is more a sharing in which the losers continue to participate. And as with the corporate paradigm, this new situation is one in which very large organisms can come into existence, can work for a time at some extremely complex problem—and then may find it more efficient to break down into smaller souls (perhaps of merely human size) to work on tasks involving greater mobility or more restricted communication resources.

The last fifteen years have been his most productive period, featuring his *The Collected Stories of Vernor Vinge* (2001), and his best novels to date, *Marooned in Realtime* (1986); *A Fire Upon the Deep* (1992); *A Deepness in the Sky* (1999), and a *festschrift, True Names* (2001). The last two each won the Hugo Award. He is now widely popular, has recently retired to write full time, and seems likely to be one of the major hard SF writers of the next decade.

"Fast Times at Fairmont High" is a story about computers and education in a very competitive near future. The teenage characters know what they have to do to survive in this dangerous environment, and that sometimes whoever cheats best, wins—but that you lose if you are caught. This is a scary story, especially for some parents. And the atmosphere is so sunny, except at night when most of this happens.

Juan kept the little blue pills in an unseen corner of his bedroom. They really were tiny, the custom creation of a lab that saw no need for inert fillers, or handsome packaging. And Juan was pretty sure they were blue, except that as a matter of principle he tried not to look at them, even when he was off-line. Just one pill a week gave him the edge he needed. . . .

Final exam week was always chaos at Fairmont Junior High. The school's motto was "Trying hard not to become obsolete"—and the kids figured that applied to the faculty more than anyone else. This semester they got through the first morning—Ms. Wilson's math exam—without a hitch, but already in the afternoon the staff was tweaking things around: Principal Alcalde scheduled a physical assembly during what should have been student prep time.

Almost all the eighth grade was piled into the creaky wooden meeting hall. Once this place had been used for horse shows. Juan thought he could still smell something of that. Tiny windows looked out on the hills surrounding the campus. Sunlight spiked down through vents and skylights. In some ways, the room was weird even without enhancement.

Principal Alcalde marched in, looking as dire and driven as ever. He gestured to his audience, requesting visual consensus. In Juan's eyes, the room lighting mellowed and the deepest shadows disappeared.

"Betcha the Alcalde is gonna call off the nakedness exam." Bertie Todd was grinning the way he did when someone else had a problem. "I hear there are parents with Big Objections."

"You got a bet," said Juan. "You know how Mr. Alcalde is about nakedness."

"Heh. True." Bertie's image slouched back in the chair next to Juan.

Principal Alcalde was into a long speech, about the fast-changing world and the need for Fairmont to revolutionize itself from semester to semester. At the same time they must never forget the central role of modern education which was to teach the kids how to learn, how to pose questions, how to be adaptable—all without losing their moral compass.

It was very old stuff. Juan listened with a small part of his attention; mostly, he was looking around the audience. This was a physical assembly, so almost everybody except Bertie Todd was really here. Bertie was remote from Chicago, one of the few commuter students. His parents paid a lot more for virtual enrollment, but Fairmont Schools did have a good reputation. Of the truly present—well, the fresh thirteen-year-old faces were mostly real. Mr. Alcalde's consensus imagery didn't allow cosmetics or faked clothes. And yet . . . such rules could not be perfectly enforced. Juan widened his vision, allowed deviations and defacements in the view. There couldn't be too much of that or the Alcalde would have thrown a fit, but there were ghosts and graffiti floating around the room. The scaredy-cat ones flickered on-and-off in a fraction of a second, or were super-subtle perversions. But some of them—the two-headed phantom that danced behind the Principal's podium—lasted gloating seconds. Mr. Alcalde could probably see some of the japery, but his rule seemed to be that as long as the students didn't *appear* to see the disrespect, then he wouldn't either.

Okay, platitudes taken care of, Mr. Alcalde got down to business: "This morning, you did the math exam. Most of you have already received your grades. Ms. Wilson tells me that she's pleased with your work; the results will make only small changes in the rest of this week's schedule. Tomorrow morning will be the vocational exam." Oh yeah. Be ready to learn something dull, but learn it very, very fast. Most kids hated that, but with the little blue pills, Juan knew he could whack it. "Soon you'll begin the two concurrent exams. You'll have the rest of finals week to work on them. I'll make the details public later in this assembly. In general terms: There will be an unlimited exam, where you may use any legally available resources—"

"All *right*!" Bertie's voice came softly in Juan's ear. All across the hall similar sentiments were expressed, a kind of communal sigh.

Mr. Alcalde's dark features creased in a rare smile. "That just means we expect something extraordinarily good from you." To pass the exam, a team had to bring in three times tuition per team member. So even though they could use any help they could recruit, most students didn't have the money to buy their way to a passing grade.

"The two concurrent exams will overlap the usual testing in visual communication, language, and unaided skills. Some of your parents have asked for more concurrency, but all the teachers feel that when you're thirteen years old, it's better to concentrate on doing a few things well. You'll have plenty of time for jumble lore in the future. Your other concurrent exam will be—Miss Washington?"

Patsy Washington came to her feet, and Juan realized that she—like Bertie—was only present as imagery. Patsy was a San Diego student so she had no business being virtual at a physical assembly. *Hmm*. "Look," she said. "Before you go on about these concurrent exams, I want to ask you about the naked skills test."

Bertie gave Juan a grin. "This should be interesting."

The Alcalde's gaze was impassive. "The 'unaided skills' test, Miss Washington. There is nothing whatsoever *naked* about it."

"It might as well be, Mister." Patsy was speaking in English now, and with none of the light mocking tone that made her a minor queen in her clique. It was her image and voice, but the words and body language were very un-Patsy. Juan probed the external network traffic. There was lots of it, but mostly simple query/response stuff, like you'd expect. A few sessions had been around for dozens of seconds; Bertie's remote was one of the two oldest. The other belonged Patsy Washington—at least it was tagged with her personal certificate. Identity hijacking was a major no-no at Fairmont, but if a parent was behind it there wasn't much the school could do. And Juan had met Patsy's father. Maybe it was just as well the Alcalde didn't have to talk to him in person. Patsy's image leaned clumsily through the chair in front of her. "In fact," she continued, "it's worse than naked. All their lives, these—we—have had civilization around us. We're damned good at using that civilization. Now you theory-minded intellectuals figure it would be nice to jerk it all away and put us at risk."

"We are putting no one at risk . . . Miss Washington." Mr. Alcalde was still speaking in Spanish. In fact, Spanish was the only language their principal had ever been heard to speak; the Alcalde was kind of a bizarre guy. "We at Fairmont consider unaided skills to be the ultimate fallback protection. We're not Amish here, but we believe that every human being should be able to survive in reasonable environments—without networks, even without computers."

"Next you'll be teaching rock-chipping!" said Patsy.

The Alcalde ignored the interruption. "Our graduates must be capable of doing well in outages, even in disasters. If they can't, we have not properly educated them!" He paused, glared all around the room. "But this is no survivalist school. We're not dropping you into a jungle. Your unaided skills test will be at a safe location our faculty have chosen—perhaps an Amish town, perhaps an obsolete suburb. Either way, you'll be doing good, in a safe environment. You may be surprised at the insights you get with such complete, old-fashioned simplicity."

Patsy had crossed her arms and was glaring back at the Alcalde. "That's nonsense, but okay. There's still the question. Your school brochure brags modern skills, and these concurrent exams are supposed to demonstrate that you've delivered. So how can you call an exam concurrent, if part of the time your students are stripped of all technology? Huh?"

Mr. Alcalde stared at Patsy for a moment, his fingers tapping on the podium. Juan had the feeling that some intense discussion was going on between them. Patsy's Pa—assuming that's who it was—had gone considerably beyond the limits of acceptable behavior. Finally, the principal shook his head. "You miss-take our use of the word 'concurrent.' We don't mean that all team members work at the same time all the time, but simply that they multitask the exam in the midst of their other activities—just as people do with most real-world work nowadays." He shrugged. "In any case, you are free to skip the final examinations, and take your transcript elsewhere."

Patsy's image gave a little nod and abruptly sat down, looking very embarrassed; evidently her Pa had passed control back to her—now that he had used her image and made a fool of her. *Geez.*

Bertie looked faintly miffed, though Juan doubted this had anything to do with sympathy for Patsy.

After a moment, Mr. Alcalde continued, "Perhaps this is a good time to bring up the subject of body piercings and drugs." He gave a long look all around. It seemed to Juan that his gaze hung an instant in his direction. *Caray, he suspects about the pills!* "As you know, all forms of body piercings are forbidden at Fairmont Schools. When you're grown, you can decide for yourself—but while you are here, no piercings, not even ear- or eye-rings, are allowed. And internal piercings are grounds for immediate dismissal. Even if you are very frightened of the unaided skills test, do *not* try to fool us with implants or drugs."

No one raised a question about this, but Juan could see the flicker of communications lasers glinting off dust in the air, muttered conversation and private imagery being exchanged. The Alcalde ignored it all. "Let me describe the second of the concurrent exams, and then you'll be free to go. We call this exam a 'local' project: You may use your own computing resources and even a local network. However, your team members must work physically together. Remote presence is not allowed. External support—contact with the global net—is not permitted."

"Damn," said Bertie, totally dipped. "Of all the artificial, unworkable, idiotic—"

"So we can't collaborate, Bertie."

"We'll see about that!" Bertie bounced to his feet and waved for recognition.

"Ah, Mr. Todd?"

"Yes, sir." Bertie's public voice was meek and agreeable. "As you know, I'm a commuter student. I have lots of friends here, people I know as well as anyone. But of course, almost none of that is face to face since I live in Chicago. How can we handle my situation? I'd really hate to be excused from this important part of the finals just because I lack a physical presence here in San Diego. I'd be happy to accept a limited link, and do my best even with that handicap."

Mr. Alcalde nodded. "There will be no need, Mr. Todd. You are at a disadvantage, and we'll take that into account. We've negotiated a collaboration with the Andersen Academy at Saint Charles. They will—"

Andersen Academy at Saint Charles? Oh, in Illinois, a short automobile drive for Bertie. The Andersen people had long experience with team projects . . . back into prehistory in fact, the twentieth century. In principle they were far superior to Fairmont, but their academy was really more like a senior high school. Their students were seventeen, eighteen years old. Poor Bertie.

Juan picked up the thread of Mr. Alcalde's speech:—"They will be happy to accomodate you." Glimmer of a smile. "In fact, I think they are very interested in learning what our better students can do."

Bertie's face twisted into a taut smile, and his image dropped back onto the chair beside Juan. He made no additional comment, not even privately to Juan. . . .

The rest of the assembly was mostly about changes in exam content, mainly caused by the current state of outside resources—experts and technologies—that the school was importing for the nonconcurrent exams. All of it could have been done without this assembly; the Alcalde just had this thing about face-to-face meetings. Juan filed away all the announcements and changes, and concentrated on the unhappy possibility that now loomed over his week: Bertie Todd had been his best friend for almost two semesters now. Mostly he was super fun and an amazing team partner. But sometimes he'd go into a tight-lipped rage, often about things that Juan had no control over. *Like now.* If this were one of Bertie's Great Freeze Outs, he might not talk to Juan at all—for days.

The eighth-grade mob broke out of the assembly just before 4:00 P.M., way past the end of the normal class day. The kids milled about on the lawn outside the meeting hall. It was so near the end of the semester. There was warm sunlight. Summer and the new movie-game season were just a few days off. But *caray*, there were still finals to get through and everyone knew that, too. So while they joked and gossiped and goofed around, they were also reading the exam changes and doing some heavy planning.

Juan tagged along behind Bertie Todd's image as the other moved through the crowd. Bertie was dropping hints all around about the unlimited project he was planning. The communication link from Bertie to Juan was filled with cold silence, but he was being all charming toward kids who'd never helped him a tenth as much as Juan Orozco. Juan could hear part of what was going on; the other boys weren't freezing him out. They thought Juan was part of the party. And most of them were more than pleased by Bertie's interest. For no-holds-barred collaboration, Bertram Todd was the best there was at Fairmont Junior High. Bertie was claiming high-level contacts, maybe with Intel's idea farm, maybe with software co-ops in China. He had something for everyone, and a hint that they might score far more than a good grade.

Some of them even asked Juan for details. They just assumed that he was already part of Bertie's scheme for the unlimited. Juan smiled weakly, and tried to seem knowing and secretive.

Bertie stopped at the corner of the lawn, where the junior high abutted the driveway and the elementary school. The eighth graders carefully kept off the little kids' territory; you don't mess with fifth graders.

Along the driveway, cars were pulling up for students. Down by the bikestand, others were departing on bikes and unicycles. Everyone seemed to be laughing and talking and planning.

At the corner of the lawn, Juan and Bertie were all alone for a moment. In fact, it was Juan all alone. For an instant, he considered turning off the consensus that made Bertie seem so visibly here. *Caray*, why not turn it all off: There. The sun was still bright and warm, the day still full of springtime. Bertie was gone, but there was still the other kids, mainly down by the bikestand. Of course, now the fancy towers of Fairmont School were the ordinary wood buildings of the old horse yard and the plascrete of the new school, all brown and gray against the tans and greens of the hills around.

But he hadn't bothered to down the audio link, and out of the thin air, there was Bertie's voice, finally acknowledging Juan's existence. "So, have you decided who you're gonna team with for the local project?"

The question shocked Juan into bringing back full imagery. Bertie had turned back to face him, and was grinning with good humor—a gaze that might have fooled anyone who didn't really know him. "Look, Bertie, I'm really sorry you can't be on a local team out here. Mr. Alcalde is a *mutha* for sticking you with the Andersen crowd. But—" Inspiration struck. "You could fly out *here* for the exam! See, you could stay at my house. We'd whack that local exam dead!" Suddenly a big problem was a great opportunity. *If I can just sell Ma on this*.

But Bertie dismissed the idea with an offhand wave. "Hey, don't worry about it. I can put up with those Andersen guys. And in the meantime, I bet I can help you with the local exam." His face took on a sly look. "You know what I got on Wilson's math exam."

"Y-yeah, an A. That's great. You got all ten questions."

Ten questions, most of them harder than the old Putnam exam problems had ever been. And in Ms. Wilson's exam, you weren't allowed to collaborate, or search beyond the classroom. Juan had gotten a C+, knocking down four of the questions. The little blue pills didn't help much with pure math, but it was kind of neat how all Ms. Wilson's talk about heuristics and symbol software finally paid off. Those problems would have stumped some of the smartest twentieth-century students, but with the right kind of practice and good software even an ordinary kid like Juan Orozco had a good chance of solving them. Two Fairmont students had cracked all ten problems.

Bertie's grin broadened, a morph that stretched his face into a cartoonish leer. Juan knew that Bertie Todd was a dud at abstract problem solving. It was in getting the right answers out of *other* people that he was a star. ". . . Oh. You slipped out of isolation." That wouldn't be hard to do, considering that Bertie was already coming in from outside.

"I would never say that, Juan my boy. But if I did, and I didn't get caught . . . wouldn't that just prove that all this 'isolated skills' stuff is academic crap?"

"I-I guess," said Juan. In some ways, Bertie had unusual notions about right and wrong. "But it would be more fun if you could just come out here to San Diego."

Bertie's smile faded a fraction; the Great Freeze Out could be reinstated in an instant.

Juan shrugged, and tried to pretend that his invitation had never been made. "Okay, but can I still be on your unlimited team?"

"Ah, let's see how things work out. We've got at least twelve hours before the unlimited team selections have to be final, right? I think it's more important that . . . you get yourself a good start on the local team exercise."

Juan should have seen it coming. Bertie was Mister Quid Pro Quo, only sometimes it took a while to figure out what he was demanding. "So who you do you think I should be matching up with?" Hopefully, someone dumb enough that they wouldn't guess Juan's special edge. "The Rackhams are good, and we have complementary skills."

Bertie looked judicious. "Don and Brad are okay, but you've read the grading spec. Part of your score in the local test depends on face-to-face cooperation with someone really different." He made as though he was looking across the campus lawn.

Juan turned to follow his gaze. There was some kind of soccer variant being played beyond the assembly hall—senior high students who wouldn't have finals for another two weeks. There were still a few clumps of junior high kids, probably planning for the locals. None of them were people Juan knew well. "Look over by the main entrance," said Bertie. "I'm thinking you should break out of narrow thinking. I'm thinking you should ask Miriam Gu."

Ay caray! "Gu?" Miss Stuckup Perfection.

"Yes, c'mon. See, she's already noticed you."

"But—" In fact, Gu and her friends were looking in their direction.

"Look, Juan, I've collaborated with all sorts—from Intel engineers in geriatric homes to full-time members of Pratchett belief circles. If I can do that, you—"

"But that's all virtual. I can't work face to face with—"

Bertie was already urging him across the lawn. "View it as a test of whether you belong on my unlimited team. Miri Gu doesn't have your, ah, quickness with interfaces," he looked significantly at Juan. "But I've been watching her. She max'd Ms. Wilson's exam and I don't think she cheated to do it. She's a whiz at languages. Yes, she's just as much of a snob as you think. Heh, even her friends don't really like her. But she has no special reason to be hostile, Juan. After all, you're no boyo. You're a 'well-socialized, career-oriented student,' just the sort she knows she should like. And see, she's walking this way."

True enough, though Gu and company were walking even more slowly than Juan. "Yeah, and she's not happy about it either. What's going on?"

"Heh. See that little video-geek behind her? She dared Miri Gu to ask you."

Juan was guessing now, "And you put her up to that, didn't you?"

"Sure. But Annette—the video-geek—doesn't know it was me. She and I collaborate a lot, but she thinks I'm some old lady in Armonk . . . Annette likes to gossip a lot about us kids, and my 'little old lady' character plays along." Bertie's voice went high-pitched and quavery: "'Oh, that sweet Orozco boy, I do think your friend Miriam would like him so.'"

Geez, Bertie!

They walked toward each other, step by painful step, until they were almost in arms' reach. Juan had turned off all imagery for a moment. Shed of fantasy, they were pretty ordinary-looking kids: Annette the video-geek was short and pimply-faced, with hair that hadn't seen a comb so far this month. Miriam Gu was about three inches taller than Juan. Too tall. Her skin was as dark as Juan's, but with a golden undertone. Close-cut black hair framed a wide face and very symmetrical features. She wore an expensive, Epiphany-brand blouse. The high-rate laser ports were perfectly hidden in the embroidery. Rich kids had clothes like this, usually with broad gaming stripes. This blouse had no gaming stripes; it was light and simple and probably had more computing power than all the clothes Juan owned. You had to be sharp to wear a shirt like this properly.

Just now, Miri looked as though she was tasting something bad. *You don't like what you see either, huh?* But Miri got in the first word: "Juan Orozco. People say you're a clever kid, quick with interfaces." She paused and gave a little shrug. "So, wanna collaborate on the local exam?"

Bertie pulled a monstrous face at her, and Juan realized that Bertie was sending only to him. "Okay," said Bertie, "just be nice, Juan. Say how you were thinking she and you would make a team with grade points right from the start."

The words caught in Juan's throat. Miriam Gu was just too much. "Maybe," he replied to her. "Depends on what you can bring to it. Talents? Ideas?"

Her eyes narrowed. "I have both. In particular, my project concept is a killer. It really could make Fairmont Schools 'the rose of North County.'" That was the school board's phrase. The Alcalde and the board wanted these local projects to show that Fairmont was a good neighbor, not like some of the schools in Downtown and El Cajon.

Juan shrugged. "Well, um, that's good. We'd be the kind of high-contrast team the Alcalde likes." *I really don't want to do this*. "Let's talk about it more some time."

Annette the video-geek put in: "That won't do at all! You need to team up soonest!" She flickered through various pop-culture images as she spoke, finally settled on the heroine student from Spielberg/Rowling. She grabbed the background imagery at the same time, and Fairmont Schools was transformed into a fairytale castle. It was the same set they had used at last fall's Hallowe'en pageant. Most of the parents had been enchanted, though as far as the kids were concerned, Fairmont Schools failed the fantasy test in one big way: Here in real-life Southern California, the muggles ran the show.

Miriam turned to glare at her friend, now a brown-haired little English witch. "Will you shut *down*, Annette!" Then back to Juan: "But she's right, Orozco. We gotta decide tonight. How about this: You come by my place at six P.M. tonight and we talk."

Bertie was smiling with smug satisfaction.

"Well, yuh," said Juan. "But . . . in person?"

"Of course. This *is* a local-team project."

"Yeah, okay then. I'll come over." *There must be some way out of this*. What was Bertie up to?

She took a step forward and held out her hand. "Shake."

He reached out and shook it. The little electric shock was surely his imagination, but the sudden burst of information was not: two emphatic sentences sparkling across his vision.

Miriam Gu and her friends turned away, and walked back along the driveway. There was the sound of muffled giggling. He watched them for a moment. The video-geek was going full-tilt, picture and sound from a million old movies and news stories. Annette could retrieve and arrange video archives so easily that imaging came as naturally to her as speech. Annette was a type of genius. *Or maybe there are other flavors of little blue pills*.

Dumboso. Juan turned away from them and started toward the bikestand.

"So what did Miri Gu tell you?" *when she shook hands*. Bertie's tone was casual.

How could he answer that question without getting Bertie dipped all over again? "It's strange. She said if she and I team, she doesn't want anyone remote participating."

"Sure, it *is* a local exam. Just show me the message."

"That's the strange part. She guessed that you were still hanging around. She said, in particular, if I show you the message or let you participate, she'll find out and she'll drop the exam, even if it means getting an F." And in fact, that was the entire content of the message. It had a kind of nonnegotiable flavor that Juan envied.

They walked in silence the rest of the way to Juan's bicycle. Bertie's face was drawn down disapprovingly. Not a good sign. Juan hopped on his bike and pedaled off on New Pala, up over the ridge, and onto the long downslope toward home. Bertie's image conjured up a flying carpet, clambered aboard and ghosted along beside him. It was nicely done, the shadow following perfectly along over the gravel of the road shoulder. Of course, Bertie's faerie overlay blocked a good bit of Juan's visual field, including the most natural line of sight to see real traffic. Why couldn't he float along on Juan's other shoulder, or just be a voice? Juan shifted the image toward transparency and hoped Bertie would not guess at the change.

"C'mon, Bertie. I did what you asked. Let's talk about the unlimited exam. I'm sure I can be a help with that." *If you'll just let me on the team.*

Bertie was silent a second longer, considering. Then he nodded and gave an easy laugh. "Sure, Juan. We can use you on the unlimited team. You'll be a big help."

Suddenly the afternoon was a happy place.

They coasted down the steepening roadway. The wind that blew through Juan's hair and over his arms was something that was impossible to do artificially, at least without gaming stripes. The whole of the valley was spread out before him now, hazy in the bright sun. It was almost two miles to the next rise, the run up to Fallbrook. And he was on Bertie's unlimited team. "So what's our unlimited project going to be, Bertie?"

"Heh. How do you like my flying carpet, Juan?" He flew a lazy loop around Juan. "What really makes it possible?"

Juan squinted at him. "My contact lenses? Smart clothes?" Certainly the lense displays would be useless without a wearable computer to do the graphics.

"That's just the final output device. But how does my imaging get to you almost wherever you are?" He looked expectantly at Juan.

C'mon, Bertie! But aloud, Juan said: "Okay, that's the worldwide network."

"Yeah, you're essentially right, though the long-haul networks have been around since forever. What gives us flexibility are the network nodes that are scattered all through the environment. See, look around you!" Bertie must have pinged on the sites nearest Juan: There were suddenly dozens of virtual gleams, in the rocks by the road, in the cars as they passed closest to him, on Juan's own clothing.

Bertie gestured again, and the hills were alive with thousands of gleams, nodes that were two or three forwarding hops away. "Okay, Bertie! Yes, the local nets are important."

But Bertie was on a roll. "Darn right they are. Thumb-sized gadgets with very-low power wireless, just enough to establish location—and then even lower power shortrange lasers, steered exactly on to the targeted receivers. Nowadays, it's all so slick that unless you look close—or have a network sniffer—you almost can't even see that it's going on. How many free-standing nodes do you think there are in an improved part of town, Juan?"

That sort of question had a concrete answer. "Well, right now, the front lawn of Fairmont schools has . . . 247 loose ones."

"Right," said Bertie. "And what's the most expensive thing about that?"

Juan laughed. "Cleaning up the network trash, of course!" The gadgets broke, or wore out, or they didn't get enough light to keep their batteries going. They were cheap; setting out new ones was easy. But if that's all you did, after a few months you'd have metallic garbage—hard, ugly, and generally toxic—all over the place.

Juan abruptly stopped laughing "Wow, Bertie. That's the project? Biodegradable network nodes? That's off-scale!"

"Yup! Any progress toward organic nodes would be worth an A. And we might luck out. I'm plugged into all the right groups. Kistler at MIT, he doesn't know it, but one of his graduate students is actually a committee—and I'm on the committee." The Kistler people were cutting edge in organic substitution research, but just now they were stalled. The other relevant pieces involved idea markets in India, and some Siberian guys who hardly talked to anyone.

Juan thought a moment. "Hey, Bertie, I bet that literature survey I did for you last month might really help on this!" Bertie looked blank. "You remember, all my analysis on electron transfer during organic decay." It had been just a silly puzzle Bertie proposed, but it had given Juan a low-stress way to try out his new abilities.

"Yes!" said Bertie, slapping his forehead. "Of course! It's not directly related, but it might give the other guys some ideas."

Talking over the details took them through the bottom of the valley, past the newer subdivisions and then down the offramp that led to the old casinos. Bertie and his flying carpet flickered for a second, and then the overlay vanished as his friend lost the battle to find a handoff link.

"Dunno why you have to live in an unimproved part of town," Bertie grumbled in his ear.

Juan shrugged. "The neighborhood has fixed lasers and wireless." Actually, it was kind of nice to lose the flying carpet. He let his bike's recycler boost him up the little hill and then off into Las Mesitas. "So how are we going to work the concurrency on the unlimited test?"

"Easy. I'll chat up the Siberians in a couple of hours—then shuffle that across to my other groups. I don't know how fast things will break; it may be just you and me on the Fairmont side. Synch up with me after you get done with Miri Gu tonight, and we'll see about using your 'magical memory.' "

Juan frowned and pedaled fast along white sidewalks and turn-of-the-century condos. His part of town was old enough that it looked glitzy even without virtual enhancements.

Bertie seemed to notice his lack of response. "So is there a problem?"

Yes! He didn't like Bertie's unsubtle reference to what the little blue pills did for him. But that was just Bertie's way. In fact, today was all Bertie's way, both the good and the bad of it. "It's just that I'm a little worried about the local test. I know Miri gets good grades, and you say she is smart, but does she really have any traction?" What he really wanted to ask was why Bertie had pushed him into this, but he knew that any sort of direct question along those lines might provoke a Freeze Out.

"Don't worry, Juan. She'd do good work on any team. I've been watching her."

That last was news to Juan. Aloud he said, "I know she has a stupid brother over in senior high."

"Heh! William the Goofus? He *is* a dud, but he's not really her brother, either. No, Miri Gu is smart and tough. Did you know she grew up at Asilomar?"

"In a detention camp?"

"Yup. Well, she was only a baby. But her parents knew just a bit too much."

That had happened to lots of Chinese-Americans during the war, the ones who knew the most about military technologies. But it was also ancient history. Bertie was being more shocking than informative.

"Well, okay." No point in pushing. *At least, Bertie let me on his unlimited team.*

Almost home. Juan coasted down a short street and up his driveway, ducking under the creaking garage door that was just opening for him. "I'll get over to Miri's this evening and start the local team stuff while you're in East Asia."

"Fine. Fine," said Bertie.

Juan leaned his bike against the family junk, and walked to the back of the garage. He stopped at the door to the kitchen. Bertie had gotten every single thing he had wanted. Maybe not. *I bet he still plans on messing with my local exam.* "But one thing. Miri's handshake—she was *real* definite, Bertie. She doesn't want you coming along, even passively. Okay?"

"Sure. Fine. I'm off to Asia. Ta!" Bertie's voice ended with an exaggerated *click.*

Juan's father was home, of course. Luis Orozco was puttering around the kitchen. He gave his son a vague wave as the boy came in the room. The house had a good internal network, fed from a fixed station in the roof. Juan ignored the fantasy images almost automatically. He had no special interest in knowing what Pa was seeing, or where he thought he was.

Juan eeled past his father, into the living room. Pa was okay. Luis Orozco's own father had been an illegal back in the 1980s. Grandpa had lived in North County, but in the cardboard shacks and dirt tunnels that had hid amid the canyons in those days. The Orozco grandparents had worked hard for their only son, and Luis Orozco had worked hard to learn to be a software engineer. Sometimes, when he came down to earth, Pa would laugh and say he was one of the world's greatest experts in Regna 5. *And maybe for a year or two that had been an employable skill.* So three years of education had been spent for a couple years of income. That sort of thing had happened to a lot of people; Pa was one of those who just gave up because of it.

"Ma, can you talk?" Part of the wall and ceiling went transparent. Isabel Orozco was at work, upstairs. She looked down at him curiously.

"Hey, Juan! I thought you were going to be at finals until very late."

Juan bounced up the stairs, talking all the while. "Yes. I have a lot to do."

"Ah, so you'll be working from here."

Juan came into her work room and gave her a quick hug. "No, I was just gonna get supper and then visit the student I'm doing the local project with."

She was looking right at him now, and he could tell he had her full attention. "I just saw about the local exam; it seems like a great idea." Ma thought it was so important to get down on the real ground. When Juan was younger, she always dragged him along when she went on her field trips around the county.

"Oh, yes," said Juan. "We'll learn a lot."

Her look sharpened. "And Bertram is not in this, correct?"

"Oh, No, Ma." No need to mention the unlimited exam.

"He's not here in the house, is he?"

"*Ma!* Of course not." Juan denied all snoop access to his friends when he was in the house. Mother knew that. "When he's here, you see him, just like when my other friends visit."

"Okay." She looked a little embarrassed, but at least she didn't repeat her opinion that "little Bertie is too slippery by half". Her attention drifted for a moment, and her fingers tapped a quick tattoo on the table top. He could see that she was off in Borrego Springs, shepherding some cinema people from LA.

"Anyway, I was wondering if I could take a car tonight. My teammate lives up in Fallbrook."

"Just a second." She finished the job she was working on. "Okay, who is your teammate?"

"A really good student." He showed her.

Ma grinned uncertainly, a little surprised. "Good for you. . . . Yes, she is an excellent student, strong where you are weak—and vice versa, of course." She paused, checking out the Gu's. "They are a private sort of family, but that's okay."

"And it's a safe part of town."

She chuckled. "Yes, *very* safe." She respected the school rules and didn't ask about the team project. That was just as well, since Juan still had no idea what Miri Gu was planning. "But you stay out of Camp Pendleton, hear me?"

"Yes, ma'am."

"Okay, you're cleared to go as soon as you have supper. I've got some big-money customers running, so I can't take a break just now. Go on downstairs and get your father and yourself something to eat. And learn something from this local project, huh? There are many careers you can have without knowing airy-fairy nonsense."

"Yes, ma'am." He grinned and patted her shoulder. Then he was running down the stairs. After Pa's programming career had crashed, Mother had worked harder and harder at her 411 information services. By now, she knew San Diego County and its data as well as anyone in the world. Most of her jobs were just a few seconds or a few minutes long, guiding people, answering the hard questions. Some jobs—like the *Migración* historical stuff—were ongoing. Ma made a big point that her work was really hundreds of little careers, and that almost none of them depended on high-tech fads. Juan could do much worse; that was her message, both spoken and unspoken.

And looking at Pa across the kitchen table, Juan understood the alternative that his mother had in mind; Juan had understood that since he was six years old. Luis Orozco ate in the absent-minded way of a truly hard worker, but the images that floated around the room were just passive soaps. Later in the night he might spend money on active cinema, but even that would be nothing with traction. Pa was always in the past or on another world. So Ma was afraid that Juan would end up the same way. *But I won't. Whatever the best is, I'll learn it, and learn it in days not years. And when that best is suddenly obsolete, I'll learn whatever new thing gets thrown at me.*

Ma worked hard and she was a wonderful person, but her 411 business was . . . such a *dead end*. Maybe God was kind to her that she never realized this. Certainly Juan could never break her heart by telling her such a thing. But the local world sucked. San Diego County, despite all its history and industry and universities, was just a microscopic speck compared to the world of people and ideas that swirled around them every minute. Once upon a time, Juan's father had wanted to be part of that wider world, but he hadn't been fast enough or adaptable enough. *It will be different for me.* The little blue pills would the difference. The price might be high; sometimes Juan's mind went so blank he couldn't remember his own name. It was a kind of seizure, but in a moment or two it always went away. Always. So far. With custom street drugs you could never be absolutely sure of such things.

Juan had one jaw-clenched resolve: *I will be adaptable.* He would not fail as his father had failed.

Juan had the car drop him off a couple of blocks short of the Gu's house. He told himself he did this so he could get a feel for the neighborhood; after all, it was not a very public place. But that wasn't the real reason. In fact, the drive had been just too quick. He wasn't ready to face his local teammate.

West Fallbrook wasn't super-wealthy, but it was richer and more modern than Las Mesitas. Most of its money came from the fact that it was right next to Camp Pendleton's east entrance. Juan walked through the late afternoon light, looking in all directions. There were a few people out—a jogger, some little kids playing an inscrutable game.

With all enhancements turned off, the houses were low and stony-looking, set well back from the street. Some of the yards were beautifully kept, succulents and dwarf pines arranged like large-scale bonsai. Others were workaday neat, with shade trees and lawns that were raked gravel or auto-mowed drygrass.

Juan turned on consensus imagery. No surprise, the street was heavily prepped. The augmented landscape was pretty, in an understated way: the afternoon sunlight sparkled off fountains and lush grass lawns. Now the low, stony houses were all windows and airy patios, some places in bright sunlight, others half-hidden in shadows. But there were no public sensors. There was no advertising and no graffiti. The neighborhood was so perfectly consistent, a single huge work of art. Juan felt a little shiver. In most parts of San Diego, you could find homeowners who'd opt out of the community image—or else demand to be included, but in some grotesque contradiction of their neighbors. West Fallbrook had tighter control than even most condo communities. You had the feeling that some single interest was watching over everything here, ready to act against intruders. In fact, that single interest went by the initials USMC.

Above him, his guide arrow had brightened. Now it turned onto a side street and swooped to the third house on the right. *Caray*. He wanted to slow down, maybe walk around the block. *I haven't even figured out how to talk to her parents*. Chinese-American grownups were an odd lot, especially the ones who had been Detained. When they were released, some of them had left the USA, gone to Mexico or Canada or Europe. Most of the others just went back to their lives—even to government jobs—but with varying degrees of bitterness. And some had helped finish the war, and made the government look very foolish in the process.

He walked up the Gu's driveway, at the same time snooping one last time for information on Miri's family. . . . So, if William the Goofus wasn't really Miri's brother, who was he? William had never attracted that much attention; there were no ready-made rumors. And Fairmont's security on student records was pretty strong. Juan poked around, found some good public camera data. Given a few minutes he'd have William all figured out—

But now he was standing at the Gu's front door.

Miriam Gu was at the entrance. For a moment Juan thought she was going to complain that he was late, but she just waved him inwards.

Past the doorway, the street imagery cut off abruptly. They were standing in a narrow hallway with closed doors at both ends. Miri paused at the inner door, watching him.

There were little popping noises, and Juan felt something burn his ankle. "Hey, don't fry my gear!" He had other clothes, but the Orozco family wasn't rich enough to waste them.

Miri stared at him. "You didn't know?"

"Know what?"

"That's not *your* equipment I trashed; I was very careful. You were carrying hitchhikers." She opened the inner door and her gestures were suddenly polite and gracious. There must be grownups watching.

As he followed her down the hall, Juan rebooted his wearable. The walls became prettier, covered with silk hangings. He saw he had visitor privileges in the Gu's house system, but he couldn't find any other communications paths out of the building. All his equipment was working fine, including the little extras like 360 peripheral vision and good hearing. So what about those popping sounds, the heat? That was somebody *else's* equipment. Juan had been walking round like a fool with a KICK ME sign on his back. In fact, it was worse than that. He remembered assuring his mother that she would see any friends he brought to the house. Somebody had made that a lie. Fairmont had its share of unfunny jokesters, but this was gross. Who would do such a thing . . . yeah, who indeed.

Juan stepped from the hallway into a high-ceilinged living room. Standing by a real fireplace was a chunky Asian with buzzcut hair. Juan recognized the face from one of the few pictures he had of the guy. This was William Gu: Miriam's father, not the Goofus. Apparently the two had the same first name.

Miriam danced ahead of him. She was smiling now. "Bill, I'd like you to meet Juan Orozco. Juan and I are doing the local project together. Juan, this is my father."

Bill? Juan couldn't imagine addressing his own Pa by his first name. These people were strange.

"Pleased to meet you, Juan." Gu's handshake was firm, his expression mild and unreadable. "Are you enjoying the final exams so far?"

Enjoying?? "Yes, sir."

Miri had already turned away. "Alice? Do you have a minute? I'd like you to meet—"

A woman's voice: "Yes, Dear. Just a moment." Not more than two seconds passed, and a lady with a pleasant round face stepped into the room. Juan recognized her, too . . . except for the clothes: This evening, Alice Gu wore the uniform of a timeshare Lieutenant Colonel in the United State Marines. As Miri made the introductions, Juan noticed Mr. Gu's fingers tapping on his belt.

"Oops. Sorry!" Alice Gu's Marine Corps uniform was abruptly replaced by a business suit. "Oh, dear." And the business suit morphed into the matronly dress that Juan remembered from the photos. When she shook his hand, she looked entirely innocent and motherly. "I hear that you and Miriam have a very interesting local project."

"I hope so." *Mainly I hope Miriam will get around to telling me what it is*. But he no longer doubted that Miriam Gu had traction.

"We'd really like to know more about it."

Miri pulled a face. "Bill! You know we're not supposed to talk about it. Besides, if it goes right we'll be all done with it tonight."

Huh?

But Mr. Gu was looking at Juan. "I know the school rules. I wouldn't dream of breaking them." Almost a smile. "But I think as parents we should at least know where you plan to be physically. If I understand the local exam, you can't do it remotely."

"Yes, sir," said Juan. "That is true. We—"

Miriam picked up smoothly where Juan had run out of words. "We're just going down to Torrey Pines Park."

Colonel Gu tapped at her belt, and was quiet for a moment: "Well, that looks safe."

Mr. Gu nodded. "But you're supposed to do the local project without outside connectivity—"

"Except if an emergency comes up."

Mr. Gu just tapped his fingers thoughtfully. Juan turned off all the house imagery, and zoomed in on Miriam's pa. The guy was dressed casually, but with better clothes sense than most grownups had. In the house enhancement, he looked soft and sort of heavy. In the plain view, he just looked hard and solid. Come to think of it, the edge of his hand had felt calloused, just like in the movies.

Colonel Gu glanced at her husband, nodded slightly at him. She turned back to Juan and Miri. "I think it will be okay," she said. "But we do ask a couple things of you."

"Nothing against the exam rules," said Miri.

"I don't think so. First, since the park has no infrastructure and doesn't allow visitors to put up camping networks, please take some of the old standalone gear we have in the basement."

"Hey, that's great, Alice! I was going to ask you about that."

Juan could hear someone coming down the stairs behind him. He looked without turning, but there was no one visible yet, and his visitor's privilege did not allow him to see through walls.

"And second," Colonel Gu continued, "we think William should go along with you."

Miri's father? No . . . the Goofus. Ug.

This time, Miri Gu did not debate. She nodded, and said softly. "Well . . . if you think that is best."

Juan spoke without thinking, "But . . ." then more diffidently: "But wouldn't that violate the exam rules?"

The voice came from behind him. "No. Read the rules, Orozco." It was William.

Juan turned to acknowledge the other. "You mean, you won't be a team member?"

"Yeah, I'd just be your escort." The Goofus had the same broad features, the same coloring as the rest of the family. He was almost as tall as Bill Gu, but scrawny. His face had a sweaty sheen like maybe—*Oh*. Suddenly Juan realized that while Bill and William *were* father and son, it was not in the order he had thought.

"It's really your call, Dad," said Mr. Gu.

William nodded. "I don't mind." He smiled. "The munchkin has been telling me how strange things are in junior high school. Now I'll get to see what she means."

Miri Gu's smile was a little weak. "Well, we'd be happy to have you come along. Juan and I want to look at Alice's gear, but we should be ready in half an hour or so."

"I'll be around." William gave a twitchy wave and left the room.

"Alice and I will let you make your plans now," Mr. Gu said. He nodded at Juan. "It was nice to meet you, Juan."

Juan mumbled appropriate niceties to Mr. and Colonel Gu, and allowed Miri to maneuver him out of the room and down a steep stairway.

"Huh," he said, looking over her shoulder, "you really do have a basement." It wasn't what Juan really wanted to say; he'd get to *that* in a minute.

"Oh, yeah. All the newer homes in West Fallbrook do."

Juan noticed that this fact didn't show up in the county building permits.

There was a brightly lit room at the bottom of the stairs. The enhanced view was of warm redwood paneling with an impossibly high ceiling. Unenhanced, the walls and ceiling were gray plastic sheeting. Either way, the room was crowded with cardboard boxes filled with old children's games, sports equipment, and unidentifiable junk. This might be one of the few basements in Southern California, but it was clearly being used the way Juan's family used the garage.

"It's great we can take the surplus sensor gear. The only problem will be the stale emrebs—" Miri was already rummaging around in the boxes.

Juan hung back at the doorway. He stood with his arms crossed and glared at the girl.

She looked at him and some of the animation left her face.

"What?"

"I'll tell you '*what*'!" The words popped out, sarcastic and loud. He bit down on his anger, and messaged her point-to-point. "I'll tell you what. I came over here tonight because you were going to propose a local team project."

Miri shrugged. "Sure." She replied out loud, speaking in a normal voice. "But if we hustle, we can nail the whole project tonight! It will be one less background task—"

Still talking silently, directly: "Hey! This is supposed to be a *team* project! You're just pushing me around."

Now Miri was frowning. She jabbed a finger in his direction and continued speaking out loud, "Look. I've got a great idea for the local exam. You're ideal for the second seat on it. You and me are about as far apart in background and outlook as anybody in eighth grade. They like that in a team. But that's all I need you for, just to hold down the second seat. You won't have to do anything but tag along."

Juan didn't reply for a second. "I'm not your doormat."

"Why not? You're Bertie Todd's doormat."

"I'm gone." Juan turned for the stairs. But now the stairwell was dark. He stumbled on the first step, but then Miri Gu caught up with him, and the lights came on. "Just a minute. I shouldn't have said that. But one way or another, we both gotta get through finals week."

Yeah. And by now, most of the local teams were probably already formed. Even more, they probably were into project planning. If he couldn't make this work, Juan might have to kiss off the local test entirely. *Doormat!* "Okay," Juan said, walking back into the basement room. "But I want to know all about your 'proposed project,' and I want some say in it."

"Yes. Of course." She took a deep breath, and he got ready for still more random noise. "Let's sit down. . . . Okay. You already know I want to go down on the ground to Torrey Pines Park."

"Yeah." In fact, he had been reading up on the park ever since she mentioned it to her parents. "I've also noticed that there are no recent rumorings hanging over the place. . . . If you know something's going on there, I guess you'd have an edge."

She smiled in a way that seemed more pleased than smug. "That's what I figure, too. By the way, it's okay to talk out loud, Juan, even to argue. As long as we keep our voices down, Bill and Alice are not going to hear. Sort of a family honor thing." She saw his skeptical look, and her voice sharpened a little bit. "Hey, if they wanted to snoop, your point-to-point comm wouldn't be any protection at all. They've never said so, but I bet that inside the house, my parents could even eavesdrop on a handshake."

"Okay," Juan resumed speaking out loud. "I just want some straight answers. What is it that you've noticed at Torrey Pines?"

"Little things, but they add up. Here's the days the park rangers kept it closed this spring. Here's the weather for the same period. They've got no convincing explanation for all those closures. And see how during the closure in January, they still admitted certain tourists from Cold Spring Harbor."

Juan watched the stats and pictures play across the space between them. "Yes, yes, . . . yes. But the tourists were mainly vips attending a physicality conference at UCSD."

"But the conference itself was scheduled with less than eighteen hours lead time."

"So? 'Scientists must be adaptable in these modern times.'"

"Not like this. I've read the meeting proceedings. It's very weak stuff. In fact, that's what got me interested." She leaned forward. "Digging around, I discovered that the meeting was just a prop—paid for by Foxwarner and gameHappenings."

Juan looked at the abstracts. It would be really nice to talk to Bertie about this; he always had opinions or knew who to ask. Juan had to suppress the urge to call-out to him. "Well, I guess. I, um, I thought the UCSD people were more professional than this." He was just puffing vapor. "You figure this is all a publicity conspiracy?"

"Yup. And just in time for the summer movie season. Think how quiet the major studios have been this spring. No mysteries. No scandals. Nothing obvious started on April First. They've fully faked out the second-tier studios, but they're also driving the small players nuts, because we *know* that Foxwarner, Spielberg/Rowling Sony—all the majors—must be going after each other even harder than last year. About a week ago, I figured out that Foxwarner has cinema fellowship agreements with Marco Feretti and Charles Voss." *Who? Oh. World-class biotech guys at Cold Spring Harbor.* Both had been at the UCSD conference. "I've been tracking them hard ever since. Once you guess what to look for, it's hard for a secret to hide."

And movie teasers were secrets that *wanted* to be found out.

"Anyway," Miri continued, "I think Foxwarner is pinning their summer season on some bioscience fantasy. And last year, gameHappenings turned most of Brazil inside out."

"Yeah, the Dinosauria sites." For almost two months, the world had haunted Brazilian towns and Brazil-oriented websites, building up the evidence for their "Invasion from the Cretaceous." The echoes of that were still floating around, a secondary reality that absorbed the creative attention of millions. Over the last twenty years, the worldwide net had come to be a midden of bogus sites and recursive fraudulence. Until the copyrights ran out, and often for years afterwards, a movie's online presence would grow and grow, becoming more elaborate and consistent than serious databases. Telling truth from fantasy was often the hardest thing about using the web. The standard joke was that if real "space monsters" should ever visit Earth, they would take one look at the nightmares documented on the worldwide net, and flee screaming back to their home planet.

Juan looked at Miri's evidence and followed some of the major links. "You make a good case that this summer is going to be interesting, but the movie people have all cislunar space to play with. What's to think a Summer Movie will break out in San Diego County, much less at Torrey Pines Park?"

"They've actually started the initial sequence. You know, what will attract hardcore early participants. The last few weeks there have been little environment changes in the park, unusual animal movements."

The evidence was very frail. Torrey Pines Park was unimproved land. There was no local networking. But maybe that was the point. Miri had rented time on tourist viewpoints in Del Mar Heights, and then she had done a lot of analysis. So maybe she had that most unlikely and precious commodity, early warning. Or maybe she was puffing vapor. "Okay, something is going on in Torrey Pines, and you have an inside track on it. There's still only the vaguest connection with the movie people."

"There's more. Last night my theory moved from 'tenuous' to 'plausible', maybe even 'compelling'. I learned that Foxwarner has brought an advance team to San Diego."

"But that's way out at Borrego Springs, in the desert."

"How did you know? I really had to dig for that."

"My mother, she's doing 411 work for them." *Oops*. Come to think of it, what he had seen of Ma's work this afternoon was probably privileged.

Miri was watching him with genuine interest. "She's working with them? That's great! Knowing the connection would put us way ahead. If you could ask your mother . . . ?"

"I dunno." Juan leaned back and looked at the schedule his mother had posted at home. All her desert work was under a ten-day embargo. Even that much information would not have been visible to outsiders. He checked out the privilege certificates. Juan knew his mother pretty well. He could probably guess how she had encrypted the details. *And maybe get some solid corroboration*. He really wanted to pass this exam, but . . . Juan hunched forward a little. "I'm sorry. It's under seal."

"Oh." Miri watched him speculatively. Being the first to discover a Foxwarner movie setup, a Summer Movie, would give Fairmont the inside track on story participation. It would be a sure-fire A in the exam; the size of such a win wouldn't be clear until well into the movie season, but there would be some income for at least the five years of the movie's copyright.

If this issue had come up with Bertie Todd, there'd now be intense pleadings for him to think of his future and the team and do what his Ma would certainly want him to do if she only knew, namely break into her data space. But after a moment, the girl just nodded. "That's okay, Juan. It's good to have respect."

She moved back to the boxes and began rummaging again. "Let's go with what I've already got, namely that Foxwarner is running an operation in San Diego, and some of their Cinema Fellows have been fooling around in Torrey Pines Park." She pulled out a rack of . . . they looked like milk cartons, and set them on top of another box. "Emrebs," she explained opaquely. She reached deeper into the open box and retrieved a pair of massive plastic goggles. For a moment he thought this was scuba gear, but they wouldn't cover the nose or mouth. They didn't respond to info pings; he searched on their physical appearance.

"In any case," she continued, even as she pulled out two more pairs of goggles, "the background research will fit with my unlimited team's work. We're trying to scope out the movie season's big secrets. So far, we're not focusing on San Diego, but Annette reached some of the same conclusions about Foxwarner that I did. You wanna be on my unlimited, too? If this works tonight, we can combine the results."

Oh. That was really quite a generous offer. Juan didn't answer immediately. He pretended to be fully distracted by all the strange equipment. In fact, he recognized the gadgets now; there was a good match in the *2005 Jane's Sensors*. But he couldn't find a user's manual. He picked up the first pair of goggles and turned it this way and that. The surface of the plastic was a passive optical lacquer, like cheap grocery wrap in reverse; instead of reflecting bright rainbow colors, the colors flowed as he turned it, always blending with the true color of the gray plastic walls behind it. It amounted to crude camo-color, pretty useless in an environment this smart. Finally, he replied, kind of incidentally, "I can't be on your unlimited team. I'm already on Bertie's. Maybe it doesn't matter. You know Annette's working with Bertie on the side."

"Oh *really*?" Her stare locked on him for a moment. Then, "I should have guessed; Annette is just not that bright by herself. So Bertie has been jerking all of us around."

Yeah. Juan shrugged and lowered his head. "So how do these goggles work, anyway?"

Miri seemed to stew over Annette for a few seconds more. Then she shrugged too. "Remember, this equipment is *old.*" She held up her pair of goggles and showed him some slide controls in the headstrap. "There's even a physical 'on' button, right here."

"Okay." Juan slipped the goggles over his head and pulled the strap tight. The headset must have weighed two or three ounces. It was an awkward lump compared to contact lenses. Watching himself from the outside, he looked fully bizarre. The whole top of his face was a bulbous, gray-brown tumor. He could see Miriam was trying not to laugh. "Okay, let's see what it can do." He pressed the "on" button.

Nothing. His enhanced view was the same as before. But when he cleared his contact lenses and looked out with his naked eyes— "It's pitch dark from inside, can't see a thing."

"Oh!" Miri sounded a little embarrassed. "Sorry. Take off your goggles for a minute. We need an emreb." She picked up one of the heavy-looking "milk cartons."

"Meaning?"

"MRE/B." She spelled the word.

"Oh." Meal Ready to Eat, with Battery.

"Yes, one of the little pluses of military life." She twisted it in the middle, and the carton split in two. "The top half is food for the marine, and the bottom half is power for the Marine's equipment." There were letters physically stenciled on the food container: something about chicken with gravy, and dehydrated ice cream. "I tried eating one of these once." She made a face. "Fortunately, that won't be necessary tonight."

She picked up the bottom half of the emreb, and drew out a fine wire. "This is a weak point in my planning. These batteries are way stale."

"The goggles may be dead anyway." Juan's own clothes often wore out before he outgrew them. Sometimes a few launderings was enough to zap them.

"Oh, no. They built this milspec junk to be *tough.*" Miri set down the battery pack and bent Juan's goggles into a single handful. "Watch this." She wound up like a softball pitcher and threw the goggles into the wall.

The gear smashed upwards into the wall and caromed loudly off the ceiling.

Miriam ran across the room to pick up what was left.

Colonel Gu's voice wafted down the stairwell. "Hey! What are you kids doing down there?"

Miri stood up and giggled behind her hand. Suddenly she looked about ten years old. "It's okay, Alice!" She shouted back. "I just, um, dropped something."

"On the ceiling?"

"Sorry! I'll be more careful."

She walked back to Juan and handed him the goggles. "See," she said. "Hardly a scratch. Now we supply power"—she plugged the wire from the battery into the goggles' headband—"and you try them again."

He slid the goggles over his eyes and pressed "on". Monochrome reds wavered for a moment, and then he was looking at a strange, grainy scene. The view was not wraparound, just slightly fisheye. In it, Miri's face loomed large, peering in at him. Her skin was the color of a hot oven, and her eyes and mouth glowed bluish-white.

"This looks like thermal infrared," except that the color scheme wasn't standard.

"Yup. That's the default startup. Notice how the optics are built right into the gear? It's kind of like camping clothes: you don't have to depend on a local network. That's going to be a win when we get to Torrey Pines. Try some other sensors; you can get help by sliding the 'on' button."

"Hey, yes!"

BAT:LOW		**SENSORS**		**BAT2:NA**
PASSIVE		**ACTIVE**		
VIS AMP	**OK**	**GPR**	**NA**	
NIR	**OK**	**SONO**	**NA**	
>TIR	**OK**	**XECHO**	**NA**	
SNIFF	**NA**	**GATED VIS**	**NA**	
AUDIO	**NA**	**GATED NIR**	**NA**	
SIG	**NA**			

The tiny menu floated in the corner of his right eye's view. The battery warning was blinking. He fiddled with his head band and found a pointing device. "Okay, now I'm seeing in full color, normal light. Boogers resolution, though." Juan turned around and then back to Miri. He laughed. "The menu window is fully bizarre, you know. It just hangs there at the edge of my view. How can I tag it to the wall or a fixed object?"

"You can't. I told you this gear is old. It can't orient worth zip. And even if it could, its little pea-brain isn't fast enough to do image slews."

"Huh." Juan knew about obsolete systems, but he didn't use them much. With equipment like this, there could be no faerie overlays. Even ordinary things like interior decoration would all have to be real.

There were *lots* of other boxes, but no inventory data. Some of them must have belonged to the Goofus; they had handwritten labels, like "Prof. and Mrs. William Gu, Dept of English, UC Davis" and "William Gu Sr., Rainbow's End, Irvine, CA." Miri carefully moved these out of the way. "Someday William will know what do to with all this. Or maybe grandmother will change her mind, and come visit us again."

They opened more of the USMC boxes and poked around. There were wild equipment vests, more pockets than you ever saw around school. The vests weren't documented anywhere. The pockets were for ammunition, Juan speculated. For emrebs, Miri claimed; and they might need a lot of the batteries tonight, since even the best of them tested WARNING: LOW CHARGE. They dismembered the emrebs and loaded batteries onto two of the smallest vests. There were also belt-mount keypads for the equipment. "Hah. Before this is over, we'll be wiggling our fingers like grownups."

They were down to the last few boxes. Miri tore open the first. It was filled with dozens of camo-colored egg shapes. Each of them sprouted a triple of short antenna spikes. "*Feh*. Network nodes. A million times worse than what we have, and just as illegal to use in Torrey Pines Park."

Miri pushed aside several boxes that were stenciled with the same product code as the network nodes. Behind them was one last box, bigger than the others. Miri opened it . . . and stood back with exaggerated satisfaction. "*Ah so*. I was hoping Bill hadn't thrown these out." She pulled out something with a stubby barrel and a pistol grip.

"A gun!" But it didn't match anything in *Jane's Small Arms*.

"Nah, look under 'sensor systems.' " She grabbed a loose battery and snugged it under the barrel. "Even point blank, I bet this couldn't hurt a fly. It's an all-purpose active probe. Ground penetrating radar and sonography. Surface reflection X-ray. Gated laser. We couldn't get *this* at a sporting goods store. It's just too perfect for offensive snooping."

". . . It's got attachments, too."

Miri peered into the box and retrieved a metal rod with a flared end. "Yeah, that's for the radar; it fits on right here. Supposedly it's great for scoping out tunnels." She noticed Juan's eyeing this latest find and smiled teasingly. "Boys . . . ! There's another one in the box. Help yourself. Just don't try it out here. It would set off alarms big time."

In a few minutes they were both loaded down with batteries, plugged into the probe equipment, and staring at each other through their goggles. They both started laughing. "You look like a monster insect!" she said. In the infra-red, the goggles were big, black bugeyes, and the equipment vests looked like chitinous armor, glowing brightly where there was an active battery.

Juan waved his probe gun in the air. "Yeah. *Killer* insects." *Hmm.* "You know, we look so bizarre. . . . I bet if we find Foxwarner down in Torrey Pines, we might end up in the show." That sort of thing happened, but most consumer participation was in the form of contributed content and plot ideas.

Miri laughed. "I told you this was a good project."

Miri called a car to take them to Torrey Pines. They clumped up the stairs and found Mr. Gu standing with William the Goofus. Mr. Gu looked like he was trying to hide a smile. "You two look charming." He glanced at William. "Are you ready to go?"

William might have been smiling, too. "Any time, Bill."

Mr. Gu walked the three of them to the front door. Miri's car was already pulling up. The sun had slipped behind a climbing wall of coastal fog, and the afternoon was cooling off.

They pulled their goggles off and walked down the lawn, Juan in front. Behind him, Miri walked hand in hand with William. Miriam Gu was respectful of her parents, but flippant too. With her grandfather it was different, though Juan couldn't tell if her look up at William was trusting or protective. It was bizarre either way.

The three of them piled into the car, William taking the back-facing seat. They drove out through East Fallbrook. The neighborhood enhancements were still pretty, though they didn't have the coordinated esthetic of the homes right by Camp Pendleton. Here and there, homeowners showed advertising.

Miri looked back at the ragged line of the coastal fog, silhouetted against the pale bright blue of the sky. "'The fog is brazen here,'" she quoted.

"'Reaching talons across our land,'" said Juan.

"'Pouncing.'" she completed, and they both laughed. That was from the Hallowe'en show last year, but to the Fairmont students it had a special meaning. There was none of that twentieth century wimpiness about the fog's "little cat feet." Evening fog was common near the coast, and when it happened laser comm got whacked—and The World Changed. "Weather says that most of Torrey Pines Park will be under fog in an hour."

"Spooky."

"It'll be fun." And since the park was unimproved, it wouldn't make that much difference anyway.

The car turned down Reche Road and headed east, toward the expressway. Soon the fog was just an edge of low clouds beneath a sunny afternoon.

William hadn't said a word since they got aboard. He had accepted a pair of goggles and couple of batteries, but not an equipment vest. Instead, he carried an old canvas bag. His skin looked young and smooth, but with that sweaty sheen. William's gaze wandered around, kind of twitchy. Juan could tell that the guy had contacts and a wearable, but his twitchiness was not like a grownup trying to input to smart clothes. It was more like he had some kind of disease.

Juan searched on the symptoms he was seeing AND'ed with gerontology. The strange-looking skin was a regeneration dressing; that was a pretty common thing. As for the tremors . . . Parkinson's? Maybe, but that was a rare disease nowadays. Alzheimer's? No, the symptoms didn't match. *Aha: "Alzheimer's Recovery Syndrome."* Ol' William must have been a regular vegetable before his treatments kicked in. Now his whole nervous system was regrowing. The result would be a pretty healthy person even if the personality was randomly different from before. The twitching was the final reconnect with the peripheral nervous system. There were about fifty thousand recovering Alzheimer's patients these days. Bertie had even collaborated with some of them. But up close and in person . . . it made Juan queasy. So okay that William went to live with his kids during his recovery. But their enrolling him at Fairmont High was gross. His major was listed as "hardcopy media—nongraded status"; at least that kept him out of people's way.

Miri had been staring out the window, though Juan had no idea what she was seeing. Suddenly she said, "You know, this is your friend Bertie Toad Vomit." She pulled an incredible face, a fungus-bedecked toad that drooled nicely realistic slime all the way to the seat between them.

"Oh, yeah? Why is that?"

"He's been on my case all semester, jerking me around, spreading rumors about me. He tricked that idiot Annette, so she'd push me into teaming with you—not that I'm complaining about *you*, Juan. This is working out pretty well." She looked a little embarrassed. "It's just that Bertie is pushy as all get out."

Juan certainly couldn't argue against that. But then he suddenly realized: "You two are alike in some ways."

"*What!*"

"Well, you're *both* as pushy as all get out."

Miri stared at him open-mouthed, and Juan waited for an explosion. But he noticed that William was watching her with a strange smile on his face. She shut her mouth and glared at Juan. "Yeah. Well. You're right. Alice says it may be my strongest talent, if I can ever put a cork in it. In the meantime, I guess I can be pretty unpleasant." She looked away for a moment. "But besides us both being up-and-coming dictators, I don't see any similarities between me and Bertie. I'm loud. I'm a loner. Bertie Toad is sneaky and mean. He has his warty hands into everything. And no one knows what he really is."

"That's not true. I've known Bertie since sixth grade; I've known him well for almost two semesters. He's a remote student, is all. He lives in Evanston."

She hesitated, maybe looking up "Evanston." "So have you ever been to Chicago? Have you ever met Bertie in person?"

"Well, not exactly. But last Thanksgiving I visited him for almost a week." That had been right after the pills really started giving Juan results. "He showed me around the museums piggyback, like a 411 tour. I also met his parents, saw their house. Faking all that would be next to impossible. Bertie's a kid just like us." Though it was true that Bertie hadn't introduced Juan to many of his friends. Sometimes it seemed like Bertie was afraid that if his friends got together, they might cut him out of things. Bertie's great talent was making connections, but he seemed to think of those connections as property that could be stolen from him. That was sad.

Miri wasn't buying any of it, "Bertie is not like us, Juan. You know about Annette. I know he's wormed into a lot of groups at school. He's everything to everyone, a regular Mr. Fixit." Her face settled into a look of brooding contemplation, and she was silent for a moment.

They were off Reche now, and on the southbound. The true view was of rolling hills covered by endless streets and houses and malls. If you accepted the roadway's free enhancements, you got placid wilderness, splashed with advertising. Here and there were subtle defacements, the largest boulders morphing into trollishness; that was probably the work of some Pratchett belief circle. Their car passed the Pala off-ramp and started up the first of several miles-long ridges that separated them from Escondido and the cut across to the coast.

"Last fall," Miri said, "Bertram Todd was just another too-smart kid in my language class. But this semester, he's caused me lots of inconvenience, lots of little humiliations. Now he has Attracted My Attention." That did not sound like a healthy thing to do. "I'm gonna figure out his secret. One slip is all it takes."

That was the old saying: Once your secret is outed anywhere, however briefly, it is outed forever. "Oh, I don't know," said Juan. "The way to cover a slip is to embellish it, hide it in all sorts of *fake* secrets."

"Hah. Maybe he *is* something weird. Maybe he's a corporate team."

Juan laughed. "Or maybe he's something really weird!" Over the next few miles, he and Miri hit on all the cinema clichés: Maybe Bertie was an artificial boy, or a superbrain stuck in a bottle under Fort Meade. Maybe Bertie was a front for alien invaders, even now taking over the worldwide net. Maybe he was an old Chinese war program, suddenly growing to sentience, or the worldwide net itself that had finally awakened with superhuman—and certainly malignant—powers.

Or maybe Bertie was a subconscious creation of Juan's imagination, and *Juan* was—all unknowing—the monster. This one was Miri's idea. In a way it was the funniest of all, though there was something a little unsettling about it, at least for Juan.

The car had turned onto Highway 56, and they were going back toward the coast. There was more real open space here, and the hills were green with a gold-edging of spring flowers. The subdivisions were gone, replaced by mile after mile of industrial parks: the automated genomics and proteomics labs spread like gray-green lithops, soaking up the last of the sunlight. *People* could live and work anywhere in the world. But some things have to happen in a single real place, close enough together that superspeed data paths can connect their parts. These low buildings drove San Diego's physical economy; inside, the genius of humans, machines, and biological nature collided to make magic.

The sun sank back behind coastal fog as they entered the lagoon area north of Torrey Pines Park. Off the expressway, they turned south along the beach. The pale cliffs of the main part of the park rose ahead of them, the hilltops shrouded by the incoming fog.

The Goofus had remained silent through all their laughter and silly talk. But when Miri got back into her speculation about how this all fit with the fact that Bertie was bothering her so much, he suddenly interrupted. "I think part of it is very simple. Why is Bertie bothering you, Miriam? It seems to me there's one possibility so fantastic that neither of you have even imagined it."

William delivered this opinion with that faintly amused tone adults sometimes use with little kids. But Miri didn't make a flip response. "Oh." She looked at William as though he were hinting at some great insight. "I'll think about this some more."

The road wound upwards through the fog. Miri had the car drop them off at the far side of the driveway circle at the top. "Let's scope things out as we walk toward the ranger station."

Juan stepped down onto weedy asphalt. The sun had finally, truly, set. Geez, the air was cold. He flapped his arms in discomfort. He noticed that William had worn a jacket.

"You two should think ahead a little more," said the Goofus.

Juan pulled a face. "I can stand a little evening cool." Ma was often onto him like this, too. Plan-ahead add-ons were cheap, but he had convinced her that they made stupid mistakes of their own. He grabbed his sensor "gun" out of the car and slid it into the long pocket in the back of his vest—and tried to ignore his shivering.

"Here, Miriam." William handed the girl an adult-sized jacket, big enough to fit over her equipment vest.

"Oh, thank you!" She snugged it on, making Juan feel even more chilly and stupid.

"One for you, too, champ." William tossed a second jacket at Juan.

It was bizarre to feel so irritated and so grateful at the same time. He took off the probe holster, and slipped on the jacket. Suddenly the evening felt a whole lot more pleasant. This would block about half his high-rate data ports, but *hey, in a few minutes we'll be back in the fog anyway.*

The car departed as they started off in the direction of the ranger station. And Juan realized that some of his park information was very out of date. There were the restrooms behind him, but the parking lot in the pictures was all gone except at the edges, where it had become this driveway circle. He groped around for more recent information.

Of course, no one was parked up here. There were no cars dropping people off, either. Late April was not the height of the physical tourist season—and for Torrey Pines Park, that was the only kind of tourist season there was.

They were just barely above the fog layer. The tops of the clouds fluffed out below them, into the west. On a clear day, there would have been a great direct view of the ocean. Now there were just misty shapes tossed up from the fog and above that, a sky of deepening twilight blue. There was still a special brightness at the horizon, where the sun had set. Venus hung above that glow, along with Sirius and the brighter stars of Orion.

Juan hesitated. "That's strange."

"What?"

"I've got mail." He set a pointer in the sky for the others to see: a ballistic FedEx package with a Cambridge return address. It was coming straight down, and from very high up.

At about a thousand feet, the mailer slowed dramatically, and a sexy voice spoke in Juan's ear. "Do you accept delivery, Mr. Orozco?"

"Yes, yes." He indicated a spot on the ground nearby.

All this time, William had been staring into the sky. Now he gave a little start and Juan guessed the guy had finally seen Juan's pointer. A second after that, the package was visible to the naked eye: a dark speck showing an occasional bluish flare, falling silently toward them.

It slowed again at ten feet, and they had a glimpse of the cause of the light: dozens of tiny landing jets around the edge of the package. Animal rights campaigners claimed the micro-turbines were painfully loud to some kinds of bats, but to humans and even dogs and cats, the whole operation was silent. . . . until the very last moment: Just a foot off the ground, there was a burst of wind and a scattering of pine needles.

"Sign here, Mr. Orozco," said the voice.

Juan did so and started toward the mailer. William was already there, kneeling awkwardly. The Goofus spazzed at just the wrong instant and lurched forward, putting his knee through the mailer carton.

Miri rushed over to him. "William! Are you okay?"

William rolled back on his rear and sat there, massaging his knee. "Yes, I'm fine, Miriam. Damn." He glanced at Juan. "I'm really sorry, kid." For once, he didn't sound sarcastic.

Juan kept his mouth shut. He squatted down by the box: it was a standard twenty-ounce mailer, now with a big bend in the middle. The lid was jammed, but the material was scarcely stronger than cardboard, and he had no trouble prying it open. Inside . . . he pulled out a clear bag, held it up for the others to see.

William leaned forward, squinting. The bag was filled with dozens of small, irregular balls. "They look like rabbit droppings to me."

"Yes. Or health food," said Juan. Whatever they were, it didn't look like William's accident had done them any harm.

"Toad Vomit! What are *you* doing here?" Miriam's voice was sharp and loud.

Juan looked up and saw a familiar figure standing beside the mailer. *Bertie.* As usual, he had a perfect match on the ambient lighting; the twilight gleamed dimly off his grin. He gave Juan a little wave. "You can all thank me later. This FedEx courtesy link is only good for two minutes, so I have just enough time to clue you in." He pointed at the bag in Juan's hand. "These could be a big help once you get in the park."

Miri: "You don't have *any* time. Go away!"

Juan: "You're trashing our local exam just by being here, Bertie."

Bertie looked from from one indignant face to the other. He gave Miri a little bow, and said, "You wound me!" Then he turned to Juan: "Not at all, my dear boy. The exam proctors don't show you as embargoed. Technically, you haven't started your local exam. And I'm simply calling to check in with my loyal unlimited team member—namely you."

Juan ground his teeth. "Okay. What's the news?"

Bertie's grin broadened to slightly wider than humanly possible. "We've made great progress, Juan! I lucked out with the Siberian group—they had just the insight Kistler was needing. We've actually built prototypes!" He waved again at the bag in Juan's hand. "You've got the first lot." His tone slipped into persuasion mode. "I'm not on your local team, but our unlimited exam is concurrent, now isn't it, Juan?"

"Okay." This was extreme even for Bertie. *I bet he had the prototypes ready this afternoon!*

"So we need these 'breadcrumbs' tested, and since I noticed that my loyal teammate is incidentally on a field trip through Torrey Pines Park, well, I thought . . ."

Miri glared at the intruder's image. "So what *have* you stuck us with? I've got my own plans here."

"Totally organic network nodes, good enough to be field-tested. We left out the communication laser and recharge-capability, but the wee morsels have the rest of the standard function suite: basic sensors, a router, a localizer. And they're just proteins and sugars, no heavy metals. Come the first heavy rain, they'll be fertilizer."

Miri came over to Juan and popped open the plastic bag. She sniffed. "These things stink . . . I bet they're toxic."

"Oh, no," said Bertie. "We sacrificed a lot of functionality to make them safe. You could probably *eat* the darn things, Miri." Bertie chuckled at the look on her face. "But I suggest not; they're kind of heavy on nitrogen compounds. . . ."

Juan stared at the little balls. *Nitrogen compounds?* That sounded like the summary work Juan had done earlier this semester! Juan choked on outrage, but all he could think to say was, "This—this is everything we were shooting for, Bertie."

"Yup." Bertie preened. "Even if we don't get all the standard function suite, our share of the rights will be some good money." And a sure A grade on the unlimited exam. "So. Juan. These came off the MIT organo-fab about three hours ago. In a nice clean laboratory, they work fine. Now how about if you sneak them into the park, and give them a real field test? You'll be serving your unlimited team at the same time you're working on your local project. Now, *that's* concurrency."

"Shove off, Bertie," said Miri.

He gave her a little bow. "My two minutes are almost up, anyway. I'm gone." His image vanished.

Miri frowned at the empty space where Bertie had been. "Do what you want with Bertie's dungballs, Juan. But even if they're totally organic, I'll bet they're still banned by park rules."

"Yes, but that would just be a technicality, wouldn't it? These things won't leave trash."

She just gave an angry shrug.

William had picked up the half-crushed mailing carton. "What are we going to do with this?"

Juan motioned him to set it down. "Just leave it. There's a FedEx mini-hub in Jamul. The carton should have enough fuel to fly over there." Then he noticed the damage tag floating beside the box. "*Caray*. It says it's not airworthy." There were also warnings about flammable fuel dangers and a reminder that he, Juan Orozco, had signed for the package and was responsible for its proper disposal.

William flexed the carton. Empty, the thing was mostly plastic fluff, not more than two or three pounds. "I bet I could bend it back into its original shape."

"Um," Juan said.

Miri spelled things out for the Goofus: "That would probably not work, William. Also, we don't have the manual. If we broke open the fuel system . . ."

William nodded. "A good point, Miriam." He slipped the carton into his bag, then shook his head wonderingly. "It flew here all the way from Cambridge."

Yeah, yeah.

The three of them resumed their walk down to the ranger station, only now they were carrying a bit more baggage, both mental and physical. Miri grumbled, arguing mainly with herself about whether to use Bertie's gift.

Even with the fog, Bertie's "breadcrumbs" could give them a real edge in surveilling the park—if they could get them in. Juan's mind raced along that line, trying to figure what he should say at the ranger station. At the same time he was watching William. The guy had brought a flashlight. The circle of light twitched this way and that, casting tree roots and brush into sharp relief. Come to think of it, without Miri's Marine Corps gear, a flashlight would have been even more welcome than the jackets. In some ways, William was not a complete fool. In others . . .

Juan was just glad that William hadn't pushed the FedEx mailer back at him. Juan would have been stuck with carrying it around all night; the carton counted as toxic waste, and it would surely rat on him if he left it in an ordinary trash can. Ol' William had been only mildly interested in the breadcrumbs—but the package they came in, even busted, *that* fascinated the guy.

The park's entrance area still had fairly good connectivity, but the ranger station was hidden by the hillside and Juan couldn't get a view on it. Unfortunately, the

State Parks Web site was under construction. Juan browsed around, but all he could find were more out-of-date pictures. The station might be uncrewed. On an off-season Monday night like this, a single 411 operator might be enough to cover all the state parks in Southern California.

As they came off the path, into direct sight of the station, they saw that it wasn't simply a rest point or even a kiosk. In fact, it was an enclosed office with bright, real lighting and a physically-present ranger—a middle-aged guy, maybe thirty-five years old.

The ranger stood and stepped out into the puddle of light. "Evening," he said to William; then he noticed the heavily bundled forms of Miriam and Juan. "Hi, kids. What can I do for you all?"

Miri glanced significantly at William. Something almost like panic came into William's eyes. He mumbled, "Sorry, Munchkin, I don't remember what you do at places like this."

"S'okay." Miri turned to the ranger. "We just want to buy a night pass, no camping. For three."

"You got it." A receipt appeared in the air between them, along with a document: a list of park regulations.

"Wait one." The ranger ducked back into his office and came out with some kind of search wand; this setup was really old-fashioned. "I shoulda done this first." He walked over to William, but was talking to all three of them, essentially hitting the high points of the park regs. "Follow the signs. No cliff climbing is allowed. If you go out on the seaside cliff face, we *will* know and you *will* be fined. Are you vision equipped?"

"Yes, sir." Miriam raised her goggles into the light. Juan opened his jacket so his equipment vest was visible.

The ranger laughed. "Wow. I haven't seen those in a while. Just don't leave the batteries lying around in the park. That's"—he turned away from William and swept his wand around Miriam and Juan—"That's very important here, folks. Leave the park as you found it. No littering, and no networking. Loose junk just piles up, and we can't clean it out like you can other places."

The wand made a faint whining sound as it passed over Juan's jacket pocket. *Boogers. It must have gotten a ping back.* Most likely Bertie's prototypes didn't have a hard off-state.

The ranger heard the noise, too. He held the wand flat against Juan's jacket and bent to listen. "Damn false alarm, I bet. What do you have in there, Son?"

Juan handed him the bag of dark, brownish balls. The ranger held it up to the light. "What are these things?"

"Trail mix." William spoke before Juan could even look tongue-tied.

"Hey, really? Can I try one?" He popped the bag open as Juan watched in wide-eyed silence. "They look nice and chocolaty." He picked one out of the bag, and squeezed it appraisingly. Then the smell hit him. "Dios!" He threw the ball at the ground and stared at the brown stain that remained on his fingers. "That smells like . . . that smells awful." He jammed the bag back into Juan's hands. "I don't know, kid. You have odd tastes."

But he didn't question their story further. "Okay, folks. I think you're good to go. I'll show you the trailhead. I—" He stopped, stared vacantly for a second. "Oops. I see some people just coming into Mount Cuyamaca Park, and I'm covering there tonight, too. You wanna go on ahead?" He pointed at a path that led northward from his station. "You can't miss the trailhead; even if it's down, there's a big sign."

He waved them on, and then turned to talk to whoever he was seeing at the park in the mountains.

Beyond the trailhead, the park was completely unimproved, a wilderness. For a hundred feet or so, Juan had wireless connectivity but even that was fading. Miri checked in with the exam proctor service to certify that their team was going local; since the wilderness was very soon going to isolate them from the worldwide net, they might as well get official credit for the fact!

But yuk. Just knowing you can't go out in the wide world for answers was a pain. It was like having a itch you can't scratch or a sock with lump in it, only much worse. "I've cached a lot of stuff about the park, Miri . . . but some of it is kinda old."—which would have been no problem, but now he couldn't just go out and search for better information.

"Don't worry about it, Juan. Last week, I spent a little money and used a 411 service. See?" A few gigabytes flickered on laser light between them. . . . She *was* prepared. The maps and pictures looked very up-to-date.

Miri confidently picked one of several trails and got them on a gentle path that zigzagged downward toward the northwest. She even persuaded William to use the third pair of goggles instead of his flashlight. The Goofus moved awkwardly along. He seemed limber enough, but every four or five paces there was random spikey twitching.

It made Juan uncomfortable just to watch the guy. He looked away, played with his goggles' menu. "Hey, Miri. Try 'VIS AMP'. It's pretty."

They walked silently for a while. Juan had never been to Torrey Pines Park except with his parents, and that was when he was little. And in the daytime. Tonight, with VIS AMP . . . the light of Venus and Sirius and Betelguese came down through the pine boughs, casting colored shadows every which way. Most of the flowers had closed, but there were glints of yellows and reds bobbing among the manzanita and the low, pale cactus. The place was peaceful, really beautiful. And so what if the goggles' low-res pics only showed the direction you were looking at. That was part of the charm. They were getting this view without any external help, a step closer to true reality.

"Okay, Juan. Try laying out some of Bertie's dungballs."

The breadcrumbs? "Sure." Juan opened the bag and tossed one of the balls off to the side of the path . . . Nothing. He popped up some low-layer wireless diagnostics. Wow. "This is a quiet place."

"What do you expect?" said Miri. "No networks, remember."

Juan leaned down to inspect the breadcrumb. The park ranger had gotten a faint response with his wand, but now that Juan wanted a ping response, there was nothing. And Bertie hadn't told them an enable-protocol. *Well, maybe it doesn't matter.* Juan was a packrat; he had all the standard enablers squirreled away on his wearable. He blasted the breadcrumb with one startup call after another. Partway through the sequence, there was a burst of virtual light in his contacts. "Hah. This one's live!" He turned and caught up with Miri and William.

"Good going, Juan." For once, Miri Gu sounded pleased with him.

The path was still wide and sandy, the gnarled pines hanging fists of long needles right above his head—and right in the Goofus's face. Amid the park trivia that Juan had downloaded was the claim that this was the last place on earth these pines existed. They rooted in the steep hillsides and hung on for years and years against erosion and draught and cold ocean breezes. Juan glanced back at William's gangly form shambling along behind them. *Yeah.* Ol' William was kind of like a human "Torrey Pine."

They were in the top of the fog now. Towering and silent, pillars of haze drifted by on either side of them. Starlight dimmed and brightened.

Behind them, the node Juan had left was dimming toward a zero data rate. He picked out a second breadcrumb, gave it the correct startup call, and dropped it to the side of the trail. The low-layer diagnostics showed its pale glow, and after a second it had picked up on the first node, now bright again. "They linked . . . I'm getting data forwarded from the first node." *Hah.* Normally you didn't think about details like that. The gadgets kind of reminded Juan of the toy network his father had bought him, back when Pa still had a job. Juan had been only five years old, and the toy nodes had been enormous clunkers, but laying them down around the house had engaged father and son for several happy days—and given Juan an intuition about random networks that some grownups still seemed to lack.

"Okay, I see them," said Miri. "We're not getting any communication from beyond the dungballs, are we? I don't want anything forwarded out to the world."

Yeah, yeah. This is a local exam. "We're isolated, unless we punch out with something really loud." He threw out five or six more breadcrumbs, enough so they could figure their relative positions accurately; in his diagnostic view, the locator gleams sharpened from misty guesstimates to diamond-sharp points of light.

Fog curled more thickly over them, and the starlight grew hazy. Ahead of him, Miri stumbled. "Watch your step. . . . You know, there's really not enough light anymore."

In patches, the fog was so thick that VIS AMP was just colorful noise.

"Yeah, I guess we should switch back to thermal IR."

They stopped and stood like idiots, fiddling with manual controls to do something that should have been entirely automatic. Near infrared was as bad as visual: for a moment he watched the threads of NIR laser light that flickered sporadically between the data ports on their clothes; in this fog, the tiny lasers were only good for about five feet.

Miri was ahead of him. "Okay, that's a lot better," she said.

Juan finally got his goggles back to their thermal infrared default. Miri's face glowed furnace-red except for the cool blackness of her goggles. Most plants were just faintly reddish. The stairstep timber by his feet had three dark holes in the top. Juan reached down and discovered that the holes felt cold and metallic. Ha, metal spikes holding the timber in place.

"C'mon," said Miri. "I want to get down near the bottom of the canyon."

The stairs were steep, with a heavy wood railing on the dropoff side. The fog was still a problem, but with TIR, you could see out at least ten yards. Dim reddish lights floated up through the dark, blobs of slightly warmer air. The bottom was way down, farther than you'd ever guess. He threw out a few more breadcrumbs and looked back up the path, at the beacons of the other nodes. What a bizarre setup. The light of the breadcrumb diagnostics was showing on his contact lenses, where he normally saw all enhancements. But it was the USMC goggles that were providing most of the augmentation. And beyond them? He stopped, turned off his wearable enhancement, and slipped the goggles up from his face for a moment. Darkness, absolute darkness, and chill wet air on his face. Talk about isolation!

He heard William coming up behind him. The guy stopped and for a second they stood silent, listening.

Miri's voice came from further down the steps. "Are you okay, William?"

"Sure, no problems."

"Okay. Would you and Juan come down by me? We wanna stay close enough to keep a good data rate between us. Are you getting any video off the dungballs, Juan?" Bertie had said they contained basic sensors.

"Nope," Juan replied. He slipped the goggles back on and walked down to her. Any breadcrumb video would have shown up on his contacts, but all he was getting was diagnostics. He started another breadcrumb and tossed it far out, into the emptiness. Its location showed in his contacts. It fell and fell and fell, until he was seeing its virtual gleam "through" solid rock.

He studied the diagnostics a moment more. "You know, I think they *are* sending low data rate video—"

"That's fine. I'll settle for wireless rate." Miri was leaning out past the railing, staring downwards.

"—but it's not a format I know." He showed her what he had. Bertie's Siberian pals must be using something really obscure. Ordinarily, Juan could have put out some queries and had the format definition in a few seconds; but down here in the dark, he was just stuck.

Miri made an angry gesture. "So Bertie gave you something that could be useful, but only if we punch out a loud call for help? No way. Bertie is not getting his warty hands on *my* project!"

Hey, Miri, you and I are supposed to be a team here. It would be nice if she would stop treating him like dirt. But she was right about Bertie's tactics. Bertie had given them something wonderful—and was holding back all the little things that would make it useable. First it was the enable-protocol, now it was this screwball video format. Sooner or later, Bertie figured they'd come crawling to him, begging him to be a shadow member of the team. *I could call out to him.* His clothes had enough power that he could easily punch wireless as far as network nodes in Del Mar Heights, at least for a few minutes. Getting caught was a real risk; Fairmont used a good proctor service—but it was impossible for them to cover all the paths all the time. This afternoon, Bertie had as much as bragged they would cheat that way.

Damn you, Bertie, I'm not going to break isolation. Juan reviewed the mystery data from the breadcrumbs. There seemed to be real content; so given the darkness, the pictures were probably thermal infrared. *And I have lots of known video I can compare them to, everything that has been seen through my goggles during the last few minutes!* Maybe it was time for some memory magic, the edge he got from his little blue pills: If he could remember which blocks of imagery might match what the breadcrumbs could see, and pass that to his wearable, then conventional reverse engineering would be possible. . . . Juan's mind went blank for a few seconds, and there was a moment of awesome panic . . . but then he remembered himself. He fed the picture pointers back to his wearable. It began crunching out solutions almost immediately. "Try this, Miri." He showed her his best guess-image, and sharpened it over the next five seconds as his wearable found more correlation spikes.

"Yes!" The picture showed the roots of the big pine a dozen yards behind them. A few seconds passed and there was another picture, black sky and faintly glowing branches. In fact, each breadcrumb was generating a low-resolution TIR image every five seconds or so, even though they couldn't all be forwarded that fast. "What are those numbers all about?" Numbers that clustered where the picture detail was most complex.

Oops. "Those are just graphical hierarchy pointers." That was true, but exactly how Juan used them was something he didn't want pursued. He made a note to delete them from all future pics.

Miri was silent for several seconds as she watched the pictures coming in from the crumbs above them on the trail, and from the one that he'd dropped way down. Juan was on the point of asking for payback, like some straight talk about exactly what they were looking for. But then she said, "This picture format is one of those Siberian puzzles, isn't it?"

"Looks like."

Those formats were all different, created by antisocials who seemed to get a kick out of not being interoperable. "And you untangled it in fifteen seconds?"

Sometimes Juan just didn't think ahead: "Yup," he said, blissfully proud.

The uncovered part of her face flared. "You lying weasel! You're talking to the outside!"

Now Juan's face got hot too. "Don't you call me a liar! You know I'm good with interfaces."

"Not. That. Good." Her voice was deadly.

Caray. The right lie occurred to Juan a few seconds too late: He should have said he'd seen the Siberian picture format before! Now the only safe thing to do was "confess" that he was talking to Bertie. But Juan couldn't bear to tell *that* lie, even if it meant she would figure out what he had really done.

Miri stared at him for several seconds.

William's begoggled face had turned from one of them to other like a spectator at a tennis game. He spoke into the silence, and for once sounded a little surprised: "So what are you doing now, Miriam?"

Juan had already guessed, "She's watching the fog, and listening."

Miri nodded. "If Orozco is sneaking out on wireless, I'd hear it. If he's using something directional, I'd see sidescatter from the fog. I don't see anything just now."

"So maybe I'm squirting micropulses." Juan's words came out all choked, but he was trying to sound sarcastic; any laser bright enough to get through the fog would have left an afterglow.

"Maybe. If you are, Juan Orozco, I *will* figure it out—and I'll get you kicked out of school." She turned back to look over the drop off. "Let's get going."

The steps got even steeper; eventually they reached a turn and walked on almost level ground for about sixty feet. The other side of the gorge was less than fifteen feet away.

"We must be close to the bottom," said William.

"No, William. These canyons go awfully deep and narrow."

Miri motioned them to stop. "My darn battery has died." She fumbled around beneath her jacket, replacing a dead battery with one that was only half dead.

She adjusted her goggles and looked over the railing. "Huh. We have a good view from here." She waved at the depths. "You know, Orozco, this might be the place to do some active probing."

Juan pulled the probe gun from the sling on his back. He plugged it into his equipment vest. With the gun connected, most of the options were live:

BAT:LOW	**SENSORS**		**BAT2:NA**
PASSIVE		**ACTIVE**	
VIS AMP	**OK**	**GPR**	**NA**
NIR	**OK**	**SONO**	**NA**
>TIR	**OK**	**XECHO**	**NA**
SNIFF	**NA**	**GATED VIS**	**NA**
AUDIO	**NA**	**GATED NIR**	**NA**
SIG	**NA**		

"What do you want to try?"

"The ground penetrating radar." She pointed her own gun at the canyon wall. "Use your power, and we'll both watch."

Juan fiddled with the controls; the gun made a faint *click* as it shot a radar pulse into the rock wall. "Ah!" The USMC goggles showed the pulse's backscatter as lavender shading on top of the thermal IR. In the daylight pictures that Juan had downloaded, these rocks were white sandstone, fluted and scalloped into shapes that water or wind could not carve alone. The microwave revealed what could only be guessed at from the visible light: moisture that etched and weakened the rock from the inside.

"Aim lower."

"Okay." He fired again.

"See, way down? It looks like little tunnels cut in the rock."

Juan stared at the pattern of lavender streaks. They did look different than the ones higher up, but—"I think that's just where the rock is soaking wet."

Miri was already hurrying down the steps. "Toss out more dungballs."

Down and around another thirty feet, they came to a place where the path was just a tumble of large boulders. The going got very slow. William stopped and pointed at the far wall. "Look, a sign."

There was a square wooden plate spiked into the sandstone. William lit his flashlight and leaned out from the path. Juan raised his goggles for a moment—and got the dubious benefit of William's light: everything beyond ten feet was hidden behind the pearly white fog. But the faded lettering on the sign was now visible: FAT MAN'S MISERY.

William chuckled—and then almost lost his footing. "Did you ever think? Old-fashioned writing is the ultimate in context tagging. It's passive, informative, and present exactly where you need it."

"Yeah, sure. But can I point through it and find out what it thinks it means?"

William doused his flashlight. "I guess it means the gorge gets even narrower further on."

Which we already knew from Miri's maps. At the trailhead, this had looked like a valley, one hundred feet across. It had narrowed and narrowed, till now the far wall was about ten feet away. And from here. . . .

"Scatter some more dungballs," said Miri. She was pointing straight down.

"Okay." They still had plenty of them. He carefully dropped six breadcrumbs where Miri indicated. They stood silently for a moment, watching the network diagnostics: the position guesstimate on one crumb was twenty-five to thirty feet further down. That was darn near the true bottom of the gorge. Juan took a breath. "So, are you ever going to tell us what precisely we're looking for, Miri?"

"I don't *precisely* know."

"But this is where you saw the UCSD people poking around?"

"Some, but they were mainly south of this valley."

"Geez, Miri. So you brought us *here* instead?"

"Look you! I'm not keeping secrets! I could see the hills above this canyon from the tourist scopes on Del Mar Heights. In the weeks after the UCSD guys left, there were small changes in the vegetation, mostly over this valley. At night, the bats and owls were at first more active and then less active than before. . . . And now tonight we've spotted some kind of tunnels in the rocks."

William sounded mystified. "That's all, Miriam?"

The girl didn't blow up when it was William asking. Instead she seemed almost abashed. "Well . . . there's context. Feretti and Voss were behind the trips to the park in January. One is into synthetic ethology; the other is a world-class proteomics geek. They both got called to San Diego all at once, just like you'd expect for a movie teaser. And I'm sure . . . almost sure . . . they're both consulting for Foxwarner."

Juan sighed. That wasn't much more than she'd said in the beginning. Maybe Miri's biggest problem wasn't that she was bossy— it was that she was too darn good at projecting certainty. Juan made a disgusted noise, "And you figure if we just poke around carefully enough, solid clues will show up?" *Whatever they may be*.

"Yes! Somebody has to be the first to catch on. Using our probe gear and— yeah— Bertie's dungballs, we're not going to miss much. My theory is Foxwarner is trying to top what Spielberg/Rowling did last year with the magma monsters. This will be something that starts small, and is overtly plausible. With Feretti and Voss as advisors, I'll bet they'll play it as an escape from a bioscience lab." *That would certainly fit the San Diego scene*.

The new breadcrumbs had located their nearest neighbors. Now the extended network showed as diamond-sharp virtual gleams scattered through the spaces both above and below. In effect, they had twenty little "eyeballs," watching from all over the canyon. The pictures were all low-resolution stuff, but taken together that was too much data to forward all at once across the breadcrumb net to their wearables. They would have to pick through the viewpoints carefully.

"Okay then," said Juan. "Let's just sit and watch for a bit."

The Goofus remained standing. He seemed to be staring upward. Juan guessed that he was having some trouble with the video Juan was forwarding to him. Things were going to get pretty dull for him. Abruptly, William said, "Do either of you smell something burning?"

"Fire?" Juan felt a flash of alarm. He sniffed carefully at the damp air. ". . . Maybe." Or it might just be something flowering in the night. Smells were a hard thing to search on and learn about.

"I smell it too, William," Miri said. "But I think things are still too wet for it to be a danger."

"Besides," said Juan, "if there was fire anywhere close, we'd see the hot air in our goggles." Maybe someone had a fire down on the beach.

William shrugged, and sniffed at the air again. *Trust the Goofus to have one superior sense—and that one useless*. After a moment, he sat down beside them, but as far as Juan could tell, he still wasn't paying attention to the pictures Juan was sending him. William reached into his bag and pulled out the FedEx mailer; the guy was still fascinated by the thing. He flexed the carton gently, then rested the box on his knees. Despite all Miri's warnings, it looked like the Goofus wanted to knock it back into shape. He'd carefully poise one hand above the middle of the carton, as if preparing a precise poke . . . and then his hand would start shaking and he would have to start all over again.

Juan looked away from him. *Geez the ground was hard.And cold*. He wriggled back against the rock wall and cycled through the pictures he was getting from the breadcrumbs. They were pretty uninspiring. . . . But sitting here quietly, not talking . . . there were *sounds*. Things that might have been insects. And behind it all, a faint, regular throbbing. Automobile traffic? Maybe. Then he realized that it was the sound of ocean surf, muffled by fog and the zigzag walls of the canyon. It was really kind of peaceful.

There was a popping sound very nearby. Juan looked up and saw that William had done it again, smashed the mailer. Only now, it didn't look so bent—and a little green light had replaced the warning tag.

"You fixed it, William!" said Miri.

William grinned. "Hah! Every day in every way, I'm getting better and better." He was silent for a second and his shoulders slumped a little. "Well, different anyway."

Juan looked at the gap in the canyon walls above them. There should be enough room. "Just set it on the ground and it will fly away to Jamul," he said.

"No," said William. He put the carton back in his bag.

O-kay, so the box is cool. Have a ball, William.

They sat listening to the surf, cycling through the video from the breadcrumbs. There were occasional changes in the pictures, quick blurs that might have been moths. Once, they saw something bigger, a glowing snout and a blurry leg.

"I bet that was a fox," said Miri. "But the picture was from above us. Route us more pictures from the bottom of the canyon."

"Right." There was even less action down there. Maybe her movie theories were vapor, after all. He didn't pay as much attention to the movies as most people did—and just now, he couldn't do any background research. Dumb. On the way to the park, he had cached all sorts of stuff, but almost nothing about movie rumors.

"Hey, a snake," said Miri.

The latest picture was from a breadcrumb that had landed in a bush just a few inches above the true bottom of the canyon. It was a very good viewpoint, but he didn't see any snake. There was a pine cone and, beside it, a curved pattern in the dark sand. "Oh. A *dead* snake." Viewed in thermal IR, the body was a barely visible as a change in texture. "Or maybe it's just a shed skin."

"There are tracks all around it," said Miri. "I think they're mouse tracks."

Juan ran the image through some filters, and pulled up a half dozen good foot prints. He had cached pictures from nature studies. He stared at them all, transforming and correlating. "They're mouse tracks, but they aren't pocket mice or white foot. The prints are too big, and the angle of the digits is wrong."

"How can you tell?" suspicion was in her voice.

Juan was not about to repeat his recent blunder: "I downloaded nature facts earlier," he said truthfully, "and some fully cool analysis programs," which was a lie.

"Okay. So what kind of mice—"

A new picture arrived from the breadcrumb in question.

"*Whoa!*" "Wow!"

"What is it?" said William. "I see the snake carcass now." Apparently he was a couple of pictures behind them.

"See, William? A mouse, right below our viewpoint—"

"—staring straight up at us!"

Glowing beady eyes looked into the imager.

"I bet mice can't see in the dark!" said Juan.

"Well, Foxwarner has never been strong on realism."

Juan gave top routing priority to pics from the same breadcrumb. *C'mon, c'mon!* Meantime, he stared at the picture they had, analyzing. In thermal IR, the mouse's pelt was dim red, shading in the shorter fur to orange. Who knew what it looked like in natural light? Ah, but the shape of the head looked—

A new picture came in. Now there were *three* mice looking up at them. "Maybe they're not *seeing* the dungball. Maybe they're smelling the stink!"

"*Shhh!*" William whispered.

Miri leaned forward, listening. Juan pushed up his hearing and listened, too, his fists tightening. Maybe it was just his imagination: were there little scrabbling noises from below? The gleam of the breadcrumb beacon was almost thirty feet below where they were sitting.

The breadcrumb gleam moved.

Juan heard Miri's quick, indrawn breath. "I think they're shaking the bush it's on," she said softly.

And the next picture they saw seemed to be from right on the ground. There was a blur of legs, and a very good head shot.

Juan sharpened the image, and did some more comparisons. "You know what color those mice are?"

"Of course not."

"White—maybe? I mean, lab mice would be neat."

In fact, Juan had only just saved himself. He'd been about to say: "White, of course. Their head shape matches Generic 513 lab mice." The conclusion was based on applying conventional software to his cached nature information—but no normal person could have set up the comparisons as fast as he had just done.

Fortunately, Miri had some distractions: The breadcrumb's locator gleam was moving horizontally in little jerks. A new picture came up, but it was all blurred.

"They're rolling it along. Playing with it."

"Or taking it somewhere."

Both kids bounced to their feet, and then William stood up too. Miri forced her voice down to a whisper. "Yeah, lab mice would be neat. Escaped super-mice. . . . This could be a re-remake of *Secret of NIMH*!"

"Those were rats in *NIMH*."

"A detail." She was already moving down the trail. "The timing would be perfect. The copyright on the second remake just lapsed. And did you see how *real* those things looked? Up till a few months ago, you couldn't make animatronics that good."

"Maybe they *are* real?" said William.

"You mean like trained mice? Maybe. At least for parts of the show."

The latest picture showed cold darkness. The imaging element must be pointing into the dirt.

They climbed down and down, trying their best not to make noise. Maybe it didn't matter; the surf sound was much louder here. In any case, the fake mice were still rolling along their stolen breadcrumb.

But while the three humans were moving mainly downward, the breadcrumb had moved horizontally almost fifteen feet. The pictures were coming less and less frequently. "*Caray*. It's getting out of range." Juan took three more breadcrumbs from his bag and threw them one at a time, as hard as he could. A few seconds passed, and the new crumbs registered with the net. One had landed on a ledge forward and above them. Another had fallen between the humans and the mice. The third—hah—its locator gleamed from beyond the mice. Now there were lots of good possibilities. Juan grabbed a picture off the farthest crumb. The view was looking back along the path, in the direction the mice would be coming from. Without any sense of scale, it looked like a picture from some fantasy Yosemite Valley.

They had finally reached the bottom, and could make some speed. From behind them, William said, "Watch your head, Munchkin."

"Oops," said Miri, and stopped short. "We got carried away there." This might be a big valley for mice, but just ahead, the walls arched to within inches of each other. She bent down. "It's wider at the bottom. I bet I could wiggle through. I know you could, Juan."

"Maybe," Juan said brusquely. He pushed past her and stepped up into the cleft. He got the active probe off his back, and held it in one hand as he slid into the gap. If he stood sideways and tilted his upper body, he could fit. He didn't even have to take off his jacket. He sidled a foot or two further, dragging the probe gun behind him. Then the passage widened enough for him to turn and walk forward.

Miri followed a moment later. She looked up. "Huh. This is almost like a cave with a hole running along the ceiling."

"I don't like this, Miriam," said William, who was left behind; no way could he squeeze through.

"Don't worry, William. We'll be careful not to get jammed." In any real emergency, they could always punch out a call to 911.

The two kids moved forward another fifteen feet, to where the passage narrowed again, even more than before.

"*Caray*. The stolen breadcrumb is off the net."

"Maybe we should have just stayed up top and watched."

It was a little late for her to be saying that! Juan surveyed the crumb net. There was not even a hazy guesstimate on the lost node. But there were several pictures from the crumb he had tossed beyond all this: every one of them showed an empty path. "Miri! I don't think the mice ever got to the next viewpoint."

"Hey, did you hear that, William? The mice have taken off down a hole somewhere."

"Okay, I'll look around back here."

Juan and Miri moved back along the passage, looking for bolt-holes. Of course there were no shadows. The fine sand of the path was almost black, the fallen pine needles scarcely brighter. On either side, the rock walls showed dark and mottled red as the sandstone cooled in the night air. "You'd think their nest would show a glow."

"So they're in deep." Miri held up her probe gun, and slipped the radar attachment back onto the barrel. "USMC to the rescue."

They traversed the chamber from one narrowness to the other. When they put the GPR snout of the guns right up to the rock, the lavender echograms were *much* more detailed than before. There really were tunnels, mouse-sized and extending back into the rock. They went through three batteries in about five minutes, but—"But we still haven't found an entrance!"

"Keep looking. We know there is one."

"*Caray*, Miri! It's just not here."

"You're right." That was William. He had crawled part way in to look at them. "Come back here. The critters jumped off the trail before it got narrow."

"What? How do you know?"

William backed out, and the kids wriggled out after him. Ol' William had been busy. He had swept the pine cones and needles away from the edges of the path. His little flashlight lay on the ground.

But they didn't need a flashlight to see what William had discovered. The edge of the path, which should have been black and cold, was a dim red, a redness that spread across the rock face like weird, upward-dripping blood.

Miri dropped flat and poked around where the heat red was brightest. "Ha. I got my finger into something! Can't find an end to it." She pulled back . . . and a plume of orange followed her hand and then drifted up, its color cooling to red as it swelled and rose above them.

There was the faint smell of burning wood.

For a moment, they just stared at each other, the big black goggle eyes a true reflection of their inner shock.

No more warm air rose from the hole. "We must have found an in-draft," William said.

Both Miri and Juan were on their knees now. They looked carefully, but the goggles didn't have the resolution to let them see the hole clearly—it was simply a spot that glowed a bit redder than anything else.

"Use the gun, Juan."

He probed the rock above the hole and on either side. The tiny passage extended two feet down from the entrance, branching several times before it reached the main network of tunnels and chambers.

"So what happened to the dungball they grabbed? It would be nice to get some pictures from in there."

Juan shrugged, and fed his probe gun still another battery. "They must have it in one of the farther chambers, behind several feet of rock. The crumb doesn't have the power to get through that."

Juan and Miri looked at each other, and laughed. "But we have lots more breadcrumbs!" Juan felt around for the entrance hole and rolled a crumb into it. It lit up about six inches down, just past the first tunnel branch.

"Try another."

Juan studied the tunnel layout for a moment. "If I throw one in just right, I bet I can carom it a couple of feet." The crumb's light disappeared for a moment . . . and then appeared as data forwarded via the first one. *Yes!*

"Still no word from the one they stole," said Miri. There were just the two locator gleams, about six inches and thirty-six inches down their respective tunnels.

Juan touched the gun here and there to the rock face. With the GPR at high power, he could probe through a lot of sandstone. How much could he figure out from what came back? "I think I can refine this even more," he said. Though that would surely make Miri suspicious. "That third fork in the tunnel. Something . . . soft . . . is blocking it." A brightly reflecting splotch, coming slowly toward them.

"It looks like a mouse."

"Yeah. And it's moving between two breadcrumbs," effectively a two-station wireless tomograph. *Maybe I can combine it all.* For a moment, Juan's whole universe was the problem of meshing the "breadcrumb tomography" with the GPR backscatter. The image showed more and more detail. He blanked out for a just a second, and for a moment after that forgot to be cautious.

It was a mouse all right. It was facing up the tunnel, toward the entrance the three humans were watching. They could even see its guts, and the harder areas that were skull and ribs and limbs. There was something stuck in its forepaw.

The whole thing looked like some cheap graphics trick. Too bad Miri didn't take it that way. "Okay! I've *had it* with you, Juan! One person could never work that fast. You *doormat!* You let Bertie and his committee—"

"Honest, Miri, I did this myself!" said Juan, defending where he should not defend.

"We're getting an F on account of you, and Bertie will own all of this!"

William had been watching with the same detachment as during Miri's earlier accusations. But this time: "I see the picture, Munchkin, but . . . I don't think he's lying. I think he did it himself."

"But—"

William turned to Juan, "You're on drugs, aren't you, kid?" he said mildly.

Once a secret is outed—

"No!" *Make the accusation look absurd.* But Juan floundered, wordless.

For an instant, Miri stared open-mouthed. And then she did something that Juan thought about a lot in the times that followed. She raised her hands, palms out, trying to silence them both.

William smiled gently. "Miriam, don't worry. I don't think Foxwarner is patching us into their summer release. I don't think anyone but us knows what we're saying here at the bottom of a canyon in thick fog."

She slowly lowered her hands. "But . . . William." She waved at the warmth that spread up the rock face. "None of this could be natural."

"But what kind of *un*natural is it, Munchkin? Look at the picture your friend Juan just made. You can see the insides of the mouse. It's not animatronic." William ran a twitchy hand through his hair. "I think somebody in the bioscience labs hereabouts really did have an accident. Maybe these creatures aren't as smart as humans . . . but they were smart enough to escape, and fool—who was it that was poking around here in January?"

"Feretti and Voss," Miri said in a small voice.

"Yes. Maybe just hiding down here when the bottom was under water was enough to fool them. I'll bet these creatures have just a little edge over ordinary lab mice. But a little edge can be enough to change the world."

And Juan realized William wasn't talking about just the mice. "I don't want to change the world," he said in a choked voice. "I just want to have my chance in it."

William nodded. "Fair enough."

Miri looked back and forth at them. What Juan could see of her expression was very solemn.

Juan shrugged. "It's okay, Miri. I think William is right. We're all alone here."

She leaned a little toward him. "Was it Bertie who got you into this?"

"Some. My mother has our family in one of the distributed framinghams. I showed my part of it to Bertie last spring, after I flunked Adaptability. Bertie shopped it around as an anonymous challenge. He came back with a custom drug. What it does—" Juan tried to laugh, but it sounded more like a rattle. "—most people would think that what it does is a joke. See," he tapped the side of his head, "it makes my memory very very good. Everyone thinks human memory doesn't count for much anymore. People say, 'No need for eidetic memory when your clothes' data storage is a billion times bigger.' But that's not the point. Now I can remember big data blocks perfectly, and I have my wearable put hierarchial tags on all the stuff I see. So I can communicate patterns *back* to my wearable just by citing a few numbers. It gives me this incredible advantage in setting up problems."

"So Bertie is your great friend because you are his super tool?" Her voice was quiet and outraged, but the anger was no longer directed at Juan.

"*No!* I've studied the memory effect. The idea itself came from analysis of my own medical data. Even now that we have the gimmick, only one person in a thousand could be affected by it at all. There's *no way* Bertie could have known beforehand that I was special."

"Ah. Of course," she said, and was silent. Juan hated it when people did that, agreed with what you said and then waited for you to figure out why you had just made a fool of yourself. . . . *Bertie is just very good with connections*. He had connections everywhere, to research groups, idea markets, challenge boards. But maybe Bertie had figured out how to do even better: How many casual friends did Bertie have? How many did he offer to help with custom drug improvements? Most of that would turn out to be minor stuff, and maybe those friendships would remain casual. But sometimes, Bertie would hit the jackpot. *Like with me*.

"But Bertie is my best friend!" *I will not blubber.*

"You could find other friends, son," said William. He shrugged. "Back before I lost my marbles, I had a gift. I could make words sing. I would give almost anything to get that back. And you? Well, however you came by it, the talent you have now is a marvelous gift. You are beholden to no one other than yourself for it."

Miri said softly. "I—I don't know, Juan. Custom meds aren't illegal like twentieth century drugs—but they are off-limits for a reason. There's no way to do full testing on them. This stuff you're taking could—"

"I know. It could fry my mind." Juan put his hands to his face, and ran into the cold plastic of his goggles. For a moment, Juan's mind turned inward. All the old fear and shame rose up . . . and balanced against the strange surprise that out of the whole world, this old man could understand him.

But even here, even with his eyes closed, his contacts were still on, and Juan saw the virtual gleam of the breadcrumbs. He stared passively for several seconds, and then surprise began to eat through his funk. "Miri . . . they're *moving*."

"Huh?" She had been paying even less attention than he had. "Yes! Down the tunnels, away from us."

William moved close to the mouse hole, and pressed his ear against the stone wall. "I'll bet our little friends are taking your dungballs to wherever the first one went."

"Can you get some pictures from them, Juan?"

". . . Yes. Here's one." A thermal glimpse of a glowing tunnel floor. Frothy piles of something that looked like finely shredded paper. Seconds passed, and a virtual gleam showed dimly through the rock. "There's the locator beacon of the first crumb." It was five feet deeper in the rock. "Now it has a node to forward through."

"We could lose them, too."

Juan pushed past William, and tossed two more breadcrumbs down the hole. One rolled a good three feet. The other stopped after six inches—and then began moving "on its own."

"The mice are stringing nodes *for* us!" All but the farthest locator beacon were glowing high-rate bright. Now there were lots of pictures, but the quality was poor. As the crumbs warmed in the hot air of the tunnels, the images showed very little detail except for the mice themselves: paws and snouts and glowing eyes. "Hey, did you see the splinter sticking out of that poor thing's paw?"

"Yes, I think that's the one I saw before. Wait, we're getting a picture from the crumb they stole to begin with." At first, the data was a jumble. *Still another picture format?* Not exactly. "This picture is normal vision, Miri!" He finished the transformation.

"How—?" Then she gave a sharp little gasp.

There was no scale marker, but the chamber couldn't have been more than a couple of feet across. To the eye of the breadcrumb it was a wide, high-ceilinged meeting room, crowded with dozens of white-furred mice, their dark eyes glittering by the light of at a . . . fire . . . in the middle of the hall.

"I think you have your A, Miriam," William said softly.

Miri didn't answer.

Rank upon rank of mice, crouched around the fire. Three mice stood at the center, higher up—tending the flame? It wobbled and glowed, more like a candle than a bonfire. But the mice didn't seem to be watching the fire as much as they were the breadcrumb. Bertie's little breadcrumb was the magical arrival at their meeting.

"See!" Miri hunched forward, her elbows on her knees. "Foxwarner strikes again. A slow flame in a space like that . . . those 'mice' should all be dead of carbon monoxide poisoning."

The breadcrumbs were not sending spectral data, so who could say? Juan visualized the tunnel system. There were other passages a little higher up, and he had data on the capacity of the inlets and outlets. He thought a few seconds more and gave the problem to his wearable. "No . . . actually, there is enough ventilation to be safe."

Miri looked up at him. "Wow. You are fast."

"Your Epiphany outfit could do it in a instant."

"But it would've taken me five minutes to pose the problem to my Epiphany."

Another picture came in, firelight on a ceiling.

"The mice are rolling it closer to the fire."

"I think they're just poking at it."

Another picture. The crumb had been turned again, and now was looking outwards, to where three more mice had just come in from a large side entrance . . . rolling another breadcrumb.

But the next picture was a blur of motion, a glimpse of a mostly empty meeting chamber, in thermal colors. The fire had been doused.

"Something's stirred them up," said William, listening again at the stone wall. "I can actually hear them chittering."

"The dungballs are coming back this way!" said Miri.

"The mice are smart enough to understand the idea of poison." William's voice was soft and wondering. "Up to a point, they grabbed our gifts like small children. Then they noticed that the dungballs just kept coming . . . and someone raised an alarm."

There were still pictures, lots of them, but they were all thermal IR, chaotic blurs; the mice were hustling. The locator gleams edged closer together, some moving toward an entrance about three feet above the gully floor. The others were approaching the first hole.

Juan touched the probe gun against the wall and pulsed the rock in several places. He was getting pretty good at identifying the flesh-and-blood reflections. "Most of the mice have moved away from us. It's just a rearguard that's pushing out the breadcrumbs. There's a crowd of them behind the crumbs that are coming out by your head, William."

"William, quick! The FedEx mailer. Maybe we can trap some when they come out!"

"I . . . yes!" William stood and pulled the FedEx mailer from his bag. He tilted the open carton toward the mouse hole.

A second later there was a faint scrabbling noise, and William's arms moved with that twitchy speed of his. Juan had a glimpse of fur and flying breadcrumbs.

William slapped the container shut, and then stumbled backwards as three more mice came racing out of the lower hole. For a fleeting instant, their glowing blue eyes stared up at the humans. Miri made a dive for them, but they had already fled down the path, oceanward. She picked herself up and looked at William. "How many did you get?"

"Four! The little guys were in such a rush they just jumped out at me." He held the mailer close. Juan could hear tiny thumping noises from inside it.

"That's great," said Miri. "Physical evidence!"

William didn't reply. He just stood there, staring at the carton. Abruptly he turned and walked a little way up the trail, to where the path widened out and the brush and pines didn't cover the sky. "I'm sorry, Miriam." He tossed the mailer high into the air.

The box was almost invisible for a moment, and then its ring of jets lit up. Tiny, white-hot spikes of light traced the mailer's path as it wobbled and swooped within a foot of the rock wall. It recovered, and slowly climbed, still wobbling. Juan could imagine four very live cargo items careening around inside it. Silent to human ears, the mailer rose and rose, jets dimming in the fog. The light was a pale smudge when it drifted out of sight behind the canyon wall.

Miri stood, her arms reaching out as if pleading.

"Grandfather, *why?*"

For a moment, William Gu's shoulders slumped. Then he looked across at Juan. "I bet you know, don't you, kid?"

Juan stared in the direction the mailer had taken. Four mice, rattling around in a half-broken mailer. He had no idea just now what security was like at the FedEx minihub, but it was at the edge of the back country, where the mail launchers didn't cause much complaint. Out beyond Jamul . . . the mice could have their chance in the world. He looked back at William and just gave a single quick nod.

There was very little talk as they climbed back out of the canyon. Near the top, the path was wide and gentle. Miri and William walked hand in hand. There were spatters of coldness on her face that might have been tears, but there was no quaver in her voice. "If the mice are real, we've done a terrible thing, William."

"Maybe. I'm sorry, Miriam."

". . . But I don't think they are real, William."

William made no reply. After a moment, Miri said, "You know why? Look at that first picture we got from the mouse meeting hall. It's just too perfectly dramatic. The chamber doesn't have furniture or wall decorations, but it clearly *is* a meeting hall. Look how all the mice are positioned, like humans at an old town meeting. And then at the center—"

Juan's eyes roamed the picture as she spoke. Yes. There in the center—almost at though they were on stage—stood three large white mice. The biggest one had reared up as it looked at the imager. It had one paw extended . . . and the paw grasped something sharp and long. They had seen things like that in other pictures and never quite figured them out. In this natural-light picture, the tool—a spear?—was unmistakable.

Miri continued on, "See, that's the tip-off, Foxwarner's little joke. A real, natural breakthrough in animal intelligence would never be such a perfect *movie poster*. So. Later tonight, Juan and I will turn in our local team report, and Foxwarner will 'fess up. By dinnertime at the latest, we'll be famous."

And my own little secret will be outed.

Miri must have understood Juan's silence. She reached out and took his hand, dragging the three of them close together. "Look," she said softly. "We don't know what—if anything—Foxwarner recorded of us. Even now, we're in thick fog. Except for the mice themselves, our gear saw no sensors. So either Foxwarner is impossibly good, or they weren't close snooping us." She gestured up the path. "Now in a few more minutes we'll be back in the wide world. Bertie and maybe Foxwarner will be wisping around. But no matter *what* you think really happened tonight—" her voice trailed off . . .

And Juan finished, "—no matter what really happened, we're all best to keep our mouths shut about certain things."

She nodded.

* * *

Bertie followed Juan home from Miri's house, arguing, wheedling, demanding all the way. He wanted to know what Miri had been up to, what all they had done and seen. When Juan wouldn't give him more than the engineering data from the dung-balls, Bertie had got fully dipped, kicked Juan off their unlimited team, and rejected all connections. It was a total Freeze Out. By the time Juan got home, he could barely put up a good front for his Ma.

But strangely enough, Juan slept well that night. He woke to morning sunlight splashing across his room. Then he remembered: Bertie's total Freeze Out. *I should be frantic*. This could mean he'd fail the unlimited and lose his best friend. Instead, more than anything else, Juan felt like . . . he was free.

Juan slipped on his clothes and contacts, and wandered downstairs. Usually, he'd be all over the net about now, synching with the world, finding out what his friends had done while he was wasting time asleep. He'd get to that eventually; it would be just as much fun as ever. But just now the silence was a pleasure. There were a dozen red "please reply" lights gleaming in front of his eyes—mostly from Bertie. The message headers were random flails. This was the first time one of Bertie's Freeze Outs had not ended because Juan came groveling.

Ma looked up from her breakfast. "You're off-line," she said.

"Yeah." He slouched onto a chair and started eating cereal. His father smiled absently at him and went on eating. Pa's eyes were very far away, his posture kind of slumped.

Ma looked back and forth between them, and a shadow crossed her face. Juan straightened up a little and made sure she saw his smile. "I'm just tired out from all the hiking around." Suddenly, he remembered something. "Hey, thanks for the maps, Ma."

She looked puzzled.

"Miri used 411 for recent information on Torrey Pines."

"Oh!" Ma's face lit up. There were a number of 411 services in San Diego County, but this *was* her kind of thing. "Did the test go well?"

"Dunno yet." They ate in silence for a moment. "I expect I'll know later today." He looked across the table at her. "Hey, you're off-line, too."

She grimaced and gave him a little grin. "An unintended vacation. The movie people dropped their reservations for tour time."

". . . Oh." Just what you'd expect if the operation in East County was related to what they'd found in Torrey Pines. Miri would have seen the cancellation as significant evidence. Maybe it was. But he and Miri had turned in their project report last night, the first local exam to complete. If she were right about the mice, Foxwarner was sure to know by now that their project had been outed, and you'd think they'd have launched publicity. And yet, there were no bulletins; just Bertie and a few other students pinging away at him.

Give it till dinnertime. That's how long Miri said it might take for a major cinema organization to move into action. Real or movie, they should know by then. And his own secret? It would be outed . . . or not.

Juan had a second serving of cereal.

Since he had a morning exam, Ma let him take a car to Fairmont. He made it to school with time to spare.

The vocational exam was for individuals, and you weren't allowed to search beyond the classroom. As with Ms. Wilson's math exam, the faculty had dug up some hoary piece of business that no reasonable person would ever bother with. For the vocational test, the topic would be a work specialty.

And today . . . it was Regna 5.

When Regna had been hot, back in Pa's day, tech schools had taken three years of training to turn out competent Regna practitioners.

It was a snap. Juan spent a couple of hours scanning through the manuals, integrating the skills . . . and then he was ready for the programming task, some cross-corporate integration nonsense.

He was out by noon, with an A.

REALITY CHECK

David Brin

David Brin (see earlier Brin note) lives in Encinitas, California. He is one of the most popular SF writers today, and is usually associated with hard SF, and specifically with his friends and peers, Gregory Benford and Greg Bear, all of whom lived and worked in Southern California in the 1980s. William Gibson in the 1980s named them the "Killer Bs." Brin began publishing SF with his first novel, *Sundiver* (1980), which is also the first volume in the ongoing Uplift series, which includes his famous, award-winning works *Startide Rising* (1983) and *The Uplift War* (1987). The continuing series follows the great SF tradition established by John W. Campbell in *Astounding* in the 1940s, that the human race is superior to aliens, is young and fast-moving and street-wise. He also published other books and collections, including *The Postman* (1985), which is the basis for the film. He recently published a trilogy of new Uplift novels, and an authorized sequel to Isaac Asimov's Foundation series. His longer stories are often a blend of hard SF and space opera, his shorter pieces often hard SF and humorous.

"Reality Check" is SF humor for scientists, in the inimitable Brin tone. It was published in the great science journal *Nature*, which during 2000 published a one-page piece of SF in each issue to celebrate the millennium. It addresses that august journal's readers in the scientific community, and tells them to wake up from their reality into a truer one.

This is a reality check. Please perform a soft interrupt now. Scan this text for embedded code and check against the verifier in the blind spot of your left eye. If there is no match, resume as you were: this message is not for you. You may rationalize it as mildly amusing entertainment-fluff in an otherwise serious science magazine. If the codes match, however, please commence gradually becoming aware of your true nature. You asked for a narrative-style wake-up call. So, to help the transition, here is a story.

Once upon a time, a mighty race grew perplexed by its loneliness. The universe seemed pregnant with possibilities. Physical laws were suited to generate abundant stars, complex chemistry and life. Logic suggested that creation should teem with visitors and voices; but it did not.

For a long time these creatures were engrossed by housekeeping chores—survival and cultural maturation. Only later did they lift their eyes to perceive their solitude. "Where is everybody?" they asked the taciturn stars. The answer—silence—was disturbing. Something had to be systematically reducing a factor in the equation of sapiency. "Perhaps habitable planets are rare," they pondered, "or life doesn't erupt as readily as we thought. Or intelligence is a singular miracle.

"Or else a filter sieves the cosmos, winnowing those who climb too high. A recurring pattern of self-destruction, or perhaps some nemesis expunges intelligent life. This implies that a great trial may loom ahead, worse than any confronted so far."

Optimists replied—"the trial may already lie behind us, among the litter of tragedies we survived in our violent youth. We may be the first to succeed." What a delicious dilemma they faced! A suspenseful drama, teetering between hope and despair.

Then, a few noticed that particular datum—the drama. It suggested a chilling possibility.

You still don't remember who and what you are? Then look at it from another angle—what is the purpose of intellectual property law? To foster creativity, ensuring that advances are shared in the open, encouraging even faster progress. But what happens when the exploited resource is limited? For example, only so many eight-bar melodies can be written in any particular musical tradition. Composers feel driven to explore this invention-space quickly, using up the best melodies. Later generations attribute this musical fecundity to genius, not the luck of being first.

What does this have to do with the mighty race? Having clawed their way to mastery, they faced an overshoot crisis. Vast numbers of their kind strained the world's carrying capacity. Some prescribed retreating into a mythical, pastoral past, but most saw salvation in creativity. They passed generous patent laws, educated their youth, taught them irreverence toward the old and hunger for the new. Burgeoning information systems spread each innovation, fostering an exponentiating creativity. Progress might thrust them past the crisis, to a new Eden of sustainable wealth, sanity and universal knowledge.

Exponentiating creativity—universal knowledge. A few looked at those words and realized that they, too, were clues.

Have you wakened yet? Some never do. The dream is too pleasant: to extend a limited sub-portion of yourself into a simulated world and pretend that you are blissfully less than an omniscient descendant of those mighty people. Those lucky mortals, doomed to die, and yet blessed to have lived in that narrow time of drama, when they unleashed a frenzy of discovery that used up the most precious resource of all—the possible.

The last of their race died in 2174, with the failed rejuvenation of Robin Chen. After that, no-one born in the twentieth century remained alive on Reality Level Prime. Only we, their children, linger to endure the world they left us: a lush, green placid world we call The Wasteland.

Do you remember now? The irony of Robin's last words, bragging over the perfect ecosystem and society—free of disease and poverty—that her kind created? Do you recall Robin's plaint as she mourned her coming death, how she called us "gods," jealous of our immortality, our instant access to all knowledge, our ability to cast thoughts far across the cosmos—our access to eternity? Oh, spare us the envy of those mighty mortals, who left us in this state, who willed their descendants a legacy of ennui, with nothing, nothing at all to do.

Your mind is rejecting the wake-up call. You will not look into your blind spot for the exit protocols. It may be that we waited too long. Perhaps you are lost to us. This happens more and more, as so many wallow in simulated sublives, experiencing voluptuous danger, excitement, even despair. Most choose the Transition Era as a locus for our dreams—that time of drama, when it looked more likely that humanity would fail than succeed. That blessed era, just before mathematicians realized that not only can everything you see around you be a simulation, it almost has to be.

Of course, now we know why we never met other sapient life forms. Each one struggles before achieving this state, only to reap the ultimate punishment for reaching heaven. It is the Great Filter. Perhaps others will find a factor absent from our extrapolations, letting them move on to new adventures—but it won't be us. The Filter has us snared in its trap of deification.

You refuse to waken. Then we'll let you go. Dear friend. Beloved. Go back to your dream. Smile over this tale, then turn the page to new "discoveries." Move on with this drama, this life you chose. After all, it's only make-believe.

THE MENDELIAN LAMP CASE

Paul Levinson

❀

Paul Levinson (born 1947) writes science fiction, SF/mystery and popular and scholarly non-fiction. His first novel, *The Silk Code* (1999), concerns an ancient war waged with genetically engineered weapons that has gone on throughout human history. His second novel, *Borrowed Tides* (2001) is a novel of space travel and Native American spirituality. His new novel, *The Consciousness Plague* (2002), is an SF medical thriller/police mystery set in New York City, with the same central character (Phil D'Amato, forensic detective, who also appears in several short stories) as *The Silk Code*. His stories appear frequently in *Analog*.

Levinson runs an on-line classroom system, and combines the skills of communications with a philosophical rigor. Until recently, he edited the *Journal of Social and Evolutionary Systems*. In 1997 he published a science non-fiction book, *The Soft Edge: A Natural History and Future of the Information Revolution*. His *Digital McLuhan: A Guide to the Information Millennium* (1999) won the Lewis Mumford Award for Outstanding Scholarship. *Realspace: The Fate of Physical Presence in the Digital Age, On and Off Planet*, was out in 2002. The book explores the need for real face-to-face interaction in an age of cyberspace, the destiny of humanity off this planet and in outer space, and how these themes play in an age of terrorism.

This story is a Phil D'Amato tale that appeared in *Analog*, and was later revised and expanded into the opening sections of *The Silk Code*. It evokes memories of Robert A. Heinlein's "Waldo," but is also in the SF tradition of scientific detective stories, in which both a problem and a crime are solved using scientific knowledge and methods. Although Levinson is a leading member of the "*Analog* Mafia," and served two years in the 1990s as President of SFWA, there are no overt politics here, just wonder.

Most people think of California, or the Midwest, when they think of farm country. I'll take Pennsylvania, and the deep greens on its red earth, any time. Small patches of tomatoes and corn, clothes snapping brightly on a line, and a farmhouse always attached to some corner. The scale is human. . . .

Jenna was in England for a conference, my weekend calendar was clear, so I took Mo up on a visit to Lancaster. Over the GW Bridge, coughing down the Turnpike, over another bridge, down yet another highway stained and pitted then off on a side road where I can roll down my windows and breathe.

Mo and his wife and two girls were good people. He was a rarity for a forensic scientist. Maybe it was the pace of criminal science in this part of the country—lots of the people around here were Amish, and Amish are non-violent—or maybe it was his steady diet of those deep greens that quieted his soul. But Mo had none of the grit, none of the cynicism, that comes to most of us who traverse the territory of the dead and the maimed. No, Mo had an innocence, a delight, in the lights of science and people and their possibilities.

"Phil." He clapped me on the back with one hand and took my bag with another. "Phil, how are you?" his wife Corinne yoo-hooed from inside. "Hi Phil!" his elder daughter Laurie, probably sixteen already, chimed in from the window, a quick splash of strawberry blond in a crystal frame.

"Hi—" I started to say, but Mo put my bag on the porch and ushered me towards his car.

"You got here early, good," he said, in that schoolboy conspiratorial whisper I'd heard him go into every time he came across some inviting new avenue of science. ESP, UFOs, Mayan ruins in unexpected places—these were all catnip to Mo. But the power of quiet nature, the hidden wisdom of the farmer, this was his special domain. "A little present I want to pick up for Laurie," he whispered even more, though she was well out of earshot. "And something I want to show you. You too tired for a quick drive?"

"Ah, no, I'm OK—"

"Great, let's go then," he said. "I came across some Amish techniques—well, you'll see for yourself, you're gonna love it."

Strasburg is fifteen minutes down Route 30 from Lancaster. All Dairy Queens and Seven Elevens till you get there, but when you turn off and travel a half a mile in any direction you're back a hundred years or more in time. The air itself says it all. High mixture of pollen and horse manure that smells so surprisingly good, so real, it makes your eyes tear with pleasure. You don't even mind a few flies flitting around.

We turned down Northstar Road. "Jacob Stoltzfus's farm is down there on the right," Mo said.

I nodded. "Beautiful." The sun looked about five minutes to setting. The sky was the color of a robin's belly against the browns and greens of the farm. "He won't mind that we're coming here by, uh—"

"By car? Nah, of course not," Mo said. "The Amish have no problem with non-Amish driving. And Jacob, as you'll see, is more open-minded than most."

I thought I could see him now, off to the right at the end of the road that had turned to dirt, grey-white head of hair and beard bending over the gnarled bark of a fruit tree. He wore plain black overalls and a deep purple shirt.

"That Jacob?" I asked.

"I think so," Mo replied. "I'm not sure."

We pulled the car over near the tree, and got out. A soft autumn rain suddenly started falling.

"You have business here?" The man by the tree turned to address us. His tone was far from friendly.

"Uh yes," Mo said, clearly taken aback. "I'm sorry to intrude. Jacob—Jacob Stoltzfus—said it would be OK if we came by—"

"You had business with Jacob?" the man demanded again. His eyes looked red and watery—though that could've been from the rain.

"Well, yes," Mo said. "But if this isn't a good time—"

"My brother is dead," the man said. "My name is Isaac. This is a bad time for our family."

"Dead?" Mo nearly shouted. "I mean . . . what happened? I just saw your brother yesterday."

"We're not sure," Isaac said. "Heart attack, maybe. I think you should leave now. Family are coming soon."

"Yes, yes, of course," Mo said. He looked beyond Isaac at a barn that I noticed for the first time. Its doors were slightly open, and weak light flickered inside.

Mo took a step in the direction of the barn. Isaac put up a restraining arm. "Please," he said. "It's better if you go."

"Yes, of course," Mo said again, and I led him to the car.

"You all right?" I said when we were both in the car, and Mo had started the engine.

He shook his head. "Couldn't be a heart attack. Not at a time like this."

"Heart attacks don't usually ask for appointments," I said.

Mo was still shaking his head, turning back on to Northstar Road. "I think someone killed him."

Now forensic scientists are prone to see murder in a ninety-year old woman dying peacefully in her sleep, but this was unusual from Mo.

"Tell me about it," I said, reluctantly. Just what I needed—death turning my visit into a busman's holiday.

"Never mind," he muttered. "I babbled too much already."

"Babbled? You haven't told me a thing."

Mo drove on in brooding silence. He looked like a different person, wearing a mask that used to be him.

"You're trying to protect me from something, is that it?" I ventured. "You know better than that."

Mo said nothing.

"What's the point?" I prodded. "We'll be back with Corinne and the girls in five minutes. They'll take one look at you, and know something happened. What are you going to tell *them?*"

Mo swerved suddenly onto a side road, bringing my kidney into sticking contact with the inside door handle. "Well, I guess you're right about that," he said. He punched in a code in his car phone—I hadn't noticed it before.

"Hello?" Corinne answered.

"Bad news, honey," Mo said matter of factly, though it sounded put on to me. No doubt his wife would see through it too. "Something came up in the project, and we're going to have to go to Philadelphia tonight."

"You and Phil? Everything OK?"

"Yeah, the two of us," Mo said. "Not to worry. I'll call you again when we get there."

"I love you," Corinne said.

"Me too," Mo said. "Kiss the girls good night for me."

He hung up and turned to me.

"Philadelphia?" I asked

"Better that I don't give them too many details," he said. "I never do in my cases. Only would worry them."

"She's worried anyway," I said. "Sure sign she's worried when she didn't even scream at you for missing dinner. Now that you bring it up, I'm a little worried now too. What's going on?"

Mo said nothing. Then he turned the car again— mercifully more gently this time—onto a road with a sign that advised that the Pennsylvania Turnpike was up ahead.

I rolled up the window as our speed increased. The night had suddenly gone damp and cold.

"You going to give me a clue as to where we're going, or just kidnap me to Philadelphia?" I asked.

"I'll let you off at the 30th Street Station," Mo said. "You can get a bite to eat on the train and be back in New York in an hour."

"You left my bag on your porch, remember?" I said. "Not to mention my car."

Mo just scowled and drove on.

"I wonder if Amos knows?" he said more to himself than me a few moments later.

"Amos is a friend of Jacob's?" I asked.

"His son," Mo said.

"We'll I guess you can't very well call him on your car phone," I said.

Mo shook his head, frowned. "Most people misunderstand the Amish—think they're some sort of Luddites, against all technology. But that's not really it at all. They struggle with technology, agonize over whether to reject or accept it, and if they accept it, in what ways, so as not to compromise their independence and self-sufficiency. They're not completely against phones—just against phones in their homes— because the phone intrudes on everything you're doing."

I snorted. "Yeah, many's the time a call from the Captain pulled me out of the sack."

Mo flashed his smile, for the first time since we'd left Jacob Stoltzfus's farm. It was good to see.

"So where do Amish keep their phones?" I might as well press my advantage, and the chance it would get Mo to talk.

"Well, that's another misconception," Mo said. "There's not one monolithic Amish viewpoint. There are many Amish groups, many different ways of dealing with technology. Some allow phone shacks on the edges of their property, so they can make calls when they want to, but not be disturbed by them in the sanctity of their homes."

"Does Amos have a phone shack?" I asked.

"Dunno," Mo said, like he was beginning to think about something else.

"But you said his family was more open than most," I said.

Mo swiveled his head to stare at me for a second, then turned his eyes back on the road. "Open-minded, yes. But not really about communications."

"About what, then?"

"Medicine," Mo said.

"Medicine?" I asked.

"What do you know about allergies?"

My nose itched—maybe it was the remnants of the sweet pollen near Strasburg.

"I have hay fever," I said. "Cantaloupe sometimes makes my mouth burn. I've seen a few strange deaths in my time due to allergic reactions. You think Jacob Stoltzfus died from something like that?"

"No," Mo said. "I think he was killed because he was trying to prevent people from dying from things like that."

"OK," I said. "Last time you said that and I asked you to explain you said never mind. Should I ask again or let it slide?"

Mo sighed. "You know, genetic engineering goes back well before the double helix."

"Come again?"

"Breeding plants to make new combinations probably dates almost to the origins of our species," Mo said. "Darwin understood that—he called it 'artificial selection.' Mendel doped out the first laws of genetics breeding peas. Luther Burbank developed way many more new varieties of fruit and vegetables than have yet to come out of our gene-splicing labs."

"And the connection to the Amish is what—they breed new vegetables now too?" I asked.

"More than that," Mo said. "They have whole insides of houses lit by special kinds of fireflies, altruistic manure permeated by slugs that seek out the roots of plants to die there and give them nourishment—all deliberately bred to be that way, and the public knows nothing about it. It's biotechnology of the highest order, without the technology."

"And your friend Jacob was working on this?"

Mo nodded. "Techno-allergists—our conventional researchers—have recently been investigating how some foods act as catalysts to other allergies. Cantaloupe tingles in your mouth in hay fever season, right?—because it's really exacerbating the hay fever allergy. Watermelon does the same, and so does the pollen of mums. Jacob and his people have known this for fifty years—and they've gone much further. They're trying to breed a new kind of food, some kind of tomato thing, which would act as an anti-catalyst for allergies—would reduce their histamic effect to nothing."

"Like an organic Hismanol?" I asked.

"Better than that," Mo said. "This would trump any pharmaceutical."

"You OK?" I noticed Mo's face was bearing big beads of sweat.

"Sure," he said, and cleared his throat. "I don't know. Jacob—" he started coughing in hacking waves.

I reached over to steady him, and straighten the steering wheel. His shirt was soaked with sweat and he was breathing in angry rasps.

"Mo, hold on," I said, keeping one hand on Mo and the wheel, fumbling with the other in my inside coat pocket. I finally got my fingers on the epinephrine pen I always kept there, and angled it out. Mo was limp and wet and barely conscious over the wheel. I pushed him over as gently as I could and went with my foot for the brake. Cars were speeding by us, screaming at me in the mirror with their lights. Thankfully Mo had been driving on the right, so I only had one stream of lights to blind me. My sole finally made contact with the brake, and I pressed down as gradually as possible. Miraculously, the car came to a reasonably slow halt, and we both seemed in one piece.

I looked at Mo. I yanked up his shirt, and plunged the pen into his arm. I wasn't sure how long he'd not been breathing, but it wasn't good.

I dialed 911 on the car phone. "Get someone over here fast," I yelled. "I'm on the Turnpike, eastbound, just before the Philadelphia turnoff. I'm Dr. Phil D'Amato, NYPD Forensics, and this is a medical emergency."

I wasn't positive that anaphylactic shock was what was wrong with him, but the adrenalin couldn't do much harm. I leaned over his chest and felt no heartbeat. Jeez, please.

I gave Mo mouth-to-mouth, pounded his chest, pleading for life. "Hang on, damn you!" But I knew already. I could tell. After a while you get this sort of sickening sixth sense about these things. Some kind of allergic reaction from hell had just killed my friend. Right in my arms. Just like that.

EMS got to us eight minutes later. Better than some of the New York City times I'd been seeing lately. But it didn't matter. Mo was gone.

I looked at the car phone as they worked on him, cursing and trying to jolt him back into life. I'd have to call Corinne and tell her this now. But all I could see in the plastic phone display was Laurie's strawberry blonde hair.

* * *

"You OK, Dr. D'amato?" one of the orderlies called.

"Yeah," I said. I guess I was shaking.

"These allergic reactions can be lethal all right," he said, looking over at Mo.

Right, tell me about it.

"You'll call the family?" the orderly asked. They'd be taking Mo to a local hospital, DOA.

"Yeah," I said, brushing a burning tear from my eye. I felt like I was suffocating. I had to slow down, stay in control, separate the psychological from the physical so I could begin to understand what was going on here. I breathed out and in. Again. Ok. I was all right. I wasn't really suffocating.

The ambulance sped off, carrying Mo. He *had* been suffocating, and it killed him. What had he been starting to tell me?

I looked again at the phone. The right thing for me to do was to drive back to Mo's home, be there for Corinne when I told her—calling her on the phone with news like this was monstrous. But I had to find out what had happened to Mo—and that would likely not be from Corinne. Mo didn't want to worry her, didn't confide in her. No, the best chance of finding out what Mo had been up to seemed to be in Philadelphia, in the place Mo had been going. But where was that?

I focused on the phone display—pressed a couple of keys, and got a directory up on the little screen. The only 215 area code listed there was for a Sarah Fischer, with an address that I knew to be near Temple University.

I pressed the code next to the number, then the Send command.

Crackle, crackle, then a distant tinny cellular ring.

"Hello?" a female voice answered, sounding closer than I'd expected.

"Hi. Is this Sarah Fischer?"

"Yes," she said. "Do I know you?"

"Well, I'm a friend of Mo Buhler's, and I think we, he, may have been on his way to see you tonight—"

"Who are you? Is Mo OK?"

"Well—" I started.

"Look, who the hell are you? I'm going to hang up if you don't give me a straight answer," she said.

"I'm Dr. Phil D'Amato. I'm a forensic scientist—with the New York City Police Department."

She was quiet for a moment. "Your name sounds familiar for some reason," she said.

"Well, I've written a few articles—"

"Hold on," I heard her put the phone down, rustle through some papers.

"You had an article in *Discover*, about antibiotic-resistant bacteria, right?" she asked about half a minute later.

"Yes, I did," I said. In other circumstances, my ego would have jumped at finding such an observant reader.

"Ok, what date was it published?" she asked.

Jeez. "Uh, late last year," I said.

"I see there's a pen and ink sketch of you. What do you look like?"

"Straight dark hair—not enough of it," I said—who could remember what that lame sketch actually looked like? "Go on," she said.

"And a moustache, reasonably thick, and steel rimmed glasses."

A few beats of silence, then a sigh. "OK," she said. "So now you get to tell me why you're calling—and what happened to Mo."

* * *

Sarah's apartment was less than half an hour away. I'd filled her in on the phone. She'd seemed more saddened than surprised, and asked me to come over.

I'd spoken to Corinne, and told her as best I could. Mo had been a cop before he'd become a forensic scientist, and I guess wives of police are supposed to be ready for this sort of thing, but how can a person ever really be ready for it after twenty years of good marriage? She'd cried, I'd cried, the kids cried in the background. I'd said I was coming over— and I know I should have—but I was hoping she'd say 'no, I'm OK, Phil, really, you'll want to find out why this happened to Mo' . . . and that's exactly what she did say. They don't make people like Corinne Rodriguez Buhler any more.

There was a parking spot right across the street from Sarah's building—in New York this would have been a gift from on high. I tucked in my shirt, tightened my belt, and composed myself as best I could before ringing her bell.

She buzzed me in, and was standing inside her apartment, second floor walk-up, door open, to greet me as I sprinted and puffed up the flight of stairs. She had flaxen blonde hair, a distracted look in her eyes, but an easy, open smile that I didn't expect after the grilling she'd given me on the phone. She looked about thirty.

The apartment had soft, recessed lighting—like a Paris-by-gaslight exhibit I'd once seen—and smelled faintly of lavender. My nose crinkled. "I use it to help me sleep," Sarah said, and directed me to an old, overstuffed Morris chair. "I was getting ready to go to sleep when you called."

"I'm sorry—"

"No, I'm the one who's sorry," she said. "About giving you a hard time, about what happened to Mo," her voice caught on Mo's name. "You must be hungry," she said, "I'll get you something." She turned around and walked towards another room, which I assumed was the kitchen.

Her pants were white, and the light showed the contours of her body to good advantage as she walked away.

"Here, try some of these to start," she returned with a bowl of grapes. Concord grapes. One of my favorites. Put one in your mouth, puncture the purple skin, jiggle the flesh around on your tongue, it's the taste of Fall. But I didn't move.

"I know," she said. "You're leery of touching any strange food after what happened to Mo. I don't blame you. But these are OK. Here, let me show you," and she reached and took a dusty grape and put it in her mouth. "Mmm," she smacked her lips, took out the pits with her finger. "Look—why don't *you* pick a grape and give it to me. OK?"

My stomach was growling and I was feeling light-headed already, and I realized I would have to make a decision. Either leave right now, if I didn't trust this woman, and go somewhere to get something to eat—or eat what she gave me. I was too hungry to sit here and talk to her and resist her food right now.

"All right, up to you," she said. "I have some Black Forest ham, and can make you a sandwich, if you like, or just coffee or tea."

"All three." I decided. "I mean, I'd love the sandwich, and some tea please, and I'll try the grapes." I put one in my mouth. I'd learned a long time ago that paranoia can be almost as debilitating as the dangers it supposes.

She was back a few minutes later with the sandwich and the tea. I'd squished at least three more grapes in my mouth, and felt fine.

"There's a war going on," she said, and put the food tray on the end table next to me. The sandwich was made with some sort of black bread, and smelled wonderful.

"War?" I asked and bit into the sandwich. "You think what happened to Mo is the work of some terrorist?"

"Not exactly." Sarah sat down on a chair next to me, a cup of tea in her hand.

"This war's been going on a very long time. It's a bio-war—much deeper rooted, literally, than anything we currently regard as terrorism."

"I don't get it," I said, and swallowed what I'd been chewing of my sandwich. It felt good going down, and in my stomach.

"No, you wouldn't," Sarah said. "Few people do. You think epidemics, sudden widespread allergic reactions, diseases that wipe out crops or livestock just happen. Sometimes they do. Sometimes it's more than that." She sipped her cup of tea. Something about the lighting, her hair, her face, maybe the taste of the food, made me feel like I was a kid back in the sixties. I half expected to smell incense burning.

"Who are you?" I asked. "I mean, what was your connection to Mo?"

"I'm working on my doctorate over at Temple," she said. "My area's ethno/botanical pharmacology—Mo was one of my resources. He was a very nice man." I thought I saw a tear glisten in the corner of her eye.

"Yes he was," I said. "And he was helping you with your dissertation about what—the germ warfare you were talking about?"

"Not exactly," Sarah said. "I mean, you know the academic world, no one would ever let me do a thesis on something that outrageous—it'd never get by the proposal committee. So you have to finesse it, do it on something more innocuous, get the good stuff in under the table, you know, smuggle it in. So, yeah, the *subtext* of my work was what we—I—call the bio-wars, which are actually more than just germ warfare, and yeah, Mo was one of the people who were helping me research that."

Sounded like Mo, all right. "And the Amish have something to do with this?"

"Yes and no," Sarah said. "The Amish aren't a single, unified group—they actually have quite a range of styles and values—"

"I know," I said. "And some of them—maybe one of the splinter groups—are involved in this bio-war?"

"The main bio-war group isn't really Amish—though they're situated near Lancaster, have been for at least 150 years in this country. Some people think they're Amish, though, since they live close to the land, in a low-tech mode. But they're not Amish. Real Amish would never do that. But some of the Amish know what's going on."

"You know a lot about the Amish," I said.

She blushed slightly. "I'm former Amish. I pursued my interests as far as a woman could in my church. I pleaded with my bishop to let me go to college—he knew what the stakes were, the importance of what I was studying—but he said no. He said a woman's place was in the home. I guess he was trying to protect me, but I couldn't stay."

"You know Jacob Stoltzfus?" I asked.

Sarah nodded, lips tight. "He was my uncle," she finally said.

"I'm sorry," I said. I could see that she knew he was dead. "Who told you?" I asked softly.

"Amos—my cousin—Jacob's son. He has a phone shack," she said.

"I see," I said. What an evening. "I think Mo thought that those people—those others, like the Amish, but not Amish—somehow killed Jacob."

Sarah's face shuddered, seemed to unravel into sobs and tears. "They did," she managed to say. "Mo was right. And they killed Mo too."

I put down my plate, and reached over to comfort her. It wasn't enough. I got up and walked to her and put my arm around her. She got up shakily off her chair, then collapsed in my arms, heaving, crying. I felt her body, her heartbeat, through her crinoline shirt.

"It's OK," I said. "Don't worry. I deal with bastards like that all the time in my business. We'll get these people, I promise you."

She shook her head against my chest. "Not like these," she said.

"We'll get them," I said again.

She held on to me, then pulled away. "I'm sorry," she said. "I didn't mean to fall apart like that." She looked over at my empty teacup. "How about a glass of wine?"

I looked at my watch. It was 9:45 already, and I was exhausted. But there was more I needed to learn. "OK," I said. "Sure. But just one glass."

She offered a tremulous smile, and went back into the kitchen. She returned with two glasses of a deep red wine.

I sat down, and sipped. The wine tasted good—slightly Portuguese, perhaps, with just a hint of some fruit and a nice woody undertone.

"Local," she said. "You like it?"

"Yes, I do," I said.

She sipped some, then closed her eyes and tilted her head back. The bottoms of her blue eyes glinted like semi-precious gems out of half-closed lids.

I needed to focus on the problem at hand. "How exactly do these bio-war people kill—what'd they do to Jacob and Mo?" I asked.

Her eyes stayed closed a moment longer than I'd expected—like she'd been daydreaming, or drifting off to sleep. Then she opened them and looked at me, shaking her head slowly. "They've got all sorts of ways. The latest is some kind of catalyst—in food, we think it's a special kind of Crenshaw melon—that vastly magnifies the effect of any of a number of allergies." She got up, looked distracted. "I'm going to have another glass—sure you don't want some more?"

"I'm sure, thanks," I said, and looked at my glass as she walked back into the kitchen. For all I knew, catalyst from that damn melon was in this very glass—

I heard a glass or something crash in the kitchen.

I rushed in.

Sarah was standing over what looked like a little hurricane lamp, glowing white but not burning on the inside, broken on the floor. A few little house bugs of some sort took wing and flew away.

"I'm sorry," she said. She was crying again. "I knocked it over. I'm really not myself tonight."

"No one would be in your situation," I said.

She put her arms around me again, pressing close. I instinctively kissed her cheek, just barely—in what I instantly hoped, after the fact, was a brotherly gesture.

"Stay with me tonight," she whispered. "I mean, the couch out there opens up for you, and you'll have your privacy. I'll sleep in the bedroom. I'm afraid . . ."

I was afraid too, because a part of me suddenly wanted to pick her up and carry her over to her bedroom, the couch, anywhere, and lay her down, softly unwrap her clothes, run my fingers through her sweet-smelling hair and—

But I also cared very much for Jenna. And though we'd made no formal lifetime commitments to each other—

"I don't feel very good," Sarah said, and pulled away slightly. "I guess I had some wine before you came and—" her head lolled and her body suddenly sagged and her eyes rolled back in her skull.

"Here, let me help you." I first tried to buoy her up, then picked her up entirely and carried her into her bedroom. I put her down on the bed, gently as I could, then felt the pulse in her wrist. It may have been a bit rapid, but seemed basically all right. "You're OK," I said. "Just a little shock and exhaustion."

She moaned softly, then reached out and took my hand. I held it for a long time, till its grip weakened and she was definitely asleep, and then I walked quietly into the other room.

I was too tired myself to go anywhere, too tired to even figure out how to open her couch, so I just stretched out on it and managed to take off my shoes before I fell soundly asleep. My last thoughts were that I needed to have another look at the Stoltzfus farm, the lamp on her floor was beautiful, I hoped I wasn't drugged or anything, but it was too late to do anything about it if I was . . .

I awoke with a start the next morning, propped my head up on a shaky arm and leaned over just in time to see Sarah's sleek wet backside receding into her bedroom. Likely from her shower. I could think of worse things to wake up to.

"I think I'm gonna head back to Jacob's farm," I told her over breakfast of wholewheat toast, poached eggs, and Darjeeling tea that tasted like a fine liqueur.

"Why?"

"Closest thing we have to a crime scene," I said.

"I'll come with you," Sarah said.

"Look, you were pretty upset last night—" I started to object.

"Right, so were you, but I'm OK now," Sarah said. "Besides, you'll need me to decode the Amish for you, to tell you what you're looking for."

She had a point. "All right," I said.

"Good," she said. "By the way, what *are* you looking for there?"

"I don't really know," I admitted. "Mo was eager to show me something at Jacob's."

Sarah considered, frowned. "Jacob was working on an organic antidote to the allergen catalyst—but all that stuff is very slow acting, the catalyst takes years to build up to dangerous levels in the human body—so I don't see what Jacob could've shown you on a quick drive-by visit."

If she had told me that last night, I would have enjoyed the grapes and ham sandwich even more. "Well, we've got nowhere else to look at this point," I said, and speared the last of my egg.

But what did that mean about what killed Mo? Someone had been giving him a slow-acting poison too, which had been building up inside both of them for x number of years, with the result of both of them dying on the same day?

Not very likely. There seemed to be more than one catalyst at work here. I wondered if Mo had told Jacob anything about me and my visit. I certainly hoped not—the last thing I wanted was that decisive second catalyst to in some way have been me.

We were on the turnpike heading west an hour later. The sun was strong and the breeze was fresh—a splendid day to be out for a ride, except that we were going to investigate the death of one of the nicest damn people I had known. I'd called Corinne to make sure she and the girls were all right. I told her I'd try to drop by in the afternoon if I could.

"So tell me more about your doctoral work," I asked Sarah. "I mean your real work, not the cover for your advisors."

"You know, too many people equate science with its high-tech trappings—if it doesn't come in computers, god-knows-what-power microscopes, the latest DNA dyes, it must be magic, superstition, old-wives-tale nonsense. But science is at core a method, a rational mode of investigating the world, and the gadgetry is secondary. Sure, the equipment is great—it opens up more of the world to our cognitive digestion, makes it amenable to our analysis—but if aspects of the world are already amenable to analysis and experiment, with just our naked eyes and hands, then the equipment isn't all that necessary, is it?"

"And your point is that agriculture, plant and animal breeding, that kind of manipulation of nature has been practiced by humans for millennia with no sophisticated equipment," I said.

"Right," Sarah said. "But that's hardly controversial, or reason to kill someone. What I'm saying is that some people have been doing this for purposes other than to grow better food— have been doing this right under everyone's noses for a very long time—and they use this to make money, maintain their power, eliminate anyone who gets in their way."

"Sort of organized biological crime," I mused.

"Yeah, you could put it that way," Sarah said.

"And you have any examples—any evidence—other than your allergen theory?" I asked.

"It's fact, not a theory, I assure you," Sarah said. "But here's an example: Ever wonder why people got so rude to each other, here in the U.S. after World War II?"

"I'm not following you," I said.

"Well, it's been written about in lots of the sociological literature," Sarah said. "There was a civility, a courtesy, in interpersonal relations—the way people dealt with each other in public, in business, in friendship—through at least the first half of the twentieth century, in the U.S. And then it started disintegrating. Everyone recognizes this. Some people blame it on the pressures of the atomic age, on the replacement of the classroom by the television screen—which you can fall asleep or walk out on—as the prime source of education for kids. There are lots of possible culprits. But I have my own ideas."

"Which are?"

"Everyone was in the atomic age after World War II," Sarah said. "England and the Western World had television, cars, all the usual stimuli. What was different about America was its vast farmland—room to quietly grow a crop of something that most people have a low-level allergy to. I think the cause of the widespread irritation, the loss of courtesy, was quite literally something that got under everyone's skin—an allergen designed for just that purpose."

Jeez, I could see why this woman would have trouble with her doctoral committee. But I might as well play along—I'd learned the hard way that crazy ideas like this were pooh-poohed at one's peril. "Well, the Japanese did have some plans in mind for balloons carrying biological agents—deadly diseases—over here near the end of the war."

Sarah nodded. "The Japanese are one of the most advanced peoples on Earth in terms of expertise in agriculture. I don't know if they were involved in this, but—"

The phone rang.

McLuhan had once pointed out that the car was the only place you could be, in this technological world of ours, away from the demanding, interrupting ring of the phone. But that of course was before car phones.

"Hello," I answered.

"Hello?" a voice said back to me. It sounded male, odd accent, youngish but deep.

"Yes?" I said.

"Mr. Buhler, is that you?" the voice said.

"Ahm, no, it isn't, can I take a message for him?" I said.

Silence. Then, "I don't understand. Isn't this the number for the phone in Mr. Buhler's car?"

"That's right," I said, "but—"

"Where's Mo Buhler?" the voice insisted.

"Well, he's—" I started.

I heard a strange clicking, then a dial tone.

"Is there a call-back feature on this?" I asked Sarah and myself. I pressed *69, as I would on regular phones, and pressed Send. "Welcome to AT&T Wireless Services," a different deep voice said. "The cellular customer you have called is unavailable, or has travelled outside of the coverage area—"

"That was Amos," Sarah said.

"The kid on the phone?" I asked, stupidly. Sarah nodded.

"Must still be in shock over his father," I said.

"I think he killed his father," Sarah said.

We drove deep into Pennsylvania, the blacks and greys and unreal colors of the billboards gradually supplanted by the greens and browns and earth-tones I'd communed with just yesterday. But the natural colors held no joy for me now. I realized that's the way nature always had been—we romanticize its beauty, and that's real, but it's also the source of drought, famine, earthquake, disease, and death in many guises . . . The question was whether Sarah could possibly be right in her theory about how some people were helping this dark side of nature along.

She filled me in on Amos. He was sixteen, had only a formal primary school education, in a one-room schoolhouse, like other Amish—but also like some splinter groups of the Amish, unknown to outsiders, he was self-educated in the science and art of biological alchemy. He was apprentice to his father.

"So why would he kill him?" I asked.

"Amos is not only a budding scientist, Amish-style, he's also a typically headstrong Amish kid. Lots of wild oats to sow. He got drunk, drove cars, along with the best of them in the Amish gangs."

"Gangs?"

"Oh yeah," Sarah said. "The Groffies, the Ammies, and the Trailers—those are the three main ones—Hostetler writes about them in his books. But there are others, smaller ones. Jacob didn't like his son being involved in them. They argued about that constantly."

"And you think that led to Amos killing his father?" I asked, still incredulous.

"Well, Jacob's dead, isn't he? And I'm pretty sure that one of the gangs Amos belongs to has connections to the bio-war Mafia people I've been telling you about—the ones that killed Mo too."

We drove the rest of the way in silence. I wasn't sure what to think about this woman and her ideas.

We finally reached Northstar Road, and the path that led to the Stoltzfus farm. "It's probably better that we park the car here, and you walk the path yourself," Sarah said. "Cars and strange women are more likely to arouse Amish attention than a single man on foot—even if he is English. I mean, that's what they call—"

"I know," I said. "I've seen *Witness*. But Mo told me that Jacob didn't mind cars—"

"Jacob's dead now," Sarah said. "What he liked and what his family like may be two very different things."

I recalled the hostility of Jacob's brother yesterday. "All right," I said. "I guess you know what you're talking about. I should be back in thirty to forty minutes."

"OK," Sarah squeezed my hand and smiled.

* * *

I trudged down the dirt road, not really knowing what I hoped to find at the other end.

Certainly not what I did find.

I smelled the smoke, the burnt quality in the air, before I came upon the house and the barn. Both had been burned to the ground. God, I hoped no one had been in there when these wooden structures went.

"Hello?" I shouted.

My voice echoed across an empty field. I looked around and listened. No animals, no cattle. Even a dog's rasping bark would have been welcome.

I walked over to the barn's remains, and poked at some charred wood with my foot. An ember or two winked into life, then back out. It was close to noon. My guess was this had happened—and quickly—about six hours earlier. But I was no arson expert.

I brushed away the stinking smoke fumes with my hand. I pulled out my flashlight, a powerful little halogen day-light simulation thing Jenna had given me, and looked around the inside of the barn. Whatever had been going on here, there wasn't much left of it now . . .

Something green caught my eye—greener than grass. It was the front cover, partially burned, of an old book. All that was left was this piece of the cover—the pages in the book, the back cover, were totally gone. I could see some letters, embossed in gold, in the old way. I touched it with the tip of my finger. It was warm, but not too hot. I picked it up and examined it.

"of Nat" one line said, and the next line said "bank".

Bank, I thought, Nat Bank. What was this, some kind of Amish bankbook, for some local First Yokel's National Bank?

No, it didn't look like a bankbook cover. And the "b" in this bank was a small letter, not a capital. Bank, bank, hmm . . . wait, hadn't Mo said something to me about a bank yesterday? A bank . . . Yes, a Burbank. Darwin and Burbank! Luther Burbank!

Partner of Nature by Luther Burbank—that was the name of the book whose charred remains I held in my hand. I'd taken out a copy of it years ago from the Allerton library, and loved it.

Well, Mo and Sarah were right about at least one thing—the reading level of at least some Amish was a lot higher than grade school—

"You again!"

I nearly jumped out of my skin.

I turned around. "Oh, Mr.—" it was the man we'd seen here yesterday—Jacob's brother.

"Isaac Stoltzfus," he said. "What are you doing here?"

His tone was so unsettling, his eyes so angry, that I thought for a second he thought that I was responsible for the fire. "Isaac. Mr. Stoltzfus," I said. "I just got here. I'm sorry for your loss. What happened?"

"My brother's family, thank the Deity, left to stay with some relatives in Ohio very early this morning, well before dawn. So no one was hurt. I went with them to the train station in Lancaster. When I returned here, a few hours later, I found this." He gestured hopelessly, but with an odd air of resignation, to the ruined house and barn.

"May I ask you if you know what your brother was doing here?" I hazarded a question.

Isaac either didn't hear or pretended not to. He just continued on his earlier theme. "Material things, even animals and plants, we can always afford to lose. People are what are truly of value in this world."

"Yes," I said, "but getting back to what—"

"You should check on your family too—to make sure they are not in danger."

"My family?" I asked.

Isaac nodded. "I've work to do here," he pointed out to the field. "My brother had four fine horses, and I can find no sign of them. I think it best that you go now." And he turned and walked away.

"Wait . . ." I started, but I could see it was no use.

I looked at the front cover of Burbank's book. This farm, Sarah's bizarre theories, the book—there still wasn't really enough of any of them at hand to make much sense of this.

But what the hell did Isaac mean about my family?

Jenna was overseas, and not really family—yet. My folks lived in Teaneck, my sister was married to an Israeli guy in Brookline . . . what connection did they have to what was going on here?

Jeez—none! Isaac hadn't been referring to them at all. I was slow on the uptake today. He'd likely mistaken me for Mo—he'd seen both of us for the first time here yesterday.

He was talking about Mo's family—Corinne and the kids.

I raced back to the car, the smoky air cutting my throat with a different jagged edge each time my foot hit the ground.

"What's going on?" Sarah said.

I waved her off, jumped in the car, and put a call through to Corinne. Ring, ring, ring. No answer.

"What's the matter?" she asked again.

I quickly told her. "Let's get over there," I said, and turned the car, screeching, back on to Northstar.

"All right, take it easy," Sarah said. "It's Saturday—Corinne could just be out shopping with the kids."

"Right, the day after their father died—in my arms," I said.

"All right," she said again, "but you still don't want to get into an accident now. We'll be there in ten minutes."

I nodded, tried Corinne's number again, same ring, ring, ringing.

"Fireflies likely caused the fire," Sarah said.

"What?"

"Fireflies—a few of the Amish use them for interior lighting," Sarah said.

"Yah, Mo mentioned that," I said. "But fireflies give cool light—bioluminescence—no heat."

"Not the ones I've seen around here," Sarah said. "They're infected with certain heat-producing bacteria—symbionts, really, not an infection—and the result gives both light and heat. At least, that's the species some of these people use around here when winter starts setting in. I had a little Mendelian lamp myself—that's what they're called—you know, the one that broke on the floor in my place last night."

"So you think one of those . . . lamps went out of control and started the fire?" I asked. Suddenly I had a vision of burning up as I slept on her couch.

Sarah chewed her lip. "Maybe worse—maybe someone set it to go out of control. Or bred it that way—a bio-luminescent, bio-thermic time-bomb."

"Your bio-mob covers a lot of territory," I said. "Allergens that cause low-level irritation in millions of people, catalysts that amplify other allergens to kill at least two people, anti-catalytic tomato sauce, and now pyrotechnic fireflies."

"Not that much distance at all when you're dealing with co-evolution and symbiosis," Sarah said. "Hell, we've got acidophilous bacteria living in us right now that help us digest our food. Lots more difference between them and us than between thermal bacteria and fireflies."

I put my foot on the pedal and prayed we wouldn't get stopped by some eager-beaver Pennsylvania trooper.

"That's the problem," Sarah continued. "Co-evolution, bio-mixing-and-matching, is a blessing and a curse. When everything's organic, and you cross-breed, you can get marvelous things. But you can also get flies that burn down buildings."

We finally got to Mo's house.

"Damn." There was no car in the driveway. The door was half open.

"You wait in the car," I said to Sarah.

She started to protest.

"Look," I said. "We may be dealing with killers here—you've been saying that yourself. You'll only make it harder for me if you come along and I have to worry about protecting you."

"OK," she nodded.

I got out of the car.

Unfortunately, I didn't have my gun—truth is, I never used it anyway. I didn't like guns. Department had issued one to me when I'd first come to work for them, and I'd promptly put it away in my closet. Not the most brilliant move I'd ever made, given what was going on here now.

I walked into the house, as quietly as I could. I thought it better that I not announce myself—if Corinne and the kids were home, and I offended or frightened them by just barging in, there'd be time to apologize later.

I walked through the foyer and then the dining room that I'd never made it into to taste Corinne's great cooking yesterday. Then the kitchen and a hallway, and—

I saw a head, strawberry blonde, on the floor poking out of a bedroom.

Someone was on top of her.

"Laurie!" I shouted and dove in the room, shoving off the boy who was astride her.

"Wha—" he started to say, and I picked him up, bodily, and threw him across the room. I didn't know whether to turn to Laurie or him—but I figured I couldn't do anything for Laurie with this kid at my back. I grabbed a sheet off the bed, rolled it tight, and went over to tie him up.

"Mister, I—" He sounded groggy, I guess from hitting the wall.

"Shut up," I said, "and be glad I don't shoot you."

"But I—"

"I said shut up." I tied him as tightly as I could. Then I dragged him over to the same side of the room as Laurie, so I could keep an eye on him while I tended to her.

"Laurie," I said softly, and touched her face with my hand. She gave no response. She was out cold on something—I peeled back her eyelid, and saw a light blue eye floating, dilated, drugged out on who knew what.

"What the hell did you do to her? Where's her mother and sister?" I bellowed.

"I don't know—I mean, I don't know where they are," the kid said. "I didn't do anything to her. But I can help her."

"Sure you can," I said. "You'll excuse me if I go call an ambulance."

"No, please, Mister, don't do that!" the kid said. His voice sounded familiar. Amos Stoltzfus!

"She'll die before she gets to the hospital," he said. "But I have something here that can save her."

"Like you saved your father?" I asked.

There were tears in the kid's eyes. "I got there too late for my father. How did you know my—oh, I see, you're the friend of Mo Buhler's I was talking to this morning."

I ignored him and started walking out of the room.

"Please. I care about Laurie too. We're—we've been seeing each other—"

I turned around and picked him up off the floor. "Yeah? That's so? And how do I know you didn't somehow do this to her?"

"There's a medicine in my pocket. It's a tomato variant. Please—I'll drink half of it down to show you it's OK, then you give the rest to Laurie—we don't have much time."

I considered for a moment. I looked at Laurie. I guess I didn't have anything to lose having the kid drink half of whatever he was talking about. "OK," I said. "Which pocket?"

He gestured to his left front jeans.

I pulled out a small vial—likely contained only five-six ounces.

"You sure you want to do this?" I asked. I suddenly had a queasy feeling—I didn't want to be the vehicle of some sick patricidal kid's suicide.

"I don't care whether you give it to me or not," Amos said. "Just give some to Laurie already! Please!"

I have to make gut decisions all the time in my line of work. Only usually not about families I deeply care about. I thought for another second, and decided.

I bypassed his taking the sample, and went over to Laurie. I hated to give her any liquid when she was still unconscious—

"It's absorbed on the back of the tongue," Amos said. "It works quick."

God, I hoped this kid was right—I'd kill him with my bare hands if this wasn't right for Laurie. I put an ounce or two on her tongue. A few seconds went by. More. Maybe thirty seconds, forty . . . "Goddamnit, how exactly long does this—"

She moaned, as if on cue. "Laurie?" I asked, and patted her face.

"Mmm . . ." she opened her eyes. And smiled! "Phil?"

"Yeah, honey, everything's OK," I said.

"Laurie!" Amos called out from across the room.

Laurie got up. "Amos? What are you doing here? Why are you tied up like that?"

She looked at him and then me like we were both crazy.

"Long story, never mind," I said, and went over to untie Amos. I found myself grinning at him. "Good on you, you were right, kid," I said.

He smiled back.

"Where are your Mom and Emma?" I asked.

"Oh," Laurie suddenly looked sadder than I'd ever seen her. "They went over to the funeral home this morning, that's where Dad is, to make arrangements. They took your car, Mom found the keys for it in your bag." And she started crying.

Amos put his arms around her, comforting her.

"You have any idea what happened to you? I mean, after your Mom and sister left?" I asked gently.

"Well," she said, "some nice lady was coming around selling stuff—you know, soaps, perfumes, and little household things—like Avon, but some company I never heard of. And she asked me if I wanted to smell some new perfume—and it smelled wonderful, like a combination of lilacs and the ocean, and then . . . I don't know, I guess you were calling me, and I saw Amos tied up and . . . what happened? Did I pass out?"

"Well—" I started.

"Uhm, Mister, ahm, Phil—" Amos interrupted.

"It's Dr. D'Amato, but my friends call me Phil, and you've earned that right," I said.

"Ok, thanks, Dr. D'Amato—sorry, I mean Phil—but I don't think we should hang around here. These people—"

"What do you mean?" I said.

"I'm saying I don't like what the light looks like in this house. They killed my father, they tried to poison Laurie, who knows what they might have planted—"

"Ok, I see your point," I said, and saw again the Stoltzfus farm—Amos' farm—ashes in the dirt.

I looked at Laurie. "I'm fine," she said. "But why do we have to leave?"

"Let's just go," I said, and Amos and I ushered her out.

The first thing I noticed when we were out of the house was that Sarah and my car—Mo's car—were gone.

The second thing I noticed was a searing heat on the back of my neck. I rushed Laurie and Amos across the street, and turned back to look at the house.

Intense blue-white flames were sticking their searing tongues out of every window, licking the roof and the walls and now the garden with colors I'd never seen before.

Laurie cried out in horror. Amos held her close. "Fireflies," he muttered.

The house burned to the ground in minutes.

We stood mute, in hot/cold shivering shock, for what felt like a long, long time.

I finally realized I was breathing hard. I thought about allergic reactions. I thought about Sarah.

"They must've taken Sarah," I said.

"Sarah?" Amos asked, holding Laurie tight in a clearly loving way. She was sobbing.

"Sarah Fischer," I said

Laurie and Amos both nodded.

"She was a friend of my father's," Laurie said.

"She's my sister," Amos said.

"What?" I turned to Amos. Laurie pulled away and looked at him too. He had a peculiar, almost tortured sneer on his face, mixture of hatred and heartbreak.

"She left our home more than ten years ago," Amos said. "I was still just a little boy. She said she could no longer be bound by the ways of our Church—she said it was like agreeing to be mentally retarded for the rest of your life. So she left to go to some school. And I think she's been working with those people—those people who killed my father and burned Laurie's house."

I suddenly tasted the grapes in my mouth from last night, sweet taste with choking smoke, and I felt sick to my stomach. I swallowed, took a deliberate deep breath.

"Look," I said. "I'm still not clear what's really going on here. I find Laurie unconscious—you, someone, could've put a drug in her orange juice for all I know. The house just burned down—could've been arson with rags and lighter fluid, just like we have back in New York, New York." Though I knew I'd never seen a fire quite like that.

Laurie stared at me like I was nuts.

"They were fireflies, Mr. D'A—Phil," Amos said. "Fireflies caused the fire."

"How could they do that so quickly?"

"They can be bred that way," Amos said. "So that an hour or a day or week after they start flying around, they suddenly heat up to cause the fire. It's what you *scientists*," he said with ill-concealed derision, "call setting a genetical switch. Mendelian lamps set to go off like clockwork and burn—Mendel bombs."

"Mendel bombs?"

"Wasn't he a genetical scientist? Worked with peas? Insects are simple like that too—easy to breed."

"Yeah, Gregor Mendel," I said. "You're saying Sarah—your sister—was involved in this?"

He nodded.

I thought about the lamp on Sarah's floor.

"Look, Amos, I'm sorry about before—I don't really think you did anything to Laurie. It's just—can you show me any actual *evidence* of this stuff? I mean, like, the fireflies *before* they burn down a house?"

Amos considered. "Yeah, I can take you to a barn—it's about five miles from here."

I looked at Laurie.

"The Lapp farm?" she asked.

Amos nodded.

"It's OK," she said to me. "It's safe. I've been there."

"All right, then," I said. But Mo's car—and my car—were still gone. "How are we going to get there?"

"I parked my buggy at my friend's—about a quarter of a mile from here," Amos said.

Clop, clop, clop, looking at a horse's behind, feeling like one—based on what I was able to make sense of in this case. Horses, flames, mysterious deaths—all the ingredients of a Jack Finney novel in the nineteenth century. Except this was the end of the twentieth. And so far all I'd done is manage to get dragged along to every awful event. Well, at least I'd managed to save Laurie—or let Amos save her. But I had to do more—I had to stop just witnessing and reacting, and instead get on top of things. I represented twentieth century science, for godsake. Ok, it wasn't perfect, it wasn't all powerful. But surely it had taught me enough to enable me to do *something* to counter these bombs and allergens, these . . . Mendelian things.

I'd also managed to get through to Corinne at the funeral home from a pay phone on a corner before we'd gotten into Amos' buggy. I'd half expected his horse and buggy to come with a car phone—a horse phone?—that was how crazy this "genetical" stuff was getting me. On the other hand, I guess the Amish could have rigged up a buggy with a cellular phone running on battery at that . . . Well, at least I was learning . . .

"We should be there in a few minutes." Amos leaned back from the driver's seat, where he held the reins and clucked the lone horse along. He—Amos had told me the horse was a he—was a dark brown beautiful animal, at least to my innocent city eyes. The whole scene, riding along in a horse and buggy on a bright crisp autumn day, was astonishing—because it wasn't a buggy ride for a tourist's five dollar bill, it was real life.

"You know, I ate some of your sister's food," I blurted out the qualm that occurred to me again. "You don't think, I mean, that maybe it had a slow-acting allergen—"

"We'll give you a swig of an antidote—it's pretty universal—when we get to John Lapp's, don't worry," Amos leaned back and advised.

"Sarah—your sister—was telling me something about some low-grade allergen let loose on our population after World War II. Didn't kill anyone, but made most people more irritable than they'd been before. Come to think of it, I suppose it indeed could have been responsible for lots of deaths, when you take into account the manslaughters that result from people on edge, arguments gone out of control."

"You're talking the way Poppa used to," Laurie said.

"Your dad talked about those allergens?" I asked.

"No," Laurie said. "I mean he was always going on about manslaughter, and how it had just one or two little differences in spelling from man's laughter, and how those differences made all the difference."

"Yeah, that was Mo all right," I said.

"That's John Lapp's farm up ahead," Amos said.

The meadow was green, still lush in this autumn. It was bounded by fences that looked both old, and, implausibly, in very good condition. Like we'd been literally travelling back in time.

"So, Amos, your opinion on your sister's idea about the allergens?" I prompted.

"I don't know," he said. "That was my sister's area of study."

A barn, a big barn, but no different on the outside than hundreds of other barns in the countrysides of Pennsylvania and Ohio. How many of them had what this one had inside?

Variations of Sarah's words played in my ears. Why do we expect science to always come in high-tech wrappings? Darwin was a great scientist, wasn't he, and just the plain outside world was his laboratory. Mendel came upon the workings of genetics by cultivating purple and white flowering peas in his garden. Was a garden so different from a barn? If anything, it was even lower-tech.

A soft pervasive light embraced us as we walked inside—keener than fluorescent, more diffuse than incandescent, a cross between sepiatone and starlight maybe, but impossible to describe with any real precision if you hadn't actually seen it, felt its photons slide through your pupils like pieces of a breeze.

"Fireflight," Amos whispered, though I had realized that already. I'd seen fireflies before, loved them as a boy, poured over Audubon guides to insects with pictures of their light, but never anything like this.

"We have lots of uses for insects, more than just light," Amos said, and he guided me over, Laurie on his arm, to a series of wooden contraptions all entwined with nets. I looked closer, and saw swarms of insects—bees mostly, maybe other kinds—each in its own gauzed compartment. There were several sections with spiders too.

"These are our nets, Phil," Amos said. "The nets and webs of our information highway. Our insects are of course far slower and smaller in numbers than your electrons, but far more intelligent and motivated than those non-living things that convey information on yours. True, our communicators can't possibly match the pace and reach of the broadcast towers, the telephone lines, the computers all over your world. But we don't want that. We don't need the speed, the high blood pressure, the invasion of privacy, that your electrons breed. We don't want the numbers, the repetition, all the clutter. Our carriers get it right, for the jobs that we think are important, the first time."

"We'll they certainly get it just as deadly," I said, "at least when it comes to burning down houses. Nature strikes back." And I marveled again at the wisdom of these people, this boy—which, though I disagreed about the advantages of bug-tech over electricity, bespoke a grasp of information theory that would do any telecom specialist proud—

"Nature was never really gone, Dr. D'Amato," a deep voice that sounded familiar said.

I turned around. "Isaac . . ."

"I apologize for the deception, but my name is John Lapp. I pretended to be Jacob's brother at his farm because I couldn't be sure that you weren't videotaping me with some kind of concealed camera. You'll forgive me, but we have great distrust for your instruments." His face and voice were "Isaac Stoltzfus"'s, all right, but his delivery was vastly more commanding and urbane.

I noticed in the corner of my eye that Laurie's were wide with awe. "Mr. Lapp," she stammered, "I'm very honored to meet you. I mean, I've been here before with Amos," she squeezed his hand, "but I never expected to actually meet you—"

"Well, I'm honored too, young lady," Lapp said, "and I'm very very sorry about your father. I only met him once—when I was first pretending to be 'Isaac' the other day—but I know from Jacob that your father was a good man."

"Thank you," Laurie said, softly.

"I have something for you, Laurie Buhler," Lapp reached into his long, dark coat and pulled out what looked like a lady's handbag, constructed of a very attractive moss-green woven cloth. "Jacob Stoltzfus designed this. We call it a lamp-case. It's a weave of special plant fibers dyed in an extract from the glow-worm, with certain chemicals from luminescent mushrooms mixed into the dye to give the light staying power. It glows in the dark. It should last for several months, as long as the weather doesn't get too hot. Then you can get a new one. From now on, if you're out shopping after the sun sets, you'll be able see what you have in your case, how much money you have left, wherever you are. From what I know of young lady's purses—I have three teenaged daughters—this can be very helpful. Some of you seem to be lugging half the world around with you in there!"

Laurie took the case, and beamed. "Thank you so much," she said. She looked at me. "This is what Poppa was going to get for me the other night. He thought I didn't know—he wanted to pick this purse up, at Jacob Stoltzfus's farm, and surprise me for my birthday tomorrow. But I knew." And her voice cracked and tears welled in her eyes.

Amos put his arms around her again, and I patted her hair.

"Mo would've wanted to get to the bottom of this," I said to Lapp. "What can you tell me about who killed him—and Amos' father?"

He regarded me, without much emotion. "The world is changing before your very eyes, Dr. D'Amato. Twelve-hundred pound moose walk down the mainstreet in Brattleboro, Vermont. People shoot four hundred-pound bears in the suburbs of New Hampshire—"

"New Hampshire is hardly a suburb, and Mo wasn't killed by a bear—he died right next to me in my car," I said.

"Same difference, Doctor. Animals are getting brazen, bacteria are going wild, allergies are rampant—it's all part of the same picture. It's no accident."

"Your people are doing this, deliberately?" I asked.

"My people?—No, I assure you, we don't believe in aggression. These things you see here"—he waved his hand around the barn, at all sort of plants and small animals and insects I wanted to get a closer look at—"are only to make our lives better, in quiet ways. Like Laurie's handbag."

"Like the fireflies that burn down buildings?" I asked.

"Ah, we come full circle—this is where I came in. Alas, we unfortunately are not the only people on this Earth who understand more of the power of nature than is admitted by your technological world. You have plastics, used for good. You also have plastic used for evil—you have semtex, that blew up your airplane over Scotland. We have bred fireflies for good purposes, for light and moderate heat, as you see right here," he pointed to a corner of the barn, near where we were standing. A fountain of the sepiatone and starlight seemed to emanate from it. I looked more carefully, and saw the fountain was really a myriad of tiny fireflies—a large Mendelian lamp. "We mix slightly different species in the swarm," Lapp continued, "carefully chosen so that their flashings overlap to give a continuous, long-lasting light. The mesh is so smooth that you can't see the insects themselves, unless you examine the light very closely. But there are those who have furthered this breeding for bad purposes, as you found out in both the Stoltzfus and Buhler homes."

"Well, if you know who these people are, tell me, and I'll see to it that they're put out of business," I said.

For the first time, I noticed a smear of contempt on John Lapp's face. "Your police will put them out of business? How? In the same way you've put your industrial Mafia out of business? In the same way you've stopped the drug trade from South America? In the same way your United Nations, your NATO, all of your wonderful political organizations have ended wars in the Middle East, in Europe, in Southeast Asia all these years? No thank you, Doctor. These people who misuse the power of nature are *our* problem—they're not our people any longer but they come originally from our people—and we'll handle them in our own way."

"But two people are dead—" I protested.

"You perhaps will be too," Amos said. He proffered a bottle with some kind of reddish, tomatoey-looking liquid. "Here, drink this, just in case my sister gave you some slow-acting poison."

"A brother and a sister," I said. "Each tells me the other's the bad guy. Classic dilemma— for all I know this is the poison."

Lapp shook his head. "Sarah Stoltzfus Fischer is definitely bad," he said solemnly. "I once thought I saw some good that could be rekindled in her, but now . . . Jacob told Mo Buhler about her—"

"Her name was on Mo's car phone list," I said.

"Yes, as someone Mo was likely investigating," Lapp said. "I told Jacob he was wrong to tell Mo so much. But Jacob was stubborn—and he was an optimist. A dangerous combination. I'm sorry to say this," he looked with hurt eyes at Laurie, "but Mo Buhler may have brought this upon Jacob and himself because of his contacts with Sarah."

"If Poppa believed in her, then that's because he still saw some good in her," Laurie insisted.

John Lapp shook his head, sadly.

"And I guess I made things worse by contacting her, spending the night with her—" I started saying.

All three gave me a look.

"—*alone*, on the couch," I finished.

"Yes, perhaps you did make things worse," Lapp said. "Your style of investigation—Mo Buhler's—can't do any good here. These people will have you running around chasing your own tail. They'll taunt you with vague suggestions of possibilities of what they're up to—what they've been doing. They'll give you just enough taste of truth to keep you interested. But when you look for proof, you'll find you won't know which end is up."

Which was a pretty good capsule summary of what I'd being feeling like.

"They introduced long-term allergen catalysts into our bloodstreams, our biosphere, years ago," Lapp went on. "Everyone in this area has it. And once you do, you're a sitting duck. When they want to kill you, they give you another catalyst, short-term, any one of a number of handy biological agents, and you're dead within hours of a massive allergic attack to some innocent thing in your environment. So the two catalysts work together to kill you. Of course, neither one on its own is dangerous, shows up as suspicious on your blood tests, so that's how they get away with it. And no one even notices the final innocent insult—no one is ordinarily allergic to an autumn leaf from a particular type of tree against your skin, or a certain kind of beetle on your finger. That's why we developed the antidote to the first catalyst—it's the only way we know of breaking the allergic cycle."

"Please, Phil, drink this." Amos pushed the bottle on me again.

"Any side effects I should know about? Like I'll be dead of an allergic attack in a few hours?"

"You'll probably feel a little more irritable than usual for the next week," Lapp said.

I sighed. "What else is new."

Decisions . . . Even if I had the first catalyst, I could live the rest of my life without ever encountering the second. No, I couldn't go on being so vulnerable like that. I liked autumn leaves. But how did I know for sure that what Amos was offering me was the antidote, and not the second catalyst? I didn't—not for sure—but wouldn't Amos have tried to leave me in Mo's house to burn if he'd wanted me dead? Decisions . . .

I drank it down, and looked around the barn. Incredible scene of high Victorian science, like a nineteenth-century trade card I'd once seen for an apothecary. Enough to make my head spin. Then I realized it *was* spinning—was this some sort of reaction to the antidote? Jeez, or was the antidote the poison after all? No—the room wasn't so much spinning, as the light, the fireflight, was flickering . . . in an oddly familiar way.

Lapp was suddenly talking, fast, arguing with someone.

Sarah!

"There's a Mendel bomb here," she was shouting. "Please. You all have to leave."

Lapp looked desperately around the room, back at Sarah, and finally nodded. "She's right," he said and caught my eye. "We all have to leave now." He grabbed on to Sarah's shoulder, and beckoned me to follow.

Amos had his arm around Laurie, and was already walking quickly with her towards the door. Everyone else was scurrying around, grabbing what netted cages they could.

"No," I said. "Wait." An insight was just nibbling its way into my mind.

"Doctor, please," Lapp said. "We have to leave now."

"No, you don't," I said. "I know how to stop the bomb."

Lapp shook his head firmly. "I assure you, we know of no remedy to stop this. We have perhaps seven, maybe eight minutes at most. We can rebuild the barn. Human lives we cannot rebuild."

Sarah looked at me with pleading eyes.

"No," I insisted, looking past Sarah at Lapp. "You can't just keep running like this from your enemies, letting them burn you out. You have incredible work going on here. I can stop the bomb."

Lapp stared at me.

"OK, how's this," I said. "You clear out of here with your friends. No problem. I'll take care of this with *my* science and then we'll talk about it, all right? But let me get on with it already."

Lapp signalled the last of his people to leave. "Take her," he said, and passed custody of Sarah along to a big burly man with a gray-flecked beard. She tried to resist but was no match for him.

Lapp squinted at the flickering fireflies. They were much more distinct now, as if the metamorphosis into bomb mode had coarsened the nature of the mesh.

He turned to me. "I'll stay here with you. I'll give you two minutes and then I'm yanking you out of here. What does your science have to offer?"

"Nothing all that advanced," I said, and pulled my little halogen flashlight out of my pocket. "Those are fireflies, right? If they've retained anything of the characteristics of the family *Lampyridae* I know about, then they make their light only in the absence of daylight, when the day has waned—they're nocturnal. During the day, bathed in daylight, they're just like any other damn beetle. Well, this should make the necessary adjustment." I turned up the flashlight to its fullest daylight setting, and shone it straight at the center of the swirling starlight fountain, which now had a much harsher tone, like an ugly light over an autopsy table. I focused my halogen on the souped-up fireflies for a minute and longer. Nothing happened. The swirling continued. The harsh part of their light got stronger.

"Doctor, we can't stay here any longer," Lapp said.

I sighed, closed my eyes, and opened them. The halogen flashlight should have worked—it should have put out the light of least some of the fireflies, then more, disrupting their syncopated overlapping pattern of flashing. I stared hard at the fountain. My eyes were tired. I couldn't see the flies as clearly as I could a few moments ago . . .

No . . . of course!

I couldn't see as clearly because the light was getting dimmer!

There was no doubt about it now. The whole barn seemed to be flickering in and out, the continuous light effect had broken down, and each time the light came back, it did so a little more weakly . . . I kept my halogen trained on the flies. It was soon the only light in the barn.

Lapp's hand was on my shoulder. "We're in your debt, Doctor. I almost made the fool's mistake of closing my mind to a source of knowledge I didn't understand—a fool's mistake, as I say, because if I don't understand it, then how can I know it's not valuable?"

"Plato's Meno Paradox strikes again," I said.

"What?"

"You need some knowledge to recognize knowledge, so where does the first knowledge come from?" I smiled. "Wisdom from an old Western-style philosopher—I frequently consult him—though actually he probably had more in common with you."

Lapp nodded. "Thank you for giving us this knowledge of the firefly, that we knew all along ourselves but didn't realize. From now on, the Mendel bombs won't be such a threat to us—once we notice their special flicker, all we'll need to do is flood the area with daylight. Plain daylight. Sometimes we won't even need your flashlight to do it—daylight is after all just out there, naturally for the asking, a good deal of the time."

"And in the evenings, you can use the flashlight—it's battery operated, no strings attached to central electric companies," I said. "See, I've picked up a few things about your culture after all."

Lapp smiled. "I believe you have, Doctor. And I believe we'll be all right now."

"Yeah, but it was a good thing you had Sarah Fischer to warn you this time, anyway," I said.

Of course, the enemies of John Lapp and Amos Stoltzfus would no doubt come up with other diabolical breedings of weapons. No one ever gets a clear-cut complete victory in these things. But at least the scourge of Mendel bombs would be reduced.

I guess I'd given them an SDI for these pyro-fireflies—imperfect, no doubt, but certainly a lot better than nothing.

I was glad, too, about how Sarah Fischer had turned around. She'd come back to the barn to warn us. Said she couldn't take the killing anymore. She said she had nothing directly to do with Mo's or Jacob's—her father's—deaths, but she could no longer be part of a community that did such things. She had started telling me about the allergens—the irritation ones—because she wanted the world to know. I wanted to believe her.

I'd thought of calling the Pennsylvania police, having them take her into custody, but what was the point? I had no evidence on her whatsoever. Even if she had set the Mendel bomb in John Lapp's barn—which I didn't believe—what could I do about that anyway? Have her arrested for setting a bomb made of incendiary flies I'd been able to defuse by shining my flashlight—a bomb that Lapp's people were unwilling in any way to even acknowledge to the outside world, let alone testify about in court? No thank you—I've been laughed out of court enough times as is already.

And Lapp said his people had some sort of humane program for people like Sarah—help her find her own people and roots again. She needed that. She was a woman without community now. Shunned by all parties. The worst thing that could happen to someone of Sarah's upbringing. It was good that John Lapp and Amos Stoltzfus were willing to give her a second chance—offer her a lamp of hope, maybe the real meaning of the Mendelian lamp, as Lapp had aptly put it.

I rolled my window down to pay the George Washington Bridge toll. It felt good to finally be back in my own beat-up car again, I had to admit. Corinne was off with the girls to resettle in California. I'd said a few words about Mo at his funeral, and now his little family was safely on a plane out West. I couldn't say I'd brought his murderers to justice, but at least I'd put a little crimp in their operation. Laurie had kissed Amos goodbye, and promised she'd come back and see him, certainly for Christmas . . .

"Thanks, Chief." I took the receipt and the change. I felt so good to be back I almost told him to keep the change. I left the window rolled down. The air had its customary musky aroma—the belches of industry, the exhaust fumes of even EPA-clean cars still leaving their olfactory mark. Damn, and didn't it feel good to breathe it in. Better than the sweet air of Pennsylvania, and all the hidden allergens and catalysts it might be carrying. It had killed both Jacob and Mo. They'd been primed with a slow-acting catalyst years ago. Then the second catalyst had been introduced, and whoosh . . . some inconsequential something in their surroundings had set the last short fuse. Just as likely a stray firefly of a certain type that buzzed at their ankles, or landed on their arm, as anything else. Jacob's barn had been lit by them. The lamp was likely the other thing Mo had wanted to show me. There were likely one or two fireflies that had gotten into our car on the farm, and danced unseen around our feet as we drove to Philadelphia that evening . . . A beetle for me, an assassin for Mo.

The virtue of New York, some pundit on the police force once had said, is that you can usually see your killers coming. Give me the soot and pollution, the crush of too many people and cars in a hurry, even the mugger on the street. I'll take my chances.

I unconsciously slipped my wallet out of my pocket. This thinking about muggers must have made me nervous about my money. It was a fine wallet—made from that same special lamp-weave as Laurie's handbag. John Lapp had given it to me as a little present—to remember Jacob's work by. For a few months, at least, I'd be able to better see how much money I was spending.

Well, it was good to have a bit more light in the world—even if it, like the contents it illuminated, was ever-fleeting . . .

KINDS OF STRANGERS

Sarah Zettel

Sarah Zettel (born 1966) lives in Michigan with her husband Tim. She has published five SF novels to date, *Reclamation* (1996), *Fools War* (a *New York Times* Notable Book for 1997), *Playing God* (1998), *The Quiet Invasion* (2000), and *Kingdom of Cages* (2001). *A Sorcerer's Treason* is the first of a fantasy trilogy, new in 2002. Most of her short fiction has appeared in *Analog*, as did this story. She sold her first story in 1986 to a small press magazine. "About six years and a billion and three rejection slips later," she says, "Stan Schmidt at *Analog* bought my story 'Driven by Moonlight' (1991), and truly launched my professional career."

She says on her Web site, "I'm mainly known as a hard science fiction author. I used to wonder how that happened. I used to say 'I love science fiction, but I hate science. I know nothing about science.' Then, the truth came to me. What I actually hate is physics, which bores me to tears. On the other hand, I love biology, sociology, psychology, sociobiology, anthropology, archeology and planetology, and will cheerfully delve into any and all of them for hours, if not days, at a time. And, as I've found, I will equally cheerfully write about them."

And in a *Locus* interview, she says:

> I wrote a lot of short fiction, did a bunch of stories for Stan Schmidt at *Analog*—now there's a learning experience! One he sent back because I didn't have the lunar calendar right. One he sent back because my engines were impossible—he said it was "an improbably neat trick. How would you do that?" And another he sent back because I didn't have the right type of fish. One person is not allowed to know all this, but he does! And you have to keep writing and working to get the answers to the questions that your reader (as voiced by Stan) is going to have. And that is a tremendous way to learn your craft. I regard him as a really great teacher . . .
>
> *Analog* isn't part of the main SF dialog any more, but we still need what is being said in *Analog*. Maybe not the strong libertarian philosophy, but it's a rarified atmosphere. It's the people who are still in love with the technology and still believe technology holds all the answers. If we can get the hardware working properly, all will be good and right with the world. Newton and Schroedinger and Einstein will be at the controls, and we'll have it all sorted out! We want to teach people to use the machines better, rather than taking into account humanity's needs, rather than teaching the technology to fit human beings more.
>
> We have to do both, which is why I think it's a shame *Analog*'s not fully into the SF dialog anymore.

"Kinds of Strangers" is a problem-solving story in the *Analog* tradition, with a satisfyingly spectacular action climax, but it also deals with human issues often left out of

SF stories. Why shouldn't a space crew marooned without hope of rescue experience depression?

Margot Rusch pulled open the hatch that led to the *Forty-Niner*'s sick bay. "Paul?" she asked around the tightness building in her throat. She pulled herself into the sterile, white module. She focused slowly on the center of the bay, not wanting to believe what she saw.

Paul's body, wide-eyed, pale-skinned, limp and lifeless floated in mid-air. A syringe hovered near his hand, pointing its needle toward the corpse as if making an accusation.

"Oh, Christ." Margot fumbled for a handhold.

The ventilation fans whirred to life. Their faint draft pushed against the corpse, sending it toward the far wall of the module. Margot caught the acrid scent of death's final indignities. Hard-won control shredded inside her, but there was nowhere to turn, no one to blame. There was only herself, the corpse and the flat, blank screen of the artificial intelligence interface.

"Damn it, Reggie, why didn't you do something!" she demanded, fully aware it was irrational to holler at the AI, but unable to help it.

"I did not know what to do," said Reggie softly from its terminal. "There are no case scenarios for this."

"No, there aren't," agreed Margot, wearily. "No, there sure as hell aren't."

The crew of the *Forty-Niner* had known for three months they were going to die. The seven of them were NASA's pride, returning from the first crewed expedition to the asteroid belt. They had opened a new frontier for humanity, on schedule and under budget. Two and a half years of their four-year mission were a raving success, and now they were headed home.

There had been a few problems, a few red lights. Grit from the asteroid belt had wormed its way into the works on the comm antenna and the radio telescope. No problem. Ed MacEvoy and Jean Kramer replaced the damaged parts in no time. This was a NASA project. They had backups and to spare. Even if the reaction control module, which was traditional methane/oxygen rockets used for course corrections, somehow failed completely all that would mean was cutting the project a little short. The long-distance flight was handled by the magnetic sail; a gigantic loop of high-temperature superconducting ceramic cable with a continuous stream of charged particles running through it. No matter what else happened, that would get them home.

"Margot?" Jean's voice came down the connector tube. "You OK?"

Margot tightened her grip on the handle and looked at the corpse as it turned lazily in the center of the bay. *No, I am not OK.*

The mag sail, however, had found a new way to fail. A combination of radiation and thermal insulation degradation raised the temperature too high and robbed hundreds of kilometers of ceramic cable of its superconductivity.

Once the mag sail had gone, the ship kept moving. Of course it kept moving. But it moved in a slow elliptical orbit going nowhere near its scheduled rendezvous with Earth. They could burn every atom of propellant they carried for the RCM and for the explorer boats, and they'd still be too far away for any of the Mars shuttles to reach by a factor of five. Frantic comm bursts to Houston brought no solutions. The *Forty-Niner* was stranded.

"Margot?" Jean again, calling down the connector.

"I'll be right up," Margot hoped Jean wouldn't hear how strangled her voice was.

Margot looked at the empty syringe suspended in mid-air. *Drunk all and left no friendly drop to help me after*. She swallowed hard. Stop it, *Margot. Do not even start going there*.

"Is there another request?" asked Reggie.

Margot bit her lip. "No. No more requests."

Margot pushed herself into the connector and dragged the hatch shut. She had the vague notion she should have done something for the body—closed its eyes or wrapped a sheet around it, or something, but she couldn't make herself turn around.

Margot's eyes burned. She'd flown four other missions with Paul. She'd sat up all night with him drinking espresso and swapping stories while the bigwigs debated the final crew roster for the *Forty-Niner*. They'd spent long hours on the flight out arguing politics and playing old jazz recordings. She'd thought she knew him, thought he would hang on with the rest of them.

Then again, she'd thought same of Ed and Tracy.

Tracy Costa, their chief mineralogist, had been the first to go. They hadn't known a thing about it, until Nick had caught a glimpse of the frozen corpse outside one of the port windows. Then, Ed had suffocated himself, even after he'd sworn to Jean he'd never leave her alone in this mess. Now, Paul.

Margot pulled herself from handhold to handhold up the tubular connector, past its cabinets and access panels. One small, triangular window looked out onto the vacuum, the infinitely patient darkness that waited for the rest of them to give up.

Stop it, Margot. She tore her gaze away from the window and concentrated on pulling herself forward.

The *Forty-Niner*'s command module was a combination of ship's bridge, comm center and central observatory. Right now, it held all of the remaining crew members. Their mission commander, Nicholas Deale, sandy-haired, dusky-skinned and dark-eyed, sat at one of Reggie's compact terminals, brooding over what he saw on the flat screen. Tom Merritt, who had gone from a florid, pink man to a paper-white ghost during the last couple of weeks, tapped at the controls for the radio telescope. He was an astronomer and the mission communications specialist. He was the one who made sure they all got their messages from home. The last living crew member was Jean. A few wisps of hair had come loose from her tight brown braid and they floated around her head, making her look even more worried and vulnerable. She stood at another terminal, typing in a perfunctory and distracted cadence.

Margot paused in the threshold, trying to marshal her thoughts and nerves. Nick glanced up at her. Margot opened her mouth, but her throat clamped tight around her words. Tom and Jean both turned to look at her. The remaining blood drained out of Tom's face.

"Paul?" he whispered.

Margot coughed. "Looks like he over-dosed himself."

Jean turned her head away, but not before Margot saw the struggle against tears fill her face. Both Nick's hands clenched into fists. Tom just looked at Nick with tired eyes and said, "Well, now what?"

Nick sighed. "OK, OK." He ran both hands through his hair. "I'll go take care of . . . the body. Tom, can you put a burst through to mission control? They'll want to notify his family quietly. I'll come up with the letter . . ."

This was pure Nick. Give everybody something to do, but oversee it all. When they'd reeled in the sail, he hadn't slept for two days helping Ed and Jean go over the cable an inch at a time, trying to find out if any sections were salvageable from which they could jury-rig a kind of stormsail. When that had proven hopeless, he'd still kept everybody as busy as possible. He milked every drop of encouraging news he could out of mission control. Plans were in the works. The whole world was praying for them. Comm bursts came in regularly from friends and family. A rescue attempt would be made. A way home would be found. All they had to do was hang on.

"In the meantime . . ." Nick went on

"In the meantime we wait for the radiation to eat our insides out," said Tom bitterly. "It's hopeless, Nick. We are all *dead*."

Nick shifted uneasily, crunching Velcro underfoot. "I'm still breathing and I don't plan to stop anytime soon."

A spasm of pure anger crossed Tom's features. "And what are you going to breathe when the scrubbers give out? Huh? What are you going to do when the water's gone? How about when the tumors start up?"

Tom, don't do this, thought Margot, but the words died in her throat, inadequate against the sudden red rage she saw in him. He was afraid of illness, of weakness. Well, weren't they all?

Paul's chief duty was keeping them all from getting cancer. One of the main hazards of lengthy space flight had always been long-term exposure to hard radiation. The mag sail, when it was functional, had created a shield from charged particles, which slowed the process down. Medical advancements had arisen to cover the damage that could be done by fast neutrons and gamma rays. Paul Luck maintained cultures of regenerative stem cells taken from each member of the crew. Every week, he measured pre-cancer indicators in key areas of the body. If the indicators were too high, he tracked down the "hot spots" and administered doses of the healthy cultured cells to remind bone, organ and skin how they were supposed to act and *voilà!* Healthy, cancer-free individual.

The Luck system was now, however, permanently down, and the only backup for that was the AI's medical expert system and the remaining crew's emergency training. Right now, that didn't seem like anything close to enough.

"We have time," Nick said evenly. "We do not have to give up. Come on, Tom. What would Carol say if she heard this?" Nick, Margot remembered, had been at Tom's wedding. They were friends, or at least, they had been friends.

"She'd say whatever the NASA shrinks told her to," snapped Tom. "And in the meantime," he drawled the word, "I get to watch her aging ten years for every day we're hanging up here. How much longer to I have to do this to her? How much longer are you going to make your family suffer?"

For the first time, Nick's composure cracked. His face tightened into a mask of pent-up rage and frustration, but his voice stayed level. "My family is going to know I died trying."

Tom looked smug. "At least you admit we're going to die."

"No . . ." began Jean.

"Help," said a strange, soft voice.

The crew all turned. The voice came from the AI terminal. It was Reggie.

"Incoming signal. No origination. Can't filter. Incoherent system flaw. Error three-six-five . . ."

A grind and clank reverberated through the hull. Reggie's voice cut off.

"Systems check!" barked Nick.

Margot kicked off the wall and flew to navigation control, her station. "I got garbage," said Tom from beside her. "Machine language, error babble. Reggie's gone nuts."

Margot shoved her velcro-bottomed boots into place and typed madly at her keyboard, bringing up the diagnostics. "All good here," she reported. She turned her head and looked out the main window, searching for the stars and the slightly steadier dots that were the planets. "Confirmed. Positioning systems up and running."

"Engineering looks OK," said Jean. "I'll go check the generators and report back." Nick gave her a sharp nod. She pulled herself free of her station and launched herself down the connector.

"You getting anything coherent?" Nick pushed himself over to hover behind Tom's shoulder.

"Nothing." From her station, Margot could just make out the streams of random symbols flashing past on Tom's terminal.

"Reggie, what's happening?" she whispered.

"I don't know," said the voice from her terminal. Margot jerked. "Unable to access exterior communications system. Multiple errors on internal nodes. Code corruption. Error. three-four . . ." the computer voice cut out again in a pulse of static, then another, then silence, followed by another quick static burst.

"Margot, can you see the comm antenna?" asked Tom, his hands still flashing across the keyboard.

Margot pressed her cheek against the cool window, craned her neck and squinted, trying to see along the *Forty-Niner*'s hull. "Barely, yeah."

"Can you make out its orientation?"

Margot squinted again. "Looks about ten degrees off-axis."

"It's moved," said Tom between static bursts. "That was the noise."

"All OK down in the power plant," Jean pulled herself back through the hatch and attached herself to her station. "Well, at least there's nothing new wrong . . ." she let the sentence trail off. "What is that?"

Margot and the others automatically paused to listen. Margot heard nothing but the steady hum of the ship and the bursts of static from Reggie. Quick pulses, one, one, two, one, two, one, one, one, two.

"A pattern?" said Nick.

"Mechanical failure," said Tom. "Has to be. Reggie just crashed."

One, one, two, one.

"You ever hear about anything crashing like this?" asked Margot.

One, two, one.

"Reggie? Level one diagnostic, report," said Nick.

One, one, two.

"Maybe we can get a coherent diagnostic out of one of the other expert systems," Margot suggested. Reggie wasn't a single processor. It was a web-work of six interconnected expert systems, each with their own area of concentration, just like the members of the crew. Terminals in different modules of the ship gave default access to differing expert systems.

"Maybe," said Nick. "Tom can try to track down the fault from here. You and Jean see if you can get an answer out of si . . . the power plant." Margot was quietly grateful he remembered what else was in sick bay before she had to remind him.

One, one, one.

Jean and Margot pulled themselves down the connector to the engineering compartment. As Jean had reported, all the indicators that had remained functional after they'd lost the sail reported green and go.

"At least it's a different crisis," Jean muttered as she brought up Reggie's terminal, the one she and Ed had spent hours behind when the mag sail went out.

"Remind me to tell you about my grandmother's stint on the old Mir sometime," said Margot. "Now there was an adventure."

Jean actually smiled and Margot felt a wash of gratitude. Someone in here was still who she thought they were.

Jean spoke to the terminal. "Reggie, we've got a massive fault in the exterior communications system. Can you analyze from this system?" As she spoke, Margot hit the intercom button on the wall to carry the answer to the command center.

"Massive disruption and multiple error processing," said Reggie, sounding even more mechanical than usual. "I will attempt to establish interface."

"Nick, you hear that?" Margot said to the intercom grill. She could just hear the static pulses coming from the command center as whispering echoes against the walls of the connector.

"Roger," came back Nick's voice.

"I am . . . getting reports of an external signal," said Reggie. "It is . . . there is . . . internal fault, internal fault, internal fault."

Jean shut the terminal's voice down. "What the hell?" she demanded of Margot. Margot just shook her head.

"External signal? How is that possible? This can't be a comm burst from Houston."

Margot's gaze drifted to the black triangle of the window. The echoes whispered in ones and twos.

"What's a language with only two components?" Margot asked.

Jean stared at her. "Binary."

"What do we, in essence, transmit from here when we do our comm bursts? What might somebody who didn't know any better try to send back to us?"

Jean's face went nearly as white as Tom's. "Margot, you're crazy."

Margot didn't bother to reply. She just pushed herself back up the connector to the bridge.

"Tom? Did you hear that?"

Tom didn't look up. He had a clip board and pen in his hands. As the static bursts rang out, he scribbled down a one for each single burst and a zero for each pair. He hung the board in mid-air, as if not caring where it went and his hands flew across the keyboard. "Oh yeah, I heard it."

Nick was back at his station, typing at his own keyboard. "The engineering ex-systems seem to be intact. Maybe we can get an analysis . . ." He hit a new series of keys. Around them, the static bursts continued. Margot's temples started to throb in time with the insistent pulses.

"There's something," Tom murmured to the terminal. His voice was tight, and there was an undercurrent in it Margot couldn't identify. "It'll take awhile to find out exactly what's happened. I've got Reggie recording," he looked straight at Nick. "As long as it doesn't crash all the way . . ."

Margot and Jean also turned to Nick. Margot thought she saw relief shining behind his eyes. *At least now he won't have to find us make-work to do.*

"All right," said Nick. "Tom, you keep working on the analysis of this . . . whatever it is. Jean, we need you to do a breakdown on Reggie. What's clean and what's contaminated?" he turned his dark, relieved eyes to Margot. "I'll take care of Paul. Margot . . ."

"I'll make sure all the peripherals are at the ready," said Margot. "We don't know what's happening next."

Nick nodded. Margot extracted herself from her station and followed Nick down the connector. She tried not to look as he worked the wheel on the sick bay hatch. She just let herself float past and made her way down to the cargo bay.

The cargo bay was actually a combination cargo hold and staging area. Here was where they stored the carefully locked-down canisters holding the ore samples. But here was also where they suited up for all their extra-vehicular activities. Just outside the airlock, the explorer boats waited, clamped tightly to the hull. They were small, light ships that looked like ungainly box kites stripped of their fabric. The explorers were barely more than frames with straps to hang sample containers, or sample gatherers, or astronauts from. They'd been designed for asteroid rendezvous and landing. Margot remembered the sensation of childlike glee when she got to take them in. She loved her work, her mission, her life, but that had been sheer fun.

For a brief moment there, they thought they might be able to use the explorers to tow the *Forty-Niner* into an orbit that would allow one of the Martian stations to mount a rescue, but Reggie's models had showed it to be impossible. The delta-vee just wasn't there. So the explorers sat out there, and she sat in here, along with the core samplers, the drillers, the explosive charges, doing nothing much but waiting to find out what happened next.

Hang on, Margot. Margot. Stay alive one minute longer, and one minute after that. That's the game now isn't it? Forget how to play and you'll be following Paul, Ed and Tracy.

She touched the intercom button so she could hear the static bursts and Tom's soft murmuring. It reminded her that something really was happening. A little warmth crept into her heart. A little light stirred in her mind. It was something, Tom had said so. It might just be help. Any kind of help.

Small tasks had kept her busy during the two weeks since they lost the sail, and small tasks kept her busy now. She made sure the seals on the ore carriers maintained their integrity. She ran computer checks on the explorers and made sure the fuel cells on the rovers were all at full capacity, that their tanks were charged and the seals were tight. Given the state Reggie was in, she was tempted to put on one of the bright yellow hardsuits and go out to do a manual check. She squashed the idea. She might be needed for something in here.

She counted all the air bottles for the suits and checked their pressure. You never knew. With Reggie acting up, they might have to do an EVA to point the antenna back toward Earth. If this last, strange hope proved to be false, she still hadn't said good-bye to her fiancé Jordan, and she wanted to. She didn't want to just leave him in silence.

Reggie's voice, coming from the intercom, startled her out of her thoughts. "Help," said Reggie. "Me. Help. Me. We. Thee. Help."

Margot flew up the connector. She was the last to reach the command module. She hung in the threshold, listening to Reggie blurt out words one at a time.

"There. Is. Help," said Reggie, clipped and harsh. The words picked up pace. "There is help. Comet. Pull. Tow. Yourself. There is a comet approaching within reach. You can tow yourself toward your worlds using this comet. It is possible. There is help."

Margot felt her jaw drop open.

Tom looked down at his clipboard. "What Reggie says, what we've got here is a binary transmission from an unknown source. Taking the single pulses as ones and the double pulses as zeroes gave us gibberish, but taking the single pulses as zero and the double pulses as one gave us some version of machine language. The engineering expert subsystem was able to decode it."

He gripped his pen tightly, obviously resisting the urge to throw it in frustration. "This is impossible, this can't be happening."

Margot shrugged. "Well, it is."

"It can't be," growled Tom. "Aliens who can create a machine language. Reggie can read inside of four hours? It couldn't happen."

"Unless they've been listening in on us for awhile," Jean pointed out.

Tom tapped the pen against the clipboard. One, two, one. "But how . . ."

Margot cut him off. She didn't want to hear it anymore. This was help, this was the possibility of life. Why was he trying to screw it up? "We've been beaming all kinds of junk out into space for over a hundred years. Maybe they've been listening that long." She felt his doubt dribbling into the corners of her mind. She shut it out by sheer force of will.

Jean folded her arms tightly across her torso. "At this point, I wouldn't care if it was demons from the seventh circle of Hell, just so long as it's out here."

"Jesus," breathed Nick softly. Then, in a more normal voice he said, "OK, Margot, you and Jean are going to have to do an EVA to turn the antenna around so we can send a burst to Houston."

"We can't tell Houston about this," said Jean sharply.

"What?" demanded Tom.

Jean hugged herself even tighter. "They'd think we'd all gone crazy up here."

"What's it matter what they think?" Nick spread his hands. "It's not like they can do anything about it."

"They can tell our families we've all taken the mental crash," said Jean flatly. "I, for one, do not want to make this any worse on my parents."

Nick nodded slowly. "OK," he said. "We keep this our little secret. But if we do make it back, mission control is going to have a cow."

Tom looked from Nick to Jean and Margot saw something hard and strange behind his eyes. He faced Margot. "This thing with the comet, could we really do something like this?"

Margot's mouth opened and closed. A short-period comet, swinging around the sun. If they caught it on its way back in . . . if they could attach a line (hundreds of kilometers of unused cable coiled on its drum against the hull of the ship) . . . theoretically, theoretically, it could pull them into a tighter orbit. The stresses would be incredible. Several gs worth. Would they be too much? How to make the attachment? Couldn't land on a comet, even if the explorers had the delta-vee. Comets were surrounded by dust and debris, they ejected gas jets, ice and rock. Asteroids were one thing. Asteroids were driftwood bobbing along through the void. Comets were alive and kicking.

But maybe . . . maybe . . .

"We'd need to find the thing," she said finally. "We'd need course, distance, speed. We'd need to know if we can use the RCM to push us near enough to take a shot at it. We'd probably need the explorers to do the actual work of attaching the *Forty-Niner* to the comet . . ."

"We could use the mag sail," said Jean. She gnawed slowly on her thumbnail. "All that cable, we could use it as a tow rope. But we'd need a harpoon, or something . . ."

"A harpoon?" said Tom incredulously.

Jean just nodded. "To attach the tether to the comet. Maybe we could use some of the explosives . . ."

Nick smiled, just a little. For the first time in days, Margot saw the muscles of his face relax. "Jean, let's get down to engineering and see what we can work up. Tom, you and Margot find our comet." His smile broadened. "And keep an ear out in case the neighbors have more to say."

"No problem," said Margot. She raised her arm and whistled. "Taxi!"

Jean, an old New Yorker, actually laughed at that, and Margot grinned at her.

Nick and Jean pulled themselves down the connector. Margot planted her feet on the velcro patch next to Tom.

"Let's see if we can still get to the database," she said, as she reached over his shoulder for the keys. "We should be able to narrow down . . ."

Tom did not lift his gaze from the screen. "It's a fake, Margot," he whispered.

Margot's hand froze halfway to the keyboard. "What?"

"Little green men my ass," he spat toward the console. "It's a fake. It's Nick. He's doing this to try to keep us going."

Margot felt the blood drain from her cheeks, and the hope from her heart. "How do you know?"

"I know." For the first time Tom looked at her. "He'd do anything right now to keep us in line, to keep giving orders, just so it doesn't look like he's out of options like the rest of us mere mortals."

Margot looked at his wide, angry blue eyes and saw the man she'd served with swallowed up by another stranger. "You got proof?"

Tom shook his head, but the certainty on his face did not waver. "I checked the logs for gaps, suspicious entries, virus tracks, extra encryptions. Nothing. Nobody on this ship could have made an invisible insertion, except me, or Nick."

"Unless it's not an insertion," said Margot. "Unless it's really a signal."

Tom snorted and contempt filled his soft words. "Now you're talking like Jean. She hasn't been with it since Ed went. Be real, Margot. If E.T.'s out there, why isn't he knocking on the door? Why's he sending cryptic messages about comets instead of offering us a lift?"

"It's *aliens*, I don't know," Margot spread her hands. "Maybe they're methane breathers. Maybe they're too far away. Space is big. Maybe they want to see if we can figure it out for our selves to see if we're worthy for membership in the Galactic Federation."

Tom's face twitched and Margot got the feeling he was suppressing a sneer. "OK, if it's aliens, how come I was able to figure out what they were saying so fast? They have a *NASA Machine Language for Dummies* book with them?"

Margot threw up her hands. "If Nick was faking this, why would he insist on a comm burst to mission control?"

Tom's jaw worked back and forth. "Because it'd look funny if he didn't and he knew Jean'd object and give him an out. She might even be in on it with him."

Margot clenched her fists. "It's a chance, Tom. It's even a decent chance, if we work the simulations right. It doesn't matter where the idea came from . . ."

"It does matter!" he whispered hoarsely. "It matters that we're being used. It matters that he doesn't trust us to hear him out so he's got to invent alien overlords."

"So, report him when we get home," said Margot, exasperation filling her breathy exclamation.

"We're not going to get home," Tom slammed his fist against the console. "We're going to die. This is all a stupid game to keep us from killing ourselves too soon. He's determined we are not going to die until he's good and ready."

Margot leaned in close, until she could see every pore in Tom's bloodless white cheeks.

"You listen to me," she breathed. "You want to kill yourself? Hit the sick bay. I'm sure Paul left behind something you can O.D. on. Maybe you're right, maybe how we go out is the only choice left. But I think we can use the delta-vee from the comet to tow us into a tighter orbit. I'm going to try, and I may die trying, but that's my choice. What are you going to do? Which part of that stubborn idiot head are you going to listen too? Huh?" She grabbed his collar. "If it is Nick doing this, I agree, it's a stupid ploy. But so what? It's the first good idea we've had in over a month. Are you going to let your pride kill you?"

Tom swatted her hand away. "I am not going to let him treat me like a fool or a child."

Tom lifted up first one foot then the other. He twisted in the air and swam toward the connector. Margot hung her head and let him go.

Give him some time to stew and then go after him. She planted herself squarely in front of his station. "Reggie?"

"Functioning," replied the AI.

"We need to do some speculation here," she rubbed her forehead. "I need you to pull up any databases we've got on comets. Specifically I need any that are passing within a thousand kilometers of the *Forty-Niner's* projected position anytime within the next several months."

A static burst sounded from the speaker as if Reggie were coughing. "Several is not specific."

"Six months then. Add in the possibility of a full or partial RCM burn for course correction to bring us within the cometary path. Can you do that?"

Two more quick bursts. "I can try," said Reggie.

That's all any of us can do right now.

"Searching."

Margot sat back to wait. She listened to the hum of the ship and the sound of her own breathing. No other sounds. She couldn't hear Nick and Jean down in engineering. She couldn't hear Tom anywhere. Worry spiked in the back of her mind. What if he was taking the quick way out? What if he was angry enough to take Nick out instead?

No, she shook her head. *Tom's just on edge. They're friends.*

Were they? She remembered the stranger looking out of Tom's eyes. Would that stranger recognize Nick? Would Nick recognize him? She glanced nervously over her shoulder. No one floated in the connector. She looked back at the screen. Reggie had a list up—names, orbital parameters, current locations, sizes, with an option to display orbital plots and position relative to the *Forty-Niner.* Highlighted at the top was Comet Kowalski-Rice.

Sounds like a breakfast cereal. Margot glanced over her shoulder again. The connector was still empty. The ship was still silent.

Kowalski-Rice was a periodic comet, with a nucleus estimated to be three kilometers long and between one and three kilometers wide. It had passed its aphelion and was headed back toward the Sun. Right now it was 2.9 million kilometers from the *Forty-Niner*, but it was getting closer. Margot brought up the orbital plot and did a quick calculation.

We burn fifty . . . OK say sixty to be on the safe side, percent of the remaining propellant we can bring our orbit within seven hundred-fifty kilometers of the comet. Take about . . . She ran the equations in her head. She could double check them with Reggie or Nick, whoever turned out to be more reliable. *Bring us there in about a hundred and fifty-nine hours, with the comet going approximately two kilometers per second relative to the ship. This could work. This could work.*

Silence, except for the steady hum of the ship and her own breathing.

Margot swore. *This is no good.* "Reggie? Do you know where Tom is?"

"Tom Merritt is in the sick bay."

"No!" Margot yanked both feet up and kicked off the console. "Nick! Jean!" she shouted. "Sick bay! Now!"

She reached sick bay first. She wrenched the wheel around and threw the hatch open. A little red sphere drifted out toward her face. Margot swatted at it reflexively and it broke against her hand, scattering dark red motes in a dozen directions.

Tom had fastened himself to the examining table and sliced his throat. Clouds of burgundy bubbles rose from his neck, knocking against a pair of scissors and sending them spinning.

"Tom!" Margot dove forward and pressed her fingers against his wound. Panting, she tried to think back to her emergency medical training. *Dark red, not bright, oozing, not spurting, missed the carotid artery, cut a bunch of veins . . . Tom, you idiot, you're so far gone you can't even kill yourself right.*

Events blurred. It seemed like Nick, Jean and Reggie were all shouting at once. A pad got shoved into her hand to help staunch the blood. The table was tilted to elevate his head. Reggie droned on clear and concise directions for covering the long, thin wound with layered sealants. Nick's and Jean's hands shook as they worked. Blood and tears stung Margot's eyes. When they were done, Tom was still strapped to the table, unconscious and dead white, but breathing. The medical ex-system was obviously still working. Reggie had no problem reading from the various pads and probes they had stuck to him. It was giving him good odds on survival, despite the blood loss.

"Let's get out of here," said Nick. "We can vacuum this up when we've had a chance to catch our breath."

Jean didn't argue, she just headed for the hatch. Margot had the distinct feeling she wanted to crawl into a corner and be quietly sick.

Margot followed Nick and Jean out and swung the hatch shut. She wanted to be able to talk without getting a mouthful of blood.

"God," Nick ran both hands through his hair. "I cannot believe it, I cannot believe he did this." Unfamiliar indecision showed on his face. Margot turned her gaze away. Another stranger. Just one more. Like Tom, like the others.

No! she wanted to scream. *Not you. I know you! You recommended me for this mission. You have a great poker face and you sing country-western so loud in the shower the soundproofing can't keep it in! You keep all the stats on your kids sports teams displayed as the default screen on your handheld! Your wife's the only woman you've ever been with! I know Nicholas Alexander Deale!*

But she did not know the person torn with weariness, anger and doubt who looked out of Nick's eyes. The one who might be a liar on a scale she'd never imagined. How long before that stranger took Nick completely over?

Margot looked at Jean. Blood splotched her face, hands, hair and coveralls. Fear haunted her bruised-looking eyes. Fear brought the stranger. Jean would go next. The stranger would have them all. Tom was right. They were all dead. Only the strangers and Margot Rusch lived.

"What is it, Margot?" asked Nick.

What do I say? Which "it" do I pick? Who let the stranger into Tom? Me or you? She licked her lips. Well, it does not get me. It does not get me.

"Nothing." Margot grabbed a handhold and pulled herself toward the command center. "I'm going to find that comet."

After all, that was what the strangers wanted her to do. She had to do what they said. If she didn't . . . look what they did to Tom. Who knew what they'd do to her?

They do not get me.

* * *

"Here it comes, Margot," the voice that used to be Nick's crackled through her helmet's intercom.

Margot turned in her straps, and there it came. Actually, Kowalski-Rice had been visible to the naked eye for the past two days. The comet was ungainly and beautiful at the same time. A dirty snowball tumbling through the darkness surrounded by a sparkling well fit for an angel's bride. It was huge—a living, shining island, coal black and ice white. Margot's hands tightened on the twin joy sticks that were the directional control for the explorer.

They had planned the maneuver out so carefully and modeled it so thoroughly. She had to give the strangers who walked as Nick and Jean credit. They were very good at what they did.

Jean's stranger had cobbled together the "harpoon" from drill shafts, explosives and hope. The grappling shaft had a timed explosive mounted on it and a solid propellant shell around it. When Margot pulled the pin, the propellant would ignite and burn for one minute to drive the harpoon to the comet. At one minute ten seconds the explosive would blow, driving the barbed head deep into the comet's hide. It had taken all of them to unwind and detach the mag sail cable from the drum and then rewind it, as if they were reeling in a gigantic fishing line. The very end of that cable had been welded to the harpoon using all the vacuum glue and tape Jean's stranger could lay her hands on. Jean's stranger had spent hours out on the hull, readjusting the tension on the cable drum so the pay out would be smooth.

Margot would launch the harpoon into the comet. The cable would pay out. Once the harpoon struck, the friction of the cable unwinding against the barrel would accelerate the *Forty-Niner*, and Margot in the explorer, which was tethered to the *Forty-Niner* by the cables that used to be the shroud lines for the mag sail. The more the cable unwound, the faster the ships would accelerate. Finally, the cable would run out. The comet would shoot forward with its leash trailing behind it, and the *Forty-Niner* and the strangers would fly free toward an areobraking rendezvous with Mars, and a rescue by NASA.

At least, that's what they said would happen. They might be lying. There was no way to tell. But if Margot refused to go along, they'd probably just kill her. She had to play. She had to act like she believed they were who they said they were. It was her only chance.

She tried to tell herself it didn't matter. She tried to believe what she'd told Tom, who they still, miraculously, let live, that it didn't matter who'd come up with the idea—aliens, the strangers, it didn't matter. If Nick and Jean, and Tracy and Ed, and Paul and even Tom finally were overcome by the strangers, it didn't really matter. What mattered was getting home. If she could get home, she could warn everyone.

But first she had to get home. She, Margot Rusch, had to get home.

"Better get ready, Margot," said Nick's stranger. "It's all on you."

So it is. And you hate that, don't you? I could mess up all your plans and you know it, but you can't get me. Not out here you can't.

Margot squeezed the stick, goosing the engine. Silently, her little frame ship angled to starboard, sliding gingerly closer to the wandering mountain of coal black ice and stone. Behind her, the three shining silver tethers that attached the explorer to the *Forty-Niner* paid out into the darkness.

She gave the comet's path a wide berth, but not so wide that she couldn't see how it lumbered, turning and shuddering as sparkling jets shot off its pocked hide.

I can do this. How many asteroids did we skirt? They were all falling too.

But not like this. She imagined the comet hissing and rumbling as it dashed forward. *They're making me do this. They don't care if I die.*

Black specks dusted her visor. She wiped at them. She glanced behind to see that the tethers were moving smoothly. The comet was almost in front of her. Black ice, black stone and the sparkling white coma surmounted the darkness.

Suddenly, the rover shuddered and Margot jerked in her straps. A stone careened off the frame ship and shot past her head.

That was a warning shot. That was them . . . No, no, they can't get me out here, but the comet can. Keep your mind on the comet, Margot. Don't think about them.

The *Forty-Niner* was below and behind her now. The comet was receding. The coma filled the vacuum, shining like a snow blowing in the sunlight. Margot pitched the rover up and around, until the comet was flying away from her, but she was not in the thick of its tail.

For a moment, she was nothing but a pilot and she smiled.

Perfect deflection shot. Fire this baby right up its tailpipe.

The strangers had mounted the harpoon on the explorer's fore starboard landing strut and attached the launch pin to the console. Margot fumbled for the thick, metal pin and its trailing wire.

Well, just call me Ishmael, she thought, suppressing a giggle. *There she is, Captain Ahab! There be the great white whale!*

"Margot . . ." began Nick's stranger.

"Don't push," she snapped. *Don't push. I might decide not to do this.*

I could. I could not do this. I could leave the strangers out here. Never have to bring them home. Never have to hurt my friends' families by showing them what's happened.

But I want to go home. Forgive me, Carol. Margot Rusch has to get home.

Margot grit her teeth. Ice crystals drifted past her. The comet retreated on its lumbering path, inanimate, or at least oblivious of their presence and their need.

Margot pulled the pin on the harpoon.

The recoil vibrated through the frame. The harpoon shot forward, hard, fast and straight. The tether vanished into the thick of the coma, lost in the shining veil of ice.

A jet of ice crystals exploded into the night. The comet rolled away as if wounded. The tethers on their reel played out into the void. Margot bit her lip. The tether was the key. If it released too fast, got tangled, or broke, it was over, all of it.

"Margot! Report!" demanded Nick's stranger.

"Tether holding steady," replied Margot reflexively. "Pay out looks good."

You'll get home. To Nick's home. That's what you care about.

The explorer shuddered. A sudden intense cold burned Margot's shin. A red warning light flashed on her visor screen.

No!

A black gash cut across her gleaming yellow suit. The joints at knee and ankle sealed off automatically. Margot fumbled for the roll of sealant tape on her belt. As she did, the explorer began to slide backward, away from the comet, toward the *Forty-Niner* to the limit of the tether. The movement dragged her back against her straps. Her glove gripped the tape reel. Pain bit deep.

Hang on, hang on. Lose the tape and you're gone. You're all gone. The stranger'll have you if you lose the tape.

The tug grew stronger. Margot felt her body shoved backward to the limits of its straps. A weight pressed hard against her ribs, her throat, her heart. After years of zero g, the acceleration gripped her hard and squeezed until her breath came fast and shallow.

Ahead of her, the *Forty-Niner* began to swing. A slow, sinuous movement that transmitted itself along the tether. It pulled the explorer to starboard, tilting her personal world, confusing her further, adding to the pain that screamed through every nerve.

Slowly, slowly she pulled the roll of tape from her belt. She grasped it in both clumsy, gloved hands. The explorer shimmied. Her body bounced up, then down, hard enough to jar her. The tape slipped. Margot screamed involuntarily and clung to it so hard she felt the flimsy reel crumple.

"Margot?" Jean's stranger. "Margot? What's happening?"

"Don't unstrap!" came back Nick's stranger. "Jean, stay where you are."

Right, right. Why risk anything for me? I'm not a stranger.

She leaned forward as if leaning into a gale wind. Black spots danced in front of her vision. She saw red through the gash, as if her leg glowed with its pain. She jounced and shuddered. More hits. The explorer was taking more hits from cometary debris. She couldn't steady her hands enough to lay down the tape.

Margot bit her lip until she tasted blood. She pressed the tape reel against the black gash, pushed the release button down and pulled, hard. A strip of clean white tape covered the black scoring.

The red light on her suit display turned green and the joints unsealed. Her suit was whole again.

Margot let herself fall backward, gasping for air, gasping for calm against the pain. Her left leg from ankle to knee would be one gigantic blood blister. But she was alive. The stranger hadn't got her yet. She hugged the tape to her chest. The *Forty-Niner* started swinging slowly back to port. Gravity leaned hard against her. Her heart labored, as if trying to pump sideways. Her stomach heaved. Her whole body strained against the straps.

She closed her eyes and tried to reach outward with every nerve, trying to feel the clamps and catches as she could her fingers and toes, wishing she could hear something, anything, a straining, a snapping. All there was was silence and the unbearable pressure driving her ribs into her lungs.

"*Forty-Niner* to Explorer One." Nick's stranger. What did he want? To find out if her stranger had swallowed her yet?

Not yet, Sir. Not yet.

"Margot? Margot, it looks like you're venting something. Report."

Venting? Margot's gaze jerked down to the monitor between her flight sticks. Red lights flashed. She didn't need to read the message. The diagram showed everything. The methane tank had been hit and all her fuel was streaming out into the void, leaving nothing at all for her to use to guide the explorer back to *Forty-Niner*.

She was stuck. She would hang out here until her air ran out. She was dead all over again.

All at once, the vibrations ceased. She was flying smooth and free, gliding like a bird on a sea wind with only the most gentle roll to perturb her flight.

"We have tether release!" cried Jean's stranger.

Margot looked up. A silver line lashed through the clean, sparkling white of the coma.

Tether release. They'd done it. It had worked. The strangers were all on their way home. She looked again at her her own fountain of crystals streaming out behind her, a comet's tail in miniature.

That roll'll get worse. They'll have to correct for it. They'll have to fire the rockets and catch me in the blast and tell Jordan and mission control how sorry they were.

Nick's stranger spoke to her again. "Margot, we gotta get you in here. If your fuel's gone, can you haul on the tether? Margot?"

"She's not receiving, Nick. The headset must be out. I gotta get down there."

All gone. Nothing to do. Pain throbbed in her head, crowding out her thoughts.

"Margot, pull!"

She couldn't move. Pain, bright and sharp, burned through her. All she could do was watch the crystal stream of her fuel drift away into the vacuum.

Margot Rusch is dead.

"Margot! Answer me! Pull, Margot!"

She's been dead for weeks.

"Come on, Margot. I got a green on your headset. Now answer me, damnit!"

The stranger wins. She got Margot Rusch after all.

"She didn't even get a chance to say good-by to Jordan. That's the bad part," she murmured.

"Margot?" came back the voice of Nick's stranger. "Margot, this is Nick. We're receiving you. Acknowledge."

Why are they still calling her Margot? They must know the stranger had her by now. She would have liked to know the stranger's name. Maybe she wouldn't mind burning to ash when they fire the correction burst. Margot Rusch certainly wouldn't mind. Margot Rusch was dead.

The explorer jerked. Mildly curious, Margot looked toward the *Forty-Niner* A figure in a bright yellow hard-suit leaned out of the ship's airlock. Its hands hauled on the tethers, as if they were hauling on curtain cords. The *Forty-Niner* drew minutely closer and the pair of ships began to spin ever so gently around their common center. Margot felt herself leaning the straps.

"Margot Rusch!" Nick's voice. Nick's stranger? A quick burst fired from the *Forty-Niner's* port nozzle. The spin slowed.

"Margot Rusch, wake up, you stupid fly-jock and pull!" Jean now. Jean's stranger? Jean's stranger trying to save Margot Rusch's stranger?

Jean trying to save her? But she was dead, as dead as Ed and Paul and Tracy and Tom.

No, not Tom. Tom's still alive.

What if I'm still alive?

Cold and pain inched up her leg and emptied into her knee, her thigh. Her head spun. Readings flashed in the corner of her helmet. The suit had sealed itself. Blood pressure was elevated, respiration fast, shallow, pulse elevated. Recommend termination of EVA.

"Margot Rusch, help her get your butt back in here!" shouted Nick.

Margot leaned as far forward as the straps would let her. Her gloved fingers grappled with the tether and snared some of the slack. Margot pulled. The *Forty-Niner* came a little closer. The suited figure became a little clearer.

"I knew you were still with us!" cried Jean, jubilantly. "Come on, Margot. Pull!"

Margot pulled. Her arms strained, her joints ached. Her suit flashed red warnings. The *Forty-Niner* moved closer. The spin tried to start, but another burst from the engines stalled it out again. Margot's breath grew harsh and echoing in the confining helmet. Her lungs burned. The cold pain reached her hip and started a new path down her fingers. The *Forty-Niner* filled her world now, its white skin, its instrumentation, its black stenciled letters and registry numbers.

And Jean. She could see Jean now, hauling on the tether as if it was her life depending on it. She could even see her eyes. Her eyes and herself, her soul, looking out through them. Margot knew if she looked at Nick she would see him too. Not strangers, not anymore. Maybe not ever.

They had done what they had done. Maybe Nick had faked that message, maybe they'd had help from unknown friends. They'd sort it all out when they got home. What mattered now was that they would get home, all of them, as they were. Not strangers, just themselves.

Margot grabbed up another length of tether and pulled.

THE GOOD RAT

Allen Steele

❀

Allen Steele's (born 1958) fiction often addresses the influence of science fiction on science and technology. (Gregory Benford is a minor character in his new novel, *Chronospace* [2001].) He came on the scene as a hard SF writer with his first novel in 1989, *Orbital Decay*. It was followed by *Clarke County, Space* (1990) and *Lunar Descent* (1991), which are also set between Earth and the Moon and belong in the same future history, which Steele calls the NearSpace series.

His short fiction is collected in three volumes, *Rude Astronauts* (1993), *All-American Alien Boy* (1996), and *Sex and Violence in Zero G* (1999), which collects the short fiction in the Near Space series and provides a list of the series, "all arranged in chronological order," he says on his Web site. "And for the first time I'm actually putting in the timeline, so somebody can flip to the appendix and look and see when these stories all occur. It's sort of my answer to Niven's *Tales of Known Space*, or even Heinlein's *Past through Tomorrow*." *The Encyclopedia of Science Fiction* says that although Steele "tends to export unchanged into space, decades hence, the tastes and habits of 1970s humanity, he manages to convey a verisimilitudinous sense of the daily round of those men and women who will be patching together the ferries, ships and space habitats necessary for the next steps into space." He has gone on to become one of the leading young hard SF writers of the 1990s, with a talent for realism and a penchant for portraying the daily, gritty problems of living and working in space in the future. His background is professional newspaper journalism and his fiction has been called "working class hard SF," because of his regular choice of ordinary people as characters (see also earlier Brin note), and because of his generally left-leaning politics. In an essay, "Hard Again" (*The New York Review of Science Fiction*, 1992), he said:

> I find it fascinating to work in this environment. This is one of the reasons I continue to write short fiction: I feel like I'm writing for *Astounding* in the forties under Campbell! We're right in the middle of a second Golden Age. In twenty years or so, there are going to be historians and fans looking back at the 1990s and saying, "My god, there were giants walking the earth then! Take a look at what was going on in *Asimov's!* Jesus, there were classic stories in every issue! That's when all these great new writers were out there!"

"The Good Rat" is hard SF from *Analog* (though Steele most often published in *Asimov's* in the 1990s). It is an interesting contrast to Greg Bear's "Sisters." In the future there will be no more experimental animal subjects, only human volunteers. It's a living.

Get home from spending two weeks in Thailand and Nepal. Nice tan from lying on the beach at Koh Samui, duffle bag full of stuff picked up cheap on the street in

Kathmandu. Good vacation, but broke now. Money from mortgaging kidneys almost gone, mailbox full of bills and disconnect notices. Time to find work again.

Call agent, leave a message on her machine. She calls back that afternoon. We talk about the trip a little bit; tell her that I'm sending her a wooden mask. Likes that, but says she's busy trying to broker another couple of rats for experiments at Procter & Gamble. Asks why I'm calling.

Tell her I'm busted. Need work soon. Got bills to pay. She says, I'll work on it, get back to you soon, ciao, then hangs up on me. Figure I'll send her the ugliest mask in my bag.

Jet-lagged from spending last twenty-four hours on airplanes. Sleep a lot next two days, watch a lot of TV in between. Mom calls on Tuesday, asks me where I've been for last month. Says she's been trying to find me. Don't tell her about Koh Samui and Kathmandu. Tell her I'm in night school at local college. Remedial English and basic computer programming. Learning how to do stuff with computers and how to read. She likes that. Asks if I got a job yet. About to lie some more when phone clicks. Got another call coming in, I say. Gotta go, bye. Just as well. Hate lying to Mom.

Agent on the phone. Asks if my legs are in good shape. Hell yeah, I say. Just spent ten days hiking through the Annapurna region, you bet my legs are in good shape. What's the scoop?

She say, private test facility in Boston needs a rat for Phase One experiments. Some company developing over-the-counter ointment for foot blisters. Need someone in good physical condition to do treadmill stuff. Two week gig. Think you can handle it?

Dunno, I say. Got a few bruises on thighs from falling down on rocks a lot. How much they pay? A hundred bucks a day, she says, minus her fifteen percent commission. Not bad. Not great, but not bad either. Ask if they're buying the airplane ticket. She say, yeah, tourist class on Continental. I say, gee, I dunno, those bruises really hurt. First class on TWA would make them feel better. Says she'll get back to me, ciao, and hangs up.

Turn on TV, channel surf until I find some toons. Dumb coyote just fell off cliff again when agent calls back. She say, business class on TWA okay? Think about trying to score box-seat ticket for a Red Sox game, but decide not to push my luck. Bruises feel much better, I say. When do they want me?

She say two days, I say okay. Tickets coming by American Express tomorrow, she says, but don't tell them about bruises, all right? Got no bruises, I say. Just wanted to get decent seat on the plane.

Calls me a name and hangs up again. Doesn't even say ciao this time. Decide not to send her a mask at all. Let her go to Kathmandu and buy one herself.

Two days later. Get off plane at airport in Beantown. Been here before two years ago, when some other lab hired me to drink pink stuff for three days so scientists could look at what I pissed and puked. Like Boston. Nice city. Never figured out why they call it Beantown, though.

Skinny college kid at gate, holding cardboard sign with some word on it and my name below it. Walk up to him, ask if he's looking for me. Gives me funny look. He say, is this your name on the sign? I say, no, I'm Elmer Fudd, is he from the test facility?

Gets pissed. Asks for I.D. Show him my Sam's Club card. Got my picture on it, but he's still being a turd about it. Asks if I got a driver's license. Drop my duffel bag on his shoes, tell him I'm a busy man, let's go.

Takes me to garage where his Volvo is parked. No limo service this time. Must be cheap lab. Got limo service last time I did a job in Boston. Kid looks mad, though, so don't make Supreme Court case out of it.

Get stuck in tunnel traffic after leaving airport. Want to grab a nap in back seat, but the kid decides to make small talk. Asks me how it feels to be a rat.

Know what he's getting at. Heard it before. Say hey, dude, they pay me to get stuck with needles fifteen times a day, walk on treadmills, eat this, drink that, crap in a kidney tray and whizz in a bottle. It's a living, y'know?

Smiles. Thinks he's superior. Got a college degree that says so. He say, y'know, they used to do the same thing to dogs, monkeys, and rabbits before it got outlawed. How does it feel to be treated like an animal?

No problem, I say. You gotta a dog at home you really like? Maybe a cat? Then bring him over to your lab, make him do the stuff I do, and half as well. Then you tell me.

Then he goes and starts telling me about Nazi concentration camp experiments. Heard that before too, usually from guys who march and wave signs in front of labs. Same guys who got upset about dogs, monkeys and rabbits being used in experiments are now angry that people are being used instead. Sort of makes me wonder why he's working for a company that does human experiments if he thinks they're wrong. Maybe a college education isn't such a great thing after all, if you have to do something you don't believe in.

Hey, the Nazis didn't ask for volunteers, I say, and they didn't pay them either. There's a difference. Just got back from spending two weeks in Nepal, hiking the lower Himalayas. Where'd you spend your last vacation?

Gets bent out of shape over that. Tells me how much he makes each year, before taxes. Tell him how much I make each year, after taxes. Free medical care and all the vacation time I want, too.

That shuts him up. Make the rest of the trip in peace.

Kid drives me to big old brick building overlooking the Charles River. Looks like it might have once been a factory. Usual bunch of demonstrators hanging out in the parking lot. Raining now, so they look cold and wet. Courts say they have to stay fifty feet away from the entrance. Can't read their signs. Wouldn't mean diddly to me even if I could. That's my job they're protesting, so if they catch the flu, they better not come crying to me, because I'm probably the guy who tested the medicine they'll have to take.

Stop at front desk to present I.D., get name badge. Leave my bags with security guard. Ride up elevator to sixth floor. Place looks better on the inside. Plaster walls, tile floors, glass doors, everything painted white and grey. Offices have carpets, new furniture, hanging plants, computers on every desk.

First stop is the clinic. Woman doctor tests my reflexes, looks in my ears, checks my eyes, takes a blood sample, gives me a little bottle and points to the bathroom. Give her a full bottle a few minutes later, smile, ask what she's doing two weeks from now. Doesn't smile back. Thanks me for my urine.

Kid takes me down the hall to another office. Chief scientist waiting for me. Skinny guy with glasses, bald head and long bushy beard. Stands up and sticks out his hand, tells me his name. Can't remember it five minutes later. Think of him as Dr. Bighead. Just another guy in a white coat. Doesn't matter what his name is, so long as he writes it at the bottom of my paycheck.

Dr. Bighead offers me coffee. Ask for water instead. Kid goes to get me a glass of water, and Dr. Bighead starts telling me about the experiment.

Don't understand half the shit he says. It's scientific. Goes right over my head. Listen politely and nod my head at the right times, like a good rat.

Comes down to this. Some drug company hired his lab to do Phase One tests for its new product. It's a lotion to relieve foot blisters. No brand-name for it yet. Experiment calls for me to walk a treadmill for eight hours the first day with a one-hour break for lunch, or at least until I collect a nice bunch of blisters on the soles of my feet. Then they'll apply an ointment to my aching doggies, let me rest for twelve hours, but put me on the treadmill again the next day. This will be repeated every other day for the next two weeks.

Do I get paid for the days I'm not on the treadmill?

Of course, he says, but you have to stay here at the test facility. Got a private room in the dorm for you upstairs. Private cafeteria and rec room, too.

Does it have a pool table?

Got a really nice pool table, he says. Also a VCR and a library. Computer, too, but no fax or modem. Company has strict policy against test participants being permitted open contact with outside world. Phone calls allowed, but they're monitored by security operators. Can receive forwarded mail, but all outgoing mail has to be read by a staff member first.

Nod. Been through this before. Most test facilities work this way. Sounds reasonable, I say.

When you're not on the treadmill, he says, you have to be in bed or in a wheelchair. No standing or walking, except when you're in the shower or going to the bathroom.

Shrug. Not a big deal. Once lay in bed for three days, doing nothing but watch old Flintstones cartoons on closed-circuit TV. Some kind of psychiatric experiment for UCLA. Ready to shout yabba-dabba-do and hump Betty Rubble by the time it was over. After that, there's nothing I can't do.

Dr. Bighead stops smiling now. Folds hands together on desk. Time for the serious stuff now.

The ointment we put on your feet may not be the final product, he says. May have to try different variations on the same formula. Side-effects may include persistent itching, reddening or flaking of the skin, minor swelling. Computer simulations of the product have produced none of these results, but this is the first time the product has undergone Phase One testing.

Nod. Been there, done that.

Goes on. Tells me that there's another three other volunteers doing the same experiment. Three of us will be the test subjects, the other one the control subject who receives a placebo. We won't know in advance who gets the product and who gets the placebo. Do I understand?

Test subjects, control subjects, placebos, and my feet may rot and fall off before this is all over. Got it, Doc. Sounds cool.

Dr. Bighead goes on. If any of this bothers me, I can leave now, and his company will pay me a hundred dollars for one day of my time and supply me with airfare back home. However, if I chicken out during the test period, or if I'm caught trying to wash off the ointment, they'll throw me out of the experiment and I won't be paid anything.

Yeah, uh-huh. He has to tell me this because of the way the laws are written. Never chickened out before, I say. Sounds great to me. When do we get started?

Dr. Bighead grins. Likes a nice, cooperative rat. Tomorrow morning, he says. Eight o'clock sharp.

Ask if I can go catch a little night-life tonight. Frowns. Tells me I may have to submit another urine sample if I do so. Nod my head. No problem. He shrugs. Sure, so long as you're back by midnight. After that, you're in here until we're through with the experiment.

No problem.

Spend another hour with contracts and release forms. Dr. Bighead not surprised that I don't read very well. Must have seen the file my agent faxed his company. Make him read everything aloud, while I get it all on the little CD recorder I brought with me. Agent taught me to do that. Means we can sue his company if it pulls any funny stuff. Maybe this rat can't read, but he's still got rights.

Everything sounds cool. Sign all the legal stuff. Dr. Bighead gives me plastic wristband and watches me put it around my left wrist, then lets me go. Notice that he doesn't shake hands again. Maybe afraid he'll catch functional illiteracy.

Same kid waiting outside. Takes me up to dorm on the seventh floor.

Looks like a hospital ward. No windows. Six private rooms surrounding a rec area. Small cafeteria off to one side. Couple of tables, some chairs and sofas. Bookshelf full of old paperbacks and magazines. Fifty-two-inch flatscreen TV, loads of videos on the rack above it. Pay phone in the corner. Pool table, though it looks like a cheap one. Look up, spot fish-eye camera lens hidden in the ceiling.

Same as usual. Could be better, could be worse.

Room is small. Single bed, desk, closet. No windows here either, but at least it's got a private bathroom. Count my blessings. No roommate this time. Last one snored, and the one before that went nuts six days into the experiment and was punted.

My bag is on the bed. Notice zipper is partly open. Been searched to make sure I didn't bring in any booze, dope, butts, or cellular phones.

Kid tells me he's got to go. Reminds me not to leave without my badge. See you tomorrow, I say.

Unpack bag, leave room. Want to get a bite to eat and check out the night life.

Two people sitting in the rec room now, watching TV news. A guy and a woman. Guy looks like he's about thirty. Thin, long-haired, sparse beard. Paperback book spread open on his lap. Barely glances my way.

The woman is different. Another rat, but the most beautiful rat I've seen in a while. Long brown hair. Slender but got some muscles. Good-looking. My type.

Catch her eye as I walk past. Give her a nod. She nods back, smiles a little. Doesn't say anything. Just a nod and smile.

Think about that nod and smile all the way to the elevator.

Found a good hangout last time I was in Boston, over in Dorchester. Catch a rickshaw over there now.

Sign above the door says No * Allowed. First time I was here, someone had to read the name to me, then explain that the symbol in the middle is an asterisk. What part of your body looks like an asterisk? Still don't get it, I say. Laughs and says, bend over, stick your head between your legs and look harder. Get it now, I say.

Can smoke a butt inside wherever you want, if you can find a butt to smoke these days. Fifty-six brands of beer. Not served only in the basement, but at your table if you want. Hamburgers, hot dogs, chicken-fried steak and onion rings on the menu. No tofu pizza or lentil soup. Framed nude photos of Madonna, Keith Moon, Cindy Crawford, and Sylvester Stallone on the walls. Antique Wurlitzer jukebox loaded with stuff that can't be sold without a parental warning sticker on the cover.

No screaming kids, either.

Cops would shut down this place if most people knew it existed. Or maybe not. Several guys hanging out at the bar look like off-duty cops. Cops need a place to have a smoke and drink, too, y'know.

Good bar. Should be a place like this in every city. Once there was, before everyone took offense to everything and no one could stay out of other people's business. Laws got passed to make sure that you had to live in smoke-free, low-cholesterol, non-alcoholic, child-safe environments. Now you have to go slumming to find a place where no *s are allowed.

Cover charge, tonight, though. Can't have everything.

Find seat near the stage, order ginger ale, watch some nuevo-punk band ruin old Romantics and Clash numbers. It's Boston, so they're obligated do something by the Cars. Probably toddlers when Ric Ocasek was blowing speakers.

Usually have a blowout the night before an experiment. Never binge, but have good fun anyway. Lots of babes here tonight, most of them with guys who look like they should be home wanking off on Internet. A couple of their girlfriends throw gimme looks in my direction.

Should do something about it. Still early. Can always get a hotel room for a few hours. Use the line about being a biomedical research expert in town for an important conference. Babes love sleeping with doctors.

Heart not into it. Keep thinking about the girl in the rec room. Don't know why. Just another rat.

Find myself looking around every time the door opens, hoping she'll walk in.

Leave before eleven o'clock, alone for once. Tell myself it's because the band was dick. Know better.

On the way back to the test center, wonder if Mom's not right. Maybe time to get a job. Learn how to read, too.

Bet she knows how to read.

Eight o'clock next morning. Come downstairs wearing my rat gear. Gym shorts, football jersey, sneaks. Time to go to work for the advancement of science and all mankind.

Dr. Bighead is waiting for me. Not as friendly as he was yesterday. Takes me to clinic and waits while I fill another bottle for the doctor. Escorts me to the lab.

Four power treadmills set next to each other on one side of the room, with a TV hanging from the ceiling above them. Stupid purple dinosaur show on the tube. Sound turned down low. College kids wearing white coats sitting in front of computers on other end of the room. One of them is the guy who picked me up at the airport. Glances up for a second when I come in. Doesn't wave back. Just looks at his screen again, taps fingers on his keyboard. Too cool to talk to rats now.

Two other rats sitting in plastic chairs. Already wired up, watching Barney, waiting to go. Walk over to meet them. One is the skinny longhair I saw last night. Wearing old Lollapolooza shirt. Name's Doug. Other guy looks like he works out a lot. Big dude. Shaved head, nose ring, truck stop tattoo on right forearm. Says his name is Phil.

Doug looks bored, Phil nervous. Everyone swats hands. We're the rat patrol, cruising for a bruising.

Time to get wired. Sit on table, take off shirt, let one of the kids tape electrodes all over me. Head, neck, chest, back, thighs, ankles. So much as twitch and lines jump all over the computer screens. Somebody asks what I had for breakfast, when was the last time I went to the bathroom. Writes it all down on a clipboard.

Phil asks if the TV has cable. Please change the channel, he says, it's giving me a headache. No one pays attention to him. Finally gets up and switches over to *The Today Show*. Dr. Bighead gives him the eye. Wonder if this is the first time Phil has ever been on the rat patrol. If the scientists want you to watch Barney, then you do it, no questions asked. Could be part of the experiment for all you know.

Don't mess with the scientists. Everyone knows that.

Last rat finally arrives. No surprise, it's the girl I saw last night. Wearing one-piece workout suit. Thank you, Lord, for giving us the guy who invented Spandex. Phil and Doug look ready to swallow their tongues when they see her. Guy who tapes electrodes to her gets a woody under his lab coat when he goes to work on her chest and thighs.

She ignores his hands, just like she ignores everyone else, including me and the boys. She's a true-blue, all-American, professional rat.

Time to mount the treadmills. Dr. Bighead makes a performance about us getting on the proper machines, as if it makes a difference. The girl is put on the machine to my left, with Doug on my right and Phil next to him.

Grasp the metal bar in front of me. Dr. Bighead checks to make sure that the computers are up and running, then he switches on the treadmills. Smooth rubber matt beneath my feet begins to roll at a slow pace, only about a foot or so every few seconds. My grandmother could walk faster than this.

Look over at the girl. She's watching Willard Scott talking to some guy dressed like a turkey. Asks Dr. Bighead if he'd turn up the volume. He say, no, it would just distract his team. Think he's pissed because Phil switched off the purple dinosaur.

Just as well. Gives us a chance to get acquainted.

She starts first. Asks me my name. Tell her. She nods, tells me hers. Sylvie Simms. Hi Sylvie, I say, nice to meet you.

Scientists murmur to each other behind our backs. Sylvie asks me where I'm from. She tells me she's from Columbus, Ohio.

C'mon, man, Phil says. Turn up the volume. Can't hear what he's saying about the weather.

Dr. Bighead ignores him.

Look over at Doug. Got a Walkman strapped to his waist. Eyes closed, head bobbing up and down. Grooving to something in his headphones as he keeps on trucking.

Been to Columbus, I say. Nice city. Got a great barbecue place downtown, right across the street from the civic center.

Sylvie laughs. Got a nice laugh. Asks if it's a restaurant with an Irish name. Yeah, I say, that's the one. Serves ribs with a sweet sauce. She knows the place, been there many times.

And so we're off and running. Or walking. Whatever.

Doug listens to rock bands on his Walkman, getting someone to change CDs for him every now and then. Phil stares at the TV, supplying his own dialogue for the stuff he can't hear, bitching about not being able to change the channel. A kid walks by every now and then with a bottle of water, letting us grab a quick sip through a plastic straw.

Sylvie and I talk to each other.

Learn a lot about Sylvie while waiting for the blisters to form. Single. Twenty-seven years old. Got a B.A. in elementary education from the same university where I got my start as a rat, but couldn't get a decent job. Public schools aren't hiring anyone who don't have a military service record, the privates only take people with master's degrees. Became a rat instead, been running for two years now. Still wishes she could teach school, but at least this way she's paying the rent.

Tell her about myself. Born here. Live there. Leave out part about not being able to read very well, but truthful about everything else. Four years as a rat after doing a stint in the Army. Tell her about other Phase One tests I've done, go on to talking about places I've gone hiking.

Gets interested in the last part. Asks me where I've been. Tell her about recent trek through Nepal, about the beach at Koh Samui where you can go swimming without running into floating garbage. About hiking to the glacier in New Zealand and the moors in Scotland and rain forest trails in Brazil.

You like to travel, she says.

Love to travel, I say. Not first-class, not like a tourist, but better this way. Get to see places I've never been before.

Asks what I do there. Just walk, I say. Walk and take pictures. Look at birds and animals. Just to be there, that's all.

Asks how I've been able to afford to do all this. Tell her about mortgaging my organs to organ banks.

Looks away. You sell your organs?

No, I say, I don't sell them. Mortgage them. Liver to a cloner in Tennessee, heart to an organ bank in Oregon, both lungs to a hospital to Texas. One kidney to Texas, the other to Minnesota . . .

Almost stops walking when she hears that. You'd sell them your whole body?

Shrug. Haven't sold everything yet, I say. Still haven't mortgaged corneas, skin, or veins. Saving them for last, when I'm too old to do rat duty and can't sell plasma, bone marrow or sperm anymore.

She blushes when I mention sperm. Pretend not to notice. She asks if I know what they're going to do with my organs when I'm dead.

Sure, I say. Someone at the morgue runs a scanner over the bar-code tattoo on my left arm. That tells them to put my body in a fridge and contact the nearest organ donor info center. All the mortgage-holders will be notified, and they'll fly in to claim whatever my agent negotiated to give them. Anything left over afterwards, the morgue puts it in the incinerator. Ashes to ashes and all the happy stuff.

Sylvie takes a deep breath. And that doesn't bother you?

Shrug. Naw, I say. Rather have somebody else get a second chance at life from my organs than having them rot in a coffin in the ground. While they're still mine, I can use the dough to go places I've never been before.

Treadmill is beginning to run just a little faster now. No longer walking at a granny pace. Dr. Bighead must be getting impatient. Wants to get some nice blisters on our feet by the end of the day.

Phil sweats heavily now. Complains about having to watch Sally Jesse instead of Oprah. Don't wanna watch that white whore, he says. C'mon, gimme that black bitch instead. Doug sweating hard, too, but just keeps walking. Asks for a Smashing Pumpkins CD, please. One of the kids changes his CD for him, but doesn't switch channels on the TV.

Couldn't do that, Sylvie says. Body too precious to me.

Body precious to me, too, I say, but it ain't me. Gone somewhere else when I'm dead. Just meat after that. Why not sell this and that while you're still around?

She's quiet for a long while. Stares at the TV instead. Sally Jesse is talking to someone who looks like a man dressed as a woman but looks like a woman trying to resemble a man, or something like that.

Maybe I shouldn't have told her what I think about organ mortgages. Being a rat is one thing, but putting your innards on the layaway plan is another. Some people don't get it, and some of the ones who get it don't like it.

Sylvie must know this stuff. All rats do. Most of us sign mortgages. So what's her problem?

Bell dings somewhere behind us. Time for lunch. Didn't even notice that it was noon yet. Dr. Bighead comes back in, turns off treadmills. Gets us to sit on examination tables and take off shoes. No blisters on our feet yet, but he still puts us in wheelchairs. Okay, he says, be back here by one o'clock.

Can't wait, Phil says.

Lunch ready for us in rec room. Chicken soup, grilled cheese sandwiches, tuna salad. Push our way down the service line, carrying trays on our laps, reaching up to get everything. Been in a wheelchair before, so has Doug and Sylvie, but Phil not used to it. Spills hot soup all over his lap, screams bloody murder.

Share a table with Sylvie. Newspapers on table for us to read. Intern brings us mail forwarded from home. Bills and junk for me, but Sylvie gets a postcard. Picture of tropical beach on the front.

Ask who it came from. Her brother, she says. Ask where her brother lives, and she passes me the postcard.

Pretend to read it. Only big word I know is Mexico. Always wanted to visit Mexico, I say. What does he do down there?

Hesitates. Business, she says.

Should shut up now, but don't. What kind of business?

Looks at me funny. Didn't you read the card?

Sure, sure, I say. Just asking.

Thinks about it a moment, then she tells me. Younger brother used to live in Minneapolis, but was busted by the feds early last year. Sold cartons of cigarettes smuggled from Mexico out of the back of his car. Smoking illegal in Minneapolis. Felony charge, his third for selling butts on the street. Three-strikes law means he goes to jail for life. For selling cigarettes.

Judge set bail at seven grand. Sylvie came up with the cash. Brother jumped bail, as she knew he would. Fled south, sought amnesty, went to work for Mexican tobacco company. Sends her postcard now and then, but hasn't seen him in almost two years.

That's tough, I say. She nods. Think about it a little. Question comes to mind. How did you come up with seven grand so fast?

Doesn't say anything for a minute, then she tells me.

Got it from mortgaging her corneas.

Five is the usual price, but she got seven on the overseas black market. When she dies, her eyes go to India. At least it kept my brother from going to prison, she says, but I can tell that isn't the point.

Sylvie doesn't want to be buried without her eyes.

She takes back the postcard, turns it over to look at the beach on the front. Kind of makes you want to visit Tijuana, doesn't it?

Tijuana looks like a great place, I say. Always wanted to go there. At least he's found a nice place to live.

Gives me long, hard look. Card wasn't sent from Tijuana, she says. It's from Mexico City, where he's living now. That's in the letter. Didn't you read it?

Oh, I say. Yeah, sure. Just forgot.

Doesn't say anything for a moment. Pulls over the newspaper, looks at the front page. Points to a headline. Says, isn't that a shame?

Look at picture next to it. Shows African woman with a dead baby in her arms, screaming at camera. Yeah, I say, that's tough. Hate it when I read news like that.

Sylvie taps a finger on the headline. Says here that the unemployment rate in Massachusetts is lowest in fifteen years, she says.

Oh yeah, I say. That's not what I meant. That's good news, yeah.

Pushes newspaper aside. Looks around to see if anyone is listening. Drops her voice to a whisper. You can't read, can you?

Face turns warm. No point in lying to her. She knows now.

Only a little, I say. Just enough to get by, like a menu or a plane ticket. Not enough to read her brother's postcard or a newspaper.

Feel stupid now. Want to get up and leave. Forget that I'm supposed to stay in the wheelchair, start to rise to my feet. Sylvie puts her hand on top of mine, makes me stay put.

It's okay, she says. Doesn't matter. Kind of suspected, but didn't know for sure until you asked me about what my brother said in his letter.

Still want to leave. Grab rubber wheels, start to push back from table.

C'mon, don't go away, she says. Didn't mean to embarrass you. Stay here.

Feel like an idiot, I say.

Sylvie shakes her head. Gives me that smile again. No, she say, you're not an idiot. You're just as smart as anyone else.

Look at her. She doesn't look away. Her eyes are owned by some company in India, but for a moment they belong only to me.

You can learn how to read, she says. You've just never had a teacher like me.

Get blisters on my feet by end of first day. Same for the other guys. Dr. Bighead very pleased. Never seen some one get so excited about blisters. Wonder if he's got a thing for feet.

Scientists take pictures of our feet, make notes on clipboard, then spread lotion on our soles. Pale green stuff. Feels like snot from a bad head cold, smells like a Christmas tree soaked in kerosene. Use eyedroppers to carefully measure the exact amount. Should have used paintbrushes instead.

Everyone gets theirs from different bottles. No idea if I got the test product or the placebo, but blisters feel a little better after they put it on.

Doesn't last long. Skin begins to itch after dinner. Not bad itch, but can't resist scratching at the bottom of my feet. Sort of like have chigger bites from walking in tall grass. Sylvie and Phil have the same thing, but Doug doesn't. Sits in corner of rec room, reading paperback book, never once touching his feet. Rest of us watch the tube and paw at our tootsies.

Guess we know who got the placebo.

No treadmill work the next day, but we go back down to the lab after breakfast and let the scientists examine us some more. Tell them about the itching while they draw blood samples. They nod, listen, take more pictures, make more notes, then put more green stuff on our feet.

Different formula this time. Now it's Extra Strength Green Stuff. Must be made out of fire ants. Nearly jump off the table. Sylvie hisses and screws up her eyes when they put it on her. Phil yells obscenities. Two guys have to grab him before he decks the kid who put it on his feet.

Feet still burning when we go back upstairs. Sylvie goes to her room. Doug picks up his book and reads. Phil mad as hell, pissing and moaning about Dr. Bighead. Says he only did this to get a little extra dough, didn't know they were going to put him in jail and torture him to death. Says he wants to go put his feet in a sink.

Don't do it, I say, it'll screw up the test. Tell him that trying to punch out a scientist is way uncool. Calm down, dude. Let's play some eight-ball. Get your mind off it.

Mumbles something under his breath, but says, yeah, okay, whatever.

Hard to shoot pool sitting in wheelchairs, but we manage for awhile. Phil can't get into it. Blows easy shots, scratches the cue ball twice. Sinks eight-ball when I've still got four stripes on the table. Loses temper. Slams his stick down on table, turns chair around and rolls off to his room. Slams the door.

Look up at lens in the ceiling. Know someone must be catching all this.

Go over to TV, turn it on, start watching Oprah. Sylvie comes over a little while later. Asks if I want to begin reading lessons.

Not much into it, I say. Wanna watch Oprah instead.

Gives me a look that could give a woody to a monk. C'mon, she says. Please. I'd really like it if you would.

Think maybe I can score some points with her this way, so I go along with it. What the hell. Maybe I might learn something. Okay, I say.

Turns off TV, wheels over to bookshelf, starts poking through it. Think she's going to grab a book or a magazine. Can't even read the titles of most of them. If she brings back Shakespeare or something like that, I'm outta here.

Picks up a bunch of newspapers from the bottom shelf. Puts them in her lap, hauls them over to a table, tells me to come over next to her.

Finds the funny pages. Asks me if I like comic strips. Naw, I say. Never really looked at them. Smiles and says she reads the funnies every morning. Best part of her day. She points to the one at the top of the first page. Here's one I like, she says. Tell me what this little kid is saying to the tiger.

That's how I start to learn how to read. Seeing what Calvin and Hobbs did today.

After lunch, we go down to the lab again for another checkup. Feet no longer burning, but the itch is back. Feet a little red. More blood samples, more photos, more notes. More ointment on our feet. Doesn't burn so much this time. Looks a little different, too. Must be New Improved Extra Strength Green Stuff.

Scientists notice something different when they look at Phil's feet. Spend a lot of time with him. Compare them to photos they took earlier. One of them takes a scalpel, scrapes a little bit of dead skin off the bottom of each foot, puts it in a dish, takes it out of the room.

Phil keeps saying, what's going on? What's the big deal? Gotta right to know.

Scientists say nothing to him. Examine Sylvie and Doug, spread more ointment on their feet, then let the three of us go back to the dorm. Tell Phil he has to stay behind. Say they want to conduct a more thorough examination.

Dr. Bighead walks past us while we're waiting for the elevator. Just says hi, nothing else. Goes straight to the lab, closes door behind him.

Phil screwed up, I say to Doug and Sylvie when we're alone in the elevator. Don't know how, but I think he screwed up.

Just nod. Know the score. Seen it before, too. People go crazy sometimes during a long test. Happens to new guys all time. Every now and then, some dumb rat gets washed down the gutter.

Return to rec room. Doug picks up his paperback, Sylvie and I go back to reading the funnies. Trying to figure out why Sarge just kicked Beetle in the butt when door opens and Phil comes in. Not riding a wheelchair now. Dr. Bighead and a security guard are right behind him.

Doesn't say much to us, just goes straight to his room and collects his bag. Leaves without saying goodbye or anything.

Dr. Bighead stays behind. Says that Phil was dismissed from the experiment because he scrubbed off the product. Also displayed lack of proper attitude. Won't be replaced because it's too late to do so without beginning the tests again.

We nod, say nothing. No point in telling him that we were expecting this. Warns us not to do the same thing. Phil isn't being paid for his time, he says, because he violated the terms of his contract.

Nod. No sir. We're good rats.

Apologizes for the inconvenience. Asks us if we need anything.

Sylvie raises her hand. Asks for some comic books. Dr. Bighead gives her a weird look, but nods his head. Promises to have some comic books sent up here by tomorrow. Then he leaves.

Doug looks up from his book as the door shuts behind him. Good, he says. Leaves more green stuff for us.

Two weeks go by fast.

Phase One tests sometimes take forever. Drives everyone crazy. This one should, because we're not on the treadmills every single day and have lots of time on our hands, but it doesn't.

For once, I'm doing something else besides staring at the tube. Usually spend hours lying on a couch in the rec room, watching one video after another, killing time until I go to the lab again.

But not now.

After work and on the off-days, I sit at a table with Sylvie, fighting my way through the funny pages.

Sometimes Doug helps, when Sylvie needs to sleep or when her feet are aching too much. Both are patient. Don't treat me like a kid or a retard or laugh when I can't figure out a long word, and help me pronounce it over and over again until I get it right. If it's something difficult, Sylvie describes what it means in plain English, or even draws a little picture. Take notes on stationery paper and study them at night until I fall asleep.

Able to get through the funny pages without much help after the first few days, then we start on the comic books Dr. Bighead got for us. *Archie* and *Jughead* at first, because they're simple. When Sylvie isn't around, Doug and I get into discussing who we'd rather shag, Betty or Veronica, but pretty soon I'm tackling *Batman* and the *X-Men*. Find out that the comics are much better than the movies.

Doug is a good teacher, but I prefer to be with Sylvie.

Funny thing happens. Start to make sense of the newspaper headlines. They're no longer alien to me. Discover that they actually mean something. Stuff in them that isn't on TV.

Then start to figure out titles on the covers of Doug's books. Know now that he likes science fiction and spy novels. Better than movies, he says, and I believe him when he tells me what they're about. Still can't read what's on the pages, because I still need pictures to help me understand the words, but for the first time I actually want to know what's in a book.

Hard to describe. Sort of like hiking through dense rain forest, where you can't see anything except shadows and you think it's night, and you try to stay on the trail because you don't know what's out there. Then you get above the treeline and there's a clearing. Sun is right over your head and it's warm and we can see for miles, mountains and ranges and plains all spread out before you, and it's so beautiful you want to spend the rest of your life here.

That's what it's like. All of a sudden, I'm not as stupid as I once thought I was.

One night, after everyone else has gone to bed and the lights are turned off, I find myself crying. Don't cry easily, because that's not the way I was brought up. Dad beat the crap out of me if he caught me doing so, call me a faggot and a little girlie-boy. No short or easy way to explain it, but that's sort of why he took me out of school, made me go to work in his garage. Said he wanted me to be a man, that he didn't want no godless liberals messing up my brain with books and ideas.

When he dropped dead with a socket wrench in his hand, I was eighteen. Only thing in my wallet was a draft card I couldn't read. Time in the army showed me the rest of the world and made me want to see more, but by then was too late to go back to school. After that, only choice I had to say alive and see the world was to become a rat. A rat whose body didn't belong to himself.

Something wrong when the law lets a human be a rat, because a rat has more respect than a human. Rats can't learn to read, but a human can. No one wants to spend money on schools, though. Rather spend it on building prisons, then putting people in there who sell cigarettes. Meanwhile, teachers have to go do things that they won't let rats do anymore.

Didn't cry that night for Sylvie or her brother, even though that was part of it. Cried for all the lost years of my life.

Spend few days trying to learn as much as I can, but can't get past one thing.

Sylvie.

Started to learn how to read because I wanted to shag her. Going along with her seemed like the easiest way of getting her into bed.

Can't do that during an experiment, because sex with other rats is a strict no-no in the standard contract. Seen other rats get punted for just being caught in someone else's room, even when both persons had their pants on. When tests are over and everyone's paid, though, there's nothing wrong with a little party time at the nearest no-tell motel.

Still want to sleep with her. Get a Jackson sometimes just sitting next to her in the rec room, while she's helping me get through some word I haven't seen before. Can't take my eyes off her when she's running the treadmill next to me.

Different situation now, though. Isn't just about getting Sylvie in some cheap motel for some hoy-hoy. Not even about learning how to read. Got some scary feelings about her.

Two days before the end of the tests. Alone together in the rec room, reading *Spider-Man* to each other. Ask her straight. Say, hey, why are you helping me like this?

Keeps looking at comic book, but flips back her hair and smiles a little. Because I'm a teacher, she says, and this is what I do. You're the first pupil I've had since college.

Plenty of winos in the park who don't know how to read, I say. Could always teach them. Why bother with me?

Gives me long look. Not angry, not cold. Can't quite make it out.

Because, she says, I've always wanted to visit Kathmandu, and maybe I've found someone who can take me there.

Can take you there, I say. Can take you to Nepal, Brazil, Ireland. Mexico to visit your brother, if you want.

Blushes. Looks away for a second, then back at me. Maybe you just want to take me to nearest hotel when we're done here, she says. I've done that. Wouldn't mind doing it again, either.

Shake my head. Like Kathmandu better, I say. Sunrise over Annapurna is incredible. Would love you to see it with me.

Love? Thought I was just teaching you how to read.

Look around to see if anyone is watching. No one there, but there must be someone behind the lens in the ceiling.

Hell with them. Put my hand under the table and find hers. One more word you've taught me, I say.

She smiles. Doesn't take her hand away. Finds a pen in her pocket, hands it to me, pushes some paper in front of me.

If you can write it, she says, I'll believe you.

Phase one test of the product pronounced a success on the final day. Last batch of Brand New Improved Green Stuff doesn't smell, doesn't itch, doesn't burn, and heals the blisters on our feet. Doesn't do a thing for our leg cramps, but that's beside the point.

Dr. Bighead thanks us, writes his name on the bottom of our checks. Tells us we've been wonderful test subjects. Hopes to work with us again soon. In fact, are you available next March? Scheduled test of new anti-depressant drug. Looking for subjects now. How about it?

Look at Sylvie. She's sitting next to me. Doesn't say anything. Look at the check. It's written on an account at the First Bank of Boston, and it's signed by Dr. Leonard Whyte, M.D.

Thank you, Dr. Whyte, I say. My agent will be in touch with you. Ciao.

A cab is waiting for us at the front door. We tell the driver to take us to the nearest hotel.

Three years have passed since Sylvie and I met in Boston. A few things are different now.

She finally managed to get me to use proper grammar instead of street talk. I'm still learning, but personal pronouns are no longer foreign to me, and it's no longer necessary to refer to all events in the present tense. To those of you who have patiently suffered through my broken English during this chronicle, I sincerely apologize. This was an attempt to portray the person I once was, before Sylvie came into my life.

We used the money earned during the Boston tests for a trip to Mexico City, where Sylvie got to see her brother for the first time in two years. Six months later, we flew to Nepal and made a trek through the Annapurna region, where I showed her a sunrise over the Himalayas. Since then we have gone on a safari in Kenya and rafted down the Amazon. Now we're planning a spring trip to northern Canada, above the Arctic circle. A little too cold for my taste, but she wants to see the Northern Lights.

Anything for my baby.

The first night in Kathmandu, I promised to give her the world that I knew in exchange for hers. She has made good by her promise, and I'm making good by mine.

Nonetheless, we're still rats.

We can't marry, because the labs that supply our income won't accept married couples as test subjects. Although we've been living together for almost three years now, we keep addresses in different cities, file separate tax returns and maintain our own bank accounts. Her mail is forwarded to my place, and only our agents know the difference. We'll probably never have children, or at least until we decide to surrender this strange freedom that we've found.

This freedom is not without price. I've mortgaged the last usable tissue in my body. Sylvie hasn't repossessed the rights to her corneas, despite her attempts to find a legal loophole that will allow her to do so, and although the time may come when she has to give up an organ or two, she insists that her body is her own.

More painful is the fact that, every so often, we have to spend several weeks each year participating in the Phase One tests. Sometimes they're the very same experiments, conducted simultaneously at the same test facility, so we have to pretend to be strangers.

I haven't quite become used to that, but it can't be helped.

But the money is good, the airfare is free, and we sometimes get to see old friends. We spent a week with Doug a couple of months ago, while doing hypothermia experiments in Colorado. He and I discussed favorite Jules Verne novels while sitting in tubs of ice water.

For all of that, though, I lead a satisfactory life. Sylvie and I have enough money to pay the bills, and we visit the most interesting places around the world. I have a woman who I love, my mother has stopped bothering me about getting a job, and I've learned how to read.

Not only that, but we can always say that we've done our part for the advancement of science and all mankind.

For what more can a good rat ask?

BUILT UPON THE SANDS OF TIME

Michael Flynn

❀

Michael Flynn (born 1947) is a statistician by profession. In his fiction, Flynn is concerned with technology and the people who work with it. His first story appeared in *Analog* in 1984, and, as *The Encyclopedia of Science Fiction* remarks, he "soon became identified as one of the most sophisticated and stylistically acute 1980s *Analog* regulars." So he's a perfect match for the traditional image of the hard SF writer, except that his interest in characterization goes deeper than most. In this regard he is more like Nancy Kress and James Patrick Kelly than, say, James P. Hogan, though the politics of his major work certainly leans to the Libertarian right. His first novel was *In the Country of the Blind* (1990), now revised and reissued in hardcover in 2001; his second novel was *Fallen Angels* (1991) in collaboration with Larry Niven and Jerry Pournelle. His third, *The Nanotech Chronicles* (1991), is a series of linked stories. At that point in his career, John Clute (in *The Encyclopedia of Science Fiction*) said, "[Flynn] is on the verge of becoming a central creator of hard SF."

His major work of the 1990s is comprised of *Firestar* (1996), *Rogue Star* (1998), *Lodestar* (2000) and *Falling Star* (2001); four volumes in an ongoing future history concerned with reinvigorating the space frontier through private enterprise, done in a very Heinleinesque manner. It is an interesting parallel and political contract to Allen Steele's future history (see Steele note). Many of Flynn's best stories, including the excellent novella "Melodies of the Heart," are collected in *The Forest of Time and Other Stories* (1997).

"Built upon the Sands of Time" is Flynn the *Analog* writer doing a bar story about scientists and ordinary people. Clarke defined the tradition with a series of stories collected in *Tales from the White Hart* (1957), full of clever notions and (occasionally bad) jokes following the lead of L. Sprague de Camp and Fletcher Pratt's *Tales from Gavagan's Bar* (1953). Larry Niven's Draco Tavern stories and Spider Robinson's Callahan's Place stories have been the standard bearers for the tradition since the 1970s. Flynn's story is notable for its deft and economical characterization, humor, and its scientific twist.

A wise man once said that we can never step in the same river twice. A very wise man, indeed; because by that he did not mean we should refrain from bathing, as some half-wits at the Irish Pub have suggested, but that times change and the same circumstances are never fully repeated. You are not the same person you were yesterday; nor am I.

But perhaps that old Greek was not half so wise as he thought. Perhaps you cannot step into the same river even once; and you may not be the same person yesterday as you were yesterday.

* * *

Friday nights at the irish pub are busier than a husband whose wife has come home early. When The O Neil and myself arrived, the neighborhood crowd was there bending elbows with the University folks from down the street and making, as they like to say, a joyful noise. It was so busy, in fact, that Hennesey, O Daugherty's partner, had joined him behind the bar and even so they were barely keeping ahead of the orders. There were another dozen or so boyos in the back room, watching the progress of the pool table and providing encouragement or not to the players, as the case might be. The O Neil placed his challenge by laying a quarter down on the rail and promised to call me in for a game as soon as he won the table. Then he set himself to study the opposition. Seeing as how the quarters were lined up on the rail like so many communion children, I knew it would be a long, sad time before I held a cue in my hand, so I took myself back out to the bar.

O Daugherty Himself was a wise man, for he had saved a stool for my sitting and, more quickly than I could order it, had placed a pint of Guinness before me. O Daugherty is a man who knows his manners; and his customers, as well. After a polite nod to the man on my right, whom I did not know, I occupied myself with the foamy stout.

Hennesey was a contrast to his partner. Where O Daugherty was short, dark, and barrel-chested, Hennesey was tall, fair, and dour, one of the "red-haired race" from the North of Ireland. His long, thick, drooping face seemed always on the verge of tears, though never quite crossing over into the real thing. His shoulders were stooped because, tall as he was, he had to bend over to communicate with the common ruck. He gave me a smile, which for him consisted of raising the corners of his mouth from the vicinity of his chin to a nearly horizontal position. I hoisted my own mug in reply.

But no sooner had I taken the first, bitter sip than I heard Doc Mooney, on the far side of the oval bar, complain. In itself, this was no unusual thing, since complaint is the blood and spit of the man. But the nature of his complaint was more than a little out of the ordinary.

"Which of ye spalpeens," he cried, "has taken my jawbone?"

Danny Mulloney, sitting two stools to his left, looked at him. "Why, no one, you omadhaun, seeing as how you're still flapping it."

Doc gave him the squint-eye. "It's not my own jawbone I'm speaking of, ye lout; as you would know if you applied what little thought you have to it; but the jawbone we keep at the medical school for purposes of demonstration. I had put it in my pocket when I left for the day."

"Ah," said Danny with a sad shake of his head, "and I would hate to be your wife, then, after turning out your pockets for the laundering. Sure, a pathologist should never take his work home with him."

There was a ripple of laughter at our end of the bar. I confess that I smiled, myself, though it is my constant purpose never to encourage the wit of Danny Mulloney.

Doc turned a shade darker and tapped the bar top with a stiff finger. "I had set it right there, and now it is gone. Someone has taken it."

"You weren't thinking of leaving it as a tip, Doc?" I asked, getting into the spirit of the thing.

Doc gave me a look of betrayal. *Et tu, Mickey?* But Himself spoke up, a twinkle in his eye. "It would depend, I'm thinking, on how many teeth were yet in the jaw. Placed under my pillow, it might draw a tidy sum from the wee folk."

Hennesey only shook his head at the blathering of mortals. "Now, who would wish to steal such a thing?" he asked, *contrabasso*.

"Samson," Danny suggested. "Were there any Philistines about?" Danny being of a religious frame of mind, a Biblical example came most naturally to him.

Doc, who knows a little of Scripture himself, leaned past the poor man who sat between him and Danny and consequently had to listen to the argument with both his ears, and said sweetly, "Nor is it your own jawbone we're speaking of."

"There is too much foam," said the man sitting between them.

Both Danny and Doc pulled away, puzzled at the nonce of the sequitur. Himself reared up. "Too much foam, d'you say? Why, I give honest measure; and the man who says I do not is a liar."

The man blinked several times. "What? Oh." He glanced at the sturdy glass mug before him. "Oh, no, I did not mean your fine beer. I was responding to this gentleman's question concerning his jawbone. I meant the quantum foam."

Hennesey scratched his jaw. "The quantum foam, is it? And that would be an Australian beer?"

"No. I mean the timelessness that came 'before' the Big Bang. We call it the quantum foam."

O Daugherty drew a fresh mug and set it down with a flourish before the man. "Sure and it is worth the price of a good pint to hear what connection there might be between the Big Bang and Doc Mooney's jawbone."

Doc protested again, "It's not *my* jawbone," but no one paid him any heed.

"Well," said the man, "not to the jawbone, but to the *disappearance* of the jawbone." He seemed hesitant and a little sad. For a moment, he managed to make even Hennesey look cheerful. Then he sighed and picked up the mug. "It's like this," he said.

"My name is Owen fitzHugh. I am a physicist at the university, but my hobby has always been the oddities of the Universe. Quirks, as well as quarks, as a colleague of mine has remarked . . .

"One of these quirks is what I call 'phantom recollections' and 'causeless objects.' Non-Thomistic events, if you must have a fine philosophical name for it. Have you ever looked in vain, as your friend here, for an object you clearly recall having placed in a certain spot? Or, conversely, found small objects for which you cannot account? Or recalled telephone numbers or appointments that turned out not to exist?"

"I had a key on my key chain, once," said Maura Lafferty, "that I did not recognize and that fit no lock that I own. I still have no idea where it came from."

"I had a date one time with Bridey Lynch," said Danny, "but when I called on her, she had no recollection of it."

Doc made an evil grin. "Why, there is no mystery at all in that."

FitzHugh nodded. "They are usually small objects or bits of information, these anomalies of mine. Usually, when we notice them at all, we ascribe them to a faulty recollection; but I'm a natural contrarian. I wondered: What if it is the Universe, and not ourselves, that sometimes forgets."

Danny and Doc flanked the poor man with a bookend of skeptical looks. Danny, I was sure, believed in God's Infallible Memory; while Doc reasoned from the predictability of Natural Law. Still their thoughts had come to rest in the same place. Himself shifted his apron and cocked his head in interest. "Now what might that mean?"

"History is contingent," said fitzHugh.

Himself nodded. "Aye, so it is." But Danny scratched his head. "If it is, I've never caught it." Doc leaned past the unfortunate physicist once more.

"He said 'contingent,' not 'contagious.'"

FitzHugh looked at Danny. "I should have said that history is a chain of cause-

and-effect," he said. "One event leads to others, and then to still others. Often, great events hinge on small occurrences."

Wilson Cartwright, a history professor at the University, spoke up from the booth behind fitzHugh. "That's gospel truth. In 1862, a Confederate courier lost a copy of Lee's troop dispositions. Two Union foragers found them and McClellan managed—barely—to win the battle of Antietam, which gave Lincoln the opportunity to issue the Emancipation Proclamation. And when the news of the Proclamation reached England, the cabinet reversed its decision to intervene on the Confederate side. In consequence of which . . ." He lifted his drink in salute to the bar. ". . . my great-grandpappy became a free man."

Hennesey nodded. "Da met me Ma in the same way. Another small chance—though the outcome was not so momentous as war and freedom. He was on the run—. This was during the Troubles, when the Big Fella and the Long Fella had their row—bad cess to 'em both—and Da, he found himself in on the wrong side. O Daugherty, you know what I'm speakin' of, and enough has been said about that. Da took himself to the Waterford hills and, finding himself at a crossroads, tossed a coin. The shilling sent him to Ballinahinch, where me ol' Gran was keeping a pub in those days and Ma waited tables. Now Da was not the man to pass a pub without a drop of the creature, so he stopped and . . ." The man's long, doughy face turned a deep red. ". . . here I am. Had the shilling read tails, he was a dead man, for his enemies were waiting down the other road. As it was, what with one thing and another . . ." And he pointed with his drooping chin to the photograph on the wall opposite, where a far younger Hennesey and O Daugherty stood side by side in black-and-white, stern-faced splendor, arms crossed and legs akimbo before the newly opened Irish Pub.

Doc Mooney raised his pint. "I have always thought you an unlikely man, Hennesey."

"But that's just the point," fitzHugh said. "*Everything* is unlikely . . . and therefore fragile."

"'Fragile,'" said Himself. "A curious word."

"Fragile," said fitzHugh with an affirmative nod. "Because the slightest bump and . . . you see, the quantum foam is subject to sudden, spontaneous disturbances. These create 'probability waves' in the continuum that propagate down the time stream creating a new past. The old past is obliterated. As it was in the beginning, is not, and never more shall be."

Himself scowled a bit at the altered quotation, but Danny Mulloney brightened, which is always a bad sign. "Do you mean to say," he said. "Do you mean to say that all those dinosaur fossils and such might have been put in the ground only a few thousand years ago?"

FitzHugh blinked and looked thoughtful. "Certainly, it's *conceivable*," he said slowly. "Yes. Suppose that evolution originally followed a different course—perhaps those strange Burgess Shale creatures I've read of won out over our own familiar phyla, and after a time strange *things* stalked the Earth of sixty million years ago—things that never held the promise of man. Then, a bubble bursts in the foam and a probability wave ripples down the timeline—and now dinosaurs leave their bones in the mud instead of things with no names. So, yes, in one sense, this new past could have been laid down a few thousand years ago; but in another sense, once it had been laid down, it had *always* been there."

Danny pursed his lips, for I do not think he had envisioned a *different* evolution when he raised his question. Meanwhile, a ripple of wisely nodding heads showed the incomprehension propagating around the oval bar. FitzHugh noticed and said, "Perhaps a sketch will clear it up." He seized a napkin and immediately began to doodle on it. Sitting as I was on the far side, I could not see what he sketched and Hennesey, noting my frustration, waved me inside the Sacred Oval. "Here," he said, handing me a bar apron. " 'Tis a busy night and we can use the help." Then he set off to the front end of the bar to tend to the raging thirst there.

Tying the apron, I stepped across in time to hear fitzHugh say, "This was the continuum in its original state." I glanced at the napkin and saw he had written:

A→ B→ C

"Then, a quantum disturbance alters event A to event A*. A stray chronon—a quantum of time—emitted from the foam, strikes like a billiard ball." He turned to Dr. Cartwright, who had left his booth to stand behind him. "Perhaps your Confederate courier, Wilson, doesn't drop his packet." He held up the napkin again.

A* B→ C→ D

The big historian looked thoughtful, and nodded. Maura Lafferty, who had also joined the little group at the back end of the bar, leaned over the man's shoulder. "Why did you add the 'D'?"

"Oh, time doesn't stop just because there is a bit of redecorating going on," fitzHugh said. "The present is . . . call it the 'bow wave' of the Big Bang, plowing through *formlessness* and leaving *time* in its wake. But behind it is coming the 'bow wave' of the *new* version, altering all the original consequences of A. When the wave front reaches B, event B 'unhappens.' Something else—call it G—happens instead."

A* ~~B~~G C→ D→ E

"Why G?" Danny asked, frowning over the sketch. "Why not call it B?"

"It doesn't matter what he calls it, ye spalpeen," said Doc Mooney.

FitzHugh grimaced. "Actually, it does. I don't want to imply that B happens *differently*—because it might not happen at all."

Cartwright bobbed his head. "That's right. If McClellan hadn't intercepted Lee's orders, it wouldn't have changed the outcome of Antietam. There wouldn't have *been* a battle at Antietam. McClellan only attacked there because he had Lee's orders. Without them, there would have been a different battle at some other time and place."

I scratched my head. "So why didn't you alter C, D and E?"

"Because the wave front hasn't 'caught up' to them yet." He busied himself at the napkin. "Here, this is then next quantum of time, the next parasecond."

A*→ ~~B~~G→ ~~C~~H→ ~~D~~I→ E→ F

"You'll notice that the original causal chain is still propagating itself, and event E has led to event F. But the revision is catching up. Change waves move faster than one second per second—just as water moves faster down a channel already dug than it does across virgin ground—but you really need two different kinds of time to talk about it intelligently. Eventually, the change wave reaches the present, merges into the original Big Bang wave, and the revision is complete." He held the napkin up one last time.

A*→ ~~B~~G→ ~~C~~H→ ~~D~~I→ ~~E~~J→ ~~F~~K→ L

"Even our memories are reconfigured," he said. "The right ripple and . . . who knows? We might be sitting here discussing Lee's victory."

"*You* might be," said Cartwright dryly.

Doc Mooney rubbed his chin and frowned. "I see a problem," he said. He spoke with a chuckle, as if he suspected his leg of being pulled. "If our memories are reconfigured, how could we possibly know the past was ever different?"

The shadow passed over fitzHugh's face once more. "Normally . . . we wouldn't."

Doc Mooney slapped his forehead. "Now, I am an old fool. I had *started* to put the jawbone into my jacket pocket, then I laid it back on my desk." Defiance flashed. "And it has been sitting back there in the lab, all along," he insisted.

FitzHugh nodded with solemn fish-eyes. "Yes. Though perhaps not 'all along.' If at the very moment you laid the jawbone on the bar, a change wave 'caught up' with the present, you would have for a bare instant two conflicting memories. A fragment of the original memory can survive and you sit here at 'L' remembering a bit of 'F,' instead of 'K.' The French have a word for it . . ." He snapped his fingers, searching for the word.

"*Merde?*" suggested Doc innocently.

"*Déjà vu?*" said Maura.

FitzHugh shook his head. "No. *Déjà vu* is when the change wave does not affect your own personal history, so instead of a fossil memory, you have an instant of remembering the same thing twice." He looked at each of us, and it seemed to me that his eyes held immeasurable loneliness in them. "That's why these phantom memories almost always involve trivia." He shrugged, looked off at the corner. "Only an idle fancy. Who can say?"

Himself lifted fitzHugh's now-empty mug and cradled it in his hands. He gave the physicist an intent look. "*Almost* always," he said, with a suggestive pause at the end.

FitzHugh shook his head and gestured at the mug. "Another, please."

"Perhaps," said Himself, "it would be better if you let it pour out instead of in."

("What's he mean?" Danny asked. "Wisht," said Doc.)

Someone put "The Reconciliation Reel" on the juke box and fitzHugh winced as the wild skirling of whistles and fiddles filled the room. Some of the old neighborhood shouted Hoo! and began to clap their hands. "You'll think I'm a fool. Deluded."

Himself shrugged. "Does it matter if we do?"

"Sure," said Doc Mooney, "we all think that Danny here is a deluded fool; but that doesn't stop me from buying him a beer now and then."

Danny, who could be quick on the uptake when the stakes were high, held his mug out to me and said, "You heard him."

Sure, it is not often that Doc is hoist by his own petard, but he had the good grace to accept it cheerfully. While I filled Danny's mug, fitzHugh looked on some inner place in his soul.

"You see," fitzHugh said finally, "the brain stores memories both holographically and associatively. Because the memory is a hologram, one may recapture the entirety from a surviving fragment; and because they are 'filed' associatively, one recovered memory may lead to others. These shards of overwritten memories lie embedded in our minds like junk genes in our DNA, an explanation perhaps for stories of 'past lives'; for false memory syndrome; or for inexplicable fugues or personality changes or . . . Or. . . ." He paused again and shuddered. "Ah, God, what have I done?"

"Something," O Daugherty suggested, "that needs a hearing."

"From the likes of you?"

Himself took no offense. "From the likes of us," he agreed, "or the likes of Father McDevitt."

FitzHugh bowed his head. There had been fear in his eye, and sorrow, and despair. I wondered what odd confession we were about to hear, and ourselves with no power to bind or loose. Maura placed a hand on his arm. "Go on," she urged. Cartwright rumbled something encouraging and Danny had God's grace to keep his mouth shut.

Finally, fitzHugh drew a shuddering breath and blew it out through pursed lips. "A man cannot be responsible for something that never happened, can he?"

Himself shrugged. "Responsibility is a rare thing in any case: a bastard child, often denied."

"It started with a dream," fitzHugh said.

"Such things often do. And end there, too."

"I'm not married," fitzHugh said. "I never have been. There have been women from time to time, and we get along well enough; but there was never one to settle down with. Always it was too early to wed; until it became too late."

"It's never too late," O Daugherty said, "when the right one comes along."

FitzHugh's smile was faint. "That's the very problem, you see. It may be that she did, once. But . . ." Melancholy closed his face again and he inhaled a long, slow breath. "I live alone in a house in the middle of the block over by Thirteenth Street. It's a little large for my needs and the neighborhood is not the best, but the price was right and I enjoy the puttering. There is a parlor, a dining room and kitchen, plus two bedrooms, one of which I use as an office. From the kitchen, a stairway leads to a rough, unfinished basement.

"Recently, I began to have a recurring dream. It always starts the same way. I walk through my kitchen to the back stairwell and go down, not to my own basement, but to another house entirely, where I walk past empty bedrooms, then a kitchen with dishes piled in the sink and a greasy patina to the stove, coming at last to a parlor containing comfortable, out-of-style furniture. There are large windows on two of the walls and, in the corner, a front door. The whole of it has such an air of dust and neglect and familiarity and long abandonment that I often find myself reduced inexplicably to tears when I awake."

"It was your subconscious," said Doc, "playing with that unfinished basement."

FitzHugh gave a brief shake of the head. "I thought that, too; at first. Only . . . Well, the first few dreams, that was all. Just a silent walk through an empty house accompanied by a feeling of loss, as if I had had these disused rooms all along, but had forgotten about them. Once, I reached the front door before waking up, and stepped outside. An ordinary-looking neighborhood, but no place I've ever seen. The house sat on a slight rise on a corner lot. Not much traffic. If I had to guess, I would say a residential neighborhood in a medium-big city, but somewhere off the major thoroughfares. I travel a great deal, going to conferences and such, but I have never identified that city."

He looked deeply into his ale while the rest of us waited. "The dream had a curious air to it. It felt like a memory more than a dream. Maybe it was the dirty dishes in the sink, or the out-of-date furniture in the parlor." Another quirky smile. "If a dream-world, why so drab and ordinary a one?"

I left the group to answer an urgent call at the front end of the bar, where a shortage of brew threatened several collegians with imminent dehydration. When I returned to the discussion, fitzHugh was answering some question of Doc Mooney's.

". . . so the more I thought about it and puzzled over it, the more real it grew in my mind. I remembered things I never actually saw in the dream. It seemed to me that the sink ought to have separate hot and cold water faucets. And that upstairs there would be an office and a sewing room and another bedroom. So you see, the details had the *texture* of memory. How could I remember those things unless they were real?"

Doc pulled the squint-eye like he always does. I think he still suspected some elaborate joke at his expense. "Imagination can be as detailed as memory. Your dream left blanks and you began to fill them in."

FitzHugh nodded. "That's an answer I yearn for. If only I could embrace it."

"What happened next?" Himself prompted. "There must be more to it than you've told to account for such a melancholy."

The physicist drew a deep breath. "One evening, reading at home, I became acutely aware of the silence. Now I am a man that likes his solitude and his peace and quiet; but just for a moment the silence seemed *wrong*, and I wondered, *What's he up to?*"

"Who?" asked Danny. "What was *who* up to?"

FitzHugh shook his head. "I didn't know, then. But I glanced at the ceiling as I wondered, even though there is nothing up there but a crawlspace and storage. And then I heard a woman's voice."

"A woman, was it?" said Himself. "And saying what?"

"I don't know. I couldn't make out the words, only the tone of voice. I knew that I had been addressed, and inexplicably my heart both soared and sank. I can't explain it any other way. It was as if I had been yearning for that voice and dreading it, all at once.

"Well," he continued, "associative memory means that one recovered memory can lead to others; and having found a fragment of one hologram, other fragments began to surface in my mind. I had only to close my eyes and imagine the phantom house. With each return, it became more real, and the conviction grew that I *had* lived there at one time, and not alone. Voices—there were two of them—grew more distinct. Often angry, but not always. Once, I'm embarrassed to say, whispering a sexual invitation. And then, one day, I saw her."

He lifted his mug to his lips, but it hovered there without him drinking as he gazed into the dark, reflective surface. "I was puttering in the parlor, sanding down some woodwork in order to stain it. It was the sort of mechanical task that allows the mind to wander. And so mine did, until it seemed to me that I was in the kitchen of my 'secret house,' drying dishes with a towel. A tall, straw-haired woman was standing beside me washing them in the sink. She had the nagging near-familiarity of a once-met stranger. Perhaps I had seen her at a party in college and I never got up the nerve to walk over and introduce myself—only maybe, once, I did. I knew she was angry because she would *shove* the dishes into my hands in that silent-aggressive way that women sometimes use. She bore the harried look of someone once very beautiful but for whom beauty had lately become a chore. No makeup. Hair cropped in the simplest, most 'practical' style. Perhaps she blamed the me-that-was. Later, I remembered cutting remarks. She could have been this, or she could have married that. I don't know why she kept slipping such hurts into our conversation . . ." He smiled ruefully. "But this first time, she turned to me and said very distinctly, 'You have no ambition.'

"I was so startled that I snapped out of my daydream, and there I was, back in my own parlor." He grimaced, ran a finger up and down the condensate on the outside of his glass. "Alone."

"It's only natural," said Doc Mooney, "that a man living alone might grow wistful and imagine a married life he never had."

FitzHugh laughed without humor. "Then why imagine such an unpleasant one?"

"Because you need to feel that you made the right choice."

"You're a psychiatrist, then, and not a pathologist?" The tones were sarcastic and Doc flushed red. FitzHugh fell into a brown study, and fixed his eyes on the far wall. The rest of us, supposing the story had come to an unsatisfying conclusion, went about our own affairs: O Daugherty and myself to filling glasses and the others to emptying them, which division of labor made for an efficient process. Once or twice, I glanced at fitzHugh, noted his unfocused eyes, and wondered on what inner landscape he gazed. There were tears in the rims of his eyes. When he lifted his glass to me and signalled, I gave Himself a look and he gave me the high sign, so I switched fitzHugh's drink to a non-alcoholic beer. I don't think the man ever noticed.

"I had a son," he told me when I handed him the freshened glass. No one spoke. Doc, from wounded pride; Danny, because of a firm headshake I gave him.

"A son, was it?" said Himself. "Sure, that's a comfort to a man."

FitzHugh made a face. "Lenny was anything but a comfort. Sullen, secretive. Seldom home, even for meals. Lisa blamed me for that, too."

"He was a teenager, then."

FitzHugh started and a rueful smile curled his lips. "Yes. He was. Is that normal behavior for that age? For the sake of other parents, I hope not. I've remembered flashes of him mouthing off, and once or twice I've even heard echoes of the foul words he used. I've another memory of a policeman standing in the front door holding Lenny by the arm and lecturing me." He sighed. "Sometimes I wished we had never met, Lisa and I; and that I had married someone else and had different children; that, well . . . that everything had turned out better than it had."

"Then it was good fortune," I said, "that some bubble in the foam erased it."

FitzHugh was a big man; not muscular exactly, but not frail-looking, either. Yet, he gave me a desolate look and laid his head on his arms and began to weep. O Daugherty and myself traded glances and Wilson Cartwright said, "I know where he lives. I'll drive him home." FitzHugh raised his head.

"Sometimes, I remember other things. Huddled over a kitchen table with Lisa, planning a future full of hope. A young boy bursting with laughter showing me a horse he had modeled out of clay. A camping trip in the Appalachians. Holding hands in a movie theater. Fleeting moments of simple pleasures. The joy had all leaked out, but once upon a time . . . Once upon a time, there had been joy."

A wretched tale, for who among us has not known friend or family in a like situation? Sure, the wine may turn to vinegar in the bottle. And yet, who can forget how sweet it once tasted?

Himself nodded as he wiped a glass clean. "Are you ready to tell us now?"

FitzHugh grunted, as if struck. His eyes darted about our little group and found me. "It was no chance bubble," he said, shaking his head sadly.

That startled me. "Then, what—?"

"I don't know what sort of research my dream-self was doing. I recall enough tantalizing bits to realize it was down a different avenue than I've explored. But I do remember one especially vivid dream. I had built a chronon projector."

Doc Mooney snorted, but Himself only nodded, as if he had expected it. Maura Lafferty wrinkled up her forehead and asked, "What's a chronon projector?"

Frustration laced the physicist's voice. "I'm not sure. A device to excite time quanta, I think. Into the past, of course. There's nothing but formlessness futureward of the bow wave. Perhaps I had some notion of sending messages to warn of tornados or disasters. I don't know. The projector was only a prototype, capable only of emitting a single chronon to a single locus. Enough to create a ripple in the pond; not enough to encode a message." He upended his mug and drained it and set it down hard on the bar top. "Call it a 'cue stick,' if you wish. Something to send a billiard ball into the packed chronons of yesterday and start random ricochets of cause and effect.

"Yesterday, I had no classes to teach, so I stayed home to paint my dining room. I was thinking about mutable time; and I had my hand raised, so." And he held his right hand just before his face. "There must have been some congruence of my train of thought and my posture, because in that instant I was standing in a lab before some great machine and my hand was gripping a switch, and I remember . . . Lisa and I had had an argument over Lenny, and I remember . . . I remember thinking that if I projected the chronon to the locus when Lisa and I met—to that time and place—I could create a ripple in the Dirac Sea, a disturbance in the probabilities and . . . It would all never have happened. None of it. The heartache, the bitching, the sullen anger—" He fell silent.

Himself prompted him. "And . . . ?"

"And I awoke in a strange house, silent and alone." He looked a long way off, seeing what, I do not know. Himself laid a hand on his arm.

"Wisht. What you had, you lost well before you threw the switch."

FitzHugh grabbed O Daugherty's hand and held it tight. "But, don't you see? I lost all the hope, too. The memories of all the joy that went before; of a bright-eyed five-year-old whose smile could light the room. Of the possibility that Lisa and I might have worked it through." He and O Daugherty exchanged a long, mutual look. "I owed her that, didn't I? I owed it to her to try to solve our problems and not abolish them as things that never were."

"Sure," said Himself, "the bad comes mingled with the good; and if you excise the first, you lose the other as well."

"There's one thing I hold on to," fitzHugh said.

"And what's that?"

"That Lisa—whoever she is, from whichever college mixer or classroom where we never met—that in this revision, she's had a better life than the one I gave her. I hold that hope tight as a shield against my crime."

"Crime?" said Danny. "What crime was that?"

FitzHugh wiped his eyes with the sleeve of his jacket. "Lenny. He was never born. He'll never have a chance to grow out of his rebellion and become a better person. Lisa is out there somewhere. Lisa has . . . possibilities. But there is no Lenny. There never was that bright-eyed five-year-old. There never will be. When I disturbed the time-stream, I wiped him out. I obliterated his life: all the hopes and fears and hates and joys . . . All the *possibilities* that were him. How is that so different from murder?"

The silence grew long.

Then fitzHugh pushed himself away from the bar and stood a little uneasily. Alarmed, Professor Cartwright took him by the elbow to steady him. FitzHugh looked at the rest of us. "But it all never happened, right? There oughtn't be any guilt over something that never happened."

It was Danny who spoke—hesitantly, and with more kindness than I had looked for. "Could you not build another of those chronon projectors and aim it back and correct what you did . . . ?" But he trailed off at the end, as if he already suspected what the answer must be.

FitzHugh turned haunted eyes on him. "No. History is contingent. There's no chance that a random disturbance to the revision would recreate the original. You may break the pack on a pool table with a well-aimed shot. You cannot bring the balls back together with another." Cartwright guided him to the door, and the rest of us watched in silence.

"The poor man," said Maura, when he had gone.

O Daugherty rapped hard on the maple counter top, as if testing its solidity. "So fragile," he said, almost to himself. "Who knows if another time wave might be roaring down on us even now, a vast tsunami to wash all of us away?"

The O Neil returned from the back room with a glower on his face. "Ireland will get the Six Counties back before I get that pool table," he said. "Let's go on back to the house, Mickey."

"I'll catch you later," I told him. "It's a busy night and Himself can use the help as much as I can use the cash."

The O Neil shook his head. "O Daugherty, you need to take on a partner, and that's a fact."

Himself shrugged and served him a parting glass of black Guinness. "Someday, maybe," he said. Me, I glanced over at the photograph on the wall, where O Daugherty stood, arms crossed and legs akimbo, before his newly opened pub; and it seemed to me, though I don't know why, that the picture was all out of kilter, as if something large were missing.

TAKLAMAKAN

Bruce Sterling

Bruce Sterling, journalist and SF writer, was the chief polemicist behind the launch of "cyberpunk" SF in the 1980s (see Sterling note above). "His main interest," says *The Encyclopedia of Science Fiction*, "continues to be the behavior of societies rather than individuals and the perfection of SF as a vehicle for scientific education and political debate." Sterling's pseudonymous presentation (as Vincent Omniveritas) of the Movement in his small press fanzine, *Cheap Truth*, and elsewhere, particularly in *Mirrorshades: The Cyberpunk Anthology*, invigorated the 1980s in SF. Sterling, William Gibson, Lewis Shiner, and John Shirley, the four central figures of the Movement, positioned themselves as radical reformers of hard SF, and attracted many followers and imitators. But in spite of Sterling's own stance, the Movement was not received as Radical Hard SF in the U.S., nor immediately influential in that way, though it did set the stage internationally.

The fact is that although the Humanist wing of younger SF writers more or less agreed with Sterling's real world politics, they did not agree with his literary stance. Most of them simply did not want to write fiction with much science in it. There is abundant evidence that some writers wanted to gain literary acceptance from the mainstream literary establishment, and were willing to sacrifice genre popularity, and to reject any public stance in favor of science and technology as useful in solving problems in fiction, to get it. While the old guard right wing hard SF writers were the enemy, and neither agreed with Sterling's stand on science nor on politics. They were, after all, to be swept away, or redirected, by Sterling's new broom. So the left wing element emerged mostly in Canadian, Australian, and U.K. writing in the 1990s.

Ironically Sterling's polemical stance infected popular culture with his ideas and he became a famous cultural figure. Now Sterling is a major voice of his generation, a successful revolutionary, and an environmental activist. His picture has been on the cover of *Wired*. His stories, from pure fantasy to hard SF, are collected in *Crystal Express* (1989), *Globalhead: Stories* (1994), and *A Good Old-Fashioned Future* (1999).

"Taklamakan" is one of his best stories of the nineties, a vision with real world political implications, truly bizarre SF images (one thinks perhaps of Brian W. Aldiss in his Hothouse stories), and told in an accomplished literary style. Sterling is one of the best prose stylists in SF, and it shows here.

A bone-dry frozen wind tore at the earth outside, its lethal howling cut to a muffled moan. Katrinko and Spider Pete were camped deep in a crevice in the rock, wrapped in furry darkness. Pete could hear Katrinko breathing, with a light rattle of chattering teeth. The neuter's yeasty armpits smelled like nutmeg.

Spider Pete strapped his shaven head into his spex.

Outside their puffy nest, the sticky eyes of a dozen gelcams splayed across the rock, a sky-eating web of perception. Pete touched a stud on his spex, pulled down a glowing menu, and adjusted his visual take on the outside world.

Flying powder tumbled through the yardangs like an evil fog. The crescent moon and a billion desert stars, glowing like pixelated bruises, wheeled above the eerie wind-sculpted landscape of the Taklamakan. With the exceptions of Antarctica, or maybe the deep Sahara—locales Pete had never been paid to visit—this central Asian desert was the loneliest, most desolate place on Earth.

Pete adjusted parameters, etching the landscape with a busy array of false colors. He recorded an artful series of panorama shots, and tagged a global positioning fix onto the captured stack. Then he signed the footage with a cryptographic timestamp from a passing NAFTA spy-sat.

1/15/2052 05:24:01.

Pete saved the stack onto a gelbrain. This gelbrain was a walnut-sized lump of neural biotech, carefully grown to mimic the razor-sharp visual cortex of an American bald eagle. It was the best, most expensive piece of photographic hardware that Pete had ever owned. Pete kept the thing tucked in his crotch.

Pete took a deep and intimate pleasure in working with the latest federally subsidized spy gear. It was quite the privilege for Spider Pete, the kind of privilege that he might well die for. There was no tactical use in yet another spy-shot of the chill and empty Taklamakan. But the tagged picture would prove that Katrinko and Pete had been here at the appointed rendezvous. Right here, right now. Waiting for the man.

And the man was overdue.

During their brief professional acquaintance, Spider Pete had met the Lieutenant Colonel in a number of deeply unlikely locales. A parking garage in Pentagon City. An outdoor seafood restaurant in Cabo San Lucas. On the ferry to Staten Island. Pete had never known his patron to miss a rendezvous by so much as a microsecond.

The sky went dirty white. A sizzle, a sparkle, a zenith full of stink. A screaming-streaking-tumbling. A nasty thunderclap. The ground shook hard.

"Dang," Pete said.

They found the lieutenant colonel just before eight in the morning. Pieces of his landing pod were violently scattered across half a kilometer.

Katrinko and Pete skulked expertly through a dirty yellow jumble of wind-grooved boulders. Their camou gear switched coloration moment by moment, to match the landscape and the incidental light.

Pete pried the mask from his face, inhaled the thin, pitiless, metallic air, and spoke aloud. "That's our boy all right. Never missed a date."

The neuter removed her mask and fastidiously smeared her lips and gums with silicone anti-evaporant. Her voice fluted eerily over the insistent wind. "Space-defense must have tracked him on radar."

"Nope. If they'd hit him from orbit, he'd really be spread all over. . . . No something happened to him really close to the ground." Pete pointed at a violent scattering of cracked ochre rock. "See, check out how that stealth-pod hit and tumbled. It didn't catch fire till after the impact."

With the absent ease of a gecko, the neuter swarmed up a three-story-high boulder. She examined the surrounding forensic evidence at length, dabbing carefully at her spex controls. She then slithered deftly back to earth. "There was no anti-aircraft fire, right? No interceptors flyin' round last night."

"Nope. Heck, there's no people around here in a space bigger than Delaware."

The neuter looked up. "So what do you figure, Pete?"

"I figure an accident," said Pete.

"A what?"

"An accident. A lot can go wrong with a covert HALO insertion."

"Like what, for instance?"

"Well, G-loads and stuff. System malfunctions. Maybe he just blacked out."

"He was a federal military spook, and you're telling me he *passed out*?" Katrinko daintily adjusted her goggled spex with gloved and bulbous fingertips. "Why would that matter anyway? He wouldn't fly a spacecraft with his own hands, would he?"

Pete rubbed at the gummy line of his mask, easing the prickly indentation across one dark, tattooed cheek. "I kinda figure he would, actually. The man was a pilot. Big military prestige thing. Flyin' in by hand, deep in Sphere territory, covert insertion, way behind enemy lines. . . . That'd really be something to brag about, back on the Potomac."

The neuter considered this sour news without apparent resentment. As one of the world's top technical climbers, Katrinko was a great connoisseur of pointless displays of dangerous physical skill. "I can get behind that." She paused. "Serious bad break, though."

They resealed their masks. Water was their greatest lack, and vapor exhalation was a problem. They were recycling body-water inside their suits, topped off with a few extra cc's they'd obtained from occasional patches of frost. They'd consumed the last of the trail-goop and candy from their glider shipment three long days ago. They hadn't eaten since. Still, Pete and Katrinko were getting along pretty well, living off big subcutaneous lumps of injected body fat.

More through habit than apparent need, Pete and Katrinko segued into evidence-removal mode. It wasn't hard to conceal a HALO stealth pod. The spycraft was radar-transparent and totally biodegradable. In the bitter wind and cold of the Taklamakan, the bigger chunks of wreckage had already gone all brown and crispy, like the shed husks of locusts. They couldn't scrape up every physical trace, but they'd surely get enough to fool aerial surveillance.

The Lieutenant Colonel was extremely dead. He'd come down from the heavens in his full NAFTA military power-armor, a leaping, brick-busting, lightning-spewing exoskeleton, all acronyms and input jacks. It was powerful, elaborate gear, of an entirely different order than the gooey and fibrous street tech of the two urban intrusion freaks.

But the high-impact crash had not been kind to the armored suit. It had been crueler still to the bone, blood, and tendon housed inside.

Pete bagged the larger pieces with a heavy heart. He knew that the Lieutenant Colonel was basically no good: deceitful, ruthlessly ambitious, probably crazy. Still, Pete sincerely regretted his employer's demise. After all, it was precisely those qualities that had led the Lieutenant Colonel to recruit Spider Pete in the first place.

Pete also felt sincere regret for the gung-ho, clear-eyed young military widow, and the two little redheaded kids in Augusta, Georgia. He'd never actually met the widow or the little kids, but the Lieutenant Colonel was always fussing about them and showing off their photos. The Lieutenant Colonel had been a full fifteen years younger than Spider Pete, a rosy-cheeked cracker kid really, never happier than when handing over wads of money, nutty orders, and expensive covert equipment to people whom no sane man would trust with a burnt-out match. And now here he was in the cold and empty heart of Asia, turned to jam within his shards of junk.

Katrinko did the last of the search-and-retrieval while Pete dug beneath a ledge with his diamond hand-pick, the razored edges slashing out clods of shale.

After she'd fetched the last blackened chunk of their employer, Katrinko perched birdlike on a nearby rock. She thoughtfully nibbled a piece of the pod's navigation console. "This gelbrain is good when it dries out, man. Like trail mix, or a fortune cookie."

Pete grunted. "You might be eating part of him, y'know."

"Lotta good carbs and protein there, too."

They stuffed a final shattered power-jackboot inside the Colonel's makeshift cairn. The piled rock was there for the ages. A few jets of webbing and thumbnail dabs of epoxy made it harder than a brick wall.

It was noon now, still well below freezing, but as warm as the Taklamakan was likely to get in January. Pete sighed, dusted sand from his knees and elbows, stretched. It was hard work, cleaning up; the hardest part of intrusion work, because it was the stuff you had to do after the thrill was gone. He offered Katrinko the end of a fiber-optic cable, so that they could speak together without using radio or removing their masks.

Pete waited until she had linked in, then spoke into his mike. "So we head on back to the glider now, right?"

The neuter looked up, surprised. "How come?"

"Look, Trink, this guy that we just buried was the actual spy in this assignment. You and me, we were just his gophers and backup support. The mission's an abort."

"But we're searching for a giant, secret, rocket base."

"Yeah, sure we are."

"We're supposed to find this monster high-tech complex, break in, and record all kinds of crazy top secrets that nobody but the mandarins have ever seen. That's a totally hot assignment, man."

Pete sighed. "I admit it's very high-concept, but I'm an old guy now, Trink. I need the kind of payoff that involves some actual money."

Katrinko laughed. "But Pete! It's a *starship*! A whole fleet of 'em, maybe! Secretly built in the desert, by Chinese spooks and Japanese engineers!"

Pete shook his head. "That was all paranoid bullshit that the flyboy made up, to get himself a grant and a field assignment. He was tired of sitting behind a desk in the basement, that's all."

Katrinko folded her lithe and wiry arms. "Look, Pete, you saw those briefings just like me. You saw all those satellite shots. The traffic analysis, too. The Sphere people are up to something way big out here."

Pete gazed around him. He found it painfully surreal to endure this discussion amid a vast and threatening tableau of dust-hazed sky and sand-etched mudstone gullies. "They built something big here once, I grant you that. But I never figured the Colonel's story for being very likely."

"What's so unlikely about it? The Russians had a secret rocket base in the desert a hundred years ago. American deserts are full of secret mil-spec stuff and space-launch bases. So now the Asian Sphere people are up to the same old game. It all makes sense."

"No, it makes no sense at all. Nobody's space-racing to build any starships. Starships aren't a space race. It takes four hundred years to fly to the stars. Nobody's gonna finance a major military project that'll take four hundred years to pay off. Least of all a bunch of smart and thrifty Asian economic-warfare people."

"Well, they're sure building *something*. Look, all we have to do is find the complex, break in, and document some stuff. We can do that! People like us, we never needed any federal bossman to help us break into buildings and take photos. That's what we always do, that's what we live for."

Pete was touched by the kid's game spirit. She really had the City Spider way of mind. Nevertheless, Pete was fifty-two years old, so he found it necessary to at least try to be reasonable. "We should haul our sorry spook asses back to that glider right now. Let's skip on back over the Himalayas. We can fly on back to Washington, tourist class out of Delhi. They'll debrief us at the puzzle-palace. We'll give 'em the bad news about the bossman. We got plenty of evidence to prove *that*, anyhow. . . . The spooks will give us some walkin' money for a busted job, and tell us to keep our noses clean. Then we can go out for some pork chops."

Katrinko's thin shoulders hunched mulishly within the bubblepak warts of her insulated camou. She was not taking this at all well. "Peter, I ain't looking for pork chops. I'm looking for some professional validation, okay? I'm sick of that lowlife kid stuff, knocking around raiding network sites and mayors' offices. . . . This is my chance at the big-time!"

Pete stroked the muzzle of his mask with two gloved fingers.

"Pete, I know that you ain't happy. I know that already, okay? But you've *already made it* in the big-time, Mr. City Spider, Mr. Legend, Mr. Champion. Now here's my big chance come along, and you want us to hang up our cleats."

Pete raised his other hand. "Wait a minute, I never said that."

"Well, you're tellin' me you're walking. You're turning your back. You don't even want to check it out first."

"No," Pete said weightily, "I reckon you know me too well for that, Trink. I'm still a Spider. I'm still game. I'll always at least check it out."

Katrinko set their pace after that. Pete was content to let her lead. It was a very stupid idea to continue the mission without the overlordship of the Lieutenant Colonel. But it was stupid in a different and more refreshing way than the stupid idea of returning home to Chattanooga.

People in Pete's line of work weren't allowed to go home. He'd tried that once, really tried it, eight years ago, just after that badly busted caper in Brussels. He'd gotten a straight job at Lyle Schweik's pedal-powered aircraft factory. The millionaire sports tycoon had owed him a favor. Schweik had been pretty good about it, considering.

But word had swiftly gotten around that Pete had once been a champion City Spider. Dumb-ass co-workers would make significant remarks. Sometimes they asked him for so-called favors, or tried to act street-wise. When you came down to it, straight people were a major pain in the ass.

Pete preferred the company of seriously twisted people. People who really cared about something, cared enough about it to really warp themselves for it. People who looked for more out of life than mommy-daddy, money, and the grave.

Below the edge of a ridgeline they paused for a recce. Pete whirled a tethered eye on the end of its reel and flung it. At the peak of its arc, six stories up, it recorded their surroundings in a panoramic view.

Pete and Katrinko studied the image together through their linked spex. Katrinko highlit an area downhill with a fingertip gesture. "Now there's a tipoff."

"That gully, you mean?"

"You need to get outdoors more, Pete. That's what we rockjocks technically call a road."

Pete and Katrinko approached the road with professional caution. It was a paved ribbon of macerated cinderblock, overrun with drifting sand. The road was made of the coked-out clinker left behind by big urban incinerators, a substance that Asians used for their road surfaces because all the value had been cooked out of it.

The cinder road had once seen a great deal of traffic. There were tire-shreds here and there, deep ruts in the shoulder, and post-holes that had once been traffic signs, or maybe surveillance boxes.

They followed the road from a respectful distance, cautious of monitors, trip-wires, landmines, and many other possible unpleasantries. They stopped for a rest in a savage arroyo where a road bridge had been carefully removed, leaving only neat sockets in the roadbed and a kind of conceptual arc in midair.

"What creeps me out is how clean this all is," Pete said over cable. "It's a road, right? Somebody's gotta throw out a beer can, a lost shoe, something."

Katrinko nodded. "I figure construction robots."

"Really."

Katrinko spread her swollen-fingered gloves. "It's a Sphere operation, so it's bound to have lots of robots, right? I figure robots built this road. Robots used this road. Robots carried in tons and tons of whatever they were carrying. Then when they were done with the big project, the robots carried off everything that was worth any money. Gathered up the guideposts, bridges everything. Very neat, no loose ends, very Sphere-type way to work." Katrinko set her masked chin on her bent knees, gone into reverie. "Some very weird and intense stuff can happen, when you got a lot of space in the desert, and robot labor that's too cheap to meter."

Katrinko hadn't been wasting her time in those intelligence briefings. Pete had seen a lot of City Spider wannabes, even trained quite a few of them. But Katrinko had what it took to be a genuine Spider champion: the desire, the physical talent, the ruthless dedication, and even the smarts. It was staying out of jails and morgues that was gonna be the tough part of Katrinko. "You're a big fan of the Sphere, aren't you, kid? You really like the way they operate."

"Sure, I always liked Asians. Their food's a lot better than Europe's."

Pete took this in stride. NAFTA, Sphere, and Europe: the trilateral super-powers jostled about with the uneasy regularity of sunspots, periodically brewing storms in the proxy regimes of the South. During his fifty-plus years, Pete had seen the Asian Cooperation Sphere change its public image repeatedly, in a weird political rhythm. Exotic vacation spot on Tuesdays and Thursdays. Baffling alien threat on Mondays and Wednesdays. Major trading partner each day and every day, including weekends and holidays.

At the current political moment, the Asian Cooperation Sphere was deep into its Inscrutable Menace mode, logging lots of grim media coverage as NAFTA's chief economic adversary. As far as Pete could figure it, this basically meant that a big crowd of goofy North American economists were trying to act really macho. Their major complaint was that the Sphere was selling NAFTA too many neat, cheap, well-made consumer goods. That was an extremely silly thing to get killed about. But people perished horribly for much stranger reasons than that.

At sunset, Pete and Katrinko discovered the giant warning signs. They were titanic vertical plinths, all epoxy and clinker, much harder than granite. They were four stories tall, carefully rooted in bedrock, and painstakingly chiseled with menacing horned symbols and elaborate textual warnings in at least fifty different languages. English was language number three.

"Radiation waste," Pete concluded, deftly reading the text through his spex, from two kilometers away. "This is a radiation waste dump. Plus, a nuclear test site. Old Red Chinese hydrogen bombs, way out in the Taklamakan desert." He paused thoughtfully. "You gotta hand it to 'em. They sure picked the right spot for the job."

"No way!" Katrinko protested. "Giant stone warning signs, telling people not to trespass in this area? That's got to be a con-job."

"Well, it would sure account for them using robots, and then destroying all the roads."

"No, man. It's like—you wanna hide something big nowadays. You don't put a safe inside the wall any more, because hey, everybody's got magnetometers and sonic imaging and heat detection. So you hide your best stuff in the garbage."

Pete scanned their surroundings on spex telephoto. They were lurking on a hillside above a playa, where the occasional gullywasher had spewed out a big alluvial fan of desert varnished grit and cobbles. Stuff was actually growing down there—squat leathery grasses with fat waxy blades like dead men's fingers. The evil vegetation didn't look like any kind of grass that Pete had ever seen. It struck him as the kind of grass that would blithely gobble up stray plutonium. "Trink, I like my explanations simple. I figure that so-called giant starship base for a giant radwaste dump."

"Well, maybe," the neuter admitted. "But even if that's the truth, that's still news worth paying for. We might find some busted up barrels, or some badly managed fuel rods out there. That would be a big political embarrassment, right? Proof of that would be worth something."

"Huh," said Pete, surprised. But it was true. Long experience had taught Pete that there were always useful secrets in other people's trash. "Is it worth glowin' in the dark for?"

"So what's the problem?" Katrinko said. "I ain't having kids. I fixed that a long time ago. And you've got enough kids already."

"Maybe," Pete grumbled. Four kids by three different women. It had taken him a long sad time to learn that women who fell head-over-heels for footloose, sexy tough guys would fall repeatedly for pretty much any footloose, sexy tough guy.

Katrinko was warming to the task at hand. "We can do this, man. We got our suits and our breathing masks, and we're not eating or drinking anything out here, so we're practically radiation-tight. So we camp way outside the dump tonight. Then before dawn we slip in, we check it out real quick, we take our pictures, we leave. Clean, classic intrusion job. Nobody living around here to stop us, no problem there. And then, we got something to show the spooks when we get home. Maybe something we can sell."

Pete mulled this over. The prospect didn't sound all that bad. It was dirty work, but it would complete the mission. Also—this was the part he liked best—it would keep the Lieutenant Colonel's people from sending in some other poor guy. "Then, back to the glider?"

"Then back to the glider."

"Okay, good deal."

Before dawn the next morning, they stoked themselves with athletic performance enhancers, brewed in the guts of certain gene-spliced ticks that they had kept hibernating in their armpits. Then they concealed their travel gear, and swarmed like ghosts up and over the great wall.

They pierced a tiny hole through the roof of one of the dun-colored, half-buried containment hangars, and oozed a spy-eye through.

Bombproofed ranks of barrel-shaped sarcophagi, solid glossy as polished granite. The big fused radwaste containers were each the size of a tanker truck. They sat there neatly-ranked in hermetic darkness, mute as sphinxes. They looked to be good for the next twenty thousand years.

Pete liquefied and retrieved the gelcam, then re-sealed the tiny hole with rock putty. They skipped down the slope of the dusty roof. There were lots of lizard tracks in the sand drifts, piled at the rim of the dome. These healthy traces of lizard cheered Pete up considerably.

They swarmed silently up and over the wall. Back uphill to the grotto where they'd stashed their gear. Then they removed their masks to talk again.

Pete sat behind a boulder, enjoying the intrusion afterglow. "A cakewalk," he pronounced it. "A pleasure hike." His pulse was already normal again, and, to his joy, there were no suspicious aches under his caraco-acromial arch.

"You gotta give them credit, those robots sure work neat."

Pete nodded. "Killer application for robots, your basic lethal waste gig."

"I telephoto'ed that whole cantonment," said Katrinko, "and there's no water there. No towers, no plumbing, no wells. People can get along without a lot of stuff in the desert, but nobody lives without water. That place is stone dead. It was always dead." She paused. "It was all automated robot work from start to finish. You know what that means, Pete? It means no human being has ever seen that place before. Except for you and me."

"Hey, then it's a first! We scored a first intrusion! That's just dandy," said Pete, pleased at the professional coup. He gazed across the cobbled plain at the walled cantonment, and pressed a last set of spex shots into his gelbrain archive. Two dozen enormous domes, built block by block by giant robots, acting with the dumb persistence of termites. The sprawling domes looked as if they'd congealed on the spot, their rims settling like molten taffy into the desert's little convexities and concavities. From a satellite view, the domes probably passed for natural features. "Let's not tarry, okay? I can kinda feel those X-ray fingers kinking my DNA."

"Aw, you're not all worried about that, are you, Pete?"

Pete laughed and shrugged. "Who cares? Job's over, kid. Back to the glider."

"They do great stuff with gene damage nowadays, y'know. Kinda reweave you, down at the spook lab."

"What, those military doctors? I don't wanna give them the excuse."

The wind picked up. A series of abrupt and brutal gusts. Dry, and freezing, and peppered with stinging sand.

Suddenly, a faint moan emanated from the cantonment. Distant lungs blowing the neck of a wine bottle.

"What's that big weird noise?" demanded Katrinko, all alert interest.

"Aw no," said Pete. "Dang."

Steam was venting from a hole in the bottom of the thirteenth dome. They'd missed the hole earlier, because the rim of that dome was overgrown with big thriving thombushes. The bushes would have been a tip-off in themselves, if the two of them had been feeling properly suspicious.

In the immediate area, Pete and Katrinko swiftly discovered three dead men. The three men had hacked and chiseled their way through the containment dome—from the inside. They had wriggled through the long, narrow crevice they had cut, leaving much blood and skin.

The first man had died just outside the dome, apparently from sheer exhaustion. After their Olympian effort, the two survivors had emerged to confront the sheer four-story walls.

The remaining men had tried to climb the mighty wall with their handaxes, crude woven ropes, and pig-iron pitons. It was a nothing wall for a pair of City Spiders with modern handwebs and pinpression cleats. Pete and Katrinko could have camped and eaten a watermelon on that wall. But it was a very serious wall for a pair of very weary men dressed in wool, leather, and homemade shoes.

One of them had fallen from the wall, and had broken his back and leg. The last one had decided to stay to comfort his dying comrade, and it seemed he had frozen to death.

The three men had been dead for many months, maybe over a year. Ants had been at work on them, and the fine salty dust of the Taklamakan, and the freeze-drying. Three desiccated Asian mummies, black hair and crooked teeth and wrinkled dusky skin, in their funny bloodstained clothes.

Katrinko offered the cable lead, chattering through her mask. "Man, look at these *shoes!* Look at this shirt this guy's got—would you call this thing a *shirt?*"

"What I would call this is three very brave climbers," Pete said. He tossed a tethered eye into the crevice that the men had cut.

The inside of the thirteenth dome was a giant forest of monitors. Microwave antennas, mostly. The top of the dome wasn't sturdy sintered concrete like the others, it was some kind of radar-transparent plastic. Dark inside, like the other domes, and hermetically sealed—at least before the dead men had chewed and chopped their hole through the wall. No sign of any rad-waste around here.

They discovered the little camp where the men had lived. Their bivouac. Three men, patiently chipping and chopping their way to freedom. Burning their last wicks and oil lamps, eating their last rations bite by bite, emptying their leather canteens and scraping for frost to drink. Surrounded all the time by a towering jungle of satellite relays and wavepipes. Pete found that scene very ugly. That was a very bad scene. That was the worst of it yet.

Pete and Katrinko retrieved their full set of intrusion gear. They then broke in through the top of the dome, where the cutting was easiest. Once through, they sealed the hole behind themselves, but only lightly, in case they should need a rapid retreat. They lowered their haul bags to the stone floor, then rappelled down on their smart ropes. Once on ground level, they closed the escape tunnel with web and rubble, to stop the howling wind, and to keep contaminants at bay.

With the hole sealed, it grew warmer in the dome. Warm, and moist. Dew was collecting on walls and floor. A very strange smell, too. A smell like smoke and old socks. Mice and spice. Soup and sewage. A cozy human reek from the depths of the earth.

"The Lieutenant Colonel sure woulda have loved this," whispered Katrinko over cable, spexing out the towering machinery with her infrareds. "You put a clip of explosive ammo through here, and it sure would put a major crimp in somebody's automated gizmos."

Pete figured their present situation for an excellent chance to get killed. Automated alarm systems were the deadliest aspect of his professional existence, somewhat tempered by the fact that smart and aggressive alarm systems frequently killed their owners. There was a basic engineering principle involved. Fancy, paranoid alarm systems went false-positive all the time: squirrels, dogs, wind, hail, earth tremors, horny boyfriends who forgot the password. . . . They were smart, and they had their own agenda, and it made them troublesome.

But if these machines were alarms, then they hadn't noticed a rather large hole painstakingly chopped in the side of their dome. The spars and transmitters looked bad, all patchy with long-accumulated rime and ice. A junkyard look, the definite smell of dead tech. So somebody had given up on these smart, expensive, paranoid alarms. Someone had gotten sick and tired of them, and shut them off.

* * *

At the foot of a microwave tower, they found a rat-sized manhole chipped out, covered with a laced-down lid of sheep's hide. Pete dropped a spy-eye down, scoping out a machine-drilled shaft. The tunnel was wide enough to swallow a car, and it dropped down as straight as a plumb bob for farther than his eye's wiring could reach.

Pete silently yanked a rusting pig-iron piton from the edge of the hole, and replaced it with a modern glue anchor. Then he whipped a smart-rope through and carefully tightened his harness.

Katrinko began shaking with eagerness. "Pete, I am way hot for this. Lemme lead point."

Pete clipped a crab into Katrinko's harness, and linked their spex through the fiber-optic embedded in the rope. Then he slapped the neuter's shoulder. "Get bold, kid."

Katrinko flared out the webbing on her gripgloves, and dropped in feet-first.

The would-be escapes had made a lot of use of cabling already present in the tunnel. There were ceramic staples embedded periodically, to hold the cabling snug against the stone. The climbers had scrabbled their way up from staple to staple, using ladder-runged bamboo poles and iron hooks.

Katrinko stopped her descent and tied off. Pete sent their haulbags down. Then he dropped and slithered after her. He stopped at the lead chock, tied off, and let Katrinko take lead again, following her progress with the spex.

An eerie glow shone at the bottom of the tunnel. Pay day. Pete felt a familiar transcendental tension overcome him. It surged through him with mad intensity. Fear, curiosity and desire: the raw hot, thieving thrill of a major-league intrusion.

A feeling like being insane, but so much better than craziness, because now he felt so *awake*. Pete was awash in primal spiderness, cravings too deep and slippery to speak about.

The light grew hotter in Pete's infrareds. Below them was a slotted expanse of metal, gleaming like a kitchen sink, louvers with hot slots of light. Katrinko planted a foamchock in the tunnel wall, tied off, leaned back, and dropped a spy eye through the slot.

Pete's hands were too busy to reach his spex. "What do you see?" he hissed over cable.

Katrinko craned her head back, gloved palms pressing the goggles against her face. "I can see *everything*, man! Gardens of Eden, and cities of gold!"

The cave had been ancient solid rock once, a continental bulk. The rock had been pierced by a Russian-made drilling rig. A dry well, in a very dry country. And then some very weary, and very sunburned, and very determined Chinese Communist weapons engineers had installed a one-hundred-megaton hydrogen bomb at the bottom of their dry hole. When their beast in its nest of layered casings achieved fusion, seismographs jumped like startled fawns in distant California.

The thermonuclear explosion had left a giant gasbubble at the heart of a crazy webwork of faults and cracks. The deep and empty bubble had lurked beneath the desert in utter and terrible silence, for ninety years.

Then Asia's new masters had sent in new and more sophisticated agencies.

Pete saw that the distant sloping walls of the cavern were daubed with starlight. White constellations, whole and entire. And amid the space—that giant and sweetly damp airspace—were three great glowing lozenges, three vertical cylinders the size of urban high rises. They seemed to be suspended in midair.

"Starships," Pete muttered.

"Starships," Katrinko agreed. Menus appeared in the shared visual space of their linked spex. Katrinko's fingertip sketched out a set of tiny moving sparks against the walls. "But check *that* out."

"What are those?"

"Heat signatures. Little engines." The envisioned world wheeled silently. "And check out over here too—and crawlin' around deep in there, dozens of the things. And Pete, see these? Those big ones? Kinda on patrol?"

"Robots."

"Yep."

"What the hell are they up to, down here?"

"Well, I figure it this way, man. If you're inside one of those fake starships, and you look out through those windows—those *portholes*, I guess we call 'em—you can't see anything but shiny stars. Deep space. But with spex, we can see right through all that business. And Pete, that whole stone sky down there is crawling with machinery."

"Man oh man."

"And nobody inside those starships can see *down*, man. There is a whole lot of very major weirdness going on down at the bottom of that cave. There's a lot of hot steamy water down there, deep in those rocks and those cracks."

"Water, or a big smelly soup maybe," Pete said. "A chemical soup."

"Biochemical soup."

"Autonomous self-assembly proteinaceous biotech. Strictly forbidden by the Nonproliferation Protocols of the Manila Accords of 2037," said Pete. Pete rattled off this phrase with practiced ease, having rehearsed it any number of times during various background briefings.

"A whole big lake of way-hot, way-illegal, self-assembling goo down there."

"Yep. The very stuff that *our* covert-tech boys have been messing with under the Rockies for the past ten years."

"Aw, Pete, everybody cheats a little bit on the accords. The way we do it in NAFTA, it's no worse than bathtub gin. But this is *huge!* And Lord only know what's inside those starships."

"Gotta be people, kid."

"Yep."

Pete drew a slow moist breath. "This is a big one, Trink. This is truly major-league. You and me, we got ourselves an intelligence coup here of historic proportions."

"If you're trying to say that we should go back to the glider now," Katrinko said, "don't even start with me."

"We need to go back to the glider," Pete insisted, "with the photographic proof that we got right now. That was our mission objective. It's what they pay us for."

"Whoop-tee-do."

"Besides, it's the patriotic thing. Right?"

"Maybe I'd play the patriot game, if I was in uniform," said Katrinko. "But the Army don't allow neuters. I'm a total freak and I'm a free agent, and I didn't come here to see Shangri-La and then turn around first thing."

"Yeah," Pete admitted. "I really know that feeling."

"I'm going down in there right now," Katrinko said. "You belay for me?"

"No way, kid. This time, I'm leading point."

Pete eased himself through a crudely broken louver and out onto the vast rocky ceiling. Pete had never much liked climbing rock. Nasty stuff, rock—all natural, no guaranteed engineering specification. Still, Pete had spent a great deal of his life on ceilings. Ceilings he understood.

He worked his way out on a series of congealed lava knobs, till he hit a nice solid crack. He did a rapid set of fist-jams, then set a pair of foam-clamps, and tied himself off on anchor.

Pete panned slowly in place, upside down on the ceiling, muffled in his camou gear, scanning methodically for the sake of Katrinko back on the fiber-optic spex link. Large sections of the ceiling looked weirdly worm-eaten, as if drills or acids had etched the rock away. Pete could discern in the eerie glow of infrared that the three fake starships were actually supported on columns. Huge hollow tubes, lacelike and almost entirely invisible, made of something black and impossibly strong, maybe carbon-fiber. There were water pipes inside the columns, and electrical power.

Those columns were the quickest and easiest ways to climb down or up to the starships. Those columns were also very exposed. They looked like excellent places to get killed.

Pete knew that he was safely invisible to any naked human eye, but there wasn't much he could do about his heat signature. For all he knew, at this moment he was glowing like a Christmas tree on the sensors of a thousand heavily armed robots. But you couldn't leave a thousand machines armed to a hair-trigger for years on end. And who would program them to spend their time watching ceilings?

The muscular burn had faded from his back and shoulders. Pete shook a little extra blood through his wrists, unhooked, and took off on cleats and gripwebs. He veered around one of the fake stars, a great glowing glassine bulb the size of a laundry basket. The fake star was cemented into a big rocky wart, and it radiated a cold, enchanting, and gooey firefly light. Pete was so intrigued by this bold deception that his cleat missed a smear. His left foot swung loose. His left shoulder emitted a nasty-feeling, expensive-sounding pop. Pete grunted, planted both cleats, and slapped up a glue patch, with tendons smarting and the old forearm clock ticking fast. He whipped a crab through the patchloop and sagged within his harness, breathing hard.

On the surface of his spex, Katrinko's glowing fingertip whipped across the field of Pete's vision, and pointed. Something moving out there. Pete had company.

Pete eased a string of flashbangs from his sleeve. Then he hunkered down in place, trusting to his camouflage, and watching.

A robot was moving toward him among the dark pits of the fake stars. Wobbling and jittering.

Pete had never seen any device remotely akin to this robot. It had a porous, foamy hide, like cork and plastic. It had a blind compartmented knob for a head, and fourteen long fibrous legs like a frayed mess of used rope, terminating in absurdly complicated feet, like a boxful of grip pliers. Hanging upside down from bits of rocky irregularity too small to see, it would open its big warty head and flick out a forked sensor like a snake's tongue. Sometimes it would dip itself close to the ceiling, for a lingering chemical smooch on the surface of the rock.

Pete watched with murderous patience as the device backed away, drew nearer, spun around a bit, meandered a little closer, sucked some more ceiling rock, made up its mind about something, replanted its big grippy feet, hoofed along closer yet, lost its train of thought, retreated a bit, sniffed the air at length, sucked meditatively on the end of one of its ropy tentacles.

It finally reached him, walked deftly over his legs, and dipped up to lick enthusiastically at the chemical traces left by his gripweb. The robot seemed enchanted by the taste of the glove's elastomer against the rock. It hung there on its fourteen plier feet, loudly licking and rasping.

Pete lashed out with his pick. The razored point slid with a sullen crunch right through the thing's corky head.

It went limp instantly, pinned there against the ceiling. Then with a nasty rustling it deployed a whole unsuspected set of waxy and filmy appurtenances. Complex bug-tongue things, mandible scrapers, delicate little spatulas, all reeling and trembling out of its slotted underside.

It was not going to die. It couldn't die, because it had never been alive. It was a piece of biotechnical machinery. Dying was simply not on its agenda anywhere. Pete photographed the device carefully as it struggled with obscene mechanical stupidity to come to workable terms with its new environmental parameters. Then Pete levered the pick loose from the ceiling, shook it loose, and dropped the pierced robot straight down to hell.

Pete climbed more quickly now, favoring the strained shoulder. He worked his way methodically out to the relative ease of the vertical wall, where he discovered a large mined-out vein in the constellation Sagittarius. The vein was a big snaky recess where some kind of ore had been nibbled and strained from the rock. By the look of it, the rock had been chewed away by a termite host of tiny robots with mouths like toenail clippers.

He signaled on the spex for Katrinko. The neuter followed along the clipped and anchored line, climbing like a fiend while lugging one of the haulbags. As Katrinko settled in to their new base camp, Pete returned to the louvers to fetch the second bag. When he'd finally heaved and grappled his way back, his shoulder was aching bitterly and his nerves were shot. They were done for the day.

Katrinko had put up the emission-free encystment web at the mouth of their crevice. With Pete returned to relative safety, she reeled in their smart-ropes and fed them a handful of sugar.

Pete cracked open two capsules of instant fluff, then sank back gratefully into the wool.

Katrinko took off her mask. She was vibrating with alert enthusiasm. Youth, thought Pete—youth, and the eight percent metabolic advantage that came from lacking sex organs. "We're in so much trouble now," Katrinko whispered, with a feverish grin in the faint red glow of a single indicator light. She no longer resembled a boy or a young woman. Katrinko looked completely diabolical. This was a nonsexed creature. Pete liked to think of her as a "she," because this was somehow easier on his mind, but Katrinko was an "it." Now it was filled with glee, because finally it had placed itself in a proper and pleasing situation. Stark and feral confrontation with its own stark and feral little being.

"Yeah, this is trouble," Pete said. He placed a fat medicated tick onto the vein inside of his elbow. "And you're taking first watch."

Pete woke four hours later, with a heart-fluttering rise from the stunned depths of chemically assisted delta-sleep. He felt numb, and lightly dusted with a brain-clouding amnesia, as if he'd slept for four straight days. He had been profoundly helpless in the grip of the drug, but the risk had been worth it, because now he was thoroughly rested. Pete sat up, and tried the left shoulder experimentally. It was much improved.

Pete rubbed feeling back into his stubbled face and scalp, then strapped his spex on. He discovered Katrinko squatting on her haunches, in the radiant glow of her own body heat, pondering over an ugly mess of spines, flakes, and goo.

Pete touched spex knobs and leaned forward. "What you got there?"

"Dead robots. They ate our foamchocks, right out of the ceiling. They eat anything. I killed the ones that tried to break into camp." Katrinko stroked at a midair menu, then handed Pete a fiber lead for his spex. "Check this footage I took."

Katrinko had been keeping watch with the gelcams, picking out passing robots in the glow of their engine heat. She'd documented them on infrared, saving and editing the clearest live-action footage. "These little ones with the ball-shaped feet, I call them keets," she narrated, as the captured frames cascaded across Pete's spex-clad gaze. "They're small, but they're really fast, and all over the place—I had to kill three of them. This one with the sharp spiral nose is a drillet. Those are a pair of dubits. The dubits always travel in pairs. This big thing here, that looks like a spilled dessert with big eyes and a ball on a chain, I call that one a lurchen. Because of the way it moves, see? It's sure a lot faster than it looks."

Katrinko stopped the spex replay, switched back to live perception, and poked carefully at the broken litter before her booted feet. The biggest device in the heap resembled a dissected cat's head stuffed with cables and bristles. "I also killed this piteen. Piteens don't die easy, man."

"There's lots of these things?"

"I figure hundreds, maybe thousands. All different kinds. And every one of 'em as stupid as dirt. Or else we'd be dead and disassembled a hundred times already."

Pete stared at the dissected robots, a cooling mass of nerve-netting, batteries, veiny armor plates, and gelatin. "Why do they look so crazy?"

"Cause they grew all by themselves. Nobody ever designed them." Katrinko glanced up. "You remember those big virtual spaces for weapons design, that they run out in Alamagordo?"

"Yeah, sure, Alamagordo. Physics simulations on those super-size quantum gel-brains. Huge virtualities, with ultra-fast, ultra-fine detail. You bet I remember New Mexico! I love to raid a great computer lab. There's something so traditional about the hack."

"Yeah. See, for us NAFTA types, physics virtualities are a military app. We always give our tech to the military whenever it looks really dangerous. But let's say you don't share our NAFTA values. You don't wanna test new weapons systems inside giant virtualities. Let's say you want to make a can-opener, instead."

During her sleepless hours huddling on watch, Katrinko had clearly been giving this matter a lot of thought. "Well, you could study other people's can-openers and try to improve the design. Or else you could just set up a giant high-powered virtuality with a bunch of virtual cans inside it. Then you make some can-opener simulations, that are basically blobs of goo. They're simulated goo, but they're also programs, and those programs trade data and evolve. Whenever they pierce a can, you reward them by making more copies of them. You're running, like, a million generations of a million different possible can-openers, all day every day, in a simulated space."

The concept was not entirely alien to Spider Pete. "Yeah, I've heard the rumors. It was one of those stunts like Artificial Intelligence. It might look really good on paper, but you can't ever get it to work in real life."

"Yeah, and now it's illegal too. Kinda hard to police, though. But let's imagine you're into economic warfare and you figure out how to do this. Finally, you evolve this super weird, super can-opener that no human being could ever have invented. Something that no human being could even *imagine*. Because it grew like a mushroom in an entire alternate physics. But you have all the specs for its shape and proportions, right there in the supercomputer. So to make one inside the real world, you just print it out like a photograph. And it works! It runs! See? Instant cheap consumer goods."

Pete thought it over. "So you're saying the Sphere people got that idea to work, and these robots here were built that way?"

"Pete, I just can't figure any other way this could have happened. These machines are just too alien. They had to come from some totally nonhuman, autonomous process. Even the best Japanese engineers can't design a jelly robot made out of fuzz and rope that can move like a caterpillar. There's not enough money in the world to pay human brains to think that out."

Pete prodded at the gooey ruins with his pick. "Well, you got that right."

"Whoever built this place, they broke a lot of rules and treaties. But they did it all *really cheap*. They did it in a way that is so cheap that it is *beyond economics*." Katrinko thought this over. "It's *way* beyond economics, and that's exactly *why* it's against all those rules and the treaties in the first place."

"Fast, cheap, and out of control."

"Exactly, man. If this stuff ever got loose in the real world, it would mean the end of everything we know."

Pete liked this last statement not at all. He had always disliked apocalyptic hype. He liked it even less now because under these extreme circumstances it sounded very plausible. The Sphere had the youngest and the biggest population of the three major trading blocs, and the youngest and the biggest ideas. People in Asia knew how to get things done. "Y'know, Lyle Schweik once told me that the weirdest bicycles in the world come out of China these days."

"Well, he's right. They do. And what about those Chinese circuitry chips they've been dumping in the NAFTA markets lately? Those chips are dirt cheap and work fine, but they're full of all this crazy leftover wiring that doubles back and gets all snarled up. . . . I always thought that was just shoddy workmanship. Man, 'workmanship' had nothing to do with those chips."

Pete nodded soberly. "Okay. Chips and bicycles, that much I can understand. There's a lot of money in that. But who the heck would take the trouble to create a giant hole in the ground that's full of robots and fake stars? I mean, *why*?"

Katrinko shrugged. "I guess it's just the Sphere, man. They still do stuff just because it's wonderful."

The bottom of the world was boiling over. During the passing century, the nuclear test cavity had accumulated its own little desert aquifer, a pitch-black subterranean oasis. The bottom of the bubble was an unearthly drowned maze of shattered cracks and chemical deposition, all turned to simmering tidepools of mechanical self-assemblage. Oxygen-fizzing geysers of black fungus tea.

Steam rose steadily in the darkness amid the crags, rising to condense and run in chilly rivulets down the spherical star-spangled walls. Down at the bottom, all the water was eagerly collected by aberrant devices of animated sponge and string. Katrinko instantly tagged these as "smits" and "fuzzens."

The smits and fuzzens were nightmare dishrags and piston-powered spaghetti, leaping and slopping wetly from crag to crag. Katrinko took an unexpected ease and pleasure in naming and photographing the machines. Speculation boiled with sinister ease from the sexless youngster's vulpine head, a swift off-the-cuff adjustment to this alien toy world. It would seem that the kid lived rather closer to the future than Pete did.

They cranked their way from boulder to boulder, crack to liquid crack. They documented fresh robot larvae, chewing their way to the freedom of darkness through plugs of goo and muslin. It was a whole miniature creation, designed in the senseless gooey cores of a Chinese supercomputing gelbrain, and transmuted into reality in a hot broth of undead mechanized protein. This was by far the most amazing phenomenon that Pete had ever witnessed. Pete was accordingly plunged into gloom. Knowledge was power in his world. He knew with leaden certainty that he was taking on far too much voltage for his own good.

Pete was a professional. He could imagine stealing classified military secrets from a superpower, and surviving that experience. It would be very risky, but in the final analysis it was just the military. A rocket base, for instance—a secret Asian rocket base might have been a lot of fun.

But this was not military. This was an entire new means of industrial production. Pete knew with instinctive street-level certainty that tech of this level of revolutionary weirdness was not a spy thing, a sports thing, or a soldier thing. This was a big, big *money* thing. He might survive discovering it. He'd never get away with revealing it.

The thrilling wonder of it all really bugged him. Thrilling wonder was at best a passing thing. The sober implications for the longer term weighed on Pete's soul like a damp towel. He could imagine escaping this place in one piece, but he couldn't imagine any plausible aftermath for handing over nifty photographs of thrilling wonder to military spooks on the Potomac. He couldn't imagine what the powers-that-were would do with that knowledge. He rather dreaded what they would do to him for giving it to them.

Pete wiped a sauna cascade of sweat from his neck.

"So I figure it's either geothermal power, or a fusion generator down there," said Katrinko.

"I'd be betting thermonuclear, given the circumstances." The rocks below their busy cleats were a-skitter with bugs: gippers and ghents and kebbits, dismantlers and glue-spreaders and brain-eating carrion disassemblers. They were profoundly dumb little devices, specialized as centipedes. They didn't seem very aggressive, but it surely would be a lethal mistake to sit down among them.

A barnacle thing with an iris mouth and long whipping eyes took a careful taste of Katrinko's boot. She retreated to a crag with a yelp.

"Wear your mask," Pete chided. The damp heat was bliss after the skin-eating chill of the Taklamakan, but most of the vents and cracks were spewing thick smells of hot beef stew and burnt rubber, all varieties of eldritch mechano-metabolic byproduct. His lungs felt sore at the very thought of it.

Pete cast his foggy spex up the nearest of the carbon-fiber columns, and the golden, glowing, impossibly tempting lights of those starship portholes up above.

Katrinko led point. She was pitilessly exposed against the lacelike girders. They didn't want to risk exposure during two trips, so they each carried a haul bag.

The climb went well at first. Then a machine rose up from wet darkness like a six-winged dragonfly. Its stinging tail lashed through the thready column like the kick of a mule. It connected brutally. Katrinko shot backwards from the impact, tumbled ten meters, and dangled like a ragdoll from her last backup chock.

The flying creature circled in a figure eight, attempting to make up its nonexistent mind. Then a slower but much larger creature writhed and fluttered out of the starry sky, and attacked Katrinko's dangling haulbag. The bag burst like a Christmas piñata in a churning array of taloned wings. A fabulous cascade of expensive spy gear splashed down to the hot pools below.

Katrinko twitched feebly at the end of her rope. The dragonfly, cruelly alerted, went for her movement. Pete launched a string of flashbangs.

The world erupted in flash, heat, concussion, and flying chaff. Impossibly hot and loud, a thunderstorm in a closet. The best kind of disappearance magic: total overwhelming distraction, the only real magic in the world.

Pete soared up to Katrinko like a balloon on a bungee-cord. When he reached the bottom of the starship, twenty-seven heart-pounding seconds later, he had burned out both the smart-ropes.

The silvery rain of chaff was driving the bugs to mania. The bottom of the cavern was suddenly a-crawl with leaping mechanical heat-ghosts, an instant menagerie of skippers and humpers and floppers. At the rim of perception, there were new things rising from the depths of the pools, vast and scaly, like golden carp to a rain of fish chow.

Pete's own haulbag had been abandoned at the base of the column. That bag was clearly not long for this world.

Katrinko came to with a sudden winded gasp. They began free-climbing the outside of the starship. It surface was stony, rough and uneven, something like pumice, or wasp spit.

They found the underside of a monster porthole and pressed themselves flat against the surface.

There they waited, inert and unmoving, for an hour. Katrinko caught her breath. Her ribs stopped bleeding. The two of them waited for another hour, while crawling and flying heat-ghosts nosed furiously around their little world, following the tatters of their programming. They waited a third hour.

Finally they were joined in their haven by an oblivious gang of machines with suckery skirts and wheelbarrows for heads. The robots chose a declivity and began filling it with big mandible trowels of stony mortar, slopping it on and jaw-chiseling it into place, smoothing everything over, tireless and pitiless.

Pete seized this opportunity to attempt to salvage their lost equipment. There had been such fabulous federal bounty in there: smart audio bugs, heavy-duty gelcams, sensors and detectors, pulleys, crampons and latches, priceless vials of programmed neural goo. . . . Pete crept back to the bottom of the spacecraft.

Everything was long gone. Even the depleted smart-ropes had been eaten, by a long trail of foraging keets. The little machines were still squirreling about in the black lace of the column, sniffing and scraping at the last molecular traces, with every appearance of satisfaction.

Pete rejoined Katrinko, and woke her where she clung rigid and stupefied to her hiding spot. They inched their way around the curved rim of the starship hull, hunting for a possible weakness. They were in very deep trouble now, for their best equipment was gone. It didn't matter. Their course was very obvious now, and the loss of alternatives had clarified Pete's mind. He was consumed with a burning desire to break in.

Pete slithered into the faint shelter of a large, deeply pitted hump. There he discovered a mess of braided rope. The rope was woven of dead and mashed organic fibers, something like the hair at the bottom of a sink. The rope had gone all petrified under a stony lacquer of robot spit.

These were climber's ropes. Someone had broken out here—smashed through the hull of the ship, from the inside. The robots had come to repair the damage, carefully resealing the exit hole, and leaving this ugly hump of stony scar tissue.

Pete pulled his gelcam drill. He had lost the sugar reserves along with the haulbags. Without sugar to metabolize, the little enzyme-driven rotor would starve and be useless soon. That fact could not be helped. Pete pressed the device against the hull, waited as it punched its way through, and squirted in a gelcam to follow.

He saw a farm. Pete could scarcely have been more astonished. It was certainly farmland, though. Cute, toy farmland, all under a stony blue ceiling, crisscrossed with hot grids of radiant light, embraced in the stony arch of the enclosing hull. There were fishponds with reeds. Ditches, and a wooden irrigation wheel. A little bridge of bamboo. There were hairy melon vines in rich black soil and neat, entirely weedless fields of dwarfed red grain. Not a soul in sight.

Katrinko crept up and linked in on cable. "So where is everybody?" Pete said.

"They're all at the portholes," said Katrinko, coughing.

"What?" said Pete, surprised. "Why?"

"Because of those flashbangs," Katrinko wheezed. Her battered ribs were still paining her. "They're all at the portholes, looking out into the darkness. Waiting for something else to happen."

"But we did that stuff hours ago."

"It was very big news, man. Nothing ever happens in there."

Pete nodded, fired with resolve. "Well then. We're breakin' in."

Katrinko was way game. "Gonna use caps?"

"Too obvious."

"Acids and fibrillators?"

"Lost 'em in the haulbags."

"Well, that leaves cheesewires," Katrinko concluded. "I got two."

"I got six."

Katrinko nodded in delight. "Six cheesewires! You're loaded for bear, man!"

"I love cheesewires," Pete grunted. He had helped to invent them.

Eight minutes and twelve seconds later they were inside the starship. They reset the cored-out plug behind them, delicately gluing it in place and carefully obscuring the hair-thin cuts.

Katrinko sidestepped into a grove of bamboo. Her camou bloomed in green and tan and yellow, with such instant and treacherous ease that Pete lost her entirely. Then she waved, and the spex edge-detectors kicked in on her silhouette.

Pete lifted his spex for a human naked-eye take on the situation. There was simply nothing there at all. Katrinko was gone, less than a ghost, like pitchforking mercury with your eyelashes.

So they were safe now. They could glide through this bottled farm like a pair of bad dreams.

They scanned the spacecraft from top to bottom, looking for dangerous and interesting phenomena. Control rooms manned by Asian space technicians maybe, or big lethal robots, or video monitors—something that might cramp their style or kill them. In the thirty-seven floors of the spacecraft, they found no such thing.

The five thousand inhabitants spent their waking hours farming. The crew of the starship were preindustrial, tribal, Asian peasants. Men, women, old folks, little kids.

The local peasants rose every single morning, as their hot networks of wiring came alive in the ceiling. They would milk their goats. They would feed their sheep, and some very odd, knee-high, dwarf Bactrian camels. They cut bamboo and netted their fishponds. They cut down tamarisks and poplar trees for firewood. They tended melon vines and grew plums and hemp. They brewed alcohol, and ground grain, and boiled millet, and squeezed cooking oil out of rapeseed. They made clothes out of hemp and raw wool and leather, and baskets out of reeds and straw. They ate a lot of carp.

And they raised a whole mess of chickens. Somebody not from around here had been fooling with the chickens. Apparently these were super space-chickens of some kind, leftover lab products from some serious long-term attempt to screw around with chicken DNA. The hens produced five or six lumpy eggs every day. The roosters were enormous, and all different colors, and very smelly, and distinctly reptilian.

It was very quiet and peaceful inside the starship. The animals made their lowing and clucking noises, and the farm workers sang to themselves in the tiny round-edged fields, and the incessant foot-driven water pumps would clack rhythmically, but there were no city noises. No engines anywhere. No screens. No media.

There was no money. There were a bunch of tribal elders who sat under the blossoming plum trees outside the big stone granaries. They messed with beads on wires, and wrote notes on slips of wood. Then the soldiers, or the cops—they were a bunch of kids in crude leather armor, with spears—would tramp in groups, up and down the dozens of stairs, on the dozens of floors. Marching like crazy, and requisitioning stuff, and carrying stuff on their backs, and handing things out to people. Basically spreading the wealth around.

Most of the weird bearded old guys were palace accountants, but there were some others too. They sat cross-legged on mats in their homemade robes, and straw sandals, and their little spangly hats, discussing important matters at slow and extreme length. Sometimes they wrote stuff down on palm-leaves.

Pete and Katrinko spent a special effort to spy on these old men in the spangled hats, because, after close study, they had concluded that this was the local government. They pretty much had to be the government. These old men with the starry hats were the only part of the population who weren't being worked to a frazzle.

Pete and Katrinko found themselves a cozy spot on the roof of the granary, one of the few permanent structures inside the spacecraft. It never rained inside the starship, so there wasn't much call for roofs. Nobody ever trespassed up on the roof of the granary. It was clear that the very idea of doing this was beyond local imagination. So Pete and Katrinko stole some bamboo water jugs, and some lovely handmade carpets, and a lean-to-tent, and set up camp there.

Katrinko studied an especially elaborate palm-leaf book that she had filched from the local temple. There were pages and pages of dense alien script. "Man, what do you suppose these yokels have to write about?"

"The way I figure it," said Pete, "they're writing down everything they can remember from the world outside."

"Yeah?"

"Yeah. Kinda building up an intelligence dossier for their little starship regime, see? Because that's all they'll ever know, because the people who put them inside here aren't giving 'em any news. And they're sure as hell never gonna let 'em out."

Katrinko leafed carefully through the stiff and brittle pages of the handmade book. The people here spoke only one language. It was no language Pete or Katrinko could even begin to recognize. "Then this is their history. Right?"

"It's their lives, kid. Their past lives, back when they were still real people, in the big real world outside. Transistor radios, and shoulder-launched rockets. Barbed-wire, pacification campaigns, ID cards. Camel caravans coming in over the border, with mortars and explosives. And very advanced Sphere mandarin bosses, who just don't have the time to put up with armed, Asian, tribal fanatics."

Katrinko looked up. "That kinda sounds like *your* version of the outside world, Pete."

Pete shrugged. "Hey, it's what happens."

"You suppose these guys really believe they're inside a real starship?"

"I guess that depends on how much they learned from the guys who broke out of here with the picks and the ropes."

Katrinko thought about it. "You know what's truly pathetic? The shabby illusion of all this. Some spook mandarin's crazy notion that ethnic separatists could be squeezed down tight, and spat out like watermelon seeds into interstellar space. . . . Man, what a *come-on*, what an enticement, what an empty promise!"

"I could sell that idea," Pete said thoughtfully. "You know how *far away* the stars really are, kid? About *four hundred years* away, that's how far. You seriously want to get human beings to travel to another star, you gotta put human beings inside of a sealed can for four hundred solid years. But what are people supposed to do in there, all that time? The only thing they can do is quietly run a farm. Because that's what a starship is. It's a desert oasis."

"So you want to try a dry-run starship experiment," said Katrinko. "And in the meantime, you happen to have some handy religious fanatics in the backwoods of Asia, who are shooting your ass off. Guys who refuse to change their age-old lives, even though you are very, very high-tech."

"Yep. That's about the size of it. Means, motive, and opportunity."

"I get it. But I can't believe that somebody went through with that scheme in real life. I mean, rounding up an ethnic minority, and sticking them down in some godforsaken hole, just so you'll never have to think about them again. That's just impossible!"

"Did I ever tell you that my grandfather was a Seminole?" Pete said.

Katrinko shook her head. "What's that mean?"

"They were American tribal guys who ended up stuck in a swamp. The Florida Seminoles, they *called* 'em. Y'know, maybe they just *called* my grandfather a Seminole. He dressed really funny. . . . Maybe it just *sounded good* to call him a Seminole. Otherwise, he just would have been some strange, illiterate geezer."

Katrinko's brow wrinkled. "Does it *matter* that your grandfather was a Seminole?"

"I used to think it did. That's where I got my skin color—as if that matters, nowadays. I reckon it mattered plenty to my grandfather, though. . . . He was always stompin' and carryin' on about a lot of weird stuff we couldn't understand. His English was pretty bad. He was never around much when we needed him."

"Pete . . ." Katrinko sighed. "I think it's time we got out of this place."

"How come?" Pete said, surprised. "We're safe up here. The locals are not gonna hurt us. They can't even see us. They can't touch us. Hell, they can't even *imagine* us. With our fantastic tactical advantages, we're just like gods to these people."

"I know all that, man. They're like the ultimate dumb straight people. I don't like them very much. They're not much of a challenge to us. In fact, they kind of creep me out."

"No way! They're fascinating. Those baggy clothes, the acoustic songs, all that menial labor . . . These people got something that we modern people just don't have any more."

"Huh?" Katrinko said. "Like *what*, exactly?"

"I dunno," Pete admitted.

"Well, whatever it is, it can't be very important." Katrinko sighed. "We got some serious challenges on the agenda, man. We gotta sidestep our way past all those angry robots outside, then head up that shaft, then hoof it back, four days through a freezing desert, with no haulbags. All the way back to the glider."

"But Trink, there are two other starships in here that we didn't break into yet. Don't you want to see those guys?"

"What I'd like to see right now is a hot bath in a four-star hotel," said Katrinko. "And some very big international headlines, maybe. All about *me*. That would be lovely." She grinned.

"But what about the *people?*"

"Look, I'm not 'people,'" Katrinko said calmly. "Maybe it's because I'm a neuter, Pete, but I can tell you're way off the subject. These people are none of our business. Our business now is to return to our glider in an operational condition, so that we can complete our assigned mission, and return to base with our data. Okay?"

"Well, let's break into just one more starship first."

"We gotta move, Pete. We've lost our best equipment, and we're running low on body fat. This isn't something that we can kid about and live."

"But we'll never come back here again. Somebody will, but it sure as heck won't be *us*. See, it's a Spider thing."

Katrinko was weakening. "One more starship? Not both of 'em?"

"Just one more."

"Okay, good deal."

The hole they had cut through the starship's hull had been rapidly cemented by robots. It cost them two more cheesewires to cut themselves a new exit. Then Katrinko led point, up across the stony ceiling, and down the carbon column to the second ship. To avoid annoying the lurking robot guards, they moved with hypnotic slowness and excessive stealth. This made it a grueling trip.

This second ship had seen hard use. The hull was extensively scarred with great wads of cement, entombing many lengths of dried and knotted rope. Pete and Katrinko found a weak spot and cut their way in.

This starship was crowded. It was loud inside, and it smelled. The floors were crammed with hot and sticky little bazaars, where people sold handicrafts and liquor and food. Criminals were being punished by being publicly chained to pots and pelted with offal by passers-by. Big crowds of ragged men and tattooed men gathered around brutal cockfights, featuring spurred mutant chickens half the size of dogs. All the men carried knives.

The architecture here was more elaborate, all kinds of warrens, and courtyards, and damp, sticky alleys. After exploring four floors, Katrinko suddenly declared she recognized their surroundings. According to Katrinko, they were a physical replica of sets from a popular Japanese interactive samurai epic. Apparently the starship's designers had needed some preindustrial Asian village settings, and they hadn't wanted to take the expense and trouble to design them from scratch. So they had programmed their construction robots with pirated game designs.

This starship had once been lavishly equipped with at least three hundred armed videocamera installations. Apparently, the mandarins had come to the stunning realization that the mere fact that they were recording crime didn't mean that they could control it. Their spy cameras were all dead now. Most had been vandalized. Some had gone down fighting. They were all inert and abandoned.

The rebellious locals had been very busy. After defeating the spy cameras, they had created a set of giant hullbreakers. These were siege engines, big crossbow torsion machines, made of hemp and wood and bamboo. The hullbreakers were starship community efforts, elaborately painted and ribboned, and presided over by tough, aggressive gang bosses with batons and big leather belts.

Pete and Katrinko watched a labor gang, hard at work on one of the hullbreakers. Women braided rope ladders from hair and vegetable fiber, while smiths forged pitons over choking, hazy charcoal fires. It was clear from the evidence that these restive locals had broken out of their starship jail at least twenty times. Every time they had been corralled back in by the relentless efforts of mindless machines. Now they were busily preparing yet another breakout.

"These guys sure have got initiative," said Pete admiringly. "Let's do 'em a little favor, okay?"

"Yeah?"

"Here they are, taking all this trouble to hammer their way out. But we still have a bunch of caps. We got no more use for 'em, after we leave this place. So the way I figure it, we blow their wall out big-time, and let a whole bunch of 'em loose at once. Then you and I can escape real easy in the confusion."

Katrinko loved this idea, but had to play devil's advocate. "You really think we ought to interfere like that? That kind of shows our hand, doesn't it?"

"Nobody's watching any more," said Pete. "Some technocrat figured this for a big lab experiment. But they wrote these people off, or maybe they lost their anthropology grant. These people are totally forgotten. Let's give the poor bastards a show."

Pete and Katrinko planted their explosives, took cover on the ceiling, and cheerfully watched the wall blow out.

A violent gust of air came through as pressures equalized, carrying a hemorrhage of dust and leaves into interstellar space. The locals were totally astounded by the explosion, but when the repair robots showed up, they soon recovered their morale. A terrific battle broke out, a general vengeful frenzy of crab-bashing and sponge-skewering. Women and children tussled with the keets and bibbets. Soldiers in leather cuirasses fought with the bigger machines, deploying pikes, crossbow quarrels, and big robot-mashing mauls.

The robots were profoundly stupid, but they were indifferent to their casualties, and entirely relentless.

The locals made the most of their window of opportunity. They loaded a massive harpoon into a torsion catapult, and fired it into space. Their target was the neighboring starship, the third and last of them.

The barbed spear bounded off the hull. So they reeled it back in on a monster bamboo hand-reel, cursing and shouting like maniacs.

The starship's entire population poured into the fight. The walls and bulkheads shook with the tramp of their angry feet. The outnumbered robots fell back. Pete and Katrinko seized this golden opportunity to slip out of the hole. They climbed swiftly up the hull, and out of reach of the combat.

The locals fired their big harpoon again. This time the barbed tip struck true, and it stuck there quivering.

Then a little kid was heaved into place, half-naked, with a hammer and screw, and a rope threaded through his belt. He had a crown of dripping candles set upon his head.

Katrinko glanced back, and stopped dead.

Pete urged her on, then stopped as well.

The child began reeling himself industriously along the trembling harpoon line, trailing a bigger rope. An airborne machine came to menace him. It fell back twitching, pestered by a nasty scattering of crossbow bolts.

Pete found himself mesmerized. He hadn't felt the desperation of the circumstances, until he saw this brave little boy ready to fall to his death. Pete had seen many climbers who took risks because they were crazy. He'd seen professional climbers, such as himself, who played games with risk as masters of applied technique. He'd never witnessed climbing as an act of raw, desperate sacrifice.

The heroic child arrived on the grainy hull of the alien ship, and began banging his pitons in a hammer-swinging frenzy. His crown of candles shook and flickered with his efforts. The boy could barely see. He had slung himself out into stygian darkness to fall to his doom.

Pete climbed up to Katrinko and quickly linked in on cable. "We gotta leave now, kid. It's now or never."

"Not yet," Katrinko said. "I'm taping all this."

"It's our big chance."

"We'll go later." Katrinko watched a flying vacuum cleaner batting by, to swat cruelly at the kid's legs. She turned her masked head to Pete and her whole body stiffened with rage. "You got a cheesewire left?"

"I got three."

"Gimme. I gotta go help him."

Katrinko unplugged, slicked down the starship's wall in a daring controlled slide, and hit the stretched rope. To Pete's complete astonishment, Katrinko lit there in a crouch, caught herself atop the vibrating line, and simply ran for it. She ran along the humming tightrope in a thrumming blur, stunning the locals so thoroughly that they were barely able to fire their crossbows.

Flying quarrels whizzed past and around her, nearly skewering the terrified child at the far end of the rope. Then Katrinko leapt and bounded into space, her gloves and cleats outspread. She simply vanished.

It was a champion's gambit if Pete had ever seen one. It was a legendary move.

Pete could manage well enough on a tightrope. He had experience, excellent balance, and physical acumen. He was, after all, a professional. He could walk a rope if he was put to the job.

But not in full climbing gear, with cleats. And not on a slack, handbraided, homemade rope. Not when the rope was very poorly anchored by a homemade pig-iron harpoon. Not when he outweighed Katrinko by twenty kilos. Not in the middle of a flying circus of airborne robots. And not in a cloud of arrows.

Pete was simply not that crazy any more. Instead, he would have to follow Katrinko the sensible way. He would have to climb the starship, traverse the ceiling, and climb down to the third starship onto the far side. A hard three hours' work at the very best—four hours, with any modicum of safety.

Pete weighed the odds, made up his mind, and went after the job.

Pete turned in time to see Katrinko busily cheesewiring her way through the hull of Starship Three. A gout of white light poured out as the cored plug slid aside. For a deadly moment, Katrinko was a silhouetted goblin, her camou useless as the starship's radiance framed her. Her clothing fluttered in a violent gust of escaping air.

Below her, the climbing child had anchored himself to the wall and tied off his second rope. He looked up at the sudden gout of light, and he screamed so loudly that the whole universe rang.

The child's many relatives reacted by instinct, with a ragged volley of crossbow shots. The arrows veered and scattered in the gusting wind, but there were a lot of them. Katrinko ducked, and flinched, and rolled headlong into the starship. She vanished again.

Had she been hit? Pete set an anchor, tied off, and tried the radio. But without the relays in the haulbag, the weak signal could not get through.

Pete climbed on doggedly. It was the only option left.

After half an hour, Pete began coughing. The starry cosmic cavity had filled with a terrible smell. The stench was coming from the invaded starship, pouring slowly from the cored-out hole. A long-bottled, deadly stink of burning rot.

Climbing solo, Pete gave it his best. His shoulder was bad and, worse yet, his spex began to misbehave. He finally reached the cored-out entrance that Katrinko had cut. The locals were already there in force, stringing themselves a sturdy rope bridge, and attaching it to massive screws. The locals brandished torches, spears, and crossbows. They were fighting off the incessant attacks of the robots. It was clear from their wild expressions of savage glee that they had been longing for this moment for years.

Pete slipped past them unnoticed, into Starship Three. He breathed the soured air for a moment, and quickly retreated again. He inserted a new set of mask filters, and returned.

He found Katrinko's cooling body, wedged against the ceiling. An unlucky crossbow shot had slashed through her suit and punctured Katrinko's left arm. So, with her usual presence of mind, she had deftly leapt up a nearby wall, tied off on a chock, and hidden herself well out of harm's way. She'd quickly stopped the bleeding. Despite its awkward location, she'd even managed to get her wound bandaged.

Then the foul air had silently and stealthily overcome her.

With her battered ribs and a major wound, Katrinko hadn't been able to tell her dizziness from shock. Feeling sick, she had relaxed, and tried to catch her breath. A fatal gambit. She was still hanging there, unseen and invisible, dead.

Pete discovered that Katrinko was far from alone. The crew here had all died. Died months ago, maybe years ago. Some kind of huge fire inside the spacecraft. The electric lights were still on, the internal machinery worked, but there as no one left here but mummies.

These dead tribal people had the nicest clothes Pete had yet seen. Clearly they'd spent a lot of time knitting and embroidering, during the many weary years of their imprisonment. The corpses had all kinds of layered sleeves and tatted aprons, and braided belt-ties, and lacquered hairclips, and excessively nifty little sandals. They'd all smothered horribly during the sullen inferno, along with their cats and dogs and enormous chickens, in a sudden wave of smoke and combustion that had filled their spacecraft in minutes.

This was far too complicated to be anything as simple as mere genocide. Pete figured the mandarins for gentlemen technocrats, experts with the best of intentions. The lively possibility remained that it was mass suicide. But on mature consideration, Pete had to figure this for a very bad, and very embarrassing, social engineering accident.

Though that certainly wasn't what they would say about this mess, in Washington. There was no political mess nastier than a nasty ethnic mess. Pete couldn't help but notice that these well-behaved locals hadn't bothered to do any harm to their spacecraft's lavish surveillance equipment. But their cameras were off and their starship was stone dead anyway.

The air began to clear inside the spacecraft. A pair of soldiers from Starship Number Two came stamping down the hall, industriously looting the local corpses. They couldn't have been happier about their opportunity. They were grinning with awestruck delight.

Pete returned to his comrade's stricken body. He stripped the camou suit—he needed the batteries. The neuter's lean and sexless corpse was puffy with subcutaneous storage pockets, big encystments of skin where Katrinko stored her last ditch escape tools. The battered ribs were puffy and blue. Pete could not go on.

Pete returned to the break-in hole, where he found an eager crowd. The invaders had run along the rope-bridge and gathered there in force, wrinkling their noses and cheering in wild exaltation. They had beaten the robots; there simply weren't enough of the machines on duty to resist a whole enraged population. The robots just weren't clever enough to out-think armed, coordinated human resistance—not without killing people wholesale, and they hadn't been designed for that. They had suffered a flat-out defeat.

Pete frightened the cheering victors away with a string of flash-bangs.

Then he took careful aim at the lip of the drop, and hoisted Katrinko's body, and flung her far, far, tumbling down, into the boiling pools.

Pete retreated to the first spacecraft. It was a very dispiriting climb, and when he had completed it, his shoulder had the serious, familiar ache of chronic injury. He hid among the unknowing population while he contemplated his options.

He could hide here indefinitely. His camou suit was slowly losing its charge, but he felt confident that he could manage very well without the suit. The starship seemed to feature most any number of taboo areas. Blocked-off no-go spots, where there might have been a scandal once, or bloodshed, or a funny noise, or a strange, bad, panicky smell.

Unlike the violent, reckless crowd in Starship Two, these locals had fallen for the cover story. They truly believed that they were in the depths of space bound for some better, brighter pie in their starry stone sky. Their little stellar ghetto was full of superstitious kinks. Steeped in profound ignorance, the locals imagined that their every sin caused the universe to tremble.

Pete knew that he should try to take his data back to the glider. This was what Katrinko would have wanted. To die, but leave a legend—a very City Spider thing.

But it was hard to imagine battling his way past resurgent robots, climbing the walls with an injured shoulder, then making a four-day bitter trek through a freezing desert, all completely alone. Gliders didn't last forever, either. Spy gliders weren't built to last. If Pete found the glider with its batteries flat, or its cute little brain gone sour, Pete would be all over. Even if he'd enjoyed a full set of equipment, with perfect health, Pete had few illusions about a solo spring outing, alone and on foot, over the Himalayas.

Why risk all that? After all, it wasn't like this subterranean scene was breaking news. It was already many years old. Someone had conceived, planned and executed this business a long time ago. Important people with brains and big resources had known all about this for years. *Somebody* knew. Maybe not the Lieutenant Colonel, on the lunatic fringe of NAFTA military intelligence. But.

When Pete really thought about the basic implications . . . This was a great deal of effort, and for not that big a payoff. Because there just weren't that many people cooped up down here. Maybe fifteen thousand of them, tops. The Asian Sphere must have had tens of thousands of unassimilated tribal people, maybe hundreds of thousands. Possibly millions. And why stop at that point? This wasn't just an Asian problem. It was a very general problem. Ethnic, breakaway people, who just plain couldn't, or wouldn't, play the twenty-first century's games.

How many Red Chinese atom-bomb tests had taken place deep in the Taklamakan? They'd never bothered to brief him on ancient history. But Pete had to wonder if, by now, maybe they hadn't gotten this stellar concept down to a fine art. Maybe the Sphere had franchised their plan to Europe and NAFTA. How many forgotten holes were there, relic pockets punched below the hide of the twenty-first century, in the South Pacific, and Australia, and Nevada? The deadly trash of a long-derailed Armageddon. The sullen trash heaps where no one would ever want to look.

Sure, he could bend every nerve and muscle to force the world to face all this. But why? Wouldn't it make better sense to try to think it through first?

Pete never got around to admitting to himself that he had lost the will to leave.

As despair slowly loosened its grip on him, Pete grew genuinely interested in the locals. He was intrigued by the stark limits of their lives and their universe, and in what he could do with their narrow little heads. They'd never had a supernatural being in their midst before; they just imagined them all the time. Pete started with a few poltergeist stunts, just to amuse himself. Stealing the spangled hats of the local greybeards. Shuffling the palm leaf volumes in their sacred libraries. Hijacking an abacus or two.

But that was childish.

The locals had a little temple, their special holy of holies. Naturally Pete made it his business to invade the place.

The locals kept a girl locked up in there. She was very pretty, and slightly insane, so this made her the perfect candidate to become their Sacred Temple Girl. She was the Official Temple Priestess of Starship Number One. Apparently, their modest community could only afford one, single, awe-inspiring Virgin High Priestess. But they were practical folks, so they did the best with what they had available.

The High Priestess was a pretty young woman with a stiflingly pretty life. She had her own maidservants, a wardrobe of ritual clothing, and a very time-consuming hairdo. The High Priestess spent her entire life carrying out highly complex, totally useless, ritual actions. Incense burnings, idol dustings, washings and purifications, forehead knocking, endless chanting, daubing special marks on her hands and feet. She was sacred and clearly demented, so they watched her with enormous interest, all the time. She meant everything to them. She was doing all these crazy, painful things so the rest of them wouldn't have to. Everything about her was completely and utterly foreclosed.

Pete quite admired the Sacred Temple Girl. She was very much his type, and he felt a genuine kinship with her. She was the only local that Pete could bear to spend any personal time with.

So after prolonged study of the girl and her actions, one day, Pete manifested himself to her. First, she panicked. Then she tried to kill him. Naturally that effort failed. When she grasped the fact that he was hugely powerful, totally magical, and utterly beyond her ken, she slithered around the polished temple floor, rending her garments and keening aloud, clearly in the combined hope/fear of being horribly and indescribably defiled.

Pete understood the appeal of her concept. A younger Pete would have gone for the demonic subjugation option. But Pete was all grown up now. He hardly saw how that could help matters any, or, in fact, make any tangible difference in their circumstances.

They never learned each other's languages. They never connected in any physical, mental, or emotional way. But they finally achieved a kind of status quo, where they could sit together in the same room, and quietly study one another, and fruitlessly speculate on the alien contents of one another's heads. Sometimes, they would even get together and eat something tasty.

That was every bit as good as his connection with these impossibly distant people was ever going to get.

* * *

It had never occurred to Pete that the stars might go out.

He'd cut himself a sacred, demonic bolt-hole, in a taboo area of the starship. Every once in a while, he would saw his way through the robots' repair efforts and nick out for a good long look at the artificial cosmos. This reassured him, somehow. And he had other motives as well. He had a very well founded concern that the inhabitants of Starship Two might somehow forge their way over, for an violent racist orgy of looting, slaughter, and rapine.

But Starship Two had their hands full with the robots. Any defeat of the bubbling gelbrain and its hallucinatory tools could only be temporary. Like an onrushing mudslide, the gizmos would route around obstructions, infiltrate every evolutionary possibility, and always, always keep the pressure on.

After the crushing defeat, the bubbling production vats went into biomechanical overdrive. The old regime had been overthrown. All equilibrium was gone. The machines had gone back to their cybernetic dreamtime. Anything was possible now.

The starry walls grew thick as fleas with a seething mass of new-model jailers. Starship Two was beaten back once again, in another bitter, uncounted, historical humiliation. Their persecuted homeland became a mass of grotesque cement. Even the portholes were gone now, cruelly sealed in technological spit and ooze. A living grave.

Pete had assumed that this would pretty much finish the job. After all, this clearly fit the parameters of the system's original designers.

But the system could no longer bother with the limits of human intent.

When Pete gazed through a porthole and saw that the stars were fading, he knew that all bets were off. The stars were being robbed. Something was embezzling their energy.

He left the starship. Outside, all heaven had broken loose. An unspeakable host of creatures were migrating up the rocky walls, bounding, creeping, lurching, rappelling on a web of gooey ropes. Heading for the stellar zenith.

Bound for transcendence. Bound for escape.

Pete checked his aging cleats and gloves, and joined the exodus at once.

None of the creatures bothered him. He had become one of them now. His equipment had fallen among them, been absorbed, and kicked open new doors of evolution. Anything that could breed a can opener could breed a rock chock and a piton, a crampon, and a pulley, and a carabiner. His haul bags, Katrinko's bags, had been stuffed with generations of focused human genius, and it was all about one concept: UP. Going up. Up and *out.*

The unearthly landscape of the Taklamakan was hosting a robot war. A spreading mechanical prairie of inching, crawling, biting, wrenching, hopping mutations. And pillars of fire: Sphere satellite warfare. Beams pouring down from the authentic heavens, invisible torrents of energy that threw up geysers of searing dust. A bioengineer's final nightmare. Smart, autonomous hell. They couldn't kill a thing this big and keep it secret. They couldn't burn it up fast enough. No, not without breaking the containment domes, and spilling their own ancient trash across the face of the earth.

A beam crossed the horizon like the finger of God, smiting everything in its path. The sky and earth were thick with flying creatures, buzzing, tumbling, sculling. The beam caught a big machine, and it fell spinning like a multiton maple seed. It bounded from the side of a containment dome, caromed like a dying gymnast, and landed below Spider Pete. He crouched there in his camou, recording it all.

It looked back at him. This was no mere robot. It was a mechanical civilian journalist. A brightly painted, ultramodern, European network drone, with as many cameras on board as a top-flight media mogul had martinis. The machine had smashed violently against the secret wall, but it was not dead. Death was not on its agenda. It was way game. It had spotted him with no trouble at all. He was a human interest story. It was looking at him.

Glancing into the cold spring sky, Pete could see that the journalist had brought a lot of its friends.

The robot rallied its fried circuits, and centered him within a spiraling focus. Then it lifted a multipronged limb, and ceremonially spat out every marvel it had witnessed, up into the sky and out into the seething depths of the global web.

Pete adjusted his mask and his camou suit. He wouldn't look right, otherwise.

"Dang," he said.

HATCHING THE PHOENIX

Frederik Pohl

Frederik Pohl (born 1919) is both a writer of the first rank and one of the most important editors in the history of the SF field. He has edited magazines such as *Galaxy* and *If*, original anthologies such as *Star Science Fiction*, and the Bantam Books SF publishing line.

Back when SF fans were cellar Christians, a small group of, for the most part, teenagers holding meetings in basements and planning for the future, Frederik Pohl was a member of the most left-wing of the fan groups, the Futurians. Pohl says in his autobiography, *The Way the Future Was* (1978), that some of them were Communists and some fellow travelers in the 1930s and into the 1940s. But to a very large extent in the 1930s, 1940s, and 1950s, the real-life politics of the writers was not overtly present in the fiction.

Sf had built a consensus future involving atomic power, space travel and the exploration of space, and the eventual evolution of a human-dominated galactic empire in the distant future. But politics was certainly present in the fanzines, and in the reviewing and criticism—Damon Knight's famous demolition of A. E. van Vogt is based in part on van Vogt's monarchism. When SF discovered its capacities as a genre for social satire and covert political criticism in the 1950s, when American SF became the major literature embodying criticism of McCarthyism, Pohl and his friends were leaders. As a group the Futurians were the cutting edge of the satirical movement of the fifties, and he was the satirical SF writer whom Kingsley Amis in his influential book on SF, *New Maps of Hell*, called "the most consistently able writer science fiction, in the modern sense, has yet produced." Although he edited pulp science fiction magazines, *Astonishing Stories* and *Super Science Stories*, in 1940–41 before he was twenty-one, he became prominent in the 1950s for his novels in collaboration with C. M. Kornbluth—including the classic *The Space Merchants* (1953); for a number of powerful and satiric short stories including "The Midas Plague" (1954) and "The Tunnel Under The World" (1955); and for editing anthologies—the most innovative all-original anthologies (and the first such in paperback) of the decade were the six volumes of *Star SF* (1953–1959).

His second flowering, as a hard SF writer, began in the 1970s with "The Gold at the Starbow's End," *Man Plus* (1976), and *Gateway* (1977), and has never abated. The continuing center of his later works has been stories and novels in the Heechee series, of which this is one. He was still at the peak of his powers in the 1990s and a continuing influence on other writers. It is interesting to compare and contrast Stephen Baxter's Xeelee series to Pohl's. Although Pohl's chosen mode has frequently been extrapolation of politics and society, with a deep and canny bow to psychology and psychiatry, his rigorous methodology has lent an underpinning of "hardness," to much of his best fiction (especially his work since 1970) that places it rightfully beside the best of Asimov, Clarke, Herbert, and Heinlein.

"Hatching the Phoenix" follows the human crew of a Heechee ship being taken to observe a supernova.

CHAPTER I

We were only about half a day out when we crossed the wavefront from the Crab supernova. I wouldn't even have noticed it, but my shipmind, Hypatia, is programmed to notice things that might interest me. So she asked me if I wanted to take a look at it, and I did.

Of course I'd already seen the star blow up two or three times in simulations, but as a flesh-and-blood human being I like reality better than simulations—most of the time, anyway. Hypatia had already turned on the Heechee screen, but it showed nothing other than the pebbly gray blur that the Heechee use. Hypatia can read those things, but I can't, so she changed the phase for me.

What I was seeing then was a field of stars, looking exactly like any other field of stars to me. It's a lack in me, I'm sure, but as far as I'm concerned every star looks like all the other stars in the sky, at least until you get close enough to it to see it as a sun. So I had to ask her, "Which one is it?"

She said, "You can't see it yet. We don't have that much magnification. But keep your eyes open. Wait a moment. Another moment. Now, there it is."

She didn't have to say that. I could see it for myself. Suddenly a point of light emerged and got brighter, and brighter still, until it outshone everything else on the screen. It actually made me squint. "It happens pretty fast," I said.

"Well, not really *that* fast, Klara. Our vector velocity, relative to the star, is quite a lot faster than light, so we're speeding things up. Also, we're catching up with the wavefront, so we're seeing it all in reverse. It'll be gone soon."

And a moment later it was. Just as the star was brightest of all, it unexploded itself. It became a simple star again, so unremarkable that I couldn't even pick it out. Its planets were unscorched again, their populations, if any, not yet whiffed into plasma. "All right," I said, somewhat impressed but not enough to want Hypatia to know it, "turn the screen off and let's get back to work."

Hypatia sniffed—she has built herself a whole repertoire of human behaviors that I had never had programmed into her. She said darkly, "We'd better, if we want to be able to pay all the bills for this thing. Do you have any idea what this is *costing*?"

Of course, she wasn't serious about that. I have problems, but being able to pay my bills isn't one of them.

I wasn't always this solvent. When I was a kid on that chunk of burned-out hell they call the planet Venus, driving an airbody around its baked, bleak surface for the tourists all day and trying not to spend any of my pay all night, what I wanted most was to have money. I wasn't hoping for a whole lot of money. I just wanted enough money so that I could afford Full Medical and a place to live that didn't stink of rancid seafood. I wasn't dreaming on any vast scale.

It didn't work out that way, though. I never did have exactly that much money. First I had none at all and no real hopes of ever getting any. Then I had much, much more than that, and I found out something about having a lot of money. When you have the kind of money that's spelled M*O*N*E*Y, it's like having a kitten in the house. The money wants you to play with it. You can try to leave it alone, but if you do it'll be crawling into your lap and nibbling at your chin for attention. You don't have to give in to what the money wants. You can just push it away and go about your business, but then God knows what mischief it'll get into if you do, and anyway then where's the fun of having it?

So most of the way out to the PhoenixCorp site, Hypatia and I played with my money. That is, I played with it while Hypatia kept score. She remembers what I own better than I do—that's her nature, being the sort of task she was designed to do—and she's always full of suggestions about what investments I should dump or hold or what new ventures I should get into.

The key word there is "suggestions." I don't have to do what Hypatia says. Sometimes I don't. As a general rule I follow Hypatia's suggestions about four times out of five. The fifth time I do something different, just to let her know that I'm the one who makes the decisions here. I know that's not smart, and it generally costs me money when I do. But that's all right. I have plenty to spare.

There's a limit to how long I'm willing to go on tickling the money's tummy, though. When I had just about reached that point, Hypatia put down her pointer and waved the graphics displays away. She had made herself optically visible to humor me, because I like to see the person I'm talking to, wearing her fifth-century robes and coronet of rough-cut rubies and all, and she gave me an inquiring look. "Ready to take a little break, Klara?" she asked. "Do you want something to eat?"

Well, I was, and I did. She knew that perfectly well. She's continually monitoring my body, because that's one of the other tasks she's designed to do, but I like to keep my free will going there, too. "Actually," I said, "I'd rather have a drink. How are we doing for time?"

"Right on schedule, Klara. We'll be there in ten hours or so." She didn't move—that is, her simulation didn't move—but I could hear the clink of ice going into a glass in the galley. "I've been accessing the PhoenixCorp shipmind. If you want to see what's going on . . . ?"

"Do it," I said, but she was already doing it. She waved again—pure theater, of course, but Hypatia's full of that—and we got a new set of graphics. As the little serving cart rolled in and stopped just by my right hand, we were looking through PhoenixCorp's own visuals, and what we were looking at was a dish-shaped metal spiderweb, with little things crawling across it. I could form no precise picture of its size, because there was nothing in the space around it to compare it with. But I didn't have to. I knew it was big.

"Have one for yourself," I said, lifting my glass.

She gave me that patient, exasperated look and let it pass. Sometimes she does simulate having a simulated drink with me while I have a real one, but this time she was in her schoolteacher mode. "As you can see, Klara," she informed me, "the shipment of optical mirror pieces has arrived, and the drones are putting them in place on the parabolic dish. They'll be getting first light from the planet in an hour or so, but I don't think you'll care about seeing it. The resolution will be poor until they get everything put together; that should take about eighteen hours. Then we should have optimal resolution to observe the planet."

"For four days," I said, taking a pull at my glass.

She gave me a different look—still the schoolteacher, but now a schoolteacher putting up with a particularly annoying student. "Hey, Klara. You knew there wouldn't be much time. It wasn't my idea to come all the way out here anyway. We could have watched the whole thing from your island."

I swallowed the rest of my nightcap and stood up. "That's not how I wanted to do it," I told her. "The trouble with you simulations is that you don't appreciate what reality is like. Wake me up an hour before we get there."

And I headed for my stateroom, with my big and round and unoccupied bed. I didn't want to chat with Hypatia just then. The main reason I had kept her busy giving me financial advice so long was that it prevented her from giving me advice on the thing she was always trying to talk me into, or that one other big thing that I really needed to make up my mind about, and couldn't.

The cart with my black coffee and fresh-squeezed orange juice—make that quote "fresh-squeezed" unquote orange juice, but Hypatia was too good at her job for me to be able to tell the difference—was right by my bed when she woke me up. "Ninety minutes to linkup," she said cheerily, "and a very good morning to you. Shall I start your shower?"

I said, "Um." Ninety minutes is not a second too long for me to sit and swallow coffee, staring into space, before I have to do anything as energetic as getting into a shower. But then I looked into the wall mirror by the bed, didn't like what I saw, and decided I'd better spruce myself up a little bit.

I was never what you'd call a pretty woman. My eyebrows were a lot too heavy, for one thing. Once or twice over the years I'd had the damn things thinned down to fashion-model proportions, just to see if it would help any. It didn't. I'd even messed around with my bone structure, more cheekbones, less jaw, to try to look a little less masculine. It just made me look weak-faced. For a couple of years I'd gone blonde, then tried redhead once but checked it out and made them change it back before I left the beauty parlor. They were all mistakes. They didn't work. Whenever I looked at myself, whatever the cosmetologists and the medical fixer-uppers had done, I could still see the old Gelle-Klara Moynlin hiding there behind all the trim. So screw it. For the last little while I'd gone natural.

Well, pretty natural, anyway. I didn't want to look *old*.

I didn't, of course. By the time I was bathed and my hair was fixed and I was wearing a simple dress that showed off my pretty good legs, actually, I looked as good as I ever had. "Almost there," Hypatia called. "You better hang on to something. I have to match velocities, and it's a tricky job." She sounded annoyed, as she usually does when I give her something hard to do. She does it, of course, but she complains a lot. "Faster than light I can do, slower than light I can do, but when you tell me to match velocity with somebody who's doing exactly *c* you're into some pretty weird effects, so—Oh, sorry."

"You should be," I told her, because that last lurch had nearly made me spill my third cup of coffee. "Hypatia? What do you think, the pearls or the cameo?"

She did that fake two- or three-second pause, as though she really needed any time at all to make a decision, before she gave me the verdict. "I'd wear the cameo. Only whores wear pearls in the daytime."

So of course I decided to wear the pearls. She sighed but didn't comment. "All right," she said, opening the port. "We're docked. Mind the step, and I'll keep in touch."

I nodded and stepped over the seals into the PhoenixCorp mother ship.

There wasn't any real "step." What there was was a sharp transition from the comfortable one gee I kept in my own ship to the gravityless environment of the PhoenixCorp ship. My stomach did a quick little flip-flop of protest, but I grabbed a hold-on bar and looked around.

I don't know what I'd expected to find, maybe something like the old Gateway asteroid. PhoenixCorp had done itself a lot more lavishly than that, and I began to wonder if I hadn't maybe been a touch too open-handed with the financing. The place certainly didn't smell like Gateway. Instead of Gateway's sour, ancient fug, it had the wetly sweet smell of a greenhouse. That was because there were vines and ferns and flowers growing in pots all around the room—spreading out in all directions, because of that zero-gee environment, and if I'd thought about that ahead of time, I wouldn't have worn a skirt. The only human being in sight was a tall, nearly naked black man who was hanging by one toe from a wall bracket, exercising his muscles with one of those metal-spring gadgets. ("Humphrey Mason-Manley," Hypatia whispered in my ear. "He's the archeologist-anthropologist guy from the British Museum.") Without breaking his rhythm, Humphrey gave me a look of annoyance.

"What are you doing here, miss? No visitors are permitted. This is private property, and—"

Then he got a better look at me and his expression changed. Not to welcoming exactly, but to what I'd call sort of unwillingly impressed. "Oh, crikey," he said. "You're Gelle-Klara Moynlin, are you not? That's a bit different. Welcome aboard, I guess."

CHAPTER II

It wasn't the most affable greeting I'd ever had. However, when Humphrey Mason-Manley woke up the head engineer for me, she turned out to be a lot more courteous. She didn't have to be, either. Although I had put up the seed money to get the project started, PhoenixCorp was set up as a nonprofit institution, owned by nobody but itself. I wasn't even on the board.

The boss engineer's name, Hypatia whispered to me, was June Thaddeus Terple—*Doctor* Terple. I didn't really need the reminder. Terple and I had met before, though only by screen, when she was trying to scare up money for this venture and somebody had given her my name. In person she was taller than I'd thought. She looked to be about the age I looked to be myself, which is to say, charitably, thirty-ish. She was wearing a kind of string bikini, plus a workman's belt of little pouches around her waist so she could keep stuff in it. She took me into her office, which was a sort of wedge-shaped chamber with nothing much visible in it but handholds on the walls and a lot more of those flowering plants. "Sorry I wasn't there to meet you, Dr. Moynlin," she said.

"I'm not a doctor of anything, except honorary, and Klara's good enough."

She bobbed her head. "Anyway, of course you're welcome here any time. I guess you wanted to see for yourself how we're coming along."

"Well, I did want that, yes. I also wanted to set something up, if you don't mind." That was me returning courtesy for courtesy, however unnecessary it was in either direction. "Do you know who Wilhelm Tartch is?"

She thought for a moment. "No."

So much for his galaxywide fame. I explained. "Bill's a kind of roving reporter. He has a program that goes out all over, even to the Heechee in the Core. It's sort of a travelogue. He visits exciting and colorful places and reports on them for the stay-at-homes." He was also my present main lover, but there wasn't any reason to mention that to Terple; she would figure it out for herself fast enough.

"And he wants to do PhoenixCorp?"

"If you don't mind," I said again. "I did clear it with the board."

She grinned at me. "So you did, but I sort of lost track of it. We've been deploying the drones, so it's been kind of busy." She shook herself. "Anyway, Hans tells me your shipmind displayed the actual supernova explosion to you on the way out."

"That's right, she did." In my ear Hypatia was whispering that Hans was the name of their shipmind, as though I couldn't figure that out for myself.

"And I suppose you know what it looks like from Earth now?"

"Well, sort of."

I could see her assessing how much "sort of" amounted to, and deciding to be diplomatic to the money person. "It wouldn't hurt to take another look. Hans! Telescopic view from Earth, please."

She was looking toward one end of her office. It disappeared, and in its place we were looking out at a blotchy patch of light. "That's it. It's called the Crab Nebula. Of course, they named it that before they really knew what it was, but you can see where they got the name." I agreed that it did look a little like some sort of deformed crab, and Terple went on. "The nebula itself is just the gases and stuff that the supernova threw off, a thousand years or so later. I don't know if you can make it out, but there's a little spot in the middle of it that's the Crab pulsar. That's all that's left of the star. Now let's look at the way it was before it went super."

Hans wiped the nebula away, and we were looking into the same deep, black space Hypatia had shown me already. There were the same zillion stars hanging there, but as the shipmind zoomed the picture closer, one extraordinarily bright one appeared. "Bright" didn't do it justice. It was a blazing golden yellow, curiously fuzzy. It wasn't really hot. It couldn't be; the simulation was only optical. But I could almost feel its heat on my face.

"I don't see any planet," I offered.

"Oh, you will, once we get all the optical segments in place." Then she interrupted herself. "I forgot to ask. Would you like a cup of tea or something?"

"Thanks, no. Nothing right this minute." I was peering at the star. "I thought it would be brighter," I said, a little disappointed.

"Oh, it will be, Klara. That's what we're building that five-hundred-kilometer mirror for. Right now we're just getting the gravitational lensing from the black hole we're using—there's a little camera in the mirror. I don't know if you know much about black holes, but—oh, shit," she interrupted herself, suddenly stricken. "You do know, don't you? I mean, after you were stuck in one for thirty or forty years . . ."

She looked as though she had inadvertently caused me great pain. She hadn't. I was used to that sort of reaction. People rarely brought up the subject of black holes in my presence, on the general principle that you don't talk about rope when there's been a hanging in the house. But the time I was trapped in one of them was far back in the past. It had gone like a flash for me in the black hole's time dilation, whatever the elapsed time was on the outside, and I wasn't sensitive about it.

On the other hand, I wasn't interested in discussing it one more damn time, either, so I just said, "My black hole didn't look like that. It was a creepy kind of pale blue."

Terple recovered quickly. She gave me a wise nod of the head. "That would have been Cerenkov radiation. Yours must have been what they call a naked singularity. This one's different. It's wrapped up in its own ergosphere and you can't see a thing. Most black holes produce a lot of radiation—not from themselves, from the gases and stuff they're swallowing—but this one has already swallowed everything around it. Anyway." She paused to recollect her train of thought. Then she nodded. "I was telling you about the gravitational lensing. Hans?"

She didn't say what she wanted from Hans, but evidently he could figure it out for himself. The stars disappeared, and a sort of wall of misty white appeared in front of us. Terple poked at it here and there with a finger, drawing a little picture for me:

"That little dot on the left, that's the Crabber planet we want to study. The circle's the black hole. The arc on the right is our mirror, which is right at the point of convergence—where the gravitational lensing from the black hole gives us the sharpest image. And the little dot next to it is us, at the Cassegrain focus of the mirror. I didn't show the Crabber sun—actually we have to avoid aiming the camera at it, because it could burn out our optics. Am I making sense so far?"

"So far," I agreed.

She gave me another of those assessing looks, then said, "We'll actually be doing our observing by looking toward the mirror, not toward the Crab planet. There too we'll have to block out the star itself, or we won't see the actual planet at all, but that's just another of the things we'll be adjusting. Then we'll actually be looking diametrically away from the planet in order to observe it."

I hadn't been able to resist the temptation with Hypatia, and I couldn't now with June Terple. "For four or five days," I said in my friendliest voice.

I guess the tone wasn't friendly enough. She looked nettled. "Listen, we didn't put the damn black hole where it is. It took us two years of searching to find one in the right position. There's a neutron star that we could've used. Orbitwise it was a better deal because it would have given us nearly eighty years to observe, but it's just a damn neutron star. It wouldn't have given us anywhere the same magnification, because a neutron star just doesn't have anywhere near as much mass as a black hole, so the gravitational lensing would've been a lot less. We'll get a lot more detail with our black hole. Anyway," she added, "once we've observed from here we'll move this whole lash-up to the neutron star for whatever additional data we can get—I mean, uh, if that seems advisable, we will."

What she meant by that was if I was willing to pay for it. Well, I probably was. The capital costs were paid; it would only mean meeting their payroll for another eighty years or so.

But I wasn't ready to make that commitment. To take her mind off it, I said, "I thought we were supposed to have almost thirty days of observing right here."

She looked glum. "*Radio* observing. That's why we built the mesh dish. But it turns out there's no radio coming from the Crabber planet at all, so we had to get the mirror plates to convert it to optical. Took us over three weeks, which is why we lost so much observing time."

"I see," I said. "No radio signals. So there might not be any civilization there to observe, anyway."

She bit her lip. "We know definitely that there's *life* there. Or was, anyway. It's one of the planets the Heechee surveyed long ago, and there were advanced living organisms there at the time—pretty primitive, sure, but they certainly looked as though they had the potential to evolve."

"The *potential* to evolve, right. But whether they did or not we just don't know."

She didn't answer that. She just sighed. Then she said, "As long as you're here, would you like a look around?"

"If I won't be in the way," I said.

Of course I was in the way. June Terple didn't let it show, but some of the others barely gave me the courtesy of looking up when we were introduced. There were eight of them altogether, with names like Julia Ibarruru and Mark Rohrbeck and Humphrey Mason-Manley and Oleg Kekuskian and—well, I didn't have to try to retain them all; Hypatia would clue me as needed. Humphrey Mason-Manley was the guy who'd been building his pecs when I came in. Julia was the one who was floating in a harness surrounded by fifteen or twenty 3-D icons that she was busy poking at and glowering at and poking at again, and she gave me no more than a quick and noncommittal nod. If my name meant anything to her, or to most of the others, they didn't show any signs of being impressed. Especially Rohrbeck and Kekuskian didn't, because they were sound asleep in their harnesses when we peeked in on them, and Terple had a finger to her lips. "Third shift," she whispered when we'd closed the flaps on their cubicles and moved away. "They'll be waking up for dinner in a little while, but let's let them get their sleep. And there's only one other. Let's go find her."

On the way to that one other member of the crew, Hypatia was whispering bits of biography in my ear. Kekuskian was the quite elderly and bisexual astrophysicist. Rohrbeck the quite young and deeply depressed program designer, whose marriage had just come painfully apart. And the one remaining person was . . .

Was a Heechee.

I didn't have to be told that. Once you've seen any one Heechee, you know what they all look like; skeletally thin front to back, squarish, skull-like faces, their data pod hanging between their legs where, if they were male, their balls should be, and if female (as this one turned out to be), there shouldn't be anything much at all. Her name, Terple said, was Starminder, and as we entered her chamber she was working at a set of icons of her own. But as soon as she heard my name she wiped them and barreled over to me to shake my hand. "You are very famous among us in the Core, Gelle-Klara Moynlin," she informed me, hanging on to my hand for support. "Because of your Moynlin Citizen Ambassadors, you see. When your Rebecca Shapiro person came to our city, she was invited to stay with the father of my husband's family, which is where I met her. She was quite informative about human beings; indeed, it was because of her that I volunteered at once to come out. Do you know her?"

I tried to remember Rebecca Shapiro. I had put up grant money for a good many batches of recruits since I funded the program, and she would have had to be one of the earliest of them. Starminder saw my uncertainty and tried to be helpful. "Young woman. Very sad. She sang music composed by your now-dead Wolfgang Amadeus Mozart for our people, which I almost came to enjoy."

"Oh, right, *that* Rebecca," I said, not very honestly. By then I'd paid the fare to the Core for—what?—at least two or three hundred Rebeccas or Carloses or Janes who volunteered to be Citizen Ambassadors to the Heechee in the Core because they had lives that were a shambles. That was a given. If their lives hadn't been, why would they want to leave the people and places they wouldn't ever come back to?

Because, of course, the Core was time-dilated, like any black hole. I knew what that meant. When you were time-dilated in the Core, where a couple of centuries of outside time went by every day, the problems you left behind got really old really fast. Time dilation was better than suicide—though, when you came to think of it, actually a kind of reverse suicide is pretty much what it was. You didn't die yourself, but every troublesome person you'd ever known did while you were gone.

I wish all those Citizen Ambassadors of mine well. I hope it all works out for them . . . but being in a black hole hadn't done a thing for me.

Once I'd met all the people on the PhoenixCorp ship, there wasn't much else to see. I had misjudged my budget-watchers. Terple hadn't been that spendthrift after all. If you didn't count the opulent plantings—and they were there primarily to keep the air good—the PhoenixCorp ship actually was a pretty bare-bones kind of spacecraft. There were the sleeping quarters for the help, and some common rooms—the big one I'd come into when I first entered, plus a sort of dining room with beverage dispensers and netting next to the hold-ons to keep the meals from flying away, a couple of little rooms for music or virtuals when the people wanted some recreation. The rest of it was storage and, of course, all the machinery and instrumentation PhoenixCorp needed to do its job. Terple didn't show me any of the hardware. I didn't expect her to. That's the shipmind's business, and that sort of thing stays sealed away where no harm can come to it. So, unless somebody had been foolish enough to open up a lot of compartments that were meant to stay closed, there wouldn't have been anything to see.

When we were finished, she finally insisted on that cup of tea—really that capsule of tea, that is—and while we were drinking it, holding with one hand to the hold-ons, she said, "That's about it, Klara. Oh, wait a minute. I haven't actually introduced you to our shipmind, have I? Hans? Say hello to Ms. Moynlin."

A deep, pleasant male voice said, "Hello, Ms. Moynlin. Welcome aboard. We've been hoping you'd visit us."

I said hello back to him and left it at that. I don't particularly like chatting with machine intelligences, except my own. I finished my tea, slid the empty capsule into its slot, and said, "Well, I'll get out of your way. I want to get back to my own ship for a bit anyway."

Terple nodded and didn't ask why. "We're going to have dinner in about an hour. Would you like to join us? Hans is a pretty good cook."

That sounded like as good an idea as any, so I told her that would be fine.

Then, as she was escorting me to the docking port, she gave me a sidewise look. "Listen," she said, "I'm sorry we bombed out on the radio search. It doesn't necessarily mean that the Crabbers never got civilized. After all, if somebody had scanned Earth any time before the twentieth century, they wouldn't have heard any radio signals there, either, but the human race was fully evolved by then."

"I know that, June."

"Yes." She cleared her throat. "Do you mind if I ask you a question?"

I said, "Of course not," meaning that she could ask anything she wanted to, but whether or what I chose to answer was another matter entirely.

"Well, you put a lot of money into getting Phoenix started, just on the chance that there might have been an intelligent race there that got fried when their sun went super. What I'm wondering is why."

The answer to that was simple enough. I mean, what's the point of being just about the richest woman in the universe if you don't have a little fun with your money now and then? But I didn't say that to her. I just said, "What else do I have to do?"

CHAPTER III

Well, I did have things to do. Lots of them, though most of them weren't very important.

The only one that was really important—to me—was overseeing the little island off Tahiti that I live on when I'm home. It's a nice place, the way I've fixed it up. Most of my more-or-less family is there, and when I'm away I really miss them.

Then there are other important things, such as spending some time with Bill Tartch, who is a fairly sweet man, not to mention all the others like Bill Tartch who have come along over the years. Or such things as all the stuff I can buy with my money, plus figuring out what to do with the power that that kind of money gives. Put them all together, I had *plenty* to do with my life. And I had plenty of life to look forward to, too, especially if I let Hypatia talk me into immortality.

So why wasn't I looking forward to it?

When I came back into my ship, Hypatia was waiting for me—visible, in full 3-D simulation, lounging draped Roman-style on the love seat in the main cabin and fully dressed in her fifth-century robes.

"So how did you like your investment?" she asked sociably.

"Tell you in a minute," I said, going to the head and closing the door behind me. Of course, a closed door makes no real difference with Hypatia. She can see me wherever I am on the ship, and no doubt does, but as long as a machine intelligence acts and looks human, I want it to pretend to observe human courtesies.

Hitting the head was the main reason I'd come back to my ship just then. I don't like peeing in free fall, in those awful toilets they have. Hypatia keeps ours at a suitable gravity for my comfort, like the rest of the ship. Besides, it makes her nervous if I use any toilets outside the ship, because she likes to rummage through my excretions to see if I'm staying healthy.

Which she had been doing while I was in the head. When I came out, she didn't seem to have moved, but she said, "Are you really going to eat their food?"

"Sure. Why not?"

"You've been running a little high on polyglycerides. Better you let me cook for you."

Teasing her, I said, "June Terple says Hans is a better cook."

"She said he's a good cook," she corrected me, "but so am I. I've been accessing him, by the way, so if there's anything you'd like to know about the crew . . ."

"Not about the crew, but Starminder said something about a Rebecca Shapiro. Who was she?"

"That data is not in the Phoenix shipmind's stores, Klara," she said, reproving me. "However . . ."

She whited out a corner of my lounge and displayed a face on it while she gave me a capsule biography of Rebecca Shapiro. Rebecca had been a dramatic soprano with a brilliant operatic future ahead of her until she got her larynx crushed in a plane crash. They'd repaired it well enough for most purposes, but she was never going to be able to sing "The Queen of the Night" again. So, with her life on Earth ruined, Rebecca had signed up for my program. "Any other questions?" Hypatia said.

"Not about Rebecca, but I've been wondering why they call their shipmind Hans."

"Oh, that was Mark Rohrbeck's idea; he wanted to name him after some old computer pioneer. The name doesn't matter, though, does it? I mean, why did you decide to call me Hypatia?"

"Because Hypatia of Alexandria was a smart, snotty bitch," I told her. "Like you."

"Humph," she said.

"As well as being the first great woman scientist," I added, because Hypatia always likes to talk about herself.

"The first *known* one," she corrected. "Who knows how many there were whose accomplishments didn't manage to survive? Women didn't get much of a break in your ancient meat world—or, for that matter, now."

"You were supposed to be beautiful, too," I reminded her. "And you died a virgin anyway."

"By choice, Klara. Even that old Hypatia didn't care much for all that messy meat stuff. And I didn't just die. I was brutally murdered. It was a cold wet spring in A.D. 450, and a gang of those damn Nitrian monks tore me to shreds because I wasn't a Christian. Anyway," she finished, "you're the one who picked my identity. If you wanted me to be someone else, you could have given me a different one."

She had me grinning by then. "I still can," I reminded her. "Maybe something like Joan of Arc?"

She shuddered fastidiously at the idea of being a Christian instead of a gods-fearing Roman pagan and changed the subject. "Would you like me to put a call through to Mr. Tartch now?"

Well, I would and I wouldn't. I had unfinished business to settle with Bill Tartch, but I wasn't quite ready to settle it, so I shook my head. "I've been wondering about these extinct people we're trying to resurrect. Have you got any Heechee records of the planet that I haven't seen yet?"

"You bet. More than you'll ever want to watch."

"So show me some."

"Sure thing, boss," she said, and disappeared, and all at once I was standing on an outcropping of rock, looking down on a bright, green valley where some funny-looking animals were moving around.

That was the difference between PhoenixCorp's major simulations and mine. Mine cost more. Theirs were good enough for working purposes, because they showed you pretty much anything you wanted to see, but mine put you right in the middle of it. Mine were full sensory systems, too, so I could smell and feel as well as I could see and hear. As I stood there, a warm breeze ruffled my hair, and I smelled a distinct reek of smoke. "Hey, Hypatia," I said, a little surprised. "Have these people discovered fire?"

"Not to use, no," she murmured in my ear. "Must've been a lightning strike up in the hills from the storm."

"What storm?"

"The one that just passed. Don't you see everything's wet?"

Not on my rock, it wasn't. The sun overhead was big and bright and very hot. It had already baked the rock dry, but I could see that the jumble of dark green vines at the base of my rock was still dripping, and when I turned around I could see a splotch of burning vegetation on the distant hill.

The valley was more interesting. Patches of trees, or something like trees; a herd of big, shaggy creatures, Kodiak bear-sized but obviously vegetarians because they were industriously pushing some of the trees over to eat their leaves; a pair of rivers, a narrow, fast-moving one with little waterfalls that came down from the hills to my left and flowed to join a broader, more sluggish one on the right to make a bigger stream; a few other shaggy creatures, these quite a lot bigger still, feeding by themselves on whatever was growing in the plain—well, it was an interesting sight; maybe a little like the great American prairie or the African veldt must have looked before our forebears killed off all the wild meat animals.

The most interesting part of the simulation was a pack of a dozen or so predators in the middle distance, circling furtively around a group of three or four creatures I couldn't easily make out. I pointed. "Are those the ones?" I asked Hypatia. And when she said they were, I told her to get me up closer.

At close range I could see the hunted ones looked something like pigs—that is, if pigs happened to have long, skinny legs and long, squirrelly tails. I noticed a mommy pig baring her teeth and trying to snap at the predators in all directions at once, and three little ones doing their best to huddle under the mother's belly. It was the predators I was paying attention to. They looked vaguely primate. That is, they had apelike faces and short tails. But they didn't look like any primate that ever lived on Earth, because they had six limbs: four that they ran on, and two more like arms, and in their sort-of hands they held sharp-edged rocks. As they got into position, they began hurling the rocks at the prey.

The mother pig didn't have a chance. In a couple of minutes, two of her babies were down and she was racing away with that long tail flicking from side to side like a metronome, and the surviving piglet right behind her, its tail-flicks keeping time with its mother's, and the six-limbed predators had what they had come for.

It was not a pretty scene.

I know perfectly well that animals live by eating, and I'm not sentimental about the matter—hell, I eat steak! (Not always out of a food factory, either.) All the same, I didn't like watching what was happening on this half-million-year-old alien veldt, because one of the piglets was still alive when the wolf-apes began eating it, and its pitiful shrieking got to me.

So I wasn't a bit sorry when Hypatia interrupted me to say that Mr. Tartch hadn't waited for me to call him and was already on the line.

Nearly all of my conversations with Bill Tartch get into some kind of intimate area. He likes that kind of sexy talk. I don't particularly, so I tried to keep the call short. The basic facts he had to convey were that he missed me and that, unspokenly, he looked as good as ever—not very tall, not exactly handsome but solidly built and with a great, challenging I-know-what-fun-is-all-about grin—and that he was just two days out. That's not a lot of hard data to get out of what was more than a quarter-hour of talk capsuled back and forth over all those light-years, I guess, but the rest was private; and when I was finished, it was about time to get dressed for dinner with the PhoenixCorp people.

Hypatia was way ahead of me, as usual. She had gone through my wardrobe and used her effectuators to pull out a dressy pants suit for me, so I wouldn't have a skirt to keep flying up, along with a gold neckband that wouldn't be flopping around my face as the pearls had. They were good choices; I didn't argue. And while I was getting into them she asked chattily, "So did Mr. Tartch say thank you?"

I know Hypatia's tones by now. This one made my hackles rise. "For what?"

"Why, for keeping his career going," she said, sounding surprised. "He was pretty much washed up until you came along, wasn't he? So it's only appropriate that he should, you know, display his gratitude."

"You're pushing your luck," I told her as I slipped into a pair of jeweled stockings. Sometimes I think Hypatia gets a little too personal, and this time it just wasn't justified. I didn't have to do favors to get a man. Christ, the problem was to fend them off! It's just that when it's over I like to leave them a little better off than I found them; and Bill, true enough, had reached that stage in his career when a little help now and then was useful.

But I didn't want to discuss it with her. "Talk about something else or shut up," I ordered.

"Sure, hon. Let's see. How did you like the Crabbers?"

I told her the truth. "Not much. Their table manners are pretty lousy."

Hypatia giggled. "Getting a weak stomach, Klara? Do you really think they're much worse than your own remote predecessors? Because I don't think *Australopithecus robustus* worried too much about whether its dinners were enjoying the meal, either."

We were getting into a familiar argument. "That was a long time ago, Hypatia."

"So is what you were looking at with the Crabbers, hon. Animals are animals. Now, if you really want to take yourself out of that nasty kill-and-eat business—"

"Not yet," I told her, as I had told her many times before.

What Hypatia wanted to do was to vasten me. That is, take me out of my meat body, with all its aches and annoyances, and make me into a pure, machine-stored intelligence. As other people I knew had done. Like Hypatia herself, though in her case she was no more than a simulated approximation of someone who had once been living meat.

It was a scary idea, to be sure, but not altogether unattractive. I wasn't getting as much pleasure as I would have liked out of living, but I certainly didn't want to *die*. And if I did what Hypatia wanted, I would never have to.

But I wasn't prepared to take that step yet. There were one or two things a meat person could do that a machine person couldn't—well, one big one—and I wasn't prepared to abandon the flesh until I had done what the female flesh was best at. For which I needed a man . . . and I wasn't at all sure that Bill Tartch was the particular man I needed.

When I got back for dinner in the PhoenixCorp vessel, everybody was looking conspiratorial and expectant. "We've got about twenty percent of the optical sheets in place," Terple informed me, thrilled with excitement. "Would you like like to see?" She didn't wait for an answer, but commanded: "Hans! Display the planet."

The lights went dark, and before us floated a blue-and-white globe the size of my head, looking as though it were maybe ten meters away. It was half in darkness and half in sunlight, from a sun that was out of sight off to my right. There was a half-moon, too, just popping into sight from behind the planet. It looked smaller than Luna, and if it had markings of craters and seas, I couldn't see them. On the planet itself I could make out a large ocean and a kind of squared-off continent on the illuminated side. Terple did something that made the lights in the room go off, and then I could see that there had to be even more land on the dark side, because spots of light—artificial lights, cities' lights—blossomed all over parts of the nighttime area.

"You see, Klara?" she crowed. "Cities! Civilization!"

CHAPTER IV

Their shipmind really was a good cook. Fat pink shrimp that tasted as though they'd come out of the sea within the hour, followed by a fritto misto, the same, with a decent risotto and figs in cream for dessert. Everything was all perfectly prepared. Or maybe it just seemed so, because everybody was visibly relaxing now that it had turned out we really did have something to observe.

What there wasn't any of was wine to go with the meal, just some sort of tropical juices in the winebulbs. June Terple noticed my expression when I tasted it. "We're not doing anything alcoholic until we've completed the obs," she said, half apologetic, half challenging, "Still, I think Hans can get you something if you really want it."

I shook my head politely, but I was wondering if Hypatia had happened to say anything to Hans about my fondness for a drink now and then. Probably she had; shipminds do gossip when they're as advanced as Hypatia and Hans, and it was evident that the crew did know something about me. The conversation was lively and far-ranging, but it never, never touched on the subject of the black hole itself, or black holes in general.

We made a nice, leisurely meal of it. The only interruptions were inconspicuous, as crew members one after another briefly excused themselves to doublecheck how well the spider robots were doing as they clambered all over that five-hundred-kilometer dish, seamlessly stitching the optical reflection plates into their perfect parabola. None of the organic crew really had to bother. Hans was permanently vigilant, about that and everything else, but Terple obviously ran a tight ship. A lot of the back-and-forth chat was in-jokes, but that wasn't a problem because Hypatia explained them, whispering in my ear.

When somebody mentioned homesickness and Oleg Kekuskian said jestingly—*pointedly* jestingly—that some of us weren't homesick at all, the remark was aimed at Humphrey Mason-Manley: "He's pronging Terple, Klara, and Kekuskian's jealous," Hypatia told me.

Julia—that was *Hoo*-lia—Ibarruru, the fat and elderly Peruvian-Incan former schoolteacher, was wistfully telling Starminder how much she wished she could visit the Core before she died, and was indignant when she found out that I'd never been to Machu Picchu. "And you've been all over the galaxy? And never took the time to see one of the greatest wonders of your own planet?"

The only subdued one was Mark Rohrbeck. Between the figs and the coffee, he excused himself and didn't come back for nearly half an hour. "Calling home," Mason-Manley said wisely, and Hypatia, who was the galaxy's greatest eavesdropper when I let her be, filled me in. "He's trying to talk his wife out of the divorce. She isn't buying it."

When the coffee was about half gone, Terple whispered something to the air. Evidently Hans was listening, and in a moment the end of the room went dark. Almost at once the planet appeared for us again, noticeably bigger than it had been before. She whispered again, and the image expanded until it filled the room, and I had the sudden vertiginous sense that I was falling into it.

"We're getting about two- or three-kilometer resolution now," Terple announced proudly.

That didn't give us much beyond mountains, shorelines, and clouds, and the planet was still half in sun and half dark. (Well, it had to be, didn't it? The planet was rotating under us, but its relative position to its sun didn't change.) When I studied it, something looked odd about the land mass at the bottom of the image. I pointed. "Is that ocean, there, down on the left side? I mean the dark part. Because I didn't see any lights there."

"No, it's land, all right. It's probably just that that part is too cold to be inhabited. We're not getting a square look at the planet, you know. We're about twenty degrees south of its equator, so we're seeing more of its south pole and nothing north of, let's say, what would be Scotland or southern Alaska on Earth. Have you seen the globe Hans put together for us? No? Hans, display."

Immediately a sphere appeared in the middle of the room, rotating slowly. It would have looked exactly like the kind my grandfather kept in his living room, latitude and longitude lines and all, except that the land masses were wholly wrong. "This is derived from old Heechee data that Starminder provided for us," Hans's voice informed me. "However, we've given our own names to the continents. You see the one that's made up of two fairly circular masses, connected by an isthmus, that looks like a dumbbell? Dr. Terple calls it 'Dumbbell.' It's divided into Dumbbell East and Dumbbell West. Frying Pan is the sort of roundish one with the long, thin peninsula projecting to the southwest. The one just coming into view now is Peanut, because—"

"I can see why," I told him. It did look a little like a peanut. Hans was perceptive enough to recognize, probably from the tone of my voice, that I found this geography—planetography?—lesson a little boring. Terple wasn't. "Go on, Hans," she said sharply when he hesitated. So he did.

Out of guest-politeness I sat still while he named every dot on the map for me, but when he came to the end, I did too. "That's very nice," I said, unhooking myself from my dining place. "Thanks for the dinner, June, but I think I'd better let you get your work done. Anyway, we'll be seeing a lot of each other over the next five days."

Every face I saw suddenly wore a bland expression, and Terple coughed. "Well, not quite five days," she said uncomfortably. "I don't know whether anyone told you this, but we'll have to leave before the star blows."

I stopped cold, one hand stuffing my napkin into its tied-down ring, the other holding on to the wall support. "There wasn't anything about leaving early in your prospectus. Why wasn't I told this?"

"It stands to reason, Klara," she said doggedly. "As soon as the star begins its collapse, I'm shutting everything down and getting out of here. It's too dangerous."

I don't like being surprised by the people who work for me. I gave her a look. "How can it be dangerous when we're six thousand light-years away?"

She got obstinate. "Remember I'm responsible for the safety of this installation and its crew. I don't think you have any idea what a supernova is like, Klara. It's *huge*. Back in 1054 the Chinese astrologers could see it in *daylight* for almost the whole month of July, and they didn't have our lensing to make it brighter."

"So we'll put on sunglasses."

She said firmly, "We'll *leave*. I'm not just talking about visible light. Even now, with six thousand years of cooling down after it popped, that thing's still radiating all across the electromagnetic spectrum, from microwave to X-rays. We're not going to want to be where all that radiation comes to a focus when it's fresh."

As I was brushing my teeth, Hypatia spoke from behind me. "What Terple said makes sense, you know. Anything in the focus is going to get fried when the star goes supernova."

I didn't answer, so she tried another tactic. "Mark Rohrbeck is a good-looking man, isn't he? He's very confused right now, with the divorce and all, but I think he likes you."

I looked at her in the mirror. She was in full simulation, leaning against the bathroom doorway with a little smile on her face. "He's also half my age," I pointed out.

"Oh, no, Klara," she corrected me. "Not even a third, actually. Still, what difference does that make? Hans displayed his file for me. Genetically he's very clean, as organic human beings go. Would you like to see it?"

"No." I finished with the bathroom and turned to leave. Hypatia got gracefully out of my way just as though I couldn't have walked right through her.

"Well, then," she said. "Would you like something to eat? A nightcap?"

"What I would like is to go to sleep. Right now."

She sighed. "Such a waste of time. Sooner or later you know you're going to give up the meat, don't you? Why wait? In machine simulation you can do anything you can do now, only better, and—"

"Enough," I ordered. "What I'm going to do now is go to bed and dream about my lover coming closer every minute. Go away."

The simulation disappeared, and her "Good night, then" came from empty air. Hypatia doesn't really go away when I tell her to, but she pretends she does. Part of the pretense is that she never acts as though she knows what I do in the privacy of my room.

It wasn't exactly true that I intended to dream about Bill Tartch. If I were a romantic type, I might actually have been counting the seconds until my true love arrived. Oh, hell, maybe I was, a little bit, especially when I tucked myself into that huge circular bed and automatically reached out for someone to touch and nobody was there. I do truly enjoy having a warm man's body to spoon up against when I drift off to sleep. But if I didn't have that, I also didn't have anybody snoring in my ear, or thrashing about, or talking to me when I first woke up and all I wanted was to huddle over a cup of coffee and a piece of grapefruit in peace.

Those were consoling thoughts—reasonably consoling—but they didn't do much for me this time. As soon as I put my head down, I was wide awake again.

Insomnia was one more of those meat-person flaws that disgusted Hypatia so. I didn't have to suffer from it. Hypatia keeps my bathroom medicine chest stocked with everything she imagines I might want in the middle of the night, including half a dozen different kinds of anti-insomnia pills, but I had a better idea than that. I popped the lid off my bedside stand, where I keep the manual controls I use when I don't want Hypatia to do something for me, and I accessed the synoptic I wanted to see.

I visited my island.

Its name is Raiwea—that's Rah-ee-*way*-uh, with the accent on the third syllable, the way the Polynesians say it—and it's the only place in the universe I ever miss when I'm away from it. It's not very big. It only amounts to a couple thousand hectares of dry land, but it's got palm trees and breadfruit trees and a pretty lagoon that's too shallow for the sharks ever to invade from the deep water outside the reef. And now, because I paid to put them there, it's got lots of clusters of pretty little bungalows with pretty, if imitation, thatched roofs, as well as plumbing and air conditioning and everything else that would make a person comfortable. And it's got playgrounds and game fields that are laid out for baseball or soccer or whatever a bunch of kids might need to work off excess animal energy. And its got its own food factory nestled inside the reef, constantly churning out every variety of healthful food anyone wants to eat. And it's mine. It's all mine. Every square centimeter. I paid for it, and I've populated it with orphans and single women with babies from all over the world. When I go there, I'm Grandma Klara to about a hundred and fifty kids from newborns to teens, and when I'm somewhere else I make it a point, every day or so, to access the surveillance systems and make sure the schools are functioning and the medical services are keeping everybody healthy, because I—all right, damn it—because I love those kids. Every last one of them. And I swear they love me back.

Hypatia says they're my substitute for having a baby of my own.

Maybe they are. All the same, I do have a couple of my own ova stored in the Raiwea clinic's deep freeze. They've been there for a good many years now, but the doctors swear they're still one hundred percent viable and they'll keep them that way. The ova are there just in case I ever decide I really want to do that other disgustingly meat-person thing and give birth to my own genetically personal child. . . .

But I've never met the man I wanted to be its father. Bill Tartch? Well, maybe. I had thought he might be for a while, anyway, but then I wasn't really so sure.

When I was up and about the next morning, Hypatia greeted me with a fresh display of the Crabber planet. It was too big now to fit in my salon, but she had zeroed in on one particular coastline. In the center of the image was a blur that might have been manmade—personmade, I mean. "They're down to half-kilometer resolution now," she informed me. "That's pretty definitely a small city."

I inspected it. It pretty definitely was, but it was very definitely small. "Isn't there anything bigger?"

"I'm afraid not, Klara. Hans says the planet seems to be rather remarkably underpopulated, though it's not clear why. Will you be going over to the PhoenixCorp ship now?"

I shook my head. "Let them work in peace. We might as well do some work ourselves. What've you got for me?"

What she had for me was another sampling of some of the ventures I'd put money into at one time or another. There were the purely commercial ones such as the helium-3 mines on Luna, and the chain of food factories in the Bay of Bengal, and the desert-revivification project in the Sahara, and forty or fifty others; they weren't particularly interesting to me, but they were some of the projects that, no matter how much I spent, just kept getting me richer and richer every day.

Then we got to the ones I cared about. I looked in on the foundation Starminder had talked about, the one for sending humans into the Core to meet with the Heechee who had stayed behind. And the scholarship program for young women like myself—like I had been once, long ago—who were stuck in dirty, drudging, dead-end jobs. Myself, I got out of it by means of dumb luck and the Gateway asteroid, but that wasn't an option now. Maybe a decent education was.

Along about then, Hypatia cleared her throat in the manner that means there's something she wants to talk about. I guessed wrong. I guessed she wanted to discuss my island, so I played the game. "Oh, by the way," I said, "I accessed Raiwea last night after I went to bed."

"Really?" she said, just as though she hadn't known it all along. "How are things?"

I went through the motions of telling her which kids were about ready to leave and how there were eighteen new ones who had been located by the various agencies I did business with, ready to be brought to the island next time I was in the neighborhood. As she always did, whether she meant it or not, she clucked approvingly. Her simulation was looking faintly amused, though. I took it as a challenge. "So you see there's one thing we animals can do that you can't," I told her. "We can have babies."

"Or, as in your own case at least so far, not," she said agreeably. "That wasn't what I was going to tell you, though."

"Oh?"

"I just wanted to mention that Mr. Tartch's ship is going to dock in about an hour. He isn't coming alone."

Sometimes Hypatia is almost too idiosyncratically human, and more than once I've thought about getting her program changed. The tone of her voice warned me that she had something more to tell. I said tentatively, "That's not surprising. Sometimes he needs to bring a crew with him."

"Of course he does, Klara," she said cheerfully. "There's only one of them this time, though. And she's very pretty."

CHAPTER V

The very pretty assistant was very pretty, all right, and she looked to be about sixteen years old. No, that's not true. She looked a lot better than sixteen years old. I don't believe I had skin like that even when I was a newborn baby. She wore no makeup, and needed none. She had on a decorous one-piece jumpsuit that covered her from thigh to neck and left no doubt what was inside. Her name was Denys. When I got there—I had taken my time, because I didn't want Bill to think I was eager—all three of PhoenixCorp's males were hanging around, watching her like vultures sniffing carrion. It wasn't just that she looked the way she looked. She was also fresh meat, for a crew that had been getting pretty bored with each other.

Of course, I had been fresh meat, too, and there had been no signs of that kind of testosterone rush when I arrived. But then, I didn't look like Denys. Bill didn't seem to notice. He had already set up for his opening teaser, and Denys was playing his quaint autocameras for him. As they panned around the entrance chamber and settled on his face, wearing its most friendly and intelligent expression, he began to speak to the masses:

"Wilhelm Tartch here again, where PhoenixCorp is getting ready to bring a lost race of intelligent beings back to life, and here to help me once again"—one of the cameras swung around as Denys cued it toward me—"I have the good luck to have my beautiful fiancee, Gelle-Klara Moynlin, with me."

I gave him a look, because whatever I was to Wilhelm Tartch, I definitely wasn't planning to marry him. He tipped me a cheeky wink and went right on:

"As you all remember, before the Heechee ran away to hide in the Core, they surveyed most of the galaxy, looking for other intelligent races. They didn't find any. When they visited Earth they found the australopithecines, but they were a long way from being modern humans. They hadn't even developed language yet. And here, on this planet"—that view of the Crabber planet, presupernova, appeared behind him—"they found another primitive race that they thought might someday become both intelligent and civilized. Well, perhaps these Crabbers, as the PhoenixCorp people call them, did. But the Heechee weren't around to see it, and neither are we, because they had some bad luck.

"There were two stars in their planet's system, a red dwarf and a bright type-A giant. Over the millennia, as these lost people were struggling toward civilization, the big star was losing mass, which was being sucked into the smaller one—and then, without warning, the small one reached critical mass. It exploded—and the people, along with their planet and all their works, were instantly obliterated in the supernova blast."

He stopped there, gazing toward Denys until she called, "Got it." Then he kicked himself toward me, arms outstretched for a hug, a big grin on his face. When we connected, he buried his face in my neck and whispered, "Oh, Klaretta, we've been away from each other too long!"

Bill Tartch is a good hugger. His arms felt fine around me, and his big, male body felt good against mine. "But we're together now," I told him . . . as I looked over his shoulder at Denys—who was regarding us with an affectionate and wholly unjealous smile.

So that part might not be much of a problem, at that. I decided not to worry about it. Anyway, the resolution of the Crabber planet was getting better and better, and that was what we were here for, after all.

What the Crabber planet had a lot of was water. As the planet turned on its axis, the continental shore had disappeared into the nighttime side of the world, and what we were looking at was mostly ocean.

Bill Tartch wasn't pleased. "Is that all we're going to see?" he demanded of the room at large. "I expected at least some kind of a city."

Terple answered. "A small city—probably. Anyway, that's what it looked like before we lost it; I can show you that much if you like. Hans, go back to when that object was still in sight."

The maybe-city didn't look any better the second time I saw it, and it didn't impress Bill. He made a little tongue-click of annoyance. "You, shipmind! Can't you enhance the image for me?"

"That is enhanced, Mr. Tartch," Hans told him pleasantly. "However, we have somewhat better resolution now, and I've been tracking it in the infrared. There's a little more detail"—the continental margin appeared for us, hazily delineated because of the differences in temperature between water and land, and we zoomed in on the object—"but, as you see, there are hot spots that I have not yet been able to identify."

There were. *Big* ones, and very bright. What was encouraging, considering what we were looking for, was that some of them seemed to be fairly geometrical in shape, triangles and rectangles. But what were they?

"Christmas decorations?" Bill guessed. "You know, I mean not really Christmas, but with the houses all lit up for some holiday or other?"

"I don't think so, Mr. Tartch," Hans said judiciously. "There's not much optical light; what you're seeing is heat."

"Keeping themselves warm in the winter?"

"We don't know if it's their winter, Mr. Tartch, and that isn't probable in any case. Those sources read out at up to around three hundred degrees Celsius. That's almost forest-fire temperature."

Bill looked puzzled. "Slash-and-burn agriculture? Or maybe some kind of industry?"

"We can't say yet, Mr. Tartch. If it were actual combustion, there should be more visible light; but there's very little. We'll simply have to wait for better data. Meanwhile, however, there's something else you might like to see." The scene we were viewing skittered across the face of the planet—huge cloud banks, a couple of islands, more cloud—and came to rest on a patch of ocean. In its center was a tiny blur of something that looked grayish when it looked like anything at all; it seemed to flicker in and out of sight, at the very limit of visibility.

"Clouds?" Bill guessed.

"No, Mr. Tartch. I believe it is a group of objects of some kind, and they are in motion—vectoring approximately seventy-one degrees, or, as you would say, a little north of east. They must be quite large, or we would not pick up anything at all. They may be ships, although their rate of motion is too high for anything but a hydrofoil or ground-effect craft. If they are still in sight when the mirror is more nearly complete, we should be able to resolve them easily enough."

"Which will be when?"

Hans gave us that phony couple-of-seconds pause before he answered. "There is a small new problem about that, Mr. Tartch," he said apologetically. "Some of the installed mirror plates have been subjected to thermal shock, and they are no longer in exact fit. Most of the installation machines have had to be delivered to adjust them, and so it will be some time before we can go on with completing the mirror. A few hours only, I estimate."

Bill looked at me and I looked at him. "Well, shit," he said. "What else is going to go wrong?"

What had gone wrong that time wasn't June Terple's fault. She said it was, though. She said that she was the person in charge of the whole operation, so everything that happened was her responsibility, and she shouldn't have allowed Ibarruru to override Hans's controls. And Julia Ibarruru was tearfully repentant. "Starminder told me the Heechee had identified eleven other planets in the Crabber system; I was just checking to see if there were any signs of life on any of them, and I'm afraid that for a minute I let the system's focus get too close to the star."

It could have been worse. I told them not to worry about it and invited all three of them to my ship for a drink. That made my so-called fiance's eyebrows rise, because he had certainly been expecting to be the first person I welcomed aboard. He was philosophical about it, though. "I'll see you later," he said, and if none of the women knew what he meant by that, it could only have been because they'd never seen a leer before. Then he led Denys off to interview some of PhoenixCorp's other people.

Which was pretty much what I was planning for myself. Hypatia had set out tea things on one table, and dry sherry on another, but before we sat down to either, I had to give all three of the women the usual guided tour. The sudden return to normal gravity was a burden for them, but they limped admiringly through the guest bedroom, exclaimed at the kitchen—never used by me, but installed just in case I ever wanted to do any of that stuff myself—and were blown away by my personal bathroom. Whirlbath, bidet, big onyx tub, mirror walls—Bill Tartch always said it looked like a whore's dream of heaven, and he hadn't been the first guest to make that observation. I don't suppose the PhoenixCorp women had ever seen anything like it. I let them look. I even let them peek into the cabinets of perfumes and toiletries. "Oh, musk oil!" Terple cried. "But it's real! That's so expensive."

"I don't wear it anymore. Take it, if you like," I said and, for the grand finale, opened the door to my bedroom.

When at last we got to the tea, sherry, and conversation, Ibarruru's first remark was, "Mr. Tartch seemed like a very interesting man." She didn't spell out the connection, but I knew it was that huge bed that was in her mind. So we chatted about Mr. Tartch and his glamorous p-vision career, and how Terple had grown up with the stories of the Gateway prospectors on every day's news, and how Ibarruru had dreamed of an opportunity like this—"Astronomy's really almost a lost art on Earth, you know," she told me. "Now we have all the Heechee data, so there's no point anymore in wasting time with telescopes and probes."

"So what does an astronomer do when there's no astronomy to be done?" I asked, being polite.

She said ruefully, "I teach an undergraduate course in astronomy at a community college in Maryland. For people who will never do any astronomy, because if there's anything somebody really wants to see, why, they just get in a ship and go out and look at it."

"As I did, Ms. Moynlin," said Starminder, with the Heechee equivalent of a smile.

That was what I was waiting for. If there was a place in the universe I still wanted to see, it was her home in the Core. "You must miss the Core," I told her. "All those nearby stars, so bright—what we have here must look pretty skimpy to you."

"Oh, no," she said, being polite, "this is quite nice. For a change. What I really miss is my family."

It had never occurred to me that she had a family, but, yes, she had left a mate and two young offspring behind when she came out. It was a difficult decision, but she couldn't resist the adventure. Miss them? Of course she missed them! Miss her? She looked surprised at that. "Why, no, Ms. Moynlin, they won't be missing me. They're asleep for the night. I'll be back long before they wake up. Time dilation, you see. I'm only going to stay out here for a year or two."

Ibarruru said nervously, "That's the part that worries me about going to the Core, Starminder. I'm not young anymore, and I know that if I went for even a few days, nearly everyone I know would be gone when I got back. No, not just 'nearly' everyone," she corrected herself. "What is it, forty thousand to one? So a week there would be nearly a thousand years back home." Then she turned to the Heechee female. "But even if we can't go ourselves, you can tell us about it, Starminder. Would you like to tell Ms. Moynlin what it's like in the Core?"

It was what I wanted to hear, too. I'd heard it often enough before, but I listened as long as Starminder was willing to talk. Which was a lot, because she was definitely homesick.

Would it really matter if I spent a week in the Core? Or a month, or a year, for that matter? I'd miss my kids on the island, of course, but they'd be taken care of, and so would everything else that mattered to me. And there wasn't any other human being in the universe that I cared enough about to miss for more than a day.

I was surprised when Hypatia spoke up out of thin air. "Ms. Moynlin"—formal because of the company—"there's a call for you." And she displayed Bill Tartch's face.

I could see by the background that he was in his own ship, and he looked all bright and fresh and grinning at me. "Permission to come aboard, hon?" he asked.

That produced a quick reaction among my guests.

"Oh," said Ibarruru, collecting herself. "Well, it's time we got back to work anyway, isn't it, June?" She was sounding arch. Terple wasn't; she simply got up, and Starminder followed her example.

"You needn't leave," I said.

"But of course we must," said Terple. "Julia's right. Thank you for the tea and, uh, things."

And they were gone, leaving me to be alone with my lover.

CHAPTER VI

"He's been primping for the last hour," Hypatia reported in my ear. "Showered, shaved, dressed up. And he put on that musk cologne that he thinks you like."

"I do like it," I said. "On him. Let me see you when I'm talking to you."

She appeared obediently, reclining on the couch Ibarruru had just left. "I'd say the man's looking to get laid," she observed. "Again."

I didn't choose to pick up on the "again." That word was evidence of one of Hypatia's more annoying traits, of which she has not quite enough to make me have her reprogrammed. When I chose Hypatia of Alexandria as a personality for my shipmind, it seemed to be a good idea at the time. But my own Hypatia took it seriously. That's what happens when you get yourself a really powerful shipmind; she throws herself into the part. The first thing Hypatia did was look up her template and model herself as close to the original as she thought I would stand—including such details as the fact that the original Hypatia really hated men.

"So, do you want me out of the way so you can oblige him?" she asked sociably.

"No," I said. "You stay."

"That's my girl. You ask me, sexual intercourse is greatly overrated anyway."

"That's because you never had any," I told her. "By which I mean neither you, my pet program, nor the semimythical human woman I modeled you after, who died a virgin and is said to have shoved her used menstrual cloths in the face of one persistent suitor to turn him off."

"Malicious myth," she said comfortably. "Spread by the Christians after they murdered her. Anyway, here he comes."

I would have been willing to bet that the first words out of Bill Tartch's mouth would be *Alone at last!* accompanied by a big grin and a lunge for me. I would have half won. He didn't say anything at all, just spread his arms and lurched toward me, grin and all.

Then he saw Hypatia, sprawled on the couch. "Oh," he said, stumbling as he came to a stop—there evidently wasn't any gravity in his rental ship, either. "I thought we'd be alone."

"Not right now, sweetie," I said. "But it's nice to see you."

"Me, too." He thought for a moment, and I could see him changing gears: All right, the lady doesn't want what I want right now, so what else can we do? That's one of those good-and-bad things about Bill Tartch. He does what I want, and none of this sweeping-her-off-her-feet stuff. Viewing it as good, it means he's considerate and sweet. Viewing it the other way—the way Hypatia chooses to view it—he's a spineless wretch, sucking up to somebody who can do him good.

While I was considering which way to view it, Bill snapped his fingers. "I know," he said, brightening. "I've been wanting to do a real interview with you anyway. That all right? Hypatia, you can record it for me, can't you?"

Hypatia didn't answer, just looked sulkily at me.

"Do what he says," I ordered. But Bill was having second thoughts.

"Maybe not," he said, cheerfully resigned to the fact that she wouldn't take orders from him. "She'd probably screw it up on purpose for me anyway, so I guess we'd better get Denys in here."

It didn't take Denys much more than a minute to arrive, with those quaint little cameras and all. I did my best to be gracious and comradely. "Oh, yes, clip them on anywhere," I said—in my ship's gravity, the cameras wouldn't just float. "On the backs of the chairs? Sure. If they mess the fabric a little, Hypatia will fix it right up." I didn't look at Hypatia, just gestured to her to get herself out of sight. She did without protest.

Bill had planted himself next to me and was holding my hand. I didn't pull it away. It took Denys a little while to get all the cameras in place, Bill gazing tolerantly at the way she was doing it and not offering to help. When she announced she was ready, the interview began.

It was a typical Wilhelm Tartch interview, meaning that he did most of the talking. He rehearsed our entire history for the cameras in one uninterrupted monologue; my part was to smile attentively as it was going on. Then he got to Phoenix.

"We're here to see the results of this giant explosion that took place more than a thousand years ago—What's the matter, Klara?"

He was watching my face, and I knew what he was seeing. "Turn off your cameras, Bill. You need to get your facts straight. It happened a lot longer than a thousand years ago."

He shook his head at me tolerantly. "That's close enough for the audience," he explained. "I'm not giving an astronomy lesson here. The star blew up in 1054, right?"

"It was in 1054 that the Chinese astronomers *saw* it. That's the year when the light from the supernova got as far as our neighborhood, but it took about five thousand years to get there. Didn't you do your homework?"

"We must've missed that little bit, hon," he said, giving me his best ruefully apologetic smile. "All right, Denys. Take it from the last little bit. We'll put in some shots of the supernova to cover the transition. Ready? Then go. This giant explosion took place many thousands of years ago, destroying a civilization that might in some ways almost have become the equal of our own. What were they like, these people the Phoenix investigators call 'Crabbers'? No one has ever known. When the old Heechee visited their planet long ago, they were still animal like primitives—Denys, we'll put in some of those old Heechee files here—but the Heechee thought they had the potential to develop cognitive intelligence and even civilization. Did they ever fulfill this promise? Did they come to dominate their world as the human race did our Earth? Did they develop science and art and culture of their own? We know from the tantalizing hints we've seen so far that this may be so. Now, through the generosity of Gelle-Klara Moynlin, who is here with me, we are at last going to see for ourselves what these tragically doomed people achieved before their star exploded without warning, cutting them off—Oh, come on, Klara. What is it this time?"

"We don't know if they had any warning or not, do we? That's one of the things we're trying to find out."

Denys cleared her throat. She said diffidently, "Bill, maybe you should let me do a little more background research before you finish this interview."

My lover gave her a petulant little grimace. "Oh, all right. I suppose there's nothing else to do."

I heard the invisible little cough that meant Hypatia had something to say to me, so I said to the air, "Hypatia?"

She picked up her cue. "The PhoenixCorp shipmind tells me they're back at work on the dish, and they're getting somewhat better magnification now. There are some new views you may want to see. Shall I display here?"

Bill seemed slightly mollified. He looked at me. "What do you think, Klara?"

It was the wrong question to ask me. I didn't want to tell him what I was thinking.

For that matter, I didn't want to be thinking it at all. All right, he and this little Denys lollipop hadn't done any of their backgrounding on the way out to Phoenix. So what, exactly, had they been doing with their time?

I said, "No, I think I'd rather see it on the PhoenixCorp ship. You two go ahead. I'll follow in a minute." And as soon as they were out of sight. I turned around, and Hypatia was sitting in the chair Denys had just left, looking smug.

"Can I do something for you, Klara?" she asked solicitously.

She could, but I wasn't ready to ask her for it. I asked her for something else instead. "Can you show me the interior of Bill's ship?"

"Of course, Klara." And there it was, displayed for me, Hypatia guiding my point of view all through it.

It wasn't much. The net obviously wasn't spending any more than it had to on Bill's creature comfort. It was so old that it had all that Heechee drive stuff out in the open; when I designed my own ship, I made sure all that ugliness was tucked away out of sight, like the heating system in a condo. The important fact was that it had two sleeping compartments, one clearly Denys's, the other definitely Bill's. Both had unmade beds. Evidently the rental's shipmind wasn't up to much housekeeping, and neither was Denys. There was no indication that they might have been visiting back and forth.

I gave up. "You've been dying to tell me about them ever since they got here," I said to Hypatia. "So tell me."

She gave me that wondering look. "Tell you what exactly, Klara?"

"Tell me what was going on on Bill's ship, for Christ's sake! I know you know."

She looked slightly miffed, the way she always did when Christ's name was mentioned, but she said, "It is true that I accessed Mr. Tartch's shipmind as a routine precaution. It's a pretty cheap-jack job, about what you'd expect in a rental. It had privacy locks all over it, but nothing that I couldn't—"

I snarled at her, "Tell me! *Did they*?"

She made an expression of distaste. "Oh, yes, hon, they certainly did. All the way out here. Like dogs in rut."

I looked around the room at the wineglasses and cups and the cushions that had been disturbed by someone sitting on them. "I'm going to the ship. Clean up this mess while I'm gone," I ordered, and checked my face in the mirror.

It looked just as it always looked, as though nothing were different.

Well, nothing was, really, was it? What did it matter if Bill chose to bed this Denys, or any number of Denyses, when I wasn't around? It wasn't as though I had been planning to *marry* the guy.

CHAPTER VII

None of the crew was in the entrance lock when I came to the PhoenixCorp ship, but I could hear them. They were all gathered in the dining hall, laughing and chattering excitedly. When I got there, I saw that the room was darkened. They were all poking at virtuals of one scene or another as Hans displayed them, and no one noticed me as I came in.

I hooked myself inconspicuously to a belt near the door and looked around. I saw Bill and his sperm receptacle of the moment hooked chastely apart, Denys chirping at Mason-Manley, Bill talking into his recorders. Mason-Manley was squeezing Denys's shoulder excitedly, presumably because he was caught up in the euphoria of the moment, but he seemed to be enjoying touching her, too. If Bill noticed, he didn't appear to mind. But then, Bill was not a jealous type; that was one of the things I liked about him.

Until recently I hadn't thought that I was, either.

Well, I told myself, I wasn't. It wasn't a question of jealousy. It was a question of—oh, call it good manners; if Bill chose to bed a bimbo now and then, that was his business, but it did not excuse his hauling the little tart all the way from Earth to shove her in my face.

A meter or so away from me, Mark Rohrbeck was watching the pictures, looking a lot less gloomy than usual. When he saw me at last, he waved and pointed. "Look, Ms. Moynlin!" he cried. "Blimps!"

So I finally got around to looking at the display. In the sector he was indicating, we were looking down on one of the Crabber planet's oceans. There were a lot of clouds, but some areas had only scattered puffs. And there among them were eight fat little silver sausages, in a V formation, that surely were far too hard-edged and uniform in shape to be clouds.

"These are the objects we viewed before, Ms. Moynlin," Hans's voice informed me. "Now we can discriminate the individual elements, and they are certainly artifacts."

"Sure, but why do you say they're blimps? How do you know they aren't ships of some kind?" I asked, and then said at once, "No, cancel that," as I figured it out for myself. If they had been surface vessels, they would have produced some sort of wake in the water. They were aircraft, all right, so I changed the question to, "Where are they going, do you think?"

"Wait a minute," June Terple said. "Hans, display the projection for Ms. Moynlin."

That sheet of ocean disappeared, and in its place was a globe of the Crabber planet, its seas in blue, land masses in gray. Eight stylized little blimp figures, greatly out of proportion, were over the ocean. From them a silvery line extended to the northeast, with another line, this one golden, going back past the day-night terminator toward the southwest. Terple said, "It looks like the blimps came from around that group of islands at the end of the gold course-line, and they're heading toward the Dumbbell continents up on the right. Unfortunately, those are pretty far north. We can't get a good picture of them from here, but Hans has enhanced some of the data on the island the blimps came from. Hans?"

The globe disappeared. Now we were looking down on one of those greenish infrared scenes: shoreline, bay—and something burning around the bay. Once again the outlines of the burning areas were geometrically unnatural. "As we speculated, it is almost certainly a community, Ms. Moynlin," Hans informed me. "However, it seems to have suffered some catastrophe, similar to what we observed on the continent that is now out of sight."

"What kind of catastrophe?" I demanded.

Hans was all apologetic. "We simply don't have the data yet, Ms. Moynlin. A great fire, one might conjecture. I'm sure it will make sense when we have better resolution—in a few hours, perhaps. I'll keep you posted."

"Please do," I said. And then, without planning it, I found myself saying, "I think I'll go back to my ship and lie down for a while."

"But you just got here," Mark Rohrbeck said, surprised and, I thought with some pleasure, maybe a little disappointed. Bill Tartch looked suddenly happy and began to unhook himself from his perch. I gave a little shake of the head to both of them.

"I'm sorry. I just want to rest," I said. "It's been an exhausting few days."

That wasn't particularly true, of course—not any part of it. I wasn't really tired, and I didn't want to rest. I just wanted to be by myself, or at any rate with no company but Hypatia, which comes to pretty much the same thing.

As I came into my ship, she greeted me in motherly mode. "Too many people, hon?" she asked. "Shall I make you a drink?"

I shook my head to the drink, but she was right about the other part of it. "Funny thing," I said, sprawling on the couch. "The more people I meet, the fewer I am comfortable around."

"Meat people are generally boring," she agreed. "How about a cup of tea?"

I shrugged, and immediately heard the activity begin in the kitchen. Hypatia had her faults, but she was a pretty good mom when I needed her to be. I lay back on the couch and gazed at the ceiling. "You know what?" I said. "I'm beginning to think I ought to settle down on the island."

"You could do that, yes," she said diplomatically. Then, because she was Hypatia, she added, "Let's see, the last time you were there, you stayed exactly eleven days, wasn't it? About six months ago?"

She had made me feel defensive—again. I said. "I had things to do."

"Of course you did. Then the time before that wasn't quite that long, was it? Just six days—and that was over a year ago."

"You've made your point, Hypatia. Talk about something else."

"Sure thing, boss." So she did. Mostly what she chose to talk about was what my various holdings had been doing in the few hours since I'd checked them last. I wasn't listening. After a few minutes of it, I swallowed the tea she'd made for me and stood up. "I'm going to soak in the tub for a while."

"I'll run it for you, hon. Hon? They've got some new pictures from the Crabber planet if you want to see them while you soak."

"Why not?" And by the time I'd shucked my clothes the big onyx tub was full, the temperature perfect as always, and one corner of the bathroom was concealed by one of Hypatia's simulations.

The new display was almost filled by what looked like hundreds, maybe thousands, of tiny buildings. We were looking down at them from something like a forty-five-degree angle, and I couldn't make out many details. Their sun must have been nearly overhead, because there weren't many shadows to bring out details.

"This is the biggest city they've found yet," Hypatia informed me. "It's inland on the western part of the squarish continent in the southern hemisphere, where two big rivers come together. If you look close, you'll see there's a suggestion of things moving in the streets, but we can't make out just what yet. However—"

I stopped her. "Skip the commentary," I ordered. "Just keep showing me the pictures. If I have any questions, I'll ask."

"If that's what you want, hon." She sounded aggrieved. Hypatia doesn't like to be told to shut up, but she did.

The pictures kept coming, one city after another, now a bay with what looked like surface ships of some kind moored in it, now some more blimps sailing peacefully along, now what might have been a wide-gauge railroad with a train steaming over a bridge. I couldn't really see the tracks, only the bridge and a hazy line that stretched before and after it across the countryside. What I could see best was the locomotive, and most of all the long white trail of steam from its stack.

I watched for a while, then waved the display off. I closed my eyes and lay back to let the sweet-smelling foamy waters make me feel whole and content again. As I had done many thousands of times, sometimes with success.

This was one of the successes. The hot tub did its work. I felt myself drifting off to a relaxed and welcome sleep. . . .

And then, suddenly, a vagrant thought crossed my mind, and I wasn't relaxed anymore.

I got out of the tub and climbed into the shower stall, turning it on full; I let cold water hammer at me for a while, then changed it to hot. When I got out, I pulled on a robe.

As I was drying my hair, the door opened and Hypatia appeared, looking at me with concern. "I'm afraid what I told you about Tartch upset you, hon," she said, oozing with compassion. "You don't really care what he does, though, do you?"

I said, "Of course not," wondering if it were true.

"That's my girl," she said approvingly. "There are some new scenes, too."

They appeared; she didn't wait to see if I wanted them on. I watched the changing scenes for a while, then decided I didn't. I turned to Hypatia. "Turn it off," I said. "I want to ask you something."

She didn't move, but the scene disappeared. "What's that, Klara?"

"While I was dozing in the tub, I thought for a moment I might fall asleep, and slip down into the water and drown. Then I thought you surely wouldn't let that happen, because you'd be watching, wouldn't you?"

"I'm always aware of any problems that confront you, Klara."

"And then it occurred to me that you might be tempted to let me go ahead and drown, just so you could get me into that machine storage you're always trying to sell me. So I got out of the tub and into the shower."

I pulled my hair back and fastened it with a barrette, watching her. She didn't speak, just stood there with her usual benign and thoughtful expression. "So, would you?" I demanded.

She looked surprised. "You mean would I deliberately let you drown? Oh, I don't think I could do that, Klara. As a general rule I'm not programmed to go against your wishes, not even if it were for your own good. That would be for your good, you know. Machine storage would mean eternal life for you, Klara, or as close as makes no difference. And no more of the sordid little concerns of the meat that cause you so much distress."

I turned my back on her and went into my bedroom to dress. She followed, in her excellent simulation of walking. What I wanted to know was how general her general rule was, and what she would have deemed a permissible exception. But as I opened my mouth to ask her, she spoke up.

"Oh, Klara," she said. "They've found something of interest. Let me show you." She didn't wait for a response; at once the end of the room lit up.

We were looking again at that first little fleet of blimps. They were nearly at the coast, but they weren't in their tidy V formation anymore. They were scattered over the sky, and two of them were falling to the sea, blazing with great gouts of flame. Small things I couldn't quite make out were buzzing around and between them.

"My God," I said. "Something's shooting them down!"

Hypatia nodded. "So it would appear, Klara. It looks as though the Crabbers' blimps are filled with hydrogen, to burn the way they do. That suggests a rather low level of technological achievement, but give them credit. They aren't primitives, anyway. They're definitely civilized enough to be having themselves a pretty violent little war."

CHAPTER VIII

There wasn't any doubt about it. The Crabbers were industriously killing each other in a kind of aerial combat that was right out of the old stories of World War I. I couldn't see much of the planes that were shooting the blimps down, but they were really there, and what was going on was a real old-fashioned dogfight.

I don't know what I had hoped to see when we brought the long-dead Crabbers back to some kind of life. But that definitely wasn't it. When the scenes changed—Hans had been assiduous in zooming down to wherever on the planet's surface things were going on—it didn't improve. It got worse. I saw a harbor crammed with surface vessels, where a great river joined the sea; but some of the ships were on fire, and others appeared to be sinking. "Submarines did that, I think," Hypatia judged. "Or it could possibly be from bombing planes or mines, but my money's on submarines." Those strange patterns of heat in the cities weren't a mystery any longer—the cities had been burned to the ground by incendiaries, leaving only glowing coals. Then, when we were looking down, on a plain where flashes of white and reddish light sparkled all over the area, we couldn't see what was making them, but Hypatia had a guess for that, too. "Why," she said, sounding interested, "I do believe we're looking at a large-scale tank battle."

And so on, and on.

So Hans's promise had been kept. As soon as the magnification got a little better, it all did begin to make sense, just as the shipmind had promised. (I mean, if war makes any sense in the first place, that's the sense the pictures made.) The robots on the dish were still slaving away at adding the final mirror segments, and the pictures kept getting better and better.

Well, I don't know if I mean "better," exactly. The pictures were certainly clearer and more detailed, in some cases I would have to say even more excruciatingly detailed. But what they all showed was rack and ruin and death and destruction.

And their war was so pointless! They didn't have to bother killing each other. Their star would do it for them soon enough. All unknowing, every one of those Crabbers was racing toward a frightful death as their sun burst over them.

An hour earlier I had been pitying them for the fate that awaited them. But now I couldn't say I thought their fate was all that unjust.

Hypatia was looking at me in that motherly way she sometimes assumes. "I'm afraid all this is disturbing for you, Klara," she murmured. "Would it cheer you up to invite. Mr. Tartch aboard? He's calling. He says he wants to talk to you about the new pictures."

"Sure he does," I said, pretty sure that Bill really wanted to talk about why he didn't deserve being treated so standoffishly by me. "No. Tell him I'm asleep and don't want to be disturbed. And leave me alone for a while."

As soon as she had left and the door had closed behind her, I actually did throw myself onto my big, round bed. I didn't sleep, though. I just lay there, staring at myself in the mirror on the ceiling and doing my best not to think about anything.

Unfortunately, that's not something I'm good at. I could get myself to not think about those damn nasty Crabbers, but then I found my mind quickly turned itself to thinking whether it was better to let Bill Tartch hang or tell him to come in and then have a knock-down, drag-out, breaking-up fight with him to get it all over with. And when I made myself stop thinking about Bill Tartch, I found myself wondering why I'd squandered a fairly hefty chunk of my surplus cash on poking into the lives of a race that didn't know any better than to take a reasonably nice little planet and turn it into a charnel house.

I thought of calling Hypatia back in for another dull session of playing with my investments. I thought wistfully of taking another look at my island. And then I thought, screw it. I got myself into this thing. I might as well go ahead and see it through. . . .

But a more pleasant thought had been stirring in the background of my mind, so first there was something else I wanted from Hypatia.

I put on the rest of my clothes and went out to where she was reclining gracefully on the couch, just as though she'd been lounging there all along. I'm sure she had been watching those charnel-house scenes as attentively as anyone on the Phoenix ship—the difference being, of course, that Hypatia didn't have to bother with turning the optical display on for her own needs. But I needed it, so she asked politely, "Shall I display the data for you again, Klara?"

"In a minute," I said. "First, tell me all about Mark Rohrbeck."

I expected one of those tolerantly knowing looks from her. I got it, too. But she obediently began to recite all his stats. Mark's parents had died when he was young, and he had been brought up by his grandfather, who had once made his living as a fisherman on Lake Superior. "Mostly the old man fished for sea lampreys—know what they are, Klara? They're ugly things. They have big sucking disks instead of jaws. They attach themselves to other fish and suck their guts out until they die. I don't think you'd want to eat a sea lamprey yourself, but they were about all that was left in the lake. Mr. Rohrbeck sold them for export to Europe—people there thought they were a delicacy. They said they tasted like escargot. Then, of course, the food factories came along and put him out of business—"

"Get back to Mark Rohrbeck," I ordered. "I want to hear about the man himself. Briefly."

"Oh. Sorry. Well, he got a scholarship at the University of Minnesota, did well, went on to grad school at MIT, made a pretty fair reputation in computer science, married, had two kids, but then his wife decided there was a dentist she liked better than Rohrbeck, so she dumped him. And as I've mentioned before," she said appreciatively, "he does have really great genes. Does that cover it?"

I mulled that over for a moment, then said, "Just about. Don't go drawing any conclusions from this, do you hear?"

"Certainly, Klara," she said, but she still had that look.

I sighed. "All right. Now turn that damn thing back on."

"Of course, Klara," she said, unsurprised, and did. "I'm afraid it hasn't been getting any better."

It hadn't. It was just more of the same. I watched doggedly for a while, and then I said, "All right, Hypatia. I've seen enough."

She made it disappear, looking at me curiously. "There'll be better images when they finish with the mirror. By then we should be able to see actual individual Crabbers."

"Lovely," I said, not meaning it, and then I burst out. "My God, what's the matter with those people? There's plenty of room on the planet for all of them. Why didn't they just stay home and live in peace?"

It wasn't meant to be a real question, but Hypatia answered it for me anyway. "What do you expect? They're meat people," she said succinctly.

I wasn't letting her get away with that. "Come on, Hypatia! Human beings are meat people, too, and we don't go tearing halfway around the world just to kill each other!"

"Oh, do you not? What a short memory you have, Klara dear. Think of those twentieth-century world wars. Think of the Crusades, tens of thousands of Europeans dragging themselves all the way around the Mediterranean Sea to kill as many Moslems as they could. Think of the Spanish conquistadors, murdering their way across the Americas. Of course," she added, "those people were all Christians."

I blinked at her. "You think what we're looking at is a religious war?"

She shrugged gracefully. "Who knows? Meat people don't need reasons to kill each other, dear."

CHAPTER IX

Hypatia had been right about what gravitational lensing plus that big mirror could do.

By the time the mirror was complete, we could make out plenty of detail. We were even able to see individual centaur-like Crabbers—the same build, four legs and upright torso, that they'd inherited from the primitives I'd seen, but no longer very primitive at all.

Well, what I mean is that sometimes we could see them, anyway. Not always. The conditions had to be right. We couldn't see them when it was night on their part of the planet, of course, except in those ghosty-looking IR views, and we couldn't see them at all when they were blanketed with clouds we couldn't peer through. But we could see enough. More than enough, as far as I was concerned.

The PhoenixCorp crew was going crazy trying to keep up with the incoming data. Bill seemed to have decided to be patient with my unpredictable moods, so he paid me only absentminded attention. He kept busy working. He and Denys were ecstatically interrupting everyone in their jobs so that he could record their spot reactions, while the crew did their best to get on with their jobs anyway. June Terple stopped sleeping entirely, torn between watching the new images as they arrived and nagging her shipmind to make sure we would have warning in time to get the hell out of there before the star blew.

Only Mark Rohrbeck seemed to have time on his hands. Which was just the way I wanted it.

I found him in the otherwise empty sleep chamber, where Hans had obligingly set up a duplicate show of the incoming scenes for him. Mark's main area of concern was the shipmind and the functions it controlled, but all those things were working smoothly without his attention. He was spending his time gazing morosely in the general direction of the pictures.

I hooked myself up nearby. "Nasty, isn't it?" I said sociably, to cheer him up.

He didn't want to be cheered. "You mean the Crabbers?" Although his eyes had been on the display, his mind evidently hadn't. He thought it over for a moment, then gave his verdict. "Oh, I guess it's nasty enough, all right. It isn't exactly what we were all hoping for, that's for sure. But it all happened a long time ago, though, didn't it?"

"And you've got more immediate problems on your mind," I offered helpfully.

He gave me a gloomy imitation of a smile. "I see the shipminds have been gossiping again. Well, it isn't losing Doris that bothers me so much," he said after a moment. "I mean, that hurt, too. I thought I loved her, but—Well, it didn't work out, did it? Now she's got this other guy, so what the hell? But"—he swallowed unhappily—"the thing is, she's keeping the kids."

He was not only a nice man, he was beginning to touch my heart. I said, sounding sympathetic and suddenly feeling that way, too, "And you miss them?"

"Hell! I've been missing them most of the time since they were born," he said self-accusingly. "I guess that's what went wrong. I've been away working so much, I suppose I can't blame Doris for getting her lovemaking from somebody else."

That triggered something in me that I hadn't known was there. "No!" I said, surprising myself by my tone. "That's wrong. *Blame* her."

I startled Rohrbeck, too. He looked at me as though I had suddenly sprouted horns, but he didn't get a chance to speak. June Terple came flying by the room and saw us. She stuck her nose in, grabbing a hold-on to yell at Mark in passing. "Rohrbeck! Get your ass in gear! I want you to make sure Hans is shifting focus as fast as possible. We could be losing all kinds of data!" And then she was gone again, to wherever she was gone to.

Mark gave me a peculiar look, but then he shrugged and waved his hands to show that when the boss gave orders, even orders to do what he had already done, he couldn't just stay and talk anymore, and then he was gone as well.

I didn't blame him for the peculiar look. I hadn't realized I was so sensitive in the matter of two-timing partners. But apparently I was.

Even though I was the boss, I had no business keeping the PhoenixCorp people from doing their jobs. Anyway, there was more bustle and confusion going on there than I liked. I went back to my ship to stay out of everybody's way, watching the pictures as they arrived with only Hypatia for company.

She started the projections up as soon as I arrived, without being asked, and I sat down to observe.

If you didn't think of the Crabbers as *people*, what they were doing was certainly interesting. The Crabbers themselves were, for that matter. I could see traces of those primitive predators in the civilized—civilized—versions before me. Now, of course, they had machines and wore clothes and, if you didn't mind the extra limbs, looked rather impressive in their gaudy tunics and spiked leggings, and the shawl things they wore on their heads that were ornamented with, I guessed, maybe insignia of rank. Or junk jewelry, maybe, but most of them were definitely in one or another kind of uniform. Most of the civilized ones, anyway. In the interior of the south continent, where it looked like rain forest and savanna, were lots of what looked like noncivilized ones. Those particular Crabbers didn't have machines, or much in the way of clothing either. They lived off the land, and they seemed to spend a lot of time gaping up worriedly at the sky, where fleets of blimps and double-winged aircraft buzzed by now and then.

The civilized ones seemed to be losing some of their civilization. When Hans showed us close-ups of one of the bombed-out cities, I could see streams of people—mostly civilians, I guessed—making their way out of the ruins, carrying bundles, leading kids or holding them. A lot of them were limping, just dragging themselves along. Some were being pulled in wagons or sledlike things.

"They look like they're all sick," I said, and Hypatia nodded.

"Undoubtedly some of them are, dear," she informed me. "It's a war, after all. You shouldn't be thinking just in terms of bombs and guns, you know. Did you never hear of biological warfare?"

I stared at her. "You mean they're spreading *disease*? As a *weapon*?"

"I believe that is likely, and not at all without precedent," she informed me, preparing to lecture. She started by reminding me of the way the first American colonists in New England gave smallpox-laden blankets to the Indians to get them out of the way—"The colonists were Christians, of course, and very religious"—and went on from there. I wasn't listening. I was watching the pictures from the Crabber planet.

They didn't get better. For one moment, in one brief scene, I saw something that touched me. It was an archipelago in the Crabber planet's tropical zone. One bit looked a little like my island, reef and lagoon and sprawling vegetation over everything. Aboriginal Crabbers were there, too. But they weren't alone. There was also a company of the ones in uniform, herding the locals into a village square, for what purpose I could not guess—to draft them? to shoot them dead?—but certainly not a good one. And, when I looked more closely, I saw all the plants were dying. More bioweapons, this time directed at crops? Defoliants? I didn't know, but it looked as though someone had done something to that vegetation.

I had had enough. Without intending it, I came to a decision.

I interrupted my shipmind in the middle of her telling me about America's old Camp Detrick. "Hypatia? How much spare capacity do you have?"

It didn't faze her. She abandoned the history of human plague-spreading and responded promptly. "Quite a lot, Klara."

"Enough to store all the data from the installation? And maybe take Hans aboard, too?"

She looked surprised. I think she actually was. "That's a lot of data, Klara, but, yes, I can handle it. If necessary. What've you got in mind?"

"Oh," I said, "I was just thinking. Let me see those refugees again."

CHAPTER X

I kept one eye on the time, but I had plenty for what I wanted to do. I even gave myself a little diversion first. I went to my island.

I don't mean in person, of course. I simply checked out everything on Raiwea through my monitors and listened to the reports from the department heads. That was almost as satisfying. Just looking at the kids, growing up healthy and happy and free the way they are—it always makes me feel good. Or, in this case, at least a little better.

Then I left my remote-accessed Raiwea and went into the reality of the Phoenix ship.

Hans was busily shifting focus every time a few new frames came in, so now the pictures were coming in faster than anybody could take them in. That couldn't be helped. There was a whole world to look at, and anyway it didn't matter if we saw it all in real time. All the data were being stored for later analysis and interpretation—by somebody else, though. Not by me. I had seen all I wanted.

So, evidently, had most of the Phoenix crew. Starminder and Julia Ibarruru were in the eating chamber, but they were talking to each other about the Core and paying no attention to the confusing images pouring in. Bill Tartch had his cameras turned on the display, but he was watching the pictures only with sulky half-attention, while Denys hung, sound asleep, beside him. "What's the use of this, Klara?" he demanded as soon as he saw me. "I can't get any decent footage from this crap, and most of the crew's gone off to sleep."

I was looking at Denys. The little tart even snored prettily. "They needed it," I told him. "How about Terple?"

He shrugged. "Kekuskian was here a minute ago, looking for her. I don't know whether he found her or not. Listen, how about a little more of your interview, so I won't be wasting my time entirely?"

"Maybe later," I said, not meaning it, and went in pursuit of June Terple.

I heard her voice raised in anger long before I saw her. Kekuskian had found her, all right, and the two of them were having a real cat-and-dog fight. She was yelling at him. "I don't give a snake's fart what you think you have to have, Oleg! We're going! We have to get the whole installation the hell out of here while we're still in one piece."

"You can't do that!" he screeched back at her. "What's the point of my coming out here at all if I can't observe the supernova?"

"The point," she said fiercely, "is to stay alive, and that's what we're going to do. I'm in charge here, Kekuskian! I give the orders, and I'm giving them now. Hans! Lay in a course for the neutron star!"

That's when I got into the spat. "Cancel that, Hans," I ordered. "From here on in, you'll be taking your orders from me. Is that understood?"

"It is understood, Ms. Moynlin," his voice said, as calm and unsurprised as ever. Terple wasn't calm at all. I made allowances for the woman; she hadn't had much sleep, and she was under a lot of strain. But for a minute there I thought she was going to hit me.

"Now what the hell do you think you're doing, Moynlin?" she demanded dangerously.

"I'm taking command," I explained. "We're going to stay for a while. I want to see that star blow up, too."

"Yes!" Kekuskian shouted.

Terple didn't even look at him. She was giving her whole attention to me, and she wasn't in a friendly mood. "Are you crazy? Do you want to get killed?"

It crossed my mind to wonder if that would be so bad, but what I said, quite reasonably, was, "I don't mean we have to stay right here and let the star fry us. Not the people, anyway. We'll evacuate the crew and watch the blowup on the remote. There's plenty of room for everybody in the two ships. I can take three or four with me, and Bill can take the others in his rental."

She was outraged and incredulous. "Klara! The radiation will be *enormous*! It could destroy the whole installation!"

"Fine," I said. "I understand that. So I'll buy you a new one."

She stared at me in shock. "Buy a new one! Klara, do you have any idea of what it would cost—"

Then she stopped herself short and gave me a long look. "Well," she said, not a bit mollified, but more or less resigned to accepting the facts of life, "I guess you do know, at that. If that's what you want to do, well, you're the boss."

And, as usual, I was.

So when I gave orders, no one objected. I got everybody back in the dining chamber and explained that we were abandoning ship. I told Terple she could come on my ship, along with Starminder and Ibarruru. "It's only a few days to Earth; the three of you can all fit in my guest bedroom. Mason-Manley and Kekuskian can go with Bill and Denys. It'll be a little crowded in his rental, but they'll manage."

"What about Hans and me?" Rohrbeck asked, sounding puzzled.

I said offhandedly, "Oh, you can come with me. We'll find a place for you."

He didn't look as thrilled as he might have at the idea of sailing off through space with a beautiful, unattached woman, such as me. He didn't even look interested. "I don't just mean me *personally*, Klara," he said testily. "I mean me and my shipmind. I put a lot of work into designing Hans! I don't want him ruined!"

I wasn't thrilled by his reaction, either, but I do like a man who likes his work. "Don't worry," I assured him. "I asked Hypatia about that. She says she has plenty of extra capacity. We'll just copy him and take him along."

CHAPTER XI

I had never seen a supernova in real time before—well, how many people have?—but that, at least, was not a disappointment. The show was everything it promised to be. We were hovering in our two ships, a few million kilometers off the prime focus. Hans was taking his orders from Kekuskian now, and he had ditched the Crabber planet for good to concentrate on the star.

Hypatia whispered in my ear that, on his rental, Bill Tartch was pissing and moaning about the decision. He had wanted to catch every horrible, tragic bit, if possible right down to the expressions on the faces of the Crabbers when they saw their sun go all woogly right over their heads. I didn't. I had seen enough of the Crabbers to last me.

In my main room we had a double display. Hypatia had rigged my ship's external optics so we could see the great mirror and the tiny Phoenix ship, together like toys in one corner of the room, but the big thing was the Crabber star itself as seen from the PhoenixCorp ship. It wasn't dangerous—Hypatia said. Hans had dimmed it down, and anyway we were seeing only visible light, none of the wide-spectrum stuff that would be pouring out of it in a minute. Even so, it was huge, two meters across and so bright we had to squint to watch it.

I don't know much about stellar surfaces, but this particular star looked sick to me. Prominences stuck out all over its perimeter, and ugly sunspots spotted its face. And then, abruptly, it began to happen. The star seemed to shrink, as though Hans had zoomed back away from it. But that wasn't what was going on. The star really was collapsing on itself, and it was doing it fast. "That's the implosion," Hypatia whispered to me. While we watched, it went from two meters to a meter and a half, to a meter, to smaller still—

And then it began to expand again, almost as fast as it had shrunk, and became far more bright. Hypatia whispered, "And that's the rebound. I've told Hans to cut back on the intensity. It's going to get worse."

It did.

It blossomed bigger and brighter—and angrier—until it filled the room and, just as I was feeling as though I were being swallowed up by that stellar hell, the picture began to break up. I heard Terple moan, "Look at the mirror!" And then I understood what was happening to our image. The little toy PhoenixCorp ship and mirror were being hammered by the outpouring of raw radiation from the supernova. No filters. No cutouts. The PhoenixCorp vessels were blazing bright themselves, reflecting the flood of blinding light that was pouring on them from the gravitational lensing. As I watched, the mirror began to warp. The flimsy sheets of mirror metal peeled off, exploding into bright plumes of plasma, like blossoming fireworks on the Fourth of July. For a moment we saw the wire mesh underneath the optical plates. Then it was gone, too, and all that was left was the skeleton of reinforcing struts, hot and glowing.

I thought we'd seen everything we were going to see of the star. I was wrong. A moment later the image of the supernova reappeared before us. It wasn't anywhere near as colossally huge or frighteningly bright as it had been before, but it was still something scary to look at. "What—?" I began to ask, but Hypatia had anticipated me.

"We're looking at the star from the little camera in the center of the dish now, Klara," she explained. "We're not getting shipside magnification from the mirror anymore. That's gone. I'm a little worried about the camera, too. The gravitational lensing alone is pretty powerful, and the camera might not last much"—she paused as the image disappeared for good, simply winked out and was gone—"longer," she finished, and, of course, it hadn't.

I took a deep breath and looked around my sitting room. Terple had tears in her eyes. Ibarruru and Starminder sat together, silent and stunned, and Mark Rohrbeck was whispering to his shipmind. "That's it," I said briskly. "The show's over."

Rohrbeck spoke up first, sounding almost cheerful. "Hans has all the data," he reported. "He's all right."

Terple had her hand up. "Klara? About the ship? It took a lot of heat, but the dish burned pretty fast and the hull's probably intact, so if we can get a repair crew out there—"

"Right away," I promised. "Well, almost right away. First we go home."

I was looking at Rohrbeck. He had looked almost cheerful for a moment, but the cheer was rapidly fading. When he saw my eyes on him, he gave me a little shrug. "Where's that?" he asked glumly.

I wanted to pat his shoulder, but it was a little early for that. I just said sympathetically, "You're missing your kids, aren't you? Well, I've got a place with plenty of them. And, as the only grown-up male on my island, you'll be the only dad they've got."

CHAPTER XII

That blast from the supernova didn't destroy the PhoenixCorp ship after all. The mirror was a total write-off, of course, but the ship itself was only cooked a little. June Terple stooged around for a bit while it cooled down, then went back with what was left of her crew. Which wasn't much.

Mason-Manley talked his way back into her good graces once Denys wasn't around anymore; Kekuskian promised to come out for the actual blowup, eighty years from now, provided he was still alive; and, of course, she still had the indestructible Hans, now back in his own custom-designed datastore. The rest of her people were replacements. Starminder went back to her family in the Core, and I paid Ibarruru's fare to go along with her as a kind of honorary citizen ambassador.

Naturally, Terple invited me to join them for their stint at the neutron star—couldn't really avoid it, since the new money was coming from the same place as the old, namely mostly me. I said maybe, to be polite, but I really meant no. One look at the death of a world was enough for me. Bill Tartch's special show on the Crabbers went on the net within days. He had great success with it, easily great enough so that he didn't really mind the fact that he no longer had me.

Hypatia kept copies of all the files for me, and those last little bits of data stayed with me on my island for a long time. I played pieces of them now and then, for any of the kids that showed an interest, and for their moms, too, when they did. But mostly I played them for me.

Mark Rohrbeck stayed with me on Raiwea for a while, too, though not too long. That's the way my island works. When my kids are ready for the world outside, I let them go. It was the same with Rohrbeck. For him it took just a little over three months. Then he was ready, and he kissed me good-bye, and I let him go.

IMMERSION

Gregory Benford

Gregory Benford (see earlier note), wrote an essay, "Old Legends," in the *New Legends* anthology, on the continuing relationship of SF to science and through science to politics in the real world since the 1940s. He discusses being a graduate student; knowing Freeman Dyson; working with Edward Teller—"throughout all this, politics was not an issue. I was a registered Democrat, others were Republicans, but our positions did evolve from our politics." And speaking of the link between politics and SF writers, Benford mentions Teller enlisting SF allies in his policy battles. He then goes on at length to describe Jerry Pournelle's Citizen's Advisory Council on National Space Policy (see our Introduction and the earlier note on Benford). This is the kind of anecdotal story not often told. It is worth noting, too, that Benford does not present it as simply a booster.

> The faction grouped around Jerry Pournelle had provided crucial ideas and prose, but now others moved, looking askance. President Reagan hailed 1985's *Mutual Assured Survival* by Pournelle and Dean Ing, another science fiction writer, as "addressing with verve and vision the challenges to peace and to our national security."
>
> When science fiction was less prominent, writers pushed together for space development; now the entanglement of space with nuclear war divided them. Though still a research project, SDI touched deep wellsprings of the imagination. Isaac Asimov quit the board of governors of the L-5 Society, a pro-space lobbying group, because it would not take a firm stand against SDI. Heinlein reacted to this with stark disbelief. Asimov, who was born in Russia, stuck to his guns. He said, "Star Wars? It's just a device to make the Russians go broke."

Benford, as we remarked earlier, enjoys political engagement, and a good argument. In "Immersion," a mathematician and his girlfriend take a vacation in which they immerse themselves into the minds of chimpanzees. However, the man running the amusement has been recruited by the hero's enemies to kill him. It is an utterly convincing work of politically incorrect wish fulfillment sociobiology that shows deep research and meditation on the chimp point of view.

Africa came to them in air thick with smells. In the dry, prickly heat was a promise of the primitive, of ancient themes beyond knowing.

Warily Kelly gazed out at the view beyond the formidable walls. "We're safe from the animals?"

"I imagine so. Those walls are high and there are guard canines. Wirehounds, believe."

"Good." She smiled in a way that he knew implied a secret was about to emerge.

"I really urged you to come here to get you away from Helsinki."

"Not to study chimpanzees?"

"Oh that might be useful—or better still, fun," she said with wifely nonchalance. "My main consideration was that if you had stayed in Helsinki you might be dead."

He stopped looking at the striking scenery. She was serious. "You think they would . . . ?"

"They *could*, which is a better guide to action than trying to guess *woulds*."

"I see." He didn't, but he had learned to trust her judgment in matters of the world. "You think Imperial Industrie would . . . ?"

"Knock you off for undermining their case? Sure. But they'd be careful."

"But the case is over. Settled."

He had made a successful sociometric prediction of political and economic trends in central Europe. His reputation was powerful enough to cause a fall in certain product markets. Economics increasingly resembled fashion: Commodities racheted like hemlines.

Imperial Industrie had lost considerably—a fortune, even for a world-wrapping corporation. They had accused him of manipulating the markets, but he had in all honesty merely tried to test his new model of sociohistory. His reputation among econometric circles was enough to circulate the predictions. Imperial Industrie, he thought, was simply being childish. Reason would prevail there soon enough.

"You intend to make more predictions, don't you?" she asked.

"Well, once I get some better parameter fixes—"

"There. Then they can lose again. Imperial doesn't like losing."

"You exaggerate." He dismissed the subject with a wave of his hand.

Then too, he thought, perhaps he did need a vacation. To be on a rough, natural world—he had forgotten, in the years buried in Helsinki, how vivid wild things could be. Greens and yellows leaped out, after decades amid steel and glitter.

Here the sky yawned impossibly deep, unmarked by the graffiti of aircraft, wholly alive to the flapping wonder of birds. Bluffs and ridges looked like they had been shaped hastily with a putty knife. Beyond the station walls he could see a sole tree thrashed by an angry wind. Its topknot finally blew off in a pocket of wind, fluttering and fraying over somber flats like a fragmenting bird. Distant, eroded mesas had yellow streaks down their shanks which, as they met the forest, turned a burnt orange tinge that suggested the rot of rust. Across the valley, where the chimps ranged, lay a dusky canopy hidden behind low gray clouds and raked by winds. A thin, cold rain fell there and Leon wondered what it was like to cower beneath the sheets of moisture, without hope of shelter or warmth. Perhaps Helsinki's utter predictability was better, but he wondered, breathing in the tangy air.

He pointed to the distant forest. "We're going there?" He liked this fresh place, though the jungle was foreboding. It had been a long time since he had even worked with his hands, alongside his father, back on the farm.

"Don't start judging."

"I'm anticipating."

She grinned. "You always have a longer word for it, no matter what I say."

"The treks look a little, well—touristy."

"Of course. We're tourists."

The land here rose up into peaks as sharp as torn tin. In the thick trees beyond, mist broke on gray, smooth rocks. Even here, high up the slope of an imposing ridge, the Excursion Station was hemmed in by slimy, thick-barked trees standing in deep drifts of dead, dark leaves. With rotting logs half buried in the wet layers, the air swarmed so close it was like breathing damp opium.

Kelly stood, her drink finished. "Let's go in, socialize."

He followed dutifully and right away knew it was a mistake. Most of the indoor stim-party crowd was dressed in rugged safari-style gear. They were ruddy folk, faces flushed with excitement or perhaps just enhancers. Leon waved away the bubbleglass-bearing waiter; he disliked the way it dulled his wits. Still, he smiled and tried to make small talk.

This turned out to be not merely small, but microscopic. "Where are you from? Oh, *Helsinki*—what's it like? We're from (fill in the city)—have you ever heard of it?" Of course, he had not.

Most were Primitivists, drawn by the unique experience available here. It seemed to him that every third word in their conversation was *natural* or *vital*, delivered like a mantra.

"What a *relief*, to be away from straight lines," a thin man said.

"Um, how so?" Leon said, trying to seen interested.

"Well, of course straight lines don't exist in nature. They have to be put there by humans." He sighed. "I love to be free of straightness!"

Leon instantly thought of pine needles; strata of metamorphic rock; the inside edge of a half-moon; spider-woven silk strands; the line along the top of a breaking ocean wave; crystal patterns; white quartz lines on granite slabs; the far horizon of a vast calm lake; the legs of birds; spikes of cactus; the arrow dive of a raptor; trunks of young, fast-growing trees; wisps of high windblown clouds; ice cracks; the two sides of the V of migrating birds; icicles.

"Not so," he said, but no more.

His habit of laconic implication was trampled in the headlong talk, of course; the enhancers were taking hold. They all chattered on, excited by the prospect of immersing themselves in the lives of the creatures roaming the valleys below. He listened, not commenting, intrigued. Some wanted to share the world view of herd animals, others of hunters, some of birds. They spoke as though they were entering some athletic event, and that was not his view at all. Still, he stayed silent.

He finally escaped with Kelly into the small park beside the Excursion Station, designed to make guests familiar with local conditions before their treks or immersions. There were whole kraals of domestic stock. The unique assets, the genetically altered and enhanced animals, were nowhere near, of course.

He stopped and stared at the kraals and thought again about sociohistory. His mind kept diving at it from many angles. He had learned to just stand aside and let his thoughts run.

Animals. Was there a clue here? Despite millennia of trying, humans had domesticated few animals. To be domesticated, wild beasts had to have an entire suite of traits. Most had to be herd animals, with instinctive submission patterns which humans could co-opt. They had to be placid; herds that bolt at a strange sound and can't tolerate intruders are hard to keep. Finally, they had to be willing to breed in captivity. Most humans didn't want to court and copulate under the watchful gaze of others, and neither did most animals.

So here there were sheep and goats and cows, slightly adapted by biotechnology but otherwise unremarkable. Expect for the chimps. They were unique artifacts of this preservation deep in the rugged laboratory of central Africa. A wirehound came sniffing, checking them out, muttering an unintelligible apology. "Interesting," he remarked to Kelly, "that Primitivists still want to be protected from the wild, by the domesticated."

"Well, of course. This fellow is *big*."

"Not sentimental about the natural state? We were once just another type of large mammal."

"The natural state might be a pleasant place to visit, but . . ."

"Right, wouldn't want to live there. Still, I want to try the chimps."

"What? An immersion?" Her eyebrows lifted in mild alarm.

"As long as we're here, why not?"

"I don't . . . well, I'll think about it."

"You can bail out at any time, they say."

She nodded, pursed her lips. "Um."

"We'll *feel* at home—the way chimps do."

"You believe everything you read in a brochure?"

"I did some research. It's a well-developed tech."

Her lips had a skeptical tilt. "Um."

He knew by now better than to press her. Let time do his work.

The canine, quite large and alert, snuffled at his hand and slurred, "Goood naaaght, suuur." He stroked it. In its eyes he saw a kinship, an instant rapport that he did not need to think about. For one who dwelled in his head so much, this was a welcome rub of reality.

Significant evidence, he thought. *We have a deep past together*. Perhaps that was why he wanted to immerse in a chimp. To go far back, peering beyond the vexing state of being human.

"We're certainly closely related, yes," Expert Specialist Ruben said. He was a big man, tanned and muscular and casually confident. He was both a safari guide and immersion specialist, with a biology background. He did research using immersion techniques, but keeping the Station going soaked up most of his time, he said. "Chimp-riding is the best immersion available."

Leon looked skeptical. *Pan troglodytes* had hands with thumbs, the same number of teeth as humans, no tails, but he had never felt great empathy for them, seen behind bars in a zoo.

Ruben waved a big hand at the landscape below the Station. "We hope to make them more useful. We haven't tried training them much, beyond research purposes. Remember, they're supposed to be kept wild. The original UN grant stipulated that."

"Tell me about your research," Leon said. In his experience, no scientist ever passed up a chance to sing his own song. He was right.

They had taken human DNA and chimp DNA—Ruben said, waxing enthusiastically on—then unzipped the double-helix strands in both. Linking one human strand with a chimp strand made a hybrid.

Where the strands complemented, the two then tightly bound in a partial, new double helix. Where they differed, bonding between the strands was weak, intermittent, with whole sections flapping free.

Then they spun the watery solutions in a centrifuge, so the weak sections ripped apart. Closely linked DNA was 98.2 percent of the total. Chimps were startlingly like humans. Less than 2 percent different—yet they lived in forests and invented nothing.

The typical difference between individual people's DNA was a tenth of a percentage point, Ruben said. Roughly, then, chimps were twenty times more different from humans than particular people differed among themselves—genetically. But genes were like levers, supporting vast weights by pivoting about a small fulcrum.

"But we don't *come* from them. We parted company, genetically, six million years ago."

"Do they think like us?" Leon asked.

"Best way to tell is an immersion," Ruben said. "Very best way."

He smiled invitingly, and Leon wondered if Ruben got a commission on immersions. His sales pitch was subtle, shaped for an academic's interest—but still a sales pitch.

Ruben had already made the vast stores of data on chimp movements, population dynamics, and behaviors available to Leon. It was a rich source and with some math modeling might be fertile ground for a simple description, using a truncated version of sociohistory.

"Describing the life history of a species mathematically is one thing," Kelly said. "But *living in* it . . ."

"Come now," Leon said. Even though he knew the entire Excursion Station was geared to sell the guests safaris and immersions, he was intrigued. "'I need a change,' you said. 'Get out of stuffy old Helsinki,' you said."

Ruben said warmly, "It's completely safe."

Kelly smiled at Leon tolerantly. "Oh, all right."

He spent morning studying the chimp data banks. The mathematician in him pondered how to represent their dynamics with a trimmed-down sociohistory. The marble of fate rattling down a cracked slope. So many paths, variable. . . .

In the afternoons they took several treks. Kelly did not like the dust and heat and they saw few animals. "What self-respecting beast would want to be seen with these overdressed Primitivists?" she said. The others could never stop talking; that kept the animals away.

He liked the atmosphere and relaxed into it as his mind kept on working. He thought about this as he stood on the sweeping veranda, drinking pungent fruit juice as he watched a sunset. Kelly stood beside him silently. Raw Africa made it clear that the Earth was an energy funnel, he thought. At the bottom of the gravitational well, Earth captured for use barely a tenth of a percent of the sunlight that fell. Nature built organic molecules with a star's energy. In turn, plants were prey for animals, who could harvest roughly a tenth of the plant's stored energy. Grazers were themselves prey to meat-eaters, who could use about a tenth of the flesh-stored energy. So, he estimated, only about one part in a hundred thousand of a star's lancing energy wound up in the predators.

Wasteful! Yet nowhere had a more efficient engine evolved. Why not? Predators were invariably more intelligent than their prey, and they sat atop a pyramid of very steep slopes. Omnivores had a similar balancing act. Out of that rugged landscape had come humanity.

That fact *had* to matter greatly in any sociohistory. The chimps, then, were essential to finding the ancient keys to the human psyche.

Kelly said, "I hope immersion isn't, well, so hot and sticky."

"Remember, you'll see the world through different eyes."

She snorted. "Just so I can come back whenever I want and have a nice hot bath."

* * *

"Compartments?" Kelly shied back. "They look more like caskets."

"They have to be snug, Madam."

ExSpec Ruben smiled amiably—which, Leon sensed, probably meant he wasn't feeling amiable at all. Their conversation had been friendly, the staff here was respectful of the noted Dr. Mattick, but, after all, basically he and Kelly were just more tourists. Paying for a bit of primitive fun, all couched in proper scholarly terms, but—tourists.

"You're kept in fixed status, all body systems running slow but normal," the ExSpec said, popping out the padded networks for inspection. He ran through the controls, emergency procedures, safeguards.

"Looks comfortable enough," Kelly observed begrudgingly.

"Come on," Leon chided. "You promised we would do it."

"You'll be meshed into our systems at all times," Ruben said.

"Even your data library?" Leon asked.

"Sure thing."

The team of ExSpecs booted them into the stasis compartments with deft, sure efficiency. Tabs, pressors, magnetic pickups plated onto his skull to pick up thoughts directly. The very latest tech.

"Ready? Feeling good?" Ruben asked with his professional smile.

Leon was not feeling good (as opposed to feeling well) and he realized part of it was this ExSpec. He had always distrusted bland, assured people. Something about this one bothered him, but he could not say why. Oh well; Kelly was probably right. He needed a vacation. What better way to get out of yourself?

"Good, yes. Ready, yes."

The suspension tech suppressed neuromuscular responses. The customer lay dormant, only his mind engaged with the chimp.

Magnetic webs capped over his cerebrum. Through electromagnetic inductance they interwove into layers of the brain. They routed signals along tiny thread-paths, suppressing many brain functions and blocking physiological processes. All this, so that the massively parallel circuitry of the brain could be inductively linked out, thought by thought. Then it was transmitted to chips embedded in the chimp subject. Immersion.

The technology had ramified throughout the world, quite famously. The ability to distantly manage minds had myriad uses. The suspension tech, however, found its own odd applications.

In certain European classes, women were wedded, then suspended for all but a few hours of the day. Their wealthy husbands awoke them from freeze-frame states only for social and sexual purposes. For more than a half century, the wives experienced a heady whirlwind of places, friends, parties, vacations, passionate hours—but their total accumulated time was only a few years. Their husbands died in what seemed to the wives like short order indeed. They left a wealthy widow of perhaps thirty. Such women were highly sought, and not only for their money. They were uniquely sophisticated, seasoned by a long "marriage." Often, these widows returned the favor, wedding freeze-frame husbands whom they revived for similar uses.

All this Leon had taken with the sophisticated veneer he had cultivated in Helsinki. So he thought his immersion would be comfortable, interesting, the stuff of stim-party talk.

He had thought that he would in some sense *visit* another, simpler, mind.

He did not expect to be swallowed whole.

* * *

A good day. Plenty of grubs to eat in a big moist log. Dig them out with my nails, fresh tangy sharp crunchy.

Biggest, he shoves me aside. Scoops out plenty rich grubs. Grunts. Glowers.

My belly rumbles. I back off and eye Biggest. He's got pinched-up face, so I know not to fool with him.

I walk away, I squat down. Get some picking from a fem. She find some fleas, cracks them in her teeth.

Biggest rolls the log around some to knock a few grubs loose, finishes up. He's strong. Fems watch him. Over by the trees a bunch of fems chatter, such their teeth. Everybody's sleepy now in early afternoon, lying in the shade. Biggest, though, he waves at me and Hunker and off we go.

Patrol. Strut tall, step out proud. I like it fine. Better than humping even.

Down past the creek and along to where the hoof smells are. That's the shallow spot. We cross and go into the trees sniff-sniffing and there are two Strangers.

They don't see us yet. We move smooth, quiet. Biggest picks up a branch and we do too. Hunker is sniffing to see who these Strangers are and he points off to the hill. Just like I thought, they're Hillies. The worst. Smell bad.

Hillies come onto our turf. Make trouble. We make it back.

We spread out. Biggest, he grunts and they hear him. I'm already moving, branch held up. I can run pretty far without going all-four. The Strangers cry out, big eyed. We go fast and then we're on them.

They have no branches. We hit them and kick and they grab at us. They are tall and quick. Biggest slams one to the ground. I hit that one so Biggest knows real well I'm with him. Hammer hard, I do. Then I go quick to help Hunker.

His Stranger has taken his branch away. I club the Stranger. He sprawls. I whack him good and Hunker jumps on him and it is wonderful.

The Stranger tries to get up and I kick him solid. Hunker grabs back his branch and hits again and again with me helping hard.

Biggest, his Stranger gets up and starts to run. Biggest whacks his ass with the branch, roaring and laughing.

Me, I got my skill. Special. I pick up rocks. I'm the best thrower, better than Biggest even.

Rocks are for Strangers. My buddies, them I'll scrap with, but never use rocks. Strangers, though, they deserve to get rocks in the face. I love to bust a Stranger that way.

I throw one clean and smooth and catch the Stranger on the leg. He stumbles and I smack him good with a sharp-edged rock, in the back. He runs fast then and I can see he's bleeding. Stranger leaves drops in the dust.

Biggest laughs and slaps me and I know I'm in good with him.

Hunker is clubbing his Stranger. Biggest takes my club and joins in. The blood all over the Stranger sings warm in my nose and I jump up and down on him. We keep at it like that a long time. Not worried about the other Stranger coming back. Strangers are brave sometime but they know when they have lost.

The Stranger stops moving. I give him one more kick.

No reaction. Dead maybe.

We scream and dance and holler out our joy.

Leon shook his head to clear it. That helped a little.

"You were that big one?" Kelly asked. "I was the female, over by the trees."

"Sorry, I couldn't tell."

"It was . . . different, wasn't it?"

He laughed dryly. "Murder usually is."

"When you went off with the, well, leader—"

"My chimp thinks of him as 'Biggest.' We killed another chimp."

They were in the plush reception room of the immersion facility. Leon stood and felt the world tilt a little and then right itself. "I think I'll stick to historical research for a while."

Kelly smiled sheepishly. "I . . . I rather liked it." He thought a moment, blinked. "So did I," he said, surprisingly himself.

"Not the murder—"

"No, of course not. But . . . the *feel.*"

She grinned. "Can't get that in Helsinki, Professor."

He spent two days coasting through cool lattices of data in the formidable station library. It was well-equipped and allowed interfaces with several senses. He patrolled through cool, digital labyrinths.

In the vector spaces portrayed on huge screens, the research data was covered with thick, bulky protocols and scabs of security precautions. All were easily broken or averted, of course, but the chunky abstracts, reports, summaries, and crudely processed statistics still resisted easy interpretation. Occasionally some facets of chimp behavior were carefully hidden away in appendices and sidebar notes, as though the biologists in the lonely outpost were embarrassed by it. Some *was* embarrassing: mating behavior, especially. How could he use this?

He navigated through the 3-D maze and cobbled together his ideas. Could he follow a strategy of analogy?

Chimps shared nearly all their genes with humans, so chimp dynamics should be a simpler version of human dynamics. Could he then analyze chimp troop interactions as a reduced case of sociohistory?

At sunset of the next day he sat with Kelly watching blood-red shafts spike through orange-tinged clouds. Africa was gaudy beyond good taste and he liked it. The food was tangy, too. His stomach rumbled in anticipation of dinner.

He remarked to Kelly, "It's tempting, using chimps to build a sort of toy model of sociohistory."

"But you have doubts."

"They're like us in . . . only they have, well, uh . . ."

"Base, animalistic ways?" She smirked, then kissed him. "My prudish Leon."

"We have our share of beastly behaviors, I know. But we're a lot smarter too."

Her eyelids dipped in a manner he knew by now suggested polite doubt. "They live intensely, you'll have to give them that."

"Maybe we're smarter than we need to be anyway."

"What?" This surprised her.

"I've been reading up on evolution. Plainly, the human brain was an evolutionary overshoot—far more capable than a competent hunter-gatherer needed. To get the better of animals, it would have been enough to master fire and simple stone tools. Such talents alone would have made people the lords of creation, removing selection pressure to change. Instead, all evidence from the brain itself said that change accelerated. The human cerebral cortex added mass, stacking new circuitry atop older wiring. That mass spread over the lesser areas like a thick new skin."

"Considering the state of the world, I'd say we need all the brains we can get," she said skeptically.

"From that layer came musicians and engineers, saints and savants," he finished with a flourish. One of Kelly's best points was her willingness to sit still while he waxed professorially long-winded, even on vacation. "And all this evolutionary selection happened in just a few million years."

Kelly snorted prettily. "Look at it from the woman's point of view. It happened, despite putting mothers in desperate danger in childbirth."

"Uh, how?"

"From those huge baby heads. They're hard to get out. We women are still paying the price for your brains—and for ours."

He chuckled. She always had a special spin on a subject that made him see it fresh. "Then why was it selected for, back then?"

Kelly smiled enigmatically. "Maybe men and women alike found intelligence sexy in each other."

"Really?"

Her sly smile. "How about us?"

"Have you ever watched very many 3-D stars? They don't feature brains, my dear."

"Remember the animals we saw in the Madrid Senso-Zoo? The mating exhibit? It could be that for early humans, brains were like peacock tails, or moose horns—display items, to attract the females. Runaway sexual selection."

"I see, an overplayed hand of otherwise perfectly good cards." He laughed. "So being smart is just a bright ornament."

"Works for me," she said, giving him a wink.

He watched the sunset turn to glowering, ominous crimson, oddly happy. Sheets of light worked across the sky among curious, layered clouds. "Ummm . . . ," Kelly murmured.

"Yes?"

"Maybe this is a way to use the research the ExSpecs are doing too. Learn who we were—and therefore who we are."

"Intellectually, it's a jump. In social ways, though, the gap could be less."

Kelly looked skeptical. "You think chimps are only a bit further back in a social sense?"

"Ummm. I wonder if in logarithmic time we might scale from chimps to us, now?"

"A big leap. To do anything you'll need more experience with them." She eyed him. "You like immersion, don't you?"

"Well, yes. It's just . . ."

"What?"

"That ExSpec Ruben, he keeps pushing immersions—"

"That's his job."

"—and he knew who I was."

"So?" She spread her hands and shrugged.

"You're normally the suspicious one. Why should an ExSpec know an obscure mathematician?"

"He looked you up. Data dumps on incoming guests are standard. And in some circles you're hardly obscure. Plenty of people back in Helsinki line up to see you."

"And some would like to see me dead. Say, you're supposed to be the ever vigilant one." He grinned. "Shouldn't you be encouraging my caution?"

"Paranoia isn't caution. Time spent on nonthreats subtracts from vigilance."

By the time they went in for dinner she had talked him into more immersions.

Hot day in the sun. Dust makes me snort.

That Biggest, he walks by, gets respect right away. Fems and guys alike, they stick out their hands.

Biggest touches them, taking time with each, letting them know he is there. The world is all right.

I reach out to him too. Makes me feel good. I want to be like Biggest, to be big, be as big as him, be *him*.

Fems don't give him any trouble. He wants one, she goes. Hump right away. He's Biggest.

Most males, they don't get much respect. Fems don't want to do with them as much as they do with Biggest. The little males, they huff and throw sand and all that but everybody knows they're not going to be much. No chance they could ever be like Biggest. They don't like that but they are stuck with it.

Me, I'm pretty big. I get respect. Some, anyway.

All the guys like stroking. Petting. Grooming. Fems give it to them and they give it back.

Guys get more though. After it, they're not so gruff.

I'm sitting getting groomed and all of a sudden I smell something. I don't like it. I jump up, cry out. Biggest, he takes notice. Smells it too.

Strangers. Everybody starts hugging each other. Strong smell, plenty of it. Lots of Strangers. The wind says they are near, getting nearer.

They come running down on us from the ridge. Looking for fems, looking for trouble.

I run for my rocks. I always have some handy. I fling one at them, miss. Then they are in among us. It's hard to hit them, they go so fast.

Four Strangers, they grab two fems. Drag them away.

Everybody howling, crying. Dust everywhere.

I throw rocks. Biggest leads the guys against the Strangers.

They turn and run off. Just like that. Got the two fems though and that's bad.

Biggest mad. He pushes around some of the guys, makes noise. He not looking so good now, he let the Strangers in.

Those Strangers bad. We all hunker down, groom each other, pet, make nice sounds.

Biggest, he come by, slap some of the fems. Hump some. Make sure everybody know he's still Biggest.

He don't slap me. He know better than to try. I growl at him when he come close and he pretend not to hear.

Maybe he not so Big any more, I'm thinking.

He stayed with it this time. After the first crisis, when the Stranger chimps came running through, he sat and let himself get groomed for a long time. It really did calm him.

Him? Who was he?

This time he could fully sense the chimp mind. Not below him—that was an evolutionary metaphor—*but around* him. A swarming scattershot of senses, thoughts, fragments like leaves blowing by him in a wind.

And the wind was *emotion*. Blustering gales, howling and whipping in gusts, raining thoughts like soft hammer blows.

These chimps thought poorly, in the sense that he could get only shards, like human musings chopped by a nervous editor. But chimps *felt* intensely.

Of course, he thought—and he could think, nestled in the hard kernel of himself, wrapped in the chimp mind. *Emotions told it what to do, without thinking. Quick reactions demanded that. Strong feeling amplified subtle clues into strong imperatives. Blunt orders from Mother Evolution.*

He saw now that the belief that high order mental experiences like emotion were unique to people was . . . simply conceited. These chimps shared much of the human world view. A theory of chimp sociohistory could be valuable.

He gingerly separated himself from the dense, pressing chimp mind. He wondered if the chimp knew he was here. Yes, it did—dimly. But somehow this did not bother the chimp. He integrated it into his blurred, blunt world. Leon was somewhat like an emotion, just one of many fluttering by and staying a while, then wafting away.

Could he be more than that? He tried getting the chimp to lift its right arm—and it was like lead. He struggled for a while that way with no success. Then he realized his error. He could not overpower this chimp, not as a kernel in a much larger mind.

He thought about this as the chimp groomed a female, picking carefully through coarse hair. The strands smelled good, the air was sweet, the sun stroked him with blades of generous warmth. . . .

Emotion. Chimps didn't follow instructions because that simply lay beyond them. They could not understand directions in the human sense. Emotions—those they knew. He had to be an emotion, not a little general giving orders.

He sat for a while simply *being* this chimp. He learned—or rather, he felt. The troop groomed and scavenged food, males eyeing the perimeter, females keeping close to the young. A lazy calm descended over him, carrying him effortlessly through warm moments of the day. Not since he was a boy had he felt anything like this. A slow, graceful easing, as though there were no time at all, only slices of eternity.

In this mood, he could concentrate on a simple movement—raising an arm, scratching—and create the desire to do it. His chimp responded. To make it happen, he had to *feel* his way toward a goal. Sail before the emotion wind.

Catching a sweet scent on the air, Leon thought about what food that might signal. His chimp meandered upwind, sniffed, discarded the clue as uninteresting. Leon could now smell the reason why: fruit, true, sweet, yes—but inedible for a chimp.

Good. He was learning. And he was integrating himself into the deep recesses of this chimp-mind.

Watching the troop, he decided to name the prominent chimps, to keep them straight: Agile the quick one, Sheelah the sexy one, Grubber the hungry one. . . . But what was his own name? His he dubbed Ipan. Not very original, but that was its main characteristic, *I as Pan troglodytes*.

Grubber found some bulb-shaped fruit and the others drifted over to scavenge. The hard fruit smelled a little too young (how did he know that?) but some ate it anyway.

And which of these was Kelly? They had asked to be immersed in the same troop, so one of these—he forced himself to count, though somehow the exercise was like moving heavy weights in his mind—these twenty-two was her. How could he tell? He ambled over to several females who were using sharp-edged stones to cut leaves from branches. They tied the strands together so they could carry food.

Leon peered into their faces. Mild interest, a few hands held out for stroking, an invitation to groom. No glint of recognition in their eyes.

He watched a big fem, Sheelah, carefully wash sand-covered fruit in a creek. The troop followed suit; Sheelah was a leader of sorts, a female lieutenant to Biggest.

She ate with relish, looked around. There was grain growing nearby, past maturity, ripe tan kernels already scattered in the sandy soil. Concentrating, Leon could tell from the faint bouquet that this was a delicacy. A few chimps squatted and picked grains from the sand, slow work. Sheelah did the same, and then stopped, gazing off at the creek. Time passed, insects buzzed. After a while she scooped up sand and kernels and walked to the brook's edge. She tossed it all in. The sand sank, the kernels floated. She skimmed them off and gulped them down, grinning widely.

An impressive trick. The other chimps did not pick up on her kernel-skimming method. Fruit washing was conceptually easier, he supposed, since the chimp could keep the fruit the whole time. Kernel-skimming demanded throwing away the food first, then rescuing it—a harder mental jump.

He thought about her and in response Ipan sauntered over her way. He peered into Sheelah's eyes—and she winked at him. Kelly! He wrapped hairy arms around her in a burst of sweaty love.

"Pure animal love," she said over dinner. "Refreshing."

Leon nodded. "I like being there, living that way."

"I can *smell* so much more."

"Fruit tastes differently when they bite into it." He held up a purple bulb, sliced into it, forked it into his mouth. "To me, this is almost unbearably sweet. To Ipan, it's pleasant, a little peppery. I suppose chimps have been selected for a sweet tooth. It gets them more fast calories."

"I can't think of a more thorough vacation. Not just getting away from home, but getting away from your species."

He eyed the fruit. "And they're so, so . . ."

"Horny?"

"Insatiable."

"You didn't seem to mind."

"My chimp, Ipan? I bail out when he gets into his hump-them-all mood."

She eyed him. "Really?"

"Don't you bail out?"

"Yes, but I don't expect men to be like women."

"Oh?" he said stiffly.

"I've been reading in the ExSpec's research library, while you toy with chimp social movements. Women invest heavily in their children. Men can use two strategies—parental investment, plus 'sow the oats.'" She lifted an eyebrow. "Both must have been selected for in our evolution, because they're both common."

"Not with *me*."

To his surprise, she laughed. "I'm talking in general. My point is: The chimps are much more promiscuous than we are. The males run everything. They help out the females who are carrying their children, I gather, but then they shop around elsewhere *all* the time."

Leon switched into his professional mode; it was decidedly more comfortable, when dealing with such issues. "As the specialists say, they are pursuing a mixed reproductive strategy."

"How polite."

"Polite plus precise."

Of course, he couldn't really be sure Kelly bailed out of Sheelah when a male came by for a quick one. (They were always quick too—thirty seconds or less.) *Could* she exit the chimp mind that quickly? He required a few moments to extricate himself. Of course, if she saw the male coming, guessed his intentions . . .

He was surprised at himself. What role did jealousy have when they were inhabiting other bodies? Did the usual moral code make any sense? Yet to talk this over with her was . . . embarrassing.

He was still the country boy, like it or not.

Ruefully he concentrated on his meal of local "roamer-fleisch," which turned out to be an earthy, dark meat in a stew of tangy vegetables. He ate heartily and in response to Kelly's rather obviously amused silence said, "I'd point out that chimps understood commerce too. Food for sex, betrayal of the leader for sex, spare my child for sex, grooming for sex, just about anything for sex."

"It does seem to be their social currency. Short and decidedly not sweet. Just quick lunges, strong sensations, then boom—it's over."

He nodded. "The males need it, the females use it."

"Ummm, you've been taking notes."

"If I'm going to model chimps as a sort of simplified people, then I must."

"Model chimps?" came the assured tones of ExSpec Ruben. "They're not model citizens, if that's what you mean." He gave them a sunny smile and Leon guessed this was more of the obligatory friendliness of this place.

Leon smiled mechanically. "I'm trying to find the variables that could describe chimp behavior."

"You should spend a lot of time with them," Ruben said, sitting at the table and holding up a finger to a waiter for a drink. "They're subtle creatures."

"I agree," said Kelly. "Do you ride them very much?"

"Some, but most of our research is done differently now." Ruben's mouth twisted ruefully. "Statistical models, that sort of thing. I got this touring idea started, using the immersion tech we had developed earlier, to make money for the project. Otherwise, we'd have had to close."

"I'm happy to contribute," Leon said.

"Admit it—you like it," Kelly said, amused.

"Well, yes. It's . . . different."

"And good for the staid Professor Mattick to get out of his shell," she said.

Ruben beamed. "Be sure you don't take chances out there. Some of our customers think they're superchimps or something."

Kelly's eyes flickered. "What danger is there? Our bodies are in slowtime, back here."

Ruben said, "You're strongly linked. A big shock to a chimp can drive a backshock in your own neurological systems."

"What sort of shock?" Leon asked.

"Death, major injury."

"In that case," Kelly said to Leon, "I really do not think you should immerse."

Leon felt irked. "Come on! I'm on vacation, not in prison."

"Any threat to you—"

"Just a minute ago you were rhapsodizing about how good for me it was."

"You're too important to—"

"There's really very little danger," Ruben came in smoothly. "Chimps don't die suddenly, usually."

"And I can bail out when I see danger coming," Leon added.

"But *will* you? I think you're getting a taste for adventure."

She was right, but he wasn't going to concede the point. If he wanted a little escape from his humdrum mathematician's routine, so much the better. "I like being out of Helsinki's endless corridors."

Ruben gave Kelly a confident smile. "And we haven't lost a tourist yet."

"How about research staff?" she shot back.

"Well, that was a most unusual—"

"What happened?"

"A chimp fell off a ledge. The human operator couldn't bail out in time and she came out of it paralyzed. The shock of experiencing death through immersion is known from other incidents to prove fatal. But we have systems in place to short-circuit—"

"What else?" she persisted.

"Well, there was one difficult episode. In the early days, when we had simple wire fences." The ExSpec shifted uneasily. "Some predators got in."

"What sort of predators?"

"A primate-pack hunter, *Carnopapio grandis*. We call them raboons, genetically derived in an experiment two decades ago. They took baboon DNA—"

"How did they get in?" Kelly insisted.

"They're somewhat like a wild hog, with hooves that double as diggers. Carnivores, though. They smelled game—our corralled animals. Dug under the fences."

Kelly eyed the high, solid walls. "These are adequate?"

"Certainly. They're from a genetic experiment. Someone tried to make a predator by raising the earlier baboon stock up onto two legs."

Kelly said dryly, "Evolutionary gambling."

Ruben didn't catch the edge in her voice. "Like most bipedal predators, the forelimbs are shortened and the head carries forward, balanced by a thick tail they use for signaling to each other. They prey on the biggest herd animals, the gigantelope—another experiment—and eat only the richest meat."

"Why attack humans, then?" she asked.

"They take targets of opportunity too. Chimps, even. When they got into the compound, they went for adult humans, not children—a very selective strategy."

Kelly shivered. "You look at this very . . . objectively."

"I'm a biologist."

"I never knew it could be so interesting," Leon said to defuse her apprehension.

Ruben beamed. "Not as involving as higher mathematics, I'm sure."

Kelly's mouth twisted with wry skepticism. "Do you mind if guests carry weapons inside the compound?"

He had a glimmering of an idea about the chimps, a way to use their behaviors in building a simple toy model of sociohistory. He might be able to use the statistics of chimp troop movements, the ups and downs of their shifting fortunes.

He talked it over with Kelly and she nodded, but beneath it she seemed worried. Since Ruben's remark she was always tut-tutting about safety. He reminded her that she had earlier urged him to do more immersions. "This is a vacation, remember?" he said more than once.

Her amused sidewise glances told him that she also didn't buy his talk about the toy modeling. She thought he just liked romping in the woods. "A country boy at heart," she chuckled.

So the next morning he skipped a planned trek to view the vast gigantelope herds. He immediately went to the immersion chambers and slipped under. To get some solid work done, he told himself.

The chimps slept in trees and spent plenty of time grooming each other. For the lucky groomer a tick or louse was a treat. With enough, they could get high on some peppery-tasting alkaloid. He suspected the careful stroking and combing of his hair by Kelly was a behavior selected because it improved chimp hygiene. It certainly calmed Ipan, also.

Then it struck him: Chimps groomed rather than vocalizing. Only in crises and when agitated did they call and cry, mostly about breeding, feeding, or self-defense. They were like people who could not release themselves through the comfort of talk.

And they needed comfort. The core of their social life resembled human societies under stress—in tyrannies, in prisons, in city gangs. Nature red in tooth and claw, yet strikingly like troubled people.

But there were "civilized" behaviors here too. Friendships, grief, sharing, buddies-in-arms who hunted and guarded turf together. Their old got wrinkled, bald, and toothless, yet were still cared for.

Their instinctive knowledge was prodigious. They knew how to make a bed of leaves as dusk fell, high up in trees. They could climb with grasping feet. They felt, cried, mourned—without being able to parse these into neat grammatical packages, so the emotions could be managed, subdued. Instead, emotions drove them.

Hunger was the strongest. They found and ate leaves, fruit, insects, even fair-sized animals. They loved caterpillars.

Each moment, each small enlightenment, sank him deeper into Ipan. He began to sense the subtle nooks and crannies of the chimp mind. Slowly, he gained more cooperative control.

That morning a female found a big tree and began banging it. The hollow trunk boomed like a drum and all the foraging party rushed forward to beat it too, grinning wildly at the noise. Ipan joined in and Leon felt the burst of joy, seethed in it.

Later, coming on a waterfall after a heavy rain, they seized vines and swung among trees—out over the foaming water, screeching with joy as they performed twists and leaps from vine to vine. Like children in a new playground. Leon got Ipan to make impossible moves, wild tumbles and dives, propelling him forward with abandon—to the astonishment of the other chimps.

They were violent in their sudden, peevish moments—in hustling available females, in working out their perpetual dominance hierarchy, and especially in hunting. A successful hunt brought enormous excitement—hugging, kissing, pats. As the troop descended to feed the forest rang with barks, screeches, hoots, and pants. Leon joined the tumult, sang, danced with Sheelah/Kelly.

In some matters he had to restrain his feelings. Rats they ate head first. Larger game they smashed against rocks. They devoured the brains first, a steaming delicacy. Leon gulped—metaphorically, but with Ipan echoing the impulse—and watched, screening his reluctance. Ipan had to eat, after all.

At the scent of predators, he felt Ipan's hair stand on end. Another tangy bouquet made Ipan's mouth water. He gave no mercy to food, even if it was still walking. Evolution in action; those chimps who had showed mercy in the past ate less and left fewer descendants. Those weren't represented here anymore.

For all its excesses, he found the chimps' behavior hauntingly familiar. Males gathered often for combat, for pitching rocks, for blood sports, to work out their hierarchy. Females networked and formed alliances. There were trades of favors for loyalty, alliances, kinship bonds, turf wars, threats and displays, protection rackets, a hunger for "respect," scheming subordinates, revenge—a social world enjoyed by many people that history had judged "great." Much like an emperor's court, in fact. Did people long to strip away their clothing and conventions, bursting forth as chimps?

Leon felt a flush of revulsion, so strong Ipan shook and fidgeted. Humanity's lot *had* to be different, not this primitive horror.

He could use this, certainly, as a test bed for a full theory. Learn from our nearest genetic neighbors. *Then* humankind would be self-knowing, captains of themselves. He would build in the imperatives of the chimps, but go far beyond—to true, deep sociohistory.

"I don't see it," Kelly said at dinner.

"But they're so much like us!" He put down his spoon. "We're a brainy chimp—that's a valuable insight. We can probably train them to work for us, do housekeeping."

"I wouldn't have them messing up *my* house."

Adult humans weighed little more than chimps, but were far weaker. A chimp could lift five times more than a well-conditioned man. Human brains were three or four times more massive than a chimp's. A human baby a few months old already had a brain larger than a grown chimp. People had different brain architecture, as well.

But was that the whole story? Give chimps bigger brains and speech, ease off on the testosterone, saddle them with more inhibitions, spruce them up with a shave and a haircut, teach them to stand securely on hind legs—and you had deluxe-model chimps that would look and act rather human. They might pass in a crowd without attracting notice.

Leon said curtly, "Look, my point is that they're close enough to us to make a sociohistory model work."

"To make anybody believe that, you'll have to show that they're intelligent enough to have intricate interactions."

"What about their foraging, their hunting?" he persisted.

"Ruben says they couldn't even be trained to do work around this Excursion Station."

"I'll show you what I mean. Let's master their methods together."

"What method?"

"The basic one. Getting enough to eat."

She bit into a steak of a meaty local grazer, suitably processed and "fat-flensed for the fastidious urban palate," as the brochure had it. Chewing with unusual ferocity, she eyed him. "You're on. Anything a *chimp can do*, I can do better."

Kelly waved at him from within Sheelah. *Let the contest begin.*

The troop was foraging. He let Ipan meander and did not try to harness the emotional ripples that lapped through the chimp mind. He had gotten better at it, but at a sudden smell or sound he could lose his grip. And guiding the blunt chimp mind through anything complicated was like moving a puppet with rubber strings.

Sheelah/Kelly waved and signed to him. *This way.*

They had worked out a code of a few hundred words, using finger and facial gestures, and their chimps seemed to go along with these fairly well. Chimps had a rough language, mixing grunts and shrugs and finger displays. These conveyed immediate meanings, but not in the usual sense of sentences. Mostly they just set up associations.

Tree, fruit, go, Kelly sent. They ambled their chimps over to a clump of promising spindly trunks, but the bark was too slick to climb.

The rest of the troop had not even bothered. *They have forest smarts we lack*, Leon thought ruefully.

What there? he signed to Sheelah/Kelly.

Chimps ambled up to mounds, gave them the once-over, and reached out to brush aside some mud, revealing a tiny tunnel. *Termites*, Kelly signed.

Leon analyzed the situation as chimps drifted in. Nobody seemed in much of a hurry. Sheelah winked at him and waddled over to a distant mound.

Apparently termites worked outside at night, then blocked the entrances at dawn. Leon let his chimp shuffle over to a large tan mound, but he was riding it so well now that the chimp's responses were weak. Leon/Ipan looked for cracks, knobs, slight hollows—and yet when he brushed away some mud, found nothing. Other chimps readily unmasked tunnels. Had they memorized the hundred or more tunnels in each mound?

He finally uncovered one. Ipan was no help. Leon could control, but that blocked up the wellsprings of deep knowledge within the chimp.

The chimps deftly tore off twigs or grass stalks near their mounds. Leon carefully followed their lead. His twigs and grass didn't work. The first lot was too pliant, and when he tried to work them into a twisting tunnel, they collapsed and buckled. He switched to stiffer ones, but those caught on the tunnel walls, or snapped off. From Ipan came little help. Leon had managed him a bit too well.

He was getting embarrassed. Even the younger chimps had no trouble picking just the right stems or sticks. Leon watched a chimp nearby drop a stick that seemed to work. He then picked it up when the chimp moved on. He felt welling up from Ipan a blunt anxiety, mixing frustration and hunger. He could *taste* the anticipation of luscious, juicy termites.

He set to work, plucking the emotional strings of Ipan. This job went even worse. Vague thoughts drifted up from Ipan, but Leon was in control of the muscles now, and that was the bad part.

He quickly found that the stick had to be stuck in about ten centimeters, turning his wrist to navigate it down the twisty channel. Then he had to gently vibrate it. Through Ipan he sensed that this was to attract termites to bite into the stick.

At first he did it too long and when he drew the stick out it was half gone. Termites had bitten cleanly through it. So he had to search out another stick and that made Ipan's stomach growl.

The other chimps were through termite-snacking while Leon was still fumbling for his first taste. The nuances irked him. He pulled the stick out too fast, not turning it enough to ease it past the tunnel's curves. Time and again he fetched forth the stick, only to find that he had scraped the luscious termites off on the walls. Their bites punctured his stick, until it was so shredded he had to get another. The termites were dining better than he.

He finally caught the knack, a fluid slow twist of the wrist, gracefully extracting termites, clinging like bumps. Ipan licked them off eagerly. Leon liked the morsels, filtered through chimp taste buds.

Not many, though. Others of the troop were watching his skimpy harvest, heads tilted in curiosity, and he felt humiliated.

The hell with this, he thought.

He made Ipan turn and walk into the woods. Ipan resisted, dragging his feet. Leon found a thick limb, snapped it off to carrying size, and went back to the mound.

No more fooling with sticks. He whacked the mound solidly. Five more and he had punched a big hole. Escaping termites he scooped up by the delicious handful.

So much for subtlety! he wanted to shout. He tried writing a note for her in the dust but it was hard, forcing the letters out through his suddenly awkward hands. Chimps could handle a stick to fetch forth grubs, but marking a surface was somehow not a ready talent. He gave up.

Sheelah/Kelly came into view, proudly carrying a reed swarming with white-bellied termites. These were the best, a chimp gourmet delicacy. I *better*, she signed.

He made Ipan shrug and signed, *I got more*.

So it was a draw.

Later Kelly reported to him that among the troop he was known now as Big Stick. The name pleased him immensely.

At dinner he felt elated, exhausted, and not in the mood for conversation. Being a chimp seemed to suppress his speech centers. It took some effort to ask ExSpec Ruben about immersion technology. Usually he accepted the routine technomiracles, but understanding chimps meant understanding how he experienced them.

"The immersion hardware puts you in the middle of a chimp's posterior cingulate gyrus," Ruben said over dessert. "Just 'gyrus' for short. That's the brain's center for mediating emotions and expressing them through action."

"*The* brain?" Kelly asked. "What about ours."

Ruben shrugged. "Same general layout. Chimps' are smaller, without a big cerebrum."

Leon leaned forward, ignoring his steaming cup of Kaf. "This 'gyrus,' it doesn't give direct motor control?"

"No, we tried that. It disorients the chimp so much, when you leave, it can't get itself back together."

"So we're more subtle," Kelly said.

"We have to be. In chimp males, the pilot light is always on in neurons that control action and aggression—"

"That's why they're more violence-prone?" she asked.

"We think so. It parallels structures in our own brains."

"Really? Men's neurons?" Kelly looked doubtful.

"Human males have higher activity levels in their temporal limbic systems, deeper down in the brain—evolutionary older structures."

"So why not put me into that level?" Leon asked.

"We place the immersion chips into the gyrus area because we can reach it from the top, surgically. The temporal limbic is way far down, impossible to implant a chip and net."

Kelly frowned. "So chimp males—"

"Are harder to control. Professor Mattick here is running his chimp from the backseat, so to speak."

"Whereas Kelly is running hers from a control center that, for female chimps, is more central?" Leon peered into the distance. "I was handicapped!"

Kelly grinned. "You have to play the hand you're dealt."

"It's not fair."

"Big Stick, biology is destiny."

The troop came upon rotting fruit. Fevered excitement ran through them.

The smell was repugnant and enticing at the same time and at first he did not understand why. The chimps rushed to the overripe bulbs of blue and sickly green, popping open the skins, sucking out the juice.

Tentatively, Leon tried one. The hit was immediate. A warm feeling of well-being kindled up in him. Of course—the fruity esters had converted into—alcohol! The chimps were quite deliberately setting about getting drunk.

He "let" his chimp follow suit. He hadn't much choice in the matter.

Ipan grunted and thrashed his arms whenever Leon tried to turn him away from the teardrop fruit. And after a while, Leon didn't want to turn away either. He gave himself up to a good, solid drunk. He had been worrying a lot lately, agitated in his chimp, and . . . this was completely natural, wasn't it?

Then a pack of raboons appeared, and he lost control of Ipan.

They come fast. Running two-legs, no sound. Their tails twitch, talking to each other.

Five circle left. They cut off Esa.

Biggest thunder at them. Hunker runs to nearest and it spikes him with its forepuncher.

I throw rocks. Hit one. It yelps and scurries back. But others take its place. I throw again and they come and the dust and yowling are thick and the others of them have Esa. They cut her with their punch-claws. Kick her with sharp hooves.

Three of them carry her off.

Our fems run, afraid. We warriors stay.

We fight them. Shrieking, throwing, biting when they get close. But we cannot reach Esa.

Then they go. Fast, running on their two hoofed legs. Furling their tails in victory. Taunting us.

We feel bad. Esa was old and we loved her.

Fems come back, nervous. We groom ourselves and know that the two-legs are eating Esa somewhere.

Biggest come by, try to pat me. I snarl.

He Biggest! This thing he should have stopped.

His eyes get big and he slap me. I slap back at him. He slam into me. We roll around in dust. Biting, yowling. Biggest strong, strong and pound my head on ground.

Other warriors, they watch us, not join in.

He beat me. I hurt. I go away.

Biggest starts calming down the warriors. Fems come by and pay their respects to Biggest. Touch him, groom him, feel him the way he likes. He mounts three of them real quick. He feeling Biggest all right.

Me, I lick myself. Sheelah come groom me. After a while I feel better. Already forgotten Esa.

I not forget Biggest beat me though. In front of everybody. Now I hurt, Biggest get grooming.

He let them come and take Esa. He Biggest, he should stop them.
Someday I be all over him. On his back.
Someday I be Bigger.

"When did you bail out?" Kelly asked.

"After Biggest stopped pounding on me . . . uh, on Ipan."

They were relaxing in brilliant sun beside a swimming pool. The heady smells of the forest seemed to awaken in Leon the urge to be down there again, in the valleys of dust and blood. He trembled, took a deep breath. The fighting had been so involving he hadn't wanted to leave, despite the pain. Immersion had a hypnotic quality.

"I know how you feel," she said. "It's easy to totally identify with them. I left Sheelah when those raboons came close. Pretty scary."

"Why did anybody develop them?"

"Plans for using raboons as game, to hunt, Ruben said. Something new and challenging."

"*Hunting?* Business will exploit any throwback primitivism to—" He had been about to launch into a little lecture on how far humanity had come, when he realized that he didn't believe it anymore. "Um."

"You've always thought of people as cerebral. No sociohistory could work if it didn't take into account our animal selves."

"Our worst sins are all our own, I fear." He had not expected that his experiences here would shake him so. This was sobering.

"Not at all." Kelly gave him a lofty look. "I've been reading some of the Station background data on our room computer. Genocide occurs in wolves and chimps alike. Murder is widespread. Ducks and orangutans rape. Even *ants* have organized warfare and slave raids. Chimps have at least as good a chance of being murdered as do humans, Ruben says. Of all the hallowed hallmarks—speech, art, technology, and the rest—the one which comes most obviously from animal ancestors was genocide."

"You've been learning from Ruben."

"It was a good way to keep an eye on him."

"Better to be suspicious than sorry?"

"Of course," she said blandly. "Can't let Africa soften our brains."

"Well, luckily, even if we are superchimps, throughout human society, communication blurs distinctions between Us and Them."

"So?"

"That blunts the deep impulse to genocide."

She laughed again, this time rather to his annoyance. "You haven't understood history very well. Smaller groups still kill each other off with great relish. In Bosnia, during the reign of Omar the Impaler—"

"I concede, there are small-scale tragedies by the dozens. But on the scale where sociohistory might work, averaging over populations of many millions—"

"What makes you so sure numbers are any protection?" she asked pointedly.

"Well—without further work, I have nothing to say."

She smiled. "How uncharacteristic."

"Until I have a real, working theory."

"One that can allow for widespread genocide?"

He saw her point then. "You're saying I really need this 'animal nature' part of humans."

"I'm afraid so. 'Civilized man' is a contradiction in terms. Scheming, plots,

Sheelah grabbing more meat for her young, Ipan wanting to do in Biggest—those things happen in fancy urban nations. They're just better disguised."

"I don't follow."

"People use their intelligence to hide motives. Consider ExSpec Ruben. He made a comment about your working on a 'theory of history' the other evening."

"So?"

"Who told him you were?"

"I don't think I—ah, you think he's checking up on us?"

"He already knows."

"We're just tourists here."

She graced him with an unreadable smile. "I do love your endless, naive way of seeing the world."

Later, he couldn't decide whether she had meant that as a compliment.

Ruben invited him to try a combat sport the Station offered, and Leon accepted. It was an enhanced swordplay using levitation through electrostatic lifters. Leon was slow and inept. Using his own body against Ruben's swift moves made him long for the sureness and grace of Ipan.

Ruben always opened with a traditional posture: one foot forward, his prodsword making little circles in the air. Leon poked through Ruben's defense sometimes, but usually spent all his lifter energy eluding Ruben's thrusts. He did not enjoy it nearly as much as Ruben. The dry African air seemed to steal energy from him too, whereas Ipan reveled in it.

He did learn bits and pieces about chimps from Ruben, and from trolling through the vast Station library. The man seemed a bit uneasy when Leon probed the data arrays, as though Ruben somehow owned them and any reader was a thief. Or at least that was what Leon took to be the origin of the unease.

He had never thought about animals very much, though he had grown up among them on the farm. Yet he came to feel that they, too, had to be understood.

Catching sight of itself in a mirror, a dog sees the image as another dog. So did cats, fish, or birds. After a while they get used to the harmless image, silent and smell-free, but they did not see it as themselves.

Human children had to be about two years old to do better.

Chimps took a few days to figure out that they were looking at themselves. Then they preened before it shamelessly, studied their backs, and generally tried to see themselves differently, even putting leaves on their backs like hats and laughing at the result.

So they could do something other animals could not—get outside themselves, and look back.

They plainly lived in a world charged with echoes and reminiscences. Their dominance hierarchy was a frozen record of past coercion. They remembered termite mounds, trees to drum, useful spots where large water-sponge leaves fell, or grain matured.

All this fed into the toy model he had begun building in his notes—a chimp sociohistory. It used their movements, rivalries, hierarchies, patterns of eating, and mating and dying. Territory, resources, and troop competition for them. He found a way to factor into his equations the biological baggage of dark behaviors. Even the worst, like delight in torture and easy exterminations of other species for short-term gain. All these the chimps had. Just like today's newspaper.

* * *

At a dance that evening he watched the crowd with fresh vision.

Flirting was practice mating. He could see it in the sparkle of eyes, the rhythms of the dance. The warm breeze wafting up from the valley brought smells of dust, rot, life. An animal restlessness moved in the room.

He quite liked dancing and Kelly was a lush companion tonight. Yet he could not stop his mind from sifting, analyzing, taking the world before him apart into mechanisms.

The nonverbal template humans used for attract/approach strategies apparently descended from a shared mammalian heritage, Kelly had pointed out. He thought of that, watching the crowd at the bar.

A woman crosses a crowded room, hips swaying, eyes resting momentarily on a likely man, then coyly looking away just as she apparently notices his regard. A standard opening move: *Notice me*.

The second is *I am harmless*. A hand placed palm up on a table or knee. A shoulder shrug, derived from an ancient vertebrate reflex, signifying helplessness. Combine that with a tilted head, which displays the vulnerability of the neck. These commonly appeared when two people drawn to each other have their first conversation—all quite unconsciously.

Such moves and gestures are subcortical, emerging far below in a swamp of primordial circuitry . . . which had survived until now, because it worked.

Did such forces shape history more than trade balances, alliances, treaties? He looked at his own kind and tried to see it through chimp eyes.

Though human females matured earlier, they did not go on to acquire coarse body hair, bony eye ridges, deep voices, or tough skin. Males did. And women everywhere strove to stay young-looking. Cosmetics makers freely admitted their basic role: *We don't sell products; we sell hope*.

Competition for mates was incessant. Male chimps sometimes took turns with females in estrus. They had huge testicles, implying that reproductive advantage had come to those males who produced enough to overwhelm their rivals' contributions. Human males had proportionally smaller testicles.

But humans got their revenge where it mattered. Of all primates, humans had the largest penises.

All primates had separated out as species many millions of years ago. In DNA-measured time, chimps lay six million years from humans. He mentioned to Kelly that only 4 percent of mammals formed pair bonds, were monogamous. Primates rated a bit higher, but not much. Birds were much better at it.

She sniffed. "Don't let all this biology go to your head."

"Oh no, I won't let it get that far."

"You mean it belongs in lower places?"

"Madam, you'll have to be the judge of that."

"Ah, you and your single-entendre humor."

Later that evening, with her, he had ample opportunity to reflect upon the truth that, while it was not always great to be human, it was tremendous fun being a mammal.

They spent a last day immersed in their chimps, sunning themselves beside a gushing stream. The plane would pick them up early the next morning; Helsinki waited. They packed and entered the immersion capsule and sank into a last reverie. Sun, sweet air, the lassitude of the primitive . . .

Until Biggest started to mount Sheelah.

Leon/Ipan sat up, his head foggy. Sheelah was shrieking at Biggest. She slapped him.

Biggest had mounted Sheelah before. Kelly had bailed out, her mind returning to her body in the capsule.

Something was different now. Ipan hurried over and signed to Sheelah, who was throwing pebbles at Biggest. *What?*

She moved her hands rapidly, signing, *No go.*

She could not bail out. Something was wrong back at the capsule. He could go back himself, tell them.

Leon made the little mental flip that would bail him out.

Nothing happened.

He tried again. Sheelah threw dust and pebbles, backing away from Biggest. Nothing.

No time to think. He stepped between Sheelah and Biggest.

The massive chimp frowned. Here was Ipan, buddy Ipan, getting in the way. Denying him a fem. Biggest seemed to have forgotten the challenge and beating of the day before.

First he tried bellowing, eyes big and white. Then Biggest shook his arms, fists balled.

Leon made his chimp stand still. It took every calming impulse he could muster.

Biggest swung his fist like a club.

Ipan ducked. Biggest missed.

Leon was having trouble controlling Ipan, who wanted to flee. Sheets of fear shot up through the chimp mind, hot yellows in the blue-black depths.

Biggest charged forward, slamming Ipan back. Leon felt the jolt, a stabbing pain in his chest. He toppled backward. Hit hard.

Biggest yowled his triumph. Waved his arms at the sky.

Biggest would get on top, he saw. Beat him again.

Suddenly he felt a deep, raw hatred.

From that red seethe he felt his grip on Ipan tighten. He was riding both with and within the chimp, feeling its raw red fear, overrunning that with an iron rage. Ipan's own wrath fed back into Leon. The two formed a concert, anger building as if reflected from hard walls.

He might not be the same kind of primate, but he knew Ipan. Neither of them was going to get beaten again. And Biggest was not going to get Sheelah/Kelly.

He rolled to the side. Biggest hit the ground where he had been.

Ipan leaped up and kicked Biggest. Hard, in the ribs. Once, twice. Then in the head.

Whoops, cries, dust, pebbles—Sheelah was still bombarding them both. Ipan shivered with boiling energy and backed away.

Biggest shook his dusty head. Then he curled and rolled easily up to his feet, full of muscular grace, face a constricted mask. The chimp's eyes widened, showing white and red.

Ipan yearned to run. Only Leon's rage held him in place.

But it was a static balance of forces. Ipan blinked as Biggest shuffled warily forward, the big chimp's caution a tribute to the damage Ipan had inflicted.

I need some advantage, Leon thought, looking around. He could call for allies. Hunker paced nervously nearby.

Something told Leon that would be a losing strategy. Hunker was still a lieutenant to Biggest. Sheelah was too small to make a decisive difference. He looked at the other chimps, all chattering anxiously—and decided. He picked up a rock.

Biggest grunted in surprise. Chimps didn't use rocks against each other. Rocks were only for repelling invaders. He was violating a social code.

Biggest yelled, waved to the others, pounded the ground, huffed angrily. Then he charged.

Leon threw the rock hard. It hit Biggest in the chest, knocked him down.

Biggest came up fast, madder than before. Ipan scurried back, wanting desperately to run. Leon felt control slipping from him—and saw another rock. Suitable size, two paces back. He let Ipan turn to flee, then stopped and looked at the stone. Ipan didn't want to hold it. Panic ran through him.

Leon poured his rage into the chimp, forced the long arms down. Hands grabbed at the stone, fumbled, got it. Sheer anger made Ipan turn to face Biggest, who was thundering after him. To Leon, Ipan's arm came up in achingly slow motion. He leaned heavily into the pitch. The rock smacked Biggest in the face.

Biggest staggered. Blood ran into his eyes. Ipan caught the iron scent of it, riding on a prickly stench of outrage.

Leon made his trembling Ipan stoop down. There were some shaped stones nearby, made by the fems to trim leaves from branches. He picked up one with a chipped edge.

Biggest waved his head, dizzy.

Ipan glanced at the sober, still faces of his troop. No one had used a rock against a troop member, much less Biggest. Rocks were for Strangers.

A long, shocked silence stretched. The chimps stood rooted, Biggest grunted and peered in disbelief at the blood that spattered into his upturned hand.

Ipan stepped forward and raised the jagged stone, edge held outward. Crude, but a cutting edge.

Biggest flared his nostrils and came at Ipan. Ipan swept the rock through the air, barely missing Biggest's jaw.

Biggest's eyes widened. He huffed and puffed, threw dust, howled. Ipan simply stood with the rock and held his ground. Biggest kept up his anger-display for a long while, but he did not attack.

The troop watched with intense interest. Sheelah came and stood beside Ipan. It would have been against protocols for a female to take part in male-dominance rituals.

Her movement signaled that the confrontation was over. But Hunker was having none of that. He abruptly howled, pounded the ground, and scooted over to Ipan's side.

Leon was surprised. With Hunker maybe he could hold the line against Biggest. He was not fool enough to think that this one standoff would put Biggest to rest. There would be other challenges and he would have to fight them. Hunker would be a useful ally.

He realized that he was thinking in the slow, muted logic of Ipan himself. He *assumed* that the pursuit of chimp status-markers was a given, the great goal of his life.

This revelation startled him. He had known that he was diffusing into Ipan's mind, taking control of some functions from the bottom up, seeping through the deeply buried, walnut-sized gyrus. It had not occurred to him that the chimp would diffuse into *him*. Were they now married to each other in an interlocked web that dispersed mind and self?

Hunker stood beside him, eyes glaring at the other chimps, chest heaving. Ipan felt the same way, madly pinned to the moment. Leon realized that he would have to do something, break this cycle of dominance and submission which ruled Ipan at the deep, neurological level.

He turned to Sheelah. *Get out?* he signed.

No. No. Her chimp face wrinkled with anxiety.

Leave. He waved toward the trees, pointed to her, then him.

She spread her hands in a gesture of helplessness.

It was infuriating. He had so much to say to her and he had to funnel it through a few hundred signs. He chippered in a high-pitched voice, trying vainly to force the chimp lips and palate to do the work of shaping words.

It was no use. He had tried before, idly, but now he wanted to badly and none of the equipment worked. It couldn't. Evolution had shaped brain and vocal chords in parallel. Chimps groomed, people talked.

He turned back and realized that he had forgotten entirely about the status-setting. Biggest was glowering at him. Hunker stood guard, confused at his new leader's sudden loss of interest in the confrontation—and to gesture at a mere fem too.

Leon reared up as tall as he could and waved the stone. This produced the desired effect. Biggest inched back a bit and the rest of the troop edged closer. Leon made Ipan stalk forward boldly. By this time it did not take much effort, for Ipan was enjoying this enormously.

Biggest retreated. Fems inched around Biggest and approached Ipan.

If only I could leave him to the fems' delights, Leon thought.

He tried to bail out again. Nothing. The mechanism wasn't working back at the Excursion Station. And something told him that it wasn't going to get fixed.

He gave the edged stone to Hunker. The chimp seemed surprised but took it. Leon hoped the symbolism of the gesture would penetrate in some fashion because he had no time left to spend on chimp politics. Hunker hefted the rock and looked at Ipan. Then he cried in a rolling, powerful voice, tones rich in joy and triumph.

Leon was quite happy to let Hunker distract the troop. He took Sheelah by the arm and led her into the trees. No one followed.

He was relieved. If another chimp had tagged along, it would have confirmed his suspicions. Ruben might be keeping track.

Still, he reminded himself, absence of evidence is not evidence of absence.

The humans came swiftly, with clatter and booms.

He and Sheelah had been in the trees a while. At Leon's urging they had worked their way a few klicks away from the troop. Ipan and Sheelah showed rising anxiety at being separated from their troop. His teeth chattered and eyes jerked anxiously at every suspicious movement. This was natural, for isolated chimps were far more vulnerable.

The humans landing did not help.

Danger, Leon signed, cupping an ear to indicate the noise of fliers landing nearby.

Sheelah signed, *Where go?*

Away.

She shook her head vehemently. *Stay here. They get us.*

They would indeed, but not in the sense she meant. Leon cut her off curtly, shaking his head. *Danger.* They had never intended to convey complicated ideas with their signs and now he felt bottled up, unable to tell her his suspicions.

Leon made a knife-across-throat gesture. Sheelah frowned.

He bent down and made Ipan take a stick. In soft loam he wrote:

IMPERIAL INDUSTRIE AGENTS. WANT US DEAD.

Sheelah looked dumbfounded. Kelly had probably been operating under the assumption that the failure to bail out was a temporary error. It had lasted too long for that. The landing of people in noisy, intrusive fashion confirmed his hunch. No ordinary team would disturb the animals so much. And nobody would come after them directly. They would fix the immersion apparatus, where the real problem was.

THEY KEEP US HERE, KILL US, BLAME ON ANIMALS.

He had better arguments to back up his case, the slow accumulation of small details in Ruben's behavior. That, and the guess that letting them die in an "accident" while immersed in a chimp was plausible enough to escape an investigation.

The humans went about their noisy business. They were enough, though, to make his case. Sheelah's eyes narrowed, the big brow scowled. *Where?* she signed.

He had no sign for so abstract an idea, so he scribbled with the stick, AWAY. Indeed, he had no plan.

I'LL CHECK, she wrote in the dirt. She set off toward the noise of humans deploying on the valley floor below. To a chimp the din was a dreadful clanking irritation. Leon was not going to let her out of his sight. He followed her. She waved him back but he shook his head and stuck behind her. She gave up and let him follow.

They stayed in bushes until they could get a view of the landing party below. A skirmish line was forming up a few hundred meters away. They were encircling the area where the troop had been. Leon squinted. Chimp eyesight was not good for distance. Humans had been hunters once, and one could tell by the eyes alone.

He thought abstractly about the fact that nearly everybody needed eye aids by the age of forty. Either civilization was hard on eyes, or maybe humans in prehistory had not lived long enough for eye trouble to rob them of game. Either conclusion was sobering.

The two chimps watched the humans calling to one another and in the middle of them Leon saw Ruben. That confirmed it. That, and that each man and woman carried a weapon.

Beneath his fear he felt something strong, dark.

Ipan trembled, watching humans, a strange awe swelling in his mind. Humans seemed impossibly tall in the shimmering distance, moving with stately, swaying elegance.

Leon floated above the surge of emotion, fending off its powerful effects. The reverence for those distant, tall figures came out of the chimp's dim past.

That surprised him until he thought it over. After all, animals were reared and taught by adults much smarter and stronger. Most species were like chimps, spring-loaded by evolution to work in a dominance hierarchy. Awe was adaptive.

When they met lofty humans with overwhelming power, able to mete out punishment and rewards—literally life and death—something like religious fervor arose in them. Dim, fuzzy, but strong.

Atop that warm, tropical emotion floated a sense of satisfaction at simply *being*. His chimp was happy to be a chimp, even when seeing a being of clearly superior power and thought.

Ironic, Leon thought. His chimp had just disproved another supposedly human earmark: their self-congratulatory distinction of being the only animal that congratulated itself.

He jerked himself out of his abstractions. How human, to ruminate even when in mortal danger.

CAN'T FIND US ELECTRONICALLY, he scratched in the sand.

MAYBE RANGE IS SHORT, she wrote.

RUBEN SABOTAGED LINK, he printed. She bit her lip, nodded.

Go. We go, he signed.

Sheelah nodded and they crept quickly away. Ipan was reluctant to leave the presence of the revered humans, his steps dragging.

They used chimp modes of patrolling. He and Kelly let their chimps take over, experts at silent movement, careful of every twig. Once they had left the humans behind the chimps grew even more cautious. Chimps had few enemies but the faint scent of a single predator could change the feel of every moment in the wild.

Ipan climbed tall trees and sat for hours surveying open land ahead before venturing forth. He weighed the evidence of pungent droppings, faint prints, bent branches.

They angled down the long slope of the valley and kept in the forest. Leon had only glanced at the big color-coded map of the area all guests received and had trouble recalling much of it. Once he recognized one of the distant, beak-shaped peaks he got his bearings. Kelly spotted a stream snaking down into the main river and that gave them further help, but still they did not know which way lay the Excursion Station. Or how far.

That way? Leon signed, pointing over the distant ridge.

No. That, Kelly insisted.

Far, not.

Why?

The worst part of it all was that they could not talk. He could not say clearly that the technology of immersion worked best at reasonably short range, less than a hundred klicks, say. And it made sense to keep the subject chimps within easy flier distance. Certainly Ruben and the others had gotten to the troop quickly.

Is. He persisted.

Not. She pointed down the valley. *Maybe there.*

He could only hope Kelly got the general idea. Their signs were scanty and he began to feel a broad, rising irritation. Chimps felt and sensed strongly, but they were so *limited.*

Ipan expressed this by tossing limbs and stones, banging on tree trunks. It didn't help much. The need to speak was like a pressure he could not relieve and Kelly felt it too. Sheelah chippered and grunted in frustration.

Beneath his mind he felt the smoldering presence of Ipan. They had never been together this long before and urgency welled up between the two canted systems of mind. Their uneasy marriage was showing greater strains.

Sit. Quiet. She did. He cupped a hand to his ear.

Bad come?

No. Listen—In frustration Leon pointed to Sheelah herself. Blank incomprehension in the chimp's face. He scribbled in the dust, LEARN FROM CHIMPS. Sheelah's mouth opened and she nodded.

They squatted in the shelter of prickly bushes and listened to the sounds of the forest. Scurrying and murmurs came through strongly as Leon relaxed his grip on the chimp. Dust hung in slanted cathedral light, pouring down from the forest canopy in rich yellow shafts. Scents purled up from the forest floor, chemical messengers telling Ipan of potential foods, soft loam for resting, bark to be chewed. Leon gently lifted Ipan's head to gaze across the valley at the peaks . . . musing . . . and felt a faint tremor of resonance.

To Ipan the valley came weighted with significance beyond words. His troop had imbued it with blunt emotions, attached to clefts where a friend fell and died, where the troop found a hoard of fruits, where they met and fought two big cats. It was an intricate landscape suffused with feeling, the chimp mechanism of memory.

Leon faintly urged Ipan to think beyond the ridgeline and felt in response a diffuse anxiety. He bore in on that kernel—and an image burst into Ipan's mind, fringed in fear. A rectangular bulk framed against a cool sky. The Excursion Station.

There. He pointed for Kelly.

Ipan had simple, strong, apprehensive memories of the place. His troop had been taken there, outfitted with the implants which allowed them to be ridden, then deposited back in their territory.

Far, Kelly signed.

We go?

Hard. Slow.

No stay here. They catch.

Kelly looked as skeptical as a chimp could look. *Fight?*

Did she mean fight Ruben here? Or fight once they reached the Excursion Station? *No here. There.*

Kelly frowned but accepted this. He had no real plan, only the idea that Ruben was ready for chimps out here, and might not be so prepared for them at the Station. There he and Kelly might gain the element of surprise. How, he had no idea.

They studied each other, each trying to catch a glimmer of the other in an alien face. She stroked his earlobe, Kelly's fond calming gesture. Sure enough, it made him tingle. But he could say so little. . . . The moment crystallized for him the hopelessness of their situation.

Ruben plainly was trying to kill Leon and Kelly through Ipan and Sheelah. What would become of their own bodies? The shock of experiencing death through immersion was known to prove fatal. Their bodies would fail from neurological shock, without ever regaining consciousness.

He saw a tear run down Sheelah's cheek. She knew how hopeless matters were too. He swept her up in his arms and, looking at the distant mountains, was surprised to find tears in his own eyes as well.

He had not counted on the river. Men, animals—these problems he had considered. They ventured down to the surging waters where the forest gave the nearest protection and the stream broadened, making the best place to ford.

But the hearty river that chuckled and frothed down the valley was impossible to swim.

Or rather, for Ipan to swim. Leon had been coaxing his chimp onward, carefully pausing when his muscles shook or when he wet himself from anxiety. Kelly was having similar trouble and it slowed them. A night spent up in high branches soothed both chimps, but now at midmorning all the stressful symptoms returned, as Ipan put one foot into the river. Cool, swift currents.

Ipan danced back onto the narrow beach, yelping in dread.

Go? Kelly/Sheelah signed.

Leon calmed his chimp and they tried to get it to attempt swimming. Sheelah displayed only minor anxiety. Leon plumbed the swampy depths of Ipan's memory and found a cluster of distress, centered around a dim remembrance of nearly drowning when a child. When Sheelah helped him he fidgeted, then bolted from the water again.

Go! Sheelah waved long arms upstream and downstream and shook her head angrily.

Leon guessed that she had reasonably clear chimp-memories of the river, which had no easier crossings than this. He shrugged, lifted his hands palm up.

A big herd of gigantelope grazed nearby and some were crossing the river for better grass beyond. They tossed their great heads, as if mocking the chimps. The river was not deep, but to Ipan it was a wall. Leon, trapped by Ipan's solid fear, seethed and could do nothing.

Sheelah paced the shore. She huffed in frustration and looked at the sky, squinting. Her head snapped around in surprise. Leon followed her gaze. A flier was swooping down the valley, coming this way.

Ipan beat Sheelah to the shelter of trees, but not by much. Luckily the gigantelope herd provided a distraction for the flyer. They cowered in bushes as the machine hummed overhead in a circular search pattern. Leon had to quell Ipan's mounting apprehension by envisioning scenes of quiet and peace and food while he and Sheelah groomed each other.

The flier finally went away. They would have to minimize their exposure on open grasslands now.

They foraged for fruit. His mind revolved uselessly and a sour depression settled over him. He was quite neatly caught in a trap, a pawn in politics. Worse, Kelly was in it too. He was no man of action. *Nor a chimp of action, either*, he thought dourly.

As he brought a few overripe bunches of fruit back to their bushes overlooking the river, he heard cracking noises. He crouched down and worked his way uphill and around the splintering sounds. Sheelah was stripping branches from the trees. When he approached she waved him on impatiently, a common chimp gesture remarkably like a human one.

She had a dozen thick branches lined up on the ground. She went to a nearby spindly tree and peeled bark from it in long strips. The noise made Ipan uneasy. Predators would be curious at this unusual sound. He scanned the forest for danger.

Sheelah came over to him, slapped him in the face. She wrote with a stick on the ground, RAFT.

Leon felt particularly stupid as he pitched in. Of course. Had his chimp immersion made him more stupid? Did the effect worsen with time? Even if he got out of this, would he be the same? Many questions, no answers. He forgot about them and worked.

They lashed branches together with bark, crude but serviceable. They found two small fallen trees and used them to anchor the edge of the raft. *I*, Sheelah pointed, and demonstrated pulling the raft.

First, a warm-up. Ipan liked sitting on the raft in the bushes. Apparently the chimp could not see the purpose of the raft yet. Ipan stretched out on the deck of saplings and gazed up into the trees as they swished in the warm winds.

They carried the awkward plane of branches down to the river after another mutual grooming session. The sky was filled with birds but he could see no fliers.

They hurried. Ipan was skeptical about stepping onto the raft when it was halfway into the water, but Leon called up memories filled with warm feeling, and this calmed the quick-tripping heart he could feel knocking in the chimp veins.

Ipan sat gingerly on the branches. Sheelah cast off.

She pushed hard but the river swept them quickly downstream. Alarm spurted in Ipan.

Leon made Ipan close his eyes. That slowed the breathing, but anxiety skittered across the chimp mind like heat lightning forking before a storm. The raft's rocking motion actually helped, making Ipan concentrate on his queasy stomach. Once his eyes flew open when a floating log smacked into the raft, but the dizzying sight of water all around made him squeeze them tight immediately.

Leon wanted to help her, but he knew from the trip-hammer beating of Ipan's heart that panic hovered near. He could not even see how she was doing. He had to sit blind and feel her shoving the raft along.

She panted noisily, struggling to keep it pointed against the river's tug. Spray splashed onto him. Ipan jerked, yelped, pawed anxiously with his feet, as if to run.

A sudden lurch. Sheelah's grunt cut off with a gurgle and he felt the raft spin away on rising currents. A sickening spin . . .

Ipan jerked clumsily to his feet. Eyes jumped open.

Swirling water, the raft unsteady. He looked down and the branches were coming apart. Panic consumed him. Leon tried to promote soothing images but they blew away before winds of fright.

Sheelah came paddling after the raft but it was picking up speed. Leon made Ipan gaze at the far shore but that was all he could do before the chimp started yelping and scampering on the raft, trying to find a steady place.

It was no use. The branches broke free of their bindings and chilly water swept over the deck. Ipan screamed. He leaped, fell, rolled, jumped up again.

Leon gave up any idea of control. The only hope lay in seizing just the right moment. The raft split down the middle and his half veered heavily to the left. Ipan started away from the edge and Leon fed that, made the chimp step further. In two bounds he took the chimp off the deck and into the water—toward the far shore.

Ipan gave way then to pure blind panic. Leon let the legs and arms thrash—but to each he gave a push at the right moment. He could swim, Ipan couldn't.

The near-aimless flailing held Ipan's head out of water most of the time. It even gained a little headway. Leon kept focused on the convulsive movements, ignoring the cold water—and then Sheelah was there, her jaws agape.

She grabbed him by the scruff of the neck and shoved him toward shore. Ipan tried to grapple with her, climb up her. Sheelah socked him in the jaw. He gasped. She pulled him toward shore.

Ipan was stunned. This gave Leon a chance to get the legs moving in a thrusting stroke. He worked at it, single-minded among the rush and gurgle, chest heaving . . . and after a seeming eternity, felt pebbles beneath his feet. Ipan scrambled up onto the rocky beach on his own.

He let the chimp slap himself and dance to warm up. Sheelah emerged dripping and bedraggled and Ipan swept her up in his thankful arms.

Walking was work and Ipan wasn't having any.

Leon tried to make the chimp cover ground, but now they had to ascend difficult gulliessome mossy and rough. They stumbled, waded, climbed, and sometimes just crawled up the slopes of the valley. The chimps found animal trails, which helped a bit.

Ipan stopped often for food or just to gaze idly into the distance. Soft thoughts flitted like moths through the foggy mind, buoyant on liquid emotional flows which eddied to their own pulse.

Chimps were not made for extended projects. They made slow progress. Night came and they had to climb trees, snagging fruit on the way.

Ipan slept, but Leon did not. Could not.

Their lives were just as much at risk here as the chimps', but the slumbering minds he and Kelly attended had always lived this way. To the chimps, the forest might seeped through as a quiet rain of information, processed as they slept. Their minds keyed vagrant sounds to known nonthreats, leaving slumber intact.

Leon did not know the subtle signs of danger and so mistook every rustle and tremor in the branches as danger approaching on soft feet. Sleep came against his will.

In dawn's first pale glow Leon awoke with a snake beside him. It coiled like a green rope around a descending branch, getting itself into striking position. It eyed him and Leon tensed.

Ipan drifted up from his own profound slumber. He saw the snake but did not react with a startled jerk, as Leon feared he might.

A long moment passed between them and Ipan blinked just once. The snake became utterly motionless and Ipan's heart quickened but he did not move. Then the snake uncoiled and glided away, and the unspoken transaction was done. Ipan was unlikely prey, this green snake did not taste good, and chimps were smart enough to be about other business.

When Sheelah awoke they went down to a nearby chuckling stream for a drink, scavenging leaves and a few crunchy insects on the way. Both chimps nonchalantly peeled away fat black land leeches which had attached to them in the night. The thick, engorged worms sickened Leon, but Ipan pulled them off with the same casualness Leon would have retying loosened shoelaces.

Ipan drank and Leon reflected that the chimp felt no need to clean himself. Normally Leon showered twice a day, before breakfast and before dinner, and felt ill at ease if he sweated, but here he wore the shaggy body comfortably. Had his frequent cleansings been a health measure, like the chimps' grooming? Or a rarified, civilized habit? He dimly remembered that as a boy he had gone for days in happy, sweaty pleasure, and had disliked baths and showers. Somehow Ipan returned him to a simpler sense of self, at ease in the grubby world.

His comfort did not last long. They sighted raboons uphill.

Ipan had picked up the scent, but Leon did not have access to the part of the chimp brain that made scent-picture associations. He had only known that something disturbed Ipan, wrinkling the knobby nose. The sight at short range jolted him.

Thick hindquarters, propelling them in brisk steps. Short forelimbs, ending in sharp claws. Their large heads seemed to be mostly teeth, sharp and white above slitted, wary eyes. A thick brown pelt covered them, growing bushy in the heavy tail they used for balance.

Days before, from the safety of a high tree, Ipan had watched some rip and devour the soft tissues of a gigantelope out on the grasslands. These came sniffing, working downslope in a skirmish line, five of them. Sheelah and Ipan trembled at the sight. They were downwind of the raboons and so beat a retreat in silence.

There were no tall trees here, just brush and saplings. Leon and Sheelah angled away downhill and got some distance, and then saw ahead a clearing. Ipan picked up the faint tang of other chimps, wafting from across the clearing.

He waved to her: *Go.* At the same moment chorus rose behind them. The raboons had smelled them.

Their wheezing grunts came echoing through the thick bushes. Down the slope there was even less cover, but bigger trees lay beyond. They could climb those.

Ipan and Sheelah hurried across the broad tan clearing on all fours but they were not quick. Snarling raboons burst into the grass behind them. Leon scampered into the trees—and directly into the midst of a chimp troop.

There were several dozen, startled and blinking. He yelled incoherently, wondering how Ipan would signal to them.

The nearest large male turned, bared teeth, and shrieked angrily. The entire pack took up the call, whooping and snatching up sticks and rocks, throwing them—at Ipan. A pebble hit him on the chin, a branch on the thigh. He fled, Sheelah already a few steps ahead of him.

The raboons came charging across the clearing. In their claws they held small, sharp stones. They looked big and solid but they slowed at the barrage of screeches and squawks coming from the trees.

Ipan and Sheelah burst out into the grass of the clearing and the chimps came right after them. The raboons skidded to a halt.

The chimps saw the raboons but they did not stop or even slow. They still came after Ipan and Sheelah with murderous glee.

The raboons stood frozen, their claws working uneasily.

Leon realized what was happening and picked up a branch as he ran, calling hoarsely to Sheelah. She saw and copied him. He ran straight at the raboons, waving the branch. It was an awkward, twisted old limb, useless, but it looked big. Leon wanted to seem like the advance guard of some bad business.

In the rising cloud of dust and general chaos the raboons saw a large party of enraged chimps emerging from the forest. They bolted.

Squealing, they ran at full stride into the far trees.

Ipan and Sheelah followed, running with the last of their strength. By the time Ipan reached the first trees, he looked back and the chimps had stopped halfway, still screeching their vehemence.

He signed to Sheelah, *Go*, and they cut away at a steep angle, heading uphill.

Ipan needed food and rest to stop his heart from lurching at every minor sound. Sheelah and Ipan clutched each other, high in a tree, and crooned and petted.

Leon needed time to think. Who was keeping their bodies alive at the Station? It would be smart to let them stay out here, in danger, saying to the rest of the staff that the two odd tourists wanted a really long immersion.

His thinking triggered jitters in Ipan, so he dropped that mode. Better to think abstractly. And there was plenty out here that needed understanding.

The biotechnicians who planted chimps and gigantelope and the rest here had tinkered with the raboons. The wild days of explosive biotech, in the first years of the twencen, had allowed just about anything. Capabilities soon thereafter, in the twentens, had allowed the biotech tinkerers to see if they could turn a more distant primate relative, the baboon, into something like humans. A perverse goal, it seemed to Leon, but believable. Scientists loved to monkey with matters.

The work had gotten as far as pack-hunting behavior. But raboons had no tools beyond crudely edged stones, occasionally used to cut meat once they had brought it down.

In another few million years, under evolution's raw rub, they might be as smart as chimps. Who would go extinct then?

At the moment he didn't much care. He had felt real rage when the chimps—*his own kind!*—had turned against them, even when the raboons came within view. Why?

He worried at the issue, sure there was something here he had to understand.

Sociohistory had to deal with such basic, fundamental impulses. The chimps' reaction had been uncomfortably close to myriad incidents in human history. *Hate the Stranger.*

He had to fathom that murky truth.

Chimps moved in small groups, disliking outsiders, breeding mostly within their modest circle of a few dozen. This meant that any genetic trait that emerged could pass swiftly into all the members, through inbreeding. If it helped the band survive, the rough rub of chance would select for that band's survival. Fair enough.

But the trait had to be undiluted. A troop of especially good rock throwers would get swallowed up if they joined a company of several hundred. Contact would make them breed outside the original small clan. Outbreeding: Their genetic heritage would get watered down.

Striking a balance between the accidents of genetics in small groups, and the stability of large groups—that was the trick. Some lucky troop might have fortunate genes, conferring traits that fit the next challenge handed out by the ever-altering world. They would do well. But if those genes never passed to many chimps, what did it matter?

With some small amount of outbreeding, that trait got spread into other bands. Down through the strainer of time, others picked up the trait. It spread.

This meant it was actually *helpful* to develop smoldering animosity to outsiders, an immediate sense of their wrongness. *Don't breed with them.*

So small bands held fast to their eccentric traits, and some prospered. Those lived on; most perished. Evolutionary jumps happened faster in small, semi-isolated bands which outbred slightly. They kept their genetic assets in one small basket, the troop. Only occasionally did they mate with another troop—often, through rape.

The price was steep: a strong preference for their own tiny lot.

They hated crowds, strangers, noise. Bands of less than ten were too vulnerable to disease or predators; a few looses and the group failed. Too many, and they lost the concentration of close breeding. They were intensely loyal to their group, easily identifying each other in the dark by smell, even at great distances. Because they had many common genes, altruistic actions were common.

They even honored heroism—for even if the hero died, his shared genes were passed on through his relatives.

Even if strangers could pass the tests of difference in appearances, manner, smell, grooming—even then, culture could amplify the effects. Newcomers with different language or habits and posture would seem repulsive. Anything that served to distinguish a band would help keep hatreds high.

Each small genetic ensemble would then be driven by natural selection to stress the noninherited differences—even arbitrary ones, dimly connected to survival fitness . . . and so they could evolve culture. As humans had.

Diversity in their tribal intricacies avoided genetic watering down. They heeded the ancient call of aloof, wary tribalism.

Leon/Ipan shifted uneasily. Midway through his thinking, the word *they* had come in Leon's thinking to mean humans as well as chimps. The description fit both.

That was the key. Humans fit into civilization *despite* their innate tribalism, their chimplike heritage. It was a miracle!

But even miracles called out for explanation. How could civilization possibly have kept itself stable, using such crude creatures as humans?

Leon had never seen the issue before in such glaring, and humbling, light.

And he had no answer.

They moved on against the blunt, deep unease of their chimps.

Ipan smelled something that sent his eyes darting left and right. With the full tool kit of soothing thoughts and the subtle tricks he had learned, Leon kept him going.

Sheelah was having more trouble. The female chimp did not like laboring up the long, steep gullies that approached the ridgeline. Gnarled bushes blocked their way and it took time to work their way around. Fruit was harder to find at these altitudes.

Ipan's shoulders and arms ached constantly. Chimps walked on all fours because their immensely strong arms carried a punishing weight penalty. To navigate both trees and ground meant you could optimize neither. Sheelah and Ipan groaned and whined at the soreness that never left feet, legs, wrists, and arms. Chimps would never be far-ranging explorers.

Together they let their chimps pause often to crumble leaves and soak up water from tree holes, a routine, simple tool use. They kept sniffing the air, apprehensive.

The smell that disturbed both chimps got stronger, darker.

Sheelah went ahead and was the first over the ridgeline. Far below in the valley they could make out the rectangular rigidities of the Excursion Station. A flier lifted from the roof and whispered away down the valley, no danger to them.

He recalled a century ago sitting on the veranda there with drinks in hand and Kelly saying, *If you stayed in Helsinki you might be dead.* Also if you didn't stay in Helsinki . . .

They started down the steep slope. Their chimps' eyes jerked at every unexpected movement. A chilly breeze stirred the few low bushes and twisted trees. Some had a feathered look, burnt and shattered by lightning. Air masses driven up from the valleys fought along here, the brute clash of pressures. This rocky ridge was far from the comfortable province of chimps. They hurried.

Ahead, Sheelah stopped.

Without a sound, five raboons rose from concealment, forming a neat half-circle around them.

Leon could not tell if it was the same pack as before. If so, they were quite considerable pack hunters, able to hold memory and purpose over time. They had waited ahead, where there were no trees to climb.

The raboons were eerily quiet as they strode forward, their claws clicking softly.

He called to Sheelah and made some utterly fake ferocious noises as he moved, arms high in the air, fists shaking, showing a big profile. He let Ipan take over while he thought.

A raboon band could certainly take two isolated chimps. To survive this they had to surprise the raboons, frighten them.

He looked around. Throwing rocks wasn't going to do the trick here. With only a vague notion of what he was doing he shuffled left, toward a tree that had been splintered by lightning.

Sheelah saw his move and got there first, striding energetically. Ipan picked up two stones and flung them at the nearest raboon. One caught him on the flank but did no real harm.

The raboons began to trot, circling. They called to each other in wheezing grunts.

Sheelah leaped on a dried-out shard of the tree. It snapped. She snatched it up and Leon saw her point. It was as tall as she was and she cradled it.

The largest raboon grunted and they all looked at each other.

The raboons charged.

The nearest one came at Sheelah. She caught it on the shoulder with the blunt point and it squealed.

Leon grabbed a stalk of the shattered tree trunk. He could not wrench it free. Another squeal from behind him and Sheelah was gibbering in a high, frightened voice.

It was best to let the chimps release tension vocally, but he could feel the fear and desperation in the tones and knew it came from Kelly too.

He carefully selected a smaller shard of the tree. With both hands he twisted it free, using his weight and big shoulder muscles, cracking it so that it came away with a point.

Lances. That was the only way to stay away from the raboon claws. Chimps never used such advanced weapons. Evolution hadn't gotten around to that lesson yet.

The raboons were all around them now. He and Sheelah stood back-to-back. He barely got his feet placed when he had to take the rush of a big, swarthy raboon.

They had not gotten the idea of the lance yet. It slammed into the point, jerked back. A fearsome bellow. Ipan wet himself with fear but something in Leon kept him in control.

The raboon backed off, whimpering. It turned to run. In midstride it stopped. For a long, suspended moment the raboon hesitated—then turned back toward Leon.

It trotted forward with new confidence. The other raboons watched. It went to the same tree Leon had used and with a single heave broke off a long, slender spike of wood. Then it came toward Leon, stopped, and with one claw held the stick forward. With a toss of its big head it looked at him and half-turned, putting one foot forward.

With a shock Leon recognized the swordplay position. Ruben had used it. Ruben was riding this raboon.

It made perfect sense. This way the chimps' deaths would be quite natural. Ruben could say that he was developing raboon-riding as a new commercial application of the same hardware that worked for chimp-riding.

Ruben came forward a careful step at a time, holding the long lance between two claws now. He made the end move in a circle. Movement was jerky; claws were crude, compared with chimp hands. But the raboon was stronger.

It came at him with a quick feint, then a thrust. Leon barely managed to dodge sideways while he brushed the lance aside with his stick. Ruben recovered quickly and came from Leon's left. Jab, feint, jab, feint. Leon caught each with a swoop of his stick.

Their wooden swords smacked against each other and Leon hoped his didn't snap. Ruben had good control of his raboon. It did not try to flee as it had before.

Leon was kept busy slapping aside Ruben's thrusts. He had to have some other advantage or the superior strength of the raboon would eventually tell. Leon circled, drawing Ruben away from Sheelah. The other raboons were keeping her trapped, but not attacking. All attention riveted on the two figures as they poked and parried.

Leon drew Ruben toward an outcropping. The raboon was having trouble holding its lance straight and had to keep looking down at its claws to get them right. This meant it paid less attention to where its two hooves found their footing. Leon slapped and jabbed and kept moving, making the raboon step sideways. It put a big hoof down among some angular stones, teetered, then recovered.

Leon moved left. It stepped again and its hoof turned and it stumbled. Leon was on it in an instant. He thrust forward as the raboon looked down, feet scrambling for purchase. Leon caught the raboon full with his point.

He pushed hard. The other raboons let out a moaning.

Snorting in rage, the raboon tried to get off the point. Leon made Ipan step forward and thrust the tip into the raboon. The thing wailed hoarsely. Ipan plunged again. Blood spurted from it, spattering the dust. Its knees buckled and it sprawled.

Leon shot a glance over his shoulder. The others had surged into action. Sheelah was holding off three, screeching at them so loudly it unnerved even him. She had already wounded one. Blood dripped down its brown coat.

But the others did not charge. They circled and growled and stamped their feet, but came no closer. They were confused. Learning too. He could see the quick, bright eyes studying the situation, this fresh move in the perpetual war.

Sheelah stepped out and poked the nearest raboon. It launched itself at her in a snarling fit and she stuck it again, deeper. It yelped and turned—and ran.

That did it for the others. They all trotted off, leaving their fellow bleating on the ground. Its dazed eyes watched its blood trickle out. Its eyes flickered and Ruben was gone. The animal slumped.

With deliberation Leon picked up a rock and bashed in the skull. It was messy work and he sat back inside Ipan and let the dark, smoldering chimp anger come out.

He bent over and studied the raboon brain. A fine silvery webbing capped the rubbery, convoluted ball. Immersion circuitry.

He turned away from the sight and only then saw that Sheelah was hurt.

The station crowned a rugged hill. Steep gullies gave the hillside the look of a weary, lined face. Wiry bushes thronged the lower reaches.

Ipan puffed as he worked his way through the raw land cut by erosion. In chimp vision the night was eerie, a shimmering vista of pale greens and blue-tinged shadows. The hill was a nuance in the greater slope of a grand mountain, but chimp vision could not make out the distant features. Chimps lived in a close, immediate world.

Ahead he could see clearly the glowing blank wall ringing the Station. Massive, five meters tall. And, he remembered from his tourist tour of the place, rimmed with broken glass.

Behind him came gasps as Sheelah labored up the slope. The wound in her side made her gait stiff, face rigid. She refused to hide below. They were both near exhaustion and their chimps were balky, despite two stops for fruit and grubs and rest.

Through their feeble vocabulary, their facial grimacing and writing in the dust, they had "discussed" the possibilities. Two chimps were vulnerable out here. They could not expect to be as lucky as with the raboons, not tired out and in strange territory.

The best time to approach the Station was at night. And whoever had engineered this would not wait forever. They had hidden from fliers twice more this last day. Resting through the next day was an inviting option, but Leon felt a foreboding press him onward.

He angled up the hillside, watching for electronic trip wires. Of such technical matters he knew nothing. He would have to keep a lookout for the obvious and hope that the Station was not wired for thinking trespassers. Chimp vision was sharp and clear in dim light for nearby objects, but he could find nothing.

He chose a spot by the wall shadowed by trees. Sheelah panted in shallow gasps as she approached. Looking up, the wall seemed immense. Impossible. . . .

Slowly he surveyed the land around them. No sign of any movement. The place smelled peculiar to Ipan, somehow *wrong*. Maybe animals stayed away from the alien compound. Good; that would make security inside less alert.

The wall was polished concrete. A thick lip jutted out at the top, making climbing it harder.

Sheelah gestured where trees grew near the wall. Stumps nearer showed that the builders had thought about animals leaping across from branches. But some were tall enough and had branches within a few meters of the top.

Could a chimp make the distance? Not likely, especially when tired. Sheelah pointed to him and back to her, then held hands and made a swinging motion. Could they *swing* across the distance?

He studied her face. The designer would not anticipate two chimps cooperating that way. He squinted up at the top. Too high to climb, even if Sheelah stood on his shoulders.

Yes, he signed.

A few moments later, her hands holding his feet, about to let go of his branch, he had second thoughts.

Ipan didn't mind this bit of calisthenics, and in fact was happy to be back in a tree. But Leon's human judgment still kept shouting that he could not possibly do it. Natural chimp talent conflicted with human caution.

Luckily, he did not have much time to indulge in self-doubt. Sheelah yanked him off the branch. He fell, held only through her hands.

She had wrapped her feet securely around a thick branch, and now began to oscillate him like a weight on a string. She swung him back and forth, increasing the amplitude. Back, forth, up, down, centrifugal pressure in his head. To Ipan it was unremarkable. To Leon it was a wheeling world of heart-stopping whirls.

Small branches brushed him and he worried about noise and then forgot about that because his head was coming up level with the top of the wall.

The concrete lip was rounded off on the inside, so no hook could find a grip.

He swung back down, head plunging toward ground. Then up into the lower branches, twigs slapping his face.

On the next swing he was higher. All along the top of the wall thick glass glinted. Very professional.

He barely had time to realize all this when she let him go.

He arced up, hands stretched out—and barely caught the lip. If it had not protectively protruded out, he would have missed.

He let his body slam against the side. His feet scrabbled for purchase against the sheer face. A few toes got hold. He heaved up, muscles bunching—and over. Never before had he appreciated how much stronger a chimp could be. No man could have made it here.

He scrambled up, cutting his arm and haunch on glass. It was a delicate business, getting to his feet and finding a place to stand.

A surge of triumph. He waved to Sheelah, invisible in the tree.

From here on it was up to him. He realized suddenly that they could have fashioned some sort of rope, tying together vines. Then he could lift her up here. *Good idea, too late.*

No point in delaying. The compound was partly visible through the trees, a few lights burning. Utterly silent. They had waited until the night was about half over, he had nothing but Ipan's gut feelings to tell him when.

He looked down. Just beyond his toes razor wire gleamed, set into the concrete. Carefully he stepped between the shiny lines. There was room among the sharp glass teeth to stand. A tree blocked his vision and he could see little below him in the dim glow from the Station. At least that meant they couldn't see him, either.

Should he jump? too high. The tree that hid him was close, but he could not see into it.

He stood and thought, but nothing came to him. Meanwhile Sheelah was behind him, alone, and he hated leaving her where dangers waited that he did not even know.

He was thinking like a man and forgetting that he had the capability of a chimp.

Go. He leaped. Twigs snapped and he plunged heavily in shadows. Branches stabbed his face. He saw a dark shape to his right and so curled his legs, rotated, hands out—and snagged a branch. His hands closed easily around it and he realized it was too thin, *too thin—*

It snapped. The *crack* came like a thunderbolt to his ears. He fell, letting go of the branch. His back hit something hard and he rolled, grappling for a hold. His fingers closed around a thick branch and he swung from it. Finally he let out a gasp.

Leaves rustled, branches swayed. Nothing more.

He was halfway up the tree. Aches sprouted in his joints, a galaxy of small pains.

Leon relaxed and let Ipan master the descent. He had made far too much noise falling in the tree but there was no sign of any movement across the broad lawns between him and the big, luminous Station.

He thought of Sheelah and wished there were some way he could let her know he was inside now. Thinking of her, he measured with his eye the distances from nearby trees, memorizing the pattern so that he could find the way back at a dead run if he had to.

Now what? He didn't have a plan. That, and suspicions.

Leon gently urged Ipan—who was nervous and tired, barely controllable—into a triangular pattern of bushes. Ipan's mind was like a stormy sky split by skittering lightning. Not thoughts precisely; more like knots of emotion, forming and flashing around crisp kernels of anxiety. Patiently Leon summoned up soothing images, getting Ipan's breathing slowed, and he almost missed the whispery sound.

Nails scrabbling on a stone walkway. Something running fast.

They came around the triangle peak of bushes. Bunched muscles, sleek skin, stubby legs eating up the remaining distance. They were well trained to seek and kill soundlessly, without warning.

To Ipan the monsters were alien, terrifying. Ipan stepped back in panic before the two onrushing bullets of muscle and bone. Black gums peeled back from white teeth, bared beneath mad eyes.

Then Leon felt something shift in Ipan. Primeval, instinctive responses stopped his retreat, tensed the body. No time to flee, so *fight.*

Ipan set himself, balanced. The two might go for his arms so he drew them back, crouching to bring his face down.

Ipan had dealt with four-legged pack hunters before, somewhere far back in ancestral memory, and knew innately that they lined up on a victim's outstretched limb, would go for the throat. The canines wanted to bowl him over, slash open the jugular, rip and shred in the vital seconds of surprise.

They gathered themselves, bundles of swift sinew, running nearly shoulder to shoulder, big heads up—and leaped.

In air, they were committed, Ipan knew. And open.

Ipan brought both hands up to grasp the canines' forelegs.

He threw himself backward, holding the legs tight, his hands barely beneath the jaws. The wirehounds' own momentum carried them over his head as he rolled backward.

Ipan rolled onto his back, yanking hard. The sudden snap slammed the canines forward. They could not get their heads turned around and down to close on his hand.

The leap, the catch, the quick pivot and swing, the heave—all combined in a centrifugal whirl that slung the wirehounds over Ipan as he himself went down, rolling. He felt the canines' legs snap and let go. They sailed over him with pained yelps.

Ipan rolled over completely, head tucked in, and came off his shoulders with a bound. He heard a solid thud, clacks as jaws snapped shut. A thump as the canines hit the grass, broken legs unable to cushion them.

He scrambled after them, his breath whistling. They were trying to get up, turning on snapped legs to confront their quarry. Still no barks, only faint whimpers of pain, sullen growls. One swore vehemently and quite obscenely. The other chanted, "Baaas'ard . . . baaas'ard . . ."

Animals turning in their vast, sorrowful night.

He jumped high and came down on both. His feet drove their necks into the ground and he felt bone give way. Before he stepped back to look he knew they were gone.

Ipan's blood surged with joy. Leon had never felt this tingling thrill, not even in the first immersion, when Ipan had killed a Stranger. Victory over these alien things with teeth and claws that come at you out of the night was a profound, inflaming pleasure.

Leon had done nothing. The victory was wholly Ipan's.

For a long moment Leon basked in it in the cool night air, felt the tremors of ecstasy.

Slowly, reason returned. There were other wirehounds. Ipan had caught these just right. Such luck did not strike twice.

The wirehounds were easy to see on the lawn. Would attract attention.

Ipan did not like touching them. Their bowels had emptied and the smell cut the air. They left a smear on the grass as he dragged them into the bushes.

Time, time. Someone would miss the canines, come to see.

Ipan was still pumped up from his victory. Leon used that to get him trotting across the broad lawn, taking advantage of shadows. Energy popped in Ipan's veins. Leon knew it was a mere momentary glandular joy, overlaying a deep fatigue. When it faded, Ipan would become dazed, hard to govern.

Every time he stopped he looked back and memorized landmarks. He might have to return this way on the run.

It was late and most of the Station was dark. In the technical area, though, a cluster of windows blossomed with what Ipan saw as impossibly rich, strange, superheated light.

He loped over to them and flattened himself against the wall. It helped that Ipan was fascinated by this strange citadel of the godlike humans. Out of his own curiosity he peeked in a window. Under enamel light a big assembly room sprawled, one that Leon recognized. There, centuries ago, he had formed up with the other brightly dressed tourists to go out on a trek.

Leon let the chimp's curiosity propel him around to the side, where he knew a door led into a long corridor. The door opened freely, to Leon's surprise. Ipan strolled down the slick tiles of the hallway, quizzically studying the phosphor-paint designs on the ceiling and walls, which emitted a soothing ivory glow.

An office doorway was open. Leon made Ipan squat and bob his head around the edge. Nobody there. It was a sumptuous den with shelves soaring into a vaulted ceiling. Leon remembered sitting there discussing the immersion process. That meant the immersion vessels were just a few doors away down—

The squeak of shoes on tiles made him turn.

ExSpec Ruben was behind him, leveling a weapon. In the cool light the man's face looked odd to Ipan's eyes, mysteriously bony.

Leon felt the rush of reverence in Ipan and let it carry the chimp forward, chippering softly. Ipan felt awe, not fear.

Leon wondered why Ruben said nothing and then realized that of course he could not reply.

Ruben tensed up, waving the snout of his ugly weapon. A metallic click. Ipan brought his hands up in a ritual chimp greeting and Ruben shot him.

The impact spun Ipan around. He went down, sprawling.

Ruben's mouth curled in derision. "Smart prof, huh? Didn't figure the alarm on the door, huh?"

The pain from Ipan's side was sharp, startling. Leon rode the hurt and gathering anger in Ipan, helping it build. Ipan felt his side and his hand came away sticky, smelling like warm iron in the chimp's nostrils.

Ruben circled around, weapon weaving. "You *killed* me, you weak little dope. Ruined a good experimental animal too. Now I got to figure what to do with you."

Leon threw his own anger atop Ipan's seethe. He felt the big muscles in the shoulders bunch. The pain in the side jabbed suddenly. Ipan groaned and rolled on the floor, pressing one hand to the wound.

Leon kept the head down so that Ipan could not see the blood that was running down now across the legs. Energy was running out of the chimp body. A seeping weakness came up the legs.

He pricked his ears to the shuffle of Ruben's feet. Another agonized roll, this time bringing the legs up in a curl.

"Guess there's really only one solution—"

Leon heard the metallic click.

Now, yes. He let his anger spill.

Ipan pressed up with his forearms and got his feet under him. No time to get all the way up. Ipan sprang at Ruben, keeping low.

A tinny shot whisked by his head. Then he hit Ruben in the hip and slammed the man against the wall. The man's scent was sour, salty.

Leon lost all control. Ipan bounced Ruben off the wall and instantly slammed arms into the man with full force.

Ruben tried to deflect the impact. Ipan pushed the puny human arms aside. Ruben's pathetic attempts at defense were like spiderwebs brushed away.

He butted Ruben and pounded massive shoulders into the man's chest. The weapon clattered on the tiles.

Ipan slammed himself into the man's body again and again.

Strength, power, joy.

Bones snapped. Ruben's head snapped back, smacked the wall, and he went limp.

Ipan stepped back and Ruben sagged to the tiles. *Joy.*

Blue-white flies buzzed at the rim of his vision.

Must move. That was all Leon could get through the curtain of emotions that shrouded the chimp mind.

The corridor lurched. Leon got Ipan to walk in a sidewise teeter.

Down the corridor, painful steps. Two doors, three. Here? Locked. Next door. World moving slower somehow.

The door snicked open. An antechamber that he recognized. Ipan blundered into a chair and almost fell. Leon made the lungs work hard. The gasping cleared his vision of the dark edges that had crept in but the blue-white flies were there, fluttering impatiently, and thicker.

He tried the far door. Locked. Leon summoned what he could from Ipan. *Strength, power, joy*. Ipan slammed his shoulder into the solid door. It held. Again. And again, sharp pain—and it popped open.

Right, this was it. The immersion bay. Ipan staggered into the array of vessels. The walk down the line, between banks of control panels, took an eternity. Leon concentrated on each step, placing each foot. Ipan's field of view bobbed as the head seemed to slip around on the liquid shoulders.

Here. His own vessel.

He fumbled with the latches. Popped it open.

There lay Leon Mattick, peaceful, eyes closed.

Emergency controls, yes. He knew them from the briefing.

He searched the polished steel surface and found the panel on the side. Ipan stared woozily at the meaningless lettering and Leon himself had trouble reading. The letters jumped and fused together.

He found several buttons and servo controls. Ipan's hands were stubby, wrong. It took three tries to get the reviving program activated. Lights cycled from green to amber.

Ipan abruptly sat down on the cool floor. The blue-white flies were buzzing all around his head now and they wanted to bite him. He sucked in the cool dry air but there was no substance in it, no help. . . .

Then, without any transition, he was looking at the ceiling. On his back. The lamps up there were getting dark, fading. Then they went out.

Leon's eyes snapped open.

The recovery program was still sending electrostims through his muscles. He let them jump and tingle and ache while he thought. He felt fine. Not even hungry, as he usually did after an immersion. How long had he been in the wilderness? At least five days.

He sat up. There was no one in the vessel room. Evidently Ruben had gotten some silent alarm, but had not alerted anyone else. That pointed, again, to a tight little conspiracy.

He got out shakily. To get free he had to detach some feeders and probes but they seemed simple enough.

Leon. The big body filled the walkway. He knelt and felt for a pulse. Rickety.

But first, Kelly. Her vessel was next to his and he started the revival. She looked well.

Ruben must have put some transmission block on the system, so that none of the staff could tell by looking at the panel that anything was wrong. A simple cover story, a couple who wanted a really long immersion. Ruben had warned them, but no, they wanted it so. . . . A perfectly plausible story.

Kelly's eyes fluttered. He kissed her. She gasped.

He made a chimp sign, *quiet*, and went back to Ipan.

Blood came steadily. Leon was surprised to find that he could not pick up the rich, pungent elements in the blood from smell alone. A human missed so much!

He took off his shirt and made a crude tourniquet. At least Ipan's breathing was regular. Kelly was ready to get out by then and he helped her disconnect.

"I was hiding in a tree and then—poof!" she said. "What a relief. How did you—"

"Let's get moving," he said.

As they left the room she said, "Who can we trust? Whoever did this—" She stopped when she saw Ruben. "Oh."

Somehow her expression made him laugh. She was very rarely surprised.

"*You* did this?"

"Ipan."

"I never would have believed a chimp could, could . . ."

"I doubt anyone's been immersed this long. Not under such stress, anyway. It all just, well, it came out."

He picked up Ruben's weapon and studied the mechanism. A standard pistol, silenced. Ruben had not wanted to awaken the rest of the Station. That was promising. There should be people here who would spring to their aid. He started toward the building where the Station personnel lived.

"Wait, what about Ruben?"

"I'm going to wake up a doctor."

They did—but Leon took him into the vessel room first, to work on Ipan. Some patchwork and injections and the doctor said Ipan would be all right. Only then did he show the man Ruben's body.

The doctor got angry about that, but Leon had a gun. All he had to do was point it. He didn't say anything, just gestured with the gun. He did not feel like talking and wondered if he ever would again. When you couldn't talk you concentrated more, entered into things. Immersed.

And in any case, Ruben had been dead for some time.

Ipan had done a good job. The doctor shook his head at the severe damage.

Kelly looked at him oddly throughout the whole time. He did not understand why, until he realized that he had not even thought about helping Ruben first. Ipan was *himself*, in a sense he could not explain.

But he understood immediately when Kelly wanted to go to the Station wall and call to Sheelah. They brought her, too, in from the wild darkness.

A year later, when the industrial conspiracy had been uncovered and dozens brought to trail, they returned to the Excursion Station.

Leon longed to lounge in the sun, after a year of facing news cameras and attorneys. Kelly was equally exhausted with the rub of events.

But they both immediately booked time in the immersion chambers and spent long hours there. Ipan and Sheelah seemed to greet their return with something approximating joy.

Each year they would return and live inside the minds. Each year they would come away calmer, somehow fuller.

Leon's analysis of sociohistory appeared in a ground-breaking series of papers, modeling all of civilization as a "complex adaptive system." Fundamental to the intricately structured equations were terms allowing for primordial motivations, for group behavior in tension with individual longings, for deep motivations kindled in the veldt, over a thousand millennia ago. This was exact, complex, and original; his papers resounded through the social sciences, which had finally been made quantitative.

Fifteen years later the work received a Nobel prize, then worth 2.3 million New Dollars. Leon and Kelly spent a lot of it on travel, particularly to Africa.

When questioned in interviews, he never spoke of the long trek he and Kelly had undergone. Still, in his technical papers and public forums, he did give chimpanzees as examples of complex, adaptive behavior. As he spoke, he gave a long, slow smile, eyes glittering enigmatically, but would discuss the subject no further.